sleeping
beauties

STEPHEN KING

sleeping beauties

OWEN KING

HODDER &
STOUGHTON

Copyright © 2017 by Stephen King and Owen King

First published in Great Britain in 2017
by Hodder & Stoughton
An Hachette UK company

The right of Stephen King and Owen King to be identified
as the Authors of the Work has been asserted by them in accordance
with the Copyright, Designs and Patents Act 1988.

1

First Hodder hardcover edition September 2017

A CIP catalogue record for this title is available from the British Library

ISBN 978 1 473 66519 4
Ebook 978 1 473 66521 7

Typeset in Bembo 12/15 pt by Palimpsest Book Production Ltd, Falkirk, Stirlingshire

Printed and bound in Great Britain by Clays Ltd, St Ives plc

Hodder & Stoughton policy is to use papers that are natural, renewable
and recyclable products and made from wood grown in sustainable forests.
The logging and manufacturing processes are expected to conform to the
environmental regulations of the country of origin.

Hodder & Stoughton
Carmelite House
50 Victoria Embankment
London
EC4Y 0DZ

www.hodder.co.uk

In Remembrance
of Sandra Bland

CHARACTERS

TOWN OF DOOLING, SEAT OF DOOLING COUNTY

- Truman 'Trume' Mayweather, 26, a meth cook
- Tiffany Jones, 28, Truman's cousin
- Linny Mars, 40, a dispatcher, Dooling Sheriff's Department
- Sheriff Lila Norcross, 45, of the Dooling Sheriff's Department
- Jared Norcross, 16, a junior at Dooling High School, son of Lila and Clint
- Anton Dubcek, 26, owner and operator of Anton the Pool Guy, LLC
- Magda Dubcek, 56, Anton's mother
- Frank Geary, 38, Animal Control Officer, Town of Dooling
- Elaine Geary, 35, a Goodwill volunteer and Frank's spouse
- Nana Geary, 12, a sixth grader at Dooling Middle School
- Old Essie, 60, a homeless woman
- Terry Coombs, 45, of the Dooling Sheriff's Department
- Rita Coombs, 42, Terry's spouse
- Roger Elway, 28, of the Dooling Sheriff's Department
- Jessica Elway, 28, Roger's spouse
- Platinum Elway, 8 months old, daughter of Roger and Jessica
- Reed Barrows, 31, of the Dooling Sheriff's Department
- Leanne Barrows, 32, Reed's spouse
- Gary Barrows, 2, son of Reed and Leanne
- Drew T. Barry, 42, of Drew T. Barry Indemnity

- Vern Rangle, 48, of the Dooling Sheriff's Department
- Elmore Pearl, 38, of the Dooling Sheriff's Department
- Rupe Wittstock, 26, of the Dooling Sheriff's Department
- Will Wittstock, 27, of the Dooling Sheriff's Department
- Dan 'Treater' Treat, 27, of the Dooling Sheriff's Department
- Jack Albertson, 61, of the Dooling Sheriff's Department (ret.)
- Mick Napolitano, 58, of the Dooling Sheriff's Department (ret.)
- Nate McGee, 60, of the Dooling Sheriff's Department (ret.)
- Carson 'Country Strong' Struthers, 32, an ex–Golden Gloves boxer
- Coach JT Wittstock, 64, Dooling High School Warriors varsity football team
- Dr Garth Flickinger, 52, a plastic surgeon
- Fritz Meshaum, 37, a mechanic
- Barry Holden, 47, a public defender
- Oscar Silver, 83, a judge
- Mary Pak, 16, a junior at Dooling High School
- Eric Blass, 16, a junior at Dooling High School
- Curt McLeod, 16, a junior at Dooling High School
- Kent Daley, 16, a junior at Dooling High School
- Willy Burke, 75, a volunteer
- Dorothy Harper, 80, retired
- Margaret O'Donnell, 72, sister of Gail, retired
- Gail Collins, 68, sister of Margaret, a secretary at a dentist's office
- Mrs Ransom, 77, a baker
- Molly Ransom, 10, the granddaughter of Mrs Ransom
- Johnny Lee Kronsky, 41, a private investigator
- Jaime Howland, 44, a communications professor
- Eve Black, appearing about 30 years of age, a stranger

THE PRISON

- Janice Coates, 57, Warden, Dooling Correctional Facility for Women
- Lawrence 'Lore' Hicks, 50, Vice-Warden, Dooling Correctional Facility for Women

- Rand Quigley, 30, Officer, Dooling Correctional Facility for Women
- Vanessa Lampley, 42, Officer, Dooling Correctional Facility for Women, and 2010 & 2011 Ohio Valley Arm-Wrestling Champion, 35–45 Age Group
- Millie Olson, 29, Officer, Dooling Correctional Facility for Women
- Don Peters, 35, Officer, Dooling Correctional Facility for Women
- Tig Murphy, 45, Officer, Dooling Correctional Facility for Women
- Billy Wettermore, 23, Officer, Dooling Correctional Facility for Women
- Scott Hughes, 19, Officer, Dooling Correctional Facility for Women
- Blanche McIntyre, 65, Secretary, Dooling Correctional Facility for Women
- Dr Clinton Norcross, 48, Senior Psychiatric Officer, Dooling Correctional Facility for Women, and Lila's spouse
- Jeanette Sorley, 36, Inmate #458251-1, Dooling Correctional Facility for Women
- Ree Dempster, 24, Inmate #4602597-2, Dooling Correctional Facility for Women
- Kitty McDavid, 29, Inmate #4603241-2, Dooling Correctional Facility for Women
- Angel Fitzroy, 27, Inmate #4601959-3, Dooling Correctional Facility for Women
- Maura Dunbarton, 64, Inmate #4028200-1, Dooling Correctional Facility for Women
- Kayleigh Rawlings, 40, Inmate #4521131-2, Dooling Correctional Facility for Women
- Nell Seeger, 37, Inmate #4609198-1, Dooling Correctional Facility for Women
- Celia Frode, 30, Inmate #4633978-2, Dooling Correctional Facility for Women
- Claudia 'the Dynamite Body-a' Stephenson, 38, Inmate #4659873-1, Dooling Correctional Facility for Women

OTHERS

- Lowell 'Little Low' Griner, 35, an outlaw
- Maynard Griner, 35, an outlaw
- Michaela Morgan née Coates, 26, National Reporter, NewsAmerica
- Kinsman Brightleaf (Scott David Winstead Jr), 60, Pastor-General, the Bright Ones
- A common fox, between 4 and 6 years of age

It makes no difference if you're rich or poor
Or if you're smart or dumb.
A woman's place in this old world
Is under some man's thumb,
And if you're born a woman
You're born to be hurt.
You're born to be stepped on,
Lied to,
Cheated on,
And treated like dirt.
> — Sandy Posey, 'Born a Woman'
> Lyrics by Martha Sharp

I say you can't *not* be bothered by a square of light!
> — Reese Marie Dempster, Inmate #4602597-2
> Dooling Correctional Facility for Women

She was warned. She was given an explanation.
Nevertheless, she persisted.
> — Sen. Addison 'Mitch' McConnell,
> speaking of Sen. Elizabeth Warren

sleeping
beauties

SLEEPING BEAUTIES

The moth makes Evie laugh. It lands on her bare forearm and she brushes her index finger lightly across the brown and gray waves that color its wings. 'Hello, gorgeous,' she tells the moth. It lifts away. Upward, upward, and upward the moth goes, and is swallowed by a slice of the sun tangled amid the glossy green leaves twenty feet above Evie's place among the roots on the ground.

A coppery red rope leaks from a black socket at the center of the trunk and twists between plates of bark. Evie doesn't trust the snake, obviously. She's had trouble with him before.

Her moth and ten thousand others surge from the treetop in a crackling, dun-colored cloud. The swarm rolls across the sky in the direction of the sickly second-growth pines on the other side of the meadow. She rises to follow. Stalks crunch under her steps and the waist-high grass scrapes her bare skin. As she approaches the sad, mostly logged-over wood, she detects the first chemical smells — ammonia, benzene, petroleum, so many others, ten thousand nicks on a single patch of flesh — and relinquishes the hope she had not realized she harbored.

Webs spill from her footprints and sparkle in the morning light.

PART ONE

THE AULD TRIANGLE

In the female prison
There are seventy women
I wish it was with them that I did dwell,
Then that old triangle
Could jingle jangle
Along the banks of the Royal Canal.

                                  – Brendan Behan

CHAPTER 1

1

Ree asked Jeanette if she ever watched the square of light from the window. Jeanette said she didn't. Ree was in the top bunk, Jeanette in the bottom. They were both waiting for the cells to unlock for breakfast. It was another morning.

It seemed that Jeanette's cellmate had made a study of the square. Ree explained that the square started on the wall opposite the window, slid down, down, down, then slopped over the surface of their desk, and finally made it out onto the floor. As Jeanette could now see, it was right there in the middle of the floor, bright as anything.

'Ree,' Jeanette said. 'I just can't be bothered with a square of light.'

'I say you can't *not* be bothered by a square of light!' Ree made the honking noise that was how she expressed amusement.

Jeanette said, 'Okay. Whatever the fuck that means,' and her cell-mate just honked some more.

Ree was okay, but she was like a toddler, how silence made her anxious. Ree was in for credit fraud, forgery, and drug possession with intent to sell. She hadn't been much good at any of them, which had brought her here.

Jeanette was in for manslaughter; on a winter night in 2005 she had stabbed her husband Damian in the groin with a clutchhead screwdriver and because he was high he'd just sat in an armchair and let himself bleed to death. She had been high, too, of course.

'I was watching the clock,' Ree said. 'Timed it. Twenty-two minutes for the light to move from the window to there on the floor.'

'You should call *Guinness*,' said Jeanette.

'Last night I had a dream about eating chocolate cake with Michelle Obama and she was pissed: "That's going to make you fat, Ree!" But she was eating the cake, too.' Ree honked. 'Nah. I didn't. Made that up. Actually I dreamed about this teacher I had. She kept telling me I wasn't in the right classroom, and I kept telling her I was in the right classroom, and she'd say okay, and then teach some, and tell me I wasn't in the right room, and I'd say no, I was in the right room, and we went around like that. It was more exasperating than anything. What'd you dream, Jeanette?'

'Ah . . .' Jeanette tried to remember, but she couldn't. Her new medication seemed to have thickened her sleep. Before, sometimes she had nightmares about Damian. He'd usually look the way he did the morning after, when he was dead, his skin that streaky blue, like wet ink.

Jeanette had asked Dr Norcross if he thought the dreams had to do with guilt. The doctor squinted at her in that are-you-fucking-serious way that used to drive her nuts but that she had come around on, and then he had asked her if she was of the opinion that bunnies had floppy ears. Yeah, okay. Got it. Anyhow, Jeanette didn't miss those dreams.

'Sorry, Ree. I got nothing. Whatever I dreamed, it's gone.'

Somewhere out in the second-floor hall of B Wing, shoes were clapping along the cement: an officer making some last minute check before the doors opened.

Jeanette closed her eyes. She made up a dream. In it, the prison was a ruin. Lush vines climbed the ancient cell walls and sifted in the spring breeze. The ceiling was half-gone, gnawed away by time so that only an overhang remained. A couple of tiny lizards ran over a pile of rusty debris. Butterflies tumbled in the air. Rich scents of earth and leaf spiced what remained of the cell. Bobby was impressed, standing beside her at a hole in the wall, looking in. His mom was an archeologist. She'd discovered this place.

'You think you can be on a game show if you have a criminal record?'

The vision collapsed. Jeanette moaned. Well, it had been nice while it lasted. Life was definitely better on the pills. There was a calm, easy place she could find. Give the doc his due; better living through chemistry. Jeanette reopened her eyes.

Ree was goggling at Jeanette. Prison didn't have much to say for it, but a girl like Ree, maybe she was safer inside. Out in the world, she'd just as likely walk into traffic. Or sell dope to a narc who looked like nothing but a narc. Which she had done.

'What's wrong?' Ree asked.

'Nothing. I was just in paradise, that's all, and your big mouth blew it up.'

'What?'

'Never mind. Listen, I think there should be a game show where you can only play if you *do* have a criminal record. We could call it *Lying for Prizes*.'

'I like that a lot! How would it work?'

Jeanette sat up and yawned, shrugged. 'I'll have to think about it. You know, work out the rules.'

Their house was as it always had been and always would be, world without end, amen. A cell ten steps long, with four steps between the bunks and the door. The walls were smooth, oatmeal-colored cement. Their curling snapshots and postcards were held (little that anyone cared to look) with blobs of green sticky-tack in the single approved space. There was a small metal desk set against one wall and a short metal shelving unit set against the opposite wall. To the left of the door was the steel toilet where they had to squat, each looking away to lend a poor illusion of privacy. The cell door, its double-paned window at eye level, gave a view of the short corridor that ran through B Wing. Every inch and object within the cell were sauced in the pervasive odors of prison: sweat, mildew, Lysol.

Against her will, Jeanette finally took note of the sun square between the beds. It was almost to the door – but it wouldn't get any farther, would it? Unless a screw put a key in the lock or opened the cell from the Booth, it was trapped in here just as they were.

'And who would host?' Ree asked. 'Every game show needs a host. Also, what kind of prizes? The prizes have to be good. Details! We gotta figure out all the details, Jeanette.'

Ree had her head propped up and was winding a finger around in her tight bleached curls as she looked at Jeanette. Near the top of Ree's forehead there was a patch of scar tissue that resembled a grill mark, three deep parallel lines. Although Jeanette didn't know what had caused the scar, she could guess *who* had made it: a man. Maybe her father, maybe her brother, maybe a boyfriend, maybe a guy she'd never seen before and never would see again. Among the inmates of Dooling Correctional there was, to put it lightly, very little history of prize-winning. Lots of history with bad guys, though.

What could you do? You could feel sorry for yourself. You could hate yourself or you could hate everyone. You could get high sniffing cleaning products. You could do whatever you wanted (within your admittedly limited options), but the situation wouldn't change. Your next turn to spin the great big shiny Wheel of Fortune would arrive no sooner than your next parole hearing. Jeanette wanted to put as much arm as she could into hers. She had her son to think about.

There was a resounding thud as the officer in the Booth opened sixty-two locks. It was 6:30 A.M., everyone out of their cells for head-count.

'I don't know, Ree. You think about it,' Jeanette said, 'and I'll think about it, and then we'll exchange notes later.' She swung her legs out of bed and stood.

2

A few miles from the prison, on the deck of the Norcross home, Anton the pool guy was skimming for dead bugs. The pool had been Dr Clinton Norcross's tenth anniversary present to his wife, Lila. The sight of Anton often made Clint question the wisdom of this gift. This morning was one of those times.

Anton was shirtless, and for two good reasons. First, it was going to be a hot day. Second, his abdomen was a rock. He was ripped, was Anton the pool guy; he looked like a stud on the cover of a romance novel. If you shot bullets at Anton's abdomen, you'd want to do it from an angle, in case of a ricochet. What did he eat? Mountains of pure protein? What was his workout? Cleaning the Augean Stables?

Anton glanced up, smiling from under the shimmering panes of his Wayfarers. With his free hand he waved at Clint, who was watching from the second-floor window of the master bathroom.

'Jesus Christ, man,' Clint said quietly to himself. He waved back. 'Have a heart.'

Clint sidled away from the window. In the mirror on the closed bathroom door there appeared a forty-eight-year-old white male, BA from Cornell, MD from NYU, modest love handles from Starbucks Grande Mochas. His salt and pepper beard was less woodcutter-virile, more lumpen one-legged sea captain.

That his age and softening body should come as any kind of a surprise struck Clint as ironic. He had never had much patience with male vanity, especially the middle-aged variety, and cumulative professional experience had, if anything, trimmed that particular fuse even shorter. In fact, what Clint thought of as the great turning point of his medical career had occurred eighteen years earlier, in 1999, when a prospective patient named Paul Montpelier had come to the young doctor with a 'crisis of sexual ambition.'

He had asked Montpelier, 'When you say "sexual ambition," what do you mean?' Ambitious people sought promotions. You couldn't really become vice-president of sex. It was a peculiar euphemism.

'I mean . . .' Montpelier appeared to weigh various descriptors. He cleared his throat and settled on, 'I still want to do it. I still want to go for it.'

Clint said, 'That doesn't seem unusually ambitious. It seems normal.'

Fresh from his psych residency, and not yet softening, this was only Clint's second day in the office and Montpelier was just his second patient.

(His first patient had been a teenager with some anxieties about her college applications. Pretty quickly, however, it had emerged that the girl had received a 1570 on her SATs. Clint pointed out that this was excellent, and there had been no need for treatment or a second appointment. *Cured!* he had dashed off on the bottom of the yellow legal pad he used to take notes on.)

Seated in the leatherette armchair opposite Clint, Paul Montpelier had that day worn a white sweater vest and pleated pants. He sat in a hunch with an ankle over his knee, hanging onto his dress shoe with one hand as he spoke. Clint had seen him park a candy-red sports car in the lot outside the lowslung office building. Working high up the food chain of the coal industry had made it possible for him to buy a car like that, but his long, careworn face reminded Clint of the Beagle Boys, who used to bedevil Scrooge McDuck in the old comic strips.

'My wife says – well, not in so many words, but, you know, the meaning is clear. The, uh, *subtext*. She wants me to let it go. Let my sexual ambition go.' He jerked his chin upward.

Clint followed his gaze. There was a fan rotating on the ceiling. If Montpelier sent his sexual ambition up there, it was going to get cut off.

'Let's back up, Paul. How did the subject come up between you and your wife in the first place? Where did this start?'

'I had an affair. That was the precipitating incident. And Rhoda – my wife – kicked me out! I explained it wasn't about her, it was about – I had a need, you know? Men have needs women do not always understand.' Montpelier rolled his head around on his neck. He made a frustrated hiss. 'I don't want to get divorced! There's a part of me that feels like she's the one who needs to come to terms with this. With me.'

The man's sadness and desperation were real, and Clint could imagine the pain brought on by his sudden displacement – living out of a suitcase, eating watery omelets by himself in a diner. It wasn't clinical depression, but it was significant, and deserving of respect and care even though he might have brought the situation on himself.

Montpelier leaned over his growing stomach. 'Let's be frank. I'm pushing fifty here, Dr Norcross. My best sex days are already gone. I gave those up for her. *Surrendered* them to her. I changed diapers. I drove to all the games and competitions and built up the college funds. I checked every box on the questionnaire of marriage. So why can't we come to some sort of agreement here? Why does it have to be so terrible and divisive?'

Clint hadn't replied, just waited.

'Last week, I was at Miranda's. She's the woman I've been sleeping with. We did it in the kitchen. We did it in her bedroom. We almost managed a third time in the shower. I was happy as heck! Endorphins! And then I went home, and we had a good family dinner, and played Scrabble, and everyone else felt great, too! Where is the problem? It's a *manufactured* problem, is what I think. Why can't I have some freedom here? Is it too much to ask? Is it so outrageous?'

For a few seconds no one spoke. Montpelier regarded Clint. Good words swam and darted around in Clint's head like tadpoles. They would be easy enough to catch, but he still held back.

Behind his patient, propped against the wall, was the framed Hockney print that Lila had given Clint to 'warm the place up.' He planned to hang it later that day. Beside the print were his half-unpacked boxes of medical texts.

Someone needs to help this man, the young doctor found himself thinking, and they ought to do it in a nice, quiet room like this. But should that person be Clinton R. Norcross, MD?

He had, after all, worked awfully hard to become a doctor, and there had been no college fund to help Clint along. He had grown up under difficult circumstances and paid his own way, sometimes in more than money. To get through he had done things he had never told his wife about, and never would. Was this what he had done those things for? To treat the sexually ambitious Paul Montpelier?

A tender grimace of apology creased Montpelier's wide face. 'Oh, boy. Shoot. I'm not doing this right, am I?'

'You're doing it fine,' Clint said, and for the next thirty minutes, he consciously put his doubts aside. They stretched the thing out; they looked at it from all sides; they discussed the difference between desire and need; they talked about Mrs Montpelier and her pedestrian (in Montpelier's opinion) bedroom preferences; they even took a surprisingly candid detour to visit Paul Montpelier's earliest adolescent sexual experience, when he had masturbated using the jaws of his little brother's stuffed crocodile.

Clint, according to his professional obligation, asked Montpelier if he'd ever considered harming himself. (No.) He wondered how Montpelier would feel if the roles were reversed? (He insisted that he'd tell her to do what she needed to do.) Where did Montpelier see himself in five years? (That's when the man in the white sweater vest started to weep.)

At the end of the session, Montpelier said he was already looking forward to the next, and as soon as he departed, Clint rang his service. He directed them to refer all of his calls to a psychiatrist in Maylock, the next town over. The operator asked him for how long.

'Until snow flurries are reported in hell,' said Clint. From the window he watched Montpelier back up his candy-red sports car and pull out of the lot, never to be seen again.

Next, he called Lila.

'Hello, Dr Norcross.' The feeling her voice gave him was what people meant – or should have meant – when they said their hearts sang. She asked him how his second day was going.

'The least self-aware man in America dropped in for a visit,' he said.

'Oh? My father was there? I bet the Hockney print confused him.'

She was quick, his wife, as quick as she was warm, and as tough as she was quick. Lila loved him, but she never stopped bumping him off his mark. Clint thought he probably needed that. Probably most men did.

'Ha-ha,' Clint had said. 'Listen, though: that opening you mentioned at the prison. Who did you hear about that from?'

There was a second or two of silence while his wife thought over the question's implications. She responded with a question of her own: 'Clint, is there something you need to tell me?'

Clint had not even considered that she might be disappointed by his decision to dump the private practice for the government one. He was sure she wouldn't be.

Thank God for Lila.

3

To apply the electric shaver to the gray stubble under his nose, Clint had to twist his face up so he looked like Quasimodo. A snow-white wire poked out from his left nostril. Anton could juggle barbells all he wanted, but white nostril hairs waited for every man, as did those that appeared in the ears. Clint managed to buzz this one away.

He had never been built like Anton, not even his last year in high school when the court granted him his independence and he lived on his own and ran track. Clint had been rangier, skinnier, stomach toneless but flat, like his son Jared. In his memory, Paul Montpelier was pudgier than the version of himself that Clint saw this morning. But he looked more like one than the other. Where was he now, Paul Montpelier? Had the crisis been resolved? Probably. Time healed all wounds. Of course, as some wag had pointed out, it also wounds all heels.

Clint had no more than the normal — i.e., healthy, totally conscious, and fantasy-based — longing to screw outside of his marriage. His situation wasn't, contra Paul Montpelier, a crisis of any kind. It was normal life as he understood it: a second look on the street at a pretty girl; an instinctive peek at a woman in a short skirt exiting a car; an almost subconscious lunging of lust for one of the models decorating *The Price Is Right*. It was a doleful thing, he supposed, doleful and perhaps a bit comic, the way age dragged you farther and farther from the body you liked the best and left those old instincts (not ambitions, thank God) behind, like the smell of cooking long after dinner has been consumed. And was he judging all men by himself? No. He was a member of the tribe, that was all. It was women who were the real riddles.

Clint smiled at himself in the mirror. He was clean-shaven. He was alive. He was about the same age as Paul Montpelier had been in 1999.

To the mirror he said, 'Hey, Anton: go fuck yourself.' The bravado was false, but at least he made the effort.

From the bedroom beyond the bathroom door he heard a lock click, a drawer open, a thump as Lila deposited her gunbelt in the drawer, shut it, and clicked it locked again. He heard her sigh and yawn.

In case she was already asleep, he dressed without speaking, and instead of sitting on the bed to put on his shoes, Clint picked them up to carry downstairs.

Lila cleared her throat. 'It's okay. I'm still awake.'

Clint wasn't sure that was entirely true: Lila had gotten as far as unsnapping the top button of her uniform pants before flopping on the bed. She hadn't even climbed under the blankets.

'You must be exhausted. I'll be right out. Everyone all right on Mountain?'

The previous night she'd texted that there was a crack-up on the Mountain Rest Road – *Don't stay up.* While this wasn't unheard of, it was unusual. He and Jared had grilled steaks and polished off a couple of Anchor Steams on the deck.

'Trailer came unhitched. From Pet-Whatever. The chain store? Went over on its side, blocked the whole road. Cat litter and dog food all over. We ended up having to bulldoze it out of the way.'

'That sounds like a shit-show.' He bent down and put a kiss on her cheek. 'Hey. You want to start jogging together?' The idea had just occurred to him and he was immediately cheered. You couldn't stop your body from breaking down and thickening, but you could fight back.

Lila opened her right eye, pale green in the dimness of the room with the curtains pulled. 'Not this morning.'

'Of course not,' Clint said. He hung over her, thinking she was going to kiss him back, but she just told him to have a good day, and make sure Jared took out the trash. The eye rolled closed. A flash of green . . . and gone.

4

The smell in the shed was almost too much to bear.

Evie's bare skin pebbled up and she had to fight not to retch. The stench was a mingling of scorched chemicals, old leaf smoke, and food that had spoiled.

One of the moths was in her hair, nestled and pulsing reassurance against her scalp. She breathed as shallowly as she could and scanned around.

The prefab shed was set up for cooking drugs. In the center of the space was a gas stove attached by yellowish tubes to a pair of white canisters. On a counter against the wall there were trays, jugs of water, an open package of Ziploc bags, test tubes, pieces of cork, countless dead matches, a one-hitter with a charred bowl, and a utility sink connected to a hose that ran away and out under the netting that Evie had pulled back to enter. Empty bottles and dented cans on the floor. A wobbly-looking lawn chair with a Dale Earnhardt Jr logo stamped on the back. Balled up in the corner, a gray checked shirt.

Evie shook the stiffness and at least some of the filth from the shirt, then drew it on. The tails hung down over her bottom and thighs. Until recently, this garment had belonged to someone disgusting. A California-shaped stain running down the chest area reported that the disgusting person liked mayonnaise.

She squatted down by the tanks and yanked the yellowing tubes loose. Then she turned the knobs on the propane tanks a quarter inch each.

Outside the shed again, netting drawn closed behind her, Evie paused to take deep breaths of the fresher air.

Three hundred feet or so down the wooded embankment stood a trailer fronted by a gravel apron with a truck and two cars parked on it. Three gutted rabbits, one of which was still dripping, hung from a clothesline alongside a few faded pairs of panties and a jean jacket. Puffs of woodsmoke rose from the trailer's chimney.

Back the way she came, through the thin forest and across the field, the Tree was no longer visible. She wasn't alone, though: moths furred the roof of the shed, fluttering and shifting.

Evie started down the embankment. Deadwood branches stabbed her feet, and a rock cut her heel. She didn't break stride. She was a fast healer. By the clothesline, she paused to listen. She heard a man laughing, a television playing, and ten thousand worms in the little patch of ground around her, sweetening the soil.

The rabbit that was still bleeding rolled its foggy eyes at her. She asked it what the deal was.

'Three men, one woman,' the rabbit said. A single fly flew from its tattered black lips, buzzed around, and zoomed into the cavity of a limp ear. Evie heard the fly pinging around in there. She didn't blame the fly – it was doing what a fly was made to do – but she mourned the rabbit, who did not deserve such a dirty fate. While Evie loved all animals, she was especially fond of the smaller ones, those creepers of meadow and leapers of deadfall, the fragile-winged and the scuttling.

She cupped her hand behind the dying rabbit's head, and gently brought its crusted black mouth to hers. 'Thank you,' Evie whispered, and let it be quiet.

5

One benefit of living in this particular corner of Appalachia was that you could afford a decent-sized home on two government salaries. The Norcross home was a three-bedroom contemporary in a development of similar houses. The houses were handsome, spacious without being grotesque, had lawns adequate for playing catch, and views that, in the green seasons, were lush, hilly and leafy. What was a little depressing about the development was that even at reduced prices almost half of its rather attractive houses were empty. The demonstrator home at the top of the hill was the one exception; that one was kept clean and shiny and furnished. Lila said it was just a matter of time before a meth-head broke into it and tried to set up shop. Clint had told her not to worry, he knew the sheriff. In fact, they had a semi-regular thing.

('She's into old guys?' Lila had replied, batting her eyes and pressing herself to his hip.)

The upstairs of the Norcross house contained the master bedroom, Jared's room, and a third bedroom, which the two adults used as a home office. On the first floor the kitchen was wide and open, separated from the family room by a counter bar. At the right side of the family room, behind closed French doors, was their little-used dining room.

Clint drank coffee and read the *New York Times* on his iPad at the kitchen bar. An earthquake in North Korea had caused an untold number of casualties. The North Korean government insisted that the damage was minor due to 'superior architecture,' but there was cell phone footage of dusty bodies and rubble. An oil rig was burning in the Gulf of Aden, probably as a result of sabotage, but no one was claiming responsibility. Every country in the region had done the diplomatic equivalent of a bunch of boys who knock out a window playing baseball and run home without looking back. In the New Mexico desert the FBI was on day forty-four of its standoff with a militia led by Kinsman Brightleaf (née Scott David Winstead Jr). This happy band refused to pay its taxes, accept the legality of the Constitution, or surrender its stockpile of automatic weapons. When people learned that Clint was a psychiatrist, they often entreated him to diagnose the mental diseases of politicians, celebrities, and other notables. He usually demurred, but in this instance he felt comfortable making a long distance diagnosis: Kinsman Brightleaf was suffering from some kind of dissociative disorder.

At the bottom of the front page was a photo of a hollow-faced young woman standing in front of an Appalachian shack with an infant in her arms: 'Cancer in Coal Country.' This made Clint recall the chemical spill in a local river five years ago. It had caused a week-long shutdown of the water supply. Everything was supposedly fine now, but Clint and his family stuck to bottled drinking water just to be sure.

Sun warmed his face. He looked out toward the big twin elm trees at the back of the yard, beyond the edge of the pool deck. The elms made him think of brothers, of sisters, of husbands and wives – he was sure that, beneath the ground, their roots were mortally entwined. Dark green mountains knuckled up in the distance. Clouds seemed to be melting on the pan of the fair blue sky. Birds flew and sang. Wasn't it a hell of a shame, the way good country got wasted on folks. That was another thing that an old wag had told him.

Clint liked to believe it wasn't wasted on him. He had never expected to own a view like this one. He wondered how decrepit and soft he'd have to grow before it made sense, the good luck that some people got, and the bad luck that saddled others.

'Hey, Dad. How's the world? Anything good happening?'

Clint turned from the window to see Jared stroll into the kitchen zipping up his backpack.

'Hold on—' He flicked through a couple of electronic pages. He didn't want to send his son off to school with an oil spill, a militia, or cancer. Ah, just the thing. 'Physicists are theorizing that the universe might go on forever.'

Jared pawed through the snack cabinet, found a Nutribar, stuck it in his pocket. 'And you think that's good? Can you explain what you mean?'

Clint considered for a second before he realized that his son was busting his balls. 'I see what you did there.' As he looked over at Jared he used his middle finger to scratch at his eyelid.

'You don't have to be shy about this, Dad. You have son–father privilege. It all stays between us.' Jared helped himself to the coffee. He took it black, the way Clint used to when his stomach was young.

The coffeemaker was near the sink, where the window opened on to the deck. Jared sipped and took in the view. 'Wow. Are you sure you should leave Mom here alone with Anton?'

'Please go,' Clint said. 'Go to school and learn something.'

His son had grown up on him. 'Dog!' had been Jared's first word, spoken so that it rhymed with *brogue*. 'Dog! Dog!' He had been a likable boy, inquisitive and well-intentioned, and he had developed into a likable young man, still inquisitive and well-intentioned. Clint took pride in how the safe, secure home they had provided Jared had allowed him to become more and more himself. It hadn't been like that for Clint.

He had been toying with the idea of giving the kid condoms, but he didn't want to talk to Lila about it and he didn't want to encourage anything. He didn't want to be thinking about it at all. Jared insisted he and Mary were just friends, and maybe Jared even believed it. Clint saw how he looked at the girl, though, and it was the way you looked at someone you wanted to be your very, very close friend.

'Little League Shake,' Jared said, and held out his hands. 'You still know it?'

Clint did: bump fists, pop and lock thumbs, twist hands, *smooth* down the palms, then clap them together twice overhead. Though it had been a long time, it went perfectly, and they both laughed. It put a shine on the morning.

Jared was out and gone before Clint remembered that he was supposed to tell his son to take out the trash.

Another part of getting older: you forgot what you wanted to remember, and remembered what you wanted to forget. He could be the old wag that said that. He should get a pillow stitched with it.

6

Having been on Good Report for sixty days, Jeanette Sorley had common room privileges three mornings a week, between eight and nine in the morning. In reality that meant between eight and eight fifty-five, because her six-hour shift in the carpentry shed began at nine. There she would spend her time inhaling varnish through a thin cotton mask and turning out chair legs. For this she made three dollars an hour. The money went into an account that would be paid to her by check when she got out (inmates called their work accounts Free Parking, like in Monopoly). The chairs themselves were sold in the prison store across Route 17. Some went for sixty dollars, most for eighty, and the prison sold a lot of them. Jeanette didn't know where that money went, and didn't care. Having common room privileges, though, she did care about. There was a big TV, boardgames, and magazines. There was also a snack machine and a soda machine that only worked on quarters, and

inmates did not *have* quarters, quarters were considered contraband
– Catch-22! – but at least you could window-shop. (Plus, the
common room became, at appointed times of the week, the visitors'
room, and veteran visitors, like Jeanette's son Bobby, knew to bring
lots of quarters.)

This morning she was sitting beside Angel Fitzroy, watching the
morning report on WTRF, Channel 7 out of Wheeling. The news
was the usual stew: a drive-by shooting, a transformer fire, a woman
arrested for assaulting another woman at the Monster Truck Jam,
the state legislature having an argle-bargle over a new men's prison
that had been built on a mountaintop removal site and appeared
to have structural problems. On the national front, the Kinsman
Brightleaf siege continued. On the other side of the globe, thousands
were thought dead in a North Korean earthquake, and doctors in
Australia were reporting an outbreak of sleeping sickness that seemed
to affect only women.

'That'd be meth,' Angel Fitzroy said. She was nibbling a Twix she
had found in the snack machine's dispenser tray. Making it last.

'Which? The sleeping women, the chick at the Monster Truck
Jam, or the reality show-type guy?'

'Could be all, but I was thinking of the chick at the Jam. I was
at one of those once, and damn near everbody oncept the kiddies
was coked up or smoked up. You want some of this?' She cupped
the remains of the Twix in her hand (in case Officer Lampley was
currently monitoring one of the common room cameras), and
offered it to Jeanette. 'It ain't so stale as some of them in there.'

'I'll pass,' Jeanette said.

'Sometimes I see something makes me wish I was dead,' Angel
said matter-of-factly. 'Or wish everbody else was. Lookit that.' She
pointed to a new poster between the snack machine and the soft
drink dispenser. It showed a sand dune with footprints leading away,
seemingly into infinity. Below the photo was this message: THE
CHALLENGE IS GETTING THERE.

'The guy got there, but where did he go? Where *is* that place?'
Angel wanted to know.

'Iraq?' Jeanette asked. 'He's probably at the next oasis.'

'Nope, he's dead of heatstroke. Just a-layin out there just where you can't see, eyes all buggin out and skin black as a top hat.' She didn't smile. Angel was a tweaker, and serious country: bark-chewing, baptized-in-a-moonshine-still country. Assault was what they got her for, but Jeanette guessed Angel could have hit most of the categories on a criminal scorecard. Her face was all bones and angles – it looked hard enough to break up pavement. She had spent a goodly amount of time in C Wing during her stay at Dooling. In C Wing you only got out two hours a day. It was bad-girl country, was C Wing.

'I don't think you turn black even if you die of heatstroke in Iraq,' Jeanette said. It could be a mistake to disagree (even humorously) with Angel, who had what Dr Norcross liked to call 'anger issues,' but this morning Jeanette felt like living dangerously.

'My point is, that's a crock of shit,' Angel said. 'The challenge is just livin through fuckin today, as you probly well know.'

'Who do you think put it up? Dr Norcross?'

Angel snorted. 'Norcross has got more sense. No, that's Warden Coates. *Jaaaanice*. Honey's big on motivation. Seen the one in her office?'

Jeanette had – an oldie, but not a goodie. It showed a kitten hanging from a tree branch. Hang in there, baby, indeed. Most of the kitties in this place had already fallen off their branches. Some were out of their trees.

The TV news was now showing the mug shot of an escaped convict. 'Oh man,' Angel said. 'He put the lie to black is beautiful, don't he?'

Jeanette did not comment. The fact was, she still liked guys with mean eyes. She was working on it with Dr Norcross, but for the time being she was stuck with this attraction to fellows who looked like they might at any moment decide to take a wire whisk to your bare back while you were in the shower.

'McDavid's in one of Norcross's babysitting cells in A Wing,' Angel said.

'Where did you hear that?' Kitty McDavid was one of Jeanette's favorite people – smart and feisty. Rumor was that Kitty had rolled with a heavy crowd on the outside, but there was no real meanness in her, except for the kind that was self-directed. She had been a deeply dedicated cutter at some point in the past; the scars were on her breasts, sides, upper thighs. And she was prone to periods of depression, although whatever meds Norcross had her on seemed to have been helping with that.

'You want all the news, you got to get in here early. I heard it from her.' Angel pointed at Maura Dunbarton, an elderly trustee who was in for life. Maura was now placing magazines from her wheelie cart on the tables, doing it with infinite care and precision. Her white hair stood out around her head in a filmy corona. Her legs were clad in heavy support hose the color of cotton candy.

'Maura!' Jeanette called – but low. Shouting in the common room was strictly *verboten*, except by kids on visiting days and inmates on the monthly Party Nites. 'Walk this way, girlfriend!'

Maura rolled her cart slowly toward them. 'Got a *Seventeen*,' she said. 'Either of you interested?'

'I wasn't interested when I was seventeen,' Jeanette said. 'What's up with Kitty?'

'Screaming half the night,' Maura said. 'Surprised you didn't hear her. They pulled her out of her cell, gave her a needle, and put her in A. Sleeping now.'

'Screaming what?' Angel asked. 'Or just screaming?'

'Screaming that the Black Queen is coming,' Maura said. 'Says she'll be here today.'

'Aretha coming to put on a show?' Angel asked. 'She's the only black queen I know.'

Maura paid no attention. She was gazing at the blue-eyed blonde on the cover of the magazine. 'Sure neither of you wants this *Seventeen*? There's some nice party dresses.'

Angel said, 'I don't wear no dress like that unless I have my tiara,' and laughed.

'Has Dr Norcross seen Kitty?' Jeanette asked.

'Not in yet,' Maura said. 'I had a party dress once. Real pretty blue, poofy. My husband burned a hole in it with the iron. It was an accident. He was trying to help. No one ever taught him how to iron, though. Most men never learn. And he won't now, that's for sure.'

Neither of them replied. What Maura Dunbarton did to her husband and two children was well known. It happened thirty years ago, but some crimes are unforgettable.

7

Three or four years earlier – or maybe five or six; the aughts had sort of sprinted away on her and the landmarks were hazy – in a parking lot behind a Kmart in North Carolina a man told Tiffany Jones she was headed for trouble. Vaporous as the last decade and a half had been, this moment had stayed with her. Seagulls were screeching and picking at the trash around the Kmart loading dock. Drizzle streaked the window glass of the Jeep she was sitting in, which belonged to the guy who said she was headed for trouble. The guy was mall fuzz. She had just given him a blowjob.

What happened was he caught her shoplifting deodorant. The *quid pro quo* they'd agreed on had been fairly straightforward and unsurprising; she gave him oral sex, he let her go. He was a beefy son of a bitch. It had been quite an operation, getting access to his dick while negotiating his gut and thighs and the steering wheel of his car. But Tiffany had done a lot of things and this was so minor by comparison it wouldn't even have made the long list, except for what he said.

'Gotta be a bummer for you, huh?' A sympathetic grimace spread across his sweaty face as he wiggled around in his seat, trying to yank up his bright red plastic jogging pants that were probably the only thing he could get in his pig size. 'You know you are headed for trouble when you find yourself in a situation like this here where you have to cooperate with somebody like me.'

Until this point Tiffany had assumed that abusers – people like her cousin Truman – must live in denial. If not, how could they go on? How could you hurt or degrade a person when you were fully cognizant of what you were doing? Well, it turned out you could – and men like the pig of a security guard did. It had been a real shock, this realization that abruptly explained so much of her entire shitty life. Tiffany was not sure she had ever gotten over it.

Three or four moths rattled around inside the bubble of the light fixture set above the counter. The bulb was burned out. It didn't matter; there was plenty of morning light in the trailer. The moths binged and fluttered, their little shadows bickering. How did they get in there? And by the way, how did she get *here*? For awhile, after some rough times in her late teens, Tiffany had managed to build a life. She had been waiting tables at a bistro in 2006, and making good tips. She had a two-room apartment in Charlottesville and grew ferns on the balcony. Doing pretty good for a high school drop out. On the weekends she had liked to rent a big bay horse named Moline who had a sweet disposition and an easy canter, and go riding at Shenandoah. Now she was in a trailer in East Shitballs, Appalachia, and she was no longer just headed for trouble; she was there. At least the trouble was wrapped in cotton, though. It didn't sting the way you expected trouble to sting, which was maybe the worst thing about it, because you were so far inside, trapped all the way back in the last row of yourself, where you couldn't even—

Tiffany heard a thump and all at once she was on the floor. Her hip throbbed where it had banged against the edge of the counter.

Cigarette dangling off his lip, Truman stared down at her.

'Earth to crack whore.' He was in his cowboy boots and boxer shorts and nothing else. The flesh of his torso was as tight as plastic wrap over his ribs. 'Earth to crack whore,' Truman repeated and clapped his hands in front of her face like she was a bad dog. 'Can't you hear? Someone's knocking on the door.'

Tru was such an asshole that, in the part of Tiffany where she was still alive – the part where she occasionally felt the urge to brush her hair or call that Elaine woman from the Planned Parenthood clinic who wanted her to agree to sign up on a list for a lockdown detox – she sometimes regarded him with scientific amazement. Tru was an asshole standard. Tiffany would ask herself, 'Is so-and-so a bigger asshole than Truman?' Few could compare – in fact, so far, officially, there was only Donald Trump and cannibals.

Truman's record of malfeasance was lengthy. As a boy he had stuck his finger up his butt and jammed it into the nostrils of smaller kids. Later, he had stolen from his mother, pawned her jewelry and her antiques. He had turned Tiffany on to meth that afternoon he'd swung by to see her at the nice apartment in Charlottesville. His idea of a prank was to poke you in the bare flesh of your shoulder with a lit cigarette while you were sleeping. Truman was a rapist, but had never done time for it. Some assholes just struck lucky. His face was patterned with an uneven growth of red-gold beard, and his eyes were enormous with pupil, but the sneering, unapologetic boy he'd always been was there in the jut of his jaw.

'Crack whore, come in.'

'What?' Tiffany managed to ask.

'I told you to answer the door! Jesus Christ!' Truman feinted a punch and she covered her head with her hands. She blinked tears.

'Fuck you,' she said half-heartedly. She hoped Dr Flickinger didn't hear. He was in the bathroom. Tiffany liked the doctor. The doc was a trip. He always called her Madame and threw a wink to let her know he wasn't making fun.

'You are a toothless deaf crack whore,' Truman announced, over-looking the fact that he was himself in need of cosmetic dental surgery.

Truman's friend came out of the trailer's bedroom, sat down at the foldout table, and said, 'Crack whore phone home.' He giggled at his joke and did an elbow jig. Tiffany couldn't remember his name, but she hoped his mother was super proud of her son who had the *South Park* poop tattooed on his Adam's apple.

A knock at the door. This time Tiffany did register it, a firm double-rap.

'Never mind! Wouldn't want to trouble you, Tiff. Just sit right there on your dumb ass.' Truman yanked open the door.

A woman was standing there in one of Truman's checked shirts, a length of olive-toned leg visible beneath.

'What's this?' Truman asked her. 'What you want?'

The voice that answered him was faint. 'Hello, man.'

From his seat at the table Truman's friend called out, 'Are you the Avon Lady, or what?'

'Listen, honey,' Truman said to her. 'You're welcome to come in
– but I believe I'm going to need that shirt back.'

That made Truman's friend laugh. 'This is amazing! I mean, this
your birthday or what, Tru?'

From the bathroom, Tiffany heard the flush of the toilet. Dr
Flickinger had finished his business.

The woman at the door shot a hand out and grabbed Truman's
neck. He made a little wheezing noise; his cigarette popped from
his mouth. He reached up and dug his fingers into the visitor's
wrist. Tiffany saw the flesh of the woman's hand whiten under the
pressure, but she didn't let go.

Red spots appeared on Truman's cheekbones. Blood trickled from
the gashes his fingernails were making in the woman's wrist. She
still didn't let go. The wheezing noise narrowed to a whistle. Truman's
free hand found the grip of the Bowie knife tucked into his belt
and pulled it loose.

The woman stepped into the room, her other hand catching the
forearm of Truman's knife hand in mid-stab. She backed him up,
slamming him against the opposite wall of the trailer. It happened
so quickly that Tiffany was never able to capture the stranger's face,
only the screen of her tangled, shoulder-length hair, which was so
dark it seemed to have a green tint.

'Whoa, whoa, whoa,' said Truman's friend, scrabbling for the pistol
behind a roll of paper towels and rising up from his chair.

On Truman's cheeks the red spots had expanded into purple
clouds. He was making a noise like sneakers squeaking on hardwood,
his grimace slipping into a sad clown droop. His eyes rolled. Tiffany
could see his heartbeat pulsing in the taut skin to the left of his
breastbone. The woman's strength was astonishing.

'Whoa,' Truman's friend said yet again, as the woman head-butted
Truman. Tru's nose broke with a firecracker snap.

A thread of blood lashed across the ceiling, a few droplets splashing
on the bubble of the light fixture. The moths were going crazy,
battering themselves against the fixture, the sound like an ice cube
being shaken around in a glass.

When Tiffany's eyes slipped back down, she saw the woman

swinging Truman's body toward the table. Truman's friend stood and pointed his gun. The crash of a stone bowling ball boomed through the trailer. An irregular-shaped puzzle piece appeared in Truman's forehead. A ragged handkerchief fell across Truman's eye, skin with a section of eyebrow attached, torn loose and hanging down. Blood overspread Truman's sagging mouth and slid down his chin. The flap of skin with his eyebrow on it flopped against his cheek. Tiffany thought of the mop-like sponges at the carwash that swabbed the windshield.

A second shot ripped a hole through Truman's shoulder, blood misted over Tiffany's face, and the woman barreled Truman's corpse into Truman's friend. The table collapsed under the weight of the three bodies. Tiffany couldn't hear her own screaming.

Time jumped.

Tiffany found herself in the corner of the closet, a raincoat pulled up to her chin. A series of muffled, rhythmic thuds made the trailer sway back and forth on its foundation. Tiffany was cast back to a memory of the Charlottesville bistro's kitchen all those years earlier, the chef using a mallet to pound veal. The thuds were like that, except much, much heavier. There was a pop of ripping metal and plastic, then the thuds ceased. The trailer stopped moving.

A knock shook the closet door.

'Are you okay?' It was the woman.

'Go 'way!' Tiffany howled.

'The one in the bathroom got out the window. I don't think you have to worry about him.'

'What did you do?' Tiffany sobbed. Truman's blood was on her and she didn't want to die.

The woman didn't answer right away. Not that she needed to. Tiffany had seen what she had done, or seen enough. And heard enough.

'You should rest now,' said the woman. 'Just rest.'

A few seconds later Tiffany thought she heard, through the sound baffles left by the gunfire, the click of the exterior door shutting.

She huddled under the raincoat and moaned Truman's name.

He had taught her how to smoke dope – take small sips, he said.

'You'll feel better.' What a liar. What a bastard he had been, what a monster. So why was she crying over him? She couldn't help it. She wished she could, but she couldn't.

8

The Avon Lady who was not an Avon Lady walked away from the trailer and back toward the meth lab. The smell of propane grew stronger with each step until the air was rancid with it. Her footprints appeared behind her, white and small and delicate, shapes that came from nowhere and seemed to be made of milkweed fluff. The hem of her borrowed shirt fluttered around her long thighs.

In front of the shed she plucked up a piece of paper caught in a bush. At the top, in big blue letters, it announced EVERYTHING IS ON SALE EVERY DAY! Below this were pictures of refrigerator units both large and small, washing machines, dishwashers, microwave ovens, vacuum cleaners, Dirt Devils, trash compactors, food processors, more. One picture showed a trim young woman in jeans smiling knowingly down upon her daughter, who was blond like Mom. The pretty tyke held a plastic baby in her arms and smiled down upon it. There were also large TVs showing men playing football, men playing baseball, men in racing cars, and grill set-ups beside which stood men with giant forks and giant tongs. Although it did not come right out and say so, the message of this advertising circular was clear: women work and nest while men grill the kill.

Evie rolled the advertising circular into a tube and began to snap the fingers of her left hand beneath the protruding end. A spark jumped at each snap. On the third one, the paper flared alight. Evie could grill, too. She held the tube up, examined the flame, and tossed it into the shed. She walked away at a brisk pace, cutting through the woods toward Route 43, known to the locals as Ball's Hill Road.

'Busy day,' she said to the moths once more circling her. 'Busy, busy day.'

When the shed blew she did not turn around, nor did she flinch when a piece of corrugated steel whickered over her head.

CHAPTER 2

1

The Dooling County sheriff's station dozed in the morning sun. The three holding cells were empty, barred doors standing open, floors freshly washed and smelling of disinfectant. The single interview room was likewise empty, as was Lila Norcross's office. Linny Mars, the dispatcher, had the place to herself. Behind her desk hung a poster of a snarling, buffed-out con wearing an orange jumpsuit and curling a couple of hand barbells. THEY NEVER TAKE A DAY OFF, the poster advised, AND NEITHER SHOULD YOU!

Linny made a practice of ignoring this well-meant advice. She had not worked out since a brief fling with Dancercise at the YWCA, but did take pride in her appearance. Now she was absorbed in an article in *Marie Claire* about the proper way to put on eyeliner. To get a stable line, one began by pressing one's pinky against one's cheekbone. This allowed more control and insured against any sudden twitches. The article suggested starting in the middle and working one's way to the far corner of the eye, then going to the nose side and working one's way in to complete the look. A thin line for daywear; a thicker, more dramatic one for that important night out with the guy you hoped would—

The phone rang. Not the regular line, but the one with the red stripe on the handset. Linny put *Marie Claire* down (reminding herself to stop by the Rite Aid and get some L'Oreal Opaque) and picked up the phone. She had been catching in Dispatch for five years now, and at this time of the morning it was apt to be a cat up a tree, a lost dog, a kitchen mishap, or – she hoped not – a choking incident with a toddler involved. The weapons-related shit almost always happened after the sun went down, and usually involved the Squeaky Wheel.

'911, what is your emergency?'

'The Avon Lady killed Tru!' a woman shouted. 'She killed Tru and Tru's friend! I don't know his name, but she put his fuckin head right through the fuckin wall! If I look at that again, I'll go blind!'

'Ma'am, all 911 calls are recorded,' Linny said, 'and we do not appreciate pranks.'

'I ain't prankin! Who's prankin? Some random bitch just came in here, killed Tru! Tru and the other guy! There's blood ever'where!'

Linny had been ninety percent sure that this was a prank or a crank when the slurry voice mentioned the Avon Lady; now she was eighty percent sure that it was for real. The woman was blubbering almost too hard to be understood, and her piney woods accent was as thick as a brick. If Linny hadn't come from Mink Crossing in Kanawha County, she might have thought her caller was speaking a foreign language.

'What is your name, ma'am?'

'Tiffany Jones, but ne'mine me! They's dead and I don't know why she let me live, but what if she comes back?'

Linny hunched forward, studying today's duty sheet – who was in, who was on patrol. The sheriff's department had only nine cars, and one or two were almost always in the shop. Dooling County was the smallest county in the state, although not quite the poorest; that dubious honor went to neighboring McDowell County, splat in the middle of nowhere.

'I don't see your number on my screen.'

'Course you don't. It's one of Tru's burners. He does somethin to em. He—' There was a pause, a crackle, and Tiffany Jones's voice at once receded and pitched higher. '—oh my Christ, the lab just blew! Why'd she do that for? Oh, my Christ, oh, my Christ, oh—'

Linny started to ask what she was talking about, and then heard a rumbling boom. It wasn't particularly loud, it didn't rattle the windows, but it was a boom, all right. As if a jet from Langley over in Virginia had broken the sound barrier.

How fast does sound travel? she wondered. Didn't we learn that formula in physics class? But high school physics had been a long time ago. Almost in another life.

'Tiffany? Tiffany Jones? Are you still there?'

'You get someone out here before the woods catch afire!' Tiffany screamed this so loudly that Linny held the phone away from her ear. 'Follow your damn nose! Watch the smoke! It's pilin up already! Out Ball's Hill, past the Ferry and the lumberyard!'

'This woman, the one you called the Avon Lady—'

Tiffany began to laugh as she cried. 'Oh, cops goan know her if they see her. She'll be the one covered in Truman Mayweather's blood.'

'May I have your ad—'

'Trailer don't have no address! Tru don't take mail! Just shut your gob and get someone out here!'

With that, Tiffany was gone.

Linny crossed the empty main office and went out into the morning sun. A number of people were standing on the Main Street sidewalks, shading their eyes and looking east. In that direction, maybe three miles distant, black smoke was rising. Nice and straight, not ribboning, and thank God for that. And yes, it was near Adams Lumberyard, a place she knew well, first from pickup truck trips out there with her daddy and then from pickup truck trips out there with her husband. Men had many strange fascinations. Lumberyards seemed to be one of them, probably falling somewhere just ahead of bigfoot trucks but well behind gun shows.

'What do we got?' called Drew T. Barry of Drew T. Barry Indemnity, standing outside his storefront across the street.

Linny could practically see the columned figures of premiums scrolling across the backs of Drew T. Barry's eyes. She returned inside without answering him, first to call the fire department (where phones would already be ringing, she guessed), then Terry Coombs and Roger Elway in Unit Four, then the boss. Who was probably asleep after calling in sick the previous night.

2

But Lila Norcross wasn't asleep.

She had read in a magazine article, probably while waiting to have her teeth cleaned or her eyes checked, that it took the average person fifteen to thirty minutes to fall asleep. There was a caveat, however, of which Lila hardly needed to be informed: one needed to be in a calm state of mind, and she was not in that state. For one thing, she was still dressed, although she had unsnapped her pants and unbuttoned her brown uniform shirt. She had also taken off her utility belt. She felt guilty. She wasn't used to lying to her husband about little things, and had never lied about a really big thing until this morning.

Crack-up on Mountain Rest Road, she had texted. *Don't try calling, we need to get the mess cleaned up.* This morning she had even added a bit of verisimilitude that now pricked her like a thorn: *Cat litter all over the highway! Needed a bulldozer!* But a thing like that would be in Dooling's weekly paper, wouldn't it? Only Clint never read it, so perhaps that would be all right. But people would talk about such a humorous happenstance, and when they didn't, he'd wonder . . .

'He wants to be caught,' she had said to Clint when they were watching an HBO documentary – *The Jinx*, it was called – about a rich and eccentric serial killer named Robert Durst. This was early in the second of six episodes. 'He would never have agreed to talk to those documentary guys if he didn't.' And sure enough, Robert Durst was currently back in jail. The question was, did *she* want to be caught?

If not, why had she texted him in the first place? She told herself at the time it was because if he called and heard the background noise in the Coughlin High School gymnasium – the cheering crowd, the squeak of sneakers on the hardwood, the blare of the horn – he would naturally ask where she was and what she was doing there. But she could have let his call go to voicemail, right? And returned it later?

I didn't think of it, she told herself. I was nervous and I was upset.

True or false? This morning she leaned toward the latter. That she had been weaving a tangled web on purpose. That she wanted to force Clint to force her to confess, and for him to be the one to pull the unraveling string.

It occurred to her, ruefully, that for all her years of experience in law enforcement, it was her husband, the psychiatrist, who would make the far better criminal. Clint knew how to keep a secret.

Lila felt as though she'd discovered that there was a whole other floor in her home. Quite by accident she had pressed a certain scuffed spot on the wall and a stairwell had been revealed. Just inside the secret passage was a hook and draped on that hook was a jacket of Clint's. The shock was bad, the pain was worse, but neither compared to the shame: How could you fail to perceive? And once you did become aware, once you did wake up to the reality of your life, how could you live a second longer without screaming it out loud? If the discovery that your husband, a man you had spoken to every day for over fifteen years, the father of your child, had a daughter that he had never mentioned – if that didn't warrant a scream, a throat-ripping howl of rage and hurt, then what did? Instead, she had wished him a good day, and lain down.

Weariness at last began to catch up and iron out her distress. She was finally going down, and that was good. This would look simpler after five or six hours of sleep; she would feel more settled; she would be able to talk to him; and maybe Clint could help her understand. That was his job, wasn't it? Making sense of life's messes. Well, did she ever have a mess for him! Cat litter all over the road. Cat shit in the secret passage, cat litter *and* cat shit on the basketball court, where a girl named Sheila dropped her shoulder, making the defender scramble back, then crossed over and headed for the hoop.

A tear dripped down her cheek and she exhaled, close to the escape of sleep.

Something tickled her face. It felt like a strand of hair or maybe an errant thread from the pillowcase. She brushed it away, slipped a little deeper toward true sleep, and was almost there when her phone bugled at her from the utility belt laid across the cedar chest at the foot of the bed.

She opened her eyes and swam into a sitting position. That thread or hair or whatever it was brushed her cheek; she swatted it away. Clint, if that's you—

She got the phone, stared at the screen. Not Clint. The single word was BASE. The clock read 7:57 A.M. Lila thumbed ACCEPT.

'Sheriff? Lila? Are you up?'

'No, Linny, this is all a dream.'

'I think we might have a big problem.'

Linny was clipped and professional. Lila gave her full marks for that, but her accent had crept back into her voice, not *I think* we have a big problem but *Ah thank*, which meant she was serious and worried. Lila popped her eyes wide, as if that would help her wake up faster.

'Caller reported multiple homicides out by Adams Lumberyard. She might have been wrong about that, or lying, or even hallucinating, but there certainly was one hell of a bang. You didn't hear it?'

'No. Tell me exactly what you got.'

'I can play the call—'

'Just tell me.'

Linny told her: stoned woman, hysterical, says there's two dead, Avon Lady did the deed, explosion, visible smoke.

'And you sent—'

'Unit Four. Terry and Roger. According to their last call-in, they're less than a mile away.'

'Okay. Good.'

'Are you—'

'On my way.'

3

She was halfway to the cruiser parked in the driveway when she became aware of Anton Dubcek staring at her. Shirtless, pecs gleaming, pants riding (barely) the spars of his hipbones, the pool guy appeared to be auditioning for the position of May pin-up boy on a Chippendales calendar. He was at the curb by his van, retrieving some piece of pool cleaning equipment. '*Anton the Pool Guy*' written on the side in Florentine script.

'What are you looking at?'

'Morning glory,' Anton said, and favored her with a radiant smile that had probably charmed every barmaid in the Tri-Counties.

She looked down and saw that she had neither tucked in nor buttoned her shirt. The plain white bra beneath showed a lot less than either of her two bikini tops (and a lot less glamorously), but there was something about men and underwear; they saw a girl in a bra, and it was like they had just won fifty on a five-buck Dollars 'N' Dirt scratch ticket. Hell, Madonna had made a career of it back in the day. Probably before Anton was born, she realized.

'Does that line work, Anton?' Buttoning and tucking in. 'Ever?'

The smile widened. 'You'd be surprised.'

Ah, such white teeth. She wouldn't be surprised.

'Back door's open, if you want a Coke. Lock it behind you when you leave, okay?'

'Roger-wilco.' He snapped off a half-assed salute.

'And no beer. It's too early even for you.'

'It's always five o'clock somewh—'

'Spare me the lyrics, Anton. It was a long night and if I don't manage some shut-eye down the line, it's going to be a long day.'

'Roger that, too. But hey, Sheriff, I got bad news: pretty sure you got Dutch Elm out back. You want me to leave you the phone number for my tree guy? You're not going to want to let that—'

'Whatever, thanks.' Lila didn't care about the trees, not this morning, although she had to appreciate the thoroughness of the bad timing: her lies, Clint's omissions, exhaustion, fire, corpses, and now infested trees, all before nine o'clock. The only thing missing was Jared breaking an arm or something, and Lila would have no choice but to go to St Luke's and beg for Father Lafferty to take her confession.

She backed down the driveway, headed east on Tremaine Street,

did a California stop that would have earned her a ticket if she
hadn't been the sheriff, saw the smoke rising out Route 17 way,
and hit the jackpot lights. She'd save the siren for the three blocks
that constituted downtown Dooling. Give everyone a thrill.

4

At the traffic light across from the high school, Frank Geary tapped
his fingers against the steering wheel. He was on his way to Judge
Silver's house. The old judge had called him on his cell phone; by
the sound he'd barely been holding it together. His cat, Cocoa, had
been struck by a car.

A familiar homeless woman, bundled in so many layers of garments
that you couldn't see her feet, crossed in front of his truck, pushing
her shopping cart. She was talking to herself with a bright, amused
expression. Maybe one of her personalities was planning a surprise
birthday party for one of her other personalities. He sometimes
thought it would be nice to be crazy, not crazy like Elaine seemed
to think he was, but actually crazy, talking-to-yourself-and-pushing-
a-shopping-cart-full-of-garbage-bags-and-the-top-half-of-a-male-
mannequin crazy.

What reason did insane people have to worry? Crazy reasons,
probably, though in his fantasy of madness, Frank liked to imagine
it was simpler. Do I pour the milk and cereal over my head, or do
I pour it all into the mailbox? If you were bonkers, perhaps that
was a stressful decision. For Frank, there was the stress of the
upcoming annual cutbacks in the Dooling Municipal Budget that
might put him out of work, and there was the stress of trying to
hold it together for the weekends when he saw his daughter, and
then there was the stress of knowing that Elaine expected him not
to be able to hold it together. His own wife rooting against him,
how was that for stress? Milk and cereal over the head or into the
mailbox, by comparison, he thought he could handle with no
problem. Cereal over the head, milk in the mailbox. There. Problem
solved.

The light turned green and Frank swung left onto Malloy.

5

On the opposite side of the street the homeless woman – Old Essie to the volunteers at the shelter, Essie Wilcox once upon a time – jounced her shopping cart up the short, grassy embankment that surrounded the high school parking lot. After she had gained the plateau of the pavement, she pushed toward the athletic fields and the scrub woods beyond, where she kept house in the warm months.

'Hurry along, children!' Essie spoke forward, as if to the rattling contents of her shopping cart, but actually addressing her invisible family of four identical little girls, who trailed behind in a row, like ducklings. 'We need to be home for supper – or else we might end up *as* supper! In a witch's pot!'

Essie chuckled but the girls began to weep and fuss.

'Oh, you silly-billy girls!' she said. 'I was only kidding.'

Essie reached the edge of the parking lot and pushed her cart onto the football field. Behind her, the girls had cheered up. They knew that Mother would never let anything happen to them. They were good girls.

6

Evie was standing between two pallets of freshly cut pine boards on the left side of Adams Lumberyard when Unit Four shot past. She was screened from the rubberneckers standing outside the main building, but not from the highway. The responders paid no attention to her, however, although she was still wearing nothing but Truman Mayweather's shirt on her body and Truman Mayweather's blood on her face and arms. The cops had eyes only for the smoke rising on the edge of some extremely dry woods.

Terry Coombs sat forward and pointed. 'See that big rock with TIFFANY JONES SUCKS spray-painted on it?'

'Yeah.'

'You'll see a dirt road just past it. Turn there.'

'You sure?' Roger Elway asked. 'The smoke looks at least a mile further on.'

'Trust me. I've been out here before, back when Tru Mayweather considered himself a full-time trailer pimp and a part-time gentleman pot grower. I guess he moved up in the world.'

Unit Four skidded on the dirt, and then the tires caught hold. Roger bucketed along at forty, the county car sometimes bottoming out in spite of the heavy suspension. High weeds growing up the center hump whickered against the undercarriage. Now they could smell the smoke.

Terry grabbed the mic. 'Unit Four to Base, Base, this is Four.'

'Four, this is Base,' Linny responded.

'We'll be at the scene in three, as long as Roger doesn't put us in the ditch.' Roger raised one hand from the wheel long enough to flash his partner the finger. 'What's the status on the FD?'

'They're rolling all four engines, plus the ambo. Some of the volunteer guys, too. Should be right behind you. Watch out for the Avon Lady.'

'Avon Lady, got it. Four is out.'

Terry racked the mic just as the cruiser took a bounce that rendered them momentarily airborne. Roger brought the car to a skidding halt. The road ahead was littered with scraps of corrugated roofing, shattered propane canisters, plastic jugs, and shredded paper, some of it smoldering. He spotted a black and white disc that looked like a stove dial.

One wall of a shed was leaning against a dead tree that was blazing like a Tiki torch. Two pine trees close to what had been the rear of the shed were also on fire. So were the scrub bushes lining the side of the road.

Roger popped the trunk, grabbed the fire extinguisher, and began spraying white foam onto the undergrowth. Terry got the fire blanket and began flapping at the flaming debris in the road. FD would be here soon; the job right now was containment.

Roger trotted over, holding the extinguisher. 'I'm empty, and you're not doing shit. Let's scat out of here before we get rear-ended, what do you think?'

'I think that's an excellent idea. Let's see what's up at *chez* Mayweather.'

Sweat beaded across Roger's forehead and glimmered in the sparse hairs of his pale yellow flattop. He squinted. 'Shay what?'

Terry liked his partner all right, but he wouldn't have wanted Roger on his Wednesday Quiz Bowl team down at the Squeaky Wheel. 'Never mind. Drive.'

Roger threw himself behind the wheel. Terry scooted to the passenger side. A Dooling FD pumper came swaying around the turn forty yards behind them, its high sides brushing the boughs of the trees crowding the road. Terry waved to them, then unlocked the shotgun beneath the dash. Better safe than sorry.

They arrived in a clearing where a trailer painted the hideous turquoise of aquarium pebbles sat on jacklifters. The steps were concrete blocks. A rust-eaten F-150 sat on a pair of flat tires. A woman slumped on the tailgate, mousy brown hair hiding her face. She wore jeans and a halter top. Much of the skin on display was decorated with tattoos. Terry could read LOVE running down her right forearm. Her feet were bare and caked with dirt. She was scrawny to the point of emaciation.

'Terry . . .' Roger inhaled and made a throat-clearing noise that was close to a retch. 'Over there.'

What Terry saw made him think of a county fair midway game he'd played as a boy. A man stuck his head through a cardboard cutout of Popeye, and for a dime you could throw three plastic bags of colored water at him. Only that wasn't colored water below the head protruding from the trailer's wall.

An immense weariness filled Terry. His entire body seemed to gain weight, as if his innards had been turned to concrete. He had suffered this before, mostly at the scene of bad car accidents, and knew the feeling was transitory, but while it lasted, it was hellish. There was that moment when you looked at a child still strapped into his car seat but with his little body torn open like a laundry bag – or when you looked at a head sticking out of a trailer wall, the skin peeled down the cheeks by its cataclysmic passage – and you wondered why in the hell the world had been created in the first place. Good things were in short supply, and so much of the rest was downright rancid.

The woman sitting on the tailgate raised her head. Her face was pale, her eyes ringed with dark circles. She held out her arms to them, then immediately lowered them to her thighs again as if they were too heavy, just too heavy. Terry knew her; she'd been one of Tru Mayweather's girls before he had gone into the meth business. Perhaps she was still here because she had been promoted to quasi-girlfriend – if you could call that a promotion.

He got out of the cruiser. She slid down from the tailgate, and would have gone to her knees if Terry hadn't caught her around the middle. The skin under his hands was chilly, and he could feel every rib. This close, he saw that some of her tattoos were actually bruises. She clung to him and began to cry.

'Hey, now,' Terry said. 'Hey, now, girl. You're okay. Whatever happened here, it's over.'

Under other circumstances, he would have considered the sole survivor the prime suspect, and all that blather about the Avon Lady so much bullshit, but the bag of bones in his arms could never have put that guy's head through the trailer wall. Terry didn't know how long Tiffany had been getting high on Truman's supply, but in her current condition he thought just blowing her nose would have taken a major effort.

Roger strolled over, looking oddly cheerful. 'Did you make the call, ma'am?'

'Yes . . .'

Roger took out his notebook. 'Your name?'

'This is Tiffany Jones,' Terry said. 'That's right, isn't it, Tiff?'

'Yeah. I seen you before, sir. When I come get Tru out of jail that time. I remember. You were nice.'

'And that guy? Who's he?' Roger waved his notebook at the protruding head, a casual gesture, as if he were pointing out an interesting local landmark, and not a ruined human being. His casualness was appalling – and Terry envied it. If he could learn to adjust to such sights as easily as Roger, he thought he'd be a happier man, and maybe better police.

'Don't know,' Tiffany said. 'He was just Trume's friend. Or cousin, maybe. He come up from Arkansas last week. Or maybe it was the week before.'

From down the road, firemen were shouting and water was whooshing – presumably from a tanker truck; there was no city water out here. Terry saw a momentary rainbow in the air, floating in front of smoke that was now turning white.

Terry took Tiffany gently by her stick-thin wrists and looked into her bloodshot eyes. 'What about the woman who did this? You told the dispatcher it was a woman.'

'Tru's friend called her the Avon Lady, but she sure wasn't one of those.' A little emotion surfaced through Tiffany's shock. She straightened up and looked around fearfully. 'She gone, ain't she? She better be.'

'What did she look like?'

Tiffany shook her head. 'I don't remember. But she stole Tru's shirt. I think she was nekkid beneath.'

Her eyes slipped shut, then slowly rolled open again. Terry recognized the signs. First the trauma of some unexpected violent event, next the hysterical call to 911, and now the post-event shock. Add to that whatever drugs she had been taking, and how long she had been taking them. Elevator up, elevator down. For all he knew, Truman Mayweather, Tiffany, and Truman Mayweather's Arkansas cuz had been on a three-day run.

'Tiff? I want you to sit in the cruiser while my partner and I have a look around. Sit right here in back. Rest up.'

'Sleepytime gal,' Roger said, grinning, and for a moment Terry felt a well-nigh irresistible urge to kick his country ass.

Instead of doing that, he held open the cruiser's back door for her, and this called up another memory: the limousine he'd rented to go to the prom in with Mary Jean Stukey. Her in a pink strapless dress with puffy sleeves, the corsage he'd brought her at her wrist, him in a rented tuxedo. This was in the golden age before he had ever seen the white-eyed corpse of a pretty girl with the crater of a shotgun blast in her chest, or a man who had hung himself in his hayloft, or a hollow-eyed meth-addicted prostitute who looked as if she had less than six months to live.

I am too old for this job, Terry thought. I should retire.

He was forty-five.

7

Although Lila had never actually shot anyone, she had drawn her gun on five occasions and fired it into the air once (and *oy vey*, the paperwork just for doing that). Like Terry and Roger and all the others in her small band of blue knights, she had cleaned up the human wreckage from plenty of mishaps on the county roads (usually with the smell of alcohol still hanging in the air). She had dodged flying objects, broken up family disagreements that turned physical, administered CPR, and splinted broken limbs. She and her guys had found two children lost in the woods, and on a handful of occasions she had been puked upon. She had experienced a great deal during her fourteen years in law enforcement, but she had never encountered a bloodstained woman in nothing but a flannel shirt strolling up the centerline of Dooling County's main highway. That was a first.

She crested Ball's Hill doing eighty, and the woman was less than a hundred feet from the cruiser. She made no effort to dodge either right or left, but even in that hair-thin moment Lila saw no deer-in-the-headlights expression on her face, just calm observation. And something else: she was gorgeous.

Lila couldn't have stopped in time even if she'd had a full night's sleep – not at eighty. She swung the wheel to the right instead, missing the woman in the road by mere inches, and not entirely missing her, at that; she heard a *clup* sound, and suddenly the outside mirror was reflecting Lila herself instead of the road behind.

Meanwhile, she had Unit One to contend with, a projectile now barely under her control. She hit a mailbox and sent it flying into the air, the post twirling like a majorette's baton before it crashed to the earth. Dust spumed up behind her, and she could feel the heavy cruiser wanting to slide ditchward. Braking wouldn't save her, so she stepped down on the accelerator instead, increasing her speed, the cruiser tearing up the rightside shoulder, gravel pinging off the undercarriage. She was riding at a severe slant. If the ditch captured her she would roll, and chances that she would ever see Jared graduate high school would shrink drastically.

Lila feathered the wheel to the left. At first the car slid, but then it caught hold and roared back onto the highway. With tar under her again she hit the brakes hard, the nose of the cruiser dipping, the deceleration pushing her so hard against her seatbelt that she could feel her eyes bulging.

She stopped at the end of a long double track of burned rubber. Her heart was hammering. Black dots floated in front of her eyes. She forced herself to breathe so she wouldn't faint, and looked into the rearview mirror.

The woman hadn't run into the woods, nor was she beating feet up Ball's Hill, where another road forked off toward the Ball Creek Ferry. She was just standing there, gazing over her shoulder. That glance-back, coupled with the woman's bare butt protruding from under the tail of her shirt, was strangely coquettish; she looked like a pin-up on an Alberto Vargas calendar.

Breathing fast, her mouth metallic with the taste of spent adrenalin, Lila backed into the dirt driveway of a neat little ranch home. A woman was standing on the porch with a toddler cradled in her arms. Lila powered down her window and said, 'Go back inside, ma'am. Right now.'

Without waiting to see if the bystander would do as ordered, Lila shifted to drive and rolled back up Ball's Hill toward where the woman stood, being careful to swerve around the dead mailbox. She could hear her bent front fender scraping one of her tires.

The radio blurped. It was Terry Coombs. 'Unit One, this is Four. You there, Lila? Come back. We got a couple of dead meth cookers out here past the lumberyard.'

She grabbed the mic, said, 'Not now, Ter,' and dropped it on the seat. She stopped in front of the woman, unsnapped the strap on her holster, and, as she got out of Unit One, pulled her service weapon for the sixth time in her career as a law enforcement officer. As she looked at those long, tanned legs and high breasts she flashed back to her driveway — could it only have been fifteen minutes ago? *What are you looking at?* she had asked. Anton had replied, *Morning glory*.

If this woman standing in the middle of Dooling Town Road wasn't morning glory, Lila had never seen it.

'Hands up. Put them up, right now.'

The Avon Lady, aka Morning Glory, raised her hands.

'Do you know how close you just came to being dead?'

Evie smiled. It lit up her whole face. 'Not very,' she said. 'You had it all the way, Lila.'

8

The old man spoke with a slight tremble. 'I didn't want to move her.'

The cat, a brown tabby, was in the grass. Judge Oscar Silver was down on the ground beside her, staining the knees of his khakis. Sprawled on its side, the cat almost appeared normal, except for its right front leg, which hung loose in a grotesque V-shape. Up close you also saw the curls of blood in her eyes, washing up around the pupils. Her breath was shallow and she was, according to the counter-intuitive instinct of wounded felines, purring.

Frank squatted beside the cat. He propped his sunglasses back on his head and squinted against the harsh morning light. 'I'm sorry, Judge.'

Silver wasn't crying now, but he had been. Frank hated to see that, although it didn't surprise him: people loved their pets, often with a degree of openness they couldn't allow themselves to express toward other people.

What would a shrink call that? Displacement? Well, love was hard. All Frank knew was that the ones you really had to watch out for in this world were the ones that couldn't love even a cat or a dog. And you had to watch out for yourself, of course. Keep things under control. Stay cool.

'Thank you for coming so quickly,' said Judge Silver.

'It's my job,' Frank said, although it wasn't exactly. As the county's sole full-time animal control officer, his department was more raccoons and stray dogs than dying cats. He considered Oscar Silver a friend, though, or something close to it. Before the judge's kidneys had put him on the wagon, Frank had shared more than a few beers with him at the Squeaky Wheel, and it was Oscar Silver who had given him the name of a divorce lawyer and suggested he make an appointment. Silver had also suggested 'some kind of counseling' when Frank admitted he sometimes raised his voice to his wife and daughter (taking care not to mention the time he'd put a fist through the kitchen wall).

Frank hadn't seen either the lawyer or the therapist. In regard to the former, he still believed he could work things out with Elaine. In regard to the latter, he felt he could control his temper quite well if people (Elaine, for instance, but also Nana, his daughter) would only realize he had their best interests at heart.

'I've had her since she was a kitten,' Judge Silver was saying now. 'Found her out behind the garage. This was just after Olivia, my wife, passed. I know it's ridiculous to say, but it seemed like . . . a message.' He drew his forefinger through the valley between the cat's ears, rubbing gently. Although the cat continued to purr, it did not extend its neck toward the finger, or react. Its bloody eyes gazed steadily into the green grass.

'Maybe it was,' said Frank.

'My grandson was the one who named her Cocoa.' He shook his head and twisted his lips. 'It was a damn Mercedes. I saw it. I was coming out for the paper. Had to be going sixty. In a residential neighborhood! Now what reason is there for that?'

'No reason. What color was the Mercedes?' Frank was thinking about something Nana had mentioned to him months earlier. A fellow on her paper route who lived in one of the big houses at the top of Briar had some kind of fancy ride. A green Mercedes, he thought she had said, and now:

'Green,' said Judge Silver. 'It was a green one.'

A gurgle had entered the cat's purr. The rise and fall of its flank had quickened. She was really hurting.

Frank put a hand on Silver's shoulder, squeezed it. 'I should do this now.'

The judge cleared his throat, but must not have trusted himself to speak. He just nodded.

Frank unzipped the leather pouch that contained the needle and the two vials. 'This first one relaxes her.' He poked the needle into the vial, drew it full. 'The second one lets her sleep.'

9

There came a time, long before the events recounted here, when the Tri-Counties (McDowell, Bridger, and Dooling) petitioned to have the defunct Ash Mountain Juvenile Reformatory converted into a badly needed women's prison. The state paid for the land and the buildings, and it was named after the county – Dooling – that provided most of the money for refurbishing the institution. Its doors opened in 1969, staffed by Tri-County residents who badly needed jobs. At the time it had been declared 'state of the art' and 'a benchmark in female corrections.' It looked more like a suburban high school than a prison – if one ignored the rolls of razor wire that topped the acres of chainlink surrounding the place.

Nearly half a century later, it still looked like a high school, but one that had fallen on hard times and a diminishing tax base. The buildings had begun to crumble. The paint (lead-based, it was rumored) was flaking. The plumbing leaked. The heating plant was badly outdated, and in the depths of winter, only the admin wing could maintain temperatures above sixty-five degrees. In summer, the inmate wings roasted. The lighting was dim, the elderly electrical wiring a disaster in waiting, and the vital inmate monitoring equipment went dark at least once a month.

There was, however, an excellent exercise yard with a running track, a basketball court in the gym, shuffleboard, a midget softball diamond, and a vegetable garden adjacent to the admin wing. It was there, close to the flourishing peas and corn, that Warden Janice Coates sat on a blue plastic milk box, her beige-colored knit purse collapsed on the ground beside her shoes, smoking an unfiltered Pall Mall and watching Clint Norcross approach.

He flashed his ID card (unnecessary since everyone knew him, but it was protocol) and the main gate rumbled open on its track. He drove into the dead space beyond, waiting for the outer gate to shut. When the officer on duty – this morning it was Millie Olson – got a green on her board, indicating the main gate was locked, she opened the inner gate. Clint brought his Prius trundling alongside the fence to the employees' parking lot, which was also gated. Here a sign cautioned MAINTAIN SECURITY! ALWAYS LOCK YOUR CAR!

Two minutes later he was standing beside the warden, leaning a shoulder against the old brick, his face turned up to the morning sun. What followed was akin to the call-and-response in a fundamentalist church.

'Good morning, Dr Norcross.'

'Good morning, Warden Coates.'

'Ready for another day in the wonderful world of corrections?'

'The real question is, is the wonderful world of corrections ready for me? That's how ready I am. How about you, Janice?'

She shrugged faintly and blew smoke. 'The same.'

He nodded to her cigarette. 'Thought you quit.'

'I did. I enjoy quitting so much I do it once a week. Sometimes twice.'

'All quiet?'

'This morning, yes. We had a meltdown last night.'

'Don't tell me, let me guess. Angel Fitzroy.'

'Nope. Kitty McDavid.'

Clint raised his eyebrows. 'That I would not have expected. Tell me.'

'According to her roommate – Claudia Stephenson, the one the other ladies call—'

'Claudia the Dynamite Body-a,' Clint said. 'Very proud of those implants. Did Claudia start something?'

Nothing against Claudia, but Clint hoped that was the case. Doctors were human, they had their favorites, and Kitty McDavid was one of his. Kitty had been in rough shape when she arrived – a self-harm habit, yo-yo moods, high anxiety. They'd come a long way since then. Anti-depressants had made a huge difference and,

Clint liked to believe, the therapy sessions had helped a bit, too. Like him, Kitty was a product of the foster systems of Appalachia. In one of their first meetings, she had asked him, sourly, if he had any idea in his big suburban head what it felt like not to have a home or a family.

Clint hadn't hesitated. 'I don't know what it felt like for you, Kitty, but it made me feel like an animal. Like I was always on the hunt, or being hunted.'

She had stared, wide-eyed. 'You . . . ?'

'Yes, me,' he had said. Meaning, *Me too.*

These days Kitty was almost always on Good Report, and, better still, she had made an agreement with the prosecutors' office to testify in the Griner brothers case, a major drug bust that Dooling's own Sheriff Lila Norcross had pulled off that winter. If Lowell and Maynard Griner went away, parole for Kitty was a distinct possibility. If she got it, Clint thought she might do all right. She understood now that while it was going to be up to her to find a place in the world, it was also going to take continued support – both medical and community – to meet that responsibility. He thought Kitty was strong enough to ask for that support, to fight for it, and she was getting stronger every day.

Janice Coates's view was less sanguine. It was her attitude that, when dealing with convicts, you were better off not letting your hopes rise too high. Maybe that was why she was the warden – the bull goose – and he was just the resident shrink in this stone hotel.

'Stephenson says McDavid woke her up,' Janice said. 'First talking in her sleep, then yelling, then screaming. Something about how the Black Angel was coming. Or maybe the Black Queen. It's in the incident report. *With cobwebs in her hair and death in her fingertips.* Sounds like it could be a pretty good TV show, doesn't it? Syfy channel.' The warden chuckled without smiling. 'I'm sure you could have a field day with that one, Clint.'

'More like a movie,' Clint said. 'Maybe one she saw in her child-hood.'

Coates rolled her eyes. 'See? To quote Ronnie Reagan, "There you go again."'

'What? You don't believe in childhood trauma?'

'I believe in a nice quiet prison, that's what I believe in. They took her over to A Wing, Land of the Loonies.'

'Politically incorrect, Warden Coates. The preferred term is Nutbar Central. Did they have to put her in the restraint chair?' Though it was sometimes necessary, Clint loathed the restraint chair, which looked like a sports car bucket seat that had been converted into a torture device.

'No, gave her a Yellow Med, and that quieted her down. I don't know which one, and don't much care, but it'll be in the incident report, if you care to look.'

There were three med levels at Dooling: red, that could only be dispensed by medical personnel; yellow, that could be dispensed by officers; and green, that inmates not in C Wing or currently on Bad Report could keep in their cells.

'Okay,' Clint said.

'As of now, your girl McDavid is sleeping it off—'

'She's not *my* girl—'

'And that is your morning update.' Janice yawned, scrubbed her cigarette out on the brick, and popped it under the milk box, as if once out of sight it would somehow disappear.

'Am I keeping you up, Janice?'

'It's not you. I ate Mexican last night. Had to keep getting up to use the can. What they say is true – the stuff that comes out looks suspiciously like the stuff that went in.'

'TMI, Warden.'

'You're a doctor, you can handle it. You going to check on McDavid?'

'This morning for sure.'

'Want my theory? Okay, here's my theory: she was molested as a toddler by some lady calling herself the Black Queen. What do you think?'

'Could be,' Clint said, not rising to the bait.

'*Could be.*' She shook her head. 'Why investigate their childhoods, Clint, when they're still children? That's essentially why most of them are here – childish behavior in the first degree.'

This made Clint think of Jeanette Sorley, who had ended years of escalating spousal abuse by stabbing her husband with a screwdriver and watching him bleed to death. Had she not done that, Damian Sorley would eventually have killed her. Clint had no doubt of it. He did not view that as childish behavior, but as self-preservation. If he said so to Warden Coates, however, she would refuse to hear it: she was old-school that way. Better to simply finish the call-and-response.

'And so, Warden Coates, we begin another day of life in the women's prison along the Royal Canal.'

She hoisted her purse, stood up, and brushed off the seat of her uniform pants. 'No canal, but there's always Ball's Ferry down the road apiece, so yeah. Let the day begin.'

They went in together on that first day of the sleeping sickness, pinning their IDs to their shirts.

10

Magda Dubcek, mother of that handsome young pool-polisher-about-town known as Anton the Pool Guy (he had incorporated, too, so please make out your checks to Anton the Pool Guy, LLC), tottered into the living room of the duplex she shared with her son. She had her cane in one hand and a morning pick-me-up in the other. She flumped into her easy chair with a fart and a sigh and fired up the television.

Normally at this hour of the day she would have tuned into the second hour of *Good Day Wheeling*, but this morning she went to NewsAmerica instead. There was a breaking story that interested her, which was good, and she knew one of the correspondents covering it, which was even better. Michaela Coates, Michaela Morgan she called herself now but little Mickey to Magda, forever and always, whom she had babysat all those years ago. Back then Jan Coates had just been a guard at the women's lockup on the south end of town, a widowed single mom only trying to hang in there. Now she was the warden, boss of the whole shebang, and her daughter Mickey was a nationally known news correspondent working out of DC, famous for her tough questions and short skirts. Those Coates women had really made something of themselves. Magda was proud of them, and if she felt a flicker of melancholy because Mickey never called or wrote, or because Janice never stopped in to chew the fat, well, they had jobs to do. Magda didn't presume to understand the pressures that they operated under.

The news anchor on duty this morning was George Alderson. With his glasses and stooped shoulders and thinning hair, he didn't look anything like the matinee idol types that usually sat behind the big desks and read the news. He looked like a mortuary attend- ant. Also, he had an unfortunate voice for a TV person. Sort of quacky. Well, Magda supposed there was a reason NewsAmerica was number three behind FOX and CNN. She was eager for the day when Michaela would move up to one of those. When it happened, Magda wouldn't have to put up with Alderson anymore.

'At this hour we're continuing to follow a breaking story that began in Australia,' Alderson said. The expression on his face attempted to combine concern with skepticism but landed closer to constipated.

You should retire and go bald in the comfort of your home, Magda thought, and toasted him with the first rum and Coke of the day. Go Turtle Wax your head, George, and get out of the way for my Michaela.

'Medical officials in Oahu, Hawaii, are reporting that the outbreak of what some are calling Asian Fainting Sickness and others are calling Australian Fainting Flu continues to spread. No one seems to be sure where it actually originated, but so far the only victims have been women. Now we're getting word that cases have popped up on our shores, first in California, then in Colorado, and now in the Carolinas. Here's Michaela Morgan with more.'

'Mickey!' Magda cried, once more toasting the television (and slopping some of her drink onto the sleeve of her cardigan). Magda's voice held only a trace of Czech this morning, but by the time Anton got home at five P.M., she would sound as if she had just gotten off the boat instead of living in the Tri-Counties for almost forty years. 'Little Mickey Coates! I chased your bare ass all around your mother's living room, both of us laughing fit to split our sides! I changed your poopy diapers, you little kook, and look at you now!'

Michaela Morgan née Coates, in a sleeveless blouse and one of her trademark short skirts, was standing in front of a rambling building complex painted barn red. Magda thought those short skirts served Mickey very well. Even big-deal politicians were apt to become mesmerized by a glimpse of upper thigh, and in such a state, the truth sometimes popped out of their lying mouths. Not always, mind you, but sometimes. On the issue of Michaela's new nose, Magda was conflicted. She missed that sassy stub that her girl had when she was a kiddo, and in a way, with her sharp new nose, Mickey didn't look so much like Mickey anymore. On the other hand, she did look terrific! You couldn't take your eyes off her.

'I'm here at the Loving Hands Hospice in Georgetown, where the first cases of what some are calling the Australian Fainting Flu were noticed in the early hours of the morning. Almost a hundred patients are housed here, most geriatric, and over half of them female. Administrators refuse to confirm or deny the outbreak, but I talked to an orderly just minutes ago, and what he had to say, although brief, was disquieting. He spoke on condition of anonymity. Here he is.'

The taped interview was indeed brief – little more than a sound bite. It featured Michaela speaking to a man in hospital whites with his face blurred and his voice electronically altered so he sounded like a sinister alien overlord in a sci-fi movie.

'What's going on in there?' Michaela asked. 'Can you fill us in?'

'Most of the women are asleep and won't wake up,' the orderly said in his alien overlord voice. 'It's just like in Hawaii.'

'But the men . . . ?'

'The men are dandy. Up and eating their breakfast.'

'In Hawaii there have been some reports of – *growths*, on the faces of the sleeping women. Is that the case here?'

'I . . . don't think I should talk about that.'

'Please.' Michaela batted her eyes. 'People are concerned.'

'That's it!' Magda croaked, saluting the television with her drink and slopping a bit more on her cardigan. 'Go sexy! Once they want to stir your batter, you can get anything out of em!'

'Not growths in the tumor sense,' the overlord voice said. 'It looks more like they've got cotton stuck to em. Now I gotta go.'

'Just one more question—'

'I gotta go. But . . . it's growing. That cotton stuff. It's . . . kinda gross.'

The picture returned to the live shot. 'Disquieting information from an insider . . . if true. Back to you, George.'

As glad as Magda was to have seen Mickey, she hoped the story wasn't true. Probably just another false scare, like Y2K or that SARS thing, but still, the idea of something that not only put women to sleep but caused stuff to grow on them . . . like Mickey said, that was disquieting. She would be glad when Anton got home. It was lonely with only the TV for company, not that she was one to complain. Magda wasn't about to worry her hardworking boy, no, no. She'd loaned him the money to start the business, but he was the one who'd made it go.

But now, for the time being, maybe one more drinky, just a little one, and then a nap.

CHAPTER 3

1

Once Lila had the woman cuffed, she wrapped her in the space blanket she kept in the trunk of the cruiser, and thrust her into the backseat. At the same time, she recited the Miranda. The woman, now silent, her brilliant grin faded to a dreamy smile, had limply accepted Lila's grip on her upper arm. The arrest was completed and the suspect secured in less than five minutes; the dust sprayed up from the cruiser's tires was still settling as Lila strode back around to the driver's side.

'They call moth watchers *moth*-ers, spelled like mothers, but not said like that.'

Lila was turning the cruiser around and pointing it back down Ball's Hill toward town when her prisoner shared this bit of information. She caught the woman's eyes, looking at her in the rearview. Her voice was soft, but not especially feminine. There was a wandering quality to her speech. It was unclear to Lila if she was being addressed, or if the woman was talking to herself.

Drugs, Lila thought. PCP was a good bet. So was ketamine.

'You know my name,' Lila said, 'so where do I know you from?'

There were three possibilities: the PTA (unlikely), the newspaper, or Lila had arrested her at some point in the last fourteen years and didn't remember. Door number three seemed the best bet.

'Everyone knows me,' said Evie. 'I'm sort of an It Girl.' Her cuffs clinked as she hiked one shoulder to scratch her chin. 'Sort of. It and Girl. Me, myself, and I. Father, Son, and Holy Eve. Eave, a roof underhang. Eve, short for evening. When we all go to sleep. Right? Moth-er, get it? Like mother.'

Civilians had no idea how much nonsense you had to listen to when you were a cop. The public loved to salute police officers for their bravery, but no one ever gave you credit for the day-in, day-out fortitude required to put up with the bullshit. While courage was an excellent feature in a police officer, a built-in resistance to gibberish was, in Lila's opinion, just as important.

As it happened, this was why filling the latest open position for a full-time deputy had proved so difficult. It was the reason she had ultimately passed on the application from the animal control guy, Frank Geary, and hired a young vet named Dan Treat instead, even though Treater had almost no experience in law enforcement. Smart and well-spoken as Geary obviously was, his job-file was too big – he'd generated too much paperwork, written up too many fines. The message between the lines was one of confrontation; this was not the kind of guy who could let the small shit slide. That was no good.

Not that her staff as a whole was some kind of crackerjack crime-fighting squad, and so what, big deal, welcome to real life. You got the best people you could, then tried to help them along. Roger Elway and Terry Coombs, for instance. Roger had probably absorbed one hit too many as a lineman for Coach Wittstock's Dooling High School football team in the early aughts. Terry was smarter, but could become dispirited and sullen if things weren't going his way, and he drank too much at parties. On the other hand, both men had fairly long fuses, which meant she could trust them. Mostly.

Lila harbored an unspoken belief that motherhood was the best possible rehearsal for a prospective police officer. (Unspoken especially to Clint, who would have had a field day with it; she could picture how he'd cock his head and twist his mouth in that rather tiresome way of his and say, 'That's interesting,' or 'Could be.')

Mothers were naturals for law enforcement, because toddlers, like criminals, were often belligerent and destructive.

If you could get through those early years without losing your cool or blowing your top, you might be able to deal with grown-up crime. The key was to not react, to stay adult – and was she thinking about the naked woman covered in blood who had something to do with the violent deaths of two, or was she thinking about how to handle someone closer to home, much closer, the fellow who rested his head on the pillow next to hers? (When the clock clicked to 00:00, the gymnasium horn had blared, and the boys and girls cheered. The final score: Bridger County Girls AAU 42 – Fayette Girls AAU 34.) As Clint might say, 'Huh, that's interesting. Want to tell me a bit more?'

'So many good sales right now,' Evie rattled on. 'Washer-dryer. Grills. Babies that eat plastic food and poop it out again. Savings galore all over the store.'

'I see,' said Lila, as if the woman was making sense. 'What's your name?'

'Evie.'

Lila twisted around. 'And a last name? How about that?'

The woman's cheekbones were strong and straight. The pale brown eyes glowed. Her skin had what Lila thought of as a Mediterranean tint, and that dark hair, ooh. A splotch of blood had dried on her forehead.

'Do I need one?' Evie asked.

As far as Lila was concerned, that carried the motion: her new acquaintance was definitively, catastrophically high.

She faced forward, tapped the gas, and popped loose the mic. 'Base, this is Unit One. I've got a woman in custody, found her walking north from the area of the lumberyard on Ball's Hill. She's got a lot of blood on her, so we need the kit to take some samples. She also needs a Tyvek suit. And call for an ambulance to meet us. She's on something.'

'Roger that,' said Linny. 'Terry says it's a real mess at that trailer.'

'Roger that.' Evie laughed cheerily. 'A real mess. Bring extra towels. Not the good ones, though, ha-ha-ha. Roger that.'

'One, out.' Lila racked the mic. She glanced at Evie in the mirror. 'You should sit quiet, ma'am. I'm arresting you on suspicion of murder. This is serious.'

They were approaching the town line. Lila rolled the cruiser to a pause at the stop sign that brokered the Ball's Hill–West Lavin intersection. West Lavin led to the prison. Visible on the opposite side of the road was a sign that warned against stopping for hitch-hikers.

'Are you injured, ma'am?'

'Not yet,' said Evie. 'But, hey! Triple-double. Pretty good.'

Something flickered in Lila's mind, the mental equivalent of a glittering fleck in the sand, quickly washed over by a frothing wave.

She looked in the rearview again. Evie had shut her eyes and settled back. Was she coming down?

'Ma'am, are you going to be sick?'

'You better kiss your man before you go to sleep. You better kiss him goodbye while you still have the chance.'

'Sure thi—' Lila began, but then the woman bolted forward, headfirst into the dividing mesh. Lila flinched away instinctively as the impact of Evie's head caused the barrier to rattle and vibrate.

'Stop that!' she cried, just before Evie smashed against the mesh a second time. Lila caught the flash of a grin on her face, fresh blood on her teeth, and then she battered against the mesh a third time.

Hand on the door, Lila was about to get out and go around to the rear, tase the woman for her own safety, settle her down, but the third strike was the last. Evie had crumpled down to the seat, gasping in a happy way, a runner who had just ripped through the finish line. There was blood around her mouth and nose, and a gash on her forehead.

'Triple-double! All right!' Evie cried out. 'Triple-double! Busy day!'

Lila unracked the mic and radioed Linny: change of plans. The public defender needed to meet them at the station just as soon-as. And Judge Silver, too, if the old fellow could be persuaded to come down and do them a favor.

2

Belly-deep in a clutch of sweet-fern, a fox watched Essie unpack her cart.

He did not think of her as Essie, of course, did not have a name for her at all. She was just another human. The fox had in any case been observing her for a long while – moons and suns – and recognized clearly her ramshackle lean-to of plastic sheeting and canvas draping for the foxhole that it was. The fox also understood that the four chunks of green glass that she organized in a semi-circle and referred to as 'The Girls' held great meaning to her. At times when Essie was not present, the fox had smelled them – no life there – and sifted through her possessions, which were negligible, except for a few discarded cans of soup that he had licked clean.

He believed that she represented no threat, but he was an old fox, and one did not become an old fox by proceeding too confidently on any matter. One became an old fox by being careful and opportunistic, by mating as frequently as possible while avoiding entanglements, by never crossing roads in daylight, and by digging deeply in good soft loam.

This morning, his prudence appeared to be unnecessary. Essie's behavior was entirely in character. After she removed the bags and sundry mysterious items from her cart, she informed the glass fragments that mother needed a snooze. 'No tomfoolery, you girls,' Essie said, and entered the lean-to to lie on the pile of mover's quilts she used as a mattress. Though the lean-to covered her body, her head poked out into the light.

While Essie was settling into her sleep, the fox silently bared his teeth at the male mannequin top that she had set in the leaves beside the lean-to, but the mannequin did nothing. It was probably dead like the green glass. The fox chewed his paw and waited.

Soon the old woman's breath settled into a sleeping rhythm, each deep intake followed by a shallow whistle of exhalation. The fox stretched slowly up from the bed of sweet-fern and slunk a few steps toward the lean-to, wanting to be absolutely sure about the mannequin's intent or lack thereof. He bared his teeth more widely. The mannequin did not move. Yes, definitely dead.

He trotted to within a few lengths of the lean-to, and stopped. A whitish fluttering was appearing over the sleeping woman's head – white strands, like cobwebs, lifting from her cheeks, unfurling breezily and settling on her skin, coating it. New strands spun out from the laid strands and they quickly covered her face, forming a mask that would soon extend all the way around her head. Moths circled in the dimness of the lean-to.

The fox retreated a few steps, sniffing. He didn't like the white stuff – the white stuff was definitely alive, and it was definitely a different creature altogether from those he was familiar with. Even at a distance, the scent of the white stuff was strong, and disturbingly mingled: there was blood and tissue in the scent, and intelligence and hunger, and an element of the deep, deep earth, of the Foxhole of Foxholes. And what slept in that great bed? Not a fox, he was certain.

His sniffs became whines, and he turned and began to trot away west. A sound of movement – someone else coming – carried through the woods behind him, and the fox's trot became a run.

3

After helping Oscar Silver inter Cocoa the cat – wrapped in a threadbare terrycloth bath towel – Frank drove the two short blocks to the house at 51 Smith Lane that he paid the mortgage on, but where, since he and Elaine had separated, only she and their eleven-year-old daughter still resided.

Elaine had been a social worker until two state budgets ago, but now she worked part-time at the Goodwill and volunteered at a couple of food pantries and at the Planned Parenthood in Maylock. The upside of this was that they didn't have to find money for childcare. When the school day ended no one minded if Nana hung around at the Goodwill with her mother. The downside was that they were going to lose the house.

This bothered Frank more than Elaine. In fact, it didn't seem to bother her at all. Despite her denials, he suspected that she planned to use the sale as an excuse to depart the area altogether, maybe take off for Pennsylvania where her sister lived. If that happened, Frank's every other weekend would become a weekend every other month, at best.

Except for visiting days, he made a concerted effort to avoid the place. Even then, if he could arrange for Elaine to bring Nana to him, that was his preference. The memories that went with the house – the sense of unfairness and failure, the patched hole in the kitchen wall – were too raw. Frank felt as though he had been tricked out of his entire life and the best part of that life had been lived at 51 Smith Lane, the neat, plain ranch house with the duck on the mailbox, painted by his daughter.

The matter of the green Mercedes, however, made a stop-in imperative.

As he jerked over to the curb, he spied Nana drawing with chalk in the driveway. It was an activity you'd normally associate with a much younger child, but his daughter had a talent for illustration. The previous school year she had won second prize in a bookmark-designing contest held by the local library. Nana's had shown a bunch of books flying like birds across a cloudbank. Frank had framed it and hung it in his office. He looked at it all the time. It was a beautiful thing, imagining books flying around inside his little girl's head.

She sat cross-legged in the sunshine, butt planted in an inner tube and her rainbow of implements arrayed around her in a fan. Along with her drawing ability, or maybe in accordance with it, Nana had a gift for making herself comfortable. She was a slow-moving, dreamy child, taking more after Frank than her vibrant mother, who never messed around about anything, was always straight-to-the-point.

He leaned over, popped the door of his truck. 'Hey, Brighteyes. Come here.'

She squinted up at him. 'Daddy?'

'Last I heard,' he said, working hard to keep the corners of his mouth turned up. 'Come here, okay?'

'Right now?' She had already glanced down to her picture.

'Yes. Right now.' Frank took a deep breath.

He hadn't started to get what Elaine called 'that way' until he was leaving the judge. By which El meant losing his temper. Which he rarely did, no matter what she thought. And today? At first he had been fine. Then, about five steps across Oscar Silver's grass, it was as if he had tripped some invisible trigger. Sometimes that just happened. Like when Elaine had kept after him about yelling at the PTA meeting and he'd punched that hole in the wall and Nana had run upstairs, crying, not understanding that sometimes you punched a *thing* so you wouldn't punch a *person*. Or that business with Fritz Meshaum, where he had been a little out of control, granted, but Meshaum deserved it. Anyone who would do a thing like that to an animal deserved it.

That cat could have been my kid was what he had been thinking as he crossed the grass. And then, *boom*! Like time was a shoelace and the length of it, between him walking and getting into the truck, had been knotted off. Because suddenly he was in his truck, he was driving for the house on Smith, and he couldn't recall getting in the truck at all. His hands were sweaty on the wheel and his cheeks hot, and he was still thinking about how the cat could have been his kid, except it wasn't a thought. More like an urgent flashing message on an LED screen:

error   error   error
my kid   my kid   my kid

Nana carefully placed a stub of purple chalk in the empty spot between an orange and a green. She pushed up from her inner tube and stood for a couple of seconds, dusting off the rear end of her flowered yellow shorts and rubbing her chalky fingertips contemplatively.

'Honey,' said Frank, fighting not to scream. Because, look, she had been right there, in the driveway, where some drunk asshole in a fancy car could drive right over her!

my kid   my kid   my kid

Nana took a step, stopped, studied her fingers again, apparently with dissatisfaction.

'Nana!' Frank, still twisted into a lean across the console. He slapped the passenger seat. Slapped it hard. 'Get over here!'

The girl's head yanked up, her expression startled, as if she had just been awakened from sleep by a thunderclap. She shuffled forward, and when she reached the open door, Frank grabbed the front of her tee-shirt and tugged her up close.

'Hey! You're stretching my shirt,' Nana said.

'Never mind that,' Frank said. 'Your shirt's not the big deal here. I'll tell you what the big deal is, so listen to me. Who drives the green Mercedes? Which house does it go with?'

'What?' Nana pressed at his grip on the front of her shirt. 'What are you talking about? You're going to ruin my shirt.'

'Didn't you hear me? Forget the fucking shirt!' The words were out and he hated them, but he was also satisfied to see her eyes jump from her shirt to him. He finally had her attention. Nana blinked and inhaled.

'Okay, now that your head's out of the clouds, let's get together on this. You told me about some guy on your paper route who drove a green Mercedes. What's his name? Which house does he live in?'

'Can't remember his name. I'm sorry, Daddy.' Nana bit her lower lip. 'It's the house beside the one with the big flag, though. It's got a wall. On Briar. Top of the hill.'

'Okay.' Frank let go of the shirt.

Nana didn't move. 'Are you done being mad?'

'Honey, I wasn't mad.' And when she said nothing: 'Okay, I was. A little. But not at you.'

She wouldn't look at him, just kept rubbing her goddam fingers together. He loved her, she was the most important thing in his life, but sometimes it was hard to believe she had all four wheels on the road.

'Thank you.' Some of the heat was draining from his face, some of the sweat cooling on his skin. 'Thank you, Brighteyes.'

'Sure,' said Nana. The girl retreated a small step, the sound of her sneaker sole against the pavement impossibly loud in Frank's ear.

Frank straightened up in his seat. 'One more thing. Do me a favor and stay out of the driveway. For the rest of the morning, anyway, till I can sort something out. There's a man driving around crazy. Draw inside with your paper, all right?'

She was biting at her lower lip. 'All right, Daddy.'

'You're not going to cry, are you?'

'No, Daddy.'

'All right. That's my girl. I'll see you next weekend, okay?'

He realized his lips were incredibly dry. He asked himself what else he was supposed to have done, and a voice inside him replied, 'Well, gee, what else *could* you have done? Maybe you could have, I don't know, this will probably sound totally wild, Frank, but hey, maybe you could have *not freaked the fuck out*?' The voice was like an amused version of Frank's own voice, the voice of a man who was kicked back in a lawn chair and wearing sunglasses and maybe sipping on an iced tea.

'Okay.' The nod she gave him was robotic.

Behind her, on the pavement, she had drawn an elaborate tree, its canopy spreading up one side of the driveway, its gnarled trunk cutting across. Moss hung from the branches and flowers bearded the base. Roots trailed down to the outline of an underground lake.

'I like what you got there,' he said and smiled.

'Thank you, Daddy,' Nana said.

'I just don't want you to get hurt.' The smile on his face felt like it was nailed on.

His daughter sniffed and gave him another robotic nod. He knew she was sucking back tears.

'Hey, Nana . . .' He started, but the words he wanted dispersed as the interior voice piped up again, telling him she'd had enough. To just leave it the hell alone.

'Bye, Daddy.'

She reached out and pushed his truck door gently shut. Spun and jogged up the driveway, scattering her chalks, striding across her tree, smudging the greens and blacks of the treetop. Head down. Shoulders shaking.

Kids, he told himself, can't always appreciate when you're trying to do the right thing.

4

There were three overnight filings on Clint's desk.

The first was predictable, but concerning: one of the officers on staff the previous night speculated that Angel Fitzroy seemed to be ramping up to something. At lights-out Angel had attempted to engage the officer over an issue of semantics. The authorities at Dooling were all strictly to be referred to as 'Officer.' Synonyms such as 'guard,' or 'screw,' let alone — obviously! — slurs like 'asshole' or 'motherfucker,' were unacceptable. Angel had asked Officer Wettermore if he understood English. Of *course* they were guards, Angel said. They could be officers, too, that was fine, but they couldn't not be guards, because they guarded. Weren't they guarding the prisoners? If you baked a cake, weren't you a baker? If you dug a hole, weren't you a digger?

Warned the inmate that she had arrived at the end of reasonable discussion and could expect consequences if she didn't lock it down immediately, Wettermore wrote. *Inmate relented and entered her cell, but further asked, How could we expect prisoners to follow the rules when the words of the rules did not make any sense? Inmate's tone was threatening.*

Angel Fitzroy was one of the few women in the prison whom Clint regarded as genuinely dangerous. Based on his interactions with her, he believed she might be a sociopath. He had never glimpsed any empathy in her, and her record inside was fat with infractions: drugs, fighting, threatening behavior.

'How do you suppose you'd have felt if the man you attacked had died from his injuries, Angel?' he had asked her during a group session.

'Aw,' Angel had said, sunken down in the chair, her eyes roaming his office walls. 'I'd have felt, oh, pretty bad — I guess.' Then, she'd smacked her lips, gaze fastening on the Hockney print. 'Looka that picture, girls. Wouldn't you like to visit where it is?'

While her assault conviction was bad enough — a man in a truck stop had said something to Angel that she hadn't liked and she'd broken his nose with a ketchup bottle – there were indications that she'd gotten away with much worse.

A detective from Charleston had driven to Dooling to solicit Clint's help with a case relating to Fitzroy. What the detective wanted was information concerning the death of a former landlord of Angel's. This had happened a couple of years before her current incarceration. Angel had been the only suspect, but there was nothing except vicinity to tie her to the crime, and no apparent motive. The thing was (as Clint himself knew), Angel had a history of not needing much of a motive. Twenty cents off in her change could be enough to blow her up. The Charleston detective had been nearly gleeful in his description of the landlord's corpse: 'Looked like the old boy just fell down the stairs, got his neck broke. But the coroner said someone had been to work on his package premortem. Balls was – I forget how the coroner put it, exactly, if he said fractured or whatever. But, layman's terms, he said, "They were basically squished."'

Clint wasn't in the business of flipping on his patients and told the detective so, but he had mentioned the inquiry to Angel later.

With an expression of glassy wonderment she responded, 'Balls can fracture?'

Now he made a note to himself to drop in on Angel that day, take a seismology reading.

The second filing was about an inmate on janitorial duty who claimed that there was an infestation of moths in the prison kitchen. A check by Officer Murphy found no moths. *Inmate willingly submitted to a urine drop – clean for drugs and alcohol.*

That one seemed to translate as a case of an inmate working hard to drive an officer crazy and an officer working hard to return the favor. Clint had no interest in continuing the circle by following up. He filed it.

Kitty McDavid was the last incident.

Officer Wettermore had jotted some of her ranting: *The Black Angel came up from the roots and down from the branches. Her fingers are death and her hair is full of cobwebs and dream is her kingdom.* After the administration of a dose of Haldol, she had been moved to A Wing.

Clint left his office and passed through admin toward the east section of the prison, which contained the cell wings. The prison was shaped roughly like a lowercase 't,' with the long central line of the corridor known as Broadway parallel to Route 17/West Lavin Road outside. The administration offices, the communications center, the officers' room, the staff lounge, and the classrooms were all situated at the west end of Broadway. The other corridor, Main Street, ran perpendicular to West Lavin. Main Street went from the prison's front door straight ahead to the craft shop, the utility room, the laundry, and the gymnasium. On the other side of Main Street, Broadway continued eastward, passing the library, the mess hall, the visitors' room, the infirmary, and intake, before arriving at the three cell wings.

A security door separated the cells from Broadway. Clint stopped here and pressed the button that notified the Booth that he wanted to enter. A buzzer sounded and the bolts of the security door retracted with a clunk. Clint pushed through.

These wings, A, B, and C, were arranged in a pincer shape. In the center of the pincer was the Booth, a shed-like structure armored in bulletproof glass. It contained the officers' monitors and communication board.

Although most of the prison population mixed in the yard and elsewhere, the wings were organized according to the theoretical danger presented by each inmate. There were sixty-four cells in the prison; twelve in A Wing, twelve in C Wing, and forty in B Wing. A and C were set entirely on ground level; B Wing was stacked with a second level of cells.

A Wing was medical, although some inmates considered 'tranquil' were also housed there, at the far end of the corridor. Inmates not necessarily tranquil but 'settled,' such as Kitty McDavid, were housed in B Wing. C Wing was for the troublemakers.

C was the least populous residence, with half of the twelve cells currently empty. When there was a breakdown or a severe disciplinary issue, it was official procedure to remove the inmate from her cell and place her in one of the 'Eye' cells in C Wing. Inmates called these the Jerk-Off Cells, because ceiling cameras allowed the officers to observe what the inmate was doing at all times. The implication was that male officers got their jollies by spying on them. The cameras were essential, though. If an inmate might attempt to harm or even kill herself, you needed to be able to see it to prevent it.

The officer in the Booth today was Captain Vanessa Lampley. She leaned over from the board to open the door for him. Clint sat beside her and asked if she could bring up Unit 12 on the monitor so he could check on McDavid. '*Let's go to the videotape!*' he yelled cheerily.

Lampley gave him a look.

'*Let's go to the videotape!* You know, it's what Warner Wolf always says.'

She shrugged and opened Unit 12 for visual inspection.

'The sportscaster?' Clint said.

Vanessa shrugged again. 'Sorry. Must be before my time.'

Clint thought that was bizarre, Warner Wolf was a legend, but he dropped it so he could study the screen. Kitty was in a fetal position, face twisted down into her arms. 'Seen anything out of line?'

Lampley shook her head. She'd come in at seven and McDavid had been snoozing the entire time.

That didn't surprise Clint. Haldol was powerful stuff. He was worried about Kitty, though, a mother of two who had been convicted of forging prescriptions. In an ideal world, Kitty would never have been put in a correctional facility in the first place. She was a bipolar drug addict with a junior high school education.

The surprise was how her bipolarity had manifested on this occasion. In the past, she had withdrawn. Last night's outburst of violent raving was unprecedented in her history. Clint had been fairly confident that the course of lithium he had prescribed for her was working. For over half a year Kitty had been levelheaded, generally upbeat – no sizable peaks or valleys. And she'd made the decision to testify for the prosecution in the Griner brothers case, which was not only courageous, but had a strong potential for advancing her own cause. There was every reason to believe that she could be paroled soon after the trial. The two of them had started to discuss the halfway house environment, what Kitty would do the first time that she became aware that someone was holding, how she would reintroduce herself to her children. Had it all started to look too rosy for her?

Lampley must have read his concern. 'She'll be all right, Doc. It was a one-off, that's what I think. The full moon, probably. Everything else is screwy, you know.'

The stocky veteran was pragmatic but conscientious, exactly what you wanted in a head officer. It also didn't hurt that Van Lampley was a competitive arm wrestler of some renown. Her biceps swelled the gray sleeves of her uniform.

'Oh, yeah,' Clint said, remembering the highway smash-up that Lila had mentioned. A couple of times he had attended Van's birthday party; she lived on the back of the mountain. 'You must have had to come to work the long way. Lila told me about the truck that crashed. Had to bulldoze the whole heap, she said.'

'Huh,' Van said. 'I didn't see any of that. Must've got it cleaned up before I left. I meant West and Ryckman.' Jodi West and Claire Ryckman were the regular day PAs. Like Clint they were nine-to-fivers. 'They never showed. So we got no one on medical. Coates is pissed. Says she's going to—'

'You didn't see anything on Mountain?' Hadn't Lila said that it was Mountain Rest Road? Clint was sure – almost sure, anyhow – she had.

Van shook her head. 'Wouldn't be the first time, though.' She grinned, displaying a big set of yellowing choppers. 'There was a truck that flipped on that road last fall. What a disaster. It was from PetSmart, you know? Cat litter and dog food all over the road.'

5

The trailer belonging to the late Truman Mayweather had not looked good the last time Terry Coombs was out here (to cool down a domestic disturbance involving one of Truman's many 'sisters,' who had vacated the residence shortly thereafter), but this morning it looked like high tea in hell. Mayweather was sprawled beneath the eating table with some of his brains on his bare chest. The furniture (mostly purchased at roadside rummage sales, Dollar Discount, or Chapter 11, Terry guessed) was scattered everywhere. The television was upside down in the rust-scaled shower stall. In the sink a toaster was making friends with a Converse sneaker mended with friction tape. Blood was splashed all over the walls. Plus, of course, there was a hunched-over body with his head sticking out through the side of the trailer and his plumber's crack showing above his beltless jeans. A wallet on the floor of the trailer contained an ID for Mr Jacob Pyle, of Little Rock, Arkansas.

How much strength did it take to pound a man's head through a wall like that? Terry wondered. The trailer walls were thin, granted, but still.

He duly photographed everything, then did a three-sixty panning shot with one of the department's iPads. He stood just inside the door long enough to send the photographic evidence to Linny Mars at the station. She would print off a set of pics for Lila and start two files, one digital and one hard copy. To Lila, Terry texted a brief message.

Know you're tired, but you better get out here.

Faint but approaching came the recognizable sound of St Theresa's one and only fully equipped ambulance, not a full-throated *WHOOP-WHOOP-WHOOP*, but a somehow prissy *whink-whink-whink*.

Roger Elway was stringing yellow CRIME SCENE DO NOT CROSS tape with a cigarette hanging from the corner of his mouth. Terry called to him from the trailer's steps.

'If Lila finds out you've been smoking at a crime scene, she'll tear you a new one.'

Roger removed the cigarette from his mouth, examined it as if he'd never seen such a thing before, put it out on the sole of his shoe, and tucked the butt into his shirt pocket. 'Where is Lila, anyway? Assistant DA's on his way, he'll expect her.'

The ambo pulled up, the doors sprang open, and Dick Bartlett and Andy Emerson, two EMTs that Terry had worked with before, got out fast, already gloving up. One carried a backboard, the other toted the portable hospital they called First In Bag.

Terry grunted. 'Only the Assistant Duck's Ass, huh? Two dead and we still don't rate the top guy.'

Roger shrugged. Bartlett and Emerson, meanwhile, after the initial hustle, had come to a halt beside the trailer, where the head stuck out of the wall.

Emerson said, 'I don't think that gentleman is going to benefit too much from our services.'

Bartlett was pointing a rubber-gloved finger at the place where the neck protruded. 'I believe he's got Mr Hankey tattooed on his neck.'

'The talking turd from *South Park?* Seriously?' Emerson came around to look. 'Oh, yeah. So he does.'

'*Howdy-ho!*' Bartlett sang.

'Hey,' Terry said. 'That's great, guys. Someday you should put your routine on YouTube. Right now we got another corpse inside, and there's a woman in our cruiser who could use a little help.'

Roger said, 'You sure you want to wake her up?' He jerked his head at Unit Four. A swatch of lank, dirty hair was plastered against the rear window. 'Girlfriend be crashing. Christ knows what she's been on.'

Bartlett and Emerson came across the junked-out yard to the cruiser, and Bartlett knocked on the window. 'Ma'am? Miss?' Nothing. He knocked harder. 'Come on, wakey-wakey.' Still nothing. He tried the doorhandle, and looked back at Terry and Roger when it didn't give. 'I need you to unlock it.'

'Oh,' Roger said. 'Right.' He thumbed the unlock button on his key fob. Dick Bartlett opened the back door, and Tiffany Jones spilled out like a load of dirty laundry. Bartlett grabbed her just in time to keep the top half of her body from hitting the weedy gravel.

Emerson sprang forward to help. Roger stayed put, looking vaguely irked. 'If she eighty-sixed on us, Lila's gonna be pissed like a bear. She's the only wit—'

'Where's her face?' Emerson asked. His voice was shocked. 'Where's her goddam *face?*'

That got Terry moving. He moved next to the cruiser as the two EMTs eased Tiffany gently to the ground. Terry grabbed her hanging hair — why, he wasn't sure — but let go in a hurry when something greasy squelched between his fingers. He wiped his hand on his shirt. Her hair was shot through with white, membranous stuff. Her face was also covered, her features now just dimly visible, as if seen through the kind of veil some older ladies still wore on their hats when they went to church out here in thank-you-Jesus country.

'What is that stuff?' Terry was still rubbing his hand. The stuff felt nasty, slippery, a little tingly. 'Spiderwebs?'

Roger was looking over his shoulder, eyes wide with a mixture of fascination and revulsion. 'It's coming out of her nose, Ter! And her eyes! What the fuck?'

EMT Bartlett pulled a swatch of the goo away from Tiffany's jawline and wiped it on his own shirt, but before he did, Terry saw that it appeared to be melting as soon as it was off her face. He looked at his own hand. The skin was dry and clear. Nothing on his shirt, either, although there had been a moment ago.

Emerson had his fingers on the side of Tiffany's throat. 'I have a pulse. Nice and steady. And she's breathing fine. I can see that crap billowing out and then sucking in. Let's get the MABIS.'

Bartlett hauled the orange MABIS all-in-one kit out of the First In Bag, hesitated, then went back into the bag for disposable glove packs. He gave one set to Emerson and took another for himself. Terry watched, wishing mightily he hadn't touched the webby stuff on Tiffany's skin. What if it was poisonous?

They got a blood pressure that Emerson said was normal. The EMTs went back and forth about whether or not to clear her eyes and check her pupils and, although they didn't know it then, made the best decision of their lives when they decided not to.

While they talked, Terry saw something he didn't like: Tiffany's web-encrusted mouth slowly opening and closing, as if she were chewing on air. Her tongue had gone white. Filaments rose from it, wavering like plankton.

Bartlett rose. 'We should get her to St Theresa's, stat, unless you have a problem with that. Say so if you do, because she seems stable . . .' He looked at Emerson, who nodded.

'Look at her eyes,' Roger said. 'All white. Gag me with a spoon.'

'Go on, take her,' Terry said. 'It's not like we can question her.'

'The two decedents,' Bartlett said. 'Is this stuff growing on them?'

'No,' Terry said, and pointed to the protruding head. 'On that one you can see for yourselves. Not Truman, the guy inside, either.'

'Any in the sink?' Bartlett asked. 'The toilet? The shower? I'm talking about wet places.'

'The TV is in the shower stall,' Terry said, which wasn't an answer, was in fact a total non sequitur, but all he could think of to say at first. Another non sequitur: Was the Squeak open yet? It was early, but you were allowed a beer or two on mornings like this; there was a special dispensation for gruesome corpses and creepy shit on people's faces. He kept looking at Tiffany Jones, who was slowly but steadily being buried alive under a diaphanous white fog of . . . something. He forced himself to speak to the question. 'Just on her.'

Roger Elway now said what they were all thinking. 'Fellas, what if it's contagious?'

No one replied.

Terry caught movement in the corner of his eye and swung back to look at the trailer. At first he thought the flock lifting off from its roof was butterflies, but butterflies were colorful, and these were plain brown and gray. Not butterflies but moths. Hundreds of them.

6

A dozen years before, on a muggy day in later summer, a call came in to animal control about a raccoon under the floor of the converted barn that the local Episcopalian church used as a 'pastoral center.' The concern was possible rabies. Frank had driven right over. He put on his facemask and elbow-length gloves, crawled under the barn, shone a flashlight on the animal, and it had darted, just the way a healthy raccoon should. That would have been that – rabid raccoons were serious, trespassing raccoons not so much – except that the pretty twenty-something woman who had shown him the hole under the barn had offered him a glass of blue Kool-Aid from the bake sale going on in the parking lot. It had been pretty nasty

– watered down, not enough sugar – but Frank drank three dollars' worth in order to stay there in the yellowing churchyard grass talking to the woman, who had a wonderful big laugh and a way of standing with her hands on her hips that made him feel tingly.

'Well, are you going to do your duty, Mr Geary?' Elaine finally asked in her patented way, abruptly chopping the head off the small talk, and getting to the point. 'I'd be happy to let you take me out if you put a lid on that critter that keeps killing things under the church floor. That's my offer. Your lips have turned blue.'

He had come back after work and nailed a piece of scrap over the hole under the barn – sorry, raccoon, a man's gotta do what a man's gotta do – and then he had taken his future wife to the movies.

Twelve years ago.

So what had happened? Was it him, or did marriage simply have a shelf-life?

For a long time, Frank had thought they were doing all right. They had the kid, the house, their health. Not everything was hunky-dunky, of course. Money was touch-and-go. Nana wasn't the most engaged student. Sometimes Frank got . . . well . . . things wore him down, and when he was worn down, a certain *edge* emerged. But everyone had failings, and over the course of twelve years, you were bound to spring an occasional leak. Only his wife didn't see it that way. Eight months ago she'd told him exactly how she saw it.

She had shared her insight after the famous kitchen wall punch. Shortly before the famous kitchen wall punch, she told him she'd given eight hundred dollars to her church, part of a fund drive to feed starving kids in some abysmally fucked-up part of Africa. Frank wasn't heartless; he grasped the suffering. But you didn't give away money you couldn't afford to give away. You didn't risk your own child's situation to help someone else's kids. Crazy as that had been – an entire mortgage payment zooming its way across the ocean – it hadn't prompted the famous wall punch. That was prompted by what she had said next, and the look on Elaine's face when she'd said it, simultaneously insolent and closed off: *It was my decision because it was my money.* As if her marriage vows meant nothing to her eleven years on, as if she could do anything she wanted without putting him in the loop. So he had punched the wall (not *her*, the *wall),* and Nana had run upstairs, wailing, and Elaine had made her declaration:

'You're going to snap on us, baby. One of these days it won't be the wall.'

Nothing Frank said or did could change her mind. It was either a trial separation or divorce, and Frank chose the former. And her prediction had been wrong. He hadn't snapped. Never would. He was strong. He was a protector.

Which left a fairly important question: What was she trying to prove? What benefit was she getting by putting him through this? Was it some unresolved childhood issue? Was it plain old sadism?

Whatever it was, it was fucking unreal. And fucking senseless. You did not, as an African-American man in the Tri-Counties (or any county in the United States), arrive at the age of thirty-eight without encountering far more than your fair share of senselessness – racism was the epitome of senselessness, after all. He recalled a miner's kid back in first or second grade, her front teeth fanned out like a poker hand, her hair in pigtails so short they looked like finger stubs. She had pressed a finger against his wrist and observed, 'You are the color of rottened, Frank. Like under my poppa's nails has.'

The girl's expression had been half-amused, half-impressed, and cataclysmically dumb. Even as a child Frank had recognized that black hole of incurable stupid. It amazed him and left him flabbergasted. Later, when he saw it in other faces, it would come to scare him, and anger him, but he was awestruck then. Stupid like that had its own gravitational field. It *pulled* at you.

Only Elaine wasn't dumb. You couldn't get farther from dumb than Elaine.

Elaine knew what it was like to be followed around a department store by some white kid who didn't even have a GED, playing like he's Batman and is going to catch her shoplifting a jar of peanuts. Elaine had been cursed by protestors outside Planned Parenthood, consigned to hell by people who didn't even know her name.

So what did she want? Why inflict this pain on him?

One nagging possibility: she was right to be worried.

As he went after the green Mercedes, Frank kept seeing Nana moving away from him, kicking her neatly arranged pieces of chalk and tracking through her drawing.

Frank knew he wasn't perfect, but he also knew that he was basically good. He helped people, he helped animals; he loved his daughter and he would do anything to protect her; and he had never put an abusive hand on his wife. Had he made mistakes? Was the famous wall punch one of them? Frank admitted as much. He would have stated it in a court of law. But he had never hurt anyone who didn't deserve to be hurt and he was just going to talk to the Mercedes guy, right?

Frank pulled his truck through a fancy wrought iron gate and parked behind the green Mercedes. The front fender on the left side was road-dusty, but the right side was sparkling clean. You could see where the sonofabitch had taken a rag to it.

Frank walked up the slate path connecting the driveway to the door of the big white house. Garden berms planted with sassafras lined the path, and the canopies created a corridor. Birds twittered in the branches above him. At the end of the path, by the foot of the steps, was a young lilac tree in a stone planter, near full bloom. Frank resisted the urge to uproot it. He climbed to the porch. On the face of the solid oak door was a brass knocker in the shape of a caduceus.

He told himself to turn around and drive straight home. Then he grabbed the knocker and banged it over and over against the plate.

7

It took awhile for Garth Flickinger to extricate himself from the couch. 'Hold on, hold on,' he said — pointlessly: the door was too thick and his voice too raspy. He had been smoking dope non-stop since he returned home from his visit to Truman Mayweather's stately pleasure trailer.

If anyone had asked him about the drugs, Garth would have made it a point to impress upon the questioner that he was merely an occasional, recreational user, but this morning had been an exception. An emergency, in fact. It wasn't every day that you were taking a whiz in your drug dealer's trailer and World War III broke out on the other side of the flimsy shithouse door. Something had happened – crashing, shooting, screaming – and, in a moment of incomprehensible idiocy, Garth had actually opened the door to check out what was going on. What he saw would be hard to forget. Perhaps impossible. At the far end of the trailer was a black-haired woman, naked from the waist down. She had hoisted up Truman's Arkansas buddy by his hair and the belt of his jeans, and was pounding him face-first into the wall – *whomp! whomp! whomp!*

Picture a siege engine, slamming a massive tree against castle gates. The man's head was awash in blood and his arms were ragdoll-flopping around at his sides.

Meanwhile, there was Truman, slumped on the floor with a bullet hole in his forehead. And the strange woman? Her expression was horrifyingly placid. It was as if she were just going about her business with no particular concern, except that her business was using a man's head as a battering ram. Garth had gently closed the door, hopped on the toilet lid, and climbed out the window. He had then sprinted for his car and driven home at the speed of light.

The experience had shaken his nerves a bit, and that was not a common occurrence. Garth Flickinger, Board Certified Plastic Surgeon, member in good standing of the American Society of Plastic Surgeons, was usually a pretty steady-handed fellow.

He was feeling better now, the rock that he'd smoked had helped with that; but the banging on the door was unwelcome.

Garth navigated his way around the couch and through the living room, crunching through a small sea of fast food boxes on the way.

On the flatscreen, an extremely sexy reporter was being extremely serious about a bunch of comatose old ladies at a nursing home in DC. Her seriousness only enhanced her sexiness. She was an A-cup, Garth thought, but her frame begged for a B.

'Why only women?' the reporter on the flatscreen wondered

aloud. 'At first we thought just the very elderly and the very young were vulnerable, but now it appears that women across age groups—'

Garth rested his forehead against the door and slapped it. 'Stop! Quit it!'

'Open up!'

The voice was deep and pissed off. He tapped some reserve strength and lifted his head to peer through the spyhole. An African-American man stood outside, mid-thirties, broad shoulders, face with terrific bone structure. The man's beige uniform momentarily caused Garth's pulse to accelerate – cop! – but then he noticed the patch read ANIMAL CONTROL.

Ah, you are a dogcatcher – a handsome dog of a dogcatcher to be sure, but a dogcatcher nonetheless. No fugitive canines here, sir, so no problem.

Or was there? Hard to be completely sure. Could this fellow be a friend of the half-naked harpy from the trailer? Better to be her friend than her enemy, Garth supposed, but far, far better to avoid her altogether.

'Did she send you?' Garth asked. 'I didn't see anything. Tell her that, okay?'

'I don't know what you're talking about! I came here on my own! Now open up!' the man yelled again.

'Why?' Garth asked, adding 'No way' for good measure.

'Sir! I just want to talk to you.' The dogcatcher had made an effort to lower his voice, but Garth could see him twisting his mouth around, fighting the need – yes, a need – to continue yelling.

'Not right now,' Garth said.

'Someone ran over a cat. The person was driving a green Mercedes. You have a green Mercedes.'

'That's unfortunate.' Meaning the cat, not the Mercedes. Garth liked cats. He had liked his Flamin' Groovies tee-shirt, as well, which was balled up on the floor by the stairs. Garth had used it to clean some blood off the fender of his car. Tough times all around. 'But I don't know anything about that, and I'm having a difficult morning, and so you'll have to leave. Sorry.'

A thud and the door shook in its frame. Garth backed up. The guy had kicked it.

Through the spyhole, Garth could see that the cords on the dogcatcher's neck were taut. 'My kid lives down the hill, you dumbfuck! What if that had been her? What if you drove over my kid instead of that cat?'

'I'm calling the cops,' Garth said. He hoped he sounded more convincing to the guy than he did to himself.

He retreated to the living room, sank into the couch, and picked up his pipe. The bag of dope was on the coffee table. Glass began to shatter outside. There was a metallic crunch. Was Señor Dogcatcher molesting his Mercedes? Garth didn't care, not today. (It was insured anyway.) That poor junkie girl. Tiffany was her name and she was so ruined and so sweet. Was she dead? Had the people who'd attacked the trailer (he assumed the strange woman was part of a gang) killed her? He told himself that Tiff, sweet as she was, wasn't his problem. Better not to fixate on what couldn't be changed.

The bag was blue plastic so the rocks appeared blue until you removed them. This was probably Tru Mayweather's half-assed tribute to *Breaking Bad*. There would be no more tributes from Truman Mayweather, half-assed or otherwise, not after this morning. Garth picked a rock, dropped it in the cup of his pipe. Whatever Señor Dogcatcher was doing to the Mercedes now caused the car alarm to go off: *beep, beep, beep.*

The television showed footage of a bright hospital room. Two female shapes lay under hospital sheets. Wispy cocoons covered the women's heads. It looked like they wore beehives that started at their chins. Garth fired up, sucked down a lungful, held it.

Beep, beep, beep.

Garth had a daughter, Cathy. She was eight, hydrocephalic, lived in a facility, a very nice one, near the coast of North Carolina, close enough to catch salt on the breeze. He paid for it all, which he could do. It was better for the girl if her mother looked after the details. Poor Cathy. What had he told himself about the junkie girl? Oh, right: better not to fixate on what couldn't be changed. Easier said than done. Poor Garth. Poor old ladies with their heads stuck in beehives. Poor cat.

The beautiful reporter was standing on a sidewalk in front of a gathering crowd. Honestly, she was fine with the A-cup. The B was just a thought. Had she had a nose job? Wow, if she had — and Garth wasn't quite certain, he'd need to see up close — it was a superb one, really natural with a pretty little button tip.

'The CDC has put out a bulletin,' she announced. '"Do not under any circumstances attempt to remove the growth."'

'Call me crazy,' Garth said, 'but that just makes me want to.'

Tired of the news, tired of the animal control guy, tired of the car alarm (although he supposed he would shut it off once the animal control guy decided to take his bad temper somewhere else), tired of fixating on what couldn't be changed, Garth channel surfed until he found an infomercial about building yourself an abdominal six-pack in just six days. He attempted to take down the 800 number, but the only pen he could find didn't work on the skin of his palm.

CHAPTER 4

1

The total population of McDowell, Bridger, and Dooling counties amounted to roughly seventy-two thousand souls, fifty-five percent male, forty-five percent female. This was down five thousand from the last full US census, officially making the Tri-Counties an 'out-migration area.' There were two hospitals, one in McDowell County ('Great gift shop!' read the only post in the comment section of the McDowell Hospital's website) and a much bigger one in Dooling County, where the largest population – thirty-two thousand – resided. There were a total of ten walk-in clinics in the three counties, plus two dozen so-called 'pain clinics' out in the piney woods, where various opioid drugs could be obtained with prescriptions written on the spot. Once, before most of the mines had played out, the Tri-Counties had been known as the Republic of Fingerless Men. These days it had become the Republic of Unemployed Men, but there was a bright side: most of those under fifty had all their fingers, and it had been ten years since anyone had died in a mine cave-in.

On the morning Evie Doe (so recorded by Lila Norcross because her prisoner would give no last name) visited Truman Mayweather's trailer, most of the fourteen thousand or so females in Dooling County awoke as usual and started their day. Many of them saw the television reports about the spreading contagion that was first called Australian Sleeping Sickness, then the Female

Sleeping Flu, and then the Aurora Flu, named for the princess in the Walt Disney retelling of the *Sleeping Beauty* fairy tale. Few of the Tri-County women who saw the reports were frightened by them; Australia, Hawaii, and Los Angeles were faraway places, after all, and although Michaela Morgan's report from that old folks' home in Georgetown was mildly alarming, and Washington, DC, was geographically close – not even a day's drive – DC was still a city, and for most people in the Tri-Counties, that put it in an entirely different category. Besides, not many people in the area watched NewsAmerica, preferring *Good Day Wheeling* or Ellen DeGeneres.

The first sign that something might be wrong even out here in God's country came shortly after eight o'clock A.M. It arrived at the doors of St Theresa's in the person of Yvette Quinn, who parked her elderly Jeep Cherokee askew at the curb and came charging into the ER with her infant twin girls crooked in her arms. A tiny, cocoon-swaddled face rested against each of her breasts. She was screaming like a fire siren, bringing doctors and nurses running.

'Someone help my babies! They won't wake up! They won't wake up for anything!'

Tiffany Jones, much older but similarly swaddled, arrived soon thereafter, and by three o'clock that afternoon, the ER was full. And still they came: fathers and mothers carrying daughters, girls carrying little sisters, uncles carrying nieces, husbands carrying wives. There was no *Judge Judy*, no *Dr. Phil*, and no game shows on the waiting room TV that afternoon. Only news, and all of it was about the mysterious sleeping sickness, the one that affected only those with the XX chromosome.

The exact minute, half-minute, or second, when sleeping female *Homo sapiens* stopped waking up and began to form their coverings was never conclusively determined. Based on the cumulative data, however, scientists were eventually able to narrow the window to a point between 7:37 A.M. EST and 7:57 A.M. EST.

'We can only wait for them to wake up,' said George Alderson on NewsAmerica. 'And so far, at least, none of them have. Here's Michaela Morgan with more.'

2

By the time Lila Norcross arrived at the square brick building that housed the Dooling County sheriff's station on one side and Municipal Affairs on the other, it was all hands on deck. Deputy Reed Barrows was waiting at the curb, ready to babysit Lila's current prisoner.

'Be good, Evie,' she said, opening the door. 'I'll be right back.'

'Be good, Lila,' Evie said. 'I'll be right here.' She laughed. Blood from her nose was drying to a crack-glaze on her cheeks; more blood, from the gash on her forehead, had stiffened her hair in front, forming a small peacock fan.

As Lila exited the car, making way for Reed to slide in, Evie added, 'Triple-double,' and laughed some more.

'Forensics is on the way to that trailer,' Reed said. 'Also the ADA and Unit Six.'

'Good,' Lila said, and trotted toward the door of the station.

'Triple-double, she thought. Ah, there it was: at least ten points, ten assists, and ten rebounds. And that was what the girl had done last night at the basketball game, the one Lila had come to see.

The girl, she thought of her. Her name was Sheila. It wasn't the girl's fault. *Sheila's* fault. Her name was the first step toward . . . What? She didn't know. She just didn't know.

And Clint. What did *Clint* want? She knew she shouldn't care, given the circumstances, but she did. He was a true mystery to her. A familiar image came: her husband, sitting at the kitchen counter, staring out at the elms in the backyard, running his thumb over his knuckles, vaguely grimacing. Long ago she'd stopped asking him if he was all right. Just thinking, he always said, just thinking. But about what? And about whom? These were obvious questions, weren't they?

Lila couldn't believe how tired she felt, how weak, as if she had dribbled out of her uniform and all over her shoes in the twenty or so paces between the cruiser and the steps. It suddenly seemed as though everything was open to question, and if Clint wasn't Clint, then who was she? Who was anybody?

She needed to focus. Two men were dead and the woman who had probably killed them was in the back of Lila's cruiser, higher than a kite. Lila could be tired and weak, but not now.

Oscar Silver and Barry Holden were standing in the main office. 'Gentlemen,' she said.

'Sheriff,' they said, almost in unison.

Judge Silver was older than God and shaky on his pins, but suffered from no shortage in the brains department. Barry Holden eked out a living for himself and his tribe of female dependents (one wife, four daughters) writing wills and contracts, and negotiating insurance settlements (mostly with that notorious dragon Drew T. Barry of Drew T. Barry Indemnity). Holden was also one of the half a dozen Tri-County lawyers who served as public defenders on a rotating basis. He was a good guy, and it didn't take long for Lila to explain what she wanted. He was agreeable, but needed a retainer. He said a dollar would do.

'Linny, do you have a dollar?' Lila asked her dispatcher. 'It might look funny if I hired representation for a woman I've arrested on two counts of capital murder.'

Linny handed Barry a dollar. He put it in his pocket, turned to Judge Silver, and spoke in his best courtroom voice. 'Having been retained by Linnette Mars on behalf of the prisoner Sheriff Norcross has just taken into custody, I request and petition that . . . what's her name, Lila?'

'Evie, no last yet. Call her Evie Doe.'

'That Evie Doe be remanded to the custody of Dr Clinton Norcross for psychiatric examination, said examination to take place at Dooling Correctional Facility for Women.'

'So ordered,' Judge Silver said smartly.

'Um, what about the district attorney?' Linny asked from her desk. 'Doesn't Janker get a say?'

'Janker agrees in absentia,' Judge Silver replied. 'Having saved his incompetent bacon in my courtroom on more than one occasion, I can say that with complete confidence. I order Evie Doe to be transported to Dooling Correctional immediately, and held there for a period of . . . how about forty-eight hours, Lila?'

'Make it ninety-six,' Barry Holden said, apparently feeling that he ought to do something for his client.

'I'm okay with ninety-six, Judge,' Lila said. 'I just want to get her someplace where she won't hurt herself anymore while I get some answers.'

Linny spoke up. In Lila's opinion, she was becoming a bit of a pain. 'Will Clint and Warden Coates be okay with a guest camper?'

'I'll handle that,' Lila said, and thought again about her new prisoner. Evie Doe, the mystery killer who knew Lila's name, and who babbled about triple-doubles. Obviously a coincidence, but an unwelcome and badly timed one. 'Let's get her in here long enough to roll some fingerprints. Also, Linny and I need to take her into one of the holding cells and put her into some County Browns. The shirt she's got on has to be marked as evidence, and it's all she's wearing. I can't very well take her up to the prison buck-ass naked, can I?'

'No, as her lawyer, I couldn't approve of that at all,' Barry said.

3

'So, Jeanette — what's going on?'

Jeanette considered Clint's opening gambit. 'Hmm, let's see. Ree said she had a dream last night about eating cake with Michelle Obama.'

The two of them, prison psychiatrist and patient–inmate, were making slow circuits of the exercise yard. It was deserted at this time of the morning, when most of the inmates were busy at their various jobs (carpentry, furniture manufacture, maintenance, laundry, cleaning), or attending GED classes in what was known in Dooling Correctional as Dumb School, or simply lying in their cells and stacking time.

Pinned to the top of Jeanette's beige smock top was a Yard Pass, signed by Clint himself. Which made him responsible for her. That was okay. She was one of his favorite patient–inmates (one of his *pets*, Warden Janice Coates would have said, annoyingly), and the least troublesome. In his opinion, Jeanette belonged on the outside

– not in another institution, but outside altogether, walking free. It wasn't an opinion he would have offered to Jeanette, because what good would that do her? This was Appalachia. In Appalachia, you didn't get a free pass on murder, it didn't matter if it was second degree. His belief in Jeanette's lack of culpability in the death of Damian Sorley was the sort of thing that he wouldn't express to anyone except his wife and maybe not even to her. Lately Lila seemed a little off. A little preoccupied. This morning, for instance, although that was probably because she needed some sleep. And there was that thing Vanessa Lampley had said about an overturned pet food truck on Mountain Rest Road last year. How likely was it that there had been two identical, bizarre accidents months apart?

'Hey, Dr N., are you there? I said that Ree—'

'Had a dream about eating with Michelle Obama, got it.'

'That's what she said at *first*. But she just made that up. She actually had a dream about a teacher telling her she was in the wrong classroom. Total anxiety dream, wouldn't you say?'

'Could be.' It was one of about a dozen default positions he kept ready for answering patient questions.

'Hey, Doc, you think Tom Brady might come here? Give a speech, sign some autographs?'

'Could be.'

'You know, he could sign some of those little toy footballs.'

'Sure.'

Jeanette stopped. 'What did I just say?'

Clint thought about it, then laughed. 'Busted.'

'Where are you this morning, Doc? You're doing that thing you do. Pardon me for, like, barging in on your personal space, but is everything okay at home?'

With a nasty internal start, Clint realized he was no longer sure that was true, and Jeanette's unexpected question – her insight – was unsettling. Lila had lied to him. There hadn't been a crash on the Mountain Rest Road, not last night. He was suddenly sure of that.

'Everything's fine at home. What's the thing I do?'

She made a frowny face and held up her fist and ran her thumb back and forth over her knuckles. 'When you do that, I know you're out there picking daisies or something. It's almost like you're remembering a fight you were in.'

'Ah,' said Clint. That was too close for comfort. 'Old habit. Let's talk about you, Jeanette.'

'My favorite subject.' It sounded good, but Clint knew better. If he let Jeanette lead the conversation, they would spend this entire hour in the sun talking about Ree Dempster, Michelle Obama, Tom Brady, and whomever else she could free associate. When it came to free association, Jeanette was a champ.

'Okay. What did *you* dream about last night? If we're going to talk about dreams, let's talk about yours, not Ree's.'

'I can't remember. Ree asked me, and I told her the same thing. I think it's that new med you put me on.'

'So you did dream something.'

'Yeah . . . probably . . .' Jeanette was looking at the vegetable garden rather than at him.

'Could it have been about Damian? You used to dream about him quite a bit.'

'Sure, about how he looked. All blue. But I haven't had the blue man dream in a long time. Hey, do you remember that movie, *The Omen*? About the son of the devil? That kid's name was Damien, too.'

'You have a son . . .'

'So?' She was looking at him now, and a bit distrustfully.

'Well, some people might say your husband was the devil in your life, which would make Bobby—'

'The son of the devil! *Omen Two*!' She pealed laughter, pointing a finger at him. 'Oh, that's too funny! Bobby is the sweetest kid in the world, takes after my momma's side of the family. He comes all the way from Ohio with my sister to see me every other month. You know that.' She laughed some more, a sound not common to this fenced and strictly monitored acre of ground, but very sweet. 'You know what I'm thinking?'

'Nope,' Clint said. 'I'm a shrink, not a mind-reader.'

'I'm thinking this might be a classic case of *transference*.' She wiggled the first two fingers of each hand in the air to make quotation marks around the key word. 'As in you're worried that *your* boy is the devil's child.'

It was Clint's turn to laugh. The idea of Jared as the devil's anything, Jared who brushed mosquitoes off his arms rather than swatting them, was surreal. He worried about his son, yes, but not that he would ever wind up behind bars and barbed wire, like Jeanette and Ree Dempster and Kitty McDavid and the ticking time-bomb known as Angel Fitzroy. Hell, the kid didn't even have enough nerve to ask Mary Pak to go to the Spring Dance with him.

'Jared's fine, and I'm sure your Bobby is, too. How's that medication doing with your . . . what do you call them?'

'My blurries. That's when I can't see people just right, or hear them just right. It's all kinds of better since I started the new pills.'

'You're not just saying that? Because you have to be honest with me, Jeanette. You know what I always say?'

'*HPD,* honesty pays dividends. And I'm being straight with you. It's better. I sometimes still get down, though, then I start to drift and the blurries come back.'

'Any exceptions? Anyone who comes through loud and clear even when you're depressed? And can maybe bootstrap you out of it?'

'Bootstrap! I like that. Yeah, Bobby can. He was five when I came in here. Twelve now. He plays keyboards in a group, can you believe that? And sings!'

'You must be very proud.'

'I am! Yours must be about the same age, right?'

Clint, who knew when one of his ladies was trying to turn the conversation, made a noncommittal noise instead of telling her that Jared was approaching voting age, weird as that seemed to him.

She thumped his shoulder. 'Make sure he's got condoms.'

From the umbrella-shaded guard post near the north wall, an amplified voice blared, 'PRISONER! NO PHYSICAL CONTACT!'

Clint tossed the officer a wave (hard to tell because of the loud-hailer, but he thought the uni in the lawn chair was that asshole Don Peters) to show all was cool and then said to Jeanette, 'Now I'm going to have to discuss this with *my* therapist.'

She laughed, pleased.

It occurred to Clint, not for the first time, that if circumstances were entirely different, he would have wanted Jeanette Sorley for a friend.

'Hey, Jeanette. You know who Warner Wolf is?'

'Let's go to the videotape!' she responded promptly, a spot-on imitation. 'Why do you ask?'

It was a good question. Why *did* he ask? What did an old sports-caster have to do with anything? And why should it matter if his pop culture frame of reference (like his physique) was a little out of date?

Another, better question: Why had Lila lied to him?

'Oh,' Clint said, 'someone mentioned him. Struck me funny.'

'Yeah, my dad loved him,' Jeanette said.

'Your dad.'

A snatch of 'Hey Jude' came from his phone. He looked at the screen and saw his wife's picture. Lila, who should have been deep in dreamland; Lila, who might or might not remember Warner Wolf; Lila, who had lied.

'I need to take this,' he told Jeanette, 'but I'll keep it brief. You should stroll over there to the garden, pull some weeds, and see if you can remember what you dreamed last night.'

'Little privacy, got it,' she said, and walked toward the garden.

Clint waved toward the north wall again, indicating to the officer that Jeanette's move was sanctioned, then pushed ACCEPT. 'Hey, Lila, what's going on?' Aware as it came out of his mouth that it was how he had started many a patient conference.

'Oh, the usual,' she said. 'Meth lab explosion, double homicide, doer in custody. I collared her strolling up Ball's Hill pretty much in her altogether.'

'This is a joke, right?'

'Afraid not.'

'Holy shit, are you okay?'

'Running on pure adrenalin, but otherwise fine. I need some help, though.'

She filled in the details. Clint listened, not asking questions.

Jeanette was working herself along a row of peas, pulling weeds and singing something cheerful about going uptown to the Harlem River to drown. At the north end of the prison yard, Vanessa Lampley approached Don Peters's lawn chair, spoke to him, then took the seat as Don trudged toward the admin wing, head down like a kid who has been called to the principal's office. And if anyone deserved to be called in, it was that bag of guts and waters.

'Clint? Are you still there?'

'Right here. Just thinking.'

'Just thinking,' Lila repeated. 'About what?'

'About the process.' The way she pressed him took Clint aback. It almost seemed like she had been mocking him. 'In theory it's possible, but I'd have to check with Janice—'

'Then do it, please. I can be there in twenty minutes. And if Janice needs convincing, convince her. I need help here, Clint.'

'Calm down, I'll do it. Fear of self-harm is a valid concern.' Jeanette had finished one row and was working her way back toward him along the next. 'I'm just saying that ordinarily, you'd take her to St Terry's first to get her checked out. Sounds like she whammed her face pretty good.'

'Her face isn't my immediate concern. She nearly tore one man's head off, and stuck another guy's head through a trailer wall. Do you really think I should put her in an exam room with some twenty-five-year-old resident?'

He wanted to ask again if she was all right, but in her current mood she'd go ballistic, because when you were tired and ragged, that's what you did, lashed out at the person who was safe. Sometimes – often, even – Clint resented having to be the safe one. 'Perhaps not.'

Now he could hear street sounds. Lila had left the building. 'It's not just that she's dangerous, and it's not just that she's off her gourd. It's like – Jared would say, "My Spidey Sense is tingling."'

'Maybe when he was seven.'

'I've never seen her before in my life, I'd swear to that on a pile of Bibles, but she knows me. She called me by name.'

'If you're wearing your uniform shirt, and I assume you are, there's a name tag on your breast pocket.'

'Right, but all it says is NORCROSS. She called me Lila. I have to get off the phone. Just tell me that when I get there with her, the welcome mat will be out.'

'It will be.'

'Thank you.' He heard her clear her throat. 'Thank you, honey.'

'You're welcome, but you have to do something for me. Don't bring her alone. You're beat.'

'Reed Barrows will be driving. I'm riding shotgun.'

'Good. Love you.'

There was the sound of a car door opening, probably Lila's cruiser. 'Love you, too,' she said, and clicked off.

Was there a slight hesitation there? No time to think about that now, to pick at it until it turned into something it probably wasn't, which was just as well.

'Jeanette!' And when she turned to him: 'I'm going to have to cut our session short. Something has come up.'

4

Bullshit was Coates's arch-enemy. Not that most people were friends with it, or even liked it, but they put up with bullshit, came to an understanding with it, and they dished up their fair share. Warden Janice Tabitha Coates didn't bullshit. It wasn't in her disposition and it would have been counterproductive anyway. Prison was basically a bullshit factory, call it the Dooling Bullshit Manufacturing Facility for Women, and it was her job to keep production from raging out of control. Waves of bullshit memos came down from the state that demanded she simultaneously cut costs and improve services. A steady stream of bullshit flowed from the courts – inmates and defense attorneys and prosecutors bickering over appeals – and Coates always seemed to get drawn in somehow. The health department loved to drop in for bullshit inspections. The engineers who came to repair the prison electrical grid always promised that this would be the last time – but their promises were bullshit. The grid kept right on crashing.

And the bullshit didn't stop while Coates was at home. Even as she slept, it piled up, like a drift in a snowstorm, a brown drift made of bullshit. Like Kitty McDavid going nuts, and the two physicians' assistants picking the exact same morning to go AWOL. That stinking pile had been waiting for her the moment she stepped through the door.

Norcross was a solid shrink, but he produced his share of bovine excrement, too, requesting special treatments and dispensations for his patients. His chronic failure to recognize that the vast majority of his patients, the inmates of Dooling, were themselves bullshit geniuses, women who had spent their lives nurturing bullshit excuses, was almost touching, except that it was Coates who had to wield the shovel.

And hey, underneath their bullshit, some of the women did have real reasons. Janice Coates wasn't stupid and she wasn't heartless. Lots of the women of Dooling were, above all else, luckless. Coates knew that. Bad childhoods, horrible husbands, impossible situations, mental illnesses medicated with drugs and alcohol. They were victims of bullshit as well as purveyors of it. However, it wasn't the warden's job to sort any of that out. Pity could not be allowed to compromise her duty. They were here, and she had to take care of them.

Which meant she had to deal with Don Peters, who appeared before her now, the bullshit artist supreme, just finishing his latest bullshit story: the honest workingman, unfairly accused.

When he had put on the finishing touches, she said, 'Don't give me that union crap, Peters. One more complaint and you're out. I got one inmate saying you grabbed her breast, I've got another saying you squeezed her butt, and I've got a third saying you offered her half a pack of Newports to suck you off. The union wants to go to the mattresses for you, that's their choice, but I don't think they will.'

The squat little officer sat on her couch with his legs spread wide (as if his basket was something she wanted to look at) and his arms crossed. He blew at the Buster Brown bangs that hung down over his eyebrows. 'I never touched anyone, Warden.'

'No shame in resigning.'

'I'm not quitting, and I'm not ashamed of anything I've done!' Red suffused his normally pale cheeks.

'Must be nice. I've got a list of things I'm ashamed of. Signing off on your application in the first place is near the top of it. You're like a booger I can't get off my finger.'

Don's lips took on a crafty twist. 'I know you're trying to make me angry, Warden. It won't work.'

He wasn't stupid, was the thing. That was the reason no one had nailed him so far. Peters was canny enough to make his moves when no one else was around.

'Guess not.' Coates, seated on the edge of her desk, pulled her bag into her lap. 'Can't blame a girl for trying.'

'You know they lie. They're criminals.'

'Sexual harassment's a crime, too. You've had your last warning.' Coates rummaged in her bag, searching for her ChapStick. 'By the way, only half a pack? Come on, Don.' She yanked out tissues, her lighter, her pill bottle, her iPhone, wallet, and finally found what she was looking for. The cap had fallen off and the stick was flecked with bits of lint. Janice used it anyway.

Peters had fallen silent. She looked at him. He was a punk and an abuser and incredibly fortunate that another officer hadn't stepped forward as a witness to any of the abuses. She'd get him, though. She had time. Time was, in fact, another word for prison.

'What? You want some?' Coates held out her ChapStick. 'No? Then get back to work.'

The door rattled in the frame when he slammed it and she heard him thudding flat-footed out of the reception area, like a teen doing a tantrum. Satisfied that the disciplinary session had gone about as she had expected, Coates returned to the matter of her linty ChapStick, and began to stir around in her bag for the cap.

Her phone vibrated. Coates set her bag on the floor and walked to the vacated couch. She considered how much she disliked the person whose ass had last been planted there, and sat down to the left of the dent in the center cushion.

'Hi, Mom.' Behind Michaela's voice was the sound of other voices, some shouting, and sirens.

Coates put aside her initial impulse to skin her daughter for not calling in three weeks. 'What's wrong, honey?'

'Hold on.'

The sounds became muffled and Janice waited. Her relationship with her daughter had had its ups and downs. Michaela's decision to quit law school and go into television journalism (as big a bullshit factory in its own way as the prison system, and probably just as full of criminals) had been a valley, and the nose job that followed had taken them way, way below sea level for awhile. There was a persistence to Michaela, however, which Coates had gradually come to respect. Maybe they weren't as different as it seemed. Daffy Magda Dubcek, the local woman who had babysat for Janice when Michaela was a toddler, once said, 'She's like you, Janice! She cannot be denied! Tell her one cookie, she make it her personal mission to eat three. Smile and giggle and sweet you up until you cannot say no.'

Two years ago, Michaela had been doing puff pieces on the local news. Now she was on NewsAmerica, where her rise had been rapid.

'Okay,' Michaela said, coming back on. 'Had to get someplace quiet. They've got us outside the CDC. I can't talk long. Have you been watching the news?'

'CNN, of course.' Janice loved this jab and never missed a chance to use it.

This time Michaela ignored it. 'You know about the Aurora Flu? The sleeping sickness?'

'Something on the radio. Old women who can't wake up in Hawaii and Australia—'

'It's real, Mom, and it's any woman. Elderly, infant, young, middle-aged. Any woman who sleeps. So: *don't go to sleep.*'

'Pardon?' Something wasn't tracking here. It was eleven in the morning. Why would she go to sleep? Was Michaela saying she should never sleep again? If so, it wasn't going to work out. Might as well ask her to never pee again. 'That doesn't make any sense.'

'Turn on the news, Mom. Or the radio. Or the Internet.'

The impossibility lingered between them on the line. Janice didn't know what else to say except, 'Okay.' Her kid might be wrong, but her kid wouldn't lie to her. Bullshit or not, Michaela believed it was the truth.

'The scientist I just talked to – she's with the feds, and a friend, I trust her – is on the inside. She says that they're estimating that eighty-five percent of women in the Pacific standard time zone are already out. Don't tell anyone that, it's going to be pandemonium as soon as it hits the Internet.'

'What do you mean *out*?'

'I mean, they aren't waking up. They're forming these – they're like cocoons. Membranes, coatings. The cocoons seem to be partly cerumen – ear wax – partly sebum, which is the oily stuff on the sides of your nose, partially mucus, and . . . something else no one understands, some kind of strange protein. It re-forms almost as quick as it comes off, but don't try to take it off. There have been – reactions. Okay? *Do-not-attempt-to-remove-the-stuff.*' On this last matter, which made no more sense than the rest, Michaela seemed uncharacteristically severe. '*Mom?*'

'Yes, Michaela. I'm still right here.'

Her daughter sounded excited now – keen. 'It started happening between seven and eight our time, between four and five Pacific standard, which is why the women west of us got hit so hard. So we've got all day. We've got just about a full tank.'

'A full tank – of waking hours?'

'Bingo.' Michaela heaved a breath. 'I know how crazy this thing sounds, but I am in no way kidding. You've got to keep yourself awake. And you're going to have some hard decisions to make. You need to figure out what you're going to do with your prison.'

'With my prison?'

'Your inmates are going to start falling asleep.'

'Oh,' Janice said. She suddenly did see. At least sort of.

'Have to go, Mom, I've got a stand-up and the producer's going crazy. I'll call when I can.'

Coates stayed on the couch. Her gaze found the framed photograph on her desk. It showed the late Archibald Coates, grinning in surgical scrubs, holding his infant daughter in the crook of his arm. Dead of a coronary at the impossibly unfair age of thirty,

Archie had been gone now almost as long as he had lived. In the picture there was a bit of whitish afterbirth on Michaela's forehead, like a scrap of web. The warden wished she'd told her daughter that she loved her — but the regret only held her still for a few seconds. There was work to be done. It had taken a few seconds to get a hold on the problem, but the answer — what to do with the women of the prison — did not seem to Janice to be multiple-choice. For as long as she could, she needed to keep on doing what she had always done: maintain order and keep ahead of the bullshit.

She told her secretary, Blanche McIntyre, to buzz their PAs again at their homes. After that, Blanche was to call Lawrence Hicks, the vice-warden, and inform him that his recovery time from wisdom tooth surgery was being curtailed; he was required on the premises immediately. Finally, she needed Blanche to notify each of the officers on duty in turn: due to the national situation everyone was pulling a double. The warden had serious concerns about whether or not she could count on the next rotation coming in. In an emergency people were reluctant to leave their loved ones.

'What?' Blanche asked. '*The national situation*? Did something happen to the president? And you want everyone for a double? They aren't going to like that.'

'I don't care what they like. Turn on the news, Blanche.'

'I don't understand. What's happening?'

'If my daughter's right, you'll know it when you hear it.'

Next, Coates went to get Norcross in his office. They were going to check on Kitty McDavid together.

5

Jared Norcross and Mary Pak were sitting on the bleachers during Period Three PE, their tennis rackets put aside for the time being. They and a bunch of Silly Sophomores on the lower tiers were watching two seniors playing on the center court, grunting like Monica Seles with each hit. The skinny one was Curt McLeod. The muscular redhead was Eric Blass.

My nemesis, Jared thought.

'I don't think it's a good idea,' he said.

Mary looked at him, eyebrows raised. She was tall, and (in Jared's opinion) perfectly proportioned. Her hair was black, her eyes were gray, her legs long and tanned, her lowtops immaculately white. Immaculate was, in fact, the best word for her. In Jared's opinion. 'And that would be apropos what?'

As if you don't know, Jared thought. 'Apropos you going to see Arcade Fire with Eric.'

'Um.' She appeared to think this over. 'Lucky you're not the one going with him, then.'

'Hey, remember the field trip to the Kruger Street Toy and Train Museum? Back in fifth grade?'

Mary smiled and brushed her hand, the nails painted a velvety blue, through her long hair. 'How could I forget? We almost didn't get in, because Billy Mears wrote some nasty ink on his arm. Mrs Colby made him stay on the bus with the driver, the one who had the stutter.'

Eric lofted the ball, went up on his toes, and whacked a killer serve that barely topped the net. Instead of trying to return it, Curt flinched back. Eric raised his arms like Rocky at the top of the Philadelphia Museum of Art steps. Mary clapped. Eric turned toward her and bowed.

Jared said, 'It was MRS COLBY EATS THE BIG ONE on his arm, and Billy didn't put it there. Eric did. Billy was fast asleep when he did it, and kept his mouth shut because staying on the bus was better than getting beaten up by Eric at a later date.'

'So?'

'So Eric's a bully.'

'Was a bully,' Mary said. 'Fifth grade was a long time ago.'

'As the twig is bent, so the bough is shaped.' Jared heard the pedantic tone his father sometimes adopted, and would have taken it back if he could.

Mary's gray eyes were on him, appraising. 'Meaning what?'

Stop, Jared told himself, just shrug and say *whatever* and let it go. He often gave himself such good advice, and his mouth usually overrode him. It did so now.

'Meaning people don't change.'

'Sometimes they do. My dad used to drink too much, but he stopped. He goes to AA meetings now.'

'Okay, some people do. I'm glad your father was one of them.'

'You better be.' The gray eyes were still fixed on him.

'But most people don't. Just think about it. The fifth grade jocks – like Eric – are still the jocks. You were a smart kid then, and you're a smart kid now. The kids who got in trouble in fifth are still getting in trouble in eleventh and twelfth. You ever see Eric and Billy together? No? Case closed.'

This time Curt managed to handle Eric's serve, but the return was a bunny and Eric was vulturing the net, almost hanging over it. His return – a clear net-foul – hit Curt in the belt-buckle. 'Quit it, dude!' Curt shouted. 'I might want to have kids someday!'

'Bad idea,' Eric said. 'Now go get that, it's my lucky ball. Fetch, Rover.'

While Curt shuffled sulkily to the chainlink fence where the ball had come to rest, Eric turned to Mary and took another bow. She gave him a hundred-watt smile. It stayed on when she turned back to Jared, but the wattage dimmed considerably.

'I love you for wanting to protect me, Jere, but I'm a big girl. It's a concert, not a lifelong commitment.'

'Just . . .'

'Just what?' The smile was all gone now.

Just watch out for him, Jared wanted to say. Because writing on Billy's arm was a minor thing. A grade-school thing. In high school there have been ugly locker room stunts I don't want to talk about. In part, because I never put a stop to any of them. I just watched.

More good advice, and before his traitor mouth could disregard it, Mary swiveled in her seat, looking toward the school. Some movement must have caught her eye, and now Jared saw it, too: a brown cloud lifting off from the gymnasium roof. It was large enough to scare up the crows that had been roosting in the oaks surrounding the faculty parking lot.

Dust, Jared thought, but instead of dissipating, the cloud banked sharply and headed north. It was flocking behavior, but those weren't birds. They were too small even for sparrows.

'An eclipse of moths!' Mary exclaimed. 'Wow! Who knew?'

'That's what you call a whole bunch of them? An eclipse?'

'Yes! Who knew they flocked? And most moths leave daytime to the butterflies. Moths are fly-by-nights. At least, usually.'

'How do you know all that?'

'I did my eighth grade science project on moths – *mott*, in Old English, meaning *maggot*. My dad talked me into doing it, because I used to be scared of them. Someone told me when I was little that if you got the dust from a moth's wings in your eyes, you'd go blind. My dad said that was just an old wives' tale, and if I did my science project on moths, I might be able to make friends with them. He said that butterflies are the beauty queens of the insect world, they always get to go to the ball, and the poor moths are the ones who get left behind like Cinderella. He was still drinking then, but it was a fun story just the same.'

Those gray eyes on him, daring him to disagree.

'Sure, cool,' Jared said. 'Did you?'

'Did I what?'

'Make friends with them.'

'Not exactly, but I found out lots of interesting stuff. Butterflies close their wings over their backs when they're at rest. Moths use theirs to protect their bellies. Moths have frenulums – those are wing-coupling devices – but butterflies don't. Butterflies make a chrysalis, which is hard. Moths make cocoons, which are soft and silky.'

'Yo!' It was Kent Daley, riding his bike across the softball field from the tangle of waste ground beyond. He was wearing a back-pack and his tennis racket was slung over his shoulder. 'Norcross! Pak! You see all those birds take off?'

'They were moths,' Jared said. 'The ones with frenulums. Or maybe it's frenula.'

'Huh?'

'Never mind. What are you doing? It's a school day, you know.'

'Had to take out the garbage for my ma.'

'Must have been a lot of it,' Mary said. 'It's already Period Three.'

Kent smirked at her, then saw Eric and Curt on the center court and dropped his bike into the grass. 'Take a seat, Curt, let a man take over. You couldn't hit Eric's serve if your dog's life depended on it.'

Curt ceded his end of the court to Kent, a bon vivant who did not seem to feel any pressing need to visit the office and explain his late arrival. Eric served, and Jared was delighted when the newly arrived Kent smashed it right back at him.

'The Aztecs believed that black moths were omens of bad luck,' Mary said. She had lost interest in the tennis match going on below. 'There are people out in the hollers who still believe a white moth in the house means someone's going to die.'

'You are a regular moth-matician, Mary.'

Mary made a sad trombone noise.

'Wait, you've never been in a holler in your life. You just made that up to be creepy. Good job, by the way.'

'No, I didn't make it up! I read it in a book!'

She punched him in the shoulder. It kind of hurt, but Jared pretended it didn't.

'Those were brown ones,' Jared said. 'What do brown ones mean?'

'Oh, that's interesting,' Mary said. 'According to the Blackfeet Indians, brown moths bring sleep and dreams.'

6

Jared sat on a bench at the far end of the locker room, dressing. The Silly Sophomores had already departed, afraid of getting whipped with wet towels, a thing for which Eric and his cohorts were famous. Or maybe the right word was infamous. You say frenulum, I say frenula, Jared thought, putting on his sneakers. Let's call the whole thing off.

In the shower, Eric, Curt, and Kent were hooting and splashing and bellowing all the standard witticisms: fuck you, fuck ya mother, I already did, fag, bite my bag, your sister's a scag, she's on the rag, et cetera. It was tiresome, and there was so much high school left before he could escape.

The water went off. Eric and the other two slapped wet-footed into the area of the locker room they considered their private preserve – seniors only, please – which meant Jared only had to suffer a brief glimpse at their bare butts before they disappeared around the corner. Fine with him. He sniffed his tennis socks, winced, stuffed them into his gym bag, and zipped it up.

'I saw Old Essie on my way here,' Kent was saying.

Curt: 'The homeless chick? The one with the shopping cart?'

'Yeah. Almost rode over her and fell into that shithole where she lives.'

'Someone ought to clean her out of there,' Curt said.

'She must have busted open her stash of Two Buck Chuck last night,' Kent said. 'Totally out cold. And she must have rolled in something. She had cobwebby crud all over her face. Fucking nasty. I could see it moving when she breathed. So I give her a yell, right? "Hey Essie, what's up, girl? What's up, you toothless old cunt?" Nothing, man. Fuckin flatline.'

Curt said, 'I wish there was a magic potion to put girls to sleep so you could bang em without having to butter them up first.'

'There is,' Eric said. 'It's called roofies.'

As they bellowed laughter, Jared thought, That's the guy taking Mary to see Arcade Fire. That guy right over there.

'Plus,' Kent said, 'she's got all kinds of weird shit in that little ravine she sleeps in, including the top half of a department store mannequin. I'll fuck just about anything, man, but a drunk-ass homeless bitch covered in spiderwebs? That's where I draw the line, and that line is thick.'

'My line is totally dotted right now.' There was a wistful note in Curt's voice. 'The situation is desperate. I'd bone a zombie on *The Walking Dead.*'

'You already did,' Eric said. 'Harriet Davenport.'

More prehistoric laughter. Why am I listening to this? Jared asked himself, and it occurred to him again: Mary is going to a concert with one of these sickos. She has no idea what Eric is actually like, and after our conversation on the bleachers, I'm not sure she'd believe me if I told her.

'You would not bone this chick,' Kent said. 'But it's funny. We ought to go by after school. Check her out.'

'Never mind after school,' Eric said. 'Let's cut out after sixth period.'

Whacking sounds as they slapped hands, sealing the deal. Jared grabbed his gym bag and left.

It wasn't until lunch that Frankie Johnson sat down next to Jared and said the weird female sleeping sickness that used to be only in Australia and Hawaii had shown up in DC, Richmond, and even in Martinsburg, which wasn't that far away. Jared thought briefly of what Kent had said about Old Essie — spiderwebs on her face — then decided it couldn't be. Not here. Nothing that interesting ever happened in Dooling.

'They're calling it Aurora,' Frankie said. 'Hey, is that chicken salad? How is it? Want to trade?'

CHAPTER 5

1

Unit 12 of A Wing was bare except for the single bunk, the steel toilet, and the camera bulbs in the corners of the ceiling. No painted square on the wall for posting pictures, no desk. Coates had dragged in a plastic chair to sit on while Clint examined Kitty McDavid, who lay on the bunk.

'So?' asked Coates.

'She's alive. Her vitals are strong.' Clint stood from his crouch. He unsnapped his surgical gloves and carefully placed them in a plastic bag. From his jacket pocket he took out a small pad and a pen and began to jot notes.

'I don't know what that stuff is. It's tacky, like sap, and it's also tough, and yet it's evidently permeable because she's breathing through it. It smells – earthy, I guess. And a little waxy. If you pressed me, I'd say it was some kind of a fungus, but it's not behaving like any fungus I've ever seen or heard of.' To even attempt to discuss the situation made Clint feel as if he were climbing up a hill made of pennies. 'A biologist could take a sample and put it under a microscope—'

'I've been told that it's a bad idea to remove the stuff.'

Clint clicked his pen, stuck it and the pad back in his coat. 'Well, I'm not a biologist, anyway. And since she seems comfortable . . .'

The growth on Kitty's face was white and gauzy, tight to her skin. It made Clint think of a winding sheet. He could tell that her eyes were shut and he could tell that they were moving in REM. The idea that she was dreaming under the stuff troubled him, although he wasn't sure why.

Little wisps of the gauzy material unspooled from her limp hands and wrists, wafting out as if breeze-blown, catching onto the waist area of McDavid's uniform, forming connections. Based on the way the stuff was spreading, Clint extrapolated that it would eventually create a full body covering.

'It looks like a fairy handkerchief.' The warden had her arms crossed. She didn't appear upset, just thoughtful.

'Fairy handkerchief?'

'Grass spiders make them. You see them in the morning, while it's still dewy.'

'Oh. Right. I see them in the backyard sometimes.'

They were quiet for a moment, watching the little tendrils of gauzy material. Beneath the coating, Kitty's eyelids fluttered and shifted. What kind of trip was she on in there? Was she dreaming of scoring? Kitty told him once that she liked the prospect even better than the high – the sweet anticipation. Was she dreaming of cutting herself? Was she dreaming of Lowell Griner, the drug dealer who promised to kill her if she ever talked about his operation? Or was her brain gone, blacked out by the virus (if it was a virus) of which the webbing was the foremost manifestation? Her rolling eyes the neural equivalent of a torn power line shooting off sparks?

'This is fucking scary,' Janice said. 'And that's not a phrase I use lightly.'

Clint was glad Lila was coming. Whatever was going on between them, he wanted to see her face. 'I ought to call my son,' Clint said, mostly to himself.

Rand Quigley, the officer on the floor, poked his head in. He darted a quick, uneasy glance at the incapacitated woman with the shrouded face before shifting toward the warden and clearing his throat. 'The sheriff's ETA is twenty or thirty minutes with her prisoner.' He hung there a moment. 'Got the word about the double shifts from Blanche, Warden. I'm here as long as you need me.'

'Good man,' she said.

On the walk over Clint had briefly filled Coates in about the woman from the murder scene, and that Lila was bringing her in. The warden, far more concerned about what Michaela had told her, had been uncharacteristically nonchalant about such a breach of protocol. Clint had been relieved by that, but only for a few seconds, because then she'd hit him with everything she knew about Aurora.

Before Clint could ask if she was joking, she'd shown him her iPhone, which was set to the front page of the *New York Times*: **EPIDEMIC** howled the twenty-point headline. The corresponding article said that women were forming coatings in their sleep, that they weren't waking up, that there were mass riots in the western time zones, and fires in Los Angeles and San Francisco. Nothing about bad shit happening if the gauze was removed, Clint noticed. Possibly because that was just a rumor. Possibly because it was true, and the press was trying not to ignite full-scale panic. At this point, who could tell?

'You can call your son in a few minutes, but Clint, this is a big goddam deal. We've got six officers on the shift, plus you, me, Blanche in the office, and Dunphy from maintenance. And there are one hundred and fourteen female inmates with one more on the way. Most of the officers, they're like Quigley, they recognize they've got a duty, and I expect they'll hold tight for a bit. For which I thank God, because I don't know when we can expect reinforcements, or what they'll amount to. You see?'

Clint saw.

'All right. To start with, Doc, what do we do about Kitty?'

'We contact the CDC, ask them to send some boys in hazmat suits to come in and take her out, get her examined, but . . .' Clint opened his hands in expression of how pointless that would be. 'If this is as widespread as you've told me, and the news certainly seems to agree that it is, we're not going to get any help until there's help to get, right?'

Coates still had her arms crossed. Clint wondered if she was holding herself to keep from showing the shakes. The idea made him feel simultaneously better and worse.

'And I suppose we can't expect St Theresa's or anyone else to take her off our hands right now, either? They probably have their hands full, too.'

'We should call around, but that's my expectation,' Clint said. 'So let's lock her up tight, keep her quarantined. We don't want anyone else getting close to her or touching her even with gloves on. Van can monitor her from the Booth. If anything changes, if she appears distressed, if she wakes up, we'll come running.'

'Sounds like a plan.' She brushed at the air where a moth was flitting around. 'Stupid bug. How do these things get in here? Goddammit. Next item: What about the rest of the population? How do we treat them?'

'What do you mean?' Clint flapped a hand at the moth, but missed. It circled up to the florescent bank in the ceiling.

'If they fall asleep . . .' The warden gestured at McDavid.

Clint touched his forehead, half-expecting to find it burning with fever. A demented multiple-choice question came to him.

How do you keep the inmates of a prison awake? Select from the following:
A) *Play Metallica over the prison's public address system on an infinite loop.*
B) *Give every prisoner a knife and tell them to cut themselves when they start to feel sleepy.*
C) *Give every prisoner a sack of Dexedrine.*
D) *All of the above.*
E) *You don't.*

'There's medication that can keep people awake, but Janice, I'd say a near majority of the women here are drug addicts. The idea of pumping them all up with what's basically speed doesn't strike me as safe or healthy. Anyhow, something like, say, Provigil, it's not like I could write a prescription for a hundred tablets. I think the pharmacist at Rite Aid would look askance, you know? Bottom line, I don't see *any* way to help them. All we can do is keep things as normal as possible and try to tamp down any panic, hope for some kind of explanation or breakthrough in the meantime, and—'

Clint hesitated for a moment before dispensing the euphemism that seemed like the only way to put it and yet totally wrong. 'And let nature take her course.' Although this was no form of nature he was familiar with.

She sighed.

They went out into the hall and the warden told Quigley to pass the word: no one was to touch the growth on McDavid.

2

The woodshop inmates ate in the carpentry shed instead of the mess hall, and on nice days they were allowed to have lunch outside in the shade of the building. This one was nice, a thing for which Jeanette Sorley was grateful. She had begun sprouting a headache in the garden while Dr Norcross was on the phone, and now it was boring deeper, like a steel rod working its way inward from her left temple. The stink of the varnish wasn't helping. Some fresh outside air might blow the pain away.

At ten minutes of twelve, two Red Tops – trustees – rolled in a table with sandwiches, lemonade, and chocolate pudding cups. At twelve, the buzzer went. Jeanette gave a final twist to the chair leg she was finishing and then flicked off her lathe. Half a dozen inmates did the same. The decibel level dropped. Now the only sound in the room – hot in here already and not even June – was the steady high-pitched whine of the Power Vac, which Ree Dempster was using to clean up the sawdust between the last row of machines and the wall.

'Turn that off, inmate!' Tig Murphy bellowed. He was a newer hire. Like most new hires, he bellowed a lot because he was still unsure of himself. 'It's lunch! Did you not hear the buzzer?'

Ree started, 'Officer, I just got this one more little—'

'Off, I said, off!'

'Yes, Officer.'

Ree turned off the Power Vac, and the silence gave Jeanette a shiver of relief. Her hands ached inside her work gloves, her head ached from the stink of the varnish. All she wanted was to go back to good old B-7, where she had aspirin (an approved Green Med, but only a dozen allowed per month). Then maybe she could sleep until B Wing chow at six.

'Line up, hands up,' Officer Murphy chanted. 'Line up, hands up, let me see those tools, ladies.'

They lined up. Ree was in front of Jeanette and whispered, 'Officer Murphy is kind of fat, isn't he?'

'Probably been eating cake with Michelle Obama,' Jeanette whispered back, and Ree giggled.

They held up their tools: hand-sanders, screwdrivers, drills, chisels. Jeanette wondered if male inmates would have been allowed access to such potentially dangerous weapons. Especially the screwdrivers. You could kill with a screwdriver, as she well knew. And that's what the pain in her head felt like: a screwdriver. Pushing in. Finding the soft meat and disarranging it.

'Shall we eat *al fresco* today, ladies?' Someone had mentioned that Officer Murphy had been a high school teacher until he lost his job when the faculty was downsized. 'That means—'

'Outside,' Jeanette mumbled. 'That means eating outside.'

Murphy pointed at her. 'We have a Rhodes Scholar among us.' But he was smiling a little, so it didn't sound mean.

The tools were checked off and collected and put into a steel floor chest that was then locked. The furniture crew shuffled to the table, grabbed sandwiches and Dixie cups of drink, and waited for Murphy to do the count. 'Ladies, the great outdoors awaits you. Someone grab me a ham and cheese.'

'You got it, cutie,' Angel Fitzroy murmured under her breath. Murphy gave her a sharp glance, which Angel returned with an innocent gaze. Jeanette felt a little sorry for him. But sorry don't buy no groceries, as her mother used to say. She gave Murphy three months. At most.

The women filed out of the shed, sat down on the grass, and leaned against the wall of the building.

'What'd you get?' Ree asked.

Jeanette peered into the depths of her sandwich. 'Chicken.'

'I got tuna. Want to trade?'

Jeanette didn't care what she had, she wasn't a bit hungry, so she swapped. She made herself eat, hoping it might make her head feel a little better. She drank the lemonade, which tasted bitter, but when Ree brought her a pudding cup, Jeanette shook her head. Chocolate was a migraine trigger, and if her current headache turned into one of those, she would have to go to the infirmary for a Zomig, which she would only get if Dr N. was still here. Word had gone around that the regular PAs hadn't come in.

A cement path ran toward the main prison building, and someone had decorated it with a fading hopscotch grid. A few women got up, found stones, and started to play, chanting rhymes they must have learned as kids. Jeanette thought it was funny, what stuck in a person's head.

She pounded down the last bite of sandwich with the last swallow of bitter lemonade, leaned back and closed her eyes. Was her head getting a little better? Maybe. In any case, they had another fifteen minutes, at least. She could nap a little . . .

That was when Officer Peters popped out of the carpentry shed like a bouncy little Jack-in-the-box. Or a troll who had been hiding under a rock. He looked at the women playing hopscotch, then at the women sitting against the side of the building. His eyes settled on Jeanette. 'Sorley. Get in here. I got a job for you.'

Fucking Peters. He was a tit-squeezer and an ass-patter, always managing to do it in one of the multiple blind spots the cameras couldn't quite reach. He knew them all. And if you said anything, you were apt to get your tit wrung instead of just squeezed.

'I'm on my lunch break, Officer,' she said, as pleasantly as she could.

'Looks like you're finished to me. Now get off your duff and come along.'

Murphy looked uncertain, but one rule about working in a women's prison had been drummed into his head: male officers were not allowed to be one-on-one with any inmate. 'Buddy system, Don.'

Color suffused Peters's cheeks. He was in no mood for ticky-tack from Teach, not after the one-two combination of Coates's harassment, and the call he'd just received from Blanche McIntyre that he 'had' to pull a double because of 'the national situation.' Don had checked his phone: 'the national situation' was that a bunch of old ladies in a nursing home had a fungus. Coates was out of her mind.

'I don't want any of her buddies,' Don said. 'I just want her.'

He's going to let it go, Jeanette thought. In this place he's just a baby. But Murphy surprised her:

'Buddy system,' he repeated. Perhaps Officer Murphy would be able to hack it after all.

Peters considered. The women sitting against the shed were looking at him, and the hopscotch game had stopped. They were inmates, but they were also witnesses.

'*Yoo-hoo.*' Angel gave a queenly wave. '*Oh, yoo-hoo.* You know me, Officer Peters, I'm always happy to help.'

It occurred to Don, alarmingly – absurdly – that Fitzroy somehow knew what he had in mind. Of course, she didn't, she was just trying to be irritating, like every other minute of the day. While he would have liked five minutes alone with that lunatic sometime, he did not care at all for the idea of having his back turned to her for so much as one second.

No, not Fitzroy, not for this.

He pointed at Ree. 'You. Dumpster.' Some of the women giggled.

'*Dempster,*' Ree said, and with actual dignity.

'Dempster, Dumpster, Dimplebutt, I don't give a fuck. Both of you, come on. Don't make me ask again, not with the day I'm having.' He glanced at Murphy, the smartass. 'See you later, Teachergator.'

This provoked more giggles, these of the ass-licking variety. Murphy was new and out of his depth and none of them wanted to be on Officer Peters's shit list. They weren't totally stupid, Don thought, the women in this place.

3

Officer Peters marched Jeanette and Ree a quarter of the way down Broadway and halted them outside the common room/visitors' room, which was deserted with everyone at lunch. Jeanette was starting to get a very bad feeling about this. When Peters opened the door, she didn't move.

'What do you want us to do?'

'Are you blind, inmate?'

No, she wasn't blind. She saw the mop bucket with the mop leaning against it, and, on one of the tables, another plastic bucket. This one was full of rags and cleaning products instead of pudding cups.

'This is supposed to be our lunchtime.' Ree was trying for indignant, but the tremor in her voice spoiled it. 'Besides, we've already *got* work.'

Peters bent toward her, lips pulled back to show the pegs of his teeth, and Ree shrank back against Jeanette. 'You can put it on your TS list and give it to the chaplain later, okay? Right now just get in there, and if you don't want to go on Bad Report, don't argue the point. I'm having a shitty day, I'm in an extremely shitty mood, and unless you want me to share the wealth, you better step to it.'

Then, moving to his right to block the sightline of the nearest camera, he grabbed Ree by the back of her smock, hooking his fingers into the elastic strap of her sports bra. He shoved her into the common room. Ree stumbled and grabbed the side of the snack machine to keep from falling.

'Okay, okay!'

'Okay, what?'

'Okay, Officer Peters.'

'You shouldn't push us,' Jeanette said. 'That's not right.'

Don Peters rolled his eyes. 'Save your lip for someone who cares. Visitation Day tomorrow, and this place looks like a pigsty.'

Not to Jeanette, it didn't. To her it looked fine. Not that it mattered. If the man in the uniform said it looked like a pigsty, it looked like a pigsty. That was the nature of corrections as it existed in little Dooling County, and probably all over the world.

'You two are going to clean it from top to bottom and stem to stern, and I'm going to make sure you do the job right.'

He pointed to the bucket of cleaning supplies.

'That's yours, Dumpster. Miss That's Not Right gets to mop, and I want that floor so clean I could eat my dinner off it.'

I'd like to feed you your dinner off it, Jeanette thought, but she went to the rolling mop bucket. She did not want to go on Bad Report. If that happened, she would very likely not be in this room when her sister arrived with her son to visit her this coming weekend. That was a long bus ride, and how she loved Bobby for never complaining about making it. But her headache was getting worse and all she wanted in this world was her aspirin and a nap.

Ree inspected the cleaning supplies and selected a spray can and a rag.

'You want to sniff that Pledge, Dumpster? Shoot some up your snoot and get high?'

'No,' Ree said.

'You'd like to get high, wouldn't you?'

'No.'

'No what?'

'No, Officer Peters.'

Ree began to polish a table. Jeanette filled the mop bucket from the sink in the corner, wet the mop, squeegeed it, and began to do the floor. Through the chainlink fence in front of the prison, she could see West Lavin, where cars filled with free people traveled back and forth, to work, to home, to lunch at Denny's, to someplace.

'Get over here, Sorley,' Peters said. He was standing between the snack machine and the soda machine, a camera blind spot where inmates sometimes exchanged pills and cigarettes and kisses.

She shook her head and kept mopping. Long wet streaks on the linoleum that dried quickly.

'Get over here if you want to see your boy next time he's here.'

I ought to say no, she thought. I ought to say you leave me alone or I'll report you. Only he's been getting away with it a long time, hasn't he? Everyone knew about Peters. Coates had to know, too, but in spite of all her big talk about having zero tolerance for sexual harassment, it kept going on.

Jeanette trudged to the little alcove between the machines and stood before him, head down, mop in one hand.

'In there. Back against the wall. Never mind the mop, you can leave that.'

'I don't want to, Officer.' Her headache was really bad now, throbbing and throbbing. B-7 was just down the corridor, with her aspirin on her little shelf.

'You get in here or you go on Bad Report and lose your visitation. Then I'll make sure you get another Bad Report, and poof, there goes your Good Time.'

And my chance of parole next year, Jeanette thought. No Good Time, no parole, back to square one, case closed.

She squeezed past Peters and he rocked his hips into her so she could feel his boner. She stood against the wall. Peters moved in. She could smell his sweat and aftershave and hair tonic. She was taller than he was and over his shoulder she could see her cellie. Ree had stopped polishing. Her eyes were filled with fear, dismay, and what might have been anger. She was gripping the can of Pledge and slowly raising it. Jeanette gave her head a minute shake. Peters didn't see; he was busy unzipping his fly.

Ree lowered the can and resumed polishing the table that needed no more polishing, hadn't needed any in the first place.

'Now cop my joint,' Peters said. 'I need some relief. You know what I wish? I wish you was Coatsie. I wish I had her old flat ass backed up against this wall. If it was her, it wouldn't be just a pull-off, either.'

He gasped as she grasped him. It was sort of ridiculous, really. He had no more than three inches, nothing he'd want other men to see unless it was absolutely unavoidable, but it was hard enough. And she knew what to do. Most women did. Guys had a gun; you unloaded it; they went about their business.

'Easy, Jesus!' he hissed. His breath was rotten with some spicy meat, maybe a Slim Jim or a pepperoni stick. 'Wait, give me your hand.' She gave it to him and he spat in her palm. '*Now* do it. And tickle my balls a little.'

She did as she was told, and while she did it, she kept her eyes on the window beyond his shoulder. This was a technique she had begun learning at eleven, when her stepfather touched her, and had perfected with her late husband. If you found something to lock onto, a point of focus, you could almost leave your body behind, and pretend it was doing its own thing while you were visiting whatever it was you suddenly found so fascinating.

A county sheriff's car stopped outside, and Jeanette watched it first wait in the dead space and then roll into the yard once the inner gate rumbled open. Warden Coates, Dr Norcross, and Officer Lampley walked out to meet it. Officer Peters's breath panting in her ear was far away. Two cops got out of the car, a woman from behind the wheel and a man from the passenger side. They both drew their sidearms, which suggested that their prisoner was a bad sugarpop, probably bound for C Wing. The woman officer opened the back door, and another woman got out. She didn't look dangerous to Jeanette. She looked beautiful in spite of the bruises on her face. Her hair was a dark flood down her back, and she had enough curves to even make the baggy County Browns she was wearing look cool. Something was fluttering around her head. A big mosquito? A moth? Jeanette tried to see, but she couldn't be sure. Peters's gasps had taken on a squeaky edge.

The male officer took the dark-haired woman by the shoulder and got her walking toward intake, where Norcross and Coates met her. Once inside, the process would begin. The woman brushed at the flyer circling her hair and as she did so, her wide mouth opened and she tilted her head to the sky, and Jeanette saw her laugh, saw her bright, straight teeth.

Peters began to buck against her, and his ejaculate pumped into her hand.

He stepped back. His cheeks were flushed. There was a smile on his fat little face as he zipped up his fly. 'Wipe that on the back of the Coke machine, Sorley, and then finish mopping the fucking floor.'

Jeanette wiped his semen away, then pushed the mop bucket back down to the sink so she could rinse off her hand. When she came back, Peters was sitting at one of the tables and drinking a Coke.

'You okay?' Ree whispered.

'Yes,' Jeanette whispered back. And she would be, as soon as she got some aspirin for her head. The last four minutes hadn't even happened. She had been watching the woman get out of the police cruiser, that was all. She didn't need to think about the last four minutes ever again. She just needed to see Bobby on his next visit.

Hsst-hsst, went the shooter of the polish can.

Three or four seconds of blessed silence elapsed before Ree checked in again. 'Did you see the new one?'

'Yes.'

'Was she beautiful, or was that just me?'

'She was beautiful.'

'Those County Mounties drew their guns, you see that?'

'Yes.' Jeanette glanced at Peters, who had clicked on the television and was now staring at some news report. The picture showed someone slumped behind the wheel of a car. It was hard to tell if it was a man or woman, because he or she seemed to be wrapped in gauze. On the bottom of the screen, BREAKING NEWS was flashing on and off in red, but that meant nothing; they called it breaking news if Kim Kardashian farted. Jeanette blinked back the water that had suddenly welled up in her eyes.

'What do you think she did?'

She cleared her throat, sucking back the tears. 'No idea.'

'You sure you're all right?'

Before Jeanette could reply, Peters spoke without turning his head. 'You two ladies stop gossiping or you're both going on Bad Report.'

And because Ree couldn't stop talking – it just wasn't in her – Jeanette mopped her way down to the far end of the room.

On TV, Michaela Morgan said, 'The president so far has declined to declare a state of emergency, but informed sources close to the crisis say that . . .'

Jeanette tuned her out. The new fish had raised her cuffed hands to the circling moths, and laughed when they alit.

You'll lose that laugh in here, sister, Jeanette thought.

We all do.

4

Anton Dubcek returned home for lunch. This was customary, and though it was only twelve thirty, it was actually a late lunch by Anton's standards – he had been hard at work since six that morning. What people didn't understand about pool maintenance was that it was not a business for softies. You had to be driven. If you wanted to succeed in pools, you couldn't sleep in, dreaming about blintzes and blowjobs. To stay ahead of the competition you had to stay ahead of the sun. At this point in his day, he had swept and adjusted the levels and cleaned out the filters of seven different pools, and replaced the gaskets on two pumps. He could save the remaining four appointments on his schedule for late afternoon and early evening.

In between: lunch, a short nap, a short workout, and perhaps a brief visit to Jessica Elway, the bored married chick he was currently boning. That her husband was a local Deputy Dog made it all the sweeter. Cops sat in their cars all day and snarfed donuts and got their jollies harassing black guys. Anton controlled the motherfucking waters and made money.

Anton dropped his keys in the bowl by the door and proceeded straight to the fridge to get his shake. He shifted around the soy milk, the bag of kale, the container of berries – no shake.

'Mom! Mom!' he cried out. 'Where's my shake?'

There was no answer, but he heard the television going in the living room. Anton poked his head through the open doorway. The evidence on display – television playing, empty rocks glass – suggested that Magda had retired for a snooze of her own. As much as he loved his mother, Anton knew she drank too much. It made her sloppy, and that pissed him off. Since his dad died it was Anton who paid the mortgage. Upkeep and sustenance was her end of the bargain. If he didn't have his shakes, Anton couldn't dominate pools the way he needed to, or excel to the maximum in his workouts, or slam a juicy ass as forcefully as the ladies wanted him to slam it.

'Mom! This is bullshit! You gotta do your part!' His voice echoed through the house.

From the cabinet under the silverware drawer he yanked out his blender, creating as much of a racket as possible as he thumped it down on the counter and pieced together jar, blade, and base. Anton dropped in a good bunch of greens, some berries, a handful of nuts, a spoonful of organic peanut butter, and a cup of *Mister Ripper Protein Powder*. While he performed this assembly he found himself pondering Sheriff Lila Norcross. She was attractive for an older chick, extremely fit — a true Yummy Mummy, no donuts for her — and he liked the way she rallied when he gave her a line. Did she want him? Or did she want to commit acts of police brutality against him? Or — and this was the truly intriguing possibility — did she both want him *and* want to commit acts of police brutality against him? The situation bore monitoring. Anton set the blender to the highest speed and watched the mix blur. Once it was a smooth pea color, he flicked off the power, removed the jar, and headed into the living room.

And on the screen, what did you know: his old playmate Mickey Coates!

He liked Mickey, although the sight of her induced uncharacteristically melancholy feelings in the president, CEO, CFO, and sole employee of Anton the Pool Guy, LLC. Would she even remember him? His mother used to babysit her, so in their early years they had been thrust together quite a lot. Anton remembered Mickey exploring his bedroom, looking through his drawers, flipping through the comics, tossing out one inquiry after another: Who gave you this? Why is this G.I. Joe your favorite? Why don't you have a calendar? Your dad's an electrician, right? Do you think he'll teach you how to do wires and stuff? Do you want him to? They must have been about eight and it was like she was planning to write his biography. That was okay, though. Good, in fact. Her interest had made Anton feel special; before that, before her, he had never even wanted someone else's interest, had been happy just being a kid. Of course, Mickey'd gone off to private school early on, and from junior high onward they'd hardly spoken.

Probably as an adult, she was into briefcase-and-cufflink types who read the *Wall Street Journal*, who understood whatever the hell the appeal of opera was, who watched shows on PBS, that sort of guy. Anton shook his head. Her loss, he assured himself.

'I want to warn you that the footage you're about to see is disturbing, and we haven't confirmed its authenticity.'

Mickey was reporting from a seat in the rear of a news van with the door open. Beside her was a man in a headset working on a laptop. Mickey's blue eye shadow was visibly damp. It must have been hot in the van. Her face looked different somehow. Anton took a large foamy gulp of his shake and studied her.

'However,' she continued, 'in light of everything surrounding Aurora, and the rumors of adverse reactions by sleepers who have been aroused, we've decided to run it because it would seem to confirm that those reports are accurate. Here's the section of footage recorded from the streaming site maintained by the self-proclaimed Bright Ones from their compound outside of Hatch, New Mexico. As you know, this militia group has been at odds with federal authorities over water rights . . .'

Good to see Mickey, but the news bored Anton. He picked up the controller and clicked over to the Cartoon Network, where an animated horse and rider were galloping through dark woods, chased by shadows. When he set the controller back on the side table he noticed the empty bottle of gin on the floor.

'Goddammit, Mom.' Anton took another gulp of shake and crossed the living room. He needed to make sure she was sleeping on her side in case of a sudden ejection; she was not going to die like a rock star on his watch.

On the kitchen counter, his cell phone chirruped. It was a text message from Jessica Elway. Now that she finally had the baby down for a nap, she planned to smoke a jay and take off her clothes and avoid the TV and the Internet, both of which were utterly freaky-bizarro today. Was Anton interested in joining her? Her poor husband was stuck at a crime scene.

5

Frank Geary thought the guy currently starring in the New Mexico footage looked like an elderly refugee from Woodstock Nation, someone who should be leading the Fish Cheer instead of a freaky-deaky cult.

Kinsman Brightleaf was what he called himself – how about that for a mouthful? He had a wild spread of curly gray hair, a curly gray beard, and wore a serape patterned in orange triangles that fell to his knees. Frank had followed the story of the Bright Ones as it developed over the spring, and come to the conclusion that beneath the pseudo-religious, quasi-political trappings, they were just another bunch of trumped-up tax dodgers, emphasis on the Trump.

Bright Ones, they called themselves, and oh, the fucking irony of that. There were about thirty of them, men and women and a few kids, who had declared themselves an independent nation. Besides refusing to pay taxes or send their kids to school or give up their automatic weapons (which they apparently needed to protect their ranch from the tumbleweeds), they had illegally diverted the only stream in the area onto the scrubland they owned. The FBI and the ATF had been parked outside their fences for months, attempting to negotiate a surrender, but nothing much had changed.

The Bright Ones' ideology disgusted Frank. It was selfishness costumed in spirituality. You could draw a straight line from the Bright Ones to the endless budget cutting that threatened to turn Frank's own job into part-time employment or outright volunteer work. Civilization required a contribution – or a sacrifice, if that's what you wanted to call it. Otherwise, you ended up with wild dogs roaming the streets and occupying the seats of power in DC. He wished (without, admittedly, a great deal of conviction) there were no kids in that compound so that the government could just roll on them and clean them out like the scum they were.

Frank was at his desk in his small office. Crowded in on all sides by animal cages of various sizes and shelves of equipment, it wasn't much of a space, but he didn't mind. It was okay.

He sipped a bottle of mango juice and watched the TV as he held an ice pack against the side of the hand that he'd used to pound on Garth Flickinger's door. The light on his cell phone was blinking: Elaine. He wasn't sure how he wanted to play that, so he let her go to voicemail. He'd pushed too hard with Nana, he saw that now. Potentially, there could be blowback.

A wrecked green Mercedes now sat in the driveway of a rich doctor. Frank's fingerprints were all over the painted paving stone he'd used to break the Merc's windows and beat on the Merc's body, as well as on the planter of the lilac tree that, at the height of his rage, he'd stuffed into the careless motherfucker's backseat. It was exactly the sort of incontrovertible evidence – felony vandalism – that a family court judge (all of whom favored the mother, anyway) would need to fix it so he could only see his daughter for a super-vised hour every other full moon. A felony vandalism rap would also take care of his job. What was obvious in retrospect was that Bad Frank had stepped in. Bad Frank had, in fact, had a party.

But Bad Frank wasn't entirely bad, or entirely wrong, because, check it: for the time being his daughter could safely draw in the driveway again. Maybe Good Frank could have handled it better. But maybe not. Good Frank was a bit of a weakling.

'I will not – *we* will not – stand idly by while the *so-called* United States government perpetrates this hoax.'

On the television screen, Kinsman Brightleaf made his address from behind a long, rectangular table. On the table lay a woman in a pale blue nightgown. Her face was shrouded in white stuff that looked like the fake webby crap they sold at the drugstore around Halloween. Her chest rose and fell.

'What is that shit?' Frank asked the mongrel stray currently visiting with him. The mongrel looked up, then went back to sleep. It was a cliché, but for all-weather company, you couldn't do better than a dog. Couldn't do better than a dog, period. Dogs didn't know any better; they just made the best of it. They made the best of you. Frank had always had one growing up. Elaine was allergic to them – she claimed. Another thing he'd given up for her, far bigger than she could ever understand.

Frank gave the mongrel a rub between the ears.

'We have observed their agents tampering with our water supply. We know that they have used their chemicals to act on the most vulnerable and treasured part of our Family, the females of the Bright, in order to sow chaos and fear and doubt. They poisoned our sisters in the night. That includes my wife, my loving Susannah. The poison worked on her and our other beautiful women while they slept.' Kinsman Brightleaf's voice bottomed out in a tobacco-scarred rattle that was oddly homey. It made you think of old men gathered around a diner table for breakfast, good-humored in their retirement.

In attendance to the high priest of tax-evasion were two younger men, also bearded, though less impressively, and also draped in serapes. All wore gunbelts, making them look like extras in an old Sergio Leone spaghetti western. On the wall behind them was a Christ on the cross. The video from the compound was clear, marred only by the occasional line scrolling across the image.

'While they slept!

'Do you see the cowardice of the current King of Lies? See him in the White House? See his many fellow liars on the useless green paper they want us to believe is worth something? Oh, my neighbors. Neighbors, neighbors. So wily and so cruel and so many faces.'

All his teeth abruptly appeared, flashing from amid the wild crop of his beard. *'But we will not succumb to the devil!'*

Hey now, thought Frank. Elaine thinks she has a problem with me, she should get a load of Jerry Garcia here. This guy's nuttier than a Christmas fruitcake.

'The parlor tricks of Pilate's descendants are no match for the Lord we serve!'

'Praise God,' murmured one of the militiamen.

'That's right! Praise Him. Yessir.' Mr Brightleaf clapped his hands. 'So let's get this stuff off my missus.'

One of his men passed him a set of poultry shears. Kinsman bent and began to carefully snip at the webbing that coated his wife's face. Frank leaned forward in his chair.

He felt an uh-oh coming.

6

When he entered the bedroom and saw Magda lying under the covers, masked in what looked sort of like Marshmallow Fluff, Anton dropped to his knees beside her, banged the jar with his shake down on the nightstand and, spying the trimmers – probably she had been clipping her eyebrows using her iPhone camera again – went right to work cutting it off.

Had someone done this to her? Had she done it to herself? Was it some kind of bizarre accident? An allergic reaction? Some crazy beauty treatment gone wrong? It was confounding, it was scary, and Anton didn't want to lose his mother.

Once the webbing was sliced open, he cast the bathroom trimmers aside, and dug his fingers into the opening in the material. It was sticky, but the stuff peeled, stretching and separating from Magda's cheeks in gummy white whorls. Her worn face with its choppy wrinkles around the eyes, her dear face that Anton had momentarily been certain would be melted beneath the weird white coating (it was kind of like the fairy handkerchiefs he saw glistening in the grass in the dawn yards of the first couple of pools each day), emerged unharmed. The skin was a bit flushed and warm to the touch, but otherwise she appeared no different than before.

A low grumble began to come from inside her throat, almost a snore. Her eyelids were working, trembling from the movement of her eyes beneath the skin. Her lips opened and shut. A little spittle dripped from the corner of her mouth.

'Mama? Mama? Can you wake up for me?'

It seemed she could, because her eyes opened. Blood clouded the pupils, wafting across the sclera. She blinked several times. Her gaze shifted around the room.

Anton slipped an arm under his mother's shoulders and raised her to a sitting position in the bed. The noise from her throat grew louder; not a snore now but more like a growl.

'Mama? Should I call an ambulance? You want an ambulance? You want me to get a glass of water for you?' The questions came out in a rush. Anton was relieved, though. She continued to look around the bedroom, seeming to regain her bearings.

Her gaze stopped on the nightstand: faux Tiffany lamp, half-drunk jar of power shake, Bible, iPhone. The growling noise was louder. It was like she was building up to a yell or maybe a scream. Was it possible she didn't recognize him?

'That's my drink, Mama,' Anton said, as she reached out and grabbed hold of the jar with the shake. 'No thanks to you, ha-ha. You forget to make it, you goose.'

She swung it, belting him across the side of his head, the connection a dull bonk of plastic finding bone. Anton tumbled backward, feeling pain and wet and bafflement. He landed on his knees. His sight focused on a green splatter on the beige carpet beneath him. Red dripped into the green. What a mess, he thought, just as his mother hit him with the jar again, this time flush against the back of his skull. There was a sharper crack upon impact – the thick plastic of the blender jar splitting. Anton's face slammed forward into the shake splatter on the bristly mat of the beige carpet. He inhaled blood and shake and carpet fiber, and threw out a hand to pull himself away, but every part of him, every wonderful muscle, had gone heavy and limp. A lion was roaring behind him and if he was going to help his mother get away from it, he needed to get up and find the back of his head.

He tried to call for Magda to run but what came out was a gurgle and his mouth was full of carpet.

A weight fell on his spine and as this new pain added itself to the old pain, Anton hoped that his mother had heard him, that she might yet escape.

7

A homeless dog started barking in one of the holding cages, and two others joined in. The nameless mongrel at his feet – so like the one Fritz Meshaum had smashed up – whined. It was now sitting up. Frank absently ran a hand along its spine, calming it. His eyes stayed locked on the screen. One of the young men attending

Kinsman Brightleaf – not the one who'd handed him the poultry shears, the other one – grabbed his shoulder. 'Dad? Maybe you shouldn't do it.'

Brightleaf shrugged the hand away. 'God says come into the light! Susannah – Kinswoman Brightleaf – God says come into the light! Come into the light!'

'Come into the light!' echoed the man who'd passed the shears, and Brightleaf's son reluctantly joined in. 'Come into the light! Kinswoman Brightleaf, come into the light!'

Kinsman Brightleaf slid his hands into the cut cocoon covering his wife's face and thundered, *'God says come into the light!'*

He pulled. There was a ripping sound that reminded Frank of a Velcro strip letting go. The face of Mrs Susannah Kinsman Brightleaf appeared. Her eyes were closed but her cheeks were flushed, and the threads at the edges of the cut fluttered with her breath. Mr Brightleaf leaned close, as if to kiss her.

'Don't do that,' Frank said, and although the TV sound wasn't high and he had spoken barely above a whisper, all the caged dogs – half a dozen of them this afternoon – were now barking. The mongrel made a low, worried sound. 'Buddy, don't do that.'

'Kinswoman Brightleaf, awake!'

She awoke, all right. And how. Her eyes flew open. She lunged upward and battened on her husband's nose. Kinsman Brightleaf screamed something that was bleeped out, but Frank thought it might have been *motherfucker.* Blood sprayed. Kinswoman Brightleaf fell back onto the table with a sizable chunk of her husband's beak caught in her teeth. Blood dotted the bodice of her nightie.

Frank recoiled. The back of his head struck the file cabinet crammed in behind his desk. One thought – irrelevant but very clear – filled his mind: the news network had bleeped out *motherfucker* but had permitted America to see a woman tear off a goodly portion of her husband's nose. Something in those priorities was badly screwed up.

Cacophony in the room where the nose-amputation had occurred. Shouts off-camera, and then the camera tipped over, showing nothing but a wooden floor upon which a spatter of blood droplets was accumulating. Then it was back to Michaela Morgan, who looked grave.

'Again, we apologize for the disturbing nature of this footage, and I want to repeat that we have not *absolutely* confirmed its authenticity, but we have late word that the Bright Ones have opened their gates, and the siege is over. This *would* seem to confirm that what you just saw really happened.' She shook her head, as if to clear it, listened to something coming from the little plastic button in her ear, then said, 'We are going to repeat this footage again on top of every hour, not out of sensationalism—'

Yeah, right, Frank thought. As if.

'—but as a public service. If this is happening, people need to know one thing: if you have a loved one or a friend in one of these cocoons, *do not attempt to remove it.* Now back to George Alderson in the studio. I've been told he has a very special guest who may be able to shed a bit more light on this terrible—'

Frank used the remote to kill the TV. What now? What the fuck now?

In Frank's little holding compound, dogs that had yet to be shipped to the Harvest Hills Animal Shelter continued to bark madly at the moth that fluttered and danced in the narrow corridor between their cages.

Frank stroked the mongrel by his feet. 'It's okay,' he said. 'Everything's all right.' The dog stilled. Not knowing any better, it believed him.

8

Magda Dubcek sat astride her son's corpse. She had finished him off by sliding a green-streaked shard of the blender jar into the side of his neck, and made sure of it by driving another shard into the opening of his ear and all the way down his auditory canal until it buried itself in his brain. Blood continued to spurt from the wound in his neck, soaking the beige carpet in a larger and larger pool.

Tears began to roll down her cheeks. Magda, at some strange distance, was dimly aware of them. Why is that woman crying? she asked herself, not certain who it was that was crying, or where. Come to think of it, where was Magda herself? Hadn't she been watching television and decided to have a rest?

She wasn't in her bedroom now. 'Hello?' she asked the darkness that surrounded her. There were others in that darkness, many others, she thought she sensed them, but she couldn't see them – maybe over here? Over there? Somewhere. Magda probed outward.

She needed to find them. She couldn't be alone in here. If there were others, maybe they could help her get back home, to her son, to Anton.

Her body rose from the corpse, elderly knees cracking. She stumbled to the bed and flopped down on it. Her eyes closed. New white filaments began to unfurl from her cheeks, wavering, then falling gently down to the skin.

She slept.

She searched for the others, in that other place.

CHAPTER 6

1

It was a hot afternoon, one that felt more like summer than spring, and all across Dooling telephones were beginning to ring, as some of those who had been keeping up with the news called friends and relatives who had not. Others held back, sure the whole thing would turn out to be a tempest in a teapot, like Y2K, or an outright hoax, like the Internet rumor that Johnny Depp was dead. As a result, many women who preferred music to TV put their infants and toddlers down for their afternoon naps, as always, and once their fussing had ceased, they lay down themselves.

To sleep, and dream of other worlds than their own.

Their female children joined them in these dreams.

Their male children did not. The dream was not for them.

When those hungry little boys awakened an hour or two later to find their mothers still slumbering, their loving faces enveloped in a sticky white substance, they would scream and claw, and tear through the cocoons – and that *would* rouse the sleeping women.

Ms Leanne Barrows of 17 Eldridge Street, for example: wife of Deputy Reed Barrows. It was her habit to lie down for a nap with her two-year-old son Gary around eleven each day. That's just what she must have done on the Thursday of Aurora.

A few minutes after two o'clock, Mr Alfred Freeman, the Barrowses' neighbor at 19 Eldridge Street, a retired widower, was spraying his curbside hostas with deer repellant. The door of 17 Eldridge banged open and Mr Freeman observed Ms Barrows as she staggered from her front door, carrying young Gary under her arm, like a piece of siding. The boy, wearing only a diaper, was screaming and waving his arms. An opaque white mask covered most of his mother's face, except for a flap of material hanging loose from one corner of her mouth to her chin. It can be presumed that it was this rip that awakened the boy's mother and gained her far-from-pleasant attention.

Mr Freeman did not know what to say as Ms Barrows made a beeline for him, as he stood thirty feet away just on the other side of the property line. For most of that morning he had been gardening; he had not seen or heard the news. His neighbor's face − or absence of it − shocked him to silence. For some reason, at her approach, he removed his Panama hat and pressed it against his chest, as if the National Anthem were about to be played.

Leanne Barrows dropped her bawling child into the plants at Alfred Freeman's feet, then swung around and returned across the lawn the way she had come, swaying drunkenly. White bits, like shreds of tissue paper, trailed from her fingertips. She re-entered her home and closed the door behind her.

This phenomenon proved to be one of the most curious and most analyzed enigmas of Aurora − the so-called 'Mother's Instinct' or 'Foster Reflex.' While reports of violent interactions between sleepers and other adults ultimately numbered in the millions, and unreported interactions millions more, few if any occurrences of aggression between a sleeper and her pre-adolescent child were ever confirmed. Sleepers handed over their male infants and toddlers to the closest person they could find, or simply put them out of doors. They then returned to their places of slumber.

'Leanne?' Freeman called.

Gary rolled around on the ground, weeping and kicking the leaves with his fat pink feet. 'Mama! Mama!'

Alfred Freeman looked at the boy, then at the hosta he had sprayed, and asked himself, *do I bring him back?*

He was not a fan of children; he'd had two, and the feeling was mutual. He certainly had no use for Gary Barrows, an ugly little terrorist whose social graces seemed to extend no farther than waving around toy rifles and yelling about *Star Wars*.

Leanne's face, screened in that white crap, made it seem that she wasn't really human at all. Freeman decided he would hang onto the kid until Leanne's deputy husband could be contacted to take charge.

This was a life-saving choice. Those who challenged the 'Mother's Instinct' regretted it. Whatever disposed Aurora mothers to peacefully cede their young male offspring, it was not receptive to questions. Tens of thousands learned this to their detriment, and then learned no more.

'Sorry, Gary,' Freeman said. 'I think you might be stuck with old Uncle Alf for a little bit.' He lifted the inconsolable child up by his armpits and brought him inside. 'Would it be too much to ask you to behave?'

2

Clint stayed with Evie through most of the intake process. Lila did not. He wanted her with him, wanted to keep emphasizing that she couldn't go to sleep, even though he'd started in on her as soon as she'd stepped out of her car in the prison parking lot. He'd told her half a dozen times already, and Clint knew his concern was testing her patience. He also wanted to ask her where she'd been the previous night, but that would have to wait. Considering developments both here and in the wider world, he wasn't sure it even mattered. Yet he kept coming back to it, like a dog licking a sore paw.

Assistant Warden Lawrence 'Lore' Hicks arrived shortly after Evie was escorted into lockdown. Warden Coates left Hicks to handle the new intake's paperwork while she worked the phone, seeking guidance from the Bureau of Corrections and putting in calls to everybody on the off-duty roster.

As it happened, there wasn't much to handle. Evie sat with her hands chained to the interview room table, still dressed (for the moment) in the County Browns Lila and Linny Mars had given her. Though her face was battered from repeated collisions with the mesh guard in Lila's cruiser, her eyes and mood were incongruously merry. To questions about her current address, relatives, and medical history, she gave back only silence. When asked for her last name, she said, 'I've been thinking about that. Let's say Black. Black will do. Nothing against Doe, a deer, a female deer, but Black seems a better one for black times. Call me Evie Black.'

'So it's not your real name?' Fresh from the dentist, Hicks spoke from a mouth that was still mushy from Novocain.

'You couldn't even pronounce my real name. *Names.*'

'Give it to me anyway,' Hicks invited.

Evie only looked at him with those merry eyes.

'How old are you?' tried Hicks.

Here, the woman's cheerful expression drooped into what appeared to Clint to be a look of sorrow. 'No age have I,' she said – but then gave the assistant warden a wink, as if to apologize for something so orotund.

Clint spoke up. There would be time for a full interview later, and in spite of everything that was going on, he could hardly wait. 'Evie, do you understand why you are here?'

'To know God, to love God, and to serve God,' Evie replied. Then she raised her cuffed hands as far as the chain would allow, made a show of crossing herself, and laughed. She would say no more.

Clint went to his office where Lila had said she'd wait for him.

He found her talking into her shoulder mic. She replaced it and nodded at Clint. 'I've got to go. Thanks for taking her.'

'I'll walk you out.'

'Don't want to stick with your patient?' Lila was already headed down the hall to the inner main door and lifting her face so Officer Millie Olson's monitors could see she was a citizen – Joan Law, in fact – and not an inmate.

Clint said, 'The strip search and delousing is ladies only. Once she's dressed, I'll rejoin.'

But you know all this, he thought. Are you too tired to remember, or do you just not want to talk to me?

The door buzzed, and they went into the airlock-sized room between the prison and the foyer, a space so small it always gave Clint a mild case of claustrophobia. Another buzz, and they re-entered the land of free men and women, Lila leading.

Clint caught up with her before she could go outside. 'This Aurora—'

'Tell me again that I have to stay awake, and I may scream.' She was trying to look good-humored about it, but Clint knew when she was struggling to keep her temper. It was impossible to miss the lines of strain around her mouth and the bags under her eyes. She had picked a spectacularly luckless time to work the night shift. If luck had anything to do with it.

He followed her to the car, where Reed Barrows was leaning with his arms folded across his chest.

'You're not just my wife, Lila. When it comes to law enforcement in Dooling County, you're the big kahuna.' He held out a hand with a piece of folded paper. 'Take this, and get it filled before you do anything else.'

Lila unfolded the piece of paper. It was a prescription. 'What's Provigil?'

He put an arm over her shoulder and held her close, wanting to be certain Reed didn't overhear their conversation. 'It's for sleep apnea.'

'I don't have that.'

'No, but it'll keep you awake. I'm not screwing around, Lila. I need you *awake*, and this town needs you awake.'

She stiffened under his arm. 'Okay.'

'Do it fast, before there's a run.'

'Yes, sir.' His orders, well meant as they might have been, clearly irritated her. 'Just figure out my lunatic. If you can.' She managed a smile. 'I can always hit the evidence locker. We've got mountains of little white pills.'

This hadn't occurred to him. 'That's something to keep in mind.'

She pulled away. 'I was kidding, Clint.'

'I'm not telling you to tamper with anything. I'm just telling you to . . .' He held up his palms. '. . . keep it in mind. We don't know where this is going.'

She looked at him doubtfully, and opened the passenger door of the cruiser. 'If you talk to Jared before I do, tell him I'll try to get home for dinner, but the chances are slim approaching none.'

She got in the car, and before she rolled up the window to take full advantage of the air conditioning, he almost popped the question, in spite of Reed Barrows's presence and in spite of the sudden, impossible crisis that the news insisted *was* possible. It was a question he supposed men had been asking for thousands of years: *Where were you last night?* But instead he said, and momentarily felt clever, 'Hey, hon, remember Mountain Rest? It might still be blocked up. Don't try the shortcut.' Lila didn't flinch, just said, uh-huh, okay, flapped a hand goodbye, and swung the cruiser toward the double gate between the prison and the highway. Clint, not so clever after all, could only watch her drive away.

He got back inside just in time to see Evie 'You Couldn't Even Pronounce My Real Name' Black get a photo snapped for her inmate ID. Don Peters then filled her arms with bedding.

'You look like a stoner to me, darling. Don't puke on the sheets.'

Hicks gave him a sharp look but kept his Novocain-numbed mouth shut. Clint, who'd had enough of Officer Peters to last a lifetime, did not. 'Cut the shit.'

Peters swiveled his head. 'You don't tell me—'

'I can write up an incident report, if you want,' Clint said. 'Inappropriate response. Unprovoked. Your choice.'

Peters glared at him, but only asked, 'Since you're in charge of this one, what's her assignment?'

'A-10.'

'Come on, inmate,' Peters said. 'You're getting a soft cell. Lucky you.'

Clint watched them go, Evie with her arms full of bedding, Peters close behind. He watched to see if Peters would touch her, but of course he didn't. He knew Clint had an eye on him.

3

Lila had surely been this tired before, but she couldn't remember when. What she could remember – from Health class in high school, for God's sweet sake – were the adverse consequences of long-term wakefulness: slowed reflexes, impaired judgment, loss of vigilance, irritability. Not to mention short-term memory problems, such as being able to recall facts from Sophomore Health but not what the fuck you were supposed to do next, today, this minute.

She pulled into the parking lot of the Olympia Diner (MY OH MY, TRY OUR EGG PIE, read the easel sign by the door), turned off her engine, got out, and took long slow deep breaths, filling her lungs and bloodstream with fresh oxygen. It helped a little. She leaned in her window, grabbed her dash mic, then thought better of it – this was not a call she wanted going out over the air. She replaced the mic and pulled her phone from its pocket on her utility belt. She punched one of the dozen or so numbers she kept on speed dial.

'Linny, how are you doing?'

'Okay. Got seven hours or so last night, which is a little more than usual. So, all good. I'm worried about you, though.'

'I'm fine, don't worry about—' She was interrupted by a jaw-cracking yawn. It made what she was saying a bit ludicrous, but she persevered. 'I'm fine, too.'

'Seriously? How long have you been awake?'

'I don't know, maybe eighteen, nineteen hours.' To reduce Linny's concern she added, 'I cooped some last night, don't worry.' Lies kept falling out of her mouth. There was a fairy tale that warned about this, about how one lie led to other lies, and you eventually turned into a parakeet or something, but Lila's worn-out brain couldn't come up with it. 'Never mind me right now. What's the deal with Tiffany what's-her-face, from the trailer? Did the EMTs transport her to the hospital?'

'Yes. Good thing they got her there fairly early.' Linny lowered her voice. 'St Theresa's is a madhouse.'

'Where are Roger and Terry now?'

Linny's response to this question was embarrassed. 'Well . . . They waited for the Assistant DA for awhile, but he never showed, and they wanted to check on their wives—'

'So they left the crime scene?' Lila was furious for a moment, but her anger had dissipated by the time her disbelief was expressed. Probably the reason the ADA hadn't shown was the same reason that Roger and Terry had left – to check on his wife. It wasn't just St Theresa's that was a madhouse. It was everywhere.

'I know, Lila, I know, but Roger's got that baby girl, you know—' If it's his, Lila thought. Jessica Elway liked to bed-hop, that was the word around town. '—and Terry was panicking, too, and neither of them could get an answer when they called home. I told them you'd be pissed.'

'All right, get them back. I want them to go to all three drug-stores in town and tell the pharmacists . . .'

Pinocchio. That was the fairy tale about lying, and he didn't turn into a parakeet, his nose grew until it was as long as Wonder Woman's dildo.

'Lila? Are you still there?'

Pull it together, woman.

'Tell the pharmacists to use discretion on all the speedy stuff they've got. Adderall, Dexedrine . . . and I know there's at least one prescription methamphetamine, although I can't remember the name.'

'Prescription meth? Shut up!'

'Yes. The pharmacists will know. Tell them to use *discretion*. Prescriptions are going to be pouring in. The fewest number of pills they can give people until we understand what in the hell is going on here. Got it?'

'Yes.'

'One other thing, Linny, and this is just between us. Look in Evidence. See what *we've* got in there for speed-up stuff, and that includes the coke and Black Beauties from the Griner brothers bust.'

'Jeepers, are you sure? There's almost half a pound of Bolivian marching powder! Lowell and Maynard, they're due to go on trial. Don't want to mess that up, we've been after them like *forever!*'

'I'm not sure at all, but Clint put the idea in my head and now I can't get it out. Just inventory the stuff, okay? No one's going to start rolling up dollar bills and snorting.' Not this afternoon, anyway.

'Okay.' Linny sounded awed.

'Who's out at that trailer where the meth lab exploded?'

'Just a minute, let me check Gertrude.' Linny called her office computer Gertrude for reasons Lila did not care to understand. 'Forensics and the FD units have departed. I'm surprised they left the scene so soon.'

Lila wasn't. Those guys probably had wives and daughters, too.

'Um . . . looks like a couple of AAH dudes might still be around, putting out the last of the hot spots. Can't say for sure which ones, all I've got is a note saying they rolled out of Maylock at eleven thirty-three. Willy Burke's probably one of them, though. You know Willy, he never misses.'

AAH, an acronym that came out sounding like a sigh, was the Tri-Counties' Adopt-A-Highway crew, mostly retirees with pickup trucks. They were also the closest thing the Tri-Counties had to a volunteer fire department, and often came in handy during brush-fire season.

'Okay, thanks.'

'Are you going out there?' Linny sounded faintly disapproving, and Lila wasn't too tired to catch the subtext: *With all this other stuff going on?*

'Linny, if I had a magic wake-up wand, believe me, I'd use it.'

'Okay, Sheriff.' Subtext: *Don't bite my head off.*

'Sorry. It's just that I've got to do what I *can* do. Presumably someone – a bunch of someones – is working on this sleeping sickness thing at the Disease Control Center in Atlanta. Here in Dooling, I've got a double murder, and I need to work on that.'

Why am I explaining all this to my dispatcher? Because I'm tired, that's why. And because it's a distraction from the way my husband was looking at me back at the prison. And because it's a distraction from the possibility – fact, really, Lila, not a possibility, but a fact, and that fact's name is Sheila – that the husband you're so concerned about isn't anybody you really knew anyway.

Aurora, they were calling it. If I fall asleep, Lila thought, will that be the end? Will I die? Could be, as Clint might say. Could fucking be.

The good-natured back-and-forth they had always had, the ease of their collaborations on projects and meals and parenting responsibilities, the comfortable pleasure they'd taken from each other's bodies – these repeated experiences, the marrow of their daily life together, had turned crumbly.

She pictured her husband smiling and it made her stomach sick. It was the same smile that Jared had, and it was Sheila's smile, too.

Lila remembered how Clint had quit his private practice without a word of discussion. All the work they'd done planning his office, the care that they had put into choosing not just the location but also the town, ultimately selecting Dooling because it was the biggest population center in the area that didn't have a psychiatrist with a general practice. But Clint's second patient had annoyed him, so he had decided, on the spot, that he needed to make a change. And Lila had just gone along. The wasted effort had bothered her, the resultant lowering of their financial prospects had meant a lot of recalculating, and all things being equal she would much rather have lived closer to a city than in the rural Tri-Counties, but she had wanted Clint to be happy. She had just gone along. Lila hadn't wanted a pool. She had gone along. One day Clint had decided that they were switching to bottled water and filled up half of the refrigerator with the stuff. She had gone along. Here was a prescription for Provigil that he had decided she needed to take. She would probably go along. Maybe sleep was her natural state. Maybe that was why she could accept Aurora, because for her, it was not much of a change. Could be. Who the hell knew?

Had Evie been there last night? Was that possible? Watching the AAU game in the Coughlin High gym as the tall blond girl went in for lay-up after lay-up, cutting through Fayette's defense like a sharp blade? That would explain the triple-double thing, wouldn't it?

Kiss your man before you go to sleep.

Yes, this is probably how you started to lose your mind.

'Linny, I have to go.'

She ended the call without waiting for a reply and re-holstered her phone.

Then she remembered Jared, and pulled the phone back out. Only what to tell him, and why bother? He had the Internet on his phone; they all did. By now Jere probably knew more about what was going on than she herself. Her son – at least she had a son, not a daughter. That was something to be thankful for today. Mr and Mrs Pak must be going crazy. She texted Jere to come straight home from school, and that she loved him, and left it at that.

Lila turned her face up to the sky and took more deep breaths. After almost a decade and a half of cleaning up the results of bad behavior, much of it drug-related, Lila Norcross was confident enough in her status and position to know that, although she would do her job to the best of her ability, she had very little personal stake in obtaining justice for a couple of dead meth chefs who, one way or another, had probably been destined to electrocute themselves on the great Bug Light of Life. And she was politically savvy enough to know that nobody was going to be yelling for a quick solve, not with this panic-inducing Aurora thing going on. But the trailer out by Adams Lumberyard was where Evie Doe had made her Dooling County debut, and Lila did have a personal stake in Freaky Evie. She hadn't dropped out of thin air. Had she left a car out there? Possibly one with an owner's registration in the glove compartment? The trailer was less than five miles away; no reason not to have a look-see. Only something else needed doing first.

She went into the Olympia. The place was nearly deserted, both waitresses sitting at a corner booth, gossiping. One of them saw Lila and started to get up, but Lila waved her back. Gus Vereen, the owner, was planted on a stool by the cash register, reading a Dean Koontz paperback. Behind him was a small TV with the sound muted. Across the bottom of the screen ran a crawl reading AURORA CRISIS DEEPENS.

'I read that one,' Lila said, tapping his book. 'The dog communicates using Scrabble tiles.'

'Now you gone and spalled it fur me,' Gus said. His accent was as thick as red-eye gravy.

'Sorry. You'll like it, anyway. Good story. Now that we've got the literary criticism out of the way, coffee to go. Black. Make it an XL.'

He went to the Bunn and filled a large go-cup. It was black, all right: probably stronger than Charles Atlas and as bitter as Lila's late Irish granny. Fine with her. Gus slipped a cardboard heat-sleeve to the halfway point, snapped on a plastic cap, and handed it to her. But when she reached for her wallet, he shook his head.

'No charge, Shurf.'

'Yes, charge.' It was an unbreakable rule, one summarized by the plaque on her desk reading NO FAT COPS STEALING APPLES. Because once you started taking stuff on the arm, it never stopped ... and there was always a *quid pro quo*.

She laid a five on the counter. Gus pushed it back.

'It ain't the badge, Shurf. Free coffee fur all the womenfolk today.' He glanced at his waitresses. 'Ain't that so?'

'Yes,' one of them said, and approached Lila. She reached into the pocket of her skirt. 'And dump this in your coffee, Sheriff Norcross. It won't help the taste any, but it'll jump-start you.'

It was a packet of Goody's Headache Powder. Although Lila had never used it, she knew Goody's was a Tri-Counties staple, right up there with Rebel Yell and cheese-covered hash browns. When you tore open the envelope and poured out the contents, what you had looked pretty much like the Baggies of coke they'd found in the Griner brothers' back shed, wrapped in plastic and stored in an old tractor tire – which was why they, and plenty of other dealers, used Goody's to cut their product. It was cheaper than Pedia-Lax.

'Thirty-two milligrams of caffeine,' the other waitress said. 'I had two already today. I ain't going to sleep until the bright boys solve this Aurora shit. No way.'

4

One of the great benefits of being Dooling County's one and only animal control officer – maybe the only benefit – was having no boss lording it over him. Technically, Frank Geary answered to the mayor and the town council, but they almost never came to his little corner around the rear side of the nondescript building that also housed the historical society, the recreation department, and the assessor's office, which was fine with him.

He got the dogs walked and quieted down (there was nothing like a handful of Dr. Tim's Chicken Chips for that), made sure they were watered, and checked that Maisie Wettermore, the high school volunteer, was due in at six to feed them and take them out again. Yes, she was on the board. Frank left her a note concerning various medications, then locked up and left. It did not occur to him until later that Maisie might have more important things on her mind than a few homeless animals.

It was his daughter he was thinking about. Again. He'd scared her that morning. He didn't like to admit it, even to himself, but he had.

Nana. Something about her had started to nag him. Not the Aurora, exactly, but something related to the Aurora. What was it?

I'll return El's call, he thought. *I'll do it just as soon as I get home.*

Only what he did first when he got to the little four-room house he was renting on Ellis Street was to check the fridge. Not much going on in there: two yogurt cups, a moldy salad, a bottle of Sweet Baby Ray's barbecue sauce, and a case of Miner's Daughter Oatmeal Stout, a high-calorie tipple which he assumed must be healthy – it had oatmeal in it, didn't it? As he grabbed one, his phone went. He looked at Elaine's picture on the little screen and had a moment of clarity he could have done without: he feared the Wrath of Elaine (a little) and his daughter feared the Wrath of Daddy (only a little . . . he hoped). Were these things any basis for a family relationship?

I'm the good guy here, he reminded himself, and took the call. 'Hey, El! Sorry I didn't get back to you sooner, but something came up. Pretty sad. I had to put Judge Silver's cat down, and then—'

Elaine wasn't about to be put off by the subject of Judge Silver's cat; she wanted to get right into it with him. And as usual, she had her volume turned up to ten right from the jump. 'You scared the crap out of Nana! Thank you very much for that!'

'Calm down, okay? All I did was tell her to draw her pictures inside. Because of the green Mercedes.'

'I have no idea what you're talking about, Frank.'

'Remember when she first got the paper route, and she said she had to swerve onto the Nedelhafts' lawn because some guy driving a big green car with a star on the front went up onto the sidewalk? You told me to let it go, and I did. I let it go.'

The words were spilling out faster and faster, soon he'd be *spitting* them if he didn't get control of himself. What Elaine didn't understand was that sometimes he had to shout to be heard. With her, at least.

'The car that took out Judge Silver's cat was also a big green car with a star on the front. A Mercedes. I was pretty sure I knew who it belonged to when Nana had her close call—'

'Frank, she said it swerved onto the sidewalk half a block down!'

'Maybe so, or maybe it was closer and she didn't want to scare us. Didn't want us to take away her paper route right after she got it. Just listen, okay? I let it go. I'd seen that Mercedes around the neighborhood many times, but I let it go.' How many times had he said that? And why did it remind him of that song from *Frozen*, the one Nana had gone around singing until he'd been quite sure it would drive him mad? He was clutching the can of stout so hard he'd dented it, and if he didn't stop, he'd pop it wide open. 'But not this time. Not after he ran over Cocoa.'

'Who's—'

'Cocoa! Cocoa, Judge Silver's cat! That could have been my kid, Elaine! *Our* kid! Long story short, that Mercedes belongs to Garth Flickinger, right up the hill.'

'The doctor?' Elaine sounded engaged. At last.

'That's him. And when I talked to him, guess what? He was *high*, Elaine. I'm almost positive. He could barely form sentences.'

'Instead of reporting him to the police, *you went to his house*? Like you went to Nana's school that time and shouted at her teacher when all the kids – *including* your daughter – could hear you ranting like a crazy person?'

Go ahead, drag it up, Frank thought, clenching the can harder. You always do. That, or the famous wall punch, or the time I told your father he was full of shit. Drag it up, drag it out, Elaine Nutting Geary's Greatest Hits. When I'm in my coffin you'll be telling somebody about the time I hollered at Nana's second grade teacher after she made fun of Nana's science project and made my daughter cry in her room. And when that one gets tired, you can reminisce about the time I yelled at Mrs Fenton for spraying her weed killer where my daughter had to breathe it in while she was riding her trike. Fine. Make me the bad guy if that's what gets you through the day. But right now I will keep my voice calm and level. Because I can't afford to let you push my buttons this time, Elaine. Somebody has to watch out for our daughter, and it's pretty clear you're not up to the job.

'It was my duty as a father.' Did that sound pompous? Frank didn't care. 'I have no interest in seeing him arrested on a misdemeanor charge of feline hit-and-run, but I *do* have an interest in making sure he doesn't run down Nana. If scaring him a little accomplished that—'

'Tell me you didn't go all Charles Bronson.'

'No, I was very reasonable with him.' That was at least close to true. It was the car he hadn't been reasonable with. But he was sure a hot-shit doc like Flickinger had mucho insurance.

'Frank,' she said.

'What?'

'I hardly know where to start. Maybe with the question you didn't ask when you saw Nana drawing in the driveway.'

'What? What question?'

'"Why are you home from school, honey?" *That* question.'

Not in school. Maybe that was what had been nagging at him.

'It was so sunny this morning, I just – seemed like summer, you know? I forgot it was May.'

'You have got your head so far the wrong way around, Frank. You're so concerned about your daughter's safety, and yet you can't even remember that it's the school year. Think about that. Haven't you noticed the homework she does at your house? You know, those notebooks she writes in, and the textbooks she reads? With God and His only son Jesus as my witness—'

He was willing to take a lot – and he was willing to admit he maybe deserved some – but Frank drew the line with the Jesus-as-my-witness shit. God's only son wasn't the one who had gotten that raccoon out from under the Episcopalian church all those years ago and nailed the board over the hole, and He didn't put clothes on Nana's back or food in her stomach. Not to mention Elaine's. Frank did those things and there had been no magic to it.

'Cut to the chase, Elaine.'

'You don't know what's going on with anyone but yourself. It's all about what's pissing Frank off today. It's all about who doesn't understand that only Frank knows how to do things right. Because those are your default positions.'

I can take it. I can take it I can take it I can take it but oh God Elaine what a high-riding bitch you can be when you set your mind to it.

'Was she sick?'

'Oh, *now* you're all Red Alert.'

'Was she? Is she? Because she looked all right.'

'She's fine. I kept her home because she got her period. Her *first* period.'

Frank was thunderstruck.

'She was upset and a little scared, even though I'd explained all about what was going to happen last year. And ashamed, too, because she got some blood on the sheets. For a first period, it was pretty heavy.'

'She can't be . . .' For a moment the word stuck in his throat. He had to cough it out like a bite of food that had gone down wrong. 'She can't be *menstruating*! She's *eleven*, for Christ's sake!'

'Did you think she was going to stay your little princess in fairy wings and sparkly boots forever?'

'No, but . . . eleven?'

'*I* started when I was eleven. And that's not the point, Frank. Here's the point. Your daughter was crampy and confused and low-spirited. She was drawing in the driveway because that's a thing that always cheers her up, and here comes her daddy, all riled up, bellowing—'

'*I was not bellowing!*' That was when the can of Miner's Daughter finally gave way. Foam ran down his fisted hand and pattered to the floor.

'—bellowing and yanking her shirt, her favorite shirt—'

He was appalled to feel the prickle of tears. He had cried several times since the separation, but never while actually talking to Elaine. Deep down he was afraid she would seize any weakness he showed, turn it into a crowbar, pry him wide open, and eat his heart. His tender heart.

'I was scared for her. Don't you understand that? Flickinger is a drunk or a doper or both, he's got a big car, and he killed Judge Silver's cat. I was afraid for her. I had to take action. I *had* to.'

'You behave like you're the only person who ever feared for a child, but you're not. *I* fear for her, and you're the main thing that makes me afraid.'

He was silent. What she'd just said was almost too monstrous to comprehend.

'Keep this up and we'll be back in court, re-evaluating your weekends and visiting privileges.'

Privileges, Frank thought. *Privileges!* He felt like howling. This was what he got for telling her how he actually felt.

'How is she now?'

'Okay, I guess. Ate most of her lunch, then said she was going to take a nap.'

Frank actually rocked back on his heels, and dropped the dented can of suds to the floor. *That* was what had been nagging him, not the question of what Nana was doing home from school. He *knew* what her response to being upset was: she slept it off. And he had upset her.

'Elaine . . . haven't you been watching TV?'

'What?' Not understanding this sudden U-turn in the conversation. 'I caught up on a couple of *Daily Show* episodes on TiVo—'

'The news, El, the *news*! It's on all the channels!'

'What are you talking about? Have you gone cr—'

'Get her up!' Frank roared. 'If she's not asleep yet, get her up! Do it now!'

'You're not making sen—'

Only he was making perfect sense. He wished he wasn't.

'Don't ask questions, just do it! Right now!'

Frank killed the call and ran for the door.

5

Jared was set up undercover when Eric, Curt, and Kent came tromping through the woods from the direction of the high school, making plenty of noise, laughing and bantering.

'It's gotta be a hoax.' That was Kent, he thought, and there was less enthusiasm in his voice than earlier, when Jared had overheard him in the locker room.

Word had gotten around about Aurora. Girls had been crying in the hallways. A few guys, too. Jared had observed one of the math teachers, the burly one with the beard who wore the cowboy snap shirts and coached the debate team, telling a couple of weeping sophomores that they needed to compose themselves, and that everything was going to be okay. Mrs Leighton who taught civics stalked up and stuck her finger into his shirt, right between two of the fancy snaps. 'Easy for you to say!' she had yelled. 'You don't know anything about this! It's not happening to *men!*'

It was weird. It was more than weird. It gave Jared the staticky feeling that accompanied a major storm, the sickly purple clouds piling up and flashing with inner lightning. The world didn't seem weird then; the world didn't seem like the world at all, but like another place that you had been flipped into.

It was a relief to have something else to focus on. At least for a little while. He was on a solo mission. Call it Operation Expose These Pricks.

His father had told him that shock therapy – ECT was what they called it these days – was actually an effective treatment for some mentally ill people, that it could produce a palliative effect in the brain. If Mary asked Jared what he thought he was accomplishing by doing this, he would tell her it was like ECT. Once the whole school got a look and a listen at Eric and his stooges trashing poor Old Essie's place and cracking wise about her boobs – which was,

Jared was certain, exactly what they would do – it might 'shock' them into being better people. Moreover, it might 'shock' some other people into being a little more careful about who they went on dates with.

Meanwhile, the trolls had almost arrived at Ground Zero.

'If it's a hoax, it's the supreme hoax of all time. It's on Twitter, Facebook, Instagram, everywhere. Ladies are going to sleep and pulling some caterpillar shit. And you're the one who said you saw it on the old bag.' This one was definitely Curt McLeod, swinging dick that he was.

Eric was the first to appear on the screen of Jared's phone, hopping over a tumble of loose stones at the edge of Old Essie's area. 'Essie? Baby? Honey? You around? Kent wants to crawl inside your cocoon and warm you up.'

The spot that Jared had selected for his stakeout was a thicket of fern about thirty feet from the lean-to. It appeared dense from the outside, but was mostly bare earth in the middle. There were a few bits of orange-white fur on the ground where some animal had camped. Probably a fox. Jared had stretched out, iPhone at arms' length. The camera was pointed through a gap in the leaves and centered on Old Essie lying in the opening of her lean-to. Just as Kent had said, there was a growth on her face – and if it had been like cobwebs earlier, it was solid now, a white mask, exactly like the ones that everyone had now seen on their phones, on news and social media sites.

That was the one part that made him uncomfortable: the home-less woman sprawled out there, defenseless, sick with the Aurora stuff. If Jared gave Lila his ECT explanation, he wondered what she would say about him just videoing it instead of putting a stop to it. That was where the structure of his logic began to creak. His mother had taught him to stand up for himself and for others, especially girls.

Eric squatted at the opening of the lean-to beside Old Essie's white-wrapped face. He had a stick in his hand. 'Kent?'

'What?' Kent had stopped a few steps away. He was scratching the neck of his tee-shirt and looking anxious.

Eric touched the stick against Essie's mask then drew away. Strands of the whitish material trailed from the stick. '*Kent!*'

'I said what?' The other boy's voice had lifted to a higher pitch. Almost a squeak.

Eric shook his head at his friend, as if he were surprised, surprised and disappointed. 'This is a hell of a load you blew on her face.'

The roar of laughter that came from Curt made Jared twitch and the bush rattled a little around him. No one was paying attention, though.

'Fuck you, Eric!' Kent stormed over to Essie's mannequin torso and kicked it tumbling into the deadfall.

This display of pique didn't divert Eric. 'But did you have to leave it to dry? That's low-class, just leaving your splat on the face of a fine old babe like this.'

Curt strolled over beside Eric to take a closer look. He cocked his head this way and that, licking his lips in a thoughtless way as he appraised Essie, considering her as if he were deciding between a box of Junior Mints and a packet of Sour Patch Kids at a checkout counter.

A sick tremble found its way to Jared's stomach. If they did something to hurt her, he was going to have to try to stop them. Except that there was no way he *could* stop them, because there were three of them and only one of him, and this wasn't about doing what was right or social media ECT, or making people think, this was about Mary and about proving to her that he was better than Eric and really, given the circumstances, was that true? If he were so much better than these guys, he wouldn't be in this fix. He'd already have done something to make them quit.

'I'd give you fifty bucks to bone her,' said Curt. He turned to Kent. 'Either of you. Cash on the line.'

'Whatever,' said Kent. In his sulk he had followed the mannequin torso to where he had kicked it and now he was stomping on it, cracking up the chest cavity with little *pop-pop-pops* of shattering plastic.

'Not for a million.' Eric, still perched in a squat by the mouth of the lean-to, pointed the stick at his friend. 'But, for a hundred,

I'll poke a hole right here—' He lowered the stick to tap Essie's right ear. '—and I'll piss into it.'

Jared could see Essie's chest rise and fall.

'Seriously? A hundred?' It was clear that Curt was tempted, but a hundred dollars was a significant amount of bread.

'Nah. I'm just teasing.' Eric winked at his buddy. 'I wouldn't make you pay for that. I'll do it for free.' He leaned over Essie; probing with the tip of the stick to dig through the webbing to her ear.

Jared needed to do something; he couldn't just watch and record and let them do this to her. So why aren't you moving? he asked himself, even as his iPhone, squeezed tight in his damp hand, popped up – *whoops!* – and landed with a crunch in the brush.

6

Even with the pedal to metal, the little animal control pickup would do no more than fifty. Not because of a governor on the engine; the pickup was just old, and on its second trip around the clock. Frank had petitioned the town council for a new one on several occasions, and the answer had always been the same: 'We'll take it under advisement.'

Driving hunched over the wheel, Frank imagined pounding several of those smalltown politicians to a pulp. And what would he say when they begged him to stop? 'I'll take it under advisement.'

He saw women everywhere. None of them were alone. They were clustered in groups of three and four, talking together, embracing, some of them crying. None of them looked at Frank Geary, even when he blew through stop signs and red lights. This is the way Flickinger must drive when he's stoned, he thought. Watch out, Geary, or you'll run over someone's cat. Or someone's kid.

But Nana! *Nana!*

His phone went. He pushed ANSWER without looking. It was Elaine, and she was sobbing.

'She's asleep and won't wake up and there's *goo* all over her face! White goo like cobwebs!'

He passed three women hugging it out on a street corner. They looked like guests on some therapy show. 'Is she breathing?'

'Yes . . . yes, I can see the stuff moving . . . fluttering out and then kind of sucking in . . . oh, Frank, I think it's in her *mouth* and on her *tongue*! I'm going to get my nail scissors and cut it off!'

An image filled his mind, one so brilliant and ghastly-real that for a moment the street ahead of him was blotted out: Kinswoman Susannah Brightleaf, battening on her husband's nose.

'No, El, don't do that.'

'Why not?'

Watching *The Daily Show* instead of the news when the biggest thing in history was happening, how stupid could you get? But that was the former Elaine Nutting of Clarksburg, West Virginia. That was Elaine right down to the ground. High on judgmental pronouncements, low on information. 'Because it wakes them up, and when they wake up, they're crazy. No, not crazy. More like rabid.'

'You're not telling me . . . Nana would never . . .'

If she's even Nana anymore, Frank thought. Kinsman Brightleaf sure didn't get the sweet and docile woman he was no doubt used to.

'Elaine . . . honey . . . turn on the television and you'll see it for yourself.'

'*What are we going to do?*'

Now you ask me, he thought. Now that your back is to the wall, it's Oh Frank, what are we going to do? He felt a sour, dismaying satisfaction.

His street. Finally. Thank God. The house was ahead. This was going to be all right. He would *make* it all right.

'We're going to take her to the hospital,' he said. 'By now they probably know what's going on.'

They'd better. They'd just better. Because this was Nana. His little girl.

CHAPTER 7

1

While Ree Dempster was chewing her thumbnail bloody, deciding whether or not to drop a dime on Officer Don Peters, a Heathrow to JFK flight, a 767 three hours southwest of London at cruising speed over the Atlantic, radioed to air traffic control to report an outbreak of some sort and consult on the proper course of action.

'We've got three passengers, one's a young girl, and they seem to have developed a – we're not sure. Doctor on board is saying that it's possibly a fungus or a growth. They're asleep, or at least, they seem to be asleep, and the doctor is telling us their vitals are normal, but there's concern about their airways being – ah, blocked, so I guess he's going to—'

The exact nature of the interruption that occurred next was unclear. There was a commotion, metallic clattering and screeching, shouts – 'They can't be in here! Get them out of here!' – and the roar of what sounded like an animal. The cacophony continued for almost four minutes, until the 767's radar trail broke off, presumably at the moment it made impact with the water.

2

Dr Clinton Norcross strode down Broadway toward his interview with Evie Black, notepad in his left hand and clicking his pen in his right. His body was in Dooling Correctional, but his mind was wandering around in the dark on Mountain Rest Road and worrying over what it was Lila was lying about. And – maybe – who she was lying about.

A few yards away, upstairs in a B Wing cell, Nell Seeger – Dooling Correctional inmate #4609198-1, five-to-ten (Class B possession with intent to distribute) – sat up in her top bunk to thumb off the television.

The small TV, a flatscreen about as thick as a closed laptop, rested on the ridge at the foot of the bunk. It had been showing the news. Nell's cellie and off-again on-again lover, Celia Frode, not quite halfway through her one-to-two years (Class D possession, second offense), had been watching from her place at their unit's single steel desk. She said, 'Thank goodness. I can't take any more of this madness. Now what are you going to do?'

Nell lay back down and rolled over on her side, facing the painted square on the wall where the school pictures of her three kids were pasted in a row. 'Nothing personal, darling, but I'm going to take a rest. I'm awful beat.'

'Oh.' Celia understood right away. 'Well. All right. Sweet dreams, Nell.'

'I hope so,' said Nell. 'Love you. You can have any of my stuff that you want.'

'Love you, too, Nell.' Celia put her hand on Nell's shoulder. Nell patted it once and then curled up. Celia sat down at their cell's small desk to wait.

When Nell was snoring softly, Celia stood up and peeked at her. Strands were curling around her cellie's face, fluttering and falling and splitting into more strands, waving like seaweed in a gentle tide. Nell's eyes were rolling under her eyelids. Was she dreaming about them, together, on the outside, sitting on a picnic blanket somewhere, maybe the beach? No, probably not. Probably Nell was dreaming about her kids. She wasn't the most demonstrative partner that Celia had ever taken up with, sure wasn't much of a conversationalist, but Nell had a good heart, and she loved her kids, was always writing to them.

It would be awfully lonely without her.

What the hell, thought Celia, and decided to take a liedown herself.

3

Thirty miles east of Dooling Correctional, and at about the same time Nell was drifting off, two brothers sat handcuffed to a bench in the Coughlin County Courthouse. Lowell Griner was thinking about his father and about suicide, which might be preferable to thirty years in State. Maynard Griner was dreaming about a slab of barbecued ribs that he'd eaten a few weeks earlier, right before the bust. Neither man had any idea what was going on in the wider world.

The bailiff on guard duty was sick of waiting around. 'What the fuck. I'm going to see if Judge Wainer plans to pee or get off the pot. I don't get paid enough to babysit you murdering little pecker-woods all day.'

4

As Celia decided to join Nell in sleep; as the bailiff entered a conference room to consult with Judge Wainer; as Frank Geary sprinted across the lawn of the house he had once lived in, his only child in his arms and his estranged wife steps behind him; while these things were happening, thirty or so civilians attempted an impromptu assault on the White House.

The vanguard, three men and one woman, all young, all to the naked eye unarmed, began to climb the White House fence. 'Give us the antidote!' bellowed one of the men as he dropped to the ground inside the fence. He was scrawny, ponytailed, and wore a Cubs cap.

A dozen Secret Service agents, pistols at the ready, quickly surrounded the trespassers, but at that point a second, much larger surge of people from the crowd that had massed on Pennsylvania Avenue pushed over the barricades and charged the fence. Police officers in riot gear swept in from behind, hauling them down from the fence. Two shots came in quick succession, and one of the cops stumbled and fell loose-bodied to the ground. After that the gunfire turned into a wall of sound. A teargas canister burst somewhere close by and a pall of ashy smoke began to unravel across the pavement, erasing most of the people running past.

Michaela Morgan, née Coates, viewed the scene on a monitor in the back of the NewsAmerica van parked across the street from the CDC, and rubbed her hands together. They had acquired a noticeable shake. Her eyes were itchy and watery from the three bumps she'd just snorted off the control deck with a ten-dollar bill.

A woman in a dark blue dress appeared in the foreground of the White House shot. She was around Michaela's mother's age, her black shoulder-length hair fissured with streaks of gray, a string of pearls bouncing at her neck. Straight out in front of her, like a hot platter, she held a baby, its lolling head swaddled in white. The woman strode smoothly by, never turning her profile, and vanished beyond the edge of the shot.

'I think I could use a little more. You mind?' Michaela asked her tech guy. He told her to knock herself out (perhaps a poor choice of words under the circumstances), and handed her the Baggie.

5

While the furious, terrified crowd was attacking 1600 Pennsylvania Avenue, Lila Norcross was driving toward Dooling. Her mind was on Jared, on her son, and on the girl, on Sheila, her son's half-sister, her husband's daughter, what an interesting new family tree they had! Wasn't there something similar around their mouths, Sheila's and Clint's, that crafty little upturn at the corners? Was she a liar, too, like her father? *Could be.* And was the girl tired like Lila was tired, still feeling the effects of all that running and jumping she'd done the previous night? If she was, well then, that was something else they had in common, something besides just Clint and Jared.

Lila wondered if she should just go to sleep, abdicate from the whole mess. It would certainly be easier. She wouldn't have thought that a few days ago; a few days ago she would have seen herself as strong and decisive and in control. When had she ever challenged Clint? Not once, it seemed to her in the light of her new understanding. Not even when she'd found out about Sheila Norcross, the girl who bore his last name, and her last name, too.

Pondering these things, Lila turned onto Main Street. She hardly registered the tan compact that swung left past her, and went blasting up the hill in the direction from which she'd just come.

The compact's driver, a middle-aged woman, was taking her mother to the hospital in Maylock. In the backseat of the automobile, the middle-aged woman's elderly father – never the most cautious of men, a tosser of young children into swimming pools, a bettor of trifectas, a cavalier gobbler of pickled sausages in foggy jars on the counters of roadside general stores – was using the edge of an ice scraper to separate the webbing covering his wife's face. 'She'll suffocate!' he yelled.

'The radio said not to!' the middle-aged woman yelled back, but her father was his own man, right to the end, and continued to carve apart the growth on his wife's face.

6

And Evie was almost everywhere. She was a fly in the 767, crawling down to the bottom of a highball glass and dabbing her legs in the residue of a whiskey and Coke moments before the plane's nose connected with the ocean's surface. The moth that fluttered around the fluorescent bar in the ceiling of Nell Seeger and Celia Frode's prison cell was also Evie. She was visiting the Coughlin Courthouse, behind the grid of the air duct in the corner of the conference room, where she peered through the shiny black eyes of a mouse. On the White House lawn, as an ant, she moved through the still-warm blood of a dead teenage girl. In the woods where Jared ran from his pursuers, she was a worm beneath his shoes, nosing in the soil, blind and many-segmented.

Evie got around.

CHAPTER 8

1

Memories of freshman track came back to Jared as he fled through the trees. Coach Dreifort had said Jared was a 'comer.'

'I got plans for you, Norcross, and they involve winning a whole mess of shiny medals,' Coach Dreifort had said. At the end of that season Jared finished fifth out of fifteen in his group at regionals in the 8,000 meter – outstanding for a frosh – but then he'd ruined Coach D.'s plans, quitting to take a job on the Yearbook Committee.

Jared had relished those late race moments when he found a fresh lung and regained the pace and felt a sense of ecstasy, loving his own strength. The reason he'd quit was that Mary was on the Yearbook Committee. She had been elected sophomore sales and distribution chairwoman, and needed a vice-chair. Jared's dedication to track was summarily abandoned. Sign me up, he told Mary.

'Okay, but there's two things,' she explained. 'Number one, if I die, which I might because I ate one of those mystery meat hot pockets at the cafeteria today, then you have to take over as chair and fulfill my duties and make sure there's a full page tribute to my memory in the yearbook senior year. And you have to make sure that the photo of me isn't something stupid that my mother picked.'

'Got it,' Jared had said, and thought, I really love you. He knew he was too young. He knew she was too young. How could he not, though? Mary was so beautiful, and she was so on the ball, but she made it seem completely natural, no stress, no strain. 'What's the second thing?'

'The second thing—' She grabbed his head with both hands and shook it back and forth and up and down. '—is that *I am the Boss!*'

As far as Jared was concerned, that was also no problem.

Now his sneaker came down on a flat rock sitting high and loose, and that, as it happened, *was* a problem, actually a pretty big one, because he felt a wobble and a sharp sting in his right knee. Jared gasped and drove forward with his left foot, concentrating on his breathing like they taught you in track, keeping his elbows working.

Eric was thundering behind him. 'We just want to talk to you!'

'Don't be a fucking pussy!' That was Curt.

Down into a gully, and Jared felt his hurt knee slide around and thought he heard a little *ping* somewhere under the thudding of his pulse and the crackle of dry leaves under his sneaker heels. Malloy Street, the one behind the high school, was up ahead, a yellow car flickering past in the gaps between the trees. His right leg buckled at the bottom of the gully, and the pain was unprecedented, hand-on-a-red-burner pain only on the inside, and he grabbed a thorny branch to yank himself staggering up the opposite bank.

The air was momentarily disturbed behind him, as if a hand had swiped right past his scalp, and he heard Eric swearing and the tumult of bodies tangling. They'd lost it while sliding down the gully behind him. The road was twenty feet on; he could hear the burr of a car engine. He was going to make it!

Jared lurched, closing the gap to the road, feeling a burst of that old track euphoria, the air in his lungs suddenly carrying him, thrusting him forward and holding off the agony of his distorted knee.

The hand on his shoulder spun him off-balance at the edge of the road. He caught onto a birch tree to keep from falling.

'Give me that phone, Norcross.' Kent's face shone bright red, the acne field on his forehead purple. His eyes were wet. 'We were kidding around, that's all.'

'No,' said Jared. He couldn't even remember picking his phone up again, but there it was in his hand. His knee felt enormous.

'Yes,' Kent said. 'Give it.' The other two had gathered themselves and were running to catch up, only a few feet off.

'You were going to pee in an old lady's ear!' cried Jared.

'Not me!' Kent blinked away sudden tears. 'I couldn't, anyway! I got a shy bladder!'

You weren't going to try to stop them, though, Jared might have replied, but instead felt his arm cock and his fist shoot out to connect with Kent's dimpled chin. The impact produced a satisfying *clack* of teeth slamming together.

As Kent tumbled down into the weeds, Jared shoved his phone in his pocket and got moving again. Three agonizing hops and he was at the yellow centerline, waving down a speeding tan compact with a Virginia plate. He didn't register that the driver was turned around in her seat – and Jared certainly didn't see what was happening in the rear of the car, where a bellowing old woman with tattered webbing hanging from her face was repeatedly gouging the edge of an ice scraper into the chest and throat of her husband who had cut said webbing from her face – but he did note the compact's erratic progress, as it jerked right-left-right-left, almost out of control.

Jared tried to twist away, wishing himself small, and was just congratulating himself on his evasion technique when the compact hit him and sent him flying.

2

'Hey! Get your hands off my Booth!' Ree had gotten Officer Lampley's attention by knocking on the front window of the Booth, a major no-no. 'What do you want, Ree?'

'The warden, Officer,' said Ree, elaborately and unnecessarily mouthing the words, which Vanessa Lampley could hear perfectly fine via the vents situated under the panes of bulletproof glass. 'I need to see the warden about something wrong. Her and no one else. I'm sorry, Officer. That's the only way. How it's got to be.'

Van Lampley had worked hard to cultivate her reputation as a firm but fair officer. For seventeen years she'd patrolled the cellblocks of Dooling Correctional, and she'd been stabbed once, punched several times, kicked even more times, choked, had drippy shit flung at her, and been invited to go and fuck herself in any number of ways and with a variety of objects, many of them unrealistically large or dangerously sharp. Did Van sometimes draw on these memories during her arm-wrestling matches? She did indeed, although sparingly, usually only during significant league bouts. (Vanessa Lampley competed in the Ohio Valley Slammers League, Women's A Division.) The memory of the time that a deranged crack addict dropped a chunk of brick from the second level of B Wing down onto Vanessa's skull (resulting in a skull contusion and a concussion), had, in fact, helped her take it 'over-the-top' in both of her championship victories. Anger was excellent fuel if you refined it correctly.

In spite of these regrettable experiences, she was forever conscious of the responsibility that went with her authority. She understood that no one wanted to be in prison. Some people, however, needed to be. It was unpleasant, both for them and for her. If a respectful attitude was not maintained, it would be more unpleasant – for them, and for her.

And although Ree was all right – poor kid had a big scar on her forehead that told you she hadn't had the easiest ride through life – it was disrespectful to make unreasonable requests. The warden wasn't available for on the spot one-on-ones, especially with a medical emergency happening.

Van had serious worries of her own concerning what she'd read on the Internet about Aurora on her last break, and the directive from above that everyone needed to stay for a second shift. Now McDavid, looking on the monitor like she belonged not in a cell but in a sarcophagus, had been put under quarantine. Van's husband Tommy, when she called him at their house, insisted he would be fine on his own for as long as she needed to stay, but she didn't believe it for a second. Tommy, on disability for his hips, couldn't make a grilled cheese sandwich for himself; he'd be eating pickles out of a jar until she got home. If Van wasn't allowed to lose her head about any of that, then neither was Ree Dempster or any other inmate.

'No, Ree, you need to lower your sights. You can tell me, or you tell no one. If it's important enough, I'll take it to the warden. And why'd you touch my Booth? Dammit. You know you can't do that. I should put you on Bad Report for that.'

'Officer . . .' Ree, on the other side of the window, put her hands together in supplication. 'Please. I'm not lying. Something wrong happened and it's too wrong to let go, and you're a lady, so please understand that.' Ree wrung her clasped hands in the air. '*You're a lady.* Okay?'

Van Lampley studied the inmate, who was on the raised concrete apron in front of the Booth and praying to her like they had anything in common besides their double X chromosomes. 'Ree, you're right up against the line here. I'm not kidding.'

'And I'm not lyin for prizes! Please believe me. It's about Peters, and it's serious. Warden needs to know.'

Peters.

Van rubbed her immense right bicep, as was her habit when a matter called for consideration. The bicep was inked with a gravestone for **YOUR PRIDE**. Under the words on the stone was a picture of a flexed arm. It was a symbol of all the opponents she'd bent back: knuckles on the table, thank you for playing. A lot of men wouldn't arm-wrestle her. They didn't want to risk the embarrassment. They made excuses, shoulder tendinitis, bad elbow, etc. 'Lying for prizes' was a funny way to put it, but somehow apt. Don Peters was the lying-for-prizes type.

'If I hadn't jacked my arm pitching high school ball, I hope you understand that I'd break you down right quick, Lampley,' the little asswipe had explained to her once when a group of them were having beers at the Squeaky Wheel.

'I don't doubt it, Donnie,' she'd replied.

Ree's big secret was probably bunk. And yet . . . Don Peters. There had been loads of complaints about him, the kind that maybe you did have to be a woman to truly relate to.

Van raised the cup of coffee that she'd forgotten she had. It was cold. Okay, she supposed she could walk Ree Dempster down to see the warden. Not because Vanessa Lampley was going soft, but because she needed a fresh cup. After all, as of now her shift was open-ended.

'All right, inmate. This once. I'm probably wrong to do it, but I will. I just hope you've thought this through.'

'I have, Officer, I have. I've thought and thought and thought.'

Lampley buzzed Tig Murphy to come down and spell her in the Booth. Said she needed to take ten.

3

Outside the soft cell, Peters was leaning against the wall and scrolling through his phone. His mouth curled into a perplexed frown.

'I hate to bother you, Don—' Clint chinned toward the cell door. '—but I need to talk to this one.'

'Oh, it's no bother, Doc.' Peters clicked his phone off and summoned a *pal-ole-pal-o'mine* grin that they both knew was as real as the Tiffany lamps that got sold at the bi-weekly flea market in Maylock.

A couple of other things that they both knew to be true: 1) it was a violation of policy for an officer to be screwing around with his phone while on deck in the middle of the day; and 2) Clint had been trying to get Peters transferred or outright fired for months. Four different inmates had personally complained of sexual harassment to the doctor, but only in his office, under the seal of confidentiality. None of them were willing to go on record. They were afraid of payback. Most of these women had experienced a lot of payback, some inside the walls, even more outside them.

'So McDavid's got this stuff, too, huh? From the news? Any reason I need to be personally concerned here? Everything I'm seeing says it's ladies only, but you're the doc.'

As he'd predicted to Coates, a half-dozen attempts to get through to the CDC had failed – nothing but a busy signal. 'I don't have any more particulars than you, Don, but yes, so far, to the best of my knowledge, there's no indication that any man has contracted the virus – or whatever it is. I need to talk to the inmate.'

'Right, right,' Peters said.

The officer unlocked the upper and lower bolts, then buttoned his mic. 'Officer Peters, letting the doc into A-10, over.' He swung the cell door wide.

Before stepping out of Clint's way, Peters pointed at the inmate seated on the foam bunk against the back wall. 'I'm going to be right here, so it would be unwise to try anything on the doc, all right? That clear? I don't want to use force on you, but I will. We clear?'

Evie didn't look at him. Her attention was fixed on her hair; she was dragging her fingers through it, picking at the tangles. 'I understand. Thank you for being such a gentleman. Your mother must be very proud of you, Officer Peters.'

Peters hung in the doorway, trying to decide if he was being dicked with. Of course his mother was proud of him. Her son served on the frontlines of the war on crime.

Clint tapped him on the shoulder before he could figure it out. 'Thanks, Don. I'll take it from here.'

4

'Ms Black? Evie? I'm Dr Norcross, the psychiatric officer at this facility. Are you feeling calm enough to have a talk? It's important that I get a sense of where your head is at, how you're feeling, whether you understand what's going on, what's happening, if you have any questions or concerns.'

'Sure. Let's chat. Roll the old conversational ball.'

'How are you feeling?'

'I feel pretty good. I don't like the way this place smells, though. There's a certain chemical aroma. I'm a fresh air person. A Nature Girl, you could say. I like a breeze. I like the sun. Earth under my feet. Cue the soaring violins.'

'I understand. Prison can feel very close. You understand that you're in a prison, right? This is the Correctional Facility for Women in the town of Dooling. You haven't been charged with any crime, let alone convicted, you're just here for your own safety. Do you follow all that?'

'I do.' She lowered her chin to her chest and dropped her voice to a whisper. 'But that guy, Officer Peters. You know about him, don't you?'

'Know what about him?'

'He takes things that don't belong to him.'

'What makes you say that? What sort of things?'

'I'm just rolling the conversational ball. I thought you wanted to do that, Dr Norcross. Hey, I don't want to tell you how to do your job, but aren't you supposed to sit behind me, where I can't see you?'

'No. That's psychoanalysis. Let's get back to—'

'The great question that has never been answered and which I have not yet been able to answer, despite my thirty years of research into the feminine soul, is "What does a woman want?"'

'Freud, yes. He pioneered psychoanalysis. You've read about him?'

'I think most women, if you asked them, if they were truly honest, what they would say is, they want a nap. And possibly earrings that go with everything, which is impossible, of course. Anyhow, big sales today, Doc. Fire sales. In fact, I know of a trailer, it's a little banged up — there's a little hole in one wall, have to patch that — but I bet you could have the place for free. Now that's a deal.'

'Are you hearing voices, Evie?'

'Not exactly. More like — signals.'

'What do the signals sound like?'

'Like humming.'

'Like a tune?'

'Like moths. You need special ears to hear it.'

'And I don't have the right ears to hear the moths humming?'

'No, I'm afraid you don't.'

'Do you remember hurting yourself in the police car? You hit your face against the safety grille. Why did you do that?'

'Yes, I remember. I did it because I wanted to go to prison. This prison.'

'That's interesting. Why?'

'To see you.'

'That's flattering.'

'But it gets you nowhere, you know. Flattery, I mean.'

'The sheriff said you knew her name. Was that because you've been arrested before? Try and remember. Because it would really help if we could find out a little more about your background. If there's an arrest record, that could lead us to a relative, a friend. You could use an advocate, don't you think, Evie?'

'The sheriff is your wife.'

'How did you know that?'

'Did you kiss her goodbye?'

'Beg your pardon?'

The woman who called herself Eve Black leaned forward, looking at him earnestly. 'Kiss: an osculation requiring – hard to believe, I know – a hundred and forty-seven different muscles. Goodbye: a word of parting. Do you need any further elucidation?'

Clint was thrown. She was really, really disturbed, going in and out of coherence, as if her brain were in the neurological equivalent of an ophthalmologist's chair, seeing the world through a series of flicking lenses. 'No need of elucidation. If I answer your question, will you tell me something?'

'Deal.'

'Yes. I kissed her goodbye.'

'Oh, that's sweet. You're getting old, you know, not quite The Man anymore, I get that. Probably having some doubts now and then. "Do I still have it? Am I still a powerful ape?" But you haven't lost your desire for your wife. Lovely. And there are pills. "Ask your doctor if it's right for you." I sympathize. Really. I can relate! If you think getting old is tough for men, let me tell you, it's no picnic for women. Once your tits fall, you become pretty much invisible to fifty percent of the population.'

'My turn. How do you know my wife? How do you know me?'

'Those are the wrong questions. But I'm going to answer the right one for you. "Where was Lila last night?" That's the right question. And the answer is: not on Mountain Rest Road. Not in Dooling. She found out about you, Clint. And now she's getting sleepy. Alas.'

'Found out about what? I have nothing to hide.'

'I think you believe that, which shows how well you've hidden it. Ask Lila.'

Clint rose. The cell was hot and he was sticky with sweat. This exchange had gone nothing at all like any introductory talk with an inmate in his entire career. She was schizophrenic – had to be, and some of them were very good at picking up cues and clues – but she was unnervingly quick in a way that was unlike any schizophrenic he had ever met.

And how could she know about Mountain Rest Road?

'*You* wouldn't have happened to be on Mountain Rest Road last night, would you, Evie?'

'Could be.' She winked at him. '*Could be.*'

'Thank you, Evie. We'll talk again soon, I'm sure.'

'Of course we will, and I look forward to it.' Through their conversation her focus on him had been unfaltering – again, nothing like any unmedicated schizophrenic he'd ever dealt with – but she now returned to pulling haphazardly at her hair. She drew down, grunting at a knot that came loose with an audible tearing sound. 'Oh, Dr Norcross—'

'Yes?'

'Your son's been injured. I'm sorry.'

CHAPTER 9

1

Dozing in the shade of a sycamore, his head propped on his balled-up yellow fire jacket, faintly smoldering pipe resting on the chest of his faded workshirt, Willy Burke, the Adopt-A-Highway man, was a picture. Well known for his poaching of fish and game on public lands as well as for the potency of his small-batch moonshine, renowned for never having been caught poaching fish and game or cooking corn, Willy Burke was a perfect human evocation of the state motto, a fancy Latin phrase that translated as *mountaineers are always free*. He was seventy-five. His gray beard fluffed up around his neck and a ratty Cason with a couple of lures snagged in the felt rested on the ground beside him. If someone else wanted to try to catch him for his various offenses, that was life, but Lila turned a blind eye. Willy was a good man who worked a lot of town services for free. He'd had a sister who had died of Alzheimer's, and before she'd passed, Willy had cared for her. Lila used to see them at firehouse chicken dinners; even as Willy's sister had stared off with her glazed eyes, Willy had kept up a patter, talking to her about this and that while he cut up her chicken and fed her bites.

Now Lila stood over him and watched his eyes move under the lids. It was nice to see that at least one person wasn't about to allow a worldwide crisis to disturb his afternoon. She just wished she could lie down under a neighboring tree and take a snooze herself.

Instead of doing that, she nudged one of his rubber boots. 'Mr Van Winkle. Your wife filed a missing persons report. She says you've been gone for decades.'

Willy's lids parted. He blinked a couple of times and picked his pipe off his chest and levered himself upright. 'Chief.'

'What were you dreaming about? Starting a forest fire?'

'I been sleeping with a pipe on my chest since I was a boy. It's perfectly safe if you've mastered the skill. I was dreaming about a new pickup, for your information.' Willy's truck, a rusty dinosaur from the Vietnam era, was parked at the edge of the gravel apron in front of Truman Mayweather's trailer. Lila had drawn her cruiser up beside it.

'What's the story here?' She chinned at the surrounding woods, the trailer surrounded by yellow tape. 'Fires all out? Just you?'

'We sprayed down the meth shack that exploded. Also watered down the pieces. Lotta pieces. It's not too dry here, which was lucky. Be awhile before the smell goes, though. Everyone else split. Thought I'd better wait, preserve the scene and whatnot.' Willy groaned as he got to his feet. 'Do I even want to know why there's a hole the size of a bowling ball in the side of that trailer?'

'No,' said Lila. 'Give you nightmares. You can go on, Willy. Thanks for making sure the fire didn't spread.'

Lila crunched across the gravel to the trailer. The blood caked around the hole in its side had darkened to maroon. Beneath the smell of burn and ozone from the explosion, there was the turned-over tang of living tissue left to cook in the sun. Before ducking under the police tape, Lila shook out a handkerchief and pressed it over her nose and mouth.

'All right, then,' said Willy, 'I'll get. Must be past three. Ought to get a bite. Oh, one other thing. Might be some chemical reaction going on up there beyond what's left of that shed. That's all I can figure.' Willy seemed in no hurry to go, despite his avowed intention of doing so; he was packing a new pipe, selecting cuts from his front shirt pocket.

'What do you mean?'

'Look in the trees. On the ground. Fairy handkerchiefs, it looks like to me, but, well, it's also sticky. Tacky. Thick, too. Fairy hand-kerchiefs aren't like that.'

'No,' Lila said. She had no idea what he was talking about. 'Of course they're not. Listen, Willy, we've got someone in custody for the murders—'

'Yep, yep, heard it on my scanner. Hard to believe a woman could've killed those men and torn up that trailer like she did, but the women are getting stronger, that's my opinion. Stronger and stronger. Just look at that Ronda Rousey, for instance.'

Lila had no idea who Ronda Rousey was, either. The only unusually physically strong woman she knew from these parts was Vanessa Lampley, who supplemented her income at the prison with competitive arm-wrestling. 'You know these parts . . .'

'Well, not like the back of my hand, but I know em a-country fair,' he agreed, tamping the fresh load in his pipe with a nicotine-yellowed thumb.

'That woman had to get here somehow, and I doubt if she walked. Can you think of anyplace she might have parked a car? Somewhere off the road?'

Willy set a match to his pipe and considered. 'Well, you know what? The Appalachian Power Company lines go through about half a mile yonder.' He pointed up the hill in the direction of the meth shed. 'Run all the way to Bridger County. Someone with a four-wheel drive might could get into that cut from Pennyworth Lane, though I wouldn't try it in any vehicle I'd paid for myself.' He glanced up at the sun. 'Time for me to roll. If I hurry back to the station, I'll be in time for *Dr. Phil*.'

2

There was nothing to see in the trailer that Terry Coombs and Roger Elway would not have already photographed, and nothing which might have helped to place Evie Black at the scene. No purse, no wallet.

Lila wandered through the wreckage until she heard the sound of Willy's pickup rattling down to the main highway. Then she crossed the relic-laden gravel in front of the trailer, ducked under the yellow tape, and walked back to the meth shed.

Half a mile yonder, Willy had said, and although the overgrowth was too thick for Lila to see the power pylons from where she was standing (and wishing for an air mask; the reek of chemicals was still strong), she could hear the steady *bzzz* they made as they carried their high-voltage load to the homes and businesses of this little corner of the Tri-Counties. People who lived near those pylons claimed they caused cancer, and from what Lila had read in the papers there was some convincing evidence. What about the sludge from the strip mines and the holding ponds that had polluted the ground water, though? Maybe one of those was the culprit. Or was it a kind of poison casserole, the various man-made spices combining into various flavorful illnesses, cancers, lung diseases, and chronic headaches?

And now a new illness, she thought. What had brought this one about? Not coal effluent, if it was happening all over the world.

She started toward the *bzzz* sound, and hadn't gone half a dozen steps before she saw the first of the fairy handkerchiefs, and understood what Willy had been talking about. You saw them in the morning; mostly, spiderwebs jeweled with dew. She dropped to one knee, reached for the patch of filmy whiteness, then thought better of it. She picked up a twig and poked it with that, instead. Thin strands stuck to the end of the twig and seemed to either evaporate or melt into the wood. Which was impossible, of course. A trick of her tired eyes. There could be no other explanation.

She thought about the cocoons that were growing on women who fell asleep, and wondered if this could possibly be the same stuff. One thing seemed obvious, even to a woman as exhausted as she was: it looked like a footprint.

'At least it does to me,' she said out loud. She took her phone from her belt and photographed it.

There was another beyond the first, then another and another. No doubt about it now. They were tracks, and the person who'd made them had been walking toward the meth shed and the trailer. White webbing also clung to a couple of tree trunks, each forming the vague outline of a hand, as if someone had either touched them going by or leaned against them to rest or to listen. What, exactly, was this shit? If Evie Black had left webwork tracks and handprints out here in the woods, how come there was no sign of the stuff in Lila's cruiser?

Lila followed the tracks up a rise, then down into the sort of narrow dip that country fellows like Willy Burke called a brake or a holler, then up another hill. Here the trees were thicker – scrub pines fighting for space and sunlight. The webby stuff hung from some of the branches. She took a few more pictures with her phone and pushed on toward the power pylons and the bright sunlight ahead. She ducked under a low-hanging branch, stepped into the clearing, and just stared. For a moment all her tiredness was swept away by amazement.

I am not seeing this, she thought. I've fallen asleep, maybe in my cruiser, maybe in the late Truman Mayweather's trailer, and I'm dreaming it. I must be, because nothing like this exists in the Tri-Counties, or east of the Rockies. Nothing like this exists anywhere, actually, not on earth, not in this epoch.

Lila stood frozen at the edge of the clearing, her neck craned, staring upward. Flocks of moths fluttered around her, brown in the shade, seeming to turn an iridescent gold in the late afternoon sunshine.

She had read somewhere that the tallest tree on earth – a redwood – was just under four hundred feet high. The tree in the center of the clearing looked taller than that, and it was no redwood. It was like no tree she'd ever seen. The closest she could come to a comparison were the banyan trees she and Clint had seen in Puerto Rico on their honeymoon. This . . . thing . . . stood on a great gnarled podium of roots, the largest of them looking twenty or thirty feet thick. The trunk was comprised of dozens of intertwined boles, rising into huge branches with fernlike leaves. The tree seemed to glow with its own light, a surrounding aura. That was probably an illusion caused by the way the westering sun flashed through the gaps in the twisting sections of the trunk, but . . .

But the whole thing was an illusion, wasn't it? Trees did not grow to a height of five hundred feet, and even if this one had — supposing it was real — she would have seen it from Mayweather's trailer. Terry and Roger would have seen it. Willy Burke would have seen it.

From the cloud of ferny leaves far above her, a flock of birds exploded into the sky. They were green, and at first Lila thought they were parrots, only they were too small. They flocked west, forming a V — like ducks, for Christ's sake — and were gone.

She pulled her shoulder mic, thumbed the button, and tried to raise Linny in dispatch. She got nothing but a steady wash of static and somehow wasn't surprised. Nor was she when a red snake — thicker than one of Van Lampley's pumped-up biceps and at least three yards long — slithered from a vertical split in the amazing tree's gray trunk. The split was as big as a doorway.

The snake lifted its spade-shaped head in her direction. Black eyes surveyed her with cold interest. Its tongue tested the air, then withdrew. The snake slid rapidly up a crevasse in the trunk and coiled over a branch in a series of neat loops. Its head pendulumed. The impenetrable eyes still regarded Lila, now viewing her upside down.

There was a low, rippling growl from behind the tree, and a white tiger emerged from the shadows, its eyes bright and green. A peacock strutted into view, head bobbing, fanning its glorious tail, making a noise that sounded like a single hilarious question, repeated over and over: *Heehh? Heehh? Heehh? Heehh?* Moths swirled around it. Lila's family had owned an illustrated New Testament, and those swirling insects made her think of the diadem Jesus always seemed to have, even as a baby lying in a manger.

The red snake slithered down from its branch, dropped the last ten feet, and landed between the peacock and the tiger. The three of them came toward Lila at the edge of the clearing, the tiger padding, the snake slithering, the peacock prancing and cackling.

Lila felt a deep and profound sense of relief: Yes. Yes. It was a dream — it definitely was. It had to be. Not just this moment, and not just Aurora, but the rest of it, everything since the spring meeting of the Tri-Counties Curriculum Committee, in the Coughlin High School auditorium.

She closed her eyes.

3

Joining the Curriculum Committee had been Clint's doing (which was ironic; he had, in the end, been hoisted by his own petard). This was back in 2007. There had been an article in the *Tri-Counties Herald* about the parent of a junior high student in Coughlin who was determined to see *Are You There God? It's Me, Margaret* banned from the school library. The parent was quoted saying that it was 'a dammed atheist tract.' Lila couldn't believe it. She had adored the Judy Blume novel as a thirteen-year-old and related intensely to its portrait of what it was like to be an adolescent girl, how adulthood suddenly loomed up in front of you like some strange and terrifying new city and demanded you go through the gates whether you wanted to or not.

'I loved that book!' Lila said, extending the paper to Clint.

She had roused him from his usual daydream, sitting at the counter and staring through the glass doors at the yard, lightly rubbing the fingers of his left hand over the knuckles on his right. Clint looked at the article. 'Sorry, hon, it's too bad, but the book's gotta burn. Orders direct from General Jesus.' He handed the paper back to her.

'It's not a joke, Clint. The reason that guy wants to censor that book is exactly the reason girls need to read it.'

'I agree. And I know it's not a joke. So why don't you do something about it?'

Lila had loved him for that, for challenging her. 'All right. I will.'

The paper mentioned a hastily formed group of parents and concerned citizens called the Curriculum Committee. Lila enlisted. And to bolster her cause, she did what a good police officer knows to do: she went to her community for assistance. Lila rallied every like-minded local she could think of to come out and support the book. She was unusually well-positioned to raise such a group. Years of settling noise complaints, cooling down property disputes, letting speeders go with warnings, and generally showing herself to be a conscientious and reasonable representative of the law, had created a lot of good will.

'Who are all these damn women?' the father who had started it all exclaimed at the outset of the Curriculum Committee's next gathering, because, one-and-all, they were women, and there were far more of them than of him. *Margaret* was saved. Judy Blume sent a thank-you note.

Lila stayed on the Curriculum Committee, but there had never been another *Margaret*-sized controversy. The members read new books that were being added to the syllabi and the libraries at high schools and middle schools around the Tri-Counties, and listened to lectures by local English teachers and librarians. It was more like a book club than a political assembly. Lila enjoyed it. And, like most book clubs, though a man or two occasionally showed up, it remained primarily an XX affair.

There had been a meeting on the previous Monday night. Afterward, on the way to her car in the high school parking lot, Lila fell into step with an elderly woman named Dorothy Harper, a member of something called the First Thursday Book Club, and one of the townsfolk Lila had originally drafted to help defend *Margaret*.

'You must be so proud of your niece Sheila!' Dorothy remarked, leaning on a cane, a flowered purse large enough to contain a baby looped over her shoulder. 'People are saying she might go to a Division I school on a basketball scholarship. Isn't that wonderful for her?' Then Dorothy added, 'Of course, I suppose you don't want to get too excited yet – I know she's only a sophomore. But very few girls make headlines at fifteen.'

It was on the tip of Lila's tongue to say that Dotty had made a mistake: Clint didn't have a brother and Lila didn't have a niece. But Dorothy Harper was at the age where names often got mixed up. She wished the old lady a nice day and drove home.

Lila was a police officer, though, and paid to be curious. During an idle moment at her desk at the sheriff's station the next morning, she thought of Dorothy's comment, and typed *Sheila Norcross* into Firefox. A sports article with the headline, **COUGHLIN PHENOM LEADS TIGERS TO TOURNEY FINALS,** was the top result, fifteen-year-old Sheila Norcross being said phenom. So Dorothy

Harper had been right about the name, after all. There were other Norcrosses in the Tri-Counties – who knew? She certainly hadn't. Down toward the bottom of the article there was a mention of Sheila's proud mother, who bore a different surname, Parks. Shannon Parks.

That creaked a board in Lila's memory. A couple of years earlier, when Jared had gone out for track, Clint had mentioned the name in passing – had said that a friend named Shannon Parks was the person who convinced him to go out for track at the same age. Given the context, Lila had assumed that Shannon Parks was a male saddled with a rather preppy name. She remembered because her husband hardly ever talked about his childhood and teenage years, and the rare occasions when he did made an impression on Lila.

He had grown up in foster care. Lila didn't know many details . . . and hey, who was she kidding? She didn't know *any* details. What she knew was that it had been difficult. You could feel Clint's temperature spike when the subject arose. If Lila ever brought up a case that involved a child being removed from its parents' custody and put into care, Clint went quiet. He claimed it didn't make him uncomfortable. 'Just ruminative.' Lila, acutely conscious of the necessity of not being a cop in her marriage, let it go.

Not that it had been easy, or that she had never felt tempted. Her resources as a police officer could have gained her access to all manner of court records. She resisted, though. If you loved a person, didn't you have to allow them their quiet places? The rooms they didn't want to visit? Also, she believed that Clint would tell her someday, all of it.

But.

Sheila Norcross.

In the room he did not want to visit and where Lila had blithely assumed that he would someday invite her, was a woman – not a man but a woman – named Shannon, and a photograph of a teenage girl whose smile, sly and curled at the right corner, resembled not just one person that Lila knew well, but two – her husband and her son.

4

The rest was a simple two-part investigation.

In part one, Lila broke the law for the first time not only in her career but in her entire life. She contacted the principal of Coughlin High School and, sans warrant, requested a copy of Sheila Norcross's records. The Coughlin principal had long been grateful for her help in putting a pin in the brief *Margaret* hullabaloo, and Lila reassured him that it was actually nothing about Sheila Norcross, and had to do rather with an identity theft ring. The principal faxed her the records without hesitation, his trust in Lila such that he was happy to break the law, too.

According to the records, Sheila Norcross was smart, strong in English, even stronger in math and science. She carried a 3.8 grade average. Her teachers described her as a little arrogant, but appealing, a natural leader. Shannon Parks, her mother, was listed as her sole guardian. Clinton Norcross was listed as her father. She had been born in 2002, making her a little over a year younger than Jared.

Until the AAU game on Wednesday night, Lila told herself she wasn't sure. Uncertainty made no sense, of course, the truth was right there on the enrollment papers, and plain as the Norcross nose on the girl's face, but she had to get through the days somehow. She told herself that she had to see the girl, see Sheila Norcross, standout point guard, slightly arrogant but likable 3.8 student, to be sure.

Lila pretended that she was undercover, that it was her job to convince Clint that she was still the woman he was married to.

'You seem preoccupied,' Clint said to her on Tuesday night.

'I'm sorry. It's probably because I'm having an affair with someone at work,' she said, which was just the sort of thing that Lila would have said, if she was still the Lila he was married to. 'It's very distracting.'

'Ah. I understand,' Clint said, 'It's Linny, isn't it?' and he pulled her close for a kiss, and she even kissed him back.

5

Then, the second step of the investigation: the stakeout.

Lila found a seat high up in the bleachers of the gymnasium and watched the Tri-Counties AAU team go through their warm-ups. Sheila Norcross was immediately identifiable, number 34, darting in to flick a lay-up off the corner of the backboard, then reversing on her heels, laughing. Lila studied the girl with a detective's eye. Maybe 34 didn't have Clint's jaw, and maybe the way she held herself was different, too, but so what? Kids had two parents.

In the second row near the home team's bench, several adults were standing, clapping along with the pre-game music. The players' parents. Was the slim one in the cableknit sweater Shannon? Or was the girl's mother the dyed blonde in the hip newsboy cap? Or some other woman? Lila couldn't tell. How could she? She was the stranger at the party, after all, the uninvited. People talked about how their marriages fell apart, and they said, 'It didn't feel real.' Lila thought the game felt real enough, though – the crowd sounds, the gymnasium smells. No, it was her. She was what felt unreal.

The horn sounded. It was game time.

Sheila Norcross trotted to the huddle, and then did something that erased all doubt, all self-denial. It was awful and simple and convincing, so much more conclusive than any physical resemblance or any school record. Lila witnessed it from her place on the bleachers and understood that she and Clint were ruined.

6

As soon as Lila closed her eyes on the approaching animals, she felt the onset of true sleep – not padding, slithering, or bobbing, but rushing at her like a driverless sixteen-wheeler. Bright panic sparked her nerves, and she slapped herself. Hard. Her eyes flew open. There was no snake, no white tiger, no gabbling peacock. There was no gigantic banyanesque tree. Where it had loomed in the center of the clearing was an oak, a fine old eighty-footer, magnificent in its own way but normal. A squirrel crouched on one of its lower limbs, chittering at her crossly.

'Hallucinating,' she said. 'This is bad.'

She buttoned her shoulder mic. 'Linny? Are you there? Come back.'

'Right here, Sheriff.' The voice was tinny, a little broken up, but there was no static. 'What . . . do for you?'

The sound of the power lines – *bzzz* – was discernible again. Lila hadn't realized it had disappeared. *Had* it disappeared? Boy, she was messed up.

'Never mind, Lins, I'll get back to you when I'm in the clear.'

'You . . . right, Lila?'

'Fine. Talk soon.'

She took another look over her shoulder. Just an oak. A big one, but still just an oak. She started to turn away, and then another brilliant green bird exploded upward from the tree, heading west into the lowering sun. In the direction the other birds had gone.

Lila closed her eyes tight, then fought them open again. No bird. Of course not. She had imagined the whole thing.

But the tracks? They led me here.

Lila decided she would not let herself care about the tracks, or the tree, or the strange woman, or anything else. What she needed to do right now was get back to town without falling asleep. It might be time to visit one of Dooling's fine pharmacies. And if all else failed, there was the evidence locker. And yet . . .

And yet what? She'd had a thought, but exhaustion had melted it away. Or almost. She caught it just before it could go completely. King Canute, that was the thought. King Canute commanding the tide to run backward.

Some things just couldn't be done.

7

Lila's son was also awake. He was lying in a muddy ditch on the far side of the road. He was wet, he was in pain, and something was digging into his back. It felt like a beer can. All that was bad enough, but he also had company.

'Norcross.'

That was Eric.

Eric fucking Blass.

Jared kept his eyes closed. If they thought he was unconscious – maybe even dead – they would run away like the chickenshit cowardly assholes they were.

Maybe.

'Norcross!' This time his name was followed by a boot prodding him in the side.

'Eric, let's get out of here.' Another country heard from. Kent Daley, sounding whiney and on the edge of panic. 'I think he's out cold.'

'Or in a coma.' Curt's tone seemed to indicate that this wouldn't be such a tragic outcome.

'He's not in a coma. He's faking.' But Eric sounded nervous himself. He bent down. Jared's eyes were closed, but he could smell Eric's Axe cologne getting stronger. Jesus, did the guy bathe in the stuff? *'Norcross!'*

Jared lay still. God, if only a cop car would come by, even one driven by his mother, embarrassing as the explanations that followed might be. But the cavalry arrived only in the movies.

'Norcross, I'm going to kick you in the balls if you don't open your eyes, and I mean really fucking hard.'

Jared opened his eyes.

'Okay,' Eric said, smiling. 'No harm and no foul.'

Jared, who felt he had been badly fouled – both by the car that had creased him and by these guys – said nothing. It seemed the wisest course.

'We didn't hurt the skeevy old lady, and you don't look too bad, either. No legbones sticking out through your pants, at least. So we're going to call it even. After you give me your phone, that is.'

Jared shook his head.

'You are such an asshole.' Eric spoke with kindly indulgence, as if to a puppy that had just piddled on the rug. 'Curt? Kent? Hold him.'

'Jesus, Eric, I don't know,' Kent said.

'I do. Hold him.'

Curt said, 'What if he's got, like, internal injuries?'

'He doesn't. Car barely skinned him. Now hold him.'

Jared tried to squirm away, but Curt pinned one of his shoulders and Kent pinned the other. He hurt all over, his knee was only the worst of it, and there was really no point in fighting these guys. He felt strangely listless. He supposed that might be shock setting in.

'Phone.' Eric snapped his fingers. 'Hand it over.' This was the guy Mary was going to a concert with. This guy right here.

'I lost it in the woods.'

Jared looked up at him, trying not to cry. Crying would be the worst.

Eric sighed, dropped to his knees, and squeezed Jared's pockets. He felt the rectangle of the iPhone in the right front and pulled it out. 'Why do you have to be such a dick, Norcross?' Now he sounded petulant and put-upon, like *why are you ruining my day?*

'There's a dick here, but it's not me,' Jared said. He blinked hard to keep the tears from falling. 'You were going to pee in her ear.'

'No, he wasn't. You're disgusting to even think that, Norcross. It was a joke,' Curt said. 'Guy talk.'

Kent piped up eagerly, as if they were actually having a reasonable discussion, and not sitting on him and holding him down. 'Yeah, it was just guy talk! We were just playing around. You know, like in the locker room. Don't be ridiculous, Jared.'

'I'm going to let this go,' Eric declared. As he spoke, he tapped away at the screen of Jared's phone. 'Because of Mary. I know that she's your friend, and she's going to be a lot more than my friend. So it's a draw. We all walk away.' He finished tapping. 'There: erased the video from your cloud, then emptied it out. All gone.'

A gray rock stuck out of the ditch, looking to Jared like a gray tongue going *nyah-nyah-nyah*. Eric hammered Jared's iPhone on it half a dozen times, shattering the screen and sending pieces of black plastic flying. He tossed what was left onto Jared's chest. It slid off into the muddy ditchwater.

'Since the video is gone, I didn't have to do that, but Mary aside,

I need you to understand that there are consequences for being a sneaky bitch.' Eric stood up. 'Got me?'

Jared said nothing, but Eric nodded as if he had.

'Right. Let him go.'

Kent and Curt stood and backed away. They looked wary, as if they expected Jared to spring up and start swinging like Rocky Balboa.

'This is over for us,' Eric said. 'We don't want anything more to do with that moldy old cunt back there, okay? It better be over for you, too. Come on, you guys.'

They left him there in the ditch. Jared held on until they were gone. Then he put an arm over his eyes and wept. When that part was over, he sat up, slid the remains of his phone in his pocket. (Several more pieces fell off as he did so.)

I am a loser, he thought. That Beck song, it must have been written with me in mind. It was three against one, but still – I am such a loser.

He began to limp home, because home was where you went when you were hurt and beaten.

CHAPTER 10

1

Until 1997, St Theresa's had been a butt-ugly cinderblock building that looked more like an urban housing project than a hospital. Then, after an outcry had arisen over the leveling of Speck and Lookout mountains to get at the coal deposits beneath, the Rauberson Coal Company had endowed an ambitious expansion. The local paper, run by a liberal Democrat – a phrase synonymous with communist, for most of the Republican electorate – called this 'no better than hush money.' Most of the people in the Tri-Counties just appreciated it. Why, customers at Bigbee's Barber Shop had been heard to say, it's even got a helicopter landing pad!

On most weekday afternoons, the two parking lots – a small one in front of the Urgent Care wing, a larger one in front of the hospital proper – were half-full at most. When Frank Geary turned into Hospital Drive on this afternoon, both were loaded, and the turnaround in front of the main entrance was also jammed. He saw a Prius with its trunk-lid crumpled from where it had been struck by the Jeep Cherokee that had pulled in behind it. Broken taillight glass shone on the pavement like drops of blood.

Frank didn't hesitate. They were in Elaine's Subaru Outback, and he bounced it over the curb and onto the lawn, which was empty (at least so far) save for the statue of St Theresa that had graced the lobby of the old hospital, and the flagpole, where the Stars and

Stripes flew above the state flag, with its two miners flanking what looked like a gravestone.

Under any other conditions, Elaine would have given him the rough side of her tongue, which could be rough indeed: *What are you doing? Are you crazy? This car isn't paid off!* Today she said nothing. She was cradling Nana in her arms, rocking her as she had when Nana was a baby, feverish with teething. The gunk covering their daughter's face trailed down to her tee-shirt (her favorite, the one she wore when she was feeling a little blue, the one Frank had stretched eons ago, that morning) like the strands of some skeevy old prospector's beard. It was hideous. All Frank wanted in the world was to rip it away, but the memory of Kinswoman Brightleaf restrained him. When Elaine tried to touch it on their gallop across town, he had snapped *'Don't!'* and she had yanked her hand back. Twice he had asked if Nana was breathing. Elaine said she was, she could see that awful white stuff going in and out like a bellows, but that wasn't good enough for Frank. He had to reach out his right hand and put it on Nana's chest and make sure for himself.

He brought the Outback to a grass-spraying halt and raced around to the passenger side. He hoisted Nana and they started toward Urgent Care, Elaine running ahead. Frank felt a momentary pang as he saw the side-zipper of her slacks was open, revealing a glimpse of her pink underwear. Elaine, who under ordinary circumstances was so perfectly put together – tucked and plucked, smoothed down, mixed and matched to a fare-thee-well.

She stopped so abruptly he almost ran into her. A large crowd was milling in front of the Urgent Care doors. She uttered a strange, horse-like whinny that was part frustration and part anger. 'We'll never get in!'

Frank could see the Urgent Care lobby was already filled to capacity. A mad image flashed through his mind: shoppers racing into Walmart on Black Friday.

'Main lobby, El. It's bigger. We can get in there.'

Elaine wheeled in that direction at once, almost bowling him over. Frank chugged after her, panting a little now. He was in good shape, but Nana seemed to weigh more than the eighty pounds she

had registered at her last physical. They couldn't get into the main
lobby, either. There was no crowd in front of the doors, and Frank
had a moment of hope, but the lobby itself was packed. The foyer
was as deep as they could penetrate.

'Let us through!' Elaine yelled, pounding the shoulder of a husky
woman in a pink housedress. 'It's our daughter! Our daughter has
got a *growth!*'

The woman in the pink dress seemed to do no more than flex
one of those linebacker shoulders, but that was enough to send El
staggering backward. 'You ain't the only one, sister,' she said, and
Frank glimpsed the stroller in front of the husky woman. He couldn't
see the face of the child inside, and didn't need to. The limply
splayed legs and one small, trailing foot – clad in a pink sock with
Hello Kitty on it – were enough.

Somewhere ahead, beyond the milling people, a man's voice
bellowed, '*If you are here because you read Internet reports of an antidote
or a vaccine, go home! Those reports are false! There is no antidote and no
vaccine at this time! Let me repeat, THERE IS NO ANTIDOTE OR
VACCINE AT THIS TIME!*'

Cries of dismay greeted this, but no one left. More people were
already crowding in behind them, rapidly filling the foyer.

Elaine turned, her face sweaty, her eyes wide and frantic and
sheened with tears. 'The Women's Center! We can take her there!'

She pushed her way through the scrum, head down, arms out
and flailing at the people in her way. Frank followed with Nana in
his arms. One of her feet lightly bumped against a man holding a
teenager with long blond hair and no visible face.

'Watch it, buddy,' the man said. 'We're all in this together.'

'Watch it yourself,' Frank snarled, and forced his way back into
the open air, his mind once more flashing like a computer with a
defective circuit.

my kid   my kid   my kid

Because right now, nothing mattered but Nana. Nothing on God's
green earth. He would do what he needed to do to make her better.

He would dedicate his life to making her better. If that was crazy, he didn't want to be sane.

Elaine was already crossing the lawn. There was a woman sitting with her back against the flagpole now, holding a baby to her breasts and keening. This was a noise Frank was familiar with; it was the sound a dog made with its foot caught and broken in a trap. She held the baby out to Frank as he passed, and he could see white filaments trailing from the back of its covered head. 'Help us!' she cried. 'Please, mister, help us!'

Frank made no reply. His eyes were fixed on Elaine's back. She was heading for one of the buildings on the far side of Hospital Drive. WOMEN'S CENTER, read the white-on-blue sign in front. OBSTETRICS AND GYNECOLOGY, DRS ERIN EISENBERG, JOLIE SURATT, GEORGIA PEEKINS. There were a few people with cocooned family members sitting in front of the doors, but only a few. This was a good idea. Elaine actually had them pretty often when she took time off from her busy schedule of busting his ass — only why were they sitting? That was odd.

'Hurry!' she said. 'Hurry up, Frank!'

'I'm hurrying . . . as fast as . . . I can.' Panting hard now.

She was looking past him. 'Some of them saw us! We have to stay ahead!'

Frank looked over his shoulder. A ragged scrum was charging across the lawn, past the beached Outback. The ones who only had babies or small children were in the lead.

Gasping for breath, he staggered up the walk behind Elaine. The caul over Nana's face fluttered in the breeze.

'Won't do you no good,' said a woman leaning against the side of the building. She looked and sounded exhausted. Her legs were spread so she could hold her own little girl, one about Nana's age, against her.

'What?' Elaine asked. 'What are you talking about?'

Frank read the sign posted on the inside of the door: CLOSED DUE TO AURORA EMERGENCY.

Stupid chick doctors, he thought as Elaine grabbed the doorhandle and yanked. Stupid *selfish* chick doctors. You should be *open* due to the Aurora emergency.

'They probably got kids of their own,' said the woman holding the little girl. There were dark brown circles beneath her eyes. 'Can't blame them, I guess.'

I blame them, Frank thought. I blame the shit out of them.

Elaine turned to him. 'What do we do now? Where can we go?'

Before he could reply, the mob from Urgent Care arrived. A geezer with a kid slung over his shoulder grainsack-style – a grand-daughter, maybe – thrust Elaine roughly away from the door so he could try it himself.

What happened next had a kind of speedy inevitability. The man reached beneath his untucked shirt, pulled a pistol from his belt, aimed it at the door, and pulled the trigger. The report was deafening, even in the open air. Glass blew inward.

'Who's closed now?' the geezer cried in a high, cracked voice. A fleck of the blasted glass had come back at him, embedding itself in his cheek. 'Who's closed now, ya shits?'

He raised the gun to fire again. People drew back. A man holding a sleeping girl in a corduroy romper tripped over the outstretched legs of the woman leaning against the building. He put out his hands to break his fall, dropping his burden. The sleeping girl fell to the pavement with a thud. As her father went down beside her, one of his hands tore straight through the caul covering the face of the sitting woman's daughter. There was no pause; the child's eyes flew open and she sat up ramrod straight. Her face was a goblin's mask of hate and fury. She dropped her mouth to the man's hand, chomped down on his fingers, and writhed forward, snake-like, from her mother's grasp so she could dig her thumb into the man's right cheek and her fingers into his left eye.

The geezer turned and aimed his gun – a long-barreled revolver that looked like an antique to Frank – at the writhing, snarling child.

'*No!*' the mother cried, attempting to shield her daughter. '*No, not my baby!*'

Frank turned to protect his own daughter, and drove one foot backward into the geezer's crotch. The geezer gasped and tottered backward. Frank kicked his gun away. The people who had run over here from Urgent Care were now fleeing in all directions. Frank had sent the geezer stumbling into the foyer of the Women's Center, where he overbalanced and sprawled amid the littered glass. His hands and face were bleeding. The man's granddaughter lay facedown (*what* face, Frank thought).

Elaine seized Frank's shoulder. 'Come on! This is crazy! We need to go!'

Frank ignored her. The little girl was still clawing at the man who had inadvertently woken her from her unnatural sleep. She had torn open the flesh under his right eye, and the eyeball bulged out, the cornea filling with blood. Frank couldn't help the guy, not with Nana in his arms, but the man didn't need help. He seized the little girl with one hand and hurled her away.

'*No! Oh, no!*' the girl's mother cried, and scrambled after her daughter.

The man fixed on Frank and spoke in a matter-of-fact voice. 'I think that child blinded me in one of my eyes.'

This is a nightmare, Frank thought. It must be.

Elaine was yanking at him. 'We need to go! Frank, we *have* to!'

Frank followed her toward the Outback, plodding now. As he passed the woman who had been leaning against the side of the Women's Center, he saw that the little girl's caul was re-knitting itself over her face with amazing speed. Her eyes had closed. The expression of fury disappeared. A look of untroubled serenity took its place. Then she was gone, buried in white fluff. The child's mother picked her up, cradled her, and began to kiss her bloody fingers.

Elaine was almost back to the car, yelling for him to keep up. Frank broke into a shambling run.

2

At the kitchen counter, Jared collapsed onto one of the bar seats and dry-swallowed a couple of aspirin from the bottle that his mother left beside the loose change dish. There was a note on the counter from Anton Dubcek about the elm trees in the backyard and the name of a tree surgeon he recommended. Jared stared at this piece of paper. What manner of surgery could one perform on a tree? Who taught Anton Dubcek, who presented as a near imbecile, how to spell, and to do so in such nice, clear handwriting? And wasn't he the *pool* guy? But he knew about *trees,* too? Would the state and health of the Norcross family yard ever be a matter of any significance again? Was Anton still going to clean pools if all the women in the world were asleep? Well, fuck, why wouldn't he? Guys liked to swim, too.

Jared ground his dirty fists into his eyesockets and took deep breaths. He needed to get it together, get showered, get changed. He needed to talk to his parents. He needed to talk to Mary.

The house phone went off, the sound strange and unfamiliar. It hardly ever rang except in election years.

Jared reached for it, and of course he knocked it from the cradle and onto the tile on the other side of the counter. The handset broke apart, the backing popping loose with a plastic snap, and the batteries scattered across the floor.

He picked his way across the living room, supporting himself on furniture as he went, and grabbed up the other phone from the occasional table beside the armchair. 'Hello?'

'Jared?'

'None other.' He sat in the leather armchair with a groan of relief. 'How's it going, Dad?' No sooner had he asked it than it struck him what a dumb question that was.

'Are you okay? I've been calling your cell phone. Why didn't you answer?'

His father's voice was tight, which wasn't all that surprising. Things probably weren't too super at the prison. It was, after all, a *women's* prison. Jared had no intention of letting his father worry about him. The ostensible reason for this choice was something anyone ought to be able to understand: in the middle of an unprecedented crisis, his father didn't need anything else on his plate. The true reason, barely submerged, was that he was ashamed. He'd gotten his ass kicked by Eric Blass, his phone had been destroyed, and before limping his way home, he'd lain in the ditch and sobbed. It wasn't something he wanted to talk to his dad about. He didn't want anyone telling him it was all right, because it wasn't. And he didn't want to be asked how he *felt* about it. How did he feel? *Shitty* pretty well covered it.

'I fell down the steps at school.' He cleared his throat. 'I wasn't watching where I was going. Broke my phone in the process. That's why you couldn't get through. I'm sorry. I think it's still under warranty, though. I'll go over to the Verizon place myself and—'

'Are you hurt?'

'I twisted my knee pretty good, actually.'

'That's all? You didn't hurt anything besides your knee? Tell me the truth.'

Jared wondered if his father knew something. What if someone had seen? It made his stomach hurt to consider. He knew what his father would say if he knew; he'd say he loved him and that he hadn't done anything wrong; he'd say it was the other guys who had done something wrong. And yes, he would want to be sure Jared was *in touch with his feelings*.

'Of course that's all. Why would I lie?'

'I'm not accusing you, Jere, I only wanted to be sure. I'm just relieved to finally have you on the phone, hear your voice. Things are bad. You know that, right?'

'Yeah, I heard the news.' More than that, he'd seen the news: Old Essie in the lean-to, the gossamer white mask welded to her face.

'Have you talked to Mary?'

'Not since before lunch.' He said he planned to check in with her shortly.

'Good.' His father explained that he wasn't sure when he'd be home, that Lila was on call, and Jared should stay put. 'If this situation doesn't resolve quickly, it's going to get weird out there. Lock the doors, keep the phone handy.'

'Yeah, sure, Dad, I'll be safe, but do you really need to stay any longer?' How to put it was tricky. It seemed somehow in bad taste, to point out the simple math; it was akin to saying aloud that a dying person was dying. 'I mean, all the inmates at the prison are women. So . . . they're just going to fall asleep . . . right?' There was a little crack at the end of the last word that Jared hoped his father hadn't caught.

Another question – *And what about Mom?* – formed in his mouth, but Jared didn't think he could get it out without crying.

'I'm sorry, Jared,' Clint said after a few seconds of dead line. 'I can't leave yet. I'd like to, but the staff is shorthanded. I'll be home as soon as I can, though. I promise.' Then, perhaps sensing the question that Jared had been thinking, he added, 'And so will your mom. I love you. Be safe and stay put. Call me right away if you need me.'

Jared sucked up all the anxiety that seemed to be centered at the back of his throat and managed a goodbye.

He closed his eyes and took deep breaths. No more crying. He needed to get out of his filthy, torn clothes, take a shower. That would make things at least a little better. Jared levered himself to his feet and limped toward the stairs. A rhythmic thumping echoed from outside, followed by a rickety tin clatter.

Through the windowed panel at the top of the front door, he could see across the street. The last occupied house on the street belonged to Mrs Ransom, a seventy-something woman who ran a baking and sweets business out of her home, benefitting from Dooling's lack of zoning laws. It was a neat, pale green house, set off by window boxes alive with merry clusters of spring flowers. Mrs Ransom was sitting in a plastic lawn chair in the driveway, sipping a Coke. A girl of ten or eleven – a granddaughter surely, Jared thought he'd seen her over there before – was bouncing a basketball on the pavement, taking shots at the freestanding basket-ball hoop at the side of the driveway.

Brown ponytail swinging out of the gap at the back of a dark baseball cap, the girl dribbled around in a circle, cut one way then another, evading invisible defenders, and pulled up for a mid-range jumper. Her feet weren't quite set and the shot went high. The ball hit the top of the backboard and ricocheted up, the crooked spin carrying it away into the next yard, a weed- and hay-strewn expanse in front of the first of their development's unoccupied houses.

She went to retrieve her ball, crunching across the hay. The ball had rolled up near the porch of the empty house, which was all bare wood, windows with the brand stickers still plastered against the glass. The girl stopped and gazed up at the structure. Jared tried to guess what she might be thinking. That it was sad, the house with no family? Or spooky? Or that it would be fun to play in, to dribble around in the bare halls? Shoot pretend lay-ups in the kitchen?

Jared really hoped his father or his mother would come home soon.

3

After listening to Ree Dempster's story twice – the second time to sniff out the inconsistencies most inmates could not avoid when they were lying – Janice Coates determined the young woman was telling the stone truth, and sent her back to the cellblock. Tired as Janice was from last night's argument with her Mexican dinner, she was also oddly elated. Here at last was something she could deal with. She had been waiting a long, long time for a reason to give Don Peters his walking papers, and if a crucial detail of Ree's story proved out, she would finally be able to nail him.

She called in Tig Murphy and told him exactly what she wanted. And when the officer didn't immediately jump to: 'What's the problem? Grab some rubber gloves. You know where they are.'

He nodded and slouched off to do her little bit of nasty forensic work.

She phoned Clint. 'Would you be available in twenty minutes or so, Doc?'

'Sure,' Clint said. 'I was about to go home and check on my son, but I was able to raise him.'

'Was he taking a nap? Lucky him, if he was.'

'Very funny. What's up?'

'What's up is one good thing in this screwed-up, fucked-over day. If all goes well, I'm going to fire Don Peters's ass. I don't expect him to do anything physical, bullies usually only get physical when they smell weakness, but I wouldn't mind having a man in the room. Better safe than sorry.'

'That's a party I'd love to attend,' Clint said.

'Thanks, Doc.'

When she told him what Ree had seen Peters do to Jeanette, Clint groaned. 'That bastard. Has anyone talked to Jeanette yet? Tell me that no one has.'

'No,' said Coates. 'In a way, that's the beauty of it.' She cleared her throat. 'Given the godawful circumstances, we don't need her.'

She had no more than ended the call when her phone rang again. This time it was Michaela, and Mickey didn't waste time. For the women of the world on Aurora Day One, there was no time to waste.

4

During her twenty-two months at NewsAmerica, Michaela 'Mickey' Morgan had seen plenty of guests grow flustered under the hot studio lights, struggling to answer questions they hadn't prepared for or trying to justify rash statements they'd made years ago that were preserved on video. There was, for instance, the representative from Oklahoma who had been forced to watch a clip of himself saying, 'Most of these unwed mothers have limp leg muscles. That's why they spread so easy.' When the moderator of NewsAmerica's Sunday interview show asked him to comment on the clip, the representative blurted, 'That was fore I got Jeepers in my harp.' For the remainder of his term he had been referred to by his colleagues (once during a roll-call vote) as Representative Harp.

Such prized 'gotcha moments' were common enough, but Michaela never saw an actual freak-out until the late afternoon of Aurora Day One. And it wasn't the guest who freaked.

She was at the console in the location van, bright-eyed and bushy-tailed thanks to her tech guy's blow. Relaxing in an air-conditioned roomette at the rear of the van was her next guest, one of the women who'd been tear-gassed in front of the White House. The woman was young and pretty. Michaela thought she'd make a strong impression, partly because she was articulate, mostly because she was still showing the effects of the gas. Michaela had decided to interview her in front of the Peruvian embassy up the street. The building stood in strong sunlight, which would make the young woman's red, raw-looking eyes stand out.

In fact, if I position her just right, Michaela thought, she'll look like she's crying bloody tears. The idea was disgusting; it was also how NewsAmerica did business. Keeping up with FOX News was no job for sissies.

They were scheduled to go live at 4:19, after the current in-studio conversation concluded. George Alderson, his pate shining greasily through the strands of his combover, was interviewing a clinical psychiatrist named Erasmus DiPoto.

'Has there ever been an outbreak like this in the history of the world, Dr DiPoto?' George asked.

'An interesting question,' DiPoto said. He wore round rimless glasses and a tweed suit that must have been hotter than hell under the lamps. Pro that he was, though, he didn't appear to be sweating.

'Look at that prissy little mouth,' her tech said. 'If he had to shit out of a hole that small, he'd explode.'

Michaela laughed heartily. Some of it was the coke, some of it was tiredness, some of it was plain old terror, suppressed by profes-sionalism for the time being, but just waiting to come out.

'Let's hope you have an interesting answer,' George Alderson said.

'I was thinking of the Dancing Plague of 1518,' DiPoto said. 'That was also an event that affected only the ladies.'

'The ladies,' said a voice from behind Michaela. It was the White House protestor, who had come over to watch. 'The *ladies*. Jesus please us.'

'That outbreak began with a woman named Mrs Troffea, who danced madly in the streets of Strasbourg for six days and nights,' DiPoto said, warming to his subject. 'Before collapsing, she was joined by many others. This dance mania spread across all of Europe. Hundreds, perhaps thousands, of women danced in cities and towns. Many died of heart attacks, strokes, or exhaustion.' He essayed a small, smug smile. 'It was simple hysteria, and eventually died out.'

'Are you saying that Aurora is similar? I suspect many of our viewers will find that hard to accept.' Michaela was pleased to see that George couldn't keep the disbelief out of his face or his voice. George was mostly blather, but he did have a small, beating news-ie's heart somewhere under his Oxford shirt. 'Sir, we've got news footage of thousands of women and girls with this fibrous material – these cocoons – covering their faces and bodies. This is affecting millions of females.'

'I am not making light of the situation, by any means,' DiPoto said. 'Absolutely not. But physical symptoms or actual physical changes as a result of mass hysteria are not uncommon. In Flanders, for instance, dozens of women exhibited stigmata – bleeding hands and feet – during the late eighteenth century. Sexual politics and political correctness aside, I feel we must—'

That was when Stephanie Koch, the producer of *Afternoon Events*, charged onto the set. She was a leathery chain-smoker in her fifties who had seen it all, and put most of it on television. Michaela would have said Steph was armored against any and all crazy guest opinions. But it seemed her armor had a chink, and Dr DiPoto with his round spectacles and prissy little mouth had found it.

'What the fuck are you talking about, you penis-equipped gerbil?' she shouted. 'I have two granddaughters with that shit growing all over them, they're in *comas*, and you think that's *female hysteria*?'

George Alderson groped out a restraining hand. Stephanie batted it away. She was crying angry tears as she loomed over Dr Erasmus DiPoto, who was cringing back in his chair and staring up at this lunatic Amazon who had appeared from nowhere.

'Women all over the world are struggling not to go to sleep because they're afraid they'll never wake up, and you think that's *female hysteria*?'

Michaela, the tech guy, and the woman from the protest were staring at the monitor, fascinated.

'Go to commercial!' George called, looking over Stephanie Koch's shoulder. 'We just need to take a break, folks! Sometimes things get a little tense. That's live television, though, and—'

Stephanie whirled, looking at the off-camera control booth. 'Don't you *dare* go to commercial! Not until I'm done with this chauvinist piece of shit!' She was still wearing her headset. Now she tore it

off and began to clobber DiPoto with it. When he raised his hands
to protect the top of his skull, she slashed at his face. His nose began
to bleed.

'*This* is female hysteria!' Stephanie shouted, whapping him with
her headset. Now the little doctor's mouth was bleeding, as well.
'*This* is what female hysteria *really looks like, you . . . you . . . you
RUTABAGA!*'

'Rutabaga?' the protestor woman said. She began to laugh. 'Did
she just call him a rutabaga?'

A couple of stagehands rushed out to restrain Stephanie Koch.
While they struggled and DiPoto bled and George Alderson gaped,
the studio disappeared and was replaced by an ad for Symbicort.

'Baby-now,' the protestor woman said. 'That was *great.*' Her gaze
shifted. 'Say, can I have some of that?' She was eyeballing the small
pile of blow sitting on top of the tech guy's laminated day-part schedule.

'Yeah,' he said. 'It's open bar today.'

Michaela watched the protestor take some on her fingernail and
ingest it.

'Whee!' She smiled at Michaela. 'I am officially ready to rock.'

'Go on back and sit down,' Michaela said. 'I'll call you.' But she
wouldn't. Combat-hardened Stephanie Koch utterly losing her shit
had brought a realization to Mickey Coates. She wasn't just looking
through a lens at this story; it was her story. And when she finally
went to sleep, she didn't want it to be among strangers.

'Hold the fort, Al,' she said.

'You bet,' the tech guy said. 'Hey, that was priceless, wasn't it?
Live TV at its best.'

'Priceless,' she agreed, and went out to the sidewalk. She powered
up her cell. If the traffic wasn't too bad, she could be in Dooling
before midnight.

'Mom? It's me. I can't do this anymore. I'm coming home.'

5

At 3:10 P.M., ten minutes past the end of Don Peters's 6:30 A.M.
to 3:00 P.M. shift, he sat in the Booth, watching the Unit 10 monitor,

watching the madwoman nod off. She slumped on the bunk with her eyes closed. Lampley had been called off for some reason, and then Murphy, and so now Don had the Booth, and that was fine with him – he'd rather sit. Actually, what he'd rather do was go home, like usual, but in the interests of not riling Coatsie up, he'd decided to stick it out for the time being.

The crazy cunt was a hot little number, Don wouldn't hesitate to grant her that. Even in scrubs her legs went for miles.

He pressed the button on the mic that piped directly to the cell and was about to tell her to wake up. Only what was the point? They were all going to fall asleep and grow that shit on their faces and bods, apparently. Christ, what a world it would be if that happened. On the plus side, it would be safer on the roads. That was a good one. He'd have to remember that for later, try it on the boys at the Squeaky Wheel.

Peters let go of the button. Ms Unit 10 swung her legs up onto the bunk and stretched out. Don, curious, waited to see how it would happen, the webbing weirdness he'd read about on his phone.

6

Once there had been hundreds of rats in the prison and dozens of colonies; now just forty remained. As Evie lay with her eyes closed, she spoke with the alpha – an old female, a long-clawed fighter with thoughts like rusty grinding wheels. Evie imagined the alpha's face as a lattice of scar tissues, very lean and beautiful.

'Why so few of you, my friend?'

'Poison,' this warrior queen told her. 'They lay poison. It smells like milk, but it kills us.' The rat was in a crease between the cinderblocks that divided Unit 10 from Unit 9. 'The poison is supposed to make us seek water, but often we become confused and die without reaching any. It's a miserable death. These walls are filled with our bodies.'

'No more of you need to suffer that way,' said Evie. 'I can promise that. But I may need you to do certain things for me, and some of them may be dangerous. Is that acceptable to you?'

As Evie expected, danger meant nothing to the queen rat. To gain her position the queen had fought her king. She had torn off his forelegs, and instead of finishing him she had sat on her haunches and watched him bleed out. The queen expected, eventually, to die in a similar manner.

'It is acceptable,' said the mother rat. 'Fear is death.'

Evie didn't agree – in her view, death was death, and it was well worth fearing – but she gave it a pass. Though rats were limited, they were sincere. You could work with a rat. 'Thank you.'

'You're welcome,' said the queen rat. 'There is only one question I need to ask you, Mother. Do you keep your word?'

'Always,' said Evie.

'Then what do you want us to do?'

'Nothing now,' said Evie, 'but soon. I will call you. For now, you only need to know this: your family will no longer want to eat the poison.'

'True?'

Evie stretched, and smiled, and gently, with her eyes still closed, kissed the wall.

'True,' she said.

7

Evie's head snapped up and her eyes snapped open. She was staring directly at the camera – and, seemingly, at Don.

In the Booth, he jerked in the chair. The pointedness of the look, the way she'd fastened on the camera lens the instant she awoke, unnerved him. What the hell? How had she woken up? Weren't they supposed to get covered in webs if they fell asleep? Had the bitch been dekeing him? If so, she'd been doing a heck of a job: face slack, body totally still.

Don pushed down the mic. 'Inmate. You're staring at my camera. It's rude. You got a rude look on your face. Do we have some kind of problem?'

Ms Unit 10 shook her head. 'I'm sorry, Officer Peters. Sorry about my face. There's no problem.'

'Your apology is accepted,' said Don. 'Don't do it again.' And then: 'How did you know it was me?'

But Evie didn't answer the question. 'I think the warden wants to see you,' she said, and right on cue, the intercom buzzed. He was needed in Administration.

CHAPTER 11

1

Blanche McIntyre let Don into the warden's office and told him Coates would be along in about five minutes. It was a thing Blanche shouldn't have done, and wouldn't have, had she not been distracted by the strange events that seemed to be happening in the prison, and in the world at large.

His hands were shaking a bit as he helped himself to coffee from the pot in the corner of the office, situated right under the stupid fucking poster of the kitten: HANG IN THERE. Once he had his coffee, he spat into the black liquid that remained in the urn. Coates, the vicious old bitch, smoked and drank coffee all day. He hoped he had a cold coming on and his spit gave it to her. Christ, why couldn't she die of lung cancer and leave him alone?

The timing, added to the unnerving prediction by the freaky female in Unit 10, left Don with no doubt that either Sorley or Dempster had snitched on him. This was not good. He should not have done what he had done. They had been waiting for him to slip and he had gone right from seeing Coates that morning and done exactly that.

No reasonable man, of course, could have blamed him. When you considered the kind of pressure that he was subjected to by Coates, and the amount of whining that he dealt with every single day from the criminals he was supposed to babysit, it was a wonder that he hadn't *murdered* anyone, just from the frustration.

Was it so wrong to grab a handful now and then? For Christ's sake, it used to be if you didn't pat a waitress on the ass, she'd be disappointed. If you didn't whistle at a woman on the street, she'd wonder what the hell she'd bothered getting dressed up for. They got dressed up to be messed up, that was just a fact. When did the whole female species get so turned around? You couldn't even compliment a woman in these PC days. And that's what a pat on the ass or a squeeze on the tit was, wasn't it, a kind of compliment? You needed to be pretty stupid not to see that. If Don squeezed a woman's rear, he didn't do it because it was an ugly rear. He did it because it was a quality rear. It was a playful thing, that was all.

Did stuff sometimes go a little farther? Okay. Now and again. And here Don would take some of the blame. Prison was hard on a woman with healthy sexual feelings. There were more bushes than a jungle and no spearmen. Attractions were inevitable. Needs couldn't be denied. The Sorley girl, for instance. It might be entirely subconscious on her part, but on some level, she had wanted him. She had sent plenty of signals: a swing of the hip in his direction on the way to mess hall; the tip of her tongue sweeping over her lips as she carried an armful of chair legs; a dirty little come-on glance over her shoulder.

Sure, the burden rested on Don not to give in to these sorts of invitations, made as they were by felons and degenerates, who would seize any opportunity to set you up and get you in trouble. But he was human; you couldn't blame him for succumbing to his normal masculine urges. Not that a flea-bitten nag like Coates would ever understand.

There was no danger of a criminal action, he was certain – the word of a crack whore, or even of two crack whores, would never count for more than his in any court of law – but his job was definitely in jeopardy. The warden had promised to take action after another complaint.

Don paced. He wondered, darkly, if the whole campaign against him might even be Coates's way of expressing a kind of fucked-up jealous love for him. He'd seen that movie with Michael Douglas and Glenn Close. It had scared the living shit out of him. A scorned woman would go to any length to fuck you over and that was a fact.

(His consideration briefly flickered to his mother, and how she had confessed to telling Don's ex, Gloria, not to marry him, because 'Donnie, I know how you are with girls.' The hurt of that went all the way to the bone, for Don Peters loved his mother, had loved her cool hand on his feverish forehead when he was a little boy, and remembered how she used to sing that he was her sunshine, her only sunshine, and how could your own mother turn on you? What did that say about *her?* Talk about controlling females, there it was in a nutshell.

(It occurred to him that he ought to call and check on his mother, but then he thought, forget it. She was a big girl.)

The current situation stank of female conspiracy: seduction and entrapment. That the loony in Unit 10 had somehow known the warden would be calling him in pretty much sealed the deal. He wouldn't say they were all in it together, no, he wouldn't go that far (it would be crazy), but he wouldn't say they weren't, either.

He sat on the edge of the warden's desk and accidentally jarred a small leather bag off the edge, onto the floor.

Don bent to pick the bag up. It looked like what you might use to put your toothbrush in if you were traveling, but it was nice leather. He unzipped it. Inside the bag was a bottle of dark red nail polish (like that was going to distract anyone from noticing that Coates was a hideous witch), a pair of tweezers, a pair of nail clippers, a small comb, a few unopened tabs of Prilosec, and . . . a prescription pill bottle.

Don read the label: *Janice Coates, Xanax, 10 mg.*

2

'Jeanette! You believe this?'

It was Angel Fitzroy, and the question made Jeanette clench up inside. Was what true? That Peters had taken her into the corner by the Coke machine and made her beat him off? Her headache wasn't just a headache anymore; it was a series of explosions, *bang-bang-bang.*

But no, that wasn't what Angel was talking about. Couldn't be.

Ree would never tell anyone, Jeanette tried to comfort herself, her thoughts like shouts inside her skull, yet barely discernible over the detonations set off by her migraine. Then she guessed – hoped – what Angel was talking about.

'You mean – the sleep thing?'

Angel stood in the doorframe of the cell. Jeanette was on her bunk. Ree was off somewhere. The floor of the wing was open in the late afternoon, everyone on Good Report free to roam.

'Yeah, course that's what I mean.' Angel slid smoothly into the cell, pulled up the single chair. 'You can't sleep. None of us can. Won't be too much of a problem for me, because I don't sleep much, anyway. Never did, not even as a kid. Sleepin's like bein dead.'

The news of Aurora had struck Jeanette as preposterous. Women cocooned in their sleep? Had the migraine ruined her mind somehow? She wanted to take a shower, but she didn't want to talk to a guard. They wouldn't let her, anyway. A prison had rules. The guards – oh excuse me, the *officers* – were the rules incarnate. You had to do what they said or bingo, Bad Report.

'My head really hurts, Angel. I have a migraine. I can't handle the crazy.'

Angel inhaled, deeply and loudly, through her long, bony nose. 'Listen, sis—'

'I'm not your sister, Angel.' Jeanette was in too much pain to worry about how Angel would take a rebuke.

But Angel just rolled right along. 'This thing's crazy but it's real. I just seen Nell and Celia. What's left of em, anyway. They went to sleep and now they wrapped up like fuckin Christmas presents. Someone said McDavid's got it, too. Gone baby gone. I watched it grow on Nell and Celia. The stuff. It crawls right up. Covers up their faces. It's like a fuckin science experiment.'

Crawls right up. Covers up their faces.

So it was true. You could tell by the way Angel said it. Well, why not. It didn't matter to Jeanette. There was nothing she could do about it, or anything else. She closed her eyes, but a hand fell on her shoulder and Angel began to shake her.

'What?'

'You goin to sleep?'

'Not while you're asking me questions and shaking me like I was popcorn. Quit it.'

The hand lifted away. 'Don't go to sleep. I need your help.'

'Why?'

'Because you're all right. You ain't like most of the rest of em. You got a head on your shoulders. You're as cool as a fool in a swimmin pool. Aren't you even gonna let me tell you?'

'I don't care.'

Although Angel didn't respond immediately, Jeanette felt her looming over the side of the bed.

'That your boy?'

Jeanette opened her eyes. Angel was peering at the photograph of Bobby fixed on the painted square on the wall beside her bunk. In the photo Bobby was drinking from a straw out of a paper cup and wearing a cap with Mickey ears. His expression was adorably suspicious, like he thought maybe somebody was going to try to snatch his drink and his hat and make a break for it. It was from when he was little, four or five.

'Yeah,' said Jeanette.

'Cool hat. Always wanted one a them. Jealous of the kids that had em. Photo looks pretty old. How old's he now?'

'Twelve.'

It must have been about a year before the bottom completely fell out, when she and Damian took Bobby to Disney World. The boy in the photograph didn't know that his father was going to punch his mother one time too many and that his mother was going to bury a clutchhead screwdriver in his father's thigh and that his aunt was going to become his guardian while his mother did her time for second-degree murder. The boy in the photograph just knew that his Pepsi tasted great and his Mickey hat was cool.

'What's his name?'

While she thought of her son, the explosions in Jeanette's head receded. 'Bobby.'

'Nice name. You like that? Bein a mom?' The question slipped out without Angel knowing she meant to ask it. A mom. Being a mom. The idea made her heart stutter. She didn't let it show, though. Angel had her secrets, and she kept them close.

'Never been much good at it,' said Jeanette and forced herself to sit up. 'But I love my son. So what is it, Angel? What do you need me to do?'

3

Later, Clint would reflect that he should have known Peters was up to something.

The officer was too placid at first, the smile on his face entirely inappropriate to the charges being leveled. Clint was angry, though, angry as he hadn't been since he was Jared's age, and he didn't see what he should have seen. It was as if there was a rope in his head, binding shut a box containing a lot of bad stuff from his childhood. His wife's lie had been the first cut in the fiber, Aurora had been the second, the interview with Evie had been the third, and what had happened to Jeanette had snapped it. He found himself considering the damage he could inflict on Peters with various objects. He could shatter his nose with the phone on the desk, he could cave in the abusing fuck's cheek with the warden's Correctional Official of the Year plaque. Clint had worked hard to exorcise that kind of violent thinking, had largely gone into psychiatric medicine in the first place in reaction to it.

What had Shannon said that time? 'Clint, sweetie, if you keep fighting, someday you're going to win too good.' She'd meant that he'd kill someone, and maybe she had been right. It wasn't much later that the court granted him his independence and Clint didn't have to fight anymore. After that, his senior year, he had consciously funneled his rage into running track. That had been Shannon's idea, too, and a damn good one. 'You want to exercise,' she had said, 'you should run. There's less bleeding.' He'd run from that old life, run like the Gingerbread Man, run all the way to medical school, to marriage, to fatherhood.

Most of the system kids didn't make it; foster care was a true case of odds-against. Many of them had ended up in jailhouses like

Dooling Correctional or Lion Head Prison up the road, which, according to the engineers, was in danger of sliding down the hill. Indeed, there were plenty of system girls in Dooling, and they lived at the mercy of Don Peters. Clint had been lucky. He had beaten the odds. Shan had helped him. He hadn't thought of her in a long while. But this day was like a broken water main, there was stuff coming up, a flood in the streets. It seemed that days of disaster were also days of remembering.

4

Clinton Richard Norcross had entered the foster system for good in 1974, when he was six, but the records he'd seen later said he'd been in and out even before that. A typical story: teenage parents, drugs, poverty, criminal records, probably mental health issues. The nameless social worker that interviewed Clint's mother had recorded, 'She is worried about passing her sad feelings along to her son.'

He had no memories of his father, and the only scrap he retained of his mother was of a long-faced girl grabbing his hands, swallowing them up in hers, shaking them up and down, pleading to him to stop chewing his nails. Lila had asked him once if he was interested in attempting to make contact with either of them, if they were alive. Clint was not. Lila said she understood, but, really, she had no idea, and he liked it that way. He didn't want her to. The man she married, the cool and able Dr Clinton Norcross, had, quite consciously, put that abandoned life behind him.

Except you couldn't put anything behind you. Nothing was lost until death or Alzheimer's took it all. He knew that. He saw it confirmed in every session he held with every prisoner; you wore your history like a necklace, a smelly one made of garlic. Whether you tucked it under your collar or let it dangle loose, nothing was lost. You fought the fight over and over, and you never won the milkshake.

He had passed through a half-dozen homes during his youth and adolescence, none of them like a home if that meant a place where you felt safe. Perhaps it was no wonder that he had ended up working in a penitentiary. The feelings in prison were the feelings of his youth and young adulthood: a sense of being always on the verge of suffocation. He wanted to help people who felt that way, because he knew how bad it was, how it struck at the center of your humanity. That was the core of Clint's decision to leave his private practice before it had really started.

There were good foster homes out there, more than ever in this day and age, but Clint had never landed in any. The best he could say was that a few had been clean, run by foster parents who were efficient and unobtrusive, doing only what was required to collect their fee from the state. They were forgettable. But forgettable was great. You'd take forgettable.

The worst were the worst in particular ways; the places where there wasn't enough to eat, the places where the rooms were cramped and dirty and cold in the winter, where the parents had non-paying jobs for you, the places where they hurt you. Girls in the system got hurt the most; of course they did.

Some of his foster siblings, Clint couldn't find their faces now, but a few remained clear. There was Jason, for instance, who killed himself at thirteen by drinking a bottle of off-brand drain cleaner. Clint could summon up Live Jason, and he could summon up Dead Jason lying in his coffin. That was when Clint had lived with Dermot and Lucille Burtell, who boarded their fosters not in their pretty Cape Cod house, but in a long shed-like structure out back with bare, splintery plywood floors and no insulation. The Burtells held what they called 'Friday Night Fights,' with their half-dozen wards as the pugilists, and a chocolate milkshake from McDonald's for the prize. Clint and Jason had been matched up once, fighting for the amusement of the Burtells and their friends. The arena was a little patch of broken-up concrete patio and the spectators gathered around the edges to watch and lay bets. Jason had been a longshot, scared and slow, and Clint had wanted that milkshake. In the open casket Jason had a nickel-sized bruise under his eye that Clint had given him a few evenings earlier.

The next Friday, after Jason drank Gunk-O and retired from boxing forever, Clint won the milkshake again and then, without thinking about any possible consequences (at least not that he could remember), he threw it in Dermot Burtell's face. That had resulted in a tremendous beating for Clint, and it hadn't brought Jason back, but it had gotten him out of that house.

At the next place, or maybe the one after that, was where he'd shared a dismal basement room with good old Marcus. Clint remembered his foster brother Marcus's wonderful cartoons. Marcus drew people so that they were eighty percent nose, pretty much just noses with wee legs and wee arms. *The Nose-It-Alls* was what he called his strip; he was really good, and dedicated, too. Then one day after school, without any explanation, Marcus told Clint he'd thrown all his notebooks away somewhere, and he was lighting out. Clint could picture the cartoons, but not Marcus.

Shannon, though, Shannon he could see; she was too beautiful to fade.

'Hey. I'm Shannon. Don't you want to know me?' She introduced herself that way without glancing over at Clint, who was walking past on his way to the park. Sunbathing across the hood of a Buick that was parked at the curb outside the group home in Wheeling, blue tank top and black jeans, and smiling right up into the sun. 'You're Clint, aren't you?'

'Yeah,' he said.

'Uh-huh. Well, isn't it nice to meet us?' she replied, and Clint, despite everything, had laughed, really laughed for the first time in who knew how long.

The group home in Wheeling where he met her was the last stop on his grand tour of the state foster system. For most, it was basically a connecting point to places like Dooling Correctional and Weston State. Weston, a monumental Gothic asylum, closed in 1994. Now, in 2017, it was open for ghost tours. Was that where his father ended up? Clint wondered. His mother? Or Richie, who got his nose and three fingers broken by some prep school boys at a mall because he said they shouldn't make fun of his purple jacket that had come from a donation box? Or Marcus? He knew they couldn't all be dead or in prison, and yet it didn't seem like any of them could still be breathing and free. Did they all float around the dark halls of Weston after hours? Did they ever talk about Clint? Were they glad for him — or did he shame them by still living?

5

The Wheeling home was preferable to many of the stops that had preceded it. The sneering administrator, thumbs popping the pockets of his gray polyester vest, admonished each new arrival, 'Enjoy your last year on the state's tit, younker!' But he, the sneering adminis-trator, didn't want any trouble. So long as you managed not to get arrested, he let you sign in and out all day long. You could fight, fuck, or shoot up. Just keep it out of the house, younker.

He and Shan were both seventeen then. She had taken notice of Clint's reading habit, how he slipped off to a park down the street and sat on a bench to catch up on his homework, despite the cold late fall weather. Shannon had also seen the bloody scrapes on his hands from the trouble he found — and sometimes searched for — between the home and school. They got to be friends. She gave him advice. Most of it was good.

'You've almost made it out, you know,' she said. 'Just need to keep from killing anyone a little while longer,' she said. 'Let your brain make you rich,' she said. Shan spoke as if the world didn't matter too much to her, and somehow that made Clint want to make it matter — to her, to himself.

He went out for track and stopped fighting. That was the short version. The long one was Shannon, Shannon in the sun, Shannon prodding him to run faster, to apply for scholarships, to stick to his books and stay off the sidewalks. Shannon at night, jimmying the lock on the door of the boys' floor with a celluloid-backed playing card (the queen of spades), and slipping into Clint's room.

'Hey now,' she said at the sight of him in his team uniform, tank top and high shorts. 'If I ruled the world, all the boys would have to wear shorts like that.'

Shannon had been gorgeous and she'd been clever and she had her own boatload of problems and Clint thought maybe she'd saved his life.

He went to college. She advised him to go, and when he hesitated (talking about the army), she demanded. She said, 'Don't be no fool, get your ass to school.'

He did and they fell out of touch, phone calls too expensive and letters too time-consuming. It was eight or nine years between when he left for college before they reconnected that New Year's in DC. 2001? 2002? He'd been in town to attend a seminar at Georgetown and stayed on for a night because of car trouble. Lila had told him he was allowed to go out and get drunk, but he was forbidden to kiss any desperate women. He could kiss a desperate man if he absolutely had to, but no more than one.

The bar where he'd run into Shan was boiling with college kids. She was waitressing. 'Hey, pal,' she said to Clint, stepping up beside him at the bar, bumping him with her hip. 'I used to know a guy in the joint who looked just like you.'

They had embraced for a long time, swaying back and forth in each other's arms.

She looked tired, but she seemed all right. They managed to get a minute alone in a corner underneath a flashing Molson sign. 'Where y'all?' she had asked.

'Out in the sticks: Tri-Counties. Place called Dooling. A day's drive from here. It's a beauty spot.'

He had shown her a photo of four-month-old Jared.

'Oh, look at him. Now wasn't it all worth it, Clint? I need to get me one of those.'

Dew shone on Shannon's eyelashes. People were screaming all around them. It was almost a new year. 'Hey,' he'd said to her, 'Hey, it's all right.'

She had looked up at him and the years had narrowed and it was like they were kids again. 'Is it?' Shannon asked. 'Is it all right, Clint?'

6

Over the warden's shoulder, on the other side of the glass, late afternoon shadows were staining the garden, where there were rows of lettuce and peas climbing trellises built of scrap wood. Coates cupped her hands around her coffee cup as she spoke.

The coffee cup! Clint could upend it on Don Peters's crotch and then smash it against his ear!

There was a time, before he knew Shannon Parks, when he would have done so. He reminded himself that he was a father and a husband, a doctor, a man with too much gray in his hair to fall into the trap of violence. Sometime soon he was going to clock out and go home to his wife, his son, and a nice view out the glass doors to a pool in the backyard. Fighting for milkshakes had been in another life. Still, he wondered what that coffee cup was made of, if it was that heavy ceramic that sometimes didn't even crack when you dropped it on hard tile.

'You're taking this rather well,' observed Janice Coates.

Peters brushed a finger along his mustache. 'I'm just enjoying thinking about how my lawyer is going to make me a millionaire off this wrongful firing, Warden. I think I'll buy a boat. Also, I was raised to be a gentleman no matter how I was mistreated. So, fire me. Fine, but you got no proof. I'm going to roll you up in court.' He glanced at Clint, who was standing by the door. 'You okay? I see you standing there and making fists, you need to pinch a loaf or something, Doc?'

'Fuck you,' Clint said.

'See? That's not nice,' said Peters. Smiling, showing teeth the color of shoepeg corn.

Coates sipped from the coffee cup she'd just refilled. It was bitter. She took another sip anyway. She was feeling optimistic. The day was an apocalypse, but her daughter was driving home and she was finally ridding herself of Don Peters. Amid the fecal mounds there occasionally glimmered a pearl or two of satisfaction.

'You're a scumbag, and you're lucky we can't deal with you to the extent you deserve right now.' From the pocket of her suit jacket she produced a Baggie. She held it up and gave it a shake. Inside the Baggie were two Q-tips. 'Because, you see, we do have proof.'

Peters's grin faltered, tried to come on strong, didn't quite make it.

'It's your squirt, Donnie Boy. From the Coke machine.' Coates took a big swig of the lousy coffee and smacked her lips. 'Once everything settles down and we *can* deal with you as you deserve, you're going to jail. Good news is, they keep the sex offenders in a special wing, so you might survive, but the bad news is, even with a good lawyer you'll be in there for quite awhile. Don't worry, though, you'll still get to see me at your parole hearings. I'm on the board, you know.' The warden twisted to her intercom and pressed the call button. 'Blanche, can you rustle up a fresh bag of coffee? This stuff is dreadful.' She waited a moment for a response and then pressed the button again. 'Blanche?' Coates released the button. 'She must have stepped out.'

Coates returned her attention to Peters on the couch. His grin had given up entirely. The officer was breathing hard, running his tongue around under his lips, clearly working through the impli- cations of the DNA evidence that had just been waved in his face.

'For now,' the warden said, 'just turn in your uniform and bug out. Telling you we have the goods on you was probably a mistake on my part, but I couldn't resist the opportunity to gloat. It gives you a few extra days until the hammer falls. You could hop in your car, head for Canada. Who knows, maybe you can keep your head down, become an ice fisherman.'

'Set-up!' Peters leaped to his feet. 'This is a set-up!'

Clint could no longer hold back. He stepped forward, grabbed the shorter man by the throat, and pushed him against the wall. Don batted at Clint's shoulders and face, scraping Clint's cheeks with his nails. Clint squeezed. Under his fingers Clint could feel Peters's pulse squirming, could feel his Adam's apple shrinking, could feel the impossibility and frustration and fright of the entire day pooling out around his hands like juice from a grapefruit. A moth was fluttering around his head. It planted a ghost-kiss on one temple and was gone.

'*Dr Norcross!*'

Clint drove a fist into the soft sack of Peters's belly and then let go. The officer fell onto the couch and slid off, onto the floor on his hands and knees. He made a choked animal noise: '*Hee-hee-hee.*'

The warden's door banged open. Tig Murphy stepped in, holding a Taser. Damp glistened on Tig's cheeks and his color was poor; he'd told Clint he was fine, but he wasn't fine, nothing was fine and nobody was fine.

'*Hee-hee-hee.*' Peters began to crawl away from Clint. The moth had lost interest in Clint and now it was circling the crawling man, seemingly ushering him out.

'We were just going to call for you, Officer Murphy.' Coates, still at her desk, proceeded as if nothing had happened at all. 'Mr Peters was about to exit the premises and he tripped over a fold in the rug. Help him up, would you? He can leave his things in the locker room.' The warden toasted Tig Murphy with her coffee cup and drank it down.

CHAPTER 12

1

'Now, Officer, you know I'm prone to fits of temper, right?'

Angel, standing at a respectful distance from the Booth, presented this rhetorical question to Vanessa Lampley. Jeanette, beside her, had no illusions: they were facing an uphill battle.

Behind the plastic shield of the Booth, seated at the board, Lampley's broad shoulders were curled dangerously forward. She looked prepared to leap straight through the shield. Jeanette figured that in a fight Angel could dish out plenty despite her narrow frame – but not enough to handle Lampley.

'Fitzroy, is that some kind of half-assed threat? With the shit that's going on today? Now I got three inmates covered in cobwebs, I'm way past when I should have clocked out, I'm weary as hell, and you want to test me? That is a bad idea, I promise you.'

Angel held up her palms. 'No, no, no, Officer. I'm just sayin, I wouldn't trust me in a situation like this either, okay? My felony record speaks for itself and there's lots else I got away with, though you understand I can't share specifics.'

Jeanette touched her forehead and studied the ground. If there had ever been a plan for Angel, post-parole, to move into the area of international diplomacy, someone needed to revamp it.

'Get out of here, you fucking nitwit,' Lampley said.

'Which is why I brought Jeanette.' With this, Angel threw out an arm: *ta-da!*

'Well, that changes everything.'

'Don't mock.' The arm that Angel had raised dropped to her side. What had been collegial in her expression flattened. 'Don't you mock me, Officer.'

'Don't you don't me, inmate.'

Jeanette decided it was now or never. 'Officer Lampley, I'm sorry. We're not trying to make any trouble.'

Van, who had started to rise, imposingly, from her chair, settled back. Unlike Fitzroy, who basically lived on Bad Report, owning it like a damn property in Monopoly, Sorley was known for her friendly attitude. And according to Ree Dempster, Sorley had been molested by that poisonous toad Peters. Van supposed she could hear her out.

'What is it?'

'We want to cook up some coffee. Some special coffee. To help everyone stay awake.'

Van held her finger on the intercom for a second or two before she spoke, then asked the obvious: 'What do you mean by *special*?'

'Stronger than regular coffee,' Jeanette said.

'You can have some, too,' Angel said, and tried for a magnanimous smile. 'It'll sharp you right up.'

'Oh, that's just what I need! A whole prison full of hopped-up inmates! That would be wonderful! Let me guess, Fitzroy: the secret ingredient is crack cocaine.'

'Well . . . not exactly. Since we don't have any. And let me ask you this: What's the alternative?'

Lampley admitted she didn't know.

Jeanette spoke up. 'Officer, unless this Aurora gets solved pronto, people in here are going to get restless.' This fully dawned on her even as she articulated it. Except for Maura Dunbarton and a couple of other lifers, there was at least a distant beacon of hope: the end of their sentence. Freedom. For all intents and purposes, the Aurora Flu was a sudden dousing of that hope. No one knew what came after sleep, or if anything did. It was like heaven that way. 'They're going to get worried and they're going to get upset and scared, and you could have a serious . . . problem.' Jeanette was careful not to employ the word *riot*, but that was the problem she was envisioning. 'They're *already* worried and upset and scared. You said it yourself, there's already been three of us that have come down with this thing.

'And we got the ingredients right in the kitchen. You just have to let us in and we'll do the rest. Look, I'm not trying to be pushy here or cause a ruckus. You know me, right? I try to get along. My time has been clean. I'm just telling you what my concern is and proposing an idea.'

'And your *special* coffee is going to fix that? Some accelerant is going to make everyone copacetic with the situation?'

'No, Officer,' said Jeanette. 'That is not what I think.'

Lampley's hand found her bicep tattoo of the gravestone, **YOUR PRIDE**. She let her fingers wander over the lines. The focus of her gaze drifted up, to something above the screen of the Booth.

A clock, Jeanette thought, most likely there's a clock hanging there. Lampley was morning shift. She probably went to bed around nine to get up at five or five thirty A.M. and drive to work. From the clock in her cell Jeanette knew it was around five P.M. now – getting late.

The officer rolled her head around on her thick neck. There were circles under her eyes, Jeanette noticed. That was what a double shift did to you. 'Fuck,' said Lampley.

Jeanette couldn't hear it through the soundproofed barrier, but she saw the officer mouth it.

Lampley leaned back into the intercom. 'Tell me more, inmate. Sell me.'

'I think it'll give everyone a little hope. Make them feel like they're doing something. And buy a little extra time for this thing to blow over.'

Van's gaze darted upward again. The discussion went on for awhile longer, eventually turning into a negotiation, and finally into a plan, but that was the moment when Jeanette knew she'd won Officer Lampley over – there was no denying the clock.

2

Clint and Coates had the warden's office to themselves again, but at first neither of them spoke. Clint had gotten his breath back, but his heart was still going *bang-bang-bang*, and he guessed his blood pressure, borderline at his last physical (a fact he had neglected to share with Lila; no need to worry her, she had enough on her plate) was red-lining.

'Thanks,' he said.

'For what?'

'Covering for me.'

She knuckled her eyes. To Clint she looked like a tired child back from a play date that had gone on too long. 'I just got rid of the bad apple in our basket, Doc. That had to be done, but I'm not getting rid of anyone else, not when I'm already shorthanded. At least everyone else has stayed on so far.'

Clint opened his mouth to say *I wanted to kill him,* closed it again.

'I will say . . .' Janice opened her mouth in a jaw-cracking yawn. '. . . that I was a little surprised. You went after him like Hulk Hogan back in his steroid-assisted heyday.'

Clint lowered his head.

'But I need you for at least the time being. My assistant warden is AWOL again, so you get the job until Hicks turns up.'

'I imagine he went home to check on his wife.'

'I imagine he did, too, and while I understand, I don't approve. We've got over a hundred women locked up in here, and those women have to be our priority. I don't need you losing your grip.'

'I'm not.'

'I hope that's true. I know you come from a difficult background – I've read your file – but there's nothing in there about a talent for choking people to death. Of course, juvenile records get sealed.'

Clint forced himself to meet the warden's eyes. 'That's right. They do.'

'Tell me what I just saw with Peters was an aberration.'

'It was an aberration.'

'Tell me you'd never lose it that way with one of the women.

Fitzroy, for instance. Or one of the others. The new one, maybe. Evie the Weirdo.'

Clint's shocked expression must have been answer enough for her, because she smiled. As it turned into another yawn, her phone rang.

'Warden.' She listened. 'Vanessa? Why are you *calling* me when you have a perfectly good intercom at your dispo—'

She listened some more, and as she did, Clint observed a queer thing. The phone kept sliding up from her ear and toward her hairline. She'd bring it down, and then it would start that upward journey again. It could be simple tiredness, but it didn't exactly look like tiredness. He wondered briefly if Janice had a bottle in her desk, and dismissed the idea. He and Lila had been out to dinner with Coates a few times, and he'd never seen her order anything stronger than a glass of wine, which she usually left unfinished.

He told himself to stop jumping at shadows, but that was hard to do. If Warden Coates went down, who would that leave until Hicksie got back? *If* Hicksie got back. Lampley? Him? Clint thought about what it would be like to become acting warden, and had to suppress a shudder.

'Okay,' Coates said into the phone. Listened. '*Okay*, I said. *Yes.* Let them do it. Go ahead and put it on the intercom. Tell gen-pop that the coffee wagon will be rolling.'

She ended the call, tried to put the phone back in the cradle, missed, and had to do it again. 'Shoot,' she said, and laughed.

'Janice, are you all right?'

'Oh, couldn't be better,' she said, but *couldn't* came out in a slur: *coont.* 'I just gave Van the go-ahead to let Fitzroy, Sorley, and a couple of others make super-coffee in the kitchen. Essentially a form of crank.'

'Say *what*?'

Coates spoke with deliberate care, reminding Clint of how drunks spoke when they were trying to appear sober. 'According to Van – who got it from Angel, our own Walter White – our coffee is light roast instead of dark, which is good because it has more caffeine.

Then, instead of one bag per pot, they're going to use three. Gonna make *gallonsh*.' She looked surprised, and licked her lips. 'Gallons, I mean. My lips feel all numb.'

'Are you kidding?' He didn't know if he was talking about the coffee or her lips.

'Oh, you haven't heard the bes part, Doc. They're gonna dump all the Sudafed from the infirmary into the coffee, and we've got quite a stock. But before they drink the coffee . . . the inmaitches . . . *inmates* . . . have to chug a mixshure of grapefruit juice and butter. Speeds up the abshorpshun. That's what Angel claims, and I don't shee the harm . . .'

Coates tried to get up and fell back into her chair with a little laugh. Clint hurried to her side. 'Jan, have you been drinking?'

She stared at him, eyes glassy. 'No, of coursh not. Thish isn't like being drunk. Thish is like . . .' She blinked and reached out to touch a small leather bag beside the IN/OUT basket on her desk. '. . . my pillsh? They were here on the desk, in my clutch.'

'What pills? What are you taking?' Clint looked for a bottle, but saw nothing on the desk. He bent and looked beneath. Nothing but a few dust bunnies left behind by the last trustee who had cleaned the place.

'Zhan . . . Zhan . . . ah, fuck.' She lolled back in her chair. 'Goin bye-bye, Doc. Goin shleep.'

Clint looked in the wastebasket, and there, among some tissues and a few crumpled Mars bar wrappers, he found a brown prescription bottle. The label said JANICE COATES and XANAX and 10 MG. It was empty.

He held it up so Janice could see it, and they spoke the same word at the same time; Coates slurring her half of the duet: 'Peters.'

Making an effort – surely a supreme effort – Janice Coates sat up and fixed Clint's gaze with her own. Though her eyes were glassy, when she spoke, she was hardly slurring at all. 'Get him, Doc. Before he leaves the building. Slam that molesting son of a bitch into a C Wing cell and throw away the key.'

'You need to vomit,' Clint said. 'Raw eggs. I'll get some from the kitch—'

'Too late. I'm going down. Tell Mickey . . .' Her eyes closed. She forced them open again. 'Tell Mickey I love her.'

'You'll tell her that yourself.'

Coates smiled. Her eyelids were rolling down again. 'You're in charge now, Doc. At least until Hicks comesh back. You . . .' She uttered a huge sigh. 'Keep them shafe until they all go to sheep . . . and then . . . ah, keep them shafe, keep us shafe until . . .'

Warden Coates crossed her arms on her desk blotter and pillowed her head on them. Clint watched in fascination and horror as the first strands of white began to spin out of her hair, her ears, and the skin of her flushed cheeks.

So fast, he thought. So goddam fast.

He hurried from the office, meaning to tell Coates's secretary to get on the horn and make sure Peters was kept on-site, but Blanche McIntyre was gone. Lying on her blotter was a single piece of prison stationery with a note written on it in black Sharpie. Clint read the big block letters twice before he could believe what his eyes told him he was seeing.

I HAVE GONE TO MY BOOK CLUB.

Book club?

Book club?

Really?

Blanche went to her fucking *book* club?

Clint ran down Broadway toward the entrance lobby, dodging a few wandering inmates in their baggy Brown Tops, aware that some were regarding him with surprise. He got to the locked main doors and hammered on the intercom button until Millie Olson, still on the board at the lobby security station, answered. 'Jesus, Doc, don't wear it out. What's wrong?'

Through the double glass panes, he could see Don Peters's battered Chevrolet beyond the inner gate, inside the dead zone, but now passing through the outer gate. He could even see Don's stubby fingers, holding out his ID card for the reader.

Clint pushed the intercom button again and said, 'Never mind, Millie. Never mind.'

CHAPTER 13

1

On her way back to town, an impudent little nonsense jingle began to run through Lila Norcross's mind, one she and her friends had chanted when they were downstreet and their parents couldn't hear. She began to chant it now, in the dying daylight.

'In Derby Town, in Derby Town, the streets are made of glass; in Derby Town, in Derby Town, the girls will kick your bumpty-bump, bumpty-bump, bumpty-bumpa-tee-bump-bump-bump . . .'

What came next? Oh yes.

'In Derby Town, in Derby Town, my brother had a fit; in Derby Town, in Derby Town, my sister's full of bumpty-bump, bumpty-b—'

Almost too late, she realized she was off the road and running into the underbrush, bound for a steep slope down which her cruiser would roll at least three times before reaching the bottom. She stood both feet on the brake and stopped with the front end of the car hanging over that gravelly drop. She threw the gearshift into park, and as she did, she felt tendrils of something brush gently against her cheeks. She tore at them, had time to see one melting away even as it lay across her palm, then shouldered open her door and tried to get out. Her harness was still on, and it yanked her back.

She opened the clasp, got out, and stood taking deep breaths of the air, which was finally cooling. She slapped herself across the face once, then twice.

'Close one,' she said. Far below, one of the little creeks – *cricks,* in the local patois – that fed the Ball River went flowing and chuckling east. 'That was a close one, Lila Jean.'

Too close. She would fall asleep eventually, she knew that, and the white crap would spin itself out of her skin and enclose her when she did, but she would not let that happen until she had kissed and hugged her son at least one more time. That was a dead-red promise.

She got back behind the wheel and grabbed her mic. 'Unit Four, this is Unit One. Come back?'

Nothing at first, and she was about to repeat when Terry Coombs replied. 'One, this is Four.' He sounded wrong, somehow. As if he had a cold.

'Four, have you checked the drugstores?'

'Yeah. Two looted, one on fire. FD is on the scene, so it won't spread. I guess that's one good thing. The pharmacist at the CVS was shot dead, and we think there's at least one body inside the Rite Aid. That's the one that's burning. FD doesn't know how many vics for sure.'

'Oh, no.'

'Sorry, Sheriff. It's true.'

No, not as if he had a cold – as if he'd been crying.

'Terry? What is it? Something else is wrong.'

'Went home,' he said. 'Found Rita covered in that cocoon crap. She nodded off at the table, just like she always does before I come home from my shift. Grab fifteen or twenty minutes for herself. I warned her not to, and she said she wouldn't, and then I zipped home to see how she was doing and—'

Now he did begin to cry.

'So I put her in bed and I came back out to check the drugstores, like you said. What else could I do? I tried calling my daughter and there's no answer in her room. Rita tried calling, too, early, a bunch of times.' Diana Coombs was a freshman in college at USC. Her father made a gaspy, watery sound. 'Most of the West Coast women are asleep, never woke up. I hoped maybe she was up all night, studying or something, partying even, but . . . I know she's not, Lila.'

'Maybe you're wrong.'

Terry ignored this. 'But hey, they're *breathing*, right? All the women and girls are still *breathing*. So maybe . . . I don't know . . .'

'Is Roger with you?'

'No. I spoke with him, though. He found Jessica covered with it. Head to toe. Must have gone to sleep naked, because she looks like a mummy in one of those old horror movies. Baby, too. Right there in the crib, wrapped up, same as the ones they've been showing on television. Roger lost it. He was bawling and howling his damn head off. I tried to get him to come with me, but he wouldn't.'

This made Lila unreasonably angry, probably because she was so goddam wrung out herself. If she wasn't allowed to give up, then no one else was, either. 'It'll be night soon, and we're going to need every cop we've got.'

'I told him that—'

'I'll go get Roger. Meet me at the station, Terry. Tell everyone you can reach to join us. Seven o'clock.'

'Why?'

Even with the world going to hell in a handbasket, Lila would not put that out over the air – but they were going to break into the evidence locker and have a nice little drug party – uppers only.

'Just be there.'

'I don't think Roger will come.'

'He will, even if I have to handcuff him.'

She backed away from the drop she'd almost gone over and headed into town. She was using her lightbar, but still paused at every intersection. Because with everything that was happening, jackpot lights might not be enough. By the time she reached Richland Lane, where Roger and Jessica Elway lived, that damned little earworm was going through her head again: In Derby Town, in Derby Town, when your daddy's got an itch . . .

A Datsun trundled slowly across her path, ignoring both her flashing lights and the four-way stop at the intersection. On an ordinary day, she would have been on the careless son of a bitch like white on rice. If she hadn't been fighting sleep, she might even have noticed the bumper sticker on the back deck – WHAT'S SO

FUNNY ABOUT PEACE, LOVE, AND UNDERSTANDING – and identified it as belonging to Mrs Ransom, who lived just up the street and a little way down from where all those unoccupied houses were. Had she been wide awake, she surely would have recognized the driver as her son and the passenger beside him as Mary Pak, the girl he was so crazy about.

But it wasn't an ordinary day, and she was far from wide awake, so she continued onward to the Elway house on Richland Lane, where she found herself in the next act of that day's continuing nightmare.

2

Jared Norcross had an earworm of his own, but it had nothing to do with Derby Town, where the streets were made of glass. It was *coincidence, serendipity, predestination, fate*. Pick one or pick none, it was probably all the same to the universe. *Coincidence, serendipity, predestination, fa—*

'You blew that stop sign,' Mary said, temporarily breaking the spell. 'And I saw a cop.'

'Don't tell me that,' Jared said. He was upright behind the wheel, sweating, his speeding heart sending bolts of pain directly to his hurt knee. He could still flex the knee, which made him believe he hadn't actually torn anything, just sprained it, but it was badly swollen and aching. The idea of getting bagged by a cop when he had no legal right to drive, at least not without a licensed driver beside him, was a nasty one. His mother had told him time and again that the worst thing for her, as sheriff, would be if he got picked up for anything illegal – *anything*, even so much as walking out of Fenton's Newsstand with a candy bar he'd forgotten to pay for. 'And believe me,' Lila'd said, 'if it's the worst thing for me, I'll make it the worst thing for you.'

Mrs Ransom's granddaughter, Molly, was perched on her knees in the backseat, looking out the rear window. 'No problem,' she reported. 'Five-oh went right across.'

Jared relaxed a little, but he still couldn't believe he was doing this. Less than half an hour ago he had been at home, waiting for the next word from one of his parents. Then he called Mary. Who started shouting at him before he could get three words beyond hello.

'Where *are* you? I've been trying to get you for *years!*'

'You have?' This might not be too bad. A girl didn't shout like that unless she cared, did she? 'My cell phone's broken.'

'Well, get *over* here! I need *help!*'

'What do you need? What's wrong?'

'You *know* what's wrong! *Everything*, if you're a girl!' She caught her breath and brought it down a notch. 'I need a ride to Shopwell. If my dad were here I'd ask him, but he's in Boston for work, and he's trying to get home, but that doesn't do us any good right now.'

Shopwell was the town's big supermarket, but it was on the far side of town. He had adopted his most reasonable, adult voice. 'Dooling Grocery is a lot closer to where you are, Mary. I know it doesn't have the best selection—'

'Will you *listen?*'

He fell silent, scared by the controlled hysteria in her voice.

'It has to be Shopwell because there's this woman who works there in the produce section. A lot of the kids know about her. She sells . . . study aids.'

'Are you talking about speed?'

Silence.

'Mary, that stuff is illegal.'

'*I don't care!* My mom's okay for now, but my little sister's only twelve, her bedtime's at nine, and she's usually a zombie even before then.'

And there's you, Jared had thought.

'Plus there's me. I don't want to go to sleep. I don't want to go into a cocoon. I'm *scared to fucking death.*'

'I get that,' Jared said.

'Oh no you don't. You're a *guy*. No guy can understand.' She drew in a deep, wet breath. 'Never mind. I don't know why I waited to hear from you. I'll call Eric.'

'Don't do that,' Jared said, panicked. 'I'll come and get you.'

'You will? Really?' Oh God, the gratitude. It had weakened his knees.

'Yes.'

'Your parents won't mind?'

'No,' Jared said, which wasn't precisely untrue. How could they mind if he never told them? They probably would have minded a lot, of course – even putting aside, you know, the world crisis – because Jared didn't have a driver's license. He *would* have had it if he hadn't bumped a trashcan while trying to parallel park during his first test. Up to then, everything had been going fine.

Had Jared given Mary the impression that he had actually passed the test? Well, only insofar as that Jared had told her he had. Dammit! The lie had seemed harmless at the time. It seemed so dorky to have failed the test. He was scheduled to take it again next month, and since he didn't have his own car anyway, she'd never know. That had been his logic. Somehow Jared didn't think driver's license exams were going to be a priority in Dooling County for awhile. Or anywhere.

'How long will it take you to get here?'

'Fifteen minutes. Twenty at the most. Just wait for me.'

It was only after he hung up that he realized how far ahead of himself he'd gotten. Not only did he have no driver's license, he had no car. His father had taken the Prius to the prison, and his mom's Toyota was parked behind the sheriff's station. In terms of vehicles, the Norcross cupboard was bare. Either he had to borrow some wheels, or he had to call Mary back and tell her to let Eric drive her, after all. The former alternative seemed unlikely, but after all that had gone on this afternoon, the latter was unthinkable.

That was when the doorbell had rung.

Coincidence, serendipity, predestination, fate.

3

Mrs Ransom had been hunched over a hospital cane and wearing a cruel-looking metal brace on her right leg. Seeing her thus made Jared, even in his current predicament, feel that he had been taking his own sprained knee far too seriously.

'I saw you come home,' Mrs Ransom said. 'Jared, isn't it?'

'Yes, ma'am.' Jared, a boy who would have remembered his manners even on the sinking *Titanic*, held out his hand, scraped from his earlier run through the underbrush.

Mrs Ransom smiled and shook her head. 'I better not. Arthritis. And you must excuse me if I skip the amenities, which I ordinarily would never do, but time is of the essence this evening, it seems. Young man, do you have a driver's license?'

Jared found himself remembering some movie where the suave villain had said, *You can only hang me once.* 'Yes, but I don't have a car.'

'That is not a problem. I have one. It's a Datsun, old but in excellent repair. I drive it seldom these days, because of my arthritis. Also, my leg brace makes it difficult to operate the pedals. I make my customers pick up from the house. They're usually okay with that – oh, never mind. It's not relevant, is it? Jared – I need a favor.'

Jared was quite sure he knew what the requested favor was going to be.

'I sleep badly these days under the best of circumstances, and since my granddaughter came to stay with me while my son and daughter-in-law work out their . . . their *differences* . . . I've hardly slept at all. I have gone in debt to sleep, you might say, and in spite of all my painful ailments, I believe that tonight that debt may be called in. Unless, that is . . .' She raised her cane so she could scratch the spot between her eyebrows. 'Oh, this is hard. I am ordinarily a private person, a *decorous* person, not one to spill my problems on a complete stranger, but I saw you arrive home and I thought . . . I thought perhaps . . .'

'You thought I might know someone, be able to get something that would help you stay awake a little while longer.' He spoke it as a statement, not a question, thinking *coincidence, serendipity, predestination, fate.*

Mrs Ransom's eyes had widened. 'Oh, no! Not at all! *I* know someone. At least I think I do. All I've ever purchased from her is marijuana – it helps my arthritis and my glaucoma – but I do believe she sells other things. And it isn't just me. There's Molly to think about. My granddaughter. She's as lively as a flea right now, but by ten o'clock she'll be—'

'Getting soupy,' Jared said, thinking of Mary's sister.

'Yes. Will you help me? The woman's name is Norma Bradshaw. She works at the Shopwell store, on the other side of town. In the produce section.'

4

Now here he was, driving to Shopwell on his permit with one traffic violation – a blown stop sign – already to his credit, and the lives of two people in his inexperienced hands. Mary he had been counting on; ten-year-old Molly Ransom not so much. She had already been sitting in the elderly Datsun's backseat when Jared assisted her grandmother back to the house, and Mrs Ransom insisted that he take the girl. Getting out of the house 'would help keep the poor mite's juices flowing.' The news reports said that there was unrest in the cities, but Mrs Ransom wasn't the least bit concerned about sending her granddaughter on an errand in little old Dooling.

Jared was in no position to refuse an extra passenger. The car belonged to the old lady, after all, and if he refused in spite of that, it might raise that pertinent question again – he *was* a licensed driver, wasn't he? Mrs Ransom might let him go even if he admitted the truth, she was pretty desperate, but he didn't want to take the risk.

They were at last approaching the supermarket, thank God. Molly was sitting down again with her seatbelt fastened, but she had a motor mouth, and it was currently in high gear. So far Jared and Mary had learned that Molly's best friend was Olive, and Olive could be a puke when she didn't get her own way, it was like her superpower, except who would even want it, and Molly's parents were seeing a *marritch* counselor, and Gram smoked special medicine because it helped her eyes and her arthritis, and she had a great big smoker thing with an American eagle on it, and usually smoking was bad, but it was different for Gram, although Molly wasn't

supposed to talk about that, because then people might think
smoking that wasn't okay—

'Molly,' Mary said, 'do you ever shut up?'

'Usually just when I'm sleeping,' Molly said.

'I don't want you to go to sleep, but your thoughts are a little
overwhelming. Also, you should stop breathing your grandmother's
pot smoke. It's not good for you.'

'Fine.' Molly folded her arms across her chest. 'Can I just ask one
thing, Miss Bossy Mary?'

'I suppose,' Mary said. Her hair, usually pulled back smoothly and
tied in a ponytail, was loose on her shoulders. Jared thought she
looked beautiful.

'Are you guys boyfriend and girlfriend?'

Mary looked at Jared, and opened her mouth to say something.
Before she could, he dared to take one hand off the wheel and
point ahead at a huge parking lot bathed in a bowl of halogen light.
It was crammed with cars.

'Shopwell ahoy.'

5

'This is *crazy*,' Mary said.

'*Crazy-crazy*,' Molly agreed.

Jared parked on the grass at the far end of the Shopwell lot. That
was probably another violation, but not one that would count for
much when the lot itself was a demo derby. Cars sped recklessly
up and down the few lanes that were still clear, honking at shoppers
who were wheeling full carts. As they surveyed the scene, two carts
collided and the men pushing them started yelling at each other.

'Maybe you better stay in the car, Molly.'

'No way.' She seized Jared's hand. 'You're not leaving me. Either
of you. *Please*. My mother left me in a parking lot once and—'

'Come on, then,' Mary said. She pointed to one of the middle
lanes. 'Let's go that way. Less chance of getting run down.'

The three of them weaved through a snarl of abandoned auto-
mobiles. They had just passed one of these orphans when a Dodge

Ram pickup backed out of its space and struck it, driving it back-ward until there was enough room to escape. The Ram roared past them, its newly dented tailgate flapping like a loose jaw.

Inside, Shopwell was pandemonium. Voices babbled. Voices roared. There were screams and the sound of breaking glass. Men were yelling. As they hung back beside the stacks of shopping baskets and the few remaining carts, a skinny man in a suit coat and tie went sprinting past, pushing a cart full of Red Bull, Blast-O Cola, and Monster Energy drinks. Chasing after him was a burly guy in jeans and a tee-shirt, stomping in motorcycle boots.

'You can't have all of those!' Motorcycle Boots shouted.

'First come, first served!' Suitcoat and Tie shouted back without turning. 'First come, first ser—'

He tried a hard right into Aisle 7 (Pet Food and Paper Products), but weight and momentum carried his overloaded cart into a display of dog cookies. They went flying. Motorcycle Boots was on the cart at once, grabbing six-packs of energy drink. When Suitcoat and Tie tried to reclaim his cart, Boots shoved him. Suitcoat went down.

Jared looked at Mary. 'Where's Produce? I've never been in here before.'

'Over there, I think.' She pointed to the left.

He carried Molly on his back, stepping over Suitcoat, who was propped on one hand and rubbing his head with the other.

'The guy was crazy,' he said to Jared. 'All that over some energy drinks.'

'I know.' Not stating the obvious, which was Suitcoat and Tie had been trying to escape with a shitload of same.

'*Everyone* is crazy. What do they think it is? A *hurricane*? A fucking *snowstorm*?' He glanced at Molly and said, 'Excuse me.'

'Oh, don't worry, my parents say that all the time,' Molly said. She clung to Jared even tighter.

Fish and Meat, running all along the back wall, was relatively calm, but Aisle 4 – Vitamins, Health Supplements, and Pain Relievers – was a war zone. Battle had raged for the brown bottles of Genestra, Lumiday, Natrol, and half a dozen other over-the-counter brands.

The middle shelves were completely stripped, and Jared guessed that was where the supplements designed to promote wakefulness had been.

An elderly lady in a blue patterned muumuu hustled up the aisle toward them, pursued by JT Wittstock, the coach of the football team and father of two of Jared's mother's deputies, Will and Rupe Wittstock. Jared didn't know the coach to speak to, but at the department's Labor Day party Will and Rupe had won the sack race and then nearly had a fistfight over who got to keep the five-dollar trophy. (Lila, ever diplomatic about her crew and their families, described them as 'very young and very energetic.')

The muumuu lady was slowed by her shopping basket, which was filled with bottles of something called Vita-Caff. Coach Wittstock grabbed her by the collar of her dress and hauled her backward. Her basket went flying and the bottles scattered, several rolling toward Jared, Mary, and Molly.

'No!' she shouted. 'No, please! We can share! We can sh—'

'You scarfed up everything that was left,' Coach Wittstock snarled. 'You call that sharing? I need some of these for my wife.'

The coach and the muumuu lady grubbed on the floor after the bottles. He shoved her into one of the shelves, sending down a cascade of aspirin cartons. 'You bully!' she cried. 'You big mean bully!'

Jared stepped forward without thinking about it, put his foot on top of Coach Wittstock's balding head, and drove it sideways. Coach Wittstock went sprawling. The lady began to refill her basket. Coach crouched behind her for a moment: three-point stance, eyes shifting from side to side. The tread of Jared's sneaker was faintly printed on his pate. Then he sprang forward and snatched the half-filled basket with the spry athleticism of a monkey stealing an orange. He sprinted past Jared (sparing him a stinkeye glare that said *I'll remember your face, bud*), bumping his shoulder and sending him spinning down with Molly still on his back. They hit the floor and Molly wailed.

Mary started toward them. Jared shook his head. 'We're all right. Make sure *she* is.' Looking at the muumuu lady, who was gathering up the few bottles of Vita-Caff Coach Wittstock had missed.

Mary dropped to one knee. 'Ma'am, are you okay?'

'I think so,' she said. 'Just shaken up. Why would that man . . . I suppose he said he had a wife . . . maybe a daughter . . . but I also have a daughter.'

Her purse had ended up halfway down the littered aisle. It was ignored by the shoppers squabbling over the few remaining bottles of supplements. Jared helped Molly up and returned the purse to the lady. She put the Vita-Caff bottles inside.

'I shall pay for these another day,' she said. And, as Mary assisted her to her feet: 'Thank you. I shop here all the time, and some of these people are my neighbors, but I don't know any of them tonight.'

She limped away, holding her purse tight against her chest.

'I want to go back to Gram's!' Molly cried.

'You get the stuff,' Mary said to Jared. 'Her name is Norma, and she's got a lot of frizzy blond hair. I'll take Molly back to the car.'

'I know. Mrs Ransom told me,' Jared said. 'Be careful.'

She moved away, leading Molly by the hand, and then turned back. 'If she's reluctant to sell to you, tell her that Eric Blass sent you. That might help.'

She must have seen the hurt in his eyes, because she gave a little wince before half-running for the front of the store, bent protectively over the frightened girl.

6

A man was standing halfway down the long produce section, smoking a cigarette. He was dressed in white pants and a white smock top with **PRODUCE MANAGER** on the left breast in red thread. He wore an almost peaceful expression on his face as he watched the pandemonium that had engulfed his store.

He saw Jared approach, nodded at him, and spoke as if resuming a conversation they'd been having. 'This shit will quiet down after all the women are asleep. They cause most of the trouble, you know. You're looking at a man who knows. I'm a three-time loser in the marriage wars. Not just a loser, either. Routed I've been, each time. Like matrimony is Vicksburg, and I'm the Confederacy.'

'I'm looking for—'

'Norma, most likely,' the produce manager said.

'Is she here?'

'Nope. Left half an hour ago, after she sold the last of her product. Except for the stuff she kept for herself, I suppose. But I've got some fresh blueberries. Add em to your cereal, perks it right up.'

'Thanks, I'll pass,' Jared said.

'There is a bright side,' the produce manager said. 'My alimony payments will soon cease. The South rises again. We been kilt, but we ain't whupped yet.'

'What?'

'Just kilt, not whupped. "I'll bring you a piece of Lincoln's tail-coat, colonel." It's Faulkner. Don't they teach you kids anything in school these days?'

Jared made his way toward the front of the store, avoiding the scrum at the checkout lanes. Several stations were unattended, and shoppers were hurrying through them with loaded baskets.

Outside, a man in a checkered shirt sat on the bus bench with a shopping basket on his lap. It was loaded with cans of Maxwell House. He caught Jared's eye. 'My wife is napping,' he declared, 'but I'm sure she'll wake up soon.'

'Hope that works out for you,' Jared said, and broke into a run.

Mary was in the passenger seat of the Datsun with Molly on her lap. She gave the girl a shake as Jared got in behind the wheel, and spoke in a too-loud voice. 'Here he is, here he is, it's our pal Jared!'

'Hi, Jared,' Molly said in a hoarse, teary voice.

'Molly was getting all sleepy,' Mary said in that same too-loud, too-jolly voice. 'But she's awake now. *Wiiiiide* awake! We both are, aren't we, Mols? Tell us some more about Olive, why don't you?'

The little girl climbed out of Mary's lap and into the backseat. 'I don't want to.'

'Did you get it?' Mary's voice was low now. Low and strained. 'Did you—'

Jared started the car. 'She's gone. A lot of other people got there first. You're out of luck. Mrs Ransom, too.'

He left the Shopwell parking lot fast, wheeling effortlessly around the cars that tried to get in his way. He was too upset to worry about his driving, and thus did it better than ever before.

'Are we going to Gram's now? I want to go to Gram's.'

'Right after I drop Mary,' Jared said. 'She needs to call her bestie Eric, see if he's holding.' It felt good for a second to strike at her, to unload the fear that was running through him. Only for a second, though. It was childish crap. He hated it and yet he couldn't seem to help it.

'What do you mean "holding"?' Molly asked, but no one answered her.

It was twilight when they got to the Pak house. Jared pulled into the driveway and put Mrs Ransom's Datsun in park.

Mary peered at him in the gathering gloom of Aurora's first night. 'Jere. I wasn't going with him to see Arcade Fire. I was going to break the date.'

He said nothing. Maybe she was telling the truth, maybe she wasn't. All he knew was that she and Eric were chummy enough for Eric to have given her the name of a local dope dealer.

'You're being a baby,' Mary said.

Jared stared straight ahead.

'Okay, then,' Mary said. 'Okay, baby. Baby wants his bottle. The hell with it. And you.'

'You two are fighting like my mother and father,' Molly said, and began to cry again. 'I wish you'd stop. I wish you'd be boyfriend and girlfriend again.'

Mary got out, slammed the door, and started up the driveway.

She had almost reached the back stoop when Jared realized that there was an actual possibility that the next time he saw her, she might be buried in a white shroud of unknown origin. He looked at Molly and said, 'Keep your eyes open. If you fall asleep, I'll knock your block off.'

Jared climbed out of the car and ran after Mary. He caught her just as she was opening the back door. She turned to him, startled. A cloud of moths circled the overhead light, and her face was dappled with their weaving shadows.

'I'm sorry,' he said. 'Mary, I'm really sorry. It's just so crazy. For all I know my mother's asleep in her car somewhere, and I'm scared, and I couldn't get what you needed and I'm sorry.'

'Okay,' she said.

'Don't go to sleep tonight. Please don't.' He pulled her into his arms and kissed her. Wonder of wonders – she kissed him back, mouth open, her breath mingling with his.

'I'm officially awake,' she said, pulling back to look into his face. 'Now take Little Red Blabbing Hood back to her gram.'

He started down the steps, rethought that, went back, and kissed her again.

'Wowee,' Molly said when he returned to the car. He could hear in her voice that her mood had dramatically improved. 'You guys were really sucking face.'

'We were, weren't we?' Jared said. He felt dazed, a stranger in his own body. He could still feel her lips and taste her breath. 'Let's get you home.'

The last leg of that long, strange trip was only nine blocks, and Jared drove it without incident, finally rolling along Tremaine Street, past the empty houses. He pulled into Mrs Ransom's driveway. The headlights swept across the figure seated in a lawn chair, a body without face. Jared slammed on the brakes. Mrs Ransom sat in the glare, a mummy.

Molly began to scream and Jared doused the headlights. He threw the Datsun into reverse and banged across the street to his own driveway.

When he unfastened Molly's seatbelt, Jared drew the kid from the car and into his arms. She clung to him, and that was all right. It felt good.

'No worries,' he said, stroking her hair. It was in clumps, matted with sweat. 'You're staying with me. We're going to put on some movies and pull an all-nighter.'

CHAPTER 14

1

Maura Dunbarton – once the subject of newspaper headlines, now largely forgotten – sat on the lower bunk of B-11, the cell she had shared with Kayleigh Rawlings for the last four years. The cell door was open. On B Wing, all the cell doors were open, and Maura did not believe they would roll closed and be locked from the Booth tonight. No, not tonight. The tiny TV set in the wall was on and tuned to NewsAmerica, but Maura had muted the sound. She knew what was going on; by now even the dimmest inmate in Dooling knew. RIOTING AT HOME AND ABROAD, read the super running across the bottom of the screen. This was followed by a list of cities. Most were American, because you cared about your own before you cared about those in more distant places, but Maura had also seen Calcutta, Sydney, Moscow, Cape Town, Mexico City, Bombay, and London before she stopped looking.

It was funny, when you thought about it; what were all those men rioting about? What did they think they could accomplish? Maura wondered if there would have been riots if it had been the other half of the human race who were falling asleep. She thought it unlikely.

Kayleigh's head, swaddled in a white helmet that pulsed in and out with her breathing, lay in Maura's lap. Maura held one of Kayleigh's white-gloved hands, but she didn't attempt to tamper with the material. There had been an announcement over the prison intercom system that it could be dangerous to do so, and the same warning had been thoroughly conveyed on the news broadcasts. Though the filament was slightly sticky, and very dense, Maura could still feel Kayleigh's fingers buried inside, like pencils encased in thick plastic. She and Kayleigh had been lovers almost from the time Kayleigh, years younger, took up residence in B-11, doing time for assault with a deadly weapon. Age difference aside, they matched. Kayleigh's slightly cock-eyed sense of humor fit Maura's cynicism. Kay was good-natured, filling the dark pits that had been eaten into Maura's character by the things she had seen and the things she had done. She was a slick dancer, she was a wonderful kisser, and although they didn't make love often these days, when they did, it was still good. As they lay together with their legs entwined, there was no prison for a little while, and no confusing outside world, either. It was just them.

Kayleigh was also a fine singer; she had won the prison talent show three years running. Last October there hadn't been a dry eye in the house when she finished singing – *a capella* – 'The First Time Ever I Saw Your Face.' Maura supposed all that was over now. People talked in their sleep; few if any sang in their sleep. Even if Kayleigh should be moved to sing, it would come out all muffled. And what if that crap was all down her throat, as well? And in her lungs? It probably was, although if that were the case, how she could go on breathing was a mystery.

Maura raised one knee, then the other, back and forth, up and down, rocking her lover gently. 'Why did you have to go to sleep, honey? Why couldn't you wait?'

Jeanette and Angel came by then, pushing a cart with two large coffee urns and two large plastic pitchers of juice on it. Maura could smell their approach before she saw them because man, that brew smelled *bitter*. Officer Rand Quigley was shepherding them along. Maura wondered how many of the female guards were left. She guessed not many. And few would show up for the next shift. Maybe none.

'Coffee, Maura?' Angel asked. 'It'll pep you right the fuck up.'

'No,' Maura said. Up and down went her knees. Up and down. Rock-a-bye Kayleigh, in the treetop.

'Sure? It'll keep you goin. If I'm lyin, I'm dyin.'

'No,' Maura repeated. 'Get on.'

Quigley didn't like Maura's tone. 'Watch your mouth, inmate.'

'Or what? You'll tonk me on the head with your stick and put me to sleep? Go ahead. That might be the only way I manage it.'

Quigley didn't reply. He looked frazzled. Maura didn't see why he should be. None of this would touch him; no man would bear this cross.

'You get that insomnia, don't you?' Angel asked.

'Yeah. Takes one to know one.'

'Lucky us,' Angel said.

Wrong, Maura thought. *Un*lucky us.

'Is that Kayleigh?' Jeanette asked.

'No,' Maura said. 'It's Whoopi fucking Goldberg under that mess.'

'I'm sorry,' Jeanette said, and she looked sorry, and that hurt Maura's heart in a way she had been guarding against. She would not cry in front of Officer Quigley or these young ones, though. She would not.

'Get on, I said.'

When they were gone with their fucked-up coffee wagon, Maura bent over her sleeping cellie – if you could call it sleep. To Maura it looked more like a magic spell from a fairy tale.

Love had come late for her and it was a miracle that it had come at all, she knew that. Like a rose blooming in a bomb crater. She should be grateful for the time the two of them had had, all the greeting cards and pop songs said so. But when she looked at the grotesque membrane covering Kayleigh's sweet face, she found that her well of gratitude, always shallow, was now dry.

Not her eyes, though. With the coffee crew and Officer Quigley gone (nothing left but the trailing stink of that strange brew), she let the tears come. They fell on the white stuff enclosing Kayleigh's head and the white stuff sucked the moisture up greedily.

If she's somewhere close, and if I could just go to sleep, maybe I could catch up. Then we could go together.

But no. Because of the insomnia. She had lived with it since the night she had methodically slaughtered her entire family, finishing with Slugger, their elderly German shepherd. Petting him, soothing him, letting him lick her hand, then cutting his throat. If she got two hours of unconsciousness at night, she considered herself lucky. On many nights she got none at all . . . and nights in Dooling could be long. But Dooling was just a place. Insomnia had been her real prison across these years. Insomnia was boundless, and it never put her on Good Report.

I'll be awake after most of them are asleep, she thought. Guards and inmates both. I'll have the run of the place. Always assuming I want to stay, that is. And why would I want to go anywhere else? She might wake up, my Kayleigh. With a thing like this, anything is possible. Isn't it?

Maura couldn't sing the way Kayleigh could – hell, couldn't carry a tune in a bucket – but there was a song Kayleigh especially liked, and now Maura sang it to her as she gently raised her knees up and down, as if operating the pedals of an invisible organ. Maura's husband had listened to it all the time, and Maura had learned the words by osmosis. Kay heard her singing it to herself once, and demanded Maura teach her. 'Aw, that's naughty!' Kayleigh had exclaimed. It had been on an LP by a bunch of goofy potato eaters. That was how long Maura had been inside; her husband had owned an extensive collection of LPs. He didn't matter now. Mr Dunbarton had been put into an everlasting slumber early on the morning of January 7, 1984. She'd given him the knife first, right in the chest, plunged it like a shovel into loam, and he sat straight up, and his eyes had said, *Why?*

Because, that was why. And she'd have killed him or anyone else over and over and over again, would do it this very moment, if it would bring Kayleigh back to her.

'Listen, Kay. Listen:

*'In the female prison there are seventy women . . . I wish it was with
    them that I did dwell . . .'*

On the little TV, downtown Las Vegas appeared to be burning up.

'Then that old triangle . . . Could jingle jangle . . .'

She bent and kissed the white cocoon that had buried Kayleigh's face. The taste was sour on her lips, but she didn't mind, because Kayleigh was beneath. Her Kay.

'Along the banks . . . of the Royal Canal.'

Maura leaned back, closed her eyes, and prayed for sleep. It did not come.

2

Richland Lane curved gently to the left before dead-ending at a small park. The first thing Lila saw when she came around this curve was a couple of garbage cans lying overturned in the street. The second was a knot of yelling neighbors in front of the Elway house.

A teenage girl in a tracksuit sprinted toward the cruiser. In the light of the flashing jackpots, her face was a stuttering picture of dismay. Lila hammered on the brake and opened the door, unsnapping the strap over the butt of her pistol.

'Come quick!' the girl screamed. 'She's killing him!'

Lila ran for the house, kicking one of the garbage cans aside and pushing past a couple of men. One of them held up a bleeding hand. 'I tried to stop her, and the bitch bit me. She was like a rabid dog.'

Lila stopped at the end of the driveway, her gun hanging down beside her right thigh, trying to process what she was seeing: a woman in a frog-squat on the asphalt. She appeared to be swathed in a muslin nightgown, at once form-fitting and ragged, leaking countless loose threads. Decorative bricks, patriotically painted in red, white, and blue, lined the drive on both sides. The woman held one in her left hand and one in her right. She was chopping them down, edge first, on the body of a man wearing a blood-drenched Dooling Sheriff's Department uniform. Lila thought it must be

Roger, although it would take fingerprints or a DNA test to be sure; except for a remnant of broad chin, his face was gone, cratered like a stomped ground-apple. Blood ran down the driveway in creeks, flashing blue each time her cruiser's jackpot lights strobed.

The woman crouched over Roger was snarling. Her flushed face – Jessica Elway's face – was visible, only partially screened by the tatters of the webs that her husband must have made the lethal mistake of removing. The hands on the plunging bricks were gloved in red.

That's not Jessica Elway, Lila thought. *It can't be, can it?*

'Stop!' Lila shouted. 'Stop it right now!'

For a wonder, the woman did. She looked up, her bloodshot eyes so wide they seemed to fill half her face. She stood, holding a dripping brick in each hand. One red, one blue. God bless America. Lila saw a couple of Roger's teeth stuck in the cocoon material hanging down from her chin.

'Watch out, Sheriff,' one of the men said. 'She sure does look ray-bid to me.'

'Drop them!' She raised her Glock. Lila had never been so tired, but her arm was steady. 'Drop the bricks!'

Jessica dropped one, and appeared to consider. Then she raised the other brick and ran, not at Lila but at one of the men who had crept closer for a better look. And, hard as it was for Lila to believe, to take a picture. The man's cell phone was raised at Jessica. As she approached, he squealed and turned tail, head down and shoulders hunched. He knocked the girl in the tracksuit sprawling.

'Drop it drop it drop it!'

The Jessica-thing paid no attention. She leaped over the girl in the tracksuit and raised the remaining brick. There was no one behind her, all the neighbors had scattered. Lila fired twice, and Jessica Elway's head exploded. Chunks of scalp with yellow hair still attached flew backward.

'Oh my God. Oh my God. Oh my God.' It was the fallen girl.

Lila helped the girl to her feet. 'Go home, hon.' And when the girl started to look toward Jessica Elway, Lila turned her head away. She raised her voice. 'All of you, go home! In your houses! Now!'

The man with the cell phone was creeping back, looking for a good angle, one where he could capture every bit of the carnage. He wasn't a man, though. Beneath his sandy hair his features were soft and teenage. She recognized him from the local newspaper, some high school kid, she didn't know his name, some kind of sports star, probably. Lila pointed a shaking finger at him. 'You take a picture with that thing and I'll stuff it down your motherfucking throat.'

The kid – it was Eric Blass's friend Curt McLeod – stared at her, brows furrowing together. 'It's a free country, isn't it?'

'Not tonight,' Lila said. Then she screamed, shocking herself as much as the cluster of neighbors. *'Get out! Get out! GO!'*

Curt and the others went, a few snatching glances back over their shoulders, as if afraid she might come flying after them, as crazy as the woman she'd just shot down in the street.

'I knew they had no business putting in a lady sheriff!' one man called over his shoulder.

Lila restrained the urge to give him the finger and walked back to her cruiser. When a lock of hair fell in her eyes, she brushed it back with a panicky shudder, thinking it was that stuff, trying to spin out of her skin again. She leaned against the door, took a couple of deep breaths, keyed her mic.

'Linny?'

'I'm here, boss.'

'Is everyone coming in?'

A pause. Then Linny said, 'Well. I got five. Both Wittstocks, Elmore, Vern, and Dan Treat. And Reed's coming back soon, too. His wife – fell asleep. I guess his neighbor's going to look after little Gary, the poor kid . . .'

Lila did the addition and it came to eight officers, not much when you were hoping to fend off anarchy. None of Dooling's three female deputies had responded to Linny's calls. It made Lila wonder how they were doing at the prison. She closed her eyes, started to drift, and forced them open again.

Linny was onto the subject of the countless emergency calls. There had been more than a dozen from men like Reed Barrows who suddenly found themselves the sole guardians of small male children.

'Several of these feckless fools wanted me to explain to them how to feed their own children! This one idiot asks me if FEMA is setting up a facility to take care of kids because he's got tickets for a—'

'Any of them at the station yet?'

'Who? FEMA?'

'No, Linny. Any of the deputies.' Not Terry, though. Please not him. Lila didn't want Terry to see what was left of the man he'd most often partnered with for the last five years.

'Afraid not. The only person here is that old guy from Adopt-A-Highway and the VFD. Wanted to know if he could do anything. He's outside, smoking his pipe.'

It took a few seconds for her exhausted, shocked brain to process this. Willy Burke, who knew about fairy handkerchiefs, and who drove a rattletrap Ford pickup.

'I want him.'

'That guy? Really?'

'Yes. I'm at 65 Richland Lane.'

'Isn't that—'

'Yes. It's bad, Linny. Very. Jessica killed Roger. He must have cut open the stuff on her face. She chased him outside and – she came at a kid with a brick, some little asshole, he was trying to take her fucking picture. She was out of her mind.' What mind? Lila thought. 'I warned her to stop, and when she didn't, I shot her. She's dead. There was no choice.'

'Roger's *dead*?' Nothing about his wife being dead. Lila wasn't surprised. Linny had always had a soft spot for Roger.

'Send Willy out here. Tell him we'll be transporting two bodies to the hospital morgue. He should bring a tarp. Hold the deputies there at the station. I'll come as soon as I can. Out.'

She lowered her head and prepared to cry. No tears came. She wondered if a person could be too tired to cry. It seemed possible. Today, anything seemed possible.

Her cell phone rang in its little holster on her utility belt. It was Clint.

'Hello, Clint,' she answered. 'This isn't really the best time to talk.'

'Are you all right?' he asked. 'You don't sound all right.'

Lila wasn't sure where to begin. With Roger and Jessica Elway, dead in the yard? With the hallucination she'd had out by the power lines in the woods behind the rubble of Truman Mayweather's meth shack? With Sheila Norcross? With Shannon Parks? With the day Clint shut down his practice with no advance warning? With their marriage vows?

'You're not falling asleep, are you? Lila?'

'No, I'm right here.'

'Janice is — out of commission. Long story. Hicks has gone off. Somehow I've ended up in charge of this place.'

Lila said she was sorry. It was a difficult situation, no question about it. But maybe it would look better once he had some sleep. Her husband could do that: go to sleep, and then wake up again.

He said he was going home to check on their son. Jared had said he'd hurt his knee and it was nothing serious, but Clint wanted to see it for himself. Did Lila want to meet him there?

'I'll try.' But Lila didn't know when she'd be able to get away. All she knew was that it looked like it was going to be another late one.

3

'Do you hear that?' A woman had found Kayleigh Rawlings in the dark. The woman smelled like booze and had a soft arm. Magda, she said her name was. 'Singing, isn't it?'

'Yeah.' It was Maura singing. Maura's voice wasn't worth a shit; her sense of a tune was all seasick, up and down and creaky and broken; and to Kayleigh right then, it was incomparably sweet, carrying off the silly old words of that dirty old air.

'. . . *Royal Canal* . . .'

The singing stopped.

'Where was it coming from?'

'I don't know.'

Somewhere far away, that was about the only thing Kayleigh could tell for sure. Had it drifted all the way from Dooling? Where *was* Dooling? This was definitely not Dooling. Or was it? Hard to tell. Impossible, really.

A gentle wind circled through the darkness. The air was fresh and good and under her feet the ground felt not like cement or sticky tile, but like grass. She squatted down and touched: yes, it was grass, or weeds, about knee high. Birds chattered faintly somewhere. Kayleigh had awakened feeling strong and young and well rested.

Correctional had taken twelve years from her, the better part of her thirties, the first couple of years of her forties, and it had a claim on another ten. Maura was the best part of those lost years. It wasn't something that could ever have worked outside the walls, of course, the deal they had, but in prison you made do. If Kayleigh had been suddenly shoved out the doors of Dooling Correctional she would have remembered Maura fondly and gratefully, and moved on. You didn't carry a torch for a triple-murderer no matter how strangely charming you found them. The woman was nuts, Kayleigh had no illusions about that. She loved Kayleigh wholly, though, and Kayleigh loved to be loved. And you know, maybe she, Kayleigh, was a little nuts, too.

There had been no heedless love in the time before prison. No love of any kind, really, not since she was a little child.

On one job – not the one they clipped her for – Kayleigh and her boyfriend had knocked over a pill shop in back of an hourly motel. In the room there'd been a teenage kid in a rocking chair. The rocking chair had been nice, polished to a glow, totally out of place in the fleabag motel, a throne amid garbage. The kid who sat in it had a massive, volcanic hole in his cheek. It was a glossy, swirling mix of red and pitch black; a hot mess from which came the wafting smell of rotting flesh. How had it happened? Had it started with a scratch, a scrape, a tiny infection? Or had someone cut him with a dirty blade? Was it a disease? Kayleigh felt lucky not to have to know or care.

She put the kid at about sixteen. He scratched his pale belly and watched as she and her boyfriend kicked around, searching for the stash. What else was wrong with him that he just sat there calm as could be and watched them with no fear?

Kayleigh's boyfriend found what he was hunting for under the mattress and stuffed it into his jacket. He turned to the kid. 'Your face is putrid,' he said. 'You know that?'

'I know,' the kid said.

'Good. Now get the fuck out of the chair, son.'

The kid didn't give any trouble. He got up from the chair and dropped onto the sprung bed, lying there and scratching his stomach. They took the rocking chair along with the money and the drugs. They could do that because the boyfriend had a panel truck.

That was the kind of life she led in those days, one where she had stood by and helped the man she slept with steal the very chair a kid was sitting in. A ruined kid. And guess what? It was a life where the kid did nothing about it. He just lay down and pointed his ruined face at the ceiling and scratched his belly and did fuck-all else. Maybe because he was stoned. Maybe because he didn't give a shit. Maybe both.

There was a floral scent on the breeze.

Kayleigh felt a pang for Maura, but at the same time, she was stirred by an intuition: that this was a better place, better than prison, better than the world outside prison. It felt boundless, and there was earth beneath her feet.

'Whoever you are, I got to tell you I'm scared,' said Magda. 'And I'm worried about Anton.'

'Don't be scared,' said Kayleigh. 'I'm sure Anton's fine.' Not knowing who that was, nor caring. She felt for Magda's hand and found it. 'Let's walk toward the birdsong.' They edged forward in the blackness, finding themselves moving down a gentle grade, among trees.

And was that a glimmer of a light there? Was that a crack of sun in the sky?

It was blazing dawn when they came to the overgrown remains of a trailer. From there, they were able to follow the ghost of a dirt lane to the time-shattered pavement of Ball's Hill Road.

CHAPTER 15

1

Leaving Old Essie's den behind, the fox cut a zigzag path through the surrounding woods, pausing to rest in the damp below an overgrown shed. In his sleep he dreamed that his mother brought him a rat, but it was rotten and poison, and he realized that his mother was sick. Her eyes were red and her mouth hung crooked and her tongue lolled to the ground. That was when he remembered that she was gone, his mother was many seasons gone. He had seen her lie down in tall grass, and the next day, she still lay in the same place, but was no longer his mother.

'There's poison in the walls,' said the dead rat in his dead mother's mouth. 'She says the earth is made of our bodies. I believe her, and oh, the pain doesn't end. Even death hurts.'

A cloud of moths descended on the fox's dead mother and the dead rat.

'Don't stop, child,' said the mother fox. 'You have work.'

The fox jerked up out of his sleep and felt a sharp pain as he struck his shoulder against the edge of something jutting down, a nail or glass or a shard of board. It was early evening.

From close by came a thunderous crash: metal and wood, a gasp of steam, the tearing sound of fire catching. The fox darted from under the overgrown shed, breaking hard for the road. Beyond the road loomed the bigger woods and, he hoped, safer ground.

At the side of the road, a car was buckled against a tree. A woman on fire was dragging a man from the front seat of the car. The man was screaming. The sound the burning woman made was a dog sound. The fox understood what it meant: *I will kill you, I will kill you, I will kill you.* Tendrils of burning web fluttered away from her body.

Here was a moment of decision. High among the fox's catalog of personal statutes was Thou Shalt Not Cross the Road in Daylight. There were more cars in the day, and cars could not be intimidated or warned off, let alone defeated. As they zoomed over the pavement, they made a sound, too, and if you listened (a fox should always listen), that sound was words, and the words were *I want to kill you, I want to kill you, I want to kill you.* The hot and leaking remains of animals that had failed to heed these words had provided the fox with many excellent snacks.

On the other hand, a fox that wanted to survive needed to maintain a fluid approach to danger. He needed to balance the threat of a car that *wanted to* kill you with a woman cloaked in fire declaring that she *was going to* kill you.

The fox bolted. As he passed her, the heat of the burning woman was in his fur and in the cut on his back. The burning woman had started to pound the man's head against the pavement and the roar of her anger grew louder, but it faded as the fox scrambled down the embankment on the opposite side of the road.

In the big woods he slowed his pace. The cut in his lower back made his rear right leg hurt every time he pushed off. It was night. Last year's leaves crackled under the fox's pads. He stopped to drink from a stream. Oil swirled in the water, but he was thirsty and had to take what he could get. A hawk perched on a stump by the stream. It picked at the belly of a squirrel.

'Let me have some?' the fox called. 'I could be a friend to you.'

'A fox has no friends,' said the hawk.

It was true, but the fox would never admit it. 'What liar told you that?'

'You're bleeding, you know,' the hawk said.

The fox didn't care for the bird's chipper tone.

The fox thought it wise to change the subject. 'What's going on? Something has changed. What's happened to the world?'

'There's a tree further on. A new tree. A Mother Tree. It appeared at dawn. Very beautiful. Very tall. I tried to fly to the top, but although I could see the crown, it was beyond my wings.' A bright red knot of intestine snapped free of the squirrel's body and the hawk gulped it down.

The hawk tilted its head. A second later a smell twitched the fox's nostrils: smoke. It had been a dry season. If the burning woman had crossed the road, a few steps into the brush would have been enough to make it all go up.

The fox needed to get moving again. He panted. He was afraid and he was hurt – but he still had his wits.

'Your eyes will make a fine meal for some lucky animal,' the hawk said, and took flight, the limp squirrel locked in its talons.

2

As was hardly uncommon, the First Thursday Book Club had begun to drift away from that month's text, which happened to be *Atonement*, by Ian McEwan. The novel's story followed two lovers, sundered from one another almost before their relationship had begun, by the false accusation of a preternaturally imaginative young girl named Briony.

Dorothy Harper, at seventy-nine the group's elder stateswoman, said she was unable to forgive Briony for her crime. 'That little baggage ruined their lives. Who cares if she was sorry?'

'They say the brain doesn't fully develop until you're much older,' said Gail Collins. 'Briony was only twelve or thirteen when she told the lie. You can't blame her.' Gail held her glass of white wine in both hands, cupped around the bowl. She was situated at the nook table by the kitchen bar.

Blanche McIntyre, Warden Coates's faithful assistant (usually faithful, at least), had met Gail in a secretarial class thirty years earlier. Margaret O'Donnell, the fourth member of the First Thursday Book Club, was Gail's sister, and the only woman Blanche knew who had a stock portfolio.

'Who says that?' Dorothy asked. 'About the brain?'

'Scientists,' Gail said.

'Pish-tush!' Dorothy waved a hand, as if to make a bad smell go away. (Dorothy was the only woman Blanche knew who still said things like *pish-tush*.)

'It's true.' Blanche had heard Dr Norcross at the prison say almost exactly the same thing, that the human brain wasn't fully developed until a person reached their twenties. Was it really such a surprise, though? If you had ever known a teenager – or, for that matter, been one – wasn't it axiomatic? Teenagers didn't know what the hell they were doing, especially male ones. And a girl of twelve? Forget it.

Dorothy sat in the armchair by the front window. It was her condo, a neat second-floor unit on Malloy Street with plush slate-colored carpeting and fresh beige walls. The view was of the woods that backed up the building. Of the world's current unrest, the only visible sign was a fire – like a match flame at this distance – off in the west, toward Ball's Hill and Route 17. 'It was just so cruel. I don't care how small her brain was.'

Blanche and Margaret were seated on the couch. On the coffee table stood the open bottle of Chablis and the still-corked bottle of Pinot. There was also the plate of cookies that Dorothy had baked, and the three bottles of pills that Margaret had brought.

'I loved it,' said Margaret. 'I loved the whole book. I thought all the details about nursing during the Blitz were amazing. And everything about the big battle and France and walking to the shore, wow! A real trek! An *epic* trek, you could say! And romance, too! It was *pretty* spicy stuff.' She shook her head and laughed.

Blanche twisted to look at her, annoyed despite the fact that Margaret was on her side about liking *Atonement*. Margaret had worked for the railroads until they gave her a nifty bundle of cash to take early retirement – some people were just so darn lucky. She was a terrible giggler, was Margaret O'Donnell, especially for someone who was past seventy, and foolish about ceramic animals, dozens of which were crowded on her windowsills. For her last book pick she'd chosen the Hemingway novel about the idiot who wouldn't let go of the fish, a book that had aggravated Blanche, because it was, let's face it, just a goddam *fish*! Margaret had thought that one was romantic, too. How could a woman like that have turned her early retirement bundle into a stock portfolio? It was a mystery.

Now Blanche said, 'Come on, Midge. We're grown women. Let's not get silly about sex.'

'Oh, it's not that. It's such a *grand* book. We're just so lucky to go out on this one.' Margaret rubbed her forehead. She peered at Blanche over the tops of her horn-rimmed glasses. 'Wouldn't it have been awful to die on a bad book?'

'I suppose,' Blanche replied, 'but who says that this thing that's happening is death? Who says we're going to die?'

The meeting had been scheduled for that night long before Aurora hit – they never missed a first Thursday – and the four old friends had spent much of the day texting like teenagers, back and forth about whether, given the circumstances, they ought to cancel. No one had wanted to, though. First Thursday was First Thursday. Dorothy had texted that if it was her last night, getting dizzy with her friends sounded like the way to do it. Gail and Margaret had voted the same, and Blanche had, too, feeling a little guilty about leaving Warden Coates in the lurch but that she was well within her rights, having already gone way into overtime for which the state would not compensate her. Besides, Blanche wanted to talk about the book. Like Dorothy, she was amazed at the evil of the little girl Briony, and also, of the way that the evil child had matured into quite a different sort of adult.

Then, once they had settled in Dorothy's living room, Margaret had produced the bottles of lorazepam. The bottles were a couple of years old. When her husband passed away, the doctor gave it to her 'just to help you cope, Midge.' Margaret never took any; though she was sad to lose her husband, her nerves were fine, maybe better, actually, since once he was dead she no longer had to worry about him killing himself shoveling the driveway in the winters or climbing up on the ladder to cut tree branches that were awfully close to the power lines. But because her insurance covered the cost, she had filled the prescriptions anyway. You never knew what might come in handy, was her motto. Or when. Now it seemed that when had arrived.

'Better to do it together, was what I was thinking,' Margaret said. 'Less scary that way.'

The other three had, with no significant objections, agreed that it was a good idea. Dorothy Harper was also a widow. Gail's husband was in a nursing home and did not recognize even his children these days. And speaking of the children of the First Thursday gals, they were middle-aged adults who lived in places far from the hills of Appalachia, and no last minute reunion was feasible. Blanche, the only non-retiree among the group, had never married or had children at all, which was probably for the best, considering how things were turning out.

Now, the question Blanche had asked put the laughter to a stop.

'Maybe we'll wake up as butterflies,' Gail said. 'The cocoons I've seen on the news, they remind me a little of the cocoons that caterpillars make.'

'Spiders wrap up flies, too. I think the cocoons look more like that than like any sort of chrysalis,' Margaret said.

'I'm not counting on anything.' Blanche's full glass had at some point in the last few minutes become an empty glass.

'I hope to see an angel,' Dorothy said.

The other three looked to her. She did not seem to be joking. Her wrinkled chin and mouth tightened into a tiny fist. 'I've been pretty good, you know,' she added. 'Tried to be kind. Good wife. Good mother. Good friend. Volunteered in retirement. Why, I drove all the way to Coughlin just on Monday for my committee meeting.'

'We know,' said Margaret, and extended a hand in the air toward Dorothy, who was the very definition of a good old soul. Gail echoed this, and so did Blanche.

They passed around the pill bottles and each woman took two tablets and swallowed them. Following this act of communion, the four friends sat and looked at each other.

'What should we do now?' Gail asked. 'Just wait?'

'Cry,' Margaret said, and giggled as she pretended to rub at her eyes with her knuckles. 'Cry, cry, cry!'

'Pass the cookies around,' Dorothy said. 'I'm quitting my diet.'

'I want to get back to the book,' Blanche said. 'I want to talk about how Briony changed. *She* was like a butterfly. I thought that was lovely. It reminded me of some of the women in the prison.'

Gail had retrieved the Pinot from the coffee table. She unwrapped the foil and stuck in the corkscrew.

While she went around pouring everyone a new glass, Blanche continued, 'You know there's a lot of recidivism – fallback, I mean – breaking parole, and getting back into bad habits and such – but some of them do change. Some of them start brand new lives. Like Briony. Isn't that inspiring?'

'Yes,' Gail said. She raised her glass. 'To emerging new lives.'

3

Frank and Elaine lingered in the doorway of Nana's room. It was past nine. They'd laid her down on the bed, leaving aside the covers. There was a poster of a uniformed marching band on the wall and a bulletin board tacked with Nana's best drawings of Manga characters. A wind chime of colored pipes and glass beads hung from the ceiling. Elaine insisted on neatness so there were no clothes or toys on the floor. The blinds were pulled shut. Around Nana's head the growth was bulbous. The growths bunched around her hands were identical, only smaller. Mittens with no thumbs.

Though neither had said anything, after standing together in silence for more than a minute, Frank realized that they were both afraid to turn off the light.

'Let's come back and check on her again in a little while.' Out of habit, Frank whispered this to Elaine, as on so many occasions when they were desperate to keep from waking Nana, instead of the opposite.

Elaine nodded. As one, they retreated from their daughter's open door and went downstairs to the kitchen.

While Elaine sat at the table, Frank made a pot of coffee, filling the urn, sifting out the grounds. It was something he'd done a thousand times before, though never at so late an hour. The normality of the activity soothed him.

She was thinking along similar lines. 'It's like the old days, isn't it? Sick baby upstairs, us down here, wondering if we're doing the right things.'

Frank pressed the brew button. Elaine had her head on the table, tucked between her arms.

'You should sit up,' he said gently, and took the chair across from her.

She nodded and sat up straight. Her bangs were stuck to her forehead and she had the querulous, what's-that-who-now? look of someone who had recently absorbed a blow to the skull. He didn't suppose he looked any better.

'Anyway, I know what you mean,' said Frank. 'I remember. Questioning how we ever could have tricked ourselves into thinking we could take care of another human being in the first place.'

This brought a bright smile to Elaine's face. Whatever was happening to them now, they'd survived an infant together – no small achievement.

The coffee machine beeped. For a moment, it had seemed quiet, but Frank suddenly became aware of the noise outside. Someone was yelling. There were police sirens, a car alarm whooping. He instinctively tilted his ear toward the stairs, toward Nana.

He didn't hear anything, of course he didn't; she wasn't a baby anymore, and these weren't the old days, weren't like any days ever before. The way Nana was sleeping tonight, it was impossible to imagine what kind of racket would rouse her, cause her to open her eyes beneath that layer of white fiber.

Elaine had her head canted the same way toward the stairs.

'What is this, Frank?'

'I don't know.' He broke away from her gaze. 'We shouldn't have left the hospital.' Implying that Elaine had made them go, not sure he really believed it, but needing to share the blame, to kick a little of the dirt he felt on himself back onto her. That he knew he was doing this, knew it exactly, made him hate himself. He couldn't stop, though. 'We should have stayed. Nana needs a doctor.'

'They all do, Frank. Soon I'll need a doctor, too.' She poured herself a cup of the coffee. Years passed while she stirred in milk and Equal. He thought that part of the discussion was over, but then she said, 'You should be grateful that I made us leave.'

'What?'

'It saved you from doing whatever you might have done if we hadn't.'

'What are you talking about?'

But he knew, of course. Each marriage had its own language, its own code words, built of mutual experience. She said two of them now: 'Fritz Meshaum.'

At each rotation of her spoon, it clicked against the ceramic of the mug – *click, click, click*. Like the combination dial on a safe.

4

Fritz Meshaum.

A name of ill repute, one Frank wished he could forget, but would Elaine let him? No. Shouting at Nana's teacher that time had been bad, and the famous wall punch had been worse, but the Fritz Meshaum incident was worst of all. Fritz Meshaum was the dead rat she waved in his face whenever she felt pushed into a corner, as she did tonight. If only she could see they were in the corner together, on the same side, *Nana's* side, but no. Instead, she had to bring up Fritz Meshaum. She had to wave the dead rat.

Frank had been hunting a fox, not that unusual in the wooded Tri-County area. Someone had seen one running around in the fields south of Route 17, not far from the women's prison. It had its tongue hanging out, and the caller thought it might be rabid. Frank had his doubts, but he took rabies calls seriously. Any animal control officer worth his salt did. He drove out to the collapsing barn where the sighting had occurred, and spent a half hour stalking around in the puckies. He didn't find anything except the rusted-out skeleton of a 1982 Cutlass with a pair of rotting panties knotted to the antenna.

On the way back to the shoulder where he'd parked his truck, he cut alongside a fenced property. The fence was a mix of junk, decaying planks, hubcaps, and corrugated sheet metal so full of holes it did more to invite attention than to discourage intruders. Through the gaps, Frank took in the peeling white house and shabby yard beyond. A tire swing on a fraying rope hung from an oak tree, black tattered clothes surrounded by circling insects were piled at the base of the tree, a milk crate full of iron scraps stood guard by the porch steps, a (presumably empty) oil can was carelessly pitched aside to rest like a hat on top of an unruly growth of bougainvillea which was itself partially draped over the porch. Glass fragments from a smashed second-floor window were scattered over the bare tarpaper roof, and a brand new Toyota pickup, blue as the Pacific, stood waxed up and parked in the driveway. Littered around its rear tires were a dozen or so spent shotgun shells, once bright red, now faded to pallid pink, as if they had been there a long time.

It was so perfectly country, the wreck of a house and the shiny truck, that Frank almost laughed out loud. He strolled on, smiling to himself, his mind requiring several seconds to compute something that hadn't made sense: the black clothes had been moving. Shifting around.

Frank retraced his steps to a break in the hodgepodge fence. He watched the clothes. They breathed.

And it happened the way it always seemed to, as if in a dream. He didn't slip under the fence and actually walk across the yard so much as he seemed to teleport the distance separating him from the black shape under the tree.

It was a dog, although Frank wouldn't have wanted to guess which breed – something medium-sized, maybe a shepherd, maybe a young Lab, maybe just a country mongrel. The black fur was tattered and flea-bitten. Where the fur was gone, there were infected patches of exposed skin. The animal's only visible eye was a small white pool sunk into a vaguely head-like shape. Twisted around the dog were four limbs, all of them askew, all clearly broken. Grotesquely – since how could it possibly have run away? – a chain was looped around its neck and fastened to the tree. The dog's side lifted and fell with one breath after another.

'You are trespassin!' announced a voice behind Frank. 'Boy, I got a gun on you!'

Frank put up his hands and turned around to behold Fritz Meshaum.

A little man, gnome-like with his stringy red hillbilly beard, he wore jeans and a faded tee-shirt. 'Frank?' Fritz sounded perplexed.

They knew each other, though not well, from the Squeaky Wheel. Frank remembered that Fritz was a mechanic, and that some people said you could buy a gun from him if you wanted one. Whether that was true or not, Frank couldn't have said, but they had swapped rounds a few months earlier, seated at the bar and watching a college football game together. Fritz – this dog-torturing monster – had expressed his fondness for the option play; he didn't think the Mountaineers had the talent to air it out with any sustained success. Frank was happy to go along with that; he didn't know much about the sport. Toward the end of the game, though, once Meshaum was full of beer, he had quit harping on the merits of the option and attempted to engage Frank on the subject of Jews and the federal government. 'Them hooky-noses got the whole thing in their pocket, you know that?' Fritz had leaned forward. 'I mean, my people come from Germany. So I know.' That had been Frank's cue to excuse himself.

Now Fritz lowered the rifle he had been aiming. 'What are you doin here? Come to buy a gun? I could sell you a good one, long or short. Hey, you want a beer?'

Although Frank didn't say anything, some kind of message must have been transmitted by his body language, because Fritz added, in a tone of chagrin, 'That dog worry you? Don't let it. Sumbitch bit my *neffe*.'

'Your what?'

'*Neffe*. Nephew.' Fritz shook his head. 'Some of the old words, they stick. You'd be surprised how—'

And that was the last thing Meshaum got out.

When Frank finished, the rifle butt he had taken from the bastard and used to do most of the work had been cracked and spattered with blood. The other man sprawled in the dirt, holding his crotch where Frank had repeatedly hammered the rifle butt. His eyes were buried under swelling, and he was spitting up blood with each shaky breath that he dragged out from under the ribs that Frank had sprained or broken for him. The possibility that Fritz would die from the beating had seemed, in the immediate aftermath, not unlikely.

Maybe he had not hurt Fritz Meshaum as badly as he thought, though – that was what he had told himself, even as, for weeks, he kept an eye on the obituary section, and no one came to arrest him. But Frank was without guilt. It had been a little dog, and little dogs couldn't fight back. There wasn't any excuse for it, for torturing an animal like that, no matter how ill-tempered it might be. Some dogs were capable of killing a person. However, no dog would do to a person what Fritz Meshaum had done to that pitiful creature chained to the base of the tree. What could a dog understand of the pleasure men could take from cruelty? Nothing, and it could never learn. Frank understood, though, and he felt calm in his soul about what he had done to Fritz Meshaum.

As for Meshaum's wife, how was Frank supposed to know the man even had a wife? Although he did now. Oh, yes. Elaine made sure of that.

5

'His wife?' Frank asked. 'Is that where you're going with this? Didn't surprise me she turned up at the shelter. Fritz Meshaum's a son of a bitch.'

When there had first been talk around town, Elaine had asked if it was true, that he had put a hurting on Fritz Meshaum. He had made the mistake of telling her the truth, and she never let him forget it.

Elaine set aside the spoon and drank from her coffee. 'No argument there.'

'I hope she finally left him,' said Frank. 'Not that she's any responsibility of mine.'

'It's not your responsibility that her husband, once he was healed up enough to go home from the hospital after the beating you gave him, beat her within an inch of her life?'

'Nope, absolutely not. I never laid a hand on her. We've been over this.'

'Uh–huh. And the baby she lost,' said Elaine, 'that's not your responsibility, either, right?'

Frank sucked his teeth. He didn't know about any baby. It was the first time Elaine had mentioned it. She'd been waiting for exactly the right moment to ambush him. Some wife, some friend.

'Pregnant, huh? And lost the baby. Gee, that's a tough one.'

Elaine fixed him with an unbelieving look. 'That's what you call it? A tough one? Your compassion stuns me. None of it would have happened if you'd just called the police. None of it, Frank. He'd have gone to jail and Candy Meshaum would have kept her baby.'

Guilt trips were Elaine's specialty. But if she'd seen the dog – what Fritz had done to it – she might think twice about giving him the stinkeye. The Meshaums of the world had to pay. It was the same with Dr Flickinger . . .

Which gave him an idea.

'Why don't I go get the Mercedes man? He's a doctor.'

'You mean the guy who ran over that old man's cat?'

'Yeah. He felt really bad about driving so fast. I'm sure he'd help.'

'Did you hear any of what I just said, Frank? You go crazy and it always backfires!'

'Elaine, forget about Fritz Meshaum and forget about his wife. Forget about me. Think about Nana. Maybe that doc could help.' Flickinger might even feel he owed Frank, for taking it out on his car instead of busting his way inside and taking it out on the good doctor himself.

There were more sirens. A motorcycle passed down the street, engine roaring.

'Frank, I'd like to believe that.' Her speech, slow and careful, was intended to be sincere, but it was the same cadence Elaine adopted when she explained to Nana how important it was to keep neat drawers. 'Because I love you. But I know you. We were together for ten years. You beat a man half to death over a dog. God knows how you handled this Flickmuller, or whatever his name is.'

'*Flickinger.* His name is Garth Flickinger. *Doctor* Garth Flickinger.'

Really, how could she be so dumb? Hadn't they almost been tram-
pled – or shot! – while trying to get a doctor to see their daughter?

She drank down the rest of her coffee. 'Just be here with your
daughter. Don't try to fix what you don't even understand.'

A dismal comprehension touched Frank Geary: everything would
be easier once Elaine was asleep, too. But for now she was awake.
So was he.

'You're wrong,' he said.

She blinked at him. 'What? What did you say?'

'You think you're always right. Sometimes you are, but not this
time.'

'Thank you for that wonderful insight. I'm going upstairs to sit
with Nana. Come with me if you want, but if you go after that
man – if you go *anywhere* else – we're done.'

Frank smiled. He felt okay now. It was such a relief to feel okay.
'We already are.'

She stared at him.

'Nana's what matters to me now. Just her.'

6

Frank stopped on the way to his truck to look at the woodpile by
the back stoop, hardwood he'd split himself. Half a cord left from
the winter just past. The little Jøtul stove in the kitchen made the
place homey and welcoming in the cold weather. Nana liked to sit
near it in the rocker, doing her homework. When she was bent
over her books with her hair curtaining her face, she looked to
Frank like a little girl from the nineteenth century, back when all
these man–woman things were a lot simpler. Back then, you told
a woman what you were going to do, and she either agreed or kept
her mouth shut. He remembered something his father had told his
mother when she protested over the purchase of a new power
lawnmower: *You keep the house. I'll make the money and pay the bills.
If you got a problem with that, speak up.*

She hadn't. They'd had a good marriage that way. Almost fifty
years. No marriage counseling, no separations, no lawyers.

There was a big tarp over the woodpile and a smaller one over the chopping block. He raised the smaller and pulled the hand-ax free from the scarred wood. Flickinger didn't seem like much, but it never hurt to be prepared.

7

Dorothy went first. Head lolling back, mouth open, dentures slipping slightly and flecked with cookie crumbs, she snored. The other three watched the white strings float and untether, split and float, float and fall down against her skin. They layered like bandages in miniature, wrapping in crisscross patterns.

'I wish—' Margaret began, but whatever it was she wished, she didn't seem to be able to catch hold of the thing.

'Do you think she's suffering?' Blanche asked. 'Do you think it hurts?' Though her words felt heavy in her mouth, she herself was not in any pain.

'No.' Gail tottered to her feet, her library copy of *Atonement* dropping to the floor with a flop of paper and crinkle of plastic sheeting. She braced herself on the furniture as she crossed the room toward Dorothy.

Blanche was hazily impressed by this effort. Along with the pills, they'd dispatched the bottle of Pinot, and Gail had drunk the most. There was an officer at the prison who competed in arm-wrestling contests. Blanche wondered if there were contests for drinking wine and taking drugs and then walking around without tripping over the chairs or running into the walls. Gail might have missed her calling!

Blanche wanted to express all this to Gail, but she found that the best she could do was, 'Nice – walking – Gail.'

She watched as Gail bent down close to Dorothy's ear, which was already layered in a thin coating of web. 'Dorothy? Can you hear us? Meet me at the—' Gail stopped.

'What place do we know is in heaven, Midge? Where should I have her meet us?'

Only Margaret didn't answer. Couldn't. The threads were now circling and knitting around her head, too.

Blanche's eyes, seeming to move around of their own accord, found the window, and the fire in the west. It was bigger now, not a match but a flaming bird's head. There were still men to fight the fire, but maybe they were too busy taking care of their women to bother. What was the name of that bird, the one that changed into fire, reborn, magic bird, scary, terrible? She didn't know. All she could remember was an old Japanese monster movie called *Rodan*. She had watched it as a child, and the giant bird in it had frightened her badly. She wasn't frightened now, just . . . interested.

'We have lost my sister,' Gail announced. She had sunk to the carpet and was leaning against Dorothy's legs.

'She's just asleep,' Blanche said. 'You didn't lose her, honey.'

Gail nodded so emphatically that her hair fell into her eyes. 'Yes, yes. You're right, Blanche. We'll just have to find each other. Just look for each other in heaven. Or . . . you know . . . a reasonable facsimile.' That made her laugh.

8

Blanche was the last. She crawled over to be near Gail, asleep beneath a layer of webbing.

'I had a love,' Blanche told her. 'Bet you didn't know that. We kept it . . . as the girls at the prison like to say . . . on the down-low. Had to.'

The filaments that lay over her friend's mouth stirred as Gail exhaled. One fine thread extended itself flirtatiously in Blanche's direction.

'I think he loved me, too, but . . .' It was hard to explain. She was young. When you were young, your brain wasn't fully developed. You didn't know about men. It was sad. He had been married. She had waited. They had aged. Blanche had given up the sweetest part of her soul for a man. He had made beautiful promises and kept none of them. What a waste.

'This might be the best thing that ever happened.' If Gail had been awake, these words of Blanche's might have been too low and garbled for her to understand. Feeling had left Blanche's tongue. 'Because at least we're all together, now, at the end.'

And if there was something else, somewhere else . . .

Before Blanche McIntyre could finish the thought, she drifted away.

9

Garth Flickinger wasn't surprised to see Frank.

After having watched NewsAmerica for the last twelve hours or so, and smoking everything in the house except for his pet iguana (Gillies), probably nothing would have surprised him. Should Sir Harold Gillies himself, that long-dead pioneer of plastic surgery, have come wandering downstairs to the kitchen to toast a cinnamon Pop-Tart, it would have barely pushed the envelope on the phenomena that Garth had witnessed on television that day.

The shock of the violence that had broken out in Truman Mayweather's trailer while Garth was in the john was but a prologue to what he had absorbed in the hours since, just sitting on the couch. Rioting outside the White House, a woman gnawing off the nose of a religious cultist, a huge 767 lost at sea, bloodied nursing home orderlies, elderly women swathed in webs and handcuffed to their gurneys, fires in Melbourne, fires in Manila, and fires in Honolulu. Something very fucking bad had occurred in the desert outside Reno where there was evidently some kind of secret government nuclear facility; scientists were reporting on Geiger counters spinning and seismographs jerking up and down, detecting continuing detonations. Everywhere women were falling asleep and growing cocoons and everywhere dumbfucks were waking them up. The wonderful NewsAmerica reporter, Michaela with the first-rate nose job, had vanished in the mid-afternoon and they'd promoted a stuttering intern with a lip ring to take her place. It reminded Garth of a piece of graffiti he'd seen on some men's room wall: THERE IS NO GRAVITY, THE EARTH JUST SUCKS.

This sucked: in and out, back and forth, all the way around. Not even the meth helped. Well, it helped a little, but not as much as it should have. By the time, the doorbell began ringing – *cling-clong, cling-clong*, went the chimes – Garth was feeling glaringly sober. He felt no particular urge to answer, not tonight. Nor did he feel compelled to rise when his visitor gave up on the bell and began knocking. Then hammering. Very energetic!

The hammering ceased. Garth had time to think his unwelcome visitor had given up before the chopping began. Chopping and splintering. The door shuddered inward, broken free of its lock, and the man who had been here earlier strode in, an ax in one hand. Garth supposed the guy was here to kill him – and he didn't feel too sad about that. It would hurt, but hopefully not for too long.

Plastic surgery was a joke to many people. Not to Garth. What was funny about wanting to like your face, your body, your only skin? Unless you were cruel or stupid, there was nothing funny about it. Only now, it seemed, the joke was on him. What kind of life would it be with only half the species? A cruel and stupid life. Garth could see that right away. Beautiful women often arrived at his office with photographs of other beautiful women, and they asked, 'Can you make me look like her?' And behind many beautiful women who wanted to tinker with their perfect faces were mean fuckers who were never satisfied. Garth didn't want to be left alone in a world of mean fuckers, because there were so many of them.

'Don't stand on ceremony, come on in. I've just been catching up on the news. You didn't happen to see the part where the woman bit the man's nose off his face, did you?'

'I did,' said Frank.

'I'm great with noses, and I enjoy a challenge, but if there's nothing to work with, there's not much you can do.'

Frank stood at the corner of the couch, a few feet from Garth. The ax was a small one, but still an ax.

'Do you plan to kill me?'

'What? No. I came—'

They were both distracted by the flatscreen, where a news camera showed a view of a burning Apple Store. On the sidewalk in front of the store, a man with a fire-blackened face moved around in a dazed little circle, a smoldering fuchsia handbag looped over his shoulder. The Apple symbol above the entrance of the store suddenly came loose of its moorings and crashed to the ground.

A quick cut brought the viewing audience back to George Alderson. George's color was a wind-stripped gray, and his voice was gravelly. He'd been on all day. 'I just received a call from my – ah, son. He went to my house to check on my wife. Sharon and I have been married for—' The anchor dropped his head and traced the knot of his pink tie. There was a coffee stain on the tie. Garth thought this the most disturbing signal yet of the unprecedented nature of the situation. '—for forty-two years now. Timothy, my son, he . . . he says . . .' George Alderson began to sob. Frank picked up the controller from the side table and turned him off.

'Is your mind clear enough to understand what's going on, Dr Flickinger?' Frank indicated the pipe on the side table.

'Of course.' Garth felt a tick of curiosity. 'You really aren't here to kill me?'

Frank pinched the bridge of his nose. Garth had the impression he was watching the outside of a serious internal monologue.

'I'm here to ask a favor. You do it, and we're all square. It's my daughter. She's the only good thing in my life anymore. And now she's got it. The Aurora. I need you to come and look at her and . . .' His mouth opened and closed a few times, but that was the end of his words.

A thought of his own daughter, of Cathy, came to Garth's mind.

'Say no more,' Garth said, snipping the thought off and letting it flutter away, a bit of ribbon in a stiff wind.

'Yeah? Really?'

Garth held out a hand. He might have surprised Frank Geary, but he hadn't surprised himself. There were so many things that couldn't be helped. Garth was always glad when he could. And it would be interesting to see this Aurora business up close.

'Of course. Help me up, would you?'

Frank got him on his feet, and after a few steps Garth was fine. The doctor excused himself for a moment, stepping into a sideroom. When he emerged he carried a small black case and a medical bag. They went outside into the night. Garth brushed his hand through the branches of the lilac tree protruding from the back left passenger window of his Mercedes as they went to Frank's truck, but refrained from comment.

10

The fox limped away from the grassfire the burning woman had started, but he carried a fire inside him. It was burning inside his lower back. This was bad, because he couldn't run fast now, and he could smell his own blood. If he could smell his blood, other things could, as well.

A few mountain lions still remained in these woods, and if one caught wind of his bloody back and haunch, he was finished. It had been a long time since he had seen a mountain lion, not since his mother was full of milk and his four littermates were alive (all dead now, one from drinking bad water, one from eating a poison bait, one taken in a trap that tore her leg as she squealed and cried, one disappeared in the night), but there were also wild pigs. The fox feared them more than the mountain lions. They had escaped some farmer's pen and bred in the woods. Now there were lots of them. Ordinarily, the fox would have had no problem escaping them and might even have enjoyed teasing them a bit; they were very clumsy. Tonight, though, he could hardly run. Soon he would not even be able to trot.

The woods ended at a metal house that smelled of human blood and human death. Yellow strips hung around it. There were metal man-things in the weeds and lying on the crushed stone in front. Mixed in with the death scents was another, something he had never smelled before. Not a human smell, exactly, but *like* a human smell.

And female.

Putting aside his fear of the wild pigs, the fox moved away from the metal house, limping and occasionally collapsing on his side while he panted and waited for the pain to subside. Then he went on. He had to go on. That scent was exotic, both sweet and bitter at the same time, irresistible. Perhaps it would take him to a place of safety. It didn't seem likely, but the fox was desperate.

That exotic smell grew stronger. Mixed into it was another female smell, but this one was fresher and clearly human. The fox paused to sniff at one of Lila's shoe prints in the loam, then a patch of white stuff in the shape of a bare human foot.

A small bird fluttered down to a low-hanging branch. Not a hawk this time. This was a kind of bird the fox had never seen before. It was green. A scent drifted from it, humid and tangy, for which the fox had no context. It fluffed its wings self-importantly.

'Please don't sing,' the fox said.

'All right,' the green bird said. 'I rarely do at night, anyway. I see you are bleeding. Does it hurt?'

The fox was too tired to dissemble. 'Yes.'

'Roll in the web. It will stop the pain.'

'It will poison me,' the fox said. His back was burning, but he knew about poison, oh yes. The humans poisoned everything. It was their best talent.

'No. The poison is leaving these woods. Roll in the web.'

Perhaps the bird was lying, but the fox saw no other recourse. He fell on his side, then rolled onto his back, as he sometimes did in deer scat, to confuse his scent. Blessed coolness doused the pain in his back and haunch. He rolled once more, then sprang to his feet, looking up at the branch with bright eyes.

'What are you? Where did you come from?' the fox asked.

'The Mother Tree.'

'Where is it?'

'Follow your nose,' said the green bird, and flew off into the darkness.

The fox went from one bare webbed footprint to the next, pausing twice more to roll in them. They cooled him and refreshed him and gave him strength. The woman-scent remained quite strong, that exotic not-quite-woman-scent fainter. Together they told the fox a story. The not-woman had come first and gone east, toward the metal house and the shed that was now burned. The real woman had come later, back-trailing the not-woman to some destination ahead, and then, later, returning to the stinking metal house with the yellow strips around it.

The fox followed the entwined scents into a brushy brake, up the other side, and through a stand of stunted fir trees. Tattered webs hung from some of the branches, giving off that exotic not-woman smell. Beyond was a clearing. The fox trotted into it. He trotted easily now, and felt he could not just run if one of those pigs showed up, but glide away. In the clearing he sat, looking up at a tree that seemed made of many trunks wrapped around each other. It rose into the dark sky higher than he could see. Although there was no wind, the tree rustled, as if talking to itself. Here the not-woman smell was lost in a hundred other traces of scent. Many birds and many animals, none of which the fox knew.

A cat came padding around from the far side of the great tree. Not a wildcat; it was much bigger. And it was white. In the dark, its green eyes were like lamps. Although the instinct to run from predators was bone-deep in the fox, he did not move. The great white tiger padded steadily toward him. The grass of the clearing rustled as it bent beneath the dense fur of its belly.

When the tiger was only five feet away, the fox lay down and rolled over, showing his own belly in submission. A fox might harbor some pride, but dignity was useless.

'Get up,' the tiger said.

The fox got to his feet and timidly stretched his neck forward to touch the tiger's nose.

'Are you healed?' the tiger asked.

'Yes.'

'Then listen to me, fox.'

11

In her prison cell, Evie Black lay with her eyes closed and a faint smile on her lips.

'Then listen to me, fox,' she said. 'I have work for you.'

CHAPTER 16

1

Clint was about to ask Tig Murphy to buzz him out through the main door, but Assistant Warden Lawrence Hicks came buzzing in first.

'Where are you going, Dr Norcross?'

The question sounded like an accusation, but at least it came out clearly. Although Lore Hicks looked disheveled – his hair a mussed halo around his bald spot, stubble on his jowly cheeks, dark circles under his eyes – the Novocain from his morning dental procedure seemed to have worn off.

'To town. I need to see my wife and son.'

'Did Janice okay that?'

Clint took a beat to control his temper. It helped to remind himself that Hicks had either lost his wife to Aurora or would soon. That did not change the fact that the man standing before him was the last guy you wanted in charge of an institution like Dooling in a time of crisis. Janice had once told Clint that her second-in-command had less than thirty credit hours of Prison Management – from a degree-mill in Oklahoma – and no hours at all in Prison Administration.

'But Hicksie's sister is married to the lieutenant governor,' Janice had said. She'd had an extra glass of Pinot on that occasion. Or maybe it had been two. 'So you do the math. He's great at sched-uling and checking inventory, but he's been here sixteen months, and I'm not sure he could find his way to C Wing without a map. He doesn't like to leave his office, and he's never done a single duty tour, although that's supposed to be a monthly requirement. He's scared of the bad girls.'

You'll be leaving your office tonight, Hicksie, Clint thought, and you'll be touring, too. Strapping on a walkie and making three-wing rounds, just like the other uniforms. The ones that are left.

'Did you hear me?' Hicks asked now. 'Did Janice okay you leaving?'

'I have three things for you,' Clint said. 'First thing, I was scheduled out at three P.M., which was . . .' He checked his watch. 'About six hours ago.'

'But—'

'Wait. Here's the second thing. Warden Coates is asleep on her couch, inside a big white cocoon.'

Hicks wore thick glasses that had a magnifying effect. When he widened his eyes, as he did now, they looked ready to fall out of their sockets. *'What?'*

'Long story short, Don Peters finally tripped over his own dick. Got caught molesting an inmate. Janice canned his ass, but Don managed to load up her coffee with her prescription Xanax. It put her down fast. And before you ask, Don is in the wind. When I see Lila, I'll tell her to put out a BOLO for him, but I doubt if it will be a priority. Not tonight.'

'Oh my God.' Hicks ran his hands through his hair, further disarraying what was left of it. 'Oh . . . my . . . *God.*'

'Here's the third thing. We do still have the other four officers from the morning shift: Rand Quigley, Millie Olson, Tig Murphy, and Vanessa Lampley. You are number five. You'll need to make midnight rounds with the others. Oh, and Van will bring you up to speed on what the inmates are calling Super Coffee. Jeanette Sorley and Angel Fitzroy are pushing it.'

'Super Coffee? What's that? And what's Fitzroy doing out? She's not trustworthy, not at all! She has anger issues! I read your report!'

'She's not angry tonight, at least not yet. She's pitching in. Like you need to. And if nothing changes, all these women are going to fall asleep, Lore. Every single one. Super Coffee or no Super Coffee.

They deserve some hope. Talk to Van, and follow her lead if a situation comes up.'

Hicks grabbed Clint's jacket. His magnified eyes were panicky. 'You can't go! You can't desert your post!'

'Why not? You did.' Clint saw Hicks wince and wished he could have called those words back. He took Hicks's hand and removed it from his jacket gently. 'You checked on your wife, I need to check on Jared and Lila. And I will be back.'

'When?'

'As soon as I can.'

'I wish they'd all go to sleep!' Hicks burst out. He sounded like a petulant child. 'Every last thieving, whoring, drug-taking one of them! We ought to give them sleeping pills instead of coffee! That would solve the problem, wouldn't it?'

Clint merely looked at him.

'All right.' Hicks did his best to square his shoulders. 'I understand. You have loved ones. It's just . . . all this . . . all these women . . . we have a jail *full* of them!'

Are you just figuring that out? Clint thought, then asked Hicks how his wife was doing. He supposed he should have asked earlier. Except, hell, it wasn't as if Hicksie had asked after Lila.

'Awake, at least so far. She had . . .' Hicks cleared his throat, and his eyes shifted away from Clint's. 'She had some pep pills.'

'Good. That's good. I'll be ba—'

'Doc.' It was Vanessa Lampley, and not on the intercom. She was at his elbow in the hall by the main door. She had left the Booth unmanned, a thing almost unheard of. 'You need to come and see this.'

'Van, I can't. I need to check on Jared, and I need to see Lila—'

So I can say goodbye, Clint thought. It occurred to him suddenly. The potential finality. How much longer could she stay awake? Not much. On the phone she had sounded – far off, like she was part of the way to another world already. Once she nodded off, there was no reason to believe she could be brought back.

'I understand,' Vanessa said, 'but it won't take more than a minute. You too, Mr Hicks, sir. This . . . I don't know, but this might change everything.'

2

'Watch monitor two,' Van said when they reached the Booth.

Two was currently showing the A Wing corridor. Two women – Jeanette Sorley and Angel Fitzroy – were pushing a coffee trolley toward the soft cell, A-10, at the end. They stopped before they got there to talk to an extremely large inmate who for some reason had taken up residence in the delousing station.

'So far we've got at least ten women asleep inside that webbing crap,' Van said. 'Might be fifteen by now. Most in their cells, but three in the common room and one in the furniture shop. That shit spins out of them as soon as they fall asleep. *Except . . .*'

She punched a button on her console, and monitor two showed the interior of A-10. Their new intake lay on her bunk with her eyes shut. Her chest rose and fell in slow respirations.

'Except for her,' Van said. There was something like awe in her voice. 'New fish is sleeping like a baby, and the only thing on her face is her Camay-fresh skin.'

Camay-fresh skin. Something struck Clint about that, but it slipped away in his surprise at what he was seeing and his concern about Lila. 'She's not necessarily asleep just because her eyes are shut.'

'Listen, Doc, I've been doing this job longer than you've been doing yours. I know when they're awake and I know when they're asleep. That one is asleep, and has been for at least forty-five minutes. Somebody drops something, makes a clatter, she kind of twitches and then turns over.'

'Keep an eye on her. You can give me a full report when I get back,' Clint said. 'I need to go.' Despite Van's insistence that she could tell the difference between sleep and closed eyes, he wasn't sold. And he had to see Lila while he still had the chance. He didn't want to lose her with this – this, whatever it was, why she was lying – between them.

He was out the door and heading for his car before the thing that had been bothering him finally coalesced in his mind. Evie Black had struck her face repeatedly against the wire mesh of Lila's cruiser, and yet only a few hours later, the swelling and bruises were entirely gone. Nothing where they'd been but Camay-fresh skin.

3

Jeanette drove the coffee wagon while Angel walked beside it, banging on one of the urns with the lid and yelling, 'Coffee! Special coffee! I got a peppy brew for all of you! Keep you leapin instead of sleepin!'

They had few takers in A Wing, where most of the cells were open and empty.

Earlier, in B Wing, Ree's reaction had been a preview of what was to come. The special coffee might be a good idea, but hard to swallow. Ree had winced and handed her cup back after giving it a taste. 'Jeez, Jeanette, I'll take a juice, but this is too strong for me.'

'Strong to last long!' Angel proclaimed. Tonight she had traded her normal southern accent for a maniacally perky ghetto patois. Jeanette wondered just how many cups of their special coffee Angel had ingested herself. She seemed to have no problem drinking it down. 'It's a power batch, so down the hatch, unless you're a dummy, want to end up a mummy!'

One of the A Wing women stared at her. 'If that's rapping, honey, I say bring back disco.'

'Don't be dissing my rhymes. We're doin you a favor. If you ain't drinkin, you ain't thinkin.'

But was postponing the inevitable really a good idea? Jeanette had thought so at first, roused by the thought of her son, but she was getting tired again, and she could sense hopelessness waiting right around the corner. And they weren't postponing the inevitable by much; when they'd brought their Super Coffee proposal to Officer Lampley there had been three sleepers in the prison, but several more had gone since then. Jeanette didn't raise the issue, though. Not because she was afraid of Angel's famous temper, but because the idea of discussing anything was wearisome. She'd had three cups of the special coffee herself – well, two and a half, her stomach refused to take all of the third cup – and she was still exhausted. It seemed like years since Ree had awakened her, asking if Jeanette had ever watched the square of light from the window as it traveled across the floor.

I just can't be bothered with a square of light, Jeanette had said.

I say you can't not be bothered with a square of light, Ree had replied, and now this played over and over in Jeanette's mind, like some crazy Zen koan. *Can't not be bothered* didn't make sense, did it? Or maybe it did. Wasn't there some rule about a double negative making a positive? If so, maybe it *did* make sense. Maybe—

'Whoa! Hold up, girlfriend!' Angel bellowed, and gave the coffee wagon a hard butt-shove. It rammed into Jeanette's crotch, temporarily bringing her wide awake. The special coffee sloshed in the urns and the juice sloshed in the pitchers.

'What?' she asked. 'What the hell is it, Angel?'

'It's my homegirl Claudia!' Angel shouted. 'Hey, baby!'

They were twenty feet or so up the A Wing corridor. Sitting slumped on a bench next to the Kwell dispenser was Claudia Stephenson, known to all the inmates (and the officers, although they did not use the nickname while in gen-pop) as Claudia the Dynamite Body-a. The bod in question wasn't quite as dynamite as it had been ten months ago, however. Since her intake, starches and gallons of prison gravy had packed on thirty or forty pounds. Her hands were resting on her brown uniform pants. The top that went with them lay crumpled at her feet, revealing an XL sports bra. Claudia's boobs, Jeanette thought, were still pretty amazing.

Angel ladled coffee into a Styrofoam cup, splashing some on the floor in her amped-up enthusiasm. She held the cup out to Claudia. 'Drink it up, Ms Dynamite! Made strong to last long! Power by the hour, my sister!'

Claudia shook her head and kept staring at the tile floor.

'Claudia?' Jeanette asked. 'What's wrong?'

Some of the inmates were jealous of Claudia, but Jeanette liked her, and felt sorry for her. Claudia had embezzled a great deal of money from the Presbyterian church where she had been director of services in order to underwrite the ferocious drug habits of her husband and oldest son. And those two were both currently on the street, free as birds. I got a rhyme for you, Angel, Jeanette thought. Men play, women pay.

'Nothing's wrong, I'm just getting up my nerve.' Claudia didn't take her eyes from the floor.

'To do what?' Jeanette asked.

'To ask her to let me sleep normal, like her.'

Angel winked at Jeanette, let her tongue loll from the corner of her mouth, and made a couple of circles around one ear with her finger. 'Who you talking about, Ms Dynamite?'

'The new one,' Claudia said. 'I think she's the devil, Angel.'

This delighted Angel. 'Devil-Angel! Angel-Devil!' She made scales in the air, lifted them up and down. 'That's the story of my life, Ms Dynamite.'

Claudia droned on: 'She must be some kind of wicked, if she's the only one who can sleep like before.'

'I'm not getting you,' Jeanette said.

Claudia raised her head at last. There were purple scoops under her eyes. 'She's sleeping, but not in one of those cocoons. Go see for yourself. Ask how she's doing it. Tell her if she wants my soul, she can have it. I just want to see Myron again. He's my baby, and needs his mama.'

Angel dumped the cup of coffee she'd offered Claudia back into the urn, then turned to Jeanette. 'We are goin to see about this.' She didn't wait for Jeanette to agree.

When Jeanette arrived with the coffee wagon, Angel was gripping the bars and staring in. The woman Jeanette had glimpsed while Peters assaulted her now lay loose-limbed on her bunk, eyes closed, breathing evenly. Her dark hair spread out in a glorious fan. Her face was even more beautiful close up, and it was unblemished. Not only was she clear of the webbing, the bruises Jeanette had seen were gone. How was that possible?

Maybe she really is the devil, Jeanette thought. Or an angel, come to save us. Only that didn't seem likely. Angels didn't fly in this place. Other than Angel Fitzroy, that was, and she was more of a bat.

'Wake up!' Angel shouted.

'Angel?' She put a tentative hand on Angel's shoulder. 'Maybe you shouldn't—'

Angel shrugged Jeanette's hand off and tried to roll the cell door, but this one was locked. Angel grabbed the lid of the coffee urn and began to whang it against the bars, creating an ungodly racket that made Jeanette slap her hands over her ears.

'Wake up, bee-yatch! Wake up and smell the motherfucking coffee!'

The woman on the bunk opened her eyes, which were almond-shaped and as dark as her hair. She swung her legs down to the floor – long and lovely they were, even in her baggy intake coverall – and yawned. She stretched her arms, thrusting forward a pair of breasts that put Claudia's to shame.

'Company!' she cried.

Her bare feet hardly seemed to touch the floor as she ran across to the bars and reached through them, grasping one of Angel's hands and one of Jeanette's. Angel instinctively pulled away. Jeanette was too stunned. It felt like some mild electricity was passing from the new woman's hand and into her own.

'Angel! I'm so glad you're here! I can talk to the rats, but they're limited conversationalists. Not a criticism, just a reality. Each individual creature on its merits. My understanding is that Henry Kissinger is a fascinating discussion partner, yet consider all the blood that man has on his hands! Force me to choose, I'll take a rat, thank you, and you can print that in the newspaper, just be sure you spell my name right.'

'What in the *hail* are you talking about?' Angel asked.

'Oh, nothing really. Sorry to blabber. I was just visiting the world on the other side of the world. Scrambles my brains a little to go back and forth. And here's Jeanette Sorley! How's Bobby, Jeanette?'

'How do you know our names?' Angel asked. 'And how come you can sleep without growin that shit all over you?'

'I'm Evie. I came from the Tree. This is an interesting place, isn't it? So lively! So much to do and see!'

'Bobby's doing fine,' Jeanette said. Feeling as if she were in a dream . . . and perhaps she was. 'I'd like to see him again before I fall aslee—'

Angel yanked Jeanette back so hard she almost fell. 'Shut up, Jeanie. This ain't about your boy.' She reached into the soft cell and grabbed Evie by the admirably filled front of her coverall. 'How're you stayin awake? Tell me or I'll put a hurtin on you like you never had. I'll make your cunt and your asshole swap places.'

Evie gave a jolly laugh. 'That would be a medical marvel, wouldn't it? Why, I'd have to learn how to go to the bathroom all over again.'

Angel flushed. 'You want to play with me? You want to? You think just because you're in that cell, I cain't get at you?'

Evie looked down at the hands on her. Just looked. But Angel screamed and staggered back. Her fingers were turning red.

'Burned me! Bitch burned me somehow!'

Evie turned to Jeanette. She was smiling, but Jeanette thought there was sadness as well as good humor in those dark eyes. 'The problem is more complex than it first might appear – I see that. I do. There are feminists who like to believe that all the world's problems go back to men. To the innate aggressiveness of men. They have a point, a woman never started a war – although, trust me, some were definitely *about* them – but there are some bad, bad chickadees out there. I can't deny it.'

'What is this shit you're spouting?'

She looked back to Angel.

'Dr Norcross has his suspicions about you, Angel. About the landlord you killed in Charleston, for one thing.'

'I didn't kill *nobody*!' But the color had drained from Angel's face, and she took a step backward, bumping the coffee wagon. Her reddened hands were pressed to her chest.

Evie redirected to Jeanette, speaking in low tones of confidence. 'She's killed five men. *Five.*' And now she turned again to Angel. 'It was a kind of hobby for awhile there, wasn't it, Angel? You out hitchhiking to nowhere in particular, with a knife in your purse and a little .32 in the side pocket of that rawhide jacket you always used to wear. But that's not all, is it?'

'Shut up! *Shut up!*'

Back to Jeanette those amazing eyes went. Her voice was quiet but warm. It was the voice of a woman in a television ad, the one that told her friend that she also used to have problems with grass stains on her children's pants, only this new detergent had changed everything.

'She got pregnant when she was seventeen. Covered it up with big loose layers of clothes. Hitchhiked to Wheeling – didn't kill anyone that time, good for her – and took a room. Had the baby—'

'SHUT UP, I SAID!'

Someone with a video monitor had taken note of the confrontation: Rand Quigley and Millie Olson were pounding down the corridor, Quigley with Mace in hand, Olson with a Taser set on medium power.

'Drowned it in the sink, dropped the body down the incinerator chute.' Evie grimaced, blinked a couple of times, and added, softly, 'Pop goes the weasel.'

Quigley tried to grab Angel. She whirled instantly at his touch, threw a punch, and overturned the cart, coffee, juice, and all. A brown wash – no longer scalding, but still hot – poured over Millie Olson's legs. She screamed in pain, and fell on her behind.

Jeanette watched in amazement as Angel went full Hulk Hogan on Quigley, grasping his neck with one hand and clawing away the Mace with the other. The can hit the floor and rolled through the bars of the soft cell. Evie bent, picked it up, offered it to Jeanette.

'Want this?'

Jeanette accepted it unthinkingly.

Officer Olson was paddling around in a brown puddle, trying to get out from under the overturned coffee wagon. Officer Quigley was trying to keep from being choked out. Although Angel was skinny and Quigley outweighed her by at least fifty pounds, Angel shook him like a dog with a snake in its jaws, and tossed him into the coffee wagon just as Millie Olson was getting up, and they went down together with a thump and a splash. Angel whirled back to the soft cell, her eyes huge and glittering in her narrow little face.

Evie spread her arms as wide as the bars would allow and held them out to Angel, like a lover beckoning her beloved. Angel held her own arms out, her fingers bent into claws, and rushed at her, screaming.

Only Jeanette saw what happened next. The two officers were still trying to untangle themselves from the overturned coffee wagon, and Angel was lost in a world of fury. Jeanette had time to think, *I'm not just seeing bad temper; this is a full-blown psychotic episode.* Then Evie's mouth yawned open so widely that the entire bottom half of her face seemed to disappear. From her mouth came a flock – no, a *flood* – of moths. They swirled around Angel's head, and some caught in the peroxided up-spout of her hair. She screamed and began to beat at them.

Jeanette rapped Angel on the back of the head with the can of Mace. *I am going to make an enemy here,* she thought, *but hey, maybe she'll go to sleep before she can come back on me.*

The moths flew toward the caged overhead lights of A Wing and into the main prison. Angel turned, still tearing at her head (although all the insects in her hair now seemed to have joined their fellows), and Jeanette triggered the Mace directly into the screaming woman's face.

'You see how complex the problem is, don't you, Jeanette?' Evie said as Angel blundered into the wall, howling and furiously rubbing her eyes. 'I think it might be time to erase the whole man–woman equation. Just hit delete and start over. What do you think?'

'That I want to see my son,' Jeanette said. 'I want to see my Bobby.' She dropped the can of Mace and began to cry.

4

While this was happening, Claudia 'the Dynamite Body-a' Stephenson emerged from the delousing station and decided to seek climes more serene and vistas new. Just too noisy in A Wing this evening. Too upsetting. That special coffee was spilled everywhere, too, and it smelled really bad. You didn't want to go and attempt to parlay with the devil when your nerves were jumbled, that was common sense. She could talk to the lady in A-10 later. She passed the Booth and walked into B Wing. She left her top behind.

'Inmate!' Van Lampley leaned out of the Booth, where she had seen the fight about to break out. (Angel with her fucking Super Coffee; Van was too bushed to castigate herself, but she should never have consented to the plan.) She had sent Quigley and Olson to defuse the situation, and was about to rush out to join them when Stephenson passed through.

Claudia made no reply, just kept walking.

'You forgot something, didn't you? This is a prison, not a strip joint. Talking to you, Stephenson! Where do you think you're going?'

But did she, Van, really care? Lots of them were wandering now, probably just trying to stay awake, and meanwhile, there was a fuckaree going on down at the far end of A Wing. That was where she was needed.

She started that way, but then Millie Olson — splashed with coffee all down her front — waved her back. 'Under control,' Millie said. 'Got that crazy bitch Fitzroy locked up. Situation back to normal.'

Van, thinking that nothing was under control and nothing was normal, nodded.

She looked around for Stephenson and didn't see her. She returned to the Booth and called up the first floor of B Wing on one of the monitors in time to see Claudia entering B-7, the cell occupied by Dempster and Sorley. Only Sorley was still in A Wing, and Van hadn't seen Dempster in quite awhile. Inmates were not above a bit of petty theft if they found a cell empty (the favorite targets of opportunity were the two Ps — pills and panties), and such depredations inevitably caused trouble. She didn't have any reason to suspect Claudia, who was no nuisance in spite of being big enough to cause plenty of hassle, would do such a thing. Nonetheless, it was Van's job to be suspicious. It wouldn't do to have a rhubarb break out over a case of stolen property. Not with everything else that was going wrong.

Van decided to make a quick check. It was just a feeling, but she hadn't liked the way Claudia was walking, with her head down, her hair in her face, and her smock top cast off God knew where. It would only take a minute, and she could stand to stretch her legs. Get the blood flowing again.

5

Claudia didn't have theft on her mind. All she wanted was a bit of calm conversation. It would pass the time until A Wing settled down and she could speak to the new woman and find out how she, Claudia, could also go to sleep and wake up like on any other day. The new woman might not tell her, but then again, she might. The devil was unpredictable. He had been an angel once.

Ree was on her bunk with her face turned to the wall. Claudia noted for the first time, and not without pity, that Ree's hair was starting to turn gray. That was true of Claudia as well, but she dyed hers. When she couldn't afford the real stuff (or when none of her few visitors could be persuaded to bring her some Nutrisse Champagne Blonde, her favorite), she used ReaLemon from the kitchen. It worked pretty well, but didn't last very long.

She reached out to touch Ree's hair, then jerked back with a little cry when some of the gray stuck to her fingers. The threads wavered in the air for a second or two, then melted away to nothing.

'Oh, Ree,' Claudia mourned. 'Not you, too.'

But maybe it wasn't too late; there were only a few strands of that cocoon stuff in Ree's hair. Maybe God had sent Claudia to B-7 while there was still time. Maybe this was a test. She took Ree by the shoulder and rolled her onto her back. The webbing was spiraling out of Ree's cheeks and her poor scarred forehead, strands of it were emerging from her nostrils and eddying in her breath, but her face was still there.

Well, mostly.

Claudia used one hand to begin scrubbing the crap from Ree's cheeks, going from one side to the other, not neglecting the whitish threads emerging from her mouth and strapping themselves across her lips. With her other hand, Claudia grabbed Ree's shoulder and began to shake her.

'Stephenson?' From down the hallway. 'Inmate, what are you doing in there? That's not your cell.'

'Wake up!' Claudia cried, shaking harder. 'Wake up, Ree! Before you can't!'

Nothing.

'Inmate Stephenson? I'm talking to you.'

'That's Officer Lampley,' said Claudia, still shaking and still scraping at the relentless white threads – God, it was hard to stay ahead of them. 'I like her, don't you? Don't you, Ree?' Claudia began to cry. 'Don't go away, honey, it's too soon to go away!'

And at first she thought the woman on the bunk appeared to agree with that, because her eyes snapped open and she began to smile.

'Ree!' Claudia said. 'Oh, thank God! I thought you were—'

Only the smile continued to spread, the lips drawing back until it wasn't a smile at all but a teeth-baring snarl. Ree sat up and clamped her hands around Claudia's neck and bit off one of Claudia's favorite earrings, a little plastic kitten-face. Claudia screamed. Ree spat out the earring along with the attached scrap of earlobe, and went for Claudia's throat.

Claudia outweighed the diminutive Ree Dempster by seventy pounds, and she was strong, but Ree had gone insane. Claudia was barely able to hold her off. Ree's fingers slipped from Claudia's neck and her fingernails dug into the larger woman's bare shoulders, bringing blood.

Claudia staggered from the bunk and toward the open cell door, Ree clinging to her like a limpet, snarling and gnashing and jerking from side to side, trying to break Claudia's hold on her so she could move in and do real damage. Then they were in the hall and inmates were shouting, Officer Lampley was bellowing, and those sounds were in another galaxy, another universe, because Ree's eyes were bulging and Ree's teeth were chomping inches from Claudia's face and then, oh God, her feet tangled and Claudia went sprawling in the B Wing corridor with Ree on top of her.

'Inmate!' Van shouted. 'Inmate, let loose!'

Women were screaming. Claudia did not, at least to begin with. Screaming took strength, and she needed hers to hold the lunatic – *the demon* – away from her. Only it wasn't working. That snapping mouth was closing in. She could smell Ree's breath and see drops of Ree's spittle, with tiny white filaments dancing in each drop.

'Inmate, I have drawn my weapon! Don't make me fire it! *Please* don't make me do that!'

'Shoot her!' someone screamed, and Claudia realized the someone was her. It seemed she had enough strength, after all. '*Please, Officer Lampley!*'

There was a huge bang in the hallway. A large black hole appeared high in Ree's forehead, right in the middle of the grid of scar tissue. Her eyes swiveled up, as if she were trying to see where she'd been shot, and warm blood spattered across Claudia's face.

With a final galvanic effort, Claudia pushed Ree away. Ree hit the corridor with a limp thud. Officer Lampley stood with her legs braced and her service weapon held out before her in both hands. The smoke curling from the muzzle reminded Claudia of the white threads that had stuck to her fingers when she had brushed Ree's hair. Officer Lampley's face was dead pale save for the purple pouches under her eyes.

'She was going to kill me,' Claudia gasped.

'I know,' Van said. 'I know.'

CHAPTER 17

1

Halfway to town, Clint Norcross had a thought that caused him to pull into the lot of the Olympia Diner and park beside the easel sign reading MY OH MY, TRY OUR EGG PIE. He pulled out his phone and searched HICKS. He didn't have his number, which said everything about his relationship with Dooling Correctional's assistant warden. He scrolled further and found LAMPLEY.

Lampley picked up on the second ring. She sounded out of breath.

'Van? You okay?'

'Yeah, but you left before the fireworks. Listen, Doc, I had to shoot someone.'

'What? Who?'

'Ree Dempster. She's dead.' Van explained what had happened. Clint listened, aghast.

'Jesus,' he said when she was finished. 'Are you all right, Van?'

'Physically unhurt. Emotionally fucked to the sky, but you can psychoanalyze me later.' Van made a vast watery honking sound, blowing her nose on something. 'There's more.'

She told Clint about the violent confrontation between Angel Fitzroy and Evie Black. 'I wasn't there, but I saw part of it on the monitors.'

'Good thing you did. And Claudia. Sounds like you saved her life.'

'It wasn't a good thing for Dempster.'

'Van—'

'I liked Dempster. If you'd asked me, I would have said she was the last woman in here to go postal.'

'Where's her body?'

'In the janitor's closet.' Van sounded ashamed. 'It was all we could think of.'

'Of course.' Clint rubbed his forehead, eyes squeezed shut. He felt he ought to say more to comfort Lampley, but the words weren't there. 'And Angel? What about her?'

'Sorley, of all people, got hold of a Mace can and blasted her. Quigley and Olson bullrushed her into a cell in A Wing. She's currently beating on the walls and yelling for a doctor. Claims she's blind, which is bullshit. She's also claiming there are moths in her hair, which might not be bullshit. We've got an infestation of the bastards. You need to get back here, Doc. Hicks is having a melt-down. He asked me to surrender my weapon, which I refused to do, even though I suppose it's protocol.'

'You did the right thing. Until things settle down, protocol's out the window.'

'Hicks is useless.'

Don't I know it, Clint thought.

'I mean, he always was, but under these circumstances, he could actually be dangerous.'

Clint searched for a thread. 'You said Evie was egging Angel on. What exactly was she saying?'

'I don't know, and neither do Quigley or Millie, either. Sorley might. She was the one who slowed Angel's roll. Chick deserves a medal. If she doesn't crash out, you can get the whole story from her when you come back. Which will be soon, right?'

'ASAP,' said Clint. 'Listen, Van, I know you're upset, but I need to be clear on one thing. Angel started in on Evie because Evie wasn't in one of those cocoons?'

'That's my sense. I just saw her whacking on the bars with a lid from one of the coffee urns, and yelling her head off. Then I had my own fish to fry.'

'But she woke up?'

'Yeah.'

'*Evie woke up.*'

'Yeah. Fitzroy woke her up.'

Clint tried to make something coherent of this, and couldn't. Maybe after he got some sleep himself—

The idea caused a flush of guilt to heat his face. A wild idea came to him: What if Evie Black was male? What if his wife had arrested a guy in drag?

But no. When Lila arrested her, Evie had been buck naked. Presumably the female officers supervising her intake had seen her that way, too. And what would explain all her bruises and scrapes healing in less than half a day?

'I need you to pass on what I'm about to say to Hicks and the other officers who are still there.' Clint had come back around to the thought that had occurred to him in the first place, why he had pulled into the diner parking lot and called the prison.

'Won't take long,' she said. 'Billy Wettermore and Scott Hughes just came in, which is good news, but still, to call this a skeleton crew would be an insult to skeletons. We've got just seven warm bodies, counting Hicks. You'll make eight.'

Clint ignored this broad hint. 'It struck me as I was driving into town, this stuff about Eve Black being different from the rest of the women, on top of what you've told me now – I just don't know what to make of it. But I know that we can't let it leave the prison, not yet. True or false. It could cause a riot. Do you understand what I'm telling you?'

'Um . . .'

That *um* gave Clint a bad feeling. 'What is it?'

'Well . . .'

He liked that *well* even less.

'Just tell me.'

There was another wet honk. 'I saw Hicks using his cell phone after the free-for-all in A Wing was over, and after I refused to give him my weapon. Also, after Millie updated Scott and Billy, they were both using their phones.'

Too late, then. Clint closed his eyes. A quick fairy tale formed itself:

Once upon a time there was an obscure prison psychiatrist who dressed all in black, ran out into the night, and lay crosswise in the middle of a length of interstate. A Trailways bus came tooling along and put him out of his misery and everyone else lived happily ever after or maybe they didn't, but it was no longer the obscure prison psychiatrist's problem. The end.

'Okay, okay,' Clint said. 'Here's what we do: tell them no more calls, not to anybody. Have you got that?'

'I called my sister!' Van burst out. 'I'm sorry, Doc, but I wanted to do something good, something to make up for having to shoot Dempster! I told Bonnie not to go to sleep no matter how much she wanted to, because we might have an immune person in the prison, and *that* might mean there's a cure! Or that it cures itself!'

Clint opened his eyes. 'How long have you been up, Van?'

'Since four this morning! The goddam dog woke me up! She had to go out and p-p-*pee*!' Tough-as-nails Vanessa Lampley could hold back no longer. She began to cry.

'Just tell everyone on staff no more calls, got it?' It was almost certainly too late, but maybe they could slow the news. There might even be a way to put a pin in this. 'Call your sister back and tell her you were mistaken. Tell her it was a false rumor and you bought into it. Tell the others who made calls to do the same.'

Silence.

'Van, are you still there?'

'I don't want to, Dr Norcross. And, all due respect, I don't think that's the right way to go. Bonnie will stay awake now, at least through the night, because she believes there's a chance. I don't want to take that away.'

'I understand how you feel, but it *is* the right call. Do you want a bunch of people from town coming up to the prison like . . . like torch-carrying peasants storming the castle in an old *Frankenstein* movie?'

'Go see your wife,' Van said. 'You said she's been up even longer than me. See if you can look her in the face and not tell her there might be a little light at the end of the tunnel.'

'Van, listen—'

But Van was gone. Clint stared at the **CALL ENDED** message in the window of his phone for a long time before he put it in his pocket and drove the rest of the way into town.

Dempster was dead. Cheerful Ree Dempster. He couldn't believe it. And his heart ached for Van Lampley in spite of her insubordination. Although, really, how could she be insubordinate to him? He was just the jailhouse shrink, for God's sake.

2

Clint pulled into one of the 15 MINUTES ONLY spaces in front of the sheriff's station, and heard the last thing he would have expected: the sound of laughter spilling out through the open door.

There was quite a crew in the ready-room. Lila was sitting at the dispatch desk next to Linny. Ranged around them in a rough circle were five other deputies, all male – Terry Coombs, Reed Barrows, Pete Ordway, Elmore Pearl, and Vern Rangle. Sitting outside the circle of cops was Barry Holden, the public defender who had briefly handled Evie Black's case, and a white-bearded elderly gent that Clint knew from around town, Willy Burke.

Lila was smoking. She had stopped eight years ago, when Jared had one day remarked that he hoped she wouldn't die from lung cancer until he grew up. Linny Mars and two of the others present were also puffing away. The air was blue and fragrant.

'What's going on, guys?' he asked.

Lila saw him, and her face brightened. She snuffed her cigarette out in a coffee cup, ran across the room to him, and jumped into his arms. Literally, with her ankles hooked together at the backs of his thighs. She kissed him hard. This occasioned more laughter, a hoot from Attorney Holden, and a spatter of applause.

'Oh, am I glad to see you!' she said, and kissed him again.

'I was on my way to see Jared,' Clint said. 'I thought I'd stop and see if you were here, if you could get away.'

'Jared!' she cried. 'Can you believe what a great kid we raised, Clint? Gosh, as good a job as we did, sometimes I think it was selfish of us not to have a second one.' His wife thumped him on the chest and detached herself. Above her smile, Lila's pupils were pinpoints.

Terry Coombs came over. His eyes were red-rimmed and puffy. Terry shook Clint's hand. 'You know what happened to Roger, don't you? Tried to unwrap his wife. Bad idea. Should have waited for Christmas.' Terry burst into a peal of laughter that turned into a sob. 'My wife's gone, too. Can't get in touch with my kid.'

There was liquor on Terry's breath, but there had been none on Lila's; whatever she had ingested was a lot more up-tempo than booze. Clint thought of matching Terry by recounting what had just happened at the prison. He pushed the idea away. The death of Ree Dempster wasn't a party story, and that was exactly what this gathering looked like.

'I'm sorry, Terry.'

Pete Ordway hooked an arm over Terry's shoulder and drew him away.

Lila pointed to the bearded man. 'Hon, you know Willy Burke, don't you? He helped me transport Roger and Jessica to the morgue with his pickup truck. Except by morgue I actually mean the freezer at the Squeaky Wheel. Turns out the hospital is a no-go these days. Talk about low-rent, huh?' She giggled and clapped her hands to her face. 'I'm sorry. I can't help it.'

'Good to see you, sir,' Willy said. 'Got a fine wife there. She's well about her business, tired as she is.'

'Thanks.' And to his fine wife: 'I take it you've been into the evidence locker.'

'Just Lila and me,' Linny said. 'Terry had a little Scotch.'

Lila produced the Provigil scrip from her back pocket and gave it to Clint. 'No luck with this, or anything else. Two of the pharmacies have been looted, and the Rite Aid is nothing but ashes and embers. You probably smelled it when you came into town.'

Clint shook his head.

'We've been having what I guess you'd call a wake,' Vern said. 'Which is what I wish all the women would do.'

For a moment everyone looked puzzled. Then Barry started

laughing, and the other deputies, and Willy and Lila and Linny joined in. The sound was jarringly merry.

'A wake,' Lila said. She punched Clint on the arm. '*Awake*. Get it?'

'Got it,' Clint said. He had stepped into the law enforcement version of Wonderland.

'Sober over here,' Willy Burke said, raising his hand. 'I make a little from time to time—' He shot a wink at Lila: 'You didn't hear that, Sheriff – but I don't touch the stuff. Been teetotal for going on forty years.'

'I must admit I appropriated Mr Burke's nip for myself,' said Barry Holden. 'Seemed like the right thing to do, given all that's going on.'

Deputies Barrows, Ordway, Pearl, and Rangle declared themselves sober, Vern Rangle raising his own hand as if he were testifying in court. Clint was beginning to be angry. It was the laughter. He understood it, certainly Lila was entitled to get a little wonky after thirty or more hours of sleeplessness, and getting into the evidence locker had been his own idea, but he still didn't like it a bit. On the drive into town, he'd thought himself ready for just about anything, but he hadn't been prepared to hear about Van shooting Ree, and he hadn't been ready to walk in on an Irish wake at the sheriff's station.

Lila was saying, 'We were just talking about the time Roger rolled on a domestic and the lady of the house leaned out of an upstairs window and told him to fuck off and die. When he wouldn't do either, she poured a bucket of paint on his head. He was still scrubbing it out of his hair a month later.'

'Dutch Boy Rhumba Red!' Linny screamed with laughter and dropped her cigarette in her lap. She picked it up, almost puffed on the lit end, and dropped it on the floor trying to get it turned around. That brought on more general laughter.

'What did you take?' Clint asked. 'You and Linny? Was it the coke?'

'No, we're saving the blow for later,' Lila said.

'Don't worry, Sheriff, I'll defend you,' Barry said. 'I'll plead exigent circumstances. No jury in America will convict.'

That caused another explosion of hilarity.

'We took in over a hundred Blue Scooties in the Griner brothers bust,' Linny said. 'Lila opened one of the capsules, and we snorted the powder.'

Clint thought of Don Peters, first getting Jeanette Sorley to perform a sex act on him in the common room, then drugging Janice's java. He thought of the idiotic coffee-mix that Coates had signed off on. He thought of the strange woman in A Wing. He thought of Ree choking Claudia and trying to open her throat with her teeth. He thought of terrified inmates crying in their cells, and of Vanessa Lampley saying, *I don't want to, Dr Norcross.*

'I see it worked,' Clint said. To hold himself in took a concentrated effort. 'You seem very awake.'

Lila took Clint's hands. 'I know how it looks, honey – how *we* look – but we had no choice. The pharmacies are a bust, and anything of a speedy nature that the supermarkets sell is long gone. Jared told me. I spoke with him. He's all right, you know, you don't have to worry, you—'

'Uh-huh. Can I talk to you alone for a minute?'

'Of course.'

3

They walked outside into the cool night. Now he could smell ashes and burning plastic – all that remained of the Rite Aid, he supposed. Behind them, the conversation started up again. And the laughter.

'Now, what's going on with Jared?'

She put up a hand, like a crossing guard. Like he was an aggressive driver. 'He's babysitting a little girl named Molly. She's old Mrs Ransom's granddaughter. Mrs Ransom is cocooned, so he took charge. He's all right for now. You don't need to worry about him.'

No, he thought, don't tell me not to worry about our son. Until he turns eighteen, *our* job is to worry about him. Are you so drugged that you've forgotten that?

'Or at least, not any more than you have to,' she added after a moment.

She's tired and she's got a lot on her plate, Clint reminded himself. She just killed a woman, for God's sake. You have no reason to be angry with her. But he *was* angry, just the same. Logic had very little power over emotions. As a shrink he knew that, not that knowing it was any help at this moment.

'Any idea how long you've been awake?'

She closed one eye, calculating. It gave her a piratical aspect he didn't care for. 'Since maybe . . . one o'clock or so yesterday afternoon, I guess. That makes it . . .' She shook her head. 'Can't do the math. Boy, my heart's pounding. But I'm wide awake, there's that. And look at the stars! Aren't they pretty?'

Clint could do the math. It came to roughly thirty-two hours.

'Linny went on the Internet to see how long a person can go without sleep,' Lila said brightly. 'The record is two hundred sixty-four hours, isn't that interesting? Eleven days! It was set by a high school kid who was doing a science project. I'll tell you, that record is going *down*. There are some very determined women out there.

'Cognition declines pretty quickly, though, and then emotional restraint. In addition, there's this phenomenon called microsleep, which I myself experienced out at Truman Mayweather's trailer, whoo, that was scary, I felt the first strands of that stuff coming right out of my hair. On the bright side, humans are diurnal mammals, and that means as soon as the sun comes up, all the women who've managed to stay awake through the night will get a boost. It's apt to be gone by mid-afternoon tomorrow, but—'

'It's too bad you had to pull that graveyard shift last night,' Clint said. The words were out before he even knew they were on the way.

'Yeah.' The laughter went out of her at once. 'It is too bad I had to do that.'

'No,' said Clint.

'Pardon?'

'A pet food truck did overturn on Mountain Rest Road, that much is true, but it happened a year ago. So what were you doing last night? Where the hell were you?'

Her face was very white, but in the darkness, her pupils had grown to more or less their normal size. 'Are you sure that's something you want to get into right now? With everything else that's going on?'

He might have said no, but then another burst of that infuriating laughter came from inside, and he gripped her arms. 'Tell me.'

Lila looked at his hands on her biceps, then at him. He let go and stepped back from her.

'At a basketball game,' said Lila. 'I went to see a girl play. Number thirty-four. Her name is Sheila Norcross. Her mother is Shannon Parks. So tell me, Clint, who's been lying to who?'

He opened his mouth – to say what, he didn't know – but before he could say anything at all, Terry Coombs burst out through the door, eyes wild. 'Oh, Jesus, Lila! Jesus fuckin God!'

She turned away from Clint. 'What?'

'We forgot! How could we forget? Oh, *Jesus*!'

'Forgot what?'

'Platinum!'

'Platinum?'

She only stared at him, and what Clint saw on her face caused his rage to collapse. Her perplexed expression said she sort of knew what he was talking about, but couldn't put it in any context or frame of reference. She was too tired.

'Platinum! Roger and Jessica's baby daughter!' Terry shouted. 'She's only eight months old, and she's still at their house! *We forgot the fucking baby!*'

'Oh dear God,' Lila said. She spun and ran down the steps with Terry on her heels. Neither of them looked at Clint, or looked around when he called after them. He took the steps two at a time and caught Lila by the shoulder before she could get into her car. She was in no shape to drive, neither of them were, but he could see that wouldn't stop them.

'Lila, listen. The baby is almost certainly okay. Once they're in those cocoons, they seem to enter a kind of steady state, like life support.'

She shrugged his hand away. 'We'll talk later. I'll meet you at the house.'

Terry was behind the wheel. Terry who had been drinking.

'Hope you're right about that baby, Doc,' he said, and slammed the door.

4

Near Fredericksburg, the spare tire the warden's daughter had been driving on for several weeks blew at the least opportune time, the way her mother – maniacally dedicated, as mothers and wardens are wont to be, to the calculation of worst case scenarios – would have warned her that it inevitably would. Michaela eased her car to a stop at a McDonald's parking lot. She went inside to pee.

A biker guy, massive and bare-chested except for a leather vest with SATAN'S 7 stitched on it, and what appeared to be a Tec-9 strapped over his back, was at the counter. He was explaining to a raccoon-eyed counter girl that, no, he wouldn't be paying for any of his Big Macs. There was a special tonight; everything he wanted was free. At the hush of the door closing, the biker guy turned to see Michaela.

'Hey, sister.' His look was appreciative: *not bad.* 'I know you?'

'Maybe?' Michaela replied, not stopping as she strode up the side of the McDonald's, skipping the bathroom, and continuing right back outside again through the rear exit door. She hustled for the rear of the parking lot and pushed between the branches of a hedge. On the other side of the hedge was the parking lot for a Hobby Lobby. The store was lit and she could see people inside. Michaela wondered how goddam dedicated to your scrapbooking you had to be to go shopping at Hobby Lobby on this night of all nights.

She took a step and something closer caught her attention: a Corolla idling about twenty feet away. A white form occupied the front seat.

Michaela approached the car. The white form was a woman, of course, head and hands cocooned. Although Michaela was still high from the coke, she wished she were much, much higher. In the cocooned woman's lap was a dead dog, a poodle, the body wrung and twisted.

Oh, Fido, you shouldn't lick the webs off Mommy's face when she's snoozing in the parking lot. Mommy can be very cross if you wake her up.

Michaela gingerly transported the dead dog to the grass. Then she dragged the woman, by her driver's license Ursula Whitman-Davies, over to the front passenger side. While she didn't much like the idea of keeping the woman in the car, she was deeply uncomfortable with the alternative, which would be depositing her in the grass next to her dead poodle. And there was the utilitarian to consider: with Ursula along, she could legally use the carpool lane.

Michaela got behind the wheel and rolled onto the service road that would take her back to I-70.

As she passed the McDonald's, an evil idea struck her. It was no doubt coke-fueled, but it seemed divinely right, nevertheless. She turned around at the Motel 6 next door and went back to Mickey D's. Parked right in front and heeled over on its kickstand was a Harley Softail that looked vintage. Above the Tennessee plate on the rear fender was a skull decal with SATAN'S in one eyesocket and 7 in the other. Written across the teeth was BEWARE.

'Hang on, Ursula,' Michaela said to her cocooned co-pilot, and aimed the Corolla at the motorcycle.

She was doing less than ten miles an hour when she struck it, but it went over with a satisfying crash. The biker guy was sitting at a table by the front window, with a mountain of food stacked before him on a tray. He looked up in time to see Michaela backing away from his iron horse, which now looked like one dead pony. She could see his lips moving as he ran for the door, a Big Mac dripping Secret Sauce in one hand and a milkshake in the other, Tec-9 bouncing against his back. Michaela couldn't tell what he was saying, but she doubted if it was *shalom*. She gave him a cheerful wave before swinging back onto the service road and putting Ursula's Toyota up to sixty.

Three minutes later, she was back on the interstate, laughing wildly, knowing that the euphoria wouldn't last, and wishing for more blow so that it might.

5

Ursula's Corolla was equipped with satellite radio, and after fiddling with the buttons for awhile, Michaela found NewsAmerica. The news was not so terrific. There were unconfirmed reports of an 'incident' involving the vice-president's wife that had caused the Secret Service to be summoned to Number One, Observatory Circle. Animal rights activists had set free the inhabitants of the National Zoo; multiple witnesses had seen a lion devouring what looked like a human being on Cathedral Avenue. Hard right conservatives on talk radio were proclaiming the Aurora virus as proof that God was angry with feminism. The pope had asked everyone to pray for guidance. The Nationals had canceled their weekend interleague series against the Orioles. Michaela sort of understood this last one, but sort of didn't; all the players (the umpires, too) were men, weren't they?

In the passenger seat, the cotton-ball-headed creature that had been Ursula Whitman-Davies mimicked the rhythm of the interstate, lolling gently with the stretches of smooth macadam, jittering around when the tires found grooved, unfinished paving. She was either the absolute best or absolute worst traveling companion in the history of the world.

For awhile Michaela had dated a girl who was devoted to crystals, who believed that, with calm focus and sincere belief, you could take the form of light. That sweet, earnest girl was probably asleep now, swathed in white. Michaela thought of her own late father: good old Dad, who used to sit beside her bed when she was scared at night – or at least, that's what her mother had told her. Michaela had been three when he'd died. She couldn't remember him as a living man. Michaela – despite her nose job, despite her fake last name – was a true reporter. She knew the facts, and the one fact about Archie Coates that she did know well, was that he had been placed in a coffin and planted in the soil of the Shady Hills Cemetery in the town of Dooling, and was there still. He had not become light. She did not allow herself to fantasize that she was soon to meet her dad in some afterlife. The deal was simply this: the world was ending and a poodle-strangling woman clothed in webs was swaying beside Michaela and all she wanted was to have a few hours with her mother before sleep took them both.

At Morgantown she had to refill the Corolla's tank. It was full-service. The young guy who pumped the gas apologized; the credit card machines were down. Michaela paid him from a wad in Ursula's purse.

The guy had a short blond beard, wore a plain white tee-shirt and blue jeans. She had never been especially attracted to men, but she liked the look of this lean Viking.

'Thank you,' she said. 'You hanging in there?'

'Oh,' he said, 'forget about me, lady. You don't need to be worrying about me. You know how to use that?'

She followed the tilt of his chin to Ursula's purse, which rested at the hip of the cocooned woman. The grip of a revolver protruded from its unzipped mouth. It seemed that Ms Whitman-Davies had fancied firearms as well as canines.

'Not really,' she admitted. 'My girlfriend knew I was making a long drive and loaned it to me.'

He gave her a stern look. 'Safety'll be on the side. Make sure it's switched off if you see trouble coming. Point it at the middle of Mr Trouble's body – center mass – and pull the trigger. Don't let go or get hit in the boob when it recoils. Can you remember that?'

'Yeah,' said Michaela. 'Center mass. Don't let go or get hit in the boob. Gotcha. Thanks.' And rolled out. She heard the Viking call, 'Hey, you on TV, maybe?'

Around one o'clock on Friday morning, she finally arrived on the outskirts of Dooling. Drifts of smoke from the fire in the woods rolled across West Lavin as she piloted the Corolla toward the long, low outline of the prison in the dark. The smoke made Michaela press a hand over her mouth to keep from inhaling the reek of ash.

At the gate, she stepped from the car, and punched the red call button.

6

Maura Dunbarton sat in her B Wing cell with what remained of Kayleigh, not dead but dead to this world. Did she dream inside her shroud?

Maura sat with her hand on Kayleigh's chest, feeling the gentle rise and fall of her respiration and watching the white mat of fibrous gunk first puffing out, then pulling back in, outlining Kayleigh's open mouth with each inhalation. Twice Maura had set her nails into that thick and slightly sticky material, on the verge of ripping it open and setting Kayleigh free. Both times she thought of what the TV news had been reporting and took her hands away.

In a closed society like Dooling Correctional, both rumors and cold germs spread fast. But what had happened an hour ago in A Wing was no rumor. Angel Fitzroy was caged up, eyes swollen from Mace. Raving about how the new woman was a fucking witch.

This to Maura seemed perfectly possible, especially after Claudia Stephenson crept through B Wing, wearing bruises on her neck and deep scratches on her shoulders, telling all and sundry how Ree almost killed her, and all she had seen and overheard before that. Claudia claimed the new woman had known Jeanette and Angel's names, but that was only the least of it. She also knew – *knew!* – that Angel had killed at least five men and a newborn baby.

'The woman's name is Evie, like Eve in the Garden of Eden,' Claudia said. 'Think about that! Then Ree tried to kill me, and I bet the witch knew that was going to happen, just like she knew them others' names, and about Angel's baby.'

Claudia was not what anyone would call a reliable witness, but it still made sense. Only a witch could know such things.

Two stories came together in Maura's head and combined there to make a certainty. One was about a beautiful princess who was cursed by a wicked witch and fell into a deep sleep when she pricked her finger on a spindle. (Maura wasn't sure what a spindle was, but it must be sharp.) After countless years, a kiss awakened the princess from her slumber. The other was the story of Hansel and Gretel. Captured by a witch, they kept their cool and escaped after burning the hag alive in her own oven.

Stories were only stories, but the ones that survived over hundreds of years must contain nuggets of truth. The truth in these two could be: spells could be broken; witches could be destroyed. Popping off the witch-woman in A Wing might not wake up Kayleigh and all the other women in the world. On the other hand, it might. It really might. Even if it didn't, the woman named Evie had to have *something* to do with this plague. Why else would she be able to sleep and wake normally? How else could she know things she had no way of knowing?

Maura had been in prison for decades. She had done a lot of reading, and even made her way through the Bible. It had seemed like a fairly worthless stack of paper at the time, men creating laws and women begetting beget-me-nots, but she remembered a compelling line: *Thou shalt not suffer a witch to live.*

A plan assembled itself in Maura's mind. She would need a bit of luck to execute it. But with half the guards AWOL and the prison's ordinary nighttime routine all shot to hell, maybe not too much. Angel Fitzroy hadn't been able to do it, because all of Angel's rage was on the surface, for anyone to see. That was why she was currently in a locked cell. Maura's rage, on the other hand, was a deeply banked fire, its glowing coals masked with ashes. Which was why she was a trustee, with the run of the prison.

'I'll be back, honey,' she said, patting Kayleigh's shoulder. 'Unless she kills me, that is. If she's a real witch, I guess she might.'

Maura lifted her mattress and felt for the tiny slit she'd made. She reached in and brought out a toothbrush. The hard plastic handle had been sharpened to a point. She slid it into the elastic waistband of her pants at the small of her back, bloused her baggy top over it, and left her cell. In the B Wing corridor, she turned back, and blew her faceless cellmate a kiss.

7

'Inmate, what are you doing?'

It was Lawrence Hicks, standing in the doorway of Dooling Correctional's small but surprisingly well-stocked library. He normally favored three-piece suits and dark ties, but tonight both his jacket and vest were gone, and the tie was pulled down so that the end flapped over the top of his fly, like an arrow pointing to his no doubt shriveled junk.

'Hello, Mr Hicks,' Maura said, continuing to load paperbacks onto a rolling library cart. She gave him a smile, her one gold tooth sparkling in the overhead fluorescents. 'I'm going on a book run.'

'Isn't it a little late for that, inmate?'

'I don't think so, sir. No lights-out tonight, I don't think.'

She spoke respectfully and continued to smile. That was the way you did it; you smiled and looked harmless. It's just old, gray Maura Dunbarton, beaten down by years of prison routine and happy to lick the shoes of anyone whose shoes needed licking, whatever harpy that had possessed her to kill those people long since exorcised. That was a grift the Angel Fitzroys of the world never learned. You had to keep your powder dry in case you ever needed it.

He came in to inspect her cart, and she could almost feel sorry for him — face all pale, beard-speckled jowls hanging like dough, what little hair he had mussed up — but if he tried to stop her, she'd stick him in his fat gut. She had to save Kayleigh if she possibly could. Sleeping Beauty had been saved with a kiss; Maura might be able to save her girl with a shiv.

Don't get in my way, Hicksie, she thought. Not unless you want a hole in your liver. I know right where it is.

Hicks was examining the paperbacks Maura had culled from the shelves: Peter Straub, Clive Barker, Joe Hill.

'These are all horror stories!' Hicks exclaimed. 'We let inmates read this stuff?'

'This and the romances is about all they *do* read, sir,' Maura told him, not adding, *Which you'd know if you knew anything about the way this place works, you weasel.* She refreshed her smile. 'I figure horror stories are what will keep the ladies awake tonight, if anything will. Besides, ain't none of this stuff real; all vampires and werewolves and such. They're like fairy tales.'

For a moment he seemed to hesitate, maybe getting ready to tell her to go back to her cell. Maura reached around to the small of her back, as if scratching an itch there. Then he puffed out his cheeks in a sigh. 'Go on. At least it'll keep *you* awake.'

This time her smile was genuine. 'Oh, don't worry about me, Mr Hicks. I suffer from insomnia.'

8

Michaela had ceased pressing the button and now just held it down. Light blazed from the glassed-in front area of the prison, and there were cars parked in the lot; someone was awake in there.

'What?' The male voice that answered was the definition of weary; it was a voice with a ten o'clock shadow. 'This is Officer Quigley. Cut it out with the damn button.'

'My name is Michaela Morgan.' A second later she remembered that her TV name meant nothing here.

'So?' The voice was not impressed.

'I used to be Michaela Coates. My mother is the warden. I would like to see her, please.'

'Uh . . .'

Silence, except for a faint buzz on the line. She straightened up, her patience exhausted. She thumbed the call button as hard as she could. 'I'll also have you know that I work for NewsAmerica. Do I need to do an exposé on you, or can I speak with my mother?'

'I'm sorry, Ms Coates. She fell asleep.'

Now it was Michaela's turn to be silent. She was too late. She sagged against the chainlink. The headlights of the Corolla bounced back from the front of the gate, and dazzled her swollen eyes.

'I'm sorry,' came the voice. 'She was a good boss.'

'What do I do now?' Michaela asked. She wasn't pressing the call button so the question was only directed to the night and the smoke leaking from the woods.

Officer Quigley came back with the answer, as if he had heard. 'Go on into town, why don't you? Get a room. Or . . . I hear the Squeaky Wheel's got an open bar tonight and they're not closing till the sun rises or the beer runs out.'

9

Maura rolled her cart down B Wing, going slow, not wanting anyone to think she had any particular goal in mind.

'Books?' she inquired at each occupied cell – at least at those where the occupants weren't covered in white shit. 'Want to read some scary stuff? I got nine different flavors of boogeyman.'

She had few takers. Most of them were watching the news, which was a horror story in itself. Officer Wettermore stopped her near B Wing to have a look at the titles on her cart. Maura wasn't that surprised to see him here tonight, because Officer Wettermore was as gay as New Orleans on the first night of Mardi Gras. If he had any womenfolk at home, she'd be astounded.

'That looks like a bunch of garbage to me,' he said. 'Go on and get out of here, Maura.'

'Okay, Officer. Going down A Wing now. A couple of the ladies down there, Dr Norcross has got them in the Prozac Posse, but they still like to read.'

'Fine, but keep your distance from both Fitzroy and the soft cell at the end, right?'

Maura gave him her biggest smile. 'Absolutely, Officer Wettermore. And thank you! Thank you very much!'

Other than the new one – the witch – there were only two wakeful women in A Wing, plus the sleeping heap that had been Kitty McDavid.

'No,' said the woman in A-2. 'Can't read, can't read. The meds Norcross has me on screw up my eyes. Can't read, no. Been shouting in here. I don't like shouting.'

The other woman, in A-8, was Angel. She looked at Maura with puffy what-the-fuck-happened-to-me eyes. 'Keep rolling, Mo-Mo,' she warned when Maura, in spite of Officer Wettermore's admonition, offered her a couple of the books. That was okay. Maura was almost at the end of the corridor now. She glanced over her shoulder and saw Wettermore with his back to her, in deep conversation with Officer Murphy, the one the girls called Tigger, like in the Pooh stories.

'Maura . . .'

It was only a whisper, but penetrating. Resonant, somehow.

It was the new one. Evie. Eve. Who in the Bible had eaten from the Tree of Knowledge and gotten both her and her hubby banished into this world of pain and perplexity. Maura knew banishment, knew it well. She had been banished to Dooling for banishing her husband and her two kids (not to mention Slugger) to the vastness of eternity.

Evie stood at the barred door of the soft cell, gazing at Maura. And smiling. Maura had never seen such a beautiful smile in her life. A witch, maybe, but gorgeous. The witch put a hand through the bars and beckoned with one long and elegant finger. Maura rolled her cart onward.

'No further, inmate!' That was Officer Tig Murphy. 'Stop right there!'

Maura kept going.

'Get her, stop her!' Murphy yelled, and she heard the clatter-clap of their hard shoes on the tiles.

Maura turned the cart sideways and pitched it over, creating a temporary roadblock. Tattered paperbacks flew and skidded.

'*Stop, inmate, stop!*'

Maura hustled for the soft cell, reaching around to the small of her back and whipping out the toothbrush shiv. The witch-woman still beckoned. She doesn't see what I got for her, Maura thought.

She drew her arm back along her hip, meaning to piston it forward into the witch-woman's midsection. Into her liver. Only those dark eyes first slowed her, then stopped her. It wasn't evil Maura saw in them, but chilly interest.

'You want to be with her, don't you?' Evie asked in a rapid whisper.

'Yes,' Maura said. 'Oh my God, so much.'

'You can be. But first you must sleep.'

'I can't. Insomnia.'

Wettermore and Murphy were coming. There were only seconds to stick the witch-woman and end this plague. Only Maura didn't. The stranger's dark eyes held her fast and she found that she did not wish to struggle against that hold. They weren't eyes at all, Maura saw, but gaps, openings into a new darkness.

The witch-woman pressed her face against the bars, her eyes never leaving Maura's. 'Kiss me quick. While there's still time.'

Maura didn't think. She dropped the sharpened toothbrush and pressed her own face to the bars. Their lips met. Eve's warm breath slipped into Maura's mouth and down her throat. Maura felt blessed sleep rising from the bottom of her brain, as it had when she was a child, safe in her own bed with Freddy the Teddy curled in one arm and Gussie the stuffed dragon curled in the other. Listening to a cold wind outside and knowing she was safe and warm inside, bound for the land of dreams.

When Billy Wettermore and Tig Murphy reached her, Maura was lying on her back outside Evie's cell, the first strands spinning out of her hair, out of her mouth, and from beneath the closed lids of her dreaming eyes.

CHAPTER 18

1

Frank expected another heaping helping of bullshit from Elaine when he returned to the house, but it turned out to be a zero-bullshit situation. Like nothing else that day – or, for that matter, in the days to come – his problems solved themselves the easy way. So why didn't he feel at all cheered?

His estranged wife lay asleep in their daughter's bed with her right arm looped over Nana's shoulder. The cocoon around her face was thin, a tight first coating of papier maché, but a complete coating nonetheless. A note on the bedside table read, *I prayed for you, Frank. I hope you will pray for us. – E.*

Frank crumpled the note and threw it in the trashcan beside the bed. Tiana, the black Disney princess, danced across the side of the bin in her glittering green dress, followed by a parade of magical animals.

'There are no adequate words.' Garth Flickinger had followed him upstairs and now stood behind Frank in the doorway to Nana's room.

'Yeah,' said Frank. 'I guess that's right.'

There was a framed photo of Nana and her parents on the bedside table. Nana was holding up her prize bookmark. The doctor picked up the photo and studied it. 'She has your cheekbones, Mr Geary. Lucky girl.'

Frank didn't know how to reply to that, so he said nothing.

The doctor, untroubled by the silence, set the photo back down. 'Well. Shall we?'

They left Elaine in the bed and for the second time that day Frank took his daughter into his arms and carried her down the stairs. Her chest rose and fell; she was alive in there. But braindead coma patients had heartbeats, too. There was a good chance that their last exchange, the one Frank would take to his own death – whenever that might come – would be from the morning, him barking at her in the driveway. Scaring her.

Melancholy overtook Frank, a ground fog devouring him from the boots upward. He didn't have any reason to expect that this dope-fiend doc would actually be able to do anything to help.

Flickinger, meanwhile, spread towels across the hardwood floor in the living room and asked Frank to lay Nana down on them.

'Why not the sofa?'

'Because I want the overhead lights on her, Mr Geary.'

'Oh. Okay.'

Garth Flickinger settled on his knees beside Nana and opened his medical bag. His bloodshot and red-rimmed eyes gave him a vampiric look. His narrow nose and a high, sloping forehead, framed by auburn curls, added an elfin hint of derangement. Nonetheless, and even though Frank knew he was at least some-what fucked up, his tone was soothing. No wonder he drove a Mercedes.

'So, what do we know?'

'We know she's asleep,' Frank said, feeling singularly stupid.

'Ah, but there's so much more to it! What I've picked up from the news is basically this: the cocoons are a fibrous material that seems to be composed of snot, spit, earwax, and large amounts of some unknown protein. How is it being manufactured? Where is it coming from? We don't know, and it would seem to be impossible, given that normal female extrusions are much smaller – two table-spoons of blood in a woman's normal menstrual period, for example, no more than a cup even in a heavy one. We also know that the sleepers appear to be sustained by the cocoons.'

'And they go nuclear when the cocoons are breached,' Frank said.

'Right.' Garth laid out instruments on the coffee table: scalpel, trimmers, and, from the black case, a small microscope. 'Let's begin by taking your daughter's pulse, shall we?'

Frank said that was fine.

Flickinger carefully lifted Nana's encased wrist and held it for thirty seconds. Then he lowered it just as carefully. 'Resting heart rate is slightly muffled by the cocooning material, but it's in the normal range for a healthy girl her age. Now, Mr Geary—'

'Frank.'

'Fine. What do we *not* know, Frank?'

The answer was obvious. 'Why this is happening.'

'*Why.*' Flickinger clapped once. 'That's it. Everything in nature has a purpose. What is the purpose of this? What is the cocoon trying to do?' He picked up his trimmers and clicked the blades open and shut. 'So let us interrogate.'

2

When she had no one else to talk to, Jeanette sometimes talked to herself – or rather, to an imagined listener who was sympathetic. Dr Norcross had told her this was perfectly okay. It was *articulation*. Tonight that listener was Ree, who had to be imagined. Because Officer Lampley had killed her. Soon she might try to find where they'd put her, pay her respects, but right now just sitting in their cell was good enough. Right now it was all she needed.

'I'll tell you what happened, Ree. Damian hurt his knee playing football, that's what happened. Just a pickup game with some guys at the park. I wasn't there. Damian told me no one even touched him – he just pushed off, going to rush the quarterback I guess, heard a pop, fell down in the grass, came up limping. ACL or an MCL, I always forget which, but you know, one of those. The part that cushions between the bones.'

Ree said Uh-huh.

'At that time we were doing okay, except for we didn't have the health insurance. I had a thirty-hour-a-week job at a daycare center, and Damian had a regular off-the-books thing that paid unbelievable.

Like, twenty an hour. Cash! He was working as sort of the sideman for this small-time contractor who did cabinetry for rich people in Charleston, politicians and CEOs and stuff. Big Coal guys. Damian did a lot of lifting and so on. We were doing great, especially for a couple of kids with nothing but high school diplomas. I was proud of myself.'

Ree said You had every right to be.

'We got the apartment and it was good, nice furniture and everything, nicer than anything I had when I was a kid. He bought this motorcycle almost brand new, and we leased a car for me to drive myself and our boy Bobby around in. We drove down to Disney. Did Space Mountain, Haunted Mansion, hugged Goofy, the whole nine yards. I loaned my sister money to see a dermatologist. Gave my mother some money to get her roof fixed. But no health insurance. And Damian's got this fucked-up knee. Surgery was the best option, but . . . We just should have bit the bullet and done it. Sold the motorcycle, let go of the car, tightened up for a year. That's what I wanted to do then. I swear. But Damian didn't want to. Refused. Hard to get around that. It was his knee, so I let it alone. Men, you know. Won't stop and ask for directions, and won't go to a doc until they're just about dying.'

Ree said You got that right, girlfriend.

'"Nah," he says. "I'm going to stick it out." And I must admit we did have a party habit. We always partied. Like kids do. Ecstasy. Weed, obviously. Coke if someone had it. Damian had some downers hid away. Started taking them to keep his knee from hurting him too much. Self-medicating, Dr Norcross calls it. And you know my headaches? My Blue Meanies?'

Ree said I sure do.

'Yeah. So one night I tell Damian my head's killing me, and he gives me a pill. "Try one of these," he says. "See if it don't sand the edge off." And that's how I got hooked. Right through the bag. Easy as that. You know?'

Ree said I know.

3

The news became too much for Jared, so he switched to the Public Access channel, where an extremely enthusiastic craftswoman was giving a lesson on beading fringe. It had to be a pre-recording. If it wasn't, if this was the craftswoman's actual current mien, he wouldn't have wanted to meet her on a normal day. 'We are going to make something *bea-utiful*!' she cried, bouncing on a stool in front of a gray backdrop.

The craftswoman was his only companion. Molly had fallen asleep.

Around one he had ducked out to use the john. When he returned three minutes later she was passed out on the couch. Clutching the can of Mountain Dew he'd given her, her poor kid face already half-covered in webs.

Jared crashed out himself for a couple of hours in the leather armchair. His exhaustion had swamped his distress.

An acrid smell awakened him, drifting in through the screen doors, the sensory alert of a distant fire. He drew the glass doors shut and returned to the armchair. On the TV, the camera focused tight on the craftswoman's hands as they wove a needle in and out, over and under.

It was 2:54 on Friday morning. A new day according to the clock, but it felt like the previous day wouldn't be letting them go anytime soon, if ever.

Jared had ventured across the street to requisition Mrs Ransom's cell phone from her purse. He texted Mary on it now:

Hey, it's Jared. You ok?

Yeah, but do you know if something is on fire?

Think so, but I don't know what. How is your mother? How is your sister? How are you?

We're all fine. Drinking coffee and baking brownies. Sunrise here we come!! How's Molly?

Jared glanced at the girl on the couch. He'd draped her with a blanket. The covering on her head was round and white.

Great, he wrote. *Chugging Mountain Dew. This is her granny's phone I'm using.*

Mary said she'd text him again soon. Jared returned his attention to the television. The craftswoman was inexhaustible, it seemed.

'Now I know this'll upset some people, but I just do not care for glass. It scratches up. It's my *true conviction* you can do just as well with plastic.' The camera went tight on a pink bead she held between her thumb and forefinger. 'See, not even an expert eye's likely to tell the difference.'

'Pretty good,' Jared said. He had never been one to talk to himself, but he had never been alone in his house with a white-swathed body while the woods burned, either. And there was no denying that little pink fucker looked like glass to his eye. 'Pretty dang good, lady.'

'Jared? Who are you talking to?'

He hadn't heard the front door open. He leaped to his feet, wobbled four or five steps on his aching knee, and threw himself in his father's arms.

Clint and Jared stood, locked together between the kitchen and the living room. They both wept. Jared tried to explain to his father that he had only gone to pee, he couldn't help it about Molly, and he felt awful, but dammit he was going to have to go sometime, and she seemed all right, he was sure she'd be okay, chattering away like she was and drinking her Mountain Dew. Everything wasn't okay, but Clint said it was. He repeated it over and over, and father and son held tighter and tighter, as if by force of will they could make it so, and maybe – maybe – for a couple of seconds, they did.

4

The trimming that Flickinger had taken from an area of Nana's hand resembled, as Frank peered through the lens of the small microscope, a finely threaded piece of fabric. The threads had threads and those threads had threads.

'It actually looks like a plant fiber,' said the doctor. 'To me, at least.'

Frank imagined snapping a celery stalk, the stringy bits that hung loose.

Garth pressed and rolled the piece of white fiber between his fingertips. When he spread his fingers apart, the stuff stretched between them like bubblegum. 'Adhesive – incredibly tensile – fast-growing – somehow distorts the chemistry of the host – *fiercely* distorts it—'

While Garth continued, talking more to himself than to Frank, Frank considered the reduction of his daughter to the word *host*. It didn't make him happy.

Garth chuckled. 'I don't like the way you behave, Mr Fiber. I really don't.' He grimaced as he squished the material onto a glass microscope slide.

'You okay, Dr Flickinger?' Frank could accept that the surgeon was eccentric and stoned, and he seemed to know what he was doing so far, but the guy did have a bunch of sharp implements around Frank's incapacitated daughter.

'I'm peachy. Wouldn't mind a drink, though.' Flickinger dropped back on his haunches beside Nana's prone figure. He used the point of the trimmers to scratch beneath the rim of his nostril. 'Our friend Mr Fiber here, he's contradictory. He ought to be a fungus, but he's so busy and so aggressive and at the same time only interested in the XX chromosome. Then, you snip him from the rest of the mass and he's nothing. Nothing. He's just some sticky shit.'

Frank excused himself, rifled around in the kitchen, and settled for the crap on the top shelf between the baking powder and the cornmeal. There was enough to pour them each an inch. He brought the glasses back to the living room.

'Unless my eyes mistake me, that's cooking sherry. We're roughing it now, Frank.' Garth didn't sound disappointed in the slightest. He accepted the glass and tossed it off with a gasp of satisfaction. 'Listen, do you have any matches? A lighter?'

5

'Okay, Ree, the next part won't be news to you. Little habit became big habit, and big habits are expensive. Damian stole stuff from a rich guy's house and got away with it once, but not the second time. They didn't arrest him or anything, but he got his ass fired.'

Ree said Why am I not surprised?

'Yeah. Then I lost my job at the daycare. That was when the economy was really going bad, and the lady who owned the place, she had to make some cutbacks. Funny thing is, there were a couple of girls that hadn't been working there as long as me, weren't as experienced, she kept them on. You'll never guess what the difference was between me and those girls.'

Ree said Oh, I might have a guess, but go on and tell me.

'They were white. Hey, I'm not making an excuse. I'm not, but you know, that's how it was. And it was fucked up, and I got a little depressed. A lot depressed. Like anybody would. So, I started taking pills even when my head didn't hurt. And you know what made it especially bad? I understood what was happening. It's like, oh, so this is the part where I become a stupid fucking junkie just like people always thought I'd become. I hated myself for that. Fulfilling this destiny people gave me for growing up poor and black.'

Ree said Yeah, tough.

'Okay, so you get it. And what Damian and I had, it probably never would have lasted anyway. I know that. We were the same age, but he was way younger on the inside. Guys usually are, I think. But he was young more than most. Like, going off to play football in the park that day while our baby was home sick. That seemed normal to me then. He went off all the time like that. "I'll be back," he'd say, or "Just going over to Rick's," or whatever. I never questioned it. It didn't seem like questioning was allowed. He'd butter me up. Flowers and whatever. Candy. New shirt from the mall. Stuff that's nice for a second. But there was a part of him that was supposed to be funny, and it wasn't. It was just unkind. Like, he'd pull up beside a lady walking a dog, and yell, "You look like twins!" or he'd be strolling along and feint at some teenager going the other way like he was going to punch him, make the kid cringe. "I'm just playing around," he'd say. And the drugs, they soured him. He still did whatever he wanted, but it wasn't happy-go-lucky anymore, the way he went about it. And his meanness got loose, like a dog off its chain. "Look at this stoned bitch, Bobby," he says to our son, and laughs like it's hilarious. Like I was a clown in the circus. That kind of thing. I finally slapped him for it, and he punched me back. Then, when I punched him for that, he broke a bowl over my head.'

Ree said That must have hurt.

'Not so much as the feeling that it was what I deserved, me getting my junkie face beaten in by my junkie husband. I hate myself for that. I remember lying on the floor, seeing a nickel in the dust under the fridge, pieces of this blue bowl all around, and figuring that the next thing that would happen would be social services taking Bobby. And sure enough, they did. A cop carried Bobby out of my house, and my baby cried for me, and it should have been the saddest thing that ever happened, except I was so out of it, I didn't feel anything.'

Ree said That's sad.

6

Ten minutes had passed and Terry still hadn't come out of the house next door to the Elways. *Zolnik*, read the mailbox. Lila didn't know what to do.

Earlier, they had gone into the Elways' house, making a wide half-circle around the blood-spattered area where the bodies had been, and entering through the front door. The baby, named Platinum by the Elway brain trust with typical care and understatedness, had been in her bassinet, peaceful as could be inside the kidney-bean-shaped cocoon that had formed all around her. Lila had been able to feel the shape of the infant's body by pressing her hands against the cocoon. There had been something hilariously ghastly about that; it was like testing a new mattress, gauging it for firmness. But her smile had dried up on her face when Terry started to sob. It was after two in the morning. That made it twenty hours deep into the crisis, give or take, and thirty-five hours since her last shut-eye. Lila was blitzed, and her best deputy was drunk and maudlin.

Well, they were doing the best they could, weren't they? And there was still all that cat litter spread over Mountain Rest Road.

'No, there's not,' she corrected herself. That was months ago. Maybe a year?

'There's not what?' They were outside again, moving to the cruiser parked out in front of Roger's house.

Lila, cradling the cocoon, blinked at Terry. 'Was I talking out loud?'

'Yeah,' said Terry.

'Sorry.'

'This sucks so much.' He sniffled and started toward the Zolnik house.

Lila asked him where he was going.

'Door's open,' he said, pointing. 'It's the middle of the night and their door is open. Need to check it out. I'll just be a sec.'

Lila sat down in the passenger seat of the cruiser with the baby. It seemed like only a moment ago, but the digital readout said 2:22. She thought it read 2:11 when she had sat down. Twenty-two and eleven were not the same numbers. But eleven plus eleven made twenty-two. Which meant . . .

Eleven tumbled through her thoughts: eleven keys, eleven dollars, eleven fingers, eleven wishes, eleven tents in eleven campgrounds, eleven beautiful women in the middle of the road waiting to get run down, eleven birds on eleven branches on eleven trees – regular trees, mind you, not imaginary trees.

What *was* that tree? If things kept going like they were going, someone was going to hang that Evie woman from a tree, Lila could see that as clear as day, because it had started with her, somehow or other it had started with her and the Tree, Lila could feel it like the warmth of the cocooned infant in her lap, little baby Silver. Eleven babies in eleven lima bean cocoons.

'Platinum, Platinum,' she found herself saying. The baby's stupid name was Platinum not Silver. Silver was the name of the judge. If

Lila had ever known the name of the judge's dead cat, she didn't now. Clint's daughter's name was Sheila Norcross. Of course he hadn't admitted it, what a disappointment, the worst disappointment of the whole thing, to not even admit it, that Platinum was his kid. Or that Sheila was his kid. Lila's lips were dry and she was sweating even though it was cool in the car. The door to the Zolnik house hung open.

7

Whether Terry could have done anything for the guy or not, he wasn't sure; it never even occurred to him to try. Instead, he sat on the bed and put his hands on his knees and took a few slow, deep breaths. He needed to try to get his poor old shit together.

The sleeper was on the floor. Webs covered her head and her hands, as well as her lower body. There was a pair of slacks, knotted together with a pair of underwear, tossed off in a corner. She was small, around five feet. From the pictures on the wall and on the bureau, she appeared to be in her seventies, perhaps older.

Terry figured that the man who had tried to rape her must have yanked her from the bed and onto the floor in the process of removing the slacks.

The rapist was on the floor, too, a few feet away. Actually, he didn't look like a full-grown man; there was a teenage leanness to him. His jeans bunched around his ankles, stopped by a pair of sneakers. CURT M, read a Magic Marker label on the side of one of the sneaker soles. His face was a red slick. Breath stirred the bloody spit around his mouth. Blood continued to stream from his crotch area, adding to the swamp that had already formed in the rug. A stain colored the far wall of the room and below, on the floor, was a wad of flesh that Terry assumed were Curt M's cock and balls.

Curt M had probably figured the woman would never notice. To a son of a bitch like this, Aurora must have arrived looking like the opportunity of a lifetime, Easter morning in rapist heaven. There were probably a lot of others like him and, boy, were they in for a nasty surprise.

But how long before the word got out? If you tore the webs and tried to dip your wick, they fought back; they killed. Which seemed perfectly fair to Terry. But it was awfully easy, from there, to imagine some half-assed messiah like that batshit Kinsman What's-His-Name who was always on the news pissing and moaning about his taxes, coming along with a brand new plan. He'd announce that it was in everyone's best interest to go around shooting the cocooned women in their web-wrapped heads. They're ticking bombs, he'd say. There were men out there who'd love that idea. Terry thought of all those guys who'd been having wet dreams for years about being able to use the ridiculous arsenals they'd amassed for 'home defense,' but would never have had the guts to pull the trigger on a person who was awake, let alone armed and pointing a gun back at them. Terry didn't believe there were millions of those guys, but he'd been a cop long enough to suspect there were thousands of them.

What did that leave? Terry's wife was asleep. Could he keep her safe? What was he going to do, put her on a shelf in a cabinet, store her like a jar of preserves?

And he knew his daughter had never awakened that morning. It didn't matter that the phone lines were scrambled. Diane was a college kid. She slept in whenever she could. Plus, she'd sent them her spring semester schedule, and Terry was pretty sure she didn't have morning classes on Thursdays.

Was it possible that Roger – stupid, stupid, stupid Roger – had made an astute choice when he took those webs off Jessica? Roger got it over with before having to see anyone he loved shot in her sleep.

I should kill myself, Terry thought.

He let the idea float around. When it didn't sink, he grew alarmed and told himself not to rush into anything. He ought to get a drink, or a couple, really let himself work through it all. He thought better when he'd had a few, always had.

On the floor, Curt McLeod – the third-best player on the Dooling High School varsity tennis team, behind Kent Daley and Eric Blass – was making hitching noises. Cheyne-Stokes respiration had begun.

8

Terry's request that Lila drop him off at the Squeaky Wheel hardly jarred her. It made as much sense as anything at this point.

'What did you see in there, Terry?'

He was in the passenger seat, holding the cocooned baby between wide-open, flattened palms, like a hot casserole. 'Some kid tried to – ah – *get* with a lady in there. You know what I'm saying?'

'Yes.'

'That woke her up. She was asleep again when I entered the premises. He was – pretty much dead. Dead all the way now.'

'Oh,' said Lila.

They rolled through the dark town. The fire in the hills was red, the smoke cloud that rose from it a shade deeper than the night. A woman in a neon pink jogging suit was doing jumping jacks on a lawn. Crowds of people – predominantly women – were visible through the big windows of the Starbucks on Main Street, which was either open exceptionally late or (perhaps more likely) had been forced open by the crowd. It was 2:44 A.M.

The parking lot at the rear of the Squeak was more packed than Lila had ever seen it. There were trucks, sedans, motorcycles, compacts, vans. A new row of vehicles had begun on the grass embankment at the end of the lot.

Lila cozied the cruiser up to the back door, which was ajar and sending out light, voices, and a jukebox blare. The current song was a clattering garage band tune she'd heard a million times but wouldn't have known the name of even if she had been operating on a full night's rest. The singer's voice was iron dragged over asphalt:

'*You're gonna wake up wonderin, find yourself all alone!*' he wailed.

A barmaid had fallen asleep sitting on a milk crate beside the door. Her cowboy boots were sprawled out in a V. Terry got out of the car, put Platinum on the seat, then leaned back in. Neon from a beer sign washed over the right side of his face and gave him the acid green visage of a movie corpse. He gestured at the cocooned bundle.

'Maybe you should hide that baby somewhere, Sheriff.'

'What?'

'Think about it. They'll start wiping the girls and women out soon. Because they're dangerous. They wake up on the wrong side of the bed, so to speak.' He straightened. 'I have to get a drink. Good luck.' Her deputy shut the door carefully, as if afraid he might rouse the infant.

Lila watched Terry walk in through the back door of the bar. He didn't spare a glance for the woman asleep on the milk crate, the heels of her boots planted in the gravel, toes pointed up.

9

Officers Lampley and Murphy had cleared off the crap on the long table in the janitor's supply room so that Ree's body could lie in peace. Taking her to the county morgue in the middle of the night was out of the question, and St Theresa's was still a madhouse. Tomorrow, if things settled down, one of the officers could transport her remains to Crowder's Funeral Home on Kruger Street.

Claudia Stephenson sat at the foot of the table in a folding chair, holding an ice pack to her throat. Jeanette came in and sat in another folding chair, at the head of the table.

'I just wanted someone who'd talk to me,' Claudia said. Her voice was husky, hardly more than a whisper. 'Ree was always a good listener.'

'I know,' said Jeanette, thinking that was true even though Ree was dead.

'I'm sorry for your loss,' Van said. She was in the open door, her muscular body looking slack with weariness and sorrow.

'You should have used your Taser,' Jeanette said, but she couldn't muster any real accusation. She was also weary.

'There was no time,' Van said.

'She was going to kill me, Jeanie.' Claudia said this in a tone of apology. 'If you want to blame anyone, blame me. I was the one who tried to get the webs off her.' She repeated, 'I only wanted someone to chat with.'

At rest, Ree's uncovered face was both slack and stunned, lids low, mouth open; it was the in-between expression – between laughs, between smiles – you wore in the photograph that you threw out or deleted from your phone. Someone had scrubbed the blood from her forehead, but the bullet hole was stark and obscene. The tattered webbing hung loose around her hair, lank and wilted instead of fluttering and silken, as dead as Ree herself. The stuff had stopped growing when Ree stopped living.

When Jeanette tried to picture the living Ree, all she could find that was solid was a few moments from that morning. *I say you can't not be bothered by a square of light.*

Claudia sighed or moaned or sobbed, or maybe did all three simultaneously. 'Oh, Jesus Christ,' she said in her choked wheeze. 'I'm so sorry.'

Jeanette closed Ree's eyelids. That was better. She let her finger graze a small portion of the patch of scar tissue on Ree's forehead. *Who did that to you, Ree? I hope whoever did that hates himself, and punishes himself. Or that he's dead, and it almost certainly was a he. Ninety-nine percent.* The girl's eyelids were paler than the rest of her sandy skin.

Jeanette bent low to Ree's ear. 'I've never told anyone what I told you. Not even Dr Norcross. Thanks for listening. Now sleep well, honey. Please sleep well.'

10

The fragment of burning web rose into the air, twisting orange and black, blooming. It didn't flare. *Blooming* was the only word for the way it opened, the fire becoming so much bigger than the fuel.

Garth Flickinger, holding the lit match that he'd used to test the trimming of web, reared back against the coffee table. His medical implements skidded across it and a few clattered to the floor. Frank, watching from near the door, lowered himself to a crouch and moved quickly toward Nana, to shield her.

The flame formed a swirling circle.

Frank pressed his body over his daughter.

In Flickinger's hand, the burning match had reached his fingertips, but he continued to hold it. Frank smelled the burning skin. In the glare of the fiery circle that hovered in mid-air above the living room, the doctor's elfin features appeared to separate, as if they wished — understandably — to flee.

Because fire did not burn this way. Fire did not float. Fire did not make circles.

The last experiment on the web was delivering a conclusive answer to the question of 'Why?' and the answer was: because what was happening was not of this world, and could not be treated by the medicine of this world. This realization was on Flickinger's face for anyone to read. Frank guessed it was in his own face, as well.

The fire collapsed into a rippling brown mass that jittered into a hundred pieces. Moths spilled into the air.

Moths rose to the light fixture; they fluttered to the lampshade, to the corners of the ceiling, through the entryway to the kitchen; moths went dancing to the print of Christ walking on water on the wall and settled on the edges of the frame; a moth tumbled through the air and landed on the ground close to where Frank was draped across Nana. Flickinger was scrambling in the opposite direction on his hands and knees, toward the front hall, yelling the whole way (*screaming*, actually), his poise shattered.

Frank didn't move. He kept his eyes on one single moth. It was the color of nothing you'd notice.

The moth crept forward across the floor. Frank was afraid, terrified really, of the little creature that weighed roughly as much as a fingernail and was a living shade of mute. What would it do to him?

Anything. It could do anything it wanted — as long as it didn't hurt Nana.

'Don't touch her,' Frank whispered. Embracing his daughter like this, he could feel her pulse and her breath. The world had a way of spinning from Frank's grasp, of making him wrong or foolish when all he wanted was to be right and good, but he wasn't a coward. He was ready to die for his little girl. 'If you have to have someone, you can have me.'

Two spots of ink on the brown chevron of the moth's body, its eyes, saw into Frank's eyes, and from there into his head. He felt it flying around in his skull for God knew how long, touching down on his brain, dragging its pointed feet along the canals like a boy on a rock in the middle of a stream, drawing a stick through the water. And Frank huddled closer to his child. 'Please take me instead.'

The moth darted away.

11

Claudia, she of the Dynamite Body-a, left. Officer Lampley had offered to give Jeanette a moment alone. Now she had the actual Ree to talk to. Or what was left of her. She felt she should have told Ree these things while Ree was still alive.

'What happened – I'm not sure if it was morning or afternoon or early evening, but we'd been on the nod for days. Didn't go out. Ordered in. At one point, Damian burned me with a cigarette. I'm lying in bed and we're both looking at my bare arm and I ask, "What are you doing?" The pain was in another room from my mind. I didn't even move my arm. Damian says, "Making sure that you're real." I still have the scar, size of a penny from his pressing so hard. "Satisfied?" I asked. "You believe I'm real?" And he says, "Yeah, but I hate you more for being real. If you'd let me get my knee fixed, none of this would have happened. You are one vicious bitch. And I'm finally onto you!"'

Ree said That's pretty scary.

'Yes. It was. Because Damian said all that with an expression like this is great news, and he's delighted to get it and pass it on. It's like he was the host of some late night radio talk show, playing to his crowd of insomniac nutbags. We're in the bedroom and the curtains are drawn and nothing's been washed in days. The power's off because we didn't pay the bill. Later, I don't know how long, I find myself sitting on the floor in Bobby's room. His bed's still there, but the other furniture, the rocker and the bureau, they're gone. Damian sold them to a guy for a little cash. Maybe I was finally coming down, maybe it was because of the cigarette burn, but I felt so sad, and so awful, and so – like I was turned around and in this foreign place and there's no way home.'

Ree said I know the feeling.

'The screwdriver, now – the clutchhead screwdriver. The guy who bought the rocker must have used it to take the base off and then forgot to take it with him. That's all I can figure. I know it wasn't our screwdriver. We didn't have any tools by then. Damian had sold them off long before the furniture. But this screwdriver is lying on the floor of Bobby's room and I pick it up. I go to the living room and Damian's sitting in the folding chair that's the last seat in the house. He goes, "You here to finish the job? Well go ahead. But you better hurry up, because if you don't get to killing me in the next few seconds here, I think I'll choke you until your stupid fucking head pops off." Says it in that same late night host voice. And he holds up a little bottle with the last couple of pills we have, and then, he gives it a shake, like for a special punchline, *ta-da!* He goes, "Right here's a good spot, plenty of meat," and he pulls my hand that's holding the screwdriver over to his upper thigh, and puts the point against his jeans, and says, "Well? Now or never, Jeanie-baby, now or never."'

Ree said I guess he wanted it.

'And he got it. I drove that bastard all the way down to the handle. Damian doesn't shout, he just gives a big exhale, and goes, "Look what you did to me," and he's bleeding all over the chair and the floor. But he doesn't make a move to help himself. He says, "Fine. Watch me die. Enjoy it."'

Ree said Did you?

'No. *No!* I huddled in the corner of the room. How long, I couldn't tell. Police said it was twelve or fourteen hours. I saw the shadows change, but I didn't know how long. Damian sat there, and he talked. And he talked. Was I happy now. Had this been the plan from the beginning. Oh, and how had I rigged the ground in the park so he'd hurt his knee in the first place. What a great trick, Jeanie-baby. Eventually, he stopped talking. But I can see him – real clear, I can see him, right this minute still. I used to dream about telling Damian I was sorry, about begging his forgiveness. In those dreams he'd just sit in that chair, looking at me and turning blue. Too-late dreams, Dr Norcross says. Too late for sorry. Score one for the doc, right, Ree? Dead men don't accept apologies. Not once in the history of the world.'

Ree said Got that right.

'But, oh, honey, oh, Ree. What I wouldn't give to change everything now just this one time, because you were too good to end up like this. You didn't ever kill anyone. It should have been me. Not you. Me.'

To this Ree said nothing.

CHAPTER 19

1

Clint found Hicks's cell phone number in the address book in his desk and called it from the landline. The acting warden was disconcertingly relaxed. Maybe he'd popped a Valium or two.

'A lot of the women seem to have reached a state of, I guess you'd call it *acceptance,* Doc.'

'Acceptance isn't the same as giving up,' said Clint.

'Put it how you want to put it, but the lights have gone out on more than half of them since you left.' Hicks said this with satisfaction, noting that the officer-to-inmate ratio was once again manageable. They would still be in good shape once they lost the female officers.

This was how people in power thought of human life, wasn't it? In terms of sum benefits and ratios and manageability. Clint had never wanted to be in power. As a ward of the foster system he had, mostly by grace, survived the dominion of countless domestic tyrants; he had chosen his field in clear reaction to that experience, in order to help the helpless, people like the boy he'd been, like Marcus and Jason and Shannon – and like his own mother, that pale, worried ghost of his faintest memory.

Jared squeezed his father's shoulder. He had been listening.

'Be advised, the paperwork is going to be unprecedented,' Hicks continued. 'The state does look down on shooting prison inmates.' Ree Dempster was cooling in the janitor's closet and Hicks was already thinking of the paperwork. Clint decided he had to get off the phone before he used the slang term that referred to men who had sexual congress with the woman who'd given them birth.

Clint said he'd be in soon, and that was it. Jared offered to make fried baloney sandwiches. 'You must be hungry.'

'Thank you,' said Clint. 'Sounds like just the right thing.'

The meat sizzled and popped in the pan and his nose found the smell. It was so good tears came to his eyes. Or maybe the tears were in his eyes already.

'I need to get me one of those.' That was what Shannon had said to him that last time, looking at the picture of little Jared. And apparently she had.

Sheila, Lila had said the girl's name was, Sheila Norcross.

It was flattering, really, maybe the most flattering thing that had ever happened to him, Shannon giving her girl his last name. It was a problem now, but still. It meant that she'd loved him. Well, he had loved Shannon, too. In a way. There were things between them that other people could never understand.

He remembered that New Year's Eve. With that damp in her eyes, Shan had asked him if it was all right. The music had been blaring. Everything had smelled like beer and cigarettes. He had bent down to her ear to make sure he heard her . . .

A bite or two was all that Clint could manage. As fine as the smell was, his stomach was a hard rubber ball. He apologized to his son. 'It's not the food.'

'Yeah,' said Jared. 'My appetite's not great, either.' He was picking at the sandwich he'd made himself.

The glass door slid open with a whoosh, and Lila entered, holding a white bundle.

2

Once he'd killed his mother, Don Peters struggled to proceed.

The first step was apparent: clean up. That was going to be hard to do, however, because Don had opted to murder his mother by pressing the barrel of a Remington shotgun against her web-encrusted forehead and then pulling the trigger. This had done the job with aplomb (or maybe he meant some other word), but it had created a hell of a mess, and Don was better at making messes than cleaning them up. This was a point his mother had made often.

And what a mess it was! Blood, brains, and bits of web sprayed up the wall in the shape of a huge, ragged megaphone.

Instead of doing something about the mess, Don sat in his La-Z-Boy and wondered why he had made it in the first place. Was it his mother's fault that Jeanette Sorley had waved her perky little tail in his face and then tattled when he would only let her jerk him off? Was it? Or that Janice Coates had hounded him out of his job? Or that Norcross, the head-shrinking priss, had sucker-punched him? No, his mother had nothing to do with any of that, and yet Don had driven home, seen that she was asleep, fetched his shotgun from the pickup, returned inside, and blown her dreaming brains out. Always supposing she was dreaming – who knew?

Yes, he had been rattled. Yes, he had been mistreated. Still, loath as Don was to concede it, as bad as it was to be rattled and mistreated, you shouldn't up and kill your mother. That was overreacting.

Don drank a beer and cried. He didn't want to kill himself or go to jail.

Seated on his mother's couch, calmer with the beer in his stomach, it occurred to Don Peters that cleaning up might not present such a problem after all. The authorities were extremely busy. Things you could not normally get away with – like arson – you could probably skate on, thanks to Aurora. Forensic analysis of crime scenes was suddenly looking like a rather secondary field. Besides, it was chicks that did all that microscope-and-computer shit. On TV, at least.

He stacked a bundle of newspaper on the stovetop and flipped on the burner. While the paper got started, he squeezed a bottle of barbecue lighter fluid, scribbling the liquid over the drapes and the furniture, all the stuff that would go up fast.

As he was driving away from the burning house, Don realized that there was something else he needed to do. This part was a lot more difficult than starting a fire, but no less important: for once in his life, Don needed to cut himself some serious slack.

If it was true that Don's relationships with women had occasionally been fraught, it also had to be acknowledged that his relationship with his mother – his earliest relationship – must have been the thing that set him off on the wrong foot. Even Norcross would probably agree to that much. She had raised him on her own and he thought she did her best, but what had his mother ever done to prepare him for the likes of Jeanette Sorley, Angel Fitzroy, or Janice Coates? Don's mother had made him grilled cheese sandwiches and baked him individual strawberry pies shaped like UFOs. She had brought him ginger ale and looked after him when he had the flu. When Don was ten, she had constructed for him a black knight costume out of cardboard and strips of felt that was the envy of the entire fourth grade – the entire school!

That was all lovely, but maybe his mother had been *too* kind. Hadn't his own go-along, get-along nature gotten him in trouble more than once? For instance, when Sorley came on to him. He had known it was wrong, and yet, he had let her take advantage of him. He was weak. All men were, when it came to women. And some – many, even – were . . . were . . .

Too generous!

Yes!

Generosity was a ticking bomb handed down to him by his mother and it had exploded in her face. There was a justice to that (an incredibly cruel justice, granted), and although Don could accept it, he vowed that he would never like it. Death was a harsh punishment for generosity. The real criminals were the Janice Coates types. Death wouldn't be too harsh for Janice Coates. Instead of dosing her with the pills, he wished he'd had the chance to choke her out. Or cut her throat and watch her *bleed* out.

'I love you, Mom,' he said to the cab of his pickup truck. It was as if he were testing the words to see if they'd ricochet. Don repeated the statement a couple of more times. He added, 'I forgive you, Mom.'

Don Peters found that he didn't want to be alone with his voice. It was like – like it didn't sound right.

('Are you sure that's true, Donnie?' his mother used to ask when he was little and she thought he might be lying. 'Is it the God's-honest that you only took one cookie from the jar, sweetheart?'

('Yes,' he'd say, 'It's the God's-honest,' but it wasn't, and he supposed she had known it wasn't, but she let it slide and look what it had gotten her. How did the Bible put it? Sow the wind, reap the whirlwind.)

3

Because the lot at the Squeaky Wheel was packed, Don ended up parking at a curb down the street.

On his way inside, he passed a few men standing on the sidewalk with their beer glasses, admiring the large blaze in the hills. 'And there's another one – think that's some place in town,' one of the men noted.

Probably Mom's house, Don thought. Maybe it'll take the whole neighborhood, and who knows how many sleeping women. A few of them good, which was a shame, but the great majority either sluts or frigid. Always too hot or too cold, that was women for you.

He acquired a shot and a beer at the bar, and found a seat at the end of a long table with Deputy Terry Coombs and a black guy whose face he recognized from previous evenings at the Squeak but whose name he couldn't recall. Don gave a moment's consideration to the question of whether Terry might have heard about the doings at the prison, the false accusation and frame-up and so on. But if Coombs had heard, he was in no condition or mood to do anything about it – the deputy looked half asleep with a three-quarters-empty pitcher on the table in front of him.

'You boys mind if I join you?' Don had to yell to be heard over the commotion in the bar.

The other two shook their heads.

Big enough to handle a hundred, the barroom, at three in the morning, was handling at least that many. Although there were a few women, most of the crowd was male. Under the current circumstances, it seemed that not many women were looking to imbibe depressants. Incongruously, there were also a few teenagers lurking around, dazed expressions on their flushed faces. Don felt sorry for them, but the mama's boys of the world were going to have to grow up fast now.

'Hell of a day,' Don said. He felt better now that he was with men.

The black guy murmured an agreement. He was tall, lots of shoulder, forty or so. Sitting ramrod straight.

'I'm just trying to decide whether or not to kill myself,' Terry said.

Don chuckled. Coombs had a hell of a deadpan. 'Did you see the Secret Service putting their boots in the asses of those rioters outside the White House? Must have been like Christmas for those guys. And Jesus, look at that.'

Terry and the black guy turned their gazes to one of the televisions on the wall.

It was security footage from an underground garage. A woman, age and race rendered indeterminate by the placement of the camera and the grain of the footage, though clearly dressed in the uniform of a parking garage attendant, was atop a man in a business suit. She appeared to be stabbing him in the face with something. Black liquid pooled on the pavement, and bright white strands hung from her face. The TV news never would have shown something like that before today, but it seemed that Aurora had put Standards and Practices – that was what they called it, right? – out of business.

'Must've woke her up for his keys or something, huh?' Don mused. 'This stuff, it's, like, the ultimate P-M-S, am I right?'

The two men made no response.

The television feed cut to the anchor's desk. It was empty; George Alderson, the old dude that Don had watched earlier, had disappeared. A younger guy, wearing a sweatshirt and headphones, poked his head into the frame and made a sharp *get-out-of-here!* gesture. The feed flipped to an advertisement for a sitcom.

'That was unprofessional,' said Don.

Terry drank directly from his pitcher of beer. Foam ran down his chin.

4

Sleeper storage.

This wasn't Lila's only consideration this early Friday morning, but it was right up there. The ideal spot would be a basement, or a tunnel with a concealed entrance. A tapped-out mineshaft could serve well – their area certainly had a healthy supply of those – but there was no time to find one, no time to set it up. So, what did that leave? It left people's homes. But if groups of vigilantes – of crazies, whoever – did start to go around killing the sleeping women, homes were the first place they'd check. *Where's your wife? Where's your daughter? It's for your own safety, for everyone's safety. You wouldn't leave dynamite lying around your house, would you?*

What if there were houses that no one lived in, though, houses that had never had a single occupant? There were plenty of houses like that just up the street: the other half of the development on Tremaine Street, the ones that had gone unsold. It was the best option that Lila could think of.

Once she had explained it to her son and her husband, Lila was drained. She felt ill and scraped, like a flu was coming on her. Hadn't a stoner she'd arrested once for breaking and entering warned her about this, about the pain of drugs wearing off? 'Anything, any risk to avoid the come-down,' he'd said. 'The come-down is ruination. Death to your happy.'

Clint and Jared didn't say anything immediately. The three of them were standing in the living room.

'Is that – a baby?' Jared finally asked.

She handed the cocoon to him. 'Yes. Roger Elway's daughter.'

Her son pulled the baby close. 'This could probably get worse,' he said, 'but I don't know how.'

Lila reached up and traced the hair at Jared's temple. The difference between the way Terry had held the baby – like it might explode or shatter – and the way Jared held it made her heart pick up speed. Her son hadn't given up. He was still trying to be human.

Clint shut the sliding glass door, closing off the smell of smoke. 'I want to say you're being paranoid about hiding sleepers – or storing them, to use your word – but you might be onto something. We could bring Molly and the baby and Mrs Ransom and whoever else we find over to one of the empties.'

'There's the demo house at the top of the hill,' Jared said. 'It's actually furnished.' And, in response to his mother's reflexive glance: 'Chill. I didn't go in, just looked through the living room window.'

Clint said, 'I hope it's an unnecessary precaution, but better safe than sorry.'

She nodded. 'I think so. Because you're going to have to put me in one of those houses eventually, too. You know that, don't you?' Lila didn't say it to shock him or to hurt him. It was just a fact that had to be stated, and she was too tired to gild the lily.

5

The man seated on the toilet in the women's bathroom stall at the Squeaky Wheel was a wall-eyed character in a rock tee-shirt and dress trousers. He gawked at Michaela. Well, look on the bright side. At least his pants were up.

'Dude,' she said, 'this is the ladies'. Another few days and it'll be all yours for eternity. For now, though, out.' *Widespread Panic,* his tee-shirt read – of course.

'I'm sorry, I'm sorry. I only need a second.' He gestured at a little clutch in his lap. 'I was about to smoke some rocks, but it was too crowded in the men's room.' He grimaced. 'And the men's room smells like shit. *Big* shit. That's unpleasant. Please, if you can be a little patient, I'd appreciate it.' His voice dropped. 'I saw some magic earlier tonight. Not Disney magic. Bad magic. I'm pretty steady as a rule, but it kind of freaked me out.'

Michaela took her hand from her purse where she had been holding Ursula's pistol. 'Bad magic, huh? That does sound unsettling. I just drove all the way from DC to find out that my mother's already asleep. What's your name?'

'Garth. I'm sorry for your loss.'

'Thanks,' she said. 'My mother was a pain in the ass, but there was a lot to like about her. Can I have some of your crack?'

'It's not crack. It's meth.' Garth unfastened his clutch and took out a pipe and handed it to her. 'But you can certainly have some if you'd like.' Next, he fished out a Ziploc of rocks. 'You look just like the girl from the news, you know.'

Michaela smiled. 'People are always telling me that.'

6

The catastrophic state of the Squeaky Wheel's men's room had likewise driven Frank Geary out to the edge of the parking lot to empty his bladder. In the aftermath of what they had seen – moths born out of fire – it seemed stupid to do anything except go to a bar and drink. With his own eyes he had witnessed something that could not be accounted for. There was another side to the world. There was a deeper stratum that had been wholly invisible until that morning. It hadn't shown itself as proof of Elaine's God, though. The moths had grown from the fire, and fire was what was supposed to be waiting at the other end of the spiritual spectrum.

Brush crunched a few yards off. 'That bathroom is a fuckin hell-hole . . .' The man's slur trailed off. Frank discerned a narrow shape wearing a cowboy hat.

Frank zipped up and turned to head back to the bar. He didn't know what else to do. He'd left Nana and Elaine at home, laid out on beach towels in the basement with the door locked.

The man's voice stopped him.

'Want to hear something crazy? My buddy's wife, Millie, she works up at the prison, and she says they got a – what, some kind of *fee*-nom up there. Probably bullshit, that's my opinion, but . . .' The man's urine spattered in the brush. 'She says this honey, when she sleeps, nothin happens. Wakes up again.'

Frank stopped. 'What?'

The man was twisting back and forth in a deliberate fashion, amusing himself by spilling his piss around as widely as possible. 'Sleeps and wakes up like normal. Wakes up fine. So my buddy's wife says.'

A cloud shifted in the sky and moonlight disclosed the distinct profile of that noted dog-beater, Fritz Meshaum. The pubic scrag of hillbilly beard and the deeply sunken area beneath the right cheekbone, where Frank had used the rifle butt to permanently alter the contours of the man's face, were both clearly visible.

'Who's that I'm speakin with?' Fritz was squinting ferociously. 'That you, Kronsky? How's that .45 working out for you, Johnny Lee? Fine gun, innit? No, that's not Kronsky. Christ, I'm not seein double, I'm seein fuckin triple.'

'She wakes up?' asked Frank. 'This inmate at the prison wakes up? No cocoon?'

'That's what I heard, but take it as you will. Say, I know you, mister?'

Frank headed back to the bar without answering. He didn't have time for Meshaum. It was this woman he was thinking of, this inmate who could sleep and wake up like normal.

7

When Frank rejoined Terry and Don Peters (followed by Garth Flickinger, who came strutting back from the women's room like a new man), his drinking companions had turned around on the bench of their long table. A man in jeans, a blue chambray workshirt, and a Case gimme cap was on his feet and holding forth, gesturing with a half-full pitcher of beer, and those around him had grown silent, listening respectfully. He looked familiar, a local farmer or maybe a long-haul trucker, his cheeks speckled with beard and his teeth discolored from Red Man, but he had a preacher's self-assured delivery, his voice rising and falling in cadences that begged for return cries of *praise Jesus*. Sitting next to him was a man Frank definitely recognized, having helped him select a dog from the shelter when his old one died. Howland, that was his name. Teacher from the community college over in Maylock. Howland was looking up at the sermonizer with an expression of wry amusement.

'We shoulda seen this coming!' the trucker/preacher proclaimed. 'The women flew too high, like that fella with the wax wings, and their wings melted!'

'Icarus,' Howland said. He wore a baggy old barn jacket with patches on the elbows. His specs stuck up out of the breast pocket.

'*Ike-a-rus*, that is correct, that is a big ten-four! Want to know how far the fair sex has come? Look back a hundred years! They couldn't vote! Skirts down to their ankles! They didn't have no birth control, and if they got a 'bortion, they went down some back alley to get it and if they got caught, they went to jail for *murrr-der*! Now they can get it done any time and place they want! Thanks to Planned Fuckin Parenthood, 'bortion's easier than gettin a bucket of chicken from KFC and costs about the same! They can run for president! They join the SEALS and the Rangers! They can marry their lesbo buddies! If that ain't terroristic, I don't know what is.'

There was a rumble of agreement. Frank didn't join in. He didn't believe his problems with Elaine had anything whatsoever to do with abortion or lesbians.

'All in just one hundred years!' The trucker/preacher lowered his voice. He could do that and still be heard because someone had pulled the plug on the jukebox, killing Travis Tritt in a dying gurgle. 'They ain't just pulled even, like they said they wanted, *they done pulled ahead*. Do you want to know what proves it?'

Now, Frank had to admit, the man was getting closer to something. Elaine could never cut him any slack. It was always her way, her call. To find himself warming to this bumpkin's homily gave Frank a sick feeling – but he couldn't deny it. Nor was he alone. The whole barroom congregation was listening closely, their mouths agape. Except for Howland, who was grinning like a guy watching a monkey do a dance on a street corner.

'They can dress like *men,* that's what proves it! A hundred years ago, a woman wouldn't have been caught dead in pants unless she was ridin a hoss, and now they wear em everywhere!'

'What you got against long legs in tight pants, asshole?' a woman called, and there was general laughter.

'*Nuthin!*' the trucker/preacher shot back. 'But do you think a man – a *natural* man, not one of those New York *trannies* – would be caught dead on the streets of Dooling in a *dress*? No! They'd be called crazy! They'd be laughed at! But the women, now they get to have it both ways! They forgot what the Bible says about how a woman should follow her husband in all things, and sew, and cook, and have the kiddies, and not be out in public wearing *hot pants*! Get *even* with men, they mighta been left alone! But that wasn't enough! They had to get *ahead*! Had to make us *second best*! They flew too close to the *sun* and God *put em to sleep*!'

He blinked and rubbed a hand over his beard-scratchy face, seeming to realize where he was and what he was doing – spewing his private thoughts to a barroom filled with staring people.

'Ike-a-rus,' he said, and abruptly sat down.

'Thank you, Mr Carson Struthers, from RFD 2.' That was Pudge Marone, bartender and owner of the Squeak, hollering out from behind his bar. 'Our own local celebrity, folks: "Country Strong" Struthers. Watch out for the right hook. Carson's my ex-brother-in-law.' Pudge was a would-be comedian with saggy Rodney Dangerfield cheeks. Not all that funny, but he gave a fair pour. 'That was some real food for thought, Carson. I look forward to discussing all this with my sister at Thanksgiving dinner.'

There was more laughter at that.

Before the general conversation could start up again, or before someone could plug in the juke and reanimate Mr Tritt, Howland stood up, holding a hand in the air. History professor, Frank suddenly remembered. That's what he said he was. Said he was going to name his new dog Tacitus, after his favorite Roman historian. Frank had thought it was a lot of name for a bichon frise.

'My friends,' the professor said in rolling tones, 'with all that has happened today, it is easy to understand why we haven't yet thought of tomorrow, and all the tomorrows to come. Let us put morals and morality and hot pants aside for a moment and consider the practicalities.'

He patted Carson 'Country Strong' Struthers's burly shoulder.

'This gentleman has a point; women have indeed surpassed men in certain aspects, at least in western society, and I submit that they have done so in ways rather more important than their freedom to shop at Walmart ungirdled and with their hair in rollers. Suppose this – let's call it a *plague*, for want of a better word – suppose this plague had gone the other way, and it was the *men* falling asleep and not waking up?'

Utter silence in the Squeaky Wheel. Every eye trained on Howland, who seemed to enjoy the attention. His delivery was not that of a backwoods Bible-thumper, but it was still mesmerizing: unhesitating and practiced.

'The women could re-start the human race, could they not? Of course they could. There are millions of sperm donations – frozen babies-in-waiting – stored in facilities all across this great country of ours. Tens and tens of millions across the world! The result would be babies of *both* sexes!'

'Assuming the new male babies didn't also grow cocoons as soon as they stopped crying and fell asleep for the first time,' a very pretty young woman said. She had appeared alongside Flickinger. It occurred to Frank that the trucker/preacher/ex-boxer had missed one thing in his oration: women just naturally looked better than men. More finished, somehow.

'Yes,' Howland agreed, 'but even if that were the case, women could continue to reproduce for generations, possibly until Aurora ran its course. Can men do that? Gentlemen, where will the human race be in fifty years, if the women don't wake up? Where will it be in a hundred?'

Now the silence was broken by a man who began to bawl in great, noisy blabbers.

Howland ignored him. 'But perhaps the question of future generations is moot.' He raised a finger. 'History suggests an extremely uncomfortable idea about human nature, my friends, one that may explain why, as this gentleman here has so passionately elucidated, women have *got ahead*. The idea, baldly stated, is this: women are sane, but men are mad.'

'Bullshit!' someone called. 'Fuckin bullshit!'

Howland was not deterred; he actually smiled. 'Is it? Who makes up your motorcycle gangs? Men. Who comprises the gangs that have turned neighborhoods in Chicago and Detroit into free-fire zones? Boys. Who are the ones in power who start the wars and who are the ones who – with the exception of a few female helicopter pilots and such – fight those wars? Men. Oh, and who suffers as collateral damage? Women and children, mostly.'

'Yeah, and who shakes their asses, egging em on?' Don Peters shouted. His face was red. Veins were standing out on the sides of his neck. 'Who's pulling the motherfucking *strings*, Mr Egghead Smartboy?'

There was a spatter of applause. Michaela rolled her eyes and was about to speak. Full of meth, blood pressure red-lining, she felt like she could go on for perhaps six hours, the length of a Puritan sermon. But before she could start, Howland was off again.

'Thoughtfully put, sir, the contribution of a true intellectual, and a belief that many men advance, usually ones with a certain sense of inferiority when it comes to the fairer s—'

Don started to rise. 'Who are you calling inferior, jackwad?'

Frank pulled him down, wanting to keep this one close. If Fritz Meshaum had really gotten hold of something, he needed to talk to Don Peters about it. Because he was pretty sure Don worked at the prison.

'Let me go,' Don snarled.

Frank slid his hand up to Don's armpit and squeezed. 'You need to calm down.'

Don grimaced, but didn't say anything more.

'Here is an interesting fact,' Howland continued. 'During the second half of the nineteenth century, most deep-mining operations, including those right here in Appalachia, employed workers called *coolies*. No, not Chinese peons; these were young men, sometimes boys as young as twelve, whose job it was to stand next to machinery that had a tendency to overheat. The coolies had a barrel of water, or a pipe, if there was a spring nearby. Their task was to pour water over the belts and pistons, to keep them cool. Hence the name coolies. I would submit that women have historically served the same function, *restraining* men – at least when possible – from their very worst, most abhorrent acts.'

He looked around at his audience. The smile had left his face.

'But now it seems the coolies are gone, or going. How long before men – soon to be the only sex – fall on each other with their guns and bombs and nuclear weapons? How long before the machine overheats and explodes?'

Frank had heard enough. It wasn't the future of the entire human race he cared about. If it could be saved, that would be a side-effect. What he cared about was Nana. He wanted to kiss her sweet face, and to apologize for stretching her favorite shirt. Tell her he would never do it again. He could not do those things unless she was awake.

'Come on,' he said to Don. 'Outside. I want to talk to you.'

'About what?'

Frank leaned close to Peters's ear. 'Is there really a woman at the prison who can sleep without growing webs and then wake up?'

Don craned around to look at Frank. 'Hey, you're the town dogcatcher, aren't you?'

'That's right.' Frank let the dogcatcher bullshit slide. 'And you're Don who works at the prison.'

'Yeah,' said Don. 'That's me. So let's talk.'

8

Clint and Lila had gone out to the back porch, the overhead light turning them into actors on a stage. They were looking toward the pool where Anton Dubcek had been skimming for dead bugs less than twenty-four hours earlier. Clint wondered idly where Anton was now. Sleeping, likely as not. Dreaming of willing young women rather than preparing for an unpleasant conversation with his wife. If so, Clint envied him.

'Tell me about Sheila Norcross, honey. The girl you saw at the basketball game.'

Lila favored him with an ugly smile of which he would have thought her incapable. It showed all of her teeth. Above it, her eyes – deep in their sockets now, with dark brown circles beneath them – glittered. 'As if you don't know. *Honey.*'

Put on your therapist's hat, he told himself. Remember that she's high on dope and running on fumes. Exhausted people can slip very easily into paranoia. But it was hard. He saw the outline of it;

she thought that some girl he'd never heard of was his daughter by Shan Parks. But it was impossible, and when your wife accused you of something impossible, and everything else in the world was, by any rational standard, more important and immediate, it was very, very hard to keep from losing your temper.

'Tell me what you know. Then I'll tell you what *I* know. But let's begin with one simple fact. That girl is not my daughter, whether she has my name or not, and I have never broken our marriage vows.' She turned as if to go back inside. He caught her by the arm. 'Please. Tell me before—'

Before you go to sleep and we lose whatever chance we have to square this, he thought.

'Before it can fester any more than it already has.'

Lila shrugged. 'Does it even matter, with everything else?'

His very thought a moment ago, but he could have said *it matters to you.* He kept his mouth closed instead. Because in spite of all that was happening in the wider world, it mattered to him, too.

'You know I never even wanted this pool, don't you?' Lila asked.

'What?' Clint was baffled. What did the pool have to do with anything?

'Mom? Dad?' Jared was standing inside the screen door, listening.

'Jared, go back inside. This is between your mother and m—'

'No, let him listen,' Lila said. 'If you insist on going through this, we will. Don't you think he should know about his half-sister?' She turned to Jared. 'She's a year younger than you, she has blond hair, she's a talented basketball player, and she's as pretty as a picture. As you would be, if you were a girl. Because, see, she *looks* like you, Jere.'

'Dad?' His brow was furrowed. 'What's she talking about?'

Clint gave up. It was too late to do anything else. 'Why don't you tell us, Lila? Start from the beginning.'

9

Lila went through it, starting with the Curriculum Committee, and what Dorothy Harper had said to her afterward, how she hadn't really thought much of it, but did an Internet search the next day. The search had brought her to the article, which included a mention of Shannon Parks, whom Clint had spoken of once before, and a striking photograph of Sheila Norcross. 'She could almost be your twin, Jared.'

Jared slowly turned to his father.

The three of them now sat at the kitchen table.

Clint shook his head, but couldn't help wondering what his face was showing. Because he felt guilty. As if there had really been something to feel guilty about. It was an interesting phenomenon. That night in 2002 what he'd whispered in Shannon's ear was, 'You know, I'll always be there if you need me.' When she'd responded, 'What if I needed you tonight?' Clint had said that was the one thing he couldn't do. If he had slept with her, there would have been something to feel guilty about, but he'd refused her, so it was all good. Wasn't it?

Maybe, but why had he never told Lila about the encounter? He couldn't remember and he wasn't required to defend what happened fifteen years before. She might as well demand that he explain why he'd knocked Jason down in the Burtells' backyard for nothing more than a chocolate milkshake.

'Is that it?' Clint asked. He couldn't resist adding, 'Tell me that's not all, Lila.'

'No, that's not all,' she said. 'Are you going to tell me that you didn't know Shannon Parks?'

'You know I did,' Clint said. 'I'm sure I've mentioned her name.'

'In passing,' Lila said. 'But it was a little more than a passing acquaintance, wasn't it?'

'Yes. It was. We were both caught in the foster system. For awhile we kept each other afloat. Otherwise one or both of us would have drowned. It was Shannon who got me to stop fighting. She said if I didn't, I was apt to kill someone.' He took Lila's hands across the table. '*But that was years ago.*'

Lila pulled her hands away. 'When was the last time you saw her?'

'Fifteen years ago!' Clint cried. It was ridiculous.

'Sheila Norcross is fifteen.'

'A year younger than me . . .' Jared said. If she'd been older –
eighteen or nineteen – her birth would have pre-dated his parents'
marriage. But younger . . .

'And her father's name,' Lila said, breathing hard, 'is Clinton
Norcross. It says so right on her school enrollment.'

'How did you get her enrollment?' Clint asked. 'I didn't know
those documents were available to the general public.'

For the first time his wife looked uncomfortable rather than
angry . . . and thus somehow less like a stranger.

'You make it sound sleazy.' Lila's cheeks had flushed. 'Okay, maybe
it *was* sleazy. But I had to know the father's name. *Your* name, as it
turns out. So then I went to see her play. That's where I was last
night, in the Coughlin High gym, at an AAU game, watching your
daughter play hoops. And it's not just your face and your name she
has.'

10

The horn blasted and the Tri-Counties AAU team jogged over to
the sideline. Lila broke away from searching the stands for a sign
of Shannon.

She saw Sheila Norcross nod at one of her teammates, a taller
girl. They did an elaborate handshake: bumped fists, locked thumbs,
and clapped hands over their heads.

It was the Cool Shake.

That was it, that was when Lila's heart broke. Her husband was
a man in a beguiling mask. All her doubts and dissatisfactions
suddenly made sense.

The Cool Shake. She had seen Clint and Jared do it a hundred
times. A thousand times. Bump, lock, clap-clap. There was a precious
slideshow in her head of Jared, growing taller with each click of
the wheel, filling out, hair darkening, doing the Cool Shake with
his father. Clint had taught it to all the boys on Jared's Little League
team.

He'd taught her, too.

CHAPTER 20

1

Around midnight central time, a fracas broke out between a small group of Crips and a much larger contingent of Bloods at a Chicago bar called Stoney's Big Dipper. It spread from there, becoming a city-wide gang war that Internet news sites described variously as apocalyptic, unprecedented, and 'fucking humungous.' No one would ever know which member of which gang actually lit the match that ignited what became known as the Second Great Chicago Fire, but it started in West Englewood and spread from there. By dawn, large parts of the city were in flames. Police and fire department response was nearly nonexistent. Most of the cops and hose-jockeys were at home, either trying to keep their wives and daughters awake, or watching over their cocooned bodies while they slept, hoping against hope.

2

'Tell me what you saw,' Frank said. He and Don Peters were standing in back of the Squeaky Wheel, where things had finally begun to wind down – probably because Pudge Marone's supply of alcohol was running low. '*Exactly* what you saw.'

'I was in the Booth, right? That's the prison's nerve-center. We got fifty different cameras. I was looking into what they call the soft cell, which is where they put the new one. She's down as Eve Black, although I don't know if that's her real name or just—'

'Never mind that now. What did you *see?*'

'Well, she was in a red top, like all the new intakes are, and she was falling asleep. I was interested to see the webs come out of her skin, because I knew about it but hadn't seen it. Only they didn't.' Don grasped the sleeve of Frank's shirt. 'You hear what I'm saying? *No webs*. Not a single thread, and by then she was asleep. Only she woke up – her eyes snapped wide open – and she stared right into the camera. Like she was staring at *me*. I think she *was* staring at me. I know that sounds crazy, but—'

'Maybe she wasn't really asleep. Maybe she was faking.'

'All relaxed and sprawled out like she was? No way. Trust me.'

'How come she's there? Why not in the lockup downtown?'

'Because she's as crazy as a shithouse mouse, that's why. Killed a couple of meth cookers with her bare fucking hands!'

'Why aren't you at the prison tonight?'

'Because a couple of ratfucks framed me!' Don burst out. 'Fucking framed me and then fucking canned me! Warden Coates and her buddy the headshrinker, the sheriff's husband! Being married to her is how he probably got the job at the prison in the first place! Had to be a fucking political deal, because he doesn't know his ass from a doorknob!'

Don plunged into the story of his innocent crucifixion, but Frank didn't care what Coates and Norcross claimed this Peters had done. At that moment Frank's mind was a frog on hot rocks, leaping from one idea to the next. Leaping high.

An immune woman? Right here in Dooling? It seemed impossible, but he now had a report of her waking from two people. If there was a Patient Zero, she had to be *somewhere*, right, so why not here? And who was to say there weren't other immunes scattered around the country and the world? The important thing was that if it was true, this Eve Black might offer a cure. A doctor (maybe even his new buddy Garth Flickinger, if Flickinger could get straight and sober) might be able to find something about her blood that was different, and that might lead to . . . well . . .

A vaccine!

A cure!

'—planted evidence! Like I'd want anything to do with some husband murderer who—'

'Shut up a minute.'

For a wonder, Don did so. He stared up into the taller man's face with booze-shiny eyes.

'How many guards at the prison right now?'

'Officers is what we call em, and I dunno for sure. Not many, with everything so screwed up. Depends on who's coming and who's going, too.' He squinted while he did the math – not a pretty sight. 'Maybe seven. Eight if you count Hicks, nine if you add in Mr Shrinky Dink, but those two ain't worth a fart in a high wind.'

'What about the warden?'

Don's eyes shifted away from Frank's. 'I'm pretty sure she went to sleep.'

'Okay, and how many of the ones on duty now are female?'

'When I left, just Van Lampley and Millie Olson. Oh, and Blanche McIntyre might still be there, but she's just Coatsie's secretary, and she's like a hundred and one.'

'Which leaves mighty few, even counting Hicks and Norcross. And you know something else? The sheriff is also a woman, and if she's able to keep order another three hours, I'd be amazed. I'd be amazed if she's even awake in another three hours.' Under sober circumstances, these were thoughts that Frank would have kept to himself – he certainly wouldn't have shared them with an excitable twerp like Don Peters.

Don, computing, ran his tongue around his lips. This was another unattractive visual. 'What are you thinking?'

'That Dooling is going to need a new sheriff soon. And the new sheriff would be perfectly within his rights to remove a prisoner from Correctional. Especially one that hasn't been tried for anything, let alone convicted.'

'You think you might apply for the job?' Don asked.

As if to underline the question, a couple of gunshots went off somewhere in the night. And there was that pervasive smell of smoke. Who was seeing to that? Anyone?

'I'm pretty sure Terry Coombs is the senior man,' Frank said. The senior man currently so deep in his cups he was on the verge of getting underneath them, but Frank didn't say that. He was exhausted and high, but he finally realized he needed to be careful what he let out.

'He's going to need help picking up the slack, though. I'd certainly put my name forward if he needed a deputy.'

'I like that idea,' said Don. 'Might throw my name in the hat, too. Looks like I'll need a job. We should talk to him about going up there and getting that woman right away, don't you think?'

'Yeah,' Frank said. In an ideal world, he didn't think he'd let Don Peters wash out a dog cage, but because of his knowledge of the prison, they might need him. 'Once we all get some sleep and sober up.'

'Well all right, let me give you my cell number,' Don said. 'And let me know what you and Terry are thinking.' He took out the pen and notebook he used to write up cunts who gave him trouble and needed to go on Bad Report.

3

Not long after the first reports of Aurora, rates of male suicide ticked upward sharply, doubling, then later tripling and quadrupling. Men killed themselves loudly, jumping from the tops of buildings or putting guns into their mouths, and men killed themselves quietly, taking pills, closing garage doors and sitting in their running cars. A retired schoolteacher named Eliot Ainsley called a radio show in Sydney, Australia, to explain his intentions and his thinking before he cut his wrists and went to lie down alongside his sleeping wife. 'I just can't see the point of continuing on without the gals,' the retired teacher informed the disc jockey. 'And it's occurred to me that perhaps this is a test, of our love for them, of our devotion for them. You understand, don't you, mate?' The disc jockey replied that he did not understand, that he thought Eliot Ainsley had 'lost his fookin mind' – but a great many men did. These suicides were known by various names, but the one that became part of the common usage was coined in Japan. These were the Sleeping

Husbands, men who hoped to join their wives and daughters, wherever they had gone.

(Vain hope. No men were allowed on the other side of the Tree.)

4

Clint was aware that both his wife and son were staring at him. It was painful to look at Lila, and even more so to look at Jared, who wore an expression of complete bewilderment. Clint saw fear in Jared's face, too. His parents' marriage, a thing so seemingly secure that he had taken it for granted, appeared to be dissolving right before his eyes.

Over on the couch was a little girl cocooned in milky fibers. On the floor beside the girl was an infant, snug in a laundry basket. The infant in the basket didn't look like an infant, however. It looked like something that a spider had wrapped up for a future snack.

'Bump, lock, clap–clap,' Lila said, though she no longer sounded like she cared all that much. 'I saw her do it. Stop pretending, Clint. Stop *lying*.'

We need some sleep, Clint thought, Lila most of all. But not until this sitcom idiocy was resolved. If it could be, and there might be a way. His first thought was of his phone, but the screen wasn't big enough for what he wanted.

'Jared, the Internet's still up, right?'

'Last time I checked.'

'Get your laptop.'

'Why?'

'Just get it, okay?'

'Have I really got a sister?'

'*No.*'

Lila's head had begun to droop, but now she brought it up. 'Yes.'

'Get your laptop.'

Jared went to get it. Lila's head was sinking again. Clint patted first one of her cheeks, then the other. 'Lila. *Lila!*'

Her head rose again. 'Right here. Don't touch me.'

'Have you got any more of that stuff you and Linny took?'

She fumbled in her breast pocket and brought out a contact lens case. She popped up one of the plastic compartments. Inside was a little powder. She glanced at him.

'It's strong,' she said. 'I might claw your eyes out. Cocoon or no cocoon. I'm sad, but I'm also extremely pissed.'

'I'll chance it. Go on.'

She bent, closed one nostril, and snorted the powder up the other. Then she sat back, eyes wide. 'Tell me, Clint, was Shannon Parks a good lay? I thought I was, but she must have been better, if you had to go hot-dogging back to her when we were only married a year or so.'

Jared returned, his closed face saying *I didn't hear that last part*, and set his laptop down in front of his father. He was careful to maintain a separation from Clint when he did it. *Et tu, Brute?*

Clint powered up Jared's Mac, went on Firefox, and searched for 'Sheila Norcross Coughlin basketball.' The story came up. And the picture of the girl named Sheila Norcross. It was a damned good head and shoulders shot, showing her in her basketball jersey. Her pretty face was flushed with on-court hustle. She was smiling. Clint studied the picture for almost thirty seconds. Then, without a word, he turned the laptop so Jared could look. His son did so with a tight mouth and his fists clenched. Then they slowly relaxed. He looked at Lila, more bewildered than ever. 'Mom . . . if there's a resemblance, I don't see it. She doesn't look anything like me. *Or Dad.*'

Lila's eyes, already wide from the fresh ingestion of magic powder, widened even more. She uttered a harsh caw of a laugh. 'Jared, please, don't. Just don't. You have no idea what you're talking about.'

Jared winced as if he had been slapped, and for an awful moment Clint was on the verge of hauling off on his wife of seventeen years. What stopped him was another look at the photo of the smiling girl. Because if you wanted to find it, there *was* a faint resemblance, whether Jared saw it or not: the long jaw, the high forehead, and the dimples that punctuated the corners of her smile. None of these features really matched Clint's own, but he could see how they suggested an association.

I love your dimples, Lila had sometimes told Clint when they were first married. Often in bed, after making love. Touching them with her fingers. *All men should have dimples.*

He could have told her what he now believed, because he thought he understood everything. But there might be another way. It was four in the morning, an hour when almost everyone in the Tri-Counties would ordinarily have been sleeping, but this was no ordinary night. If his old friend from the foster system wasn't in a cocoon, she would be able to take a call. The only question was whether or not he could reach her. He considered his cell, then went to the phone hanging on the wall instead. He got the buzz of an active line; so far, so good.

'What do you think you're doing?' Lila asked.

He didn't answer, simply dialed 0. After six rings he was afraid no one was going to answer, which would hardly be surprising, but then a weary female voice said, 'Yeah? What?'

Clint very much doubted if that was the way Shenandoah Telecom instructed its operators to respond to customer calls, but he was simply grateful to get a human voice. 'Operator, my name is Clinton Norcross, from Dooling, and I badly need some help.'

'Tell you what, I doubt that,' she responded in a drawl that could (and probably did) come straight from the toolies of Bridger County. 'It's the women need help tonight.'

'It's a woman I need to reach. Her name is Shannon Parks. In Coughlin.' If she was listed at all. Single women often went the unlisted route. 'Can you look for me?'

'You could dial 611 for that information. Or check y'damn computer.'

'Please. Help me if you can.'

There was a long silence. The connection hadn't been broken, but suppose she'd gone to sleep on him?

At last the operator said, 'I have an S. L. Parks on Maple Street in Coughlin. That the lady you're looking for?'

It almost had to be. He grabbed the pencil hanging from the memo board so hard it snapped the string. 'Thank you, operator. Thank you so much. Can you give me the number?'

The operator did, then broke the connection.

'I won't believe her, even if you get her!' Lila cried. 'She'll lie for you!'

Clint dialed the number without replying, and didn't even have time to hold his breath. It was picked up halfway through the first ring. 'I'm still awake, Amber,' Shannon Parks said. 'Thanks for call—'

'It's not Amber, Shan,' Clint said. His legs suddenly felt weak, and he leaned against the refrigerator. 'It's Clint Norcross.'

5

The Internet is a bright house standing above a dark cellar with a dirt floor. Falsehoods sprout like mushrooms in that cellar. Some are tasty; many are poisonous. The falsehood that began in Cupertino – which was stated as absolute fact – was one of the latter. In a Facebook post titled AURORA TRUTH, a man who claimed to be a doctor wrote the following:

AURORA WARNING: URGENT!
By Dr. Philip P. Verdrusca

A team of biologists and epidemiologists at Kaiser Permanente Medical Center have determined that the cocoons surrounding women afflicted with the Aurora Sleeping Sickness are responsible for the spread of the disease. The respiration of those afflicted passes through the cocoon and becomes a transmission vector. **This vector is highly contagious!**
The only way to stop the spread of Aurora is to burn the cocoons and the sleeping women inside! Do this **immediately**! You will give your loved ones the rest they long for in their semiconscious state, and stop the spread of this pestilence.
Do it for the sake of the women who are still awake!
SAVE THEM!!!

There was no doctor named Philip Verdrusca on the staff of the Kaiser Permanente facility, or at any of its adjuncts. This fact was quickly posted on TV and online, along with rebuttals from dozens of reputable doctors, and the Atlanta Centers for Disease Control and Prevention. The Cupertino Hoax became the lead story on the news networks as the sun rose over the East Coast of America. But the horse was out of the barn, and Lila Norcross could have predicted what followed. In fact, she *had* predicted it. While people might hope for the best, Lila, closing in on twenty years in a blue uniform, knew that what they believed was the worst. In a terrified world, false news was king.

By the time dawn rose in the midwestern states, Blowtorch Brigades were roaming cities and towns all over America and the world beyond. Cocooned women were hauled to dumps and fields and stadium lawns, where they went up in gouts of fire.

The work of 'Philip P. Verdrusca' had already begun as Clint explained the Norcross family's current situation to Shannon, and then silently extended the telephone to his wife.

6

At first Lila said nothing, only looked mistrustfully at her husband. He nodded to her as if she had spoken, and took his son gently by the arm. 'Come on,' he said. 'Give her some privacy.'

In the living room, on the TV, the Public Access woman continued doing beadwork – would do so, it seemed, even unto the end of the world – but the sound was mercifully muted.

'You're not that girl's father, are you, Dad?'

'No,' Clint said. 'I am not.'

'But how could she have known the Cool Shake we used to do in Little League?'

Clint sat down on the couch with a sigh. Jared sat beside him. 'Like mother like daughter, they say, and Shan Parks was also a basketball player, although never in high school or on an AAU team. She wasn't into anything where they made you take a number or run through paper hoops at pep rallies. That wasn't her style. She stuck to playground pickup games. Boys and girls together.'

Jared was fascinated. 'Did you play?'

'A little, for fun, but I was no good. She could blow by me any old time she wanted, because she had a ton of game. Only she didn't have to, because we never played against each other. We were always on the same team.' In all ways, he thought. It wasn't just how we rolled, it was how we survived. Survival was the real milkshake, the one we both fought for. 'Shan *invented* the Cool Shake, Jere. She taught it to me, and I taught it to you boys when I was coaching.'

'That girl you knew invented the Shake?' Jared sounded awed, as if Shannon had pioneered not a handshake but molecular biology. It made Jared seem so terribly young. Which of course he was.

'Yep.'

The rest he didn't want to say to Jared, because it would sound wildly conceited, but he hoped Shannon was telling his wife now. He thought she would, because Shannon would know both women could be erased from the world in a matter of days, or even hours. That made telling the truth imperative, if not necessarily easier.

Shan had been his best friend, and they had been lovers, but only for a few months. She had been in love with him – head over heels. That was the truth. Clint knew it now, and he supposed in the deepest corner of his heart he had known it then and chosen to ignore it because he didn't feel the same, and couldn't let himself feel the same. Shannon had given him the lift he needed, and he would always owe her for that, but he had not wanted to spend his life with her, had never even considered it. What they had was the bald matter of survival – his survival and hers. Shannon belonged to a life where he had been hurt and scarred and almost broken. She had convinced him to stay on the path. Once he was on it, Clint needed to keep going. She would have to find someone to help her, but it couldn't be him, and was that cruel? Was that selfish? Yes to both.

Years after they parted, she had met a guy and got pregnant. What Clint believed was that the father of Shannon's daughter was a man who looked a little like the boy she had been in love with as a teenager. She had borne a child who carried a tiny bit of that resemblance.

Lila came into the living room at a slow plod and stood between the couch and the TV. She looked around as if unsure where she was.

Clint said 'Honey?' and Jared said 'Mom?' at the same time.

She smiled wanly. 'It seems that I have some apologizing to do.'

'The only thing you have to apologize for is not coming to me with this sooner,' Clint said. 'For letting it fester. I'm just glad I could get hold of her. Is she still on the line?' He nodded toward the kitchen.

'No,' Lila said. 'Oh, she wanted to talk to you, but I hung up on her. Not very nice, but I guess I'm still getting some residual vibration from my jealous bone. Besides, a lot of this is her fault. Giving her daughter your name . . .' She shook her head. 'Idiocy. God, I'm tired.'

You had no problem taking my name, or giving it to your son, Clint thought, and not without resentment.

'The real father was some guy she met at the bar where she used to waitress. All she ever knew about him was his name, and who knows if he gave her his real one. In the story Parks told the kid, it's you, except you died in a car crash during the pregnancy. Not that the girl will ever know any better.'

'She went to sleep?' Jared asked.

'Two hours ago,' Lila said. 'Parks is only staying awake herself because of her best friend, Amber somebody. Who's also a single mother. They practically grow on trees around here, don't they? Everywhere, I guess. Never mind. Let me finish this stupid little story, shall I? She moved to Coughlin for a fresh start shortly after the baby was born. Claims she didn't know you were anywhere in the area, which I don't believe for a second. My name is in the *Herald* every goddam week, and as you yourself pointed out, there are no other Norcrosses in the area. She knew, all right. She's still hoping you can work something out someday, I'd bet anything on it.' Lila's jaws cracked open in a huge yawn.

Clint considered this ragingly unfair, and had to remind himself that Lila — raised in a comfortable middle-class home, with cheery parents and siblings out of an old 1970s sitcom — could not comprehend the nine flavors of hell he and Shannon had been through. Yes, the naming business had been neurotic behavior, no argument, but there was one thing Lila either didn't see or didn't want to see: Shannon had been living only a hundred and fifty miles away, and had never tried to make contact. He could tell himself it was because she'd never known he was close, but as Lila had pointed out, that was farfetched.

'The shake,' Lila said. 'What about that?'

Clint told her.

'All right,' Lila said. 'Case closed. I'm going to make some fresh coffee, then go back to the station. Jesus, I'm so fucking tired.'

7

When she had her coffee, Lila hugged Jared and told him to take care of Molly and the baby, and to hide them well. He promised he would, and she moved from him as quickly as she could. If she hesitated she'd never be able to leave him.

Clint followed her into the vestibule. 'I love you, Lila.'

'I love you, too, Clint.' She supposed she meant it.

'I'm not angry,' he said.

'I'm glad,' Lila said, restraining herself from adding, *Whoopee-ding*.

'You know,' he said, 'the last time I saw Shannon — years ago, but after we were married — she asked me to sleep with her. I told her no.'

The vestibule was dark. Clint's glasses reflected the light through the window at the top of the door. Coats and hats hung on the hooks behind him, a row of abashed spectators.

'I told her no,' Clint said again.

She had no idea what he wanted her to say — good boy, maybe? She had no idea about anything.

Lila kissed him. He kissed her back. It was just lips, skin on skin.

She promised to call him when she got to the station. She went down the steps, then stopped and looked back at him. 'Never told me about the pool,' she said. 'Just went ahead and called a contractor. I came back one day to a hole in the yard. Happy fucking birthday.'

'I—' He stopped. What was there to say, really? That he thought she'd want it, when the truth was *he* wanted it?

'And when you decided to ditch your private practice? We never discussed that, either. You asked some questions, I thought maybe you were researching a paper, or something, and then, boom. Done deal.'

'I thought it was my decision to make.'

'I know you did.'

She waved a vague farewell and walked to her cruiser.

8

'Officer Lampley said you wanted to see me.'

Evie bounded to the bars of her cell so rapidly that Assistant Warden Hicks did a quick reverse two-step. Evie smiled radiantly, her black hair tumbling around her face. 'Lampley is the only female officer left awake, isn't she?'

'Not at all,' Hicks said. 'There's also Millie. Officer Olson, I mean.'

'No, she's asleep in the prison library.' Evie continued to smile her beauty queen smile. And she was a beauty, there could be no arguing that. 'Facedown on a copy of *Seventeen*. She was looking at the party dresses.'

The assistant warden didn't even consider Evie's claim. She couldn't know such a thing. Beautiful as she was, she was in the Romper Room, as the soft cell was sometimes called, and for a reason. 'You're messed up in the head, inmate. I'm not saying that to try and hurt your feelings, I'm saying it because it's true. Maybe you should go to sleep, see if that doesn't clear out some of the cobwebs.'

'Here's an interesting tidbit for you, Assistant Warden Hicks. Although the earth has made a little less than a single turn since what you call Aurora began, well over half of the women in the world have gone to sleep. Almost seventy percent already. Why so many? Lots of the women never woke up in the first place, of course. They were asleep when it started. And then a great number tired and drowsed off despite their best efforts to stay awake. But that's not all of them. No, there's also a significant portion of the female population that just decided to hit the hay. Because, as your Dr Norcross undoubtedly knows, dreading the inevitable is worse than the inevitable itself. Easier to let go.'

'He's a shrink, not a medical doctor,' Hicks said. 'I wouldn't trust him to treat a hangnail. And, if there's nothing else, I have a prison to run and you need a nap.'

'I understand completely. You go ahead, just leave me your cell phone.' All of Evie's teeth were on view. Her smile seemed to get bigger and bigger. Those teeth were very white, and looked very strong. The teeth of an animal, Hicks thought, and of course she was an animal. Had to be, considering what she had done to those meth cookers.

'Why do you need my cell phone, inmate? Why can't you use your own personal invisible cell phone?' He pointed to the empty corner of her cell. It was almost funny, the mix of stupid and crazy and arrogant that this woman was serving up. 'It's right over there and it has unlimited minutes.'

'A good one,' said Evie. 'Very amusing. Now your phone, please. I need to call Dr Norcross.'

'No can do. It's been a pleasure.' He turned to go.

'I wouldn't leave so soon. Your company wouldn't approve. Look down.'

Hicks did, and saw he was surrounded by rats. There were at least a dozen of them, looking up at him with marble-hard eyes. He felt a scream rising in his chest, but stifled it. A scream might set them off, make them attack.

Evie was holding a slim hand out through the bars, palm up, and even in his near panic Hicks noted a terrible thing: there were no lines on that palm. It was entirely smooth.

'You're thinking about running,' she said. 'You can do that, of course, but given your adipose condition, I doubt if you can run very fast.'

The rats were squirming over his shoes now. A pink tail caressed one ankle through his checkered dress sock, and he felt that scream rising again.

'You'll be bitten several times, and who knows what infections my small friends may be carrying? Give me your cell phone.'

'How are you doing it?' Hicks could barely hear his own words over the blood rushing from his heart.

'Trade secret.'

With a shaking hand, Hicks removed his phone from his belt and placed it in that horrible lineless palm.

'You can leave,' Evie said.

He saw that her eyes had turned a bright amber color. The pupils were black diamonds, cat pupils.

Hicks walked gingerly, high-stepping among the circling rats, and when he was beyond them, he ran for Broadway and the safety of the Booth.

'Very well done, Mother,' Evie said.

The largest rat stood on her hind paws and looked up, whiskers twitching. 'He was weak. I could smell his failing heart.' The rat dropped to the floor and scurried toward the steel door of the shower closet further down A wing. The others followed in a line, like children on a school outing. There was a gap between the wall and the floor, a flaw in the cement that the rats had widened to an entry point. They disappeared into the dark.

Hicks's cell was password protected. Evie entered the four-digit code with no hesitation, nor did she bother consulting his contacts before tapping in Clint's cell number. He answered promptly, and without saying hello.

'Cool your jets, Lore. I'm on my way back soon.'

'This isn't Lore Hicks, Dr Norcross, it's Evie Black.'

Silence at the other end.

'Situation normal at home, I hope? Or as normal as can be, under the circumstances?'

'How did you get Hicks's cell phone?'

'I borrowed it.'

'What do you want?'

'First, to give you some information. The torching has begun. Men are burning women in their cocoons by the thousands. Soon it will be by the tens of thousands. It's what many men have always wanted.'

'I don't know what your experiences with men have been. Rotten, I suppose. But whatever you may think, most men don't want to kill women.'

'We'll see, won't we?'

'Yes, I suppose we will. What else do you want?'

'To tell you that you are the one.' She laughed cheerily. 'That you are *the* Man.'

'I'm not getting you.'

'The one who stands for all mankind. As I stand for all women-kind, both those sleeping and those awake. I hate to wax apocalyptic, but in this case I must. This is where the fate of the world will be decided.' She mimicked the momentous drums of television melo-drama. '*Bum-bum-BUM!*'

'Ms Black, you are in the grip of a fantasy.'

'I told you, you can call me Evie.'

'Fine: Evie, you are in the grip of a—'

'The men of your town will come for me. They will ask me if I can revive their wives and mothers and daughters. I will say it's certainly possible, because, like young George Washington, I cannot tell a lie. They will demand that I do it, and I will refuse — as I must. They will torture me, they will rend my body, and still I'll refuse. Eventually they will kill me, Clint. May I call you Clint? I know we've only just started working together, so I don't want to overstep.'

'You might as well.' He sounded numb.

'Once I'm dead, the portal between this world and the land of sleep will close. Every woman will eventually go nighty-night, every man will eventually die, and this tortured world will breathe an enormous sigh of lasting relief. Birds will make nests in the Eiffel Tower and lions will walk through the broken streets of Cape Town and the waters will drink up New York City. The big fishies will tell the little fishies to dream big-fishie dreams, because Times Square is wide open, and if you can swim strong enough against the prevailing current there you can swim against it anywhere.'

'You're hallucinating.'

'Is what's happening all over the world a hallucination?'

She left him a gap, but he didn't take it.

'Think of it as a fairy tale. I am the fair maiden pent in the castle keep, held in durance vile. You are my prince, my knight in shining armor. You must defend me. I'm sure there are weapons in the sheriff's station, but finding men willing to use them – to perhaps die defending the creature they believe has caused all this – will be more difficult. I have faith in your powers of persuasion, though. It is why . . .' She laughed. '. . . you *are* the Man! Why not admit it, Clint? You've always wanted to be the Man.'

He flashed on that morning, his irritation at the sight of Anton, the melancholy he'd felt as he inspected his sagging stomach. As depleted as he was, her insinuating tone made Clint want to punch something.

'Your feelings are normal, Clint. Don't get down on yourself.' She turned sympathetic, gentle. 'Every man wants to be the Man. The one who rides in, says nothing but yup, nope, and draw, cleans up the town, and rides away again. After sleeping with the prettiest wench in the saloon, of course. Which ignores the central problem. You men butt your horns and the banging gives the whole planet a headache.'

'Can you really end it?'

'Did you kiss your wife goodbye?'

'Yes,' Clint said. 'Just a moment ago. We've had better ones, but I tried. She did, too.' He inhaled. 'I don't know why I'm telling you any of this.'

'Because you believe me. And I actually know you kissed her. I was watching. I'm a terrible peeper. I should stop, but I'm a sucker for romance. I'm glad you worked everything out tonight, too, got it all on the table. It's what's left unspoken that can really damage a marriage.'

'Thank you, Dr Phil. Answer my question. Can you end it?'

'Yes. Here's the deal. Keep me alive until, oh, sunrise next Tuesday. Or maybe a day or two later, I can't tell for sure. Should be at sunrise, though.'

'What happens if I – if *we* – do that?'

'I might be able to fix things. So long as they agree.'

'So long as who agrees?'

'The women, silly. The women from Dooling. But if I die, no

agreement they come to will matter. It can't be one or the other.
It has to be both.'

'I don't understand what you're talking about!'

'You will. Eventually. Perhaps I'll see you tomorrow. And by the
way, she was right. You never discussed the pool with her. Although
you did show her a few pictures. Guess you thought that would be
enough.'

'Evie—'

'I'm glad you kissed her. I'm very glad. I like her.'

Evie broke the connection and placed Hicks's cell phone carefully
on the little shelf meant for her personal belongings – of which
she had none. Then, she lay down on her bunk, rolled onto her
side, and soon fell asleep.

<h1 style="text-align:center">9</h1>

Lila fully intended to go directly to the sheriff's station, but when
she backed down the driveway and swerved onto the street, her
headlights spotted a white thing sitting in a lawn chair on the
opposite side. Old Mrs Ransom. Lila could hardly blame Jared for
leaving her there. He'd had the little girl to think about, the one
now lying upstairs in the spare bedroom. Holly? Polly? No, Molly.
A fine drizzle was falling.

She pulled into the Ransom driveway, then went around back
and rummaged through the crap in the rear seat for her Dooling
Hound Dogs baseball cap, because the drizzle was thickening to a
steady light rain. It might put the fires out, and that was good. She
checked Mrs Ransom's front door. It was unlocked. She crossed to
the lawn chair and lifted the cocooned woman into her arms. She
was prepared for a burden, but Mrs Ransom weighed no more than
ninety pounds. Lila could press more than that in the gym. And
what did it matter? Why was she even doing this?

'Because it's the decent thing,' she said. 'Because a woman is not
a lawn ornament.'

As she climbed the steps, she saw fine threads detach themselves
from the white ball surrounding Mrs Ransom's head. They wavered

as if in a breeze, but there was no breeze. They were reaching for *her*, for the sea of sleep just waiting behind her forehead. She blew them away, and struggled backward down the hall to the old lady's living room. Open on the rug was a coloring book with a scattering of markers around it. What *was* that little girl's name again?

'Molly,' Lila said as she pulled the encased woman up onto a couch. 'Her name was Molly.' She paused. '*Is* Molly.'

Lila put a throw pillow beneath Mrs Ransom's head and left her.

After locking the old lady's front door, she went to her cruiser and started the engine, reached for the gearshift, then dropped her hand. Suddenly the sheriff's station seemed like a pointless destination. Furthermore, it seemed at least fifty miles away. She could probably get there without hitting a tree (or some woman trying to jog away sleep), but what was the sense?

'If not the office, what?' she asked her car. 'What?'

She took the contact lens case from her pocket. There was another wake-up shot in the other container, the one marked **L**, but the question recurred: What was the sense in fighting it? Sleep would catch her eventually. It was inevitable, so why postpone it? According to Shakespeare, it knitted up the raveled sleeve of care. And at least she and Clint had gotten some of that fabled closure he was always going on about.

'I was a fool,' she confessed to the police car's interior. 'But Your Honor, I plead sleep deprivation.'

If that was all it was, why hadn't she confronted him sooner? With everything that happened, it seemed unforgivably small. It was embarrassing.

'All right,' she said, 'I plead fear, Your Honor.'

But she wasn't afraid now. She was too spent to be afraid. She was too spent to be anything.

Lila yanked the mic from its prongs. It actually felt heavier than Mrs Ransom — how weird was that?

'Unit One to Base. Are you still there, Linny?'

'Still here, boss.' Linny had probably been into the powdered goodies again; she sounded as chipper as a squirrel sitting on a pile of fresh acorns. Also, she had gotten a full eight hours the night before, instead of going all the way to Coughlin in McDowell County and driving aimlessly until dawn, thinking bad thoughts about a husband who had turned out to be faithful after all. Ah, but so many of them weren't, and was that a reason or only an excuse? Was it even true? Could you find statistics about fidelity on the Internet? Would they be accurate?

Shannon Parks had asked Clint to sleep with her, and he had said no. That's how faithful he was.

But . . . that was what he was supposed to be, wasn't it? Did you get medals for keeping your promises and living up to your responsibilities?

'Boss? Read me?'

'I won't be in for awhile, Linny. Got something I need to do.'

'Roger that. What's up?'

This was a question Lila chose not to answer. 'Clint needs to go back to the prison after he has a little rest. Give him a call around eight, will you? Make sure he's up and ask him to check in on Mrs Ransom on his way out. He needs to take care of her. He'll understand what that means.'

'Okay. Wake-up calls aren't my specialty, but I don't mind branching out. Lila, are you all r—'

'Unit One out.'

Lila racked the mic. In the east, a faint line of Friday morning light had appeared on the horizon. Another day was about to dawn. It would be a rainy one, the kind made for sweet afternoon naps. The litter of her trade lay on the seat beside her: camera and clipboard and Simmons radar gun, banded stacks of fliers, her citation book. She took this last, tore off the top sheet, and turned it over to the blank side. She printed her husband's name in big capital letters at the top, and then: *Put me and Platinum and Mrs Ransom and Dolly in one of the empty houses. Keep us safe. There might not be any coming back from this, but maybe there is.* She paused, thinking (it was hard to think), then added: *Love you both.* She added a heart – corny, but so what? – and signed her name. She took a paperclip from the little plastic caddy in the glove compartment, and attached the note to her breast pocket. As a small girl, her mother had attached her milk-money, sealed in a small envelope, to her shirt every Monday, in just the same way. Lila couldn't remember it, but her mother had told her.

With that chore taken care of, she sat back and closed her eyes. Sleep rushed at her like a black engine with no headlight, and oh the relief. The blessed relief.

The first delicate threads spun out of Lila's face and caressed her skin.

PART TWO

I'LL SLEEP WHEN I'M DEAD

It don't matter if I get a little tired
I'll sleep when I'm dead.

Warren Zevon

The spongy old boards of the porch bow and weep beneath Lila's shoes. A powerful spring breeze shakes the field of oxtail that used to be her own front yard, and the noise is a beautiful roar. The fabulous green of the oxtails strains credulity. She glances back in the direction she has come from and sees that saplings have risen up through the broken pavement of Tremaine Street. They rock in the wind like the hands of confused clocks, trapped between twelve and one. A blue sky covers the world. In Mrs Ransom's driveway, her cruiser, the door left ajar, is scaled with rust. All four tires are flat.

How did she get here?

Never mind, she tells herself. It's a dream. Leave it at that.

She goes inside her house and stops to consider the remains of the little-used dining room: windows broken, tattered curtains curling and uncurling in another waft of breeze, seasons and seasons' worth of leaves drifted almost to the top of the mold-spackled table. The smell of rot is pervasive. As she walks down the hall, she thinks this might be a time-traveling dream.

Chunks of the living room ceiling have fallen, littering the carpet with moon rocks. The flatscreen TV is still bolted to the wall, but the screen has gone bad somehow, warped and puffed out, as if it has been baked.

Dirt and dust have whitened the sliding glass doors to opacity. Lila pulls the right one, and it opens, moaning along its decayed rubber track.

'Jared?' she asks. 'Clint?'

They were here last night, sitting around a table that now lies on its side. Yellow weeds tower around the edges of the deck and sprout between the boards. Their barbecue, the center of many summer picnic suppers, has been engulfed.

In the pool, where the waters are the brackish color of a fish tank after a long power outage, a bobcat pauses breast-deep in its crossing. A bird is clamped in its teeth. The bobcat's eyes are bright and its teeth are large and water beads its fur. Pasted to its broad, flat nose is a white feather.

Lila rakes her fingernails down her cheek, feels the pain, and decides (reluctantly) that this might not be a dream, after all. If not, how long has she been asleep?

A good while. Or a bad one.

The animal blinks its shining eyes and begins to paddle toward her.

Where am I? she thinks, then thinks, I am home, *and then thinks the first thing again*: Where am I?

CHAPTER 1

1

Late Friday afternoon, well into the second day of the disaster (in Dooling, at least; in some parts of the world, it was already Aurora Day Three), Terry Coombs awoke to the aroma of sizzling bacon and brewing coffee. Terry's first coherent thought was: Is there any liquid left in the Squeaky Wheel, or did I drink the whole place, right down to the dishwater? His second was more basic: get to the bathroom. He did just that, arriving in time to vomit copiously into the toilet. For a couple of minutes he rested there, letting the pendulum that was making the room swing back and forth settle to a stop. When it did, he hauled himself up, found some Bayer and swallowed three with gulps of water from the faucet. Back in the bedroom, he stared at the space on the left side of the bed where he recalled that Rita had been lying, cocoon around her head, the white stuff in her mouth sucking inward and billowing out with each breath.

Had she gotten up? Was it over? Tears prickled Terry's eyes and he staggered, wearing nothing but his underwear, out into the kitchen.

Frank Geary sat at the table, dwarfing it with his broad upper body. Somehow the inherent mournfulness of that sight − a big man at a tiny table in bright sunlight − informed Terry of everything he needed to know before any words were spoken. Their gazes met. Geary had a copy of *National Geographic* folded open. He set it aside.

'I was reading about Micronesia,' said Frank. 'Interesting place. Lots of wildlife, too much of it endangered. Probably you were hoping for someone else. I don't know if you remember, but I slept over. We moved your wife into the basement.'

Ah, now it came back. They'd carried Rita downstairs, a man to each end, as if she were a rug, banging their shoulders off the railings and the walls as they descended. They'd left her on the old couch, atop the old quilt that covered it to keep the dust off. Rita was undoubtedly lying there at that moment, surrounded by the other pieces of dusty furniture they'd discarded over the years and intended to yardsale but never got around to: bar chairs with yellow vinyl seats, the VCR, Diana's old crib, the old woodstove.

Despondency sapped Terry: he couldn't even keep his head raised. His chin dropped to his chest.

In front of the empty chair on the opposite side of the table was a plate with bacon and toast on it. Beside the plate was a cup of black coffee and a bottle of Beam. Terry drew in a ragged breath and sat down.

He crunched up a piece of bacon and waited to see what would happen. His stomach made noises and swirled around some, but nothing came up. Frank wordlessly added a dollop of whiskey to Terry's coffee. Terry took a sip. His hands, which he hadn't realized were trembling, steadied.

'I needed that. Thank you.' His voice was a croak.

Though they weren't close friends, he and Frank Geary had shared a few drinks together over the years. Terry knew Frank was serious about his job as the town's animal control officer; he knew Frank had a daughter he believed was a pretty terrific artist; he remembered that a drunk had once suggested to Frank that he should leave some irritation or another up to God, and Frank had told the drunk to put a sock in it, and as well-sauced as the drunk had been, he'd caught the warning in Frank's tone and had not made a peep the rest of the night. In other words, Frank had seemed to Terry like a right enough guy, just not someone whose balls you'd ever want to bust. That Frank was black might have played into a certain sense of necessitated distance, too. Terry had never actually considered the possibility of being buddies with a black guy, although he had nothing against the idea now that he did consider it.

'It's no problem,' said Frank. His cool, straightforward manner was reassuring.

'So, everything's . . .' Terry had another swallow of the juiced coffee. 'The same?'

'As yesterday? Yeah. Which means everything's different. For one thing, you're acting sheriff. Station called looking for you a few minutes ago. The old sheriff has gone missing.'

Terry's stomach sent up a bubble of nastiness. 'Lila missing? Jeez.'

'Congratulations, huh? Big promotion. Cue the marching band.'

Frank's right eyebrow was wryly arched. They both broke into laughter, but Terry's dried up quickly.

'Hey,' Frank said. His hand found Terry's, squeezed it. 'Keep it together, okay?'

'Okay.' Terry swallowed. 'How many women are still awake?'

'Don't know. It's bad. But I'm sure you can handle this.'

Terry wasn't. He drank his doctored coffee. He chewed his bacon. His dining companion was quiet.

Frank drank from his own coffee and looked at Terry over the rim of his cup.

'*Can* I handle it?' Terry asked. 'Can I really?'

'Yes.' There was no doubt at all in Frank Geary's voice. 'But you'll need all the help you can get.'

'You want me to deputize you?' It made sense to Terry: besides Lila, they were down at least a couple of officers.

Frank shrugged. 'I'm a town employee. I'm here to pitch in. If you want to give me a star, that's fine.'

Terry took another slug of the laced coffee and got to his feet. 'Let's go.'

2

Aurora had knocked out a quarter of the department, but Frank helped Terry fill out a roster of volunteer deputies that Friday morning, and brought in Judge Silver to administer their oaths on Friday afternoon. Don Peters was one of the new hires; another was a high school senior named Eric Blass, young but enthusiastic.

On Frank's advice, Terry posted a nine P.M. curfew. Two-man teams began canvasing Dooling's neighborhoods to put up the notices. Also to settle folks down, discourage vandalism, and – another notion of Frank's – to begin cataloging the whereabouts of the sleepers. Frank Geary might have been a dogcatcher before Aurora, but he made a helluva law officer, with a terrific sense of organization. When Terry discovered he could lean on him, he leaned hard.

Almost a dozen looters were collared. This really wasn't much in the way of police work, because few bothered to hide what they were doing. They probably believed their behavior would be winked at, but soon learned better. One of these miscreants was Roger Dunphy, Dooling Correctional's AWOL janitor. On their first Sunday morning cruise around town, Terry and Frank spied Mr Dunphy blatantly toting a clear plastic bag filled with necklaces and rings that he'd lifted from the rooms of the female residents at Crestview Nursing Home, where he sometimes moonlighted.

'They don't need them now,' Dunphy had argued. 'Come on, Deputy Coombs, gimme a break. It's a clear case of salvage.'

Frank seized the janitor by the nose, squeezing hard enough to make the cartilage creak. 'Sheriff Coombs. You'll call him Sheriff Coombs from now on.'

'Okay!' Dunphy cried. 'I'll call im President Coombs, if you'll just leave go of my schnozz!'

'Return that property and we'll let this ride,' Terry said, and was gratified by Frank's approving nod.

'Sure! You bet!'

'And don't you fuck the dog on this, because we'll be checking.'

The great thing about Frank, Terry realized during those first three days, was that he grasped the enormous pressure Terry was functioning under in a way that no one else seemed to. He never pressed, but he always had a suggestion and, nearly as important, he kept that leather-encased silver hip flask – very cool, maybe it was a black thing – at the ready for when Terry got low, when it seemed the day would never end and his wheels started spinning in the awful, surreal mud of it all. He was at Terry's elbow the entire time, stalwart as hell, and he was with him on Monday, Aurora Plus Five, outside the gates of the Dooling Correctional Facility for Women.

3

Acting sheriff Coombs had tried several times over the weekend to convince Clint that he needed to release Eve Black into his custody. Rumors about the woman who had killed the meth dealers were circulating: unlike all the others, the stories went, she slept and woke. At the station, Linny Mars (still hanging in there; you go, girl) had received so many calls regarding this that she had taken to hanging up on anyone who asked. Frank said they *had* to find out if the rumors were true; it was a priority. Terry supposed he was right, but Norcross was being stubborn, and Terry was finding it increasingly difficult to even get the annoying man on the phone.

The fires had burned themselves out by Monday, but the country-side near the prison still smelled like an ashtray. It was gray and humid and the misty rain that had been falling off and on since early Friday morning was falling again. Acting sheriff Terry Coombs, feeling mildewed, stood at the intercom and monitor outside the gates of the Dooling Correctional Facility for Women.

Norcross still wasn't buying the transfer order that Judge Silver had signed for Eve Black. (Frank had assisted with that, too, explaining to the judge that the woman might possess a unique immunity to the virus, and impressing on the old jurist the need to act quickly and keep things calm before a riot started.)

'Oscar Silver's got no jurisdiction in the matter, Terry.' The doctor's voice burbled from the speaker, sounding as if it were coming from the bottom of a pond. 'I know he signed her in at my wife's request, but he can't sign her out. Once she was remanded to me for evaluation, that was the end of his authority. You need a county judge now.'

Terry couldn't fathom why Lila's husband, who had always seemed down-to-earth, was being such a pain in the ass. 'There's no one else right now, Clint. Judge Wainer and Judge Lewis are both asleep. Just our luck to've had a couple of female judges on the county circuit.'

'All right, so go ahead and call Charleston and find out who they've appointed as interim,' Clint said. As if they'd come to a happy compromise, as if he'd given even a single damn inch. 'But why bother? Eve Black is now asleep like all the rest.'

Hearing that put a lead ball in Terry's stomach. He should have known better than to believe a bunch of loose talk. Might as well try to question his own wife, a mummy in the basement dark, sprawled atop the dingy quilt on their old couch.

'She went down yesterday afternoon,' Norcross continued. 'We've only got a few inmates that are still awake.'

'Then why won't he let us see her?' Frank asked. He had been standing silently throughout the exchange.

It was a good question. Terry jabbed the call button and asked it.

'Look, here's what we'll do,' said Clint. 'I'll send you a picture on your cell phone. But I can't let anyone in. That's *lockdown protocol*. I've got the warden's book open right here in front of me. I'll read you what it says. "State authorities must *enjoin* the facility and may remove the Lockdown Order at their discretion." *State authorities.*'

'But—'

'Don't but me, Terry, I didn't write it. Those are the regulations. Since Hicks walked off on Friday morning, I'm the only adminis-trative officer this prison's got, and protocol is all I have to go on.'

'But—' He was starting to sound like a two-cycle engine: *but-but-but-but.*

'I had to put us on lockdown. I had no choice. You've seen the same news I've seen. There're people going around torching women in their cocoons. I think you'll agree that my population would be a prime target for that breed of vigilante.'

'Oh, come on.' Frank made a hissing noise and shook his head. They hadn't been able to find a uniform shirt large enough to button across his chest, so Frank wore it open to his undershirt. 'Sounds like a bunch of bureaucratic gobblydegook to me. You're the acting sheriff, Terry. That's gotta trump a doctor, especially a shrink.'

Terry held up a hand to Frank. 'I get all that, Clint. I understand your concern. But you know me, all right? I've worked with Lila for more than a decade. Since before she was sheriff. You've eaten dinner at my house and I've eaten dinner at yours. I'm not going to do anything to any of those women, so give me a break.'

'I'm trying—'

'You would not believe some of the garbage I've had to shovel up around town over the weekend. Some lady left her stove on and burned down half of Greely Street. A hundred acres of woods south of town are torched. I got a dead high school athlete who tried to rape a sleeper. I got a guy with his head smashed in by a blender. I mean, this is *stupid*. Let's put aside the rulebook. I'm acting sheriff. We're friends. Let me see she's sleeping like the others, and I'll get out of your hair.'

The security kiosk on the opposite side of the fence, where an officer ought to have been stationed, was empty. Beyond it, across the parking lot and on the opposite side of the second fence, the prison hunched its gray shoulders. There was no movement to be seen through the bulletproof glass of the front doors, no prisoners taking laps on the track or working in the garden plot. Terry thought of amusement parks in the late fall, the ramshackle appearance they took on when the rides stopped spinning and there were no kids walking around eating ice cream and laughing. Diana, his daughter, was grown now, but he'd taken her on countless amusement park trips when she was younger. Those had been fine times.

Christ, he could use a nip. Good thing Frank kept his cool flask handy.

'Check your phone, Terry,' came Clint's voice through the intercom speaker.

The train whistle that was Terry's ringtone went off. He took his cell phone from his pocket and looked at the photograph that Clint had messaged him.

A woman in a red top lay on a cell cot. There was an ID number above her breast pocket. Beside the ID number an ID card had been placed. On the card was a photograph of a woman with long black hair, tan skin, and a wide, white smile. The name of the woman was listed as 'Eve Black' and her ID number matched the number on the uniform shirt. A cocoon had blotted out her face.

Terry handed the phone to Frank so he could see the picture. 'What do you think? Do we call it good?'

It occurred to Terry, that he – the acting sheriff – was fishing for a direction from his new deputy, when it was supposed to be the other way around.

Frank studied the picture and said, 'This doesn't prove jack shit. Norcross could put one on any sleeping woman and add Black's ID.' Frank returned the phone to Terry. 'It doesn't make any sense, refusing to let us in. You're the law, Terry, and he's a goddam prison psychiatrist. He is smoother than slippery elm, I'll give him that, but it smells. I think it's a stall game.'

Frank was right, of course; the picture didn't prove anything. Why not allow them in to at least *see* the woman in the flesh, sleeping or not? The world was on the verge of losing half its population. What did some warden's rulebook matter?

'Why stall, though?'

'I don't know.' Frank took out the flat flask and offered it. Terry thanked him, took a glorious swig of the whiskey, and offered the flask back. Frank shook his head. 'Keep it handy.'

Terry pocketed the flask and thumbed the intercom. 'I got to see her, Clint. Let me in, let me see, and we can all get on with our day. People are talking about her. I need to put the talk to rest. If I don't, we might have a problem I can't control.'

4

From his seat in the Booth, Clint observed the two men on the main monitor's feed. The door to the Booth was open, as it never would have been under normal conditions, and Officer Tig Murphy was leaning in. Officers Quigley and Wettermore were just outside, also listening. Scott Hughes, the only other officer they had left, was taking a nap in an empty cell. A couple of hours after she'd shot Ree Dempster, Van Lampley had clocked out – Clint hadn't had the heart to ask her to stay. ('Good luck, Doc,' she'd said, sticking her head in the door of his office, out of uniform and in her street clothes, eyes bloodshot from tiredness. Clint had wished her the same. She hadn't thanked him.) If she wasn't asleep by now, he doubted she would have been of much use, anyway.

Clint was confident that he could put Terry off at least for awhile. What concerned him was the big guy standing beside Terry, who had given the acting sheriff the flask and was advising him between exchanges. It was like watching a ventriloquist and his talking dummy. Clint noticed the way the big guy was scanning around instead of staring at the intercom speaker, as people instinctively tended to do. It was like he was casing the place.

Clint depressed his intercom button and spoke into the mic. 'Honestly, I'm not trying to complicate things, Terry. I feel terrible about this. Not to beat a dead horse, but I swear, I've got the warden's book right here in front of me. It's in capital letters at the top of the Lockdown Ordinances!' He tapped the electronics board in front of him, on which there rested no book of any kind. 'This isn't what I was trained for, Terry, and the book is all I have.'

'Clint.' He could hear Terry's disgusted exhalation. 'What the heck, man. Am I going to have to bust down the gate? This is ridiculous. Lila would be – really disappointed. Really disappointed. She wouldn't believe this.'

'I understand you're frustrated, and I know I can't even begin to appreciate the stress you've been under the last couple of days, but you do realize there's a camera on you, right? I just watched you take a drink from a flask and we both know that it wasn't Kool-Aid. With all due respect, I knew Lila—' The mention of his wife in the past tense, realized only as soon as it was out of his mouth, caused Clint's heart to catch. To get himself a moment, he cleared his throat. 'I know Lila a little better than you, and that's what I think would disappoint her, that her go-to deputy is drinking on the job. Put yourself in my position. Would you let someone into the prison who doesn't have jurisdiction, or the right paperwork, and who's been drinking?'

They watched Terry throw up his hands and walk away from the intercom, pacing in a circle. The other man put an arm around his shoulder, and spoke to him.

Tig shook his head and chuckled. 'You should never have gone into prison medicine, Doc. You could have been rich selling shit on HSN. You just did major voodoo on that guy. He's going to need therapy now.'

Clint swiveled to the three officers standing by. 'Anybody know the other one? The big dude?'

Billy Wettermore did. 'That's Frank Geary, the local animal control officer. My niece helps out with the strays. She told me he's okay, but kind of intense.'

'Intense how?'

'He really doesn't like people who don't take care of their animals, or abuse them. There was a rumor that he put a beatdown on a redneck who tortured a dog or cat or something, but I wouldn't bet all my money on that one. High school grapevine has never been too reliable.'

It was on the tip of Clint's tongue to ask Billy Wettermore to give his niece a ring before he remembered how unlikely it was that she'd still be awake. Their own female population was down to a grand total of three: Angel Fitzroy, Jeanette Sorley, and Eve Black. The woman he'd photographed was an inmate named Wanda Denker who had a body type similar to Evie's. Denker had been conked out since Friday night. In preparation, they'd dressed her in scrubs with Evie's ID number and Evie's ID pinned to her red top. Clint was grateful – and a little stunned – that the crew of four remaining officers had bought into what he was doing.

He'd told them that since word of Evie's sleeping and waking was public knowledge, it was inevitable that someone – probably the cops – would come for her. He hadn't attempted to pitch Tig Murphy and Rand Quigley and Billy Wettermore and Scott Hughes on the idea that Evie was some sort of fantastic being whose safety, and by extension the safety of every woman in existence, depended on Clint. He had a great deal of confidence in his ability to talk a person around to a new way of seeing things – he'd been doing exactly that for nearly two decades – but this was an idea that not even he dared attempt to sell. The tack Clint had taken with Dooling Correctional's remaining officers was simpler: they couldn't hand Evie over to locals. Moreover, they couldn't play it straight with them, because as soon as they acknowledged that Evie was different, they'd only become more relentless. Whatever the deal with Evie was – whatever immunity she possessed – it needed to be sorted out by serious scientists from the federal government who knew what the hell they were doing. It didn't matter that the town authorities probably had a comparable plan in mind: to have a doctor examine her, to question her about her background, and perform every test you could perform on a person who seemed to have a unique biology. Which sounded okay.

But, as Terry might have said. *But.*

She was too precious to risk, that was the but. If they handed Evie over to the wrong people and things went sideways, if someone lost their temper and killed her – perhaps out of simple frustration, perhaps because they needed a scapegoat – what good would she be then to anyone's mothers and wives and daughters?

And forget Evie as an interview subject, Clint told his (very) thin blue line. She couldn't or wouldn't tell anyone anything. She seemed not to have the remotest idea of what was so special about her biology. Plus, immune or not, Eve Black was a psychopath who'd planted a pair of meth cookers.

'Someone could still, like, study her body and her DNA and such, couldn't they?' Rand Quigley had hopefully proposed. 'Even if her brains were blown out?' He added hastily: 'I'm just sayin.'

'I'm sure they could, Rand,' said Clint, 'but don't you think that's not optimal? It's probably better if we keep her brains in. They might be useful.'

Rand had conceded as much.

Meanwhile, for the benefit of this scenario, Clint had been making regular calls to the CDC. Since the guys in Atlanta didn't answer – repeated calls yielded nothing but a recorded announcement or the same busy signal as on the Thursday the crisis started – he was discussing matters with a branch of the CDC that happened to be located on the second floor of an empty house on Tremaine Street. Its number was Lila's cell phone, and Jared and Mary Pak were the only scientists on the staff.

'This is Norcross again at Dooling Correctional in West Virginia,' began the play that Clint performed over and over, with minor variations, for the ears of his remaining officers.

'Your son is asleep, Mr Norcross,' was how Mary replied at the start of their latest go-round. 'May I please kill him?'

'That's a negative,' Clint said. 'Black is still sleeping and waking. She's still extremely dangerous. We still need you to come and get her.'

Mrs Pak and Mary's younger sister had both fallen asleep by Saturday morning, and her out-of-town father was still attempting to make his way back from Boston. Rather than stay home alone, Mary had tucked her mother and sister into bed and gone to join Jared. To the two teenagers, Clint had been honest – mostly. He had omitted some things. He had told them that there was a woman in the prison who slept and woke, and asked them to participate in the CDC rigamarole because he said he was worried that the staff would give up and walk if it didn't seem like he was talking to someone and that help was imminent. The parts he'd left out were about Evie: her impossible knowledge, and the deal she'd offered him.

'My pee is pure Monster Energy drink, Mr Norcross. When I move my arms fast, there are, like, traces in the air – *that I see.* Does that make sense? Oh, probably not, but whatever, I think this might be my superhero origin story and Jared is in his sleeping bag missing the excitement. I am going to have to dribble spit in his ear if he doesn't wake up soon.'

This was the part where Clint increasingly flashed a show of annoyance. 'That's all fascinating, and I certainly hope you'll take whatever steps are necessary, but let me repeat: we need you to come and extract this woman and get to work on whatever makes her different. *Capisce*? Call me as soon as you have a helicopter en route.'

'Your wife is okay,' Mary said. Her euphoria had abruptly

dampened. 'Well, not changed. You know, the same. Resting . . . um . . . resting comfortably.'

'Thank you,' said Clint.

The entire structure of logic he'd constructed was so rickety that Clint wondered how much Billy and Rand and Tig and Scott truly believed, and how much of it was the officers craving something to dedicate themselves to amid an emergency that was as amorphous as it was nightmarish.

And there was another motivation in play, simple but strong: the territorial imperative. In the view of Clint's small cadre of shields, the prison was their patch, and townies had no business messing in it.

These factors had allowed them, for a few days at least, to keep doing the job they were accustomed to, albeit with fewer and fewer prisoners that needed attending. They found comfort in doing the job in familiar surroundings. The five men took shifts sleeping on the couch in the officers' break room, and cooking in the prison kitchen. It also may have helped that Billy, Rand, and Scott were young and unmarried, and that Tig, the oldest of the bunch by twenty years, was divorced without kids. They had even seemed to acclimate, after some grumbling, to Clint's insistence that everyone's safety depended on no more personal calls being made. And, accordingly, they had abetted him in the most distasteful measure he'd been forced to make: under the pretext of 'emergency security regulations' they had used tin snips to amputate the receivers from the three payphones available for the use of the prisoners, and deprived the population, in what might well be their last days, from any opportunity to communicate with their loved ones.

This precaution had led to the breaking out of a small riot on Friday afternoon when half a dozen prisoners had made a charge for the administration wing. It had not been much of a riot; the women were exhausted and, except for one inmate wielding a sock filled with dead batteries, they had been unarmed. The four officers had quickly put the insurrection down. Clint didn't feel good about it, but if anything, the attack had probably served to strengthen his officers' resolve.

How long the men would stay resolved, Clint couldn't hazard a guess. He just hoped they could be persuaded to hang on until he could either change Evie's mind and get her to cooperate in a way that made sense, or the sun rose on Tuesday or Wednesday or Thursday or whenever, and she was satisfied.

If what she claimed was true. If it wasn't . . .

Then it didn't matter. But until it didn't matter, it did.

Clint felt bizarrely energized. A lot of bad shit had happened, but at least he was doing something. Unlike Lila, who had given up.

Jared had found her in Mrs Ransom's driveway. She had let herself fall asleep in her car. Clint told himself he didn't blame her. How could he? He was a doctor. He understood the body's limits. Once you went without sleep long enough, you fragmented, lost your sense of what was important and what wasn't, lost your sense of what was even real, lost yourself. She'd broken down, that was all.

But he couldn't break down. He had to make things right. Like he'd made things right with Lila before Aurora had taken her, by staying strong and persuading her to see reason. He had to try to resolve this crisis, bring his wife home, bring them all home. Trying was the only thing left.

Evie might be able to stop it. Evie might be able to wake Lila up. She might be able to wake all of them up. Clint might get her to see reason. The world might be returned to normal. Despite everything that Clint knew about the science of medicine – everything that said that Evie Black was just a madwoman with delusions of grandeur – too much had happened for him to entirely refute her claims. Madwoman or not, she had powers. Her lacerations had healed in less than a day. She knew things she couldn't know. Unlike every other woman on the planet, she slept and woke.

The big man, Geary, slipped his fingers through the fencing of the front gate, and gave it an experimental shake. Then he crossed his arms and peered at an electronic lock the size of a boxing glove.

Clint saw this, noted how Terry had wandered off to toe the dirt at the roadside and nip at the flask, and concluded that serious trouble might be brewing down the road. And maybe not that far down.

He tapped the intercom. 'Hi there. So are we all set? Terry? And Frank? You're Frank, aren't you? Nice to meet you. You got the picture?'

Instead of responding, the new deputy and the acting sheriff went back to their police car, climbed in, and departed. Frank Geary drove.

5

There was a scenic turnout halfway between the prison and the town. Frank swung in and cut the engine. 'Isn't this a sight?' he said in a low, marveling voice. 'You'd think the world, was just the same as it was last week.'

Frank was right, Terry thought, it was a fine view. They could see all the way to Ball's Ferry and beyond – but it was hardly time to admire the countryside.

'Um, Frank? I think we should—'

'Discuss it?' Frank nodded emphatically. 'Just what I was thinking. My take's pretty simple. Norcross may be a psychiatrist or whatever, but his advanced degree must've been in bullshit. He gave us a classic runaround, and he's going to keep on doing it until we refuse to accept it.'

'I guess.'

Terry was thinking of what Clint had said about drinking on the job. He was probably right, and Terry was willing to admit (if only to himself) that he was close to being drunk right now. It was just that he felt so overwhelmed. Sheriff was no job for him. When it came to law enforcement, he was strictly deputy class.

'What we need here is closure, Sheriff Coombs. Not just for us, for everyone. We need access to the woman in the picture he sent, we need to cut open the webs over her face, and make sure it's the same face as the woman in the ID photo. If that turns out to be the case, we can go to Plan B.'

'Which is what?'

Frank reached into his pocket, produced a pack of bubblegum, peeled a piece out of its wrapper. 'Fuck if I know.'

'Cutting the cocoons is dangerous,' Terry said. 'People have died.'

'Which makes it damn lucky that you've got a certified animal control specialist on your team. I've dealt with some mean dogs in my time, Terry, and once I got called out to deal with a very pissed-off bear that managed to wrap himself up in barbed wire. To deal with Ms Black, I'll use my biggest catch-pole, the Tomahawk ten-foot. Stainless steel. Spring lock. Drop the noose around her neck before snipping the shit over her face. Yank it as tight as I have to when she starts to buck and snap. She might lose conscious-ness, but it won't kill her. The stuff'll grow back, and when it does, she'll go sleepy-bye again. All we need is a look. That's all. A quick look.'

'If it's her, and all the chatter turns out to be bullshit, everybody's gonna be disappointed,' Terry said. 'Including me.'

'Me, too.' Frank was thinking of Nana. 'But we have to know. You see that, don't you?'

Terry did: 'Yeah.'

'The question is, how do we get Norcross to give us access? We could raise a posse, and we might have to, but that's a last resort, don't you think?'

'Yes.' Terry found the idea of a posse unpleasant bordering on stomach-churning. In the current situation, a posse might well turn into a mob.

'We could use his wife.'

'Huh?' Terry stared at Frank. 'Lila? Say what?'

'Offer a swap,' he said. 'You give us Eve Black, we give you your wife.'

'Why would he go for that?' Terry asked. 'He knows we'd never hurt her.' When Frank didn't reply to this, Terry grabbed Frank by the shoulder. 'We would never hurt her, Frank. Never. You get that, right?'

Frank shook loose. 'Of course I do.' He showed Terry a smile. 'I'm talking about running a bluff. But it's one he might believe. They're burning cocoons in Charleston. Just panicky social-media-driven bullshit, I know. But lots of people believe it. And Norcross might believe *we* believe it. Also . . . he has a son, right?'

'Yeah. Jared. Nice kid.'

'*He* might believe it. He might be persuaded to call his dad and tell him to give the Black woman up.'

'Because what, we threaten to burn his mother like a mosquito on a bug light?' Terry couldn't believe the words he was hearing himself say. No wonder he was drinking on the job. Look at the kind of discussion he was being forced to have.

Frank chewed his gum.

'I don't like it,' Terry said. 'Threatening to burn up the sheriff. I don't like it a bit.'

'I don't like it, either,' Frank said, and this was the truth. 'But desperate times sometimes call for desperate measures.'

'No,' Terry said, for the moment not feeling drunk at all. 'Even if one of the teams find her, it's a flat no. And hell, for all we know, she's still awake. Put on her boogie shoes and blew town.'

'Left her husband and son? Left her *job,* with things messed up like they are? You believe that?'

'Probably not,' Terry said. 'One of the teams will find her eventually, but using her that way is still a no. Cops don't make threats, and cops don't take hostages.'

Frank shrugged. 'Message received. It was just an idea.' He turned around to face out through the windshield, started the engine and backed Unit Four onto the highway. 'I suppose somebody checked Norcross's house for her?'

'Reed Barrows and Vern Rangle, yesterday. She and Jared are both gone. Place is empty.'

'The boy, too,' Frank said thoughtfully. 'Babysitting her somewhere, maybe? Could have been the shrink's idea. He ain't dumb, I'll give him that.'

Terry didn't reply. Part of him thought having another nip was a bad idea, but part of him thought one more couldn't hurt. He fished the flask out of his pocket, unscrewed the cap, and offered it to Frank first, which was only polite, since it was his.

Frank smiled and shook his head. 'Not while I'm driving, amigo.'

Five minutes later, as they were passing the Olympia Diner (the sign out front no longer attempted to entice passersby with the promise of egg pie; now it read PRAY FOR OUR WOMEN), something the headshrinker had said over the intercom came to Frank. *Since Hicks walked off on Friday morning, I'm the only administrative officer this prison's got.*

His big hands clamped down on the wheel, and the cruiser swerved. Terry, who had been dozing, snapped awake. 'What?'

'Nothing,' Frank said.

Thinking about Hicks. Wondering what Hicks knew. Wondering what Hicks had *seen*. But for now, he would keep these questions to himself.

'Everything's fine, Sheriff. Everything's fine.'

6

What pissed Evie off about the video game were the blue stars. Multi-colored triangles, stars, and fiery orbs rained down the screen. You needed a string of four fiery orbs in order to explode one sparkling blue star. Other shapes flashed and disappeared if you linked up chains of them, but the sparkling blue stars were apparently made of some almost adamantine material that only the incendiary force of the fiery orbs could shatter. The name of the game was, for no rationale that Evie could grasp, *Boom Town*.

She was on Level 15, teetering on extinction. A pink star appeared, then a yellow triangle, and then − finally, thank fuck! − a fiery orb, which Evie tried to slide left to a stack of three fiery orbs that she'd already amassed alongside a blue star that was clogging up that area of her screen. But then came a green death-triangle, and that was all she wrote.

'SORRY! YOU DIED!' proclaimed a flashing message.

Evie groaned and flipped Hicks's phone onto the far end of her cot. She wanted as much distance as possible between herself and the wicked thing. Eventually, of course, it was going to suck her back in. Evie had seen dinosaurs; she had looked down upon the great forests of America from the eyes of a passenger pigeon. She had surfed into

Cleopatra's sarcophagus atop a flume of desert sand and caressed the glorious queen's dead face with beetle legs. A playwright, a clever Englishman, had written an amusing, if not entirely accurate, speech about Eve once. *She is the fairies' midwife, and she comes/In shape no bigger than an agate-stone/ On the fore-finger of an alderman,/Drawn with a team of little atomies/Athwart men's noses as they lie asleep . . .*

As an enchanted being, she should be able to do better than Level 15 of *Boom Town*.

'You know, Jeanette, they say the natural world is cruel and stupid, but that little machine . . . that little machine is a very good argument in and of itself that technology is a lot worse. Technology is, I would say, the *actual* Boom Town.'

7

Jeanette was nearby, pacing the short A Wing corridor. She was now, it seemed, the head trustee. She was also the only trustee, but Jeanette had paid attention during the career counseling sessions about post-prison life − when composing your resume it was incumbent upon you to make the most of your achievements, and to let the person who was doing the hiring decide what was and was not significant. The title was hers.

While the four remaining officers walked B and C wings and kept an eye on the prison's perimeter, Dr Norcross had asked if she would mind keeping an eye on the other two inmates whenever he had to step out.

'Sure,' said Jeanette. 'I'm not busy. Seems like furniture shop got canceled.'

It was good to have work; it kept her mind occupied.

She shuffled forward. In front of her, the triple-plated, wire-gridded window in the west wall showed a gray morning. There was standing water on the running track and the fields looked marshy.

'I never liked video games,' Jeanette said. It had taken her awhile to construct her response to Evie. She had been awake for ninety-six hours.

'More proof of your excellent character, my dear,' Evie said.

Angel, in the neighboring cell, now entered the discussion. 'Excellent character? *Jeanette?* Shee–yit. She kilt her fuckin husband, you know. Stabbed him. Didn't even use a knife, like a normal person would. Done it with a screwdriver, ain't that right, Jeanette?' Rapper Angel was gone; Redneck Angel was back. Jeanette figured she was too tired to make rhymes. That was good. On balance, Redneck Angel was less annoying and more (Jeanette struggled for the word) . . . more authentic.

'I do know that, Angel. And I give her credit for it.'

'Wish she'd let me kill you,' Angel said. 'I think I'd get to your juggler with my teeth. I think I would.' She made a humming noise. 'Know I would.'

'Would you like to have a turn with the phone, Angel? Jeanette, if I give you the phone through the tray slot, will you give it to Angel?' Evie's tone was conciliatory.

There was talk that the beautiful woman in the soft cell was either a sorceress or a demon. Moths had poured from her mouth; Jeanette had seen them. Whatever Evie was, it seemed that she wasn't immune to Angel's taunts.

'I bet I could make you swallow that phone,' Angel said.

'Bet you couldn't,' said Evie.

'Could.'

Jeanette stopped at the window in the wall, placed her hand against the glass, and let herself lean there. She didn't want to fantasize about sleep, and couldn't stop fantasizing about it.

Of course there were prisons even in sleep; Jeanette had on many occasions waited to be let out of a dream cell, as bored as all the times she waited in her actual life to be let out of her actual cell. But sleep was also a beach, and the waves cleaned it up every night, all the footprints and bonfires and sand castles and beer cans and scraps of trash; those cleansing waves washed most every trace into the depths. Sleep was also Bobby. He had met her in a forest that had grown over the ruins of the bad old world and everything was better.

Would Ree be in her sleep, her dreams? Damian was in there,

so why not Ree? Or was the sleep that came with the cocoons dreamless?

Jeanette remembered, some days, waking up feeling so young and strong and healthy. 'I'm ready to whip my weight in wildcats!' she sometimes told Bobby when he was just little. She couldn't imagine feeling that way now, or ever again.

When he was a newborn, Bobby had given her some hard nights. 'What do you want?' she would ask him. He just cried and cried. She imagined that he hadn't actually known what he wanted, but hoped maybe his mother might, and fix it for him. That was the hurtful part of motherhood, not being able to fix what you couldn't understand.

Jeanette wondered if she even *could* sleep now. What if she had broken her sleep-bone? Sleep-muscle? Sleep-tendon? Her eyes felt terribly dry. Her tongue felt like it was too big. Why didn't she give in?

Simple. Because she didn't want to.

She had given in to Damian and she had given in to drugs and her life had gone exactly the way everyone said it would go. She wasn't giving in to this. This wasn't going how they expected it to go.

She counted to sixty, got lost in the forties, returned to one and the second time made it up to a hundred. She shoots, she scores. *Let's go to the videotape!* What was that guy's name, the let's-go-to-the-videotape guy? Dr Norcross would remember.

Jeanette was facing the east wall, where the metal door of the shower gave on the delousing area. She walked toward the door, right-left, right-left. A man crouched on the floor, pinching buds into a cigarette paper. Behind her, Angel was explaining to Evie how she'd peel off her skin, how she'd dig out her eyes, fry them up with some ramps and eat them, ramps'd flavor up any rotten morsel. And on from there, more bibble-babble, tone and accent, angry-angry-angry, country-country-country. At this point, unless Jeanette really focused, conversation – pretty much anything anyone said – was low volume radiogab. She kept expecting to hear an 800 number.

'You know, Angel, I don't think I will be sharing my *Boom Town* video game with you, after all,' Evie said, and Jeanette went right-left, right-left, locking on the differently colored notices on the bulletin board by the Kwell dispenser, the words too bleary to read but knowing that they were lists of church services, AA meetings, crafts classes, and reminders of rules. On one piece of paper, a girl elf was dancing over the words I'M ON GOOD REPORT! Jeanette shuffled to a stop and flashed a look at the spot where the man had been squatting. There was no one.

'Hello? Hey! Where'd you go?'

'Jeanette? Are you all right?'

'Uh-huh.' Jeanette glanced back at Evie's cell door. The strange woman stood at the bars. She wore a melancholy expression, a well-of-course expression, like you did when you had a hope that you knew wasn't too realistic, and sure enough, life did what life did with unrealistic hopes. It was the face babies made after a cat scratched them and right before they cried.

'I just thought I — saw someone.'

'You're beginning to hallucinate. That's what happens when you don't sleep. You should go to sleep, Jeanette. It'll be safer for you if you're asleep when the men come.'

Jeanette shook her head. 'I don't want to die.'

'You won't. You'll sleep, and then you'll wake up somewhere else.' Evie's face lit. 'And you'll be free.'

When it came to Evie, Jeanette couldn't think straight. She seemed crazy, but not crazy like anyone else Jeanette had met in Dooling Correctional. Some insane people were so close to blowing up you could almost hear them tick. Angel was like that. Evie seemed like something else, and not just because of the moths; Evie seemed inspired.

'What do you know about free?'

'I know everything about free,' said Evie. 'Shall I give you an example?'

'If you want.' Jeanette risked another look at the spot where the man had been sitting. No one was there. No one.

'You find creatures in the dark of the earth, far below the rubble of the mountaintops that the coal-men have chopped flat, eyeless creatures, that are freer than you have ever been. Because they live as they want to, Jeanette. They are fulfilled in their darkness. They are everything they want to be.' Evie repeated this last, emphasizing it. '*They are everything they want to be.*'

Jeanette pictured herself in a warm darkness far beneath the earth's surface. Minerals glittered around her in constellations. She felt small and secure.

Something tickled her cheek. She opened her eyes, brushed at the strand of web that had started to curl up from her skin. She wobbled on her feet. She hadn't even realized she'd closed her eyes. In front of her, not halfway across the room, was the wall – bulletin board, door to the shower, Kwell dispenser, cement blocks. Jeanette took a step, then another.

There was the man. He was back, now smoking the joint he had rolled. Jeanette wasn't going to look at him. She wasn't giving in. She was going to touch the wall, and then she was going to turn around and walk to the other wall, and she wasn't giving in. Jeanette Sorley wasn't ready to be enshrouded yet.

I can go awhile, she thought. I can go awhile. You just watch me.

8

All the regular cruisers were taken, so Don Peters and the kid he was partnered with scoured the grid of suburban streets just south of the high school in Don's Dodge Ram. It had no official insignia, which was disappointing (Don planned to see about that later, maybe get some stick-on letters from the hardware store), but there was a battery-powered bubble light on the dashboard, revolving slowly, and he was wearing his prison officer's uniform. The kid didn't have any kind of uniform, of course, just a plain blue shirt with a badge on it, but the Glock on his hip carried all the additional authority he needed.

Eric Blass was only seventeen, technically four years too young to be in law enforcement. Don thought the kid had the right stuff, though. He'd been a Life Scout with a merit badge in target shooting before giving up the Scouting program the year before. ('Too many pussies,' Blass had said, to which Don replied, 'Copy that, Junior.') Besides, the kid was funny. He had invented a game to speed the hours. It was called Zombie Chicks. Don had the left side of the street, since he was driving; Eric had the right. It was five points for old chicks, ten points for middle-aged chicks, fifteen points for kiddie chicks (hardly any of those left by Saturday, none at all today), and twenty points for hotties. Blass was currently up, eighty to fifty-five, only as they turned onto St George Street, that was about to change.

'Hottie on the left at two o'clock,' Don said. 'That puts me up to seventy-five. Closing in on you, Junior.'

The kid, riding shotgun, leaned forward to scrutinize the youngish woman stumbling along the sidewalk in spandex shorts and a sports bra. Her head was down, her sweaty hair swinging back and forth in clumps. Maybe she was trying to run, but the best she could manage was a half-assed, weaving jog.

'Saggy tits and saggy ass,' Eric said. 'If that's what you call a hottie, I pity you.'

'Oh, jeez, pack your bags, we're goin on a guilt trip.' Don cackled. 'Fine, since we can't see the face, how about I call it fifteen?'

'Works for me,' Eric said. 'Give her a honk.'

As they rolled slowly by the staggering woman, Don laid on the horn. The woman's head jerked up (the face was not too bad, actually, except for the big purple circles under her hollowed-out eyes), and she stumbled. Her left foot caught on her right ankle and she sprawled on the pavement.

'She's *down*!' Eric yelled. 'Chick goes *down*!' He craned to look over his shoulder. 'But wait, she's getting up! Not even waiting for the eight-count!' He began to toot the *Rocky* theme through flapping lips.

Don glanced in the rearview mirror and saw the woman rising shakily to her feet. Her knees were scraped, and blood was trickling down her shins. He thought she might give them the finger – the teenager they'd blasted shortly after their shift began had done that – but the zombie chick didn't even look around, just went staggering off toward downtown.

Don said, 'Did you see the look on her face?'

'Priceless,' Eric said, and raised his palm.

Don high-fived him.

They had a list of streets to be canvased, tucked into a notebook where they wrote down the addresses of houses containing sleeping women, plus their names and some form of ID. If the houses were locked, they were allowed to break in, which was fun at first. Don enjoyed washing his hands with different kinds of soap in different kinds of bathrooms, and the variety of styles and colors of panties in the underwear drawers of the women of Dooling was a subject that had long called for his study. Cheap thrills wore out, though. It wasn't real action. Without an ass to fill them out, panties got old fast. When you came right down to it, he and Junior were little more than census-takers.

'This *is* Ellendale Street, right?' Don said, as he pulled the Ram to a curb.

'Roger that, El Commandante. All three blocks of it.'

'Well, let's get walking, partner. Check out some bitch-bags and write down some names.' But before Don could open the driver's side door, Eric grabbed his arm. The newbie was looking toward a patch of waste ground between Ellendale and the high school.

'You want to have some fun, boss?'

'Always up for fun,' Don said. 'It's my middle name. What have you got in mind?'

'You burned one yet?'

'A cocoon? No.' Don had seen footage on the news, though, a cell phone video of a couple of guys in hockey masks putting a match to one. The news called guys like that 'Blowtorch Brigades.' The cocoon in the video had gone up like a campfire wetted down with gasoline. *Whoosh!*

'Have you?'

'Nope,' Eric said, 'but I heard they, you know, really burn like crazy.'

'What are you thinking?'

'There's an old homeless babe who lives over there.' Eric pointed. 'If you want to call that living, that is. No good to herself or anyone else. We could give her a hotfoot. Just to see what it's like, you know. It's not like anybody would miss her.' Eric suddenly looked uneasy. 'Of course, if you don't want to . . .'

'I don't know if I do or not,' Don said. This was a lie. He wanted to, all right. Just thinking about it had gotten him a little horny. 'Let's check her out, then decide. We can do Ellendale later.'

They got out of the truck and headed for the weed-choked acre of ground where Old Essie kept her den. Don had a Zippo lighter. He took it from his pocket and began to click it open and shut, open and shut.

CHAPTER 2

1

The women started out just calling it 'the new place,' because it wasn't really Dooling anymore – not the Dooling they'd known, at least. Later, as they began to realize they might be here for the long haul, it became Our Place.

The name stuck.

2

The meat tasted strongly of the lighter fluid it took to ignite the ancient charcoal from Mrs Ransom's basement, but they ate the entire shank that Lila had hacked from the body of the bobcat she'd shot with her service revolver and dragged out of the fetid swimming pool.

'We are sick puppies,' said Molly on that first night, licking the grease from her fingers and grabbing another chunk. Being a sick puppy didn't seem to sit too badly with her.

'Got that right, m'darlin,' her grandmother said, 'but I'm damned if this isn't half-decent eatin. Grab me another piece, Missus Sheriff.'

They had taken shelter in the remains of Mrs Ransom's house, not trying anything from the dusty canned goods in the pantry because Lila was afraid of botulism. They subsisted for the next two weeks primarily on berries they picked from the bushes in their former suburban neighborhood, and tiny ears of wild corn, tough and almost tasteless, but at least edible. May was too early for berries and corn, but there it was.

From this Lila drew a conclusion, shaky at first but growing more solid: the version of Dooling where they found themselves was moving at a different pace in time from the Dooling they had been in before. Time felt the same, but it wasn't. Mrs Ransom confirmed that she had been alone for several days before Molly appeared. The hours in the old place (before?), were days in the new one (now?). Maybe more than days.

This concern with the differing time-streams most often occupied Lila in the loose minutes before sleep took her. Many of the places they slept were open to the sky – fallen trees had punched holes in some roofs, wind had snatched others away altogether – and Lila blinked at the stars as she drifted off. The stars were the same, but their glare was shocking. They were hot-white welding sparks. Was it even real, this world without men? Was it heaven? Purgatory? An alternate universe on an alternate time-stream?

More women and girls arrived. The population began to snow-ball, and although Lila didn't want the job, she found herself in charge. By default, it seemed.

Dorothy Harper of the Curriculum Committee, and her friends, three cheerful, white-haired women in their seventies, who intro-duced themselves as book club chums, emerged from the scrub forest that had risen around a condo. They made a great fuss over Molly, who enjoyed being fussed over. Janice Coates arrived strolling down Main Street, a leaf stuck in the ruins of her perm, accompan-ied by three women in prison red tops. Janice and the three former inmates – Kitty McDavid, Celia Frode, and Nell Seeger – had needed to hack their way through a thicket to get out of Dooling Correctional.

'Good afternoon, ladies,' Janice said, after embracing first Blanche McIntyre, then Lila. 'Forgive our appearance. We just broke jail. Now which one of you nicked your finger on a spindle and created this mess?'

Some of the old dwellings were habitable and salvageable. Others were fabulously overgrown or crumbled or both. On Main Street they gaped at the high school, which had been an outmoded building even in the old Dooling. In this new one, it was literally split down the middle, each half of the structure leaning to opposite sides, and open air in between jagged brick edges. Birds perched on the cliffs of classroom lino that jutted out into space. The Municipal Building, which had included the town and sheriff's department offices, was half-collapsed. A sinkhole had opened on Malloy. A car sat at the bottom, submerged to the windshield in coffee-colored water.

A woman named Kayleigh Rawlings joined the colony, and volunteered her experience as an electrician. It was no surprise to the former warden, who knew that Kayleigh had gone to vocational school to learn about wiring and voltage. That Kayleigh and her education had emerged from inside the fence of Dooling Correctional was not an issue. The woman had never committed a crime in this new place, under these too-bright stars.

Kayleigh managed to resurrect a solar-powered generator attached to what had once been a rich doctor's house, and they cooked rabbit on his electric stovetop and listened to old records on his vintage Rock-Ola jukebox.

In the evenings they talked. Most of the women had, like Lila in the cruiser in Mrs Ransom's driveway, awakened in the places where they had fallen asleep. A few others, however, remembered finding themselves in the dark, hearing nothing but wind and bird-song and – perhaps – distant voices. When the sun had risen these women had picked their way west through woods and come out either on Ball's Hill Road or West Lavin. To Lila, the picture they drew of those early moments was of a world being formed, as if the surroundings of their existence was an act of collective imagin-ation. That, she thought, was as likely as anything else.

3

Day followed day and night followed night. Exactly how many from the first day no one was sure, but weeks certainly, and then months.

A hunting and gathering group was formed. There was a great deal of game – deer and rabbit, especially – as well as plenty of wild fruits and vegetables. They never came close to starving. There was a farming group, a construction group, a healthcare group, and an education group to teach the children. Each morning a different girl stood out in front of the little school, ringing a cowbell. The sound carried for miles. Women taught; some of the older girls did, too.

No viruses afflicted them, though there were many cases of poison ivy to deal with and more than a few cuts and bruises, even broken bones brought about by the perils inherent in long-abandoned structures – sharp edges and bucklings and hidden traps. If this world was an act of imagination, Lila sometimes thought as she drifted toward sleep, it was a remarkably strong one if it could make people bleed.

In the basement of the high school, where some variety of mold had made a feast of the filing cabinets full of decades-old school board transcripts, Lila unearthed a mimeograph machine that had probably not been used since the mid-sixties. It was packed neatly away in a plastic crate. Some of the erstwhile prison inmates turned out to be remarkably crafty. They helped Molly Ransom make fresh ink from swamp redcurrants, and the girl founded a single-sheet newspaper called *Dooling Doings*. The first headline was **SCHOOL REOPENS!** and she quoted Lila Norcross as saying, 'It's nice to see the kids getting back into their routine.' Molly asked Lila what her title was, Dooling Chief of Police or plain Sheriff. Lila said to just to call her 'a local.'

And there were the Meetings. These took place once a week initially, then twice, and lasted an hour or two. Although they turned out to be extremely important to the health and well-being of the women living in Our Place, they came about almost by accident. The first attendees were the ladies who had called themselves the First Thursday Book Club in the old world. In this new one, they got together in the Shopwell supermarket, which had held up remarkably well. And they had enough to talk about without a book to get them started. Blanche, Dorothy, Margaret, and Margaret's sister Gail sat on folding chairs at the front of the store, chatting about all the things they missed. These included fresh coffee and orange juice, air conditioning, television, garbage pickup, the Internet, and being able to just power up a phone and call a friend. Mostly, though – they all agreed on this – they missed men. Younger women began to drift in, and were welcomed. They talked about the gaps in their lives, places of absence that had once been filled by their sons, nephews, fathers, grandfathers . . . and their husbands.

'Let me tell you girls something,' Rita Coombs said at a Meeting toward the end of that first summer – by then there were almost four dozen ladies in attendance. 'It may be too frank for some of you, but I don't care. I miss a good old Friday night fuck. Terry was too quick on the trigger at the start of our relationship, but once I got him trained, he was fine. I had nights when I could pop off two little ones and one big one before he fired his gun. And afterward? Slept like a baby!'

'Don't your fingers work?' someone asked, to general laughter.

'Yes, they do!' Rita retorted. She was also laughing, her cheeks as red as apples. 'But darlin, they are *not* the same!'

This earned her a hearty round of applause, although a few women – Fritz Meshaum's mousy wife, Candy, for one – abstained.

The two big questions came up, of course, in a hundred different ways. First, how had they come to be here, in Our Place? And why?

Was it magic? Was it some scientific experiment gone wrong? Was it the will of God?

Was their continued existence a reward or a punishment?

Why them?

Kitty McDavid was a frequent speaker when the discussion turned in this direction; Kitty's memory of her Aurora's eve nightmare – of the dark figure that she'd somehow recognized as a queen, and the cobwebs that had flowed from the queen's hair – remained vivid, haunting her still. 'I don't know what to do, if I should pray for forgiveness or what,' she said.

'Oh, fuck it,' Janice Coates had advised her. 'You can do what you want since the pope's not here to make a ruling, but I'm just going to keep doing my best. What else is there to do, honestly, that we know for sure can make a difference?' This had been another crowdpleaser.

The question, however – What the fuck had happened? – was renewed again and again. Without lasting satisfaction.

At one Meeting (it was at least three months after what Janice Coates liked to call the Great Displacement), a new attendee crept in, and settled on a fifty-pound bag of fertilizer at the back of the room. She kept her head down during the lively discussion of life as it was now lived, and news of a wonderful discovery at the local UPS shipping office: nine boxes of Lunapads, which were reusable sanitary napkins.

'No more cutting up tee-shirts to stuff in my underwear at that time of the month!' Nell Seeger exulted. 'Hallelujah!'

Toward the end of the Meeting, talk turned – as it always did – to those things they missed. These discussions almost always occasioned tears for the boys and men, but most of the women said they felt at least temporarily unburdened. Lighter.

'Are we done, ladies?' Blanche asked on this particular day. 'Does anyone have a burning desire to share before we get back to work?'

A small hand went up, the fingers dusted with many different colors of chalk.

'Yes, dear,' Blanche said. 'You're new, aren't you? And very short! Would you care to stand?'

'Welcome,' the women chorused, turning to see.

Nana Geary got to her feet. She brushed her hands down the front of her shirt, which was now very worn and raggedy at the sleeves . . . but still her favorite.

'My mom doesn't know I'm here,' she said, 'so I hope no one will tell her.'

'Honey,' said Dorothy Harper, 'this is like Vegas. What goes on in Women's Hour stays in Women's Hour.'

This brought a murmur of laughter, but the little girl in the faded pink tee-shirt did not even smile. 'I just want to say I miss my daddy. I went into Pearson's Barber Shop and found some of his aftershave – Drakkar Noir, it's called – and I smelled it, and it made me cry.'

The front of the supermarket was dead silent except for a few sniffles. It would turn out later that Nana hadn't been the only one to visit the aftershave shelves at Pearson's.

'I guess that's all,' Nana said. 'Just . . . I miss him, and I wish I could see him again.'

They applauded her.

Nana sat down and put her hands over her face.

4

Our Place was no utopia. There were tears, more than a few arguments, and during the first summer, a murder-suicide that shocked them all, mostly because it was utterly senseless. Maura Dunbarton, another refugee from the Dooling Correctional of the previous world, strangled Kayleigh Rawlings, then took her own life. It was Coates who fetched Lila to see.

Maura was hanging from a noose knotted to the rusty crossbar of a backyard swing set. Kayleigh had been discovered in the room the lovers had shared, dead in her sleeping bag, her face gray and the sclera of her open eyes filigreed with hemorrhages. She had been strangled, then stabbed at least a dozen times. Maura had left a note, penciled on a scrap of envelope.

This world is different, but I am the same. You will be better off without me. I have killed Kayleigh for no reason. She did not aggravate me or start anything. I still loved her, like in prison. I know she was useful to you. I could not help myself. It came on to me to kill her so I did. I was sorry I did it afterwards. – Maura

'What do you think?' asked Lila.

Janice said, 'I think it's a mystery, like everything else here. I think it's a goddam shame that when it came on to the crazy bitch to kill someone, she picked the only one in Our Place who understood how to wire a circuit and make it hot. Now I'll hold her legs while ya climb up and cut her down.'

Coates walked over and, without any ceremony, wrapped her arms around Maura Dunbarton's short legs. She looked over at Lila. 'Come on, then, don't make me wait. Smells like she loaded her pants. Suicide is so glamorous.'

They buried both the killer and her hapless victim outside the sagging ring of fencing that surrounded the prison. It was summer again by then, bright and hot, with chiggers popping around the grass tops. Coates spoke a few words about Kayleigh's contribution to the community and Maura's puzzling act of homicide. A chorus of the children sang 'Amazing Grace.' Their little girl voices made Lila weep.

She had salvaged a number of photographs of Jared and Clint from their home, and she sometimes attended the Meetings, but as time passed, her son and husband began to seem less real. At night, in her tent — Lila preferred to camp out as long as the weather was clement — she wound her crank flashlight, and scanned their faces in the beam. Who would Jared become? There was still that softness at the edges of his face, even in the most recent of the pictures. It hurt her not to know.

She looked at her husband's image, his wry smile and graying hair, and missed him, though not as much as she missed Jere. Her suspicions of Clint on that horrible last day and night embarrassed her; her lies and the pointless fears made her ashamed. But Lila also found herself regarding her husband differently now that she saw him through the lens of memory. She thought about how carefully he'd bricked up his past, the way he'd used his authority as a doctor to bolster the concealment and ward her off. Had Clint thought that only he could handle that kind of pain? That it was too much for her little mind and puny spirit to absorb? Or was it a kind of egotism masquerading as strength? She knew men were taught (primarily by other men, of course) that they were to keep their pain to themselves, but she also knew marriage was supposed to undo some of that teaching. That hadn't been the case with Clint.

And there was the pool. It still made her mad. And how he'd quit his job without a moment's notice all those years ago. And a million tiny decisions in between, taken by him, and for her to live with. It made her feel like a Stepford Wife, even with her husband in some other world.

Owls hooted in the dark, and dogs, run feral after who knew how many canine generations, howled. Lila zipped the flap of her tent. The moon shone blue through the yellow fabric. Remembering all that domestic soap opera depressed her, her parts and his parts, back and forth, he slams one door, she slams the other. The histrionic crap she had always looked down on in other people's marriages. Condescension, thy name was Lila, she thought, and had to laugh.

5

The hedges that once framed the prison had flourished into dense mounds. Lila entered through the gouge in the foliage that Coates and the other women who had awakened there had hacked out. Entry to the prison itself was through a hole in the south wall. Something – Lila was guessing the industrial gas stove in the kitchen – had exploded, blowing out the concrete as easily as a child huffing out a birthday candle. Going in, she half-expected to emerge in yet another place – a white beach, a cobbled thoroughfare, a rocky mountaintop, Oz – but when she arrived, it was only a wing of former cells. The walls were half-crumbled, some of the barred doors blown right off their hinges. She thought that the detonation must have been a doozy. Weeds grew from the floor and mold crawled across the ceiling.

She walked through the ruined wing and emerged into the central hall of the prison, what Clint called Broadway. Things looked better here. Lila followed the red line painted down the middle of the corridor. The various gates and barriers were unlocked; the wire-reinforced windows that gave onto the prison's facilities – cafeteria, library, the Booth – were fogged over. Where Broadway reached the front doors there was another section that showed signs of an explosion: busted cinderblocks, dusty shards of glass, the steel door separating the entry area from the prison proper crumpled inward. Lila skirted the junk.

Farther down Broadway she passed the open door to the staff lounge. Inside, mushrooms sprouted from the wall-to-wall carpeting. The air reeked of enthusiastic plant-life.

She eventually came to Clint's office. The corner window was blown out and a mass of overgrown shrubbery poured in, flowering with white blooms. A fleshy rat was rummaging around in the stuffing of a torn couch cushion. It gawked at Lila for a moment and darted for the safety of a pile of crumbled drywall.

The Hockney print behind her husband's desk hung askew, cocked at eleven and five. She straightened it. The picture showed a plain, sandy-colored building with rows of identically curtained windows. At ground level, the building had two doors. One door was blue, the other red: examples of Hockney's famous colors, bright like the feelings aroused by good memories, even if the memories themselves were thin – and the interpretative possibilities had appealed to Lila. She had given it to Clint all those years ago, thinking that he might point to it and say to his patients: 'See? Nothing is closed to you. There are doors to a healthier, happier life.'

The irony was as glaring as the metaphor. Clint was in another world. Jared was in another world. For all she knew, one or both of them might be dead. The Hockney print belonged to the rats and mold and weeds of this world. It was a broken world, emptied out and forgotten, but it was the one they had. It was, God save us, Our Place. Lila left the office and retraced her steps through the dead world of the prison to the hole in the foliage. She wanted out.

6

Throughout those months, more women continued to appear from what James Brown had once called a man's, man's, man's world. They reported that in Dooling, when they'd fallen asleep, the Aurora crisis was still fresh; there, only two or three days had passed. The violence and confusion and desperation they talked about seemed unreal to the earlier arrivals in this new place. More – it seemed almost unimportant. The women of this world had their own problems and concerns. One of them was the weather. Summer waned. After the fall, the winter would follow.

With the aid of manuals from the library, and overseen by the unlikely personage of Magda Dubcek, the widow of a contractor (not to mention the mother of Lila's pool boy), they were able to finish some of the work Kayleigh had begun before being murdered by her crazy ex-girlfriend. Magda's late husband had taught her quite a bit about electrical work. 'My husband, he was telling me what he was doing every day: "And look, here is the live wire, Magda, and look here is the ground wire, and so on." I listen. He never knew it, he thought he was just talking to some stupid wall, but I listen.' At this, Magda paused to make a sly face that reminded Lila, heartbreakingly, of Anton. 'Well, for the first five hundred times I listen, anyway.'

With power scavenged from a handful of solar panels that had survived the years of neglect, they were able to create a limited electrical grid for at least a few of the high-ground houses.

Regular cars were useless; it was impossible to determine how long this version of their world had spun unattended, but the state of the parked cars was a clue that it had been enough time for water and moisture to have its way with engines. A car stored in a still-standing garage might have been salvageable, except there wasn't a drop of gasoline anywhere that hadn't destabilized or evaporated. What the women did find was a small fleet of well-preserved solar-powered golf carts in the equipment shed at the country club. Once they were recharged, they started right up. Women drove them up and down streets that had been cleared of trees and foliage.

Like the Shopwell, the Olympia Diner had stood up to the passage of time remarkably well, and Rita Coombs, once the wife of Terry, reopened it on a barter basis, cooking with an old portable wood-stove that a gang of women had helped haul up from the Coombses basement.

'I always wanted to try my hand at running a restaurant,' she explained to Lila, 'but Terry never wanted me to work. He said it would make him worry. Terry could never understand how damn boring it was, to be a piece of china in a hutch.'

She said this in a light way, but kept her gaze averted in an expression of what Lila read as shame — a shame that came from being happy to have something of her own. Lila hoped Rita would get over it, and thought she would — eventually. There were a lot of them that felt changed, but in a way that might also contain that tincture of shame, as if they were playing hooky. Women like Magda and Rita, who suddenly found themselves in demand and flourishing in the light of a new world. As those unmarked weeks peeled away, they discussed not just what they missed, but also some of what they did not miss.

The leaves changed as they did in the old world, but to Lila their colors seemed more vibrant and longer-lasting.

She was in Mrs Ransom's garden one day in what felt like late October, picking pumpkins for the schoolgirls to carve. Old Essie, seated on a bench in the shade, watched her. Next to the bench was a rusty shopping cart full of things Essie had picked up, as if trying to restock her new life from memories of the old one: a radio, a cell phone, a heap of clothes, a dog collar, a calendar from 2007, a bottle of something that had no label but might have been maple syrup once upon a time, and a trio of dolls. She liked to follow Lila when she saw Lila in her big straw hat rolling the wheelbarrow piled high with gardening implements.

The old lady was silent at first, and shied away if anyone came near her, but as the weeks passed, she began to relax, at least around Lila. Sometimes she would even talk, although Lila guessed she'd never been a great conversationalist, even in her prime.

'Things are better now,' Essie said once. 'I have my very own house.' She looked fondly down at the dolls in her lap. 'My girls like it. Their names are Jingle, Pingle, and Ringle.'

Lila had asked her on that occasion what her last name was.

'Once it was Wilcox,' Essie said, 'but now it's Estabrook. I have taken back my maidenhood name just like that Elaine woman. This place is better than the old place, and not just because I have my maidenhood name and my very own house. It smells sweeter.'

Today, Essie seemed to have slipped back inside herself a bit. When Lila tried to engage her in conversation, Essie shook her head, made violent shooing motions in Lila's direction, and rummaged in her rusty shopping cart. From it she removed an ancient Philco table radio and started tossing it from hand to hand. Which was perfectly okay with Lila; let her play hot potato to her heart's content if that was what eased her mind.

As she was getting ready to break for lunch, Janice Coates rode up on a bicycle. 'Sheriff,' she said to Lila. 'A word.'

'I'm not the sheriff anymore, Janice. Don't you read the *Dooling Doings*? I'm just another local.'

Coates was undeterred. 'Fine, but you need to know there's people disappearing. Three of them now. Too many to be a coincidence. We need someone to look into this situation.'

Lila examined the pumpkin she had just torn from a vine. The top was bright orange, but the underside was black and rotten. She dropped it with a thud in the tilled earth. 'Talk to the Redevelopment Committee, or bring it up at the next Meeting. I'm retired.'

'Come on, Lila.' Coates, perched on the seat of the bike, crossed her bony arms. 'Don't give me that bullshit. You're not retired, you're depressed.'

Feelings, Lila thought. Men almost never wanted to talk about them, women almost always did. It could get boring. That came as a surprise. It came to her that she might have to re-evaluate some of her resentments about Clint's stoicism.

'I can't, Janice.' Lila walked down the row of pumpkins. 'I'm sorry.'

'I'm depressed, too,' said Janice. 'I may never see my daughter again. I think of her first thing in the morning and last thing at night. Every damn day. And I miss calling my brothers. But I'm not about to let that—'

There was a dull thump and a soft cry from behind them. Lila glanced around. The radio lay on the grass next to Jingle, Pingle, and Ringle. The dolls stared up at the cloudless sky with their flat, beatific expressions. Essie was gone. There was a single brown moth where she had been. It fluttered aimlessly for a moment, then flew up and away, trailed, faintly, by the smell of fire.

CHAPTER 3

1

'Holy fucking shit!' Eric Blass cried. He was sitting on the ground, and staring up. 'Did you *see* that?'

'I'm still seeing it,' Don replied, looking at the flock of moths winging above the tennis courts and toward the high school. 'And smelling it.'

He had given Eric his lighter, since it was Eric's idea (also so he could semi-plausibly put it all on the kid, if anyone found out). Eric had squatted, flicked the Zippo alight, and applied it to the edge of the cocoon in the littered den filled with junk. The cocoon had gone up in a crackling flash, as if it had contained gunpowder instead of a crazy homeless lady. The stench was immediate and sulphuric. It was like God himself had cut the cheese. Old Essie had sat upright – not that you could see anything more than the outline of her – and seemed to twist toward them. For an instant, her features had clarified, black and silver like a photo negative, and Don had seen her lips rolling back into a snarl. In another beat there was nothing left of her.

The fireball rose to a height of four feet, seeming to revolve as it did so. Then the fireball had turned into moths – hundreds of them. Of the cocoon or a skeleton there was no sign, and the grass where Old Essie had been lying wasn't so much as charred.

It wasn't that kind of fire, Don thought. If it had've been, we would be baked.

Eric got to his feet. His face was very white, and his eyes were frantic. 'What *was* that? What just happened?'

'I don't have a fucking clue,' Don said.

'Those Blowtorch Brigades, or whatever they call themselves . . . have there been any reports from them of burning cocoons that turned into flying bugs?'

'Not that I know of. But maybe they're not reporting it.'

'Yeah, maybe.' Eric licked his lips. 'Yeah, there's no reason why she'd be different.'

No, there wasn't any reason why Old Essie would be different from every other sleeping woman in the world. But Don could think of one reason why things in Dooling might be different. Things might be different here because there was a special woman here, one who slept without growing a cocoon around her. And who woke up again.

'Come on,' Don said. 'We've got work to do on Ellendale Street. Bitch-bags to count. Names to write down. This here . . . this never happened. Right, partner?'

'Right. Absolutely.'

'You're not going to talk about it, are you?'

'Jesus, no!'

'Good.'

But *I* might talk about it, Don thought. Not to Terry Coombs, though. It had only taken Don a couple of days to come to the conclusion that the man was next door to useless. A what-did-you-call-it, a figurehead. And he seemed to have a drinking problem, which was truly pathetic. People who couldn't control their urges repulsed Don. That guy Frank Geary, though, the one Terry had appointed his chief deputy . . . that one was a thinking cat, and he was keenly interested in the Evie Black woman. He'd have her sprung soon, if not already. *He* was the one to talk to about this, if talking had to be done.

But he needed to think about it first.

Very carefully.

'Don?'

They were back in the truck. 'Yeah, kid?'

'Did she see us? It seemed like she saw us.'

'No,' said Don. 'She didn't see nothing, just exploded. Don't be a pussy, Junior.'

2

Terry said he wanted to go home and think about their next move. Frank, who was pretty sure the acting sheriff's next move would be lying down to sleep it off, said that was a good idea. He saw Terry to his front door, then drove directly to the sheriff's station. There he found Linny Mars pacing circles with a laptop in her hands. There was a crust of white powder around her nostrils. Her cheeks were colored a hectic red. Her eyes were bleary and sunken. From the laptop came the all-too-familiar sounds of chaos.

'Hi, Pete.'

She had been calling him Pete since yesterday. Frank didn't bother correcting her. If he did, she'd remember he was Frank for a few minutes, then revert to Pete. Short-term memory loss was common among the women who were still awake. Their frontal lobes were melting like butter in a hot pan. 'What are you watching?'

'YouTube vids,' she said, not slowing her circuit of the office. 'I could watch at my desk, I know, Gertrude's screen is much bigger, but every time I sit down I start to float away. Walking is better.'

'Gotcha. What's on?' Not that he really needed an update. Frank knew what was going on: bad things.

'Clips from Al Jazeera. All the news networks are going crazy, but Al Jazeera's absolutely shitting themselves. The whole Mideast is on fire. Oil, you know. Oil wells. At least no nukes yet, but somebody over there will pop one eventually, don't you think?'

'I don't know. Linny, I wonder if you could look something up for me. I tried on my phone and couldn't get anywhere. I guess prison personnel's pretty cagey about their personal info.'

Linny was walking faster now, still staring at her laptop, which she held out in front of her like a chalice. She stumbled over a chair, almost fell, righted herself, and forged onward. 'The Shias are fighting the Sunnis, and ISIL is fighting them both. Al Jazeera had a panel of commentators on, and they seem to think it's because the women are gone. They say that without females to protect, though their idea of protection sure isn't mine, some central psychological underpinning of Judaism and Islam is gone. Like both of those things are the same. Basically still blaming the women, even after they've gone to sleep. Bonkers, huh? In England—'

Enough news of the world, Frank thought. He clapped his hands repeatedly in front of Linny's face. 'I need you to do your job for a minute, hon. Could you do that for me?'

She snapped to attention. 'Absolutely! What do you need, Pete?'

'Terry asked me to get an address for Lawrence Hicks. He's the assistant warden up at Correctional. Can you find that for me?'

'Walk in the park, piece of cake, can of corn. Got all their phone numbers and addresses. In case there's trouble up there, you know.'

But it didn't turn out to be a walk in the park, after all. Not in Linny's current state. Frank waited patiently as she sat at her desk, first trying one file and backing out, then another, then a third, shaking her head and cursing the computer as people did even when it was their own fault. Once she started to nod off and he saw a fine white thread spinning out of her ear. He clapped his hands again in front of her nose. 'Concentrate, Linny, okay? This could be important.'

Her head jerked up. The thread snapped off, floated, disappeared. She gave him a loopy smile. 'Roger that. Hey, remember that night we went line-dancing at Halls of Ivy over in Coughlin, and they kept playing that "Boot-Scootin' Boogie?"'

Frank had no idea what she was talking about. 'I sure do. Lawrence Hicks. Address.'

She finally got it. Sixty-four Clarence Court, on the south side of town. Just about as far from the prison as you could get, and still be a Dooling resident.

'Thanks, Linny. Better get some coffee.'

'I think I'll settle for Colombian marching powder instead of Colombian roast. Works better. God bless the Griner brothers.'

The phone rang. Linny grabbed the receiver. 'Police!' For about three seconds she listened, then hung up.

'They keep calling to ask. "Is it true that there's a woman up at the prison—" *Blah, blah, blah.* Do I look like the newspaper?' She gave him a desperately unhappy smile. 'I don't know why I bother staying awake. I'm just postponing the inevitable.'

He bent down and rubbed her shoulder with his fingertips, didn't know he was going to do it until it was done. 'Hang in. There might be a miracle waiting around the next bend in the road. You won't know until you get there.'

Linny started to cry. 'Thanks, Dave. That's a nice thing to say.'

'I'm a nice man,' Frank said, who did try to be nice, but found that it wasn't always possible. In the long run, he suspected niceness didn't pull the plow. Frank didn't like that. It didn't give him any pleasure. He wasn't sure Elaine had ever grasped that he didn't actually enjoy losing his temper. But he saw how it was. Someone had to pull the plow, and in Dooling, that was him.

He left, feeling sure that the next time he saw Linny Mars, she would be in a cocoon. What some of the deputies had started calling bitch-bags. He didn't approve of the term, but he didn't stop them. That was Terry's job.

He was the sheriff, after all.

3

Behind the wheel of Unit Four once more, Frank got on the horn to Reed Barrows and Vern Rangle in Unit Three. When Vern answered, Frank asked if they were still in the Tremaine Street area.

'Yup,' said Vern, 'and making fast work of it. Not many sleepers in this neighborhood once you get past the sheriff's place. You should see all the For Sale signs. Guess the so-called economic recovery never made it this far.'

'Uh-huh. Listen, you two, Terry says he wants to locate Sheriff Norcross and her son.'

'Their house is empty,' Vern said. 'We already checked it. I *told* Terry that. I think maybe he's been . . .' Vern must have suddenly realized that what he was saying was going out over the air. 'He's been, you know, a little overworked.'

'No, he knows that,' Frank said. 'He wants you to start checking the empty houses, too. I seem to remember there's a whole cul-de-sac that's unfinished a little further up. If you find them, just say howdy and move on. But then get in touch with me right away, all right?'

Reed took the mic. 'I think if Lila's not awake, Frank, then she must have wandered off into the woods or something. Otherwise she'd be in a cocoon at home or at the sheriff's station.'

'Look, I'm just passing on what Terry told me.' Frank certainly wasn't going to tell those two what seemed obvious to him: Norcross was a step ahead. If his wife was still awake, she'd still be in charge. Therefore, the doc had phoned his son and told the kid to move Lila to a safer place. It was another indication that the man was up to mischief. Frank was sure they wouldn't be far from home.

'Where is Terry, anyway?' Reed asked.

'I dropped him off at his house,' Frank said.

'Jesus.' Reed sounded disgusted. 'I hope he's up to this job, Frank. I really do.'

'Can that talk,' Frank said. 'Remember you're on the air.'

'Roger that,' Reed said. 'We'll start checking the empty houses further up Tremaine. That section's on our list, anyway.'

'Great. Unit Four is clear.'

Frank racked the mic and headed for Clarence Court. He badly wanted to know where Lila Norcross and her son were – they could be the levers he needed to end the situation bloodlessly – but that was second on his list. It was time to get some answers about Ms Eve Black.

4

Jared answered on the second ring. 'This is the CDC, Dooling branch, epidemiologist Jared Norcross speaking.'

'No need for that, Jere,' Clint said. 'I'm alone in my office. Is Mary okay?'

'Yeah, for now. She's walking around in the backyard. She says the sun perks her up.'

Clint felt vague alarm, and told himself not to be such an old biddy. Privacy fences, lots of trees; she'd be okay back there. It wasn't as if Terry and his new second-in-command could send out a drone or a helicopter.

'I don't think she can stay awake much longer, Dad. I don't know how she's managed it this long.'

'Me, either.'

'And I'm not sure why Mom wanted us up here, anyway. There's some furniture, but the bed is hard.' He paused. 'Guess that sounds pretty whiny, huh? With all that's going on?'

'People tend to focus on the small things to keep the big ones from overwhelming them,' Clint said. 'And your mom was right, Jere.'

'You don't really think a Blowtorch Brigade is going to start up in Dooling, do you?'

Clint thought of the title of an old novel – *It Can't Happen Here*. The point being that anything could happen anywhere. But no, it wasn't a Dooling Blowtorch Brigade he was currently worried about.

'There are things you don't know,' Clint said, 'but since other people do – or suspect, at least – I'll bring you up to speed tonight.' *After that I might not get many more chances*, he thought. 'I'll bring you and Mary dinner. Double hamburg, double mush from Pizza Wagon sound okay? Assuming they're still open for business?'

'Sounds awesome,' Jared said. 'How about a clean shirt, too?'

'It will have to be an officer's blueshirt,' Clint said. 'I don't want to go by the house.'

Jared didn't reply at first. Clint was about to ask if he was still there when his son said, 'Please tell me you're just being paranoid.'

'I'll explain everything when I get there. Keep Mary awake. Remind her she can't eat pizza through a cocoon.'

'I'll do that.'

'And Jared?'

'Yeah?'

'The cops aren't keeping me apprised of their strategy for dealing with the local situation – I'm not their favorite person right now

– but if I were them, I'd be grid-searching the town and keeping a master list of all the sleeping women, plus their locations. Terry Coombs might not be smart enough or on top of things enough to think of that, but I believe there's a man who's working with him who is.'

'Okay . . .'

'If they show up where you are, keep quiet and . . . is there a storage space in that house? Other than the cellar, I mean?'

'Not sure, I haven't exactly searched it, but I think there's an attic.'

'If you see cops on the street, you should get everyone up there.'

'Jesus, really? You're kind of freaking me out here, Pop. I'm not sure I'm following you. Why shouldn't I let the cops find Mom and Mrs Ransom and Molly? They're not burning women here, right?'

'No, they're not, but it could still be dangerous, Jared. For you, for Mary, and especially for your mother. Like I said, the police aren't very happy with me right now. It has to do with the woman I told you guys about, the one who's different. I don't want to get into the details now, but you have to believe me. Can you get them up to the attic or not?'

'Yeah. I hope I don't have to, but yeah.'

'Good. I love you, and I'll be there soon, hopefully bearing pizza.'

But first, he thought, I'm going to take another run at Evie Black.

5

When Clint got to A Wing, carrying a folding chair from the common room under one arm, Jeanette was standing by the door to the shower and the delousing station, having a conversation with an individual who didn't exist. It seemed to be some kind of convoluted dope deal. She said she wanted the good stuff, the Blues, because they mellowed Damian out. Evie was at the bars of her cell, watching this with what appeared to be sympathy . . . although with the mentally unbalanced, you could never be sure. And speaking of the mentally unbalanced, Angel was sitting on the bunk in a nearby cell with her lowered head propped on her hands and her hair hiding her face. She looked up briefly at Clint, said, 'Hello, cocksucker,' and lowered her head again.

'I know where you get it,' Jeanette was saying to the invisible pusher, 'and I know you can get it now. It's not like they close at midnight. Do me a favor, okay? Please? *Please?* I don't want Damian in one of those *moods*. And Bobby's teething, too. My head can't take it.'

'Jeanette,' Clint said.

'Bobby?' She blinked at him. 'Oh . . . Dr Norcross . . .' Her face seemed attenuated now, as if all muscles there had already gone to sleep and were only waiting for her stubborn brain to follow. It made Clint think of an old joke. Horse walks into a bar, and the bartender says, Hey, buddy, why the long face?

Clint wanted to explain to her why he'd ordered the officers to disable the payphones, and apologize for preventing her from calling her son to make sure the boy was all right. He wasn't certain, however, that Jeanette would be able to comprehend him at this point, and if she did, if it would achieve anything, or only distress her further. The liberties that Clint had taken with the lives of the prison's women, the lives of his *patients*, were grotesque. That he felt he had no alternative did not make it less grotesque or cruel. And that didn't cover all of it, not by a long shot. It was because of Evie that he'd had to do all of it – and he realized, suddenly, insane or not, he hated her for that.

'Jeanette, whoever you—'

'Don't bother me, Doc, I gotta do this.'

'I want you to go out to the exercise yard.'

'What? I can't do that, at least not by myself, I can't. This is a prison, you know.' She turned from him and peered into the shower. 'Oh now look, the man's gone. You scared him away.' She gave a single dry sob. 'What'll I do now?'

'None of the doors are locked, sweetheart.' Never in his life had Clint used such a term of intimacy when addressing an inmate, but now it came naturally, without thought.

'I'll get on Bad Report if I do that!'

'She's lost it, Doc,' Angel said without looking up.

'Go on, Jeanette,' Evie said. 'Out to the furniture shop, across the exercise yard, into the garden. There are new peas there, as sweet as honey. Fill your pockets and come back. Dr Norcross and I will be done by then, and we can have a picnic.'

'A *pea-pea* picnic,' Angel said through the screen of her hair, and snickered.

'Go on, now,' Evie said.

Jeanette eyed her uncertainly.

'The man may be out there,' Evie coaxed. 'In fact, I'm sure he is.'

'Or possibly up your dirty ass,' Angel said through her hair. 'He might be hiding there. Go find me a wrench and I'll help you find him.'

'You got a bad mouth, Angel,' Jeanette said. 'Bad.' She started up the short A Wing corridor, then stopped, staring fixedly down at a slanting oblong of sun on the floor as if hypnotized.

'I say you can't not be bothered by a square of light,' Evie said quietly.

Jeanette laughed, and exclaimed, 'That's right, Ree! That's right! It's all *Lying for Prizes,* isn't it?'

She went on, step by slow step, weaving left and correcting, weaving right and correcting.

'Angel?' Evie said.

She spoke in that same quiet, courteous voice, but Angel looked up at once, seemingly wide awake.

'Dr Norcross and I are going to have a brief consultation. You may listen, but you need to keep your mouth closed. If you don't, I'll stop it up with a rat and it will eat the tongue right out of your head.'

Angel stared at her for several seconds, then lowered her face into her hands again.

Officer Hughes showed up just as Clint was unfolding his chair outside Evie's cell. 'Inmate just went outside,' he said. 'Looked like she was headed for the garden. That okay?'

'It's fine, Scott. But keep an eye on her, would you? If she falls asleep out there, get her into the shade before she starts to grow a cocoon. We'll bring her in after she's completely wrapped.'

'Okay, boss.' Hughes sketched a salute and left.

Boss, Clint thought. Jesus-God, *boss*. I wasn't nominated, I didn't campaign, but I got the job, anyway.

'Uneasy lies the head that wears the crown,' Evie said. '*Henry IV, Part Two*. Not one of his best, but not bad. You know they had boys play the women's parts back then, right?'

She is not a mind-reader, Clint told himself. The men came, just as she predicted, but I could have predicted that. It's simple logic. She's got the skills of a good carnival fortune-teller, but she is *not* a mind-reader.

Yes, and he could go on believing that as long as he liked – it was a free country. Meanwhile, she was looking at him with curiosity and interest, eyes aware and totally awake. Probably the only woman alive who still looked like that.

'What shall we talk about, Clint? Shakespeare's history plays? Baseball? The last season of *Doctor Who*? Too bad it ended on a cliffhanger, huh? I'm afraid it's reruns from here on out. I have it on good authority that the doctor's companion fell asleep a couple of days ago and now she's riding in a TARDIS through her own innerspace. Maybe they can recast, though, go all male next season.'

'Sounds good,' said Clint, automatically falling into shrink mode.

'Or should we tackle something more germane to the current situation? I'd suggest the last, because time is getting short.'

'I'm interested in this idea you have about the two of us,' Clint said. 'You being the Woman, and me being the Man. Symbolic figures. Archetypes. Yin and yang. The king on one side of the chessboard, the queen on the other.'

'Oh, no,' she said, smiling. 'We're on the same side, Clint. White king and white queen. On the other side, arrayed against us, is an entire army of black pieces. All the king's horses and all the king's men. Emphasis on *men*.'

'That's interesting, that you see us on the same side. I didn't get that before. And when, exactly, did you begin to realize that?'

The smile faded. 'Don't. Don't you do it.'

'Don't do what?'

'Fall back on *DSM IV.* To deal with this, you need to let go of certain rational assumptions and rely on intuition. Embrace your female side. Every man has one. Just think of all the male authors who have put on the dress. *Mildred Pierce,* by James Cain, for example. That's a personal favorite.'

'There are a lot of female psychiatrists who would object to the idea that—'

'When we spoke on the phone, while your wife was still awake, you believed what I was telling you. I could hear it in your voice.'

'I was in . . . a strange place that night. Dealing with personal issues. Look, I'm not discounting your influence, your powers, however you want to characterize it. Let's assume you're in control. At least for today.'

'Yes, let's assume that. But tomorrow they may come for me. If not then, the next day, or the one after that. It won't be long. While in the other world, the one beyond the Tree, time is moving at a much faster pace – months are reeling by there. There are dangers, but with every one the women surmount, it becomes less likely that they will want to return to this world.'

'Let's say I understand and believe even half of what you're saying,' Clint said. 'Who sent you?'

'President Reginald K. Dinkleballs,' Angel blurted from the neighboring cell. 'Either him, or Lord Herkimer Jerkimer. Maybe—'

Then she screamed. Clint turned in time to see a large brown rat scamper though the bars and into Angel's cell. She drew her feet up on the bunk and screamed again. 'Git it out! Git it out! I *hate* rats!'

'Are you going to be quiet, Angel?' Evie asked.

'Yes! Yes! I promise! Yes!'

Evie twirled her finger, like an umpire signaling a home run. The rat reversed out of Angel's cell and squatted in the corridor, watching her with beady eyes.

Clint turned back to Evie. He'd had a series of questions in mind when he came down here, questions designed to make her face her delusions, but now they were blown away like a house of cards in a strong wind.

I am the one with the delusions, he thought. Holding onto them so I don't go completely insane.

'No one sent me,' Evie said. 'I came on my own.'

'Can we make a deal?' he asked.

'We already have one,' Evie said. 'If I live through this, if you save me, the women are free to decide their own course. But I warn you: the big guy, Geary, is very determined to have me. He thinks he can control the other men and capture me alive, but he's probably wrong about that. And if I die, it's over.'

'What are you?' he asked.

'Your only hope. I suggest you stop worrying about me and focus all your energies on the men outside these walls. They're the ones that need to concern you. If you love your wife and son, Clint, you need to work quickly to gain the upper hand. Geary isn't in complete control yet, but he will be soon. He's clever, he's motivated, and he doesn't trust anyone but himself.'

'I put him off.' Clint's lips felt numb. 'He has his suspicions, yes, but he can't be sure.'

'He will be, once he talks to Hicks, and he's on his way there now.'

Clint rocked back on his chair as if she had reached through the bars and slapped him. Hicks! He'd forgotten all about Hicks. Would he keep his mouth shut, if Frank Geary questioned him about Eve Black? Balls he would.

Evie sat forward, her eyes locked on Clint's. 'I've warned you about your wife and son, I've reminded you that there are weapons you may be able to access, and those things are more than I should have done, but I didn't expect to like you so much. I suppose I might even be *attracted* to you, because you're so damn foolhardy. You're like a dog barking at the ocean tide, Dr Norcross. Not to get off the subject, but this is another aspect of the basic problem, the man–woman equation that never balances. Never mind, subject for another time. You have a decision to make: either prepare your defenses, or clear out and let them have me.'

'I'm not going to let them have you,' Clint said.

'Big talk. Very macho.'

Her dismissive tone galled him.

'Does your all-seeing eye know I had to disable the payphones, Evie? That I kept every last woman here from saying goodbye to anyone, even to their children, because we couldn't risk letting word of you get out any further? That my own son is probably in danger, too? He's a teenage boy, and he's taking chances that I'm telling him to take.'

'I know what you've done, Clint. But I didn't *make* you do anything.'

Clint was suddenly furious with her. 'If you believe that, you're lying to yourself.'

From the shelf, she took Hicks's phone. 'We're done here, Doctor. I want to play a few games of *Boom Town*.' She dropped him the wink of a flirty teenager. 'I'm getting better all the time.'

6

'Here we are,' Garth Flickinger said, and brought his battered Mercedes to a stop in front of the late Truman Mayweather's far more battered trailer.

Michaela regarded it blankly. For the last few days she'd felt like a woman in a dream, and the rusty trailer – up on blocks, surrounded by weeds and discarded auto parts, the police tape now lying on the ground and fluttering lackadaisically – seemed like just another of the peculiar turns dreams take.

But I'm still here, she told herself. *My skin is still my skin. Right?* She rubbed a hand up one cheek and across her forehead. Right. Still clean of cobwebs. Still here.

'Come on, Mickey,' Garth said, getting out. 'If I find what I'm looking for, you'll be good to go for at least another day or two.'

She tried to open her door, couldn't find the handle, and simply sat there until Garth came around and opened it for her, with an extravagant bow. Like a boy taking his date to the prom instead of to some shitass trailer in the woods where there was a recent double murder.

'Upsa-daisy and out you come,' Garth said, seizing her arm and pulling. He was bright and lively. Why not? He wasn't the one who'd been awake for over a hundred hours.

Since that night in the Squeaky Wheel, she and Garth had become fast friends. Or drug buddies, at least. He'd had a large bag of crystal meth – his emergency stash, he said – and that had balanced off the drinks nicely. She'd been happy enough to go home with him when the Wheel finally ran out of booze and closed its doors. Under other circumstances she might even have slept with him – as little as men did for her, sometimes the novelty was appealing, and God knew, the way things were going, she appreciated the company. Not under these circumstances, though. If she slept with him, she would *really* go to sleep after, she always did, and if she did that, whoopsie, there goes your ballgame. Not that she had any idea if he would even be interested; Garth Flickinger did not present as the most sexual of beings, except in regards to dope, about which he was quite passionate.

The emergency stash turned out to be sizable, and they had kept the party going at Garth's house for the better part of the next forty-eight hours. When he finally fell asleep for a few hours on Sunday afternoon, she had explored the contents of the doctor's rolltop desk. It contained, predictably, a stack of medical journals and several scorched drug pipes. Less expected was a creased photo of a baby wrapped in a pink blanket. *Cathy* was penciled lightly on the reverse side – and in the desk's bottom cabinet, a big box of reptile vitamin supplements. Next, she played with his jukebox. It held nothing but jam bands, unfortunately; she didn't need to listen to 'Casey Jones'; she was well en route to becoming Casey Jones. Michaela flicked through what seemed like five hundred channels on his el gigantico TV, pausing only to watch those info-mercials where the hucksters had the loudest, most offensive, listen-to-me-or-die voices. She seemed to remember ordering a Shark vacuum cleaner and having it sent to her old address in DC. She doubted if it would arrive; although it had been a man who took her call, Michaela was sure that it was women who actually filled the orders. Wasn't it usually the women who got those kinds of jobs? The crap jobs?

If you see a toilet bowl without a ring, she thought, you know there's a woman somewhere in the vicinity.

'Trume told me he got hold of the best shit ever, and he wasn't lying,' Garth said, leading her toward the trailer. 'I mean, don't get me wrong, he was a maniac and he lied almost all the time, but this was the rare instance when he wasn't.'

The trailer had a hole in the side that was surrounded by a corona of what looked like dried blood – but surely that wasn't really there. She must be waking-dreaming, quite common among people who had been without sleep for a long time – so said a self-proclaimed expert in a NewsAmerica sidebar piece she'd seen before decamping for the green hills of her Appalachian home town.

'You don't see a hole in the side of that trailer, do you?' she asked. Even her voice was dreamlike now. It seemed to be issuing from a loudspeaker in the top of Michaela's head.

'Yeah, yeah,' he said. 'It's there, all right. Listen, Mickey, Trume called this new stuff Purple Lightning, and I got a sample before the wild woman came on the scene and offed Trume and his side-kick.'

Garth was momentarily diverted into reverie. 'The guy, he had the stupidest tattoo. That turd from *South Park*? The one that sings and stuff? It was on his Adam's apple. Who gets a turd tattoo on his Adam's apple? You tell me. Even if it's a witty, singing and dancing turd, it's still a turd. Everyone who looks at you sees a turd. Not my specialty, but I've consulted, and you would not believe what a pain it is to get something like that removed.'

'Garth. Stop. Rewind. The crazy lady. Is that the woman people in town are talking about? The one they're holding at the prison?'

'Uh-huh. She totally Hulked out. I was lucky to get away. But that's water under the bridge, piss down the sewer pipe, last week's news, so on and so forth. Doesn't matter. And we should be grateful for that, trust me. What does matter is this superb crystal. Trume didn't make it, he got it from Savannah or somewhere, but he was *going* to make it, dig? Analyze it and then create his own version. He had a two-gallon Baggie of the shit, and it's in there somewhere. I'm going to find it.'

Michaela hoped so, because resupply was necessary. They had smoked up Garth's reserves over the last few days, even smoked up the rug-bunnies and a couple of shards they'd found under the couch, Garth insisting that she brush her teeth after every session with the bong. 'Because that's why meth addicts have such bad teeth,' he'd told her. 'They get high and forget basic hygiene.'

The stuff hurt her throat, and the euphoric effect had long since worn off, but it kept her awake. Michaela had been almost positive she would fall asleep on the ride out here — it had seemed interminable — but somehow she had managed to stay conscious. And for what? The trailer, balanced crooked on its cement blocks, didn't exactly look like the Fountain of Awareness. She could only pray that the Purple Lightning wasn't a fantasy of Garth Flickinger's dope-addled brain.

'Go ahead,' she said, 'but I'm not going in with you. There might be ghosts.'

He looked at her with disapproval. 'Mickey, you're a reporter. A *news maven*. You know there are no such things as ghosts.'

'I do know that,' Michaela said from the loudspeaker on top of her head, 'but in my current state, I might see them anyway.'

'I don't like leaving you on your own. I won't be able to slap you if you start nodding off.'

'I'll slap myself. Go get it. Just try not to be long.'

Garth trotted up the steps, tried the door, and put his shoulder to it when it wouldn't give. It flew open and he stumbled inside. A moment later he poked his head out the maroon-stained hole in the side of the trailer, a big grin on his face. 'Don't go to sleep, you pretty thing! Remember, I'm going to touch up your nose one of these fine days!'

'In your dreams, buster,' she said, but Garth had already pulled his head back inside. Michaela heard thuds and crashes as he began his search for the elusive Purple Lightning. Which the cops had probably taken and stashed in the evidence locker at the sheriff's station, if they hadn't taken it home to their womenfolk.

Michaela wandered to the ruins of the meth-cooking shed. It was surrounded by charred bushes and blackened trees. No meth would be cooked here in the future, purple or otherwise. She wondered if the shed had blown up on its own, as meth-cooking facilities were wont to do, or if the woman who had killed the cookers had blown it up. It was a moot question at this late date, but the woman herself interested Michaela, piqued the natural, seeking curiosity that had made her investigate Anton Dubcek's dresser drawers when she was eight and eventually led her into journalism, where you got to investigate *everybody's* drawers – those in their houses, and those that they wore. That part of her mind was still active, and she had an idea it was keeping her awake as much as Flickinger's methamphetamine. She had Qs with no As.

Qs like how this whole Aurora business got rolling in the first place. And why, assuming there *was* a why. Qs about whether or not the world's women could come back, as Sleeping Beauty had. Not to mention Qs about the woman who had killed the meth dealers, and whose name was, according to some talk they'd over-heard at the Squeaky Wheel and in town, either Eve or Evelyn or Ethelyn Black, and who could supposedly sleep and wake again, which made her like no other woman anywhere, unless another existed in Tierra del Fuego or the high Himalayas. This woman might only be a rumor, but Michaela tended to believe there was an element of truth to her. When rumors came to you from different directions, it was wise to pay attention.

If I wasn't living with one foot in reality and the other in the Land of Nod, Michaela thought, starting up the path beyond the ruined meth shed, I would hie myself to the women's prison and make some inquiries.

Another Q: Who was running the place up there, now that her mother was asleep? Hicks? Her mother said he had the brain of a gerbil and the spine of a jellyfish. If memory served, Vanessa Lampley was the senior officer on the staff. If Lampley wasn't there anymore, or if she was snoozing, that left—

Was that humming just in her head? She couldn't be completely sure, but she didn't believe so. She thought it was the power lines that ran near here. No big deal. Her eyes, however, were reporting stuff that was harder to dismiss as normal. Glowing splotches like handprints on some of the tree trunks a few feet from the blasted shed. Glowing splotches that looked like footprints on the moss and mulch, as if saying, *This way, m'lady*. And clumps of moths on many of the branches, perched there and seeming to watch her.

'Boo!' she shouted at one of these clumps. The moths fluttered their wings, but did not take off. Michaela slapped one side of her face, then the other. The moths were still there.

Casually, Michaela turned and looked down the slope toward the shed and the trailer below. She expected to see herself lying on the ground, wrapped in webs, undeniable evidence that she had disconnected from her body and become a spirit. There was nothing, though, except for the ruins and the faint sounds of Garth Flickinger, treasure-hunting his ass off.

She looked back up the path – it *was* a path, the glowing footprints said so – and saw a fox sitting thirty or forty yards ahead. Its brush was curled neatly around its paws. It was watching her. When she took a hesitant three steps toward it, the fox trotted further up the path, pausing once to glance over its shoulder. It seemed to be grinning amiably.

This way, m'lady.

Michaela followed. The curious part of her was fully awake now, and she felt more aware, more with it, than she had in days. By the time she'd covered another hundred yards, there were so many moths roosting in the trees that the branches were furry with them. There had to be thousands. Hell, tens of thousands. If they attacked her (this brought a memory of Hitchcock's film about vengeful birds), she'd be smothered. But Michaela didn't think that was going to happen. The moths were observers, that was all. Sentinels. Outriders. The fox was the leader. But leading her where?

Her trail-guide brought Michaela up a rise, down a narrow dip, up another hill, and through a scrubby stand of birch and alder. The trunks were patched with that weird whiteness. She rubbed her hands over one of the spots. The tips of her fingers glowed briefly, then faded. Had there been cocoons here? Was this their residue? More Qs without As.

When she looked up from her hand, the fox was gone, but that hum was louder. It no longer sounded like power lines to her. It was stronger and more vital. The earth itself was vibrating beneath her shoes. She walked toward the sound, then stopped, awestruck just as Lila Norcross had been on this same spot a bit more than four days before.

Ahead was a clearing. In the center of it, a gnarled tree of many entwined, russet-colored trunks ascended into the heavens. Ferny, prehistoric leaves lolled from its arms. She could smell their spicy aroma, a little like nutmeg, mostly like nothing she had ever smelled in her life. An aviary's worth of exotic birds roosted in the high branches, whistling and keening and chattering. At the foot was a peacock as large as a child, its iridescent fan spread for Michaela's delectation.

I am not seeing this, or if I am, all of the sleeping women are seeing it, too. Because I'm like them now. I fell asleep back by the ruins of that meth shed, and a cocoon is weaving around me even as I admire yonder peacock. I must have overlooked myself somehow, that's all.

What changed her mind was the white tiger. The fox came first, as if leading it. A red snake hung around the tiger's neck like barbaric jewelry. The snake flicker-flicked its tongue, tasting the air. She could see shadows waxing and waning in the muscles of the tiger's flanks as it paced toward her. Its enormous green eyes fixed on hers. The fox broke into a trot, and its muzzle scraped against her shin – cool and slightly damp.

Ten minutes before, Michaela would have said she no longer had it in her to jog, let alone run. Now she turned and fled the way she had come in great bounding leaps, batting branches aside and sending clouds of brown moths whirling into the sky. She stumbled to her knees, got up, and ran on. She didn't turn around, because she was afraid the tiger would be right behind her, its jaws yawning open to bite her in two at the waist.

She emerged from the woods above the meth shed and saw Garth standing by his Mercedes, holding up a large Baggie filled with what looked like purple jewels. 'I am part cosmetic surgeon, part motherfucking drug-sniffing dog!' he cried. 'Never doubt it! The sucker was taped to a ceiling panel! We shall . . . Mickey? What's wrong?'

She turned and looked back. The tiger was gone, but the fox was there, its brush once more curled neatly around its paws. 'Do you see that?'

'What? That fox? Sure.' His glee evaporated. 'Hey, it didn't bite you, did it?'

'No, it didn't bite me. But . . . come with me, Garth.'

'What, into the woods? No thanks. Never a Boy Scout. I only have to look at poison ivy to catch it. Chemistry Club was my thing, ha-ha. No surprise there.'

'You have to come. I mean it. It's important. I need . . . well . . . verification. You won't catch poison ivy. There's a path.'

He came, but without any enthusiasm. She led him past the ruined shed and into the trees. The fox just trotted at first, then sprinted ahead, weaving between the trees until it was lost to view. The moths were also gone, but . . .

'There.' She pointed at one of the tracks. 'Do you see that? Please tell me you do.'

'Huh,' Garth said. 'I'll be damned.'

He tucked the precious Baggie of Purple Lightning into his unbuttoned shirt and took a knee, examining the luminous footprint. He used a leaf to touch it gingerly, sniffed the residue, then watched the spots fade.

'Is it that cocoon stuff?' Michaela asked. 'It is, isn't it?'

'It might have been once,' Garth said. 'Or possibly an exudation of whatever *causes* the cocoons. I'm just guessing here, but . . .' He got to his feet. He seemed to have forgotten that they had come out here searching for more dope, and Michaela glimpsed the intelligent, probing physician who occasionally roused himself from the king-sized bed of meth inside Garth's skull. 'Listen, you've heard the rumors, right? Maybe when we went downtown for more supplies at the grocery?' (Said supplies – beer, Ruffles potato chips, ramen noodles, and an economy-sized tub of sour cream – had been meager. The Shopwell had been open, but pretty much ransacked.)

'Rumors about the woman,' she said. 'Of course.'

Garth said, 'Maybe we really do have Typhoid Mary right here in Dooling. I know it seems unlikely, all the reports say Aurora started on the other side of the world, but—'

'I think it's possible,' Michaela said. All her machinery was working again, and at top speed. The feeling was divine. It might not last long, but while it did, she meant to ride it like one of those mechanical bulls. Yahoo, cowgirl. 'And there's something else. I might have found where she came from. Come on, I'll show you.'

Ten minutes later, they stood at the edge of the clearing. The fox was gone. Ditto tiger and peacock with fabulous tail. Also ditto exotic birds of many colors. The tree was still there, only . . .

'Well,' Garth said, and she could practically hear his attentiveness dwindling away, air whistling out from a punctured floatation device, 'it's a fine old oak, Mickey, I'll give you that, but otherwise I see nothing special.'

'I didn't imagine it. I *didn't*.' But already she was beginning to wonder. Perhaps she had imagined the moths, too.

'Even if you did, those glowing handprints and footprints are definitely *X-Files* material.' Garth brightened. 'I've got all those shows on disc, and they hold up remarkably well, although the cell phones they use in the first two or three seasons are *hilarious*. Let's go back to the house and smoke up and watch some, what do you say?'

Michaela did not want to watch *The X-Files*. What she wanted was to drive to the prison and see if she could score an interview with the woman of the hour. It seemed like an awful lot of work, and it was hard to imagine persuading anyone to let her in looking as she did now (sort of like the Wicked Witch of the West, only in jeans and a shell top), but after what they had seen up here, where that woman had reportedly made her first appearance . . .

'How about a real-life X-File?' she said.

'What do you mean?'

'Let's take a ride. I'll tell you on the way.'

'Maybe we could try this stuff out first?' He shook the Baggie hopefully.

'Soon,' she said. It would have to be soon, because weariness surrounded her. It was like being stuck in a suffocating black bag. But there was one tiny rip in it, and that rip was her curiosity, letting in a shaft of bright light.

'Well . . . okay. I guess.'

Garth led their return down the path. Michaela paused long enough to take a look back over her shoulder, hoping to surprise the amazing tree back into existence. But it was just an oak, broad and tall but not in the least supernatural.

The truth is out there, though, she thought. And maybe I'm not too tired to find it.

7

Nadine Hicks was of the old school; in the days before Aurora she had been wont to introduce herself as 'Mrs Lawrence Hicks,' as though by marrying her husband, she had to some degree become him. Now she was wrapped up like a wedding present and reclining at the dining room table. Set in front of her was an empty plate, an empty glass, napkin and cutlery. After letting Frank into the house, Hicks brought him into the dining room, and the assistant warden sat down at the cherrywood table across from his wife to finish his breakfast.

'I bet you think this is weird,' said Hicks.

No, Frank thought, I don't think arranging your cocooned wife at the dining table like a giant mummified doll is weird at all. I think it's, oh, what's the word? Ah, there it is: *insane.*

'I'm not going to judge you,' Frank said. 'It's been a big shock. Everyone's doing the best they can.'

'Well, Officer, I'm just trying to keep to a routine.' Hicks was dressed up in a suit and he'd shaved, but there were huge bags under his eyes and the suit was wrinkled. Of course, everyone's clothes seemed to be wrinkled now. How many men knew how to iron? Or to fold, for that matter? Frank did, but he didn't own an iron. Since the separation, he took his clothes to Dooling Dry Cleaners, and if he needed a pair of creased pants in a hurry, he put them under the mattress, lay down for twenty minutes or so, and called it good.

Hicks's breakfast was chipped beef on toast. 'Hope you don't mind if I eat. Good old shit-on-a-shingle. Moving her around works up an appetite. After this, we're going to sit out in the yard.' Hicks swiveled to his wife. 'Isn't that right, Nadine?'

They both waited a couple of pointless seconds, as if she might respond. Nadine just sat there, though, an alien statue behind her place setting.

'Listen, I don't want to take up too much of your time, Mr Hicks.'

'It's fine.' Hicks scooped up a toast point and took a bite. Droplets of white mush and beef splatted down on his knee. 'Darn it.' Hicks chuckled through his mouthful. 'Running out of clean clothes already. Nadine's the one who does the laundry. Need you to wake up and get on that, Nadine.' He swallowed his bite, and gave Frank a small, serious nod. 'I scoop the litter box and take out the trash on Friday mornings. It's equitable. A fair division of labor.'

'Sir, I just want to ask you—'

'And I gas up her car. She hates those self-service pumps. I used to tell her, "You'll have to learn if I predecease you, honey." And she'd say—'

'I want to ask you about what's going on at the prison.' Frank also wanted to get away from Lore Hicks as quickly as possible. 'There's a woman there that people are talking about. Her name's Eve Black. What can you tell me about her?'

Hicks studied his plate. 'I would avoid her.'

'So, she's awake?'

'She was when I left. But yes, I would avoid her.'

'They say that she sleeps and wakes. Is that true?'

'It seemed like she did, but . . .' Hicks, still staring at his plate, angled his head, as if he were suspicious of his shit on toast. 'I hate to beat a dead horse, but I would let that one go, Officer.'

'Why do you say that?' Frank was thinking of the moths that had burst up from the clipping of web that Garth Flickinger had lit. And the one that had seemed to fix its eyes on him.

'She took my phone,' said Hicks.

'Pardon? How did she do that?'

'She threatened me with rats. The rats are with her. They do her bidding.'

'The rats do her bidding.'

'You see the implications, don't you? Like every hotel, every prison has rodents. Cutbacks exacerbate the problem. I remember Coates complaining about having to cancel the exterminator. No room in the budget. They don't think about that at the legislature, do they? "It's just a prison. What are a few rats to an inmate, when they are rats themselves?" Well, what if one of the inmates learns to *control* the rats? What then?' Hicks pushed his plate away. Apparently his appetite had left him. 'Rhetorical question, of course. Legislature doesn't think of things like that.'

Frank hovered in the doorway of the Hickses' dining room, contemplating the likelihood that the man was suffering from hallucinations brought on by stress and grief. But there was the fragment of web that had turned into moths – what about that? Frank had seen it happen. And hadn't a moth stared Frank down? That might have been a hallucination (he himself was suffering from stress and grief, after all), but Frank didn't really think so. Who was to say that the assistant warden hadn't completely lost his marbles? And who was to say he wasn't telling the truth?

Maybe he'd lost his marbles *because* he was telling the truth. How about that for an unpleasant possibility?

Hicks stood up. 'Since you're here, would you mind helping me carry her outside? My back's aching, and I'm not exactly young anymore.'

There were few things he wanted to do less, but Frank agreed. He took Nadine Hicks's bulked-up legs and her husband gripped her under her bulked-up armpits. They hoisted her and went out the front door, down the steps, and along the side of the house, carefully carrying the woman between them. The webbing crackled like Christmas paper.

'Just hold on there, Nadine,' Hicks told the white membrane that surrounded his wife's face. 'We're going to get you set up good in the Adirondack. Get you some sun. I'm sure it filters through.'

'So who's supposed to be in charge now?' Frank asked. 'At the prison?'

'No one,' said Hicks. 'Oh, I suppose Van Lampley could make a claim, if she's still upright. She's the senior officer.'

'The psychiatrist, Dr Norcross, claims he's the acting warden,' Frank said.

'Nonsense.'

They settled Mrs Hicks in a bright yellow Adirondack chair on the stone patio. There was, of course, no sun. Not today. Just the same light rain. Instead of soaking in, the precipitation beaded on the surface of the cocoon, the way it would on the fabric of a waterproof tent. Hicks began to half-rock, half-drag over a stand-up umbrella. The umbrella's base screeched across the stone. 'Have to be careful, can't apply sunblock with that stuff on her, and she burns very easily.'

'Norcross? The psychiatrist?'

Hicks chuckled. 'Norcross is just a contractor. He doesn't have any authority. He wasn't appointed by anybody.'

This didn't surprise Frank. He'd suspected that Norcross's line of bullshit was just that – a line. It did piss him off, though. Lives were at stake. Plenty of them, but it was okay to think mostly of Nana, because she stood for all the rest. There was no selfishness in what he was doing when you looked at it that way; seen in that light, it was altruistic! Meanwhile, he needed to stay cool.

'What kind of a man is he? This shrink?'

Hicks got the umbrella situated and opened it over his wife. 'There.' He took a few deep breaths. Sweat and rain had darkened his collar. 'He's smart, I'll give him that. Too smart, actually. No business working in a prison. And think of this: he is awarded a full-time salary, almost the equal of my own, and yet we cannot afford an exterminator. This is politics as we know it in the twenty-first century, Officer Geary.'

'What do you mean when you say he has no business working in a prison?'

'Why didn't he go into private practice? I've seen his records. He's published. Got the right degrees. I've always figured there was something off about him, wanting to hang around with reprobates and drug addicts, but I couldn't say what. If it's a sex thing, he's been extremely cautious. That's your first idea when you think of a man who likes to work with female criminals. But I don't think that's it.'

'How would you deal with him? Is he reasonable?'

'Sure, he's reasonable. A very reasonable man who also happens to be a politically correct softie. And that's exactly why I hate to, as you put it, *deal* with him. We're not a rehab facility, you know. Prison's a storage center for people who won't play by the rules and suck at cheating. A garbage can, when you come right down to it, and we're paid to sit on the lid. Coates gets her jollies sparring with him, they're pally, but he exhausts me. He'll reason you right out of your shoes.' From his pocket Hicks withdrew a crumpled handkerchief. He used it to dab away some water beads from his wife's shroud. 'Big on eye contact. Makes you think he thinks you're nuts.'

Frank thanked Lawrence Hicks for his help and went back around to the front where he'd parked. What was Norcross thinking? What reason would he have to keep them from seeing the woman? Why wouldn't he trust them? The facts only seemed to support one conclusion, and it was an ugly one: for some reason, the doctor was working on the woman's behalf.

Hicks came jogging after him. 'Mr Geary! Officer!'

'What is it?'

The assistant warden's expression was tight. 'Listen, that woman—' He rubbed his hands together. The light rain stained the shoulders of his wrinkled suit jacket. 'If you do talk to her, to Eve Black, I don't want you to give her the impression that I care about getting my phone back, all right? She can keep it. I'll use my wife's if I need to make any calls.'

8

When Jared hurried out to the rear of the demo house where he and Mary were currently living (if you can call this living, he thought), Mary was leaning against the stake fence with her head in her arms. Fine white threads were spinning out of her hair.

He sprinted to her, almost tripping over the neat-as-pie doghouse (a match for the demo, right down to the miniature blue window frames), grabbed her, shook her, then pinched both earlobes, as she'd told him to do if she started to drift away. She said she'd read on the Internet that it was the quickest way to wake someone up when they were dozing off. Of course there were all sorts of stay-awake remedies on the Internet now, as many as there had once been go-to-sleep strategies.

It worked. Her eyes came back into focus. The strands of white webbing detached themselves from her and lazed upward, disappearing as they went.

'Whoa,' she said, touching her ears and trying on a smile. 'Thought I was getting my ears pierced again. There's a big purple blotch floating over your face, Jere.'

'You were probably looking into the sun.' He took her arm. 'Come on. We have to hurry.'

'Why?'

Jared didn't answer. If his dad was paranoid, then it was catching. In the living room, with its perfectly matching but somehow sterile items of furniture – even the pictures on the wall matched – he paused to look out the window at the sheriff's department cruiser parked six or seven houses down the street. As he watched, two officers emerged from one of the houses. His mom had invited all her deputies and their wives to dinner at one time or another over the years, and Jared knew most of them. Those two were Rangle and Barrows. Given that all the houses except for this one were empty of furniture, the cops would probably just give them a lick and a promise. They'd be here in no time.

'Jared, stop *pulling*!'

They had stashed Platinum, Molly, Mrs Ransom, and Lila in the master bedroom. Mary had wanted to leave them on the ground floor, said it wasn't as if they were going to care about the décor, or anything. Jared had insisted, thank God, but even the second floor wasn't enough. Because the demo house was furnished, Rangle and Barrows might decide to really search it.

He got Mary up the stairs, she muttering complaints the whole way. From the bedroom he grabbed the basket containing Platinum's swathed little body and rushed to pull down the ringbolt in the hallway ceiling. The ladder to the attic descended with a bang. It would have clocked Mary on the head if he hadn't pulled her out of the way. Jared climbed up, shoved the baby's basket up over the edge onto the attic floor, and slid back down. Ignoring her questions, he ran to the end of the hall and looked out. The cruiser was creeping along the curb. Only four houses away now. No, three.

He ran to where Mary was standing with her shoulders slumped and her head down. 'We have to carry them up there.' He pointed to the ladder.

'I can't carry anyone,' she said, sounding like a whiny child. 'I'm *tiyy-erd,* Jere!'

'I know. But you can manage Molly, she's light. I'll get her gram and my mother.'

'Why? Why do we have to?'

'Because those cops might be looking for us. My father said so.'

He expected her to ask why it would be bad for the deputies to find them, but she didn't. Jared led her to the bedroom – the women were on the double bed, Molly reposing on a fluffy towel in the en suite bathroom. He picked Molly up and put her in Mary's arms. Then he got Mrs Ransom, who seemed heavier than he remembered. But not *too* heavy, Jared thought, and remembered what his mother liked to sing when he was small: *Ack*-sen-tuate the positive, *elim*-i-nate the negative.

'And don't mess with Mr In Between,' he said, getting a better grip on what remained of the old lady.

'Huh? Wha?'

'Never mind.'

With Molly in her arms, Mary began to mount the ladder one slow step at a time. Jared (imagining the prowl car already pulling up out front, Rangle and Barrows looking at the sign on the lawn reading **COME IN AND LOOK AROUND**) socked his shoulder into Mary's butt when she stopped halfway to the top. She looked down over her shoulder.

'You're getting a little personal there, Jared.'

'Hurry up, then.'

Somehow she struggled to the top without dropping her burden on his head. Jared followed, panting, pushing Mrs Ransom through the opening. Mary had set Molly's small body on the bare boards of the attic. The space ran the length of the house. It was low and very hot.

'I'll be back,' Jared said.

'Okay, but I'm finding it very hard to care. The heat is making my head ache.'

Jared hurried back to the master bedroom. He got his arms around Lila's wrapped body and felt his sore knee give a warning twang. He had forgotten about her uniform, her heavy workshoes, and her utility belt. How much did all that add to the weight of a healthy, well-nourished female? Ten pounds? Twenty?

He got her as far as the ladder, contemplated its steep incline, and thought, I'll never be able to get her up there. No way.

Then the doorbell rang, four cheery ascending chimes, and he started to climb, not panting now but gasping. He made it three-quarters of the way up the ladder, then ran out of gas. Just as he was trying to decide if he could get down without dropping his mother, two slim arms appeared, hands open. Mary, thank God. Jared managed another two steps, and Mary was able to grab Lila.

From below, one of the deputies said, 'Not even locked. Door's wide open. Come on.'

Jared shoved. Mary pulled. Together they managed to get Lila above the level of the trapdoor. Mary collapsed on her back, yanking Lila over and in. Jared grabbed the top of the ladder and pulled. It came up, folding in on itself as it did, and he pressed against it, easing it the last couple of feet so it wouldn't bang shut.

Down below, the other deputy called, 'Yoo-hoo, anybody home?'

'Like some woman in a bitch-bag is going to answer,' the other said, and the two of them laughed.

Bitch-bags? Jared thought. Is that what you're calling them? If my mother heard something like that come out of your mouths, she'd kick your country asses right up between your shoulder blades.

They were still talking, but moving toward the kitchen side of the house, and Jared could no longer tell what they were saying. His fear had communicated itself to Mary, even in her dopey state, and she put her arms around him. He could smell her sweat, and when her cheek pressed against his, he could feel it.

The voices came back, and Jared sent the cops below a thought command: *Leave! The place is obviously empty, so just leave!*

Mary whispered in his ear. 'There's food in the fridge, Jere. In the pantry, too. A wrapper I tossed in the wastebasket. What if they—'

Big cop shoes going *clump-clump-clump*, the deputies came up the stairs to the second floor. That was bad, but they weren't talking about food in the fridge, or fresh trash in the can beside it, and that was good. (*Ack*-sen-tuate the positive.) They were discussing what to do about their lunch.

From beneath them and to the left, one of the cops – Rangle, maybe – said, 'This bedspread looks kinda rumpled to me. Does it to you?'

'Yeah,' said the other. 'Wouldn't shock me if someone's been squatting here, but more likely, people that come in to look at the place, prospective buyers, they probably sit down, too, sometimes, right? Or even try the bed. Natural thing to do.'

More footsteps, back out into the hall. *Clump-clump-clump.* Then they stopped, and this time when the voices came, they were directly below. Mary tightened her arms around Jared's neck and whispered. 'If they catch us hiding up here, they'll arrest us, won't they!'

'Shhh,' Jared whispered back, thinking, They would have arrested us even if they found us down there. Only they'd probably call it protective custody.

'Trapdoor in the ceiling,' the one who was probably Barrows said. 'You want to go up and check the attic, or should I?'

The question was followed by a moment of silence that seemed to stretch out forever. Then the one who was probably Rangle said, 'You can go up if you want to, but if Lila and her kid were in the house they'd be down here. And I got allergies. I'm not going up and breathing a lot of dust.'

'Still . . .'

'Have at it, buddy,' Rangle said, and all at once the ladder went flopping back down, spilling muted light into the attic. If Lila's cocooned body had been even six inches closer to the open trap-door, it would have been in view. 'Enjoy the heat up there, too. I bet it's a hundred and ten.'

'Fuck it,' Barrows said. 'And while I'm at it, fuck you and the horse you rode in on. *Allergies*. Come on, let's get out of here.'

The ladder came back up, this time closing with a loud bang that made Jared twitch even though he'd known it was coming. The big cop shoes went *clump-clump-clump*ing back down the stairs. Jared listened, holding his breath, as the deputies stood in the foyer, talking some more. Low tones. Impossible to catch more than a word or a phrase. Something about Terry Coombs; something about a new deputy named Geary; and something else again about lunch.

Leave! Jared wanted to scream at them. *Leave before Mary and me have fucking heatstrokes!*

At last the front door shut. Jared strained his ears to catch the sound of their cruiser starting up, but couldn't. Either he'd spent too much time listening to loud music with his headphones on, or the attic insulation was too thick. He counted to a hundred, then back down to zero. He couldn't stand to wait any longer. The heat was killing him.

'I think they're gone,' he said.

Mary didn't answer, and he realized her formerly tight grip on his neck had slackened. He had been concentrating too hard to notice until now. When he turned to look at her, her arms fell limply to her sides and she collapsed to the board floor.

'Mary! *Mary!* Don't go to sleep!'

There was no response. Jared shoved the trapdoor open, not caring about the bang the ladder made when its feet landed on the hardwood floor below. He had forgotten about the cops. Mary was what he cared about now, and all he cared about. Maybe it wasn't too late.

Only it was. Shaking did no good. Mary had fallen asleep while he was listening to make sure the cops weren't coming back. Now she was lying beside Lila, her fine features already blurring beneath the white threads that were busily knitting themselves out of nothing.

'No,' Jared whispered. 'She tried so hard.'

He sat there for almost five minutes, watching the cocoon thicken, weaving relentlessly, then called his father.

It was all he could think to do.

CHAPTER 4

1

In the world the women had somehow exited, Candy Meshaum
had resided in a house on West Lavin, in the direction of the prison.
Which was fitting, because her house had also been a prison. In
this new world, she had chosen to live with some other women,
all regular attendees of the Meeting, in an enclave they'd made out
of a storage facility. The storage facility, like the Shopwell (and unlike
the great majority of the other buildings in the area), had stayed
almost entirely water-tight over the indeterminate number of years
of abandonment. It was an L-shaped structure of two levels, box-
upon-box-upon-box, hacked out of the surrounding woods and
planted on a cement tarmac. Built of hard plastics and fiberglass,
the storage pods had admirably fulfilled the leakproof promise of
the faded advertisement on the sign outside. Grasses and trees had
encroached on the tarmac, and leaves clogged the gutter system,
but it had been an easy project to cut back the overgrowth and
clear the drainage, and the opened pods, once emptied of useless
boxes of possessions, had proven to be excellent if not exactly
beautiful housing.

Although Candy Meshaum had made a sweet try at it, hadn't
she, Lila thought.

She walked around the box, which was filled with the natural
light that came through the open bay door. There was a nicely
made bed in the middle of the room, draped in a glossy red comforter

that picked up the daylight. Hung on the windowless wall was a framed seascape: fair skies and a length of rocky coast. It had perhaps been scavenged from the original stored contents of the pod. In the corner was a rocking chair, and on the floor beside the chair was a basket of yarn punctured by two brass needles. Another basket nearby contained pairs of expertly knitted socks, examples of her work.

'What do you think?' Coates had lingered outside the box to smoke. (Cigarettes, wrapped in foil and cellophane, were another of the things that had lasted quite well.) The warden – former warden – had grown her hair out, allowing it to go white. The way it spread down to her narrow shoulders gave her a prophetic look – as if she had been wandering in the desert in search of her tribe. Lila thought it suited her.

'I like what you've done with your hair.'

'Thanks, but I was referring to the woman who ought to be here, but suddenly isn't.'

Candy Meshaum was one of four women who had lately vanished, counting Essie. Lila had interviewed a number of other women who lived in the neighboring pods. Candy had been seen happily rocking in her chair, knitting, and ten minutes afterward, she was nowhere. The pod was on the second floor of the storage complex, close to the middle, and yet not a single person had seen her slip away, a good-sized woman with a bad limp. It wasn't inconceivable that she'd managed such a disappearance, but it was improbable.

Her neighbors described Candy as cheerful and happy. One of them, who had known her before, in the old world, used the word *reborn*. She evinced great pride in her crafts, and in her pretty little decorated box of a home. More than one person mentioned that she referred to her home as 'the apartment of her dreams' without a crumb of irony.

'I don't see anything definitive. Nothing I'd want to take to court,' Lila said. She guessed, however, that what had happened was what had occurred with Essie: there one second, gone the next. Poof. Abracadabra.

'Same thing, isn't it?' Janice, who had been looking right at Essie, reported seeing a tiny flash – no bigger than a lighter flame – and then nothing. The space that the woman had filled was empty. Janice's eyes had failed to detect the transformation, or disintegration, or whatever phenomenon had occurred. It was too quick for the eye. It was, the warden said, as if Essie had been turned off like a light bulb, except not even a filament dimmed that quickly.

'Could be,' Lila said. God, she sounded like her lost husband.

'She's dead,' Janice said. 'In the other world. Don't you think so?'

A moth perched on the wall above the rocking chair. Lila held out her hand. The moth fluttered to it, landing on the fingernail of her index finger. Lila smelled a faint odor of burn.

'Could be,' she repeated. For the moment, this Clint-ism was all she dared to say. 'We ought to go back and see the ladies off.'

'Crazy idea,' Janice grumbled. 'We've got enough to do without exploring.'

Lila smiled. 'Does that mean you wish you were going?'

Mimicking Lila, ex-Warden Coates said, 'Could be.'

2

On Main Street, a patrol was about to set off for a look at the world beyond Dooling. There were a half-dozen women in the group, and they'd packed a pair of the golf carts with supplies. Millie Olson, an officer from the prison, had volunteered to take the lead. To this point, no one had ventured much beyond the old town lines. No airplanes or helicopters had flown overhead, no fires had burned in the distance, and no voices had surfaced on the bands of the emergency radios they'd cranked up. It reinforced in Lila that sense of incompleteness she'd felt from the beginning. The world they inhabited now seemed like a reproduction. Almost like a scene inside a snow globe, only without the snow.

Lila and Janice arrived in time to watch the final preparations. A former prisoner named Nell Seeger crouched on the ground by one of the golf carts, humming to herself as she checked the air

pressure on the tires. Millie was sifting through the packs loaded
onto a trailer hitched to the back, making last minute double-checks
of the supplies: sleeping bags, freeze-dried food, clean water, clothes,
a couple of toy walkie-talkies that had been found sealed in plastic
and actually functioned (somewhat), a couple of rifles that Lila
herself had cleaned up, first aid kits. There was an atmosphere of
excitement and good humor; there was laughter and high-fives.
Someone asked Millie Olson what she'd do if they ran into a bear.

'Tame it,' she deadpanned, not glancing up from the pack she
was digging through. This earned a round of laughs from the
onlookers.

'Did you know her?' Lila asked Janice. 'You know, before?' They
were under a sidewalk awning, shoulder to shoulder in winter coats.
Their breath steamed.

'Shit, I was her damn boss.'

'Not Millie, Candy Meshaum.'

'No. Did you?'

'Yes,' said Lila.

'And?'

'She was a domestic abuse victim. Her husband beat her. A lot.
That's why she limped. He was a total asshole, a mechanic who
made his real money selling guns. Ran a bit with the Griners. Or
so it was rumored – we never managed to clip him for anything.
He used his tools on her. They lived out on West Lavin in a house
that was falling down around their ears. I'm not surprised she didn't
want to try to fix the place up, wouldn't have been any point.
Neighbors called us out more than once, heard her screaming, but
she wouldn't give us a word. Afraid of reprisals.'

'Lucky he never killed her.'

'I think he probably did.'

The warden squinted at Lila. 'Do you mean what I think you
mean?'

'Walk with me.'

They strolled along the ruins of the sidewalk, stepping over
weed-choked fissures, detouring around asphalt chunks. The little
park that faced the broken remains of the Municipal Building had

been salvaged, trimmed and swept. Here the only sign of time's passage was the toppled statue of some long-deceased town dignitary. A massive elm branch – storm-tossed, surely – had knocked him off his perch. The branch had been dragged away and chipped, but the dignitary was so heavy no one had done anything about him yet. He had gone down at an acute angle from the plinth, his top hat dug into the ground and his boots to the sky; Lila had seen little girls run up him, using his backside like a ramp, laughing wildly.

Janice said, 'You think her son-of-a-bitch husband torched her in her cocoon.'

Lila didn't answer directly. 'Has anyone mentioned feeling dizzy to you? Nauseated? Comes on very suddenly, and then after a couple of hours it goes?' Lila had felt this herself a couple of times. Rita Coombs had mentioned a similar experience; so had Mrs Ransom, and Molly.

'Yes,' said Janice. 'Just about everyone I know has mentioned it. Like being spun around without being spun. I don't know if you know Nadine Hicks, wife of my colleague at the prison—'

'Met her at a couple of community potlucks,' said Lila, and wrinkled her nose.

'Yeah, she hardly ever missed. And wasn't missed when she did, if you know what I mean. Anyway, she claims to have that vertigo thing just about all the time.'

'Okay, keep that in mind. Now think about the mass burnings. You know about those?'

'Not personally. I'm like you, I came relatively early. But I've heard the newer arrivals talk about seeing it on the news: men burning women in their cocoons.'

'There you go,' Lila said.

'Oh,' Janice replied, getting the drift. 'Oh shit.'

'Oh shit covers it, all right. At first I thought – hoped – that maybe it was some sort of misinterpretation on the part of the newer arrivals. They'd been sleep-deprived, of course, and distressed, and maybe they saw something on television that they *thought* was cocoons being burned, but was actually something else.' Lila inhaled deeply of the late fall air. It was so crisp and clean it made you feel taller. No exhaust smells. No coal trucks. 'That instinct, to doubt what women say, it's always there. To find some reason not to take their word. Men do it . . . but we do, too. I do it.'

'You're too hard on yourself.'

'And I saw it coming. I talked about it with Terry Coombs not more than three or four hours before I fell asleep in the old world. Women reacted when their cocoons were torn. They were dangerous. They fought. They killed. It doesn't surprise me that a lot of men might see the situation as an opportunity, or a precaution, or the pretext they'd always wanted to light a few people on fire.'

Janice offered a slanted smile. 'And I get accused of taking a less than sunny view of the human race.'

'Someone burned Essie, Janice. Back in our world. Who knows who. And someone burned Candy Meshaum. Was her hubby upset because his punching bag fell asleep on him? He'd definitely be the first person I'd question, if I was there.'

Lila sat down on the fallen statue. 'And the dizziness? I'm pretty sure that's also because of what's happening back there. Someone moving us. Moving us around like furniture. Right before Essie was burned, she was in a low mood. I'm guessing that maybe someone moved her a bit before lighting her up and it was the vertigo that had her down.'

'Pretty sure you've got your ass on Dooling's first mayor,' said Janice.

'He can take it. Someone washed his underwear for him. This is our new honorary bench.' Lila realized she was furious. What had Essie or Candy Meshaum ever done, except finally find a few months of happiness out of the entirety of their rotten lives? Happiness that had come at the price of nothing more than a few dolls and a converted storage space with no windows.

And men had burned them. She was sure of it. That was how their story ended. When you died there, you died here, too. Men had ripped them right out of the world – right out of two worlds. Men. There seemed to be no escape from them.

Janice must have read her thoughts . . . or, more likely, her face.

'My husband Archie was a good guy. Supported everything I ever did.'

'Yeah, but he died young. You might not have felt that way if he'd stuck around.' It was an awful thing to say, but Lila didn't regret it. For some reason, an old Amish saying occurred to her: KISSIN' DON'T LAST, COOKIN' DO. You could say that about a lot of things when it came to the wedded state. Honesty. Respect. Simple kindness, even.

Coates gave no sign of offense. 'Clint was that bad a husband?'

'He was better than Candy Meshaum's.'

'Low bar,' Janice said. 'Never mind. I'll just sit here and treasure the gilded memory of my husband, who had the decency to pop off before he became a shit.'

Lila let her head loll back. 'Maybe I deserved that.' It was another sunny day, but there were gray clouds to the north, miles of them.

'Well? *Was* he that bad a husband?'

'No. Clint was a good husband. And a good father. He pulled his weight. He loved me. I never doubted that. But there was a lot he never told me about himself. Things I shouldn't have had to find out in ways that made me feel bad about myself. Clint talked the talk, about openness and support, talked until his face turned blue, but when you got below the surface, he was your basic Marlboro Man. It's worse, I think, than being lied to. A lie indicates a certain degree of respect. I'm pretty sure he was carrying a bag of stuff, real heavy stuff, that he thought I was just too delicate to help him with. I'd rather be lied to than condescended to.'

'What do you mean by a bag of stuff . . . ?'

'He grew up rough. I think he fought his way out, and I mean that literally. I've seen the way he rubs his knuckles when he's preoccupied or upset. But he doesn't talk about it. I've asked, and he does the Marlboro Man thing.' Lila glanced at Coates, and read some variety of unease in her expression.

'You know what I mean, don't you? From being around him.'

'I suppose I do. Clint has – another side. A harder side. Angrier. I didn't come to see it clearly until recently.'

'It pisses me off. But you know what's worse? It's left me feeling kind of . . . disheartened.'

Janice was using a twig to poke bits of caked mud off the face of the statue. 'I can see how that would dishearten a person.'

The golf carts started to move away, followed by their small, tarp-draped trailers of supplies. The procession moved out of sight and then reappeared for a couple of minutes where the road ascended to higher ground before disappearing for good.

Lila and Janice switched to other topics: the ongoing repairs to the houses on Smith; the two beautiful horses that had been corralled and taught — or perhaps re-taught — how to take riders; and the wonder Magda Dubcek and those two former prisoners claimed to be on the verge of bringing to fruition. If they could get more juice, more solar panels, clean running water seemed to be a fore-seeable possibility. Indoor plumbing, the American dream.

It was dusk before they were talked out, and never once did the subject of Clint, of Jared, of Archie, of Candy Meshaum's husband, of Jesus Christ, or of any other man, again arise to trouble their discourse.

3

They didn't talk about Evie, but Lila had not forgotten her. She had not forgotten about the suggestive timing of Eve Black's appear-ance in Dooling, or her strange, knowing talk, or the webbed tracks in the woods near Truman Mayweather's trailer. She had not forgotten about where those tracks had brought her, either, to the Amazing Tree, driving up into the sky on its countless roots and intertwined trunks. As for the animals that had appeared from around the Tree — the white tiger, the snake, the peacock, and the fox — Lila remembered them, too.

Her mental picture of the spiraling roots of the Tree, like the cords for a giant's sneakers, the way they wound around each other, recurred often. It was so perfect, so majestic, the plan of its being so right.

Had Evie come from the Tree? Or had the Tree come from Evie?

And the women of Our Place – were they dreamers, or were they the dream?

4

Icy rain pelted Our Place for forty-eight hours, snapping tree branches, pouring chilly slop through the holes in roofs, filling the streets and walks with cloudy puddles. Lila, stretched in her tent, occasionally put aside the book she was reading to kick at the walls and break off the frozen coating that had formed on the vinyl. The sound was like breaking glass.

Before, she'd switched from paper books to an e-reader, little suspecting that the world would break down and make such things obsolete. There were still books in her house, though, and a few of them weren't moldy. When she finished the one she was reading, she ventured from her tent in the front yard to the wreckage of her home. It was too depressing – too redolent of her son and husband – for Lila to imagine living in it, but she hadn't been able to bring herself to move away.

The slicks of rain sliding down the interior walls glistened in the beam of her crank flashlight. The rain sounded like an ocean being stirred. From a shelf at the back of the living room, Lila picked out a damp mystery novel, and started to return the way she had come. The beam caught an odd, parchment-colored leaf, lying on the rotted seat of a stool by the kitchen counter. Lila picked it up. It was a note from Anton: the information for his 'tree guy,' to deal with the Dutch Elm in the backyard.

She studied the note for a long time, stunned by it, by the sudden closeness of that other life – her real life? her previous life? – which appeared like a child darting out between parked cars and into traffic.

5

The exploration party had been gone a week when Celia Frode returned on foot, splattered in mud from head to toe. She was alone.

6

Celia said that beyond Dooling Correctional, in the direction of the little neighboring town of Maylock, the roads had become impassable; every tree they cleared from the highway only got them a few yards before they came to the next one. It was easier to leave the golf carts and hike.

There was no one in Maylock when they got there, and no sign of recent life. The buildings and houses were like the ones in Dooling – overgrown, in states of greater and lesser disrepair, a few burned by fires – and the road above Dorr's Hollow Stream, which was now a swollen river with sunken cars for shoals, had collapsed. Probably they should have turned around then, Celia conceded. They'd scavenged useful supplies from the grocery store and other businesses in Maylock. But they got to talking about the movie theater in the small town of Eagle that was another ten miles off, and how great it would be for the kids if they came back with a film projector. Magda had assured them that their big generator would be up to such tasks.

'They still had that new *Star Wars* movie playing there,' Celia said, and added, wryly, 'You know, Sheriff, the one where the girl's the hero.'

Lila didn't correct the 'Sheriff.' It had turned out to be remarkably difficult to quit being a cop. 'Go on, Celia.'

The exploring party crossed the Dorr's Hollow Stream at a bridge that was still intact, and picked up a mountain road called Lion Head Way that seemed to offer a shortcut to Eagle. The map they'd been using – borrowed from the remains of the Dooling Public Library – showed an old, unnamed coal company road curling off near the top of the mountain. The company road could take them to the interstate, and from there the going would be easy. But the map turned out to be outdated. Lion Head Way now dead-ended at a plateau, where stood that dreary place of male incarceration called Lion Head Prison. The company road they had been hoping to find had been plowed under during the construction of the prison.

Because it was late in the day, rather than attempt to backtrack the narrow, broken decline off the mountain in the dark, they had decided to camp at the prison, and start fresh in the morning.

Lila was all too familiar with Lion Head Prison; it was the maximum security facility where she had anticipated the Griner brothers would spend the next twenty-five or so years.

Janice Coates, also present for Celia's retelling, had a brief verdict on the prison. 'That place. Nasty.'

The Head, as it was called by the men imprisoned there, had been in the media a great deal before Aurora, a rare story of successful land reclamation on the site of a mountaintop removal. After Ulysses Energy Solutions finished deforesting and blasting away the top of the mountain to mine the coal beneath, it 'restored' the land by pulling debris up and flattening it out. The oft-promoted idea was that, instead of viewing the mountaintops as 'destroyed,' the public ought to see them as having been 'opened up.' Newly flattened land was newly buildable land. Although the majority of the state's population supported the coal industry, few failed to recognize this for the bunkum it was. These wonderfully useful new plateaus were generally situated in the middle of nowhere and often came attended by impoundments of slurry waste or chemical containment ponds, which were not the sort of neighbors anyone wanted.

But a prison was uniquely suitable for backwoods reclamation. And no one had been particularly concerned about the possible environmental dangers that its residents might face. That was how Lion Head Mountain had become the setting for Lion Head Maximum Security Prison.

The prison gate, Celia said, had been open, and the front doors, too. She, Millie, Nell Seeger, and the others had gone in. Most of the exploration party from Our Place consisted of recently released prison inmates and personnel, and they were curious about how the other half had lived. All things being equal, it was pretty comfortable. As much as it reeked from being shut up, and although there were some fissures in the floors and walls, it was dry; and the gear in every cell looked new. 'Some déjà vu,' conceded Celia, 'but kind of funny, too, you know.'

Their last night had been calm. In the morning, Celia had trekked down the mountain a ways, searching for a trail that might cut off some of the hike and save them having to go all the way down the longer, circuitous route to Eagle. To Celia's surprise, she'd received a call on her toy walkie-talkie.

'Celia! We think we see someone!' It was Nell.

'What?' Celia had replied. 'Say again?'

'We're inside! Inside the prison! The windows at the end of their version of Broadway are all fogged, but there's a woman in one of the solitary confinement cells! She's lying under a yellow blanket! It looks like she's moving! Millie's trying to find a way to get the door to release without the power so—' That's where the transmission ended.

A vast rumble in the earth startled Celia. She held out her hands, trying to balance. The toy walkie flew out of her hand and shattered on the ground.

Returning to the top of the road, lungs burning and legs shaking, Celia went through the prison gate. Powder sifted through the air like snow; she had to cover her mouth to keep from choking. What she saw was hard to process, and even harder to accept. The terrain was shattered, heaved up in clefts as if in the aftermath of an earthquake. Displaced dirt hung in the air. Celia stumbled to her knees several times, eyes slitted almost shut, reaching for anything solid. Gradually, the rectangular shape of the Lion Head intake unit, two stories high, emerged, and then nothing else. There was no more land behind the intake unit, and no more prison. The plateau had crumbled and given way. The new max security facility had gone down the back of the mountain like a great stone child down a slide. Intake was now no more than a film prop, all front and no back.

Celia didn't dare go all the way to the edge to look down, but she glimpsed a few pieces of wreckage far below: massive cement blocks jumbled at the foot, amid a swamp of dust particles.

'So I came back by myself,' said Celia, 'as fast as I could.'

She inhaled and scratched a clean place in the mud on her cheek. The listeners, a dozen women who had hurried to their meeting place at the Shopwell when word spread that she was back, were silent. The others weren't going to return.

'I recall reading that there was some controversy about the fill under that overgrown jailhouse,' said Janice. 'Something about how the ground was too soft for the weight. People saying the coal company cut corners when they were packing it down. State engineers were looking into it . . .'

Celia let her breath go, a long sigh, and continued absently. 'Nell and I always kept it casual. I didn't expect it to last outside of prison.' She sniffed — just once. 'So I probably shouldn't feel so blue, but there it is: I feel blue as hell.'

There was silence. Then Lila said, 'I need to go there.'

Tiffany Jones said, 'Want company?'

7

What they were doing was foolish, Coates said.

'Fucking *foolish*, Lila. To go off and play around in an avalanche.' She had walked with Lila and Tiffany Jones as far as Ball's Hill Road. The two expeditionaries were leading a pair of horses.

'We're not going to play around in an avalanche,' Lila said. 'We're going to play around in the wreckage from an avalanche.'

'And see if someone is still alive in there,' Tiffany added.

'Are you kidding?' Janice's nose was beet-red in the cold. She appeared ever more oracular, her white hair floating out behind her, the color in her rawboned cheeks as bright as road flares. All that was missing was the gnarled staff and a bird of prey to perch on her shoulder. 'They went down the side of a *mountain,* and the prison landed on *top* of them. They're *dead*. And if they saw a woman in there, she's dead, too.'

'I know that,' said Lila. 'But if they did see a woman in Lion Head, it means there are other women outside of Dooling. Knowing we're not alone in this world, Janice . . . that would be huge.'

'Don't die,' the warden called after them as they rode up Ball's Hill. Lila said, 'That's the plan,' and beside her, Tiffany Jones chimed in, more conclusively, 'We won't.'

8

Tiffany had ridden all through her girlhood. Her family had run an apple orchard with a playground, goats to feed, a hotdog stand, and a pony ride. 'I used to ride all the time, but . . . there was some other stuff with the family – downsides, you could say. It wasn't all ponies. I started to run into some trouble and got out of the habit.'

This trouble was no mystery to Lila, who had personally arrested Tiff more than once. That Tiffany Jones bore startlingly little resemblance to this one. The woman who rode astride the massive roan beside Lila's smaller white mare was a full-faced, auburn-haired woman in a white cowboy hat that would have suited any John Ford rancher. She had a self-possession about her that was utterly unlike the wretched drug addict Truman Mayweather had regularly tuned up on in the trailer next to his meth lab so long ago, and so far away.

And she was pregnant. Lila had heard Tiffany mention it at a Meeting. That, Lila thought, was where at least part of her glow came from.

It was dusk. They would have to stop soon. Maylock was visible, a spread of dim dark buildings in a valley a couple of miles distant. The exploring party had been there, and found no one, male or female. It seemed that only Dooling held human life. Unless there really had been a woman in the men's prison, that was.

'You seem like you're doing pretty well,' said Lila carefully. 'Now.'

Tiffany's laugh was amiable. 'The afterlife clears your mind. I don't want dope, if that's what you mean.'

'Is that what you think this is? The afterlife?'

'Not really,' said Tiffany, and didn't pick the subject up again until they were lying in their sleeping bags in the shell of a gas station that had been abandoned in the other world, too.

Tiffany said, 'I mean, the afterlife, it's supposed to be heaven or hell, right?' They could see the horses through the plate glass, tied up to the old pumps. The moonlight gave their coats a sheen.

'I'm not religious,' Lila said.

'Me neither,' Tiffany said. 'Anyway, there's no angels and no devils, so go figure. But isn't this some kinda miracle?'

Lila thought of Jessica and Roger Elway. Their baby, Platinum, was growing fast, crawling all over the place. (Elaine Nutting's daughter, Nana, had fallen in love with Plat – an ugly nickname, but everyone used it; the kid would probably hate them for it later – and rolled her everywhere in a rusty baby carriage.) Lila thought of Essie and Candy. She thought of her husband and her son and her whole life that was no longer her life.

'Some kind,' Lila said. 'I guess.'

'I'm sorry. Miracle's the wrong word. I'm just saying we're doin all right, right? So it's not hell, right? I'm clean. I feel good. I got these wonderful horses, which I never in my wildest dreams imagined could happen. Someone like me, takin care of animals like these? Never.' Tiffany frowned. 'I'm making this all about me, aren't I? I know you've lost a lot. I know most everybody here has lost a lot, and I'm just someone who didn't have nothing to lose.'

'I'm glad for you.' She was, too. Tiffany Jones had deserved something better.

9

They skirted Maylock and rode along the banks of the swollen Dorr's Hollow Stream. In the woods, a pack of dogs gathered on a hummock to observe them as they passed. There were six or seven of them, shepherds and Labs, tongues out, breath steaming. Lila took out her pistol. Beneath her, the white mare rolled its head and shifted its gait.

'No, no,' Tiffany said. She reached a hand across and brushed the mare's ear. Her voice was soft but steady, not cooing. 'Lila's not gonna shoot that gun.'

'She's not?' Lila had an eye on the dog in the middle. The animal's fur was a bristly gray and black. It had mismatched eyes, blue and yellow, and its mouth seemed especially large. She wasn't a person who typically let her imagination run away from her, but she thought the dog looked rabid.

'She certainly isn't. They want to chase us. But we're just doing our thing. We don't want to play chase. We're just getting along.'

Tiffany's voice was airy and certain. Lila thought that if Tiffany didn't know what she was doing, she *believed* she knew what she was doing. They paced along through the underbrush. The dogs didn't follow.

'You were right,' Lila said later. 'Thanks.'

Tiffany said she was welcome. 'But it wasn't for you. No offense, but I'm not lettin you put a fright in my horses, Sheriff.'

10

They crossed the river and bypassed the high road the others had taken up the mountain, continuing instead on the lower ground. The horses descended into a dell that formed the gap between what was left of Lion Head on the left and another cliff face on the right, which rose up at a sharp, splintery slant. There was a pervasive metallic stench that tickled the backs of their throats. Crumbles of loose earth shook down, the embedded stones echoing far too loudly in the bowl created by the rises on either side.

They tied up the horses a couple of hundred yards from the prison ruins and approached on foot.

'A woman from somewhere else,' Tiffany said. 'Wouldn't that be something?'

'Yes,' Lila agreed. 'Finding some of our own still alive would be even better.'

Fragments of masonry, some as tall and wide as moving vans, were embedded higher up along the back of Lion Head, stabbed into the earth like enormous cenotaphs. As sturdy as they appeared, Lila could easily imagine them breaking loose under their own weight and tumbling down to join the pile at the bottom.

The body of the prison had hit bottom and folded inward on itself, forming a vaguely pyramid-like shape. In a way, it was impressive, how much of the building's body had survived the slide down the mountain — and hideous, too, in its decipherability, like a dollhouse smashed by a bully. Spears of jagged steel jutted out from the cement, and massive root-knotted clods of earth had settled on other parts of the debris. At the edges of this unplanned new structure were tattered breaches in the cement that offered glimpses of the black interior. Everywhere there were smashed trees, twenty- and thirty-footers snapped into raw shards.

Lila put on a surgical mask that she'd brought. 'Stay here, Tiffany.'

'I wanna come with you. I'm not afraid. Let me have one a them.' She stuck out her hand for a surgical mask.

'I know you're not afraid. I just want someone able to go back if this place falls in on my head, and you're the horse girl. I'm just a middle-aged ex-cop. Also, we both know you're living for two.'

At the nearest opening, Lila paused to wave. Tiffany didn't see it; she'd walked back to the horses.

11

Light filtered into the interior of the prison in sabers punched through the smashed concrete. Lila found herself walking atop a wall, stepping on the closed steel doors of cells. Everything was turned one-quarter. The ceiling was on her right. What would have been the left wall was now the ceiling, and the floor was on her left. She had to lower her head to slip under an open cell door that hung down like a trap. She heard ticking noises, dripping noises. Her boots crunched against stone and glass.

A clog composed of rock, shattered pipes, and chunks of insulation obstructed her forward progress. She flicked her flashlight around. **A-Level** was stenciled in red paint on the wall above her head. Lila backtracked to where the door hung. She jumped and grabbed the doorframe, hoisting herself up into the cell. A hole had broken open in the wall on the opposite side of the hanging door. Lila made her way – carefully – to the breach. She crouched and ducked her way through. Serrations of broken concrete snagged at the back of her shirt, and the fabric tore.

Clint's voice came to her, inquiring if maybe – *just maybe*, and don't take this as an accusation, please – there was a risk-reward ratio that needed to be reconsidered here?

Let's unpack it, shall we, Lila? The risk is that you are climbing into an unsettled wreck at the bottom of an unsettled mountain. Also, there are goddam wild, deranged-looking dogs out there, and a pregnant drug addict waiting — or not waiting — with the horses. And you are — again, no criticism, merely setting down the facts, darling — forty-five. Everyone knows that the prime age for a woman to crawl around unsettled and volatile ruins is from her late teens to her late twenties. You're out of the target group. It all adds up to a significant risk of death, horrible death, or unimaginably horrible death.

In the next cell, Lila had to climb over a battered steel toilet, then slip down through another hole in the floor that had been the right wall. Her ankle bent funny when it hit the bottom, and she grabbed for purchase. Something metal slashed her hand.

The wound on her palm was a deep red gash. It probably needed a stitch or two. She ought to turn back, get some ointment and a proper bandage from the first aid kit that they'd brought.

Instead, Lila ripped off a piece of her shirt and wrapped her hand. She used the flashlight to find another stencil on the wall: Secure Wing. This was good. That sounded like exactly the place where they'd seen the woman in the cell. What was bad was that the new hall was situated above her head, a shaft going upward. What was worse was the leg in one canted corner, raggedly severed two inches above the knee. It was clad in green corduroy. Nell Seeger had been wearing green cords when the expedition had left for Eagle.

'I'm not going to tell Tiff about this,' Lila said. Hearing herself speaking out loud both startled and comforted her. 'It would do no good.'

Lila pointed her beam upward. The Lion Head's secure wing had become a great wide chimney. She shone the light from side to side, looking for a way to go, and thought she might see one. The ceiling of the wing had been of the drop-panel type; the panels had all shaken loose in the slide, but the steel gridding remained in place. It resembled a trellis. Or a ladder.

As for the reward, Clint offered, *you might find someone. Might. But be honest with yourself. You know that this wreck is empty, just like the rest of the world. There's nothing to be found but the bodies of the women who went with Nell. Let that one severed leg stand for all of them. If there were other women in the world you're calling Our Place, they would have made themselves known by now. They would at least have left some trace. What is it you think you have to prove? That women can be Marlboro Men, too?*

It seemed that even in her imagination, he couldn't just tell her he was afraid for her. He couldn't stop treating her like one of his incarcerated patients, throwing leading questions like dodgeballs in a playground game.

'Go away, Clint,' she said, and for a wonder, he did.

She reached up and grabbed the lowest trellis of ceiling gridding. The crosspiece bowed, but didn't break. Her hand sang and she felt blood leaking around the edges of her rag bandage – but she hung on and pulled herself up, and upright. She braced her boot on the crosspiece and pushed down. It bowed again – and held. Lila reached up, pulled, stepped. She began to ascend the ladder of gridding. Each time she came to the level of a cell door, Lila used her good left hand to hang on while she swung out in the air, shining the flashlight with her hurt right. There was no woman to be seen through the wired glass at the top of the first cell door, no woman in the second, no woman in the third; all she saw were bed frames sticking out from what had been the floors. Her hand pulsed. The blood was dripping down inside her sleeve. Nothing in the fourth cell and she had to stop and rest, but not for too long, and definitely no looking down into the darkness. Was there a trick to this kind of effort? Something that Jared had mentioned about cross-country, something to tell yourself? Oh, right, now she had it. 'When my lungs start tightening up,' Jared had said, 'I just pretend there are girls checking me out, and I can't let them down.'

That wasn't much use. She'd just have to keep going.

Lila climbed. The fifth cell contained just a cot, a sink, and a dangling toilet. Nothing more.

She had arrived at a **T**. Off to the left, across the channel, the length of another hall stretched away. Far off, at the end of the hall, the beam of Lila's flashlight found what appeared to be a pile of laundry – a body or bodies, she thought, the remains of the other explorers. Was that Nell Seeger's puffy red jacket? Lila wasn't sure, but as cold as it was, she could smell the beginnings of decomp. They had been tossed around until they snapped and then probably tossed around some more. There was nothing to do but leave them there.

Something moved amid the pile and she heard squeaking. The prison's rats had survived the tumult, it seemed.

Lila climbed some more. Each metal grid seemed to give more under her weight, creaking longer and higher with every push-off. The sixth cell was empty and so were the seventh and the eighth and the ninth. It's always the last place you check, isn't it? It's always on the top shelf of the closet at the very back. It's always the bottom file in the stack. It's always in the littlest, least-used pocket of the knapsack.

If she fell now, at least she'd die instantaneously.

You always – always, always, always – fall from the topmost grid of the ceiling that you're using for a ladder in the hall of the maximum security prison that has gone sliding down the unstable remains of a former coal mountain.

But she decided she was not going to quit now. She had killed Jessica Elway to defend herself. She had been the first female sheriff in the history of Dooling County. She had clapped handcuffs on the Griner brothers, and when Low Griner had told her to go fuck herself, she had laughed in his face. A few more feet wasn't going to stop her.

And it didn't.

She leaned out into the dark, swinging free as if unfurled by a dance partner, and cast the beam of her flashlight through the window of the tenth cell door.

The blow-up doll had come to rest with its face against the glass. Its cherry red lips were a bow of surprise, made for fellatio; its eyes were a thoughtless and seductive Betty Boop blue. A draft from somewhere caused it to nod its empty head and shrug its pink shoulders. A sticker on its head was printed with the label, *Happy 40th Birthday, Larry!*

12

'Come on now, Lila,' said Tiffany. Her voice drifted up from the well. 'Just take one step and then worry about the next step.'

'Okay,' Lila managed. She was glad that Tiffany hadn't listened to her. In fact, she didn't know if there were many things she'd ever been so glad about. Her throat was dry; her body felt too tight in her skin; her hand was burning. The voice below was another life, though. This dark ladder didn't have to be the end.

'That's good. Now: one step,' said Tiffany. 'You just gotta go one step. That's how you start.'

13

'A blow-up fuck-me doll,' Tiffany marveled later. 'Some a-hole's birthday present. They let em have shit like that?'

Lila shrugged. 'All I know is what I saw. There's probably a story, but we'll never know it.'

They rode all day and into the dark. Tiffany wanted one of the women in Our Place who'd had nursing experience to clean up Lila's hand pronto. Lila said she'd be okay, but Tiff was insistent. 'I told that crone who used to be warden up at the prison we wouldn't die. *We*. That means both of us.'

She told Lila about the apartment she had in Charlottesville before meth addiction had napalmed the last decade or so. She'd kept a shitload of ferns. Buggers had flourished, too.

'That's livin right, when you got big houseplants,' Tiffany said.

Slumped low in her saddle, the pace of her horse rocking her so pleasantly, Lila had to fight to keep from falling asleep and possibly slipping off. 'What?'

'My ferns,' said Tiffany. 'I'm regalin you about my ferns to keep you from passing out on me.'

This made Lila feel giggly but all that came out was a moan. Tiffany said not to be sad. 'We can get you some. Ferns all over the fuckin place. They ain't rare.'

Later, Lila asked Tiffany if she was hoping for a boy or a girl.

'Just a healthy kid,' said Tiffany. 'Either way, so long as it's healthy.'

'How about if it's a girl, you name her "Fern."'

Tiffany laughed. 'That's the spirit!'

Dooling appeared at dawn, the buildings floating through a blue haze. Smoke twisted up from the parking lot behind the remains of the Squeaky Wheel. Here a communal firepit had been set up. Electricity was still at a premium, so they cooked outside as much as possible. (The Squeak had proved an excellent source of fuel. Its roof and walls were slowly being dismantled.)

Tiffany led them toward the fire. There were a dozen women there, shapeless in their heavy coats, caps, and mittens. Two big pots of coffee were boiling over the wide fire.

'Welcome home. We got coffee.' Coates stepped from the group.

'Unlike us, we got nothing,' Lila said. 'Sorry. It was a Fuck-Me Farrah doll in the secure wing. If there's anybody else in this world, there's still no sign of them. And the others . . .' She shook her head.

'Mrs Norcross?'

They all turned to check out the new one, who'd arrived just a day earlier. Lila took a step toward her, then stopped. 'Mary Pak? Is that you?'

Mary came to Lila and hugged her. 'I was just with Jared, Mrs Norcross. I thought you'd want to know, he's all right. Or he was, the last I saw him. That was in the attic of the demo house over in your neighborhood, before I fell asleep.'

CHAPTER 5

1

Tig Murphy was the officer that Clint told first – the truth about Evie, and about what she'd said: that everything seemed to depend on whether or not Clint could keep her alive, but she would plead her case no more than Jesus had when hauled in front of Pontius Pilate. Clint finished by saying, 'I lied because I couldn't bring myself to tell the truth. The truth is so big it stuck in my throat.'

'Uh-huh. You know I used to teach high school history, Doc?' Tig was, in fact, looking at him in a way that reminded Clint intensely of high school. It was a gaze that doubted your hall pass. It was a gaze that wanted to see if your pupils were dilated.

'Yes, I know that,' Clint said. He'd pulled the officer into the laundry room where they could talk in private.

'I was the first person in my family to graduate from college. Busting chops in a women's prison wasn't exactly a step up for me. But, you know, I've seen how you care about these gals. And I know that even though a lot of them have done bad stuff, most aren't bad through and through. So, I want to help . . .' The officer grimaced and rubbed a hand through the receding hair at his temples. You could see the teacher he'd been, picture him pacing around, going on about the vast difference between the legend of the Hatfields and the McCoys and the historical facts of the feud, dragging his fingers harder and harder through his hair the more excited and enthusiastic he got about the subject.

'So help,' Clint said. If not one of the officers agreed to stay he would try to keep the prison locked down without them, and he would fail. Terry Coombs and the new guy had the remains of the police force. They could gather other men if necessary. Clint had seen the way Frank Geary had eyed the fences and the gates, looking for weak spots.

'You really believe this? You think she's — magic?' Tig said the word *magic* the way Jared said the word *seriously* — as in, 'You *seriously* want to see my homework?'

'I believe she's got some command of this thing that's happening, and more importantly, I believe that men outside this prison believe that.'

'You believe she's magic.' Tig gave him the suspicious teacher look again: *Kid, just how stoned are you?*

'Actually, I do,' Clint said, and raised a hand to stop Tig from speaking, at least for the moment. 'But even if I'm wrong, we need to hold this prison. It's our obligation. We have to protect every one of our prisoners. I do not trust Terry Coombs in his cups, or Frank Geary, or anyone else, to just *talk* to Eve Black. You've heard her. Whether she's just delusional or not, she's a genius at pissing people off. She will go on doing that until someone loses his shit and kills her. Someone or all of them. Burning at the stake isn't entirely out of the question.'

'You don't believe that.'

'Actually, I do. Blowtorch Brigades tell you anything?'

Tig leaned against one of the industrial washers. 'All right.'

Clint could have hugged him. 'Thank you.'

'Well, it's my stupid job, y'know, but okay, you're welcome. How long do you think we need to hold out?'

'Not long. A few days, at most. That's what she says, anyway.' He realized that he was talking about Eve Black like an ancient Greek talking about an angry deity. It was outrageous, and yet it felt as true as anything.

2

'Wait-wait-wait,' Rand Quigley said after Clint had gone through everything a second time. 'She's going to end the world if we let the cops have her?'

That was almost exactly what Clint believed, but he preferred to finesse it a bit. 'We just can't let the local cops carry her off, Rand. That's the bottom line.'

Rand's pale brown eyes blinked behind the thick lenses of his square-framed glasses, and his black unibrow sat on the crosspiece like a burly caterpillar. 'What about the CDC? I thought you were talking to the CDC?'

Tig handled this one head-on. 'The CDC was bullshit. The doc made it up so we'd stay.'

This is where Rand puts one foot in front of the other, Clint thought, and the whole thing ends. But Rand only glanced at Clint and then back to Tig. 'Never got through to them?'

'No,' Clint said.

'Never at all?'

'Well, I got an answering machine a couple of times.'

'Fuck,' Rand said. 'That blows.'

'You said it, buddy,' Tig said. 'Can we still count on you? If someone wants to start something?'

'Yeah,' Rand said, sounding offended. 'Of course. They run the town, we run the prison. That's how it's supposed to be.'

Wettermore was next. The whole scenario amused him in a sour but genuine way.

'It wouldn't surprise me in the slightest if Warrior Girl the Meth-Head Slayer was magic. I wouldn't be surprised if bunnies wearing pocket watches started hopping through the joint. What you're telling me is no nuttier than the Aurora. It doesn't change anything for me. I'm here for the duration.'

It was Scott Hughes, at nineteen the youngest of the bunch, who handed over his keys, his gun, his Taser, and the rest of his gear. If the CDC wasn't coming to take Eve Black, he wasn't staying. He wasn't anybody's white knight; he was just an ordinary Christian who'd been baptized at the Lutheran church right there in Dooling and hardly missed a Sunday. 'I like all you guys. You're not like Peters or some of the other dinks at this place. And I don't care that Billy's gay or that Rand's half-retarded. Those guys're okay.'

Clint and Tig had followed him past intake to the front door of the prison and out into the yard to try and change his mind.

'And Tig, you've always been cool. You seem fine, too, Dr Norcross. But I'm not dying here.'

'Who said anything about dying?' Clint asked.

The teenager arrived at his pickup, which stood on enormous bigfoot tires. 'Get real. Who do you know in this town who doesn't have a gun? Who do you know in this town who doesn't have two or three?'

It was true. Even in exurban Appalachia (and exurban might have been pushing it; they had a Foot Locker and a Shopwell in Dooling, but the nearest movie theater was in Eagle), just about everyone had a gun.

'And, I mean, I been to the sheriff's station, Dr Norcross. They got a rack of M4s. Other stuff, too. The vigilantes show up after raiding the armory, no offense, but you and Tig can take those Mossbergs we got in the gun locker and shove em up your asses.'

Tig was standing at Clint's shoulder. 'So you're just going to split?'

'Yeah,' Hughes said. 'I'm just going to split. Someone needs to open the gate for me.'

'Shit, Tig,' Clint said, which was the signal.

Tig sighed, apologized to Scott Hughes – 'I feel terrible about this, man' – and zapped his colleague with his Taser.

This was a matter that they'd discussed. There were serious problems with letting Scott Hughes leave. They couldn't allow someone telling the town folks what a short roster they had, or outlining the limitations of the prison's armaments. Because Scott was right, the prison's armory was not impressive: a dozen Mossberg 590 shotguns, birdshot to load them, and each officer's personal sidearm, a .45-caliber pistol.

The two men stood over their colleague, writhing on the parking lot pavement. Clint was queasily reminded of the Burtells' backyard, the Friday Night Fights, his foster sibling Jason, lying bare-chested on the patio cement at Clint's filthy sneakers. Under Jason's eye there had been a red quarter-shaped mark from Clint's fist. Snot had leaked out of Jason's nose, and from the ground, he had mumbled, 'It's okay, Clint.' The grownups all cheered and laughed from their lawn chairs, toasting with their cans of Falstaff. That time, Clint had won the milkshake. What had he won this time?

'Well, damn, now we done it,' said Tig. Three days ago, when they'd had to deal with Peters, Tig had looked like a man in the throes of an allergic reaction, about to pitch up a bellyful of spunky shellfish. Now he just looked like he had a touch of acid. He lowered himself to his knees, rolled Scott over, and zip-tied his wrists behind his back.

'How about we put him in B Wing, Doc?'

'Okay, I guess.' Clint hadn't even considered where to put Scott, which did not exactly increase his confidence in his ability to deal with the developing situation. He squatted to grab Hughes's armpits and help Tig hoist him to his feet so they could bring him inside.

'Gentlemen,' came a voice from just beyond the gate. It was a woman's voice, full of grit, and exhaustion . . . and delight. 'Can you hold that pose? I want to get a good picture.'

3

The two men looked up, their expressions the very essence of guilt; they could have been Mafia button men about to bury a body. Michaela was even more delighted when she checked her first photo. The camera she carried in her purse was only a bottom-of-the-line Nikon, but the image was sharp. Perfect.

'Ahoy, ye scruffy pirates!' Garth Flickinger cried. 'What are ye about, pray tell?' He had insisted on stopping at the nearby scenic lookout to sample the Purple Lightning, and he was feeling chipper. Mickey also seemed to have caught her second wind. Or maybe by now it was her fourth or fifth.

'Oh, shit, Doc,' said Tig. 'We are surely fucked.'

Clint didn't reply. He stood, holding Scott Hughes and gaping at the newcomers standing in front of a battered Mercedes. It was as if a weird reverse landslide were going on inside his head, one where things came together instead of falling apart. Maybe this was how true inspiration came to a great scientist or philosopher. He hoped so. Clint dropped Scott and the disoriented officer gave a moan of dissatisfaction.

'One more!' Michaela called. She snapped. 'And one more! Good! Great! Now exactly what are you boys doing?'

'God's blood, it's mutiny!' Garth cried, doing what might have been an imitation of Captain Jack Sparrow in *Pirates of the Caribbean*. 'They've rendered the first mate unconscious, and soon will make him walk the plank! Arrr!'

'Shut up,' said Michaela. She grasped the gate — not electrified, fortunately for her — and shook it. 'Does this have anything to do with the woman?'

'We are *so* fucked.' Tig said this as if he were impressed.

'Open the gate,' Clint said.

'What—?'

'Do it.'

Tig started toward the entry booth, pausing once to look doubtfully back over his shoulder at Clint, who nodded and motioned him on. Clint walked to the gate, ignoring the steady click of the young woman's camera. Her eyes were red, which was to be expected after four days and three nights of wakefulness, but her companion's were just as red. Clint suspected they might have been partaking of illegal stimulants. In the throes of his sudden inspiration, that was the least of his concerns.

'You're Janice's daughter,' he said. 'The reporter.'

'That's right, Michaela Coates. Michaela Morgan, to the great viewing public. And I believe you're Dr Clinton Norcross.'

'We've met?' Clint didn't remember that.

'I interviewed you for the high school newspaper. Would have been eight or nine years ago.'

'Did you like me?' he asked. Christ, he was old; and getting older by the minute.

Michaela tipped a hand. 'I thought it was a little weird that you liked working in a prison so much. *In a prison with my mom.* But never mind that, what about the woman? Is her name Eve Black? Does she really sleep and then wake up? Because that's what I'm hearing.'

'Eve Black is the name she goes by,' Clint said, 'and yes, she does indeed sleep and wake normally. Although not much else about her seems normal in the least.' He felt giddy, like a man walking a tightrope blindfolded. 'Would you like to interview her?'

'Are you kidding?' For the moment, Michaela appeared not the slightest bit sleepy. She looked feverish with excitement.

The outer and inner gates began to trundle open. Garth hooked Michaela's arm with his own and stepped into the dead space between them, but Clint held up his hand. 'There are conditions.'

'Name them,' Michaela said briskly. 'Although, given the pictures I have in my camera, you might not want to be too greedy.'

Clint asked, 'Did you see any sheriff's cruisers nearby?'

Garth and Michaela shook their heads.

No cruisers yet. No one watching the access road leading in from West Lavin. That was a trick Geary had missed, at least so far, and Clint wasn't terribly surprised. With Terry Coombs seeking refuge in a flask, his Number Two, Mr Animal Control Guy, had to be playing catch-up. But Clint didn't think he'd miss it for long. There might be someone on the way already. In fact, and on second thought, he would have to assume that was the case, which meant going for pizza and eating with Jared was out. Geary might not care about anyone entering the prison, but he surely wouldn't want anyone leaving. The problematic head-doctor, for one. Evie Black, possibly smuggled out in the back of a prison van, for another.

'Your conditions?' Michaela asked.

'It has to be quick,' Clint said. 'And if you hear what I think you're going to hear, and see what I think you're going to see, you have to help me.'

'Help with what?' asked Tig, rejoining them.

'Reinforcements,' Clint said. 'Weapons.' He paused. 'And my son. I want my son.'

4

There was no pie at the Olympia. The woman who made the pies was sleeping in a cocoon in the break room. Gus Vereen, taking the deputies' orders, said he was shorthanded all around. 'Found some ice cream cake down at the bottom of the freezer, but I can't vouch for it. Been there since Hector was a pup.'

'I'll try it,' said Don, although it was a piss-poor substitute – a diner without pie was a disgrace – but with Frank Geary on the other side of the table, he was on his best behavior.

Also present at the rear table of the diner were deputies Barrows, Rangle, Eric Blass, plus an old legal beagle named Silver. They'd just finished eating a lousy lunch. Don had the Haluski Special and it had arrived swimming in a pool of yellow grease. He'd eaten it anyway, partly out of spite, and Magic 8-Ball said that a case of the dribbling shits was in his future. The others had eaten sandwiches and burgers; none of them had finished more than half. They had also passed on dessert, which was probably smart of them. Frank had spent half an hour giving them all the rundown on what he knew about the situation at the prison.

'You think Norcross is boning her?' Don blurted at this point.

Frank turned a low-lidded gaze on him. 'That's unlikely and irrelevant.'

Don received the message and hadn't said another word until Gus Vereen came around to see if they needed anything else.

Once Gus left, Judge Silver spoke up. 'What do you see as our options, Frank? What's Terry's take on this?' His Honor's skin tone was worryingly gray. His speech was wet, as if he were talking around a knot of chewing tobacco.

'Our options are limited. We could wait Norcross out, but who knows how long that could mean. Prison's probably got quite a stock of food.'

'He's right,' Don said. 'There's no prime rib or nothing, but they got enough dry goods to last to the end of days.'

'The longer we wait,' Frank went on, 'the more talk gets around. Lot of guys around here might start thinking about taking things into their own hands.' He waited for someone to say, *Isn't that what you're doing?* But no one did.

'If we don't wait?' the judge asked.

'Norcross has got a son, and of course you know his wife.'

'Good cop,' the judge said. 'Careful, thorough. The lady goes by the book.'

Eric, busted twice by Sheriff Norcross for speeding, made a sour face.

'And we wish we had her,' Geary said. Don didn't believe that for a second. From the first, when Geary had jammed his hand under Don's armpit, treated him like a puppet, he'd seen that he wasn't the kind of fellow who accepted second position. 'But she's in the wind, and so is the son. If they were around, I'd say we should try and get them to see if they couldn't convince Norcross to break loose from whatever thing he has going with the Black woman.'

Judge Silver clucked his tongue and stared into his coffee cup. He hadn't touched it. His tie had bright yellow lemons on it and the contrast with his skin underlined the sickly look of the man. A moth fluttered around his head. The judge waved it away and it flew off to alight on one of the light-globes that hung from the diner's ceiling.

'So . . .' Judge Silver said.

'Yeah,' Don said. 'So what do we do?'

Frank Geary shook his head and swept a few crumbs from the table, catching them in his palm. 'We put together a responsible group. Fifteen, twenty reliable men. We tool up. There should be enough body armor to go around at the station. God knows what else. We haven't exactly had time to take inventory.'

'Do you really think—' Reed Barrows began doubtfully, but Frank overrode him.

'There's half a dozen assault rifles, anyway. They should go to the guys who can handle them. Everyone else carries either Winchesters or their sidearms or both. Don here gives us the layout of the prison, any particulars that might help. Then, we make a show of force, and give Norcross one more chance to send her out. I think he will.'

The judge asked the obvious. 'If he doesn't?'

'I don't think he could stop us.'

'This seems rather extreme, even under the extraordinary circumstances,' the judge said. 'What about Terry?'

'Terry is . . .' Frank brushed his crumbs onto the diner floor.

'He's drunk, Judge,' Reed Barrows said.

Which kept Frank from having to say it. What he said (pulling
a glum face) was, 'He's doing the best he can.'

'Drunk is drunk,' Reed said. Vern Rangle opined that this was a
true statement.

'Then . . .' The judge touched Frank's big shoulder, gave it a
squeeze. 'Guess it's you, Frank.'

Gus Vereen came over with Don's slice of ice cream cake. The
diner owner's expression was dubious. The slice was bearded in frost.
'You sure, Don?'

'What the fuck,' Don said. If the pie ladies of the world were
gone, and he still wanted sweet stuff, he was going to have to eat
more adventurously.

'Uh, Frank?' Vern Rangle said.

'What?' It sounded more like *What now?*

'I was just thinking maybe we ought to have a cruiser watching
the prison. In case, you know, the doc decides to take her out and
hide her somewhere.'

Frank stared at him, then slapped the side of his own head – a
good hard whack that made them all jump. 'Jesus. You're right. I
should have done that right away.'

'I'll go,' Don said, forgetting the ice cream cake. He got up fast,
his thighs striking the underside of the table and making the cups
and plates rattle. His eyes were bright. 'Me and Eric. Anyone tries
to get in or out, we'll stop them.'

Frank didn't much care for Don, and Blass was just a kid, but
maybe it would be okay. Hell, it was just a precaution. He didn't
really think Norcross would try to take the woman out. To him,
she probably seemed safer where she was, behind the prison walls.

'Okay,' he said. 'But if anyone *does* come out, just stop them. No
drawn guns, you hear? No OK Corral stuff. If they refuse to stop,
just follow them. And radio me ASAP.'

'Not Terry?' the judge asked.

'No. Me. Park at the foot of the prison access road, where it meets West Lavin. Got it?'

'Got it!' Don snapped. He was on the case. 'Come on, partner. Let's go.'

As they left, the judge mumbled, 'The unspeakable in pursuit of the uneatable.'

'What, Judge?' Vern Rangle asked.

Silver shook his head. He looked weary. 'Never mind. Gentlemen, I must say that on the whole, I don't care much for the way this is going. I wonder . . .'

'What, Oscar?' Frank asked. 'What do you wonder?'

But the judge didn't reply.

5

'How'd you know?' It was Angel. 'About the baby?'

The question drew Evie away from the Olympia Diner where, from the eyes of the moth perched on the light-globe, she'd been observing the men making their plans. And just to add to the fun, something else was going on, much closer. Clint had visitors. Soon she would have visitors, as well.

Evie sat up and inhaled Dooling Correctional. The stench of industrial cleaning products went horribly deep; she expected to die soon, and felt sad about that, but she had died before. It was never nice, but it had never been the end . . . although this time might be different.

On the bright side, she told herself, I won't have to smell this place anymore, this mixture of Lysol and despair.

She'd thought Troy stank: the corpse piles, the fires, the fish guts thoughtfully left out for the gods — gee fucking thanks, guys, just what we want — and the stupid Achaeans stomping around on the beach, refusing to wash, letting the blood cook to black in the sun and rust the joints of their armor. That was nothing compared to the inescapable reek of the modern world. She had been young and too easily impressed then, in the days before Lysol and bleach.

Meanwhile, Angel had asked a perfectly fair question, and she sounded almost sane. For the time being, at least.

'I know about your baby because I read minds. Not always. Most of the time. I'm better at reading men's minds — they are simpler — but I'm pretty good with women, too.'

'Then you know . . . I dint want to.'

'Yes, I know that. And I was too hard on you. Before. I'm sorry. There was a lot going on.'

Angel ignored the apology. She was focused on reciting something she'd clearly memorized, a little comfort she'd created to provide light when the dark was at its deepest and there was no one awake with whom to speak and take her mind off herself and the things she had done. 'I had to. Every man I killed did hurt me, or woulda hurt me if I give him a chance. I dint want to put that baby girl down, but I couldn't let that be her life.'

The sigh that Evie produced in response was thick with real tears. Angel was telling the truth, the whole truth, and nothing but the truth of an existence in a time and a place where things had just not worked out. Of course, chances were slim that they would have worked out for Angel, anyway; the woman was bad and mad. Even so, she was right: they had hurt her, and they probably would've hurt that baby girl, given time. Those men and all the men like them. The earth hated them, but it loved the fertilizer of their murderous bodies.

'Why you cryin, Evie?'

'Because I feel it all, and it's painful. Now hush. If I may once more quote *Henry IV*, the game is afoot. I have things to do.'

'What things?'

As if in answer, the door at the far end of A Wing clashed open and footfalls approached. It was Dr Norcross, Officers Murphy and Quigley, and two strangers.

'Where's they passes?' Angel shouted. 'Those two don't have no passes to be back here!'

'Hush, I said,' Evie told her. 'Or I'll make you hush. We were having a moment, Angel, don't spoil it.'

Clint stopped in front of Evie's cell. The woman pushed up beside him. There were purple pouches beneath her eyes, but the eyes themselves were bright and aware.

Evie said, 'Hello, Michaela Coates, also known as Michaela Morgan. I'm Eve Black.' She put her hand through the bars. Tig and Rand moved forward instinctively, but Clint extended his arms to hold them in place.

Michaela clasped the offered hand with no hesitation. 'You've seen me on the news, I take it.'

Evie smiled warmly. 'I'm afraid I'm not big on the news. Too depressing.'

'Then how do you know—'

'Shall I call you Mickey, as your friend Dr Flickinger does?'

Garth jumped.

'I'm sorry you didn't get to see your mother,' Evie went on. 'She was a good warden.'

'Like fuck,' Angel muttered, and when Evie cleared her throat forbiddingly: 'Okay, I'm hushin, I'm hushin.'

'How do you know—' Michaela began.

'That your mother was Warden Coates? That you took the name Morgan because some silly cockhound of a journalism professor told you that television audiences tend to remember alliterative names? Oh, Mickey, you never should have slept with him, but I think you know that now. At least the miscarriage saved you having to make a difficult choice.' Evie clucked and shook her head, making her dark hair fly.

Except for her red-rimmed eyes, Michaela was dead pale. When Garth put an arm around her shoulders, she clutched at his hand like a drowning woman clutching at a life preserver.

'How do you know that?' Michaela whispered. 'Who *are* you?'

'I am woman, hear me roar,' Evie said, and once more laughed: a merry sound, like shaken bells. She turned her attention to Garth. 'As for you, Dr Flickinger, a word of friendly advice. You need to get off the dope, and very soon. You've had one warning from your cardiologist already. There won't be another. Keep on smoking those crystals, and your cataclysmic heart attack will come in . . .' She closed her eyes like a carnival psychic, then popped them open. 'In about eight months. Nine, maybe. Most likely while watching porn with your pants around your ankles and a squeeze-bottle of Lubriderm near at hand. Still shy of your fifty-third birthday.'

'Worse ways,' Garth said, but his voice was faint.

'Of course, that's if you're lucky. If you hang around Michaela and Clint here, and try to defend poor defenseless me and the rest of the women here, you're likely to die a lot sooner.'

'You have the most symmetrical face I have ever seen.' Garth paused and cleared his throat. 'Can you stop saying scary things now?'

Apparently Evie couldn't. 'It's a shame that your daughter is hydrocephalic and must live her life in an institution, but that is no excuse for the damage you are inflicting on a formerly fine body and mind.'

The officers were goggling at her. Clint had hoped for something that would prove Evie's otherworldliness, but this was beyond his wildest expectations. As if he had spoken this aloud, Evie looked at him . . . and winked.

'How do you know about Cathy?' Garth asked. 'How *can* you?'

Looking at Michaela, Evie said, 'I have agents among the creatures of the world. They tell me everything. They help me. It's like in *Cinderella*, but different. For one thing, I like them better as rats than as coachmen.'

'Evie . . . Ms Black . . . are you responsible for the sleeping women? And if so, is it possible you can wake them up again?'

'Clint, are you sure this is smart?' Rand asked. 'Letting this lady have a jailhouse interview? I don't think Warden Coates would—'

Jeanette Sorley chose this moment to stumble down the hall, holding up her brown top so it made a makeshift pouch. 'Who wants peas?' she cried. 'Who wants fresh peas?'

Evie, meanwhile, seemed to have lost the thread. Her hands were gripping the prison bars hard enough to turn her knuckles white.

'Evie?' asked Clint. 'Are you okay?'

'Yes. And while I appreciate your need for haste, Clint, I'm multitasking this afternoon. You need to wait while I take care of something.' Then, to herself rather than the half a dozen people outside her cell: 'I'm sorry to do this, but he wouldn't have had long, anyway.' A pause. 'And he misses his cat.'

6

Judge Silver had shuffled most of the way to the Olympia's parking lot before Frank caught up with him. Gems of drizzle shone on the slumped shoulders of the old fellow's topcoat.

Silver turned at his approach – nothing wrong with his ears, it seemed – and gave him a sweet smile. 'I want to thank you again for Cocoa,' he said.

'That's all right,' he said. 'Just doing my job.'

'Yes, but you did it with real compassion. That made it easier for me.'

'I'm glad. Judge, it seemed to me that you had an idea in there. Would you like to share it with me?'

Judge Silver considered. 'May I speak frankly?'

The other man smiled. 'Since my name is Frank, I'd expect nothing less.'

Silver did not smile back. 'All right. You're a fine man, and I'm glad you've stepped up to the plate since Deputy Coombs is . . . shall we say *hors de combat* . . . and it's clear none of the other officers want the responsibility, but you have no background in law enforcement, and this is a delicate situation. Extremely delicate. Do you agree?'

'Yes,' Frank said. 'On all points.'

'I'm worried about a blow-up. A posse that gets out of control and turns into a mob. I've seen that happen, back during one of the uglier coal strikes in the seventies, and it was not a pretty thing. Buildings were burned, there was a dynamite explosion, men were killed.'

'You have an alternative?'

'I might. I – get away, dammit!' The judge waved one arthritic hand at the moth fluttering around his head. It flew away and landed on a car aerial, slowly flexing its wings in the fine drizzle. 'Those things are everywhere lately.'

'Uh-huh. Now what were you saying?'

'There's a man named Harry Rhinegold in Coughlin. Ex-FBI, retired there two years ago. Fine man, fine record, several Bureau commendations – I've seen them on the wall in his study. I'm thinking I might talk to him, and see if he'll sign on.'

'As what? A deputy?'

'As an advisor,' the judge said, and took a breath that rattled in his throat. 'And, possibly, as a negotiator.'

'A hostage negotiator, you mean.'

'Yes.'

Frank's first impulse, childish but strong, was to tell the judge no way, he was in charge. Except, technically speaking, he wasn't. Terry Coombs was, and it was always possible Terry would show up, hungover but sober, and want to take the reins. Also, could he, Frank, stop the judge, short of physical restraint? He could not. Although Silver was too much of a gentleman to say it (unless he absolutely had to, of course), he was an officer of the court, and as such far outranked a self-appointed lawman whose specialties were catching stray dogs and doing ads for Adopt-A-Pet on the Public Access channel. There was one more consideration, and it was the most important of all: hostage negotiation was actually not a bad idea. Dooling Correctional was like a fortified castle. Did it matter who pried the woman out, as long as the job got done? As long as she could be questioned? Coerced, if necessary, should they conclude that she actually might be able to stop the Aurora?

Meanwhile, the judge was looking at him, shaggy eyebrows raised.

'Do it,' Frank said. 'I'll tell Terry. If this Rhinegold agrees, we can have a skull session either here or at the station tonight.'

'So you won't . . .' The judge cleared his throat. 'You won't take any immediate steps?'

'For this afternoon and tonight, I'll just keep a car posted near the prison.' Frank paused. 'Beyond that, I can't promise, and even that depends on Norcross not trying anything funny.'

'I hardly think—'

'But I do.' Frank gravely tapped a finger against the hollow of his temple, as if to indicate thought processes hard at work. 'Position I'm in right now, I have to. He thinks he's smart, and guys like that can be a problem. To others, and to themselves. Looking at it that way, your trip to Coughlin is a mission of mercy. So drive carefully, Judge.'

'At my age, I always do,' Judge Silver said. His entry into the Land Rover was slow and painful to watch. Frank was on the verge of going to help him when Silver finally made it behind the wheel and slammed the door. The engine roared to life, Silver gunning it thoughtlessly, and then the lights came on, cutting cones through the drizzle.

Ex-FBI, and in Coughlin, Frank marveled. Wonders never ceased. Maybe he could call the Bureau and get an emergency federal order enjoining Norcross to let the woman go. Unlikely, with the government in an uproar, but not out of the question. If Norcross defied them then, no one could blame them for forcing the issue.

He went back inside to give the remaining deputies their orders. He'd already decided to send Barrows and Rangle to relieve Peters and that Blass kid. He and Pete Ordway could start making a list of guys, responsible ones, who might form a posse, should a posse be needed. No need to go back to the station, where Terry might show up; they could do it right here at the diner.

7

Judge Oscar Silver rarely drove anymore, and when he did, he no longer exceeded forty miles an hour, no matter how many cars stacked up behind him. If they began to honk and tailgate, he found a place to pull over and let them go by, then resumed his stately pace. He was aware that both his reflexes and his vision had declined. In addition, he had suffered three heart attacks, and knew that the bypass operation performed on his failing pump at St Theresa's two years ago would only hold the final infarction at bay for so long. He was at peace with that, but he had no wish to die behind the wheel, where a final swerve might take one or more innocent people with him. At only forty (less, within the city limits), he thought he would have a fair chance to apply braking and shift into park before the lights went out for good.

Today was different, however. Once he was beyond Ball's Ferry and on the Old Coughlin Road, he increased his speed until the needle hovered at sixty-five, territory it hadn't explored in five years or more. He had reached Rhinegold on his cell, and Rhinegold was willing to talk (although the judge, a crafty old soul, hadn't wanted to discuss the subject of their confab on the phone – probably a needless precaution, but discretion had ever been his byword), and that was good news. The bad news: Silver suddenly found that he did not trust Frank Geary, who talked so easily about gathering a bunch of men and storming the prison. He had *sounded* reasonable enough back at the Olympia, but the situation was utterly unreasonable. The judge didn't care for how practical Frank made such a move sound, when it ought to be an absolute last resort.

The windshield wipers clicked back and forth, clearing the thin rain. He turned on the radio and tuned in the all-news station in Wheeling. 'Most city services have been shut down until further notice,' the announcer said, 'and I want to repeat that the nine o'clock curfew will be strictly enforced.'

'Good luck with that,' the judge murmured.

'Now, recapping our top story. So-called Blowtorch Brigades, goaded by Internet-fueled fake news that respiration exhaled through the growths – or *cocoons* – surrounding the sleeping women is spreading the Aurora plague, have been reported in Charleston, Atlanta, Savannah, Dallas, Houston, New Orleans, and Tampa.' The announcer paused, and when he resumed, his flat twang had become more pronounced. Folksier. 'Neighbors, I'm proud to say none of these ignorant mobs have been operating here in Wheeling. We all have womenfolks we love like mad, and killing them in their sleep, no matter how unnatural that sleep may be, would be a terrible thing to do.'

He pronounced *terrible* as *turrible*.

Judge Silver's Land Rover was nearing the outer limits of Dooling's neighbor, Maylock. Rhinegold's house in Coughlin was on the other side, a drive of another twenty minutes or so.

'The National Guard has been called out in all the cities where those Brigades have been at work, and they have orders to shoot to kill if those superstitious fools won't cease and desist. I say amen to that. The CDC has repeated that there is no truth whatsoever to—'

The windshield was fogging up. Judge Silver leaned to his right, never taking his eyes from the road, and flipped on the defroster. The fan whooshed. On its wind, clouds of small brown moths spewed from the vents, filling the cabin and circling the judge's head. They lit in his hair and battered his cheeks. Worst of all, they spun before his eyes, and something one of his old aunts had told him long ago, when he was just an impressionable boy, recurred to him with the brilliance of a proven fact, like up is up and down is down.

'Don't ever rub your eyes after touching a moth, Oscar,' she had said. 'The dust from their wings will get in there and you'll go blind.'

'Get away!' Judge Silver yelled. He took his hands off the wheel and beat at his face. Moths continued to pour from the vents – hundreds of them, perhaps thousands. The Land Rover's cabin became a swirling brown mist. *'Get away, get away, get aw—'*

A huge weight settled on the left side of his chest. Pain hammered down his left arm like electricity. He opened his mouth to cry out and moths flew in, crawling on his tongue and tickling the lining of his cheeks. With his last struggling breath he pulled them down his throat, where they clogged his windpipe. The Land Rover veered left; an approaching truck veered right just in time to avoid it, ending up in the ditch, canted but not quite toppling. There was no ditch to avoid on the other side of the road – just the guardrails separating the Dorr's Hollow Bridge from the open air and the stream beneath. Silver's vehicle snapped the guardrails and pitched over. The Land Rover went end-for-end into the water below. Judge Silver, by then already dead, was ejected through the windshield and into Dorr's Hollow Stream, a tributary of Ball Creek. One of his loafers came off and floated downstream, shipping water and then sinking.

The moths exited the overturned vehicle, now bubbling its way down into the water, and flew back toward Dooling in a flock.

8

'I hated to do that,' Eve said – speaking not to her guests, Clint felt, but to herself. She wiped a single tear from the corner of her left eye. 'The more time I spend here, the more human I become. I had forgotten that.'

'What are you talking about, Evie?' Clint asked. 'What did you hate to do?'

'Judge Silver was trying to bring in outside help,' she said. 'It might not have made any difference, but I couldn't take the chance.'

'Did you kill him?' Angel asked, sounding interested. 'Use your special powers an all?'

'I had to. From this point forward, what happens in Dooling has to stay in Dooling.'

'But . . .' Michaela rubbed a hand down her face. 'What's happening in Dooling is happening *everywhere*. It's going to happen to me.'

'Not for awhile,' Evie said. 'And you won't need any more stimulants, either.' She extended a loose fist through the prison bars, extended a finger, and beckoned. 'Come to me.'

'I wouldn't do that,' Rand said, as Garth overlapped him, saying, 'Don't be stupid, Mickey.' He grabbed her forearm.

'What do *you* think, Clint?' Evie asked, smiling.

Knowing he was giving in – not just to this, but to everything – Clint said, 'Let her go.'

Garth released his grip. As if hypnotized, Michaela took two steps forward. Evie put her face against the bars, her eyes on Michaela's. Her lips parted.

'Lesbo stuff!' Angel crowed. 'Turn on the cameras, freaks, the muff-divin comes next!'

Michaela took no notice. She pressed her mouth to Evie's. They kissed with the hard bars of the soft cell between them, and Clint heard a sigh as Eve Black breathed into Michaela's mouth and lungs. At the same time he felt the hairs stand up on his arms and neck. His vision blurred with tears. Somewhere Jeanette was screaming, and Angel was cackling.

At last Evie broke the kiss and stepped back. 'Sweet mouth,' she said. 'Sweet *girl*. How do you feel now?'

'I'm awake,' Michaela said. Her eyes were round, her recently kissed lips trembling. 'I'm really awake!'

There was no question that she was. The purple pouches beneath her eyes had disappeared, but that was the least of it; her skin had tightened on her bones and her formerly pallid cheeks had taken on a rosy glow. She turned to Garth, who was staring at her with slack-jawed amazement.

'I'm really, really awake!'

'Holy shit,' Garth said. 'I think you are.'

Clint darted his spread fingers at Michaela's face. She snapped her head away. 'Your reflexes are back,' he said. 'You couldn't have done that five minutes ago.'

'How long can I stay this way?' Michaela clasped her shoulders, hugging herself. 'It's *wonderful*!'

'A few days,' Evie repeated. 'After that, the weariness will return, and with interest. You'll fall asleep no matter how much you struggle against it, and grow a cocoon like all the rest. Unless, that is . . .'

'Unless you get what you want,' Clint said.

'What I want is immaterial now,' Evie said. 'I thought you understood that. It's what the men of this town do with me that matters. And what the women on the other side of the Tree decide.'

'What—' Garth began, but then Jeanette hit him like a left tackle intent on sacking the quarterback, driving him into the bars. She shouldered him aside and grasped the bars, staring at Evie. 'Do *me*! Evie, do *me*! I don't want to fight it no more, I don't want to see the bud man anymore, so do *me*!'

Evie took her hands and looked at her sadly. 'I can't, Jeanette. You should stop fighting it and go to sleep like all the others. They could use someone as brave and strong as you are over there. They call it Our Place. It can be your place, too.'

'Please,' Jeanette whispered, but Evie let go of her hands. Jeanette staggered away, squashing spilled peas underfoot and crying soundlessly.

'I don't know,' Angel said thoughtfully. 'Maybe I won't kill you,

Evie. I'm thinking maybe . . . I just don't know. You're spiritual. Plus, even crazier than me. Which is goin some.'

Evie addressed Clint and the others again: 'Armed men will be coming. They want me because they think I may have caused Aurora, and if I caused it, I can put a stop to it. That's not exactly true – it's more complicated than that – just because I turned something on by myself doesn't mean I can turn it off by myself – but do you think angry, frightened men would believe that?'

'Not in a million years,' Garth Flickinger said. Standing behind him, Billy Wettermore grunted agreement.

Evie said, 'They'll kill anyone who gets in their way, and when I'm not able to awaken their sleeping beauties with a wave of my Fairy Godmother magic wand, they'll kill me. Then they'll set fire to the prison and every woman in it, just for spite.'

Jeanette had wandered into the delousing area to resume her conversation with the bud man, but Angel was paying close attention. Clint could almost hear her mood lift, like a generator first thumping to life and then whirring into gear. 'They ain't gonna kill me. Not without a fight.'

For the first time Evie looked piqued. Clint thought that whatever she'd done to awaken Mickey Coates might have drained her battery. 'Angel, they'll wash over you like a wave over a child's sand castle.'

'Maybe, but I'll take a few with me.' Angel did a couple of rusty kung fu moves that made Clint feel an emotion he had never before associated with Angel Fitzroy: pity.

'Did you bring us here?' Michaela asked. Her eyes were bright, fascinated. 'Did you *draw* us here? Garth and me?'

'No,' Evie said. 'You don't understand how powerless I am – little more than one of the drug-man's rabbits hung on a line, waiting to be skinned or set free.' She turned her gaze fully on Clint. 'Do you have a plan? I think you do.'

'Nothing so grand,' Clint said, 'but I might be able to buy some time. We've got a fortified position here, but we could use a few more men—'

'What we could use,' Tig interrupted, 'is a platoon of marines.'

Clint shook his head. 'Unless Terry Coombs and that guy Geary can get outside help, I think we can hold the prison with a dozen men, maybe as few as ten. Right now we number just four. Five, if we can get Scott Hughes on board, but I don't hold out much hope of that.'

Clint went on, speaking mostly to Mickey and the doc she'd brought with her. He didn't like the idea of sending Flickinger on a life-or-death mission — nothing about how he looked or smelled disagreed with Evie's pronouncement that he was a big-time doper — but Flickinger and Janice Coates's daughter were all he had to work with. 'The real problem is weaponry, and the big question is who lays hands on it first. I know from my wife that they've got quite the armory at the sheriff's station. Since 9/11 and all the domestic terrorism threats afterward, most towns Dooling's size do. For handguns they've got Glock 17s and, I think Lila said, Sig . . . something or others.'

'Sig Sauer,' Billy Wettermore said. 'Good weapon.'

'They've got M4 semi-autos with those big clips,' Clint went on, 'and a couple of Remington Model 700s. Also, I believe Lila said they have a forty-millimeter grenade launcher.'

'Guns.' Evie spoke to no one in particular. 'The perfect solution to any problem. The more you have, the more perfectly they solve the problem.'

'Are you shitting me?' Michaela cried. 'A *grenade* launcher?'

'Yes, but not for explosives. They use it with teargas.'

'Don't forget the bulletproof vests.' Rand sounded glum. 'Except at super-close range, those things will stop a Mossberg slug. And the Mossies are the heaviest armament we've got.'

'This sounds like a punting situation,' Tig remarked.

Billy Wettermore said, 'I sure don't want to kill anybody if I don't have to. Those are our friends, for God's sake.'

'Well, good luck,' Evie said. She went to her bunk and powered up Assistant Warden Hicks's phone. 'I'm going to play a few games of *Boom Town*, then take a nap.' She smiled at Michaela. 'I won't be taking any further questions from the press. You're a wonderful kisser, Mickey Coates, but you've worn me out.'

'Just watch that she don't decide to sic her rats on you,' Angel said to the group at large. 'They do whatever she wants. It's how she got Hicksie's cell phone.'

'Rats,' Garth said. 'This keeps getting better.'

'I need you folks to come with me,' Clint said. 'We need to talk, but it has to be quick. They'll have this place locked down soon enough.'

Billy Wettermore pointed to Jeanette, now seated cross-legged in the shower alcove of the delousing station and talking earnestly with someone only she could see. 'What about Sorley?'

'She'll be fine,' Clint said. 'Come on. Go to sleep, Jeanette. Let yourself rest.'

Without looking at him, Jeanette said a single word. 'No.'

9

To Clint, the warden's office had an archaeological appearance, as if it had been abandoned for years instead of less than a week. Janice Coates lay on the couch, wrapped in her cerements of white. Michaela went to her and knelt down. She stroked the cocoon with one hand. It gave off crackling sounds. Garth started to approach her, but Clint took his arm. 'Give her a minute, Dr Flickinger.'

It was actually more like three before Michaela got to her feet. 'What can we do?' she asked.

'Can you be persistent and persuasive?' Clint asked.

She fixed him with eyes that were no longer bloodshot. 'I came to NewsAmerica as an unpaid intern at twenty-three. By twenty-six, I was a full-time correspondent and they were talking about giving me my own evening show.' She saw Billy giving a look to Tig and Rand, and smiled at them. 'You know what they say around here, don't you? It ain't bragging if it's the truth.' She returned her attention to Clint. 'Those are my references. Are they good enough?'

'I hope so,' Clint said. 'Listen.'

He talked for the next five minutes. There were questions, but not many. They were in a bad corner, and all of them knew it.

CHAPTER 6

1

Alexander Peter Bayer, the first baby to be born on the other side of the Tree, son of a former Dooling inmate named Linda Bayer, breathed air for the first time a week after Lila and Tiffany returned from the wreck below Lion Head. It was another few days before Lila made his acquaintance at a small gathering in Elaine Nutting Geary's repaired home. He was not a traditionally attractive infant; the stacking of his many jowls produced an association not with the Gerber Baby but with a bookie that Lila had once arrested who had been known as 'Larry Large.' However, baby Alexander had an irresistibly comic way of rolling his eyes around, as if he were anxiously attempting to gain his bearings amid the flowering of female faces that loomed above him.

A plate of slightly crispy (though still pretty tasty) scones was passed around. Between bouts of the strange vertigo that afflicted her, Nadine Coombs had baked them in an outdoor oven. The oven itself had recently been hauled from the ruins of the Lowe's in Maylock, using sledges and Tiffany's horses. It flabbergasted Lila sometimes, the rate of progress they were making, the speed and efficiency with which problems were solved and advancements made.

At some point Lila ended up with the baby. 'Are you the last man on earth, or the first?' she asked him.

Alexander Peter Bayer yawned.

'Sorry, Lila. He doesn't talk to cops.' Tiffany had sidled up beside her in the corner of the living room.

'That so?'

'We teach em young around here,' Tiffany said.

Since their adventure they'd become odd friends. Lila liked how Tiffany rode around town on her horses, wearing her white cowboy hat, insisting that children come over and stroke the animals' necks, and see how soft and warm they were.

2

One day, with nothing better to do, Lila and Tiffany searched the Dooling YMCA, not knowing exactly what they were looking for, only knowing it was one of the few places that hadn't been investigated. They found plenty of stuff, some of it interesting, but nothing they really needed. There was toilet paper, but supplies of that in the Shopwell were still plentiful. There were also cartons of liquid soap, but over the years it had hardened into pink bricks. The pool had dried up; nothing remained but a faint, astringent odor of chlorine.

The men's locker room was damp and dank; luxuriant growths of mold — green, black, yellow — spanned the walls. A varmint's mummified corpse lay at the far end of the room, its legs stiff in the air, its face frozen in a savage death-gape, lips stretched away from rows of sharp teeth. Lila and Tiffany stood for a moment in silent contemplation of the first urinal in a row of six.

'Perfectly preserved,' said Lila.

Tiffany gave her a quizzical look. 'That?' Pointing at the varmint.

'No. This.' Lila patted the top of the urinal, her wedding ring clicking against the porcelain. 'We'll want it for our museum. We can call it the Museum of Lost Men.'

'Ha,' Tiffany said. 'Tell you what, this is a scary fuckin place. And believe me, that is sayin something because I have toured some real dungeons. I mean, I could write you a guidebook of the sweaty, drafty, fucked-up meth caves of Appalachia, but this is truly unpleasant. I knew men's locker rooms were creepy places, but this is worse than I could ever have imagined.'

'It was probably better before it got old,' Lila said . . . but she wondered.

They used hammers and chisels to break the combination locks off the lockers. Lila found stopped watches, wallets full of useless green paper and useless plastic rectangles, dead smart-phones thus rendered stupid, key rings, moth-eaten trousers, and a caved-in basketball. Tiffany's haul wasn't much better: an almost full box of Tic Tacs and a faded photograph of a bald man with a hairy chest standing on a beach with his little laughing daughter perched on his shoulders.

'Florida, I bet,' Tiffany said. 'That's where they go if they got the scratch.'

'Probably.' The photo made Lila think of her own son, which she increasingly felt was counterproductive – not that she could keep from doing it. Mary had filled her in on Clint, stalling to keep the officers at the prison, and Jared, hiding their bodies (*our other bodies*, she thought) in the attic of the show house up the street. Would she hear any more about either of them? A couple of other women had appeared since Mary, but none of them knew anything about her two guys, and why would they? Jared and Clint were on a spaceship and the spaceship was getting farther and farther away, so many light years, and eventually they'd slip from the galaxy entirely and that would be the end. Finito. When should she begin to mourn them? Had she already started?

'Aw,' said Tiffany. 'Don't.'

'What?'

But Tiffany had read her face somehow, seen right through to the hopelessness and the muddle. 'Don't let it get you.' Lila returned the photo to its locker and shut the door.

In the gymnasium upstairs, Tiffany challenged her to a game of H-O-R-S-E. The prize was the almost full box of Tic Tacs. They pumped up the basketball. Neither of them had any talent for the game. Clint's daughter who had turned out to not be his daughter would have dispatched them both with ease. Tiffany shot everything granny-style, underhanded, which Lila found annoyingly girly but also cute. When she had her coat off, you could see her pregnant stomach protrude, a bulb at Tiffany's waist.

'Why Dooling? Why us? Those are the questions, wouldn't you say?' Lila trotted after the basketball. Tiffany had shot it into the dusty bleachers to the right of the court. 'I've got a theory.'

'You do? Let's have it.'

Lila hurled the basketball from the bleachers. It missed the basket by a couple of car lengths and bounced into the second row of the opposite set of bleachers.

'That was pathetic,' Tiffany said.

'You're one to talk.'

'I'll admit that.'

'We've got a couple of doctors and a few nurses. We've got a veterinarian. We've got a bunch of teachers. Kayleigh knew her way around a circuit, and although she's gone, Magda isn't bad. We've got a carpenter. We've got a couple of musicians. We've got a sociologist who's already writing a book about the new society.'

'Yeah, and when it's done, Molly can print it with her berry-juice ink.' Tiffany snickered.

'We've got that retired engineering professor from the university. We've got seamstresses and gardeners and cooks out the ying-yang. The book club ladies are running an encounter group so women can talk about the stuff they miss, and get out some of the sadness and grief. We've even got a horse whisperer. See?'

Tiffany retrieved the basketball. 'See what?'

'We're all we need,' Lila said. She had descended from the bleachers and stood with her arms crossed at the baseline of the court. 'That's why we were chosen. Every basic skill we need to survive is here.'

'Okay. Maybe. Could be. Sounds about right to me.' Tiffany took off her cowboy hat and fanned herself with it. She was plainly amused. 'You are such a cop. Solving the mysteries.'

Lila wasn't done, though. 'So how do we keep things going? We've already got our first baby. And how many pregnant women are there? A dozen? Eight?'

'Could be as many as ten. That enough to jump-start a new world, you think, when half of em's apt to be girls?'

'I don't know.' Lila was riffing now, her face feeling hot as ideas came to her, 'But it's a start, and I bet you there's cold storage facilities with generators that were programmed to run and run and are still running. You'd have to go to a city to find one, I'd guess, but I bet you could. And there would be frozen sperm samples there. And that *would* be enough to get a world – a new world – going.'

Tiffany stuck her hat on the back of her head and thumped the basketball off the floor a couple of times. 'New world, huh?'

'She could have planned it this way. The woman. Eve. So we could start over again without men, at least at the beginning,' Lila said.

'Garden of Eden with no Adam, huh? Okay, Sheriff, let me ask you a question.'

'Sure.'

'Is it a *good* plan? What that woman's set up for us?'

A fair question, Lila thought. The inhabitants of Our Place had discussed Eve Black endlessly; the rumors that had started in the old world had been carried into the new world; it was a rare Meeting when her name (if it was her name) did not come up. She was an extension, and a possible answer to the original questions, the great How and Why of their situation. They discussed the likelihood that she was something more than a woman – more than human – and there was increasing unity in the belief that she was the source of everything that had happened.

On the one hand, Lila mourned the lives that had been lost – Millie, Nell, Kayleigh, Jessica Elway before them, and how many others – as well as the histories and existences from which those that still lived had been separated. Their men and boys were gone. Yet most – Lila definitely among them – could not deny the renewal before them: Tiffany Jones with full cheeks and clean hair and a second heartbeat. In the old world, there were men who had hurt Tiff, and badly. In the old world, there were men who burned women, thus incinerating them in both realities. Blowtorch Brigades, Mary said they were being called. There were bad women and there were bad men; if anyone could claim the right to make that statement, Lila, who had arrested plenty of both, felt that she could. But men fought more; they killed more. That was one way in which the sexes had never been equal; they were not equally dangerous.

So, yes, Lila thought it was probably a good plan. Merciless, but very good. A world re-started by women had a chance to be safer and fairer. And yet . . .

'I don't know.' Lila couldn't say that an existence without her son was better. She could conceptualize the idea, but she couldn't articulate it without feeling like a traitor to both Jared and to her old life.

Tiffany nodded. 'How about this, then: can you shoot backwards?' She turned away from the basket, bent her knees low, and flipped the ball over her head. It went up, caromed off the corner of the square, caught the rim – and fell off, bounce, bounce, bounce, so close.

3

An ocher gush belched from the tap. A pipe clanked loudly against another pipe. The brownish flow sputtered, stopped, and then, hallelujah, clean water began to pour into the sink.

'Well,' said Magda Dubcek to the small assembly around the work-sink set against the wall of the water treatment plant. 'Dere it is.'

'Incredible,' said Janice Coates.

'Nah. Pressure, gravity, not so complex. We be careful, turn on one neighborhood each at a time. Slow but steady win the race.'

Lila, thinking of the ancient note from Magda's son Anton, undoubtedly a dope and a cocksman, but pretty damn sharp about the ways of water in his own right, abruptly hugged the old lady.

'Oh,' said Magda, 'all right. Thanks.'

The water echoed in the long room of the Dooling County Water District plant, hushing them all. In silence, the women took turns passing their hands though the fresh stream.

4

One of the things everyone missed was the ability to just jump in a car and drive somewhere, instead of walking and getting blisters.

The cars were still there, some in pretty good shape from being parked in garages, and at least some of the batteries they found in storage still held juice. The real problem was gasoline. Every drop had oxidized during the in-between period.

'We'll have to refine some,' the retired engineering professor explained at a committee meeting. Not more than a hundred and fifty miles distant, in Kentucky, there were storage wells and refineries that might be re-started with work and luck. They immediately began to plan another journey; they assigned tasks and selected volunteers. Lila scanned the women in the room for signs of misgivings. There were none. Among the faces, she took special note of Celia Frode, the only survivor of the exploration party. Celia nodded along with the rest of them. 'Put me on that list,' Celia said. 'I'll go. Feel a need to put on my rambling shoes.'

It would be risky, but they would be more careful this time. And they would not flinch.

5

When they got to the second floor of the demo house, Tiffany announced that she wasn't climbing the ladder to the attic. 'I'll wait here.'

'If you're not coming up, why'd you come at all?' Lila asked. 'You're not that pregnant.'

'I was hoping you'd give me some of your Tic Tacs, ringer. And I'm plenty pregnant enough, believe me.' Lila had won H-O-R-S-E and the mints.

'Here.' She tossed the box to Tiffany, and climbed up the ladder.

The Pine Hills show house had, ironically, proved to be better constructed than almost every other structure on Tremaine, including Lila's own. Although dim – small windows smudged by the passage of seasons – the attic was dry. Lila paced the low room, her footfalls drawing puffs of dust from the floor. Mary had said that this was the one where she and Lila and Mrs Ransom were, back there, wherever back there was. She wanted to feel her other self, to feel her son.

She didn't feel anything.

At one end of the attic, a moth was batting against one of the dirty windows. Lila walked over to release it. The window was stuck. Lila heard creaking as, behind her, Tiffany climbed the ladder. She moved Lila aside, took out a pocket knife, worked the point around the edges, and the window went up. The moth escaped and flew away.

Below, there was snow on the overgrown lawns, on the busted-up street, on her dead cruiser in Mrs Ransom's driveway. Tiffany's horses were poking their noses around, nickering about whatever it was that horses nickered about, switching their tails. Lila could see past her own house, past the pool that she had never wanted and that Anton had tended, and past the elm tree that he had left her the note about. An orange animal trotted from the shadowy edge of the pine woods that backed the neighborhood. It was a fox. Even at this distance the luster of its winter coat was evident. How had it got to be winter so soon?

Tiffany stood in the middle of the attic. It was dry, but also cold, especially with the window open. She held out the box of Tic Tacs for Lila to take back. 'I wanted to eat them all, but it would've been wrong. I've given up my life of crime.'

Lila smiled and put them back in her own pocket. 'I declare you rehabilitated.'

The women stood about a foot apart, looking at each other, breathing steam. Tiffany pulled off her hat and dropped it on the floor.

'If you think that's a joke, it's not. I don't wanna take anything from you, Lila. I don't wanna take anything from anybody.'

'What do you want?' asked Lila.

'My very own life. Baby and a place and stuff. People that love me.'

Lila closed her eyes. She'd had all those things. She couldn't feel Jared, couldn't feel Clint, but she could remember them, could remember her very own life. It hurt, those memories. They made shapes in the snow, like the angels they'd made as children, but those shapes became fuzzier every day. God, she was lonesome.

'That's not so much,' Lila said, and reopened her eyes.

'It seems like a lot to me.' Tiffany reached out and drew Lila's face to hers.

6

The fox trotted away from the Pine Hills development, across Tremaine Street, and into the thick stands of winter wheat that had grown up on the far side. He was hunting for the smell of hibernating ground squirrels. The fox loved ground squirrels – Crunchy! Juicy! – and on this side of the Tree, unbothered for so long by human habitation, they had grown careless.

After a half hour's search he discovered a little family of them in a dug-out chamber. They never awoke, even as he was crushing them between his teeth. 'So tasty!' he said to himself.

The fox went on, entering the deep woods, making for the Tree. He paused briefly to explore an abandoned house. He pissed on a pile of books scattered on the floor and nosed fruitlessly around in a closet full of rotting linens. In the kitchen of the house there was food in the refrigerator that smelled deliciously spoiled, but his attempts to bump the door ajar accomplished nothing.

'Let me in there,' the fox demanded of the fridge, just in case it was only pretending to be a dead thing.

The fridge loomed, unresponsive.

A copperhead slid out from under the woodstove on the far side of the kitchen. 'Why are you glowing?' it asked the fox. Other animals had commented on this phenomenon and were wary of it. The fox saw it himself when he looked into still water and saw his reflection. A gold light clung to him. It was Her mark.

'I've had some good fortune,' the fox said.

The copperhead wriggled its tongue at him. 'Come here. Let me bite you.'

The fox ran from the cabin. Various birds heckled him as he loped beneath the canopy of gnarled and tangled bare branches, but their petty jibes meant nothing to the fox, whose belly was full and whose coat was thick as a bear's.

When he emerged into the clearing, the Tree was there, the centerpiece of a leafy, steaming oasis in the fields of snow. His paws crossed over from the cold ground to the rich, warm summer loam that was the Tree's forever bed. The Tree's branches were layered and blended in countless greens and beside the passage in the bole, the white tiger, flicking its great tail, watched him approach with sleepy eyes.

'Don't mind me,' said the fox, 'just passing through.' He darted by, into the black hole, and out the opposite side.

CHAPTER 7

1

Don Peters and Eric Blass had yet to be relieved at the West Lavin roadblock when a banged-up Mercedes SL600 came trundling toward them from the prison. Don was standing in the weeds, shaking off after a leak. He zipped up in a hurry and returned to the pickup that served as their cruiser. Eric was standing in the road with his gun drawn.

'Stow the cannon, Junior,' Don said, and Eric holstered his Glock.

The driver of the Mercedes, a curly-haired man with a florid face, pulled to an obedient stop when Don raised his hand. Sitting beside him was a good-looking woman. Make that *astoundingly* good-looking, especially after all the zombie chicks he and Eric had seen the last few days. Also, she was familiar.

'License and registration,' Don said. He had no orders to look at drivers' IDs, but it was what cops said when they made a stop. Watch this, Junior, he thought. See how a man does it.

The driver handed over his license; the woman rooted around in the glove compartment and found the registration. The man was Garth Flickinger, MD. From Dooling, with a listed residence in the town's fanciest neighborhood, over on Briar.

'Mind telling me what you were doing up at the prison?'

'That was my idea, Officer,' the woman said. God, she was good-looking. No bags under *this* bitch's eyes. Don wondered what she'd been taking to keep her so bushy-tailed. 'I'm Michaela Morgan. From NewsAmerica?'

Eric exclaimed, 'I *knew* I recognized you!'

It meant jack shit to Don, who didn't watch network news, let alone the blah-blah crap they put out 24/7 on the cable, but he remembered where he'd seen her. 'Right! The Squeaky Wheel. You were drinking there!'

She gave him a high-voltage smile, all capped teeth and high cheekbones. 'That's right! A man gave a speech about how God was punishing women for wearing pants. It was very interesting.'

Eric said, 'Could I have your autograph? It would be something cool to have after you . . .' He stopped in confusion.

'After I fall asleep?' she said. 'I think the bottom may have fallen out of the autograph market, at least temporarily, but if Garth — Dr Flickinger — has got a pen in his glove compartment, I don't see why n—'

'Forget that,' Don said harshly. He was embarrassed by his young partner's lack of professionalism. 'I want to know why you were up at the prison, and you aren't going anywhere until you tell me.'

'Of course, Officer.' She spotlighted him with her smile again. 'Although my professional name is Morgan, my real name is Coates, and I'm from right here in town. In fact, the warden is—'

'Coates is your *mother*?' Don was shocked, but once you got past her nose, which was arrow-sharp while old Janice's honker was crooked, he could see the resemblance. 'Well, I hate to tell you this, but your mother isn't with us anymore.'

'I know.' No smile now. 'Dr Norcross told me. We spoke to him on the intercom.'

'The man is an asshole,' the Flickinger guy said.

Don grinned, just couldn't help it. 'I'll double down on that.' He handed back the paperwork.

'Wouldn't let her in,' Flickinger marveled. 'Wouldn't even let her say goodbye to her own mother.'

'Well,' Michaela said, 'the complete truth is that wasn't the *only* reason I persuaded Garth to take me up there. I also wanted an interview with a woman named Eve Black. I'm sure you've heard the chatter about how she sleeps and wakes. It would have been quite a scoop, you know. The outside world doesn't care about much these days, but it would care about that. Only Norcross said she was inside a cocoon, like all the rest of the inmates.'

Don felt compelled to set her straight. Women – even women reporters, it seemed – could be painfully gullible. 'Pure bullshit, and everybody knows it. She's different, special, and he's holding onto her for some crazy reason of his own. But that's going to change.' He dropped her a wink ponderous enough to include Garth, who winked back. 'Be nice to me, and I might get you that interview once we spring her.'

Michaela giggled.

'I better look in your trunk, I guess,' Don said. 'Just so I can say I did.'

Garth got out and wrenched open his trunk, which rose with a weary squall – Geary had taken a few swipes here, as well. He hoped this clown wouldn't check beneath the spare tire; it was where he had sequestered the Baggie of Purple Lightning. The clown didn't bother, just took a quick look and gave a nod. Garth closed the trunk. This produced an even louder squall, the sound of a cat with its paw caught in a door.

'What happened to your car?' Eric asked as Garth got back behind the wheel.

Garth opened his mouth to tell the lad that a crazed animal control officer had laid into it, then remembered the crazed animal control officer was now, according to Norcross, the acting sheriff.

'Kids,' he said. 'Vandals. They see something nice and they just want to destroy it, don't they?'

The clown bent down to look at the pretty lady. 'I'm heading down to the Squeak when my shift is over. If you're still awake, I'd love to buy you a drink.'

'That would be wonderful,' Michaela said, just as if she meant it.

'You guys drive carefully and have a good evening,' the clown said.

Garth dropped the transmission into drive, but before he could turn onto the main road, the kid shouted, 'Wait!'

Garth stopped. The kid was bending down, hands on his knees, looking at Michaela. 'How about that autograph?'

There *was* a pen in the glove compartment, it turned out – a nice one with GARTH FLICKINGER, MD stamped in gold on the barrel. Michaela scribbled *To Eric, with best wishes* on the back of a drug rep's business card, and handed it over. Garth got rolling while the kid was still thanking her. Less than a mile down Route 31 toward town, they spotted a town cruiser coming toward them, moving fast.

'Slow down,' Michaela said. As soon as the cruiser disappeared over the hill behind them, she told him to step on it.

Garth did.

2

For two years Lila had pestered Clint to add her various contacts to his own, in case of trouble at the prison. Six months ago he had finally done it, mostly to get her off his case, and now he thanked God for her persistence. First he called Jared and told him to sit tight; if all went well, he told his son, someone would be along to pick him up before dark. Possibly in an RV. Then he closed his eyes, said a brief prayer for eloquence, and called the lawyer who had facilitated Eve Black's transfer to the prison.

After five rings, as Clint was resigning himself to voicemail, Barry Holden answered. 'Holden here.' He sounded uninterested and exhausted.

'This is Clint Norcross, Barry. Up at the prison.'

'Clint.' No more than that.

'I need you to listen to me. Very carefully.'

Nothing from Barry Holden.

'Are you there?'

After a pause, Barry replied in that same uninterested voice. 'I'm here.'

'Where are Clara and your daughters?' Four girls, ages twelve to three. A terrible thing for the father who loved them, but maybe a good thing for Clint, awful as that was to think of; he didn't have to talk about the fate of the world, only about the fate of Barry's female hostages to fortune.

'Upstairs, sleeping.' Barry laughed. Not a real laugh, though, just ha-ha-ha, like a dialogue balloon in a comic book. 'Well, you know. Wrapped up in those . . . things. I'm in the living room, with a shotgun. If anybody shows up here with so much as a lit match, I'm going to blow them away.'

'I think there might be a way to save your family. I think they could wake up. Does that idea interest you?'

'Is it the woman?' Something new crept into Barry's voice. Something alive. 'Is it true, what they're saying? That she can sleep and then wake up? If it's only a rumor, be straight with me. I can't stand to hope unless there's a reason to.'

'It's true. Now listen. Two people are coming to see you. One's a doctor, the other is Warden Coates's daughter.'

'Michaela's still awake? Even after all this time?' Barry had begun to sound like his old self. 'Not impossible, I guess – Gerda, my eldest, held out until last night – but still pretty remarkable.'

'She's not just awake, she's *totally* awake. Unlike every other woman in the Tri-Counties who's still got her eyes open. The woman we've got in custody up here did it. Just breathed down her throat and woke her up.'

'If this is a joke, Norcross, it's in extremely bad ta—'

'You'll see for yourself. They're going to tell you everything, then ask you to do some pretty dangerous stuff. I don't want to say you're our only hope, but . . .' Clint closed his eyes, rubbed at his temple with his free hand. '. . . but that might be what you are. And time is very short.'

'I would do anything for my wife and girls,' Barry said. '*Anything.*'

Clint allowed himself a long exhalation of relief. 'Buddy, I was hoping you'd say that.'

3

Barry Holden did indeed have a shotgun. It wasn't new, having been handed down through three generations of Holdens, but he had cleaned it and oiled it, and it looked lethal enough. He listened to Garth and Michaela with it laid across his thighs. Beside him, on an end table decorated with one of Clara Holden's lace doilies, was an open box of fat red shells.

Talking turn and turn about, Michaela and Garth told the lawyer what Clint had told them: how Eve Black's arrival roughly coincided with Aurora's first reported victims; how she had killed two men with her bare hands; how she had allowed herself to be taken into custody without a struggle, saying it was what she wanted; how she had banged her face repeatedly into the protective mesh of Lila's cruiser; how the bruises had healed with magical speed.

'Besides fixing me up, she knew things about me she couldn't possibly have known,' Michaela said, 'and they say she can control the rats. I know that's hard to believe, but—'

Garth interrupted. 'Another prisoner, Fitzroy, told us she used rats to get the assistant warden's cell phone. And she does have a cell phone. I saw it.'

'There's more,' Michaela said. 'She claims to have killed Judge Silver. She claimed . . .'

She paused, reluctant to say it, but Clint had told them to tell the truth, the whole truth, and nothing but the truth. *Remember that he may be grieving*, Clint had said, *but he's still a lawyer, and a damned good one. He can smell a lie at forty yards, even upwind.*

'She claimed she did it using moths. Because Silver was trying to bring in someone from out of town, and that's not allowed.'

Michaela knew that a week ago, this was where Barry Holden would have decided they were either sharing a pernicious delusion or trying on the world's worst and most stoned prank, and invited them to leave his house. But it wasn't a week ago. Instead of telling them to get out, Barry handed his grandfather's shotgun to Michaela. 'Hold this.'

There was a laptop on the coffee table. Barry sat on the couch (also liberally decorated with his wife's needlework) and began tapping away. After a moment, he looked up. 'Bridger County police are reporting an accident on the Old Coughlin Road. One fatality. No name, but the vehicle was a Land Rover. Judge Silver drives a Land Rover.'

He regarded Michaela Coates. What they were telling him, essentially, was that the fate of every woman on planet Earth depended on what happened here in Dooling over the next few days. It was mad, but Warden Coates's daughter, sitting there in Clara's favorite bentwood rocker and looking at him earnestly, was the best argument that it was true. Possibly an irrefutable argument. A news report on CNN that morning had said that less than ten percent of the world's women were estimated to still be awake on Aurora Day Five. Barry didn't know about that, but he would have been willing to bet Grampa Holden's shotgun that none of them looked like Michaela.

'She just . . . what? Kissed you? Like when the prince kissed Princess Aurora in the cartoon?'

'Yes,' said Michaela. 'Like that. And she breathed down my throat. I think that's what really did it – her breath.'

Barry switched his attention to Garth. 'You saw this?'

'Yes. It was amazing. Mickey here looked like a vampire after a fresh transfusion.' And when he caught Michaela's frowning stare: 'Sorry, darling, maybe not the best metaphor.'

'That was actually a simile,' she said coldly.

Barry was still trying to get his mind around it. 'And she says they'll come for her? The cops? The townies? And that Frank Geary's in charge?'

'Yes.' Michaela had left out everything Evie had said about the sleeping women having to make their own decision; even if true, that part was out of their hands.

'I know Geary,' Barry said. 'I never defended him, but he's been in District Court a couple of times. I remember a case where a woman complained that he threatened her for not keeping her Rottweiler on a leash. He has what you'd call anger issues.'

'Tell me about it,' Garth murmured.

Barry looked at him, eyebrows raised.

'Never mind,' Garth said. 'Not important.'

Barry took back his shotgun. 'Okay, I'm in. For one thing, I've got nothing else to do, with Clara and the girls gone. For another . . . I want to see this mystery woman with my own eyes. What does Clint want from me?'

'He said you have a Winnebago,' Michaela said. 'To go camping in with your wife and girls.'

Barry smiled. 'Not a Winnebago, a Fiesta. Sucks a ton of gas, but it sleeps six. The girls squabble almost non-stop, but we had some good times in that old thing.' His eyes abruptly filled with tears. 'Some very, very good times.'

4

Barry Holden's Fleetwood Fiesta was parked in a small lot behind the old-fashioned granite block of a building where he kept his office. The RV was a monstrous zebra-striped thing. Barry sat behind the wheel while Michaela climbed into the passenger seat. They waited for Garth to reconnoiter the cop-shop. The Holden family's heirloom shotgun lay on the floor between them.

'Does this have any chance at all, do you think?' Barry asked.

'I don't know,' Michaela replied. 'I hope so, but I really don't know.'

'Well, it's nuts, no doubt about that,' Barry said, 'but it beats sitting home and thinking bad thoughts.'

'You have to see Evie Black to really understand. Speak to her. You have to . . .' She searched for the right word. 'You have to *experience* her. She—'

Michaela's cell phone rang. It was Garth.

'There's a geezer with a beard sitting under an umbrella on one of the benches out front, but otherwise the coast is clear. No cruisers in the side lot, just a few personal vehicles. If we're going to do this, I think we'd better hurry up. That RV is not what I'd call unobtrusive.'

'Coming now,' Michaela said. She ended the call.

The alley between Barry's building and the one next to it was narrow – there couldn't have been more than five inches of clearance for the lumbering Fleetwood on either side – but Barry threaded its length with the ease of long experience. He stopped at the mouth of the alley, but Main Street was deserted. It's almost as if the men are gone, too, Michaela thought as Barry made a wide right turn and drove the two blocks to the Municipal Building.

He parked the Fleetwood in front, taking three spaces marked

OFFICIAL BUSINESS ONLY, OTHERS WILL BE TOWED. They got out and Garth joined them. The man with the beard got up and ambled over, holding the umbrella over his head. The stem of a pipe poked up from the bib of his Oshkosh overalls. He held out his hand to Barry and said, 'Hello there, Counselor.'

Barry shook with him. 'Hey, Willy. Good to see you, but I can't stop to chew the fat. We're in sort of a hurry. Urgent business.'

Willy nodded. 'I'm waiting for Lila. I know the chances are good that she's asleep, but I'm hoping not. Want to talk to her. I went back out to that trailer where those meth-heads got killed. Something funny out there. Not just fairy handkerchiefs. The trees are full of moths. Wanted to talk to her about it, maybe take her to see. If not her, then whoever's supposed to be in charge.'

'This is Willy Burke,' Barry told Garth and Michaela. 'Volunteer fire department, Adopt-A-Highway, coaches Pop Warner, all around good guy. But we're really pressed for time, Willy, so—'

'If it was Linny Mars you came to talk to, you better hurry up.' Willy's eyes flicked from Barry to Garth to Michaela. They were deep-set, caught in nets of wrinkles, but sharp. 'She was still awake the last time I popped in, but she's fadin fast.'

'No deputies around?' Garth asked.

'Nope, all out on patrol. Except maybe for Terry Coombs. I heard he's a little under the weather. Struck drunk, don't you know.'

The three of them started up the steps to the triple doors. 'Haven't seen Lila, then?' Willy called after them.

'No,' Barry said.

'Well . . . maybe I'll wait a little longer.' And Willy wandered back to his bench. 'Something funny out there, all right. All those moths. And the place has got a vibration.'

5

Linny Mars, part of the ten percent of earth's female population still holding out on that Monday, continued to walk around with her laptop, but now she was moving slowly, occasionally stumbling and bumping into the furniture. To Michaela she looked like a wind-up toy that had almost run down. Two hours ago, that was me, she thought.

Linny walked past them, staring at her laptop with her bloodshot eyes, not seeming to realize they were there until Barry tapped her on the shoulder. Then she jumped, her hands flying up. Garth caught her laptop before it could crash to the floor. On the screen was a video of the London Eye. In slow motion it tottered and rolled into the Thames again and again. Hard to tell why anyone would want to destroy the London Eye, but apparently someone had felt a need to do so.

'Barry! You scared the *dickens* out of me!'

'I'm sorry,' he said. 'Terry sent me to get some of the hardware from the weapons room. I guess he wants it up to the prison. May I have the key, please?'

'Terry?' she frowned. 'Why would *he* . . . Lila's the sheriff, not Terry. *You* know that.'

'Lila, right,' Barry said. 'It's Lila's order *via* Terry.'

Garth went to the doors and looked out, convinced that a sheriff's department cruiser would pull up at any moment. Maybe two or three. They would be thrown in jail, and this lunatic adventure would be over before it even got started. So far there was no one but the bearded guy sitting out there under his umbrella, like Patience on her monument, but that couldn't last.

'Can you help me out, Linny? For Lila?'

'Sure. I'll be glad to see her back,' Linny said. She went to her desk and put her laptop down. On the screen, the London Eye fell and fell and fell. 'That guy Dave is running things until she does. Or maybe his name is Pete. Confusing to have two Petes around. In any case, I don't know about him. He's very serious.'

She rummaged in her wide top drawer, and brought out a heavy ring of keys. She peered at them. Her eyes drifted closed. White threads immediately rose from her eyelashes, wavering in the air.

'Linny!' Barry said sharply. 'Wake up!'

Her eyes snapped open, and the threads disappeared. 'I *am* awake. Stop shouting.' She ran a finger along the keys, making them jingle. 'I know it's one of them . . .'

Barry took them. 'I'll find it. Miss Morgan, maybe you'd like to go back to the RV and wait there.'

'No, thanks. I want to help. It will be quicker that way.'

At the back of the main room was an unmarked metal door painted a particularly unappetizing shade of green. There were two locks. Barry found the key that fitted the top one easily enough. The second, however, was taking more time. Michaela thought Lila might have kept that key for herself. It might be in her pocket, buried under one of those white cocoons.

'Do you see anyone coming?' she called to Garth.

'Not yet, but hurry up. This is making me need to pee.'

There were only three keys left on the ring when Barry found the one that turned the second lock. He opened the door, and Michaela saw a small closet-sized room with rifles stowed in racks and pistols nestled in Styrofoam-lined cubbies. There were shelves stacked with boxes of ammunition. On one wall was a poster showing a Texas Ranger in a ten-gallon hat, pointing a revolver with a huge black barrel. I FOUGHT THE LAW AND THE LAW WON, read the line beneath.

'Get as much of the ammo as you can,' Barry said. 'I'll get the M4s and some of the Glocks.'

Michaela started for the ammo shelves, then changed her mind and went back into the dispatch area. She grabbed Linny's wastebasket and turned it over, dumping out a heap of crumpled paper and takeout coffee cups. Linny took no notice. Michaela loaded as many boxes of ammunition as she thought she could carry into the wastebasket and left the secure room with the basket clasped in her arms. Garth brushed past her to get his own armload of weaponry. Barry had left one of the triple entry doors open. Michaela staggered down the wide stone steps through the thickening rain in time to see Barry reach the Fleetwood. The bearded man got up from his bench, still holding his umbrella over his head. He said something to Barry, who replied. Then the bearded man, Willy, opened the RV's rear door so Barry could put in his armload of guns.

Michaela joined him, panting. Barry took the wastebasket from her and dumped the boxes of ammo on top of the jackstraw pile of guns. They went back together while Willy stood beneath his umbrella, watching. Garth came out with a second load of armament, his pants sagging under the weight of the ammo boxes he had shoved into all his pockets.

'What did the old guy say to you?' Michaela asked.

'He wanted to know if we were doing something Sheriff Norcross would approve of,' Barry replied. 'I said we were.'

They went back inside and hurried to the secure room. They had taken about half the weaponry. Michaela spotted something that looked like a submachine gun afflicted with the mumps. 'We should definitely take that. I think it's the teargas-launcher thingy. I don't know if we need it, but I don't want anyone else to have it.'

Garth rejoined them. 'I come bearing bad news, Counselor Holden. Truck with a jackpot light on the dash just pulled up behind your RV.'

They hurried to the doors and peered out through the smoked glass. Two men were getting out of the truck, and Michaela recognized them both: the clown and his autograph hound partner.

'Oh, Christ,' Barry said, 'that's Don Peters, from the prison. What's he doing pretending to be a cop? The man has the brains of an insect.'

'That particular insect was most recently seen manning a roadblock near the prison,' Garth said. 'Same bug, same truck.'

The bearded man approached the newcomers, said something, and pointed further up Main Street. Peters and his young partner ran to their truck and jumped in. The lightbars came on and they pulled out with the siren screaming.

'What's going on?' Linny asked in a distracted voice. 'Just what in the doodly-fuck is going on?'

'Everything's fine,' Garth said, and gave her a smile. 'Not to worry.' Then, to Barry and Michaela: 'May I suggest we quit while we're ahead?'

'What's going on?' Linny wailed. 'Oh, this is all just a bad dream!'

'Hang in there, miss,' Garth said. 'It might get better.'

The three of them left, running once they got to the concrete path. Michaela had the grenade launcher in one hand and a bag of teargas shells in the other. She felt like Bonnie Parker. Willy was standing beside the Fleetwood.

'How did you get those guys out of here?' Barry asked.

'Told em someone was shooting up the hardware store. They won't be long, so I think you folks better roll.' Willy snapped his umbrella closed. 'And I think I better roll with you. Those two ain't going to be happy campers when they come back.'

'Why would you help us like this?' Garth asked.

'Well, it's strange days now, and a man has got to trust his instincts. Mine have always been pretty good. Barry here's always been a friend to Lila, even though he bats for the other team in court, and I recognize this girl here from the TV news.' He peered at Garth. 'You I don't like the looks of so much, but you're with them, so what the hell. Besides, the die is cast, as they say. Where we going?'

'First to pick up Lila's son,' Barry said, 'then up to the prison. How would you like to take part in a siege, Willy? Because that may be what's shaping up.'

Willy smiled, showing tobacco-stained teeth. 'Well, I had a coon-skin cap when I was a kid, and I always like movies about the Alamo, so why not? Help me up the steps of this rig, would you? The goddam rain plays hell with my rheumatism.'

6

Jared, waiting at the door of the demo house, was getting ready to call his father again when a huge RV pulled up in front. Jared recognized the driver; like his mother's deputies and many other town officials, Barry Holden had been a dinner guest at the Norcross house on occasion. Jared met him on the stoop.

'Come on,' Barry said. 'We have to go.'

Jared hesitated. 'My mom and three others are in the attic. It was really hot up there before the rain started, and it will be hot again tomorrow. You should help me get them down.'

'It will cool off fast tonight, Jared, and we have no time.'

Barry didn't know if the cocooned women could feel heat or

cold, but he did know that their window of opportunity was rapidly closing. He also thought that Lila and the others might be better off stashed away here on this quiet street. He had insisted on bringing his own wife and daughters along, because of the RV. It was well known in Dooling, and he was afraid of reprisals.

'Can we at least tell someone—'

'That's a decision your father can make. Please, Jared.'

Jared allowed himself to be led down the walk to the idling Fleetwood. The back door opened, and his old Pop Warner coach leaned out. Jared smiled in spite of himself. 'Coach Burke!'

'Well, lookit this!' Willy exclaimed. 'The only peewee quarterback I ever had who didn't drop every other snap. Climb in here, son.'

But the first thing Jared saw was the array of guns and ammo on the floor. 'Holy shit, what are these for?'

A woman sat on the plaid couch just inside the door. She was young, extremely pretty, and vaguely familiar, but the most remarkable thing about her was how awake she looked. She said, 'Hopefully just insurance.'

A man standing in the passage in front of her laughed. 'I wouldn't bet on that, Mickey.' He held out his hand. 'Garth Flickinger.'

Behind Garth Flickinger, on a matching couch, were arranged four cocooned bodies, each smaller than the previous, like a set of separated nesting dolls.

'That's Mr Holden's wife and daughters, I'm told,' Coach Burke said.

The RV started rolling. Jared staggered. Willy Burke steadied him, and as Jared shook with Mr Flickinger, he thought that maybe all of this was a dream. Even the guy's name seemed like something out of a dream – who, in the real world, was named Garth Flickinger?

'Pleased to meet you,' he said. In his peripheral vision the Holden women rolled against one another as the RV went around a corner. Jared told himself not to see them, but there was no not seeing them, reduced to mummified dolls. 'I'm – ah – Jared Norcross.' And dream or no dream, he had a certain resentment – there had been time for Mr Holden to get *his* family, hadn't there? And why was that? Because it was his RV?

Jared's phone rang as Barry hooked them around the Tremaine Street cul-de-sac. They were leaving his mother, Molly, Mary, and Mrs Ransom behind. It felt wrong. Everything felt wrong, though, so what else was new?

The caller was his father. They spoke briefly and then Clint asked to speak to Michaela. When she took the phone, Clint said, 'Here's what you need to do.'

She listened.

7

Deputy Sheriff Reed Barrows had parked Unit Three directly across the byroad leading to the prison. This was high ground; he and Vern had a clear view down at least six miles of Route 31. Reed had expected a ration of shit from Peters about being relieved so soon after they had taken up their post, but Peters had been surprisingly agreeable. Probably eager to get an early start on the day's drinking. Maybe the kid was, too. Reed doubted if they were checking IDs at the Squeaky Wheel this week, and currently the cops had better things to do than enforce alcohol laws.

Peters reported they had stopped just a single car, some reporter who'd gone up to the prison hoping to get an interview, and been turned away. Reed and Vern had stopped no one at all. Even traffic on the main road was so sparse it was nearly nonexistent. The town was in mourning for its women, Reed thought. Hell, the *world* was in mourning.

Reed turned to his partner, who was reading something on his Kindle and picking his nose. 'You're not wiping boogers under the seat, are you?'

'Jesus, no. Don't be disgusting.' Vern raised his rump, pulled a handkerchief from his back pocket, wiped a little green treasure into it, and replaced it. 'Tell me something – what exactly are we doing here? Do they really think Norcross is stupid enough to take that woman out into the world when he's got her behind bars right now?'

'I don't know.'

'If a food truck or something comes along, what are we supposed to do?'

'Stop it and radio for instructions.'

'Radio who? Terry or Frank?'

About this Reed was less sure. 'Guess I'd try Terry's cell first thing. Leave a message just to cover our asses if he doesn't pick up. Why don't we worry about that if it happens.'

'Which it probably won't, the mess everything's in.'

'Yeah. Infrastructure's shot to hell.'

'What's infrastructure?'

'Look it up on your Kindle, why don't you?'

Vern did so. '"The basic physical and organizational structures needed for the operation of a society or an enterprise." Huh.'

'Huh? What does *huh* mean?'

'That you're right. It's shot to hell. I went to the Shopwell this morning, before I came on. Place looks like a bomb hit it.'

Down the hill, in the gray afternoon light, they could see an approaching vehicle.

'Reed?'

'What?'

'With no women, there's going to be no babies.'

'You've got a scientific mind, all right,' Reed said.

'If this doesn't end, where will the human race be in another sixty or a hundred years?'

This was something Reed Barrows did not want to think about, especially with his wife in a cocoon and his toddler being babysat (probably inadequately) by ancient Mr Freeman next door. Nor did he have to. The vehicle was now close enough to see it was a humungous zebra-striped camper, and slowing down as if it meant to turn onto the prison road. Not that it could, with Three parked across it.

'That RV belongs to Holden,' said Vern. 'The lawyer. My brother services it over in Maylock.'

The Fleetwood came to a stop. The driver's door opened, and Barry Holden got out. At the same time, the officers got out of Three.

Holden greeted them with a smile. 'Gentlemen, I come bearing good tidings of great joy.'

Neither Reed nor Vern returned the smile.

'No one goes up to the prison, Mr Holden,' Reed said. 'Sheriff's orders.'

'Now, I don't think that's strictly true,' Barry said, still smiling. 'I believe a gentleman named Frank Geary gave that order, and he's what you might call self-appointed. Isn't that so?'

Reed wasn't sure how to respond to this, so he kept silent.

'In any case,' Barry said, 'I got a call from Clint Norcross. He's decided that turning the woman over to local law enforcement is the right thing to do.'

'Well, thank God for that!' Vern exclaimed. 'The man sees reason!'

'He wants me at the prison to facilitate the deal and make it clear for the public record as to why he went outside of protocol. Just a formality, really.'

Reed was about to say, *You couldn't find a smaller vehicle to come up here in? Car wouldn't start, maybe?*, but that was when Three's dash radio blared. It was Terry Coombs, and he sounded upset. 'Unit Three, Unit Three respond! Right now! *Right now!*'

8

Just as Reed and Vern were first noticing the approach of Barry Holden's RV, Terry Coombs entered the Olympia Diner and walked to the booth where Frank and Deputy Pete Ordway were sitting. Frank was less than happy to see Coombs up and about, but concealed his displeasure as best he could. 'Yo, Terry.'

Terry nodded to both men. He had shaved and changed his shirt. He looked rocky but sober. 'Jack Albertson told me you guys were here.' Albertson was one of the retired deputies who had been pressed back into service two days before. 'I got some pretty bad news from Bridger County fifteen minutes ago.' There was no smell of booze about Terry. Frank hoped to change that. He didn't like encouraging a man who was probably an incipient alcoholic, but Coombs was easier to work with when he'd had a few.

'What's going on in Bridger?' Pete asked.

'Wreck on the highway. Judge Silver went into Dorr's Hollow Stream. He's dead.'

'*What?*' Frank's shout was loud enough to bring Gus Vereen out of the kitchen.

'It's a damn shame,' Terry said. 'He was a fine man.' He pulled up a chair. 'Any idea what he was doing over there?'

'Went to speak to an ex-FBI guy he knew in Coughlin about helping to talk sense into Norcross,' Frank said. It had to have been a heart attack. The judge had looked horrible, washed out and shaky. 'If he's dead . . . I guess that's out.' With an effort, he composed himself. He'd liked Judge Silver and had been willing to go along with him – up to a certain point. That point was erased now.

'And that woman is still at the prison.' Frank leaned forward. 'Awake. Norcross was lying about her being in a cocoon. Hicks told me.'

'Hicks's got a poor reputation,' Terry said.

Frank wasn't hearing it. 'And there's other strange things about her. She's the key.'

'If the bitch started it, she'll know how to stop it,' Pete said. Terry's mouth twitched. 'There's no proof of that, Pete. And since Aurora started halfway around the world, it seems kind of farfetched. I think we all need to take a deep breath and just—'

Frank's walkie came to life. It was Don Peters. 'Frank! Frank, come in! I need to talk to you! You better answer this thing, because they fucking—'

Frank raised the walkie to his lips. 'This is Frank. Come back. And watch the profanity, you're going out over the ai—'

'*They fucking robbed the guns!*' Don yelled. '*Some decrepit old piece of shit sent us on a wild goose chase and then they robbed the fucking guns right out of the fucking sheriff's station!*'

Before Frank could reply, Terry snatched the walkie-talkie out of his hand. 'Coombs here. Who did?'

'Barry Holden, in a big motherhumper of an RV! Your dispatcher said there were others with them, but she's three-quarters out of it and don't know who!'

'All the guns?' Terry asked, astounded. 'They took *all* the guns?'

'No, no, not all, I guess they didn't have time, but plenty of them! Jesus Christ, that RV was *huge!*'

Terry stared at the walkie in his hand, frozen. Frank told himself he ought to keep his mouth shut and let Terry work through the computation on his own – and he just couldn't do it. It seemed he never could, once he was angry. 'Do you still think we just need to take a deep breath and wait Norcross out? Because you know where they're going with those weapons, don't you?'

Terry looked up at him, his lips pressed so tightly together his mouth was almost gone. 'I think you might have forgotten who's in charge here, Frank.'

'Sorry, Sheriff.' Under the table, his hands were so tightly clenched they were shaking, the nails digging crescents into his palms.

Terry was still staring at him. 'Tell me you put someone out there on the road to the prison.'

It would be your own damn fault if I didn't, drunk as you were. Ah, but who had been plying him with the booze?

'I did. Rangle and Barrows.'

'Good. That's good. Which unit are they in?'

Frank didn't know, but Pete Ordway did. 'Three.'

Don was blabbering on, but Terry cut him off and pressed SEND. 'Unit Three, Unit Three respond! Right now! *Right now!*'

CHAPTER 8

1

At the squawk of the radio, Reed Barrows told Barry to stay put.

'No problem,' Barry said. He gave the side of the Fleetwood three knocks, a message to Willy Burke – crouched behind the curtain that separated the front of the RV from the back – that it was on to Plan B. Plan B was pretty simple: beat it while Barry provided as much of a distraction as possible. It was paramount that the guns got to the prison, and that his girls were safe from harm. Barry didn't have to think twice about it. They'd arrest him, of course, but he knew a terrific lawyer.

He placed a hand on Vern Rangle's shoulder, gently easing him past the front of the RV.

'Sounds like someone at the station's got a full diaper,' Rangle observed cheerfully, moving thoughtlessly along with the lawyer's guidance. 'Where we going?'

Where they were going was away from the RV so that, one, Rangle didn't see Willy Burke sliding into the driver's seat and, two, to give the Fleetwood room to go forward without running anyone over. Barry couldn't tell the officer that, though. A concept that he had endeavored to impress upon his girls was that the law was impersonal; it wasn't about your feelings, it was about your argument. If you could partition yourself off from personal preference entirely, that was for the best. You wanted, really, to remove your skin, and assume the skin of your client, while at the same time hanging onto your brain.

(Gerda, who had been asked on a date by a high school boy
– just a sophomore, but still much too old for her – had recently
tried to get her father to take her on as a *pro bono* client to argue
to her mother that she was old enough to go to the movies with
the guy. This had been exceptionally clever of Gerda, but Barry
had recused himself on the grounds of their familial relationship.
Also because, as her father, he had no intention of letting her go
anywhere with a boy who was almost fifteen and probably got
hard every time the wind blew. If Cary Benson wanted to spend
time with her that badly, he'd said, then Cary could buy her an
ice cream sundae at the Dairy Treet right here in town. And in
broad daylight.)

What Barry had chosen not to express to Gerda was the sticky
provision of the utterly culpable. Sometimes you pulled on your
clifent's skin only to find that they – *you* – were astoundingly,
hopelessly, no-way-to-even-pretend guilty as original sin. When this
situation arose, the only sensible tactic was to distract and disrupt,
litigate minutiae, gum up the wheels and delay. With luck, you might
wear the opposition down until they offered you an advantageous
deal just to be rid of you, or better yet, irritate or flummox them
into screwing up their case altogether.

With that in mind, he improvised with the most dumbfounding
question he could come up with on short notice:

'Listen, Vern. Wanted to take you aside and ask you something.'

'Okay . . .'

Barry leaned forward confidentially. 'Are you circumcised?'

Rain sprinkles dotted the surface of Vern Rangle's glasses,
obscuring his eyes. Barry heard the engine of the RV turn over,
heard the clunk as Willy put it into drive, but the cop paid no
mind. The circumcision question had put him in mental vapor
lock.

'Gee, Mr Holden . . .' Vern absently shook out a handkerchief
and began to refold it. '. . . kinda personal, you know.'

Behind them there was a thud and the whinge of metal grinding
against metal.

Meanwhile, Reed Barrows had scooted into the driver's side of the cruiser to take Terry's call, but the mic slipped out of his damp hand. The seconds that elapsed while he bent to retrieve it from the footwell and untangle the cord were important because that got Willy Burke settled in driving mode.

'Roger, this is Unit Three. Barrows speaking, over,' Reed said once he had the mic again.

Out the window, he saw the RV swerving around the front of the cruiser to the gravel shoulder and grassy embankment on the southbound half of the road. This vision didn't alarm Reed; it perplexed him. Why was Barry Holden moving his RV? Or was Vern moving it so someone else could get by? That didn't make sense. They needed to sort out the shyster and his Fleetwood before they dealt with anyone else who wanted to drive through.

Terry Coombs's voice blared over the radio. 'Arrest Barry Holden and confiscate his vehicle! He's got a pile of stolen guns and he's headed for the prison! You hear me—'

The front end of the RV bumped the front end of the cruiser, the mic jumped out of Reed's hand a second time, and his view through the windshield swung away as if on hinges.

'Hey!'

2

In the back of the RV, Jared lost his balance. He fell off the couch and onto the guns. 'You okay?' Garth asked. The doctor had kept his feet by pressing his back against the counter of the kitchenette and grabbing the sink.

'Yeah.'

'Thanks for asking about me!' Michaela had managed to stay on the couch, but she'd fallen over onto her side.

Garth realized that he adored Mickey. She had sand, as the old timers liked to say. He wouldn't change a thing about her. Her nose and everything else was as close to flawless as you could get. 'I didn't have to, Mickey,' he replied. 'I know you're okay because you'll always be okay.'

3

The RV rolled slowly along, hugging the sloping roadside at a tilted angle and doing about fifteen miles an hour, shoving the cruiser aside. Metal squalled against metal. Vern gaped and spun to Barry. The lawyer had pissed right down his leg. Vern therefore slugged Barry in the eye and dumped him flat on his rear end.

'Stop the RV!' bellowed Reed from the open door of the shifting cruiser. 'Shoot the tires!'

Vern drew his service weapon.

The RV broke loose from the cruiser and began to pick up speed. It was at a two o'clock angle as it moved off the shoulder, now headed back for the center of the road. Vern, aiming for the right rear tire, triggered too quickly. His shot went way high, puncturing a piece of the RV's wall. The vehicle was about fifty yards distant. Once it gained the road, it would be gone. Vern took a moment to reset and aimed again, properly, focusing again on the rear right tire . . . and fired into the air as Barry Holden tackled him to the ground.

4

Jared, on the floor, his back poked in half a dozen places by gunsights and gun barrels, was deafened by the blast. He could somehow feel the screaming around him – the woman, Michaela? Flickinger? – but he couldn't hear it. His eyes found a hole in the wall: the bullet had made an opening like a burst firecracker top. His hands, flat on the floor of the RV, felt the wheels moving below, gaining speed, thrumming on the hardtop.

Flickinger still had his feet. He was braced at the kitchen counter. Nope, it wasn't Flickinger who was screaming.

Jared looked where the doctor was looking.

The cocooned figures lay on the couch. A bloody cavity had opened at the sternum of the third in the row, the oldest of the three girls, Gerda. She stood up from the couch, and staggered forward. She was the one that was screaming. Jared saw that she was moving at Michaela, who was huddled at the end of the parallel couch. The girl's arms were raised, torn loose from the webbing that had held them fast to her torso, and the impression of the open, howling mouth under the material was vivid. Moths spilled from the hole in her sternum.

Flickinger caught Gerda. She spun, and her hands clawed at his throat as they wobbled in a circle, and went tripping over the guns on the floor. The two bodies crashed against the rear door. The latch snapped, the door flew open, and they fell out, followed by a rush of moths, and a stream of guns and bullets.

5

Evie moaned.

'What?' Angel asked. 'What's wrong?'

'Oh,' Evie said. 'Nothing.'

'Liar,' Jeanette said. She was still slumped in the shower alcove. Angel had to hand it to Jeanette: she was almost as stubborn as Angel herself.

'That's the sound you make when people die.' Jeanette inhaled. She cocked her head and addressed an invisible person. 'That's the sound she makes when people die, Damian.'

'I guess that's true, Jeanette,' Evie said. 'I guess I do that.'

'That's what I said. Didn't I, Damian?'

'You're seein shit, Jeanette,' Angel said.

Jeanette's gaze stayed on the empty air. 'Moths came from her mouth, Angel. She's got moths in her. Now let me alone – I'm trying to have a conversation with my husband.'

Evie excused herself. 'I need to make a call.'

6

Reed heard Vern's shot as he hurled himself over the police cruiser's console and jerked open the passenger door. He glimpsed the rear end of the RV as it lumbered over beyond the slope, its back door flapping back and forth.

Two bodies lay in the road. Reed unholstered his service weapon and ran toward them. Past the bodies there was a trail of three or four assault rifles and a few handfuls of ammunition scattered among them.

When he reached the bodies, he stopped. Blood and gray matter painted the pavement around the skull of the prone man who was nearest. Reed had seen his share of corpses, but the mess here was notable, maybe a prize-winner. In the course of his fall, the guy's glasses had flipped up to rest on the fringe of his curly hair. The arrangement of the glasses gave him a perversely warm and casual look, a teacherly aspect, as he lay dead in the road with his brains splattered on the asphalt.

A few steps further on, a female was sprawled on her side in the position that Reed himself often adopted when he was on the couch watching television. Her mask of webbing had been scraped away by contact with the road, and the skin that remained was tattered. From what was left of the face and of her body, Reed could determine that she was young, but not much more than that. A bullet had torn a large wound in her chest. The girl's blood flowed onto the damp pavement.

Sneakers slapped against the pavement behind Reed. 'Gerda!' someone screamed. 'Gerda!'

Reed turned and Barry Holden rushed past him, falling to his knees by the body of his daughter.

Vern Rangle, nose bloodied, staggered up the road after Holden, bellowing that he'd circumcise *him,* the fucker.

What a hill of shit: a smeared guy, a dead girl, a howling attorney, Vern Rangle with his blood up, guns and ammo in the road. Reed was relieved that Lila Norcross was not currently serving as sheriff because he would not have wanted to even begin to attempt to explain to her how it had happened.

Reed grabbed for Vern a second too late, catching just a piece of fabric at his shoulder. Vern shook him off and swatted the butt end of his pistol across the back of Barry Holden's head. There was an ugly cracking noise, like a breaking branch, and a gout of blood. Barry Holden tumbled face-first onto the ground beside his daughter.

Vern squatted beside the unconscious lawyer and began to hit him again and again with the butt of his gun. 'Fuck you, fuck you, fuck you! You broke my nose, you b—'

The young woman who should have been dead and wasn't grasped Vern's jaw, wrapped her fingers over his lower teeth, and jerked him down to her level. Her head lifted and her mouth snapped wide and she buried her teeth in Vern's throat. Reed's partner began to whack at her with the pistol butt. It didn't faze her. Arterial blood pumped out around her lips.

Reed remembered his own weapon. He raised it and shot. The bullet entered through the young woman's eye and her body went loose, but her mouth remained clamped on Vern's throat. She appeared to be drinking his blood.

On his knees, Reed dug his fingers into the hot and slippery mess where the young woman's teeth were locked to his partner's throat. He hauled and pulled, feeling tongue and enamel. Vern swung at her once more, ineffectually, his gun flying from his relaxing hand and bouncing away. Then he collapsed.

7

Last in a three-cruiser caravan, Frank drove alone. Everyone had their sirens going. Ordway and Terry were at the fore, followed by Peters and Peters's sidekick, Blass. Aloneness was not something that Frank sought, but it seemed to find him. Why was that? Elaine had taken Nana and left him alone. Oscar Silver had gone off the road and left him alone. It was grim. It had made him grim. Maybe that was how it had to be, though – how he had to be – to do what he had to do.

But could he do what he had to do? Things were going wrong. Reed Barrows had radioed that shots had been fired and there was an officer down. Frank believed he was ready to kill for his daughter; he was certain that he was ready to die for her. What occurred to him now, though, was that he was not the only one who was willing to take mortal risks. Norcross's people had stolen police armaments and broken through a barricade. Whatever their reasons, they were determined. It worried Frank that they should be so determined, that their reasons should be such an enigma. What was driving them? What was it between Eve Black and Norcross?

His cell phone rang. The caravan was speeding north on Ball's Hill. Frank pulled the phone from his pocket. 'Geary.'

'Frank, this is Eve Black.' She spoke a shade above a whisper, and her voice had a husky, flirty quality.

'It is, is it? Nice to meet you.'

'I'm calling you from my new cell phone. I didn't have one, so Lore Hicks gifted me his. Wasn't that chivalrous of him? By the way, you might as well slow down. No need to risk an accident. The RV got away. There's just four dead people and Reed Barrows.'

'How do you know that?'

'Trust me, I know. Clint was surprised it was so easy to pull off the heist. I was, too, to be honest. We had a good laugh. I thought you were a little more on top of things. My mistake.'

'You should give yourself up, Ms Black.' Frank concentrated on measuring his words. On keeping the redness that wanted to over-take his mind at bay. 'Or you should give this – thing up. Whatever it is. You should do that before anyone gets hurt.'

'Oh, we're pretty well past the getting-hurt stage. Judge Silver, for instance, got a lot more than hurt. As did Dr Flickinger, who actually wasn't such a bad fellow when his head was clear. We're in the mass extinction stage.'

Frank choked the wheel of the cruiser. 'What the fuck *are* you?'

'I could ask you the same question, but I know what you'd say: "I am the Good Father." Because with you it's all Nana-Nana-Nana, isn't it? The protective daddy. Have you thought even once about all the other women, and what you might be doing to them? What you might be putting at risk?'

'How do you know about my daughter?'

'It's my business to know. There's an old blues song that goes, "Before you accuse me, take a look at yourself." You need to widen your perspective, Frank.'

What I need, Frank Geary thought, is my hands around your throat. 'What do you want?'

'I want you to man up! I want you to man the fuck up and make this interesting! I want your precious Nana to be able to go to school and say, "My daddy isn't just a civil servant who catches feral cats, and he isn't just a guy who punches walls or pulls on my favorite shirt or yells at Mom when things aren't going his way. He's also the man who stopped that wicked old fairy who put all the women to sleep."'

'Leave my daughter out of it, you bitch.'

The teasing note evaporated from her voice. 'When you protected her at the hospital, that was brave. I admired it. I admired *you*. I truly did. I know you love her, and that's no small thing. I know, in your way, all you want is the best for her. And that makes me love you a tiny bit, even though you're part of the problem.'

Ahead, the first two vehicles were pulling to a stop beside Reed Barrows's dented cruiser. Frank could see Barrows walking to meet them. Further on, he could see the bodies in the road.

'Stop this,' said Frank. 'Let them go. Let the women go. Not just my wife and daughter, all of them.'

Evie said, 'You'll have to kill me first.'

8

Angel asked who was this Frank that Evie had been talking to.

'He's the dragonslayer,' Evie said. 'I just needed to make sure that he wasn't going to allow himself to be distracted by unicorns.'

'You are so fuckin crazy.' Angel whistled.

Evie wasn't, but it wasn't an issue to debate with Angel – who, anyway, was entitled to her opinion.

CHAPTER 9

1

The fox comes to Lila in a dream. She knows it's a dream because the fox can talk.

'Hey, babe,' he says as he pads into the bedroom of the house on St George Street she's now sharing with Tiffany, Janice Coates, and two of the docs from the Women's Center – Erin Eisenberg and Jolie Suratt. (Erin and Jolie are unmarried. The third Women's Center doctor, Georgia Peekins, lives on the other side of town, with two daughters who sorely miss their big brother.) Another reason to know this is a dream is that she's alone in the room. The other twin bed, where Tiffany sleeps, is empty and neatly made up.

The fox puts its cunning forepaws – white rather than red, as if he has walked through fresh paint to get here – on the quilt that covers her.

'What do you want?' Lila asks.

'To show you the way back,' the fox says. 'But only if you want to go.'

2

When Lila opened her eyes, it was morning. Tiffany was in the other bed where she belonged, the blankets pushed down to her knees, her belly a half-moon above the boxer shorts she slept in. She was over seven months now.

Instead of going to the kitchen to brew up a nasty-tasting mess of the chicory that served them as coffee in this version of Dooling,

Lila went straight down the hall and opened the front door to a pleasant spring morning. (Time passed with such slippery limberness here; watches kept ordinary time, but there was really nothing ordinary about it.) The fox was there as she'd known it would be, sitting on the weed-choked slate path with its brush of a tail curled neatly around its paws. It regarded Lila with bright interest.

'Hey, babe,' Lila said. The fox cocked its head and seemed to smile. Then it trotted down the path to the broken street and sat again. Watching her. Waiting.

Lila went to wake Tiffany up.

3

In the end, seventeen residents of Our Place followed the fox in six of the solar-powered golf carts, a caravan trundling slowly out of town and then along what had been Route 31 toward Ball's Hill. Tiffany rode in the lead cart along with Janice and Lila, grousing the whole way about not being allowed to ride her horse. This had been nixed by Erin and Jolie, who were concerned about the strength of Tiff's contractions when she still had six or eight weeks to go. This much they had told the mom-to-be herself. What they hadn't passed on (although Lila and Janice knew) were their worries for the baby, which had been conceived while Tiffany was still using drugs on a daily – sometimes hourly – basis.

Mary Pak, Magda Dubcek, the four members of the First Thursday Book Club, and five erstwhile Dooling Correctional inmates were going. Also along was Elaine Nutting, formerly Geary. She rode with the two lady docs. Her daughter had wanted to come, but Elaine had put her foot down and kept it down even when tears began to flow. Nana had been left with old Mrs Ransom and her granddaughter. The two girls had become fast friends, but not even the prospect of spending a day with Molly had cheered Nana up. She wanted to follow the fox, she said, because it was like something out of a fairy tale. She wanted to draw it.

'Stay with your little girl, if you want,' Lila had told Elaine. 'We've got plenty of people.'

'What I *want* is to see what that thing wants,' Elaine had replied. Although in truth, she didn't know if she did or not. The fox – now sitting in front of the slumped ruin of Pearson's Barber Shop and waiting patiently for the women to assemble and get moving – filled her with a sense of foreboding, unfocused but strong.

'Come on!' Tiffany called grumpily. 'Before I need to pee again!'

And so they followed the fox as it trotted out of town along the faded white line in the center of the highway, occasionally looking back to make sure his troop was still there. Seeming to grin. Seeming almost to say, *There sure are some fine-looking women in the audience today.*

It was an outing – a strange one, granted, but still a day off from their various chores and jobs – and there should have been talking and laughter, but the women in the trundling line of golf carts were almost silent. The headlamps of the carts came on when they were rolling, and as they went past the jungle that had once been Adams Lumberyard, the thought came to Lila that they looked more like a funeral cortege than gals on an outing.

When the fox left the highway for an overgrown track a quarter mile past the lumberyard, Tiffany stiffened and put her hands protectively on her belly. 'No, no, no, you can stop right here and let me out. I ain't going back to Tru Mayweather's trailer, not even if it ain't no more than a pile of scrap metal.'

'That's not where we're going,' Lila said.

'How do you know?'

'Wait and see.'

As it turned out, the remains of the trailer were barely visible; a storm had knocked it off its blocks and it lay on its side in high weeds and brambles like a rusty dinosaur. Thirty or forty yards from it, the fox cut left and slipped into the woods. The women in the two lead carts saw a ruddy orange flash of fur, then it vanished.

Lila dismounted and went to where it had entered the woods. The ruins of the nearby shed had been entirely overgrown, but even after all this time, a sallow chemical smell remained. The meth may be gone, Lila thought, but the memories linger on. Even here, where time seems to gallop, pause for breath, then gallop again.

Janice, Magda, and Blanche McIntyre joined her. Tiffany remained in the golf cart, holding her belly. She looked ill.

'There's a game trail,' Lila said, pointing. 'We can follow it without much trouble.'

'I'm not goin in those woods, either,' Tiffany said. 'I don't care if that fox does a tap dance. I'm havin goddam contractions again.'

'You wouldn't be going even if you weren't having them,' Erin said. 'I'll stay with you. Jolie, you can go, if you want.'

Jolie did. The fifteen women went up the game trail in single file, Lila in the lead and the former Mrs Frank Geary bringing up the rear. They had been walking for almost ten minutes when Lila stopped and raised her arms, index fingers pointing both left and right like a traffic cop who can't make up her mind.

'Holy shit,' Celia Frode said. 'I never seen nothing like that. *Never.*'

The branches of the poplars, birches, and alders on either side were furred with moths. There seemed to be millions of them.

'What if they attack?' Elaine murmured, keeping her voice low and thanking God that she hadn't given in to Nana's demands to be brought along.

'They won't,' Lila said.

'How can you know that?' Elaine demanded.

'I just do,' Lila said. 'They're like the fox.' She hesitated, searching for the right word. 'They're emissaries.'

'For who?' Blanche asked. 'Or what?'

This was another question Lila chose not to answer, although she could have. 'Come on,' she said. 'Not far now.'

4

Fifteen women stood in thigh-high grass, staring at what Lila had come to think of as the Amazing Tree. No one said anything for perhaps thirty seconds. Then, in a high, gasping voice, Jolie Suratt said, 'My good God in heaven.'

The Tree rose like a living pylon in the sun, its various knotted trunks weaving around each other, sometimes concentrating shafts of sunlight filled with dusty pollen, sometimes creating dark caves.

Tropical birds disported among its many branches and gossiped in its ferny leaves. In front of it, the peacock Lila had seen before strutted back and forth like the world's most elegant doorman. The red snake was there, too, hanging from a branch, a reptilian trapeze artist penduluming lazily back and forth. Below the snake was a dark crevasse where the various boles seemed to draw back. Lila didn't remember this, but she wasn't surprised. Nor was she when the fox popped out of it like Jack from his box and took a playful snap at the peacock, who paid him no mind.

Janice Coates took Lila's arm. 'Are we seeing this?'

'Yes,' Lila said.

Celia, Magda, and Jolie screamed shrilly, in piercing three-part harmony. The white tiger was emerging from the split in the many-boled trunk. It surveyed the women at the edge of the clearing with its green eyes, then stretched long and low, seeming almost to bow to them.

'Stand still!' Lila shouted. 'Stand still, all of you! It won't harm you!' Hoping with all her heart and soul that it was true.

The tiger touched noses with the fox. It turned to the women again, seeming to fix on Lila with particular interest. Then it paced around the Tree and out of sight.

'My God,' Kitty McDavid said. She was weeping. 'How beautiful was that? How fucking oh–my–God beautiful was *that?*'

Magda Dubcek said, 'This is *svaté místo*. Holy place.' And she crossed herself.

Janice was looking at Lila. 'Tell me.'

'I think,' Lila said, 'it's a way out. A way back. If we want it.'

That was when the walkie–talkie on her belt came to life. There was a burst of static, and no way to make out words. But it sounded like Erin to Lila, and it sounded like she was yelling.

5

Tiffany was stretched across the front seat of the golf cart. An old St. Louis Rams tee-shirt that she had scrounged somewhere lay crumpled on the ground. Her breasts, once little more than nubbins, jutted skyward in a plain D-cup cotton bra. (The Lycra ones were now totally useless.) Erin was bent between her legs with her hands splayed on that amazing mound of belly. As the women came running, some brushing twigs and the odd moth from their hair, Erin bore down. Tiffany shrieked – '*Stop that, oh for God's sake stop!*' – and her legs shot out in a V.

'What are you doing?' Lila asked, reaching her, but when she looked down, what Erin was doing and why she was doing it became obvious. Tiff's jeans were unzipped. There was a stain on the blue denim and the cotton of Tiff's underpants was a damp pink.

'The baby is coming, and its butt is where its head should be,' Erin said.

'Oh my God, a breech?' Kitty said.

'I have to turn it around,' Erin said. 'Get us back to town, Lila.'

'We'll have to straighten her up,' Lila said. 'I can't drive until you do that.'

With the help of Jolie and Blanche McIntyre, Lila got Tiffany to a half-sitting position with Erin crammed in next to her. Tiffany screamed again. '*Oh, that hurts!*'

Lila slid behind the wheel of the cart, her right shoulder tight against Tiffany's left one. Erin had turned almost sideways to fit. 'How fast will this thing go?' she asked.

'I don't know, but we're going to find out.' Lila hit the accelerator pedal, wincing at Tiff's howl of pain as the cart jerked forward. Tiffany screamed at every jounce, and there were a lot of jounces. At that moment, the Amazing Tree with its freight of exotic birds was the farthest thing from Lila Norcross's mind.

This was not true of the former Elaine Geary.

6

They stopped at the Olympia Diner. Tiffany was in too much pain to go further. Erin sent Janice and Magda back to town to get her bag while Lila and three other women carried Tiffany inside.

'Pull a couple of the tables together,' said Erin, 'and do it fast. I need to straighten this baby out now, and I need Mom lying down to do it.'

Lila and Mary pushed over the tables. Margaret and Gail hefted Tiffany atop them, grimacing and turning their faces away, as if she were throwing mud at them instead of screams of objection.

Erin went back to work on Tiffany's stomach, kneading it like dough. 'I think it's starting to move, praise God. Come on, Junior, how about a little somersault for Dr E.?'

Erin bore down on Tiff's stomach with one hand while Jolie Suratt pushed sideways.

'Stop!' Tiffany screamed. 'Stop it, you fuckers!'

'It's turning,' said Erin, ignoring the profanity. 'Really turning, thank God. Yank her pants off, Lila. Pants and underpants. Jolie, keep pressing. Don't let it turn back.'

Lila took one leg of Tiffany's jeans, Celia Frode the other. They yanked and the old denims came off. Tiffany's underpants came with them part way, leaving brushstrokes of blood and amniotic fluid on her thighs. Lila pulled them the rest of the way. They were heavy with liquid, warm and sopping. She felt her gorge rise, then settle back into place.

The screams were constant now, Tiffany's head lashing from side to side.

'I can't wait for the bag,' Erin said. 'This baby is coming right now. Only . . .' She looked at her former office-mate, who nodded. 'Somebody get Jolie a knife. A sharp one. We have to cut her a little.'

'I-gotta-push,' Tiffany panted.

'The hell you do,' Jolie said. 'Not yet. The door's open, but we need to take the hinges off. Make a little more room.'

Lila found a steak knife, and in the bathroom, an ancient bottle of hydrogen peroxide. She doused the blade, stopped to consider the hand sanitizer by the door, and tried it. Nothing. The stuff inside had evaporated long ago. She hurried back. The women had surrounded Tiffany, Erin, and Jolie in a semi-circle. All were holding hands except for Elaine Geary, who had her arms wrapped tightly around her midsection. She was directing her gaze first to the counter, then to the empty booths, then out the door. Anywhere but at the panting, screaming woman on the makeshift operating table, now mother-naked save for an old cotton bra.

Jolie took the knife. 'Did you disinfect it with something?'

'Hydrogen per—'

'That'll do,' Erin said. 'Mary, find me a Styrofoam cooler if there's one around. One of you other ladies, get towels. There'll be some in the kitchen. Put them on top of the—'

A miserable howl from Tiffany as Jolie Suratt performed a steak-knife episiotomy, *sans* anesthetic.

'Put the towels on top of the golf carts,' Erin finished.

'Oh yeah, the solar panels!' That was Kitty. 'To heat em up. Hey, that's pretty sma—'

'We want them warm but not hot,' Erin said. 'I have no intention of roasting our newest citizen. Go on.'

Elaine stood where she was, letting the other women wash around her like water around a rock, continuing to direct her gaze at any object that was not Tiffany Jones. Her eyes were shiny and shallow.

'How close is she?' Lila asked.

'Seven centimeters,' Jolie said. 'She'll be at ten before you can say Jack Robinson. Cervical effacement is complete — one thing that went right, at least. Push, Tiffany. Save a little for next time, though.'

Tiffany pushed. Tiffany screamed. Tiffany's vagina flexed, then closed, then opened again. Fresh blood flowed between her legs.

'I don't like the blood.' Lila heard Erin mutter this to Jolie from the side of her mouth, like a racetrack tout passing on a hot tip. 'There's way too much. Christ, I wish I at least had my fetoscope.'

Mary came back with the sort of hard plastic cooler Lila had toted to Maylock Lake many times, when she and Clint and Jared used to go on picnics there. Printed on the side was **BUDWEISER! THE KING OF BEERS!** 'Will this do, Dr E.?'

'Fine,' Erin said, but didn't look up. 'Okay, Tiff, big push.'

'My back is killing me—' Tiffany said, but *me* became *meeeeeeeEEEEEEE* as her face contorted and her fists beat up and down on the chipped Formica of the tabletop.

'I see its head!' Lila shouted. 'I see its fa – oh, Christ, Erin, what—?'

Erin pushed Jolie aside and seized one of the baby's shoulders before it could retreat, her fingertips pressing deep in a way that made Lila feel ill. The baby's head slid forward tilted strenuously to one side, as if it was trying to look back to where it had come from. The eyes were shut, the face ashy gray. Looped around the neck and up one cheek toward the ear – like a hangman's noose – was a blood-spotted umbilical cord that made Lila think of the red snake hanging from the Amazing Tree. From the chest down, the infant was still inside its mother, but one arm had slithered free and hung down limply. Lila could see each perfect finger, each perfect nail.

'Quit pushing,' Erin said. 'I know you want to finish it, but don't push yet.'

'I need to,' Tiffany rasped.

'You'll strangle your baby if you do,' Jolie said. She was back beside Erin, shoulder to shoulder. 'Wait. Just . . . just give me a second . . .'

Too late, thought Lila. It's already strangled. You only have to look at that gray face.

Jolie worked one finger beneath the umbilical cord, then two. She flexed the fingers in a come-on gesture, first pulling the cord away from the infant's neck and then slipping it off. Tiffany screamed, every tendon in her neck standing out in stark relief.

'Push!' Erin said. 'Just as hard as you can! On three! Jolie, don't let it face-plant on this filthy fucking floor when it comes! Tiff! One, two, *three*!'

Tiffany pushed. The baby seemed to shoot into Jolie Suratt's hands. It was slimy, it was beautiful, and it was dead.

'Straw!' Jolie shouted. 'Get a straw! Now!'

Elaine stepped forward. Lila hadn't seen her move. She already had one ready, the paper stripped off. 'Here.'

Erin took the straw. 'Lila,' Erin said. 'Open his mouth.'

His. Until then, Lila hadn't noticed the tiny gray comma below the baby's stomach.

'Open his mouth!' Erin repeated.

Carefully, Lila used two fingers to do as she was told. Erin put one end of the straw in her own mouth and the other in the tiny opening Lila's fingers had created.

'Now push up on his chin,' Jolie instructed. 'Gotta create suction.'

What point? Dead was dead. But Lila once more obeyed orders, and saw shadowy crescents appear in Erin Eisenberg's cheeks as she sucked on her end. There was an audible sound – *flup*. Erin turned her head aside to spit out what looked like a wad of phlegm. Then she nodded to Jolie, who raised the baby to her face and blew gently into its mouth.

The baby just lay there, head back, beads of blood and foam on its bald head. Jolie blew again, and a miracle happened. The tiny chest heaved; the blue eyes popped sightlessly open. He began to wail. Celia Frode started the applause, and the others joined in . . . except for Elaine, who had retreated to where she was earlier, her arms once again clasping her midsection. The baby's cries were constant now. Its hands made tiny fists.

'That's my baby,' Tiffany said, and raised her arms. 'My baby is crying. Give him to me.'

Jolie tied off the umbilical cord with a rubber band and wrapped the baby in the first thing that came to hand – a waitress's apron someone had grabbed from a coathook. She passed the wailing bundle to Tiffany, who looked into his face, laughed, and kissed one gummy cheek.

'Where are those towels?' Erin demanded. 'Get them now.'

'They won't be too warm yet,' Kitty said.

'Get them.'

The towels were brought and Mary lined the Budweiser cooler with them. While she did, Lila saw more blood gushing from between Tiffany's legs. A lot of blood. Pints, maybe.

'Is that normal?' someone asked.

'Perfectly.' Erin's voice was firm and sure, confidence personified: absolutely no problem here. That was when Lila began to suspect that Tiffany was probably going to die. 'But someone bring me more towels.'

Jolie Suratt moved to take the baby from his mother and put

him in the makeshift Budweiser bassinet. Erin shook her head. 'Let her hold him a little longer.'

That was when Lila knew for sure.

7

Sundown in what had once been the town of Dooling and was now Our Place.

Lila was sitting on the front stoop of the house on St George Street with a stapled sheaf of paper in her hands when Janice Coates came up the walk. When Janice sat down next to her, Lila caught a scent of juniper. From a pocket inside her quilted vest, the ex-warden removed the source: a pint bottle of Schenley's gin. She held it out to Lila. Lila shook her head.

'Retained placenta,' Janice said. 'That's what Erin told me. No way to scrape it out, at least not in time to stop the bleeding. And none of that drug they use.'

'Pitocin,' Lila said. 'I had it when Jared was born.'

They sat quiet for awhile, watching the light drain from what had been a very long day. At last Janice said, 'I thought you might like some help cleaning out her stuff.'

'Already done. She didn't have much.'

'None of us do. Which is sort of a relief, don't you think? We learned a poem in school, something about getting and spending laying waste to all our powers. Keats, maybe.'

Lila, who had learned the same poem, knew it was Wordsworth, but said nothing. Janice returned the bottle to the pocket it had come from and brought out a relatively clean handkerchief. She used it to wipe first one of Lila's cheeks, then the other, an action that brought back painfully sweet memories of Lila's mother, who had done the same thing on the many occasions when her daughter, a self-confessed tomboy, had taken a tumble from her bike or her skateboard.

'I found this in the dresser where she was keeping her baby things,' Lila said, handing Janice the thin pile of pages. 'It was under some nightshirts and bootees.'

On the front, Tiffany had pasted a picture of a laughing, perfectly permed mommy holding up a laughing baby in a shaft of golden sunlight. Janice was pretty sure it had been clipped from a Gerber baby food ad in an old women's magazine – maybe *Good Housekeeping*. Below it, Tiffany had lettered: **ANDREW JONES BOOK FOR A GOOD LIFE**.

'She knew it was a boy,' Lila said. 'I don't know how she knew, but she did.'

'Magda told her. Some old wives' tale about carrying high.'

'She must have been working on this for quite awhile, and I never saw her at it.' Lila wondered if Tiffany had been embarrassed. 'Look at the first page. That's what started the waterworks.'

Janice opened the little homemade book. Lila leaned close to her and they read it together.

10 RULES FOR GOOD LIVING

1 Be kind to others & they will be kind to you
2 Do not use drugs for fun EVER
3 If you are wrong, apologize
4 God sees what you do wrong but HE is kind & will forgive
5 Do not tell lies as that becomes a habit
6 Never whip a horse
7 Your body is your tempul so DO NOT SMOKE
8 Do not cheet, give everyone a SQUARE SHAKE
9 Be careful of the friends you choose, I was not
10 Remember your mother will always love you & you will be OKAY!

'It was the last one that really got me,' Lila said. 'It still does. Give me that bottle. I guess I need a nip after all.'

Janice handed it over. Lila swallowed, grimaced, and handed it back. 'How's the baby? Okay?'

'Considering he was born six weeks shy of term, and wearing his umbilical cord for a necklace, he's doing very well,' Janice said.

'Thank God we had Erin and Jolie along, or we would have lost them both. He's with Linda Bayer and Linda's baby. Linda quit nursing Alex a little while ago, but as soon as she heard Andy crying, her milk came right back in. So she says. Meanwhile, we've got another tragedy on our hands.'

As if Tiffany wasn't enough for one day, Lila thought, and tried to put her game face on. 'Tell me.'

'Gerda Holden? Oldest of the four Holden girls? She's disappeared.'

Which almost certainly meant something mortal had happened to her in that other world. They all accepted this as a fact now.

'How's Clara taking it?'

'About as you'd expect,' Janice replied. 'She's half out of her mind. She and all the girls have been experiencing that weird vertigo for the last week or so—'

'So someone's moving them around.'

Janice shrugged. 'Maybe. Probably. Whatever it is, Clara's afraid another of her girls is going to blip out of existence at any moment. Maybe all three of them. I'd be afraid, too.' She began flipping through the Andrew Jones Book for a Good Life. Every page was filled with an expansion of the 10 Rules.

'Should we talk about the Tree?' Lila asked.

Janice considered, then shook her head. 'Maybe tomorrow. Tonight I just want to sleep.'

Lila, who wasn't sure she could sleep, took Janice's hand and squeezed it.

8

Nana had asked her mother if she could sleep over with Molly at Mrs Ransom's house, and Elaine gave her permission after ascertaining that it would be all right with the old lady.

'Of course,' Mrs Ransom said. 'Molly and I love Nana.'

That was good enough for the former Elaine Geary, who was for once glad to have her little girl out of the house. Nana was her dear one, her jewel – a rare point of agreement with her estranged husband, and one that had kept the marriage together longer than it might have survived otherwise – but this evening Elaine had an important errand to run. One that was more for Nana than it was for her. For all the women of Dooling, really. Some of them (Lila Norcross, for instance) might not understand that now, but they would later.

If, that was, she decided to go through with it.

The golf carts they'd taken on the expedition to that weird tree in the woods were all neatly parked in the lot behind what was left of the Municipal Building. One good thing you could say for women, she thought – one of *many* things – was that they usually put things away when they were done with them. Men were different. They left their possessions scattered hell to breakfast. How many times had she told Frank to put his dirty clothes in the hamper – wasn't it enough that she washed them and ironed them, without having to pick them up, as well? And how many times did she still find them in the bathroom outside the shower, or littered across the bedroom floor? And could he be bothered to rinse a glass or wash a dish after a late night snack? No! It was as if dishes and glasses became invisible once their purpose had been served. (The fact that her husband kept his office immaculate and his animal cages spotless made such thoughtless behavior more irritating.)

Small things, you would say, and who could disagree? They were! But over the course of years, those things became a domestic version of an old Chinese torture she'd read about in a Time-Life book that she'd pulled out of a donation box at Goodwill. *The Death of a Thousand Cuts*, it was called. Frank's bad temper had only been the worst and deepest of those cuts. Oh, sometimes there was a present, or a soft kiss on the back of the neck, or a dinner out (with candlelight!), but those things were just frosting on a stale and hard-to-chew cake. The Cake of Marriage! She was not prepared to say every man was the same, but the majority were, because the instincts came with the package. With the penis. A man's home was his castle, so the saying went, and etched into the XY chromosome was a deep belief that every man was a king and every woman his serving maid.

The keys were still in the carts. Of course they were – there might be an occasional case of petty pilfering in Our Place, but there had been no real theft. That was one of the nice things about it. There were many nice things, but not everyone could be content with those things. Take all the whining and whingeing that went on at the Meetings, for instance. Nana had been at some of those meetings. She didn't think Elaine knew, but Elaine did. A good mother monitors her child, and knows when she is being infected by bad companions with bad ideas.

Two days ago it had been Molly at their house, and the two girls had a wonderful time, first playing outside (hopscotch and jump-rope), then inside (re-decorating the large dollhouse Elaine had felt justified in liberating from the Dooling Mercantile), then outside again until the sun went down. They had eaten a huge supper, after which Molly had walked the two blocks back to her house in the gloaming. By herself. And why could she do that? Because in this world there were no predators. No pedophiles.

A happy day. And that was why Elaine was so surprised (and a bit fearful, why not admit it) when she had paused outside her daughter's door on the way to bed and heard Nana crying.

Elaine chose a golf cart, turned the key, and toed the little round accelerator pedal. She rolled soundlessly out of the lot and down Main Street, past the dead streetlights and dark storefronts. Two miles out of town she reached a neat white building with two useless gas pumps out front. The sign on the roof proclaimed it the Dooling Country Living Store. The owner, Kabir Patel, was gone, of course, as were his three well-mannered (in public, at least) sons. His wife had been visiting her family in India when the Aurora struck, and was presumably cocooned in Mumbai or Lucknow or one of those other places.

Mr Patel had sold a bit of everything – it was the only way to compete with the supermarket – but most of it was gone now. The liquor had disappeared first, of course; women liked to drink, and who taught them to enjoy it? Other women? Rarely.

Without pausing to look in the darkened store, Elaine drove her golf cart around to the back. Here was a long metal annex with a sign out front reading Country Living Store Auto Supply Shop

Come Here First And SAVE! Mr Patel had kept it neat, she would give him points for that. Elaine's father had done small-engine repair to supplement his income as a plumber – in Clarksburg, this had been – and the two sheds out back where he worked had been dotted with cast-off parts, bald tires, and any number of derelict mowers and rototillers. An eyesore, Elaine's mother had complained. It pays for your Fridays at the beauty salon, replied the king of the castle, and so the mess had remained.

Elaine needed to put her whole weight against one of the doors before it would move on its dirty track, but eventually she got it to slide four or five feet, and that was all she needed.

'What's the matter, sweetie?' she had asked her crying daughter – before she'd known that damned tree existed, when she'd thought her child's tears were the only problem she had, and that they would end as quickly as a spring shower. 'Does your tummy hurt from supper?'

'No,' Nana said, 'and you don't need to call it my tummy, Mom. I'm not *five*.'

That exasperated tone was new, and set Elaine back on her heels a bit, but she continued to stroke Nana's hair. 'What is it, then?'

Nana's lips had tightened, trembled, and then she had burst. 'I miss Daddy! I miss Billy, he held my hand sometimes when we walked to school and that was nice, *he* was nice, but mostly I miss Daddy! I want this vacation to be over! I want to go back *home!*'

Instead of stopping, as spring showers did, her weeping had become a storm. When Elaine tried to stroke her cheek, Nana knocked her hand away and sat up in bed with her hair wild and staticky around her face. In that moment, Elaine saw Frank in her. She saw him so clearly it was scary.

'Don't you remember how he shouted at us?' Elaine asked. 'And the time he punched the wall! That was awful, wasn't it?'

'He shouted at *you!*' Nana shouted. 'At *you*, because you always wanted him to do something . . . or get something . . . or be something different . . . I don't know, but he never shouted at *me!*'

'He pulled your shirt, though,' Elaine said. Her disquiet deepened into something like horror. Had she thought Nana had forgotten

Frank? Relegated him to the junkheap along with her invisible friend, Mrs Humpty-Dump? 'It was your favorite, too.'

'Because he was afraid of the man with the car! The one who ran over the cat! He was taking care of me!'

'Remember when he yelled at your teacher, remember how embarrassed you were?'

'I don't care! I *want* him!'

'Nana, that's enough. You've made your p—'

'*I want my daddy!*'

'You need to close your eyes and go to sleep and have sweet dr—'

'I WANT MY DADDY!'

Elaine had left the room, closing the door gently behind her. What an effort it had been not to descend to the child's level and slam it! Even now, standing in Mr Patel's oil-smelling shed, she would not admit how close she had come to shouting at her daughter. It wasn't Nana's strident tone, so unlike her usual soft and tentative voice; it wasn't even the physical resemblance to Frank, which she could usually overlook. It was how much she sounded like him as she made her unreasonable and unfulfillable demands. It was almost as if Frank Geary had reached across from the other side of whatever gulf separated that violent old world from this new one, and possessed her child.

Nana had seemed her old self the next day, but Elaine had been unable to stop thinking about the tears heard through the door, and the way Nana knocked away the hand that had meant only to comfort, and that ugly, yelling voice that came from Nana's child's mouth: *I want my daddy.* Nor was that all. She had been holding hands with ugly little Billy Beeson from down the block. She missed her little boyfriend, who probably would have enjoyed taking her behind a bush so they could play doctor. It was even easy to imagine Nana and the scabrous Billy at sixteen, making out in the back of his father's Club Cab. French kissing and auditioning her for the position of first cook and bottle washer in his shitty little castle. Forget about drawing pictures, Nana, get out in the kitchen and rattle those pots and pans. Fold my clothes. Haul my ashes, then I'll burp and roll over and go to sleep.

Elaine had brought a crank flashlight, which she now shone on the interior of the auto annex, which had been left alone. With no fuel to run Dooling's autos, there was no need for fan belts and spark plugs. So what she was looking for might be here. Plenty of that stuff had been stored in her father's workshop, and the oily smell in this one was just the same, bringing back with startling vividness memories of the pigtailed girl she'd been (but not with nostalgia, oh no). Handing her father parts and tools as he called for them, stupidly happy when he thanked her, cringing if he scolded her for being slow or grabbing the wrong thing. Because she had wanted to please him. He was her daddy, big and strong, and she wanted to please him in all things.

This world was ever so much better than the old man-driven one. No one yelled at her here, and no one yelled at Nana. No one treated them like second-class citizens. This was a world where a little girl could walk home by herself, even after dark, and feel safe. A world where a little girl's talent could grow along with her hips and breasts. No one would nip it in the bud. Nana didn't understand that, and she wasn't alone; if you didn't think so, all you had to do was listen in at one of those stupid meetings.

I think it's a way out, Lila had said as the women stood in the tall grass, looking at that weird tree. And oh God, if she was right.

Elaine walked deeper into the auto supply shed, training the flashlight beam on the floor, because the floor was concrete, and concrete kept things cool. And there, in the far corner, was what she had been hoping for: three five-gallon cans with their pour-tops screwed down tight. They were plain metal, unmarked, but there was a thick red rubber band girdling one of them and blue bands around the other two. Her father had marked his tins of kerosene in exactly the same way.

I think it's a way out. A way back. If we want it.

Some of them undoubtedly would. The Meeting women who couldn't understand what a good thing they had here. What a fine thing. What a safe thing. These were the ones so socialized to generations of servitude that they would eagerly rush back into their chains. The ones from the prison would, counterintuitively, probably be the first to want to go home to the old world, and right back into the pokey from which they'd been released. So many of these childish creatures were unable or unwilling to realize that there was nearly always some unindicted male co-conspirator behind their incarceration. Some man for whom they'd degraded themselves. In her years as a volunteer, Elaine had seen it, and heard it all a million times over. 'He's got a good heart.' 'He doesn't mean it.' 'He promises he'll change.' Hell, she was vulnerable to it herself. In the midst of that endless day and night, before they fell asleep and were transported, she'd almost let herself believe, in spite of everything she'd experienced with Frank in the past, that he would do what she asked, that he would get control of his temper. Of course, he hadn't.

Elaine didn't believe Frank *could* change. It was his male nature. But he had changed her. Sometimes she thought that Frank had driven her mad. To him, she was the scold, the taskmaster, the grating alarm bell that ended recess each day. It awed her, Frank's obliviousness to the weight of her responsibilities. Did he actually believe it made her happy, having to remind him to pay bills, to pick up things, to keep his temper in check? She was certain that he actually did. Elaine was not blind: she saw that her husband was not a contented man. But he did not see her at all.

She had to act, for the sake of Nana and all the others. That was what had come into focus that very afternoon, even as Tiffany Jones was dying in that diner, giving up the last of her poor wrecked life so that a child might live.

There would be women who wanted to return. Not a majority, Elaine had to believe most of the women here were not so insane, so masochistic, but could she take that chance? Could she, when her own sweet Nana, who had shrunk into herself every time her father raised his voice—

Stop thinking about it, she told herself. Concentrate on your business.

The red band meant cheap kerosene, and would probably be of

no more use to her than the gasoline stored under the town's various service stations. You could douse a lit match in red-band kerosene once it was old. But those blue bands meant that a stabilizer had been added, and that kind might retain its volatility for ten years or more.

The Tree they'd found that day might be amazing, but it was still a tree, and trees burned. There was the tiger to reckon with, of course, but she would take a gun. Scare it away, shoot it if necessary. (She knew how to shoot; her father had taught her.) Part of her thought that might turn out to be a needless precaution. Lila had called the tiger and the fox emissaries, and to Elaine, that felt right. She had an idea that the tiger would not try to stop her, that the Tree was essentially unguarded.

If it was a door, it needed to be closed for good.

Someday Nana would understand, and thank her for doing the right thing.

9

Lila did sleep, but woke shortly after five, with the coming day just a sour line of light on the eastern horizon. She got up and used the chamber pot. (Running water had come to Dooling, but it had not yet reached the house on St George. 'A week or two, perhaps,' Magda assured them.) Lila considered going back to bed, but knew she would only toss and turn and think about how Tiffany – ashy gray at the end – had lost consciousness for the final time with her newborn baby still in her arms. Andrew Jones, whose only legacy would be a stapled-together booklet of handwritten pages.

She dressed, and left the house. She had no particular destination in mind, but wasn't entirely surprised when she saw the shattered hulk of the Municipal Building ahead of her; she had spent most of her adult life working there. It was a kind of magnetic north, even though there was nothing there now, really, to see. A fire of some sort had done the damage – started by a lightning strike, maybe, or faulty wiring. The side of the building that had contained Lila's office was blackened rubble, while years of weather had swept through the broken walls and windows and done their work on the other half, making the drywall soft for mold, blowing in debris that had gathered in layers across the floors.

So it surprised Lila to see someone sitting on the granite steps. The steps were about all the old building had going for it anymore.

As she drew closer, the figure stood and approached her.

'Lila?' Although full of uncertainty and thick with recently shed tears, the voice was familiar. 'Lila, is it you?'

New women appeared only rarely now, and if this was to be the last, there could be no better. Lila ran to her, embraced her, kissed her on both cheeks. 'Linny! Oh God, it's so good to see you!'

Linny Mars hugged her back with panicky force, then held her away so she could look at Lila's face. Making sure. Lila understood perfectly and remained still. But Linny was smiling, and the tears on her cheeks were good ones. It felt to Lila as if some divine scale had been balanced – Tiffany's departure on one side, Linny's arrival on the other.

'How long have you been sitting there?' Lila asked at last.

'I don't know,' said Linny. 'An hour, maybe two. I saw the moon go down. I . . . I didn't know where else to go. I was in the office, looking at my laptop, and then . . . how did I get here? Where *is* here?'

'It's complicated,' Lila replied, and as she led Linny back to the steps, it occurred to her that this was a thing women said often, men almost never. 'In a sense, you're still in the office, only in one of the cocoons. Or at least, that's what we think.'

'Are we dead? Ghosts? Is that what you're saying?'

'No. This is a real place.' Lila hadn't been completely sure of this at first, but now she was. Familiarity might or might not breed contempt, but it certainly bred belief.

'How long have you been here?'

'At least eight months. Maybe more. Time moves faster on this side of – well, whatever it is that we're on. I'd guess that over there – where you've come from – it's not even been a full week since Aurora started, right?'

'Five days. I think.' Linny sat back down.

Lila felt like a woman who has been long abroad, and was eager for news of home. 'Tell me what's happening in Dooling.'

Linny squinted at Lila and then gestured at the street. 'But this *is* Dooling, isn't it? Only it looks kind of cracked up.'

'We're working on that,' Lila said. 'Tell me what was going on when you left. Have you heard from Clint? Do you know anything about Jared?' That was unlikely, but she had to ask.

'I can't tell you much,' Linny said, 'because the last two days all I could think about was staying awake. I kept taking those drugs in the evidence room, the ones from the Griner brothers bust, but by the end they were hardly working at all. And there was weird stuff. People coming and going. Yelling. Somebody new in charge. I think his name was Dave.'

'Dave who?' It was all Lila could do to keep from shaking her dispatcher.

Linny frowned down at her hands, concentrating, trying to remember.

'Not Dave,' she said at last. 'Frank. A big guy. He was wearing a uniform, not a cop's uniform, but then he changed it for a cop's uniform. Frank Gearhart, maybe?'

'Do you mean Frank Geary? The animal control officer?'

'Yes,' Linny said. 'Geary, that's right. Boy, he's intense. A man on a mission.'

Lila didn't know what to make of the Geary news. She remembered interviewing him for the job that had gone to Dan Treat. Geary had been impressive in person – quick, confident – but his record as an animal control officer had troubled her. He'd been way too free with citations, and received too many complaints.

'What about Terry? He's the senior officer, he should have taken my place.'

'Drunk,' Linny said. 'A couple of the other deputies were laughing about it.'

'What do you—'

Linny raised her hand to stop her. 'But then right before I fell asleep, some men came in and said Terry wanted the guns from the armament room because of a woman up at the prison. The one who talked to me was that public defender guy, the one you say reminds you of Will Gardner on *The Good Wife.*'

'Barry Holden?' Lila didn't get it. The woman up at the prison was undoubtedly Evie Black, and Barry had helped Lila get Evie in a cell at Correctional, but why would he—

'Yes, him. And some others were with him. One was a woman. Warden Coates's daughter, I think.'

'That can't be,' Lila said. 'She works in DC.'

'Well, maybe it was someone else. By then it was like I was in a deep fog. But I remember Don Peters, because of how he tried to feel me up on New Year's Eve last year at the Squeaky Wheel.'

'Peters from the prison? He was with Barry?'

'No, Peters came after. He was furious when he found out some of the guns were gone. "They got all of the good ones," he said, I remember that, and there was a kid with him and that kid said . . . he said . . .' Linny looked at Lila with enormous eyes. 'He said, "What if they're taking them to Norcross, up at the prison? How will we get the bitch out then?"'

In her mind Lila pictured a tug-of-war rope, with Evie Black as the knot in the middle that would mean victory for one side or the other.

'What else do you remember? Think, Linny, this is important!' Although what could she, Lila, do about it, even if it was?

'Nothing,' Linny said. 'After Peters and the young guy went running out, I fell asleep. And woke up here.' She looked around doubtfully, still not sure that there was a here. 'Lila?'

'Mmm?'

'Is there anything to eat? I guess I really must not be dead, because I'm *starving.*'

'Sure,' Lila said, helping the other woman to her feet. 'Scrambled eggs and toast, how does that sound?'

'Like heaven. I feel like I could eat half a dozen eggs and have room left over for pancakes.'

But as it turned out, Linnette Mars never got breakfast; she had, in fact, eaten her last meal the day before (two cherry Pop-Tarts microwaved in the sheriff's station break room). As the two women turned onto St George Street, Lila felt Linny's hand melt away in her own. She caught just a glimpse of Linny from the corner of her eye, looking startled. Then there was nothing left but a cloud of moths, rising into the morning sky.

CHAPTER 10

1

There could be no telling, Lowell Griner Sr used to say, where a deep seam of coal might begin. 'Sometimes a single chisel's worth of difference is all there is tween the shit and the Shinola,' was how he put it. This pearl had dropped from the old crank's lips, around about the time when many of the Tri-Counties' best miners had been marching through the fucked-up, fucked-over boonies of Southeast Asia, getting jungle rot and smoking heroin-laced fatties. This was a conflict the elder Griner had missed, given a lack of two toes on his right foot and one finger on his left hand.

Few men who ever walked the green earth spoke more nonsense than the late Lowell Griner Sr – he had also believed in UFOs, vengeful spirits of the woods, and had taken as gold the empty promises of the coal companies. Big Lowell Griner, he was called, perhaps in honor of that old Jimmy Dean song about Big John. Big Low had rested snug in his coffin for ten years now, along with a full bottle of Rebel Yell and a pair of lungs that were as black as the bituminate he mined.

His son Lowell Jr (naturally known as Little Low) had recalled his father's words with rueful amusement after Sheriff Lila Norcross nipped him and his older brother Maynard with ten kilos of cocaine, a pharmacy's worth of speed, and all of their guns. It had certainly appeared that the seam of their luck had come to an abrupt end, the Shinola magically turning to shit the moment the sheriff's team used the department's bull-ram on the kitchen door of the old family manse, a creekside farmhouse for which the term *tumbledown* was too grand.

Though Little Low (who actually stood an inch over six feet and weighed in at two-forty) was not sorry about anything that he had done, he was extremely sorry that it had all not lasted longer. In the weeks that he and Maynard had spent locked up in the county jail in Coughlin awaiting transfer, he had whiled away most of his free time dreaming on the fun they'd had: the sports cars they'd drag-raced, the fine houses they'd crashed in, the girls they'd screwed, and the numerous slobs they'd stomped, outsiders who'd tried horning in on the Griner patch and had ended up buried in the hills. For the better part of five years they'd been serious players, up and down the Blue Ridge. It had been a hell of a hot ride, but now it seemed to have turned cold.

They were, in fact, fucked in every orifice. The cops had the drugs, had the weapons, had Kitty McDavid to say that she had witnessed Lowell exchanging packets of cash for bundles of coke with their cartel connection on multiple occasions, and that she had seen him shoot that Alabama fool who had tried to pass them counterfeit bills. The cops even had the bump of C4 that they had socked away for the Fourth of July. (The plan had been to put it under a silo and see if they could get the motherfucker to lift off like one of those Cape Carnival rockets.) As good as the ride had been, Lowell wasn't sure how long re-running the memories could sustain him. Thinking of those memories growing thin and then falling apart was a downer.

When they ran out, Little Low thought he would probably just have to kill himself. He wasn't afraid of that. What he was afraid of was choking on boredom in some cell the way Big Low, confined to a wheelchair and sucking on Yell and bottled oxygen for the last few years of his life, had choked to death on his own snot. Maynard, quarter-wit that he was, would probably be fine for a few decades in prison. That wasn't Little Lowell Griner Jr, though. He wasn't interested in playing out a junk hand just to stay in the game.

Then, as they were awaiting a pre-trial conference, the shit had turned back into Shinola. God bless Aurora, the vehicle of their deliverance.

Said deliverance had arrived last Thursday afternoon, the day the sleeping sickness had come to Appalachia. Lowell and Maynard were shackled to a bench outside a meeting room at the Coughlin court-house. Both the prosecutor and their lawyer should have arrived an hour earlier.

'What the fuck,' announced the prick from the Coughlin Police Department who was keeping an eye on them. 'This is stupid. I don't get paid enough to babysit you murdering peckerwoods all day. I'm going to see what the judge wants to do.'

Through the reinforced glass opposite their bench, Lowell could see that Judge Wainer, the only one of the three officials who had seen fit to show up for the hearing, had lowered her head between her arms and dropped off for a little snooze. Neither of the brothers had, at this point, any idea about Aurora. Nor had the prick cop.

'Hope she bites his head off for wakin her up,' Maynard had remarked.

This was not exactly what happened when the horrified officer tore away the mask of webbing that had grown over the Honorable Judge Regina Alberta Wainer's face, but it was, as the saying went, close enough for government work.

Lowell and Maynard, chain-locked to the bench, saw it all through the reinforced glass. It was awesome. The judge, no more than five-one in heels, rose up righteous and smote the cop, say hallelujah, in the chest with a gold-tipped fountain pen. That put the bastard on the carpet and she pressed the advantage, scooping up her nearby gavel and beating his face in before he had chance to fart sideways or holler Your Honor, I object. Then Judge Wainer tossed aside her gory gavel, sat down again, lowered her head back to her crossed arms, and resumed snoozing.

'Brother, did you see that?' Maynard asked.

'I did.'

Maynard had shaken his head, making the unwashed clots of his long hair fly. 'That was amazin. I be dog.'

'Court is fucking adjourned,' Lowell agreed.

Maynard – firstborn but named for an uncle when his parents felt sure the baby would die before the sun went down on his natal day – had a caveman beard and wide dull eyes. Even when he was dropping fists on some poor sonofabitch, he tended to look dumbfounded. 'What do we do now?'

What they did was bang around until they broke the arms of the bench they were shackled to, and enter the conference room, laying a trail of shattered wood behind them. Careful not to disturb the sleeping Judge Wainer – the webbing was spinning around her head, thickening again – they nicked the cop's keys and unlocked themselves. The brothers also requisitioned the dead prick's gun, his Taser, and the keys to his GMC pickup.

'Look at this spider shit,' Maynard whispered, gesturing at the judge's new coating.

'No time,' Little Low said.

A door at the end of the hall – opened with the prick's pass card – led to a second hall. As they passed the open door of a staff room, not a single one of the dozen-plus men and women inside – cops, secretaries, lawyers – paid them any mind. They were all focused on NewsAmerica, where bizarre and horrific footage showed some Amish chick on a table rearing up and biting the nose off a man attending to her.

At the end of this second hall was an exit into the parking lot. Lowell and Maynard strolled out into bright sunshine and free air, big as life and happy as hound dogs in a barking contest. The dead cop's GMC was parked nearby, and in the center console was a goodly supply of shitkicking music. The Brothers Griner agreed on Brooks and Dunn, followed by Alan Jackson, who was a good old boy for sure.

They boot-scooted their way to a nearby campground and parked the Jimmy-Mac behind a forest ranger outpost that had been closed in a round of cutbacks years before. The lock on the outpost door popped with one shove. A woman's uniform hung in the closet. Luckily, she had been a large lady, and at Lowell's command, Maynard squeezed into it. Dressed as such, it was easy to convince the driver of a Chevy Silverado in the campground parking lot to step away for a word.

'Is there something wrong with my camping permit?' Silverado Man asked Maynard. 'This disease news has got me all turned around, I'll tell you what. I mean, whoever heard of such a thing?' Then, with a glance at the tag on Maynard's chest: 'Say, how'd you get the name Susan?'

Little Low gave this question the answer it deserved by stepping out from behind a tree and using a junk of firewood to split Silverado Man's skull. He was approximately Lowell's height and weight. After Low dressed in Silverado Man's clothes, the brothers wrapped the body in a tarp and put it in the back of their new vehicle. They transferred the dead cop's music and drove to a hunting cabin that they had stocked for a rainy day long before. On the way, they burned through the rest of the CDs, agreeing that this James McMurtry fellow was probably a communist, but Hank III was the total package.

Once at the cabin, they alternated between the radio and the police scanner they kept there, hoping to glean intelligence concerning the police response to their escape.

Initially, Lowell found the complete inattention to said escape unnerving. By the second day, however, the snowballing events of the Aurora phenomenon – which explained the lady judge's rough treatment of the Coughlin cop and the crap on her face – were so encompassing and cataclysmic that Lowell's apprehension evaporated. Who had time for two country outlaws amid mass riots, plane crashes, nuclear meltdowns, and people incinerating chicks in their sleep?

2

On Monday, as Frank Geary was planning his assault on the women's prison, Lowell was reclining on the moldy couch in the hunting cabin, gnawing on deer jerky and visualizing their own next moves. Though the authorities were currently in disarray, they would be reestablished in some form or another before long. Moreover, if things turned out the way they appeared to be headed, those authorities would likely be all-rooster, which meant that it would be the Wild West – hang em now, hang em high, ask questions later. The Griner brothers wouldn't stay forgotten forever, and when they were remembered, the jackboots would be polished and primed to kick ass.

The news on the radio had initially caused Maynard to fall into gloom. 'Is this the end of fuckin, Lowell?' he'd asked.

A little blue at the thought himself, Low had replied that they'd think of something . . . as if there might be some alternative. He was thinking of some old song about how birds do it, bees do it, even educated fleas do it.

His older brother's mood had improved, however, at the discovery of a jigsaw puzzle in a cabinet. Now Maynard, in his camo underwear, on his knees by the coffee table, was drinking a Schlitz and working away on it. The puzzle showed Krazy Kat with his finger in a socket, getting electrocuted. Maynard enjoyed puzzles as long as they weren't too hard. (This was another reason why Lowell had felt good about his brother's possible prison future. They had a shit-ton of puzzles in prison.) The picture of Krazy Kat in the center was pretty much done, but the pale green wall surrounding the figure was giving May fits. He complained it all looked the same, which was cheating.

'We need to clean up,' Lowell announced.

'I told you,' Maynard said, 'I put that old boy's head inside a hollow log and dropped the rest of him down a hole.' (Low's older brother broke down bodies the way other folks broke down turkeys. It was eccentric, but it seemed to bring May satisfaction.)

'That's a start, May, but it's not enough. We need to clean up even better while everything is still fucked up. A clean sweep, so to speak.'

Maynard finished his beer, pitched the can away. 'How do we do that?'

'We burn down the Dooling Sheriff's Department to start with. That'll take care of the evidence,' Lowell explained. 'That's big numero uno.'

His brother's slack-faced expression of puzzlement suggested elaboration was necessary.

'Our drugs, May. They got everthing in the bust. We burn those up, they got nothing solid.' Lowell could envision it – just wonderful. He had never known how much he wanted to obliterate a police station. 'Then, just to make sure we've got our t's crossed, we make a visit to the prison up there and deal with Kitty McDavid.' Low sawed a finger across his unshaven neck to show his brother exactly how that deal would go down.

'Aw, she's probly asleep.'

Low had considered this. 'What if the scientists figure out how to wake them all up?'

'Maybe her memory will be wiped out even if they do. You know, amnesia, like on *Days of Our Lives*.'

'And what if it's not, May? When does anything work out as convenient as that? The McDavid cunt can put us away for the rest of our lives. That ain't even the important thing. She *snitched*, that's the important thing. She needs to go for that, wakin or sleepin.'

'You really think we can get to her?' asked Maynard.

In truth, Lowell didn't know, but he thought they had a shot. Fortune favored the brave – he'd seen that in a movie, or maybe on a TV show. And what better chance would they have? Practically half the world was asleep, and the rest of it was running around like a chicken with its head cut off. 'Come on. Clock's ticking, May. No time like the present. Plus, it'll be dark soon. Always a better time to move around.'

'Where do we go first?' Maynard asked.

Lowell didn't hesitate. 'To see Fritz.'

Fritz Meshaum had done some engine and detailing work for Lowell Griner, and had also moved some blow. In exchange, Lowell had connected the Kraut with a few gunrunners. Fritz, besides being a stellar mechanic and an excellent detailer, had a bee in his hat about the federal government, so he was always eager for opportunities to enhance his personal arsenal of heavy weaponry. When the inevitable day came that the FBI decided to capture all of the nation's shanty-dwelling asshole mechanics and ship them off to Guantánamo, Fritz would have to defend himself, and to the death, if need be. Each time Lowell saw him, Fritzie had to show off one cannon or another, and brag about how well it could vaporize someone. (The hilarious part: it was widely rumored that Fritz had been beaten within an inch of his life by a dogcatcher. He was tough, was li'l Fritz.) The last time Lowell had seen him, the bearded gnome had gleefully displayed his latest toy: an actual goddam bazooka. Russian surplus.

Low needed to get into the women's prison to assassinate a snitch. That was the sort of mission where a bazooka could actually come in handy.

3

Jared and Gerda Holden had not known each other well – Gerda was in her first year of middle school and Jared was in high school – but he knew her from dinners when the two families got together. Sometimes they played video games in the basement, and Jared always let her win a couple. A lot of bad had happened since the Aurora outbreak, but this was the first time Jared had seen a person shot.

'She must be dead, right, Dad?' He and Clint were in the bathroom of the administrative wing. Some of Gerda's blood had splattered Jared's face and shirt. 'From the fall on top of the shot?'

'I don't know,' Clint said. He was leaning against the tiled wall.

His son, patting water from his face with a paper towel, found Clint's eyes in the mirror over the sink.

'Probably,' Clint said. 'Yes. Based on what you've told me happened, she's almost certainly dead.'

'And the guy, too? The doctor? Flickinger?'

'Yes. Him, too, probably.'

'All because of this woman? This Evie person?'

'Yes,' Clint said. 'Because of her. We have to keep her safe. From the police and from anyone else. I know it seems crazy. She could be the key to understanding what's happened, the key to turning it around, and – just trust me, okay, Jared?'

'Okay, Dad. But one of the guards, that Rand guy, he said she's, like – magic?'

'I can't explain *what* she is, Jared,' he said.

Although he was trying to sound calm, Clint was livid – with himself, with Geary, with Evie. That bullet could have hit Jared. Could have blinded him. Left him comatose. Killed him. Clint had not beaten up his old friend Jason in the Burtells' yard so that his own son could die before him; he had not shared beds with kids who pissed themselves in their sleep for that; he had not left behind Marcus and Shannon and all the others for that; and he had not worked his way through college or medical school for it.

Shannon had told him, all those years before, that if he just hung on and kept from killing anyone, he would make it out. But to make it out of the current situation, they might have to kill people. *He* might have to kill people. The idea did not upset Clint as much as he would have expected. The situation changed, and the prizes changed, but maybe, at bottom, it was the same deal: if you wanted the milkshake, you'd better be ready to fight.

'What?' asked Jared.

Clint cocked his head.

'You look,' his son said, 'sort of tense.'

'Just tired.' He touched Jared's shoulder and excused himself. He needed to make sure everyone was placed.

4

There was no need to say I told you so.

Terry caught Frank's eye as they stepped away from the group around the bodies. 'You were right,' Terry said. He produced the flask. Frank thought about stopping him, didn't. The acting sheriff took a healthy swallow. 'You were right all the way down the line. We'll have to take her.'

'You sure?' Frank said it as if he himself wasn't.

'Are you kidding? Look at this goddam mess! Vern dead, girl there did it, she's shot to pieces and dead, too. Lawyer's skull caved in. Think he might have lived for awhile, but he's sure dead now. Other guy, driver's license says he's an MD named Flickinger—'

'Him too? Really?' If so, it was too bad. Flickinger had been a mess, but he'd had enough soul left in him to try to help Nana.

'And that's not the worst part. Norcross and the Black woman and the rest of them have got serious armaments now, most everything high-powered that we could have used to make them stand down.'

'Do we know who was with them?' Frank asked. 'Who was behind the wheel of that RV when they hauled ass out of here?'

Terry tipped the flask again, but there was nothing left inside. He swore and kicked a chunk of broken macadam.

Frank waited.

'Codger named Willy Burke.' Terry Coombs breathed out between his teeth. 'Cleaned up his act in the last fifteen or twenty years, does a lot of community stuff, but he's still a poacher. Used to be a moonshiner, too, back when he was young. Maybe he still is. Vet. Can handle himself. Lila always gave him the right-of-way, felt like it wouldn't be worth the trouble to try and get him for something. And I guess she liked him.' He inhaled. 'I felt the same.'

'All right.' Frank had decided to keep Black's phone call to himself. It had infuriated him so much, in fact, that he would have been hardpressed to recount the details of the conversation. One part had stayed with him, though, and tugged at his sleeve: how the woman had praised him for protecting his daughter at the hospital. How could she have known about that? Eve Black had been in the jail that morning. It kept coming back to him and he kept pushing it away. As with the moths that had burst from the lit fragment of Nana's cocoon, Frank could not fathom an explanation. He could only see that Eve Black had meant to tweak him – and she had succeeded. But he didn't believe she understood what tweaking him meant.

In any case, Terry was back on track – he didn't need any extra motivation. 'You want me to start putting together a group? I'm willing, if that's your pleasure.'

Although pleasure had nothing to do with it, Terry seconded the motion.

5

The prison defenders hurriedly removed the tires from the various cars and trucks in the parking lot. There were about forty vehicles altogether, counting the prison vans. Billy Wettermore and Rand Quigley rolled the tires out and arranged them in pyramids of three in the dead space between the inner and outer fences, then doused them in gasoline. The petrol stench quickly overwhelmed the ambient odor of damp, charred wood from the still-smoldering fire in the woods. They left the tires on Scott Hughes's truck but parked it crossways right behind the interior gate, as an extra barrier.

'Scott loves that truck,' Rand said to Tig.

'You want to put yours there instead?' Tig asked.

'Hell no,' said Rand. 'Are you crazy?'

The only vehicle they left untouched was Barry Holden's RV, situated in the handicap space by the cement path to the Intake doors.

6

Minus Vern Rangle, Roger Elway, and the department's female officers, all of whom had been confirmed as asleep during Frank's cataloging operation, seven deputies remained from Sheriff Lila Norcross's duty roster: Terry Coombs, Pete Ordway, Elmore Pearl, Dan 'Treater' Treat, Rupe Wittstock, Will Wittstock, and Reed Barrows. It was a solid group, in Terry's opinion. They were all force veterans of at least a year, and Pearl and Treater had both served in Afghanistan.

The three retired deputies – Jack Albertson, Mick Napolitano, and Nate McGee – made ten.

Don Peters, Eric Blass, and Frank Geary made lucky thirteen.

Frank quickly martialed a half-dozen other volunteers including Coach JT Wittstock, father of the deputies who shared his surname and the defense-first coach of the Dooling High School varsity football team; Pudge Marone, bartender at the Squeaky Wheel, who brought along his Remington shotgun from beneath the bar; Drew

T. Barry of Drew T. Barry Indemnity Company, by-the-book insurance agent and prize-winning deer hunter; Carson 'Country Strong' Struthers, Pudge's brother-in-law, who had fought to a 10–1 Golden Gloves record before his doctor told him he had to quit while he still had some brain left; and two town board members, Bert Miller and Steve Pickering, both of whom, like Drew T. Barry, knew their way around a deer stand. That was nineteen, and once they were informed that the woman inside the prison might have information related to the sleeping sickness, maybe even knowledge of a cure, every single one was eager to serve.

7

Terry was pleased, but wanted an even twenty. The sight of Vern Rangle's bleached-out face and torn neck was something he would never be able to forget. He could feel it the way he could feel Geary, silent as a shadow, following everything he did, judging every choice he made.

But never mind. The only way out was through: through Norcross to Eve Black, and through the Black woman to the end of this nightmare. Terry didn't know what would happen when they got to her, but he knew it would be the end. Once the end came, he could work at blurring the memory of Vern Rangle's bloodless face. Not to mention the faces of his wife and daughter, which no longer exactly existed. Seriously drinking his brain into submission, in other words. He was aware that Frank had been encouraging him to use the booze, and so what? So fucking what?

Don Peters had been tasked with calling around to the male officers on Dooling Correctional's roll, and it didn't take him long to figure out that Norcross had four officers on duty, max. One of those, Wettermore, was a swish, and another, Murphy, had been a history teacher. Throw in the Black woman and the old coot, Burke, plus maybe a couple or three others they didn't know about just to be generous, and that meant they were up against less than a dozen, few if any of whom could be expected to stand fast if things got hot, no matter how much armament they had acquired.

Terry and Frank stopped at the liquor store on Main Street. It was open, and busy.

'She didn't love me anyway!' one fool announced to the entire store, waving a bottle of gin. He smelled like a polecat.

The shelves were largely empty, but Terry found two pints of gin, and paid with money that would soon be worthless, he supposed, if this terrible fuck-up went on. He filled the flask with one pint, carried the other in a paper bag, and walked with Frank to a nearby alley. It opened into a courtyard piled with garbage bags and rain-softened cardboard boxes. Johnny Lee Kronsky's scuffed apartment door was here, at ground level, between two windows with plastic sheeting for glass.

Kronsky, a mythic figure in this part of West Virginia, answered and spied the bottle in the bag. 'Those who come bearing gifts may enter,' he said and took the bottle.

There was only one chair in the living room. Kronsky claimed it for himself. He drank half the pint in two ginormous swallows, his Adam's apple rolling like a bobber at the end of a hooked line, paying no attention to Terry or Frank. A muted television sat on a stand, showing footage of several cocooned women floating on the surface of the Atlantic Ocean. They looked like weird life rafts.

What if a shark decided to bite one? Terry wondered. He guessed that if that happened, the shark might be in for a surprise.

What did any of it mean? What was the point?

Terry decided the point might be gin. He got out Frank's flask and had a tug.

'Those women are from the big plane that crashed,' Johnny Lee said. 'Interesting that they float like that, isn't it? The stuff must be mighty light. Like kapok, or something.'

'Look at them all,' Terry marveled.

'Yes, yes, quite a sight.' Johnny Lee smacked his lips. He was a licensed private investigator, but not the kind that checked up on cheating spouses or solved mysteries. Until 2014, he had worked for Ulysses Energy Solutions, the coal company, cycling through their various operations, posing as a miner and listening for rumors of union organizing, working to undercut leaders who seemed particularly effective. A company dog, in other words.

Then had come trouble. A right smart of trouble, one could say. There was a cave-in. Kronsky had been the man handling the explosives. The three miners who had been buried under the rock had been talking loudly about holding a vote. Almost as damning, one had been wearing a tee-shirt with the face of Woody Guthrie on it. Lawyers hired by Ulysses had prevented the levying of charges – a tragic accident, they successfully argued before the grand jury – but Kronsky had been forced into retirement.

That was why Johnny Lee had come home to Dooling, where he had been born. Now, in his ideally located apartment – right around the corner from the liquor store – he was in the process of drinking himself to death. Each month, a check from UES arrived via Federal Express. A woman Terry knew at the bank told him that the notation on the stub was always the same: **FEES**. Whatever his **FEES** amounted to wasn't a fortune, as the crummy apartment proved, but Kronsky managed on it. The whole story was familiar to Terry because hardly a month passed that the police weren't called out to the man's apartment, by a neighbor who had heard breaking glass – a rock or a brick thrown through one of Kronsky's windows, undoubtedly by union spooks. Johnny Lee never called himself. He had let it be known that he was not overly concerned – J. L. Kronsky didn't give Shit One about the union.

One afternoon not long before the Aurora outbreak, when Terry had been partnered with Lila in Unit One, the conversation had turned to Kronsky. She said, 'Eventually some disaffected miner – probably a relative of one of the guys Kronsky got killed – is going to blow his head off, and the miserable son of a bitch will probably be glad to go.'

8

'There's a situation at the prison,' Terry said.

'There's a situation everywhere, Mister Man.' Kronsky had a beaten face, pouched and haggard, and dark eyes.

'Forget everywhere,' Frank said. 'We're here.'

'I don't give a tin shit where you are,' Johnny Lee said, and polished off the pint.

'We might need to blow something up,' Terry said.

Barry Holden and his station-robbing friends had taken a lot of firepower, but had missed the Griner brothers' bump of C4. 'You know how to work with plastic, don't you?'

'Could be I do,' Kronsky said. 'What's in it for me, Mister Man?'

Terry calculated. 'I tell you what. Pudge Marone from the Squeak is with us, and I think he'll let you run an endless tab for the rest of your life.' Which Terry guessed wouldn't be long.

'Hm,' Johnny Lee said.

'And of course, it's also a chance to do your town a great service.'

'Dooling can go fuck itself,' Johnny Lee Kronsky said, 'but still – why not? Just why the fuck not?'

That gave them twenty.

9

Dooling Correctional did not have guard towers. It had a flat tarpaper roof, piped with vents, ducts, and exhaust stems. There wasn't much in the way of cover beyond a half-foot of brick edging. After assessing this roof, Willy Burke told Clint he liked the three-hundred-and-sixty-degree perspective of the entire perimeter, but he liked his balls even more. 'Nothing up here that could stop a bullet, see. How about that shed there?' The old man pointed down below.

Although labeled EQUIPMENT SHED on the prison blueprints, it was your basic catch-all, containing the riding lawnmower that inmates (trustworthy ones) used to groom the softball field, plus gardening tools, sports equipment, and stacks of moldering newspapers and magazines bound with twine. Most importantly, it was built of cement blocks.

They had a closer look. Clint dragged a chair out behind the shed and Willy had a seat there beneath the overhang of the shed's roof.

From this position, a man would be sheltered from the view of anyone at the fence, but would still be visible at either end of a firing line that stretched between the shed and the prison. If they're just on one side, I should be all right,' said Willy. 'I'll see em from the corner of my eye and take cover.'

'Both sides at the same time?' Clint asked.

'If they do that, I'll be for it.'

'You need help. Backup.'

'When you say that, Doc, it makes me wish I'd done more churchin in the days of my youth.'

The old fellow regarded him amiably. Upon arriving at the prison, the only explanation that he had required of Clint was a further assurance that the stand they were making was what Lila would have wanted. Clint had readily given it to Willy, although at this stage he was no longer sure what Lila would have wanted. It seemed like Lila had been gone for years.

Clint tried to reflect the same amiability – a bit of lighthearted *savoir faire* in the face of the enemy – but what remained of his sense of humor seemed to have fallen out of the back of Barry Holden's RV along with Gerda Holden and Garth Flickinger. 'You were in Vietnam, weren't you, Willy?'

Willy held up his left hand. The meat of his palm was gouged with scar tissue. 'As it happens, a few bits of me are still there.'

'How did it feel?' Clint asked. 'When you were there? You must have lost friends.'

'Oh, yes,' Willy said. 'I lost friends. As to how I felt, mostly just scared. Confused. All the time. Is that how you feel right now?'

'It is,' Clint admitted. 'I never trained for this.'

They stood there in the milky afternoon light. Clint wondered if Willy sensed what Clint was really feeling – some fear and confusion, that was true, but also excitement. A certain euphoria infused the preparations, the prospect of pouring the frustration and dismay and loss and impossibility of everything into action. Clint could observe it happening to himself, a rush of aggressive adrenalin that was as old as apes.

He told himself he shouldn't be thinking that way, and maybe not, but it felt good. It was as if some guy who looked exactly like him, driving a coupe with the top down, had pulled up beside the old Clint at a stoplight, nodded once in recognition, then, at the flip of the green, his doppelganger had planted the accelerator, and the old Clint was watching him roar off. The new Clint had to hurry, because he was on a mission, and being on a mission was good.

While they were making their way to the rear of the prison, Willy told him about the moths and the fairy footprints he'd seen near Truman Mayweather's trailer. Millions of moths, it seemed, coating the branches of trees, rolling above the canopy of the woods in swarms. 'Was it from her?' Like everyone else, Willy had heard the rumors. 'That woman you got?'

'Yes,' Clint said. 'And that's not even the half of it.'

Willy said he didn't doubt it.

They dragged out a second chair and issued an auto to Billy Wettermore. It had been converted (legally or not Clint didn't know, nor did he care) to full auto. That put a man on each end of the shed. It wasn't perfect, just the best they could do.

10

Behind the front desk at the sheriff's office, the body of Linny Mars lay cocooned on the floor with her laptop beside her and still broadcasting that Vine of the falling London Eye. It appeared to Terry that she had slid out of her chair when she finally drifted off to sleep. She was in a heap, partly blocking the hallway that led to the official areas of the facility.

Kronsky stepped over her and walked down the hallway, in search of the evidence locker. Terry didn't like that. He called after him, 'Hey, you notice the fucking person here? On the floor?'

'It's okay, Terry,' Frank said. 'We'll take care of her.'

They carried Linny to a holding cell and lowered her gently to the mattress. She hadn't been out for long. The webs were thin across her eyes and mouth. Her lips were twisted up in an expression of delirious happiness – who knew why, maybe just because her struggle to stay awake was over.

Terry had another drink. He lowered the flask and the wall of the cell rushed at him and he stuck out his hand to stop it. After a moment he was able to push up straight again.

'I'm worried about you,' Frank said. 'You're — overmedicating.'

'I'm perfecto.' Terry waved his hand at a moth that was bothering his ear. 'Are you happy we're arming up, Frank? It's what you wanted, isn't it?'

Frank gave Terry a long look. It was totally unthreatening, totally blank. He stared at Terry the way that kids looked at television screens — as if they were gone from their bodies.

'No,' Frank said. 'I wouldn't say I'm too happy. It's the job, that's all. The one in front of us.'

'Do you always tell yourself that before you kick somebody's ass?' Terry asked, genuinely interested, and was surprised when Frank recoiled, as if from a slap.

Kronsky was in the waiting room when they came out. He'd found the plastic explosive, also a bundle of dynamite someone had found in a gravel pit near the Griner property and turned in for disposal. Johnny Lee looked disapproving. 'This dyno had no business back there, folksies. It gets old and cranky. The C4, now—' He shook it, making Frank wince. 'You could run it over with a truck and nothing would happen.'

'So you want to leave the dynamite?' Terry asked.

'Jesus, no.' Kronsky looked offended. 'I love me some dyno. Always have. Dyno's what you call old-school. Need to wrap it in a blanket, is all. Or maybe Sleeping Beauty there's got a nice thick sweater in the closet. Oh, and I'll need to get some items from the hardware store. I trust the sheriff's department has an open account?'

Before Terry and Frank left, they packed a duffel bag with the handguns and ammo that hadn't been looted, and carried out all the vests and helmets they could rustle up. There wasn't much, but their posse — really no sense calling it anything else — would bring plenty of armament from home.

Linny hadn't left a sweater in the closet, so Johnny Lee had wrapped the dynamite in a couple of towels from the bathroom. He held it to his chest as if carrying an infant.

'Getting late in the day for any kind of assault,' Frank observed. 'If that's what it comes to.'

Terry said, 'I know. We'll get the boys out there tonight, make sure everyone knows what's what and who's in charge.' He looked pointedly at Frank as he said this. 'Requisition a couple schoolbuses from the town motor pool and park them at the intersection of Route 31 and West Lavin, where the roadblock was, so the fellas don't have to sleep raw. Keep six or eight of em on watch, in a . . . you know . . .' He made a circle in the air.

Frank helped him out. 'A perimeter.'

'Yeah, that. If we have to go in, we'll do it tomorrow morning, from the east. We'll need a couple of bulldozers to bust through. Send Pearl and Treater to pick out a couple from the public works yard. Keys are in the office trailer there.'

'Good,' Frank said, because it was. He wouldn't have thought of bulldozers.

'First thing tomorrow morning, we bulldoze the fences and come at the main building across the parking lot. That way the sun will be in their eyes. Step one, push em deep, away from the doors and windows. Step two, Johnny Lee blows the front doors and we're inside. Press em to throw down their weapons. At that point, I think they will. Send a few around the far side to make sure they can't bolt for it.'

'Makes sense,' Frank said.

'But first . . .'

'First?'

'We talk to Norcross. Tonight. Face to face, if he's man enough. Offer him a chance to give the woman up before something happens that can't be taken back.'

Frank's eyes expressed what he felt.

'I know what you're thinking, Frank, but if he's a reasonable man, he'll see it's the right thing. He's responsible for more lives than just hers, after all.'

'And if he still says no?'

Terry shrugged. 'Then we go in and take her.'

'No matter what?'

'That's right, no matter what.' They went out, and Terry locked the glass double doors of the station behind him.

11

Rand Quigley got his toolbox and spent two hours chiseling and hammering out the small wire-reinforced window that was embedded in the concrete wall of the visitors' room.

Tig Murphy sat nearby, drinking Coke and smoking a cigarette. The no-smoking reg had been lifted. 'If you were an inmate,' he said, 'that'd get about five years added to your sentence.'

'Good thing I'm not an inmate, then, isn't it?'

Tig tapped ash on the floor and decided not to say what he was thinking: if being locked in meant you were an inmate, that's what they were now. 'Man, they really built this place, didn't they?'

'Uh-huh. Like it was a prison, or something,' Rand said. *'Hyuck-hyuck-hyuck.'*

When the glass finally fell out, Tig clapped.

'Thank ya, ladies and gentlemen,' Rand said, doing Elvis. 'Thank ya very much.'

With the window removed, Rand could stand on top of the table they had pulled below as a shooting platform, and stick his weapon through. This was his spot, with clean angles on the parking lot and the front gate.

'They think we are pussies,' Rand said. 'But we are not.'

'Got that right, Rand-o.'

Clint poked his head in. 'Tig. With me.'

The two of them walked up the stairs to the raised level of B Wing. This was the prison's highest point, the only second floor in the structure. There were windows in the cells that faced out on West Lavin. These were stronger even than the window in the visitors' room – thick, reinforced, and sandwiched between layers of concrete. It was hard to imagine Rand knocking one out of the wall with just hand tools.

'We can't defend this end,' Tig said.

'No,' Clint said, 'but it makes a helluva lookout post, and we don't need to defend it, right? There's no way through here.'

That seemed inarguable to Clint, and to Scott Hughes, too, who was relaxing a few cells down the line and listening in. 'I'm sure you guys are going to get yourselves killed one way or another, and I won't be crying any tears when it happens,' he called, 'but Shrink Boy's right. It'd take a bazooka to blow a hole in this wall.'

12

On the day two opposing groups of Dooling men armed up, preparing to make war, less than a hundred women were still awake in the Tri-Counties. One was Eve Black; one was Angel Fitzroy; one was Jeanette Sorley.

Vanessa Lampley was a fourth. Earlier that day, her husband finally nodded off in his armchair, allowing Van to do what she had decided to do. Since she had returned home from the prison after shooting and killing Ree Dempster, Tommy Lampley had tried to stay awake with her as long as he could. Van had been glad for the company. A cooking competition show had done him in, though, lulling him to dreamland with a tutorial on molecular gastronomy. Van waited to make sure he was soundly out before she left. She wasn't about to assign her husband, ten years her senior, with titanium hips and afflicted by angina, the thankless task of somehow taking care of her body for however many years remained to him. Nor did Van have any interest in becoming the world's most dismal piece of furniture.

Tired as she was, she was still light on her feet, and crept from the room without disturbing his thin sleep. In the garage she got her hunting rifle and loaded it. She yanked up the door, fired up the ATV, and rolled out.

Her plan was simple: cut through the woods to the ridge above the road, breathe in the fresh air, take in the view, jot a note to her husband, and put the barrel under her chin. Goodnight. At least there were no kids to worry about.

She went slow because she was afraid, weary as she was, of crashing. The ATV's heavy tires sent every root and rock jolting up her thick arms and deep into her bones. Van didn't mind. The thin rain was all right, too. Despite the exhaustion – her thoughts crawled – she was intensely aware of every physical sensation. Would it have been better to die without knowing you were going to, like Ree? Van could ask the question, but her brain could not break it down in a way that allowed a satisfactory answer. Any response dissolved before it could form. Why did it feel so bad, that she had shot an inmate who would have killed another inmate if she hadn't? Why did it feel so bad, just to have done her job? Those answers wouldn't coalesce, either, couldn't even begin to.

Van arrived at the top of the ridge. She shut off the ATV and dismounted. Far away, in the direction of the prison, a haze of black hovered over the dying day, damp residue from the forest fire that had burned itself out. Directly below, the land descended in a long, easy grade. At the base of the grade was a muddy stream, fattening in the rain. Above the stream a few hundred feet away was a hunting cabin with a mossy roof. Smoke scribbles pumped from the stove-pipe chimney.

She patted her pockets and realized that she had completely forgotten paper and something to write with. Van wanted to laugh – suicide really wasn't that complex, was it? – but a sigh was the best she could manage.

There was no help for it, and her reasoning ought not to be that hard to figure out. If she were found at all, that was. And if anyone cared. Van unstrapped the rifle from her back.

The door of the cabin banged open just as she located the barrel against the shelf of her chin.

'He just better still have that fucking boom-tube,' said a man, his voice carrying crisp and clear, 'or he'll wish that dogcatcher had finished the job on him. Oh, and bring along the scanner. I want to keep up on what the cops are doing.'

Van lowered her rifle and watched as two men climbed into a shiny Silverado truck and drove away. She was sure she knew them, and looking like they did – a couple of rode-hard and put-away wet woods-rats – it wasn't from any chamber of commerce awards ceremony. Their names would have come to her immediately if she hadn't been so sleep-deprived. Her mind felt full of mud. She could still feel the jouncing ATV, even though it was no longer moving. Phantom dots of light went zooming across her vision.

When the truck was gone, she decided to visit the cabin. There would be something to write on inside, if only the back of a calendar years out of date. 'And I'll need something to pin it to my shirt,' she said.

Her voice sounded foggy and foreign. The voice of someone else. And there *was* someone else, standing just beside her. Only when she turned her head, the someone was gone. That was happening more and more: watchers lurking at the farthest reach of her vision. Hallucinations. How long could you stay awake before all rational thought broke down and you lost your mind completely?

Van remounted her ATV and drove it along the ridge until the land descended and she could switchback along the rutted track that led to the cabin.

The cabin smelled of beans, beer, fried deermeat, and man-farts. Dishes cluttered the table, the sink was filled with more, and there were clotted pots on the woodburning stove. On the mantel was a picture of a fiercely grinning man with a pick over his shoulder and a countryman's battered fedora pulled so low on his head that the brim bent the tops of his ears. Looking at the sepia-toned photo, Vanessa realized exactly who it was she had seen, because her father had pointed out the man in that picture to her when she had been no more than twelve. He had been going into the Squeaky Wheel.

'That is Big Lowell Griner,' Daddy had said, 'and I want you to keep clear of him, honey. If he should ever say hello to you, say hello back, ain't it a nice day, and keep walking.'

So that's who those two were: Big Lowell's no-account boys. Maynard and Little Low Griner, big as life and driving a new pickup when they were supposed to be jugged over in Coughlin, awaiting trial for, among other things, a murder Kitty McDavid had witnessed, and agreed to testify about.

On a pine-paneled wall of the short corridor that probably led to the cabin's bedrooms, Van saw a battered notebook hanging from a piece of string. A sheet from that would do just fine for a suicide note, but she suddenly decided she wanted to stay awake and alive at least a little longer.

She left, glad to escape the stink, and drove her ATV away from the cabin as fast as she dared. After a mile or so, the track emptied into one of Dooling County's many dirt roads. Dust hung on the left – not much, on account of the drizzle, but enough to tell her which way the fugitives had turned. They had a good lead on her by the time she reached Route 7, but the land here was downsloping and open, which made it easy to see the truck, diminished by distance but clearly headed for town.

Van slapped herself briskly across each cheek and followed. She was wet through now, but the cold would help her stay awake a little while longer. If *she* were on the lam from a murder charge, she'd be halfway to Georgia by now. Not these two; they were headed back to town, no doubt to do something nasty, as was their wont. She wanted to know what it was, and maybe stop it.

Atonement for what she'd had to do to Ree was not out of the question.

CHAPTER 11

1

Fritz Meshaum didn't want to give up his bazooka, at least not without payment. When May seized him firmly by the shoulders and Low twisted his right arm nearly up to his shoulder blades, however, he changed his mind and lifted a trapdoor in the floor of his ramshackle cabin, revealing the treasure for which the Griner brothers had come.

Little Low had expected it to be green, like the ones in World War II movies, but Fritz's bazooka was painted a dusty black, with a long serial number running up the side and some of those funny Russian letters beneath. A scale of rust rimmed the mouth. Lying beside it was a duffel bag containing a dozen shells stenciled with more words in Russian. There were also eight or ten rifles and as many as twenty handguns, most semi-auto. The brothers stuffed a couple in their belts. There was nothing like pistols in a man's belt to make him feel like he had the right-of-way.

'What's that thing?' asked May, pointing to a shiny black square of plastic above the bazooka's trigger housing.

'Dunno,' Fritz said, peering at it. 'Some kind of inventory control for the bean-counters, most likely.'

'It's got words in English on it,' May said.

Fritz shrugged. 'So what? I got a John Deere cap with Chinese shit on the tag inside. Everybody sells everything to anyone. Thanks to the Jews, that's just the way the world works. The Jews, they—'

'Never you mind the damn Jews,' Little Low said. If he let Fritz get on a roll about the Jews, he'd shortly be on to the federal government, and they'd be hunkered around this fucking hole in the floor for the rest of the spring. 'All I care about is does it work. If it don't, tell me now, lest we come back here and tear off your ballsack.'

'I think we should tear off his ballsack, anyhow, Low,' May said. 'That's what I think. I bet it's small.'

'It works, it works,' Fritz said, presumably talking about the bazooka rather than his ballsack. 'Now let loose of me, you scum.'

'Got a mouth on him, don't he, brother?' Maynard observed.

'Yes,' Little Low said. 'Yes he does. But we'll forgive him this time. Get a couple of those grease-guns.'

'Those ain't grease-guns,' Fritz said indignantly. 'Those're fully automatic army—'

'It'd suit me fine if you shut up,' Low said, 'and what suits me is going to suit you. We're going now, but if this bazooka of yours don't work, we will return and make it disappear up your saggy ass all the way to the trigger housing.'

'Yessir, what he said!' May exclaimed. 'Try shittin after takin a load like that!'

'What are you going to do with my boom-tube?'

Little Low Griner smiled gently. 'Hush, now,' he said, 'and don't worry about what don't concern you.'

2

From a hilltop a quarter of a mile away, Van Lampley observed the Silverado pull into Fritz Meshaum's scabrous dooryard. She observed the Griners get out and return to their stolen truck a few minutes later, carrying stuff – no doubt more stolen goods – which they put in the truckbed. Then they took off again, once more in the direction of Dooling. She considered pulling into Meshaum's place once they left, but in her current state, she felt incapable of asking any questions that would make sense. And really, did she have to? Everyone in Dooling knew that Fritz Meshaum was in love with anything that had a trigger and went bang. The Griner brothers had stopped to gun up. It was as plain as the nose on her face.

Well, she had a gun herself, her good old .30-.06. Probably not much of a shake compared to what was now in the bed of that stolen truck, but so what? Did she really have anything to lose that she hadn't been planning, just an hour ago, to give away to the universe?

'Want to mess with me, boys?' Van said, keying the ATV and revving it (a mistake, as she had never bothered to check how much gas was in the Suzuki's tank before setting out). 'Well, why don't we see just who messes with who?'

3

The Griners had listened to their scanner only off and on during their days at the cabin, but they did so constantly on the trip to town, because the police band had gone crazy. The transmissions and crosstalk meant little to Maynard, whose brains rarely got out of first gear, but Lowell picked up the general drift.

Someone — a bunch of someones, actually — had taken a mess of guns from the armory at the sheriff's station, and the cops were just as mad as hornets in a shook-up nest. At least two of the gun-robbers had been killed, a cop had also been killed, and the rest of the gang had gotten away in a big RV. They had taken the stolen guns up to the women's prison. The cops also kept talking about some woman they wanted to pull out of the Ho Hotel, and it seemed like the gun-robbers wanted to keep her for themselves. Low couldn't follow that part. He didn't much care, either. What he cared about was the cops had raised up a posse and were preparing for a big fight, maybe starting tomorrow morning, and they planned to rendezvous at the intersection of Route 31 and West Lavin Road. That meant the station would be undefended. It also gave Lowell a brilliant idea about how they might be able to nail Kitty McDavid.

'Low?'

'Yes, brother?'

'I can't make out from all that bibble-babble who's in charge. Some say Deputy Coombs took over from the Norcross bitch, and some say a fella named Frank. Who's Frank?'

'Don't know and don't care,' Little Low said. 'But when we get into town, you keep an eye peeled for a kid by himself.'

'Which kid, brother?'

'One old enough to ride a bike and carry a tale,' said Low, just as the stolen Silverado passed the sign reading WELCOME TO DOOLING, A NICE PLACE TO RAISE YOUR FAMILY.

4

The Suzuki ATV could do sixty on the open road, but with night coming down and her reflexes shot to perdition, Van dared no more than forty. By the time she passed the WELCOME TO DOOLING sign, the Silverado containing the Griner brothers had disappeared. Maybe she'd lost them, but maybe not. Main Street was nearly deserted, and she hoped to spot it there, either parked or cruising slowly while those bad boys looked for something worth holding up. If she didn't spot it, she supposed the best she could do was pop into the sheriff's station and report them to whoever was on duty. That would be sort of an anticlimax for a woman who was hoping to do something good to make up for a shooting she still felt bad about, but it was like her daddy always said – sometimes you get what you want, but mostly you get what you get.

The beginning of downtown proper was marked by Barb's Beauty Salon and Hot Nails on one side of the road and Ace Hardware (recently visited by Johnny Lee Kronsky, in search of tools, wires, and batteries) on the other. It was between these two fine business establishments that Vanessa's ATV chugged twice, backfired, and died. She checked the gauge, and saw the needle resting on E. Wasn't that just the perfect end to a perfect fucking day?

There was a Zoney's one block up where she could buy a few gallons of gas, assuming anyone was bothering to run the place. But it was getting dark, those damn Griners could be anywhere, and even walking a block seemed like quite a trek in her current state.

It might be better to go ahead and end it, as she'd set out to do earlier . . . except she hadn't become a statewide arm-wrestling champion by giving up when the going got tough, had she? And wasn't that what she was thinking of? Giving up?

'Not until my damn hand's down on the damn table,' Van told her beached ATV, and began plodding up the deserted sidewalk toward the sheriff's.

5

The business directly across from the cop-shop was the Drew T. Barry Indemnity Company, proprietor currently out at West Lavin Road with the rest of the posse. Low parked the Silverado behind it in a space marked RESERVED FOR BARRY EMPLOYEE, ALL OTHERS WILL BE TOWED. The back door was locked, but two slams of May's beefy shoulder fixed that. Low followed him inside, dragging the kid they had found riding his bike down by the bowling alley. The kid in question happened to be Kent Daley, member of the high school tennis team and close friend of Eric Blass. Kent's bike was now in the back of the Silverado. He was sniveling, although he was really too old for such behavior; it was Low's opinion that sniveling was okay for teenage girls, but boys should start to taper off at ten and be done with it by twelve or so. He was willing to give this one a pass, however. After all, he probably thought he was going to be raped and murdered.

'You need to shut up, youngster,' he said. 'You'll be all right, if you behave.'

He frog-marched Kent into the big front room, which was filled with desks and posters telling how the right insurance policy could save your family from a life of poverty. On the front window, which faced the deserted business district, Drew T. Barry's name was printed backward in tall gold-flake letters. As Low looked out, he saw a woman come slowly up the sidewalk on the other side. Not much of a looker, heavyset, lesbo haircut, but seeing any woman today was a rarity. She glanced at the Barry establishment, but with no lights inside, could see nothing but the reflection of the streetlights, which had just flicked on. She climbed the steps to the cop-shop and tried the door. Locked, and wasn't that smalltown police for you? Low thought. Lock the front door after the guns are stolen. Now she was trying the intercom.

'Mister?' Kent whined. 'I want to go home. You can have my bike, if you want it.'

'We can have anything we want, you pimply little peckerwood,' May said.

Low twisted the boy's wrist, making him holler. 'What part of shut up don't you understand? Brother, go get Mr Bazooky. And the shells.'

May left. Low turned to the kid. 'Card in your wallet says your name is Kent Daley and you live at 15 Juniper Street. That right?'

'Yes, sir,' the boy said, wiping snot from his nose up one cheek with the heel of his hand. 'Kent Daley, and I don't want any trouble. I want to go home.'

'You're in a real pickle, Kent. My brother is an awful sick man. There is nothing he loves more than to wreck a human being. What'd you do, caused you to be so unlucky, do you suppose?'

Kent licked his lips and blinked rapidly. He opened his mouth and shut it.

'You did something, all right.' Low laughed; guilt was hilarious. 'Who's at home?'

'My dad and my mom. Only my mom's, you know . . .'

'Catchin forty winks, is she? Or four hundred and forty?'

'Yes, sir.'

'But your dad's fine?'

'Yes, sir.'

'Would you like me to go to 15 Juniper Street and blow your dad's fuckin head off?'

'No, sir,' Kent whispered. Tears rolled down his pale cheeks.

'No, course you wouldn't, but I will, unless you do just as I say. Will you do as I say?'

'Yes, sir.' Not even a whisper now, just a breeze through the boy's lips.

'How old are you, Kent?'

'Suh–Suh–Seventeen.'

'Jesus, almost old enough to vote and grizzling like a baby. Quit on it.'

Kent did his best.

'Ride that bike pretty fast, can you?'

'I guess so. I won the Tri-County 40K last year.'

Little Low didn't know a 40K from a serving tray, and didn't care. 'You know where Route 31 meets up with West Lavin Road? The road that goes to the prison?'

Maynard had returned with the bazooka and the case of shells. Across the street, the heavyset woman had given up on the intercom and was heading back the way she had come with her head hanging down. The drizzle had ceased at last.

Low gave Kent, who was staring at the bazooka with dreadful fascination, a shake. 'Know that road, do you?'

'Yes, sir.'

'Good. There are a bunch of men up there and I'm going to give you a message. You will give it to the one named Terry, or the one named Frank, or both of them. Now listen.'

6

Terry and Frank were at that moment getting out of Unit One and approaching the double gates of Dooling Correctional, where Clint and another guy stood waiting for them. Ten members of the posse were back at the intersection; the rest had taken up positions around the prison at what Terry called the compass rose: north, northeast, east, southeast, south, southwest, west, and northwest. There were woods, and they were damp, but none of the guys seemed to mind. They were high on excitement.

And they'll stay that way until the first one takes a bullet and starts screaming, Terry thought.

Someone's tricked-out truck was blocking the inner gate. The dead space had been filled with tires. And soaked in gasoline, from the smell. Not a bad move. Terry could almost admire it. He shone his light on Norcross, then on the bearded man standing next to him.

'Willy Burke,' said Terry. 'I'm sorry to see you here.'

'And I'm sorry to see you here,' Willy responded. 'Doing what you shouldn't be doing. Overstepping your authority. Playing the vigilante man.' He took his pipe from the pocket of his biballs and started to load it.

Terry had never been sure if Norcross was a doctor or just a mister, so he settled on his given name. 'Clint, this has almost gone beyond talking. One of my deputies has been killed. Vern Rangle. I think you knew him.'

Clint sighed and shook his head. 'I did, and I'm sorry. He was a fine man. I hope you feel equally sorry about Garth Flickinger and Gerda Holden.'

'The Holden girl's death was an act of self-defense,' Frank said. 'She was ripping Deputy Rangle's goddam throat out.'

'I want to talk to Barry Holden,' Clint said.

'He's dead,' Frank said. 'And it's your fault.'

Terry turned to Frank. 'You need to let me handle this.'

Frank raised his hands and stepped back. He knew Coombs was right – there was his damn temper, getting the best of him again – but he hated him for it, just the same. What he felt like doing was climbing that fence, barbed wire rolls at the top be damned, and knocking the heads of those two smug sons of bitches together. Evie Black's goading voice was still in his head.

'Clint, listen to me,' Terry said. 'I'm willing to say there's blame on both sides, and I'm willing to guarantee that no charges will be brought against any of you here if you let me take the woman into custody now.'

'Is Barry really dead?' Clint asked.

'Yes,' the acting sheriff said. 'He attacked Vern, too.'

Willy Burke reached over and gripped Clint's shoulder.

'Let's talk about Evie,' Clint said. 'What exactly do you plan to do with her? What *can* you do?'

Terry appeared stumped, but Frank was ready, speaking with assurance. 'We're going to take her to the sheriff's station. While Terry's questioning her, I'm going to get a team of doctors from the state hospital down here double-quick. Between the cops and the docs, we're going to find out what she is, what she did to the women, and whether or not she can fix it.'

'She says she did nothing,' Clint said, staring off into the distance. 'She says she's just an emissary.'

Frank turned to Terry. 'You know what? I think this man is totally full of shit.'

Terry gave him a reproachful (if slightly red-eyed) look; Frank once again raised his hands and stepped back.

'You don't have a single medical doctor in there,' Terry said, 'and you don't have any PAs you can call, because I seem to remember that they're both women and they'll be in cocoons by now. So, bottom line, you're not examining her, you're just *holding* her—'

'Holding *onto* her,' Frank growled.

'—and listening to what she tells you—'

'*Swallowing* it, you mean!' Frank shouted.

'Be quiet, Frank.' Terry spoke mildly, but when he turned back to Clint and Willy his cheeks were flushed. 'But he's right. You're swallowing it. Drinking the Kool-Aid, so to speak.'

'You don't understand,' Clint said. He sounded weary. 'She's not a woman at all, at least not in the sense we understand. I don't think she's entirely human. She has certain abilities. She can call rats, that much I'm sure of. They do what she wants. It's how she got Hicks's cell phone. All those moths people have been seeing around town have something to do with her, too, and she knows things. Things she can't know.'

'You saying she's a witch?' Terry asked. He pulled out the flask and had a sip. Probably not the best way to negotiate, but he needed something, and right now. 'Come on, Clint. Next you'll be telling me she can walk on water.'

Frank thought of the fire spinning in the air in his living room, and then exploding into moths; and of the phone call, Evie Black saying that she had seen him protect Nana. He tightened his arms across his chest, squeezing down his anger. What did it matter what Eve Black was? What mattered was what had happened, *was* happening, and how to fix it.

'Open your eyes, son,' Willy said. 'Look at what's happened to the world over the last week. All the women asleep in cocoons, and you're sticking at the idea the Black woman may be something supernatural? You boys need to do better. Need to quit on sticking your fingers where they don't belong and let this thing play out like the doc says she wants.'

Because Terry could think of no adequate reply, he took another drink. He saw the way Clint was looking at him and had a third, just to spite the bastard. Who was he to judge, hiding behind prison walls while Terry tried to hold the rest of the world together?

'What she's asked for is a few more days,' Clint said, 'and that's what I want you to give her.' He nailed Terry's eyes with his own. 'She's expecting bloodshed, she's made that much clear. Because she believes that's the only way men know how to solve their problems. Let's not give her what she expects. Stand down. Give it seventy-two hours. Then we can revisit the situation.'

'Really? And what do you think will change?' The liquor hadn't taken over Terry's mind yet, so far it was only visiting, and he thought, almost prayed: Give me an answer I can believe in.

But Clint only shook his head. 'I don't know. She says it's not entirely in her hands. But seventy-two hours without shooting would be the right first step, of that I'm sure. Oh, and she says that the women have to take a vote.'

Terry nearly laughed. 'How the fuck are sleeping women going to do that?'

'I don't know,' Clint said.

He's playing for time, Frank thought. Spouting any old made-up thing that comes into his shrinky-dink brain. Surely you're still sober enough to see that, aren't you, Terry?

'I need to think it over,' Terry said.

'All right, but you need to think clearly, so do yourself a favor and pour the rest of that liquor out on the ground.' His eyes shifted to Frank, and they were the cold ones of the orphan boy who had fought for milkshakes. 'Frank here thinks he's the solution, but I think he's the problem. I think she knew there'd be a guy like him. I think she knows there always is.'

Frank leaped forward, reached through the fence, seized Norcross by the throat, and choked him until his eyeballs first bulged, then dropped out to dangle on his cheeks . . . but only in his mind. He waited.

Terry considered, then spat in the dirt. 'Fuck you, Clint. You're no real doctor.'

And when he raised the flask and took another long, defiant swallow, Frank raised an inward cheer. By tomorrow, acting Sheriff Coombs would be in the bag. Then he, Frank, would take over. There would be no seventy-two hours, and he didn't care if Eve Black was a witch, a fairy princess, or the Red Queen of Wonderland. Everything he needed to know about Eve Black had been in that one short phone call.

Stop this, he had told her – almost begged her – when she called him on her stolen cell. *Let the women go.*

You'll have to kill me first, the woman had replied.

Which was what Frank intended to do. If it brought the women back? Happy ending. If not? Revenge for taking away the only person in his life who mattered. Either way? Problem solved.

7

Just as Van Lampley reached her stalled ATV – with no idea what to do next – a kid tore past on one of those bikes with the apehanger handlebars. He was making enough speed to blow his hair back from his forehead, and he wore an expression of stark, bug-eyed terror. It could have been caused by any one of a dozen things, the way the world was now, but Van had no doubt what had lit a fire under the boy. It wasn't an intuition; it was a rock-solid certainty.

'Kid!' she shouted. 'Kid, where are they?'

Kent Daley paid her no mind, only pedaled faster. He was thinking about the old homeless woman they had been goofing with. They never should have done it. This was God, paying them back. Paying *him* back. He pedaled faster still.

8

Although Maynard Griner had left the halls of academe while still in the eighth grade (and those halls had been delighted to see him go), he was good with machinery; when his younger brother passed him the bazooka and one of the shells, May handled them as if he had been doing so all his life. He examined the shell's high-explosive tip, the wire that ran down the side of the thing, and the fins at the base. He grunted, nodded, and aligned the shell's fins with the grooves inside the tube. It slid in easy-peasy. He pointed to a lever above the trigger and below the black plastic inventory tag. 'Pull that back. Should lock her in.'

Low did, and heard a click. 'Is that it, May?'

'Should be, as long as Fritz put in a fresh battery. I believe it's a lectric charge that fires the rocket.'

'If he didn't, I'll go on back there and ramguzzle him,' Low said. His eyes were sparkling as he faced Drew T. Barry's plate glass window and rested the bazooka on his shoulder in the best war-movie style. 'Stand clear, brother!'

The battery in the trigger housing turned out to be just fine. There was a hollow *whoosh*. Exhaust shot from the tube. The display window blew out into the street, and before either man had time to draw a breath, the front of the sheriff's station exploded. Chunks of sand-colored brick and shards of glass rained down on the street.

'*Hoooo-EEEE!*' May slapped his brother on the back. '*Did you see that, brother?*'

'I did,' Low replied. An alarm was braying somewhere deep inside the wounded station. Men were running to look. The front of the building was now a gaping mouth filled with broken teeth. They could see flames inside, and paperwork fluttering around like singed birds. 'Reload me.'

May aligned the fins of a second shell and latched it tight. 'All set!' May was hopping with excitement. This was more fun than the time they'd thrown a package of dynamite into the trout tank up at Tupelo Crossing.

'Fire in the hole!' Low shouted, and pulled the bazooka's trigger. The shell flew across the street on a trail of smoke. The men who had come out to gawk saw it and either turned tail or hit the deck. The second explosion gutted the center of the building. Linny's cocoon had survived the first blast, but not this second one. Moths flew up from where she had been, and caught fire.

'Let me have a turn!' May held out his hands for the bazooka.

'No, we need to get out of here,' Low said. 'But you'll get your chance, brother. That I promise.'

'When? Where?'

'Up to the prison.'

9

Van Lampley stood by her ATV, stunned. She had seen the first contrail cross Main Street, and knew what it meant even before the blast. Those son-of-a-bitching Griner brothers had gotten an RPG launcher or something like it from Fritz Meshaum. As the smoke from the second blast began to clear, she could see flames licking out from holes that had been windows. One of the triple doors was lying in the street, twisted into a corkscrew of chromed steel. The others were nowhere to be seen.

Woe to anyone who was in there, she thought.

Red Platt, one of the salesmen at Dooling Kia, came swaying and staggering toward her. Blood was sheeting down the right side of his face, and his lower lip no longer looked completely attached – although with all the blood, it was hard to tell.

'What was that?' Red shouted in a cracked voice. Shards of glass glittered in his thinning hair. 'What the fuck was *that?*'

'The work of two swinging dicks who need a broomhandle stuck in their spokes before they hurt anyone else,' Van said. 'You ought to get patched up, Red.'

She walked toward the Shell station, feeling like herself for the first time in days. She knew it wouldn't last, but while it did, she intended to ride the adrenalin. The gas station was open, but un-attended. Van found a ten-gallon can in the garage bay, filled it at one of the pumps, and left a twenty on the counter beside the cash register. The world might be ending, but she had been raised to pay her bills.

She toted the can back to her ATV, filled the tank, and headed out of town in the direction the Griner brothers had come from.

10

Kent Daley was having a very bad night, and it wasn't even eight o'clock. He had no more than turned off Route 31 and accelerated toward the buses blocking West Lavin Road when he was clothes-lined off his bike and driven to the ground. His head hit the asphalt and bright lights flashed in front of his eyes. When they cleared, he saw the muzzle of a rifle three inches from his face.

'Shit *fire!*' exclaimed Reed Barrows, the deputy who had taken Kent down. Reed had been placed at the southwest point of Terry's compass rose. He put his gun down and hauled Kent up by the front of his shirt. 'I know you, you're the kid who was putting firecrackers in mailboxes last year.'

Men were running toward them from the new and improved roadblock, Frank Geary in the lead. Terry Coombs brought up the rear, weaving slightly. They knew what had happened in town; there had already been a dozen calls on a dozen cell phones, and they could easily see the fire burning in the middle of Dooling from this high vantage point. Most of them wanted to go tear-assing back, but Terry, fearing it was a diversion to get the woman out, had ordered them to hold their positions.

'What are you doing out here, Daley?' Reed asked. 'You could have gotten yourself shot.'

'I've got a message,' Kent said, rubbing the back of his head. It wasn't bleeding, but a large knot was forming there. 'It's for Terry or Frank, or both of them.'

'What the fuck's going on?' Don Peters asked. He had donned a football helmet at some point; his close-set eyes, deep in the shadow of the forehead shield, looked like those of a small and hungry bird. 'Who's this?'

Frank pushed Don aside and dropped to one knee beside the kid. 'I'm Frank,' he said. 'What's the message?'

Terry also took a knee. His breath was redolent of booze. 'Come on, son. Take a beep death . . . deep breath . . . and pull yourself together.'

Kent groped among his scattered thoughts. 'That woman in the prison there, the special one, she's got friends in town. Lots of them. Two of them grabbed me. They said to tell you to stop what you're doing and go away, or the police station will only be the first thing to go.'

Frank's lips stretched in a smile that came nowhere near his eyes. He turned to Terry. 'So what do you think, Sheriff? Are we going to be good boys and go away?'

Little Low was no Mensa candidate himself, but he possessed a degree of cunning that had kept the Griner operation afloat for almost six years before he and his brother had finally been brought down. (Low blamed his generous nature; they had let the McDavid cunt, who was hardly a ten, hang around and she had repaid them by becoming a snitch.) He had an instinctive grasp of human psychology in general and male psychology in particular. When you told men they oughtn't to do a thing, that was what they did.

Terry didn't hesitate. 'Not going away. Going in at sunrise. Let them blow up the whole goddam town.'

The men who had gathered around raised a cheer so hoarse and so savage that Kent Daley flinched. What he wanted more than anything was to take his sore head home, lock all the doors, and go to sleep.

11

So far, the adrenalin was holding out; Van hammered on Fritz Meshaum's door hard enough to rattle it in its frame. A long-fingered hand that looked as if it had too many knuckles pulled aside a filthy curtain. A stubble-spackled face peered out. A moment later, the door opened. Fritz opened his mouth, but Van seized him and began to shake him like a terrier with a rat before he could utter a word.

'What did you sell them, you scrawny little shitepoke? Was it a rocket launcher? It was, wasn't it? How much did those bastards pay you so they could blow a hole in the middle of downtown?'

By then they were inside, Van roughly steering Fritz across his cluttered living room. He beat feebly at one of her shoulders with his left hand; the other arm was bound in a makeshift sling that looked as if it had been made from a bedsheet.

'Quit it!' Fritz shouted. 'Quit it, woman, I already had my damn arm dislocated by them two cretins!'

Van shoved him down in a filthy armchair with a stack of old skin magazines beside it. 'Talk.'

'It wasn't a rocket launcher, it was a vintage Russian bazooka, coulda sold it for six, seven thousand dollars at one of those parkin lot gun sales up in Wheeling, and those two country-fried fuckers *stole* it!'

'Well, of course you would say that, wouldn't you?' Van was panting.

'It's the truth.' Fritz looked at her more closely, his eyes sliding from her round face to her big breasts to her wide hips, then back up again. 'You're the first woman I've seen in two days. How long you been awake?'

'Since last Thursday morning.'

'Holy moly, that must be a record.'

'Not even close.' Van had Googled it. 'Never mind that. Those boys just blew up the sheriff's station.'

'I heard a hell of a bang,' admitted Fritz. 'Guess that bazooka works pretty good.'

'Oh, it worked fine,' Van said. 'I don't suppose you'd know where they're going next.'

'Nope, not a clue.' Fritz began to grin, exposing teeth that hadn't seen a dentist in a good long while, if ever. 'But I could find out.'

'How?'

'Damn fools looked right at it, and when I told em it was an inventory tag, they *believed* me!' His laugh sounded like a file scraping on a rusty hinge.

'What are you talking about?'

'GPS tracker. I put em on all my high-end items, case they get stolen. Which that bazooka was. I can track it on my phone.'

'Which you will give me,' Van said, and held out her hand.

Fritz looked up at her, his eyes a sly and watery blue under wrinkled lids. 'If you get my bazooka, will you give it back before you go to sleep?'

'No,' Van said, 'but I won't give you a broken arm to go with the one they dislocated. How's that?'

The little man chuckled and said, 'All righty, but it's just cause I got a soft spot for wide women.'

If she had felt more like herself Van might've had to beat the shit out of him for a comment like that – it wouldn't be hard and it would be public service – but in her exhaustion, she hardly considered it. 'Come on, then.'

Fritz pushed up from the couch. 'Phone's on the kitchen table.' She backed up, keeping the rifle on him.

He led her down a short, dark hall and into the kitchen. There was a stench of ash that made Van gag. 'What have you been cooking?'

'Candy,' Fritz said. He thumped down at a linoleum-topped table.

'Candy?' It didn't smell like any candy she knew of. Gray scraps, like bits of burned newspaper, were scattered around the floor.

'Candy's my wife,' he said. 'Now deceased. Lit the mouthy old bag up with a kitchen match. Never realized she had such a spark.' His black and brown teeth were revealed in a ferocious grin. 'Get it? Spark?'

No avoiding it now. Tired or not, she was going to have to put a hurting on the vile bastard. That was Van's first thought. The second was, there was no cell phone on the linoleum-topped table.

A gun banged and the air went out of Van. She thumped against the refrigerator and down to the floor. Blood spilled from a bullet wound at her hip. The rifle she had been holding had flown from her hands. Smoke curled from around the edge of the eating table directly in front of her. She spotted the barrel then; the pistol that Meshaum had strapped underneath the tabletop.

Fritz pulled it free of the duct tape that had held it, stood, and came around the table. 'Never can be too careful. Keep a loaded gun in every room.' He squatted down beside her and jammed the barrel of a pistol against her forehead. His breath smelled like tobacco and meat. 'This one was my opa's. What you think about that, you fat pig?'

She didn't think much of it, and didn't have to. Van Lampley's right arm – the arm that had put down Hallie 'Wrecker' O'Meara in the championship match of the 2010 Ohio Valley Women's 35–45 Year-Old Division, and snapped one of Erin Makepeace's elbow ligaments in 2011 to repeat – was like a spring trap. Her right hand swung up, catching Fritz Meshaum's wrist and squeezing with fingers made of steel, jerking down so violently that he was pitched forward on top of her. The antique pistol went off, putting a bullet into the floor between Van's arm and side. Bile rose in her throat as the weight of his body pressed into her wound, but she kept twisting his wrist, and at that angle all he could do was fire into the floor again before the gun slipped from his hand. Bones popped. Ligaments twanged. Fritz screamed. He bit her hand, but she just turned harder on his wrist, and began to methodically punch him in the back of the head with her left fist, driving down with the diamond of her engagement ring.

'Okay, okay! Uncle! Fuckin uncle! I give!' screamed Fritz Meshaum. 'That's enough!'

But Van did not think so. Her bicep flexed and the tattoo of the headstone – **YOUR PRIDE** – swelled.

She kept twisting with one hand and punching with the other.

CHAPTER 12

1

On the prison's last night, the weather cleared and the rain clouds of the day were blown south by a steady wind, leaving the sky to the stars and inviting the animals to stick their heads up, and sniff, and converse. No seventy-two hours. No second thoughts. A change was coming tomorrow. The animals felt it the way they felt oncoming thunderstorms.

2

Hunkered beside his partner in the rearmost seat of one of the schoolbuses that had been requisitioned to block Route 31, Eric Blass listened to Don Peters's snores. Any vague remorse Eric had felt about burning Old Essie had been assuaged by the fading of the day. If no one ever noticed she was gone, what did she count for, really?

Rand Quigley, a far more thoughtful man than most gave him credit for, was also hunkered down. His spot was in a plastic chair in the visitors' room. In his lap he had overturned the toddler-sized toy car from the family area. It had been a source of disappointment for as long as Rand could remember; the kids of the inmates climbed in it and pushed forward, but got frustrated because they couldn't turn. The problem was a broken axle. Rand had fetched a tube of epoxy from his toolbox and glued the break, and now he tied the pieces together to set with a bowline knot of twine. That he might be in his last hours did not elude Officer Quigley. It comforted him to do something useful with whatever time might be left.

On the wooded knoll above the prison, Maynard Griner stared up at the stars, and fantasized about shooting them out with Fritz's bazooka. If you could do that, would they pop like light bulbs? Had anyone – scientists, maybe – poked a hole in space? Did aliens on other planets ever think about shooting out stars with bazookas or death-rays?

Lowell, propped against the trunk of a cedar, commanded his brother, who was flat on his back, to wipe his mouth; the light of the stars, sent out billions of years ago, glimmered on Maynard's drool. Low's mood was sour. He did not like to wait, but it was not in their best interest to unload with the artillery until the cops made their move. The mosquitoes were biting and some hemorrhoid of an owl had been screeching since sundown. Valium would have improved his spirits greatly. Even some Nyquil would have been helpful. If Big Lowell's grave had been nearby, Little Lowell would not have hesitated to dig up the rotting corpse and relieve it of that bottle of Rebel Yell.

Down below, the T-shaped structure of the prison lay pinned in the harsh radiance that shone from the light towers. On three sides, woods surrounded the dell in which the building stood. There was an open field to the east, running up to the high ground where Low and May were camped. That field was, Low thought, an excellent firing lane. Nothing at all to impede the flight of a high-explosive bazooka shell. When the time came, it was going to be awesome.

3

Two men crouched in the space between the nose of Barry Holden's Fleetwood and the front doors of the prison.

'You want to do the honors?' Tig asked Clint.

Clint wasn't sure it was an honor, but said okay and lit the match. He placed it against the trail of gas that Tig and Rand had laid earlier.

The trail flamed, snaking from the front doors across the apron of the parking lot and under the interior fence. In the grass median that separated this fence from the second, outer fence, the piles of doused tires first smoldered and then began to flicker. Soon, the firelight had cut away much of the darkness at the perimeter of the prison. Curls of filthy smoke began to rise.

Clint and Tig went back inside.

4

In the darkened officers' break room, Michaela used a flashlight to sift the drawers. She found a pack of Bicycles, and asked Jared to play War with her. Everyone else, save the three remaining wakeful prisoners, was on watch. Michaela needed something to occupy herself. It was around ten P.M. on Monday night. Way back last Thursday morning, she had awoken at six sharp and gone running. Feeling frisky, feeling fine.

'Can't,' Jared said.

'What?' Michaela asked.

'Super busy,' he said, and gave a twitchy grin. 'Thinking about stuff I should have done, and didn't. And how my dad and mom should have waited to be mad at each other. Also about how my girlfriend – she wasn't really my girlfriend, but sort of – fell asleep while I was holding her.' He repeated, 'Super busy.'

If Jared Norcross needed mothering, Michaela was the wrong person. The world had been out of tilt since Thursday, but as long as she'd been around Garth Flickinger, Michaela had been able to treat it almost like a lark, a bender. She would not have expected to miss him so much. His stoner good cheer was the only thing that made sense once the world went wacky.

She said, 'I'm afraid, too. You'd be crazy not to be afraid.'

'I just . . .' He trailed off.

He didn't understand it, what the others around the prison had said about the woman, that she had *powers*, and that this Michaela, the warden's reporter daughter, had supposedly received a magic kiss from the special prisoner that had given her new energy. He didn't understand what had come over his father. All he understood was that people had started to die.

As Michaela had guessed, Jared missed his mother, but he wasn't angling for a substitute. There was no replacing Lila.

'We're the good guys, right?' Jared asked.

'I don't know,' Michaela admitted. 'But I'm positive we're not the bad guys.'

'That's something,' Jared said.

'Come on, let's play cards.'

Jared swiped a hand across his eyes. 'What the hell, okay. I'm a champ at War.' He came over to the café table in the middle of the break room.

'Do you want a Coke or something?'

He nodded, but neither of them had change for the machine. They went to the warden's office, emptied out Janice Coates's huge knit handbag, and crouched on the floor, sifting for silver through the receipts and notes and ChapSticks and cigarettes. Jared asked Michaela what she was smiling about.

'My mom's handbag,' said Michaela. 'She's a prison warden, but she's got, like, this hippie monstrosity for a bag.'

'Oh.' Jared chuckled. 'But what's a warden's handbag supposed to look like, do you think?'

'Something held together with chains or handcuffs.'

'Kinky!'

'Don't be a child, Jared.'

There was more than enough change for two Cokes. Before they went back to the break room, Michaela kissed the cocoon that held her mother.

War usually lasted forever, but Michaela beat Jared in the first game in less than ten minutes.

'Damn. War is hell,' he said.

They played again, and again, and again, not talking much, just flipping cards in the dark. Michaela kept winning.

5

Terry dozed in a camp chair a few yards behind the roadblock. He was dreaming about his wife. She had opened a diner. They were serving empty plates. 'But Rita, this isn't anything,' he said, and handed his plate back to her. Rita handed it right back. This went on for what seemed like years. Back and forth with the empty plate. Terry grew increasingly frustrated. Rita, never speaking, grinned at him like she had a secret. Outside the windows of the diner, the seasons were shuffling past like photographs through one of those old View-Masters — winter, spring, summer, fall, winter, spring—

He opened his eyes and Bert Miller was standing over him.

Terry's first waking thought was not of the dream, but of earlier that night, at the fence, Clint Norcross calling him out about the booze, humiliating him in front of the other two. The irritation of the dream mixed with shame, and Terry fully comprehended that he was not the man for the sheriff's job. Let Frank Geary have it if he wanted it so bad. And let Clint Norcross have Frank Geary if he wanted to deal with a sober man.

Camp lights were set up everywhere. Men stood in groups, rifles hung from straps over their shoulders, laughing and smoking, eating food from crinkly plastic MRE packages. God only knew where they'd come from. A few guys knelt on the pavement, shooting dice. Jack Albertson was using a power drill on one of the bulldozers, rigging an iron plate over the window.

Selectman Bert Miller wanted to know if there was a fire extinguisher. 'Coach Wittstock's got asthma and the smoke from those assholes' tire fires is drifting over here.'

'Sure,' Terry said, and pointed to a nearby cruiser. 'In the trunk.'

'Thanks, Sheriff.' The selectman went to fetch the extinguisher. There was a cheer from the dicing men as somebody made a hard point.

Terry lurched up from the camp chair and oriented himself toward the parked cruisers. As he walked, he unbuckled his gunbelt and let it fall into the grass. Fuck this shit, he thought. Just fuck it.

In his pocket were the keys to Unit Four.

6

From his seat on the driver's side of the animal control pickup, Frank observed the acting sheriff's silent resignation.

You did that, Frank, Elaine said from beside him. *Aren't you proud?*

'He did it to himself,' Frank said. 'I didn't tie him down and put a funnel in his mouth. I pity him, because he wasn't man enough for the job, but I also envy him, because he gets to quit.'

But not you, Elaine said.

'No,' he agreed. 'I'm in it to the end. Because of Nana.'

You're obsessed with her, Frank. Nana-Nana-Nana. You refused to hear anything Norcross said, because she's all you can think of. Can you not wait at least a little longer?

'No.' Because the men were here, and they were primed and ready to go.

What if that woman is leading you by the nose?

A fat moth sat on the pickup's wiper blades. He flicked the wand for the blades to clear it off. Then he started the engine and drove away, but unlike Terry, he intended to return.

First, he stopped at the house on Smith to check on Elaine and Nana in the basement. They were as he had left them, hidden away behind a shelving unit and tucked beneath sheets. He told Nana's body that he loved her. He told Elaine's body that he was sorry that they could never seem to agree. He meant it, too, although the fact that she continued to scold him, even in her unnatural sleep, was extremely irritating.

He relocked the basement door. In the driveway, by the headlights of his pickup, he noticed a pool had collected in the large pothole that he had planned to fix soon. Sediments of green and brown and white and blue sifted around in the water. It was the remains of Nana's chalked drawing of the tree, washed away by the rain.

When Frank reached downtown Dooling, the bank clock read 12:04 A.M. Tuesday had arrived.

As he passed the Zoney's convenience store, Frank noticed that someone had smashed out the plate glass windows.

The Municipal Building was still smoking. It surprised him that Norcross would allow his cohorts to blow up his wife's place of work. But men were different now, it seemed – even doctors like Norcross. More like they used to be, maybe.

In the park across the street, a man was, for no apparent reason, using a cutter to work on the verdigris-stained trousers of the statue of the top-hatted first mayor. Sparks fountained up, doubling in the tinted slot of the man's welding helmet. Farther along, another man, a la Gene Kelly in *Singin' in the Rain,* was hanging off a lamp post, but he had his cock in his hand and he was pissing on the pavement and bellowing some fucked-up sea chanty: '*The captain's in his cabin, lads, drinking ale and brandy! Sailors in the whorehouse, where all the tarts are handy! Way, haul away, we'll haul away, Joe!*'

The order that had existed, and which Frank and Terry had tried to shore up over the last few chaotic days, was collapsing. It was, he supposed, a savage kind of mourning. It might end, or it might be building to a worldwide cataclysm. Who knew?

This is where you should be, Frank, Elaine said.

'No,' he told her.

He parked behind his office. Each day he'd found half an hour to stop in here. He fed his strays in their cages and left a bowl of Alpo for the one that was his special pet, his office-dog. There was a mess in the holding area each time he came, and they were restless, shivering and whimpering and howling, because he usually was only able to walk them once a day, if that, and of the eight animals, probably only a couple had ever been housetrained to begin with.

He considered putting them down. If something happened to him, they would almost certainly starve; it wasn't likely a Good Samaritan would come along and take care of them. The possibility of simply releasing them did not cross his mind. You didn't let dogs run wild.

A fantasy sketched itself in Frank's mind's eye: coming in the next day with Nana, letting her help feed and walk them. She always liked to do that. He knew she would love his office-dog, a sleepy-eyed beagle-cocker mix with a stoic manner. She would love the way his head drooped down over his paws like a kid slumped over a desk, forced to listen to some never-ending school lecture. Elaine didn't like dogs, but no matter what happened, that no longer made a difference. One way or another, he and Elaine were through, and if Nana wanted a dog, it could stay with Frank.

Frank walked them on triple leashes. When he finished, he wrote a note – PLEASE CHECK ON THE ANIMALS. MAKE SURE THEY HAVE FOOD AND WATER. GRAY-WHITE PITBULL MIX IN #7 IS SKITTISH APPROACH CAREFULLY. PLEASE DON'T STEAL ANYTHING, THIS IS A GOVERNMENT OFFICE. – and fastened it to the outside door with duct tape. He stroked the office-dog's ears for a couple of minutes. 'Look at you,' he said. 'Just look at you.'

When he returned to his pickup and headed back to the road-block, the bank clock read 1:11 A.M. He'd start prepping everyone for the assault at four thirty. Dawn would come two hours later.

7

Across the prison athletic fields, on the far side of the fence, two men with bandannas over their mouths were using fire extinguishers to put out the tire fires. The extinguisher spray glowed phosphor-escent through the night vision scope and the men were limned in yellow. Billy Wettermore didn't recognize the larger man, but the smaller one he knew well. 'Yonder dingleberry in the straw hat is Selectman Miller. Bert Miller,' Billy said to Willy Burke.

There was ironic personal history here. While attending Dooling High, Billy Wettermore had, as a National Honor Society student, interned in the selectman's office. There he had been forced to silently attend to Bert Miller's frequent thoughts on homosexuality.

'It's a mutation,' Selectman Miller explained, and he dreamed of stopping it. 'If you could wipe out all the gays in an instant, Billy, perhaps you could stop the mutation from spreading, but then again, much as we might not like to admit it, they're human, too, aren't they?'

A lot had happened in the intervening decade-plus. Billy was a country boy and stubborn, and when he quit college he had returned to his Appalachian home town in spite of the politics. Around here his preference for men seemed to be the first thing on everyone's mind. This being almost two decades into the twenty-first century, that was damned annoying to Billy, not that he would ever show it, because that would be giving folks something they didn't deserve to have.

However, the thought of putting a bullet in the dirt right in front of Bert Miller and making him drop a big old bigoted shit in his pants was extremely tempting. 'I'm going to give him a jump, get him away from our tires, Willy.'

'No.' This came not from Willy Burke, but from behind him.

Norcross had materialized from the propped-open door at the rear of the prison. In the dimness, there was barely anything to his face except for the shine on the rims of his glasses.

'No?' Billy said.

'No.' Clint was rubbing the thumb of his left hand across the knuckles of his right. 'Put one in his leg. Drop him.'

'Seriously?' Billy had shot game, but never a man.

Willy Burke made a kind of humming sound through his nose. 'Bullet in the leg can kill a man, Doc.'

Clint nodded his head to show he understood. 'We have to hold this place. Do it, Billy. Shoot him in the leg. That'll be one less and it'll show them we're not playing games here.'

'All right,' Billy said.

He dropped his eye down to the scope. Selectman Miller, big as a billboard, crisscrossed the two layers of chainlink, was fanning himself with his straw hat, the extinguisher set on the grass beside him. The crosshairs settled on Miller's left knee. Billy was glad his target was such an asshole, but he hated to do it anyway.

He triggered.

8

Evie's rules were:

1) Stay undercover and no killing until daylight!
2) Cut open the cocoons enclosing Kayleigh and Maura!
3) Enjoy life!

'Yeah, that's fine,' Angel said. 'But are you sure Maura an Kay won't kill me while I'm enjoyin life?'

'Pretty sure,' Evie said.

'Good enough,' Angel said.

'Open her cell,' Evie said, and a line of rats emerged from the hole by the shower alcove. The first one stopped at the base of Angel's cell door. The second climbed atop the first, the third atop the second. A tower formed, gray rat body stacked on gray rat body like hideous ice cream scoops. Evie gasped when she felt the bottom rat suffocate. 'Oh, Mother,' she said. 'I am so, so sorry.'

'Look at this wonderful circus shit here.' Angel was entranced. 'You could make money at this, sister, you know it?'

The topmost rat was the smallest, still a pup. It squeezed into the keyhole and Evie controlled its tiny paws, searching through the mechanisms, investing it with a strength that no rat had ever possessed before. The cell door opened.

Angel fetched a couple of towels from the shower, fluffed them up, laid them on the bunk, and draped a blanket over them. She closed the cell door behind her. If anyone looked in, it would appear that she had finally lost the fight and fallen asleep.

She started up the corridor, headed for C Wing, where most of the cocooned sleepers now resided.

'Goodbye, Angel,' Evie called.

'Yeah,' Angel said. 'See ya.' She hesitated with her hand on the door. 'You hear screamin somewhere far off?'

Evie did. It was, she knew, Selectman Bert Miller, blatting about the bullet wound in his leg. His wailing carried inside the prison through the ventilation ducts. Angel didn't need to concern herself with that.

'Don't worry,' Evie said. 'It's just a man.'

'Oh,' Angel said, and left.

9

Jeanette had been sitting against the wall across from the cells during Angel and Evie's conversation, listening and observing. Now she turned to Damian, years dead and buried over a hundred miles away, and yet also sitting beside her. He had a clutchhead screwdriver in his thigh and he was bleeding onto the floor, although the blood didn't feel like anything to Jeanette, not even wet. Which was strange, because she was sitting in a pool of it.

'Did you see that?' she asked. 'Those rats?'

'Yeah,' Damian said. His tone went high-pitched and squeaky, his imitation of her voice. '*I see those ratsies, Jeanie baby.*'

Ugh, Jeanette thought. He had been all right when he first re-appeared in her life, but now he was becoming irritable.

'There's rats just like that chew on my corpse because of how you killed me, Jeanie baby.'

'I'm sorry.' She touched her face. It felt like she was crying, but her face was dry. Jeanette scratched at her forehead, digging the nails in, trying to find some pain. She hated being crazy.

'Come on. Check it out.' Damian moved over, bringing his face up close. 'They chewed me right down to the marrow.' His eyes were black sockets; the rats had eaten the eyeballs. Jeanette didn't want to look, wanted to close her own eyes, but if she did, she knew sleep would be waiting.

'What kind of a mother lets her son's daddy be done by like this? Kills him and lets the rats chew on him like he was a goddam Butterfinger?'

'Jeanette,' Evie said. 'Hey. Over here.'

'Never mind that bitch, Jeanie,' Damian said. A rat pup fell out of his mouth as he spoke. It landed in Jeanette's lap. She screamed and slapped at it, but it wasn't there. 'I need your attention. Eyes on me, moron.'

Evie said, 'I'm glad you stayed awake, Jeanette. I'm glad you didn't listen to me. Something's happening on the other side and – well, I thought I'd be happy about it, but maybe I'm getting soft in my old age. On the off-chance this thing goes on long enough, I'd like for there to be a fair hearing.'

'What are you talking about?' Jeanette's throat ached. Her everything ached.

'Do you want to see Bobby again?'

'Of course I want to see him,' Jeanette said, ignoring Damian. It was getting easier to do that. 'Of course I want to see my boy.'

'All right, then. Listen carefully. There are secret ways between the two worlds – tunnels. Each woman who goes to sleep passes through one of them, but there's another – a very special one – that begins at a very special tree. That's the only one that goes both ways. Do you understand?'

'No.'

'You will,' Evie said. 'There's a woman on the other side of that tunnel, and she's going to close it unless someone stops her. I respect her position, I think it's perfectly valid, the male species has performed abysmally on this side of the Tree, no amount of grade inflation can alter that conclusion, but everyone deserves a say. One woman, one vote. Elaine Nutting can't be allowed to make the decision for everyone.'

Evie's face was at the bars of her cell. Verdant tendrils had grown up around her temples. Her eyes were auburn-colored tiger eyes. Moths had gathered in her hair, collecting themselves into a fluttering band. She was a monster, Jeanette thought, and beautiful.

'What does that have to do with Bobby?'

'If the Tree burns, the tunnel closes. No one can ever come back. Not you, not any other woman, Jeanette. The end will become inevitable.'

'Nope, nope, nope. It's already inevitable,' Damian said. 'Go to sleep, Jeanie.'

'Can you just shut up! You're dead!' Jeanette screamed at him. 'I'm sorry I killed you, and I would do anything to take it back, but you were cruel to me, and it's done, so will you just shut your fucking mouth!'

The declaration echoed around the narrow confines of A Wing. Damian was not there.

'Well put,' Evie said. 'Courageous! Now listen to me, Jeanette: I want you to close your eyes. You'll go through the tunnel – *your* tunnel – but you won't remember.'

This part Jeanette thought she understood. 'Because I'll be sleeping?'

'Exactly! Once you're on the other side, you're going to feel better than you have in quite a long time. I want you to follow the fox. He'll take you where you need to go. Remember: Bobby and Tree. The one depends on the other.'

Jeanette let her eyes shut. Bobby, she reminded herself. Bobby and the Tree and the tunnel that went both ways. The one some woman named Elaine wanted to close by an act of burning. Follow the fox. She counted one-two-three-four-five and everything was the same. Except for Evie, that was, who had turned into a Green Lady. As if she were a tree herself.

Then she felt a tickle along her check, a swab of the lightest lace.

10

After the shot, they heard Bert Miller bellow and wail and keep wailing as his companion dragged him away. Clint borrowed Willy Burke's riflescope to take a look. The yellow-clad figure on the ground was clutching his thigh and the other guy was hauling him underneath his armpits.

'Good. Thanks.' Clint returned the rifle to Wettermore. Willy Burke was eyeing both of them with careful consideration: part admiration and part caution.

Clint went back inside. The rear door that let into the small gymnasium was propped open with a brick.

To lower visibility from the outside, they had trimmed the lights to just the red-tinted emergency bulbs. These cast small scarlet spots around the edges of the hardwood floor where inmates played half-court basketball. Clint stopped under the hoop and steadied himself against the padded wall. His heart was pumping. He wasn't scared, he wasn't happy, but he was *here*.

Clint warned himself about the euphoria he was feeling, but it didn't temper the pleasant thrumming in his limbs. He was either becoming walled off from himself or returning to himself. He didn't know which. What he knew was that he had the milkshake, and Geary wasn't going to take it away from him. That Geary was wrong almost didn't matter.

Aurora wasn't a virus, it was an enchantment, and Evie Black was like no woman – no human – who had ever existed. You couldn't fix something that was beyond human understanding with a hammer, which was what Frank Geary and Terry Coombs and the other men outside the prison presumed they could do. This required a different approach. It was obvious to Clint and should have been to them, because they weren't all stupid men, but for some reason it wasn't, and that meant he was going to have to use his own hammer to block theirs.

They started it! How childish! And how true!

The cycle of this logic went around on rusty, squalling wheels. Clint punched the padded wall several times and wished it were a man under his knuckles. He thought of pyrotherapy: the fever cure. For awhile, it had been cutting edge treatment, except giving malaria to your patients was awfully heavy medicine. Sometimes it saved them, and sometimes it finished them. Was Evie a pyrotherapist or the pyrotherapy? Was she possibly doctor and treatment both?

Or, by ordering Billy Wettermore to fire that shot to the leg of Selectman Bert Miller, had he himself administered the first dose?

11

Footsteps clicked across the floor from the direction of the gymnasium. Angel was just leaving the abandoned Booth with a set of cell keys. She gripped them in her right hand, the longest key protruding between the knuckles of her index finger and her middle finger. She had once stabbed a sloppy old cowboy in an Ohio parking lot in the ear with a sharpened key. It had not killed the cowboy, but he hadn't enjoyed it much. Angel, feeling kind, had merely taken from the man his wallet, his dimestore wedding ring, his scratch tickets, and silver belt buckle; she had allowed him to keep his life.

Dr Norcross walked by the glassed wall of the Booth without stopping. Angel weighed coming up behind him and plunging the key in the untrustworthy quack's jugular. She loved the idea. Unfortunately, she had made a promise to Evie not to kill anyone until daylight, and Angel was profoundly wary of crossing the witch.

She allowed the doctor to pass.

Angel headed for C Wing and the cell that was home to Maura and Kayleigh. The shape that was clearly Maura, short and stout, lay on the outside of the bottom bunk, where someone had placed her after she had gone night-night in A Wing. Kayleigh was on the inside of the bunk. Angel had no clue what Evie had meant when she said that 'their souls were dead,' but it encouraged caution.

She used the tip of a key to slice through the webbing that covered Maura's face. The material separated with a purr, and Maura's pudgy, red-cheeked features emerged. They could have served as the model for an illustration on the box of some 'down home' brand sold in little backwater stores – 'Mama Maura's Cornbread' or 'Dunbarton Soothing Syrup.' Angel jumped away into the hall, ready to flee if Maura went for her.

The woman on the bed sat up slowly.

'Maura?'

Maura Dunbarton blinked. She stared at Angel. Her eyes were entirely pupil. She pulled her right arm free of its cocoon, then her left arm, and then placed her hands together in her crinkly lap.

After Maura had sat like that for a couple of minutes, Angel eased into the cell again. 'I won't just harm you if you move on me, Mo-Mo. I'll kill you.'

The woman sat quietly, black eyes fixed on the wall.

Angel used the key to slice the webbing that covered Kayleigh's face. As quickly as before, she darted back out of the cell and into the hall.

The same process repeated itself: Kayleigh slipping down the top half of her cocoon as though it were a dress, looking with eyes that were all black. Shoulder to shoulder, the two women sat, torn webs hanging over their hair, their chins, their necks. They looked like ghosts in some cheap traveling carny's haunted house.

'You gals all right?' Angel asked.

They made no reply. They did not appear to be breathing.

'You know what-all you're supposed to do?' Angel asked, less nervous now, but curious.

They said nothing. No reflection of any kind stirred in their black eyes. A faint scent of turned, damp earth emanated from the two women. Angel thought (she wished she hadn't), *This is how the dead sweat.*

'Okay. Good.' Either they would do something or they wouldn't. 'I'll leave you gals to it.' She thought of adding something of an encouraging nature, like *go get em*, and decided not to.

Angel went to the woodshop and used the keys to unlock the tools. She tucked a small hand drill into her waistband, a chisel into one sock, and a screwdriver into the other.

Then, she lay down on her back beneath a table, and watched a dark window for the first sign of light. She didn't feel a bit sleepy.

12

Filaments spun and whirled around Jeanette's face, splitting and falling and rising, burying her features. Clint knelt beside her, wanting to hold her hand, but not daring. 'You were a good person,' he told her. 'Your son loved you.'

'She *is* a good person. Her son *does* love her. She is not dead, she only sleeps.'

Clint went to the bars of Evie's cell. 'So you say, Evie.'

She sat on her cot. 'You look like you're getting your second wind, Clint.'

Her bearing – the downward tilt of her head, glossy black hair falling across the side of her face – was melancholy. 'You can still hand me over. But not for much longer.'

'No,' he said.

'What a voice on that man you had Wettermore shoot! I could hear him all the way over here.'

Her tone wasn't goading. It was reflective.

'People don't like to be shot. It hurts. Maybe you didn't know that.'

'The Municipal Building was destroyed tonight. The ones who did it blamed it on you. Sheriff Coombs took a walk. Frank Geary will bring his people in the morning. Does any of that surprise you, Clint?'

It didn't. 'You're very good at getting what you want, Evie. I'm not going to congratulate you, though.'

'Now think of Lila and the others in the world beyond the Tree. Please believe me: they're doing well there. They're building something new, something fine. And there will be men. Better men, raised from infancy by women in a community of women, men who will be taught to know themselves and to know their world.'

Clint said, 'Their essential nature will assert itself in time. Their maleness. One will raise a fist against another. Believe me, Evie. You're looking at a man who knows.'

'Indeed so,' Evie agreed. 'But such aggression isn't *sexual* nature, it's *human* nature. If you ever doubt the aggressive capacity of women, ask your own Officer Lampley.'

'She'll be asleep somewhere by now,' Clint said.

Evie smiled, as if she knew better. 'I am not so foolish as to promise you the women on the far side of the Tree have utopia. What they will have is a better start, and a good chance of a better finish. You are standing in the way of that chance. You and only you, of all the men on earth. I need you to know that. If you let me die, those women will be set free to live lives of their own choosing.'

'Lives of *your* choosing, Evie.' His voice sounded parched to his own ears.

The being on the other side of the cell door tapped a rhythm on the frame of the cot with her fingertips. 'Linny Mars was in the sheriff's station when it was destroyed. She's gone forever. She didn't get a choice.'

'You took it from her,' Clint said.

'We could go on like this forever. He said, she said. The oldest story in the universe.' Evie left the cell door and sat on her cot. 'Go fight your war, Clint. That's one thing men know how to do. Make me see another sunset if you can.'

CHAPTER 13

1

As the rim of the sun appeared over the woods behind Dooling Correctional, a line of bulldozers clanked up West Lavin, end-to-end. All three were Caterpillars, two D9s and a big D11. The assault team was eighteen men in total. Fifteen of them were with the bulldozers, headed for the front gate; three of them were advancing around the backside of the prison fence. (They'd left Selectman Miller at the roadblock with a bottle of Vicodin and his bandaged leg propped on a camp chair.)

Frank had organized twelve in the forward group – his dirty dozen – into three quartets. Each quartet, in vests and masks, hunkered behind a bulldozer, using it for cover. The windows and grilles of the dozers had been jury-rigged with scrap steel. Retired Deputy Jack Albertson drove the first in line, Coach JT Wittstock drove the second, and the former Golden Gloves boxer, Carson Struthers, drove the third. Frank was with Albertson's bulldozer.

The men in the woods were Deputy Elmore Pearl, the deer hunter Drew T. Barry (his office now in ruins), and Don Peters.

2

Clint spotted the bulldozers from the high window on B Wing and bolted for the stairs, pulling on his bulletproof vest as he went. 'Have fun gettin fucked, Doc,' Scott Hughes called cheerfully as he ran past.

'Like they'll give you a pass if they get in,' Clint said. This wiped the smile from Scott's face.

Clint hurried down Broadway, stopping to put his head in the visitors' room. 'Rand, they're coming. Lay down the teargas.'

'Okay,' said Rand from the family alcove at the end of the room, and calmly donned the gas mask he had at the ready.

Clint continued to the security station at the main door.

The station was your basic bulletproof tollbooth where visitors were required to check in. The little room had a long facing window and a drawer for passing IDs and valuables through to the officer on duty. There was a communications board like the ones in the Booth and the gatehouse, with monitors that could flip through views of the various inner and outer areas of the prison. Tig was at the board.

Clint rapped on the door and Tig opened it.

'What have you got on the monitors?'

'Sunrise is flaring the lenses. If there's men behind the bulldozers, I can't see them yet.'

They had eight or nine gas grenades to go with the launcher. On the central monitor, below the spirals of glare, Clint saw several of these strike the parking lot and spew white fumes to mix with the tarry smoke still leaking from the tires. He told Tig to keep watching and ran on.

His next destination was the break room. Jared and Michaela were at a table with a deck of cards and cups of coffee.

'Make yourselves scarce. It's starting.'

Michaela toasted him with her cup. 'Sorry, Doc. I'm legal to vote and everything. I think I'll stick around. Who knows, there might be a Pulitzer in my future.'

Jared's color was chalky. He looked from Michaela to his father.

'Fine,' Clint said. 'Far be it for me to abridge the freedom of the press. Jared, hide, and don't tell me where.'

He jogged on before his son could respond. His breath was short by the time he reached the rear door that opened near the shed and the fields. The reason that, until the morning of Aurora, he'd never before suggested to Lila that they should go running was because he hadn't wanted her to have to limit her pace for him; it would have been embarrassing. What was the root here, vanity or laziness? Clint promised himself to give the question real consideration when he had a free second and, if he should be so lucky as to live through the morning, and ever get to speak to his wife again, possibly to repeat his proposal that they take up jogging together.

'Three bulldozers on the road,' Clint announced as he emerged outside.

'We know,' Willy Burke said. He walked over to Clint from his spot behind the shed. There was a weird contrast between his bulletproof vest and his festive red suspenders, now lolling in loops at his hips. 'Tig radioed. Billy's going to hold tight here, watch the north fence. I'm gonna sidle on up along this wall to the corner and see if I can get a few clean shots. You're welcome to join me, but you'll need one of these.' He handed Clint a gas mask and put on his own.

3

At the ninety-degree turn from the road to the gate, Frank pounded the metal plate over the door, a signal to Albertson to hang a right. Jack did so – slowly and carefully. The men slipped back further, keeping the mass of metal in front of them at all times as it swung around. Frank was wearing a vest, and he had a Glock in his right hand. He could see licks of smoke spilling down the road. This was expected: he'd heard the pops of the gas grenades being fired. They couldn't have too many. There had been a lot more masks than grenades in the armaments room of the sheriff's station.

The first bulldozer completed its adjustment and the four men climbed on the back, pressed together shoulder to shoulder.

In the bulldozer cockpit Jack Albertson was safe behind the steel blade, which was raised to the upper position, therefore blocking the window. He gave it plenty of gas as it headed for the gate.

Frank used his walkie, although not everyone in his attack force had them; all of this had been done on the fly. 'Get ready, everyone.

This is going to happen.' And please, he thought, with as little bloodshed as possible. He was already two men down, and the attack hadn't even started.

4

'What do you think?' Clint asked Willy.

On the other side of the double fences, the first bulldozer, blade high, was crunching forward. For a half-second there'd been a glimpse of movement slipping around to the back of the machine.

Willy didn't respond. The old moonshiner was revisiting an unnamed square meter of hell in Southeast Asia in '68. Everything had been still, swamp water up to his Adam's apple, a layer of smoke closing out the sky, him sandwiched in the middle; everything had been so still, and a bird, red and blue and yellow and massive, eagle-sized, had floated up beside him, dead, its eye clouded. The creature was so vivid and so incongruous in the strange light. Its glorious feathers had grazed Willy's shoulder, and the faint current had drawn it away, and it had vanished back into the smoke.

(Once, he had told his sister about that. 'Never saw a bird like that before. Not the whole time I was there. Never saw one since, either, of course. I wonder sometimes if it was the last of its kind.' The Alzheimer's had taken most of what made her herself by then, but there had been a small piece left, and she had said, 'Maybe it was just – hurt, Willy,' and Willy had said to her, 'I sure love you, you know.' His sister had blushed.)

The dozer blade hit the middle of the fence with a rattling crash. The links bowed inward before the whole section tore free of the ground and flopped back against the second layer of fence across the median. Ghosts of teargas broke across the front of the bulldozer as it ground forward, bashing against the second fence with the tangled fragment of the first. The inner fence buckled and collapsed, the bulldozer jouncing over the debris. It continued across the smoke-filled parking lot, a length of fencing stuck shrieking under its nose.

The second and third bulldozers followed the first through the gap.

A brown shoe, visible behind the rear left corner of the first bulldozer, appeared in Willy's sight. He fired. A man shouted and fell out from behind the bulldozer, one pinwheeling arm casting off a shotgun. It was a banty-legged little guy wearing a gas mask and a vest. (Willy wouldn't have known it was Pudge Marone, saloonkeeper of the Squeaky Wheel, even if Pudge's face had been visible. Willy hadn't drunk in bars, not for years.) While the man's torso was covered, his legs and arms were not, and that was just fine because Willy did not want to kill anyone if he could help it. He shot again, not quite where he wanted, but close enough, and the .223-caliber bullet, expressed by an M4 assault rifle that had been the property of the Dooling Sheriff's Department until the previous day, blew off Pudge Marone's thumb.

An arm reached out from behind the bulldozer to assist the prone man, an understandable and perhaps commendable attempt, though definitely unwise. The arm in question belonged to retired Deputy Nate McGee, who, having lost over a hundred dollars playing dice on the tarmac of Route 31 the previous evening, had soothed himself with a pair of false thoughts: one, that if he'd known for certain that Mrs McGee might some day reawaken, he wouldn't have bet at all; and two, that at least he had used up his bad luck for the week. Not so. Willy shot a third time, catching the elbow of the reaching arm. There was another shout and McGee tumbled from behind the bulldozer. Willy squeezed off four more quick shots, testing the steel plate that had been mounted over the bull-dozer's grille, and heard them zing off uselessly.

Frank leaned out from the cover of the first bulldozer with a pistol and fired a series of rapid shots at Willy. In 1968 Willy might have been able to judge by the angle of Geary's arm that his aim would be way off, and thus stayed in position and taken him out, but 1968 was fifty years ago, and getting shot at was something you lost your coziness with pretty swiftly. Willy and Clint scooted to cover.

As Jack Albertson's bulldozer rolled through the tangles of teargas and black smoke, straight on for the RV and the front doors, the debris under its nose grinding, the second bulldozer, driven by Coach Wittstock, barreled through the hole in the fence.

Like Albertson before him and Carson Struthers behind him, Coach Wittstock's blade was raised for protection. He could hear the shots, could hear the shouts, but he couldn't see Nate McGee clutching his elbow on the ground in front of him, and when the bulldozer rolled over the disabled man, Coach Wittstock assumed it was just one of the burned tires that the machine's crawlers were climbing.

He whooped. He was breaking through just like he taught his linebackers to do, reckless and relentless!

From his vantage at the window in the visitors' room, Rand waited to fire on the first bulldozer until it was halfway between the gatehouse and the front doors. His shots struck plating here and there, ricocheting off without effect.

Pete Ordway, the Wittstock boys, and Dan 'Treater' Treat, under cover of the second bulldozer, found themselves confronted with the crushed corpse of Nate McGee. The dead man's gas mask was full of blood and his torso had burst out around the straps of his vest. Gore sprayed up from the crawler treads; shreds of skin flapped like streamers. Rupe Wittstock screamed and leaped away from the mess, clearing himself of the viscera, but putting himself in Rand's line of fire.

Rand's first shot missed his target's head by an inch, the second by half an inch. Rand swore at himself and put his third shot square in the middle of the man's back. The slug lodged itself in the bulletproof vest the target was wearing and bowed him over. He threw his arms skyward like a fan in a stadium doing the Wave. Rand shot a fourth time, lower. It hit the target in the buttocks and sent him sprawling.

Deputy Treat was not fazed. Treater, only a year late of the 82nd Airborne, still possessed the relative comfort with being shot at that Willy Burke had lost long ago. He hopped off Dozer Two without a second thought. (He was relieved, in fact, to settle into military mode. Action was a break from the untenable reality of his daughter, Alice, at that second propped at her play table in their apartment, wrapped up in white fibers, when she ought to have just been getting up for another day of second grade. And it was a break from the thought of his year-old son, currently in a makeshift daycare run by men.) Free of cover, Treat returned suppression fire with an M4 he'd recovered on Route 31.

At the window, Rand dropped to his knees on the table he had been standing atop. Concrete fragments rained down his neck and back.

Treater hoisted Rupe Wittstock and pulled him to safety behind a stack of smoldering tires.

Dozer One crashed into the rear end of the Fleetwood RV, slamming its hood against the front doors of the prison in an explosion of glass.

5

Jared sat on the floor of the laundry room while Michaela piled sheets around him, constructing a mound to hide him. 'I feel stupid,' Jared said.

'You don't look stupid,' Michaela said, which wasn't true. She fluttered a sheet above his head.

'I feel like a pussy.'

Michaela hated that word. Even as she heard more shots ring out, it touched a nerve. A pussy was supposed to be soft, and although Michaela possessed one, there was nothing particularly soft about the rest of her. Janice Coates had not raised her to be a softie. She flipped up the sheet and gave Jared a hard – but not too hard – slap across the cheek.

'Hey!' He put a hand to his face.

'Don't say that.'

'Say what?'

'Don't say pussy when it means weak. If your mother didn't teach you better than that, she should have.' Michaela dropped the sheet over his face.

6

'It is a fucking crime that someone is not filming this for fucking reality TV,' Low said. Eye to the scope of the bazooka, he had seen the second bulldozer squash the poor sucker who had fallen in front of the treads, seen the Rambo guy jump out from behind the second dozer, start blasting, and rescue another guy. He then witnessed – not without a mixture of wonder and glee – the first bulldozer as it smashed the RV into an accordion in front of the prison doors. It was a stellar conflict, and it was only going to get better once they spiced the soup with three or four bazooka shells.

'When do we do our thing?' May asked.

'Soon as the cops have wore themselves out a bit more.'

'How are we going to be sure we got Kitty, Low? That place must be full of slags in cocoons.'

Low didn't appreciate his brother's last minute naysaying. 'We probably won't be absolutely sure, May, but we are going to fire all these shells, and blow the fuck out of the place, so I like our chances. To a certain extent, I suppose we're just going to have to hope for the best. Now are we going to enjoy this or not? Or would you rather that I do all the shooting?'

'Come on, Low, I didn't say that,' protested May. 'Be fair.'

7

On Level 32 of *Boom Town*, little pink spiders began to invade Evie's field of stars, triangles, and burning orbs. The spiders doused the orbs and turned them into the irritating sparkling blue stars that clogged up all the works – booger. In A Wing, the sound of the gunfire echoed piercingly. Evie was undisturbed; she had seen and heard men killing on numerous occasions. The pink spiders did bother her, though.

'So evil,' she said to no one, sliding her colorful shapes around, searching for connections. Evie was extremely relaxed; as she played with the phone, she floated on her back a couple of centimeters above the cot.

8

Bushes twitched on the opposite side of the north fence, directly across from Billy Wettermore's position in the alley behind the garden shed. He unleashed a dozen rounds into the mass of greenery where the twitch had come from. The bushes shook and trembled.

Drew T. Barry, a crafty insurance man who always kept to the most risk-averse course, wasn't anywhere near Billy's line of fire. Instead, with the prudence that not only made him Dooling's first stop for all your indemnification needs but also an excellent deer hunter, willing to take his time to get an ideal shot, he had halted the other two men – Pearl and Peters – in the woods behind the prison gymnasium. Peters had told him that the rear door to the prison was on the west wall of the gym. The reaction produced by the rock that Drew had thrown into the brush close to that spot had told them a lot: yes, there must be a door, and yes, it was definitely defended.

'Deputy?' Drew T. Barry asked.

They were crouched behind an oak. Fifteen feet or so ahead of them, bits of leaf were still drifting down from where the gunfire had torn up the foliage. To judge by the sound, the shooter was perhaps thirty or forty yards beyond the interior fence, near the wall of the prison.

'What?' Don Peters replied. Sweat streaked his flushed face. He had been lugging the duffel bag with their masks and the bolt cutters.

'Not you, the real deputy,' Drew T. Barry said.

'Yeah?' Pearl nodded at him.

'If I kill this guy shooting here, there's no chance of prosecution? Are you sure Geary and Coombs will swear we acted in the legal performance of our duties?'

'Yup. Scout's honor.' Elmore Pearl raised his hand in the salute of his childhood, first three fingers raised, pinky held down by his thumb.

Peters hocked some phlegm. 'You need me to hustle back and fetch you a notary, Drew?'

Drew T. Barry ignored this witless jibe, told them to stay put, and started backtracking into the woods, taking the northern incline in quick, quiet steps, his Weatherby rifle strapped to his back.

9

With the bulldozer halted, Frank continued to aim at the southwest corner of the prison, ready to pick off the rifleman there if he showed his face. The shooting had rattled him; had made it all real. He felt nauseated by the blood and the bodies on the ground, obscured and revealed as the clouds of teargas shifted in the wind, but his determination was still strong. He felt horror but no remorse. His life was Nana's life, which made the risk acceptable. So he told himself.

Kronsky joined him. 'Hurry,' Frank said. 'The sooner this is over, the better.'

'You got a point there, Mister Man,' Kronsky said, on one knee with his backpack on the ground. He unzipped the pack, removed the bundle of dynamite, and snipped off three-quarters of the fuse.

The armored door of the bulldozer swung open. Jack Albertson climbed down, carrying his old service weapon, a .38.

'Cover us from yonder shitbird down the way,' Kronsky said to Albertson, pointing in the direction of Willy Burke's position. Then Kronsky turned to Frank. 'Come on, and you'd best high-step it.'

The two men hustled along the northwest wall of the prison, ducking low. Beneath the cutout window that was one of the defenders' firing points, Kronsky stopped. He had the dynamite in his right hand and a blue plastic lighter in the other. The defender's rifle barrel that had been there before poked back out.

'Grab that thing,' he said to Frank.

Frank didn't question the order, just reached up and closed his left hand around the metal tube. He jerked it out of the grip of the man inside. He heard a muffled curse. Kronsky flicked his lighter, lit the shortened fuse on the bundle, and casually tossed it, hook-shot-style, up and through the hole. Frank released the rifle and hit the ground.

Three seconds later there was a thundercrack. Smoke and chunks of bloody flesh flew from the cutout window.

10

The earth trembled and gave an outraged roar.

Clint, shoulder to shoulder with Willy Burke at the west wall, saw a tidal wave of teargas curl from the parking lot, swept along by whatever had just exploded. Chimes rang through his skull and his joints vibrated. Beneath the noise, all he could think was that things were not going as well as he had hoped. These guys were going to kill Evie and all the rest of them. His fault, his failing. The pistol that he had been carrying around, ridiculously – never once in their fifteen years of marriage had he taken up Lila's invitation to go to the gun range with her – had nevertheless slid into his hand, begging to be fired.

He leaned around Willy Burke, scanned the pile-up at the front doors, and locked on the figure standing at the rear of the first bulldozer. This man was staring at the cloud of dust boiling from Rand Quigley's window, which had been – like everything else this morning – exploded out of its former normal shape.

(Jack Albertson had not expected the blast. It startled him and he dropped his guard to look. While the chaos did not upset him – as a miner in his youth, one who had survived a good many rumbles in the earth, his nerves were cool – it did perplex him. What was wrong with these folks, that they would prefer a shootout to surrendering some damned wild woman to the law? In his view, the world got crazier and crazier with each passing year. His personal Waterloo had been Lila Norcross's election as Dooling sheriff. A skirt in the sheriff's office! It didn't get much more ludicrous than that. Jack Albertson had put in his retirement papers there and then, and returned home to enjoy his lifelong bachelorhood in peace.)

Clint's arm lifted the pistol, the gunsight found the man behind the bulldozer, and Clint's finger pulled the trigger. The shot was followed by a succulent pop, the sound of a bullet punching through the faceplate of the man's gas mask. Clint saw the head snap back and the body crumple.

Ah, Jesus, he thought. That was probably someone I knew.

'Come on,' Willy cried, hauling him away to the rear door. Clint went, his legs doing what they needed to do. It had been easier than he might have guessed to kill someone. Which only made it worse.

CHAPTER 14

1

When Jeanette opened her eyes, a fox was lying down outside the door to Evie's cell. Its snout rested on the fissured cement floor, from which ridges of green moss sprouted.

'Tunnel,' Jeanette said to herself. Something about a tunnel. She said to the fox, 'Did I go through one? I don't remember, if I did. Are you from Evie?'

It didn't answer, as she had almost expected it might. (In dreams animals could talk, and this felt like a dream . . . yet at the same time didn't.) The fox only yawned, looked at her slyly, and pushed itself to its feet.

A Wing was empty, and a hole gaped in the wall. Beams of morning sunlight poured through. There was frost on the chunks of broken cement, beading and liquefying as the temperature rose.

Jeanette thought, I feel awake again. I believe I *am* awake.

The fox made a mewling noise and trotted to the hole. It glanced at Jeanette, mewled a second time, and went through, and was swallowed by the light.

2

She gingerly picked her way through the hole, stooping under the sharp edges of gashed cement, and found herself in a field of knee-high weeds and dead sunflowers. The morning light made Jeanette squint. Her feet crunched frozen undergrowth and the cool air raised gooseflesh under the thin fabric of her uniform.

The strong sensations of fresh air and sunshine awakened her completely. Her old body, exhausted by trauma and stress and lack of sleep, was a skin that had been shucked. Jeanette felt new.

The fox cut briskly through the grass, taking her past the east side of the prison toward Route 31. Jeanette had to walk fast to keep up as her eyes adjusted to the sharp daylight. She flashed a glance at the prison: naked brambles choked the walls; the rusted hump of a bulldozer and an RV were jammed against the front of the building, also thick with brambles; extravagant clumps of yellow grass sprouted from cracks and gashes in the parking lot; other rusted vehicles were stranded across the tarmac. Jeanette looked in the opposite direction. The fences were down – she could see flattened chainlink glinting among the weeds. Although Jeanette couldn't make sense of the how or the why, she immediately absorbed the what. This was Dooling Correctional, but the world had spun on for years.

Her guide continued up from the ditch that edged Route 31 crossed the cracked and disintegrating road, and entered the blue-green dark of the rising woods on the other side. As the fox ascended, his orange brush bobbed and flashed in the dimness.

Jeanette ran across the road, keeping her eye on the flicking tail. One of her sneakers skated in a patch of damp, and she had to snatch for a branch to keep from losing her feet. The freshness of the air – tree sap and composting leaves and wet earth – burned down her throat and into her chest. She was out of prison, and a memory of playing Monopoly as a girl surfaced: Get Out of Jail Free! This wondrous new reality excised the square of forest from time itself, and made it an island beyond reach – of industrial cleaners, of orders, of jangling keys, of cellmate snores and farts, of cellmate crying, of cellmate sex, of cell doors banging shut – where she was the sole ruler; Queen Jeanette, evermore. It was sweet, sweeter even than she'd fantasized, to be free.

But then:

'Bobby.' She whispered it to herself. That was the name she had to remember, had to bring with her, so she would not be tempted to stay.

3

Judging distance was difficult for Jeanette; she was used to the level rubber track that circled the yard at the prison, each loop about half a mile. The steady southwest climb was more demanding than that and she had to lengthen her strides, making her thigh muscles sing in a way that hurt and felt wonderful at the same time. The fox stopped once in awhile to let her close some of the distance before he trotted on. She was sweating hard despite the chill. The air felt like that knife-edge of time when winter teetered on the edge of spring. A few green-tipped buds flashed in the gray-brown of the woods, and where the earth was naked to the sky, it was squishy with melt.

Maybe it was two miles, maybe three, when the fox led Jeanette around the rear side of a fallen trailer beached in a sea of weeds. Ancient yellow police tape fluttered on the ground. She had an idea she was getting close now. She heard a faint buzz in the air. The sun was higher and it was getting toward noon. She was starting to feel thirsty and hungry, and there might be something to eat and drink at her destination – how perfect a cold pop would be just now! But never mind, Bobby was what she needed to be thinking about. Seeing Bobby again. Ahead, the fox disappeared beneath an arch of broken trees.

Jeanette hurried after, passing a pile of rubble wigged in weeds. It might once have been a small cabin or shed. Here moths covered the branches of the trees, their countless tan bodies pressed together so that they resembled strange barnacles. Which followed somehow, Jeanette thought, understanding innately that the world she found herself in was outside of all she had ever known, like a land at the bottom of the sea. The moths appeared still, but she could hear them crackling softly, as if speaking.

Bobby, they seemed to say. *It's not too late to start again*, they seemed to say.

The slope finally topped out. Through the last of the woods, Jeanette could see the fox standing in the faded grasses of a winter field. She sucked at the air. A kerosene scent, wholly unexpected and seemingly unattached to anything, tingled in her nose and mouth.

Jeanette stepped into the open and saw something that could not be. Something that made her sure she was no longer in the Appalachian country she had always known.

4

It was a white tiger, coat tipped with black, fin-shaped markings. It rolled its head and roared, sounding like the MGM lion. Behind it soared a tree – a Tree – bursting up from the earth in a tangle of a hundred trunks that twisted into a looming, sprawling fountain of branches, dripping with leaves and curling mosses, alive with the flitting bodies of tropical birds. A massive red snake, shining and glittering, coursed up the center.

The fox trotted up to a gaping split in the bole, tossed a somehow roguish look at Jeanette, and vanished into the depths. That was it, that was the tunnel that went both ways. The tunnel that would take her back to the world she had left, the one where Bobby waited. She started toward it.

'Stop where you are. And raise your hands.'

A woman in a checked yellow button-down and blue jeans stood in grass that came up to her knees, pointing a pistol at Jeanette. She had come around the side of the Tree, which was, at its base, roughly the size of an apartment building. In the hand that wasn't holding the pistol she had a canister with a blue rubber band around its middle.

'No closer. You're new, aren't you? And your clothes say you're from the prison. You must be confused.' A peculiar smile touched Ms Yellow Shirt's lips, a futile attempt to soften the oddness of the situation – the Tree, the tiger, the gun. 'I want to help you. I will help you. We're all friends here. I'm Elaine, okay? Elaine Nutting. Just let me do this one thing and we'll talk more.'

'What thing?' Jeanette asked, although she was pretty sure she knew; why else the kerosene stink? The woman was getting ready to light the Impossible Tree on fire. If it burned, the way back to Bobby burned. Evie had pretty much said so. It couldn't be allowed, but how was the woman to be stopped? She was at least six yards away, too far to rush her.

Elaine went down on one knee, watching Jeanette carefully as she laid the pistol aside in the dirt (but close at hand) and quickly unscrewed the cap of the kerosene canister. 'I already spread the first two around. I just need to finish making a circle. To be sure it'll go up.'

Jeanette took a couple of steps forward. Elaine snatched up the gun and got to her feet. 'Stay back!'

'You can't do this,' Jeanette said. 'You have no right.'

The white tiger sat near the crevice that had absorbed the fox. It thumped its tail back and forth and watched with half-closed eyes of a brilliant amber.

Elaine splashed kerosene against the Tree, staining the wood a deeper brown. 'I *have* to do this. It's better this way. It solves all the problems. How many men have hurt you? Plenty, I imagine. I've worked with women like you for my entire adult life. I know you didn't just walk into prison on your own. A man pushed you.'

'Lady,' Jeanette said, offended by the idea that one look at her could tell anyone anything that mattered. 'You don't know me.'

'Maybe not personally, but I'm right, aren't I?' Elaine dumped the last of the kerosene onto some roots and pitched the canister aside. Jeanette thought, you ain't Elaine Nutting, you're Elaine Nuts.

'There was a man who hurt me, yes. But I hurt him worse.' Jeanette took a step toward Elaine. She was about fifteen feet away now. 'I killed him.'

'Good for you, but don't come any closer.' Elaine waved the pistol back and forth, as if she could brush Jeanette away. Or erase her.

Jeanette took another step. 'Some people say he deserved it, even some who were his friends once. Okay, they can believe that. But the DA didn't believe it. More important, *I* don't believe it, although it's true I wasn't in my right mind when it happened. And it's true that no one helped me when I needed help. So I killed him, and I wish I hadn't. It's on me, not him. I have to live with that. And I do.'

Another step, just a small one.

'I'm strong enough to take my share of the blame, okay? But I've got a son who needs me. He needs to know how to grow up right, and that's something I can teach him. I'm done being pushed around by anyone, man or woman. The next time Don Peters tries to get me to give him a handjob, I won't kill him, but I . . . I'll scratch his eyes out, and if he hits me, I'll keep right on scratching. I'm done being a punching bag. So you can take what you think you know about me, and you can shove it where the sun doesn't shine.'

'I believe you may have lost your mind,' said Elaine.

'Aren't there women here who want to go back?'

'I don't know.' Elaine's eyes shifted. 'Probably. But they're misguided.'

'And you get to make that decision for them?'

'If no one else has the guts,' Elaine said (with absolutely no awareness of how like her husband she sounded), 'then yes. In that case, it's down to me.' From the pocket of her jeans, she withdrew a long-barreled trigger lighter, the kind people used to fire up the coals in a barbecue. The white tiger was watching and purring – a deep rumbling sound like an idling engine. It didn't look to Jeanette as if there would be any help from that direction.

'Guess you don't have any kids, huh?' Jeanette asked.

The woman looked hurt. 'I have a daughter. She's the light of my life.'

'And she's here?'

'Of course she is. She's safe here. And I intend to keep her that way.'

'What does she say about that?'

'What she says doesn't matter. She's just a child.'

'Okay, what about all the women who had to leave boy children behind? Don't they have a right to raise their kids and keep them safe? Even if they do like it here, don't they have that *responsibility?*'

'See,' Elaine said, smirking, 'that statement alone is enough to tell me you're foolish. *Boys* grow up to be *men.* And it's men who cause all the trouble. They're the ones who shed the blood and poison the earth. We are better off here. There are male babies here, yes, but they're going to be different. We'll teach them to be different.' She took a deep breath. The smirk spread, as if she were inflating it with crazy-gas. 'This world will be kind.'

'Let me ask you again: You mean to close the door on the life all them other ladies left behind without even asking them?'

Elaine's smile faltered. 'They might not understand, so I . . . I'm making . . .'

'What're you making, lady? Besides a mess?' Jeanette slid her hand in her pocket.

The fox reappeared and sat beside the tiger. The red snake slithered weightily across one of Jeanette's sneakers, but she did not so much as look down. These animals did not attack, she understood; they were from what some preacher, back in the dim days of her optimistic churchgoing childhood, had called the Peaceable Kingdom.

Elaine flicked the lighter's switch. Flame wavered from the tip. 'I am making *an executive decision!*'

Jeanette pulled her hand from her pocket and hurled a handful of peas at the other woman. Elaine flinched, raised her hand with the gun in an instinctive motion of defense, and stepped back. Jeanette closed the remaining distance and caught her around the waist. The gun tumbled from Elaine's hand and fell into the dirt. She hung onto the lighter, though. Elaine stretched, the flame at the tip curling toward the knot of kerosene-dampened roots. Jeanette banged Elaine's wrist against the ground. The lighter slipped from her hand and went out, but too late – guttering blue flames danced along one of the roots, moving up toward the trunk.

The red snake slithered up the Tree, wanting away from the fire. The tiger rose, lazily, went to the burning root, and planted a paw on it. Smoke rose around the paw, and Jeanette smelled singeing fur, but the tiger remained planted. When it stepped away, the blue flames were gone.

The woman was weeping as Jeanette rolled off her. 'I just want Nana to be safe . . . I just want her to grow up safe . . .'

'I know.' Jeanette had never met this woman's daughter and probably never would, but she recognized the sound of true pain, spirit pain. She had experienced plenty of that herself. She picked up the barbecue lighter. Examined it. Such a small tool to close the door between two worlds. It might have worked, if not for the tiger. Was it supposed to do that, Jeanette wondered, or had it gone beyond its purview? And if that was so, would it be punished?

So many questions. So few answers. Never mind. She whipped her arm in a circle, and watched the barbecue lighter go spinning away. Elaine gave a cry of despair as it disappeared into the grass forty or fifty feet distant. Jeanette bent and picked up the pistol, meaning to put it in her belt, but of course she was wearing her inmate browns and had no belt. Belts were a no-no. Inmates sometimes hung themselves with belts, if they had them. There was a pocket in her drawstring pants, but it was shallow and still half full of peas; the gun would fall right out. What to do with it? Throwing it away seemed to be the wisest course.

Before she could do that, leaves rustled behind her. Jeanette swung around with the pistol in her hand.

'Hey! Drop it! Drop the gun!'

At the edge of the woods stood another armed woman, her own pistol trained on Jeanette. Unlike Elaine, this one held her weapon in both hands and with her legs planted wide, as if she knew what she was doing. Jeanette, no stranger to orders, started to lower the gun, meaning to put it in the grass beside the Tree . . . but a prudent distance away from Elaine Nutball, who might make a grab for it. As she bent, the snake rustled along the branch above her. Jeanette flinched and raised the hand holding the gun to protect her head from a half-glimpsed falling object. There was a crack, then a faint *tink*, two coffee mugs clicking together in a cabinet, and she seemed to hear Evie in her head – an inarticulate cry of mingled pain and surprise. After that, Jeanette was on the ground, the sky was nothing but leaves, and there was blood in her mouth.

The woman with the gun came forward. The muzzle was smoking, and Jeanette understood she had been shot.

'Put it down!' the woman ordered. Jeanette opened her hand, not knowing she still held the pistol until it rolled free.

'I know you,' Jeanette whispered. It felt as if there was a large warm weight on her chest. It was hard to breathe, but it didn't hurt. 'You were the one who brought Evie to the prison. The cop. I seen you through the window.'

'That smells like kerosene,' Lila said. She picked up the overturned canister, sniffed at it, then dropped it.

Outside that morning's Meeting at the Shopwell, someone had mentioned that one of the golf carts was missing, and no one had signed the register for it; a girl named Maisie Wettermore had volunteered that she had seen Elaine Nutting just a few minutes earlier, driving one in the direction of Adams Lumberyard. Lila, who had come with Janice Coates, had exchanged a glance with the ex-warden. There were only two things in the direction of Adams Lumberyard these days: the desiccated ruins of a meth lab, and the Tree. It had worried both of them, the idea of Elaine Nutting going out there alone. Lila had remembered Elaine's doubts about the animals there – the tiger, especially – and it occurred to her that she might try to kill it. This, Lila was certain, would be unwise. So, the two of them had taken out a golf cart of their own, and followed.

And now Lila had shot a woman she had never seen before, who lay bleeding on the ground, badly wounded.

'What the hell were you going to do?' she asked.

'Not me,' Jeanette said, and looked over at the weeping woman. 'Her. She was the one. Her kerosene. Her gun. I stopped her.'

Jeanette knew she was dying. Coldness like well water rising up through her, taking away her toes, then the rest of her feet, then her knees, slipping up toward the heart of her. Bobby had been afraid of water when he was little.

And Bobby had been afraid someone was going to take his Coke and his Mickey Mouse hat. That was the moment captured in the photo on her little block of paint in the cell. No, honey, no, she had told him. Don't you worry. Those are yours. Your mother's not going to let anyone take them from you.

And if Bobby were here now, asking about this water? This water that his mother was sinking down into? Oh, she'd tell him, that's nothing to worry about, either. It's just a shock at first, but you get used to it.

But Jeanette was no *Lying for Prizes* champion. She wasn't that caliber of contestant. She might have been able to get a fib past Bobby, but not Ree. If Ree had been there, she'd have had to admit, though the well water didn't hurt, it didn't feel right, either.

She could hear the host's disembodied voice: *That's all for Jeanette Sorley, I'm afraid, but we're sending her home with some lovely parting gifts. Tell her about them, Ken!* The host sounded like Warner Wolf, Mr Let's-Go-to-the-Videotape himself. Hey, if you had to be sent home, you couldn't ask for a better announcer.

Warden Coates, her hair now as white as chalk, interrupted Jeanette's sky. It kind of suited her, the hair. She was too thin, though, big dents under her eyes, hollows at her cheeks.

'Sorley?' Coates went to a knee and took her hand. 'Jeanette?'

'Oh, shit,' the cop said. 'I think I just made a very bad mistake.' She dropped to her knees and put her palms against Jeanette's wound, applying pressure, knowing it was pointless. 'I only meant to wing her, but the distance . . . and I was so afraid for the Tree . . . I'm sorry.'

Jeanette felt blood leaking from both corners of her mouth. She began to gasp. 'I have a son – his name is Bobby – I have a son—'

Jeanette's last words were directed at Elaine, and the last thing she saw was that woman's face, her wide, scared eyes. '—Please – I have a son—'

CHAPTER 15

Later, when the smoke and teargas clears, there will be dozens of stories about the battle for the Dooling Correctional Facility for Women, all of them different, most conflicting, true in some of the details and false in others. Once a serious conflict commences – a fight to the death – objective reality is quickly lost in the smoke and noise.

Also, many of those who could have added their own accounts were dead.

1

As Van Lampley – hip-shot, bleeding, tired to her soul – drove her ATV slowly along a dirt road that she believed might be Allen Lane (hard to tell for sure; there were so many dirt roads curling around in these hills), she heard a distant explosion from the direction of the prison. She looked up from the screen of the tracker-equipped cell phone she had liberated from Fritz Meshaum. On that screen, the phone in her hand was represented by a red dot. The GPS gizmo on the bazooka was a green one. The two dots were now very close, and she felt she had taken the ATV as far as she could without alerting the Griners that she was after them.

Maybe that boom was them shooting off another bazooka shell, she thought. It was possible, but as a mining-country girl who had grown up to the rough music of dynamite, she didn't believe it. The explosion from the prison had been sharper and harder. It had been dyno, all right. Apparently the Griner brothers weren't the only sleazebuckets abroad with explosives.

She parked, dismounted the ATV, and staggered. The left leg of her pants was soaked with blood from hip to knee, and the adrenalin that had carried her this far was dwindling. Every part of her body ached, but her hip, where Meshaum had shot her, was agony. Something was shattered in there, she could feel the bones grinding with every step, and now she was lightheaded with blood loss as well as days upon nights of no sleep. Every part of her cried out to give up – to quit this madness and go to sleep.

And I will, she thought, grabbing her rifle and the antique pistol Meshaum had used to shoot her, but not yet. I may not be able to do anything about what's happening at the prison, but I can put a hurt on those two bastards before they make it any worse. After that, I can rack out.

Branching off from the lane and angling up through the scrubby second-growth trees were two weedy ruts that might once have been a road. Twenty yards along, she found the truck the Griners had stolen. She looked inside, saw nothing she wanted, and continued on, her leg a rake that she dragged alongside the rest of her body. She no longer needed the tracker app because she knew where she was, although she hadn't been here since her high school days, when it had been a less-than-prime makeout spot. A quarter mile up, maybe a bit more, the overgrown track ended on a knoll where there were a few tilted gravestones: the family plot of a family that had long since departed – probably the Allen family, if this really was Allen Lane. It had been the third or fourth choice for randy kids because the view from the knoll was of Dooling Correctional. Not exactly conducive to romance.

I can do this, she told herself. Another fifty yards.

She made the fifty yards, told herself she could make another fifty, and continued that way until she heard voices ahead. Then there was an explosive *whoosh*, followed by Little Lowell Griner and his brother Maynard whooping and slapping each other on the back.

'I wasn't sure it'd have the range, brother, but looka that!' one of them cried. The response was a rebel yell.

Van cocked Meshaum's pistol, and moved toward the sounds of redneck celebration.

2

Clint would have believed the phrase *his heart sank* was nothing but a poetic expression until his actually did it. Unaware that he had left the cover provided by the southwestern corner of the main building, he stared, slack-jawed, at the concrete showering down from C Wing. How many of the sleeping women in that cellblock had been killed in the blast, incinerated or torn to pieces in their cocoons? He barely heard something buzz past his left ear, and didn't feel the tug as another bullet, this one thrown by Mick Napolitano from behind the second bulldozer, tore open one of his pants pockets and spilled loose change down his leg.

Willy Burke seized him by the shoulders and yanked him back so hard Clint nearly fell over. 'You crazy, Doc? You want to get yourself killed?'

'The women,' Clint said. 'There were women up there.' He swiped at his eyes, which were smarting from the acrid gas and welling with tears. 'That son of a bitch Geary put a rocket launcher or something up on that knoll where the little graveyard is!'

'Nothing we can do about it now.' Willy bent over and gripped his knees. 'You got one of the bastards, anyway, and that's a start. We need to be inside. Let's get to the back door, pull Billy in with us.'

He was right. The front of the building was now a free-fire zone. 'Willy, are you all right?'

Willy Burke straightened up and offered a strained smile. His face was pale, his forehead dotted with sweat. 'Well, shoot a pickle. Might be having a little heart episode. Doctor told me to give up the pipe after my last checkup. Shoulda listened.'

Oh no, thought Clint. Oh . . . fucking . . . no.

Willy read the thought on Clint's face – there was nothing wrong with his eyes – and clapped him on the shoulder. 'I ain't done yet, Doc. Let's go.'

3

From his position outside the visitors' room, now most surely gutted by the dynamite blast (along with whoever had been inside), Frank saw Jack Albertson go down with his gas mask torn askew. There was nothing but blood where his face had been. His own mother wouldn't recognize him, Frank thought.

He lifted his walkie-talkie. 'Report! Everybody report!'

Only eight or so did, mostly those who had been using the bulldozers for cover. Of course not all of the men had walkies, but there should have been at least a few more responses. Frank's most optimistic guess was that he had lost four men, including Jack, who had to be as dead as dirt. In his heart, he guessed it might be five or six, and the wounded would need hospitalization. Maybe the kid, Blass, whom they had left at the roadblock with Miller, could drive them back to St Theresa's in one of the buses, although God knew who might still be on duty at St Terry's. If anyone. How had it come to this? They had the bulldozers, for God's sake. The dozers were supposed to end it fast!

Johnny Lee Kronsky grabbed his shoulder. 'We need to get on in there, buddy. Finish them off. With this.' His backpack was still unzipped. He pushed aside the towel he'd wrapped the dynamite in and showed Frank the Griner brothers' bump of C4. Kronsky had shaped it into something that looked like a child's toy football. Embedded in it was an Android.

'That's my phone,' Kronsky said. 'I'm donating it to the cause. It was a piece of shit, anyway.'

Frank asked, 'Where do we go in?' The teargas was blowing away, but he felt as if his mind was full of it, obscuring all thought. The daylight was strengthening, the sun rising red.

'Right up the gut would be best,' Kronsky said, and pointed at the half-crushed Fleetwood RV. It was tilted against the building, but there was room to squeeze through and reach the main doors, which had been smashed inward and twisted off their hinges. 'Struthers and those bulldozer guys'll give us cover. We go in, and we keep moving until we get to the bitch that caused all this.'

Frank was no longer sure who had caused all this, or who was in charge, but he nodded. There seemed to be nothing else to do.

'Gotta set the timer,' Kronsky said, and powered up the phone embedded in the C4. There was a wire plugged into the cell's headphone port. The other end was attached to a battery pack stuck in the explosive. Looking at it made Frank remember Elaine preparing Sunday dinners, pulling the roast out of the oven and sticking in a meat thermometer.

Kronsky whapped him on the shoulder, and not gently. 'How much time, do you think? And think about it careful, because when the count gets down to single numbers, I'm gonna throw it, no matter where we are.'

'I guess . . .' Frank shook his head, trying to clear it. He had never been in the prison, and had expected Don Peters would give them all the layout they needed. He just hadn't realized how useless Peters was. Now that it was too late, that seemed like a glaring oversight. How many other things had he overlooked? 'Four minutes?'

Sounding like a crabby high school teacher faced with a thick-headed pupil, Kronsky said, 'Are you asking me or telling me?'

They heard spatters of gunfire, but the attack seemed to have fallen into a lull. The next thing might be his men deciding to fall back. That could not be allowed.

Nana, Frank thought, and said: 'Four minutes. I'm sure.'

Frank thought, In four minutes I'll either be dead, or this will be on the way to being over.

Of course it was possible the woman herself would be killed in the final assault, but that was a chance he would have to take. That made him think of his caged strays, their lives held hostage to forces they did not understand.

Kronsky opened an app, tapped the screen, and 4:00 appeared. He tapped again and the numbers began to count down. Frank watched, fascinated, as 3:59 became 3:58 became 3:57.

'You ready, Geary?' Kronsky asked. In his manic grin, a gold tooth glimmered.

('What are you doing?' the sonofabitch agitator had called to

Kronsky that day in the Ulysses Energy's Graystone #7 mine. 'Quit lagging.' The sonofabitch agitator had been at least twenty yards down the hall. In the deep black of the underground, Kronsky hadn't been able to see the dumb bastard's face, let alone his Woody Guthrie tee-shirt, just his headlamp. Power in a union, the sonofabitch agitator liked to say. More power in a dollar, and the man from Ulysses Energy had given Johnny Lee Kronsky a few crisp ones to take care of their problem. 'Fuck you, your union, and the horse you rode in on,' Kronsky had told the sonofabitch agitator, before throwing the dynamite and running like hell.)

'I think we ought to—' Frank began, and that was when Lowell Griner fired the bazooka for the first time. There was a *whooshing* sound almost directly overhead. Frank had a blurred glimpse of something flying. Some projectile.

'Hit the deck!' Kronsky screamed, but didn't give Frank a chance to do so; just grabbed him around the neck and yanked him down.

The bazooka shell hit C Wing and exploded. In the world beyond the Tree, fourteen former Dooling Correctional inmates disappeared, flashing once, before clouds of moths spilled into the open air where they had stood.

4

Although he had a walkie, Drew T. Barry was one of those who had not responded to Frank's command to report in. He didn't even hear it, because he had turned the walkie off. He'd gotten as high up as he could while maintaining cover, and unslung his Weatherby. The angle wasn't quite as good as he'd hoped. Through the Weatherby's scope, he could see a corrugated metal shed. The back door to the prison was open – light spilled out in an oblong – but that guy was behind the shed, defending the way in. Barry saw an elbow . . . a shoulder . . . part of a head, but quickly withdrawn after a single peek at where Elmore Pearl and Don Peters were still stationed. Drew T. Barry had to put that guy down, and itched to take the shot – yes, his trigger finger was literally itching – but he knew that no shot was better than a bad one. He had to wait. If

Pearl or Peters would throw another rock, that might make the guy down there stick his whole head out to see what was happening, but Drew T. Barry did not expect this to happen. Elmore Pearl was too cautious, and that fat little shit Peters was as numb as a pounded thumb.

Move, you sucker, Drew T. Barry thought. Two steps would be enough. Maybe just one.

But although he cringed into a crouch when the bundle of dynamite went off, Billy Wettermore held his position behind the shed. It took the exploding bazooka shell to get him on his feet. He stepped out from behind the protection of the shed, looking toward the sound, and that gave Drew T. Barry the clean shot he had been waiting for.

Smoke was billowing above the prison. People were yelling. Guns were firing – wildly, no doubt. Drew T. Barry had no patience with wild shooting. He held his breath and squeezed the trigger of his rifle. The result was entirely satisfactory. In his scope he saw the defender fly forward, his shirt billowing out in shreds.

'Got him, by God,' Drew T. Barry said, looking at the remains of Billy Wettermore with a species of doleful satisfaction. 'Was a good shot, if I do say so myse—'

From the trees below came another gunshot, followed by the unmistakable voice of Deputy Elmore Pearl: '*Oh, you fuckin idiot, what did you do? WHAT DID YOU DO?*'

Drew T. Barry hesitated, then ran back toward his mates, keeping low, wondering what had gone wrong now.

5

Clint and Willy saw Billy Wettermore thrown in the air. When Billy came down he was boneless. One of his shoes flew from his foot, spun up, and banged off the lip of the shed roof. Clint started toward him. Willy Burke's hand pulling him back was surprisingly strong.

'Nope, nope,' Willy said. 'Back it up, Doc. That way's no good now.'

Clint tried to think. 'We might be able to get into my office through the window. The glass is reinforced, but not barred.'

'I can take care of the window,' Willy said. 'Let's go.' But instead of moving, he bent over and grasped his knees again.

6

Don Peters hardly heard Elmore Pearl shouting at him. Down on his knees, he was staring at his erstwhile Zombie Patrol partner, who was spreadeagled on the ground with blood gushing from a hole in the base of his throat. Eric Blass stared up at him, gagging on more blood.

'Partner!' Don shouted. His football helmet slid down, obscuring his eyes, and he pushed it back up with the heel of his hand. 'Partner, I didn't mean to!'

Pearl hauled him to his feet. 'You dumb asshole, didn't anybody ever teach you to see what you were shooting at before you pulled the trigger?'

Eric made a thick glugging sound, coughed out a fine spray of blood, and pawed at the ruins of his throat.

Don wanted to explain. First the roar of the dynamite, then a second explosion, then the rustling bushes behind him. He had been sure it was more of that fucking shrink's men. How was he supposed to know it was Blass? He had shot without thinking, let alone aiming. What evil brand of providence had caused the shot to hit Blass as he came through the trees to join them?

'I . . . I . . .'

Drew T. Barry appeared, his Weatherby slung over his shoulder. 'What in hell's name—'

'Wild Bill Hickok here just shot one of ours,' Pearl said. He socked Don in the shoulder, driving him down beside Eric. 'Kid was coming to help out, I guess.'

'I thought he was back at the buses!' Don gasped. 'Frank told him to stay back in case there was wounded, I heard him!' This much was true.

Drew T. Barry hauled Don to his feet. When Pearl balled up a fist to hit the weeping, white-faced man again, Barry grabbed him. 'Beat him all you want later. Beat him like a red-headed stepchild, for all of me. Right now we might need him – he knows the lay of the land in there, and we don't.'

'Did you get him?' Pearl asked. 'The guy down there by that shed?'

'I got him,' Drew T. Barry said, 'and if this ever winds up in a courtroom, remember you gave me the green light. Now let's end this.'

From a knoll above the prison, they saw a flash of bright light, and a contrail of white smoke. This was followed by another explosion on the other side of the prison.

'Who in fuck is shooting rockets from up on that hill?' Pearl asked.

'Don't know and don't care,' Barry said. 'Being as how we're behind the prison, we've got a thousand or so tons of concrete between us and them.' He pointed down the hill and across the track. 'What's inside that door, Peters?'

'The gym,' Don said, eager to atone for what he was already coming to believe had been a justifiable mistake, the sort of thing anyone might have done. I was trying to protect Pearl as well as myself, he thought, and when this madness is over, Elmore will see that. Elmore will probably thank me and buy me a drink down at the Squeak. And hey, it was just Blass, a lunatic delinquent if ever there was one, lighting that poor homeless bag on fire before Don could stop him.

'It's where the cunts play basketball and volleyball. The main corridor starts on the other side, what we call Broadway. The woman's in a cell in A Wing, down to the left. Not far.'

'Then let's go,' Pearl said. 'You lead, Quickdraw. I got clippers for the fence.'

Don didn't want to lead. 'Maybe I ought to stay here with Eric. He was my partner, after all.'

'No need,' Drew T. Barry said. 'He has expired.'

7

A year before Aurora, when Michaela had still been relegated to taping filler features for NewsAmerica – stuff like dogs that could count and twin brothers meeting by accident after fifty years of separation – she had done a story about how people with large collections of books had lower heating bills than non-readers, because books made good insulation. With this in mind, she repaired to the prison library once the shooting started, scurrying with her head low. What she discovered was mostly shelves of battered paperbacks, not exactly the insulation she'd had in mind, and when the dynamite bundle exploded in the room next door, she was pelted with Nora Roberts and James Patterson novels as the wall buckled.

She ran back onto Broadway, this time not bothering to duck but pausing, horrified, to look into the visitors' room, where what remained of Rand Quigley was puddled on the floor and dripping from the ceiling.

She was totally disoriented, on the verge of panic, and when the bazooka shell hit C Wing and a cloud of dust billowed toward her (reminding her of news footage she'd seen following the collapse of the Twin Towers), she turned to go back the way she had come. Before she managed three steps, a strong arm encircled her throat, and she felt a cold steel edge press against her temple.

'Hey there, sweetcheeks,' Angel Fitzroy said. When Michaela did not immediately respond to this greeting, Angel pressed harder with the chisel she'd borrowed from the furniture shop. 'What the fuck's going on out there?'

'Armageddon,' Michaela managed in a gasping voice that sounded nothing like her chirrupy TV tones. 'Please stop choking me.'

Angel let go and turned Michaela to face her. The smoke drifting down the corridor carried the bitter tang of teargas, making them cough, but they could see each other well enough. The woman with the chisel was pretty in a narrow, intense, predatory sort of way.

'You look different,' Michaela said. Possibly a supremely stupid comment with the prison under attack and a convict brandishing a chisel in front of her eyes, but all she could think of. 'Awake. Really awake.'

'*She* woke me up,' Angel said proudly. 'Evie. Same as she did you. Cause I had a mission.'

'What mission would that be?'

'*Them,*' Angel said, and pointed as two female creatures came shambling down the corridor, seemingly untroubled by the smoke and gunfire. To Michaela, the shreds of cocoon hanging from Maura Dunbarton and Kayleigh Rawlings looked like bits of rotted shroud in a horror movie. They passed by without looking at Michaela and Angel.

'How can they—' Michaela began, but a second bazooka shell hit out front before she could finish her question. The floor shook, and more smoke billowed in, black and stinking of diesel fuel.

'Don't know how they can do anything, and don't care,' Angel said. 'They got their job and I got mine. You can help out, or I can put this chisel in your gizzard. Which would you prefer?'

'I'll help,' Michaela said. (Journalistic objectivity aside, it would be hard to report the story later if she was, you know, dead.) She followed Angel, who at least seemed to know where she was going. 'What's the job?'

'Gonna protect the witch,' Angel said. 'Or die trying.'

Before Michaela could reply, Jared Norcross stepped out of the kitchen, which was adjacent to the prison laundry where Michaela had left him. Angel raised the chisel. Michaela grabbed her wrist. 'No! He's with us!'

Angel was giving Jared her best Stare of Death. 'Are you? Are you with us? Will you help protect the witch?'

'Well,' Jared said, 'I was planning to go clubbing and drop some E, but I guess I could change my plans.'

'I told Clint I'd protect you,' Michaela said reproachfully.

Angel brandished her chisel and bared her teeth. 'No one gets protection today but the witch. No one gets protection but Evie!'

'Fine,' Jared said. 'If it helps my dad and gets my mom and Mary back, I'm in.'

'Is Mary your girlfriend?' Angel asked. She had lowered the chisel.

'I don't know. Not exactly.'

'Not exactly.' Angel seemed to chew on that for a moment. 'You treat her right? No pushing, no hitting, no yelling?'

'We need to get out of here before we choke,' Michaela said.

'Yeah, I treat her right.'

'Damn well better,' Angel said. 'Let's get truckin. Evie's in the soft cell down on A Wing. Soft cell, but hard bars. You gotta stand in front of her. That way, anyone that wants to get to her will have to go through you.'

Michaela thought that sounded like a terrible plan, which might explain why Angel was talking 'you' instead of 'us.'

'Where will you be?'

'Commando mission,' Angel said. 'Maybe I can drop a few before they get this far.' She brandished her chisel. 'I'll be with you soon, don't fear.'

'A few guns might help, if you really—' Jared was drowned out by the loudest explosion yet. This time shrapnel – mostly pieces of wall and ceiling – rained down. When Michaela and Jared straightened up again, Angel was no longer with them.

8

'What the fuck was *that*?' Frank asked in the seconds after the first bazooka shell hit C Wing. He got to his feet, brushing dust, dirt, and a few crumbles of cement out of his hair. His ears weren't ringing, exactly; what he heard was the high, steely whine he sometimes got in his head after taking too much aspirin.

'Someone's shooting off ordinance from up on yonder knoll,' Kronsky said. 'Probably the same ones who took out the sheriff's station. Come on, Mr Acting Sheriff. Time's a-wasting.' He once more bared his teeth in a gold-twinkling grin so cheerful it looked surreal. He pointed at the screen of the phone embedded in the plastic explosive. 3:07 became 3:06 became 3:05.

'Okay,' Frank said.

'Remember, don't hesitate. He who hesitates is butt-fucked.'

They headed for the crushed front doors. In his peripheral vision, Frank could see the men who had come in behind the bulldozers, watching them. None seemed eager to join this particular assault, and Frank did not blame them. Probably some were wishing they had left with Terry Coombs.

9

As the battle for Dooling Correctional approached its climax, Terry was parked in his garage. The garage was a small one; the door was closed; Unit Four's windows were open and its big V8 engine was running. Terry inhaled exhaust in long, chest-filling gulps. It tasted bad to begin with, but you got used to it pretty fast.

It's not too late to change your mind, Rita said, taking his hand. His wife sat beside him in the passenger seat. You might still be able to take control out there. Impose a little sanity.

'Too late for that, hon,' Terry said. The garage was now blue with toxic vapor. Terry took another deep breath, stifled a cough, and inhaled again. 'I don't know how this is going to come out, but I see no good ending. This way is better.'

Rita squeezed his hand sympathetically.

'I keep thinking of every mess on the highway I ever cleaned up,' Terry said. 'And that guy's head, pushed right through the wall of that meth-cooker's trailer.'

Dimly, across the miles, from the direction of the prison, came the sound of explosions.

Terry repeated, 'This way is better,' and closed his eyes. Although he knew he was alone in Unit Four, he could still feel his wife squeezing his hand as he drifted away from Dooling and everything else.

10

Frank and Johnny Lee Kronsky were working their way between the wreckage of Barry Holden's RV and the wall of the prison. They were almost to the smashed main doors when they heard the second bazooka shell whistling toward them.

'*Incoming!*' Kronsky shouted.

Frank looked over his shoulder and saw an amazing thing: the bazooka shell struck the parking lot on its rear fin, bounced high without exploding, and dropped nose-down toward the bulldozer that had been piloted by the late Jack Albertson. The roar of its detonation was deafening. The driver's seat was blown through the thin shell of the dozer's roof. Disintegrating treads rose in the air like steel piano keys. And one of the iron shields that had been placed to guard the cockpit doors shot outward, punching through the RV ahead of it like the peen of a giant's sledgehammer.

Frank stumbled over the twisted base of one of the main doors, and thus his life was saved. Johnny Lee Kronsky, still upright, was not just decapitated by a flying wedge of the Fleetwood's siding; he was cut in two at the shoulders. Yet he staggered on two or three more steps, his heart beating long enough to send two gaudy jets of blood into the air. Then he collapsed. The C4 football fell from his hands and wobbled toward the security station. It came to rest with the embedded Android phone visible, and Frank saw 1:49 become 1:48 become 1:47.

He crawled toward it, blinking concrete dust out of his eyes, then rolled to one side and into the shelter of the half-collapsed reception desk as Tig Murphy leaped up behind the security station's bulletproof glass and fired his sidearm through the slot where visitors were supposed to surrender their IDs and phones. The angle was bad, and Tig's slug went high. Frank was okay if he stayed down, but if he tried to go forward, toward the doors leading into the prison proper, he'd be a sitting duck. Going back, ditto.

The lobby was filling with diesel smoke from the burning bull-dozer. Added to this was the high, nauseating stench of Kronsky's spilled blood – gallons of it, from the look. Beneath Frank was one of the reception desk's legs, its splintered end digging into his back between his shoulder blades. Lying just out of Frank's reach was the C4. 1:29 became 1:28 became 1:27.

'There's men all around the prison!' Frank shouted. 'Give up and you won't be hurt!'

'Suck shit! This is our prison! You're trespassing, and you got no authority!' Tig fired another shot.

'There's explosive! C4! It's going to blow you to pieces!'

'Right, and I'm Luke fucking Skywalker!'

'Look out! Look down! You'll see it!'

'So you can try putting one in my gut through the slot? Think I'll pass.'

Desperate, Frank looked around toward the doors he'd come through, partially blocked by the remains of the RV. '*You guys out there!*' he shouted. '*I need some covering fire!*'

No covering fire came. No reinforcements, either. Two of the men – Steve Pickering and Will Wittstock – were in full retreat, carrying the wounded Rupe Wittstock between them.

On the littered floor of the lobby, almost at the base of the security station manned by Tig Murphy, the cell phone continued to count down toward zero.

11

Seeing Billy Wettermore undeniably dead made Don Peters feel a little better. Don had gone bowling with him once. The little princess had rolled a 252 and taken twenty bucks off Don. It was pretty obvious that he'd used some sort of doctored bowling ball, but Don had let it pass, the way he let so many things pass, because that was the kind of easygoing guy he was. Well, sometimes the world tilted the right way, and that was a fact. One less fag in the world, he thought, and we all say hooray.

He hustled toward the gymnasium. Maybe I'll be the one to get her, he thought. Put a bullet right into Evie Black's quacking mouth and end this for good. They'd forget all about that mistake with Junior, and I wouldn't have to buy a drink down at the Squeak for the rest of my life.

He stepped toward the door, already imagining Evie Black in his sights, but Elmore Pearl shoved him away. 'Stand back, Quickdraw.'

'Hey!' Don bleated. 'You don't know where you're going!'

He started forward again, but Drew T. Barry grabbed him and shook his head. Barry himself had no intention of being first inside, not when he didn't know what was waiting. Probably the one he'd shot had been their only rearguard, but if there *was* someone, Pearl had a better chance of knocking him down than Peters, whose only kill this morning had been one of their own.

Pearl was looking over his shoulder at Don and grinning as he stepped into the gym. 'Relax, and let a man lead the w—'

That was as far as he got before Maura Dunbarton's cold hands gripped him, one by the neck and the other by the back of his head. Elmore Pearl gazed into those soulless eyes and began to screech. He didn't screech for long; the reanimated thing that had been Maura stuck her hand into his mouth, ignored his biting teeth, and yanked straight down. The sound of his upper and lower jaws parting company was like the sound of a drumstick being torn off a Thanksgiving turkey.

12

'Damn if we ain't a couple of lucky sonsabitches!' Maynard Griner exulted. 'Any more distance and them shells'd just explode in the parking lot. Did you see that last one bounce, Low?'

'I saw it,' Low agreed. 'Skipped like a stone on a pond and took out a bulldozer. Not bad, but I can do better. Reload me.'

Below, the prison was boiling smoke from the hole in the western wall. It was a glorious sight, reminiscent of the gush that came out of a mine when a blast went off, except much better obviously, because they weren't cracking rocks. They were cracking a goddam state facility. It would have been worth doing even if they hadn't needed to close Kitty McDavid's snitching mouth.

May was reaching into the ammo bag when he heard a branch snap. He whirled, reaching for the gun stuffed into his belt at the small of his back.

Van fired the pistol Fritz Meshaum had tried to kill her with. The range was short, but she was exhausted, and instead of taking Maynard in the chest, the bullet only clipped his shoulder and sent him sprawling over the depleted bag of bazooka shells. His unfired gun fell into some bushes and caught by the trigger guard. 'Brother!' he shouted. 'Shot! She shot me!'

Low dropped the bazooka and snatched up the rifle lying beside him. With one of them out of commission, Van could afford to focus. She secured the butt of the pistol at the center of her considerable bosom, and pulled the trigger. Little Low's mouth exploded, his brains exited the back of his skull, and he aspirated his teeth with his final breath.

'Low!' Maynard screamed. 'Brother!'

He grabbed the gun hanging in the bushes, but before he could bring it to bear, his wrist was gripped by something more like an iron manacle than a human hand.

'You should know better than to point a gun at an arm-wrestling champ, even when she's been awake for a week,' Van said in an oddly gentle voice, and twisted. From inside May's wrist came a sound like breaking twigs. He shrieked. The gun dropped from his hand and she kicked it away.

'You shot Low,' Maynard blubbered. 'Kilt him!'

'So I did.' Van's head was ringing; her hip was throbbing; it felt like she was standing on a deck in rough waters. She was near the end of her considerable endurance, and she knew it. But this had been a sight more useful than killing herself, no doubt about that. Only now what?

May had the same question, it seemed. 'What are you going to do with me?'

I can't tie him up, Van thought. I've got nothing to tie him up with. Am I just going to go to sleep and let him get away? Probably after he puts a few rounds in me while I'm growing my cocoon?

She looked down at the prison, where a crushed RV and a blazing bulldozer blocked the main doors. She meditated on the hole the first bazooka shell had put in C Wing, where dozens of women had been sleeping, defenseless in their cocoons. How many had been killed by these two country-fried assholes?

'Which one are you? Lowell or Maynard?'

'Maynard, ma'am.' He tried on a smile.

'You the stupid one or the smart one, Maynard?'

His smile grew. 'I'm the stupid one, no doubt. Failed out of school in the eighth grade. I just do whatever Lowell says.'

Van returned the smile. 'Well, I guess I'll just let you go, Maynard. No harm and no foul. You've got a truck down there. I took a peek, and the keys are in the ignition. Even driving one-handed, I think you could be most of the way to Pedro's South of the Border by noon, if you don't spare the horses. So why don't you get going, before I change my mind?'

'Thank you, ma'am.'

May started jogging back among the tombstones of the little country graveyard. Van briefly considered following through on her promise, but the chances were fair to good that he'd double back and discover her sleeping beside his dead brother. Even if he didn't, they'd been laughing over their dirty ambush like boys throwing baseballs at wooden bottles during county fair week. She didn't dare let him get far, either, because she no longer trusted her aim.

At least he won't know what hit him, she thought.

Van raised Meshaum's pistol and – not without regret – put a round in May's back. 'Oof,' was his final word on mother earth, as he tripped forward into a pile of dry leaves.

Van sat down with her back against a leaning gravestone – so old the name once carved thereon was almost completely worn away – and closed her eyes. She felt bad about shooting a man from behind, but this feeling was quickly smothered beneath a rising wave of sleep.

Oh, it felt so good to give in.

Threads began to spin from her skin. They blew prettily back and forth in a morning breeze. It was going to be another beautiful day in mountain country.

13

The glass was supposed to be bulletproof, but two close-range shots from the M4 Willy was toting blew Clint's office window out of its frame. Clint hauled himself in, and landed on his desk. (It seemed to him that he had sat behind it writing reports and evaluations in another lifetime.) He heard screams and shouting from the direction of the gymnasium, but that was nothing he could deal with now.

He turned to assist Willy and saw the old man leaning against the building with his head lowered. His breathing was harsh and rapid.

Willy raised his arms. 'Hope you're strong enough to pull me in, Doc, because I ain't gonna be able to give you much help.'

'Give me your gun first.'

Willy handed up the M4. Clint put it on his desk with his own weapon, atop a stack of Good Report forms. Then he seized Willy's hands and pulled. The old man was able to help after all, pedaling his workshoes against the building below the window, and he practically flew in. Clint went over on his back. Willy landed on top of him.

'This is what I'd call pretty goddam intimate,' Willy said. His voice was strained, and he looked worse than ever, but he was grinning.

'In that case, you better call me Clint.' He got Willy to his feet, handed him the M4, and grabbed his own gun. 'Let's get our asses down to Evie's cell.'

'What are we going to do when we get there?'

'I have no idea,' said Clint.

14

Drew T. Barry couldn't believe what he was seeing: two women who looked like corpses and Elmore Pearl with his mouth pulled into a yawning cavern. His lower jaw seemed to be lying on his chest.

Pearl staggered away from the creature that held him. He made almost a dozen steps before Maura caught him by the sweat-soaked collar. She drew him against her and stuck a thumb deep into his right eye. There was a pop, like a cork coming out of a bottle. Viscous liquid spilled down Pearl's cheek, and he went limp.

Kayleigh turned jerkily toward Don Peters, like a wind-up toy with a tired spring. He knew he should run, but an incredible lassitude seemed to have filled him. I have gone to sleep, he reasoned, and this is the world's worst nightmare. Has to be, because that's Kayleigh Rawlings. I put that bitch on Bad Report just last month. I'll let her get me, and that's when I'll wake up.

Drew T. Barry, whose life's work involved imagining the worst things that could happen to people, never considered the old I-must-be-dreaming scenario. This was happening, even though it seemed like something straight out of that show where rotting dead people came back to life, and he had every intention of surviving it. '*Duck!*' he shouted.

Don might not have done so if the plastic explosive hadn't detonated at that instant on the other side of the prison. It was actually more of a fall than a duck, but it did the job; instead of grasping the soft meat of his face, Kayleigh's pallid fingers slapped off the hard plastic shell of the football helmet. There was a gunshot, amplified to monstrous levels in the empty gymnasium, and a point-blank round from the Weatherby – a gun that could literally stop an elephant – did the job on Kayleigh. Her throat simply exploded and her head lolled back, all the way back. Her body crumpled.

Maura cast Elmore aside and lurched toward Don, a boogeylady whose hands opened and snapped closed, opened and snapped closed.

'Shoot her!' Don screamed. His bladder let go and warm piddle coursed down his legs, soaking his socks.

Drew T. Barry considered not doing it. Peters was an idiot, a loose cannon, and they might be better off without him. Oh well, he thought, okay. But after this, Mr Prison Guard, you're on your own.

He shot Maura Dunbarton in the chest. She flew back to center court, landing beside the late Elmore Pearl. She lay there a moment, then struggled up and started toward Don again, although her top and bottom halves no longer seemed to be working together very well.

'*Shoot her in the head!*' Don screamed. (He seemed to have forgotten that he had a gun himself.) '*Shoot her in the head like you did the other one!*'

'Will you please just shut up,' said Drew T. Barry. He sighted and blew a hole through Maura Dunbarton's head that vaporized the upper left quadrant of her skull.

'Oh God,' Don gasped. 'Oh God, oh God, oh God. Let's get out of here. Let's go back to town.'

Little as Drew T. Barry liked the pudgy ex-guard, he understood Peters's impulse to run; even sympathized with it to a degree. But he had not become the most successful insurance man in the Tri-Counties by giving up on a job before it was finished. He grabbed Don by the arm.

'Drew, they were *dead*! What if there are more?'

'I don't see any more, do you?'

'But—'

'Lead the way. We're going to find the woman we came for.' And out of nowhere, a bit of Drew T. Barry's high school French recurred to him. '*Cherchez la femme.*'

'Churchy *what*?'

'Never mind.' Drew T. Barry gestured with his high-powered rifle. Not exactly at Don, but in his general vicinity. 'You go first. Thirty feet ahead of me should be good.'

'Why?'

'Because,' Drew T. Barry said, 'I believe in insurance.'

15

While Vanessa Lampley was putting paid to Maynard Griner and Elmore Pearl was undergoing impromptu oral surgery from the reanimated corpse of Maura Dunbarton, Frank Geary was beneath the half-collapsed reception desk, watching as 0:46 became 0:45 became 0:44. There would be no help from outside, he knew that now. The remaining men out there were either hanging back or gone. If he was going to get past the goddam security station and into the prison proper, he would have to do it on his own. The only alternative was to scurry back outside on his hands and knees and hope the guy behind the bulletproof glass didn't shoot him in the ass.

He wished none of this had happened. He wished he was cruising one of the pleasant roads of Dooling County in his little truck, looking for someone's pet raccoon. If a domesticated coon was hungry, you could coax him close enough to use the net with a piece of cheese or hamburger on the end of the long pole Frank called his Treat Stick. That made him think of the shattered desk leg poked into his back. He rolled on his side, grabbed it, and pushed it along the floor. The leg was just long enough to reach the lethal football. Nice to finally catch a break.

'What are you doing?' Tig asked from behind the glass.

Frank didn't bother answering. If this didn't work, he was a dead man. He speared the football with the jagged end of the leg. Johnny Lee had assured him that even driving over the stuff wouldn't cause it to explode, and the stick didn't set it off. He lifted the desk leg and leaned it just below the window with its ID slot. 0:17 became 0:16 became 0:15. Tig fired once, and Frank felt the bullet pass just above his knuckles.

'Whoever you are in there, you better get gone,' he said. 'Do it while you've got the chance.'

Taking his own advice, Frank dove toward the front doors, expecting to take a bullet. But Tig never fired again.

Tig was peering through the glass at the white football stuck on the end of the desk leg like a big piece of gum. He got his first good look at the phone, where 0:04 became 0:03. He understood then what it was and what was going to happen. He bolted for the door giving on the prison's main corridor. His hand was on the knob when the world went white.

16

Outside the main doors, shadowed from the brightening sun by the remains of the Fleetwood RV – never to take Barry Holden and his family on camping expeditions again – Frank felt the badly mauled building shudder from the latest blast. Glass that had survived the earlier explosions thanks to reinforcing wire belched out in glittering shards.

'Come on!' shouted Frank. 'Any of you who are left, come on! *We're taking her right now!*'

For a moment there was nothing. Then four men – Carson Struthers, Deputy Treat, Deputy Ordway, and Deputy Barrows – trotted from cover and ran to the blasted front doors of the prison.

They joined Frank and disappeared into the smoke.

17

'Holy . . . fucking . . . shit,' Jared Norcross breathed.

Michaela was for the time being incapable of speech, but found herself wishing with all her heart for a film crew. Except a crew wouldn't help, would it? If you broadcast what she was seeing, the audience would dismiss it as a camera trick. You had to actually be here to believe it. You had to actually see a naked woman floating a foot over her bunk with a cell phone in her hands; you had to see the green tendrils twisting through her black hair.

'Hello, there!' Evie called cheerily, but without looking around. The better part of her attention was on the cell phone in her hands. 'I'll be with you in a minute, but right now I've got an important piece of business to finish.'

Her fingers on the phone were a blur.

'Jared?' It was Clint. He sounded both amazed and afraid. 'What are *you* doing here?'

18

Leading the way (little as he liked it) now, Don Peters had reached the halfway point of the corridor leading to Broadway when Norcross and an old bearded fellow with red suspenders appeared out of the drifting smoke. Norcross was supporting his companion. Red Suspenders was plodding slowly in a hunch. Don guessed he'd been shot, although he couldn't see any blood. You'll both be shot in a minute, Don thought, and raised his rifle.

Thirty feet behind him, Drew T. Barry raised his own rifle, although he had no idea what Peters had seen; the drifting smoke was too thick, and Peters was in the way. Then — as Clint and Willy headed past the Booth and down the short A Wing corridor leading to the soft cell — a pair of long white arms reached out of the infirmary and seized Don by the throat. Drew T. Barry watched, amazed, as, like a magic trick, Don vanished. The infirmary door slammed shut. When Barry hurried up to where Peters had been standing and tried the knob, he found the door locked. He peered through the wire-reinforced glass and saw a woman who looked like she might be high on drugs holding a chisel to Peters's throat. She had stripped away the ridiculous football helmet; it lay overturned on the floor beside his gun. Peters's thinning black hair was plastered to his skull in sweaty strings.

The woman – an inmate wearing prison browns – saw Barry looking in. She raised her chisel and motioned with it. The gesture was clear enough: *Get out of here.*

Drew T. Barry considered shooting through the glass, but that would draw any defenders who were left. He also remembered the promise he'd made to himself before shooting the second boogey-lady in the gym: *After this, Mr Prison Guard, you're on your own.*

He gave the crazy-looking inmate a little salute, plus a thumbs-up for good measure. Then he headed down the corridor. But cautiously. Before being grabbed, Peters had seen *something.*

19

'Oh, look who I found,' said Angel. 'It's the one who likes to grab girls' tits and twist their nips and rub up against their hinies until he shoots off in his underwear.'

When she had lifted her hand to wave off the insurance man, Don had slipped away, putting a little space between them. 'Put that chisel down, inmate. Put it down this instant and I won't have to write you up.'

'That ain't come on your pants this time,' Angel observed. 'Too much of it, even for a jizzhound like you. You wet yourself, didn't you? Mommy wouldn't like that, would she?'

At the mention of his sainted mother, Don threw caution to the wind and rushed forward. Angel slashed at him, and might have ended things right there, had he not stumbled over the football helmet; instead of cutting his throat, the chisel drew a deep gash across his forehead. Blood sheeted down his face as he went to his knees.

'*Ow! Ow! Stop it, that hurt!*'

'Yeah? See how this does,' Angel said, and kicked him in the stomach.

Trying to blink blood out of his eyes, Don grabbed one of Angel's legs and yanked her down. Her elbow struck the floor and jarred the chisel out of her hand. Don wriggled up her body and reached for her throat. 'I ain't gonna fuck you after you're dead,' he told her, 'that's nasty. I'll just choke you unconscious. I won't kill you until I'm fin—'

Angel grasped the football helmet, swung it in a wide-armed arc, and brought it crashing into Don's bleeding forehead. He rolled off her, clutching at his face.

'Ow, no, you stop that, inmate!'

That helmet-smashing stuff is also a big penalty in the NFL, Angel thought, but since no one's showing this on TV, I guess I won't lose any yardage.

She hit Don with the helmet twice more, perhaps breaking his nose with the second blow. It was certainly bent badly enough. He managed to turn over and get to his knees with his ass sticking up. He was shouting something that sounded like *Stop it, inmate*, but it was hard to tell because the pig was panting so hard. Also, his lips were busted and his mouth was full of blood. It sprayed out with each word, and Angel remembered what they used to say when they were kids: Do you serve towels with your showers?

'No more,' Don said. 'Please, no more. You broke my *face.*'

She cast the helmet aside and picked up the chisel. 'Here's your titty-rub, Officer Peters!'

She buried the chisel between his shoulder blades, all the way up to the wooden handle.

'Mom!' he cried.

'Okay, Officer Peters: here's one for your ma!' She ripped the chisel out and buried it in his neck, and he collapsed.

Angel kicked him a few times, then straddled him and began to stab again. She went on until she could no longer lift her arm.

CHAPTER 16

1

Drew T. Barry reached the Booth and saw what had stopped Peters before the woman grabbed him: two men, one of them possibly Norcross, the arrogant bastard who had instigated this mess. He had his arm around the other one. This was good. They had no idea he was here, and were probably on their way to the woman. To protect her. It was insane, given the size of the force Geary had mustered, but look how much damage they'd managed to inflict already. Good townspeople killed and wounded! They deserved to die just for that.

And then, two more came out of the smoke: a woman and a younger man. All with their backs to Drew T. Barry.

Better and better.

2

'Jesus Christ,' Clint said to his son. 'You were supposed to be hiding.' He looked reproachfully at Michaela. 'You were supposed to take care of that.'

Jared replied before Michaela could. 'She did what you told her, but I couldn't hide. I just couldn't. Not if there's a chance we can get Mom back. And Mary. Molly, too.' He pointed to the woman in the cell at the end of the corridor. 'Dad, look at her! She's *floating*! What is she? Is she even human?'

Before Clint could answer, a burst of music came from Hicks's phone, followed by the proclamation of a tiny electronic voice: 'Congratulations, Player Evie! You have survived! Boom Town *is yours!'*

Evie dropped to her bunk, swung her legs onto the floor, and approached the bars. Clint would have thought he was beyond surprise at this point, but was shocked to see her pubic hair was mostly green. Not hair at all, in fact – it was some kind of vegetation.

'I won!' she cried happily, 'and not a minute too soon! I was down to the last two percent of battery. Now I can die happy!'

'You're not going to die,' Clint said. He no longer believed it, though. She *was* going to die, and when what remained of Geary's force got here – which would be momentarily – it was likely that they were going to die with her. They had killed too many. Frank's men wouldn't stop.

3

Drew T. Barry slid around the side of the Booth, liking what he saw more and more. Unless some of the defenders were hiding in the cells, all that remained of Norcross's little cabal was at the end of this corridor, clustered together like pins in a bowling alley. They had no place to hide, and they were all out of running room. Excellent.

He raised the Weatherby . . . and a chisel pressed into his throat, just below the angle of his jaw.

'No-no-no,' Angel said in the voice of a cheery primary school teacher. Her face, shirt, and baggy pants were stippled with blood. 'Move and I'll cut open your juggler vein. I got the blade right on it. Only reason you're not dead already is you let me finish my business with Officer Peters. Put that elephant gun on the floor. Don't bend, just drop it.'

'This is a very valuable weapon, ma'am,' said Drew T. Barry.

'Ask me if I give a shit.'

'It might go off.'

'I'll take that chance.'

Drew T. Barry dropped it.

'Now hand me the one you got slung over your shoulder. Don't try anything weird, either.'

From behind them: 'Lady, whatever you're holding on his throat, put it down.'

Angel snatched a quick look over her shoulder and saw four or five men with their rifles pointed. She smiled at them. 'You can shoot me, but this one here will die with me. That's a stone promise.'

Frank stood, indecisive. Drew T. Barry, hoping to live a little longer, handed over Don's M4.

'Thank you,' Angel said, and hooked it over her own shoulder. She stepped back, dropped the chisel, and raised her hands to either side of her face, showing Frank and the others that they were empty. Then she backed slowly down the short hall to where Clint was standing with his arm still around Willy, supporting him. She kept her hands up the whole way.

Drew T. Barry, surprised to be alive (but grateful), picked up his Weatherby. He felt lightheaded. He supposed anyone would feel lightheaded after having a lunatic female inmate hold a chisel to his throat. She had told him to put the gun down . . . then let him pick it up again. Why? So she could be on the killing ground with her friends? It seemed the only answer. A crazy one, but *she* was crazy. They all were.

Drew T. Barry decided it was up to Frank Geary to make the next move. He had inaugurated this colossal shit-show, let him figure out how to clean it up. That was best, because to the outside world, what they had done in the last half hour would look a lot like a vigilante action. And there were parts of it – the walking corpses in the gym, for instance, or the naked green woman he spied standing at the cell bars a few steps behind Norcross – that the outside world would simply not believe, Aurora or no Aurora. Drew T. Barry felt lucky to be alive, and would be happy to fade into the background. With luck, the world might never know he'd even been here.

'What the fuck?' said Carson Struthers, who had seen the green woman down the hall. 'That ain't right nor normal. What do you want to do with her, Geary?'

'Take her and take her alive,' Frank said. He had never felt so tired in his life, but he would see this through. 'If she really is the key to Aurora, let the docs figure her out. We'll drive her to Atlanta and hand her over.'

Willy started to raise his rifle, but slowly, as if it weighed a thousand pounds. It wasn't hot in A Wing, but his round face was wet with sweat. It had darkened his beard. Clint grabbed the rifle away from him. At the end of the corridor, Carson Struthers, Treater, Ordway, and Barrows raised their own guns.

'That's it!' Evie cried. 'Here we go! Shootout at the OK Corral! Bonnie and Clyde! *Die Hard in a Women's Prison!*'

But before the short A Wing corridor could become a free-fire zone, Clint dropped Willy's rifle and yanked the M4 from Angel's shoulder. He held it over his head for Frank's group to see. Slowly, and with some reluctance, the men who had raised their guns now lowered them.

'No, no,' Evie said. 'People won't pay to see such a poor excuse for a climax. We need a rewrite.'

Clint paid no attention; he was focused on Frank. 'I can't let you take her, Mr Geary.'

In an eerily good John Wayne imitation, Evie drawled, 'If ya hurt the little lady, you're gonna have to answer to me, ya varmint.'

Frank also ignored her. 'I appreciate your dedication, Norcross, although I'll be damned if I understand it.'

'Maybe you don't want to,' Clint said.

'Oh, I think I've got the picture,' Frank said. 'You're the one who's not seeing clearly.'

'Too much shrinky-dink shit in his head,' Struthers said, and this brought a few grunts of tense laughter.

Frank spoke patiently, as if lecturing a slow pupil. 'So far as we know, she's the only woman on earth who can sleep and wake up again. Be reasonable. I only want to take her to doctors who can study her, and maybe figure out how to reverse what's happened. These men want their wives and daughters back.'

There was a rumble of agreement at this from the invaders.

'So stand aside, tenderfoot,' Evie said, still doing the Duke. 'Ah reckon—'

'Oh, shut up,' Michaela said. Evie's eyes flew wide, as if she had been unexpectedly slapped. Michaela stepped forward, fixing Frank with a stare that burned. 'Do I look sleepy to you, Mr Geary?'

'I don't care what you are,' said Frank. 'We're not here for you.' This raised another chorus of agreement.

'You ought to care. I'm wide awake. So is Angel. *She* woke us up. Breathed into us and woke us up.'

'Which is what we want for all the women,' Frank said, and this brought a louder chorus of agreement. The impatience that Michaela read on the faces of the men gathered before her was close to hate. 'If you're really awake, you should get that. It's not rocket science.'

'*You* don't get it, Mr Geary. She was able to do that because Angel and I weren't in cocoons. Your wives and daughters *are*. That's not rocket science, either.'

Silence. She finally had their attention, and Clint allowed himself to hope. Carson Struthers spoke one flat word. 'Bullshit.'

Michaela shook her head. 'You stupid, willful man. All of you, stupid and willful. Evie Black isn't a woman, she's a supernatural being. Don't you understand that yet? After all that's happened? Do you think doctors can take DNA from a supernatural being? Put her in an MRI tube and figure out how she *ticks*? All the men who have died here, it was for nothing!'

Pete Ordway raised a Garand rifle. 'I could put a bullet in you, ma'am, and stop your mouth. Tempted to do it.'

'Put it down, Pete.' Frank could feel this thing dancing on the edge of control. Here were men with guns faced with a seemingly insoluble problem. To them, the easiest way to deal with it would be to shoot it to pieces. He knew this because he felt it himself.

'Norcross? Have your people stand aside. I want a good look at her.'

Clint stepped back, one arm around Willy Burke to hold him up and one hand laced through Jared's fingers. Michaela flanked Jared on the other side. Angel stood defiantly in front of the soft cell for a moment, shielding Evie with her body, but when Michaela took her hand and pulled gently, Angel gave in and stood beside her.

'Better not hurt her,' Angel said. Her voice was trembling; tears stood in her eyes. 'Just better not, you bastards. She's a fuckin goddess.'

Frank took three steps forward, not knowing or caring if his remaining men followed. He looked at Evie so long and hard that Clint turned to look himself.

The greenery that had twined in her hair was gone. Her naked body was beautiful, but in no way extraordinary. Her pubic hair was a dark triangle above the joining of her thighs.

'What the fuck,' Carson Struthers said. 'Wasn't she – just – green?'

'It's – nice to finally make your acquaintance in person, ma'am,' Frank said.

'Thank you,' said Evie. Bold nakedness not withstanding, she sounded as shy as a schoolgirl. Her eyes were downcast. 'Do you like it, Frank, putting animals in cages?'

'I only cage those that need to be caged,' said Frank, and for the first time in days, he really smiled. If there was one thing he knew, it was that wild went two ways – the danger a wild animal presented to others, and the danger that others presented to a wild animal. In general, he cared more about keeping the animals safe from the people. 'And I've come to let you out of yours. I want to take you to doctors who can examine you. Would you allow me to do that?'

'I think not,' Evie said. 'They would find nothing, and change nothing. Remember the story of the golden goose? When the men cut it open, there was nothing inside but guts.'

Frank sighed and shook his head.

He doesn't believe her because he doesn't want to believe her, Clint thought. *Because he can't* afford *to believe her. Not after all he's done.*

'Ma'am—'

'Why don't you call me Evie,' she said. 'I don't like this formality. I thought we had a lovely little rapport when we talked on the phone, Frank.' But her eyes were still downcast. Clint wondered what was in them that she had to hide. Doubt about her mission here? That was probably wishful thinking, but possible – hadn't Jesus Christ himself prayed to have the cup taken from his lips? As, he supposed, Frank wished that scientists at the CDC would take the cup from his. That they would look at Evie's scans and bloodwork and DNA and say *aha*.

'Evie it is,' Frank said. 'This inmate . . .' He tilted his head toward Angel, who was staring at him with wrath. 'She says that you're a goddess. Is that true?'

'No,' Evie said.

At Clint's side, Willy began to cough and rub the left side of his chest.

'This other woman . . .' This time the tilt went toward Michaela. '*She* says you're a supernatural being. And—' Frank didn't like to say it aloud, to get close to the fury that it could lead to, but he had to. '—you knew things about me that you couldn't have known.'

'Plus she can float!' Jared blurted. 'You may have noticed that? She levitated! I saw it! We all did!'

Evie looked at Michaela. 'You're wrong about me, you know. I am a woman, and in most ways like any other. Like the ones these men love. Although love is a dangerous word when it comes from men. Quite often they don't mean the same thing as women do when they say it. Sometimes they mean they'll kill for it. Sometimes when they say it they don't mean much of anything. Which, of course, most women come to know. Some with resignation, many with sorrow.'

'When a man says he loves you, that means he wants to get his pecker up inside your pants,' Angel put in helpfully.

Evie returned her attention to Frank and the men standing behind him. 'The women you want to save, are at this very moment living their lives in another place. Happy lives, by and large, although of course most miss their little boys and some miss their husbands and fathers. I won't say they never behave badly, they are far from saints, but for the most part, they're in harmony. In that world, Frank, no one ever pulls your daughter's favorite shirt, shouts in her face, embarrasses her, or terrifies her by putting his fist through the wall.'

'They're alive?' Carson Struthers asked. 'Do you swear it, woman? Do you swear to God?'

'Yes,' Evie said. 'I swear to your god and every god.'

'How do we get them back, then?'

'Not by poking me or prodding me or taking my blood. Those things wouldn't work, even if I were to allow them.'

'What will?'

Evie spread her arms wide. Her eyes flickered, the pupils expanding to black diamonds, the irises roiling from pale green to brilliant amber, turning to cat's eyes. 'Kill me,' she said. 'Kill me and they'll awake. Every woman on earth. I swear this is true.'

Like a man in a dream, Frank raised his rifle.

4

Clint stepped in front of Evie.

'No, Dad, no!' Jared screamed.

Clint took no notice. 'She's lying, Geary. She wants you to kill her. Not all of her − I think part of her has changed her mind − but it's what she came here to do. What she was sent here to do.'

'Next you'll be saying she wants to be hung on a cross,' Pete Ordway said. 'Stand aside, Doc.'

Clint didn't. 'It's a test. If we pass it, there's a chance. If we don't, if you do what she expects you to do, the door closes. This will be a world of men until all the men are gone.'

He thought of the fights he'd had growing up, battling not for milkshakes, not really, but just for a little sun and space − a little room to fucking *breathe*. To grow. He thought of Shannon, his old friend, who had depended on him to pull her out of that purgatory as much as he had depended on her. He had done so to the best of his ability, and she had remembered. Why else would she have given her daughter his last name? But he still owed a debt. To Shannon, for being a friend. To Lila, for being a friend and his wife and his son's mother. And those who were with him, here in front of Evie's cell? They also had women to whom they owed debts − yes, even Angel. It was time to pay off.

The fight he'd wanted was over. Clint was punched out and he hadn't won a thing.

Not yet.

He held his hands out to either side, palms up, and beckoned.

Evie's last defenders came and stood in a line in front of her cell, even Willy, who appeared on the verge of passing out. Jared stood next to Clint, and Clint put a hand on his son's neck. Then, very slowly, he picked up the M4. He handed it to Michaela, whose mother slept in a cocoon not far from where they now stood.

'Listen to me, Frank. Evie's told us that if you don't kill her, if you just let her go, there's a chance the women can come back.'

'He's lying,' Evie said, but now that he couldn't see her, Frank heard something in her voice that gave him pause. It sounded like anguish.

'Enough bullshit,' Pete Ordway said, and spat on the floor. 'We lost a lot of good men getting this far. Let's just take her. We can decide what comes next later.'

Clint lifted Willy's rifle. He did so reluctantly, but he did it.

Michaela turned to Evie. 'Whoever sent you here thinks this is how men solve all their problems. Isn't that right?'

Evie made no reply. Michaela had an idea that the remarkable creature in the soft cell was being torn in ways she had never expected when she appeared in the woods above that rusted trailer.

She turned back to the armed men, now halfway down the corridor. Their guns were pointed. At this range, their bullets would shred the little group in front of the strange woman.

Michaela raised her weapon. 'It doesn't have to go this way. Show her it doesn't have to.'

'Which means doing what?' Frank asked.

'It means letting her go back to where she came from,' Clint said.

'Not on your life,' said Drew T. Barry, and that was when Willy Burke's knees buckled and he went down, no longer breathing.

5

Frank handed his rifle to Ordway. 'He needs CPR. I took the course last summer—'

Clint pointed his rifle at Frank's chest. 'No.'

Frank stared at him. 'Man, are you crazy?'

'Step back,' Michaela said, pointing her own gun at Frank. She didn't know what Clint was doing, but she had an idea he was playing the last card in his hand. In *our* hand, she thought.

'Let's shoot em all,' Carson Struthers said. He sounded near hysterics. 'That devil-woman, too.'

'Stand *down*,' Frank said. And, to Clint: 'You're just going to let him die? What would that prove?'

'Evie can save him,' Clint said. 'Can't you, Evie?'

The woman in the cell said nothing. Her head was lowered, her hair obscuring her face.

'Geary — if she saves him, will you let her go?'

'That old cocksucker's fakin'!' Carson Struthers shouted. 'It's all a set-up they planned!'

Frank began, 'Can I just check if—?'

'Okay, yes,' Clint said. 'But be quick. Brain damage starts after three minutes, and I don't know if even a supernatural being could reverse that.'

Frank hurried to Willy, dropped to one knee, and put his fingers to the old man's throat. He looked up at Clint. 'His clock's stopped. I should start CPR.'

'A minute ago, you were ready to kill him,' Reed Barrows grumbled.

Officer Treat, who thought he had witnessed some shit in Afghanistan, groaned. 'I don't understand any of this. Just tell me what it's going to take to get my kids back and I'll do it.' To whom, exactly, this statement was directed, was unclear.

'No CPR.' Clint turned to Evie, who stood with her head down. Which, he thought, was good, because she couldn't help seeing the man on the floor.

'This is Willy Burke,' said Clint. 'His country told him to serve, and he served. These days he goes out with the volunteer fire department to fight brushfires in the spring. They do it without pay. He helps at every bean supper the Ladies' Aid puts on for indigent families the state is too chintzy to support. He coaches Pop Warner football in the fall.'

'He was a good coach, too,' Jared said. His voice was thick with tears.

Clint continued. 'He took care of his sister for ten years when she was diagnosed with early onset Alzheimer's. He fed her, he brought her back when she took it into her head to wander, he changed her shitty diapers. He came out here to defend you because he wanted to do the right thing by you and by his conscience. He never hurt a woman in his life. Now he's dying. Maybe you'll let him. After all, he's just another man, right?'

Someone was coughing on the smoke drifting down Broadway. For a moment there was no other sound, then Evie Black shrieked. Lights burst in their overhead cages. Cell doors that had been locked slammed open and then banged shut in a sound that was like iron hands applauding. Several of the men in Frank's group screamed, one of them in a pitch so high that he sounded like a little girl of six or seven.

Ordway turned and ran. His footfalls echoed through the cinderblock halls.

'Pick him up,' Evie said. Her cell door had opened with the others. If, that was, it had ever been locked in the first place. Clint had no doubt that she could have left whenever she wished at any time during the last week. The rats had only been part of her theater.

Clint and Jared Norcross lifted Willy's limp form. He was heavy, but Evie took him as if he were no more than a bag of goose-feathers.

'You played on my heart,' she said to Clint. 'That was a cruel thing to do, Dr Norcross.' Her face was solemn, but he thought that he saw a glint of amusement in her eyes. Maybe even merriment. She encircled Willy's considerable waistline with her left arm and placed her right hand on the matted, sweat-soaked hair at the back of the old man's head. Then she pressed her mouth to his.

Willy shuddered all over. His arms lifted to encircle Evie's back. For a moment the old man and the young woman remained in a deep embrace. Then she let him go and stood back. 'How do you feel, Willy?'

'Damn good,' Willy Burke said. He sat up.

'My God,' Reed Barrows said. 'He looks twenty years younger.'

'I ain't been kissed like that since I was in high school,' said Willy.

'If ever. Ma'am, I think you saved my life. I thank you for that, but I think the kiss was even better.'

Evie began to smile. 'I'm glad you enjoyed it. I rather liked it myself, although it wasn't as good as beating *Boom Town*.'

Clint's blood was no longer up; exhaustion and Evie's latest miracle had cooled it. He looked on the rage he had felt so recently like a man looking at a stranger who has broken into his house and cluttered the kitchen while making himself an extravagant and gluttonous breakfast. He felt sad and regretful and terribly tired. He wished he could just go home, sit beside his wife, share space with her, and not have to say a word.

'Geary,' Clint said.

Frank was slow to look at him, like a man shaking off a daze.

'Let her go. It's the only way.'

'Maybe, but even that's not sure, is it?'

'No,' Clint agreed. 'What in this fucked-up life is?'

Angel spoke up then. 'Bad times and good times,' she said. 'Bad times and good. All the rest is just horseshit in the barn.'

'I thought it would take at least until Thursday, but . . .' Evie laughed, a sound like tinkling bells. 'I forgot how fast men can move when they set their minds to a thing.'

'Sure,' Michaela said. 'Just think of the Manhattan Project.'

6

At ten minutes past eight on that fine morning, a line of six vehicles drove down West Lavin Road, while behind them the prison smoldered like a discarded cigar butt in an ashtray. They turned onto Ball's Hill Road. Unit Two led the way with its flashers turning slowly. Frank was behind the wheel. Clint was in the shotgun seat. Behind them sat Evie Black, exactly where she had been sitting after Lila arrested her. Then she had been half-naked. On this return trip, she was wearing a Dooling Correctional red top.

'How we're ever going to explain this to the state police, I don't know,' Frank said. 'Lot of men dead, lot of men wounded.'

'Right now everyone's got their hands full with Aurora,' Clint said, 'and probably half of them aren't even showing up. When all the women come back — *if* they come back — no one will care.'

From behind them, Evie spoke quietly. 'The mothers will. The wives. The daughters. Who do you think cleans up the battlefields after the shooting stops?'

7

Unit Two stopped in the lane leading to Truman Mayweather's trailer, where yellow **CRIME SCENE** tape still fluttered. The other vehicles — two more police cruisers, two civilian cars, and Carson Struthers's pickup truck — pulled up behind them. 'Now what?' Clint asked.

'Now we'll see,' Evie said. 'If one of these men doesn't change his mind and shoot me after all, that is.'

'That won't happen,' Clint replied, not nearly as confident as he sounded.

Doors slammed. For the moment, the trio in Unit Two sat where they were.

'Tell me something, Evie,' Frank said. 'If you're just the emissary, who's in charge of this rodeo? Some . . . I don't know . . . life force? Big Mama Earth, maybe, hitting the reset button?'

'Do you mean the Great Lesbian in the sky?' Evie asked. 'A short, heavyset deity wearing a mauve pantsuit and sensible shoes? Isn't that the image most men get when they think a woman is trying to run their lives?'

'I don't know.' Frank felt listless, done up. He missed his daughter. He even missed Elaine. He didn't know what had happened to his anger. It was like his pocket had torn, and it had fallen out somewhere along the way. 'What comes to mind when you think about men, smartass?'

'Guns,' she said. 'Clint, there appear to be no doorhandles back here.'

'Don't let that stop you,' he said.

She didn't. One of the back doors opened, and Evie Black stepped out. Clint and Frank joined her, one on each side, and Clint was reminded of the Bible classes he'd been forced to attend at one foster home or another: Jesus on the cross, with the disbelieving bad guy on one side and the good thief on the other – the one who would, according to the dying messiah, shortly join him in paradise. Clint remembered thinking that the poor guy probably would have settled for parole and a chicken dinner.

'I don't know what force sent me here,' she said. 'I only know I was called, and—'

'You came,' Clint finished.

'Yes. And now I'll go back.'

'What do *we* do?' asked Frank.

Evie turned to him, and she was no longer smiling. 'You'll do the job usually reserved for women. You'll wait.' She drew in a deep breath. 'Oh, the air smells so fresh after that prison.'

She walked past the clustered men as if they weren't there, and took Angel by the shoulders. Angel looked up at her with shining eyes. 'You did well,' Evie said, 'and I thank you from my heart.'

Angel blurted, 'I love you, Evie!'

'I love you, too,' said Evie, and kissed her lips.

Evie walked toward the ruins of the meth shed. Beyond it sat the fox, its brush curled around its paws, panting and looking at her with bright eyes. She followed it, and then the men followed her.

8

'Dad,' Jared said in a voice that was little more than a whisper. 'Do you see it? Tell me you see it.'

'Oh my God,' Deputy Treat said. 'What is *that*?'

They stared at the Tree with its many twisting trunks and its flocks of exotic birds. It rose so high that the top could not be seen. Clint could feel a force radiating out from it like a strong electric current. The peacock spread his tail for their admiration, and when the white tiger appeared from the other side, its belly swishing in the high grass, several guns were raised.

'*Lower those weapons!*' Frank shouted.

The tiger lay down, its remarkable eyes peering at them through the high grass. The guns were lowered. All but one.

'Wait here,' Evie said.

'If the women of Dooling come back, all the women of earth come back?' Clint asked. 'That's how it works?'

'Yes. The women of this town stand for all women, and it must be all of your women who come back. Through there.' She pointed at a split in the Tree. 'If even one refuses . . .' She didn't have to finish. Moths flew and fluttered around her head in a kind of diadem.

'Why would they want to stay?' Reed Barrows asked, sounding honestly bewildered.

Angel's laugh was as harsh as a crow's caw. 'I got a better question – if they built up a good thing, like Evie says, why would they want to leave?'

Evie started toward the Tree, the long grass whickering against her red pants, but stopped when she heard the *snap-clack* of someone racking a shell into the chamber of a rifle. A Weatherby, as it happened. Drew T. Barry was the only man who hadn't lowered his gun at Frank's command, but he wasn't pointing it at Evie. He was pointing it at Michaela.

'You go with her,' he said.

'Put it down, Drew,' said Frank.

'No.'

Michaela looked at Evie. '*Can* I go with you to wherever it is? Without being in one of the cocoons?'

'Of course,' Evie said.

Michaela returned her attention to Barry. She no longer looked afraid; her brow was furrowed in puzzlement. 'But why?'

'Call it insurance,' said Drew T. Barry. 'If she's telling the truth, maybe you can persuade your mother, and your mother can persuade the rest of them. I'm a strong believer in insurance.'

Clint saw Frank raising a pistol. Barry's attention was fixed on the women, and it would have been an easy shot, but Clint shook his head. In a low voice he said, 'There's been enough killing.'

Besides, Clint thought, maybe Mr Double Indemnity is right.

Evie and Michaela walked past the white tiger to the split in the

Tree, where the fox sat waiting for them. Evie stepped in without hesitation, and was lost to sight. Michaela hesitated, and then followed.

The remaining men who had attacked the prison, and those remaining who had defended it, settled down to wait. At first they paced, but as time passed and nothing happened, most of them sat down in the high grass.

Not Angel. She strode back and forth, as if she couldn't get enough of being beyond the confines of her cell, and the woodshop, and the Booth, and Broadway. The tiger was dozing. Once Angel approached it, and Clint held his breath. She was truly insane.

It raised its head when Angel dared to stroke its back, but then the great head dropped back to its paws, and those amazing eyes closed.

'It's *purrin!*' she called to them, in what sounded like exultation.

The sun rose to the roof of the sky and seemed to pause there.

'I don't think it's going to happen,' Frank said. 'And if it doesn't, I'm going to spend the rest of my life wishing I'd killed her.'

Clint said, 'I don't think it's been decided yet.'

'Yeah? How do you know?'

It was Jared who answered. He pointed at the Tree. 'Because *that's* still there. If it disappears or turns into an oak or a weeping willow, *then* you can give up.'

They waited.

CHAPTER 17

1

In the Shopwell supermarket, where the Meetings were traditionally held, Evie spoke to a large gathering of those who now called Our Place home. It didn't take long for her to speak her piece, which boiled down to one thing: it was their choice.

'If you stay here, every woman, from Dooling to Marrakesh, will appear in this world, in the place where they fell asleep. Free to begin again. Free to raise their children the way they want to. Free to make peace. It's a good deal, or so it seems to me. But you can go. And if you do, every woman will awaken where they fell asleep in the world of men. But you all must go.'

'What are you?' Janice Coates, holding Michaela tight, spoke to Evie over her daughter's shoulder. 'Who gave you this power?'

Evie smiled. A green light hovered around her. 'I'm just an old woman who looks young for the time being. And I don't have any power. Like the fox, I'm only an emissary. It's you, all of you, who have the power.'

'Well,' Blanche McIntyre said, 'let's talk it out. Like a jury. Because I guess that's what we are.'

'Yes,' Lila said. 'But not here.'

2

It took until the afternoon to gather the inhabitants of the new world. Messengers were sent to every corner of the town to call forth the women who hadn't been at the supermarket.

They walked from Main Street in a quiet column and climbed up Ball's Hill. Blanche McIntyre's feet were bothering her, so Mary Pak drove her in one of the golf carts. Blanche held Andy Jones, the infant orphan, bundled in a blue blanket and told him a very short story: 'Once upon a time, there was a little guy, who went here and there, and every lady in the place loved him.'

Tufts of green were sprouting. It was cold, but spring was on the verge. They had almost caught up to the time of year it had been in the old world when they had left. The realization surprised Blanche. It felt to her as though a far longer period had elapsed.

When they left the road and started up the moth-lined path through the woods, the fox appeared to conduct them the rest of the way.

3

Once Evie's terms had been re-explained for those who needed to be caught up, Michaela Coates stood on a milk crate, donned her reporter's hat (perhaps for the last time, perhaps not), and told them all what had happened on the outside.

'Dr Norcross convinced the vigilantes to stand down,' she said. 'A number of men gave their lives before reason prevailed.'

'Who died?' one woman shouted out. 'Please say my Micah wasn't one of them!'

'What about Lawrence Hicks?' asked another. There was a babble of questioning voices.

Lila raised her hands. 'Ladies, ladies!'

'I ain't no lady,' grumbled an ex-inmate named Freida Elkins. 'Speak for yourself, Sheriff.'

'I can't tell you who's dead,' Michaela resumed, 'because during most of the fighting I was stuck in the prison. I know that Garth

Flickinger is dead, and . . .' She was about to mention Barry Holden, then saw his wife and remaining daughters looking at her expectantly, and lost her nerve. '. . . and that's about all I know. But I can tell you that all the boy children and infants in Dooling are fine and well.' Praying with all her heart that this was so.

The audience erupted in cheers, whoops, and applause.

When Michaela was finished, Janice Coates took her place, and explained that everyone would be given a turn to make her choice known.

'For myself,' she said, 'I vote, with some regret, to return. This is a much better place than the one we left, and I believe the sky is the limit. Without men, we make decisions fairly, and with less fuss. We share resources with less argument. There has been very little in the way of violence among the members of our community. Women have irritated me my entire life, but they have nothing on men.' Her personal irony, that her own husband, poor Archie, bounced from life by that early heart attack, was such an equable, sensible man, she did not mention. Exceptions were not the point. The point was the general case. The point was history.

Where Janice's features had once been lean, now they were burned down to the bone. Her white hair flowed down her back. Plunged in their sockets, her eyes had a distant shine. It struck Michaela that her mother, no matter how straight she stood or how clearly she spoke, had become ill. *You need a doctor, Mom.*

'However,' Janice went on, 'I also believe I owe it to Dr Norcross to go back. He risked his life, and the others risked theirs, for the women of the prison when I doubt many others would have. Related to that, I want to make it known to you women who were inmates at the prison that I will do whatever I can to see your sentences commuted, or at the very least lessened. And if you want to double-time it for the hills, I will inform the authorities in Charleston and Wheeling that I believe you were killed in the attack.'

Those former prisoners came forward in a bloc. There were fewer than there had been that morning. Kitty McDavid, among others, had vanished without a trace (except for a brief flurry of moths).

No doubt remained about what that might mean – those women were dead in both worlds. Men had killed them.

And yet every single inmate voted to go back. This might have surprised a man, but it didn't surprise Warden Janice Coates, who knew a telling statistical fact: when women escaped prison, most were recaptured almost immediately, because they did not usually double-time it for the hills, as men were wont to do. What women did was go home. First on the minds of the former inmates who spoke at that final meeting were the male children in that other world.

For example, Celia Frode: Celia said Nell's boys would need mothering, and even if Celia had to go back to lockup, Nell's sister could be counted on to stand for them. 'But Nell's sister won't be much use to them if she's asleep, will she?'

Claudia Stephenson spoke to the ground so softly that the crowd called for her to repeat herself. 'I don't want to hold anybody down,' she repeated. 'I'll go along with the majority.'

The First Thursdays also voted to return. 'It's better here,' Gail said, speaking for all of them, 'Janice is right about that. But it's not really Our Place. It's someplace else. And who knows, maybe all that's apparently happened over there will make that place better.'

Michaela thought she was probably right, but likely just in the short term. Men promised never to raise another hand to their wives or children often enough, and meant it at the time, but were only able to keep their promises for a month or two, if that. The rage came around again, like a recurring bout of malaria. Why would this be different?

Large, cool gusts rippled through the high grass. V-shaped flocks of geese, returning from the uninhabited south, crossed the blue pane above the crowd.

It feels like a funeral, Mary Pak thought. It was so undeniable – like death was – bright enough to scald your eyes, cool enough to go through your coat and your sweater and raise goosebumps along your skin.

When it was her turn, she said, 'I want to find out what it feels like to really fall in love with a boy.' This confession surely would have sundered Jared Norcross's heart, had he been present to hear it. 'I know the world's easier for men, and it's lousy, and it's stacked, but I want a chance at a regular life like I always expected to have, and maybe that's selfish, but that's what I want, okay? I might even want to have a baby. And . . . that's all I got.' These last words broke apart into sobs and Mary stepped down, waving away the women who tried to comfort her.

Magda Dubcek said that of course she had to go back. 'Anton needs me.' Her smile was terrible in its innocence. Evie saw that smile, and her heart broke.

(From a spot a few yards distant, scraping his back against a pin oak, the fox eyed the blue bundle that was Andy Jones, nestled in the rear of the golf cart. The baby was fast asleep, unguarded. There it was, the dream of dreams. Forget the hen, forget the whole fucking henhouse, forget all the henhouses that had ever been. The sweetest of all morsels, a human baby. Did he dare? Alas, he did not. He could only fantasize – but, oh, what a fantasy! Pink and aromatic flesh like butter!)

One woman spoke of her husband. He was a great guy, he really, really was, did his share, pulled for her, all that. Another woman talked about her songwriting partner. He was nobody's idea of a picnic, but there was a connection they had, a way they were in tune. He was words; she was music.

Some just missed home.

Carol Leighton, the civics teacher at the high school, said she wanted to eat a Kit Kat that wasn't stale and sit on her couch and watch a movie on Netflix and pet her cat. 'My experiences with men have been one hundred percent lousy, but I am not cut out for starting over in a new world. Maybe I'm a coward for that, but I can't pretend.' She was not alone in her wish for ordinary creature comforts left behind.

Mostly it was the sons, though, that drew them back. A new start for every woman in the world was goodbye forever to their precious sons and they couldn't bear that. This also made Evie's heart break, too. Sons killed sons. Sons killed daughters. Sons left guns out where other sons could find them and accidentally shoot themselves or their sisters. Sons burned forests and sons dumped chemicals into the earth as soon as the EPA inspectors left. Sons didn't call on birthdays. Sons didn't like to share. Sons hit children, choked girl-friends. Sons figured out they were bigger and never forgot it. Sons didn't care about the world they left for their sons or for their daughters, although they said they did when the time came to run for office.

The snake glided down the Tree and drooped into the blackness, lolling before Evie. 'I saw what you did,' she said to it. 'I saw how you distracted Jeanette. And I hate you for it.'

The snake said nothing in return. Snakes do not need to justify their behavior.

Elaine Nutting stood beside her daughter, but she wasn't present, not really. In her mind, she was still seeing the dead woman's wet eyes. They were almost gold, those eyes, and very deep. The look in them wasn't angry, just insistent. Elaine couldn't deny those eyes. A son, the woman had said, I have a son.

'Elaine?' someone asked. It was time for her to make a decision.

'I have things I need to do,' Elaine said. She put her arm around Nana. 'And my daughter loves her father.'

Nana hugged her back.

'Lila?' asked Janice. 'What about you?'

They all turned to her, and Lila understood she could talk them out of it, if she wanted to. She could insure the safety of this new world and destroy the old one. It would only take a few words. She could say, *I love you all, and I love what we made here. Let's not lose it.* She could say, *I'm going to lose my husband, no matter how heroic he may have tried to be, and I don't want to lose this.* She could say, *You women will never be what you were, and what they expect, because part of you will always be here, where you were truly free. You'll carry Our Place with you from now on, and because of that, you will always mystify them.*

Except, really, when had men not been mystified by women? They were the magic that men dreamed of, and sometimes their dreams were nightmares.

The mighty blue sky had faded. The last streaks of light were magnesium smears above the hills. Evie was watching Lila, knowing it all came down to her.

'Yeah,' she told them. 'Yeah. Let's go back and get those guys in shape.'

They cheered.

Evie cried.

4

By twos, they departed, as if from the ark beached on Ararat. Blanche and baby Andy, Claudia and Celia, Elaine and Nana, Mrs Ransom and Platinum Elway. They went hand-in-hand, carefully stepping over the giant riser of a gnarled root, and then into the deep night inside the Tree. In the space between, there was a glimmer, but it was diffuse, as if the light source came from around a corner – but the corner of what? It deepened the shadows without revealing much of anything. What each traveler did recall was noise and a feeling of warmth. Inside that faintly lit passage there was a crackling reverberation a tickling sensation over the skin, like moths' wings brushing – and then they awakened on the other side of the Tree, in the world of men, their cocoons melting away . . . but there were no moths. Not this time.

Magda Dubcek sat up in the hospital room where the police had conveyed her body after they discovered her asleep in the room with the body of her dead son. She wiped the webbing from her eyes, astonished to see a whole ward of women, rising up from their hospital beds, tearing at the shreds of their cocoons in an orgy of resurrection.

5

Lila watched the Tree shed its glossy leaves, as if it were weeping. They sifted to the ground and formed shiny mounds. Strings of moss slid down, whooshing from the branches. She watched a parrot, its marvelous green wings banded with silver marks, arise from the Tree and pierce the sky – watched it flap right into the dark and cease to be. Whorls of speckles, not unlike the Dutch Elm that Anton had warned her about, rapidly spread along the Tree's roots. There was a sick smell in the air, like rot. She knew that the Tree had become infested, that something was devouring it from the inside while it died on the outside.

'See you back there, Ms Norcross,' said Mary Pak, waving one hand, holding Molly's hand with the other.

'You can call me Lila,' said Lila, but Mary had already gone through.

The fox trotted after them.

In the end, it was Janice, Michaela, Lila, and Jeanette's body. Janice brought a shovel from one of the golf carts. The grave they made was only three feet deep, but Lila didn't think it mattered. This world wouldn't exist after they left it; there would be no animals to get at the body. They'd wrapped Jeanette in some coats, and covered her face with an extra baby blanket.

'It was an accident,' Janice said.

Lila bent down, scooped a handful of dirt, and tossed it on the shrouded figure in the hole. 'The cops always say that after they shoot some poor black man or woman or child.'

'She had a gun.'

'She didn't mean to use it. She came to save the Tree.'

'I know,' said Janice. She patted Lila's shoulder. 'But you didn't. Remember that.'

A thick branch of the Tree moaned and cracked, smashing to the ground with an explosion of leaves.

'I'd give anything to take it back,' Lila said. She wasn't crying. For now, tears were beyond her. 'I'd give my soul.'

'I think it's time to go,' said Michaela. 'While we still can.' She took her mother's hand and drew her into the Tree.

6

For a handful of minutes, Lila was the last woman in Our Place. She did not ponder this wonder, however. She had decided to be practical, starting right now. Her focus was on the dirt, on the shovel, and on filling the grave. Only when the work was done did she enter the dark of the Tree and cross over. She went without looking back. Doing that, she felt, would break her fragile heart.

PART THREE

IN THE MORNING

The maid is not dead, but sleepeth.

Matthew ix, 24

1

To most people in the weeks after the women awoke, the world seemed a bit like some dismal thrift store boardgame: there were pieces missing, not necessarily the important pieces, but definitely some you'd liked to have had. You sensed, at the very least, certain cards that might have helped you to victory were absent.

Grief was everywhere, like a disfigurement. But what did you do when you lost a wife, or a daughter, or your husband? Unless you were like Terry Coombs – and some were – you lived with the loss and went on playing the game.

Pudge Marone, bartender and owner of the Squeak, had lost a piece of himself and learned to live with it. His right thumb now ended below the knuckle. It took him awhile to lose the habit of reaching for beer taps with that hand, but he made do. Then, he received an offer for the building from a guy who wanted to open a TGI Fridays franchise. Pudge told himself the Squeaky Wheel would never have recovered from Aurora anyway, and the payday was not bad.

Certain people – Don Peters, for instance – were not missed much at all. They were so completely forgotten it was like they never existed. The wreck of the Peters property was sold at auction.

Johnny Lee Kronsky's few possessions were bagged up with the trash, but his grim apartment remains unoccupied to this day.

Van had left the door open when she left Fritz Meshaum's house that last day of Aurora, and after he had been dead a day or two, the turkey vultures came in and helped themselves to the free buffet. Smaller birds came inside to harvest Fritz's wiry red beard for nesting materials. Eventually, an enterprising bear dragged the carcass outside.

In time, insects polished his skeleton clean, and the sun bleached his overalls white. Nature made use of him and, as was her way, managed to make something beautiful: a bone sculpture.

When Magda Dubcek learned what had happened to Anton — the blood on her bedroom carpet told most of the story — she bitterly regretted her vote to come back. 'What a mistake I have made,' she said to herself too many times to count, over too many rum and Cokes to count. To Magda, her Anton wasn't a piece, or two pieces, or three pieces; to her, he was the whole game. Blanche McIntyre tried to get Magda involved in volunteering — there were so many children who had lost a parent and needed help — and she invited her to join the book club, but Magda wasn't interested. 'There is no happy ending for me here,' she said. On long, sleepless nights, she drank and watched *Boardwalk Empire*. When she finished that one, she moved on to *The Sopranos*. She filled the empty hours with stories of mean men doing mean things.

2

For Blanche, there *was* a happy ending.

She awoke in Dorothy's apartment, on the floor where she had fallen asleep a few days before, and peeled herself out of the remains of her decaying cocoon. Her friends were there, too, likewise coming around and tearing themselves free. But one thing was different: Andy Jones. The baby was not in Blanche's arms, as he had been when she entered the Tree. He was asleep in a crude crib made of woven twigs on the floor nearby.

'Holy shit,' Dorothy said. 'The kid! Yippee!'

Blanche took it as a sign. Tiffany Jones Daycare was built on the site of a home that had burned down during Aurora. The project was financed from Blanche's retirement fund, and from that of her new boyfriend (which, in Willy Burke's case, had been accruing without interest in the lining of his yellowed mattress since 1973), and from many community donations. In the wake of Aurora, it seemed that many more people were charitably inclined than had previously been the case. The Norcross family was particularly generous, in spite of their difficulties. On the sign outside, below Tiffany's name, was a picture of a crib made of woven twigs.

Blanche and her staff accepted any child between the ages of one month and four years, regardless of the parents' (or parent's) ability to pay. After Aurora, it was small community operations like Blanche's, in large part funded and staffed by men, that began the movement that led to the establishment of a universal childcare program. Many men seemed to understand that a rebalancing was necessary.

They had, after all, been warned.

Blanche thought once or twice of the novel they had met to talk about on that last night before everything changed: the story of a girl who told a lie that changed many lives. Blanche often considered the penance that weighed so heavily on that girl's life. She, Blanche, did not feel that she owed any such penance. She was a decent person, had been a decent person all along, a hard worker and a good friend. She had always been good to the inmates of the prison. The daycare was not about atonement. It was about decency. It was natural, obvious, and essential. If the boardgame was missing pieces, it was sometimes – often, even – possible to make new ones.

Blanche had met Willy when he showed up at the door of the daycare, then still undergoing renovations, with a wad of fifty-dollar bills.

'What's this now?' she asked.

'My share,' he said.

Except it wasn't. Mere money wasn't enough. If he wanted to share, he'd have to *do* his share.

'Kids crap so much,' Willy observed to Blanche one evening after they had been courting for awhile.

She was standing by her Prius, waiting for him to finish dragging two straining, translucent bags of used diapers to the bed of his truck. They would be washed at Tiny Tot Laundry in Maylock. Blanche had no intention of filling a landfill with used Pampers. Willy had lost weight and bought new suspenders. Blanche had thought he was cute before, but now, with his beard trimmed (and those pesky eyebrows), he was downright handsome.

'If you die on me, Willy,' said Blanche, 'we're going to have fun with the obituary. "Willy Burke died doing what he loved. Transporting poopy diapers across a parking lot.'" She blew him a kiss.

3

Jared Norcross volunteered at Tiffany Jones Daycare the following summer, and part-time during his senior year. He liked helping out. The kids were sort of demented – they made dirt castles and licked walls and rolled in puddles, and that was just when they were happy – but he was endlessly fascinated, like so many before him, at the easy way the boys and the girls played together. So what changed later on? Why did they suddenly split into largely separate playgroups almost as soon as they began organized school? Was it chemical? Genetic? Jared didn't accept that. People were more complex; people had root systems, and their root systems had root systems. He had an inkling that in college he might like to study child behavior and eventually become a psychiatrist, like his father.

These thoughts comforted Jared and distracted him when he needed distracting, which was, during that period of his life, almost all the time. His parents' marriage was breaking up, and Mary was dating Molly Ransom's older cousin, a lacrosse star at a high school in the next county. He had seen them together once, Mary and her guy. They had been sitting at a picnic table outside an ice cream parlor, feeding each other ice cream cones. It could only have been more horrible if they were having sex.

Molly bird-dogged him once, heading out of his house. 'What's going on, dude? Mary and Jeff are coming over. You want to hang with us?' The little girl had braces now, and it seemed like she'd grown about seven feet. Soon the boys who didn't want to play with her after school would be chasing her for maybe a kiss.

'I wish I could,' Jared said.

'So why can't you?' Molly asked.

'Broken heart,' Jared said, and winked. 'I know you'll never love me, Molly.'

'Oh, please, get a life,' she said, and rolled her eyes.

Sometimes Jared's steps carried him past the empty house where he'd hidden Mary and Molly and Mom. He and Mary had been a sweet team, he thought – but she had put all that firmly into the past. 'It's just a whole different world now, you know,' Mary had told him, as if that was any consolation, or explained anything at all. Jared told himself that she had no idea what she was missing, but decided – gloomily – that she probably wasn't missing anything.

4

Cocoons, it turned out, could float.

Three women, passengers on the flight that had crashed in the Atlantic Ocean, awoke in their webs on a rocky beach in Nova Scotia. Their cocoons were wet, but the women inside them were dry. They walked to an empty rescue station and called directory assistance for help.

This item was relegated to the back pages of newspapers and webzines, if reported at all. In the shadow of that year's major miracle, such minor ones were of little interest.

5

To find one's husband dead inside an exhaust-filled garage was a terrible way to return home.

Rita Coombs had some bad moments after that: despair, terror of a single life, and of course her own sleepless nights when it seemed the next day would never come. Terry had been steady, smart, and genial. That he had bogged down in a depression so hideous and encompassing that he had taken his own life was hard to square with her experience of the man who had been her partner and the father of her child. She wept until she was sure all the tears were gone . . . and then more tears came.

A fellow named Geary visited her one afternoon to offer his condolences. Rita knew – though there were conflicting stories, and a desire to protect everyone involved had thrown a hush over the details of the event – that it was Geary who had directed the attack on the prison, but his manner was soft-spoken and kind. He insisted she call him Frank.

'What happened to my husband, Frank?'

Frank Geary said that he believed Terry just couldn't bear it. 'Everything was out of hand and he knew it. But he couldn't stop it. The only thing he could stop was himself.'

She gathered herself and asked one of the questions that plagued her on her sleepless nights. 'Mr Geary . . . my husband . . . he had a little bit of a drinking problem. Did he . . . was he . . .'

'Sober the whole time,' Frank said. He raised his ringless left hand. 'My word on it. Hand to God.'

6

Aurora's mass outbreaks of violence and property damage, plus the disappearance of so many women, resulted in massive restructuring of the insurance industry nationwide and worldwide. Drew T. Barry, and the team at Drew T. Barry Indemnity, rode it out as well as any company in America, and managed to facilitate life insurance settlements for both Nate McGee's widow and Eric Blass's parents. Since both had died in the midst of an unauthorized assault on a penal institution, this had been no small feat, but Drew T. Barry was no mean insurance agent.

It was less difficult to achieve remuneration for the relatives, near and distant, of the Honorable Oscar Silver, Barry and Gerda Holden, Linny Mars, Officer Vern Rangle, Dr Garth Flickinger, Officer Rand Quigley, Officer Tig Murphy, and Officer Billy Wettermore, all of whom, it could be legitimately claimed, had died under circumstances covered by their respective policies. Not that the various resolutions weren't a long and involved process. It was the work of years, work that would see Drew T. Barry's hair turn salty and his skin turn gray, and in the midst of it, during early mornings of emails and late nights of filings, Drew T. Barry lost his taste for hunting. It seemed decadent in juxtaposition to the seriousness of his work on behalf of the abandoned and the aggrieved. He'd sit in a stand, and see, on the other end of his scope, a deer with a ten-point rack wander through the mist, and think to himself, Act of God Insurance. Does that buck have Act of God Insurance? Because to a deer, that's what getting shot must be, right? Will his children be taken care of? Can a dead buck with good insurance make a little dough? Of course not, the idea was even more ridiculous than the pun. So he sold his Weatherby, and even tried to become a vegetarian, although that didn't work out so well. Sometimes, after a day in the existential toils of the insurance biz, a man needed a pork chop.

Loss changes you. Sometimes that's bad. Sometimes it's good. Either way, you eat your goddam pork chop and go on.

7

Due to the absence of identification, Lowell and Maynard Griner were buried in unmarked graves. Much later, when the Aurora craziness began to subside (not that it ever did, entirely), their fingerprints were matched with the extensive sheets on file and the brothers were officially declared dead. It was doubted by many, however, especially by folk who lived out in the brakes and hollers. Rumors abounded that Little Low and Maynard had made themselves a home in the shaft of an abandoned wildcat mine, that they were running Acapulco Gold further south under assumed names, that they drove the hills in a jacked-up midnight black Ford F-150 with a severed boar's head chained to the grille and Hank Williams Jr. blasting from the stereo. An award-winning author, a man who had lived in Appalachia as a young man and fled as soon as he turned eighteen, heard some of the legends from his relatives, and used them as the basis of a children's picture book titled *The Bad Stupid Brothers*. In the picture book, they end up as miserable toads in Poopy Swamp.

8

The stream that the Bright Ones cult had dammed near their compound in Hatch, New Mexico, broke, and the waters ripped the community's buildings from their foundations. When the waters receded, the desert moved in; sand covered up the few discarded weapons that had been overlooked by the feds; a few pages of their new nation's Constitution, which declared their dominion over the lands and waters they had seized and their rights to bear arms, and the United States federal government's lack of standing to demand they pay their share of taxes, were speared on cactus needles. A graduate student studying botany, hiking to collect specimens of native desert plants, discovered several of these spiked pages.

'Thank you, God!' she cried and snatched them off the cactus. The graduate student's stomach was bothering her. She hustled off the mountain path, defecated, and used the providential papers to wipe herself.

9

To continue the march to her thirty-year pension, Van Lampley took a job at the women's prison in Curly, which was where the vast majority of Dooling's surviving prisoners were shifted. Celia Frode ended up there, though not for long (paroled), and so did Claudia Stephenson.

They were, by and large, a rough bunch at Curly Correctional – lots of tightly wired girls, lots of tough women with felony priors – but Van was up to it. One day a white girl with faux gold teeth, cornrows, and a forehead tattoo (it said **EMPTY** in bleeding letters) asked Van how she got the limp. The inmate's sneer was both piggy and jovial.

'I kicked a little too much ass,' Van said, a harmless lie. She had kicked exactly the right amount of ass. The officer rolled up her sleeve to show the tattoo on her mighty left bicep: **YOUR PRIDE**, etched on the gravestone with the wee arm. She turned the other way and rolled up the other sleeve. On her equally impressive right bicep another gravestone had been inked. **ALL YOUR FUCKING PRIDE** was etched on this one.

'Okay,' the tough girl said, losing the sneer. 'You're cool.'

'You better believe it,' Van said. 'Now move along.'

Sometimes Van prayed with Claudia, now the ordained Reverend Stephenson. They prayed for forgiveness for their sins. They prayed for Ree's soul. They prayed for Jeanette's soul. They prayed for the babies and the mothers. They prayed for whatever needed praying on.

'What was she, Claudia?' Van asked once.

'It's not what she was, Vanessa,' said Reverend Stephenson. 'It's what we are.'

'And what would that be?'

The reverend was stern – very unlike the old Claudia, who would not say boo to a goose. 'Resolved to be better. Resolved to be stronger. Ready to do whatever we have to do.'

10

It would have killed her, the cervical cancer that had been brewing in Janice Coates, but the clock on the other side of the Tree had slowed its growth somehow. Also, her daughter had seen it on the other side of the Tree. Michaela took her mother to an oncologist two days after the women awoke, and the warden was receiving chemotherapy two days after that. Janice acquiesced to Michaela's demand that she step down from her position immediately, allowing Michaela to make all the arrangements, to take care of her, to order her to the doctor, to bed, and to take her meds on a regular basis. Michaela also made sure her mother stopped smoking.

In Michaela's humble opinion, cancer was horseshit. She had lost her father at a young age, and she was still working through some of the emotional horseshit that had come with that. But horseshit abounded. Horseshit was something you had to shovel pretty much non-stop if you were a woman, and if you were a woman in television, you had to shovel it double-time. Michaela could shovel it triple-time. She had not driven home from DC, rammed a bad biker's vintage ride, stayed awake for days smoking Garth Flickinger's meth, and survived a gruesome armed conflict in order to succumb to any variety of horseshit whatsoever, even if that horseshit was a disease that actually belonged to her mother.

Following her course of chemo, when the clean scan came back that told them Janice was in remission, Michaela said to her mother, 'All right. What are you going to do now? You need to stay active.'

Janice said Mickey was absolutely right. Her first plan: to drive Michaela to DC. Her daughter needed to go back to work.

'Are you ever going to try and report on what happened?' Janice asked her daughter. 'Personal experience type of thing?'

'I've thought about it, but . . .'

'But?'

There were problems, that was the but. First, most people would say that the adventures of the women on the far side of the Tree were horseshit. Second, they would say that no such supernatural creature as 'Evie Black' had ever existed, and that Aurora had been caused by perfectly natural (if as yet undiscovered) means. Third, if certain authorities decided Michaela *wasn't* spouting horseshit, questions would be raised that the authorities in Dooling – especially former Sheriff Lila Norcross – could not answer.

For a couple of days Janice stayed with her daughter in the capital. The cherry blossoms were long gone. It was hot, but they did a lot of walking anyway. On Pennsylvania Avenue they saw the president's motorcade, a train of gleaming black limos and SUVs. It went straight through without stopping.

'Look.' Michaela pointed.

'Who gives a shit?' Janice said. 'Just another swinging dick.'

11

In Akron, Ohio, at the apartment he lived in with his Aunt Nancy, checks began to arrive made out to Robert Sorley. The amounts were never large – twenty-two dollars here, sixteen dollars there – but they added up. These checks were drawn from the account of a woman named Elaine Nutting. In the cards and letters that accompanied the checks, Elaine wrote to Bobby about his late mother, Jeanette, about the life of kindness and generosity and achievement that she had envisioned for him.

Though Bobby had not known her as well as he had wanted,

and because of her crime, had never quite been able to trust her while she was alive, Bobby had loved his mother. The impression she seemed to have made on Elaine Nutting convinced him that she had been good.

Elaine's daughter, Nana, included drawings with some of her mother's letters. She was really talented. Bobby asked her to please draw him a picture of a mountain so he could look at it and think of the world beyond Akron, which wasn't such a bad place but was, you know, Akron.

She did. It was a beauty – streams, a monastery in a crook of a valley, birds circling, clouds lit from above, a winding footpath leading to the unseen far side.

Because you said please, Nana wrote.

Of course I said please, he wrote back to her. *Who doesn't say please?*

In her next letter, she wrote, *I know a lot of boys who don't say please. I don't have room on this paper to write the names of all the boys I know who don't say please.*

In response, he wrote, *I'm not one of those boys.*

They became regular correspondents, and eventually planned to meet.

Which they did.

12

Clint never asked Lila if she'd taken a lover during her time on the other side of the Tree. It was as though there was a universe inside her husband, an arrangement of meticulously detailed and landscaped planets hanging down from wires. The planets were ideas and people. He explored them and studied them and came to know them. Except they didn't move, didn't rotate, didn't change over time, the way actual bodies, astral and otherwise, did. Lila sort of understood that, knowing that once he'd lived a life where there had been nothing *but* movement and uncertainty, yet that didn't mean she had to like it. Or accept it.

And how it felt to have killed Jeanette Sorley, accident though it had been? That was something he could never understand, and the few times he tried, she walked away fast, fists clenched, hating him. She did not know exactly what it was that she wanted, but it was not to be understood.

Upon waking that first afternoon, Lila drove her cruiser from Mrs Ransom's driveway directly to the still-smoldering prison. Tiny bits of dissolving cocoon were still clinging to her skin. She organized the removal of the attackers' bodies and the sweeping up and disposal of police weapons and gear. The helpers she martialed in this task were, primarily, the inmates of Dooling Correctional. These women, convicted criminals who had surrendered their freedom – virtually all of whom were survivors of domestic abuse, or survivors of addiction, or survivors of poverty, or survivors of mental illness, or some combination of all four – were not unaccustomed to distasteful labor. They did what they had to. Evie had given them a choice and they had made it.

When the state authorities finally turned their attention to Dooling Correctional, the cover story had been spread and codified among the people of the town and the prison. Marauders – a heavily armed Blowtorch Brigade – had laid siege, and Dr Clinton Norcross and his officers had defended their position heroically, assisted by the police and by volunteers such as Barry Holden, Eric Blass, Jack Albertson, and Nate McGee. Given the overarching, inexplicable fact of Aurora, this story held a little less interest than the floating women who'd washed up in Nova Scotia.

After all, it was only Appalachia.

13

'His name's Andy. His mother died,' Lila said.

Andy was crying when she introduced him to Clint. She had retrieved him from Blanche McIntyre. His face was red and he was hungry. 'I'm going to say that he was mine, that I gave birth to him. It'll be simpler that way. My friend Jolie is a doctor. She's already filed the paperwork.'

'Hon, people are going to know you weren't pregnant. They won't believe it.'

'Most will,' she said, 'because time was different, over there. For the rest . . . I don't care.'

Because he saw she meant it, he held out his arms and accepted the wailing child. He rocked Andy back and forth. The baby's screams became howls. 'I think he likes me,' Clint said.

Lila didn't smile. 'He's constipated.'

Clint didn't want a child. He wanted a nap. He wanted to forget it all, the blood and death and Evie, especially Evie, who had bent the world, who had bent him. But the videotape was in his head; any time he wanted to do a Warner Wolf and go to it, it ran on a loop.

He remembered Lila, on that awful night when the world was burning down, informing him that she had never wanted the pool.

'Do I get a say in this?' he asked.

'No,' Lila said. 'I'm sorry.'

'You don't sound sorry.' Which was true.

14

Sometimes – usually at night when she lay wakeful, but sometimes even on the brightest afternoons – names would go through Lila's head. They were the names of white police officers (like her) who had shot innocent black civilians (like Jeanette Sorley). She thought of Richard Haste, who had shot eighteen-year-old Ramarley Graham in the bathroom of the youth's Bronx apartment. She thought of Betty Shelby, who killed Terence Crutcher in Tulsa. Most of all she thought of Alfred Olango, shot dead by Officer Richard Gonsalves when Olango playfully pointed a vaping device at him.

Janice Coates and other women from Our Place had tried to convince her that she'd had perfectly valid reasons for what she had done. These exhortations might or might not be true; either way, they were of no help. One question recurred like a maddening earworm: Would she have given a white woman more time? She was terribly, dreadfully afraid she knew the answer to that . . . but knew she would never be sure. The question would haunt her for the rest of her life.

Lila stayed on the job until the situation at the prison was sorted, then handed in her resignation. She brought baby Andy to Tiffany Jones Daycare and stayed to help out.

Clint was commuting to Curly, an extra hour in travel. He was fixated on his patients, especially on those inmates transferred from Dooling who had crossed over, because he was the only person they could talk to about what they'd seen and experienced who wouldn't label them as crazy.

'Do you regret your choice?' he asked them.

They all said no.

Their selflessness astounded Clint, shrank him, kept him awake, sitting in his armchair in the A.M. gloom. He had risked his life, yes, but the inmates had handed their new ones over. Had made a gift of them. What group of men would ever have made such a unanimous sacrifice? No group of men was the answer, and if you recognized that, then Christ, hadn't the women made an awful mistake?

He ate drive-thru food at both ends of his day and the softening he had worried about that spring became a healthy front porch by the following fall. Jared was a melancholy ghost, skimming at the edges of his perception, coming and going, sometimes offering a small salute or a *yo, Dad.* Erotic dreams of Evie rattled away any real serenity Clint might have found. She captured him in vines and blew wind across his naked body. And her body? It was a bower where he thought he could rest, but never reached before awakening.

When he was in the same room with the baby, it grinned at him, as if it wanted to make friends. Clint grinned back and found himself crying in his car on the way to work.

One night, unable to sleep, he Googled the name of his second patient, Paul Montpelier, he of the 'sexual ambition.' An obituary popped up. Paul Montpelier had died five years before, after a long battle with cancer. There was no mention of a wife or children. What had his 'sexual ambition' gained him? A very short and sad obituary, it seemed. Clint cried for him, too. He understood this was a well-known psychological phenomenon known as *transference*, and didn't care.

One rainy evening not long after reading Montpelier's obituary, exhausted from a day of group meetings and one-on-one consult-ations, Clint stopped at a motel in the little town of Eagle, where the heater rattled and everyone on the TV looked green. Three nights later, he was in the same room when Lila called his cell phone to ask if he was coming home. She didn't sound particularly concerned about his answer.

'I think I'm beat, Lila,' he said.

Lila heard his meaning, the larger encircling defeat it conveyed.

'You're a good man,' she said. This was a lot to give him right then. The baby didn't sleep much. She was beat herself. 'Better than most.'

He had to laugh. 'I believe that's known as damning with faint praise.'

'I do love you,' she said. 'It's just been a lot. Hasn't it?'

It had. It had been a hell of a lot.

15

The warden at Curly told Clint he absolutely didn't want to see his face over the Thanksgiving holiday.

'Heal thyself, Doc,' said the warden. 'Eat some vegetables, anyway. Something besides Big Macs and moon pies.'

He abruptly decided to drive to Coughlin to see Shannon, but ended up parked outside her house, unable to go in. Through the thin drapes of the ranch house he observed the shadows of female figures moving. The warmth of the lights was cheerful and inviting; snow had started to fall in huge flakes. He thought of knocking on her door. He thought of saying, *Hey, Shan, you were the milkshake that got away.* The thought of a milkshake running away on Shannon's shapely legs made him laugh, and he was still laughing when he drove off.

He ended up in a tavern called O'Byrne's with melting slush on the floor, the Dubliners on the jukebox, and a bleary-eyed, white-headed bartender who moved in slow motion between the taps and the glasses, as if he were not pouring beers, but handling radioactive isotopes. This fine fellow addressed Clint. 'Guinness, son? Tasty on a night like this.'

'Make it a Bud.'

The current Dubliners tune was 'The Auld Triangle.' Clint knew it, and sort of liked it, in spite of himself. There was a romance to the song that was nothing like his experience of prison, but it got you, those voices gathering. Someone, he thought, ought to add another verse, though. The warden, the screw, and the lag all got turns. Where was the shrink?

He was just about to take his beer to a dark corner when a finger tapped him on the shoulder. 'Clint?'

16

What did it was the hug.

Frank's daughter didn't just hug him when they were reunited, she dug her girl's hands into his upper arms so that he could feel her fingernails through his shirt. Everything that had happened, everything he had done, had made it clear that he needed to do something – anything! – about himself, but that hug had tipped the dominoes. The last time he had seen her awake, he had almost ripped her favorite shirt off her body. His daughter loved him anyway. He didn't deserve it – but he wanted to.

The anger management program was three days a week. At the first meeting, it was just Frank and the therapist in the basement of the Dooling VFW.

Her name was Viswanathan. She wore large round spectacles and was so young-looking Frank figured she didn't remember cassette tapes. She asked why he was there.

'Because I scare my kid and I scare myself. I also trashed my marriage, but that's just a side-effect.'

The therapist took notes as he explained his feelings and compulsions. It came more easily than Frank would have guessed, sort of like expressing pus from an infected wound. In a lot of ways, it was like talking about another person, because that pissed-off dogcatcher didn't feel like him. That pissed-off dogcatcher was someone who showed up and took control when Frank didn't like what was happening, when he just couldn't deal. He told her about putting animals in cages. He kept coming back to that.

'My friend,' said Dr Viswanathan, this twenty-six-year-old girl with glasses the color of Kool-Aid, 'have you ever heard of a drug called Zoloft?'

'Are you patronizing me?' Frank wanted to get himself together, not be fucked with.

The therapist shook her head and smiled. 'No, I'm being jaunty. And you're being brave.'

She introduced him to a psychopharmacologist and the psycho-pharmacologist wrote Frank a prescription. He took the prescribed dosage without feeling especially different and continued to go to the meetings. Word got around, and more men began to appear, filling half the chairs in the basement of the VFW. They said they 'wanted to make a change.' They said they 'wanted to get their shit together.' They said they 'wanted to stop being so fucking angry all the time.'

No amount of therapy or Big Pharma happy-pills could change the fact that Frank's marriage was kaput. He had broken Elaine's trust too many times (not to mention the kitchen wall). But maybe that part was okay. He discovered he didn't actually like her that much. The best thing was to let her go. He gave her full custody, and told her he was grateful for his two weekends a month with their daughter. In time, if things went well, it would be more.

To his daughter he said, 'I've been thinking about a dog.'

17

'How are you doing?' Frank asked Clint as the Dubliners played and sang.

Frank was on his way to Thanksgiving in Virginia with his former in-laws. The Zoloft and the meetings helped him control his temper, but in-laws were still in-laws, only more so when their daughter had divorced you. He'd stopped in at O'Byrne's to postpone his execution for a half hour.

'I'm hanging in there.' Clint rubbed his eyes. 'Need to lose some weight, but yeah, hanging in there.'

They took seats at a booth in a dark corner.

Frank said, 'You're drinking in an Irish dive on Thanksgiving. Is that your idea of hanging in there?'

'I didn't say I was great. Besides, you're here, too.'

Frank thought *What the hell* and just said it. 'I'm glad we didn't kill each other.'

Clint raised his glass. 'I'll drink to that.'

They toasted. Clint didn't feel any anger toward Frank. Anger wasn't something he felt toward anyone. What he felt was great disappointment in himself. He had not expected to save his family only to lose them. It was not his idea of a happy ending. It was his idea of an American shit-show.

He and Geary talked about their children. Frank's girl was in love with some kid in Ohio. He was a little worried he might be a grandfather at forty-five, but he was playing it cool. Clint said that his son was awfully quiet these days, probably couldn't wait to blow town, go to college, see what the world was like beyond coal country.

'And your wife?'

Clint waved to the bartender for another round.

Frank shook his head. 'Thanks, but not for me. Booze and Zoloft don't mix all that well. I should shove off. The outlaws are expecting me.' He brightened. 'Hey, why not come along? I'll introduce you to Elaine's folks. Gotta keep on their good side; they're my daughter's grandparents, after all. Visiting them is sort of like hell, but with slightly better food.'

Clint thanked him, but declined.

Frank started to get up, then settled back. 'Listen, that day at the Tree . . .'

'What about it?'

'Do you remember when the churchbells started ringing?'

Clint said he would never forget. The bells began when the women started to wake up.

'Yeah,' Frank said. 'Right about then I looked around for that crazy girl, and saw she was gone. Angel, I think her name was.'

Clint smiled. 'Angel Fitzroy.'

'Any idea what became of her?'

'None at all. She's not at Curly, I know that much.'

'Barry, the insurance guy? He told me he was pretty sure she killed Peters.'

Clint nodded. 'He told me the same thing.'

'Yeah? What did you say?'

'Good riddance to bad rubbish. That's what I said. Because Don Peters was the problem in a nuthell.' He paused. '*Shell*. That's what I mean. Nut*shell*.'

'My friend, I think you should go home.'

Clint said, 'Good idea. Where is it?'

18

Two months after what had become known as the Great Awakening, a Montana rancher saw a woman hitchhiking on Route 2, just east of Chinook, and pulled over. 'Hop in, young lady,' he said. 'Where you headed?'

'Not sure,' she said. 'Idaho, to start with. Maybe out to California after that.'

He offered his hand. 'Ross Albright. Got a spread two counties over. What's your name?'

'Angel Fitzroy.' Once she would have refused the shake, used an alias, and kept her hand on the knife she always stored in her coat pocket. Now there was no knife and no alias. She felt no need of either.

'Nice name, Angel,' he said, fetching third gear with a jerk. 'I'm a Christian myself. Born and born again.'

'Good,' Angel said, and without a trace of sarcasm.

'Where you from, Angel?'

'A little town called Dooling.'

'That where you woke up?'

Once Angel would have lied and said yes, because that was easier, and besides, lying came naturally to her. It was a real talent. Only this was her new life, and she had resolved to tell the truth to the best of her ability in spite of the complications.

'I was one of the few who never went to sleep,' she said.

'Wow! You must have been lucky! And strong!'

'I was blessed,' Angel said. This was also the truth, at least as she understood it.

'Just hearing you say so is a blessing,' said the rancher, and with great feeling. 'What's next, Angel, if you don't mind me asking? What are you going to do when you finally decide to nail your traveling shoes to the floor?'

Angel looked out at the glorious mountains and the never-ending western sky. At last she said, 'The right thing. That's what I'm going to do, Mr Albright. The right thing.'

He took his eyes off the road long enough to smile at her and said, 'Amen, sister. Amen to that.'

19

The women's Correctional Facility was fenced off and condemned, marked with signs warning against trespassers, and left to crumble while the government allocated funds to more pressing public works. The new fence was strong, and its base was embedded deep into the turf. It took the fox several weeks of digging, and all his reserves of patience to tunnel beneath it.

Once he had accomplished this engineering feat, he trotted into the building through the massive hole in the wall and set about constructing his new den in a cell close by. He could detect the scent of his mistress there, faded but sweet and tangy.

An emissary came from the rats. 'This is our castle,' the rat said. 'What are your intentions, fox?'

The fox appreciated how straightforward the rat was. He was a fox, but he was getting older. Perhaps it was time to quit with tricks and risks, find a mate, and stay close to his skulk. 'My intentions are humble, I assure you.'

'And they are?' pressed the rat.

'I hesitate to say aloud,' the fox said. 'It's a little embarrassing.'

'Speak,' said the rat.

'All right,' the fox said. He tipped his head shyly. 'I'll whisper it. Come up close to me and I'll whisper it to you.'

The rat came close. The fox could have bitten her head off – it was his talent, each of God's creatures has at least one – but he didn't.

'I want to be at peace,' he said.

The morning after Thanksgiving, Lila drives to the gravel turnaround on Ball's Hill and parks. She pops Andy, bundled in his infant snowsuit, into a baby carrier. She starts to hike.

Maybe they could put their Humpty-Dumpty marriage back together, Lila muses. Maybe, if she wants him to, Clint could love her again. But does she want him to? There is a mark on Lila's soul, the name of the mark is Jeanette Sorley, and she does not know how to erase it. Or if she wants to.

Andy makes small, amused noises as she walks. Her heart aches for Tiffany. An unfairness and a randomness knits into the fabric of everything and it inspires as much awe in Lila as it does resentment. The icy woods creak and tick. When she gets to Truman Mayweather's trailer, it's frosted with snow. She gives it just a passing glance and moves on. Not far to go now.

She emerges into the clearing. The Amazing Tree isn't there. Jeanette's grave is not there. There is nothing but winter grass and a haggard oak stripped of its leaves. The grass wavers, an orange shape flashes, vanishes, and the grass resettles. Her breath steams. The baby hums and expresses what sounds like a question.

'Evie?' Lila moves around in a circle, searching — woods, ground, grass, air, milky sunshine — but there's no one. 'Evie, are you there?'

She yearns for a signal, any kind of signal.

A moth flutters from the branch of the old oak tree and settles on her hand.

AUTHORS' NOTE

If a fantasy novel is to be believable, the details underpinning it must be realistic. We had plenty of help with those details while writing *Sleeping Beauties*, and we are enormously grateful. And so, before we leave you, here's a tip of our Red Sox caps to some of those who helped us find our way.

Russ Dorr was our primary research assistant. He helped us with everything from RVs to facts on how quickly kerosene degrades. He also made valuable contacts for us in the world of women's incarceration and corrections. Because we needed to visit a women's prison – get boots on the ground, so to speak – our thanks to the Honorable Gillian L. Abramson, Justice, New Hampshire Superior Court, who arranged a field trip to the New Hampshire State Prison for Women in Goffstown, New Hampshire. There we met Warden Joanne Fortier, Captain Nicole Plante, and Lieutenant Paul Carroll. They took us on a tour of the prison and answered all of our questions patiently (sometimes more than once). These are dedicated corrections officers, both tough and humane. It's quite possible that the situation at Dooling Correctional might have been resolved peacefully if any of them were on staff – lucky for us they weren't! We can't thank them enough.

We also want to express our gratitude to Mike Muise, a corrections officer with the Valley Street Jail, in Manchester, New Hampshire. Mike passed on lots of good info on intake procedure at police stations and prisons. Officer Tom Staples (retired) helped us furnish the armory at the Dooling Sheriff's Office with a fine supply of weapons.

We conceived of the shaky ground on which Lion Head Prison was built from our reading of Michael Shnayerson's superb non-fiction chronicle *Coal River*.

Where we got it right, thank those folks. Where we got it wrong, blame us . . . but don't be too quick to do so. Remember that this is a work of fiction, and from time to time we found it necessary to bend the facts a little to suit the course of our story.

Kelly Braffet and Tara Altebrando gave us enormously helpful readings of an early, much-longer version of the novel. We are much obliged to them.

Thanks are due to all the folks at Scribner, and in particular to Nan Graham and John Glynn, who co-edited the book with tireless efficiency and panache. Susan Moldow lent moral support. Mia Crowley-Hald was our in-house production editor, and we are grateful for her hard work. Angelina Krahn did a wonderful job of copyediting a long and complex manuscript. Katherine 'Katie' Monaghan is the tireless publicist who worked to get news of the book out there. Stephen's agent, Chuck Verrill, and Owen's agent, Amy Williams, both supported us through this long effort and worked together as if they had been doing it their whole lives. Chris Lotts and Jenny Meyer sold the foreign rights all over the globe, and we thank them for their efforts.

Steve wants to thank his wife, Tabitha; his daughter, Naomi; and his other son, Joe, known to his readers as Joe Hill. Owen wants to thank his mom, his sibs, Kelly, and Z. All of them understand the difficulty of the job, and made time for us to do it.

Last but hardly least, we want to thank you, sir or madam, for reading our novel. We appreciate your support more than words can say, and hope you enjoyed yourself.

Stephen King
Owen King
April 12, 2017

: : THE SPEAKERS OF : :
THE HOUSE OF COMMONS

SIR THOMAS HUNGERFORD
1376-7

From a stained-glass window in Farley Church, drawn by Stanley North

THE SPEAKERS OF
THE HOUSE OF COMMONS
FROM THE EARLIEST TIMES TO
THE PRESENT DAY WITH A
TOPOGRAPHICAL DESCRIPTION
OF WESTMINSTER AT VARIOUS
EPOCHS & A BRIEF RECORD OF
THE PRINCIPAL CONSTITUTIONAL
CHANGES DURING SEVEN CENTURIES
BY ARTHUR IRWIN DASENT
WITH NOTES ON THE ILLUSTRATIONS
BY JOHN LANE & A PORTRAIT
OF EVERY SPEAKER WHERE ONE
IS KNOWN TO EXIST   ❦   ❦   ❦

LONDON : JOHN LANE THE BODLEY HEAD
NEW YORK : JOHN LANE COMPANY MCMXI

WILLIAM BRENDON AND SON, LTD., PRINTERS, PLYMOUTH

DEDICATED WITH SINCERE REGARD

TO

ARTHUR WELLESLEY PEEL

SPEAKER OF THE HOUSE OF COMMONS

1884–1895

NOW 1ST VISCOUNT PEEL OF SANDY

PREFACE

IT is now more years ago than I care to remember since the outline of this book suggested itself to me. Undeterred by the adverse opinion of some who insisted that there was little or nothing, worth the telling, to be said of the earlier Speakers— with the possible exceptions of Coke, Lenthall and Arthur Onslow, to mention the three names which most readily occur to the superficial enquirer—I received sufficient encouragement from the late Sir Archibald Milman and other friends to induce me to supplement and revise the earlier labours of Townsend and Manning in the same field.

The outcome of these years of toil, performed in the intervals of official duty, is a blend of history and biography based on authentic records, and leavened, here and there, with topographical matter tending to throw light upon some of the obscurities which surround the origin of Parliaments. I have endeavoured to show the close nature of the ties which united the greatest of Benedictine Monasteries to the popular assembly in the earliest days of its existence, though I must admit that the allusions to Parliament remaining in the archives of the Dean and Chapter of Westminster are disappointingly few.

There are occasional entries in the carefully kept accounts of the monks of wine bought by the abbots for the entertainment of distinguished personages repairing to Westminster in obedience to the Royal summons, but, with the exception of the extremely interesting entry on page 45 of this volume, I have found little which adds to our previous knowledge of the relations of Church and State in the Middle Ages.

One minor survival of this ancient connection may be mentioned here. This is the custom, still annually observed, of opening the gate leading from Dean's Yard into Great College Street on the first day of a new session, but on no other.

This practice, far from being a mere police regulation of modern date, carries the mind back to that remote period when the Plantagenet Kings, in conjunction with the Abbots of Westminster and the Archbishops of Canterbury, watched with jealous care the growth of representative institutions.

In the middle of the fourteenth century that great ecclesiastic Simon Langham, who sleeps to-day in the chapel of St. Benedict, walked with measured steps to his place in the House of Lords, resplendent in jewelled cope and mitre, escorted by a long train of attendant priests and acolytes, and with his processional cross of gold borne high before him.

In his progress to the Palace he would have met a

throng of knights, scarcely less picturesque in their glittering armour than his own cortège, making peaceful invasion of his monastic house.

Drawn from every shire in the land, they filled the cloisters and choked the vestibules leading to the Chapter House or to some other chamber temporarily set apart for their use, there forthwith to deliver a mighty shout of assent (or the contrary, as the case might be) to the demands of their sovereign lord for the support of the realm and the maintenance of his Royal estate.

There would be little or nothing in the way of discussion. Their voices were collected then and there by some official of the Court, as they stood leaning on their swords. It is true that the carrying of arms within the Palace during the sittings of Parliament had been discountenanced by Edward II, but the prohibition was so commonly disregarded that his successor formally sanctioned the practice in the case of Earls and Barons, save only in his Royal presence. Once their duty had been performed, the Knights of the Shire were at liberty to depart to their homes, and, until they were again summoned to Westminster to repeat the process with little or no variation, save in the amount of the subsidy required of them, the monks could pursue their ordinary avocations undisturbed by the clank of spurs and the tramp of armed men.

Having very briefly outlined the nature of an early Parliamentary assembly, I may here indulge in a fragment of autobiography by way of excuse for having attempted the history of over two hundred separate elections to the Chair, covering between them a period of more than seven centuries.

Born as I was under the shadow of the Abbey—in the Broad Sanctuary—it was my good fortune to receive my first intelligent impressions of Westminster from the lips of my father's friend and neighbour, the late Dean Stanley. In a sense I may be said to have assisted at the funeral of Lord Palmerston, and, incidentally, at the inauguration of a new Parliamentary epoch, for I retain to this day a vivid recollection of being held up at a window by my nurse to see that great man's coffin carried into the Abbey by the west door. As a boy I was present at the last Westminster election fought under the old system, and I remember the hustings in Trafalgar Square.

But my most enduring memories of the Abbey and its priceless historical associations are those which I received from the holder of an ecclesiastical office, unique in its dignity in this or any other country, and it would be strange, indeed, if I had not acquired from the teachings of so fascinating a guide an abiding interest in Westminster, and all that it means to Englishmen. Somehow my life has been bound up with the place of my birth. Returning to it in 1882—on the nomination of Sir Thomas Erskine-May (Lord Farnborough), my first official chief, to devote myself to the service of the House of Commons—for more than a quarter of a century the greater part of my days, and, in the aggregate, an appalling number of hours after midnight, have been passed within the walls of St. Stephen's.

I need hardly say that this book is written in no party spirit, nor is it designed to serve any purpose other than that of accuracy.

My publisher has shown such zeal and enthusiasm in the preparation of the portraits and other illustrations, that it will be unnecessary for me to add a word concerning them. I may say, however, that, to the best of my belief, no likeness of either Catesby, Dudley, or Empson has ever been published before. The various printed authorities consulted are, in the majority of instances, indicated in the footnotes, but I desire to acknowledge here my frequent indebtedness to Messrs. Longmans' recently completed *Political History of England.*

Sir Courtenay Ilbert, K.C.B., the present Clerk of the House, gave me the benefit of his views on Mediæval Parliaments, but my especial thanks are due to Mr. T. L. Webster, the second Clerk Assistant of the House, for many valuable suggestions throughout the course of my labours, and for unreservedly placing his knowledge of the more technical questions dealt with in these pages at my disposal. Mr. M. W. Patterson, of Trinity College, Oxford, was good enough not only to help me in the revision of the proof sheets, but to save me from many errors both of omission and commission. The Rev. R. B. Rackham, of the Deanery, Westminster, searched the Sacrist's and other Rolls in the Abbey

Muniment room with a view to helping me in this branch
of my researches. Miss Lenthall, of Besselsleigh, Berks,
a descendant of the celebrated Speaker of that name,
also gave me much valuable information, as did Colonel
La Terriere, the present owner of Burford Priory.

Last, but by no means least, I must tender my grateful
acknowledgments to Mr. J. Horace Round, the first
living authority on peerage law and the most discriminating, as well as the most fascinating, genealogist of the
present age.

He kindly brought to my notice the very instructive
account of the election of Sir Thomas Lovell to the Chair
in the first year of Henry VII. Though unfortunately
received too late for incorporation in my Tudor chapter,
I trust that it will gain importance by appearing, as it
does, in an Appendix at the end of the book. The same
remark applies to the speech of Sir Thomas More, on
presentation for the Royal approval, which I have also
placed by itself, on account of the eminence of the man
who made it.

I shall be grateful for any additions or corrections
which I may be favoured with, and, especially, for any
unpublished letters or documents relating to individual
Speakers.

ARTHUR IRWIN DASENT.

THE DUTCH HOUSE, HAMPTON-ON-THAMES,
        February 5th, 1911.

CONTENTS

CHAPTER I

PAGE

WESTMINSTER IN THE REIGN OF HENRY III. THE ISLE OF THORNS. THE PALACE AND THE ABBEY. PREFERENCE OF HENRY FOR WESTMINSTER. DAWN OF THE ENGLISH CONSTITUTION. WESTMINSTER THE EARLIEST MEETING-PLACE OF THE COMPLETE PARLIAMENT . . 3

CHAPTER II

THE HOUSE OF COMMONS UNDER THE PLANTAGENETS . 22

CHAPTER III

THE HOUSE OF LANCASTER AND THE INFLUENCE OF THE WARS OF THE ROSES UPON PARLIAMENTARY INSTITUTIONS 61

CHAPTER IV

THE HOUSE OF COMMONS UNDER THE HOUSE OF YORK, A PERIOD, FOR THE MOST PART, OF SUBSERVIENCY TO THE CROWN 87

CHAPTER V

WESTMINSTER AND PARLIAMENT IN TUDOR TIMES. RESTRICTION OF THE POWERS OF THE HOUSE OF COMMONS AND INCREASED POWER OF THE PRIVY COUNCIL . 99

CHAPTER VI

THE STUARTS AND THE LIBERTIES OF THE PEOPLE . 164

CONTENTS

CHAPTER VII

PAGE

THE HOUSES OF HANOVER AND SAXE-COBURG GOTHA.
RISE OF THE SYSTEM OF CABINET GOVERNMENT, WITH
MINISTERIAL RESPONSIBILITY TO PARLIAMENT . . 251

CATALOGUE OF SPEAKERS FROM THE EARLIEST TIMES TO
THE PRESENT DAY, WITH THE PLACES THEY SAT FOR,
THE DATES OF THEIR APPOINTMENT TO AND CLOSE OF
OFFICE, ETC. 341

APPENDIX I 419

APPENDIX II 421

INDEX 425

ILLUSTRATIONS

SIR THOMAS HUNGERFORD, 1376–7 . *Frontispiece (in colour)*
From a stained-glass window in Farleigh Hungerford Church.
Drawn by Stanley North.

FACING PAGE

THE JEWEL TOWER, WESTMINSTER . . . 8
From a drawing by L. Hussell Conway.

STAIRCASE AND ANCIENT DOORWAY IN THE JEWEL TOWER . 10
From a photograph by Sir Benjamin Stone.

VAULTED CHAMBER IN THE JEWEL TOWER 12
From a photograph by Sir Benjamin Stone.

SIR THOMAS HUNGERFORD, 1376–7 52
From a drawing in the National Portrait Gallery.

SIR THOMAS HUNGERFORD, 1376–7 54
From a drawing by Stanley North of the monumental effigy in the chapel
at Farleigh Castle.

HENRY IV CLAIMING THE THRONE OF ENGLAND . . . 60
From the Harleian Manuscripts.

SIR ARNOLD SAVAGE, 1400–1, 1403–4 66
From a brass in S. Chancel of Bobbing Church, Kent.

JOHN TIPTOFT, EARL OF WORCESTER 70
From a monumental effigy in Ely Cathedral.

THOMAS CHAUCER, 1407, 1409–10, 1411, 1414, 1421 . . . 72
From a print of the memorial brass in Ewelme Church, Oxfordshire.

SIR WALTER HUNGERFORD, AFTERWARDS LORD HUNGERFORD, 1414 74
Formerly in the north side of the nave of Salisbury Cathedral. Reproduced
from Gough's *Sepulchral Mouuments*.

ROGER HUNT, 1420 76
From a memorial brass of 1473 in Great Linford Church, Bucks. It may
possibly be that of his son.

EFFIGY OF SIR RICHARD VERNON, 1425–6 78
In the Church of Tong, Shropshire.

SIR JOHN SAY, 1448–9, 1463, 1467 80
From a brass in Broxbourne Church, Herts. Reproduced from Waller's
Monumental Brasses, 1864.

WILLIAM CATESBY, 1483–4 96
From a memorial brass at Ashby St. Ledgers, Northants.

FACING PAGE

SIR THOMAS LOVELL, 1485 (*in photogravure*) 102
From the bronze medallion in Henry VII Chapel, Westminster Abbey, by
Torregiano (photogravure).

SIR JOHN MORDAUNT, 1487 105
From a monumental effigy in Turvey Church, Beds.

SIR RICHARD EMPSON, 1491, AND EDMOND DUDLEY, 1503-4,
WITH HENRY VII 106
From a painting in the possession of the Duke of Rutland.

SIR ROBERT DRURY, 1495 108
From a monumental effigy in St. Mary's Church, Bury St. Edmunds.

SIR REGINALD BRAY, 1496 110
From a drawing in the possession of Mr. Justice Bray of a window in the
Priory Church, Malvern.

SIR ROBERT SHEFFIELD, 1511-12 118
From a print.

SIR THOMAS NEVILL, 1514-15 120
From a memorial brass in Mereworth Church, Kent.

SIR THOMAS MORE, 1523 122
From a painting at the Speaker's House.

SIR THOMAS AUDLEY, 1529 124
From a painting at the Speaker's House.

SIR HUMPHREY WINGFIELD, 1533 126
From a painting in the possession of Major J. M. Wingfield, Tickencote Hall,
Stamford.

SIR RICHARD RICH, 1536 128
From a print.

SIR JOHN BAKER, 1545, 1547 130
From a drawing in the National Portrait Gallery.

SIR JAMES DYER, 1552-3 132
Reproduced from an original painting in the possession of Canon Mayo, of
Long Burton, Farley.

SIR ROBERT BROOKE, 1554 132
From a drawing at the National Portrait Gallery.

SIR CLEMENT HEIGHAM, 1554 133
From a drawing in the National Portrait Gallery.

SIR WILLIAM CORDELL, 1557-8 134
From a portrait at St. John's College, Oxford.

SIR THOMAS GARGRAVE, 1558-9 136
From a painting in the possession of Milner Gibson Gery Cullum, Esq.

THOMAS WILLIAMS, 1562-3 138
From a memorial brass at Harford Church, Devon.

FACING PAGE

SIR CHRISTOPHER WRAY, 1571 138
From a painting in the National Portrait Gallery.

RICHARD ONSLOW, 1566 140
From a painting in the Speaker's House.

SIR ROBERT BELL, 1572 140
From a print.

SIR JOHN POPHAM, 1580–1 142
From a painting in the National Portrait Gallery.

SIR JOHN PUCKERING, 1584, 1586. . . . 142
From his tomb in Westminster Abbey. From a print.

SPEAKER SNAGGE'S MONUMENT, 1588–9 . . . 144
At Marston Morteyne, Beds. From a drawing.

LETTER FROM LORD BURGHLEY TO SPEAKER SNAGGE, 1588–9 . 146

SIR EDWARD COKE, 1592–3 148
From a painting at Holkham.

SIR CHRISTOPHER YELVERTON, 1597 . . . 158
From a print.

SIR JOHN CROKE, 1601 160
From a drawing in the National Portrait Gallery.

SIR EDWARD PHELIPS, 1603–4 166
From a painting at Montacute, Somerset.

MONTACUTE, SOMERSET 168
Built by Sir Edward Phelips.

SIR RANDOLPH CREWE, 1614 170
From a painting in the Speaker's House.

SIR THOMAS RICHARDSON, 1620–1 172
From a drawing in the National Portrait Gallery.

SIR THOMAS CREWE, 1623–4, 1625 174
From a painting in the Speaker's House.

SIR HENEAGE FINCH, 1625–6 176
From a painting at Guildhall, by J. M. Wright.

SIR JOHN FINCH, 1627–8 176
From a painting by Van Dyck in the possession of Lord Barnard.

THE KNIGHTS, CITIZENS AND BURGESSES OF THE COUNTIES,
CITIES AND BOROUGH TOWNES OF ENGLAND AND WALES AND
THE BARONIE OF THE PORTS NOW SITTING IN PARLIAMENT,
HOLDEN AT WESTMINSTER THE 17 OF MARCH, 1627–8, IN THE
THIRD YEAR OF THE RAIGNE OF OUR SOVERAIGNE LORD
KING CHARLES, ETC. (SPEAKER, SIR JOHN FINCH) . . 178
From a woodcut in the possession of Sir Walter Spencer-Stanhope.

b

FACING PAGE

SIR JOHN GLANVILLE, 1640 182
From a painting at the National Portrait Gallery.

WILLIAM LENTHALL, 1640, 1647, 1654, 1659 (2), 1659–50 . . 184
From a painting in the National Portrait Gallery.

WESTMINSTER AS SPEAKER LENTHALL KNEW IT . . 186
From Hollar's etching of New Palace Yard.

JOHN RUSHWORTH, CLERK ASSISTANT OF THE HOUSE OF COMMONS, 1640 192
From a painting at the Speaker's House.

BURFORD PRIORY, FORMERLY THE RESIDENCE OF SPEAKER LENTHALL, AS RESTORED IN 1908–9 204

HENRY PELHAM, 1647 208
From a painting in the possession of the Earl of Yarborough.

FRANCIS ROUS, 1653 210
From a print.

SIR THOMAS WIDDRINGTON, 1656 . . . 212
From a drawing in the National Portrait Gallery.

BULSTRODE WHITELOCKE, 1656–7 . . . 212
From a painting in the National Portrait Gallery.

CHALONER CHUTE, 1658–9 214
From a painting at the Vyne, Basingstoke.

SIR HARBOTTLE GRIMSTON, 1660 . . . 214
From a painting in the National Portrait Gallery by Lely.

THE MACE 216
From a photograph in the possession of the Serjeant-at-Arms (Mr. H. D. Erskine, of Cardross).

SIR EDWARD TURNOUR, 1661 . . . 218
From a painting in the Speaker's House.

SIR JOB CHARLTON, 1672–3 . . . 222
From a painting in the Speaker's House.

SIR EDWARD SEYMOUR, 1672–3, 1678, 1678–9 . . 224
From a drawing in the National Portrait Gallery.

SIR ROBERT SAWYER, 1678 . . . 226
From a painting in the possession of the Earl of Carnarvon.

SIR WILLIAM GREGORY, 1678–9 . . . 228
From a painting in the Speaker's House.

SIR WILLIAM WILLIAMS, 1680, 1680–1 . . 228
From a painting in the Speaker's House.

SIR JOHN TREVOR, 1685, 1689–90 . . . 230
From a painting in the Speaker's House.

FACING PAGE

HENRY POWLE, 1688–9 232
From a print.

STOKE EDITH, HEREFORDSHIRE. BUILT BY SPEAKER FOLEY . 234

PAUL FOLEY, 1694–5, 1695 234
From a miniature in the possession of Paul Henry Foley, Esq., at Stoke Edith.

SIR THOMAS LITTLETON, 1698 236
From a print.

ROBERT HARLEY, 1700–1, 1701, 1702 238
From a painting in the National Portrait Gallery.

JOHN SMITH, 1705, 1707 240
From a drawing in the National Portrait Gallery.

SIR RICHARD ONSLOW, 1708 242
From a painting in the Speaker's House.

WILLIAM BROMLEY, 1710 244
From a print.

SIR THOMAS HANMER, 1713–14 250
From a print.

SIR SPENCER COMPTON, 1714–15, 1722 252
From a print.

ARTHUR ONSLOW, 1727–8, 1734–5, 1741, 1747, 1754 . . 254
From a painting in the National Portrait Gallery.

SPEAKER ARTHUR ONSLOW'S HOUSE IN SOHO SQUARE . . 256
No. 20, formerly Falconbergh House.

WESTMINSTER AS SPEAKER ONSLOW KNEW IT . . . 262
From Lediard and Fourdrinier's Map of 1740.

JEREMIAH DYSON, CLERK OF THE HOUSE OF COMMONS 1814–20 . 268
From a portrait by Sir Joshua Reynolds in the possession of Mrs. Myddelton.

SIR JOHN CUST, 1761, 1768 27
From a painting in the Speaker's House.

SIR FLETCHER NORTON, 1770, 1774 278
From a painting by Sir Wm. Beechy in the possession of Lord Grantley.

SIR FLETCHER NORTON 280
A caricature by Ingleby lent by Lord Grantley.

CHARLES WOLFRAN CORNWALL, 1780, 1784 282
From a painting by Gainsborough in the Speaker's House.

WILLIAM WYNDHAM GRENVILLE, 1789 286
From a painting in the National Portrait Gallery.

HENRY ADDINGTON, 1789, 1790, 1796, 1801 . . . 290
From a print.

FACING PAGE

SKETCH OF THE INTERIOR OF ST. STEPHEN'S, WITH PORTRAITS OF
ADDINGTON, SPEAKER ABBOT, AND JOHN LEY (CLERK OF THE
HOUSE) 292
From a print by Js. Gillray.

SIR JOHN MITFORD, 1801 294
From a painting in the Speaker's House.

CHARLES ABBOT, 1802 (2), 1806, 1807, 1812 . . . 298
From a print.

CHARLES MANNERS-SUTTON, 1817, 1819, 1820, 1826, 1830, 1831,
1833 304
From a print.

SPEAKER MANNERS-SUTTON. "MAKE WAY FOR MR. SPEAKER" 314
By H. B.

JAMES ABERCROMBY, 1835, 1837 318
From a print.

CHARLES SHAW-LEFEVRE, 1839, 1841, 1847, 1852 . . . 320
From a print.

JOHN EVELYN DENISON, 1857, 1859, 1866, 1868 . . . 326
From a print.

HENRY BOUVERIE WILLIAM BRAND, 1872, 1874, 1880 . . 334
From an engraving in the possession of the Serjeant-at-Arms after F. Sargent.

ARTHUR WELLESLEY PEEL, 1884, 1886 (2), 1892 . . . 336

WILLIAM COURT GULLY, 1895 (2), 1900 338

JAMES WILLIAM LOWTHER, 1905, 1906, 1910, 1911 . . . 340

A NOTE ON THE ILLUSTRATIONS
BY THE PUBLISHER

ABOUT two years ago Mr. Arthur Dasent wrote, as a stranger, offering me his book on the Speakers of the House of Commons from the earliest times to the present day, hoping that I would publish it and that I would afford the book eight or twelve illustrations. He was informed, when I replied, that if I undertook the publication I would give a picture of every Speaker of whom we could find a portrait. Later on we recollected that our common interest in prints had brought us together on several occasions many years earlier.

The present is one of the rare opportunities which a publisher interested in portraiture has of giving rein to his fancy. I certainly have never published a book which has afforded me greater interest in this direction.

It has also confirmed a conviction which I have had for many years, that there should be a Royal Commission on historical portraits on the same lines as the Royal Commission on historical manuscripts, for I have abundant proof of surprising ignorance on the part of many owners of portraits of distinguished Englishmen, who neither know the names of the subjects of the portraits they possess nor those of the artists who painted them. The head of one notable house sent me three portraits of successive ancestors, each bearing the same Christian name, but which was which and which was the man I wanted for my purpose I had to find out for myself.

I seldom wander round the picture gallery of a country house, however remote, without finding one or more unidentified portraits, and occasionally examples of what I believe to be paintings by English Primitives.

From some points of view, this is the most interesting collection of portraits known to me ; its range of date, from the close of the fourteenth century to the present day, the historical and decorative importance of the subjects and the various forms of portraiture, all but unique, make it a veritable pageant of English History.

Within these covers are gathered two portraits from church windows, eight memorial brasses, six monumental effigies ; and there is one noble example of the art of Torregiano in the beautiful medallion of Sir Thomas Lovell, now—thanks to the munificence of Sir Charles Robinson — preserved in Westminster Abbey. This is appropriately placed in Henry VII Chapel, guarding, as it were, the same artist's masterpiece, the recumbent figure of Margaret Beaufort, likewise in bronze. There is also a miniature, that of Paul Foley, reproduced by kind permission of Mr. Paul Henry Foley. There are forty-seven paintings, some of which are of rare interest ; and seventeen fine prints, mostly after famous portraits, the originals of which in many instances cannot now be traced.

It has been a difficult matter to get together so many early portraits. One obstacle has been the fact that Mr. Dasent has added sixteen important characters to the *Dictionary of National Biography :* William Alington (1429), William Alington (1472), Richard Baynard (1421), Henry Beaumont (1331-2), John Bowes (1435), Sir Robert Brooke (1554), Sir Thomas Charlton (1453-4), Sir John Cheyne (1399), John Dorewood (1399), Sir Thomas Englefield (1496-7), Sir Thomas Fitzwilliam (1488-9), John Green (1460), Sir John Guildesborough (1379-80), Peter de Montfort (1258), Henry Pelham (1647), and William Stourton (1413). It is comparatively easy to hunt up portraits when these are given in the *D.N.B.* ; but it is not always certain even then that the picture is available for reproduction. For instance, the *D.N.B.* states that a portrait of . . . . . is in the possession of a peer whose ancestor was a Speaker in the eighteenth century, but although I have written three times to the noble possessor he has not vouchsafed a reply ; which recalls the famous story about this same ancestor—a well-known Counsel before he was elected to the Chair— who was notorious for his disagreeable, abrupt manner, and broad dialect. On one occasion, when pleading before the Court on some disputed question of manorial rights, he remarked to the presiding judge that he could speak from personal experience on the subject, " for I myself

have two little manors." The judge bowed and said,
" We all know that, Sir . . . . . ."

The earliest Speaker of whom we have any kind of
portrait is Sir Thomas Hungerford, who was also the
first " Speaker for the Commons " mentioned on the
Rolls, of whom I have reproduced as frontispiece a
drawing by Mr. Stanley North from the portrait at present
in the window of the church at Farleigh Hungerford.
As Sir Walter Hungerford did not build the church until
1443, forty-five years after the death of Sir Thomas, it may
not be exactly contemporary, though experts agree in as-
signing it a very early date. It is possible, too, that the
window may have been removed from Farleigh Castle
Chapel after the church was built. A drawing, also by
Mr. North, of the freestone monumental effigy in Farleigh
Castle has been included. I have, in addition, reproduced
a drawing from an Album of the Speakers—which will be
dealt with later—in the library of the National Portrait
Gallery. This drawing is inscribed as being copied from
a picture in the possession of Richard Pollen, Esq. It
will be observed that all three portraits have a striking
resemblance to each other. The nondescript costume
of the picture is, of course, of a later date.

The son of Sir Thomas Hungerford, Sir Walter, was also
Speaker in 1414. His tomb is in Salisbury Cathedral,
where there was a monument with his effigy in brass. I
have reproduced the brassless figure in the hope that,
if the brass should be in some private collection, the
owner will see fit to restore it to its proper position. I

will now consider the other seven portraits represented by memorial brasses, namely, Thomas Chaucer at Ewelme Church, Oxon ; Sir Arnold Savage at Bobbing Church, Kent ; and William Catesby at the Church of Ashby St. Ledgers, Northants. These three names impart a strange, opalescent character to one's vision, for apart from the Speakership they suggest pilgrimages, romance, poetry, prose, and even conspiracy. There are also brasses of Sir John Say, slightly restored, in Broxbourne Church, Hertfordshire ; Sir Thomas Nevill in the church at Mereworth, Kent ; and Thomas Williams in Harford Church, Ivybridge, Devon. In this church there is also a fine brass in colours to the memory of the ancient family of Prideaux, one of whom was the mother of Thomas Williams. The epitaph on Thomas Williams is so quaint that it has been thought desirable to reproduce it :—

Here lyeth the corps of Thoms Willms esquire
Twice reader he in Court appounted was
Whose sacred minde to vertu did aspire
Of parlament he Speaker hence did passe

The comen peace he studied to preserue
And trew relygion euer to maynteyne
In place of Justyce where as he dyd serue
And nowe in heaben wth mightie Joue doth Raigne

The brass of Roger Hunt, dated 1473, in Great Linford Church, Bucks, may possibly be that of the Speaker of 1420 and 1433, but it is more probably that of his son.

Of monumental effigies and tombs the following have

been reproduced : Sir Thomas Hungerford ; Sir Richard Vernon in Tong Church, Salop ; Sir John Mordaunt in Turvey Church, Bedfordshire ; Sir Robert Drury in St. Mary's Church, Bury St. Edmunds ; Sir John Puckering, in Westminster Abbey ; Thomas Snagge, at Marston Morteyne, Beds, which has been reproduced from a drawing kindly supplied by his descendant, Sir Thomas Snagge.

In addition to the portrait of Sir Thomas Hungerford in the window of Farleigh Hungerford Church, it should be stated that the portrait of Sir Reginald Bray is from a window in the Priory Church at Malvern. Mr. Justice Bray possesses a drawing of it, from which our reproduction has been made. Sir Reginald Bray died without issue, but he left the greater part of his estates, including the manors at Shere, to the eldest son of his younger brother John ; Edmund became Lord Bray, and he gave his estates at Shere to Sir Edward Bray, his next brother, from whom Mr. Justice Bray is descended, and to whom the manors at Shere still belong. Judge Edward Bray is also descended in the same line, being a brother of Mr. Justice Bray.

It must be owned that the *pièce de résistance* of the collection is the wonderful picture at Belvoir, which the Duke of Rutland has most kindly allowed us to reproduce, of Henry VII, with Empson and Dudley on either side of him. This extraordinary picture is on panel, $37\frac{1}{4}$ by $29\frac{3}{4}$ inches, but, unhappily, the master who painted it is unknown, though there can be but little doubt that it is the work of an English artist. It is, of course, the earliest and finest representation of the painter's art in our Valhalla.

In the National Portrait Gallery are the following paintings, all of which have been used excepting the one of Sir James Dyer : William Wyndham Grenville, Arthur Onslow, Sir John Popham, Sir Christopher Wray, Sir John Glanville, William Lenthall, Sir Harbottle Grimston, Bulstrode Whitelocke, and Robert Harley. In the case of Sir James Dyer a reproduction has been made from a painting in the possession of the Rev. Canon Mayo, of Long Burton.

There is also, as mentioned above, a kind of Speakers' Album in the Reference Library of the National Portrait Gallery, which contains forty-five clever water-colour drawings copied by an early nineteenth-century anonymous artist, probably S. P. Harding or Sylvester Harding, most likely the former, who did much work of this kind. We have, however, only used the following from this interesting collection : Sir Thomas Hungerford, Sir John Baker, from an original picture in the possession of William Baker, Esq., of Norwich ; Sir Robert Brooke ; Sir Clement Heigham, from a picture in the possession of John Higham, of Bedford ; Sir John Croke ; Sir Thomas Richardson ; Sir Edward Seymour ; John Smith ; and Sir Thomas Widdrington. This last-named Speaker was buried in the Church of St. Giles-in-the-Fields, where there was an imposing monument to his memory ; but this was *broken up and, curiously enough, it is believed to have been buried in the course of some church restoration,* as was undoubtedly done in the case of a ponderous memorial of the Bellasis family in the same church which had fallen into disrepair.

I must not omit to enumerate the names of the other Speakers whose portraits figure in the Album referred to above, for in some cases the names of the contemporaneous owners of the original pictures from which the water-colour drawings were made are given : Sir Thomas More ; Sir Thomas Audley ; Sir Richard Rich, from a drawing after Hans Holbein, in the possession of Mr. Simco ; Sir James Dyer ; Richard Onslow ; Sir Christopher Wray ; Sir Robert Bell, from a miniature in the possession of J. Bell, Esq. ; Sir Edward Coke ; Sir Edward Phelips ; Sir Randolph Crewe ; Sir Thomas Crewe ; Sir Heneage Finch, from an original picture at the Guildhall ; Sir John Finch, from a picture at the Speaker's house (a similar portrait by Van Dyck is at Raby Castle) ; Francis Rous, from an original picture at Pembroke College, Oxford ; Sir Harbottle Grimston ; Sir Edward Turnour ; Sir Robert Sawyer, from an original picture at Barbers Hall ; Sir William Gregory, from an original picture in the possession of Mr. Gregory ; Henry Powle ; Paul Foley, from an original picture at Coldham ; Robert Harley ; Sir Richard Onslow ; Sir Thomas Hanmer ; Sir Spencer Compton ; Arthur Onslow ; Sir John Cust ; Sir Fletcher Norton ; Charles Wolfran Cornwall ; William Wyndham Grenville ; Henry Addington ; Sir John Mitford ; Charles Abbot, from an original picture at

Christ Church College, Oxford; and Charles Manners-
Sutton.

We are indebted to the Earl of Yarborough for permission to reproduce his portrait of Henry Pelham ;
to the Earl of Leicester for the portrait of Sir Edward
Coke ; to Lord Barnard for that of Sir John Finch ; to
Major Wingfield for the picture of Sir Humphrey Wingfield;
to Mr. George Gery Milner-Gibson Cullum for that of
Sir Thomas Gargrave ; to Mr. William Robert Phelips,
of Montacute, for the fine portrait of Sir Edward Phelips ;
to Mr. Charles Chute for the portrait of Chaloner Chute
at the Vyne ; to Lord Grantley for that of Sir Fletcher
Norton ; to the President of St. John's College, Oxford,
for the distinguished portrait of Sir William Cordell,
who was executor to the Will of Sir Thomas White,
the founder of the college ; and to Mr. Bernard Kettle,
of the Guildhall Library, for the very interesting portrait of Sir Heneage Finch, by John Michael Wright.
Finch was also one of the " Fire " Judges whom Lely
fortunately declined to paint. The Corporation then
commissioned Wright, a native of Scotland, to paint
a number at £36 each. This artist's work is not
sufficiently appreciated. He is the only man, we can
recollect, who was endowed with two Christian names
in the seventeenth century, but perhaps he felt over-
weighted by the fact, for he frequently signed himself
" Michael Ritus."

The following have been reproduced from rare engravings, a few from my own collection, but chiefly from

those loaned to me by that most intelligent and obliging of dealers, Mr. Bruen, of Greek Street : Sir Robert Sheffield ; Sir Richard Rich ; Sir Robert Bell ; Sir Christopher Yelverton ; Francis Rous ; Henry Powle ; Sir Thomas Littleton ; William Bromley ; Sir Thomas Hanmer ; Sir Spencer Compton ; Henry Addington ; Charles Abbot ; Charles Manners-Sutton ; James Abercromby ; Charles Shaw - Lefevre ; John Evelyn Denison ; and Henry Bouverie Brand. This last was kindly lent by the Serjeant-at-Arms, Mr. H. D. Erskine, of Cardross.

I have reserved till the last the important collection of portraits which adorns the Speaker's official residence. These Mr. Lowther with great kindness placed at our entire disposal. The collection is of varied interest and the pictures are of different sizes ; some are unquestionably copies. We have reproduced the following : Sir Thomas Audley ; Sir Job Charlton ; Charles Wolfran Cornwall, by Gainsborough ; Sir Randolph Crewe ; Sir Thomas Crewe ; Sir John Cust ; Sir William Gregory ; Sir John Mitford ; Sir Thomas More ; Richard Onslow ; Sir Richard Onslow ; Sir John Trevor ; Sir Edward Turnour ; and Sir William Williams.

There is also a portrait of the last-named, by Kneller, in the Members' Dining-room of the House, where a collection of paintings of English statesmen is in process of formation.

In addition to the above, the collection contains the following, which have not been used for the reasons that some were fixtures, and in a position where it was impossible to obtain satisfactory results for reproduction, whilst others, it will be seen, have been reproduced from other sources : Charles Abbot, by Lawrence ; James Abercromby ; Henry Addington, by Phillips ; Henry Brand, by Frank Holl; William Bromley; Sir Edward Coke ; Sir Spencer Compton, by Lely ; John Evelyn Denison, by Sir F. Grant ; Sir John Finch ; Sir John Glanville ; William Wyndham Grenville ; Sir Harbottle Grimston ; William Court Gully, by Sir George Reid ; Sir Thomas Hanmer ; Robert Harley ; Charles Shaw-Lefevre, by Sir Martin Archer Shee ; William Lenthall, by Van Dyck or his pupil, Henry Peart ; Arthur Onslow; Arthur Wellesley Peel, by Orchardson; Sir Edward Phelips; Francis Rous; Sir Edward Seymour ; John Smith ; Charles Manners-Sutton; and Sir Christopher Wray.

Since the time of Mr. Speaker Addington it has become a rule that each Speaker's portrait should be added to the collection on his retirement. It is a national loss that this rule has not been longer in operation. The most effectual manner to gauge that loss is to compare this collection with that great historical collection across the river at Lambeth. I shall always remember being shown after lunch one day, by Archbishop Benson, the portraits in Lambeth Palace. The Archbishop told me that Lambeth was the only official residence known to him where could be found the portraits of all the successive occupiers, at any rate for any considerable length of time. During our tour through the various rooms I well remember the

Archbishop stopping in front of the portrait of Laud, and impressively informing me that this identical portrait fell with a terrible crash from its position a few days before Laud was beheaded, and that the incident caused the gravest apprehension, for it was held by Laud's friends to be a bad omen. As we passed from this gallery into another room I was shown a large engraving (some sixteen feet long) of Rome, before which the Archbishop stood, and told me that some time previously he had had an old Oxford friend to lunch with him there, Father Edward Purbrick, the head of the Jesuit College, to whom he repeated the Laud story. As they passed out of the room into the corridor they heard a tremendous thud on the floor, and on re-entering the room the huge engraving of Rome had fallen to the ground. The Jesuit Father stood by, placing his hand over it, and cried out, " Oh, that I should live to see the fall of my beloved Rome ! " and straightway left the Palace. I hope I may be pardoned for dragging in this story, but I do not remember having seen it in print. It was certainly not in the Life, and it occurs to me that it may not be inappropriate to record it here.

In addition to the eighty-one portraits of Speakers it has been decided to add three other portraits, not of Speakers, to the series. But perhaps no apology is here necessary. The first is that of John, Earl of Worcester, and the son of the redoubtable Speaker of the same name. The magnificent portrait of this wonderful face is from the cenotaph in Ely Cathedral. He was a great

patron of learning and art. Indeed, Caxton says of him :
" he floured in vertue and cunnyng ; to whom he knew
none lyke, among the lordes of the temporalitie in science
and moral vertue," and Fuller exclaims of his beheadal,
" The axe did at one blow cut off more learning than
was left in the heads of the surviving nobility."   The
Dukes of Rutland are descended from the Tiptofts.

The next character is that of John Rushworth, Clerk-
Assistant of the House of Commons, who on that memorable day, January 3rd, 1641–2, embalmed for all time
the kingly speech, and the never-to-be-forgotten, if
equivocal, and certainly epigrammatic reply of Speaker
Lenthall.

The third portrait is that of Jeremiah Dyson, after
Sir Joshua Reynolds, the original picture being now
in the possession of his great-granddaughter, Mrs.
Myddleton, of Chirk Castle. Dyson was Clerk and afterwards a member of the House.

In the course of my researches I have discovered
the whereabouts of several portraits and monumental
effigies of Speakers, which have not been used in this
work for various reasons. As some of these may be
useful to students, it is proposed to place them on record.

In Westminster Abbey there is the fine bronze bust
of Sir Thomas Richardson, by Le Sueur, whose
equestrian statue of Charles I still stands at Charing
Cross. There is a painting of Sir Thomas Audley, by
Holbein, in the possession of Lord Braybrooke, and Lord
Onslow has portraits of his three Speaker ancestors in

c

the Speaker's Parlour at Clandon.   He has also the well-known picture of Sir Robert Walpole as Prime Minister, with Arthur Onslow in the chair.   This is partly painted by Hogarth, and partly by his father-in-law, Sir James Thornhill, who was a member of Parliament, and painted the faces.   Lord Redesdale possesses a fine portrait of Sir John Mitford by Sir Thomas Lawrence.   At Barrow Church, Bury St. Edmunds, there is the effigy of Sir Clement Heigham.   In Felstead Church, Essex, there is a monumental effigy of Lord Rich; in Claverley Church, near Wolverhampton, one of Sir Robert Brooke ; and at Checkenden, Bucks, where Sir Walter Beauchamp was buried, there is an allegorical brass, his coat of arms, and the following inscription : " Hic jacet Walterus Beauchamp filius Willi : Beauchamp Militis cujus aie ppiciet : Deus Amen."   A monument was also erected in St. Chad's Church, Shrewsbury, to Richard Onslow, the Speaker of 1566.   In Eastwell Church, Kent, where Sir Thomas Moyle is buried, there is an altar tomb with his coat of arms, and apparently it was intended to place an effigy upon it, but none exists.   There is also in the same church a bust and mural tablet of Sir Heneage Finch, who was a grandson of Sir Thomas Moyle, and at Coverham Church, Yorkshire, where Sir Geoffrey le Scrope's body was taken after his death at Ghent, there is a coloured window with the arms of the Scropes. At Wellington Church, Somerset, is a monumental effigy of Sir John Popham.   Mr. Harold St. Maur, M.P., is the possessor of a painting of Sir Edward Seymour,

and there is a fine monumental effigy of him at
Maiden Bradley.   Lord Crewe also possesses paintings
of Sir Randolph Crewe and Sir Thomas Crewe, and the
Right Hon. James Round has an oil painting of Sir
Harbottle Grimston at Birch Hall, Colchester.   At Oxford
there are portraits of Sir Thomas More (in the Bodleian),
of Francis Rous, at Pembroke (the portrait engraved by
Faithorne, 1656), of Arthur Onslow at Wadham, by
Hysing (engraved by Faber in 1728), three of William
Wyndham Grenville, one at Oriel, by Owen, another at
Christ Church also by Owen, and a third in the Bodleian,
by Phillips.   At Christ Church there is a portrait of
Charles Abbot, by Northcote (engraved by Picart,
1804), also one of William Bromley, by Dahl, at the
Bodleian.

The reproduction of the Broadside or List of Members,
in the possession of Sir Walter Spencer Stanhope, Bart.,
is one of the earliest if not the earliest known representation of the House in session.   It is dated March 17th,
1627–28, with Sir John Finch in the chair.   It is greatly
to be regretted that no earlier authentic illustration of
a sitting of "The Mother of Parliaments" is available,
for such must surely exist—either from early wood-
blocks or from still earlier miniatures.   It is hoped,
however, that this Note may prove to be the means of
bringing others to light.

Mr. Dasent has placed on record some hundred and
thirty Speakers, and there are doubtless others whose
names, when verified, will some day be added to the

list, when the State Papers shall have been exhaust-
ively examined and carefully calendared, possibly by
Americans.

When we reflect on our rough island story as portrayed
by Mr. Dasent from the Parliamentary or Speakers'
point of view for the past six and a half centuries, we
discover that, in addition to the beheading of Lord Worcester, no less than nine Speakers have lost their lives
for performing what they considered to be their public
duty, and in most cases their estates were sequestrated
and their wealth confiscated. Thus life and property
were less secure than in these democratic days. For
the Speaker of our time is known as " the first
Commoner in England," with a salary of £5000 per
annum, a palatial residence, picturesque privileges,
and a retiring pension of £4000. Surely this ought
to be some consolation, even to the most Conservative
minds. The names of the Speakers who suffered death
were : Sir John Bussy, Thomas Thorpe, William Tresham,
Sir John Wenlock, Sir Thomas Tresham, William Catesby,
Sir Richard Empson, Edmond Dudley, and Sir Thomas
More.

Unfortunately I have not been able to discover any
portraits of the following Speakers, though it is almost
certain that many of these exist in the shape of paintings,
miniatures, stained-glass windows, memorial brasses, and
monumental effigies.

William Alington (1429), William Alington (1472),
Thomas Bampfylde (1659), Sir Walter Beauchamp

(1416), Sir John Bussy (1393-8), Henry Beaumont (1331-2), William Burley (1437), John Bowes (1435), Richard Baynard (1421), Sir Thomas Charlton (1453-4), Sir John Cheyne (1399), John Dorewood (1399), Sir Thomas Englefield (1496-7), Sir Thomas Fitzwilliam (1488-9), Roger Flower (1416), Sir John Guildesborough (1379-80), Henry Green (1362-3), John Green (1460), Sir Nicholas Hare (1539), Sir Lislebone Long (1659), Sir Peter de la Mare (1377), Peter de Montfort (1258), Sir Thomas Moyle (1542), Sir William Oldhall (1450), Sir James Pickering (1378), Sir John Pollard (1553), Sir John Popham (1449), Sir Henry Redford (1402), Richard Redman (1415), Sir John Russell (1423), William Say (1659-60), Sir Geoffrey le Scrope (1332), William de Shareshull (1350-1), William Stourton (1413), Sir James Strangeways (1461), Sir William Sturmy (1404), Thomas Thorpe (1452-3), William de Thorpe (1347), Sir John Tiptoft (1405-6), William Tresham (1439), Sir Thomas Tresham (1459), William Trussell (1326-7), Sir John Tyrrell (1427), Sir Richard Waldegrave (1381), Sir Thomas Walton or Wauton (1425), Sir John Wenlock (1455), John Wood (1482-3).

After the names of the Speakers I have added the year of election to the Chair, so as to make it easier to identify the various holders of the office, and I hope that correspondents will continue to help me towards the completion of the list.

In response to a letter recently published by the editors of *The Times*, *The Daily Telegraph*, *The Standard*, *The*

Athenæum, and *Notes and Queries,* asking for information on the subject of Speaker Portraits, I was fortunate enough to obtain valuable information from the readers of each paper. It would be extremely useful too if readers would help to locate other portraits than those already reproduced or recorded in this work, especially of Speakers down to the end of the eighteenth century.

The topographical illustrations require little notice here, as they are, for the most part, fully explained in the text. The views of the interior of the Jewel Tower are from photographs kindly supplied by Sir Benjamin Stone. Hollar's view of New Palace Yard has not often been reproduced in so perfect a state. The one herein inserted is taken from the late Sir Francis Seymour Haden's own copy, now in Mr. Dasent's possession.

The view of the House of Commons in session is interesting from the idea it gives of St. Stephen's Chapel in the reign of Charles I. It will be noticed that there are two Clerks at the table, thus disproving the usually accepted belief that Rushworth was the first Clerk-Assistant. Speaker Onslow said, on the authority of Hatsell, that he had seen a print of the House in 1620 in which two Clerks were shown sitting at the table ; if his statement is correct, this is probably a re-issue of the same view.

The illustration of the Jewel Tower is from a drawing specially made by Mr. L. Hussell Conway. The map of Westminster in 1740, which Mr. Dasent discovered in the

British Museum, is valuable as showing streets projected as well as actually completed. Parliament Street was not built until many years later, nor did Abingdon Street come into existence before 1750.

The caricatures of Gillray and H. B. explain themselves, and the views of Montacute, Burford, and Stoke Edith are from photographs supplied by the present owners.

The illustration of the Mace is from a photograph kindly lent by the Serjeant-at-Arms (Mr. H. D. Erskine). The Mace dates from the Restoration. Although there is no decipherable mark upon it, in all probability it originally bore both date and hall-mark. The wear and tear have, however, been so great that these may have been obliterated, for the Mace has lost in weight, since it left the silversmith's, no less than 23 ounces. Originally it weighed 251 ounces, now it scales only 228 ounces.

Arthur Onslow's house in Soho Square is an especially interesting London view, as it stands on the site of Old Falconbergh House, once the residence of Cromwell's daughter. The author regrets that an illustration of the house in which Coke was born, still standing at Mileham, near Swaffham, has not been included, but the information only reached him at the last moment when the book was in the hands of the binders. If it should be so fortunate as to reach a second edition the omission shall be repaired.

It now only remains for me to express my thanks to : Earl Beauchamp, Earl and Countess Cairns, The Earl

of Crewe, The Earl of Iddesleigh, The Earl of Onslow, The
Earl of Radnor, Earl Waldegrave, Viscount Peel, Vis-
count Powerscourt, Lord Barnard, Lord Hylton, Lord
Redesdale, Lady Poltimore, Lady Victoria Manners, Mrs.
Stanley Lane Poole, The Rev. Charles H. Coe, The Rev.
H. H. B. Ayles, D.D., The Rev. C. T. Eland, The Rev.
J. A. Halloran, The Rev. C. W. Holland, The Rev. E.
Hutton-Hall, The Rev. John T. Steele, The Rev. C. B.
Hulton, The Rev. R. Wall, The Serjeant-at-Arms, Mr.
C. J. Holmes and Mr. J. D. Milner, of the National
Portrait Gallery, Mr. R. P. Chope, Mr. J. G. Earle, F.S.A.,
Mr. Henry Greensted, Mr. A. L. Humphreys, Mr. Geo.
Robinson, Mr. J. Horace Round, LL.D., Mr. J. L. Rutley,
Mr. Henry Yates Thompson, for much valuable aid, and
to Mr. Dasent himself for his kindness in permitting me
to append this note to his exhaustive researches.

JOHN LANE.

The Bodley Head.

34

: : THE SPEAKERS OF : :
THE HOUSE OF COMMONS

B

THE SPEAKERS OF
THE HOUSE OF COMMONS

CHAPTER I

WESTMINSTER IN THE REIGN OF HENRY III—THE ISLE OF
THORNS—THE PALACE AND THE ABBEY—PREFERENCE
OF HENRY FOR WESTMINSTER—DAWN OF THE ENGLISH
CONSTITUTION—WESTMINSTER THE EARLIEST MEETING
PLACE OF THE COMPLETE PARLIAMENT

NOTWITHSTANDING the inevitable tendency of the age to disparage the past, the
opinion is still widely held that the House of
Commons is amongst the greatest of human
institutions. The primary object of the following pages
has been to present a fuller and more accurate account
than has previously been attempted of the presiding
officers of this great instrument of popular liberty.
At the same time it has been the author's aim to describe how the Lower House of Parliament came into
existence; the place where it first held its deliberations
(with a topographical and architectural description of
Westminster at various epochs); the circumstances under
which Parliament assembled, with a brief retrospect of

its principal legislative and administrative achievements. An attempt has also been made to trace throughout the history of the House of Commons the close connection which formerly existed between the Abbey and the seat of government. These points are severally of importance not only to the student of constitutional history, but to all who value the conditions under which modern England is governed.

The cities of Oxford and Lincoln are entitled to take precedence of London as the places in the kingdom selected for the holding of the earliest known Parliaments; but to Westminster undoubtedly belongs the distinction of having witnessed the dawn of the English Constitution. King John frequently visited Oxford, and in 1204 he held a *colloquium* there for the purpose of procuring a grant in aid. In November, 1213, writs were addressed to the Sheriffs requiring them to send all knights in arms in their bailiwicks, and four knights from each county, " *ad loquendum nobiscum de negotiis regni nostri* "; and two years later the same king again came to Oxford in the vain hope that his nobles would meet him there.

Lincoln was the city chosen by Henry III in 1226, whilst he was still a minor, as the rendezvous of four knights elected by the *milites et probi homines* of the bailiwicks of eight specified counties, in order to settle long-standing disputes with the Sheriffs as to certain articles of their Charter of Liberty. But of the proceedings of these embryo Parliaments no record has been preserved.

No returns to these tentative and restricted assemblies have been discovered, and the earliest germ of popular representation is to be found in connection with the Isle of Thorns. The history of that traditionally sacred spot, revered by Edward the Confessor above all other parts of his dominions, is inextricably associated with the second founder of the Abbey.

Born at Winchester, Henry III was the first of the Plantagenet line to identify himself with Westminster. Distrusting the city of London, he felt himself secure within the sheltering walls of the great Benedictine Abbey, the re-edifying and beautifying of which was to be the darling project of his later years. Between 1245 and his death in the place of his adoption Henry is believed to have spent more than half a million of money on the rebuilding of the Confessor's church, and, according to the somewhat exaggerated view of the late Dean Stanley, his enormous exactions have left their lasting trace on the English Constitution in no less a monument than the House of Commons, which rose into existence as a protest against the lavish expenditure on the mighty Abbey which it confronts.[1]

As if to point the moral, the only contemporary memorial of Simon de Montfort is to be seen to this day, carved with the arms of other benefactors, upon the Abbey walls.[2] The tendency of modern historical research has been rather to deprive De Montfort of his

[1] Stanley's *Historical Memorials of Westminster Abbey*, 1896 edition, p. 110. At the same time a large amount of money was raised by subscriptions which entitled the donors to indulgence in purgatory, and much of the money spent in the rebuilding of the church was derived from the King's private income.

[2] Simon de Montfort's shield, a double-tailed lion, is reproduced on the outer cover of this volume.

claim to be the originator of the representative system,[1] but there can be no manner of doubt that, in the closing years of his strenuous Parliamentary life, his efforts in the cause of popular government caused his name to be regarded as a talisman among the English people.

Henry III was the first of the English kings who could properly be called a great patron of the arts. Though, in his remodelling of the Abbey, his conception of architectural effect was derived from foreign sources, yet it is to his encouragement of native art that London and the nation owe that triumph of the Early English style (happily little altered internally since the thirteenth century), the choir and transepts which replaced the church of the Confessor. Some doubt exists as to how far westward Henry carried the rebuilding of the nave, but Dean Stanley was of opinion that the beautiful diaper pattern upon the walls marked the limits of his work, leaving only the remaining bays to the westward to be completed by his successors on the throne. The vaulting of the nave was not finished till a much later date, but the junction of the thirteenth- and fourteenth-century work, where the diaper pattern ceases, is still readily discernible in the altered level of the triforium string courses.[2] The delay in the completion of the nave, as it now stands, was probably due to the fact that the first three Edwards cared less for the Abbey than did Henry III, and pre-

[1] The representative principle in England may be said to date from the introduction of the jury system for purposes of inquests, etc., by William I and its further development under Henry II.

[2] Since Dean Stanley wrote, the researches of Messrs. Micklethwaite, Lethaby, Bond and, more recently, the Rev. R. B. Rackham, have added enormously to our knowledge of the fabric of the Abbey and the exertions made by individual abbots to complete the original design of Henry III.

ferred to concentrate their attention on the rebuilding
of St. Stephen's Chapel in the palace, the building
which, as we shall show later on, was destined in after
years to become the home of the Commons, and so to
continue for well-nigh three centuries. The influence of
Amiens and Rheims, which Henry III knew and loved, is
apparent in the apse of Westminster Abbey, in the am-
bulatory, and in the nest of chapels radiating from the
central shrine, yet, to their lasting credit be it spoken,
the erection and adornment of almost the whole of the
great church was due to native craftsmen.

It was customary for the Kings of England to wear
their crowns at least once a year at Winchester, and
preferably at Eastertide. In the case of Henry III
this symbol of sovereignty was a mere circlet of gold,
for his father had lost the ancient crown with the other
regalia in the Wash. And at Winchester, the place of
his birth, Henry continued to keep his money and
his treasure. The office of the Exchequer at Westminster, where the money was in the first instance
paid in, has been frequently confused with the Winchester
Treasury, where it was permanently stored. Gradually
the Winchester storehouse was superseded for all purposes by that at Westminster, and from Plantagenet
times both Treasury and Jewel House formed part of the
appurtenances of the Palace. But little known, owing
to its remote situation, in a quiet mews of Great College
Street, the venerable Jewel Tower still stands much as
it left the builder's hands not later than the reign of
Richard II. To a chamber in this historic building
Charles I and Rushworth, the Clerk Assistant of the
House of Commons, retired to compare their respective

notes of the proceedings on the occasion of the attempted
arrest of the Five Members in 1642.

An illustration of this interesting relic of old Westminster will be found reproduced in this volume. In
it are now stored the standard weights and measures
in the custody of the Board of Trade. Surrounded
as it is on nearly every side by high modern buildings,
it is difficult to obtain a good view of the exterior. The
view here given is taken from the leads at the back
of the house lately in the occupation of Mr. Henry
Labouchere, and tradition says that under it have
been discovered the traces of an underground passage
leading from the Palace to the Abbey. It is perhaps not
known to many of those who frequent the Palace at the
present day that a portion of the outer surface of the
western wall of Westminster Hall has been preserved
precisely as it left the hands of its Norman builders,
and with their masons' marks still intact on many of
the stones.[1]

The lower storey of the cloister,[2] added to the Hall
by Mr. Pearson in 1888 on the demolition of Sir John
Soane's Law Courts, replaces, according to the views
of that capable architect, an earlier lean-to structure
on the same site. For some 800 years the outer air
has been excluded from the Norman masonry, and to
the protecting influence of this cloister and its predecessors is due the preservation of this relic of the Palace
of Rufus. Even after the great fire of 1834, one of the

[1] I give this information on the authority of Mr. Pearson, though
good judges have also been of opinion that no part of the ashlar work
of the Hall is of earlier date than Richard II.

[2] Now used as the Journal office and Private Bill office.

THE JEWEL TOWER
From a drawing by L. Hussell Conway

original Norman windows remained at the south end of
the eastern side of the Hall, immediately above the string-
course added by Richard II, and a good illustration
of it will be found in Brayley and Britton's *Palace of
Westminster*,[1] but it was most unnecessarily destroyed
in the course of some repairs to the Hall in the reign of
William IV.

By an ingenious contrivance Mr. Pearson filled the
spaces between the buttresses (added by Richard II to
support the great thrust of the incomparable roof) with
a two-storeyed gallery, which, though much criticised
at the time of its erection, should preserve for centuries
to come the only genuine fragments of Norman work
remaining in and about the Hall.   If, when Mr. Pearson's
additions were made, the sills of the windows on the
west side had been lowered to correspond with those
on the east, the symmetry of this noble building would
have been enhanced, but unfortunately the opportunity
was missed.

The same architect desired to rebuild the principal,
or northern, façade, the towers of which have a spurious
air, but a parsimonious Treasury withheld the necessary
funds, as it withheld them from Sir Charles Barry when
he proposed to cover the roof of the Hall with copper
and to carry his Victoria Tower up a hundred feet
higher than it is now.   On entering the gates of New
Palace Yard the least observant will notice that the
ground falls rapidly towards the great door of the Hall.
In the course of centuries the level of the soil has been
raised many feet in the vicinity of the Abbey, but were
the ground to be excavated to the same depth as in

[1] Plate VIII.

the ornamental garden between St. Margaret's Church and the Hall, it would at once be apparent to the most casual observer that the Abbey as originally designed stood on considerably higher ground than the ancient residence of the Saxon and Norman kings. Thus its commanding situation in the centre of Thorney Island caused it to dominate the surrounding buildings, producing a grand architectural effect which is now, unhappily, lost. Both Palace and Abbey were surrounded, not only by strong walls of defence, but by running water on every side.

A considerable stream, having its source in the wooded northern heights, ran through what is now the Green Park to join the estuary of the Thames. This was the Aye bourne, from which Hay [Aye] Hill, Tyburn, and Ebury derive their names. Eye Cross, an oft-quoted boundary in the precincts of the Abbey, stood on the same stream. Successive alterations of the surface have obliterated many of its channels, but, by carefully comparing the *terrain* with the most trustworthy maps, the limits of Thorney Island can even now be traced. A stream ran from near Storey's Gate to De La Hay Street, through Gardeners Lane, and emptied itself into the Thames near Cannon, or, as some have called it, Channel, Row. This waterway in its turn was connected with a long ditch or moat occupying the site of Princes Street, whilst another brook flowed by Great Smith Street and Great College Street to the river near Millbank. Westward of this again lay a great marsh known to the Anglo-Saxons as Bulinga Fen.[1]

It must be remembered that in Norman, and probably

[1] The name has been wisely revived by the London County Council in forming a new street by the Tate Gallery of British Art.

STAIRCASE AND ANCIENT DOORWAY IN THE JEWEL TOWER
From a photograph by Sir Benjamin Stone

much later, times the whole site of St. James's Park
and Tothill Fields was a tidal swamp, and that where
Buckingham Palace now stands bitterns boomed and
snipe drummed. St. James's Park is said to have been
formed by Henry VIII to gratify Anne Boleyn after
the Court had removed from Westminster to Whitehall. To this day there is water in the cellars of the
houses in Birdcage Walk at certain states of the tide,
and when the new building for the Office of Works
at Storey's Gate was in course of erection, a few years
ago, the greatest difficulty was experienced in procuring
a solid foundation, owing to the boggy nature of the sub-
soil at this spot. Whenever an old house on the site
of the Long Ditch is rebuilt similar difficulties are encountered, and the fact that the soil underlying the
Abbey and the Palace is composed of pure water-worn
sand is the probable explanation of there being no crypt
under the church, and no subterranean chamber under
the great Hall. The gardens and orchards, and even
the vineyards, of Westminster were famous for centuries
before the atmosphere of London became laden with
soot, and foul from the smoke of innumerable chimneys ;
and in a place called the Herbary, " between the King's
Chamber and the Church," Henry III ordered pear
trees to be planted, so that he might see the Abbey
rising in all its fairness, in the springtime, above a wealth
of white blossom.

Before the destruction of Gardeners Lane simultaneously with King Street—for centuries the only
approach to Westminster from the north, for Parliament Street is, as it were, a thing of yesterday—it was
easy to trace in its bends and curves the tortuous course

of the bed of the stream which once divided the Isle of Thorns from what we now call Whitehall.

The King Street avenue to Westminster only came into existence when the Empress Maud, at her own charge, threw a bridge across the stream at this point, additional proof, if such were needed, of the detachment of the city of London from the residence of the Norman kings. When the river was yet unembanked, the usual mode of approach to Westminster was by water, and, shifting the scene to Great College Street, it requires no great effort of imagination to picture in the mind's eye the clear, cool water flowing alongside the wall of the Infirmary garden, and the Abbot issuing from his water-gate to take barge upon the Thames. Architecturally, London may have gained by the formal alignment of the Embankment, but much that was picturesque was destroyed when, on the destruction of the foreshore, a great natural force was hemmed in between solid walls of stone, and a mighty river reduced to the commonplace proportions of the Liffey or the Seine. Before the Thames was urbanised, so to speak, Thorney Island was subject to periodical inundations, and Matthew Paris relates how the untrammelled waters swept into Westminster Hall and boats floated within its gates.[1]

The space enclosed in the thirteenth century by these various streams, of which the Gardeners Lane channel formed the northern boundary of the island, the Thames the eastern, the Long Ditch the western, and the College Street brook the southern, measured rather less than five hundred yards from north to south, and less than

---

[1] Only within the last decade a violent thunderstorm which burst over Westminster once more flooded the Hall, so that the water stood a foot deep at its principal entrance.

VAULTED CHAMBER IN THE JEWEL TOWER
From a photograph by Sir Benjamin Stone

three hundred from east to west. Yet this circumscribed area is believed to have supported a population of many thousands, if there be taken into account, in addition to all the King's dependents, those of the Abbot. Everything required for the Court was produced within the walls, and such was the profusion of the Plantagenets, that they maintained within the verge of the palace a small army of artificers.

When we remember that, in addition to the multitude of servants and men-at-arms (Richard the Second never moved without an escort of four thousand archers), the great officers of state—many of whom were in constant attendance on the Sovereign—were all housed within the Palace, and when, further, we take into account the vast establishment of the adjoining Abbey, it is probable that the total population of Thorney, at the period when it first became the meeting-place of Parliament, amounted to some twenty-five thousand souls.

The difficulty of reaching Westminster in the Middle Ages is brought home to us by numerous recorded instances of failure on the part of the Commons to comply with the royal summons. In most cases the delay was attributed to the state of the roads. Never good at the best of times, in rainy seasons and severe winters the main highways became almost impassable. The long and expensive journey to London from the northern parts of the country could only be accomplished after many halts by the way. Leaving Furness, for example, the Abbot would cross the sands at Morecambe Bay on his way to York to join the Archbishop. Five-and-twenty miles would be as much as he would accomplish in his first day's progress, and, after putting up at a rest house on the line of route, he would cross the moors separating Lancashire from Yorkshire on the next day. One or more of these ancient rest houses are still standing. There is one at Halton and another near Clitheroe. From York to London the Abbot would enjoy the protection of the Archbishop's retinue on the road. The Abbots of Abingdon and other great ecclesiastics had town houses in Westminster from a very early period. Many of the episcopal sees owned mansions in the Strand with gardens sloping to the waterside, and the Archbishops of York only lost their hold on White-hall with the fall of Wolsey.

Some of those who came from the home counties, and who dwelt within reach of the Thames, were able to make a portion of the journey to London by water. Archbishop Wake, who died in 1737, is said to have been the last Primate who habitually came from Lambeth to West-minster in his state barge. But the hardships cheerfully endured by the Knights of the Shire and the burgesses whose homes lay in remote districts must have been considerable in the thirteenth century. Such was the habitual insecurity of the roads that the faithful Commons, in their efforts to reach Westminster, were accustomed to travel in large bodies ; the knights on horseback, each with his retinue of men-at-arms, whilst the humbler burgesses in a straggling cavalcade formed their own body-guard. Wheeled vehicles were seldom, if ever, used on long journeys, and for the all-sufficient reason that there was no conveyance to be had between the clumsy waggons employed by the Sovereign on his royal progresses and the two-wheeled agricultural carts,

which were as yet little better than square boxes of
rudely-fashioned planks.

The luxury of private coaches dated from a much
later period, and their use only became practicable
when the condition of the main roads had been materially
improved. An illustration of the almost universal practice of making long journeys on horseback is afforded
by a letter written by Dame Margaret Paston to her
husband, who was lying ill of " a great dysese " in London
in the fifteenth century. She begged him to return to
Norfolk as soon as he could bestride his horse. Though
the Pastons were rich people as the times went, the idea
of his returning home in a carriage seems never to have
occurred to either of the pair.

Peers and prelates did not start on a journey without
a great train following in their wake. On such occasions
they took with them a number of body servants of
different degrees, like kings in miniature. Attended
by their squires, their men-at-arms, their jesters, and
their menial servants, they descended like locusts on the
reluctant inhabitants of the region through which they
desired to pass.

Purveyance was in the main a royal prerogative,
yet the demands of lesser men often weighed heavily
on the rural population. At sundown the traveller
of high degree, and likewise his retainers, sought shelter
for the night.[1] In the monastery hospitality was held to
be a religious duty, and as most of the greater ecclesiastical houses had been, in part at least, endowed by the
nobility, its members felt no compunction in asking for
the accommodation so freely accorded. But only people

[1] Compare Jusserand, *English Wayfaring Life in the Middle Ages.*

of exalted rank were entertained in the monastery itself. The great mass of their dependents fared less sumptuously in the guest-house.

The habits of courtesy prevailing in mediæval England ensured the knight the asylum of the guest-chamber in the house of his equal in rank. Thus, whilst the monks received the poor from charity and the rich from necessity, the country gentleman upon his travels quartered himself upon his like. The common inns were only used by the lower middle class, and they as a rule did not move far from their homes. Too expensive for the poor and too miserable in their appointments for the better class of traveller, these inns did not emerge from the chrysalis stage until the advent of the public coach in the seventeenth century. What kind of accommodation the Knights of the Shire found at Westminster it is difficult to say. Probably the evils of overcrowding were thus early in evidence. Sanitation was so far unknown that the cleansing of the streets was left to that volunteer army of scavengers—the kites. Soaring in mid-air around the Abbey they fell, like bolts from the blue, on the offal and carrion with which the narrow streets were strewn, to bear it away to their nesting-places in the wooded northern heights.

The condition of the main thoroughfares in London was not much better than that of the country roads. In 1314 several members of the Court petitioned Edward II to have the road from Temple Bar to the Palace Gate at Westminster repaired. It was said to be so dangerous that rich and poor alike, whether on horseback or on foot, were impeded in their passage to and fro. Those who were compelled to use it " en

mauvais tempz " were " desturbez de lor busoignes suire
par profoundesce del dit chemyn." Nothing was done
for some years, but Edward III ordered the road to be
paved from end to end, and the expense defrayed by a
tax on all merchandise going to the Staple at Westminster. At the same time the Staple was defined to extend
from Temple Bar to Tothill.[1] But all journeys, whether
by sea or land, must have an ending, and at last the
faithful Commons, with a perseverance only equalled
by that of the Canterbury pilgrims, came in sight of the
massive towers and frowning walls of Westminster, and
passed, awestruck at the novelty and magnificence of
the scene, within the portals of the Palace. There
in the heart of the ancient buildings stood, until the
disastrous fire of 1834, the actual room in which the
Confessor died—the painted chamber of European
renown—the very hub and centre of the governance
of England since Anglo-Saxon times.

The names of several other buildings in the old Palace
have been preserved. Marculph's Tower stood on the
river bank and overhung the water. In one of its
chambers the triers of Petitions, the precursors of legislation by Bill, met for centuries. There was the Little
Hall, in which the Commons were ordered to assemble
in the reign of Edward III.[2] The chamber of the Chaun-
tour[3] was near the Palace Gate, and here the triers
of Petitions for Gascony met.

The Star Chamber is mentioned in the Rolls for 1427,
and the Council Chamber " près la grande Chambre du
Parlement " in 1436, but both of them were probably

[1] *Rot. Parl.*, Vol. I, p. 302.   [2] *Ibid.*, Vol. II, p. 294.
[3] Of St. Stephen's Chapel.

C

in existence long before. The green chamber was another apartment, the exact position of which it is not now possible to identify. In it a miscreant secreted himself at the bidding of the Bishop of Winchester, with the intention of murdering Henry VI, when Prince of Wales, after which no more is heard of it. The Chamber of the Cross was the scene of the meeting of the first Parliament of Henry VII, and the White Hall, which must not be confused with the later palace of that name, was the usual meeting-place of the House of Lords.

Many of these time-honoured halls remained till the close of the eighteenth century, when the all-destroying Wyatt was unfortunately appointed Superintendent of the Works. What escaped his iconoclastic hand, with the exception of Westminster Hall and the crypt of St. Stephen's Chapel, perished in the great fire of 1834, to which further allusion will be made in these pages. The great bell tower which forms such a conspicuous object in Hollar's *View of Westminster* was not in existence in the thirteenth century, nor had the chapel of St. Stephen, afterwards the home of the Commons of England, thus early assumed the shape it bore for five hundred years.

What must have been the feelings of the Knight of the Shire when, having never perhaps been absent from his broad acres before, he entered Thorney, the shrine of the Confessor, and found himself for the first time in the presence of his sovereign lord the King! A visit to the Confessor's tomb in the adjoining Abbey would undoubtedly be paid during his sojourn in London, and if, by chance, any of his friends or neighbours were at legal variance, was not justice administered from the fountain head within the same precincts?

One of the greatest changes which have taken place in the Palace of Westminster since Henry III took up his abode there has been the formation of the comparatively modern thoroughfare between the Abbey and the Houses of Parliament which leads to Millbank and on to Pimlico. In the Middle Ages there was no road at all through Old Palace Yard. This open space represents the Inner Bailly, whilst New Palace Yard to the northward formed the Outer Bailly of the original structure. Access to City, Palace, or Abbey could only be obtained by one or other of the strongly fortified gates in the high wall of defence which girt alike the residence of King and Abbot. Of these there were four, and one at least—the High Gate towards London—was held to be of surpassing beauty. Nor was there then any road leading up from the river-side, along the line of the modern Great George Street, towards St. James's Park and the agricultural lands of the great Benedictine house. Until the Thames, the *fluvius maximus piscosus* of Fitz-Stephen, was bridged at Westminster the course of traffic north and south adhered to the horse ferry at Lambeth and avoided the populous suburb on the river bank.[1]

Thorney in the thirteenth century we know to have been a fortress, a prison, a palace, and a great religious house. Defended from the outer world by lofty walls and formidable battlements, upon which the royal archers

[1] The late Sir Walter Besant thought otherwise, and maintained that Thorney was a thickly populated spot long before the building of the Abbey, but unfortunately he failed to adduce any convincing evidence of his contention.

kept watch and ward night and day, the extent and magnificence of ancient Westminster must have been an impressive sight for provincial eyes. Surrounded by its great and lesser sanctuaries, its almonries, its bell towers, its chapels, gate-houses, and prisons, Thorney stood for all that was most inspiring to the average English subject, whether of high or low degree.

Mention of its prisons recalls the grim fact that the Abbots of Westminster possessed amongst their many privileges the franchise of " furca et fossa," a gallows for male offenders, and a pit filled with water for the women. In the vicinity of Dean's Yard, to call it by its modern name, the Abbot set up his tree of death on a spot known as " the Elms," whilst Old Palace Yard was for centuries the place of execution for malefactors confined in the King's prison. And, even after it ceased to be so used, the practice of exposing the heads of felons on the façade of Westminster Hall carried on the sinister traditions of the place.

In contradistinction to these sombre associations, an age of chivalry provided for the King's loyal subjects an ever-changing feast for the eye. It was, on the whole, a merry England which ushered in the dawn of the Constitution. The warmth and colour of the Middle Ages, the tramp of armed men in the Palace, the stately processions, and the gorgeous ritual of the Catholic Church in an age of almost universal piety, are gone from us, with a corresponding loss of reverence in the minds of the people, never more to be regained amidst the dull conventionalism of the twentieth century. Beauty, if perceived at all, must be felt, and the manhood of England gained enormously by the teachings of chivalry, loyalty, and honour so abundantly manifested in the period under review.

Coronation feasts, solemn jousts and tournaments in Tothill Fields held amidst the pageantry which the times produced, allegories, mystery plays, tiltings at the ring ; all these were part and parcel of the life of a Londoner in the Middle Ages. Though there were as yet no theatres, the Bankside in Southwark offered more questionable attractions to the profligate, who took boat at Stew Lane and landed on the Surrey side at Cardinal Cap Alley. The great fairs granted to the Abbots by Henry III, to the annoyance and the lasting detriment of the City of London, were another joyous feature of mediæval Westminster. There, too, could be witnessed, until it was finally superseded by Trial by Jury, the moving spectacle of the ordeal by battle.

When life's task is done, it has ever been the summit of an Englishman's ambition to sleep within the hallowed walls of St. Peter's. And, here at Westminster, within one encompassing rampart, were congregated the residence of the Sovereign, the Courts of Law, the greatest of Benedictine monasteries, and the accustomed meeting-place of the Council of the nation. Well may Thorney be called, when our purview opens, the seed-plot of sovereignty, liberty, justice, and piety !

CHAPTER II

THE HOUSE OF COMMONS UNDER THE PLANTAGENETS
(*Thirteenth and Fourteenth Centuries*)

THE EARLY SPEAKERS AND THEIR PRECURSORS

Peter de Montfort
William Trussell
Henry Beaumont
Geoffrey Le Scrope (Chief Justice)
William de Thorpe (Chief Justice)
William de Shareshulle (Chief Justice)

Henry Green (Chief Justice)
Thomas Hungerford
Peter de la Mare
James Pickering
John Guildesborough
Richard Waldegrave
John Bussy

THE Knights of the Shire, the backbone of the English representative system, were the logical outcome of the severance of the *barones minores*, or lesser tenants in chief, from the House of Lords, a body lineally descended from the feudal Norman *Curia*, and consisting of the greater tenants in chief or *barones majores*. These derived their Parliamentary existence mainly, if not wholly, from the principle of primogeniture. Sitting in the first instance by virtue of tenure, a very important modification, designed in the first instance to secure sufficient attendance on the King in Council, was in course of time introduced, which led to developments more far-reaching in their effect than their authors perhaps foresaw. This epoch-making innovation was the issue of a writ of summons, without which none could attend. Viewed by its recipients in the earliest days of its employment as an inalienable right, it gradually came to be regarded as a privilege, and especially when it was found that it could be used on occasion to exclude possible opponents as well as to include known supporters of the Crown. By a master-stroke, amounting to positive genius, Simon de Montfort so utilised this method of selection as to cause attendance on the King in Council to be regarded as a privilege by one class—the magnates of the realm—and as a burden, haply to be evaded by the other.[1]

The precise date at which the lesser tenants-in-chief ceased to attend at Westminster, in company with the greater barons, and became merged in the body of the Knights of the Shire cannot now be determined, but, once the control of the Crown over the summons was tacitly admitted, it only remained to provide for the separate representation of the under tenants and freeholders in Parliament, and the transition from tenure to selection was in all essentials complete.[2] From the ranks of the Knights of the Shire the Speakers were invariably drawn until the reign of Henry VIII, when a burgess was first selected for that honour.[3] The aristocracy of

[1] *Peerage and Pedigree*, by J. Horace Round, 1910, Vol. I, p. 357, where the origin of the House of Lords is dealt with by a master hand.

[2] For the early history of the House of Lords, the first Report of the Lords Committee on the Dignity of the Peerage, presented to the House 12 July, 1819, and further Reports printed in 1820, 1822, and 1825, are especially valuable. This Committee was presided over by the Earl of Shaftesbury, and its several voluminous Reports have been freely used, often without acknowledgment, by almost every writer on the British Constitution since the date of issue.

[3] The rural population far outnumbering the sum total of the towns, the Knights were able to control the House, while the burgesses, in many instances, were content to petition Parliament without attending it in person.

the Lower House of Parliament, they were first summoned to Westminster during Henry the Third's absence in Gascony in 1254 by Eleanor of Provence and Richard, Earl of Cornwall, the King's brother.[1]

There is no evidence that the summons was ever obeyed, yet it stands as a landmark in our Parliamentary annals from its embodying the principle of popular representation. The industrious Prynne,[2] writing in the seventeenth century, cited the terms of the writ commanding the sheriffs to cause two knights to be *elected* in every county by the counties themselves, to appear before the King in Council to report what voluntary aid each county would grant towards the defence of Gascony. " Præcipimus," the writ ran, " quod præter omnes prædictos venire faciatis coram consilio nostro, apud Westmonasterium, in quindena Pasche prox futur, quatuor legales et discretes milites de Comitatibus prædictis, quos iidem Comitatus ad hoc *eligerint* vice omnium et singulorum eorundem, videlicet duos de uno Comitatu et duos de alio." Thus the financial exigencies of the Sovereign were the primary and determining cause of a resort to popular election.

The gradual decline of the feudal aristocracy of the Norman Conquest and the expulsion of foreigners enabled the great Simon de Montfort to realise his dream of England for the English, and to stamp his name for all time upon the Constitution, by setting up a representative assembly to which the writ of summons

---

[1] Regent or Joint Guardian of England 1253–54 ; King of the Romans 1256–71.   Died 1272.

[2] The much-persecuted Prynne, the stormy petrel of debate and the arch-enemy of the stage, succeeded Selden as Custodian of the Public Records in the Tower of London.

was to be a right, instead of, as in the case of the House of Lords, a privilege, to be issued or withheld at the will of the Sovereign. The loss of Normandy and other French possessions of the Crown had the important result of rendering the Baronage essentially English, a fact which must not be lost sight of in estimating the patriotic action of De Montfort.

A further stage in the growth of Parliamentary institutions was reached in 1264-65, when, for the first time, De Montfort caused the summons to be extended to the burgesses as well as to the Knights of the Shire :—

" Item mandatum est singulis Vice Com per Angl, quod venire faciant Duos milites de legalioribus, probioribus et discretioribus militibus singulorum Comitatum ad Regem London in Octob prædict in forma prædicta. Item in forma prædicta scribitur civibus Eborum, civibus Lincoln et cœteris Burgis Angl quod mittant in forma prædicta Duos de discretioribus, legalioribus, et probioribus tam civibus quam Burgensibus suis. Item in forma prædicta mandatum est Baronibus et probis hominibus Quinque Portuum prout Continetur in Brevi inrotulato inferius."

The Cinque Ports, it will be observed, were specially directed to send representatives to Parliament, an instance of the importance already attaching to the question of maritime defence.[1]

It would appear that the writs then issued to knights, citizens, and burgesses were identical in form and substance with those addressed to the spiritual and temporal lords. None were issued to the citizens of London, as their liberties had been seized by the King, many of

---

[1] Quoted by Prynne in the second part of *A Register and Survey of the Several Kinds and Forms of Parliamentary Writs*, 1660, p. 29.

them imprisoned, and their estates confiscated, for having sided with the Barons. York and Lincoln were the only cities specially mentioned, and throughout the long reign of Henry III distrust of the City of London and a preference for Westminster were shown by the reluctant conceder of Parliaments. On the one occasion upon which he called a Parliament to assemble in the Tower of London the Barons refused to attend except at Westminster.

The transactions of these early Parliaments, all of them of brief duration, consisted for the most part of petitions to the Crown for redress of grievances, and the principal function of their presiding officers was to collect the views of the majority and to report to the King what amount of aid the assembly was willing to grant. Little or nothing in the nature of articulate protest by the minority is entered on the Rolls, nor is it definitely known at what date the practice of dividing the House and recording the names of those who dissented from the majority was instituted. In 1258 Henry III was in such pressing need of money that he announced that he must have a third of all property. In return the Barons were powerful enough to extort from him [1] a promise of direct control over the executive.

Even whilst these pages were passing through the press, portions of three writs, addressed to the sheriffs of Bedfordshire and Buckinghamshire, Surrey and Sussex, and Wiltshire, summoning both Knights of the Shire and burgesses to a Parliament to be held at West-minster at Easter, 1275, were accidentally found in the dust at the bottom of a chest transferred to the Public

[1] In the " Mad Parliament " of Oxford.

Record Office when the Chapel of the Pyx in the Abbey precincts was being cleared out, preparatory to its being thrown open to the public. This valuable historical discovery, foreshadowing to some extent the "Model Parliament,"[1] included the names of the members returned for the above-mentioned counties, for Middlesex, Somerset, and Dorset, and also for Warwickshire and Leicestershire.

It is true that in 1275 the wording of the sheriffs' instructions was "Venire facias," leaving the all-important condition of *election* unspecified, but it must be remembered that from the time of King John until the various features of our complex Parliamentary system were, so to speak, stereotyped in 1295, novelties and experiments were frequently being introduced in the form of the directions issued by the King to the returning officers. Sometimes the Knights of the Shire and the burgesses were required to be elected, sometimes the vaguer form of "venire facias" was employed, and on more than one occasion the summoning of clerical proctors was dispensed with.

The important fact revealed by these documents, unexpectedly brought to light after lying unheeded for centuries within a stone's-throw of the chamber to which they refer, is that, so early as 1275, Edward I, when he had only been on the throne for three years, had improved upon De Montfort's original idea of a summons to each borough through its mayor; that is to say, that in the form which Parliament finally assumed the representatives of the town were summoned through the sheriff of the shire.

The Parliament of 1295, which has been called the "Model Parliament," marked the end of the experimental

---

[1] Of 1295.

stage and the definite and permanent establishment of an assembly comprising the three estates of the realm. For while in the reign of King John, and at the accession of Henry III, the legislative assembly of the kingdom convened for the purpose of granting aids to the Crown may be deemed to have been wholly constituted by tenure, in and after 1295 it is clear that tenure did not constitute the qualification by which members of the Commons sat. Their qualification was henceforth constituted by election, and the earlier constitution of a legislature wholly by tenure was superseded. Besides the Lords and Prelates were now regularly included the proctors of each cathedral diocese, two knights from each shire, two citizens from each city, and two burgesses from each borough.

At the present day, when the powers and constitution of the House of Lords are being closely scrutinised, it is well to remember that in those far-off Plantagenet times the non-hereditary element in the Upper House amounted to nearly a moiety of the whole body, a condition which continued until the reign of Henry VIII. The composition of the House of Commons which met at Westminster in November, 1295, though presumably based upon the distribution of the existing population, was remarkable (with certain exceptions, to be noted hereafter) for the preponderance of representatives from the southern and western shires. It numbered 292 members. Of these no less than 219 represented the towns, whilst only 73 Knights of the Shire were returned.[1]

---

[1] In the Parliament of 1298 appear for the first time in the official returns the names of the two members for the City of London. Westminster did not obtain separate representation until the first year of Edward VI.

Cornwall, the county which in after years enjoyed the unenviable reputation of possessing the greatest number of rotten boroughs within its borders, had thus early five representative towns, Bodmin, Launceston, Liskeard, Tregony, and Truro. Dorset had four, Somerset five, Devonshire and Sussex six each, Hampshire nine, and Wiltshire, where no doubt the influence of the great territorial family of Hungerford was paramount, no less than thirteen! North of the Trent, the part of the kingdom which returned the greatest number of borough members was, as might have been expected, the county of York, which had eleven representatives, Worcester coming next to it with seven. It has, unfortunately, been impossible to discover the name of the Procurator, for such was the title given by contemporary chroniclers to the earliest leaders of the Commons, who presided over the deliberations of this Mother of Parliaments.[1]

The transactions of the important constitutional assembly which met at Westminster in February, 1304–5, have been analysed by the late Professor Maitland in his masterly introduction to the *Memoranda de Parliamento*.[2] The representatives of the people then dealt with many subjects, and amongst others the impending subjugation of Scotland. They even concerned themselves with the internal affairs of Ireland; two natives of the sister isle actually petitioning the King to be placed under English rule.

No presiding officer can be positively identified as having been chosen in 1304–5, but from the list of names

[1] The title of Procurator, one still retained by Convocation, was applied to Trussell, who exercised many of the functions associated with the Speaker's office, in the reign of Edward II.
[2] Published in the Rolls Series in 1893.

preserved in the Public Records we gather that a Lowther sat as Knight of the Shire for Westmorland exactly six hundred years before a member of the same ancient Northern family was raised to the Chair.[1] The deficiencies of the printed Rolls of Parliament, the work in the first instance of the Clerks in Chancery, are both numerous and regrettable. Chiefly concerned as they are with Petitions, to the exclusion of debate, there is some reason to believe that many interesting details of the ordinary routine of Parliament in the days of its youth remain unedited and undigested in the national archives.

Valuable as are the six folio volumes printed between 1767 and 1777, their editors only made selections from a mass of available material. Historical research at the close of the eighteenth century had not attained to the high level reached in our own day by Professor Maitland and other labourers in the same field, and it is much to be desired that the entire series of Chancery Rolls should be edited afresh and printed *in extenso* in English, after the thorough manner adopted in the case of the Registers of the Privy Council. To these should be added a transcript of the various forms of Parliamentary Writs and a précis of all such documents in the Public Record Office as relate to the early history of both branches of the legislature.

Much divergence of opinion prevails amongst constitutional writers as to the actual date of the separation of the two Houses. Hakewil, who wrote in 1641, possibly had access to documentary evidence no longer extant, and he maintained that they deliberated apart, or that at all events they gave their assents separately,

---

[1] The Right Hon. James William Lowther was first elected Speaker in 1905.

so early as 1260, and Sir Edward Coke asserted that he had seen contemporary evidence which proved that the separation of the two bodies took place at the desire of the Commons.[1] But as there is no evidence in existence to show that the Parliaments held before 1264–65 included a more popular element than the Barons and Prelates, it seems safer to assume that the division into two Houses did not actually take place until early in the reign of Edward III.[2]

Throughout this reign the Rolls record regulations for the maintenance of order within the Palace of Westminster during the sitting of Parliament. In 1331–32 it was declared that " Our Lord the King forbids, on pain of imprisonment, any child or other person from playing at bars [3] or other games, the taking off of men's caps, laying hands on them, or otherwise preventing them from peacefully following their occupations in any part of the Palace of Westminster during the sitting of Parliament."[4]

[1] See Howell's *State Trials*, Vol. XIII, p. 1410, in which a report of Coke's of XII James I (1614) is quoted.

[2] In 1332, and again in 1339, the Lords and Commons undoubtedly made separate grants. These distinct grants imply separate grantors, and it is safe to assume that after 1332 a permanent union of knights and burgesses was effected. See *Rolls of Parliament*, Vol. II, pp. 66 and 104. An ingenious view, supported by a considerable section of well-informed opinion, is that although the Lords and the Commons met together in Westminster Hall, or some other apartment in the Palace, on the opening day of a new Parliament, it has not been conclusively proved that they, at any time, deliberated in the same chamber.

[3] Bares.

[4] *Rot. Parl.*, VI Edward III, p. 64. The words of the original Norman-French are worth quoting : " Nre Seigneur le Roi defend sur peyne d'emprisonement que nul enfaunt ne autres ne jue en ul lieu du Paleys de Westminster, durant le Parlement q y est somons, a bares ne as autres jues, ne a ouster Chaperouns des gentz, ne mettre mayn en eux, ne autre empeschement fais p qoi chescun ne puisse peysible-ment sure ses basoignes.

The precise nature of the game of " bares," to which the youth of Westminster were addicted, cannot now be stated, but it was probably some form of a game known in later times as French and English or prisoner's base. The snatching of men's caps, and other forms of rough horse-play were the traditional recreations of the idle apprentice. Nearly six hundred years later the police are directed, at the beginning of each session, to secure free access to members repairing to the Palace of Westminster, though it is no longer necessary to issue regulations as to the playing of games within the precincts of Parliament.

When the Knights of the Shire first obtained representation at Westminster they acted with the Barons rather than with the citizens and burgesses, and it was not until the country gentry were fused with the new blood imported by the inclusion of the burgesses that an estate of the realm which, in the fullness of time, was destined to become the predominant partner in the Constitution, became an established fact.

Though there is conclusive proof of the Commons being thanked by the King for their services in 1304–5,[1] this does not necessarily imply that they had finally separated from the Lords, and when in 1315 one William de Ayremine, a Clerk in Chancery, was deputed by the Crown to note the business in Parliament he probably recorded the doings of both Lords and Commons. Another of this name was secretary to Edward II in 1325–26.

The Parliament held at York in May, 1322, obtained from Edward II an acknowledgment of the supremacy of a complete representative assembly. This declaration, entered on the Rolls, virtually amounted to a

---

[1] *Rot. Parl.*, Vol. I, p. 159.

written Constitution, and made it abundantly clear that, for the future, "all matters to be established for the estate of our Lord the King and his heirs, and for the estate of the realm and of the people" should require the consent of the prelates, the earls and barons, and the Commonalty of the realm. No mention is made at this time of the Knights of the Shire, who probably continued to act with the Barons until after 1332.[1]

In 1330 the Upper House had its own clerk.[2] Sire Henry de Edenestowe was the first to be appointed to the honourable position of Clerk of the Parliaments. Apparently it was from the first an office of profit under the Crown, for in 1346 the King required a loan of £100 from him![3] Not until 1388, when John de Scardesburgh was chosen, does history record the appointment of a similar officer for the Commons, yet as he was established in office at that date it is reasonable to infer that his post existed previously.

Turning aside from the conditions under which the Lower House first met at Westminster, its earliest presiding officers claim attention at our hands. The great names of Montfort, Trussell, Beaumont, Scrope, De la Mare, and Hungerford, six of the very flower of England, are associated with the popular assembly in the first years of its existence, and those, scarcely less considerable, of Pickering, Guildesborough, Waldegrave, and Bussy, completing the catalogue of Plantagenet Speakers, are all known to have played some part in the history of the country. The memory of others who filled the Chair in the turbulent times of the fourteenth century has been

---

[1] *Rot. Parl.*, Vol. I, p. 456.   [2] *Ibid.*, Vol. II, p. 52.
[3] *Ibid.*, Vol. II, p. 154.

D

obliterated in the course of the centuries which have elapsed since they voiced the opinion of the representatives of the people in free Parliament assembled. England then, as now, was governed by opinion rather than by acts of despotism, as Sir Robert Peel was wont to remark. Peter de Montfort is said[1] to have consented "*vice totius communitatis*" to the banishment of Aymer de Valence, Bishop-Elect of Winchester and half-brother to Henry the Third. These were the identical words made use of by Speaker Tiptoft in 1405–6, when he signed and sealed the entail to the Crown,[2] and yet the word *communitas* as applied by Peter de Montfort may only have been intended to convey a collective body of Crown vassals, whereas, in the latter instance, the Speaker undoubtedly referred to the House of Commons as a separate entity.

The sole authority for Hakewil's statement is the Register Book of St. Alban's Abbey, formerly in the Cottonian Library, and, as he refers to the actual page,[3] it appears that both he and Sir Symonds D'Ewes, who also quotes the Register, saw it with their own eyes. But it cannot now be traced in the British Museum, and it is to be feared that this valuable manuscript must have perished in the fire which destroyed 100 volumes of the Cottonian Collection in 1731, and rendered a like number illegible. In 1259 Pope Alexander IV was striving with all his might to procure the recall of Aymer de Valence from exile, but the answer which Peter de Montfort transmitted to Rome was couched in these uncompromising terms :—

---

[1] Again on the authority of Hakewil.
[2] VII and VIII Henry IV.   [3] Folio 207.

" Si Dominus Rex et Regni majores hoc vellent, communitas tamen, ipsius ingressorum in Anglia, jam nullatenus sustineret." [1]

From the date given by Hakewil, [2] it seems not unlikely that Peter de Montfort may have acted as presiding officer of the so-called " Mad Parliament " of 1258, when he was undoubtedly one of the twelve nominees of the Baronial, as opposed to the Court, party, entrusted with the duty of carrying out the great work of reform known to our forefathers as the " Provisions of Oxford." But, as has already been pointed out, the Knights of the Shire and the burgesses were not represented in the Parliament of 1258, therefore Peter de Montfort can only have acted as the spokesman of a restricted assembly of Barons and Prelates, nor was there any Parliament actually in session at the time of his protest against the recall of Aymer de Valence. To the Provisions of Oxford Henry III published his adhesion in the first known English Proclamation, and a copy of it still exists at Oxford. It is written chiefly in the Midland dialect and there is not a single French word in it. Probably Simon de Montfort felt the need of appealing to the nation at large, and this English confirmation of the royal acquiescence was duplicated by his orders in the Latin and French tongues.

One would naturally like to connect the name of the first Parliamentary spokesman with that of the great Simon, the originator of the principle of the House of Com-

---

[1] For an account of the whole circumstances attending Aymer de Valence's banishment, see Gasquet's *Henry III and the Church*, 1905, pp. 320–3.

[2] The forty-fourth year of Henry III.

mons, if not its actual inventor ; and some writers have gone so far as to assert that Peter was his son, and that, like his better-known father, he was killed at the battle of Evesham. But, unfortunately for the holders of this theory, it does not anywhere appear that Simon had a son called Peter. He was, in greater likelihood, Baron of Beaudesert, and of Henley in Arden, in the county of Warwick, and of a family not known to have been nearly related to the great Earl of Leicester. One of the same name, a possible relative of Simon, fought and fell at Evesham, but if, as seems certain, the earliest Parliamentary spokesman on record came of the Warwickshire stock, his death did not take place till twenty years later.[1]

We have no certain knowledge of the individuals who acted as Procurator in any of the sessions known to have been held between 1261 and 1325, yet in all of them there must have been some presiding officer, some intermediary between Parliament and the Crown. But when the last Parliament summoned by Edward the Second is reached there is documentary evidence of a Parliamentary leader who achieved sufficient notoriety to be honoured at his death by burial in Westminster Abbey, a distinction, by the way, which has been conferred on but very few of his successors in the Chair. This was William Trussell,[2] who acted as "Procurator totius Parliamenti"[3] on the deposition of Edward the

[1] See G. E. C.'s *Complete Peerage* under the title *Montfort*, where the date of his death is given as 1284.

[2] Trussell's name is not to be found in the Return of Members' Names in 1326–27, though he had been a Knight of the Shire for Leicester in 1314. Like Peter de Montfort, he probably attended Parliament in the capacity of a Minor Baron.

[3] Henry of Knighton's Chronicle, contained in Twysden's *Decem Scriptores*, 1652, p. 2549.

Second at Kenilworth, and the same man whom Marlowe
refers to in his play of *Edward II* :—[1]

" My Lord, the Parliament must have present news,
and therefore say, will you resign or not ? "

Apparently Trussell acted in a similar capacity in the
reign of Edward the Third, for in 1340 he announced a
naval victory to the House,[2] and was specially mentioned
in the Rolls as undertaking to raise wools for the King's
aid.

The Parliament which assembled at Westminster, " a
la quinzeine de la Seint Michel," in 1339,[3] whether it
was presided over or not by Trussell, was one of exceptional interest and importance, although its proceedings
have received very scant attention at the hands of constitutional writers. John Stratford, the Archbishop of
Canterbury, came from overseas with a message from
the King to his Parliament; the Proclamation calling
the Lords and Commons together was made in the
Great Hall, and the cause of summons made no secret
of the fact that the King was in urgent need of a great
sum of money for the defence of the realm.

The Abbot of Westminster, Thomas Henley, Monsieur
Hugh le Despencer, Monsieur Gilbert Talbot, Monsieur
Robert de l'Isle, and Monsieur William de la Pole are
amongst those specially named in the Rolls as assenting
forthwith to the granting of a sum sufficient to meet the
King's necessities, " ou autrement il serroit honiz [shamed]
& deshonurez et lui et son poeple destruyt à tous jours."
But when Parliament came to consider the method of

[1] Act V, scene 17.
[2] *Rot. Parl.*, Vol. II, p. 118.
[3] XIII Edward III.

raising the necessary supplies, there occurred one of those marked divergences of opinion between the two Houses which occasionally agitate the public mind in the twentieth as in the fourteenth century.

In 1339 the Lords consented to grant the King the tenth sheaf of all the corn in their demesnes, except of their bound tenants, the tenth fleece of the wool, and the tenth lamb of their own store, to be paid within two years. To this they attached a proviso to the effect that the great burden proposed to be laid upon wool ought to be revoked at no distant date, and that the grant should not be turned into a custom. But the Commons, when asked for an equivalent levy, made answer that before they were prepared to assent to this novel taxation they desired to consult their constituents, and, in effect, they prayed the King to dissolve the Parliament and call another to decide the question. *Mutatis mutandis*, the *impasse* in 1339 was not dissimilar to the deadlock of 1909, though, whereas in the former year the Commons desired to take the opinion of the country before agreeing to a new form of taxation, in 1909 it was the Upper House which refused to pass the Budget of the year without first referring it to the judgment of the people. The whole record on the Rolls is of such historical importance that no apology is needed for reproducing *in extenso* the answer of the Commons :—

" Et ceux de la Commune donnerent lour respons en un autre cedule, contenante la fourme souuzescrite.

" Seignurs, les gentz q sount cy a ce Parlement pur la Commune ount bien entendu l'estat ñ̃e Seignur le Roi, et la graunt necessite q'il ad d'estre aide de son poeple ; et molt sount leez de cuer, & grantment confortez de ce q'il est tant alez avant en les busoignes queles il ad empris, a l'honur de lui, & salvacion de son poeple ; et prient a Dieu q'il lui doigne grace de bien continuer & victorie de ses enemys a l'honur de lui, & salvacion de sa terre. Et quant a la necessite q'il ad d'estre aide de son poeple, les gentz de la Commune qi sount cy scievent bien q'il covient estre aidez grauntement, et sount en bone volente de la faire, si come ils ount este touz jours devant ces houres. Mes pur ceo q'il covient q l'aide soit graunt, en ce cas ils n'osoront assentir tant q'ils eussent conseillez & avysez les Communes de lour pais. Parquoi prient les ditz gentz q cy sount pur les Communes a Monseigneur le Duc, & as austres Seigñ q cy sount, q'il lui pleise somondre un autre Parlement au certein jour covenable, et en le meen temps chescun se trerra vers son pais, & promettent loiaument, en la ligeance q'ils deyvent a nře Seignur le Roi, q'ils mettront tut la peine q'ils purront chescun devers son pais pur aver aide bon et covenable pur nře Seignur le Roi, et quident, od l'aide de Dieu, bien exploiter. Et prient outre, qe Brief soit mande a chescun Viscont d'Engleterre, q̃ deux de mielx vanez Chivalers des Contez soient esluz & enviez at preschein Parlement pur la Commune, si qe nul de eux soit Viscomt ne autre ministre." [1]

It would seem that the request of the Commons was granted, for the King called a new Parliament to assemble at Westminster only three months later. On this occasion the infant Black Prince was the nominal guardian of the kingdom in his father's absence, while the administration of the country really lay in the hands of the Council.

Three years later, in 1343, the Rolls relate : " Et puis vindrent les Chivalers de Counteez et les Communes et

[1] *Rot. Parl.*, Vol. II, p. 104, 1339, XIII Edward III.

repondirent par Monsr William Trussell en la dite Chambre blanche " to a communication from the Pope. Dean Stanley says that he was buried in the Abbey in 1364, but, if the statement in G. E. C.'s *Peerage* that he died before 1346 is correct, Stanley's note is in all probability a misprinted date. Trussell's tomb was in St. Michael's Chapel under the image of St. George. A foliated cross remaining in the pavement may be his memorial, for, though the slab has long been supposed to mark the resting-place of one of the Abbots, a herald's roll of the reign of Edward III records that : " Monsire William Trussell port d'argent une crois de gules les bouts floretes," [1] which accords with the blazon on the stone at Westminster. The Rolls record the names of one or two more Parliamentary spokesmen of early date, though the constituencies they represented are not now in all cases to be ascertained.

Of the Parliament which met at Westminster 16 March, 1331–32, we read : " Lesqueux Contes Barons et autres Grantz puis revindrent et repondirent touz au Roi par la bouche [de] Monsr Henri de Beaumont." And in the next Parliament Sir Geoffrey Le Scrope, the King's Chief Justice, is mentioned as acting in the same capacity. Both Beaumont and Scrope, and probably others, were,

---

[1] Though summoned to a Council in 1341–42, Trussell was never a Peer of Parliament, as has been supposed by Burke and other genealogical writers. The family owned property in the county of Stafford, and other large estates in the neighbourhood of Windsor formerly belonging to Oliver of Bordeaux. Their armorial bearings are still to be seen in a south window of the beautiful Decorated chancel of Warfield Church, an old forest parish in Berkshire. Though styled " Monsieur " in the Rolls, Trussell was made a Knight of the Bath on 22 May, 1306, unless this was another man of the same name. Shottesbrooke Church, also in Windsor Forest, was built by one of the same family.

however, almost certainly the mouthpieces of both Houses
rather than the especial servants of the Commons.
It now became customary for the Chief Justice to declare the cause of summons at the opening of a new
Parliament, and instances are cited by Elsynge of this
being done by William Thorpe, Sir William Shareshull,
and Henry Green. Occasionally the King's Chamberlain
acted as his deputy.[1] Elsynge, however, misconceived
the true functions of the individual selected by the
Crown to declare the cause of summons, and he was
quite wrong in assuming that the Chief Justice performed duties analogous to those of the modern Speaker.
All the evidence which exists goes to prove that the
Commons had not as yet acquired the right of electing
the Speaker of their free choice.

It has often been stated in print that the Commons,
from the time when they began to deliberate apart,
were in the habit of assembling in the Chapter House of
Westminster Abbey. This building was begun about
1250, but it was certainly not finished in 1256, when
Dean Stanley states that the Commons met in it. He
also stated that the " Commons of London," a rather

---

[1] XXV Edward III, 1351-52. " The cause of summons was declared
by William de Shareshull, Chief Justice, and receivers and triers of
petitions being read, he willed the Commons to put their advice in
writing, and deliver it to the King, so that he was Speaker."
XXIX Edward III. " The Chief Justice declared that the King's
pleasure was that the cause of summons should be declared by Monsieur Walter de Manny, and so it was. Yet the Chief Justice managed
the Parliament business as Speaker, for presently after Monsr Manny
his discourse, he willed the Commons to advise thereof. Here you
see the Chief Justice ranked first above the Lords in delivering their
votes, so that it is plain the Chief Justice managed the Parliament
business as Speaker appointed by the King, and that he did execute
the office (not supply the place) of the Chancellor therein."—Elsynge's
Manner of Holding Parliaments in England, 1768 edition, pp. 138-46.

vague term, assembled in the cloisters in 1263, yet in
neither of these years was there a Parliament summoned.
Other writers give 1282, when Ware was Abbot, as the
year in which the Chapter House was first so used ; but,
unfortunately for the holders of this theory, no Parliament is known to have been summoned to meet at Westminster between 1275 and 1290, though an informal
assembly of ecclesiastical and civil magnates was held
there on 23 April, 1286.

A careful study of the Rolls will show that these
several assumptions are based upon a misapprehension
of the facts. The Commons' first known place of assembly
apart from the Lords was the Painted Chamber, and they
met in it at least as early as the Easter Parliament of
1343.[1] This apartment was in close proximity to the
White Hall, or Chambre Blanche, in which the Peers and
Prelates were accustomed to meet. Moreover, at the
beginning of the fourteenth century relations between
the King and the Abbot were very strained, and after a
robbery of the Royal Treasury, to be mentioned hereafter, the Abbot of Westminster and many of his monks
were committed to the Tower of London. In 1348 came
the Black Death, which reduced the income of the
monastery almost to vanishing point.

Not until 1351–52 is there any mention in the Rolls
of the Commons deliberating in the Chapter House.
But in that year Simon Langham was Abbot of Westminster, and it is conceivable that, owing to his interest
with the King, they were then induced to forsake the
Palace for a building not originally intended for lay purposes, and which lay under the iron rule of the most

[1] *Rot. Parl.*, Vol. II, pp. 136, 237a.

powerful ecclesiastic whom Westminster had yet known. From his great wealth (liberally expended on the fabric, both in his lifetime and after his decease), and his commanding personality, Simon Langham, Cardinal and Archbishop, came to be known as the third Founder of the Monastery on the Isle of Thorns.[1]

Like the earlier Simon, the still greater De Montfort, the Abbot of Westminster had his share in the development of Parliamentary institutions. Only a little while before the first definite association of the Commons with the Chapter House the representatives of the people had shown an inclination to find fault with the existing land laws, and Edward III may have thought the moment an opportune one for bringing the knights, citizens, and burgesses more directly under the influence of the Church. Yet in 1368, the forty-second year of Edward III, the Commons were back in the Palace, meeting in the Petite Salle, and the Lords in the Chambre Blanche.[2]

Abbot Langham, from his unique position at the head of a monastery with vast territorial possessions, was a most competent adviser of the Crown on all questions relating to the ownership of the soil, and, once within the sheltering walls of the sacred building, the earlier note of discontent amongst the Commons was hushed, at any rate for a time. Becoming Treasurer of England in 1360, Langham was Chancellor three years later, and in that capacity he declared the cause of summons (in the English language) at the opening of more than one

[1] Langham's benefactions rendered possible the completion of the cloisters and the nave, according to the unfinished designs of Henry III, and amounted to nearly a quarter of a million of money at the present computation of value.   [2] *Rot. Parl.*, Vol. II, p. 294.

Parliament. When, in 1366, he was promoted to the Archbishopric of Canterbury, he received the pallium from the Pope in the Royal Chapel of St. Stephen ; nor was this his last connection with the scene of his up-bringing. From far-off Avignon, where the closing years of his life were spent, his heart always turned to the Isle of Thorns beside the Thames, and his body was brought back to be buried in the Chapel of St. Benedict, the especial resting-place of his Order, where to this day his stately monument, happily uninjured by the accidents of time, is conspicuous among the older ecclesiastical tombs in the Abbey over which he formerly ruled. The fact that Trussell was buried there at a time when the right of interment at Westminster was confined, almost without exception, to members of the Royal Family and to ecclesiastics of high degree is an additional proof, if any were needed, of the bond of union which existed between Church and State in the days of the Plantagenets. Moreover, Simon Langham, though not yet Abbot, was a prominent member of the great Benedictine Monastery at least as early as 1346, in which year Trussell is believed to have died, and it may have been owing to his intervention that a new precedent was set when a Parliamentary leader's bones were laid to rest at Westminster.

Amongst the Abbey MSS. there is an entry on the Sacrists' Roll of the year 1377–78, at which date Langham was dead and had been succeeded by Abbot Litlington, which refers to certain floor coverings which had been worn out by the fretful feet of the knights and burgesses in the course of a recent session. The monks, with the care which characterised all their doings, then took note of "Mattis pro choro & Capitulo empt 16/8 quia tempore Parliamenti Mattæ erant destructæ." And, as there appears to be no earlier mention in the archives remaining in the custody of the Dean and Chapter of similar purchases for the use of the Commons, it seems reasonable to assume that the incomparable Chapter House, as it was called by Matthew Paris, was not habitually used for Parliamentary purposes before the middle of the fourteenth century.

There may have been isolated instances, owing to the close connection which existed between Henry III and the Abbey of his foundation, in which the Lords and Commons sitting together as one body assembled somewhere within the walls of St. Peter's at the earliest dawn of the English Constitution, but all the evidence goes to show that the Commons did not finally separate from the Lords until Langham sat in the Abbot's seat.

The removal of the representative Chamber from the disturbing influences of the Court to the austerer serenity of the Cloister having been found in practice to conduce to good order in debate, the Abbey became the usual home of the Commons during Litlington's beneficent rule in the Isle of Thorns, and entries in the Rolls show that they assembled in the Chapter House in 1376, 1377, 1384, and 1394–95. But the great statute of Præmunire,[1] which restrained the papal authority in England, was not, as supposed by Dean Stanley, enacted at Westminster, but at Winchester in the Parliament of 1393.

In the picturesque language of Sir Walter Besant, there lay on the other side of the wall which formed the eastern boundary of the Abbey:—

[1] XVI Richard II, c. 5.

" The Palace, the Court and Camp of the King, a place filled with noisy, racketing, even uproarious life. There were taverns without the Palace precincts where the noise of singing never ceased. There was the clashing of weapons ; there were the profane oaths of the soldiers ; there was the blare of trumpets ; there were the pipe and tabor of the minstrels and the jesters. . . . Only a low wall between a world of action and the world of prayer." [1]

Besant emphasises the gloomy side of monastic life in the Isle of Thorns, but he might have added, with equal truth, that, within the jurisdiction of the Abbot, scenes of violence and disorder were of such frequent occurrence that for a man "to take Westminster" became in after years synonymous with his flight from justice.

It is one of the boasted advantages of our Parliamentary system that the Legislature is powerless to bind its successors, yet William of Colchester, who ruled over the Abbey in 1393, could hardly have foreseen that, within fifty years of the Commons accepting the shelter of the Church, measures limiting the power of its acknowledged head, though not within the walls of St. Peter's Monastery, would be debated and placed on the Statute Book.

The Chapter House can never have been a very suitable place for the sittings of Parliament. It was inconveniently situated for the purpose of rapid communication between the two Houses ; it was required by the monks themselves every day of the week, and it is probable that the actual number of times when it was used by the Commons was much smaller than has been gene-

[1] *Westminster*, by Sir Walter Besant, 1897 edition, p. 88.

rally supposed. The use of this particular building may only have been extended to the Lower House by Abbots Langham, Litlington, and William of Colchester.

The Speaker would, no doubt, occupy the Abbot's stall facing the entrance door ; whilst the knights and burgesses seated themselves, as best they could, in the eighty stalls of the monks. Late-comers would have to be contented with standing-room, though, as the attendance of the burgesses in the fourteenth century was never large and the sessions were of brief duration, no great inconvenience may have been caused. To the central pillar supporting the roof were attached placards having reference to the business to be discussed, though there were occasions on which mischievous hands affixed libellous documents in the same conspicuous position.[1]

But there was another, and even nobler, apartment in the monastery in which the Commons of England are known to have assembled. This was the great Refectory beyond the south cloister walk. Originally of Norman construction, it was consumed by fire in 1298, but promptly rebuilt, together with other domestic offices, under Abbot Langham and his successor. It was a rectangular hall of great magnificence, 130 feet long, nearly double the length of the existing House of Commons, and 38 feet broad. If Parliament is desirous of commemorating its former association with the Abbey, it would do well to restore, as far as possible, the ruined glories of Litlington's work. Its north wall still stands, together with some of the windows and the corbels of the roof ; and on its inner face a portion of the Norman arcading of the earlier building may still

[1] *Archæologia*, Vol. XVI, 1812, pp. 80–83.

be seen. As rebuilt in the fourteenth century, it had a fine timber roof, from which hung a crown of lights the fall of which is mentioned by Caxton. Over the high table was a painting of Christ in majesty, an inspiring symbol of the union subsisting between Church and State.

The actual date at which it became ruinous is not known, but though the Commons assembled in it in 1397, 1403–4,[1] 1414, 1415, and 1416, during the whole of which period William of Colchester was Abbot of Westminster, the Rolls are silent as to the actual place of meeting after the last-mentioned date. It is almost certain that until the dissolution of the monasteries they occupied either the Little Hall or the Painted Chamber. They removed to St. Stephen's Chapel on its becoming vacant in 1547, never again to desert it except when directed to assemble at Oxford in the seventeenth century.

It would seem that too much importance has hitherto been attached to an entry in the Rolls of the year 1376, which speaks of the Chapter House as the " ancient place " of meeting for the Commons. All that the phrase was intended to convey was that, although earlier meetings had taken place within the Abbey precincts (one of them, as has been seen, in the Chapter House during the session of 1351–52), a return to the Palace had been made in 1368. Therefore, when in 1376—the year in which De la Mare first held an office practically indistinguishable from that of the later Speakers, though there is no mention in the Rolls of his having been then elected

---

[1] In 1413 the knights, citizens, and burgesses were only commanded to meet " en lour lieu accustume dens l'Abbeie de Westmn at sept del clokke a matyn pour eslier lour Commune Parlour, & de luy presenter au Roy a sept del clokke mesme le jour."—*Rot. Parl.*, Vol. IV, p. 3.

to the Chair by his fellow-members—the King directed
the Commons to repair once more to the Chapter House,
the officials whose duty it was to record the proceedings
of Parliament were only desirous of showing that a precedent existed for the alteration in the rendezvous.

The Rolls do not specify the Chapter House as having
been used for Parliamentary purposes after 1394-95.
The Refectory was probably used in its stead until it fell
into disrepair ; but after the great fire in the Palace,
which occurred in 1512, the chamber used by the Commons was found to be so inconvenient as to necessitate
a temporary removal to Black Friars, and it was there,
and not at Westminster, that Sir Thomas More was
chosen Speaker in 1523.[1]

Whilst the Lords adhered to one of the chambers in
the King's Palace, there may have been occasions when
both Houses assembled in Westminster Hall in obedience to the King's summons. But there can be no doubt
that after the middle of the fourteenth century the usual
practice was for both bodies to deliberate apart and to
transact business separately with each other and with
the King. In 1362 the opening speech was for the first
time delivered in English, though for long after the
records continued to be kept in Norman-French.

In the " Good Parliament," which met at Westminster
28 April, 1376, the names of 117 members are known, of
whom 73 sat for counties, and 44 for boroughs and cities.
The foremost man returned to it was Sir Peter de la

[1] The Rolls in 1351-52 have an interesting note on the hour of
meeting of the Commons in Plantagenet times. They were then
directed to assemble in the Painted Chamber, "toust apres le soleil
lever," a custom which it is sincerely to be hoped will not be revived
in the twentieth century.

E

Mare, Knight of the Shire for Hereford, and Seneschal to
Edmund Mortimer, Earl of March, a connection which
intensified the animosity of his relations to the House
of Lancaster.[1]

Edward III, when well stricken in years, had fallen
under the baneful influence of Alice Perrers, a squire's
daughter whose rapacity and shamelessness as the King's
mistress-in-chief is only paralleled by some of the especial
favourites of Charles II and George IV.   In one year the
King, in his senile infatuation, spent many thousands
of the public money in settling her jeweller's bill, besides
making her large grants of land and constituting her the
guardian of several rich orphans.[2]   It became expedient
for ambitious nobles to stand well with her, and even
John of Gaunt took up her cause against the Black
Prince.   The financial exigencies of the Sovereign were
now great, and the public dissatisfaction increased rapidly
after the loss of all England's French possessions with
the exception of Calais, Bordeaux, and Bayonne.   The
Commons grew uneasy concerning Alice's influence with
the King, and when, emboldened by the success of her
political intrigues, she appeared in Westminster Hall,
and presumed to lecture the presiding judge on the
duties of his office, the patience of the House was exhausted.   In a long game of give-and-take between
De la Mare and the King's mistress the former scored
the first point when he discovered that Alice was married

---

[1] De la Mare was a man " fearless of consequences in an age of
violence, one whose spirit imprisonment could not bend nor threats
overpower."—Trevelyan's *England in the Age of Wycliffe*, 1899.

[2] It is said that this insatiable *traviata* was with Edward III in his
last moments, and that she even stole the rings from his fingers when
he lay at the point of death.

and bore the legal title of Baroness of Windsor. The
King swore that he knew nothing of the marriage, and
Alice was expelled from Court. Moreover, in order to
humour the Commons he gave his assent to an Ordinance
whereby any woman thenceforward, and especially Alice
Perrers, was forbidden to prosecute the suits of others in
Courts of Justice, by way of maintenance.[1]

After protracted debates, both by themselves and in
conjunction with the Lords, the Commons appeared in
full Parliament with De la Mare at their head. His
first duty was to answer the usual demand for money,
made to the Lower House on this occasion by the Chancellor, Sir John Knyvet. Not only did De la Mare take
upon himself to refuse supplies until the grievances of the
nation were redressed, but he adopted the financial position as the text for a sermon on the required reforms.

Edward the Black Prince now lay a-dying at the Abbot
of Westminster's manor-house of Neyte, in what is now
Pimlico, and it was known that it was John of Gaunt's
intention to secure for himself the succession to the
throne. In the subsequent proceedings of the House,
perhaps the most interesting to that date, De la Mare
voiced the opinion of a nation more than he represented
the views of any one party. He was, in fact, more of
a Parliamentary autocrat, combining in his personality
many of the attributes of Pym and Lenthall, than the
mouthpiece of the Commons, and the Parliament which
he dominated resembled, more perhaps than any of its
successors down to the Revolution of 1688, the Parliament of to-day in the extent of its powers. In 1376
the Commons proceeded to impeach Lord Latimer, thus

[1] Hallam's *Middle Ages*, edition of 1834, Vol. III, p. 83.

affording the earliest recorded instance of a Minister of the Crown being arraigned by the Lower House.

For a time the fortunes of the contest inclined to the side of the reforming party in the Commons. But with the death of the Black Prince the supreme power once more fell into the hands of John of Gaunt, and a change quickly came over the scene. Alice Perrers reappeared openly at Court, De la Mare was imprisoned, without trial, in Nottingham Castle, and would have been put to death if the King's mistress could have had her way. Wykeham was deprived of his temporalities on a frivolous charge and banished from the precincts of the palace.

The new Parliament was controlled by John of Gaunt, who, by putting pressure upon the sheriffs, was able practically to pack the House with men of his own choosing. Yet some of De la Mare's old fellow-members managed to secure re-election, and though they promptly petitioned for his release, counter influences were too strong for them. One of the first acts of the reactionary assembly of 1376–77, usually known as the " Bad Parliament," was to reverse the sentence against Alice Perrers.

From the point of view of the Constitutional historian the Parliament is a memorable one, since in it the Speaker's office first emerged from the twilight which shrouds its origin into the full light of day. Summoned at the close of a year in which a King of England celebrated the jubilee of his reign, the House of Commons, for the first time in its history, is known to have been represented at Westminster by a presiding officer of its own choice. Sir Thomas Hungerford, specified in the Rolls as having " les paroles pour les Communes d'Engleterre

SIR THOMAS HUNGERFORD
1376-7
From a drawing in the National Portrait Gallery

en cest Parlement," made a daring speech to the throne at the close of the session, calling the King's attention to various grievances and alleged infringements of the liberties of his subjects, both male and female.

This, the first recorded utterance of the House of Commons to find public expression through the mouth of its responsible president, has been strangely over-looked by Parliamentary historians, as has also the interesting fact that Hungerford, on the same occasion, delivered seven " Billes " to the Clerk of the Parliament, to which, alas for the budding hopes of the representatives of the people, the Lords vouchsafed no reply, " a cause q̂ le dit Parlement s'estoit departiz & finiz a mesme le jour devant q̂ rienz y fust plus fait a ycelles."

Sir Thomas Hungerford was the head of the powerful Wiltshire family which owned Farleigh Castle. Like Chaucer's Frankleyn, " full oft tyme he was a Knight of the Schire," for his career at Westminster extended over thirty-six years. He died in 1398, and was buried at Farleigh Hungerford, in Somerset, where his tomb and a portrait in a stained-glass window are still to be seen.[1]

On the death of the King, a new Parliament was called by Richard II, in October, and De la Mare, again the most prominent figure in the popular assembly, was voted to the Chair. The sentence of the Good Parliament against Alice Perrers was re-enacted and the power of John of Gaunt was finally broken.[2]

De la Mare again represented Herefordshire in 1379–80,

[1] See frontispiece to this volume.
[2] *Rot. Parl.*, Vol. III, p. 5.

1382, and 1383, after which date his name disappears from the page of history, nor has the year of his death been ascertained.

Sir James Pickering, the head of a great Westmorland family, became Speaker in 1378.[1] His speech, asserting the right of free speech and declaring the loyalty of the House to the throne, remains upon the Rolls and is the first of its kind on record. It is interesting at the present day to recall the fact that Speaker Pickering's wife was a Lowther. To him succeeded Sir John Guildesborough, Knight of the Shire for Essex, in the Parliament which met at Northampton on 5 November, 1380. This Speaker set an important precedent which, to a certain extent, foreshadowed the modern procedure in Committee of Supply. He demanded of the Crown that a schedule of the exact sums needed, and the purposes for which they were required, should be laid before the Commons. Thus the annually recurring phrase in the King's speech " estimates for the expenditure of the year will in due course be laid before you," is the logical outcome of a procedure adopted more than five hundred years ago.

The Eastern Counties also supplied the next Speaker, Sir Richard Waldegrave of Smallbridge, Suffolk, ancestor of the present Earl Waldegrave. He begged to be excused from accepting the post, but the King charged him on his allegiance that since he was already chosen by his colleagues he should execute the office. His is the first instance of a Speaker declining appointment, and for generations after his day a similar formal excuse was put forward, only to be refused, nor was the pre-

[1] " Monsieur James de Pekeryng Chivaler, q'avoit les paroles de la cõe faisant sa Protestation si bien pur lui mesmes come pur toute la Coc d'Engl illoeq's assemble."—*Rot. Parl.*, Vol. III, p. 34.

SIR THOMAS HUNGERFORD
1376-7
From a drawing by Stanley North of the
monumental effigy in the chapel at Farleigh
Castle

cedent set in 1381 broken until the reign of Charles II, when Sir Edward Seymour, who had been chosen against the King's wish, merely said, on presenting himself for approval in the House of Lords: "The House of Commons have unanimously elected me their Speaker, and now I come hither for Your Majesty's approbation, which if Your Majesty will please to grant, I shall do them and you the best service I can." The Chancellor had been instructed to express the King's acceptance of the customary excuse, but the Speaker's unexpected utterance took him so aback that he could only falter out that the King wished to reserve him for other services and desired that the Commons would make another choice. After a heated discussion and a prorogation a compromise was arrived at, but the important principle was established that the Crown has a right to veto, but not to dictate, the Commons' choice.

Sir Richard Waldegrave's motive, as far as it is possible to analyse it, appears to have been a prudential one. Grave disputes were likely to arise between Parliament and the people respecting the enfranchisement of the villeins to whom Richard II had lately granted charters of freedom. But as the King contended that these charters had been extorted from him when he was not seized of his full kingly power, he ultimately revoked them. Waldegrave may have been apprehensive of the consequences likely to result from this evasion, hence his desire to be relieved of the post.[1]

From 1383, when Pickering was called to the Chair for the second time, the Rolls of Parliament are defective for

[1] See the *Scrope and Grosvenor Roll*, Vol. II, p. 374, and *Rot. Parl.*, Vol. III, p. 100.

about ten years, though it is highly probable that he again acted as Speaker in one or other of the Parliaments held in 1384, 1388, 1389–90, 1390, and 1397–98, in all of which he is known to have sat for Yorkshire.

The last, and in some respects the most notorious of Plantagenet Speakers was Sir John Bussy, or Bushey, the first man to be twice elected to the Chair, and also the first to be alluded to by Shakespeare.[1] He represented Lincolnshire (where his family owned land at a place called Grentewell, at Domesday), between 1383 and 1397–98. He was first chosen Speaker in 1393–94, re-elected in January, 1396–97, and again in September, 1397.[2] During his second term of office occurred the important case of Privilege arising out of the trial of Sir Thomas Haxey, a prebendary of Southwell and proctor of the Clergy attending Parliament. Haxey introduced a Bill or rather an article in a Bill complaining of maladministration, and making specific charges of extravagance against the King. Richard II, when he heard of it, called upon the Speaker to give up the name of the person responsible for the introduction of the obnoxious measure. The Commons were alarmed and made a scapegoat of Haxey. He was adjudged a traitor and condemned to death, his trial taking place in the Salle Blanche of the Palace. He was eventually pardoned, and in Henry IV's first Parliament the judgment was formally reversed. Haxey, who was an ecclesiastical pluralist of an extreme type, became Treasurer of York and was a benefactor to the Cathedral, in which he was buried in 1425.

---

[1] He is styled "Commune Parlour" in the Rolls.

[2] He was probably Speaker also in the twenty-third Parliament of Richard II, 1394–95 ; but the Rolls are defective at that period.

Hakewil calls Bussy " a special minion to the King," but this appears to have been a prejudiced opinion. On the landing of Henry, Duke of Lancaster, at Ravenspur, where the whole countryside greeted him with acclamation, Bussy took possession of the Castle at Bristol with others of Richard's ministers.

" To Bristol Castle, which they say is held by Bussy, Bagot and their complices." [1]

A little later in the same play Shakespeare writes slightingly of him as—

" A caterpillar of this Commonwealth which I [2] have sworn to weed and pluck away."

On the surrender of Bristol to the invader, Bussy, with the Lord Treasurer (William Le Scrope, Earl of Wiltshire), and Sir Henry Green were executed without trial,[3] as the first act of the new dynasty. Thus, with the possible exception of Peter de Montfort, whose end is somewhat of a mystery, the last of the Plantagenet Speakers was also the first to die a violent death, a fate which, as subsequent chapters will show, was to befall many of his successors in the Chair of the Commons. Within six weeks of Bussy's murder Henry reached London, bringing Richard with him captive, and took up his abode in St. John's Priory in Clerkenwell.

On 29 September, the day before the intended meeting of Parliament, he had an interview with his cousin in the Tower. Having obtained from him the crown and sceptre, the outward symbols of kingship which counted for so much with the populace, he hurriedly deposited

---

[1] Shakespeare, *Richard II*, act II, scene 3, line 164.
[2] Bolingbroke.   [3] 29 July, 1399.

them in the treasury of Westminster Abbey, now usually known as the Chapel of the Pyx.

This ancient building, which should not be confused with the Royal Jewel House of which there is an illustration in this book, undoubtedly formed part of the Confessor's foundation. It makes the proud claim, in common with an adjoining apartment long used as the gymnasium of Westminster School, to be the oldest building in London. Henry III spared it when he pulled down the Confessor's Church, and in it, or in the undercroft of the Chapter House hard by, the kings of England kept the regalia and other treasures, of which a list is given by Dean Stanley. The advantage of having more than one such treasure-house—and if the Jewel Tower is reckoned there were three in close proximity to one another—is obvious ; because an intending thief would be unaware in which, for the moment, the royal wealth lay hid. But the utmost secrecy will not avail against treachery from within, and in 1303 the Chapel of the Pyx, or, as some think, the undercroft, was the scene of a great robbery. The sacristan of the Abbey and two monks were involved in the rifling of the treasury by one Richard Podlicote, who contrived by their help to force an entrance and to carry off articles of priceless value. A jury empanelled to investigate the crime found that Master William Torel, the famous English sculptor who made the effigies of Henry III and Eleanor which are still to be seen in the Abbey, bought two ruby rings in good faith from the thief, and the sacristan was found to have in his possession a bowl of unknown value which he could not account for. The manner of Podlicote's punishment is not certainly known, though it was long believed that he was flayed alive. Some fragments of human skin adhering to one of the doors leading out of the east cloister walk have been thought to be his, though within the recollection of the present writer these remains, if human, indeed, they be, were confidently stated to have been portions of the skin of a Dane, executed as a terror to evil-doers at an even earlier date. The probability is that both stories are apocryphal. Towards the close of his ill-starred reign Richard II, who throughout his life had a graceful passion for extravagance, practically rebuilt Westminster Hall in the shape in which it now stands. Even the names of the royal craftsmen employed upon it are known. Robert Brassington made the shield-bearing angels of the incomparable roof. William Burgh filled the great window with " flourished glass "—would that it had escaped the ravages of time—and William Cleuderre sculptured some of the images of " grave kings " which still stand at the upper end of the hall.[1] By the irony of fate, no sooner was the vast building finished than it became the scene of Richard's deposition.

For in Westminster Hall Henry of Lancaster, aided by the dignitaries of the Church, including the Abbot of Westminster, came forward to " challenge the realm of England " on the last day of September, 1399.[2] Amongst the Harleian MSS. in the British Museum,[3] the collection of which England owes to a Speaker to be mentioned here-after, is a representation by a Frenchman named Créton (who accompanied Richard on his last journey to Ireland), of the great hall as it appeared on this momentous day.

---

[1] The south porch was added by Sir Charles Barry after the great fire of 1834.

[2] *Rot. Parl.*, Vol. III, p. 422.   [3] No. 1319, p. 57.

It shows the throne at the upper end unoccupied—
" sede regali cum pannis Auri solempnitur præposita
tunc vacua." [1]

Nearest to the throne stands Henry of Lancaster wearing a high-crowned cap of fur. On the right of the picture
are grouped the spiritual, and, on the left, the temporal
Lords and the Knights. All appear to be actual portraits,
while the figures of two men in the foreground would
seem from their dress to be officials. Neither of them can
have been intended to represent the Speaker, for with
Bussy dead, no presiding officer of the Commons existed.
For two hundred years until that September day the
doctrine of hereditary right to the throne had been
preserved without interruption, but now in Richard's
newly finished hall, far surpassing Rufus' original building
and adorned from end to end with the white hart, the
badge of his adoption, amidst a shout of acclamation
which made the rafters ring, the Plantagenet dynasty
passed away and a new era opened for England and for
Parliament. [2]

[1] See reproduction of this curious painting in this volume.
[2] William Rufus and Henry I had obtained the throne in prejudice
of the claims of their elder brother, Robert. Stephen had been advanced
to the same dignity, contrary to every opinion of hereditary succession.
John had been crowned in opposition to the claims of Arthur (the son
of his elder brother) ; but from that time till the usurpation of Henry
IV the principle of heredity had been strictly observed.

HENRY IV CLAIMING THE THRONE OF ENGLAND
From the Harleian Manuscripts

CHAPTER III

(1399–1461)

THIRTY SPEAKERS

John Cheyne	Thomas Walton
John Dorewood	Richard Vernon
Arnold Savage	John Tyrrell
Henry Redford	William Alington
William Esturmy	John Bowes
John Tiptoft	William Burley
Thomas Chaucer	William Tresham
William Stourton	John Say
Walter Hungerford	John Popham
Richard Redman	William Oldhall
Walter Beauchamp	Thomas Thorpe
Roger Flower	Thomas Charlton
Roger Hunt	John Wenlock
Richard Baynard	Thomas Tresham
John Russell	John Green

WITH almost indecent haste Henry of Lancaster, after usurping the throne, proceeded to consolidate his position. The Parliament of Richard had come to an end with the abdication of the King, and within a week Henry issued writs for a new one returnable in six

61

days. These were not, and indeed could not be, complied with ; but the same members who had deposed Richard met on 6 October and fixed the date of the usurper's coronation for eight days later.[1] Henry distributed the great offices of State amongst his personal friends, though little or no change seems to have been made in the composition of the judicial bench.

Proceeding from the Tower, where Richard was detained in close custody, on a triumphal progress through London, Henry slept for the first time in the Palace of Westminster on the night of 12 October, 1399.[2] On the following day he was crowned in the Abbey, with all the ancient ceremonial proper to the occasion, and exactly one year after he had fled the country in exile. During the Coronation banquet in Westminster Hall a fountain in Palace Yard ran continually with red and white wine ; and Dymoke, the King's champion, who had acted the same part at Richard's accession, rode into the Hall and challenged any man to appear who dared maintain that Henry was not a lawful Sovereign.

The choice of the Commons for their Speaker fell upon Sir John Cheyne, or Cheney, Knight of the Shire for Gloucester, and on the morrow of the Coronation his nomination was approved by the King. But at once a hitch arose. For Cheyne was a renegade cleric, more than suspected of Lollardy by Archbishop Arundel, the new King's principal adviser at this juncture, and the

---

[1] 13 October.
[2] According to Froissart Henry of Lancaster was escorted by a cavalcade of 6000 horsemen as he rode bareheaded through the crowded streets. Having arrived at Westminster he bathed himself, and, on the morrow, confessed, as he had good need to do, hearing three masses.

man who more than any other had been instrumental in placing him on the throne. Cheyne only filled the chair for two days; and, on his making a convenient excuse of infirmity, the Commons elected John Dorewood, Knight of the Shire for Essex, in his stead.

Little or nothing is known of this Speaker or his family beyond the fact that his father had represented the same county in the reign of Edward III; but it is a singular coincidence that on the two occasions on which the son was called to the Chair—for he was again Speaker in the first Parliament of Henry V—he owed his election to the illness of the presiding officer first chosen by the Commons. In 1413 he replaced William Stourton, Knight of the Shire for Dorset, " being sick in his bed " and unable to execute the duties of the office.

To the despotic incapacity of Richard in his later years succeeded the energetic rule of a Sovereign driven by necessity to depend—at least, outwardly— upon constitutional methods. That this was the opportunity of the Commons, and one fully recognised by them, events soon showed. But the peculiar circumstances of the time also favoured the consolidation of the Peerage, inasmuch as the inheritable right of summons was now for the first time conceded in lieu of a mere summons by custom. If henceforth there could be no taxation without consent, legislation was in future to be based upon a mutual recognition of the rights of both Houses; and while a remarkable unanimity between Lords and Commons prevailed at this period, the right of the latter to vote subsidies and to co-operate in legislation coincided with the establishment of a permanent hereditary chamber acting in civil cases as an ultimate

Court of Appeal. Whereas Richard had succeeded in obtaining the subsidy on wool and a tax on movables for life, the first Parliament of Henry IV would not grant a subsidy for more than three years. The Parliament which assembled at Westminster in January, 1400-1, proved more complaisant, and the utmost harmony prevailed between the two Houses. At the end of the session the Commons, addressing the King through the mouth of their Speaker, Sir Arnold Savage, sought to draw a parallel, more curious than convincing, between the achievements of a loyal and united Parliament and the observance of the Mass.[1]

Henry IV set an entirely new precedent, and one which has never been repeated, when, in 1402, he invited the Commons to dine with him at the close of the session.[2] Sir Henry Redford, Knight of the Shire for Lincoln, was Speaker when this novel bid for popularity was made. The Earl of Northumberland, in the absence of the King's Seneschal, begged the whole of the Lords spiritual and temporal, as well as the Commons, to assemble on Sunday, 26 November, the business of Parliament having come to an end on the previous day, in order to enjoy the King's hospitality. The place of meeting, though not specified in the Rolls, must almost certainly have been Westminster Hall, as no other apart-

---

[1] "Au fyn de chescun messe y Covient de dire : ' Ite missa est ' & ' Deo gratias.' " Semblablement les Communes, Coment ils feurent Venuz al fyn del messe pur dire : "Ite missa est." Et qu'ils, & tout le Roialme, feurent espalement tenuz de dire cel parol : " Deo gratias."
Rot. Parl., Vol. III, p. 466.

[2] In this session also occurred an early instance of the thanks of Parliament being awarded to a general (the Earl of Northumberland) for his military achievements (*Rot. Parl.*, 16 October, 1402).

ment in the Palace could have accommodated so large a number at a banquet.[1]

Advocates of a single Chamber system will note with approval this reunion of the two Houses " en pleine Parlement," although in 1402 it was contrived for a purely social purpose.   It has been thought that by somewhat similar means a Government, unsympathetic to the hereditary principle, but commanding, as in 1833 and again in 1906, an overwhelming majority in the Lower House, might despite the existing veto of the House of Lords ensure the passage of its legislative and financial proposals, were the two Chambers or a committee elected by both Peers and Commoners to meet as one deliberative body, in cases where a deadlock has arisen.   It may strike the impartial student of constitutional practice as somewhat surprising that a proposal to revert to conditions known to have prevailed under the Plantagenets should be seriously entertained in the twentieth century, but the fact remains that a return to such a method of amicably settling disputes between the two Houses has recently found considerable support in the country, and that a section of moderate opinion inclines to the belief that by some such means a final solution of an admitted difficulty may be within measurable distance.

In 1404, when Sir Arnold Savage, Knight of the Shire for Kent, and the strongest man who had filled the Chair since De la Mare, was again Speaker, the subsidies granted,

[1] " Le Cont de Northumberland, en absence du Seneschall de l'ostiel du Roi, pria as toutz les Seigneurs Espirituels & Temporelx, & as toutz les Communes suis ditz, d'estre le Dymenge ensuant a mangier ovesq le Roi nře Seigneur." Unfortunately no description of this unique gathering seems to have been preserved.

F

liberal though they were, were voted subject to the novel
condition that the money raised should be received by
Treasurers by whose appointment Parliament could feel
confidence that the supplies should not be misappro-
priated. Savage, who has been called " the great com-
prehensive symbol of the English people," made, on his
elevation to the Chair, a more elaborate complimentary
address to the King than any of his predecessors, yet in
the first of the two Parliaments which Henry called
in 1404 [1] he formulated petitions to the effect that
redress of grievances should precede the granting of
supplies.

This uncompromising attitude was due to the fact
that a modified income-tax was sought to be imposed
on all owners of land and house property, and a contemporary historian spoke of the tax as a novel one,
" galling to the people and highly oppressive." So
long as the incidence of taxation was designed to
fall on commodities, it could be cheerfully borne, but
when it was applied to individuals a new grievance was
created.

After a delay of six weeks the Commons consented to
levy a tax of a shilling in the pound on land value, but
only on the understanding that it should not be con-
strued into a precedent, and that no official record of it
should be preserved. It reads almost like the twentieth
century to find this subsidy described by one chronicler as *taxa nova et exquisita*, and by another as
taxa insolita et incolis tricabilis et valde gravis. Notwithstanding the unpopularity of land taxation, it

[1] It met at Westminster, 14 January, 1404, and remained in
session till the second week in April.

SIR ARNOLD SAVAGE
1400·1, 1403-4
From a brass in S. Chancel of Bobbing Church, Kent

was again imposed in a later Parliament at the rate of 6s. 8d. on every £20 of income from land. A valuation list for the City of London and the suburbs was prepared by a Commission over which the Lord Mayor presided. It was found that the gross rental amounted to £4220 divided amongst 1132 individuals or institutions, while the actual yield was only £70 6s. 8d.

Walter Savage Landor, who believed himself to be a lineal descendant of Sir Arnold, introduced an ingenious duologue between the Speaker and the King on the subject of this tax into his *Imaginary Conversations* :—

" Henry IV to the Speaker : This morning in another place thou declaredst that no subsidy should be granted me until every cause of public grievance was removed."

To which Savage diplomatically made answer :

" I am now in the house of the greatest man upon earth. I was then in the house of the greatest nation."

Henry then went on to say :

" I raised up the House of Commons four years ago, and placed it in opposition to my barons, with trust and confidence that I might be less hampered in my complete conquest of France. . . . Parliament speaks too plainly and steps too stoutly for a creature of four years' growth."

Savage :

" God forbid that any King of England should achieve the conquest of all France ! "

A little later he advises the King " to keep the hearts of his subjects. . . ."

> " Wars are requisite to diminish the power of your barons by keeping them long and widely separate from the main body of retainers."
>
> " In general they[1] are the worthless exalted by the weak, and dangerous from wealth ill acquired and worse expended."
>
> " The whole people is a good King's household, quiet and orderly when well treated, and ever in readiness to defend him against the malice of the disappointed, the perfidy of the ungrateful, and the usurpation of the familiar. Act in such guise, and I will promise you the enjoyment of a blessing to which the conquest of France in comparison is as a broken flagstaff—self-approbation in government and security in power."

On which the King declared that he wished he could make the Speaker a peer.[2] Savage was a party to the passing of the famous enactment, " De hæretico comburendo," which first made religious error an offence against the statute law. It had been a punishable offence before, since a renegade clerk was condemned by the Church court in 1222, and then handed over to the secular arm to be burnt. Even Sawtre was burnt in 1401, before " De hæretico comburendo " was passed.

This was the statute which Gardiner and Bonner found so convenient during the Marian persecution of 150 years later. In his second Speakership Savage

---

[1] The Barons.

[2] Walter Savage Landor's *Imaginary Conversations*, 1826, Vol. I, p. 41.

demanded from the King the dismissal of several officers of the household and many of the Queen's retinue.[1]

Henry's sixth Parliament, summoned to meet at Coventry, 6 October, 1404, was presided over by Sir William Esturmy, of Wolf Hall, near Maiden Bradley, Wilts, now the property of the Duke of Somerset. Esturmy's family intermarried with that of St. Maur, and the Dukes of Somerset quarter his coat of arms to this day. The main work of the Coventry Parliament was the attempted spoliation of the Church, and it fell to Esturmy's lot to carry a proposal to the King that the clergy should contribute largely to the expenses of the realm. As a compromise they granted the King a tenth and a half of their revenues.

The next Speaker on the roll, Sir John Tiptoft, whose tenure of the Chair was marked by a perceptible increase in the power of the Commons, and by repressive measures against the Lollards, was the first to enter what Pulteney, in the eighteenth century, called " that hospital for invalids," the House of Peers. " My Lord Bath," said Walpole, on meeting his old opponent in the Upper House, " you and I have now become two of the most insignificant fellows in England ! " Summoned as Baron Tiptoft in 1426, his son was created Earl of Worcester in 1449 ; but the precedent of conferring a peerage upon the Speaker was not renewed for many years. Tiptoft spoke more boldly to the King and to the Peers than any of his predecessors in the Chair of the Commons. He even told the King that, though

[1] Savage was also a considerable landowner in Cheshire, where he owned Frodsham Castle, and his name is perpetuated in one of the minor titles of the Marquesses of Cholmondeley.

his title to the crown was less worthy of respect, his household expenses were in excess of any previous sovereign.

The Speaker's eldest son, another John Tiptoft, has been confused by Hakewil with his father. The Earl of Worcester, who earned the lasting hatred of his countrymen for the ruthless severity with which he repressed the opponents of Edward IV, deserves separate mention at our hands. A willing instrument of the usurper's scheme of revenge, the younger Tiptoft was destined to be far more powerful under the White Rose than ever his father had been under the Red. On the outbreak of the Civil Wars he had betaken himself to the Holy Land, only returning to England after the battle of Towton had secured the crown for his patron. The flower of the English nobility had poured out their blood at Towton to an extent altogether unprecedented; but, when the semblance of peace had been restored to a distracted country, Worcester found congenial work awaiting him.

Proceeding on the Machiavellian principle of extirpating the King's foes as the only effective means of rendering them harmless, he tried and condemned in his Constable's Court within the Palace of Westminster so many of the Lancastrian party as gained him the odious sobriquet of the "Butcher of England."[1] When the headman's axe had been blunted by constant use during his reign of terror, he ordered some of Warwick's followers who fell into his power at Southampton in March, 1470,

---

[1] In the I Henry IV (1399) the Constable of England had apartments assigned to him in the "Inner Palace" of Westminster (*Rot. Parl.*, III, p. 452).

JOHN TIPTOFT, EARL OF WORCESTER
From a monumental effigy at Ely Cathedral

to be impaled, contrary to any known law of England. But the day of retribution was near. In October of the same year Edward was dispossessed and Henry temporarily restored. Thenceforth there could be little hope or chance of life for the Jeffreys of the fifteenth century. Arraigned in the White Hall of the Palace before the Earl of Oxford, who had been appointed Constable for the purpose, the Speaker's son, who in that same court had sent his Judge's father and brother to the block, was now condemned to die a traitor's death on Tower Hill.

The last Speaker of the reign was the bearer of a famous name. Had Geoffrey Chaucer, the father of English poetry, lived only a few more years than he did, he would have seen his son chosen Speaker of the House of Commons, in which he had himself served as Knight of the Shire for Kent. Thomas Chaucer, Geoffrey's son, was a Westminster man in the fullest sense of the word, for his father lived in Old Palace Yard in a house demolished to make room for Henry VII's Chapel. A man of great wealth,[1] which his father certainly was not, he owned considerable landed property at Ewelme, in Oxfordshire, where he was buried in 1434 in a tomb of great magnificence described by Leland in his Itinerary.

His only daughter and heiress, Alice, married, as her third husband, William de la Pole, Duke of Suffolk, a politician as ambitious as he was incompetent who, after being virtually Prime Minister of England, was

---

[1] His wealth was derived in part from the office of Chief Butler to the King, which he held for many years. His predecessor, Liptoft, enjoyed the same lucrative post.

impeached, and subsequently murdered, in 1450. The fact that the Duchess of Suffolk is described on her tombstone as "Serenissima Principessa" has led to a belief that Thomas Chaucer was an illegitimate son of John of Gaunt, and not Geoffrey's son, but, in the opinion of many competent authorities, the inscription on the Duchess' tomb is a forgery of later date.

Thomas Chaucer was Speaker on no less than five separate occasions,[1] in 1407, 1409-10, 1411, 1414, and in the next reign, in 1421. During his first tenure of the Chair the Commons gained the inalienable right of initiating money grants, though not without a struggle. In the Parliament held at Gloucester[2] they were required to send twelve of their number to report on the questions propounded to them for a huge increase of taxation, and to give in their answer by deputation.

Protesting as they did against this procedure as being an infringement of their privileges, the Declaration of Gloucester, entered on the Rolls, laid down once and for all that money grants, proceeding as they do from the free will of Parliament, must not be hampered by the personal intervention of the Crown in Council, whilst the Commons claimed a precedence in finance in so far as the Lords were required to assent to the money grants of the representatives of the people, instead of the process being reversed. But this was not tantamount to saying that it was beyond the power of the Lords to refuse their assent or to revise the methods by which the money was to be raised.

The King, who was nothing if not a diplomatist, knew

---

[1] Manning, in his *Lives of the Speakers*, 1851, p. 50, says, in error, that he was only chosen four times.   [2] October, 1407.

THOMAS CHAUCER
1407, 1409-10, 1411, 1414, 1421
*From a print of the Memorial Brass in
Ewelme Church, Oxfordshire*

exactly when to give way, and in 1407 he succeeded in
pleasing both parties to the dispute : the Lords by his
permission to deliberate, even in his absence, on the
state of the realm and the appropriate remedies ; the
Commons by conceding the principle that no report of a
money grant should henceforth be made to the Crown
until both Houses were agreed on its terms, such report
then to be delivered only by the mouth of their Speaker.[1]

In this connection it should be borne in mind that all
Bills granting supplies to the Crown are, after third
reading in the Lords, returned to the custody of the
Commons (unlike other Bills, which are retained by the
Lords pending the Royal Assent), and are taken up by
the Speaker when the Commons are summoned to the
Lords to hear the Royal Assent given.   If, on such
an occasion, the King should be present in person,
the Speaker addresses the Sovereign on the principal
measures awaiting his assent, not forgetting to mention
the supplies which have been granted by the Lower
branch of the legislature.

Having obtained all the money he wanted, the King did
not call Parliament together again until January, 1409–10.
By this time Archbishop Arundel, the greatest enemy
the Lollards ever had, had retired from the Chancellorship, and the reformers must have secured a majority
in the new House, for the first act of the Commons was

[1] The original words of this famous Declaration are worth quoting :
" Purveux toutes foitz qe les Seigneurs de lour part, ne les Communes
de la leur, ne facent ascun report a ñre dit Sr le Roy d'ascunt grant pr
les Communes grantez, & pr les Seigneurs assentuz, ne de les Communications du dit Graunt, aviunt ce qe mesme les Seigneurs &
Communes soient d'un assent & d'un accord en celle partie & adouges
en manore & forme como il est accustomez, c'est assever pr bouche de
Purparlour de la dite Commune par le temps estant."

to reverse their former attitude of hostility towards the Anti-Clerical movement. They now recommended to the King the wholesale confiscation of Church lands, but this revolutionary proposal was not destined to receive the Royal Assent. Though the Houses continued in session until May, no great constitutional change marked their labours.[1]

Shortly before his death, the last subsidy voted to him having nearly expired, Henry called another Parliament ; but in consequence of his serious illness no formal opening took place, and therefore no choice of a Speaker. On 20 March, 1413, the King died in the Jerusalem Chamber at Westminster, whither he had been carried by the monks after he had fallen down in a swoon before the shrine of the Confessor.

The short reign of Henry V, the greatest soldier of his age, was also the shortest since the Norman Conquest. Yet in nine years of, for the most part, glorious strife, Parliamentary institutions saw considerable development. This period has usually been associated with military achievement rather than with Constitutional progress. Yet, in 1414, when a Hungerford was again called to the Chair[2] and the Lower House met in the " Fermerie " at Leicester, the King granted to his Commons a boon which they had long desired. This was to the effect that their petitions, which now, for the first time, were be-

---

[1] Or those of the succeeding Parliament of 1411, in which Chaucer was Speaker for the third time.

[2] Sir Walter (son of the Speaker of 1377), created Lord Hungerford in 1425–26 and buried in Salisbury Cathedral in 1449, where his mutilated brass is still to be seen with its stone slab powdered with sickles, the favourite device of this family before crests came into general use.

Schnebbelie, delt.   *J. Basire, Sculpt.*

SIR WALTER HUNGERFORD, AFTERWARDS LORD HUNGERFORD
1414
Formerly in the North side of the nave of Salisbury Cathedral
Reproduced from Gough's "Sepulchral Monuments"

ginning to be replaced by bills,[1] should in future be engrossed as statutes, without garbling or alteration of any kind by way of addition or diminution, after passing from their control. And whilst the King maintained unimpaired the prerogative of refusing the Commons petitions outright, he could henceforward only accept them in the shape in which they were presented by the Speaker for the royal approval.[2]

Sir Walter Hungerford, apart from his Parliamentary career, fought bravely against the French, and, as if something of the military ardour of the King had animated his faithful Commons, the bold spectacle is next presented of a Speaker[3] buckling on his sword and armour, accompanying his Sovereign to the war, and fighting by his side at Agincourt. In domestic politics Henry's chief aim was to reassert the authority of the Church, and in his determination to crush the Lollards he was assisted once more by Archbishop Arundel, to whom repression of the reformers was a congenial task. Oldcastle, the most conspicuous of the anti-clerical party, was excommunicated, and after evading capture for four years, was dragged before Parliament as an outlaw, and summarily drawn, hanged, and burned at the New Gallows beyond the Temple Gate. Roger Flower of Oakham, Knight of the Shire for Rutland, was Speaker when the Commons petitioned for his execution.

[1] Langland, indeed, in "Piers Plowman," written in 1362, makes use of the word "bill," though scarcely in the strict Parliamentary sense.

[2] *Rot. Parl.*, Vol. IV, p. 22, where the Commons are described in an interesting passage as "Assentirs as well as Peticioners," as being desirous of "Axkynge remedie of any mischief by the mouthe of their Speaker," and as having ever been a "membre of your Parlement."

[3] Once again Thomas Chaucer.

Sir Walter Beauchamp, who sat for Wiltshire, had been Flower's predecessor. Little is known of him beyond the fact of his being the first lawyer to be chosen by the Commons themselves for this high office. But having once chosen a lawyer for their President, the Commons soon renewed their preference for the long robe. In Henry V's ninth Parliament,[1] Roger Hunt of Chalverston, Beds, Knight of the Shire for the County, an eminent lawyer, and in 1438 Baron of the Exchequer, was called to the Chair. To him succeeded Thomas Chaucer, for the fifth time, in 1421.

One further Parliament was called by Henry V before his early death. It was summoned solely to provide the money necessary for the prosecution of the war with France, and, in the King's absence, the Duke of Gloucester, as regent, issued the summons for it to meet at Westminster.[2] The length of the session has not been definitely ascertained, but it is known that the new Speaker was Richard Baynard, a member of an old East Anglian family who had intermarried with the Dorewoods.[3]

The last of the Lancastrian kings was also the weakest. Henry VI, an amiable imbecile with a saving sense of piety, as testified by the foundation of his " holy shade " at Eton, was completely overshadowed by the superior force of character of his wife.[4] When he came to be of legal age in 1442,[5]

[1] December, 1420.
[2] December, 1421.
[3] Baynard represented Essex from 1405–6 until 1433. For a pedigree of his family see Morant's *Essex*, Vol. II, pp. 176, 404.
[4] Margaret of Anjou.
[5] During his minority the Dukes of Bedford and Gloucester carried on the government.

ROGER HUNT
1420
From a memorial brass in Great Linford Church, Bucks

it was evident to thoughtful men that all the advantages gained by his illustrious father were in danger of being lost. During the early years of the King's minority, the Chair of the Commons was filled by Sir John Russell, a member of a family which has played a prominent part in the political history of this country, especially since the acquisition of the Woburn property at the dissolution of the monasteries. The Russells had no connection with the county of Bedford in the fifteenth century, and the Speaker of 1423 and 1432 sat for Herefordshire. Attempts have been made to derive the descent of the first Earl of Bedford [1] from the Speaker of Henry VI, but it seems probable that the pedigrees contained in the earlier editions of Sir Bernard Burke's *Peerage* are fabulous. The rise of the younger branch of the Russell family was really due to the successful commercial operations of a fishmonger at Poole, in the county of Dorset. One of the junior branch of this ancient race became Knight of the Shire in 1472, but the fortunes of the family were accidentally consolidated when Joanna of Castille landed at Weymouth in 1506, and was entertained at Wolfeton, near Dorchester, by Sir Thomas Trenchard, until the Earl of Arundel, who had been sent by Henry VII to escort her to Windsor, arrived. Sir Thomas summoned his kinsman, Mr. Russell, to help him to entertain his royal visitor, because he was the only gentleman of his acquaintance in the county who could speak Spanish. This Mr. Russell, having been introduced to Henry VII, who quickly discerned his merits and promise of future usefulness, became the first Earl of Bedford, and was the direct ancestor of the present Duke.

[1] So created in 1550.

The *Dictionary of National Biography* states that Sir John Russell was again chosen Speaker in 1450, but this is not accurate, as Sir William Oldhall was then called to the Chair. During Sir John's second term of office in 1432, an important concession was obtained by the Commons. The King, we read, " released the subsidy granted in the last Parliament on lands and tenements, so as it should never be mentioned again." The imposition of a land tax on the subject was then not only regarded by all parties as a thing too monstrous and unjust ever to be reimposed, but the work of one Parliament was deliberately reversed by its successor.

The Parliament which met in 1425 was presided over by Sir Thomas Walton, who had sat in the House of Commons for nearly thirty years, sometimes for Huntingdonshire and sometimes for Bedfordshire.[1] The greater part of the session was taken up with what seems at first sight to have been an irregular matter to occupy the attention of the Lower House—the settlement of a quarrel between John Mowbray, Earl Marshal of England, and Richard Beauchamp, Earl of Warwick, on a question of their relative precedence in the House of Lords.[2] Roger Hunt, whom we have already noticed as Speaker, now appeared as counsel for Mowbray, and that forensic warrior, Sir Walter Beauchamp, another former Speaker, represented his kinsman. The fact of their being so engaged as counsel may have been the reason for the contest being fought in the Commons. Walton was himself a lawyer, but the legal questions involved were rendered nugatory by the forfeited Dukedom of Norfolk

[1] Sir Thomas Walton, or Wauton as the name is sometimes spelt, was connected by marriage with the Tiptoft family, which may in part account for his advancement to the Chair.

[2] See *Rot. Parl.*, Vol. IV, pp. 267–8.

Albert Way, delt.
EFFIGY OF SIR RICHARD VERNON
1425-6
In the Church of Tong, Shropshire

being restored to the Earl Marshal, whereupon Warwick's pretensions fell to the ground.

Passing over one or two Speakers, whose names and periods of office will be found in the catalogue at the end of this volume, the Parliament of 1429-30, presided over by William Alington, Knight of the Shire for Cambridge, witnessed a great change in the county electorate by which the right to vote at the election of Knights of the Shire formerly possessed by the miscellaneous body that constituted the county-court (there is nothing in the writs of the thirteenth century to suggest that the franchise was limited to " free " men to the exclusion of villeins), was limited to the possessors of a freehold of forty shillings annual value,[1] a qualification which continued to be the basis of the English county franchise for the next four centuries.

Shortly before the outbreak of the Wars of the Roses the Chair was filled by William Tresham, who sat for his native county of Northants during a long series of years. He was Speaker on four separate occasions—in 1439, 1441-42, 1446-47, and 1449.[2] Tresham, as a prominent Yorkist, took an active part in the impeachment of William de la Pole, Duke of Suffolk. The House was in session when, on the 17th of March, 1449, Suffolk was hauled before the King and sentenced to five years' exile. Accused of having betrayed England to the French, he was done to death in 1450 ; and the Speaker, who by this time had become an object of suspicion to the Lancastrian party, was also murdered, at

[1] VIII Henry VI, c. 7.
[2] The *Dictionary of National Biography* says that Tresham was again Speaker in 1448-49, but this was not the case, as the Chair was filled by Sir John Say in that Parliament.

Thorpland, in his native county, whither he had gone to meet the Duke of York.[1] The son of William Tresham, Sir Thomas Tresham, who was brought up in Henry VI's household, was also Speaker in the packed Lancastrian Parliament of 1459. Like his father, he met with a violent death. He fought on the side of the Lancastrians at St. Albans, was proclaimed a traitor after Edward IV's return, and was beheaded at Tewkesbury, having been, in all, three times attainted.

Sir John Say, Knight of the Shire for Herts, also filled the Chair in turbulent times. During Jack Cade's insurrection[2] the rioters threatened his life, and he was indicted for treason at the Guildhall. Jack Cade, the first Radical in the history of English politics,[3] declared that the freedom of election for Knights of the Shire had been wrested from the people by the great men of the land, who directed their tenants to choose men of whom they tacitly disapproved. Cade had probably seen and read Langland's "Richard the Redeless," a poem written as a remonstrance to Richard II, for there is a passage in it positively affirming that the Knights of the Shire were the nominees of the Court. Though Sir John Say began political life as a Lancastrian, he threw in his lot later with the Yorkists.

---

[1] Lord Grey de Ruthyn, a member of Queen Margaret's faction, is said to have been responsible for his death (see *Paston Letters*, 5 May, 1450, No. 93, Vol. I, p. 124). Leland, in his Itinerary, gives a circumstantial account of the murder.

[2] 1450.

[3] This proud title should, perhaps, be conferred on John Ball, who was hanged in 1381. Adopting as his text—

"When Adam delved and Eve span,
Who was then the gentleman?"

he incited the villeins to murder all the lords and all the lawyers in the land.

SIR JOHN SAY
1448-9, 1467
From a Brass in Broxbourne Church, Herts.
Reproduced from Waller's "Monumental Brasses," 1864

Dying in 1478, he was buried in Broxbourne Church, Herts, where his memorial brass, one of the few remaining in England showing traces of colour, is still to be seen. The William Say who was Speaker *pro tem.* during Lenthall's absence from the Chair in 1659 was probably a collateral descendant.

The later Parliaments of Henry's ill-starred reign,[1] presided over respectively by Sir William Oldhall, Thomas Thorpe and his successor Sir Thomas Charlton, Sir John Wenlock, Sir Thomas Tresham, and John Green, were so overshadowed, first by Jack Cade's rebellion, and then by the Wars of the Roses, that little or no legislation was attempted, and the course of constitutional progress was arrested. As the fortunes of the faction fight between the Red Rose and the White inclined to either party, the time of the House was mainly occupied in the prosecution and attainder of the more prominent political leaders who chanced, for the moment, to be on the losing side.

It would be outside the scope of the present work to enter at any length into the causes which led to the outbreak of hostilities, but it should be borne in mind that the evils of livery and maintenance were once more rife, and when, after forty years of strife, the French wars ceased to afford occupation to the English soldiery, bands of military retainers habituated to the practice of arms were at the absolute disposal of the great landowning class, only awaiting the signal of their leaders to re-engage in acts of violence. Whilst the greater nobility for the most part ranged themselves on the Lancastrian side, a constitutional opposition, with the Duke of York at its head, com-

[1] 1450, 1453, 1455, 1459, and 1460.

G

manded the sympathies of the City of London and the bulk of the provincial municipalities.

Sir William Oldhall, a Hertfordshire magnate, had for his country home a castellated mansion, in part incorporated in Hunsdon House, the property in after years of the Calvert family ; and he was chosen Knight of the Shire for Herts on his first entry into Parliament in 1450. He had been Chamberlain to the Duke of York, and it was therefore only to be expected that he would take a strong line against the feeble occupant of the throne. Even more remarkable than Speaker Tiptoft's celebrated demand of the Sovereign was that which Oldhall now made on behalf of the Commons. He claimed the immediate dismissal of no less than twenty-eight officers of the Court, including a duke and duchess, a bishop, three barons, four knights, and one abbot. All were banished for a year, " to see," as the King said, " if in the meantime any man could truly lay anything to their charge." Being himself implicated in some way in Cade's rebellion, though the evidence against him was not very conclusive, the Speaker was attainted by the next Parliament. He took sanctuary in St. Martin's-le-Grand, for Westminster would have been too dangerous an asylum for a man of his position, and he only emerged from hiding after the first battle of St. Albans had again placed his party in power. Fortune inclining once more, after Ludlow, to the Red Rose, his name was again included in a Bill of Attainder, and though, on the accession of Edward IV, his sentence was promptly reversed, Oldhall's public career was at an end, nor did he seek to re-enter Parliament.

Dame Agnes Paston was anxious to bring about a

match between the ex-Speaker and her husband's sister Elizabeth, " if ye can think that his land standeth clear." This was in 1455, but nothing came of the project. A few years later the young lady wedded Robert Poynings, who was sword-bearer to Jack Cade. He was killed in the second battle of St. Albans, and his widow re-married Sir George Browne, of Betchworth, Surrey.

The adherents of the Red Rose once more predominated in the Parliament of 1453, and the choice of the Commons for their Speaker fell upon Thomas Thorpe, the repre- · sentative of the county of Essex, who had been brought up from his childhood in the royal service. But in August Henry VI became insane, and during his incapacity the Yorkists singled out the Speaker for attack. He became a marked man when it transpired that he had taken possession of some arms belonging to the Duke of York, and, notwithstanding the flagrant breach of privilege which his arrest involved, Thorpe was committed to the Fleet prison and fined £1000 before he was released.[1]

Dismissed from his offices of Remembrancer and Baron of the Exchequer by the " Butcher of England," Thorpe recovered his position at the next revolution of fortune's wheel, so that he was enabled to draw up Yorkist attainders in the Parliament which met at Coventry in November, 1459. But when the Yorkists came to town in 1460 he took refuge in the Tower. He was soon taken prisoner again, and, after attempting to escape in the disguise of a monk, he was recognised and beheaded by the mob at Haringay on 17 February, 1460–61.

[1] Sir Thomas Charlton was chosen Speaker in his stead on the 16th of February, 1453–54.

Nor was Sir John Wenlock, the Speaker of the 1455 Parliament, more fortunate in his end. A Knight of the Shire for Beds and a dependent of Warwick the " King Maker," he was at first a Lancastrian, only to change sides in 1455. After being wounded at the first battle of St. Albans, he was killed at Tewkesbury, fighting once again on the Lancastrian side. The manner of his death was sufficiently shocking even in this age of violence, for he was struck down and his skull cleft in two with a battle-axe by the Duke of Somerset for not coming up in time, whereby the fortunes of the day were alleged to have been lost. His murderer was beheaded on the same day.

Wenlock's life had been one of activity in the field throughout the whole period of the Civil Wars, nor does history record a more martial career than his in the annals of the Chair. After taking part, as has been seen, in the battle of St. Albans, he captured Sandwich in 1460, and entered London with Edward IV, after fighting for him at Towton. He held Calais for the usurper, but rejoined his first love at Tewkesbury, the last engagement of his chequered military career.

A Knight of the Most Noble Order of the Garter, he was raised to the Peerage as Baron Wenlock after the coronation of Edward IV. He owned property at Sommaries, at Luton, and at Houghton Conquest, all in the county of Bedford ; and he built the Wenlock mortuary chapel in Luton Church, though his bones were not destined to lie in it. His second wife, Agnes Danvers, remarried Sir John Say, the Speaker of 1449, 1463, and 1467, and a neighbour of Wenlock in the adjoining county of Herts.

The last of the Speakers of Henry VI was to witness
even more stirring scenes at Westminster than any of his
immediate predecessors. John Green, whose homely
name is not to be found in the *Dictionary of National
Biography*, was voted to the Chair in 1460, and though
this Parliament only sat for about ten days, it found
time to repeal all the Acts passed at Coventry in the previous year and to annul the attainders of the Yorkist
Lords.

After the battle of Wakefield the Wars of the Roses,
which began by an attempt to vindicate constitutional
liberty, degenerated into a savage blood feud between
two desperate and reckless factions, in which no quarter
was either given or expected. John Green, though not
himself known to fame, was probably an eye-witness,
in the momentous month of October, 1460, of a startling
scene enacted in the Palace of Westminster, when
Richard, Duke of York, the victor at St. Albans, burst
into the great hall at the head of five hundred armed
men, as if about to seize the vacant throne, declaring
that he " challenged and claimed the crown of England,"
as heir of Richard II. He proposed to an astonished
audience, much after the manner of Henry IV in 1399,
that his coronation should take place in the Abbey on
All-hallows Day following.[1] But, though the final
triumph of the White Rose was near at hand and the old
hall of Rufus and of Richard was once more to witness
the death knell of a dynasty, a compromise was arrived

[1] Parliament had met on 7 October, and the Duke of York's
invasion of the Palace was three days later. The Archbishop of
Canterbury, Thomas Bourchier, asked the intruder if he desired to
see the King, to which York made answer that he knew of no one in
the kingdom who ought not rather to wait on him.

at, whereby Henry was to retain the crown for life and Duke Richard was to be recognised as his heir. [1]

Soon news reached London that the valiant Queen Margaret had succeeded in collecting a fresh army in the north, and Richard, hastening from the Council Chamber to the camp, marched to meet her at Wakefield, only to lose his life and to defer the imminent success of his cause, in a battle unprecedented for the savagery with which it was contested. Margaret caused York's head to be cut off after death, and, adorned in cruel mockery with a paper crown, it was stuck on one of the gates of the city from which his title was derived. [2]

After Wakefield, the leadership of the Yorkists fell into the hands of the " King Maker," the greatest aristocrat in England since John of Gaunt. But not until he too had fallen at Barnet, and the triumph of the White Rose was assured at Tewkesbury, was young Edward [3] able to plant himself firmly on the throne, to restore something like peace to an exhausted and distracted England, and o open a new constitutional era for its people.

[1] During the negotiations the King retreated to his wife's apartments, and York remained in the Palace till he had gained his point. He then withdrew to Baynard's Castle, his own mansion in the city.

[2] See Shakespeare, third part of *King Henry VI* :
" So York may overlook the town of York "
(Act II, scene 4, line 180).

[3] Like Henry IV, fresh from his landing at Ravenspur.

CHAPTER IV

THE HOUSE OF COMMONS UNDER THE HOUSE OF YORK, A PERIOD, FOR THE MOST PART, OF SUBSERVIENCY TO THE CROWN

(1461–1485)

FOUR SPEAKERS

James Strangeways	John Wood
William Alington	William Catesby

ON the cessation of the Wars of the Roses the exhaustion of the English nobility coincided with an increased desire amongst the upper middle class to obtain a seat in the House of Commons. A number of new boroughs sprang into existence, and men of good birth were selected to represent them at Westminster.

It is true that early in the history of the Mother of Parliaments some of the more powerful territorial families had monopolised the borough representation in the neighbourhood of the castles and mansions in which dwelt the Knights of the Shire. Thus in East Anglia the Fastolfs and the Pastons had swooped down upon the smaller boroughs as early as the beginning of the fourteenth century, when a member of the first-named family sat for Great Yarmouth,[1] and one of the latter for Grimsby.[2]

---

[1] In 1300–1. [2] In 1325.

In the north country a Lowther sat for Appleby in
1318, and a Pickering for Carlisle in 1334 ; but these were
exceptions to the general rule, whereby the burgesses,
for the most part, were men of mean estate and humble
calling.   In 1382–83 the City of London elected Sir
Nicholas Brembre, an ex-Lord Mayor, the head of the
grocers, and a staunch supporter of the King.   The
victualling trades, the grocers and fishmongers, as a rule
supported the Court ; whereas the clothing trades, the
drapers and the mercers, mostly ranged themselves in
opposition.   Brembre came to an untimely end, being
murdered in 1388.

Between the date of his election and the year 1467
exactly fifty burgesses are described in the official returns
as being either " miles," " armiger," or " gentleman," and
the appearance of one or other of these magic words after
their names probably indicates the gradual relinquish-
ment of an obligation on the part of the constituencies to
pay wages to their representatives.   While the pay of
the burgesses was only two shillings a day, the Knights of
the Shire were remunerated at double rates.   The change
in the status of the borough member, though gradual,
was progressive, for whereas in the first Parliament of
Henry VI not one burgess is described as " armiger,"
and only one in his last,[1] no less than six Sussex borough
representatives are described in 1472 as " armiger."
One hundred years later, as the old class distinctions
were swept away, the esquires predominated over the
tradesmen and merchants.

In 1472 Sir John Paston was anxious to be chosen a
Knight of the Shire for Norfolk, which he had already

---

[1] 1460.

represented in 1467 ; but the Dukes of Suffolk and Norfolk having come to an agreement, Sir Robert Wingfield
and Sir Richard Howard were returned. Paston's
brother advised Sir John to try for the borough of Maldon,
if he could arrange matters with the Sheriff, but in the
end he was returned for Great Yarmouth in 1477–78.
When in London he lodged at the " George," by Paul's
Wharf, and, no doubt, proceeded to Westminster by
water in the performance of his Parliamentary duties.[1]

The first Parliament of Edward IV chose for its Speaker
a Yorkshire knight, Sir James Strangeways, of Whorlton.[2]
A new precedent was introduced on his presentation.
Not only did he make the customary " excuse " and a
demand for the continuance of the privileges of the
House, but he offered a formal address to the Crown,
reviewing the political situation and the events of the
recent Civil War.

" PRESENTATIO PRELOCUTORIS

" Item, die Veneris tunc prox sequent, videlicet Tertio
die Parliamenti, prefati Cões coram Domino Rege in
Parliamento prædicto comparentes, presentaverunt Domino Regi quendam Jacobum Strangways militem, pro
cõi Prelocutore suo, de quo idem Dominus Rex se bene
contentavit. Qui quiden Jacobus, post excusationem
suam coram Domino Rege factam, pro eo qd ipsa sua
excusatio ex parto Dicti Domini Regis admitti non
potuit, eidem Domino Rege humillime supplicavit, qua-
tinus omnia & singula per ipsum in Parliamento prædicto,
nomine dicte Communitatis proferend' & declarand', sub
tali posset Protestatione proferre & declarare, qd si ipse
aliqua sibi per prefatos Socios suos injuncta, aliter quam
ipsi concordati fuerint, aut in addendo vel omittendo

[1] See *Paston Letters*, 21 September, 1472.   [2] 5 November, 1461.

declaraverit, ea sic declarata per predictos Socios suos corrigere posset & emendare ; et qd Protestatio sua hujusmodi in Rotulo Parliamenti prædicti inactitaretur. Cui per prefatum Dominum cancellarium de mandato Domini Regis extitit responsum, qd idem Jacobus tali Protestatione frueretur & gauderet, quali alii Prelocutores hujusmodi antea hac tempora uti & gaudere consueverunt."[1]

The precedent set by Speaker Strangeways in 1461 is the origin of the existing custom which enables young members of the House, exchanging for this occasion only the dull conventionality of morning dress for uniformed splendour, to move and second the Address to the Throne. Strangeways received a grant from Henry VII in 1485, from which it appears that he lost no time in espousing the Tudor cause. He left a family of no less than seventeen children, and at his death, in 1516, he was buried in St. Mary Overy's, in Southwark, the cathedral of South London, in a tomb not now to be identified.

At the close of the session the young King thanked the Commons for their support, and in so doing assured them of his determination to protect them to the utmost of his power.[2] The greater part of the session, following closely the precedent of 1459, had been devoted to attainting the followers of Henry VI, alive or dead, and providing for the confiscation of their lands and possessions; the Act of Attainder not being drawn up by the House of Commons, but presented to it ready-made. It was a far more sweeping proscription than the Coventry

[1] *Rot. Parl.*, Vol. V, p. 462.
[2] Dr. S. R. Gardiner regarded this fresh departure as the beginning of a new constitutional era in which the wishes of the middle classes, both in town and country, were to prevail over those of the nobility, simultaneously with the strengthening of the kingship.

one, for it implicated no less than 133 persons, of whom 14 were peers of the realm, 7 dead and 7 living, and 100 knights, squires, and men of lesser degree.

The young King, being at this time completely under the influence of his cousin, reigned only in name while Warwick ruled. The humiliation of Henry VI was complete, and of all his former strongholds he only retained one castle, that at Harlech. When Henry again became temporarily dominant in 1470, a Parliament, the fifth of Edward's reign, was summoned to meet at Westminster in the month of November ; but if any records of it were kept, it is believed that they were destroyed by Edward's orders after Henry's deposition and subsequent murder. William Alington, son of the Speaker of the 1429 Parliament, and, like his father, Knight of the Shire for Cambridge, became Speaker in October, 1472, and held the office until March, 1474-75, the longest Parliament which England had hitherto known.

In the intervals between the summoning of his various Parliaments the King lived on confiscations and gifts extorted from opponents whose lives he had spared, and it has been estimated that nearly one-fifth of the kingdom came into his hands by forfeiture. The vast estates of Warwick, the King Maker, and of the Archbishop of York, to give but two instances out of many, should have furnished ample wealth for a ruler less extravagant and pleasure-loving than Edward proved himself to be. But Jane Shore[1] and others of her pro-

---

[1] According to Sir Thomas More, Jane Shore was a woman of a kindly disposition, possessed of a never failing wit and good humour, and as her influence was uniformly exerted in the direction of clemency and gentleness, she was generally regarded with kindly feelings by the King's subjects.

fession exerted the same evil influence over him as had
Alice Perrers over Edward III, and Fair Rosamund over
Henry II in an even earlier age, and it soon became
necessary to devise fresh methods of taxation.

The Commons were invited to consider favourably a
project for an inquisitorial assessment of private incomes.
This, not unnaturally, proved to be highly unpopular,
and a growing spirit of independence in the Lower House
is revealed in its refusal to grant money for the invasion
of France unless it received assurances that the army
would start at a given date.[1] Parliament was summoned
to meet again in January, 1477-78, and the session is
believed to have lasted about five weeks, during which
time the sole business under consideration was the trial
of the Duke of Clarence.   No grants were asked for, no
legislation was attempted, and in the course of the month
of February it was announced that Clarence was dead,
having perished in the Tower no man knew how. After
this date no Parliament was called until 1483, the King
having obtained an assured income for life from earlier
Parliamentary grants, supplemented by the " benevolences " which became so odious to the nation at large.

The eighth and last Parliament of the reign was called
together in January, 1482-83, and the cause of summons
stated that it was convened to hear Edward's complaints
against the French King.   The new Speaker was John

---

[1] "The new method of raising funds by income tax necessitated an
assessment of lands at their real value. It had been found, by experience, that to allow owners to return their own valuations, resulted in a
sum considerably below what was right. The King's financial agents
accordingly began an assessment. The King took great interest in the
process, and wrote that the progress of collection was ' one of the
things earthly that we most desire to know.' "—*Edward the Fourth*, by
Laurence Stratford, 1910, p. 217.

Wood, Knight of the Shire for Sussex, and one of the least distinguished in the long catalogue. It was in the main a humdrum session. The King graciously consented to accept the comparatively modest sum of £11,000 for the annual expenses of his household, and, in return for their liberality, the Commons were permitted to pass Acts dealing with the trade of the country, with the grievances of " livery and maintenance " which had long vexed the minds of the people, and to spend their energies on unambitious measures designed for the preservation of domestic peace. But of real redress of grievances there was none, owing, perhaps, to the fact that throughout his reign Edward acted as the head of a triumphant political party, rather than as the ruler of a contented and united nation.

On 9 April, 1483, he died in the Palace of Westminster, prematurely worn out by a life of debauchery. For a week his remains lay in St. Stephen's Chapel before being removed to Windsor for interment. Naked to the waist, in order that the civic authorities might be assured of his death, the lying-in-state of Edward IV at Westminster presents a striking contrast to the dignified ceremonial observed on the occasion of the recent death of King Edward VII, when, for the first time in its long history, the great hall was utilised for a similar purpose. In May, 1910, the two branches of the Legislature, headed by the Lord Chancellor and the Speaker in their robes of state, forgot their differences in the presence of a common sorrow, and united in honouring their departed Sovereign lying in the hall of Rufus re-edified and embellished by the last of the Plantagenet race. Edward IV was the first of the Kings of England to be buried, of his own free will, in the Royal Chapel of St. George, though to it the body of his unhappy predecessor and rival is said to have been removed by Richard III from its first resting-place, Chertsey.

The severance of the House of York from the traditional burial place of the Kings of England marks the dawn of a sentiment which led eventually to the substitution of Windsor for Westminster as the last resting-place of the Sovereign, until the Coronation remains the only indissoluble link between the Abbey and the throne.

The Kings of England, unlike their brothers of France, seem never to have feared to be reminded of death. In Anglo-Saxon times they were buried at Winchester where they lived, and where they were crowned. When they became truly English they were crowned, as they lived, at Westminster. And when they died, they were buried, almost as a matter of course, in the Abbey, and as close as possible to the shrine of the Confessor. " Their graves, like their thrones, were in the midst of their own life, and of the life of their people." [1]

In the sixteenth century the Palace of Westminster ceased to be the accustomed home of the Sovereign, from causes to be alluded to hereafter, and though the first of the Tudors was interred in the magnificent chapel originally intended as a mausoleum for the last of the Lancastrian kings, Henry VIII, turning in aversion from a spot connected in his mind with the hated marriage of his youth, directed that his bones should be laid at Windsor beside his best-loved wife Jane Seymour.

A reaction in favour of Westminster set in with the accession of Mary, and it was by her direction that the

[1] Stanley's *Memorials of Westminster.*

body of Edward VI, the last male child of the Tudor line, was interred in the Abbey. Elizabeth was the last of the royal race to whom a monument was erected there, and since her death, neither the gratitude of a successor nor the affection of a nation has gone so far as to provide either sumptuous tomb or recumbent effigy for James I, Charles II, William and Mary, Anne, or the second monarch of the House of Hanover. They all lie in the Abbey without any such memorial. While it is significant that the custom of royal interment at Westminster should scarcely have survived the Reformation, from the sixteenth century onwards the figures of other than kings meet the eye in ever-increasing numbers. Warriors, statesmen, and leaders of Parliament were freely accorded the honour of burial in the Abbey, and before Elizabeth's death the bones of a Speaker were laid to rest there, for the first time since the reign of Edward III.

Edward V was a true son of Westminster, for he was born in the Sanctuary and educated in the Abbot's school. On the flight of Edward IV from London the Queen took refuge in Westminster and accepted the hospitality of Thomas Millyng, who was Abbot from 1469 till 1474. He was one of the most capable rulers the monastery ever had, and a great benefactor to the fabric. In gratitude for his timely help, and for his having stood godfather to the infant prince, the Queen founded, after Tewkesbury, the chantry and chapel of St. Erasmus in the Abbey. It was, however, destroyed by Henry VII during the building of his own noble mausoleum. Edward and his younger brother were murdered in the Tower by Richard, Duke of Gloucester, only about six weeks after the death of Edward IV. After being proclaimed Protector by the Council, Gloucester removed from Crosby Hall, or Crosby Place, as it was then called, to Westminster, and ascended the throne as Richard III on 25 June. His first and only Parliament met at Westminster in the Painted Chamber on 23 January, 1483–84. It chose for its Speaker William Catesby, a lawyer, and the devoted adherent of Richard from the moment when he urged his master to assume the crown till he died for a lost cause only two years later.[1] " The Cat, the Rat, and Lovell the Dog," to quote a popular distich, which cost its author his life, governed all England " under the hog " for a little over a year.

There seems to be little or no evidence that Catesby was personally unpopular with the House of Commons, and it is, no doubt, largely due to the odium cast upon both him and Richard by Shakespeare that his name has acquired such a sinister reputation in after ages. In the Parliament over which he presided, short though it was, time was found to pass an Act for the abolition of those " benevolences " which had made Edward IV so unpopular at the close of his reign. The statutes of the realm were now, for the first time, printed in English that all men might read them, and no measures of repression or severity towards opponents were introduced to the House. Richard kept Christmas at Westminster in 1484 with great state, but it was destined to be his and Catesby's last. Both met their doom in the fateful thirteenth encounter between the Houses of Lancaster

---

[1] One of the Catesby family was Keeper of the Royal Palace at Westminster and also of the Fleet Prison, and Robert Catesby, the projector of the Gunpowder Plot, was a descendant of the Speaker.

WILLIAM CATESBY
1483-4
From a Memorial Brass at Ashby St. Ledgers, Northants

and York, the battle of Bosworth being the closing scene in a struggle which had cost 100,000 lives. At the time of his death Richard had not completed his thirty-fifth year, nor was Catesby much older. The ex-Speaker was beheaded without form or semblance of a trial, three days after the fighting was over, time, however, being given him to make his will.

The dynasty of York had only endured for twenty-four years, yet this short space was not without importance for the House of Commons. With the close of mediæval monarchy, and the advent of a more personal element in the relations of the throne towards Parliament, disappeared, at all events for a time, much of the sturdy independence which had animated the earlier occupants of the Chair. Patriots like De la Mare, who used their position in the House to call attention to the pressing necessity of maritime defence ; [1] independent leaders like Savage and Tiptoft, who did not shrink on occasion from admonishing the Sovereign on his shortcomings, compare very favourably with the servile tribe of lawyers who monopolised the Chair in the Tudor period.

The Dudleys and Empsons of Henry VII, the Riches and Audleys of his successor on the throne, and the Snagges and Puckerings of Elizabethan memory, would have been impossible under the Plantagenets, and it is a curious fact that the Speakers of the Irish House of Commons, down to nearly the close of the eighteenth century, were regarded as Parliamentary leaders far more than were their English prototypes at the same period. Edmond Sexten Pery, Speaker of the Irish Commons from 1772–85, used his great political power in the best

---

[1] *Rot. Parl.*, Vol. II, p. 307.

H

interests of his country to an extent unapproached by any of his predecessors in office.

Though there are great names to be found in the Tudor catalogue of Speakers, as will be shown hereafter, the fame of the two greatest amongst them was won in spheres other than Parliamentary. The tenure of the Chair by Sir Thomas More and Sir Edward Coke was in each case a mere passing incident in the life of a man who played a leading part in the history of his country. With the decay of chivalry and the growth of a more commercial spirit in England went hand in hand a lessening of the importance of the Commons. Yet the spirit of liberty was never wholly dead. It only awaited the coming of the seventeenth century, and the final struggle of the Commons with the Crown to reassert itself with added force.

CHAPTER V

THIRTY-THREE SPEAKERS

Henry VII—

    Thomas Lovell
    John Mordaunt
    Thomas Fitzwilliam
    Richard Empson
    Robert Drury
    Reginald Bray (doubtful)
    Thomas Englefield
    Edmond Dudley

Henry VIII—

    Robert Sheffield
    Thomas Nevill
    Thomas More
    Thomas Audley
    Humphrey Wingfield
    Richard Rich
    Nicholas Hare
    Thomas Moyle
    John Baker

Edward VI—

    James Dyer

Mary—

    John Pollard
    Robert Brooke
    Clement Heigham
    William Cordell

Elizabeth—

    Thomas Gargrave
    Thomas Williams
    Richard Onslow
    Christopher Wray
    Robert Bell
    John Popham
    John Puckering
    Thomas Snagge
    Edward Coke
    Christopher Yelverton
    John Croke

A T the accession of Henry VII the House of
Commons acquired an immediate, if temporary, importance as the working Chamber,
from the depletion of the numbers of the
House of Lords. Forfeiture, confiscation and attainder

had so decimated the Upper House that only twenty-nine temporal peers were entitled to sit in it. The old feudal nobility had been weakened and reduced in the Wars of the Roses, though without any violent dislocation of the Constitution ; and until the peerages created in the sixteenth century laid the foundations of an aristocracy which could never again be a serious menace to the Crown, the House of Lords, as a legislative body, virtually ceased to exist.

In the first Parliament of Henry VII sat the head of the great family of Nevill—the Earl of Westmorland. Allied in blood to the King Maker, and owning vast estates in the north, south, and midland districts, the first earl of this creation, a Lancastrian to the backbone, left four sons, all of whom were raised to the Peerage, whilst his five sons-in-law were the Dukes of Buckingham, Norfolk, and York, the Earl of Northumberland, the head of the ancient house of Percy, and Lord Dacre.

Whilst the Nevills had been for centuries an acknowledged force in English political life, the Upper House, in spite of the grievous losses it had sustained, still numbered amongst its surviving members the Berkeleys, the Courtenays, the Stanleys, the Greys, and the Veres, to mention but a few of the more notable names of the English aristocracy. The Herberts and the Howards were but newly ennobled. The hour of the Seymours, the Cavendishes, and the Cecils had not struck.

That it was Henry VII's deliberate intention to relegate the Lords to a position of legislative impotence is shown by the fact that in the whole course of his reign he created scarcely any new peers, though some few were restored

to their former rank on the reversal of their attainders.[1]
In addition to crippling the hereditary branch of the
legislature, the Tudors desired to be as far as possible
independent of the House of Commons. Tonnage and
poundage had been granted to the Crown for life since
the reign of Henry VI, and although Henry VII summoned seven Parliaments in all, their attention, with the
exception of some salutary changes in the law relating
to trade and navigation, whereby a powerful stimulus was
given to English shipping, both national and mercantile,
was in the main devoted to the raising of subsidies.
The ruling passion of Henry's life was the accumulation
of wealth, not so much from an innate love of money
for money's sake, as from a desire to secure a large reserve
to be used as a guarantee for the national peace.

Henry enlarged the powers of the Privy Council in the
new Court of Star Chamber, an assembly whose proceedings were never regulated by statute. At first a
court of summary jurisdiction, it was destined to become
in after years the favourite instrument of the Sovereign
in the illegal collection of compulsory loans. The actual
room in the Palace of Westminster in which this much-
dreaded tribunal held its sittings remained standing until
the great fire of 1834, soon after which it was taken down.
Its exact site is indicated at the present day by a brass
plate affixed to the former official residence of the Chief
Clerk of the House, the greater part of which has
now been annexed by the Prime Minister and other
members of the Cabinet, and used by them as a place of
retreat from the storm and strain of the actual chamber.

[1] Only once during the whole Tudor period did the number of the
temporal lords amount to sixty.

Another innovation affecting the independence of the House of Commons was the direct nomination of the Speaker in all cases by the Crown. No less an authority than Sir Edward Coke candidly admitted that this open interference of the Sovereign was designed to avoid loss of time in disputing.[1] In spite of the increasing powers of the royal prerogative, it remained theoretically impossible for the Crown to levy any new tax without the assent of both Houses, and it became the business of the chiefs of Henry's secret service so to manage Parliament that the outward forms of the Constitution might at least be observed. Assuming Coke to be correct, it will be of interest to consider what manner of men Henry VII selected to preside over the House of Commons, and it will be seen that they were drawn both from the landed gentry and from the legal profession.

At Bosworth there had fought by his side Sir Thomas Lovell, of ancient lineage in Norfolk, and a kinsman of Francis, Viscount Lovell of Tichmarsh, Northants, an adherent of Richard III, whose ancestors had fought for the Conqueror at Senlac. When Thomas Lovell first entered Parliament it was as Knight of the Shire for Northants. A man of great and varied attainments, the King showed his appreciation of his services by making him Chancellor of the Exchequer for life, in which capacity he seems to have had a share, in conjunction with Morton, in the fiscal policy of Dudley and Empson. This connection may in part account for his having died enormously rich. In addition to the offices already mentioned, Lovell became President of the Council, Constable of the Tower

[1] Coke, *Institutes*, Vol. IV, p. 8.

Sir Thomas Lovell.
1485.
From the bronze medallion in
Henry VII Chapel Westminster Abbey
by Torregiano.

(under Henry VIII), and High Steward of both Oxford and Cambridge.

A Bencher also of Lincoln's Inn, he deserves to be remembered as the builder of the gate-house in Chancery Lane. Though often threatened with demolition, this interesting specimen of sixteenth-century brickwork, having many points of resemblance to the gate-towers of Eton and St. James's Palace, still guards the entrance to the Law and preserves on its outer face the Lovell arms. Its appearance is, however, much spoilt by the insertion of modern sash-windows in its venerable face. Previous to its erection in 1518, Lincoln's Inn had only been entered from Holborn. In quite recent days the Inn has suffered many indignities at the hands of an ill-informed if well-meaning body of Benchers. To modernise their Chapel and to undo the work of Inigo Jones, they called in a lawyer masquerading as an architect—the late Lord Grimthorpe, whose outrageous vandalism at St. Albans stands universally condemned as the most deplorable architectural failure of modern times. His iconoclastic hand, sweeping all before it and disfiguring all that it touched, fortunately stopped just short of Lovell's gateway, and it is to be hoped that this, the oldest building in any of the Inns of Court, is now safe from the unwelcome attentions of the restorer and the amateur architect.

At Westminster Lord Grimthorpe's energies were happily confined to the erection of " Big Ben."[1] This, the largest chiming clock in the world, was completed in 1860, but the hour bell was unfortunately cracked

[1] So called from Sir Benjamin Hall, First Commissioner of Works, 1855–58.

soon after it was placed in position. Its predecessor, "Great Tom of Westminster," which hung for centuries in a detached *clochard* dating from Plantagenet times, was given by William III to St. Paul's Cathedral when the tower was taken down after it had become ruinous. It is a conspicuous feature in Hollar's view of New Palace Yard.[1] When tolled Great Tom was said to have soured all the milk in Westminster.

Sir Thomas Lovell, soldier, statesman, and lawyer, was chosen Speaker of the Parliament which met on 7 November, 1485, "in Camera communiter dicta Crucis infra Palacium Westmonasterium," and one of his first official acts must have been to put the question to the House on the Bill for the reversal of his own attainder by Richard III. This, the first Tudor Parliament, was probably dissolved in March, 1486, after granting the King a liberal subsidy and attainting many of King Richard's followers. In the same year the Speaker's kinsman, Francis, Lord Lovell, headed an abortive rising in the north, but this does not seem to have impaired Sir Thomas's influence and intimacy with his Sovereign, as he continued to shower favours upon him, and selected him to be one of the executors of his will.

It is said that Lord Lovell's widow, fearing that Henry's vengeance would extend to her, retired after her husband's attainder to a lodge in Whittlebury Forest, where she lived for a time under the protection of gipsies. One of her sons is believed to have married a Romany bride and to have become their king, whence the common occurrence of the name of Lovell amongst the tribe. There are yeomen Lovells in Northamptonshire to this day, but

[1] Reproduced in this volume.

SIR JOHN MORDAUNT
1487

From a monumental effigy at Turvey Church, Beds.

the direct line of the Speaker appears to be extinct. In Henry VII's Chapel there has recently been placed, owing to the generosity of Sir J. C. Robinson, a fine bronze medallion of Sir Thomas, by Torregiano. It was brought from his manor-house at East Harling, Norfolk, and it is the earliest pictorial representation of a Speaker of the House of Commons, other than a monumental effigy or a brass, discovered up to the present time.[1] Lovell died at Elsing, in Middlesex, and was buried with great magnificence in a chantry chapel which he had built at the Nunnery of Holywell, in Shoreditch. As the last of the martial Speakers it is fitting that he should be worthily commemorated at Westminster, and in the magnificent mausoleum built by the first of the Tudor line.

Sir John Mordaunt, Knight of the Shire for Beds, was Speaker in the Parliament which created the Court of Star Chamber, and Sir Thomas Fitzwilliam, of Aldwark, Yorkshire, an ancestor of Earl Fitzwilliam, in Henry's third Parliament. A new House of Commons was summoned to meet on 17 October, 1491, and it chose for its Speaker, or rather it had forced upon it, Sir Richard Empson, Knight of the Shire for Northants, and, by repute, the son of a sievemaker at Towcester in that county. Parliament opened with alarums and excursions of war. The King announced his intention of heading an army to recover the ancient rights of England in France, and though after the fall of Sluys he crossed the Channel, the peace of Etaples was signed[2] without any further

---

[1] A reproduction of this beautiful work of mediæval art will be found in this volume.

[2] 3 November, 1492.

fighting. Empson and his *fidus achates*, Dudley, *par ignobile fratrum*, lived in adjoining houses in Walbrook, and, according to Stow, they had a " door of intercourse " from the garden which now belongs to Salters' Hall.

It would almost seem as if there was something in the atmosphere of this corner of the City peculiarly favourable to the accumulation of colossal wealth, for within a stone's-throw of Dudley and Empson's garden, and on a site adjoining Salters' Hall, stand Messrs. Rothschild's famous London offices. But here the parallel ceases. The royal extortioners never devoted any of their ill-gotten gains to relieving the necessities of the poor, whereas St. Swithin's Lane has been for more than a century, not only the chosen home of the true aristocracy of finance, but a business centre rightly associated in the public mind with unbounded charity, freely and unceasingly dispensed without regard to class or creed.

The next Parliament of the reign met at Westminster, 14 October, 1495, and chose for its Speaker Sir Robert Drury, a member of a Suffolk family long seated at Hawstead and Horningsheath in that county, a property now merged in the estates of the Marquis of Bristol. Drury is the first Speaker definitely known to have received a University education, and in this respect Cambridge takes the pride of place. Possibly the reversion to a Speaker of knightly degree and unconnected with the law was due to the fact that no sanction was required for any war tax. Parliament dealt instead with such domestic matters as vagabondage, gaming, the licensing of ale-houses, and other non-controversial matters, for even licensing Bills were strictly uncontentious in the fifteenth century.

SIR RICHARD EMPSON, 1491, AND EDMOND DUDLEY, 1503-4,
WITH HENRY VII
From a painting in the possession of the Duke of Rutland

In an unostentatious way some of the earlier Tudor Parliaments accomplished a fair amount of useful legislation. They passed laws against usury, generally, it is to be feared, a dead letter from the day they received the Royal Assent; they attempted to fix the labourer's wages; and, in their solicitude for his welfare, they even settled the hours at which he was to rise, and the time he was to spend at his meals. From this Speaker's family Drury Lane, where their town house was situated, derives its name, and it will also be familiar to many old Etonians from the well-known dame's house, founded by the Rev. Benjamin Drury, an assistant master under the redoubtable Keate. Sir Thomas Englefield, of Englefield, a Berkshire knight with a pedigree of fabulous antiquity, presided over Henry's sixth Parliament;[1] and, by way of contrast, the notorious Dudley, a Gray's Inn lawyer with an Oxford education and an assumed name, filled the Chair in his seventh and last. Empson was Chancellor of the Duchy at the same time, and these " two ravening wolves," as they have been called by an old chronicler, acting in concert, practised extortion and intimidation to an extent hitherto unknown in England. By browbeating the sheriffs they were able to nominate whom they pleased at elections; every infraction of the law, however antiquated, was punished by a heavy fine, verdicts were dictated to judges by men who were not judges themselves, but who seem to have acted as a committee of the Privy Council. The unscrupulous policy pursued by Dudley and Empson between 1504 and the King's death brought an immense sum of money into the royal treasury, whilst the "wolves" and

[1] Held in January, 1496–97.

their friends reaped no inconsiderable share of the spoil. From Dudley's *Tree of Commonwealth*, written during his imprisonment in 1510, it would seem that some scheme for the appropriation of ecclesiastical revenues had already engaged the attention of the Privy Council, and owing to his denunciations of abuses in the Church, the idea of the Reformation may have suggested itself to Henry VIII.

In connection with the House of Commons under the first of the Tudors, there only remains to be noticed Sir Reginald Bray, of Steyne, Co. Northants (a fruitful soil for the Speakership at this period), who has been assumed by many historical writers to have presided over the House of Commons. Bray's name, however, is nowhere to be found in the Rolls as having filled that high office, and such evidence as exists favours the presumption that he acted as President of a great Council, and not a fully equipped Parliament, which assembled at Westminster on 24 October, 1496. As it was attended by the Lords spiritual and temporal, the serjeants-at-law and burgesses and merchants from the principal cities and boroughs, and as it pledged itself to an expenditure of £120,000 to be used in the invasion of Scotland, it had many of the attributes of a regular Parliament, and for that reason it has seemed desirable to include Bray's name in this catalogue of honour. Like Speaker Lovell, he had fought at Bosworth, where he plucked Richard's crown out of a hawthorn bush, into which it had been cast in the moment of defeat. The Brays adopted the hawthorn as their badge, and it was formerly to be seen in one of the painted windows of the manor house at Steyne.[1]

[1] It also reappears amongst the fragments of contemporary stained glass in Henry VII's Chapel.

SIR ROBERT DRURY
1495
From a monumental effigy in St. Mary's Church, Bury St. Edmunds

The biographical dictionaries, without exception, confidently state that Sir Reginald Bray was the architect of Henry VII's Chapel, and that he put the finishing touches to St. George's in Windsor Castle, in which latter building he lies buried without a monument. But this statement requires examination, and has too hastily been accepted as correct. Bray was undoubtedly a patron of architecture, but he was certainly not the architect, in the modern sense of the word, of the royal mausoleum at Westminster. To Robert Vertue, the greatest of a distinguished family of builders, belongs the honour of having designed that noble work.[1] All that Bray did at Windsor was to buy the materials—the stone, timber, lead, glass, etc.—and to pay the architect's salary and the wages of the men. He seems to have done the same at the royal palaces of Richmond and Greenwich, where Vertue again worked under him. Moreover, Bray died in 1503, when the great chapel at Westminster was only just beginning to rise from its foundations, nor was it fully finished at the King's death in 1509. He had been associated with the fiscal abuses of Morton, Fox, and Empson, and he appointed the last-named to be an executor of his will. Sir Reginald was a man of great wealth. He "had the greatest freedom of any councillor with the King," who granted to him, amongst others, the forfeited estates of Francis, Lord Lovell, but his claim to be considered a great master of design is unfounded. The mind is insensibly drawn from his supposed share in the beauti-

[1] See Professor Lethaby's *Westminster Abbey*, 1906, p. 225. Vertue's name has been strangely overlooked by the *Dictionary of National Biography*, and the omission is the more to be regretted as he was essentially a master of the English school.

fying of the Abbey to what was actually accomplished at Westminster by the King's craftsmen.

In private life Henry VII was a pious man and a frugal liver, but his love of art and architecture caused him to be lavish in the prosecution of his building schemes. He had amassed a fortune estimated at sixteen millions of the present value of money, and he spared no expense in the erection of the royal tomb-house, with the result that he has stamped his personality upon Westminster more than any King of England since Henry III. The last of all the great works of the Benedictine Abbey, for Wren's additions were in the nature of repairs and restorations, the magnificent chapel erected between 1502 and 1509 was originally intended as a mausoleum for the remains of Henry VI. Its exterior has been much spoilt by injudicious restoration early in the nineteenth century,[1] but the interior ranks amongst the highest achievements of Gothic art in this country.

" Far in advance," to quote the words of the Abbey's latest historian, Mr. Francis Bond, " of anything of contemporary date in England, or France, or Italy, or Spain, it shows us Gothic architecture not sinking into senile decay, as some have idly taught, but bursting forth, Phœnix-like, into new life, instinct with the freshness, originality and inventiveness of youth." The fan-vaulting of its matchless roof, pieced together with the accuracy and precision of an astronomical instrument, is, by common consent, the most wonderful achievement of masonry ever wrought by the hand of man. Its

---

[1] In the words of William Morris : " Wyatt managed to take all the romance out of the exterior of this most romantic work of the late Middle Ages."

SIR REGINALD BRAY
1496
From a drawing in the possession of Mr. Justice Bray of a window in the Priory Church,
Malvern

pendants, seeming to rest on unsubstantial air, look down upon the finest piece of embellished metal-work in all England—the gilt bronze railing, or " grate " as it is called in contemporary writings—which surrounds the tombs of Henry and Elizabeth of York.   Their recumbent effigies, on which Torregiano was engaged for many years, are admitted to be among the greatest of their kind.   Novel as was Robert Vertue's system of vaulting in England, his scheme of exterior abutment is even more strikingly original.   By substituting octagonal domed turrets for the flying buttresses of an earlier age, the architect not only economised space, but introduced into his scheme of fenestration a new and attractive feature.   The windows, no longer mere flat insertions, are here made to follow the curved lines of the exterior walls, with the happiest results of light and shade.

The beauty of Henry VII's Chapel induced Barry to adopt the Tudor style for the new Houses of Parliament. With all their imperfections, of which not the least was the selection of a stone which has proved incapable of resisting the destructive effect of the London atmosphere, they stand out by themselves as the most picturesque Gothic building, on a large scale, added to the metropolis in the nineteenth century.   The daring combination of gilding and masonry exhibited in both the Victoria and the Clock Towers has elicited nothing but commendation from qualified critics, while the design of the members' private staircase is held to equal that at Christ Church, Oxford, in lightness and elegance, than which no higher praise can be given.

The mistake of employing a Gothic architect to design

a classical building, which Lord Palmerston made when Sir Gilbert Scott was selected to build the Home and Foreign Offices, is only too apparent in Whitehall. That artistic failure should have taught a lesson to successive Commissioners of Works, but not much can be said in praise of the more recently erected Public Offices, mostly of a machine-made type, which line what ought to be the finest thoroughfare in London—the approach from Trafalgar Square to Westminster.

At the present time London happens to want a dignified and adequate memorial to King Edward VII. What an opportunity for a First Commissioner of Works to immortalise himself by reconstructing Trafalgar Square and the main approach to the Houses of Parliament on an heroic scale ! If he could obtain the necessary funds there is actually a vacant pedestal awaiting him in the finest site in Europe, whereon he might, in course of time, be exhibited to a grateful posterity as a pendant in extravagance to George IV.

The formation of a *Via Regia* from the Forum to the Senate, such as would have delighted ancient Rome, would present no insuperable difficulty to Paris, or even to Berlin. Yet the example of the New Processional Road through the Mall, which, whilst it opens up a clearer view of the hideous front of Buckingham Palace, destroyed a genuine relic of seventeenth-century London, almost makes one despair of the artistic future of metropolitan improvements. Leaving St. James's Park by a well-proportioned triple arch the scheme of the architect has been choked and strangled at its birth for want of the funds required to demolish a few insignificant business premises. To buy out the banks, clubs, hotels, and shops which dis-

figure three sides of Trafalgar Square would cost a large
sum, but a beginning might be made by sweeping away the
paltry fountains feebly spurting from amidst a waste of
sombre asphalte. And although the public sentiment
would probably not approve of any material alteration
in the central feature of the nation's memorial to Nelson,
our sympathy is rather with the survivor of the *Victory's*
crew who exclaimed, on being invited to admire the
gigantic column : " Well, I'm blessed if they haven't
mast-headed the Admiral ! "

At the accession of Henry VIII continuous Parliamentary government was neither expected nor desired
by the constituencies, and the burden of paying their
representatives at Westminster would account for no
public indignation being evoked, when nearly six years
elapsed [1] before a new Parliament was called. When at
last it did meet it sat for less than a month, and, though
at its opening the Chancellor, Archbishop Warham,
expatiated on the necessity of making good laws and
spoke of the constitutional assembly as " the stomach of
the nation," the legislative output of the session was
infinitesimal, and when, after the Houses had granted
the King a liberal subsidy, the dissolution was reached,[2]
the only concession made to popular opinion was the
condemnation of Dudley and Empson, who expiated
their crimes on Tower Hill in the following August.[3]

Assuredly, this was the only occasion in Parliamentary
history when two former Speakers died on the same day.
Yet in the seventeenth century the situation was nearly

[1] Between 1504 and January, 1509–10.
[2] On 23 February.
[3] This stop-gap Parliament was presided over by Sir Thomas
Englefield, who had preceded Dudley in the Chair during the last reign.

I

paralleled, when Chaloner Chute and Lislebone Long die
within a month of one another, and in the eighteenth
when Mr. Speaker Cornwall expired within twenty-fou
hours of his old antagonist Fletcher Norton. It would b
interesting to know, remembering his former intimacy
with the twin extortioners, what were Speaker Lovell'
feelings when he heard that Dudley and Empson wer
to be brought to the block. As it was, he lived just lon;
enough to see the profession of the law once more pre
ferred to the Chair in the person of Sir Thomas More
the gifted author of *Utopia*—that happy land which h
described as having few laws and no lawyers.

The temporary eclipse of the House of Lords a
a legislative body enabled Henry VIII to introduc
Bills into the Upper House which had previously beer
prepared by the Privy Council, in concert with the law
officers of the Crown ; to pass them rapidly through tha
complacent assembly ; and to present them cut and driec
to a packed House of Commons. The practice of referring
Government measures to the consideration of a committee
of both Houses was also initiated by the Tudors. At the
same time the power of the Crown over the legislature
was much increased by so manipulating the elections a;
to ensure the return of the King's Household officers
And while Henry was careful to lay stress upon the
independence of Parliament in his communications
with the Pope, there is abundant evidence to the effect
that, aided as the King was by Thomas Cromwell, the
constituencies had little or no free choice in the electior
of their representatives.

The earliest and crudest form of intimidating voters
was to beat them off by armed force on the day of the

poll, as related in the Paston letters, and even where no coercion was employed the preliminaries to election were often accompanied by strange and novel conditions. Some amusing instances of payment in kind for Parliamentary service occur in the fifteenth century, as when John Strange entered into an agreement with the bailiffs of Dunwich to give his attendance at Westminster " for a cade of full herring " whether the House " holds long time or short," while the borough of Weymouth at the same period was able to secure a member to watch over its interests at the even cheaper rate of five hundred mackerel. Five shillings a week was all that Ipswich was willing to pay for the services of William Worsop in 1472, whilst John Walworth, the junior member, covenanted to serve for as little as three shillings and four pence !

Though little is heard of direct bribery in the sixteenth century, instances occurred of members compounding with their constituents by agreeing to accept less than the statutory allowance for travelling expenses. Some even went so far as to offer to serve altogether without pay. This negative form of bribery became increasingly common in the reign of Henry VIII, and the city of Canterbury, overjoyed, on one occasion, at having saved the wages of one of its members who stayed away from Westminster on account of the plague, actually rewarded him for his abstention. There is this much to be said for bribery as understood and practised in olden days. The briber did at least pay the money out of his own pocket, therefore the revenues of the State did not suffer. Nowadays the would-be briber offers the money of the State in order to corrupt voters, and whilst party leaders talk grandiloquently of the great constitutional issues involved in a general election, the actual canvassing for votes in many constituencies turns mainly on the granting of pecuniary rewards by the State.

The seventeenth century brought with it increased cost to candidates, but bribery was not translated into a fine art until the division of the House of Commons into parties, each anxious to turn the other out and obtain the spoils of office, became an accomplished fact. Wasteful expenditure at contested elections attained its height towards the end of the eighteenth century, but since 1832 bribery in an acute form has tended steadily to decline. Traces of the old leaven occasionally manifested themselves far on into the nineteenth century, but under an extended franchise, and a pure and beneficent system—which substitutes cheerfully paid subscriptions and charitable donations for the wholesale treating and degrading corruption of the electorate prevailing within the memory of many still living—the cost of entering the House of Commons, and, what is often more difficult, of securing re-election at the second attempt, is now appreciably less than it was before the passing of the Corrupt Practices Act of 1883.

Although it has not been possible to discover that the measures adopted by Thomas Cromwell to secure a compliant House of Commons included anything in the nature of wholesale pecuniary corruption, the constant pressure put upon the sheriffs and mayors by the Privy Council was so stringent and so far-reaching that throughout the period of the Reformation the popular assembly was almost entirely subservient to the Sovereign, from the Speaker in his Chair to the humblest burgess. To a House so constituted was assigned the spade work of severing England from Rome and despoiling the Church, and, owing to the spirit of independence being almost wholly absent from its deliberations, it became possible for the real rulers of the country, under the thin disguise of a constitutional movement which was in reality a hollow sham, to rob the English people of a faith which, of their own free will, they had never deliberately rejected.

Henry's second Parliament, a " War Parliament " as it has been called, was presided over by Sir Robert Sheffield, of Butterwick, near Boston, in Lincolnshire, an ancestor of the Dukes of Buckingham of that family.[1] The ancient seat of the Sheffields had been at a place called Hemmeswelle, but a fortunate match with the heiress of Delves enabled the Speaker to build extensively at Butterwick, in the Isle of Axeholme.

It has been supposed that the Speakers had no official residence at Westminster until a much later period, but from the journal of a Venetian traveller, who visited England in 1512, it appears that not only did the Speaker thus early live within the precincts of the Palace, but that a certain amount of ceremonial hospitality was expected of him by the general body of members :—

" The Parliament has begun, that is to say all the gentlemen of the Kingdom have come, and are making a Parliament in the Palace of the King called *Vasmonestier*, distant from London less than two miles ; and all the gentlemen who come have houses in London, and it

[1] Speaker Sheffield was buried in 1518 in the church of the Augustinian Friars. This, which has been since 1550 the meeting-place of the Dutch Communion in London, was for centuries a favourite burying-place with the greater nobility and the wealthier City merchants.

behoves them to pass before the door of the House of the Worshipful Speaker, as well those who go by land as those who go by water ; for there is a river called the Tamixa, whereon they can go in 100 boats, made after their fashion, from London to the said *Vasmonestier*. And they are bound to pass before the said worshipful house ; and having reached the said door, these gentlemen, for the love they bear to the magnificent and worshipful speaker, visit him with 16 and more or less servants ; some come to dinner and some to breakfast (*colation*), for this is the custom of the country : they have breakfast every morning. . . . Every morning he goes to Mass with some of these gentlemen, who hold him by the arms and walk up and down with him for an hour ; then they go to the Council and he to his house."[1]

During Sheffield's tenure of the Chair [2] a disastrous fire broke out in the Palace of Westminster, and many old buildings between the Great Hall and the Abbey were destroyed. Details of the calamity, which occurred in 1512, are scanty. The Hall itself, the Painted Chamber, St. Stephen's Chapel, the Star Chamber, and the Clock Tower escaped injury, but many of the King's private apartments were burnt. This fire, by no means the first in which the Palace had been involved, was the primary cause of the removal of the Court, first to Bridewell and thence, after the fall of Wolsey, to Whitehall.

Apparently the Cloister Court of St. Stephen's, dating

[1] This delightful bit of Parliamentary anecdote will be found in *Gentlemen Errant*, by Mrs. Henry Cust, 1909, p. 512, note.

[2] The *Dictionary of National Biography*, following Manning, says that Sheffield had also been Speaker in 1510, but the Rolls conclusively prove that Englefield was Speaker from 23 January, 1509-10, until 23 February. And as under the old style the year was reckoned to begin on 25 March, Parliament was not actually in session at any time in 1510.

Hans Holbein, pinxt.   Robert Grave sculpt.

SIR ROBERT SHEFFIELD
1511-2
From a print

from the middle of the fourteenth century, was involved in the conflagration, for it is known to have been rebuilt in 1526 by Dr. John Chambers, the last Dean of the *Saint Chapelle* of the Palace. A bell tower rising on the east side of Westminster Hall escaped the flames in 1512, and was heightened when the Cloister Court was rebuilt, only to be once more practically destroyed in the still greater fire of 1834.

Its subsequent restoration by Sir Charles Barry ranks as one of the most successful achievements of that architect at Westminster.

In the library of Hatfield House are two interesting plans, drawn by John Symonds in 1593, showing in detail the various buildings between the Great Hall and the Receipt of the Exchequer as they existed when Coke sat in the Speaker's Chair.

The Palace of Bridewell was only divided from the Blackfriars by the Fleet Ditch, and in consequence of the damage caused by the fire at Westminster, the sittings of Parliament were temporarily held in the Priory.

The next Speaker after Sheffield was Sir Thomas Nevill, fifth son of the second Baron Bergavenny. He was voted to the Chair on 6 February, 1514-15, and held office till the dissolution, on 22 December. When he was presented for the royal approval in the House of Lords he had the honour of knighthood conferred upon him in the presence of the assembled Lords and Commons, "the like whereof was never known before." During the session an Act was passed which laid down that no knight, citizen, or burgess "do depart until Parliament be fully finished except he have licence of the Speaker and the same be entered in the book of the clerk," upon pain of losing his wages. An earlier statute of Richard II had dealt with the subject of absenting members and the penalties to be inflicted for non-attendance at Westminster.

In the reign of Elizabeth, and probably earlier, the House was called over at the opening of every session, and members in their places answered to their names. But in spite of all attempts to ensure regular attendance, there were frequent complaints of scanty houses in Tudor times, and even such expedients as locking the doors and forcibly preventing members who were present from leaving until the business of the day was concluded proved ineffectual; nor has it ever been possible to devise any effective machinery for securing a full attendance of members throughout the lifetime of a Parliament, or even during a single session. The accurate reporting of debates, the publication of the division lists, and the fierce light which now beats upon the doings of private members, to say nothing of ministers of the Crown, has done more to ensure constant attendance than any penal resolutions passed by the House in order to meet individual cases.

After an interval of over seven years a new Parliament met, not at Westminster, but again in the Great Chamber of the Priory at Blackfriars, where now stands the *Times* office. It chose for its Speaker a man in the prime of life, the member for Middlesex, no other than the great Sir Thomas More, the first layman, with one exception, to be Chancellor of England. It was not his first appearance in the House, for in the previous reign he had successfully resisted a grant to the King, for which temerity, as it would have been a violation

SIR THOMAS NEVILL
1514-15
From a Memorial Brass in Mereworth Church, Kent

of the Constitution to punish a member for his vote, More's aged father was imprisoned and fined. This truly great man may be said to have only flitted across the stage of the House of Commons, for the session of 1523 lasted less than four months. Short as it was, it is memorable for the wholly unconstitutional irruption of Wolsey into the Chamber to demand a grant of £800,000[1] in order to carry on the war with France.[2]

The proposed tax, which was in the nature of a graduated toll upon income and property amounting to four shillings in the pound upon land and goods, was unparalleled in amount, and was stoutly resisted, though More, who seems to have considered it justified under the circumstances, urged the House to comply with the royal demands. But when the Cardinal entered, after the question of his being admitted at all had been debated at length, he was met by a chilling and preconcerted silence. "Masters," cried Wolsey, "unless it be the manner of your House, as in likelihood it is, by the mouth of your Speaker whom you have chosen for trusty and wise (as

---

[1] About £12,000,000 at the present computation of money.

[2] In Fiddes' *Life of Wolsey*, 1724, there is a representation, at page 302, of Henry VIII sitting in Parliament (? at Blackfriars) with the Archbishop of Canterbury (Warham), Cardinal Wolsey, the mitred Abbots, the Prior of St. John of Jerusalem, and the temporal peers. The Clerk of the Parliaments and his assistant are shown kneeling behind one of the woolsacks, and the Speaker of the House of Commons with several members of the Lower House are standing at the bar.

This print, which was communicated to Fiddes by John Anstis, Garter, in 1722, bears a striking resemblance to a plate printed in Pinkerton's *Iconographica Scotica* from a drawing formerly in the Heralds' College, but not now to be found there, supposed to represent Edward I with the King of Scotland, and Llewellyn, Prince of Wales, in Parliament assembled. It is probably, however, of much later date and of little or no historical value.

indeed he is) in such cases to utter your mind, here is, without doubt, a marvellous obstinate silence." Falling upon his knees, More replied that though the Commons might entertain communications from without, it was not according to precedent to enter into debate with outsiders.

Thomas Cromwell, the man who, a few years later, was more than any other responsible for the spoliation of the Church and the degradation of the House of Commons, sat in this Parliament for the first time. Combining the unpopular profession of a solicitor with the disreputable one of a money-lender, by the double experience so gained he made himself the master of the secrets of half the aristocracy, including many members of both Houses. On the present occasion he was not acting under Henry's orders, and he delivered a telling speech against the war. Not till 13 May did the House consent to grant any portion of the land tax, and then only a much lesser sum than Wolsey would be satisfied with.

The burgesses, who declared that the tax was only intended to affect the squires and the land, declined to vote at all. A few days later the House adjourned for Whitsuntide ; but on its reassembling a proposal that, in addition to the sum derived from landed estate, one shilling in the pound should be levied on goods was supported by the squires, and vehemently opposed by the borough members. It was only by the personal intervention of the Speaker that the differences of the country party and the burgesses were composed and the tax finally voted. At the close of the session Cromwell wrote to a friend : " Ye shall understand that I,

Given by The Rt Honble Charles Abbot 1803

SIR THOMAS MORE
1523
From a painting at the Speaker's House

amongst others, have endured a Parliament which continued by the space of seventeen whole weeks where we communed of war, peace, strife, contention, debate, murmur, grudge, riches, poverty, trouble, falsehood, justice and equity. . . . Howbeit we have done as well as we might and left off where we began."

After the Great Hall of Blackfriars, the scene of Katherine of Arragon's trial before Cardinal Campeggio, ceased to be used for Parliamentary purposes, the site of the Priory was devoted to various secular uses, and many famous names are found in connection with it.

A theatre, in which no less a man than Shakespeare trod the boards, flourished in the old home of the monks from the reign of Elizabeth until all theatrical enterprise was stifled under the Commonwealth.[1]

Vandyck, on his first coming to London, took a house in the precincts, where he had been preceded by Isaac Oliver and other painters. Towards the close of the eighteenth century the first John Walter set up his logographic press in Printing House Square, and laid the foundations of a gigantic instrument of popular enlightenment—the greatest newspaper the world has ever seen. Here, almost on the identical spot where More confronted Wolsey, Delane sat in the editorial chair of *The Times* for thirty-six arduous years.

It would be superfluous, if not impertinent, to dwell in these pages upon More's subsequent career and tragic fate. There is in the Speaker's house a recently acquired portrait of the great Chancellor in the Holbein manner, but it is at best a contemporary copy. Another

---

[1] Play House Yard preserves the association of the drama with Blackfriars to this day.

Sir Thomas, cast in a very different mould, succeeded More as Speaker, and also on the Woolsack. This was Thomas Audley, a " sordid slave," according to Lord Campbell, whose promotion coincided with Wolsey's disgrace. The " Black " or Reformation Parliament, an epoch in our national history, met at Westminster in November, 1529, and was not dissolved until 1536, so that it was easily the longest known to that time. If not actually packed with the nominees of the Crown, as far as it was possible to control the elections, only candidates hostile to the Church were held to be eligible. " With the Commons it is nothing but down with the Church," said the Bishop of Rochester from his place in the House of Lords in the course of the first session. While Audley was in the Chair only the outworks of the Church were laid siege to, and not till after his transfer to the Woolsack, when Sir Humphrey Wingfield became Speaker, did the actual severance from Rome take place.[1]

Audley left no male heir, but his grandson Thomas, Earl of Suffolk, ultimately inherited his vast wealth, and built Audley End in Essex between 1603 and 1616. It is said to be the largest private house in England, and to have cost £200,000. The Chancellor died in 1544, and was buried in a chapel which he had built at Saffron Walden in his native county. An elaborate monument was

---

[1] The Acts contrived by Cromwell in 1533–34 in order to ensure the final breach with Rome were four in number : " An Act for the submission of the Clergy to the King's Majesty," " An Act restraining the payment of annates," " An Act concerning the exoneration of the King's subjects from exactions and impositions heretofore paid to the see of Rome, and for having Licences and Dispensations within this Realm without suing further for the same," and " An Act declaring the establishment of succession of the King's most Royal Majesty in the Imperial Crown of this Realm."

SIR THOMAS AUDLEY
1529
From a painting at the Speaker's House

erected to his memory. His portrait in official robes with gold-laced sleeves is in the Speaker's house. With the exception of that of Sir Thomas More it is the earliest in point of date in the collection, but the painting is not earlier than the eighteenth century, having probably been painted to order with several others of the series.

Wingfield, in early life a protégé of Wolsey, though not otherwise remarkable, deserves mention for his having been the first Speaker to sit for a borough constituency. Sir Robert Brooke, *temp*. Mary I, is said by Hakewil and others to have been the first burgess so honoured, but this is inaccurate. Wingfield represented Great Yarmouth in 1529, and Sir John Say, who was Speaker in 1448-49, had represented the borough of Cambridge before he became a Knight of the Shire. The salary received by Wingfield was £100 a year. Sprung from an old East Anglian family of Brantham Hall, in the county of Suffolk, he was educated at Gray's Inn, where his coat of arms is still to be seen in a north window of the hall.

The precedent set in Wingfield's case was soon followed, for Sir Richard Rich, of Leigh's Priory, Co. Essex, sat for Colchester when elected to the Chair in 1536. Hypocrite, perjurer, oppressor, and time-server, he is without manner of doubt the most despicable man who ever sat in the Chair of the Commons. Shrinking from no infamy so long as he was on the winning side, he had a part in the fall of Wolsey, the deaths of More (whose conviction was only obtained on Rich's perjured evidence), of Fisher, Cromwell, Wriothesley, the Protector Somerset, and his brother Lord Seymour of Sudeley and of Northumberland. A monster in human shape, Rich stretched the rack with his own hands when Anne Askew was put to torture in the Tower.[1] During the short session of 1536—for it sat little more than a month—Parliament passed an Act by which Elizabeth as well as Mary was declared illegitimate, the King having married Jane Seymour shortly before the Houses met.

Before another Parliament was summoned Edward the Confessor's golden shrine had been hacked down by sacrilegious hands, and the Abbey despoiled of its treasures, an irreparable loss to the nation as well as to the Church. At the same time the priceless jewelled shrine of Becket at Canterbury was totally destroyed, and the spoils, which are said to have filled six-and-twenty carts, were swept into the royal treasury. The " Regale of France," a large diamond which was considered to be one of its chief glories, was long worn by Henry as a ring, and it is shown on his enormous thumb in some of his later portraits. It reappeared in the inventory of Queen Mary's jewels, after which date its history cannot be traced. Rich was one of the principal gainers through the disposition of the monastic lands. Henry VIII gave him St. Bartholomew's, Smithfield, as his share of the spoils of the Reformation, and he made his town house in Cloth Fair. Long known as Warwick House, it was standing in quite recent years.

In the list of Speakers in the library of the House of Commons, the date of Rich's advancement to the Chair

---

[1] Rich was then Chancellor of the Augmentations, and Wriothesley, who was associated with him in the torture of this unfortunate woman, was Chancellor.

SIR HUMPHREY WINGFIELD
1533
From a painting in the possession of Major J. M. Wingfield, Tickencote Hall,
Stamford

is given as 1537, but this is an obvious error, as no Parliament was summoned in that year. He resigned the Great Seal in 1551, and died in 1567 or 1568.[1] There is a recumbent effigy of him in Felstead Church, but the inscription on the tomb has been destroyed.

Sir Nicholas Hare, another compliant tool of Henry VIII, was Speaker in 1539-40—in the Parliament which passed the atrocious Act known as the "Whip with six strings." Hare was also Keeper of the Great Seal, though only for fourteen days. There is some doubt as to the constituency he represented whilst he was Speaker. One of the name sat for Downton in 1529, and Hare is supposed to have been Knight of the Shire for Norfolk in 1539, though the official returns for that year are wanting. He was the ancestor of the Hares of Stow Hall in that county, having bought the hundred of Clackhouse (which included Stow Bardolph) from Lord North in 1553. Appointed Master of the Rolls in that year, he died in Chancery Lane and was buried in the Temple Church.

It should be mentioned that he was absent during part of the session of 1539-40, having been committed to the Tower for advising Sir John Skelton how to evade the Statute of Uses in his will. This was deemed to be an infringement of the royal prerogative. He was released in Easter Term, 1540, and, strange to say, his imprisonment does not seem to have been considered a

---

[1] The *Dictionary of National Biography* gives the earlier and the *Complete Peerage* the later date, and they are also at variance as to the year of his birth. The Earls of Warwick and Holland were descended from him, hence the name of Warwick House, Smithfield.

breach of privilege. To such a degree of subserviency was the House reduced that even the imprisonment of its Speaker passed without remonstrance.

The next Parliament, which passed the Act for the Reformation of Religion, chose for its Speaker Sir Thomas Moyle. Originally a Cornish family, the Moyles migrated to Kent in the fifteenth century. In Queen Mary's reign Sir Thomas posed as a true friend of the Reformation, and vacated his seat rather than support the policy of Rome. He died at Eastwell, near Ashford, in 1560, and his youngest daughter married Sir Thomas Finch, the progenitor of the Earls of Winchilsea and Nottingham, thus carrying the estate into a family which gave two subsequent Speakers to the House of Commons. During Moyle's Speakership occurs an early use of the well-known term " Member of Parliament." Henry VIII, writing to the Deputy and Council of Ireland, apropos of O'Brien, Earl of Thomond, said : " But you must remember that the heir of the Earl of Thomond from henceforth must abide his time to be admitted as a Member of our Parliament till his father or parent shall be deceased, and to be only a hearer standing bareheaded at the bar beside the Cloth of Estate as the young Lords do here in our realm of England." [1]

It has been thought that Rich again filled the Chair in Henry's ninth and last Parliament, but from an entry which the present writer found in the Registers of the Privy Council, it appears that Sir John Baker, whom previous writers have not noticed in this connection until the reign of Edward VI, was the next to hold the office. February 7, 1546–47. " Also Sir John Baker had

[1] *State Papers*, III, 395.

SIR RICHARD RICH
1536
From a print

warrant to the Treasurer and Chamberlains of the Exchequer for £100 to be given to him in consideration of his service in the room of Speaker in the last session of the Parliament as hath been heretofore accustomed." It was also customary for the Speaker to receive an allowance for his diet, five pounds for every private Bill passed by both Houses, and five pounds for every name in any Bill for denizens, unless he agreed to accept less. [*Harleian Miscellany*, Vol. IV, page 561.] On Christmas Eve, 1545, Henry made the last of his many speeches to Parliament, urging the nation to religious unity, and on 31 January, 1546–47, the day that Wriothesley announced the King's death, only just in time to save the Duke of Norfolk from a traitor's death, Parliament was dissolved.

Sir John Baker, who was re-elected Speaker in Edward VI's first Parliament, was the head of an old Kentish family seated at Sissinghurst, near Cranbrook. He erected a castle, long since dismantled, on a commanding site overlooking the Weald. Originally a quadrangular edifice of great extent and profusely ornamented in the Tudor style, it has fallen by gradual stages from its former high estate until little remains of Speaker Baker's building with the exception of one wing, now converted into cottages and stabling, and a lofty tower, of somewhat unusual design, capped by two conical turrets.

After being bred to the Law, Baker was sent Ambassador to Denmark by Henry VIII, and, in the same year in which he was called to the Chair,[1] he became Chancellor of the Exchequer, a post which he continued

[1] 1545.

K

to fill until the death of Queen Mary in 1558. His zeal for the Roman faith coinciding with a ruthless persecution of Kentish Protestants caused him to be known and execrated throughout the Weald as " Bloody Baker.' Some of his hapless neighbours, after being arraigned before him, were burnt at Maidstone for their religious convictions, and it is said that, having procured an order from the Privy Council for sending yet two more to the stake, it was only at the last moment that their lives were miraculously spared. The ex-Speaker was riding towards Cranbrook with full intent to carry his sinister purpose into effect, when, at a spot where three roads meet, known to this day as Baker's Cross, the bells of the parish church intimated to him that Elizabeth had ascended the throne.

Sir John Baker died in London in 1558, but his body was brought down to Cranbrook and buried with great ceremony in the church there. A monument erected to his memory was accidentally destroyed in 1725 when, on opening the family vault, a portion of the middle aisle fell down owing to the loosening of one of the supporting arches.

The Bakers ceased to be connected with Sissinghurst in the eighteenth century, and the dilapidated castle came into the possession of Horace Walpole's correspondent, Sir Horace Mann. During the Seven Years' War it was used as a place of confinement for French prisoners, as many as three thousand being horded together in it at one time. After their withdrawal in 1763 it was uninhabited for about twenty years, and in 1784 the parochial authorities hired the premises from Sir Horace Mann for the purpose of a poor-house.

With the dissolution of the ecclesiastical houses the

SIR JOHN BAKER
1545, 1547
From a drawing in the National Portrait Gallery

long and intimate connection between the Abbey and the House of Commons came to an end. It ceased to meet in the precincts of St. Peter's and took possession of the disused Chapel of St. Stephen in the Palace of Westminster. It met there for the first time on 4 November, 1547, and by a singular coincidence the city of Westminster now first obtained separate representation in the House.[1]

The posthumous generosity of Henry VIII involved a heavy charge on the Exchequer, and, Somerset's ambitious policy entailing great expense, such old devices as tampering with the coinage were once more resorted to, and endeavours were made to persuade Parliament to grant the King the lands held by guilds and fraternities, and to sell them in order to supply the pressing necessities of the Government.

But the new House of Commons was not quite so subservient as some of its predecessors, and it became necessary for the State to come to terms with the most determined opponents of the measure in the House. From entries in the Registers of the Privy Council we gather that systematic obstruction and many of the devices of modern Parliamentary tactics were not unknown. Lynn and Coventry were two boroughs principally affected, and the Council came to the conclusion that " the article for the guildable lands should be dashed" (this being the current phraseology for the rejection of a Bill or one of its articles or clauses), since " the time of the

[1] The Journals of the House begin with this Parliament; on the first page Baker's election to the Chair is recorded, but the appointments of several subsequent Speakers are unnoticed in their pages, and the earlier Journals are, in many respects, of a fragmentary character.

prorogation being hard at hand the whole body of the Act might sustain peril unless by some good policy the principal speakers against the passing of that article might be stayed."[1] History has a habit of repeating itself, and three hundred years later than Protector Somerset, ministers of the Crown have often had occasion to resort to very similar measures in " staying " loquacious members, so that unpopular " articles " in Government Bills should not be " dashed."

Early in 1549 the Act of Uniformity passed through both Houses and the celebration of the Mass in England was prohibited after the month of May. At the dissolution in 1552 the Privy Council directed the payment of fifty marks to John Seymour, " Clerk of the Lower House of Parliament," for his pains (and in 1554 he received the same sum), but it is not stated that the Speaker received any reward for his services.[2]

The second and last Parliament of Edward VI, like so many of its predecessors, was a packed assembly. Sir James Dyer,[3] who appears to have been the willing tool of Northumberland, then at the zenith of his power, was its Speaker. The House only sat for a month, and almost the only Act of importance which it passed was one for the suppression of the Bishopric of Durham. Speaker Dyer's portrait in judge's robes, for he became Chief Justice of the Common Pleas in 1560 in which capacity he was noted for an incorruptible integrity, has recently been added to the National Portrait Gallery.

[1] Acts of the Privy Council, 6 May, 1548.
[2] Ibid., 15 May, 1552.
[3] Youngest son of Richard Dyer, of Wincanton and Roundhill, Co. Somerset.

SIR JAMES DYER
1552-3
Reproduced from an original painting in the possession of Canon Mayo, of Long Burton, Farley

SIR ROBERT BROOKE
1554
From a drawing at the National Portrait Gallery

SIR CLEMENT HEIGHAM
1554
From a drawing in the National Portrait Gallery

Just as the country seemed to be settling down into Protestantism, a state of affairs which coincided with the apportionment of the remaining lands of the Church amongst the members of the Privy Council, Edward VI, whose health had long been precarious, grew suddenly worse, and on 6 July, 1553, he died. The Council, controlled by the Duke of Northumberland, who wished to place his daughter-in-law, Lady Jane Grey, on the throne, were anxious to keep Mary misinformed as to her brother's death. But from Kenninghall, whither she had summoned Sir Clement Heigham, a staunch Catholic and a subsequent Speaker of the House of Commons, Mary sent a spirited message to the Council in London asserting her rights, and from that moment the tide of public opinion turned in her favour. She set up her standard at Framlingham, was proclaimed Queen at Norwich, and within a month she entered London in triumph.

On 1 October she was crowned at Westminster amidst every sign of popular rejoicing. Five days later her first Parliament met and at once proceeded to repeal the laws concerning religion passed under her predecessor and to declare the Queen legitimate. The new Speaker was Sir John Pollard, the second son of Walter Pollard, of Plymouth, by Avice, daughter of Richard Pollard of Way, Co. Devon. Parliament was dissolved early in December, after requesting the Queen to marry, and suggesting that she should choose her husband from amongst the English nobility, for the possibility of union with Philip of Spain was strongly resented. Mary returned a diplomatic answer, denying the right of the House to influence her choice, but declaring that her sole wish was to secure her people's happiness as well as her own. Immediately afterwards she entered upon the final negotiations for her marriage to Philip.

Pollard was re-elected Speaker in October, 1555, and during the session an Act was passed to restore some at least of the Church property alienated by Henry VIII. It was only carried in the Lower House by 193 to 126, but in the Lords only two peers voted against it. Machyn records the burial of Sir John Pollard on 25 August, 1557, but he omits to mention the place of interment. Sir Robert Brooke was Speaker of Mary's second Parliament, summoned to ratify the Queen's contract of marriage. Of a Shropshire family, he was the first Speaker to sit for the City of London. He died in 1558, and in the chancel of Claverley Church near Wolverhampton a stately monument to his memory was erected. Sir Clement Heigham, an intimate friend of the Queen, was Speaker of her third Parliament (the first of Philip and Mary). It was opened in great state by Mary and her consort in person, who rode on horseback from Whitehall to Westminster. Two days later, his attainder having been reversed, Cardinal Pole arrived at Westminster in his state barge, bearing the Legatine emblem of a silver cross at the prow. Between the dissolution of this Parliament and the end of the reign three hundred heretics were burnt at Smithfield and other places.

Much the same precautions were taken to secure the return of members acceptable to the Court as had been taken by Henry VIII. The sheriffs were enjoined only to return such as were resident in the constituencies, a regulation well worthy of imitation at the present day, and " men given to good order, Catholic, and discreet."

SIR WILLIAM CORDELL
1557-8
From a portrait at St. John's College, Oxford

In the year in which Calais was lost, Queen Mary, sick at heart at Philip's desertion, met her last Parliament. She opened it in person after attending Mass in the Abbey. Sir William Cordell, of Long Melford, Suffolk, member for the county, was chosen Speaker. The session was not in any way remarkable, and, after granting a subsidy, the Houses were prorogued from March till November. The Commons on their reassembly were about to consider a Bill for the limitation of the powers of the Press, a new subject to engage the attention of the legislature, when the Queen's fatal illness brought the sittings to an abrupt termination. Cordell became Master of the Rolls, and held that lucrative office for nearly a quarter of a century. From that time forward the Speakership came to be regarded by ambitious lawyers as a stepping-stone to high legal preferment. The spacious days of Queen Elizabeth saw ten Parliaments and eleven Speakers; all of them without exception were lawyers.[1]

The tenure of the Chair, even for a single session, served as a bridge to higher legal honours. Nor is the reason far to seek. Whilst the majority were men in good practice at the Bar, the emoluments of the Chair at the close of the sixteenth century were so small that the natural trend of their ambition was towards the better-paid offices of the profession. Including the great Sir Thomas More, five Speakers have risen to the Woolsack either as Chancellor or Keeper of the Great Seal: Audley, Rich, Puckering, and Heneage Finch, whilst Hare, Lenthall, and Whitelocke were Commissioners during vacancy. Seven became Masters of the Rolls: Hare, Cordell, Phelips, Lenthall, Grimston, Trevor, and Powle. More numerous still have

---

[1] The same was the case in the two succeeding reigns.

been the instances in which the post of Chief Justice of the King's Bench or the Common Pleas has been conferred on a former Speaker. Sir James Dyer, Sir Robert Brooke, Sir Christopher Wray, Sir John Popham, Sir Edward Coke, Sir John Croke, Sir Randolph Crewe, Sir Thomas Richardson, and Sir Job Charlton filled one or other of these coveted places, whilst Barons of the Exchequer and Recorders of London are to be found in plenty in the catalogue. For 170 years the Speakership was farmed by the Law, and that during the least glorious period of its history. When Sir John Trevor was expelled the House in 1695 for taking bribes he was allowed to remain Master of the Rolls.

So many Speakers had lived in Chancery Lane that in the seventeenth century the Rolls House came to be looked upon as the official residence of the presiding officer of the Commons sooner or later in his career. This house, which was pulled down to make way for an extension of the Public Record Office, was designed by Colin Campbell in the reign of George I to replace an earlier structure on the same site. It was a comfortable, rambling building large enough to accommodate a big family. A good story is told of Sir William Grant in connection with it. When his successor arrived, the great Judge personally conducted him over the ground floor. " Here are two or three good rooms : this is my sitting-room ; my library and bedroom are beyond ; and I am told there are some good rooms upstairs, but I never was there myself."

The illegal system of State monopolies,[1] which originated

---

[1] A monopoly conferred the right of selling articles at a higher price than could have been obtained under a system of competition.

SIR THOMAS GARGRAVE
1558-59
From a painting in the possession of Milner Gibson Gery Cullum, Esq.

under the Tudors, was perpetuated and extended by the Stuarts. These encroachments on the liberty of the subject provided a convenient means of raising money without the consent of Parliament, and tended, as much as anything, to produce that rooted antagonism to the misuse of the royal prerogative which characterised the House of Commons in the first half of the seventeenth century. The valuable collections of Sir Symonds D'Ewes, supplemented by the Registers of the Privy Council, throw a lurid light on the proceedings of Parliament in the reign of Elizabeth.

As a rule, the Speaker was elected by the unanimous vote of the House, but the appointment of Richard Onslow is an early instance, perhaps the earliest, of a contested election to the Chair. On 1 October, 1566, he was chosen by eighty-two votes to sixty, and though he pleaded as an excuse for serving the necessity of his attendance in the House of Lords as Solicitor-General, the House decided that he might fill the two offices concurrently. Onslow, the first of three Speakers of his name and family, married Katherine Hardinge in 1559, whose father lived at Knowle, Cranley, Surrey, and from him the Earls of Onslow are descended.

His brother Fulk was Clerk of the House at the time of Richard's election, and in that capacity it fell to his lot to record the result of the division. Richard Onslow's town house was in Blackfriars, so that he was doubtless in the habit of proceeding to Westminster in his state barge, as the roads leading to the House were still unsuited to the passage of a heavy coach in bad weather.

An interesting account of the arrangement of the House of Commons as Richard Onslow knew it was prepared in

1568 by Hooker, a well-known antiquarian writer of the day, for the use of the then Speaker of the Irish Parliament. "The Lower House, as it is called, is a place distinct from the other : it is more of length than of breadth ; it is made like a theatre, having four rows of seats one above another round about the same. At the higher end, in the middle of the lower row, is a seat made for the Speaker, in which he always sitteth ; before it is a table board, at which sitteth the Clerk of the House, and thereupon layeth his books, and writeth his records. Upon the lower row, on both sides the Speaker, sit such personages as be of the King's Privy Council, or of his chief officers ; [1] but as for any other, none claimeth nor can claim any place, but sitteth as he cometh, saving that on the right hand of the Speaker, next beneath the said counsels, the Londoners and the citizens of York do sit, and so in order should sit all the citizens accordingly ; without this House is one other, in which the under clerks do sit, as also such as be suitors and attendant to that House. And whensoever the House is divided upon any Bill, then the room is voided, and the one part of the House cometh down into this place to be numbered." Here is indicated the origin of the outer lobby, and the primitive manner of taking divisions under the Tudors.

St. Stephen's Chapel, in addition to its still-existing crypt, had also an attic storey in which were kept the manuscript records of Parliament. A great clearance of these was made in the time of the Commonwealth, when Scobell, the then Clerk of the House, was found to have carried many of them away to his own house.

[1] An early mention of the front Government and Opposition benches.

THOMAS WILLIAMS
1562-3
From a memorial brass at Harford Church, Devon

SIR CHRISTOPHER WRAY
1571
From a painting in the National Portrait Gallery

Richard Onslow died of a pestilent fever in 1571, and was buried at St. Chad's Church, Shrewsbury, where a monument with the effigies of himself and his wife was erected.   Sir Robert Bell, a Norfolk gentleman, who was Speaker from 1572 to 1575–76, met with a somewhat similar end.   Having been made Chief Baron of the Exchequer, in succession to Sir Edward Saunders, he died, at the Oxford summer assizes, of gaol fever, contracted whilst presiding at the trial of a bookseller for slandering the Queen.

Of Sir John Popham, Speaker from 1580–81 to 1583, the first Balliol man to fill the Chair, a witty saying is recorded by Bacon.   The Commons had sat a long time without achieving much in the way of legislation, and when the Queen asked him : " What hath passed in the House, Mr. Speaker ? " he made answer : " May it please Your Majesty, seven weeks ! "   He acted as Prosecutor for the Crown at the trial of Mary, Queen of Scots, and only in this present year, 1910, the original document signed by Elizabeth prescribing the payment of £100 as " blood money " for his services on that occasion was sold by auction in London.

In his oration on his elevation to the Chair, Popham advised his fellow-members " to use reverent and discreet speeches, to leave curiosity of form, and to speak to the matter."   Further, as the Parliament was likely to be a short one, to avoid superfluous argument.

Increased respect was now beginning to be paid to the Chair, and a motion was made by the Comptroller of the Household and universally approved by which the residue of the House " of the better sort of calling "

were enjoined, at the conclusion of each day's sitting,
" to depart and come forth in comely and civil sort,"
curtseying to the Speaker on leaving, and not thrusting
and thronging " as of late time hath been disorderly
used." Members were further required to keep their
servants, pages, and lacqueys attending on them in good
order.[1]

In the course of the same session D'Ewes makes
mention of a concession by the House at large to the
Serjeant-at-Arms, who was infirm, but without specify-
ing the occasion. " The House being moved did grant
that the Serjeant, who was to go before the Speaker,
being weak and somewhat pained in his limbs, might ride
upon a foot-cloth nag." Although he appears to have
ruled the House wisely, Popham's attitude in the Chair
was occasionally unfavourably commented upon, a
Mr. Cope complaining, on one occasion, that Mr. Speaker
" in some such matters as he hath favoured, but without
licence of this House, hath spoken to a Bill, and in some
other cases which he did not favour and like of, he
would prejudice the speeches of other members."

Probably a descendant of the Popham who was
Speaker in 1449, his legal knowledge is embodied in his
well-known volume of " Reports and Cases." His portrait, by an unknown artist, in the National Portrait
Gallery, represents him as a benevolent-looking old man
of sixty-eight.

Sir John Puckering, Speaker from 1584–86, and again
from 1586–87, is not mentioned in the official Commons
Journals (which indeed contain no record of the proceedings of any of the later Parliaments of Elizabeth), but

---

[1] D'Ewes, *Journals of Elizabeth*, 1682 edition, p. 282.

Given By the Rev.ᵈ Sir Richard Cope *Bar.ᵗ* 1803.

RICHARD ONSLOW
1566
From a painting in the Speaker's House

W.C. EDWARDS SCULP^{SIT}.   *from an Original Drawing in Crayons*

SIR ROBERT BELL, KN^T.

OF OUTWELL, NORFOLK, CHIEF BARON OF THE EXCHEQUER, OB. 1577.

SIR ROBERT BELL
1572
From a print

deserves more than passing notice here. When he was voted to the Chair for the second time Parliament had been especially convened to consider the verdict in the trial of Mary, Queen of Scots. Elizabeth sent an order to the Commons by her Vice-Chamberlain[1] requiring that no laws should be made in the course of the session, " there being many more already than could be well executed." A compliant House was only too willing to endorse the views of the advisers of the Crown, and after the preliminaries of meeting had been disposed of, Puckering put the House in remembrance of its duty to deal forthwith with what he hypocritically described as " The Great Cause," recommended to its consideration by the Queen. In the debate which followed, Francis Bacon made his maiden speech and the Speaker was unanimously directed to wait upon Elizabeth and to urge her to comply with the findings of the House against her prisoner.

The Queen received Puckering in audience at Richmond,[2] when he submitted a petition calling for Mary's speedy execution, using many " excellent and solid reasons," in a memorial written with his own hand, why her life should be taken. Of these reasons the one which weighed most with Elizabeth was that which declared that Mary was " greedy for her death," and preferred it before her own life or safety. The House adjourned over Christmas, and before it could meet again[3] the last act in the long-drawn tragedy of Fotheringay had taken place. In after days Puckering was rewarded for his complaisant servility by being made Keeper of the Great Seal. In the Upper House he

---

[1] Sir Christopher Hatton.   [2] 13 November.
[3] On 15 February.

deserted the Commons' cause when in his reply to Coke's demand for the ancient privileges of the House he replied in overbearing terms, " Your right of free speech is not to say anything that pleaseth you and come out with whatsoever may be your thought. Your right of free speech is the right of Aye or No."

Puckering lived at Kew, where he entertained the Queen, who was graciously pleased to take away a knife and fork as a memento of her visit. When in town he lived at Russell House, near Ivy Bridge, on the south side of the Strand. The Hotel Cecil now covers the site. He was buried in Westminster Abbey, the second in the long catalogue of Speakers to be so honoured. A ponderous monument, erected by his widow in the Chapel of St. Paul, with effigies of both husband and wife, may still be seen.

Rather less than justice has been done by Parliamentary historians to Serjeant Thomas Snagge, who was Speaker in 1588-89, in the Parliament summoned by Elizabeth, after the defeat of the Armada, to place the country in a state of security in the event of a renewal of Spanish aggression. Coming as he did after Puckering, who became Keeper of the Great Seal, and immediately before Coke, whose effulgence overshadowed his more modest attainments, Snagge, though he never reached the judicial bench, seems to have been an excellent public servant and a man in advance of his time in advocating the simplification of legal phraseology in the drafting of Acts of Parliament. Though a staunch supporter of the royal prerogative, he was less subservient to the Court than the majority of his predecessors, which may account for his having been passed over,

SIR JOHN POPHAM
1580-1
From a painting in the National Portrait Gallery

F. Cole, *sculpt.*

SIR JOHN PUCKERING
1584, 1586
From his tomb in Westminster Abbey
From a print

whilst less scrupulous members of his profession were raised to hereditary honours. His speech to the throne, on presentation as Speaker for the royal approval, compares very favourably with the bombastic language employed by Coke on a similar occasion.

The son of Thomas Snagge, of Letchworth—the "garden city" of the twentieth century—a gentleman bearing arms at the Heralds' Visitation of Hertfordshire in 1572, he acquired a large landed estate by his marriage with Elizabeth, daughter and heiress of Thomas Decons, of Marston-Morteyne, in the county of Bedford, and became a wealthy man independently of his professional emoluments. He was bred to the law at Gray's Inn, where he formed the acquaintance of Walsingham, and the first mention to be found of his Parliamentary services is on 7 April, 1571, when he was appointed to serve on a Committee which met in the Star Chamber to consider the subsidy to be granted to the Queen. At this time he sat for Bedfordshire, though at the time of his promotion to the Chair he represented the borough, while his eldest son, also Thomas Snagge, sat for the county. His brother, Robert Snagge, had also been a member of the House in 1571.

In the course of the session he made speeches advocating the use of simpler language in the making of laws, " whereby all entrapments should be shunned and avoided," an enlightened view, coming from the source which it did. He also spoke at some length on the difficult question of Simony.[1] Probably through Walsingham's influence he was made Attorney-General for Ireland in 1577. The Lord Deputy, Henry Sidney, had written to the

[1] D'Ewes, *Journals of Elizabeth*, pp. 163 and 165.

Privy Council in England to say that there were no lawyers in that country capable of filling the post, with the exception of Sir Lucas Dillon, the Chief Baron.

The Queen's choice fell upon Thomas Snagge, and in a letter, dated from Oatlands in September, 1577, she wrote that she was " sufficiently persuaded of his learning and judgment," and that he was to have £100 a year in addition to his fees, and the wages of two horsemen and three footmen. Moreover, " forasmuch as for an infirmity taken by an extreme cold he hath once in the year used his body to the baynes in England, the continuance whereof was requisite to his health," he was to be at liberty to repair to Bath once a year for six weeks " at such time of vacation as may best agree with his cure and be least hindrance to the public service."

In sending Snagge's Patent of Appointment to Sidney, Walsingham wrote as follows: " The Dutye that he oweth to Her Majestie and his Countrye doth make him leave all other Respects and willinglie to dedicate himself to that Service, for the which I find him a Man so chosen both for Judgement and bould Spirit . . . as hardly all the Howses of Court could yield his like." [1]

Snagge's first letter to Walsingham is dated from Holyhead, to which he had been driven back by stress of weather. In it he mentions that his journey had already cost him forty-eight pounds, and he feared that it would cost him eight pounds more. But on 7 November he wrote from Dublin, saying that " he had seen what there is to be seen concerning the course of law in Ireland, which I find to be but a bare shadowe of Westminster Hall." A little later he is found com-

[1] Collins, *Letters and Memorials of State*, i. 228.

SPEAKER SNAGGE'S MONUMENT
1588-9
At Marston-Morteyne, Beds.
From a drawing

plaining of the conduct of the Master of the Rolls in Ireland, whom he found to be " very negligent in his office, which greatly hindereth Her Majesty. I can get nothing of him but fayre words, and he hath not delivered into the Exchequer these 3 yeares past any estreates for things which passed the seale." He also told Walsingham that the same official would, in his opinion, " do more hurt in this Commonwealth than all the rest of the counseyle can do good."

The Lord Deputy, who was then engaged in the congenial task of crushing Desmond's rebellion, appears to have thought highly of Snagge's capacity, and he wrote to the Privy Council from Dublin Castle :[1] " I find him a man well learned, sufficient stoute and well-spoken, an instrument of good service for Her Majesty, and such as is carefull to redresse by wisdome and good discretion such errors as he findeth in H.M.'s courts here, so that by his presence I find myself well assisted, and I humbly thank your Lordships for the sending of him unto me," adding, significantly enough, that more of his sort were then needed in Ireland.

In 1578 Snagge was still complaining of the disservice done to the Queen's Government by the inefficiency of the officials of Dublin Castle, and the Chief Remembrancer in particular, whose office he described as being the key of all the services touching the revenue, " the wrong turning whereof hath greatly hindered the good I would have done in my service, and, to be plain, if the place is not filled with a special man it is in vain to send over any in my place to serve here." On his return to England Snagge was rewarded by being

[1] On November 26, 1577.

L

made one of Her Majesty's Serjeants-at-Law, and resumed his attendance in Parliament. Nor were Walsingham and Sidney the only ministers of the Crown whose confidence he enjoyed.

Lord Treasurer Burghley, another celebrity hailing from Gray's Inn in its most glorious days, signed himself " Your loving friend " in a letter which he addressed to the Speaker shortly after his elevation to the Chair. This document, which is preserved in the Public Record Office, is reproduced in facsimile on the adjoining page, and deserves to be inserted here, as it contains an early allusion to the state of public business in the House of Commons, and reveals the anxiety of the Government of the day to secure the passage of the measures referred to in an accompanying schedule :—

" Mr. Speaker,
  " I praie you consider of this note which I had of my Lord Chancellor,[1] and to cause the Clerk of the Lower House to sett down how theie stande at this daie in their Readinge, etc.
                      " Your loving friend,
          " W. Burghley, xv Martii, 1588–[89]."

Fulk Onslow, brother of the Speaker of 1566, was the person referred to by the Lord Treasurer.

Speaker Snagge died in 1593, and was buried in a sumptuous alabaster tomb at Marston-Morteyne adorned with the recumbent effigies of himself and his wife. Manning, writing in 1851, erroneously supposed that the male line of the family was extinct ; but the present Sir Thomas Snagge, Judge of County Courts, is the

[1] Sir Christopher Hatton.

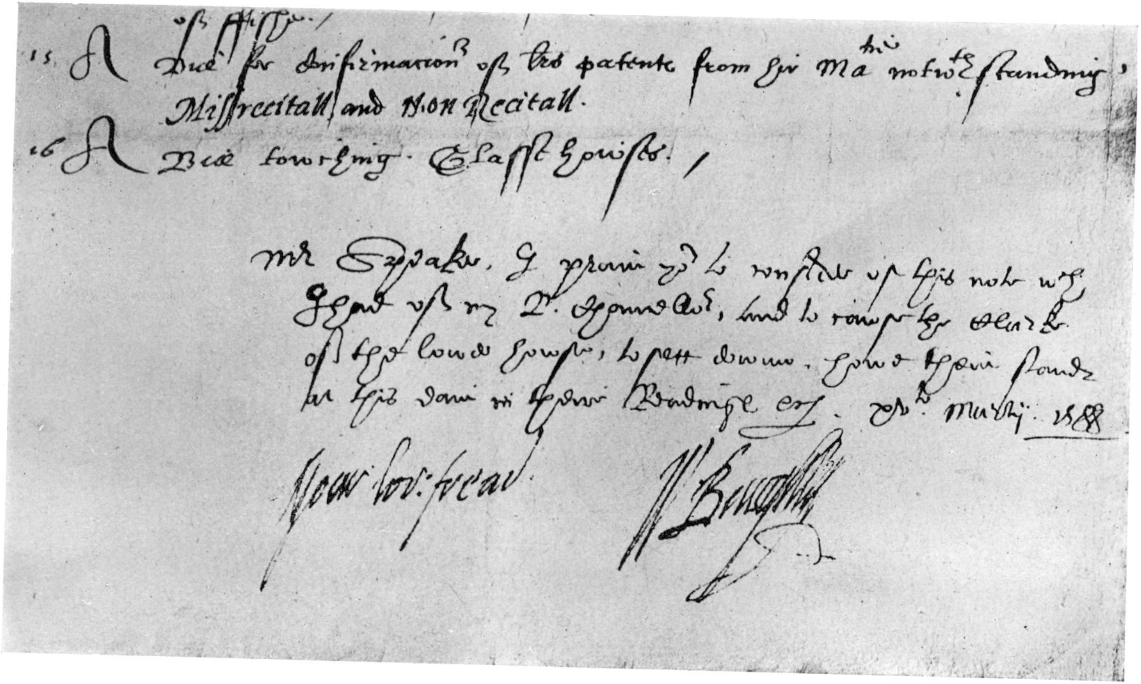

LETTER FROM LORD BURGHLEY TO SPEAKER SNAGGE, 1588-89

representative head of this ancient family and tenth in descent from the Speaker of 1588–89.[1]

Sir Edward Coke, like Sir Thomas More, now crossed the stage of Parliament. He was Speaker for less than two months, and it was not until the evening of his days, and after he had been out of the House for twenty-seven years, that he re-entered it, as an independent member, to become the foremost champion of the liberties of the subject. His Parliamentary fame therefore belongs rather to the Stuart period and will be treated of in the next chapter. What little is known of Coke's attitude in the Chair during the few weeks in which he was Speaker is mainly due to the collections of the indefatigable Sir Symonds D'Ewes. His speech (or speeches, for he made two), on presentation for the royal approval, differed in no material degree from the language of extravagant metaphor employed by most of his predecessors, and showed little of the independence and courage which marked the later years of his career. Although anxious to pose as the faithful servant of the House, he seems to have misconceived the true function of the Speaker's office, and never to have been able to forget that he was also the Queen's Solicitor-General. Likening himself with mock humility to untimely fruit " not yet ripe, but a bud scarcely blossomed," [2] he expressed the fear that Her Majesty " amongst so many fair fruit had plucked in him a shaking leaf."

The Lord Keeper, Puckering, answered him in similar

[1] The illustration of Speaker's Snagge's monument was kindly supplied to the author, together with much interesting genealogical information, by Sir Thomas Snagge, from a drawing by G. Wilson, of Messrs. Farmer and Brindley, Lambeth.

[2] Coke was now in his forty-second year.

strain, and in his second oration, the new Speaker, after a complimentary reference to Elizabeth's late successes over her enemies the Pope and the King of Spain, passed in rapid review the legislative achievements of every reign since that of Henry III. But, as Coke was notoriously careless in verifying his references, even his great and acknowledged erudition could hardly have prevented him from making many mistakes in attempting such an epitome of Parliamentary history. He also spoke of there being already so many laws that they might properly be termed *Elephantinæ Leges*, saying that to make more would seem superfluous were it not that the malice of " our arch-enemy the Devil " required the passing of measures designed to counteract his evil influence. He concluded with the usual formal requests for liberty of speech, freedom from arrest, and access to the Sovereign. To which Puckering, an even greater sycophant, having received fresh instructions from the Queen, made the singular reply already mentioned[1] in which he defined his latest interpretation of the right of free speech.

Two days later Coke was suddenly taken ill and could not attend the sittings of the House. " On Saturday 24 February the House being set, and a great number of the members of the same assembled, Mr. Speaker not then as yet being come to the House, some said to one another, they heard he was sick ; and one affirmed it to be so indeed, showing that he had been with him this morning himself, and left him sick in his bed,[2] and his physician and his wife with him ; and some others

---

[1] At page 142 of this volume.
[2] At his house in Serjeant's Inn, Fleet Street, for he did not remove to Holborn until his second marriage.

SIR EDWARD COKE
1592-3
From a painting at Holkham

supposing that he would shortly signify unto this House the cause of that his absence, moved that the Clerk [1] might in the meantime proceed to saying of the Litany and Prayers. Which being so done accordingly the Serjeant of this House, presently after the said prayers finished, brought word from Mr. Speaker unto the Rt. Hon. Sir John Woolley, Kt., one of H.M.'s most honourable Privy Council, and a member of this House and then present, that he had been this last night and also was this present forenoon so extremely pained with a wind in his stomach and looseness of body, that he could not as yet without his further great peril and danger adventure into the air at this time, which otherwise most willingly he would have done." Whereon : " all the said members of this House being very sorry for Mr. Speaker, his sickness, rested well satisfied. And so the House did rise, and every man departed away." [2]

His recovery must have been as rapid as his indisposition was sudden. On the 27th of the same month, when he returned to the Chair, he dealt a blow against the advocates of complete religious liberty by ensuring the postponement of an inconvenient debate which had been sprung upon the House in connection with the abuses prevailing in the Ecclesiastical Courts. An unequal contest was in progress between the Crown and a numerous section of the House which sought to prevent the Bishops and Ecclesiastical Judges from applying the penal laws originally directed against the Papists to the Puritan Clergy. The subtlety which he had acquired in the practice of the law enabled Coke,

[1] Fulk Onslow.
[2] Sir Symonds D'Ewes, *Journals of Queen Elizabeth's Reign*, p. 470.

knowing as he did the Queen's wishes, so to utilise and amplify the forms of the House as to serve what he conceived to be the royal interests without, at the same time, alienating from himself the confidence of the assembly over which he presided.

A Mr. Morris, Attorney of the Court of Wards, brought forward a Bill to protect the Puritans from harsh ecclesiastical jurisdiction, and its reception by the House was not unfavourable. Sir Francis Knollys, the Treasurer of the Household, and Oliver St. John [1] supported it, whilst Sir Robert Cecil [2] and Doctor William Lewin, M.P. for Rochester and a judge of the Prerogative Court of Canterbury, inveighed against it. Coke, who owed much of his early advancement to the Cecil family and to Lord Burghley in particular, dexterously prevented the House from coming to an immediate decision, by stating that the Bill was too complex for him to comprehend its full meaning on such short notice, and by asking leave to consider its provisions in private on the understanding that he would keep them secret. The Bill was accordingly left in his hands for perusal. But the House at large had not foreseen the dangers of procrastination so adroitly recommended to it by an expert in the manipulation of precedent. The Queen forthwith sent for the Speaker to St. James's Palace and commanded him to deliver a message to the Body of the Realm, as she was pleased to describe the House of Commons, peremptorily forbidding its Members

[1] Afterwards first Viscount Grandison and Lord High Treasurer of Ireland in 1625.

[2] Raised to the Peerage in the next reign as Viscount Cranborne and Earl of Salisbury, the well-known builder of Hatfield House.

to meddle in matters of State policy or in ecclesiastical causes.

That the Coke of 1593 was a wholly different man from the fearless champion of liberty which his many admirers assert that he became after his final estrangement from the atmosphere of the Court, is apparent from the speech which he made to the House in commendation of the royal message. In it he stands revealed as the docile servant of the Crown, whilst endeavouring, with scant success, to justify himself to the House for having disclosed the contents of the Bill to the Queen.

" I must be short, for Her Majesty's words were not many, and I may, perhaps, fail in the delivery of them. For though my auditors be great, yet who is so impudent whom the presence of such a Majesty could not appal ? Her Majesty did not require the Bill of me, this only she required of me, what were the things in the Bill spoken of by the House ? Which points I only delivered as they that heard me can tell. . . . Her Majesty's express commandment is that no Bill touching the said matters of State or Reformation in causes ecclesiastical be exhibited. And, upon my allegiance, I am commanded, if any such Bill be exhibited, not to read it."

Not only was the Bill quashed, but Mr. Morris, the unfortunate sponsor of it, was sent for to the Court, and committed to the custody of the Chancellor of the Exchequer.[1] Later in the same session there was a serious disagreement, perhaps the most remarkable since 1407, between the two Houses as to the amount of the subsidy to be granted to the Crown, and the means to be taken to expedite it. In a periodically

[1] Cobbett's *Parliamentary History*, Vol. I, p. 889.

recurring controversy, wherein, thirty-five years later, Coke was destined to play the foremost part in determining the questions at issue in favour of the representative Chamber, the Speaker acted once more as the instrument of the Sovereign rather than as the jealous protector of the privileges of the Commons. An animated and, from the constitutional point of view, a highly instructive debate continued for several days, touching the right of the Lords to intervene in the matter of finance. On 1 March their Lordships sent down a message to the Commons requiring them to expedite the passing of an increased supply and desiring a conference on the subject.

The great Sir Francis Bacon, Coke's lifelong rival, was foremost in opposing the adoption of such a course, declaring that it was contrary to the privileges of the Commons to join with the Lords in the granting of a subsidy : " For the custom and privilege of this House hath always been," he said, " first to make offer of the subsidies from hence, then to the Upper House. . . . And reason it is, that we should stand upon our privilege, seeing the burthen resteth upon us as the greatest number, nor is it reason the thanks should be theirs. And in joining with them in this motion, we shall derogate from ours ; for the thanks will be theirs and the blame ours, they being the first movers. Wherefore I wish that in this action we should proceed, as heretofore we have done, apart by ourselves, and not join with their Lordships." He argued further that though the Lords might give notice to the Commons what need or danger there was, they ought not to prescribe the sum to be given. It will be noted that he based his argument for the supremacy of the Commons in finance, not upon their representative character, but upon their numerical superiority. Sir Walter Raleigh spoke in favour of an increased subsidy without alluding to the constitutional aspect of the question, but Robert Beale, the representative of the Borough of Lostwithiel, an old member of the House and a well-known diplomatist and antiquarian writer, vehemently insisted on the preservation and maintenance of the ancient liberties of the House, citing the inevitable precedent of the reign of Henry IV, in the Parliament held at Gloucester in 1407, whereat it was asserted that a conference between the two Houses in the sphere of finance would be a derogation of the privileges of the representatives of the people.[1]

Sir Robert Cecil used his great influence in favour of holding the conference, but on a division being taken only 128 voted for it and 217 against it. But the matter was not even then finally disposed of. A message was sent to the Lords to acquaint them that the Commons could not join with them in cases of benevolence or contribution, but, on a later day, Mr. Beale, who seems to have been but a pinchbeck Hampden after all, receded from his former uncompromising attitude, and humbly asked leave of the House to make a personal explanation. This was to the effect that he had mistaken the precise significance of the question already put from the Chair and decided by the House, and that he now thought that if the Lords desired a conference it ought to be accorded.

" Mr. Beale desired to satisfy the House, by reason it was conceived by the Lords the other day, that upon his

---

[1] For his share in the dispute and his attitude towards the malpractices of the Ecclesiastical Courts referred to above, Beale was banished from Court and Parliament.

motion, and by his precedent showed, the House was led to deny a conference with the Lords, acknowledged he had mistaken the question propounded. For there being but a conference desired by the Lords, and no confirming of any thing they had done, he thought we might, and it was fit we should confer. And to this end only he showed the Precedent. That in the ninth year of Henry IV the Commons having granted a subsidy, which the Lords thought too little, and they agreed to a greater and would have the Commons to confirm that which they had done ; this the Commons thought they could not do without prejudice to this House. Wherefore he acknowledged himself mistaken in the question, and desired if any were led by him, to be satisfied, for that he would have been of another opinion if he had conceived the matter as it was meant."[1]

Sir Walter Raleigh, quick to see the advantage to be gained through this change of front, then proposed and carried, without a dissentient voice, a motion for a general conference with the Lords, " touching the great imminent dangers of the Realm and State, and the present necessary supply of Treasure to be provided speedily for the same according to the proportion of the necessity."

At these Conferences the Lords sat covered whilst the members of the Lower House stood uncovered. This curious Parliamentary survival lingered well into the nineteenth century, and the late Mr. Evelyn Philip Shirley, of Ettington, who died so recently as 1882, not only remembered the observance of this custom, but to have seen the carpet spread, not on the floor of the Conference room, but on the table. This usage is believed to have given rise to the phrase " on the tapis."

[1] D'Ewes, *Journals*, p. 487.

Macaulay attended one of these Conferences,[1] and made an interesting comment on the relations of the Lords and Commons in this connection.

" The two Houses had a conference on the subject in an old Gothic room called the Painted Chamber. The painting consists in a mildewed daub of a woman in the niche of one of the windows. The Lords sat in little cocked hats along a table, and we stood uncovered on the other side, and delivered in our Resolutions. I thought that before long it may be our turn to sit, and theirs to stand." [2]

The last time the Painted Chamber was ever used was on 13 August, 1834, when a Conference between the two Houses was held in it on the County Coroners Bill. In October of the same year it was destroyed by fire.

The Conference of 1593 was held in due course in the " chamber next to the Upper House of Parliament," and from that moment victory rested with the Lords. For, notwithstanding a sharp wrangle as to the wording of the preamble of the Bill of Supply, it was drawn up and finally assented to in the following terms : " We the Lords Spiritual and Temporal, and the Commons of this present Parliament assembled, do by our like assent, and authority of this Parliament, give and grant to your Highness," etc. etc. Thus, in 1593, the Commons yielded to the Lords the very point which Coke, when the question of the wording of the preamble of Bills of Supply came up for settlement in 1628, was foremost in insisting upon, namely, the right of the Commons to be exclusively named in the granting of supplies.

[1] On Indian Resolutions, June 17, 1833.
[2] Trevelyan's *Life and Letters of Macaulay*, Vol. I, p. 302.

Sir Symonds D'Ewes, whose collections are especially valuable for this period, further states that the Bill of 1593 was only passed with much difficulty, and after many days' agitation, " by reason of the greatness thereof," owing to the Speaker " *over-reaching the House in the subtle putting of the question*, by which means it had only been considered of in the Committee Chamber by eighteen members of the House appointed in the beginning of this forenoon,[1] though many of the House desired a longer time for it to have been considered in Committee." It had actually been under consideration on ten separate occasions between 26 February and 22 March, when it passed the third reading.

Some scraps of information concerning the more personal aspect of the House of Commons at this period are to be gleaned from contemporary sources. On the occasion of the great debate on the financial relations of the two Houses, it fell to Coke's lot to reprimand an unfortunate stranger,[2] who had wandered into St. Stephen's Chapel and sat there for the greater part of the morning. He was committed to the custody of the Serjeant-at-Arms and imprisoned for several days. Matthew Jones, " gentleman," was charged with a similar offence on 27 March, and appearing to the House to be a simple ignorant old man, he was pardoned after being admonished by the Speaker.

On another day Coke, perceiving some men to whisper together, said that it was not the manner of the House to talk secretly, for that only public speeches were to be used there.

Purely legal Bills were committed to the Serjeants-

[1] 22 March. [2] John Legge, a servant of the Earl of Northumberland.

at-Law who were members of the House, and were considered not in the precincts of St. Stephen's, but at Serjeant's Inn in Fleet Street, perhaps with the intention of keeping them under the direct surveillance and control of the Speaker, who had his town house there.

Coke regularly asserted his right of speaking and voting in committee, and he appears to have inaugurated a rule whereby the chairman was empowered, in the case of two or more members rising at the same time, to ask on which side they desired to speak, and to give precedence to a member who desired to oppose the arguments of the last speaker. Members who, for any good reason shown, desired leave of absence were required to leave a small sum of money with the Serjeant to be distributed amongst the poor. The amount varied from one shilling to six, but Mr. Wilfrid Lawson, Knight of the Shire for Cumberland, a direct ancestor of the late member for Cockermouth, left town without making the customary donation. In 1593 every member gave a shilling to the Serjeant for his attendance on the House, and for the cost of a clock which he had set up for the general convenience. Every Privy Councillor paid thirty shillings as a charitable contribution to the relief of the poor, every Knight of the Shire, and Serjeant or Doctor of Law twenty shillings, and every burgess five shillings. One poor burgess refused to pay more than half a crown, whereupon Coke would have committed him to the custody of the Serjeant for disobeying the order of the House. But the general sense of the House being against such harsh dealing he escaped.

The legislative harvest of the Session of 1592-93, a remarkable Parliament, owing to its standing nearly midway between the earliest Plantagenet assemblies and those of modern times, and from its having been presided over by one of the greatest intellects of his own or any age, was not a large one. It comprised only fourteen public and thirteen private Bills. In the former category, apart from the controversial Subsidy Bill, two only were of any consequence. Both of them, according to strict Tudor precedent, originated in the House of Lords, and both were penal measures, one directed against the Puritans and the other to restrain papal recusants to some certain place of abode.

On quitting the Chair, Coke apologised for the unbecoming expressions into which his natural proclivity to violent language had often led him.[1] When Sir Walter Raleigh was being tried for his life in 1603, Coke denounced him from the Bench as: " Traitor, viper and spider of hell "; nor was this the only occasion when " one of the toughest men ever made," as Carlyle described him, so far forgot himself as to descend to vulgar abuse of his political opponents.

In the person of Sir Christopher Yelverton the House once more chose a Northamptonshire man for its Speaker. His family was of Easton Mauduit and is not yet extinct in the county. In excusing himself to the House, Yelverton is reported to have said : " Your Speaker ought to be a man big and comely, stately and well-spoken, his voice great, his carriage majestical, his nature haughty, and his purse plentiful. But contrarily, the stature of

---

[1] *The Speaker's Chair*, by E. Lummis, 1900, a concise and useful contribution to the literature of the subject, to which the present author hereby acknowledges his frequent indebtedness.

Janssen, pinxt.　　　　　　　　　*R. Dumbarton, sculpt.*

SIR CHRISTOPHER YELVERTON
1597
From a print

my body is small, myself not so well-spoken, my voice low, my carriage of the common fashion, my nature soft and bashful, my purse thin, light, and never plentiful." Previous to the summoning of this Parliament the Privy Council sent out no less than fifty-two cautionary letters to the sheriffs directing them to use their utmost endeavours to procure the election of " men of understanding and knowledge for the particular estate of the places whereunto they ought to be chosen," and to select, " without partiality as sometimes hath been used," fit persons to serve, especially in the boroughs. No doubt the Council, in looking so far ahead, anticipated that by October, when the House was appointed to meet, Essex would have returned in triumph from his expedition against Spain.

Speaker Yelverton composed the prayer still in use in the Commons, and a very beautiful piece of English it is. The usual hour of assembling was then eight o'clock in the morning, and, as now, the day's proceedings were opened with prayer, but so early as 1558 it had been customary for the Clerk of the House to repeat the Litany kneeling, " answered by the whole House on their knees with divers prayers."[1] In 1571 the hour of meeting was as early as seven a.m., and the afternoon sittings of recent times had their forerunners in May of the same year, when, as an experiment, the House was appointed to meet on Mondays, Wednesdays, and Fridays at three o'clock and to sit till five. An instance of a still earlier meeting is on record, for on 28 March, 1641, the House met at six o'clock in the morning. Later in the seventeenth century nine or ten was the usual hour for assembling, and Lord

[1] Sir Symonds D'Ewes, p. 473.

Clarendon spoke of from eight till twelve as the old Parliamentary hours. To Sir Robert Walpole the House owes its Saturday holiday, and to Sir Robert Peel the short sitting on Wednesday, now altered to Friday in each week.

The last of the Elizabethan Speakers was Sir John Croke, Recorder of London, " a very black man by complexion," thus resembling the " black funereal Finches " of a later era. Fulk Onslow, the Clerk of the House, was stricken with ague, and through the Speaker he petitioned the House for one Cadwallader Tydder to be allowed to execute the duties of his office until it should please God to restore him to health. The House, which has always been careful of its officers' interests, and jealous of their privileges, at once granted Onslow's request, and Tydder took the oath of supremacy.

An interesting question of Parliamentary procedure was settled during Croke's tenure of the Chair. On a division in which the Ayes were 105 and the Noes 106 (in the discussion on a Bill for compelling attendance at church), the minority claimed the Speaker's vote to make the numbers even and secure a casting vote in their favour. Sir Walter Raleigh spoke in opposition to this view, and ultimately the House decided that the only vote a Speaker has is a casting vote between equal numbers. This precedent still obtains, and the Speaker has no right to enter the division lobby, except in committees of the whole house, and even this right has not been exercised since Speaker Denison[1] passed through the lobby in wig and gown to record his vote.[2]

[1] Lord Ossington.
[2] When the question of the Speaker's casting vote was debated Secretary Cecil said : " The Speaker hath no voice ; and, though I am sorry for it, the Bill is lost, and farewell to it."

SIR JOHN CROKE
1601
From a drawing in the National Portrait Gallery

In an address to the throne Speaker Croke was alluding to the defeat of Essex's insurrection, " by the mighty arm of our dread and sacred Queen," when Elizabeth caught him up, and interposed, " No, by the mighty hand of God, Mr. Speaker." Croke was responsible for the introduction of sundry orders tending to the general convenience of members. They were forbidden to come into the House with spurs, and a similar restriction was sought to be imposed on rapiers.[1] This Speaker was fifth in descent from Nicholas Le Blount, who changed his name to Croke in consequence of his cousin, Sir Thomas Blount, having been engaged in a conspiracy to restore Richard II to the throne.

At a dinner given by the Abbot of Westminster in December, 1399, it was agreed to surprise Henry IV at a tournament to be held at Windsor on the following Twelfth Night. But the plot was revealed within a few hours of its being carried into execution, and Sir Thomas Blount was put to death under circumstances of exceptional barbarity. Having been partially hanged, he was slowly roasted before a blazing fire, his bowels were cut out, and he was then beheaded, exclaiming, shortly before he expired, " Blessed be this day, for I shall die in the service of my sovereign lord, the noble King Richard ! "

Their estates having been forfeited to the Crown, the family fled abroad and entered the service of the Duke of Milan. Having acquired fresh wealth in foreign parts, they returned to England after the death of Henry IV, when they could appear in public in safety. They bought lands in Buckinghamshire, and on the

[1] Sir Symonds D'Ewes, p. 623.

M

marriage of Speaker Croke to the daughter of Sir Michael Blount, of Maple Durham, the name of Blount was altogether omitted by the branch of the family which had previously styled itself Croke, *alias* Blount. The direct line of the Crokes is now extinct, and their property at Studley, in Oxfordshire, where the Speaker's portrait was formerly preserved, has passed into the possession of the Henderson family.

The deep-rooted antagonism of the English people to Spain, which reached its culminating point with the coming of the Armada, resulted in the return to the House of Commons of a permanent Protestant majority, whereas, at the beginning of Elizabeth's reign, the adherents of the old faith were a preponderating element both in Parliament and in the country. The Parliament of 1571, in which Sir Christopher Wray was Speaker, was in the main a Puritan assembly. It bestowed the authority of the legislature upon the thirty-nine articles drawn up by convocation nearly ten years earlier, but, as it evinced a strong desire to amend the Prayer Book and to impose new penalties upon the Catholics, it was hastily dismissed.

The next House of Commons included many followers of Thomas Cartwright, the chief exponent of Calvinism in England, and when in 1581 the teachings of the Jesuit, Edmund Campion, inflamed the public mind against Rome, no great indignation was shown when the penal laws against the Catholics were revived. Though the fires of Smithfield were not relighted, recourse was once more had to torture, and the rack was again set up in the Tower in order to extract confessions from prisoners as in the darkest days of the Marian persecution.

Notwithstanding the sharp contrasts of Elizabeth's civil and religious legislation and her determination to regard the two Houses as mere instruments of taxation, convened for the express purpose of replenishing the royal purse, a growing spirit of self-reliance manifested itself in the House of Commons towards the close of a reign in which England became great, not so much because of, as in spite of, the popular assembly.

The fact that the responsible ministers of the Crown, Hatton and Cecil amongst the number, now sat in the House of Commons and took part in its debates on equal terms with the general body of members is conclusive proof that the right of argument was beginning to be recognised as an essential feature of a Constitution hitherto mainly controlled by prerogative.[1]

[1] Portraits of Elizabethan Speakers are not numerous. There is one of Sir Thomas Gargrave at Hardwick House, Bury St. Edmunds, the property of Mr. Gery Cullum, who has kindly allowed it to be reproduced in this volume. Of Richard Onslow and Sir John Popham there are likenesses in the Speaker's collection; and of Sir Christopher Wray there are portraits both at Westminister and in the National Portrait Gallery. Sir Edward Coke is also doubly represented, but of Thomas Williams, Sir John Puckering, and Thomas Snagge, no portraits have been traced.

CHAPTER VI

THE STUARTS AND THE LIBERTIES OF THE PEOPLE

THIRTY-TWO SPEAKERS

James I—
  Edward Phelips
  Randolph Crewe
  Thomas Richardson
  Thomas Crewe

Charles I—
  Heneage Finch
  John Finch
  John Glanville
  William Lenthall

Commonwealth—
  Henry Pelham
  Francis Rous
  Thomas Widdrington
  Bulstrode Whitelocke
  Chaloner Chute
  Lislebone Long
  Thomas Bampfylde
  William Say

Charles II—
  Harbottle Grimston
  Edward Turnour
  Job Charlton
  Edward Seymour
  Robert Sawyer
  William Gregory
  William Williams

James II—
  John Trevor

William III—
  Henry Powle
  Paul Foley
  Thomas Littleton
  Robert Harley

Anne—
  John Smith
  Richard Onslow
  William Bromley
  Thomas Hanmer

THE first of the Stuart line was an unkingl[y]
pedant who entirely failed to understan[d]
the temper of the nation over which he wa[s]
called upon to rule. The new and aggressiv[e]
spirit which showed itself in the House of Commons earl[y]

in the reign of James I was stimulated by the perverse and persistent egotism of the " wisest fool in Europe " ; and boded ill for the Crown in an age which was beginning to value privilege more than prerogative. The efforts, partial and incomplete though they were, which had been made under Elizabeth to bring about some amelioration of the hard lot of the lower classes, to promote education and to relieve the necessities of the poor, were succeeded by a period of retrogression during which Parliamentary progress was first hindered and then rendered impossible.

A plague in London, which carried off 30,000 people, caused the meeting of James's first Parliament to be delayed until March 1603-4. Sir Edward Phelips, a Somersetshire gentleman, was elected Speaker " by general acclamation," after the names of Sir Henry Nevill, Sir Francis Bacon, Sir Edward Hoby, Sir Henry Montagu, and Sir Francis Hastings had been proposed. The last of these was the colleague of Phelips in the representation of the county of Somerset. The English counties were very unequally represented in the new Parliament, for whilst the official returns give the names of 39 members for Cornwall, 34 for Wiltshire and 26 for Hampshire, Lancashire had only 12, Kent 10, Cumberland and Westmorland 4 each, and Northumberland only 2.[1] Speaker Phelips succeeded to the estate of Montacute in 1598, and soon after that date he began to build the

---

[1] The writs for the Parliament were issued under a Royal Proclamation, which in its terms directly infringed the privileges of the House of Commons. [N.B. Especially the order that the writs should be returned to the Chancery.] It assumed entire control of the elections, and threatened fines and imprisonment if its injunctions were traversed (*History of the English Parliament*, by G. Barnett Smith, 1892, Vol. I. p. 361).

magnificent Renaissance mansion which remains to this day one of the principal architectural glories of the county of Somerset. His portrait here reproduced is by permission of his lineal descendant the present owner of Montacute, where, by the way, are preserved the original minutes of the Gunpowder Plot inquiry.

As was customary at this period, the King's speech abounded in metaphor,[1] nor was Speaker Phelips' reply, in which he expressed the usual formal desire to be excused from executing the office, less free from the extravagantly flowery language then considered appropriate to the occasion. Whilst he spoke of himself as " not tasting of Parnassus' springs, nor of the honey left upon the lips of Pluto and Pindarus by the bees," he defined the duties of the Chair as being : " Managed by the absolute perfection of experience, by the profoundness of literature, and by the fullness and grace of natural gifts, which are the beauty and ornament of arts and actions." Nevertheless, the Speaker of the Gunpowder Plot Parliament deserves to be remembered for his energetic vindication of the privileges of the House of Commons. The important case of Sir Thomas Shirley, wherein the amount of protection afforded by the House to its members was carried a step further than in the well-known instances of Haxey and Strode, was determined in the opening session of James's first Parliament.

The member for Steyning, Sussex, a small borough long consigned to oblivion, had been cast into prison, after his return to, but before the meeting of Parliament, in execution of a private debt. Instead of wasting time in

---

[1] It occupies more than twelve closely printed double columns in Cobbett's *Parliamentary History*.

SIR EDWARD PHELIPS
1603-4
From a painting at Montacute, Somerset

discussing abstract matters of law, the House focused its attention on the means necessary to secure Shirley's immediate release. The Warden of the Fleet was commanded to deliver up his prisoner, and six members acting as a deputation of the whole body, to be accompanied by the Serjeant and the Mace, were empowered to free him, if need be by force, and to bring him in triumph to Westminster. The Warden of the Fleet, however, proved obdurate, whereupon he was summoned to the Bar and admonished by the Speaker in the following terms : " That, as he did increase his contempt, so the House thought fit to increase his punishment ; and that their judgment was that he be committed to the prison called Little Ease, within the Tower."

An ingeniously worded request to the King was sent through the Vice-Chamberlain desiring him to command the contumacious Warden to deliver Shirley " not as petitioned for by the House, but as if himself thought it fit out of his own gracious judgment." It was now the Warden's turn to sue for release from durance vile, and, on his making due submission for his dilatoriness in complying with the original Order of the House, the Speaker pronounced pardon, the Warden, on his knees at the Bar, expressing unfeigned regret for his offence. To legalise the position an Act was hastily passed whereby the privileges of members in cases of arrest were, for the first time, defined. A creditor was authorised to sue for a new execution against any one delivered by virtue of his Parliamentary privilege, and power was taken to discharge from liability those out of whose custody such persons should be released.[1]

---

[1] I James I, c. 13.

The Journals at this time reveal a growing tendency to make rules for the guidance of the House and its presiding officer. On 26 March, 1604, a Mr. Hext moved " against hissing to the interruption and hindrance of the speech of any man in the House," and the clerk recorded that the motion was " well approved." [1] And on 27 April it was agreed for a rule that " If any doubt arise upon a Bill, the Speaker is to explain, but not sway the House with argument or dispute."

Nor was the lighter side of Parliamentary life wholly unrepresented at this period, for on 3 July, 1604, the Merchant Taylors Company gave a solemn feast to the Speaker and a great number of members of the House of principal rate and quality to the number of one hundred. The King sent a buck and a hogshead of wine, and the Clerk of the House, not to be outdone in generosity, presented the Company with a marchpane representing the Commons in session.

Phelips was taken ill in March, 1607, and, as there was no precedent for choosing a temporary Speaker, a committee was ordered to search the records in order to avoid a Parliamentary deadlock. But, as Phelips resumed the Chair next day, nothing was done to meet the emergency, and though temporary Speakers were occasionally chosen in Commonwealth times, it was not until 1853 that the Chairman of Ways and Means was empowered to act as Deputy Speaker. Under more recent Standing Orders the Speaker may call upon the Chairman to take the Chair at any time. Phelips, who, in the opinion of Sir Julius Cæsar, was the most worthy and judicious Speaker

---

[1] *Commons Journals*, Vol. I, p. 152.

MONTACUTE, SOMERSET
Built by Sir Edward Phelips

since Sir John Popham, became Master of the Rolls, and in that capacity occupied the house in Chancery Lane which so many Speakers have inhabited. He opened the indictment of Guy Fawkes, at which the venerable Sir John Popham presided as Lord Chief Justice. Fawkes was executed in Old Palace Yard on 31 January, 1606, and from an old print published at the time some idea can be gathered of its appearance at this date.

The Crewes of Crewe Hall are said, on the authority of Ormerod, to have been a family of established position in Cheshire as early as the thirteenth century, but more discriminating genealogists have preferred to date the fortunes of the family from one John Crewe, a tanner at Nantwich in the sixteenth century. Cases of nepotism may have occurred in connection with the Speaker's office, but to John Crewe of Nantwich belongs the unique honour of having had two sons, Randolph and Thomas, both of whom sat in the Chair of the Commons. Both were bred to the law, Randolph at Lincoln's Inn and Thomas at Gray's. Both took the usual lawyer's road to notoriety by standing for Parliament. Randolph, who bought the estate of Crewe Hall from the heirs of Sir Christopher Hatton in 1608, entered the House of Commons as member for Brackley, Northants, in 1597.[1] On 5 April, 1614, he was chosen Speaker *nemine contradicente*, though there is some doubt as to the constituency he then represented.

The session opened with two separate speeches from

[1] He is called Randal in the official return, but this variation in the spelling of the Christian name has not been uncommon, especially in Cheshire.

the throne, one delivered at Westminster on the opening day, and one, a few days later, in the Banqueting House, Whitehall. The Speaker's reply has not been preserved. Two months later the Houses were dissolved without having passed a single Bill, a precedent in Parliamentary history which earned for this assembly the name of the " Addled Parliament." It is on record that Speaker Crewe's experiences in the Chair " gave him a strong distaste for politics," and well they may have done, for during his tenure of office were heard the first mutterings of the storm which was soon to break over England in the form of Civil War. In 1625 he became Chief Justice of the King's Bench, only to be dismissed a year later by Charles I for refusing to acknowledge the legality of forced loans. Sir Randolph Crewe, after his retirement from public life, lived in Westminster, where, according to Fuller, he was renowned for his hospitality; and dying there in January, 1646, he was buried in a chapel which he built at Barthomley on his Cheshire estate. The present Earl of Crewe is descended from him.

It was some years before James summoned another Parliament, and meanwhile he resorted to the old and discredited system of raising money by means of benevolences, a grievance as old as the days of Richard III, by selling patents for peerages and baronetages, and by the creation of monopolies. Before Crewe's younger brother was preferred to the Chair, Sir Thomas Richardson, the son of a country clergyman in Norfolk, became Speaker in James's third Parliament. In making his formal excuse to the House he " wept outright," an incident which points to his well-known

Given by His Descendent Amabella Baronefs Lucas 1805.

SIR RANDOLPH CREWE
1614
From a painting in the Speaker's House

tenderness of heart. His refusal, when Chief Justice of the Common Pleas, to allow Felton, the assassin of the Duke of Buckingham, to be subjected to torture, marks an epoch in the annals of the criminal law. Richardson was faced in Parliament by the redoubtable Coke, who, after an interval of twenty-seven years, now re-entered the House as member for Liskeard.

Though Richardson's tenure of the Chair was marked by many events of the highest constitutional importance, he does not seem to have been what is called a strong Speaker. The Parliament over which he presided soon showed itself active against the holders of monopolies. It impeached Sir Giles Mompesson, the chief delinquent in this category; it imprisoned a bishop who was implicated in a charge of bribery; it degraded Lord Chancellor Bacon, who was proved to have accepted money corruptly tendered, if without corrupt motive. And when the hostility between King and Commons, which characterised the entire reign, came to a crisis in December, 1621, the House addressed a Petition and Remonstrance to the King recommending that he should declare war against Spain, and that the Prince [1] "may be timely and happily married to one of our religion." James, in return, directed the Commons to forbear from meddling " with anything concerning our government and mysteries of State," warning them, at the same time, that they derived their ancient liberty of freedom of speech from " the grace and permission of his ancestors and himself."

By the dim candlelight of a winter afternoon,[2] the House forthwith resolved that " The Liberties, franchises,

---

[1] Charles I.   [2] 18 December, 1621.

privileges and jurisdictions of Parliament, are the ancient and undoubted birthright and inheritance of the subjects of England; and that the arduous and urgent affairs concerning the King, State, and the defence of the Realm, and of the Church of England, and the making and maintenance of laws, and redress of mischiefs and grievances, which daily happen within this Realm, are proper subjects and matter of counsel and debate in Parliament; and that in the handling and proceeding of those businesses every member of the House hath, and of right ought to have, Freedom of Speech, to propound, treat, reason and bring to conclusion the same; and that the Commons in Parliament have like liberty and freedom to treat of those matters, in such order as in their judgments shall seem fittest; and that every such member of the said House hath like freedom from all Impeachment, Imprisonment, and Molestation (other than by the censure of the House itself), for, or concerning any speaking, reasoning or declaring of any matter or matters, touching the Parliament, or Parliament business: and that, if any of the said members be complained of, and questioned for any thing said or done in Parliament, the same is to be shewed to the King, by the advice and assent of all the Commons assembled in Parliament, before the King give credence to any private information."

On learning of this emphatic pronouncement of its liberties, James dispersed the House by a compulsory adjournment; he sent for the Journal Book and tore the protestation out of it with his own hand.[1] At the same time Coke and Pym were committed to the

---

[1] *The Manuscript Journals of the House of Commons.* Privately printed by the late Sir Reginald Palgrave, Clerk of the House, 1897.

F. Cole, sculpt.

SIR THOMAS RICHARDSON
1620-21
From a drawing in the National Portrait Gallery

Tower. Reflections were cast upon Richardson from time to time for his conduct in the Chair. It was alleged that he curtailed discussion at a moment opportune for the King, and Sir H. Manners declared that "Mr. Speaker is but a servant to the House, not a master, nor a master's mate," while one Sir W. Herbert bade him "sit still." This much-tried man, who witnessed the earliest rise of the Court and country parties, which, in after years, so sharply divided the House, died at his house in Chancery Lane in 1635. He was accorded the honour, seldom bestowed upon a Speaker, of burial in Westminster Abbey. His monument is still to be seen in the south choir aisle,[1] surmounted by a bronze portrait bust by Le Sueur, the sculptor of King Charles I's statue at Charing Cross.

Sir Thomas Crewe, Sir Randolph's younger brother, was Speaker in James's last Parliament, which met in February, 1623–24, and was dissolved, in consequence of the death of the King, in May, 1625. Elsynge declared that Sir Thomas, on presentation for the royal approval, made the best speech, delivered on a similar occasion, since Speaker Nevill's in the sixth year of Henry VIII, that it did not consist of mere verbal praises but that it was, on the contrary, real and fit for the times. Yet it certainly was not free from the extravagant metaphor indulged in by Phelips and most of the previous Speakers, whose addresses to the Crown have been preserved. Sir Thomas, amongst other oratorical gems, likened himself to a lowly shrub planted amongst many cedars of Lebanon. He went on to express the hope that the King, "like Ahasuerus," would extend to him his sceptre of grace "to sustain him

[1] The *Dictionary of National Biography* says wrongly, "north aisle."

in his fainting." After a passing allusion to the " hellish inventions " of Guy Fawkes, he declared, in the most uncompromising Protestant manner, that it was the wish of every loyal subject of the Crown that the " generation of locusts," the Jesuits and Seminary Priests, who were wont to creep in holes and corners, but who now came openly abroad, might, as with an east wind, be blown away into the sea. He added that though the Pope cursed Queen Elizabeth, God blessed her, and that the ark of true religion would ultimately land James in Heaven, when that " hopeful Prince "[1] would sway the sceptre of England, the while his father wore a celestial crown.[2]

It has been well said that from this time forth the history of England was written at the Clerk's table of the House of Commons. Elsynge, Scobell, and Rushworth are the three best-remembered men who filled the office of Clerk or Clerk-Assistant in the seventeenth century, and the historical collections of the last-named are the most valuable record of the doings of the Long Parliament extant. It is sad to think that this zealous public servant spent the closing years of his life in straitened circumstances in the King's Bench prison in Southwark.

The animated debates on the war with Spain (for which the House voted £300,000) ; the impeachment of the Earl of Middlesex for bribery, in which Coke took the lead, whilst the prosecution ultimately devolved upon the Speaker's brother acting as Attorney-General ; the important concession by the Crown whereby Parliament

---

[1] Charles I.

[2] *Journals of the House of Lords*, Vol. III, p. 211. When reappointed in the next reign he made a somewhat similar oration, not forgetting his old enemies the Jesuit locusts.

Given by His Descendent William Ralph Cartwright Esqr. 1805.

SIR THOMAS CREWE
1623-4, 1625
From a painting in the Speaker's House

won the right of appointing its own Commissioners for the disbursement of supply : all these intricate questions were so tactfully handled by the younger Crewe, that he was once more voted to the Chair when Charles I ascended the throne. He now sat for Gatton, in Surrey, a small borough, as notorious in later times as even Old Sarum. Its political history, prior to the passing of the great Reform Bill, excited Lord Rosebery's scathing ridicule in a recent speech in the House of Lords, though he did not suggest that Gatton was corrupt when a Crewe sat for it.

Charles's first Parliament, holding that the refusal of supplies to the Crown was its most potent weapon against the abuses of prerogative, would only grant a beggarly £140,000, by way of subsidy. It was therefore dissolved after a session of less than three months. To Thomas Crewe succeeded Sir Heneage Finch, son of Sir Moyle Finch, of Eastwell, Kent, and member for the City of London.[1] His brief term of office was marked by an increasing boldness on the part of the Commons, as instanced by the impeachment of Buckingham, the King's prime favourite. It was managed by that trio of patriots, Eliot, Pym, and Dudley Digges.[2] Sir John Eliot, writing in 1625, spoke of the Speakership as being then regarded by the general body of members as " an office frequently filled by nullities, men selected for mere Court convenience," nor was the charge altogether an unjust one.

Eliot came into collision with the Chair when Sir John

---

[1] Of which he was also Recorder.

[2] Eliot and Digges were arrested, but their imprisonment was held by the Judicature to be a breach of privilege.

Finch, cousin to the Sir Heneage above mentioned, filled the post in the third Parliament of this reign; the first, by the way, in which Oliver Cromwell, then only twenty-nine years of age, had a seat. Sir John Eliot, desiring to raise a question on the subject of tonnage and poundage, Finch, who was a very nervous man, refused to put it on the ground that the King had commanded the House to adjourn. Eliot then read the remonstrance for himself, and on the Speaker rising to adjourn the debate, he was forced back into the Chair by Denzil Holles and some other members, Holles exclaiming : " That by God's wounds he should sit there till it pleased him to rise." [1] The Speaker then burst into tears, saying : " I will not say I will not, but that I dare not." Straightway the House adopted the substance of Eliot's motion, and shortly afterwards Parliament was dissolved, not to meet again for eleven years.

This was not the first occasion on which tears started to this nervous Speaker's eyes. A royal message of 5 June, 1628, commanding the Commons not to meddle with affairs of State or to asperse the King's ministers, having been read in the House, Eliot rose ostensibly to rebut the implied charge of implicating ministers. The Speaker, apprehending that he intended to make an attack upon the Duke of Buckingham, cried whilst he faltered out : " There is a command laid upon me to interrupt anyone that should go about to lay aspersion on the Ministers of State." Eliot then resumed his seat, and on the next day the Speaker brought down a conciliatory message from the King.

[1] *Parliamentary History*, Vol. II, p. 487.

SIR HENEAGE FINCH
1625-26
From a painting at Guildhall by J. M. Wright

That Finch was the creature of the Crown appears certain when it is remembered that he was mainly responsible for the judgment in the Ship Money case—that monstrous exaction never intended to be spent wholly on ships. On the other hand, he was quite unable to stem the rising tide of popular indignation, which found its adequate expression in the right of free speech so forcibly contended for by Pym, Hampden, and Coke until it became a reality, and not the sham it had been under the Tudors. But there is this much excuse to be made for Finch, that no Speaker before his time had ever been confronted with so many difficulties.

On 7 June, 1628, the very day on which Charles I gave a reluctant assent to that bulwark of English Constitutional liberty—the Petition of Right—a strong Committee of the Commons was appointed to draw up the preamble of the Bill of Supply. It numbered thirty-two members, including an ex-Speaker and a future one in Coke and Glanville, Selden, the most famous jurist in Europe,[1] Pym, Sir John Eliot, and Sir Dudley

---

[1] The "great dictator of learning of the English nation" was the title by which Selden was known, not only at home, but on the Continent. Some of his political opinions have been quoted in recent discussions of the great Constitutional question now agitating the public mind. It will, therefore, not be inappropriate to recall the views which he entertained on the relations of the two Houses.

"There be but two erroneous opinions in the House of Commons: That the Lords sit only for themselves, when the truth is, they sit as well for the Commonwealth. The second error is, that the House of Commons are to begin to give subsidies, yet if the Lords dissent, they can give no money."

In another remarkable passage, dealing with the composition of the hereditary chamber, he said:

"The Lords that are ancient we honour, because we know not whence they come; but the new ones we slight, because we know their beginning." (*Selden's Table Talk*, edited by S. W. Singer, 1847.)

N

Digges. Coke, then in his seventy-seventh year, but in full possession of his remarkable powers, was Chairman, and on the next sitting day he reported the findings of the Committee to the House. The form of words, omitting the assent of the Lords to a money grant, and requiring only their assent to the Bill founded upon such grant to clothe it with the form of law, had been altered three years before and accepted by the Upper House without demur; while in 1626 a Supply Bill, with a similarly worded preamble, was only lost owing to the premature dissolution of Parliament.

In 1628 the popular indignation against the Duke of Buckingham, who, rightly or wrongly, was believed by the Commons to be the primary cause of all the recent strainings of the Royal Prerogative, was at the flood-tide. Coke denounced him by name as " the grievance of grievances," and it was felt that the rights of the representative Chamber in the matter of finance stood in need of more explicit and emphatic assertion. A few days later [1] a free conference between the two Houses was appointed to be held in the Painted Chamber, at which Coke, Glanville, and Hakewil, the latter a legal antiquary deeply versed in the laws and customs of Parliament, were to speak on behalf of the Commons. Unfortunately the names of the Lords' representatives are, contrary to custom, not given in their own journal. On 17 June the conference took place, not in the place first appointed, but in the Star Chamber, and at it the Lords made formal complaint of the wording of the preamble, " Wherein they were excluded, contrary to ancient precedents, *though*

[1] On 13 June.

THE KNIGHTS, CITIZENS AND BURGESSES OF THE COUNTIES, CITIES AND BOROUG
IN PARLIAMENT, HOLDEN AT WESTMINSTER THE 17 OF MARCH, 1627-8, IN TI
(SPEAKER
From a woodcut in the possess.

TOWNES OF ENGLAND AND WALES AND THE BARONIE OF THE PORTS NOW SITTING
THIRD YEAR OF THE RAIGNE OF OUR SOVERAIGNE LORD KING CHARLES, ETC.
R JOHN FINCH)
of Sir Walter Spencer-Stanhope

the last were not so."[1] They intimated their desire to have the name of the Commons struck out of the preamble, requesting the Lower House to show warrant for the insertion, as they, on their part, were prepared to show cause for the omission. Lord Keeper Coventry, whose rôle in life seems to have been, though with indifferent success, to mediate between the King and the popular leaders, had previously been instructed by the Peers to signify at the conference " the great care the Lords had had, all this Parliament, to continue a good correspondency between both Houses, which is best done where nothing is intrenched upon either House ; to show them, that in the front [2] of the Bill of Subsidies, which they lately sent up, the Commons are only named ; whereas in many precedents (but[3] only in the last Parliament) it is ; [4] neither naming the Lords nor yet the Commons ; That the Lords conceived this rather to have happened by some slip, than done of set purpose ; To move them, that the word[5] may be struck out, for as the Commons give their subsidies for themselves and for the representative body of the Kingdom, so the Lords have the disposition of their own."

The Journals of the Commons state expressly that " this course was not liked, as being of a dangerous example, in point of consequence " ; and a further message was delivered to the Peers by Sir Edward Coke,

---

[1] An allusion apparently intended to refer to the alterations which had been made in 1625 and 1626.

[2] Or preamble.

[3] *i.e.* except.

[4] We, Your Majesty's most humble and loyal subjects, in your High Court of Parliament assembled, etc.

[5] " Commons "

the wording of which is so curious as to deserve quotation in full :—

"There is nothing more desired by that [1] House than the good concurrence between the Lords and them, which they esteem an Earthly Paradise. They have entered into consideration of the proposition to omit the words 'The Commons' in the Subsidy Bill, which they find to be a matter of greater consequence than can be suddenly resolved on. But to-morrow morning they will consider of it, and return an answer with all the convenient speed they can."

A dramatic surprise was in store. A deadlock between the two Houses was averted by the Lords passing the Bill as it stood,[2] and as soon as the Commons learnt of it they sent the following magnanimous message to their late opponents :—

"That, after the Conference yesterday touching the amendment of the Subsidy Bill propounded by the Lords, they took the same presently into their consideration, with a full intent to have proceeded therein this morning; but were prevented by a constant report that their Lordships had passed and voted the said Bill of Subsidies. Yet, nevertheless, the Commons have thought good to signify unto their Lordships, that they will always endeavour to continue a good correspondency with their Lordships, knowing well that the good concurrence between the two Houses is the very heartstring of the Commonwealth, and they shall be ever as zealous of their Lordships' Privileges as of their own rights."

Whilst the crisis was still undetermined the Duke of Buckingham had called the attention of the Peers to a

[1] The Commons.
[2] *Journals of the House of Lords*, 17 June, 1628, Vol. III, p. 860.

statement made by a member of the House of Commons,[1] who declared that he[2] had said at his own table : " Tush, it makes no matter what the Commons or Parliament doth ; for, without my leave and authority, they shall not be able to touch the hair of a dog." The Duke asked leave to move that the member in question should be called upon to prove his words, as not only had he never uttered them, but that they were never so much as in his thoughts.[3] The next day he returned to the charge, adding that Mr. Lewkenor had acknowledged having made use of the words attributed to him, though he refused to name his informant.

After the Conference was over, the Duke again appealed to the Peers to be allowed to make the same protest before the Commons as he had made in the House of Lords. Lord Keeper Coventry was instructed to intimate his desire to the Lower House, but he does not seem to have made any such dramatic appearance as his entrance at the Bar would have given rise to.[4] The Duke's unpopularity seems to have been at its summit all through the crisis of June, 1628, and, significantly enough, on the same day that the deadlock between Lords and Commons was averted a protégé of his, Dr. John Lambe, was fatally injured by a mob of London apprentices, and a couplet, illustrating the vindictive feeling which prevailed against his patron, was hawked about the town and passed from mouth to mouth :—

" Let Charles and George do what they can,
    The Duke shall die like Doctor Lambe."

[1] Mr. Lewkenor. [2] The Duke. [3] *Lords Journals*, 18 June, 1628.
[4] There were two members named Lewkenor in the House at this time, Richard, Knight of the Shire for Sussex, and Christopher, member for Midhurst.

As all the world knows, Buckingham fell by an assassin's knife, at Portsmouth, only two months later.

One further fact concerning this memorable dispute between the two Houses must be placed on record. The Speaker, Sir John Finch, was prevented, on the day of the prorogation, from carrying up the Subsidy Bill to the Lords for the Royal Assent, according to ancient custom. He was thus debarred from making a speech to the Throne and alluding to the victory won by the Commons in the matter of finance. To which, the Journal states, " much exception was taken." Finch's last appearance in the House of Commons — he had succeeded Lord Coventry as Lord Keeper — was when he appeared at the Bar in 1640, after being impeached by the Long Parliament. Though he spoke in his own defence, and spoke well, he did not await the conclusion of the indictment, but fled to The Hague, where he died in 1660.[1]

The Speaker of the " Short Parliament " came of a very ancient West of England family, and it is strange that Sir John Glanville's election should have received the royal approbation, for he was known to have been opposed to the Court, and, in a former House, he had prepared a protest against arbitrary dissolution. Possibly during the period of personal government his convictions had undergone modification. Great changes in popular feeling had, indeed, taken place in those eleven years in which Charles had essayed to rule without Constitutional assistance. Hampden had

[1] The first article in his impeachment was his arbitrary conduct in the Chair on the occasion of Sir John Eliot's motion on tonnage and poundage. He is buried in St. Martin's Church, near Canterbury, under a stupendous marble monument.

SIR JOHN GLANVILLE
1640
From a painting at the National Portrait Gallery

become a popular hero through his opposition to ship money ; the abuse of justice by the Court of Star Chamber had sunk deep into the public mind ; Strafford had been recalled from Ireland to give the King counsel in his dire necessity ; and, though Coke and Eliot were dead and Holles was no longer a member, Hampden and Pym remained the indomitable champions of English liberty when Glanville succeeded to the Chair.

His tenure of it was too brief for fame ; but a very singular story of his private life deserves to be rescued from oblivion. His elder brother, Francis, a profligate and a spendthrift, had been cut off with the proverbial shilling by his father, and when the will was read it had such an effect upon the son's mind that he retired from society and became a changed man. One day Sir John, seeing the alteration in his brother's mode of life, invited him to dine at his house, and placing a dish before him, requested him to take off the cover and help himself to the contents. To the surprise of all present, it was found to contain the title deeds of the family estate of Kilworthy, with a formal conveyance from the Speaker to his elder brother. Nor was this the only disinterested action of Glanville's life, for he is said to have reclaimed the celebrated Sir Matthew Hale from an idle and dissolute life to become a great pleader and a greater judge.[1]

When the Long Parliament was about to assemble,

[1] Sir John Glanville's portrait is in the Speaker's collection, and there is another likeness by an unknown artist in the National Portrait Gallery, painted at the age of sixty-two. The ex-Speaker of the Short Parliament was imprisoned in the Tower from 1645 to 1648. Some of his speeches are contained in Rushworth's *Collections*. He was buried at Broad-Hinton, Wilts.

Charles I designed the post of Speaker for Sir Thomas Gardiner, but, as he failed to obtain a seat in the House, William Lenthall, by the merest accident, was chosen in his stead; 504 members being returned to serve at Westminster, of whom more than half had sat in the previous Parliament. The remarkable man who was called to the Chair in November, 1640, was born in 1591, not at Henley-on-Thames as has been generally supposed, but at Hasely in Oxfordshire, of parents whose lineage in that county can be traced to the fifteenth century, when a Lenthall married the heiress of Pypard of Lachford. He received the early part of his education at Thame grammar school under Richard Bourchier, and before he was sixteen years old he was entered at St. Alban Hall, Oxford, was called to the Bar at Lincoln's Inn in 1616, and entered the House of Commons as Member for Woodstock in the last Parliament of James I. He therefore sat for some years in the House with the redoubtable Coke.

Having prospered at the Bar, he bought Besselsleigh, in Berkshire, from the ancient family of Fettyplace, in 1633, a property which is still enjoyed by his descendants. In the course of the next year, he paid the Cavalier Lord Falkland, it is believed under an assumed name, £7000 for Burford Priory, the house with which his name will always be chiefly associated. His wife, Elizabeth Evans, it will be remembered, was a cousin of Lord Falkland. The statement that Burford was acquired for him by the Parliament appears to be untrue. However that may be, he was living in the town for some years before he became the owner of the Priory.

Nearly every modern writer who has treated the sub-

WILLIAM LENTHALL
1640, 1647, 1654, 1659, 1659-60
From a painting in the National Portrait Gallery

ject of Parliamentary history and control has lauded Lenthall to the skies. Yet the opinion of many of his contemporaries was decidedly unfavourable. Clarendon thought him " in all respects very unequal to the work ; and not knowing how to preserve his own dignity, or to restrain the licence and exorbitance of others, his weakness contributed as much to the growing mischiefs as the malice of the principal contrivers."

D'Ewes, who sat under him from 1640 until ejected from the House by Pride's Purge, was suspicious of his honesty, and being himself a recognised authority on questions of Parliamentary procedure and etiquette, he was a vigilant and unsparing critic of his conduct in the Chair, until it was more than hinted that the Member for Sudbury, and not the Speaker, was the right man to settle questions of order, and to compose jarring discords in debate. On one occasion he reminded Lenthall that it was his duty to read to the House a message from the King, which he was about to delegate to the Clerk. Alternately patronising and criticising, D'Ewes would have been a thorn in any Speaker's side, and during the early days of the Long Parliament Lenthall must often have longed to be rid of him.

Sir H. Mildmay was another member who treated him with scant courtesy. He dared to say in his place that the Speaker should come down to the House in good time. On which Lenthall, in a sudden access of passion, threw down a shilling upon the table, this being the customary fine imposed on members who came in late. But if he was not exactly loved in the early days of his career, he was cordially hated by the Cavaliers when he continued to sit at Westminster after the death of the King.

There was, however, one responsible official of the Long Parliament whose personal scruples proved, in the hour of crisis, to be tenderer than those of its presiding officer. This was Henry Elsynge, Clerk of the House from 1640 to 1648, when he voluntarily relinquished the service of the Commons to pass the remainder of his days in grinding poverty, rather than have it said that he even tacitly concurred with Cromwell and the Army in the trial and condemnation of his Sovereign. He appears to have been esteemed by men of all shades of political opinion, and to have consistently maintained the dignity of his office, despite occasional differences of opinion with the irrepressible D'Ewes, whose egregious vanity sometimes brought him into collision with constituted authority. Such was Elsynge's acknowledged ability and discretion that in the turbulent years preceding his withdrawal from Westminster quite as much genuine respect was paid to the impersonal Clerk at the table as to the Speaker invested by the House at large with the traditional authority of the Chair.

Lenthall, a consummate opportunist throughout his career, made the utmost possible use of the tool he found ready to his hand, and, in the early days of his power, he was deeply indebted to Elsynge for guidance and advice, habitually leaning upon him as a prop to support his own inexperience in questions of procedure demanding an immediate decision from the Chair. What he thought of his colleague's unfailing devotion to duty and high character appears in the vindication

Sala Regalis cum Curia Westmonasterij vulgo Westminster hall

WESTMINSTER AS SPEAKER LENTHALL KNEW IT
From Hollar's etching of New Palace Yard

of his own conduct, which he issued at the Restoration, when the changed circumstances of the time compelled him to make tardy confession of his gains and losses in the service of the State.

Almost the only unfavourable critics, in modern times, known to the author are John Forster, who in his *Arrest of the Five Members* calls him "weak and commonplace," and the late Mr. Charles Townsend, whose *Memoirs of the House of Commons* still afford such good reading. But Townsend somewhat overstates the case when he calls Lenthall "a poor creature, the tame instrument of a worse and more vulgar tyranny, the buffeted tool of the Army and the Rump, subdued to sit or go, to remain at home or return to find the doors of St. Stephen's shut or open, according to the will of his masters, the officers, and at the bidding of Cromwell." Rather would we say, with Dr. Gardiner, that, if not a great and heroic man, he knew what his duty was, and defined it in words of singular force and dexterity. Great historical crises have been determined one way or the other, and will be determined hereafter, not so much by men of heroic degree as by men who know what duty is and are prepared to act upon the knowledge. In the case of an office like the Speaker's there can be no posthumous fame without contemporary appreciation. And this, notwithstanding the adverse opinions quoted above, was accorded to the presiding genius of the Long Parliament to an extent unparalleled in the previous history of the Chair. The Corporation of Windsor voted him a gift of wine and a sugar-loaf[1] in the early days of his Speakership, and similar presents were showered upon him from time to time by the various

---

[1] Tighe and Davis, *Annals of Windsor*, 1858, Vol. II, p. 154.

municipalities which espoused the Parliamentary cause. The inscription on his portrait in the National Collection also shows that it was painted expressly to commemorate his action in the Chair at the time of the attempted arrest of the Five Members.

Without any special gifts of oratory, Lenthall, at a time of exceptional difficulty, impressed his personality upon the House by his eminent common sense; and, although his honesty at the time of the breaking off of negotiations with the King has been called in question, there is no room to doubt that by sheer force of character he preserved, during the twenty years in which he was in and out of the Chair, the historic continuity of his office, and this at a time when the monarchy itself suffered an interruption. On the other hand, he was avaricious; obsessed by a desire for the accumulation of wealth; [1] greedy of power and rank; and, towards the close of his career, somewhat unduly impressed with a sense of his own importance. One fact emerges very clearly from his tenure of office: he made rules, with the assistance of Elsynge, for the preservation of order in debate, without which the proceedings of the Long Parliament would have been even more turbulent than they sometimes were.

The quorum of the House of Commons was fixed at its present number on 5 January, 1641, when Lenthall had not been in the Chair more than two months. As late as 1801 an attempt was made to raise the limit to sixty,

---

[1] At one time he held the Mastership of the Rolls worth £3000 a year, the Speakership for which he received £2000, a commissionership of the Great Seal £1500, the Chancellorship of the Duchy of Lancaster, £1500; and he was also Chamberlain of the City of Chester, a lucrative sinecure coveted by many lawyers, before and since Lenthall's day.

but without avail, and at forty it remains to this day.
In the "Short Parliament" Lenthall was one of the
committee on ship money and chairman of the committee on grievances. Mr. Firth, in his admirable Life
in the *Dictionary of National Biography*, states that he
had occupied the Chair, in the absence of the real Speaker,
during one or more debates in the Short Parliament, but
the official Journals[1] show that it was as Chairman of the
Committee of the whole House that he so presided.

Lenthall's first complete session was an index to the
stormy times ahead of him. In one year the House of
Commons passed the Triennial Bill, a measure which it
almost immediately ignored; it impeached Strafford
and Laud; it declared the levying of taxes without
consent to be illegal; it abolished the Star Chamber;
and, after a short recess, it sat for fifteen hours to pass
the Grand Remonstrance.[2] No wonder that the Speaker
complained in pathetic tones to the House of the unusual
length of their sittings. The unaccustomed strain of long
hours in the Chair told upon his strength; he became
irritable and petulant, and after a little more than a year
of office he had serious thoughts of tendering his resignation to the King.

Long sittings in the House itself were not the only
strain upon the Speaker's patience. On a fast day,
piously observed by Parliament in November, 1640,
Dr. Burgess and Master Marshall preached between them
before the unfortunate Commons for the space of seven
hours![3] and there were occasions when the protracted

[1] *Commons Journals*, 23 April, 1640, Vol. II, p. 9.
[2] 22 November, 1641.
[3] *Diurnal Occurrences of the Great and Happy Parliament*, 1641,
p. 4.

debates prevented the Speaker from going home to dinner.

Lenthall's personal expenditure at this time was heavy, as he entertained lavishly, amongst his guests being many courtiers as well as members of the Lower House.[1] Early in his career he lived in a house on the site of the Westminster Fire Office in King Street, Covent Garden ; but later on he took Goring House, on the site of Buckingham Palace, then a perfect *rus in urbe*, and it was there that most of his entertaining was done. Sir John Lenthall, his son, also lived in the same house and seems to have owned the freehold at one time.

On 3 January, 1641–42, that misguided monarch Charles I desired to impeach the five most prominent opponents of his government in the House of Commons,[2] and he sent a message, delivered at the Bar of the House to the Speaker, requiring from him the five members, that they might be arrested, in His Majesty's name, on a charge of high treason. Lenthall, by command of the House, enjoined them to give attendance in the House *de die in diem*. On the next day the House met early in the morning, and considered in committee the charges which the King had brought against five of its number. Notice was taken of the muster of armed men at Whitehall and in the immediate neighbourhood of the Houses of Parliament. At noon the sitting was suspended " for an hour's space," but before it had ended the King's design to seize the accused was unfolded.

---

[1] On 9 April, 1642, the House voted Lenthall a sum of £6000 in consideration of his long and strict attendance to duty.

[2] Denzil Holles, Haselrig, Pym, Hampden, and Strode.

Lenthall returned to the Chair between one and two o'clock, when the House resumed the discussion on the gathering of armed men in the precincts of Westminster. The five members were then in their places, uncertain whether to remain or to depart, when news was brought in hot haste to the Speaker by a Mr. Fiennes to the effect that the King was nearing Westminster Hall at the head of a large company of guards. Leave was given to the accused to withdraw, but they had barely quitted the House and reached the boats which lay on the river at Westminster Stairs, when a loud knock on the door announced the entrance of the only King of England who has ever penetrated into a House of Commons in session.

According to Rushworth, the Clerk-Assistant, who was, of course, an eye-witness of all the events of that memorable day : " His Majesty entered the House, and as he passed up towards the Chair, he cast his eye on the right hand near the Bar of the House, where Mr. Pym used to sit ; but His Majesty not seeing him there (knowing him well) went up to the Chair, and said, ' By your leave, Mr. Speaker, I must borrow your Chair a little ' ; whereupon the Speaker came out of the Chair, and His Majesty stepped into it. After he had stood in the Chair awhile, casting his eye upon the members as they stood up uncovered, but could not discern any of the five members to be there—nor, indeed, were they easy to be discerned (had they been there) among so many bare faces all standing up together,

"Then His Majesty made this speech :—

" ' Gentlemen,

" ' I am sorry for this occasion of coming unto you. Yesterday I sent a Serjeant-at-arms upon a very important occasion, to apprehend some that by my command were accused of High Treason ; whereunto I did expect obedience, and not a message. And I must declare unto you here, that albeit no king that ever was in England, shall be more careful of your privileges, to maintain them to the utmost of his power, than I shall be, yet you must know that in cases of treason, no person hath a privilege. And therefore I am come to know if any of these persons that were accused are here.'

"Then, casting his eyes upon all the members in the House, he said, 'I do not see any of them; I think I should know them.'

"'For I must tell you, gentlemen, that so long as these persons that I have accused (for no slight crime, but for treason) are here, I cannot expect that this House will be in the right way that I do heartily wish it. Therefore I am come to tell you, that I must have them, wheresoever I find them.'

"Then His Majesty said, 'Is Mr. Pym here?' To which nobody gave answer. 'Well, since I see all my birds are flown, I do expect from you, that you shall send them unto me, as soon as they return hither. But I assure you, on the word of a king, I never did intend any force, but shall proceed against them in a legal and fair way, for I never meant any other.

"'And now since I see I cannot do what I came for, I think this no unfit occasion to repeat what I have said formerly, That whatsoever I have done in favour, and to the good of my subjects, I do mean to maintain it.

"'I will trouble you no more, but tell you I do expect as soon as they come to the House, you will send them to me ; otherwise I must take my own course to find them.'"

When the King was looking about the House, the Speaker standing below by the Chair, His Majesty asked

JOHN RUSHWORTH, CLERK ASSISTANT OF THE HOUSE OF COMMONS
1640
From a painting at the Speaker's House

him whether any of these persons were in the House ? whether he saw any of them ? and where they were ? To which the Speaker, falling on his knees, thus answered :—

"May it please your Majesty,

"I have neither eyes to see, nor tongue to speak in this place, but as the House is pleased to direct me, whose servant I am here ; and I humbly beg Your Majesty's pardon, that I cannot give any other answer than this, to what Your Majesty is pleased to demand of me."

The King, having concluded his speech, went out of the House, which by this time was in great disorder, and many cried out, so that he might hear, " Privilege ! Privilege ! " Fortunately for posterity, Rushworth, on this occasion, disregarded the condition of his appointment on 25 April, 1640, namely : " That he shall not take any notes here without the precedent directions and command of this House, but only of the orders and reports made to this House." On the contrary, whilst the hand of Elsynge, his official superior, was stayed by doubt, Rushworth took down the King's words in shorthand, and also the memorable reply which he received from Lenthall. The accuracy of his notes is unquestionable, as the King, baffled and perplexed as he was when standing on the step of the Speaker's chair, had noticed Rushworth's pen at work and sent for the report of the words so noted down, returning it to him with corrections. The incidents of this single day inspired John Forster, the biographer of Dickens, with material for an entire volume. Soon after this unique incident in the history of the House of Commons Charles left Whitehall, never to return to it till he came there to die ; and

o

on the final disruption between Crown and Parliament the only course which remained was the arbitrament of arms.

In June, 1642, the Speaker gave a horse and fifty pounds in money in defence of the Parliament, a sufficient indication of the trend of his political convictions, and in direct contrast to the fulsome language in which he had addressed the Throne at the conclusion of the session of 1641. In that speech, reported in full in the Journals of the House of Lords for 2 December, he said :—

" Give me leave here, most gracious Sovereign, to sum up the sense of eleven months' observation, without intermission (scarce) of a day, nay an hour in that day, to the hazard of life and fortune, and to reduce all into this conclusion : The endeavours of your Commons assembled, guided by your pious and religious example, is to preserve Religion in its purity, without mixture or composition, against these subtle invaders ; and, with our lives and fortunes, to establish these Thrones to your sacred person, and those beams of Majesty your Royal progeny, against treason and rebellion."

Lenthall probably participated in the spoliation of Whitehall Palace, and he secured for his own collection a portrait of the King, by Vandyck,[1] and a group, in the manner of Holbein, of Sir Thomas More and his family. This latter picture hung at Burford Priory for many years, and after being sold in 1833, it reappeared at Christie's during the present year,[2] when it fetched 950 guineas at auction.

Some of the Speaker's biographers have assumed, quite erroneously, that he secured for the gallery at

[1] Sometimes stated, however, to have been a gift to the Speaker from the Sovereign.
[2] 1910.

Burford some of the pictures removed from Hampton Court at this period. In making this statement they were probably unaware that Lenthall owned a large landed property in Herefordshire, also called Hampton Court, which had been in the possession of his family since the reign of Henry IV. Sir Roland Lenthall, Master of the Robes to that sovereign, and who fought at Agincourt, had licence to embattle his manor-house and to impark a thousand acres, and from his brother Walter, whose will was dated in 1421, the Speaker was seventh in direct descent. A curious portrait, painted on panel, presented by Henry IV to Sir Roland, is still preserved at Besselsleigh, together with the bulk of the pictures from Burford, an interesting collection of Stuart relics, including a glove of Charles I, the Speaker's walking-stick, a portrait group of himself and his family by Dobson, and a great number of rare Civil War tracts and pamphlets. The canopy of the Chair which Lenthall filled with such distinction was presented by him to Radley Church, near his Berkshire estate, at the Restoration. Though black with age, it is still in good preservation, and is in all probability the oldest piece of Parliamentary furniture in existence.

Lenthall continued to preside over the House until 26 July, 1647, when, the Army and the Parliament having quarrelled, both Lords and Commons and the City were placed at the mercy of the military party, which had, by that time, become a highly organised political association. The Speaker, acting on a hint conveyed to him by Rushworth, abandoned his post and left London, fearing the violence of the mob. On the same day the Common Council appeared at Westminster and compelled the two Houses by threats to rescind their late votes, Cromwell and the army being the absolute masters of the situation.

" Several members having been desired by the House to repair to the Speaker's house,[1] reported that Mr. Speaker was not to be heard of, that he had not lodged at his house that night, but was gone out of town yesterday morning."[2]

On 6 August the truants returned with the army for escort, and Lenthall was back in the Chair he had so recently deserted. An ordinance annulling all orders " made or pretended to be made " in his absence was promptly passed, and Pride's Purge, the real object of which was to exclude the Presbyterians from the House as being too favourable to the King, took place on December, 1648, apparently without articulate protest from the Speaker. It has often been stated by unauthoritative writers that in the previous August Lenthall gave his casting vote in favour of breaking off negotiations with the King in the Isle of Wight on the basis of the Hampton Court proposals. Neither Dr. Gardiner, in his exhaustive *History of the Civil War*, nor Professor Firth, in the *Dictionary of National Biography*, makes any allusion to this supposed discreditable incident in his career ; and the present writer was at first disposed to regard both debate and division as the phantom of some partisan brain. However, on searching the official Journal for the year in question, he found that on 28 July—not in the month of August—the Speaker did give a casting vote, but only on a minor and immaterial issue

[1] Goring House, in Pimlico, now Buckingham Palace.
[2] *Commons Journals*, 29 July, 1647.

connected with a more important decision of the House. On the question being put: "That a Treaty be had in the Isle of Wight with the King in person, by a Committee appointed by both Houses upon all the propositions presented to him at Hampton Court, for the taking away of Wards and Liveries, and for settling of a safe and well-grounded Peace," a member, unnamed, moved that the words "and not elsewhere" be added after the words "Isle of Wight" to the question already proposed from the Chair. On a division being taken, fifty-seven were found to have voted for the inclusion of those words, and fifty-six against. A Mr. Askew, who was in the Gallery at the time, and who withdrew into the Committee Chamber without having declared upon which side he wished his vote to be recorded, was ordered by the Speaker to make his choice, and having given his vote with the Yeas,[1] the numbers became equal, fifty-seven on either side. The Speaker then gave his casting vote, but only against the addition of the words "and not elsewhere"; and on the Main Question being put, it was unanimously resolved "that a Treaty be concluded," etc. etc., in the terms of the original motion.[2]

Whilst Lenthall must therefore be acquitted of the charge of having influenced the decision of the House at a critical moment in the King's fortunes, he cannot be wholly exonerated from a suspicion of double dealing at this period in the struggle between the Crown and the Parliament, as there is evidence of his having been engaged in secret correspondence with the Prince of Wales at the very moment that the question of resuming nego-

[1] *Sic* in the original Journal, but the sense requires the substitution of the word "Noes" for "Yeas."

[2] *Commons Journals*, Vol. V, p. 650.

tiations with his royal father was hanging in the balance. Manning, though he may be presumed to have consulted the Journals of the House when he wrote his book on the lives of the Speakers, gives an inaccurate version of the facts related above, and treats Lenthall's vote as if it had turned the scales in favour of the King, which, it will be seen, it did not.

It was, however, Lenthall's casting vote which saved the life of Lord Goring; [1] and the humanity and courage which he displayed in incurring the displeasure of the more powerful party, which was in favour of sending Norwich to the scaffold, probably induced him, on his deathbed, to issue a public apology for his attitude at the King's trial. After Goring's reprieve the Speaker was invited to a banquet by the Lord Mayor, who resigned to him the civic sword, an honour usually paid to Royalty alone.

After the establishment of the Commonwealth the nation was not truly represented at Westminster, and the rift between the Army and the Parliament broadened in consequence. A Bill was brought in, with Cromwell's approval, to fix a time for the dissolution of the existing House, as many of his adherents were beginning to chafe under the uncontrolled rule of a single chamber. During the Dutch war the Army became still more disaffected, until it was rumoured that Cromwell was meditating the restoration of monarchical government under another guise. "What if a man should take upon himself to be King!" he said to Whitelocke, realising, as he did, that the rivalry between the Army and the Parliament could not be indefinitely prolonged without grave danger to the State.

[1] Afterwards Earl of Norwich.

Continuous Parliamentary government is, in all essentials, antagonistic to the supremacy of an army, and this was the condition which Cromwell had to take seriously into account when, in 1653, he determined to get rid of the existing House of Commons, lest the Army, which had made him what he was, should instal Lambert, the second man in England and the darling of the soldiery, in his place. After he had addressed a meeting of officers at the Cockpit, in the month of April, urging the reform of the realm, but not with the existing Parliament, news was brought to him at Whitehall that the House was disposed to bring its existence to a close. The rumour proved to be untrue, for the House was busily engaged in passing a Bill designed to perpetuate its authority. Once his mind was made up Cromwell acted at once. He marched a file of musketeers down to the House, and stationed them at the very spot where Charles I's guard had remained stationed on the occasion of the attempted arrest of the five members. This time they filed through the doorway, Cromwell shouting to the House that he would put an end to "their prating." The Speaker was pulled out of the Chair, the "bauble" mace was taken away, the members were dispersed by force, and Cromwell, with the keys in his pocket, returned to Whitehall. "Make way for honester men!" was the cry which rang in Lenthall's ears as he was helped out of the chair.

Scobell, the Clerk of the House, siding with the victor, put the finishing touch to the work of the Lord General by entering on the Journal page: "Wednesday, 20th April, 1653. This day his Excellency the Lord General dissolved this Parliament." He made a false entry in order to curry favour with Cromwell, well knowing that the only authority which could effect a dissolution of the House of Commons was the Crown. Though Cromwell could and did disperse the House, he could not dissolve it.

With the expulsion of the Long Parliament fell Lenthall, for a time, for he was not a member of the Barebones or Little Parliament which elected Francis Rous as its Speaker. This assembly, " the Reign of the Saints," [1] consisted of 140 nominees of Cromwell, which, after it had served the purpose of its masters by preparing the Instrument of Government, and paving the way for Oliver's assumption of the title of Protector, was cajoled by its Speaker into summary abdication.

In the first Parliament of Oliver, Protector, summoned in September, 1654, the first name put forward was that of the old Speaker. " Something was said to excuse him, by reason of his former services, and something objected as if he had served so long, that he had been outworn " ; [2] but in the end his re-election to the Chair was unanimous, " in regard of his great experience and knowledge of the orders of the House and his dexterity in the guidance of it." This Parliament came to an end on 22 January, 1654–55 ; but in the next, the second Parliament of the Protectorate, he was not re-elected to the Chair.

Lenthall now hankered after a writ of summons to Cromwell's House of Lords, and he complained that he, who had been for some years the first man of the nation, was denied to be a member of either House of Parliament ;

---

[1] *Oliver Cromwell*, by John Morley, 1900, p. 358.
[2] Burton's Diary.

for he was held to be incapable of sitting in the House of Commons by his place as Master of the Rolls, whereby he was obliged to attend merely as an assistant in the other. Cromwell eventually sent him a writ, and in the caricature of the Upper House, which met in January, 1658, he took his place, in company with Fleetwood, Monk, and Pride. Hazelrig, whom Cromwell had designed for the same dignity, refused to be promoted, and became the recognised leader of the Commons, and, after Cromwell's death, one of the most powerful men in England.

On the fall of Richard Cromwell the Army desired to restore the Long Parliament, and a deputation waited on Lenthall to urge him to return to his seat. After many excuses,[1] he consented to preside over the forty-two members of the Rump, and on 7 May, 1659, he proceeded once more to St. Stephen's Chapel with the mace in front of him. His position was now greatly increased in dignity, even commissions in the army were not valid until countersigned by him, and no Speaker before him was invested with such far-reaching authority.

> " Cut out more work than can be done
> In Pluto's year but finish none,
> Unless it be the bulls of Lenthall,
> That always pass'd for fundamental."[2]

Once more the attenuated assembly was to be violently dispersed. On 13 December Lambert drew up his forces in Westminster, obstructing all passages to the House both by land and water, setting guards at all the doors, and interrupting the members from coming to take their seats. When the Speaker appeared in his

[1] Lenthall had previously declared that he was not altogether satisfied that the death of the King had not put an end to the Parliament.
[2] Butler's *Hudibras*, and an obvious allusion to the " Rump."

coach the horses were turned back. " Do you not know me ? " he said. " If you had been with us at Winnington Bridge, we should have known you," replied the soldiers.[1] Lenthall was unceremoniously conducted to his own house, the mace was taken from him by Lambert, and the Army recovered supreme authority.

On Christmas Eve, 1659, a new revolution took place. The soldiery assembled in Lincoln's Inn Fields and resolved to restore the Parliament. They halted in Chancery Lane at the Speaker's door, for Lenthall was in residence at the Rolls House, and there they hailed him as their general and the father of their country. Two days later he was again in the Chair, and the remnants of the Long Parliament were once more restored. Pepys noted in his diary that the Speaker hesitated to sign the writs for the choice of new members in the place of the excluded, but on Monk declaring for a free Parliament in February, 1659–60, the Restoration was in sight. Military and Parliamentary rule had alike become distasteful and obnoxious to the people, and the nation at large was prepared to welcome the restoration of the Monarchy.

Lenthall, having decided to throw in his lot with Monk, declared himself to be devotedly attached to the monarchical principle, and he told a personal friend, who was present at his deathbed,[2] that Monk was able to assure Charles II that, had it not been for his secret concurrence and assistance, the Restoration could never have been brought about.

[1] Sir George Booth headed a rising in Cheshire for Charles II. Lambert marched against him and defeated him at Winnington (not " Warrington," as the *Dictionary of National Biography* has it) Bridge.

[2] Dr. Dickenson, a physician in St. Martin's Lane and a Fellow of Merton.

Lenthall was a candidate for the University of Oxford in the Convention Parliament, but, in spite of Monk's influence being cast in his favour, he was not elected, nor was he able to retain the Mastership of the Rolls at the Restoration. He was excepted from the Act of Indemnity, but, possibly on account of his having lent Charles II £3000, a sum which has never been repaid to this day, he subsequently obtained the King's pardon.[1]

His son, Sir John Lenthall, was returned for Abingdon in 1660, but his connection with Parliament on this occasion was brief. Having made an incautious speech on the Indemnity Bill, in which he said " that he that drew his sword against the King committed as high an offence as he that cut off the King's head," he was severely reprimanded at the bar by the new Speaker, Sir Harbottle Grimston, who had no great liking for the presiding genius of the Long Parliament, and, perhaps, rather welcomed the opportunity of administering a reproof to his offspring. Two days later he was expelled the House, soon after to be rewarded by the King with the Governorship of Windsor Castle.

Lenthall seems to have thought it advisable to publish a pamphlet, copies of which are now extremely rare, purporting to give a full and accurate account of his profits and gains in the public service from 1648 to 1660, but deliberately excluding all mention of sums received before the first-mentioned date. In it he declared that before he became Speaker he had an assured income of £2500 from his practice at the Bar, that when he succeeded Sir Charles Cæsar as Master of the Rolls the

[1] The original document with the royal seal and signature is still preserved by the family at Besselsleigh.

emoluments of the office were less than in the time of his predecessor by £2200, a sum equivalent to what he received in respect of private Bills and Pardons. He pointed out that as the Clerks of the House were also paid by fees these could not have been excessive, since one of the ablest men who ever executed that office [1] died in such poor circumstances that he was buried at the expense of his friends. He asserted that the Chancellorship of the Duchy of Lancaster brought him "only labour for his pains," that he was prepared to state on oath that from 1648 he never received anything from the Chair by way of fee or reward; and that, having settled the bulk of his estate on his son, he estimated his total annual income in 1660 at £800, and his personal property (including, oddly enough, his debts) at no more than £2000. The short remainder of Lenthall's life was passed in retirement at his Oxfordshire home.

In a remote situation in a fold of the Cotswold hills, in the valley of the little river Windrush, and surrounded by the most delightful sylvan scenery, Burford Priory exhibits many interesting features of the domestic architecture of the sixteenth, seventeenth, and eighteenth centuries. After years of wanton neglect, which eventually led to its becoming a melancholy ruin—the home of bats and owls—it has recently been thoroughly and lovingly repaired, rather than *restored*, under the capable supervision of its present owner, Colonel de Sales La Terriere, acting as his own architect.

In 1808 the whole of the north wing was pulled down, together with half of the eastern front. The

[1] Elsynge.

BURFORD PRIORY, FORMERLY THE RESIDENCE OF SPEAKER LENTHALL, AS RESTORED IN 1908-9

south wing, which was built by the Speaker—as was the existing but disused chapel connected with the main building by an external gallery—fell into decay and was demolished in order to provide material for new farm buildings within the last fifty or sixty years. Neither of the wings so ruthlessly destroyed has been rebuilt, but the ballroom, or great chamber, on the first floor, with a beautiful plaster ceiling and a chimney-piece enriched with the armorial bearings of the Lenthalls, presents much the same appearance as it must have done when the Speaker of the Long Parliament hung the pictorial spoils of Whitehall on its lofty walls.

An even more interesting feature of the Priory, as it stands to-day, is the rediscovery of some of the original pointed arches of the thirteenth-century religious house. These, which were found embedded in the interior walls during the repairs undertaken during the last two years, appear to have been deliberately concealed from view in the time of Henry VIII by the then owners, the Harmans, whose heraldic supporters, with the Lenthall coat of arms between them, are still to be seen over the entrance door. These arches, the very existence of which must have been quite unknown to the Speaker, have been carefully re-erected within a few feet of where they were found, and constitute, with their fine curves and time-worn edges, an enduring link between the monastic building and the Tudor dwelling-house. The stone fire-place, now in the hall, though not occupying its original site, may date from an even earlier period than the ownership of the Harmans.

Since its conversion from ecclesiastical to lay uses Burford has known many owners, most of them persons of distinction in their day, and nearly all of whom have left their mark upon the old building. After the Harmans it came into the possession of the Duchess of Somerset, but, having passed to the Crown, Queen Elizabeth sold it to Sir John Fortescue, Chancellor of the Exchequer in 1589, who, in his turn, parted with it to Sir Lawrence Tanfield, Chief Baron of the Exchequer in 1625. He rebuilt the greater part of the house in the reign of James I, and Lucius Cary, Lord Falkland, Lenthall's immediate predecessor here, was his grandson.

King James and Anne of Denmark stayed with the Tanfields at the Priory in 1603 ; Charles I refreshed himself and his troops at the Speaker's in 1644 on his way from Oxford to Bourton-on-the-Water ; Charles II dined here in 1681 with Sir John Lenthall,[1] and attended the races held on the neighbouring downs, the King being received by the Mayor and Corporation of Burford on the occasion. These time-honoured races, which gave birth to the Bibury Club of after days, were held on an upland course between Burford and Bibury for 150 years before their removal, first to Danebury, near Stockbridge, and, more recently, to Salisbury. Nell Gwynne was also an occasional visitor to the Priory in its roystering days, and it will be recollected that one of the minor titles of her son, the Duke of St. Albans, was Lord Burford.

William III slept at the Priory in 1695, when it was in the occupation of the fifth Earl of Abercorn, who married the widow of William Lenthall, only daughter

[1] The Speaker's son and a well-known profligate at the Court of Whitehall.

and heiress of James Hamilton, Lord Paisley, by his wife Catherine, daughter of a brother of the Speaker. Lord Abercorn seems to have carried on the dissipated traditions of the Priory in the days of Charles II, for he was tried at Oxford in 1697 for the murder of John Prior of Burford, his wife's steward. It is only fair to add that he was acquitted of the capital charge. Incidentally, justice was appeased by the hanging of a gardener in his stead. Numerous alterations were made to the house at the beginning of the nineteenth century, since which its history has been one of sordid disfigurement at the hands of its responsible owners until it was saved from utter ruin and destruction by Colonel La Terriere in 1908.

When Lenthall was nearing his end his conscience so troubled him that he sent to Witney to ask Dr. Ralph Brideoak, afterwards Bishop of Chichester, to come over to Burford and hear his dying confession and to absolve him from his sins. It was then that he apologised for his share in the trial and execution of the King; and though it is usually unsafe to attach much importance to deathbed confessions, admirers of the independence which he displayed earlier in his Parliamentary career can appreciate the remorse which filled his soul and induced him to make such reparation as he could when at the point of death.

Dr. Brideoak, having entreated the dying man to relieve his conscience by a full confession, invited him to say to what extent he considered that his public career had transgressed the teaching of the Ten Commandments. Laying stress upon the fact that disobedience, rebellion, and schism were the greatest

sins against the fifth of these precepts, Lenthall replied :
" Yes, sir, there is my trouble, my disobedience, not
against my natural parents, but against the Pater Patriæ,
our deceased Sovereign. I confess, with Saul, I held their
clothes whilst they murdered him ; but herein I was not
so criminal as Saul was ; for God, Thou knowest ! I never
consented to his death ; I ever prayed and endeavoured
what I could against it ; but I did too much. Almighty
God, forgive me ! "

" I then desired him to deal freely and openly on
that business, and if he knew any of those villains that
plotted or contrived that horrid murder, who were not
yet detected, now to discover them. He answered that
' he was a stranger to that business ; his soul never
entered into that secret, but what concerns myself I
will confess freely. Three things are especially laid to
my charge, wherein, indeed, I am too guilty : that I
went from the Parliament to the Army ; that I proposed
the bloody question for trying the King ; and that I
sat after the King's death. To the first I may give this
answer, that Cromwell and his agents deceived a wiser
man than myself, that excellent King, and they might
deceive me also, and so they did. I knew the Presbyterians would never restore the King to his just rights ;
those men swore they would. For the second no excuse
can be made, but I have the King's pardon, and I hope
Almighty God will show me His mercy also. Yet, sir,'
said he, ' even then, when I put the question, I hoped
the very putting the question would have cleared him,
because I believed four for one were against it ; but they
deceived me also. To the third I make this candid confession, that it was my own baseness and cowardice and

HENRY PELHAM
1647
From a painting in the possession of the Earl of Yarborough

unworthy fear to submit my life and estate to the mercy of those men that murdered the King, that hurried me on, against my own conscience, to act with them, yet then I thought also I might do some good and hinder some ill. Something I did for the Church and Universities, something for the King, when I broke the Oath of Abjuration, as Sir O. B. and yourself know ; something, also, too for his return, as my lord G., Mr. J. T., and yourself know. But the ill I did overweighed the little good I would have done. God forgive me for this also.'" Brideoak then allowed him the absolution of the Church, and Lenthall received the Sacrament the next day. Having repeated the substance of his confession to Dr. Dickenson, of Merton College, who was at Burford at the time, he spent the few remaining hours of his life in devotion and penitential meditation.[1] In his will he humbled himself to the dust, and ordered that no monument should be raised to his memory other than a plain stone with the legend "Vermis sum." The original terms of the will are worth quoting : " As to my body and burial I do leave it to the disposition and discretion of my executors hereafter named. But with this special charge : That it be done as privately as may be without any pomp or state, acknowledging myself to be unworthy of the least outward regard of this world, and unworthy of any remembrance, that have been so great a sinner. And I do further charge and desire that no monument be made for me, but at the utmost a plain stone with this superscription only :

[1] This deathbed repentance and confession was twice printed in 1662, and reissued forty years later as an appendix to the *Memoirs of the Two Last Years of the Reign of King Charles I*, by Sir Thomas Herbert and others.

P

' Vermis sum.' " The inscription was, however, placed on his coffin plate, as was discovered when the vault in which he was buried was opened to allow of another interment. There is a portrait of Lenthall, attributed to Vandyck, in the Speaker's House, but it is more probably the work of Henry Peart, one of his many pupils. Rushworth, whose name will always be associated with Lenthall, by reason of his action on the attempted arrest of the five members, is also commemorated in the Speaker's Portrait Gallery.

Some mention should be made of the temporary Cromwellian Speakers, eight in number, who sat in the Chair of the Commons between the date of Lenthall's first leaving it in 1647 and the final dissolution of the Long Parliament. Henry Pelham, of Belvoir, Lincolnshire, though not mentioned by Manning, was chosen by the Presbyterian section of the House by general approbation on 30 July, 1647, on Lenthall's joining the Army, and not long after Charles was taken prisoner.[1] The member for Grantham (who sat for the same constituency in the Short Parliament of 1640, and earlier for Great Grimsby) was conducted to the Chair by Sir Anthony Irby and Mr. Richard Lee, and there he remained until replaced by Lenthall in the month of August, when the Army and Cromwell had become the real masters of the situation. As one of the leading Presbyterians, he was secluded and imprisoned when Pride's Purge took place in 1648, but was liberated six days later.

In the " Barebones," or Little Parliament, the Chair

---

[1] He was the third son of Sir William Pelham, of Brocklesby, by Anne, daughter of Charles, second Lord Willoughby of Parham.

FRANCIS ROUS
1653
From a print

was filled by the Rev. Francis Rous, a Cornish gentleman of good family and education. His career was a most singular one, even in an age of unexpected happenings. An ordinance passed by the Lords on 10 February, 1643–44, deprived Richard Steward, the Provost of Eton, of his post and appointed Rous in his stead "for the term of his natural life." He contrived to get Eton exempted from the " Self-Denying Ordinance," in order that he might retain his emoluments, and it was probably owing to Rous's exertions that the College was also exempted from the sale of the estates of religious corporations. The Provost was rewarded for his subservience in the Chair by a writ of summons to Cromwell's short-lived House of Lords. He was buried in Lupton's Chapel at Eton, and his portrait still hangs in the Provost's Lodge.

Sir Thomas Widdrington, of an old Northumbrian family, many of whose members were Cavaliers, filled the Chair in Oliver's second Parliament, from 17 September, 1656, till it was dissolved on 4 February, 1657–58. He then became Chief Baron of the Exchequer. He was brother-in-law to Fairfax, and sat in the Commons Chair when Cromwell declined the crown. At the Restoration Widdrington was deprived of all his offices. Pepys alludes to him as " My Lord Widdrington going to seal the Patents for the Judges in January, 1659–60," he having been a Commissioner of the Great Seal on three separate occasions. Such evidence as exists as to his demeanour in the Chair shows him to have been anything but a strong Speaker, but his incompetence was perhaps partly due to his habitual ill-health. On 8 January, 1657, the adjournment of the House for a week was agreed to by reason of his indisposition. On the 12th the Speaker was brought in a sedan chair to the lobby door, and with much ado he was hoisted into the Chair, but "looked most piteously." Being asked to deal plainly with the House, he was invited to declare the cause of his sufferings. "If you please to go on," was his meek answer, "I shall sit till Twelve o'clock." But his intentions were obviously beyond his strength, and the House again adjourned for a week.

In 1657 Cromwell was an inexorable master, and, as Thurloe observes, he required "too much to have been expected" of Parliament. The House confirmed more than a hundred Bills and Ordinances in one day, nothing being read but the titles. From 24 to 30 April members were kept in attendance from eight in the morning till nine o'clock at night, and the strain of sitting dinnerless in the Chair told upon Speaker Widdrington's health. On a division, in which the numbers were equal, he rose and said, "I am a Yea, a No I should say." Amid much ill-bred laughter another member claimed that he too had been mistaken in giving his vote; but it was determined that, while some latitude might be extended to a weary Speaker, other members were not at liberty to recall their votes. Later in the same sitting Speaker Widdrington blundered in putting a question to the House for its decision, and, when the mistake was challenged, he appeared to be quite at a loss to explain his meaning. The House thereupon "fell into great confusion." During Widdrington's temporary absence from indisposition, that great lawyer, Bulstrode Whitelocke, well known from his *Memorials of English Affairs*, filled the

SIR THOMAS WIDDRINGTON
1656
From a drawing in the National Portrait Gallery

BULSTRODE WHITELOCK
1656-7
From a painting in the National Portrait Gallery

Chair for a short time.[1] When a proposal came before the House that lawyers should be precluded from practising their profession if elected to Parliament, he used the following words :—

" With respect to the proposal for compelling lawyers to suspend their practice while they sit in Parliament, I only insist that in the Act for that purpose it be provided that merchants should forbear their trading, physicians from visiting their patients, and country gentlemen from selling their corn or wool while they are members of this House."

In Richard Cromwell's only Parliament Chaloner Chute, of the Vyne (a fine property which he bought in 1653 from the sixth Lord Sandys), " a worthy gentleman of the long robe," was Speaker. He resigned from ill-health on 9 March, and died on 14 April. He had a great reputation as an advocate, and amongst other eminent men whom he defended was Archbishop Laud. Sir Lislebone Long, " by general consent of the House," was chosen in his stead ; but on 14 March he too informed the House that he was too unwell to sit, and within forty-eight hours of Chute he died. Thomas Bampfylde (M.P. Exeter) succeeded Long on 16 March, 1658–59, after one Mr. Reynell (M.P. Ashburton) had been proposed. Bampfylde was, however, preferred as being " a person of greater experience and of approved learning and gravity." From his nephew, Sir Coplestone Bampfylde, the present Lord Poltimore is descended. This Speaker's tenure of office was interrupted by the Committee of Safety. The last of Lenthall's many substitutes was

[1] He is not mentioned by Manning, but the fact of his having been Speaker is established by reference to the *Commons Journals*, Vol. VII, p. 482.

William Say, or Saye,[1] a Bencher of the Middle Temple,
and one of the Regicides, who sat in the Chair for a
few days in January, 1659–60, during Lenthall's temporary absence from indisposition. He was a member of
the Long Parliament from 1647. At the Restoration his
name was exempted from the Act of Indemnity, but he
contrived to make his escape to the Continent.

It is a curious fact that of these Cromwellian Speakers
Pelham, Rous, and Bampfylde were members of old
knightly families boasting pedigrees which satisfied that
most exclusive of genealogists, Mr. E. P. Shirley, who included their names in his *Noble and Gentle Men of England*.
Lenthall, Widdrington, Chute, and Long were all men
of good family. Whitelocke, on his mother's side, was
descended from the very ancient Buckinghamshire house
of Bulstrode of Hedgerley. Even the Regicide Speaker
could claim kinship with the Sir John Say who filled the
same office in 1449, so that in the darkest days of the
Commonwealth the House was jealous of the status and
origin of its presiding officer.

At an age somewhat older than that of most holders
of the office, Sir Harbottle Grimston was unanimously
elected Speaker at the Restoration, on the motion of Mr.
William Pierpont. Early in life he had been a strong
Presbyterian, and prominent amongst those who opposed
the rise of Cromwell and the Independents in the army.
He was excluded from the House by Pride's Purge, and,
disapproving as he did of the King's execution, he withdrew from public life. Again elected for Essex in 1656,
he was once more excluded. About 1652 he purchased
the reversion of the estate of Gorhambury, his second

[1] M.P. Camelford.

CHALONER CHUTE
1658-59
From a painting at the Vyne, Basingstoke

SIR HARBOTTLE GRIMSTON
1660
From a painting in the National Portrait Gallery by Lely

wife having been a great-niece of Sir Nicholas Bacon, the builder of the now ruined mansion. Grimston held the Mastership of the Rolls concurrently with the Speakership, and until his death in 1685.[1] At the Restoration he was living in Lincoln's Inn, and he entertained the King at his house there soon after his arrival in London.

The existing mace of the House of Commons dates from Sir Harbottle Grimston's Speakership. The earlier "fool's bauble," removed by Cromwell, was made in 1649 by Thomas Maundy, a goldsmith in Fetter Lane, and, though it was formerly supposed that it was refashioned at the Restoration, it appears certain that the one now in use is wholly of the Charles II period. It weighs upwards of 250 ounces, and is rather less than five feet in length, whereas the Commonwealth mace is known to have been considerably smaller. The tradition that a mace at Kingston, in Jamaica, is the one turned out of the House by Cromwell appears to be without foundation, as the oldest now preserved in that island is of eighteenth-century workmanship. When the House of Commons is not in session the Serjeant-at-Arms returns the emblem of his office to the custody of the Lord Chamberlain's Department, whence it is reissued after each Parliamentary recess.

The Convention Parliament met on 25 April, 1660. Charles II landed at Dover a month later, and on 29 May (his thirtieth birthday) the only one of the Stuarts who had tact and who knew when to give way entered London

---

[1] In 1803 the Speaker's lineal descendant, the third Viscount Grimston, presented Sir Harbottle's portrait to the historical series preserved at Westminster, and his coat of arms from the old Rolls Chapel is still to be seen in a window of the museum at the Public Record Office.

amidst universal rejoicing. The "Pensionary Parliament" of Charles II, though often unfavourably contrasted with the Long Parliament, showed itself extremely jealous of the privileges of the Commons, and sat for an even greater number of years than its famous predecessor. It extended over seventeen sessions, and was presided over by four Speakers.

The first of these, Sir Edward Turnour, an ancestor of the present Earl Winterton, occupied the Chair for ten whole years. Samuel Pepys, who knew him well, appeared before him on 4 March, 1668, to deliver his celebrated defence of the principal officers of the Navy. In the speech of his life he held the attention of a crowded House for over three hours in justification of himself and his colleagues. So favourable an impression did the speech produce that when Sir William Coventry, the Chief Commissioner of the Navy, met him the next day he greeted him in the following words : " Good-morrow, Mr. Pepys that must be Speaker of the Parliament House." Coventry also told this invaluable public servant that he could earn £1000 a year at the Bar ; the Solicitor-General said that he was the best speaker in England ; and the Speaker himself declared that in all his experience of the House of Commons he had never heard such a good defence. All which must have been extremely gratifying to Pepys' well-known vanity. The diarist confesses that before going to Westminster on this memorable morning of his life he drank half a pint of mulled sack and a dram of brandy, after which he felt himself " in better order as to courage." He took great interest in the House of Commons even before he became a member, and in his Diary for 27 July, 1663, he

THE MACE
From a photograph in the possession of the Serjeant-at-Arms (Mr. H. D. Erskine of Cardross)

relates how he crowded into the House of Lords, standing close behind the Speaker when he recapitulated the
Acts of the session to the King and desired the Royal
Assent. " The Speaker's speech was far from any
oratory, but was as plain (though good matter) as anything could be, and void of elocution."

No man up to this date had occupied the Chair for
anything like so long a time as Speaker Turnour. Lenthall's longest continuous term of office was, as we have
shown, under seven years ; but during the decade of
1661–71 the Speaker witnessed events as stirring and
as far-reaching in their political effect as any of his predecessors had taken part in. He saw the wreck of
Clarendon (though his policy continued to commend itself
to the majority of the House of Commons), the loss of
England's command of the sea in the disastrous war with
Holland, ending with the humiliating Treaty of Breda,
hurriedly concluded after the Dutch fleet had sailed up
the Medway, bombarded Chatham, and threatened Dover
and Harwich. And when the thunder of the enemy's
guns caused a panic in London the Speaker was hindered
from taking the Chair until after the King had proceeded
to the House of Lords, for fear anything should be resolved
upon by the Commons contrary to the wishes of the
Court.[1]

[1] Considerable light is thrown upon the temper of the House
at the time of this discreditable manœuvre by the ubiquitous Pepys.
Writing on 25 July, 1667, when details of the disaster were still wanting,
he said : " Contrary to all expectation by the King that there would
be a thin meeting, there met above 300 this first day, and all the dis-
contented party ; and indeed the whole House seems to be no other
almost. The Speaker told them, as soon as they were sat, that he
was ordered by the King to let them know he was hindered by some
important business to come to them and speak to them as he had

Speaker Turnour saw the rise of the Cabal, that inner conclave of the King's advisers, two of whose members, at least, were in favour of restoring the Roman Catholic religion in this country ; but he may never have known that by a secret treaty, which Charles concluded with Louis XIV in 1670, in return for a heavy bribe, the King was pledged to declare his own adhesion to the Church of Rome as soon as the times were deemed to be ripe for a public declaration.

Like many other public men at this period, Speaker Turnour received large grants of public money, amounting in the aggregate to £11,000, as free gifts ; nor did he altogether escape the stigma of corruption. It was found that he was in receipt of a small gratuity from the East India Company, and in 1669 it was rumoured in the House that evidence existed of corrupt dealings on his part on a much larger scale. His elevation to the Judicial Bench may have been accelerated by a desire to shield him from unpleasant consequences if these charges were found to be proven.

An order which was passed by the House shortly be-

intended, and therefore, ordered him to move that they would adjourn themselves till Monday next, it being very plain to all the House that he expects to hear by that time of the sealing of the peace." Four days later, when the signing of the peace was generally known, he wrote : " I went up to the Painted Chamber thinking to have got in to hear the King's speech, but upon second thoughts did not think it would be worth the crowd, and so went down again into the Hall. . . . But presently comes down the House of Commons, the King having made them a very short and no pleasing speech to them at all." The King informed them that he had made peace, but gave no particulars and dismissed Parliament until October. But it leaked out that the Speaker's detention had been deliberately planned " for fear they should be doing anything in the House of Commons to the further dissatisfaction of the King and his courtiers."

Given By His Descendent The Earl of Winterton, 1803.

SIR EDWARD TURNOUR
1661
From a painting in the Speaker's House

fore his retirement from the Chair—" That the Back Door of the Speaker's Chambers be nailed up and not opened during any sessions of Parliament "—has given rise to some speculation without eliciting any definite agreement as to its motive. Though backstairs influence was so much in the ascendant at this period, it does not appear that the House, in making the order, had any ulterior object in view beyond regulating the entry of its members through one, and that the main, approach to the Chamber. From a much earlier date the Speaker had been provided with private apartments in which to don his robes, but there is no evidence to show that he was required to live in the Palace in the seventeenth century. Sir Edward Turnour, when in town, lived, like so many of his predecessors, at the Rolls House in Chancery Lane. He died 4 March, 1675, at Bedford during the hearing of the assizes, and was buried with much ceremony at Little Parndon, Essex, on the south side of the chancel.

An account of St. Stephen's Chapel, as it appeared in the sixteenth century, has been given at an earlier page. In the second part of Chamberlayne's *Angliæ Notitia*, published in 1671, there is a very full and interesting account of both Houses of Parliament as Pepys saw them.

" The Commons in their House sit promiscuously, only the Speaker hath a Chair placed in the middle, and the Clerk of that House near him at the Table. They never had any robes (as the Lords ever had), but wear every one what he fancieth most, which to strangers seems very unbecoming the gravity and authority of the Great Council of England."

But few nowadays will be found to endorse the recommendation which follows :—

" During their attendance on Parliament, a robe or grave vestment would as well become the honourable members of the House of Commons, as it doth all the noble Venetians, both young and old, who hath right to sit in the Great Council of Venice, and as it doth the Senators of Rome at this day."

Though Chamberlayne only mentions one Clerk, there had been an assistant at least as early as the reign of James I. In the House of Lords, while the Clerk of the Parliament sat on the " lowermost woolsack " in 1671, his two assistants knelt behind it and wrote their minutes in the same uncomfortable posture. In another passage Chamberlayne speaks of the House of Commons as the " Grand Inquest of the Realm," an early use of a very familiar definition. But even before this the watchful eye of a foreigner had noted the general aspect of the House of Commons in the latter half of the seventeenth century. Monconys, who accompanied the Duc de Chevreuse to London, Oxford, and other places in 1663, has placed on record his impressions of St. Stephen's, and, if for no other reason, they are valuable because they contain the earliest reference of which the author is aware to the green benches of the Lower House :—

" Avant dîner je fus à Westminster, d'où les Deputez de la Chambre Basse sortoient. Le lieu où ils s'assemblent est une Chambre mediocrement grande, environnée de six ou sept rangs de degrez couverts de sarge verte, & disposez en Amphitéatre, au milieu desquels il y a un preau, au fonds duquel vis à vis de la porte est une grande Chaise à bras, avec un dossier de menuë sarge doré & ouvragé, haut de sept ou huit piés, dans lequel s'assoit le President, tournant le dos à la fenêtre, & le visage à la porte. Au dessus de la porte, bien plus haut que les derniers degrez, il y a une tribune, où il y a encore trois ou quatre rangs de ces degrés ; il y a une place pour 500 personnes. Devant la chaise du President il y a un Bureau, où sont les Griffiers, ou Secretaires."

This French traveller and his patron were lodged in Westminster during their visit to London, at a house in the immediate vicinity of Palace Yard, which appears to have been set apart for the reception of foreign ambassadors on their first coming to town.

" Il y a une assez belle place au devant, au fond de laquelle M. le Duc alla loger, à cinq pieces par semaine ou 100 Chelins, dans la maison que M. Brunetti lui avoit loüée, & où le Roi loge les Ambassadeurs extraordinaires les trois premiers jours qu'ils arrivent, & où il les défraye." [1]

The session of 1671 is memorable in the annals of Parliament for the contention then first seriously advanced by the Commons that the Lords were unable to amend a Money Bill. A slight diminution of a proposed duty on sugar having been proposed by the Peers, a deadlock ensued between the two Houses, and, as neither side was disposed to give way, the Bill was dropped. Six years later the same difficulty was experienced when the Lords amended a Bill granting money for an increase in the fleet. On this occasion, however, the Lords did not insist upon their amendment. But in the following year the struggle between the two

---

[1] Mr. de Moncony's descriptions of London, though little known, are so vivid and so evidently the results of personal experience, that they will repay careful attention. In the *National Review*, some years ago, the present author wrote an article on the French traveller's impressions of 1663, and the above extracts are taken from an edition, published in Paris in 1695, in the writer's possession.

Houses was renewed over a Money Bill for the disbandment of troops. Public opinion being found to be hostile to a reduction of the armed forces of the Crown, in view of the threatening attitude of France, the question was not fought out to a conclusion ; but the venal assembly, contemptuously known as the " Pensionary Parliament," passed the Resolution quoted in every textbook of constitutional history, which has ever since been held to debar the Lords from amending, though not of rejecting or suspending, a Money Bill originating in the Lower House.

Sir Job Charlton, whom Roger North calls " an old Cavalier, loyal, learned, grave, and wise," was the next Speaker. He is generally said to have been the son of a London goldsmith, by name Robert Charlton, and that his mother was the daughter of another, by name Thomas Harby ; but in the exhaustive list of London goldsmiths printed in Jackson's *English Goldsmiths and their Marks*, neither of these names occurs. It seems more probable that he came of a Shropshire stock, and that his father was Robert Charlton, of Whitton, in that county. He represented Ludlow in 1659, 1660, and 1661, and died at his seat at Ludford, Herefordshire, 24 May, 1697. As he only held office for eleven days, little or nothing is known of his conduct in the Chair. He became Justice of the Common Pleas, but was removed on account of his opposition to James II's dispensing power. He had also been Chief Justice of Chester, but here he was no luckier, for he had to resign the post in favour of Jeffreys, who had " laid his eye on it." Charlton was the first Speaker to be made a Baronet, and when he resigned from ill-health, the House, for the

SIR JOB CHARLTON
1672-3
From a painting in the Speaker's House

first time for 150 years, elected a Speaker who was not a lawyer. This was Sir Edward Seymour, of Maiden Bradley, Wilts, an aristocratic Tory, who held office for five years, when he too resigned on the plea of ill-health, though there is reason to believe that this was but a convenient excuse. The real reason was a difference of opinion with Danby, the master mind of the Government.

Seymour was first voted to the Chair on 18 February, 1672–3, and in October of the same year a wholly irregular debate was initiated by Sir Thomas Littleton, who declared that he was unfitted to hold the office, owing to his being a Privy Councillor and his having admission to the most secret conclaves of the Court. "You are too big for that Chair, and for us," he said; "and you, that are one of the governors of the world, to be our servant, is incongruous." A Mr. Harbord was even more uncomplimentary. "You expose the honour of the House in resorting to gaming-houses, with foreigners as well as Englishmen, and other ill places. I think you to be an unfit person to be Speaker, by your way of living." Colonel Strangways, however, came to Seymour's rescue, declaring that as for his being a gamester, exception might just as well be taken to the Judicial Bench for the same reasons.[1]

In Seymour's first session a debate arose on the printing of addresses to the King in connection with grievances concerning the billeting of soldiers. On a motion to adjourn the debate, the numbers (on a division) were found to be equal, whereupon the Speaker gave his casting vote in favour of adjournment, saying, "He would have his reason for his judgment recorded, viz.

[1] Cobbett's *Parliamentary History*, Vol. IV, p. 589.

because he was very hungry." Seymour was a very proud, not to say overbearing, man, and he was unpopular with the general body of members. A trick was once played upon him by a wag, who handed him a petition, which the Speaker began to read aloud : " The humble petition of Oliver Cromwell—the devil," whereon a shout of laughter caused him to throw down the paper and hasten from the Chair.

On 10 May, 1675, a serious disturbance arose in Committee of the whole House on the consideration of His Majesty's answer to an address for recalling British subjects from the service of the French King. The riot could only have been quelled by a strong man, and the Speaker's intervention has scarcely had a parallel since that day until Mr. Speaker Peel's memorable intervention in the Home Rule debate on 27 July, 1893.[1] Seymour " very opportunely and prudently rising from his seat near the Bar, in a resolute and slow pace, made his three respects through the crowd, and took the Chair." The mace was laid on the table and the disorder ceased on the Speaker stating that he had acted, " though not according to order, with the intent of bringing the House into order again." [2] He " maintained the dignity of the Chair after that of the House was gone " by obliging every member present to stand up in his place and engage on his honour not to resent any of that day's proceedings. As an instance of his pride it is related that when he was presented to William III the King remarked that he believed Sir Edward was of the Duke of Somerset's family, whereupon the ex-Speaker retorted " that the

[1] *Commons Journals*, Vol, CXLVIII, p. 469.
[2] Grey's *Debates*, Vol. III, p. 129.

SIR EDWARD SEYMOUR
1672-73
From a drawing in the National Portrait Gallery

Duke was rather of *his* family." Once, when his coach broke down at Charing Cross, he ordered the next gentleman's to be stopped and brought to him, and when its occupant expressed surprise, Sir Edward told him that it was more proper for him to walk in the streets than for the Speaker of the House of Commons.

The year 1675 was a memorable one in English politics. Alternately inclining to the counsels of Shaftesbury and religious toleration, and to the advice of Danby, who desired the supremacy of the Anglican Church, Charles had allowed the Nonconformists to be harried to please the Churchmen, and had assented to the Test Act of 1673 to gratify the hatred of both persuasions for the Roman Catholics. But a haunting fear in the public mind that the Protestant succession to the throne was still endangered convinced Danby that a new and more stringent test was required. The reorganisation of his supporters in the Commons which followed led to a cleavage of parties, out of which was gradually evolved the permanent division of English political opinion into two distinct bodies : the Tory and the Whig of after days.

Whilst Danby's proposals were under consideration the relations of the two Houses became once more strained. Evelyn, writing in the summer of 1675, mentions a conference of Lords and Commons in the Painted Chamber, at which the Lords accused the representatives of the people of infringing their privileges, and brought forward once more the oft-quoted precedent of Henry IV. To gain time the King suddenly prorogued Parliament for four months, and the storm blew over.

Sir Robert Sawyer, Pepys' " old chamber fellow " at Magdalene College, Cambridge, succeeded Sir Edward

Q

Seymour in the Chair on 11 April, 1678; but year
before that the same assiduous gossip had noted that "h
do very well in the world." Like his two predecessors, h
resigned from ill-health. Within a month of his electio
he was found to be suffering from a violent fit of th
stone, attributed to his long sitting one day in the Chai
Sawyer's subsequent career was a chequered one. H
became Attorney-General, defended the Seven Bishops
was expelled the House for his conduct in the cas
of Sir Thomas Armstrong in 1690, and was again re
turned (for Cambridge University) later in the year
The beautiful seat of Highclere, Hants, came to Lor
Carnarvon's family from the Sawyers. The eighth Earl o
Pembroke married Margaret Sawyer, Sir Robert's onl
daughter and heiress, in 1684, and her father built th
church at Highclere in which he lies buried. Seymour'
health being conveniently re-established, he returned t
the Chair on 6 May, 1678, and held office till th
Pensionary Parliament was dissolved, 24 January
1678-79.

On the meeting of Charles's third Parliament the Kin
wished to force Sir Thomas Meres upon the House, bu
the Commons desired to have the services of Seymou
once more. In a long dispute Seymour's re-election wa
refused by the King,[1] and, though the Commons did no
insist upon their original choice, they elected Serjean
Gregory in preference to the King's nominee. This wa
the last occasion on which the Sovereign attempted t
impose his own choice upon the House; and with Sey
mour's rejection began that period of 150 years, more o
less, ending with the Speakership of Mr. Shaw Lefevre

[1] 15 March, 1678-79.

SIR ROBERT SAWYER
1678
From a painting in the possession of the Earl of Carnarvon

during which the evolution of the non-partisan Speaker steadily proceeded. At the same time it should be noted that, though Charles failed to force Sir Thomas Meres upon the House, he was still powerful enough to procure the removal of his successor from the Judicial Bench when he gave a judgment in opposition to his personal wishes. Sir William Gregory, of How Caple, Herefordshire (a junior branch of the family of Gregory of Styvechal, in Warwickshire), like Speaker Charlton, was so removed for giving judgment against the King's dispensing power. He only sat in the Chair for four months, during which time the famous Habeas Corpus Act— the Statute which becomes more famous still when suspended—was passed into law.

Towards the close of the reign of Charles II the growth of the party system brought with it considerable expense to Parliamentary candidates, especially in the counties. Evelyn's brother George spent nearly £2000 in 1678-79 by "a most abominable custom" in carrying the county of Surrey against Lord Longford and Sir Adam Brown,[1] when most of the money was spent in eating and drinking. His colleague was Arthur Onslow, grandfather of the celebrated Speaker of the same name. In 1685 Evelyn and Onslow stood again, their opponents being Sir Adam Brown, who was stone deaf, and Sir Edward Evelyn, a cousin of the diarist. But, through a trick of the sheriff in holding the election a day before it was expected, the old members were not returned.

The new names of Whig and Tory were generally applied to the respective members of the country and the Court party at the next general election. Though

[1] Evelyn's Diary, 4 February, 1678-79.

summoned for October, 1679, Charles's fourth Parliament did not meet for the despatch of business until a year later. Sir William Williams, the Whig member for Chester, and a notable champion of the liberties of the Commons, was elected Speaker, *nemine contradicente*, on 21 October, 1680. The first Welshman to fill the Chair, he migrated from Jesus College, Oxford, the home of the leek, to Gray's Inn.[1] Luttrell tells a story of Sir Robert Peyton,[2] who had been expelled the House, going to Williams a few days after the dissolution and demanding satisfaction for a severe rebuke administered to him at the time of his expulsion. He wanted to challenge the Speaker to a duel, but thought fit to retreat in haste on the " young gentlemen of Gray's Inn " (of which Williams was a Bencher) showing signs of taking the law into their own hands on account of what they held to be Peyton's insolence to the Chair.

In this Parliament, though the Exclusion Bill was thrown out in the Lords, the Lower House set itself steadily to curtail the prerogative of the Crown. It was, in consequence, dismissed in January, 1680–81. Popular excitement ran high in London over the fate of the Bill, and the King thought it prudent to summon his fifth Parliament to meet at Oxford in the month of March. Convocation House was fitted up for the Commons, and the Lords sat in the gallery above. Williams was unanimously recalled to the Chair, but after sitting for a week the King sent it about its business, saying, " Now am I King of England, if I never was

---

[1] This Parliament ordered the Votes and Proceedings of the House of Commons to be printed, and in the Journal Office are preserved many of the earliest issues extant.

[2] Knight of the Shire for Middlesex.

SIR WILLIAM GREGORY
1678-9
From a painting in the Speaker's House

Given by Sir Watkin Williams Wynn. Bar.^t 1854.

SIR WILLIAM WILLIAMS
1680, 1680-81
From a painting in the Speaker's House

before." Relieved of the Speakership, Williams returned to the Bar and became Solicitor-General in 1687. He died at his chambers, in Gray's Inn, in 1700, and was buried at Llansilen, Denbighshire. His portrait by Sir Godfrey Kneller has recently been presented to the House by Sir Alfred Thomas, Chairman of the Welsh Parliamentary Party.

The Welsh precedent, once set, was soon followed, for in James II's only Parliament Sir John Trevor, of Bryn-kinalt, the ancestor of the present Lord Trevor, was unanimously called to the Chair, and at the accession of William III he was re-elected. Having been convicted of taking bribes, he was expelled the House in March, 1695, though he was allowed to remain Master of the Rolls, an office which he had held concurrently with the Speaker-ship. In the Speaker's Portrait Gallery at Westminster there hangs his likeness, showing him to have had a decided squint, a defect which, it might be thought, would have increased the proverbial difficulty of catching the Speaker's eye. His early days had been passed in the chambers of a kinsman in the Inner Temple—Arthur Trevor. One day a visitor observed a strange-looking boy seated at a desk, and asked his name. " Oh," said old Trevor, " he is a connection of mine whom I have allowed to sit here to learn the knavish part of the law." Being addicted to high play, he became a recognised authority in gambling disputes, and amongst his fellow-gamesters he had the authority of a judge whose decision was final.

Trevor is said to have owed his promotion to the Chair to his cousin, the notorious Judge Jeffreys; and some years before, on a motion to remove Jeffreys from the

Recordership of London, Trevor's was the only voice raised in his cousin's behalf. It was probably owing to this support that he was advanced to the position of a K.C. when Jeffreys became Chief Justice. The wits of the day declared that justice might be blind, but that bribery only squinted; and when Trevor was expelled in 1695 they added that he could no longer take an oblique view of every question from the Chair. When Archbishop Tillotson chanced to meet him some little time before his disgrace, Trevor exclaimed, in an audible whisper, " I hate a fanatic in lawn sleeves " ; whereon the Archbishop turned and faced him, saying, " And I hate a knave in any sleeves."

On the Bench he appears to have been as upright as he was unscrupulous in the House of Commons, and though he favoured the Protestant interest he remained faithful to James II. As Master of the Rolls he lived in Clement's Lane, then a fashionable street. On the erection of the New Law Courts, the greater part of it was demolished, but a small portion remains at the northern end. Dying there in May, 1717, he was buried in the Rolls Chapel, so unnecessarily pulled down some years ago to make way for an extension of the Public Record Office. In the museum erected on its site Trevor's arms, with an enlarged copy of his signature, taken from one of the windows of the old chapel, are still to be seen. The Trevor estate at Knightsbridge belonged to the ex-Speaker, and, as Master of the Rolls, he set the bad precedent of hearing suitors at his private house, in what was then a pleasant suburb of London.

With the Revolution which placed William III upon the throne, the history and importance of the Speaker-

PRESENTED by
Lord A. E. Hill Trevor, 1869

SIR JOHN TREVOR
1685, 1689-90
From a painting in the Speaker's House

ship may be said to enter upon a new phase. From that date the first Commoner of the realm has occupied his proper station at the head of English gentlemen; whilst the character and consideration of his office was then, for the first time, recognised by the legislature. By I William and Mary, c. 21, he ranks next to the peers of Great Britain, both in and out of Parliament, though not until many years later did he cease to hold, concurrently with the Speakership, any office of profit under the Crown. The great Arthur Onslow, to silence any imputations of leaning towards the ministry of the day, set an example of independence almost invariably adhered to by his successors, yet, in his case, the now customary reward of a peerage after long service in the Chair was unaccountably withheld.

The Speaker of the Convention Parliament, which assembled on 22 January, 1688–89, was naturally a member of the Whig party; and though Sir Edward Seymour, the vehement Tory of earlier days, joined the Prince of Orange at Exeter in the vain hope of once more presiding over the Commons, the choice of the House fell upon Mr. Henry Powle, the son of Henry Powle, of Shottesbrooke, and member for the royal borough of Windsor. Powle had identified himself with the opponents of the Court in the reign of Charles II, and was more than suspected of having been in the pay of Barillon; but his tact and discretion caused him to become the trusted adviser of William, who, on the first convenient opportunity, conferred on him the Mastership of the Rolls.

"I will not invade prerogative, neither will I consent to the infringement of the least liberty of my country," were the proud words in which he sought to define his Parliamentary position ; but the proudest day of his life was when, on 13 February, 1688–89, he stood at the head of the assembled Commons in the Banqueting House at Whitehall, Lord Halifax, the Speaker of the Lords, and the peers facing him, and heard the Declaration of Right asserted prior to the tender of the crown to William. In the magnificent procession which paraded the streets of London to proclaim the King and Queen, the Speaker in his coach took precedence even of the Earl Marshal and others of the great nobility. At the dissolution Powle lost his seat on petition and returned to the administration of justice at the Rolls, maintaining his wonted independence when he refused to attend the Lords at their pleasure, declaring that he was an assistant to, but not an attendant upon, the Upper House. He did not live to see Trevor's expulsion from the Chair, having died at Quenington, in Gloucestershire, in 1692. On his tombstone is inscribed the following epitaph, possibly, according to the practice of the times, his own composition :—

> " Regi et regno fidelissimus,
> Aequi rectique arbiter integerrimus,
> Pius, probus, temperans, prudens,
> Virtutum omnium
> Exemplar magnum."

The next Speaker after Trevor's fall was a man of an altogether different mould and of a different political complexion. The rise of his family was somewhat singular. Richard Foley, and his son Thomas after him, made a fortune in Stourbridge by selling nails. Thomas Foley bought Witley, in Worcestershire, for his eldest son, and Stoke Edith, the old home of the Lingens, for his second son,

G.^r Kneller Eques pinxit.   Geo. Vertue Lond. Sculp 1737.

HENRY POWLE Esqr
Speaker of the HOUSE of COMMONS & MASTER of the ROLLS.
MDCXC.

HENRY POWLE
1688-9
From a print

Paul. In 1679 Paul Foley became member for the city of Hereford, but, though a Tory, he was not a courtier, and he supported the Revolution of 1688–89. Only a year before his elevation to the Chair he showed his independent spirit, in Grand Committee on the state of the nation, and used remarkably plain language in stating his personal opinions on the King's veto. " I believe," he said, " the King hath a negative voice, and it is necessary that it should be so. But if this be made use of to turn by all bills and things the Court likes not, it is misused ; for such a prerogative is committed to him for the good of us all." [1] Roger North called him " a factious lawyer, very busy in ferreting out musty old repositories," which was another way of stating that he had a great knowledge of precedents. North was also responsible for the cryptic utterance attributed to Foley, that—" Things would never go well in England till forty heads flew for it." In 1695 he was put into the Speaker's chair in opposition to Sir Thomas Littleton, the nominee of the Court, and there he remained till within a year of his death. Foley has been styled the first non-partisan Speaker, and, though this is not a strictly accurate description, his tenure of the office undoubtedly marks a stage in the evolution of the office.

Paul Foley, like Speaker Phelips, was a mighty builder in his day. Stoke Edith, one of the best-proportioned country houses in England, a thoughtful mingling of brick and stone, was in part designed by Wren, who appears to have been consulted on most of the important houses built at the close of the seventeenth century. The harmony and proportion of Foley's house

[1] Porritt's *Unreformed House of Commons*, 1903, Vol. I, p. 444.

were somewhat marred by alterations carried out by the brothers Adam, when the windows were taken out and replaced by others less suitable to the original design. Sir James Thornhill, who was entrusted with the decoration of the great hall, introduced an allegorical figure of constitutional liberty, with Foley's own portrait in a contemplative attitude.[1]

On the occasion of Foley's first election to the Chair, Sir Thomas Littleton, the candidate of the Whigs, was defeated by 179 votes to 146; but in 1698, after his rival's retirement, having been again put forward by the Junto, he was chosen Speaker in William's third Parliament by a large majority. Shortly before the meeting of the new House in December, 1698, a curious pamphlet, *Considerations upon the Choice of a Speaker of the House of Commons in the Approaching Session*, was published by the Tories with a view to excluding Littleton. His appointment, like Sir Edward Seymour's, was a reaction from the custom of promoting lawyers, the House once more preferring to have a country gentleman to preside over their deliberations.

Sir Thomas Littleton, who was the youngest son of a poor baronet, had, however, served an apprenticeship to trade, having been trained in business habits from his youth. He is said to have been recommended to William III by the Duke of Shrewsbury, the " favourite

---

[1] Paul Foley was the ancestor of the present Lord Foley. He married Mary, daughter of John Lane, an alderman of the City of London, and dying on 11 November, 1699, was buried at Stoke Edith. The Speaker's nephew was one of the twelve emergency peers created by Queen Anne in 1712 to secure a Tory majority in the House of Lords. When they made their first appearance at Westminster, Lord Wharton ironically asked them if they desired to give their votes singly, or, as a jury, through their foreman.

STOKE EDITH, HEREFORDSHIRE.   BUILT BY SPEAKER FOLEY

PAUL FOLEY
1694-95, 1695
*From a miniature in the possession of
Paul Henry Foley, Esq., at Stoke Edith*

of the nation," according to Swift, and a statesman whose biography deserves to be written at length. Although he had but one eye, his political vision was remarkably clear, and at critical moments in the lives of both William III and Anne the Duke rendered invaluable service to the Crown.

The sessions of 1698–99 and 1700 proved to be full of humiliations for the Court. Though the ministry had succeeded in securing the election of a Whig Speaker, the new House of Commons contained a composite majority made up of avowed Tories and members who were opposed to a forward military policy. Charles Montagu, afterwards Earl of Halifax, who must not be confounded with the celebrated Trimmer, had carried all before him in the last Parliament, but he now found himself powerless to guide or control the deliberations of the House. In addition to demanding the reduction of the Dutch guards, the Commons became inquisitive in the matter of royal grants, and proposed to appoint Commissioners to inquire into the manner in which the forfeited Irish lands had been conferred on William's personal favourites. In order to force their Bill through the House of Lords the Commons deliberately tacked it on to a Bill granting the Land Tax. And though William reluctantly gave his assent to the measure, rather than throw the Constitution into the melting-pot, he prorogued Parliament [1] without making a speech from the throne, and wrote to a friend :—

" This has been the most dismal session I ever had. The members have separated in great disorder and after many extravagances. Unless one had been present, he could have no notion of their intrigues : one cannot even describe them."

[1] 11 April, 1700.

Party government was still in its infancy in 1700, and the prolonged quarrel between the two Houses having engendered a dangerous spirit in the Commons, the way was paved for a better understanding between the King and the acknowledged leaders of the Tory party. Thus was established, almost unconsciously, the general principle, ever since accepted, that ministers who cannot command a majority in the House of Commons cannot cling to office without being discredited in the country.

When his fourth Parliament was about to assemble in February, 1700–1, William intimated to Littleton, who lacked the physique necessary to the efficient performance of the duties of the Chair, his desire that he should give way to Harley, and, with the prompt compliance of a courtier, the late Speaker absented himself from the House on the day of meeting, to be rewarded with the valuable office of Treasurer of the Navy, a post which he retained till his death, unshaken by all the efforts made to remove him. On this occasion Harley was proposed by Sir Edward Seymour, the ex-Speaker of the Pensionary Parliament, but the House was by no means unanimous in his favour, 249 members voting for him and 129 against him. Bishop Burnet, who knew Littleton well, wrote of him earlier in his career :—

" I happened in looking for a house to fall accidentally on the next house to Sir Thomas Littleton, knowing nothing concerning him. But I soon found that he was one of the considerablest men in the nation. He was at the head of the opposition that was made to the Court, and living constantly in town, he was exactly informed of all that passed. He came to have an entire confidence in me, so that for six years together we were seldom two days without spending some hours together. I was by

The Honble Sr Thomas   Littleton Baronet
Treasurer of the   Navy & Speaker
of the Honourable   House of Commons.

SIR THOMAS LITTLETON
1698
From a print

this means let into all their secrets, and indeed without the assistance I had from him I could never have seen so clearly into affairs as I did. We argued all the matters that he perceived were to be moved in the House of Commons till he thought he was a master of all that could be said on the subject, and it was observed of him that in all debates in the House of Commons he reserved himself to the conclusion, and what he spoke commonly determined the matter."

Burnet and Littleton were living at the time referred to—the latter end of the reign of Charles II—near the Plough Inn, which was on the south side of Carey Street, Lincoln's Inn Fields, and convenient to the Rolls Chapel, where Burnet was then preacher. Manning gives a slightly different version of Burnet's estimate of the Speaker.[1] Burnet, however, was wrong in saying that Littleton was the first Speaker who had not been brought up in the profession of the law. Littleton had a profound antipathy to the members of the long robe in Parliament, and in the debates upon the Bill for allowing counsel to prisoners in cases of high treason, and the impeachment of Sir John Fenwick, who had asked for further time to produce witnesses, he argued, as a private member, as follows :—

" Here ye shall have cunning lawyers defending an impeachment. I hope I shall not degrade your members to argue against lawyers ; but when an impeachment is by gentlemen of his own quality, I think a cause is as well tried without counsel, and I would disagree with the Lords." He further observed, in the same contemptuous strain : " It may be the counsel have a mind to another fee."

[1] Supplement to the *History of My Own Time*, edited by Miss Foxcroft, 1902, p. 485.

He was a stout party man, and from his place in the House he declared that the principle which ever guided his vote was the party from whom the proposition emanated. " For my part, I have a way how to guide my vote always in the House, which is to vote contrary to what our enemies without doors wish." Such slavish adherence to party ties carries joy to the heart of the party whips, who dislike above everything the " independent " member, who watches the opportunity to snatch a momentary notoriety by stabbing his own side in the back.

Littleton was again put forward for the Chair on December 30, 1701, when 212 members voted in his favour and 216 against him, the closest contest on record. Harley was then re-elected without further opposition. Like Sir Thomas More and " tough old Coke," Harley's principal triumphs were achieved in other spheres than that of the Chair of the Commons, so that it is unnecessary to dwell at any length upon the career of this nimblest of politicians. Belauded by Pope and beloved of Swift, this brilliant statesman may be said to have embarked on a ministerial career whilst still Speaker of the Commons, for he was Secretary of State for the Northern Department for some months before he quitted the Chair for the third and last time.

By birth and education a Whig, by imperceptible stages he developed into the leader of the Tory and Church party. On becoming Chancellor of the Exchequer,[1] he virtually filled the position of Prime Minister, and when, at the general election of 1710, the Tory party had a large majority at the polls he was all but supreme. In King William's time, when he had only £500 a year,

[1] In 1710.

ROBERT HARLEY
1700-1, 1701, 1702
From a painting in the National Portrait Gallery

he is.said to have spent half this sum in employing clerks to copy out for him treaties and official papers, so that members were almost afraid to speak before him. His enemies said that he had spies and inspectors in every public office. In contrast to his great rival Bolingbroke, who fascinated the House as much by his handsome appearance as by his neatly turned speeches, Harley's physical proportions were unimposing ; his features were homely, and there was little that was impressive in his voice or carriage. " Can it be true," said M. Le Sac, a celebrated *maître de danse*, " that Mr. Harley has been made an Earl and Lord Treasurer ?   I wonder what the devil the Queen can see in him! He was a pupil of mine for two years, and a greater dunce I never taught."

In 1701 he was elected Speaker by 120 votes over Sir Richard Onslow ; on the second occasion he only beat Sir Thomas Littleton by four ; and in 1702 there is no mention in the Journals of his re-election, the Clerks of the House having neglected to minute the proceedings of the first two days of the session.   Harley is said to have been the inventor of the newspaper press as an engine of party warfare, and, apart from his political eminence, he deserves to be gratefully remembered for the literary taste displayed in the formation of the splendid library, of which the MS. portion is now in the British Museum, it having been acquired for the nation for the small sum of £10,000.

On the meeting of Queen Anne's second Parliament, which became the first Parliament of Great Britain by Proclamation dated 29 April, 1707, there was a furious party contest for the Chair.   The Tory candidate was Mr. William Bromley, of Baginton, who was to have his revenge later on, and the chosen of the Whigs was plain Mr. John Smith, M.P. for Andover, who carried the day by 248 votes to 205. Mr. Smith came of a respectable Hampshire family, and previous to his elevation to the Chair he had acted as a party whip. His close friendship with Godolphin also stood him in good stead.

The Scotch members sat at Westminster for the first time on 23 October, 1707, and when the ministerial crisis which drove Harley from office early in the next year necessitated a reconstitution of the ministry, the Chancellorship of the Exchequer was conferred upon the Speaker. Mr. Smith only held the post for two years, and, though he remained a member of the House until his death in 1723, his subsequent career was uneventful. He subsided into the less influential but more lucrative sinecure of a Tellership of the Exchequer. On one occasion he was indiscreet enough to inform the House that the debts of the Civil List, then stated to be £400,000, had not amounted to half that sum two months before the estimates were made. The deficiency had apparently arisen from excessive disbursements on account of secret service. Swift had a thrust at the ex-Speaker when he wrote in the *Invitation to Dismal*—

> " Wine can clear up Godolphin's cloudy face
> And fill Jack Smith with hopes to keep his place."

And keep it he did, until the accession of George I dispelled all danger of removal. As an orthodox Whig, he supported Walpole in opposition to the Stanhope Administration, and one of his last public utterances was on a curious motion to close the House of Lords against Commoners for the future.[1]

[1] Speaker Smith's portrait is in the Speaker's collection at Westminster, and his family is represented at the present day by Mr. Assheton Smith, of Vaynol, near Bangor.

JOHN SMITH
1705, 1707
From a drawing in the National Portrait Gallery

Anne's third Parliament was presided over by Sir Richard Onslow, a descendant of the man of the same name who was Speaker in 1566. The portrait of the Speaker of 1708–10 has been drawn by the infinitely greater Arthur Onslow, the third of the family to fill the Chair.

"Tall and very thin, not well shaped, and with a face exceeding plain, yet there was a certain sweetness with a dignity in his countenance, and so much of life and spirit in it, that no one who saw him ever thought him of a disagreeable aspect. His carriage was universally obliging, and he was of the most winning behaviour that ever I saw. There was an ease and openness in his address, that even at first sight gave him the heart of every man he spoke to. He had always something to say that was agreeable to everybody, and used to take as much pleasure in telling a story to a man's advantage, as others generally do to the contrary. It was this temper that made him so fit for reconciling differences between angry people, an office he frequently and readily undertook and seldom failed of succeeding in." [1]

So far it might be thought that Sir Richard possessed every qualification for the post, but less partial judges perceived in "stiff Dick," as he was irreverently called by the Tories, an unfortunate propensity to quarrelsomeness which led him on more than one occasion to challenge a fellow-member to a duel. He fought Mr. Oglethorpe, a young man of twenty-two, for something he had said in the course of a debate, and he was only restrained by an order of the House from prosecuting another affair of honour with Sir E. Seymour.

[1] Historical Manuscripts Commission Report on the MSS. of the Earl of Onslow.

R

At the time of his election many would have preferred Sir Peter King, who, missing the Chair, attained the Woolsack in the next reign.

Paul Jodrell, the Clerk of the House, was also suggested as being the most competent adviser in matters of precedent and procedure, much as the late Sir Thomas Erskine May's name was put forward in recent years as the greatest authority on Parliamentary history and the mainstay of every Speaker with whom he acted. " Stiff Dick " found himself in the uncomfortable position of being confronted with no less than three ex-Speakers, two of them sitting, comparatively negligible quantities, on the ministerial benches—Littleton and Smith, and the redoubtable Harley on the Opposition side. Lord Shaftesbury, writing in November, 1708, when Onslow was quite new to the Chair, said : " The late Speaker beset the old one ; and he will have, I fear, a hard task, if this be not an easy session."

Whatever his shortcomings, Richard Onslow ingratiated himself at Court. King William shortly before his death called him into his closet and " bade him continue the honest man he had always found him." Anne made him a Privy Councillor.[1] George I made him Chancellor of the Exchequer and a peer, and on his resigning the Chancellorship he succeeded in getting himself made Teller of the Exchequer for life, the first instance of that appointment being conferred for that period. His manner in the Chair was somewhat imperious. When the House went up to the Lords to demand judgment against Dr. Sacheverell, every complaint took the

[1] Said to be the last favour which Lord Godolphin ever procured from the Queen.

Given by the Revd Sir Richard Cope *Bar.^t* 1803.

SIR RICHARD ONSLOW
1708
From a painting in the Speaker's House

form of a threat : " My Lords, if you do not immediately order your Black Rod to " do this or that, " I will return to the House of Commons at once."

With the return of Harley to office at the head of a solid Tory majority, and a Parliament strongly attached to the Church, Mr. William Bromley, who had been disappointed of the Chair on a previous occasion, was unanimously chosen on 25 November, 1710.[1] A perfect type of the English country gentleman, Bromley was educated at Christ Church, Oxford, and at the time of his election to the Chair he represented the University. After taking his degree he made the tour of the Continent and published an account of his travels. The title-page shows that he considered printing an act of condescension :[2] " Remarks on the Grand Tour of France and Italy lately performed by a person of quality, 1692." In the Doge's Palace at Genoa he observed with approval " an excellent method for freedom in voting," and was in advance of his time and party in commending the ballot boxes which rendered it " impossible the suffrage of any particular person should be known." From Genoa he proceeded to Rome, where he was received in audience by the Pope. " In the evening I was admitted to the honour of kissing the Pope's slipper, who, though he knew me to be a Protestant, gave me his blessing, and, like a wise man, said nothing about religion."

He was sceptical as to the genuineness of the Sancta Scala at St. John Lateran, and was relieved to hear from

[1] For his speech on taking office see Boyer's *Political State of England*.

[2] Townsend, *Memoirs of the House of Commons*, 1844, second edition, p. 178.

one of the cardinals that they were not the actual stairs ascended by the Saviour, but as they were generally considered to be so it was not thought advisable to un-deceive the devout. From Rome he went to Florence. He was delighted to see the portraits of King Charles and King James, but he would not permit himself to speak of King William, except as the " Prince of Orange."

His political opponents professed to believe that he must be a Papist and Jacobite at heart, on account of his having kissed the Pope's toe ; and, in consequence of the derision cast by the Whigs on the casual impres-sions of a fairly intelligent traveller, he withdrew from circulation such copies as remained in the bookseller's hands. A second edition appeared, without Bromley's permission, just at the time when he was first proposed for the Chair. To this was added a fictitious table of contents, attributed, though we believe erroneously, to Walpole, turning Bromley's observations into ridicule.[1]

During his Speakership his house at Baginton, in Warwickshire, was burnt to the ground, and the story goes that he was informed of the catastrophe whilst sitting in the Chair, the news having been brought to town by special messenger. Very calmly, and without quitting the Chair, he is said to have given directions for the immediate rebuilding of his ruined home. This was done, and Queen Anne came to see it and planted a cedar in the garden. On the new house the inscription " Phœnix Resurgens " was placed, but none the less it was burnt down again in 1889, and nothing now remains of it but

[1] Both these little books are now rare and there is no copy of either of them in the library of the House.

WILLIAM BROMLEY
1710
From a print

the outside walls with the inscription, which has not yet been made good.

That Bromley was held in esteem by the House at large is apparent from its having adjourned for six whole days on the occasion of the death of his only son, " out of respect to the father and to give him time both to perform the funeral rites and to indulge his just affliction." He was offered, and accepted, a seat in the Government before the dissolution of August, 1713, and on quitting the Chair for the Treasury Bench he became the recognised leader of the Tory party in the House of Commons. At Harley's instigation he wrote to Sir Thomas Hanmer, asking him to allow himself to be nominated for the Chair in the new Parliament. Having secured his main object, he sought to ensure the re-election of his chaplain, Dr. Pelham. The manœuvre was not successful, and history does not record whether another and minor request weighed with his successor. Dating from Whitehall, 22 September, 1710, Bromley had written to Hanmer :—

" You'll smile at the transition from chaplain to coach horses. I have a pair that drew my great coach, and believe you cannot be better fitted, and I offer them to you before I dispose of them. One especially is a very fine horse, and better than sixteen hands high. You shall have him or them on reasonable terms."

With the death of Queen Anne Mr. Bromley's official career practically came to a close. To the end of his life he came out on Parliamentary field days with a set oration against the Whigs, emphatically denouncing such evils as Hanoverian alliances, the maintenance of a standing army, and the Septennial Act. He died at Baginton, in the summer of 1732, in his sixty-ninth year, " a not un-favourable specimen of the Tory squire in politics, having sat in twelve Parliaments and under four Sovereigns." His library was fortunately saved from the fire in 1889, as was the fine service of plate used by him as Speaker. There is a portrait of him at Westminster, and another in the possession of his descendant, Mr. William Bromley-Davenport, late M.P. for Macclesfield.

The last Speaker of Queen Anne's reign was Sir Thomas Hanmer, the Shakespearean commentator, and the head of a family which had been settled in the Welsh marches since the reign of Henry III. At the early age of twenty-one he married the widowed Duchess of Grafton, who had been first wedded to one of Charles II's illegitimate sons at the tender age of twelve. Educated at Westminster and Christ Church, Oxford, he entered the House of Commons as member for Thetford, where the Grafton interest was no doubt paramount, and took up his abode in Pall Mall at a house on the south side of the street. He soon made his mark in debate, and in a letter of Lord Berkeley of Stratton, written in 1712, he was said to " outshine all in the House."

In the course of the next year Swift, who, it was rumoured, occasionally helped him in the composition of his speeches, confided to Stella the opinion that " he was the most considerable man in the House of Commons." Though of generally Tory proclivities, he was looked upon as somewhat of a waverer about this time, and, after he had refused office under Harley, from a growing distrust of his policy, that astute minister desired to relegate him to the Chair, where he thought that he would be more safely occupied than in playing the rôle of a Parliamentary free-lance. But before this could be contrived the debates on the Commercial Treaty with France, arising out of the eighth and ninth Articles of the ill-starred Treaty of Utrecht, gave Hanmer the chance of his life.

The Articles were the work of Bolingbroke even more than of Harley, and were designed in the interests of free trade with France, at the expense of Spain, Portugal, and Italy. They proposed concessions in the importation of French wines to the certain injury of the Portuguese trade; whilst the silk and woollen manufactures of France were to enter England free. A revolt of English manufacturers and traders at once took place, and the cry of " Treat the foreigner as he treats us ! " was immediately raised. Petitions against the Treaty poured in, and for a month nothing else was talked of in London. This was the age of pamphlets, and public interest in the subject was stimulated and inflamed by the appearance of two rival periodicals, one, *The Mercator, or Commerce Retrieved*, written by Daniel Defoe, upholding the free trade clauses of the Treaty; and the other, *The British Merchant, or Commerce Preserved*, (said to have been written by General Stanhope who led the opposition in the House of Commons), which was strongly in favour of a protective tariff. A tariff reform debate in the reign of Queen Anne may seem something of an anomaly to modern readers, but the strenuous party fight which took place on 14 May, prior to the introduction of the Government Bill to make the Articles effectual, raised the whole question of free imports and the imposition of a commercial tariff with France.

General Stanhope quoted the preamble of an earlier tariff concluded between Louis XIV and Charles II in 1664, which declared :—

" That it has been found by long experience that the importing of French wines, brandy, linen, salt and paper, and other commodities of the growth, product, and manufactures of the territories and dominions of the French King, has much exhausted the treasure of this nation, lessened the value of the native commodities and manufactures thereof, and caused great detriment to the Kingdom in general."

At this point Speaker Bromley interposed, saying " that there was no such thing in that Act," but, being found to be mistaken after the Clerk of the House had read the original words, General Stanhope was allowed to proceed with his arguments, to show the disadvantages of an open trade with France.[1] When the Bill went into Committee it occupied the House for five whole days, and Hanmer, who had originally favoured the scheme of the Government, made an elaborate speech against it. He said that though he had given his vote for the bringing in of the Bill, having in the interval weighed and considered the allegations of the petitioning merchants and traders, he had been convinced that the passing of the Bill would inflict great prejudice to the home woollen and silk manufactures, increase the number of the poor, and ultimately affect the land.

" While he had the honour to sit in the House he would never be blindly led by any ministry ; neither,

[1] Boyer says, in relating this incident, " He " (General Stanhope) " and some other members animadverted with some vehemence on the Speaker's mistake." (*Political State of Great Britain*, Vol. V, p. 370.)

on the other hand, was he biased by what might weigh with some men, viz. the fear of losing their elections. The principles upon which he acted were the interests of his country and the conviction of his judgment, and upon those considerations alone he must oppose the Bill."

This speech made a great impression upon the House, and when the division was taken, " near eleven at night and after candles had been brought in," the Government was defeated by the narrow majority of nine, and the Bill was killed. Only one of the four members for the City of London voted for it ; the other three and the members for Westminster voted for its rejection. The London drapers, mercers, and weavers were over-joyed at the result, and Hanmer became for a time a popular idol. Bonfires and illuminations expressed the general satisfaction on the news becoming known.[1] The coolness which ensued between Sir Thomas Hanmer and the ministry was temporarily patched up when he consented to take the Chair in the new Parliament. The precarious session of 1714, when the chances of the Stuart and the Hanoverian dynasties were nearly equally balanced, gave the Speaker an opportunity of testifying to his regard for the Protestant succession.

The country party declared that this was in danger under Her Majesty's Government, and when ministers attempted to shelve an inconvenient topic by moving the

[1] A very interesting letter from the Tory point of view, describing the preliminary debate in the House on 14 May, will be found in the Wentworth correspondence, pp. 234, 235. Peter Wentworth, writing to his brother, Lord Strafford, who had negotiated the Treaty of Utrecht, states that he was an attentive listener to the debate from one o'clock till ten at night.

previous question, the Speaker, speaking in Committee of the whole House, baffled the attempt in a remarkable speech, in which he said that " he was sorry to see that endeavours were used to stop their mouths, but he was of opinion that this was the proper, and perhaps the only, time for patriots to speak; that though, for his own part, he had all the honour and respect imaginable for Her Majesty's ministers, he felt that he owed more to his country than to any minister; that, in the debate, so much had been said to prove that the succession was in danger, and so little to make out the contrary, that he could not but believe the first." Henceforth he became the recognised leader of the Hanoverian Tories, or, as they were nicknamed, the Whimsicals. With the death of George I the last chance of the restoration of his friends to political power disappeared, and Hanmer withdrew from public life to pursue his Shakespearean studies.[1]

[1] As recently as July, 1907, Speaker Hanmer's plate was brought to the hammer at Christie's, when it realised high prices.

I. Allen, delt.   *W. Bond, sculpt.*

SIR THOMAS HANMER

1713-4

From a print

CHAPTER VII

THE HOUSES OF HANOVER AND SAXE-COBURG-GOTHA. RISE OF THE SYSTEM OF CABINET GOVERNMENT, WITH MINISTERIAL RESPONSIBILITY TO PARLIAMENT

SEVENTEEN SPEAKERS

George I—
   Spencer Compton
George II—
   Arthur Onslow

George III—
   John Cust
   Fletcher Norton
   Charles Wolfran Corn-
     wall
   William Wyndham
     Grenville

George IV—
   Henry Addington
   John Mitford

   Charles Abbot
   Charles Manners-Sutton

William IV—
   James Abercromby

Victoria—
   Charles Shaw-Lefevre
   John Evelyn Denison
   Henry Bouverie Wil-
     liam Brand
   Arthur Wellesley Peel
   William Court Gully

Edward VII and George V—
   James William Lowther

WITH the accession of George I and the rout of the Tory party the Speakership acquired a permanent character hitherto unknown in its annals. Whilst the House of Lords was the most compact body in the State, Sir Robert Walpole, after 1721, taught the nation to look upon the House of Commons as the real seat of power in the legislature, with the result that a corresponding increase took

251

place in the importance and dignity of the Speaker's office. No longer to be regarded as a stepping-stone to rapid legal preferment, the Chair in the early days of the eighteenth century was filled more often than not by men with little or no legal training. It has been shown that in the Middle Ages instances occurred in which a Speaker was re-elected on three, four, and even five occasions; but when the House of Commons knew but one president during an entire reign (and history repeated itself under George II), new records of long service in the Chair were established which have never since been surpassed or even equalled.

An aristocrat by birth, Sir Spencer Compton, the third son of the Earl of Northampton, came of a good Tory stock, but in early life he deserted to the Whigs. This "most solemn, formal man in the world," according to Horace Walpole, entered the House as member for Eye in 1698, became Speaker in March, 1715, was re-elected in 1722 (from which date he combined the then lucrative office of Paymaster-General with the duties of the Chair), and was raised to the Peerage as Lord Wilmington on the accession of George II. The new King wished to make him his Prime Minister, but Walpole having promised the Queen £100,000 a year from Parliament, whereas Wilmington had only ventured to propose £60,000, the arrangement fell through. But on Walpole's fall and nominal replacement in 1742, he achieved his heart's desire and became First Lord of the Treasury.

Though not a strong Speaker, Compton could on occasion administer sharp reproof. When a member once called upon him to make the House quiet, declaring that he had a right to be heard, he answered, " No, sir, you

G. Kneller, pinxt   I. Faber, sculpt. 1734

SIR SPENCER COMPTON
1714-5, 1722
From a print

have a right to speak, but the House has a right to judge whether it will hear you." [1] Though often called Prime Minister, he was never so in the sense that Walpole was. Carteret, who is said to have been the only peer of Cabinet rank who could talk to the first two Georges in their native tongue, was the chief minister. In this connection it will be remembered that the late Mr. W. H. Smith, when leader of the House, was First Lord of the Treasury, though never Prime Minister. Lord Wilmington seems to have excited in an uncommon degree the mirth and ridicule of the wits of the day. Sir Charles Hanbury Williams, in his " New Ode to a great number of great men newly made," wrote :—

> " See yon old, dull important Lord
> Who at the longed-for money board
> Sits first, but does not lead."

And Lord Hervey, the " Sporus " of Pope, said of him :—

> " Let Wilmington, with grave contracted brow,
> Red tape and wisdom at the Council show,
> Sleep in the Senate, in the circle bow."

The " Broad-bottomed Administration," a remarkably aristocratic body, seeing that there were five Dukes, a Marquis, and an Earl in it, replaced Lord Carteret's, and was itself upset on Pelham's death. An arch-mediocrity in office, Lord Wilmington could make an effective speech on ceremonial occasions, and a jest of his on the Duke of Newcastle deserves to be remembered as much as the gibes of his political opponents : " The Duke always loses half an hour in the morning, which he is running after the rest of the day, without being able to overtake it." During the whole of his official career this " transient,

---

[1] Hatsell's *Precedents of Proceedings in the House of Commons*, 1818, Vol. II, p. 108.

embarrassed phantom " lived in St. James's Square, at a house erroneously supposed to have been Nell Gwynne's, and now merged in the Army and Navy Club. It had originally been built for Moll Davis, a young actress and dancer, whose professional career presented many similar features to Nelly's own. Naive and flippant on the stage, what she lacked in beauty she made up for in agility, and her antics on the stage made the pulse of Pepys beat quicker as he sat in the pit of Old Drury marking time with his foot as he applauded the measure. Lord Wilmington inherited the house from his mother, Mary, Countess of Northampton. Its last occupier was Lord De Mauley, until it was pulled down to make way for the Army and Navy Club.

The Speaker's next-door neighbour in the Square, at No. 21, was " Beau Colyear," Lord Portmore, who married James II's ugly mistress, Katherine Sidley; and before he came there Arabella Churchill, another of James's favourites, lived in the house. Lord Portmore was a great patron of horse-racing, even before the foundation of the Jockey Club in the middle of the eighteenth century. Lord Wilmington died in July, 1743, and was buried at Compton Wynyates, Warwickshire, one of the most charming country houses in the Midlands. Having never been married, his titles became extinct, and his estates passed to his brother, from whom the present Marquis of Northampton is descended. There is a good portrait of Speaker Compton, by Sir Peter Lely, at Westminster.

Throughout the whole of the next reign, during Walpole's last administration and those of Lord Carteret,

ARTHUR ONSLOW
1727-8, 1734-5, 1741, 1747, 1754
From a painting possibly by Hysing in the National Portrait Gallery

the Pelhams, the Duke of Newcastle, the elder Pitt, and the Coalition Ministry of 1757, the Chair was filled, in five successive Parliaments, by the great Arthur Onslow, the third of his family to be so honoured, and unquestionably one of the most distinguished Speakers the House has ever known. As from 1720 to 1727 he represented Guildford, and from 1728 to 1761 the county of Surrey, in the Whig interest, at the time of his retirement in the latter year there can have been very few members of the House who sat in it when he was first called to the Chair.

The story goes that having in early life conceived a great desire to become Speaker, Sir Robert Walpole wrote reminding him that " the road to that station lay through the gates of St. James's " ; but whether or not Onslow owed his selection to the direct interest of the Crown, no better choice could have been made. He was first returned for Guildford at a bye-election, and in the course of the same year, 1720, he married. He embraced, as a matter of course, the orthodox Whig creed, which professed to regard the passing of the Septennial Act as coincident with a Constitutional millennium.

This measure, although often threatened with radical curtailment of its provisions, still sets a convenient limit to the activities of a Parliament, and when Onslow made his appearance at Westminster this great constitutional landmark had not outrun its first allotted term.

The ideal Speaker, that was to be, chose for his London home a modest dwelling in Leicester Street, a narrow thoroughfare converging, at its upper end, upon Lisle Street. Despite its proximity to the abode of Royalty (in the person of the Prince of Wales at Leicester House, where the Empire Theatre now stands), it can never have been a very cheerful situation, and, at the present day, having been long since deserted by private residents of any and every rank in life, it is a singularly unattractive row of business premises. Probably no district in the West End has so changed for the worse, from the residential point of view, as the once fashionable Leicester Fields, to give it the name usually attributed to it in the reign of the first and second George.

Yet Onslow lived there for no less than thirty years, only quitting it in 1752 to take up his abode at the finest and largest house in Soho Square. No. 20 stands on the site of Old Falconbergh House, built at the end of the seventeenth century by the head of the Bellasis family.

It has a handsome façade in the Square (reproduced in this volume), and the London County Council would be well advised to place a memorial tablet on its walls, if only for the sake of an interesting link between the Commonwealth and the reign of George III.

Mary, Lady Falconbergh, was Oliver Cromwell's daughter, and is said to have borne a striking resemblance to her father. Marrying in his lifetime, she did not die until 1713, so that Arthur Onslow might well have remembered her. Sir Thomas Frankland and Mr. Anthony Duncombe also lived at No. 20, Onslow's immediate predecessor there being the Lord Tylney for whom Colin Campbell, the author of *Vitruvius Britannicus*, built Wanstead House in the Essex marshes.

In its original state Falconbergh House, to give it its earliest name, must have been well suited to the holding of the Speaker's levees, but the interior, with the exception of one room on the first floor decorated with coats

SPEAKER ARTHUR ONSLOW'S HOUSE IN SOHO SQUARE. (NO. 20, FORMERLY FALCONBERG HOUSE)

of arms and a highly enriched ceiling, was practically gutted by Messrs. Crosse and Blackwell in adapting it to business purposes. The fine staircase and a quantity of tapestry were then removed, but the well-proportioned front fortunately escaped alteration. The Duke of Argyll and Lord Bradford were other occupiers after the Speaker, and, before it was consecrated to jam and pickles, this historic mansion was used for a time as D'Almaine's pianoforte showrooms.

Next door, now No. 21 in the square and the corner house of Sutton Street, was the notorious " White House." Some years after Onslow had left the neighbourhood it became a den of infamy unexampled in the annals of disreputable London, thus affording another instance of the vicissitudes which surround the former abodes of the most impeccable citizens.

The positive identification of Speaker Onslow's house has only been arrived at after an exhaustive examination of the parochial rate-books. Much confusion has prevailed in the minds of even recent writers on Soho respecting the actual sites of houses in the square formerly occupied by distinguished men. The statement that Admiral Sir Cloudesley Shovell and the Dutch adventurer Ripperda lived at No. 20 is as inaccurate as the one frequently put forward that Onslow's mansion was one and the same with the " White House " of evil memory. As a matter of fact, Sir Cloudesley lived on the west side of the square and Ripperda on the north, in a house represented by Nos. 10 and 10A of the modern numbering.

When first called to the Chair, Onslow confessed to feeling apprehensive at being raised to so dangerous

s

a height, saying that greater men before him had tried their abilities in the same station and had found the eminence too high for them. He was then only thirty-six, a comparatively early age for a Speaker, and had sat in the House for rather less than eight years. When his re-election was proposed in 1747 he felt some compunction at accepting a further term of office, telling the House that, " painful as the situation [of Speaker] is, at any time, and worn as I am, perhaps, with its labours, since honourable gentlemen seem inclined to try my poor abilities once more . . . I do not think it decent in me to dispute their commands. I therefore resign myself to the judgment of the House, which has a right to dispose of me here in whatever manner it may think proper." And, pausing on the step of the Chair, he added, much after the manner of his immediate predecessors, " It is my duty to let honourable gentlemen know that, before I go any further, they have it in their power to call me back to the seat from whence I came, and to choose some other person to fill this place."

And not until every member then present had cried out, " No, no," did he consent to preside over the deliberations of the House for the fourth time. Onslow was the first in the long catalogue to realise the supreme importance of the independence and impartiality of the Chair. Whereas most of his predecessors had been pluralists or expectant office-holders, he raised the character of the Speakership by resigning the lucrative office of Treasurer of the Navy and contenting himself with the modest income derived from fees on private bills. Hatsell, who went to the Table of the House while Onslow was still in the Chair, wrote of him, in connection with the rules then obtaining, that the Speaker endeavoured to preserve order in debate with great strictness, yet always with civility and courtesy, saying that he had often heard, as a young man, from old and experienced members, that nothing tended more to throw power into the hands of the Administration than the neglect of or departure from these rules. That he, Onslow, was of opinion that they had been instituted by our ancestors as a check on the action of ministers, and as a protection to the minority against the arbitrary exercise of power. There can be little doubt that Speaker Onslow's rigid adherence to duty, and his detachment from political office, notwithstanding some divergence from his standard on the part of his immediate successors, paved the way for the wholly non-partisan Speaker evolved during the nineteenth century, and that the methods introduced by him have contributed to the shaping of the system of Party Government as understood at the present day. His demeanour in the Chair is said to have been firm but impartial, his voice clear and impressive, and his temper imperturbable. By way of contrast this grave and dignified man, when released from his official duties, would steal away from Westminster to enjoy his pipe and glass *incognito* in the chimney-corner of the " Jew's Harp," a famous tavern and bowling alley in Marylebone Fields, the site of which is now merged in the Regent's Park. As the great man was driving to the House of Commons one day in his state coach his identity was accidentally revealed to the landlord, who insisted, on the occasion of the Speaker's next visit, on treating him with the deference due to his exalted position. But his secret having been betrayed, Marylebone and its diversions knew the First Commoner no more.

During the forty-one years which Arthur Onslow passed at Westminster he witnessed great changes, not only in the composition and in the manners of the House, but in the actual conditions of Parliamentary life. Speaker Onslow the third saw the development of the modern system of Cabinet Government coupled with ministerial responsibility to Parliament. He saw the elder Pitt make his first entrance on the Parliamentary stage,[1] and during the most glorious period of the great Commoner's career—those two short years in which Clive laid the foundations of our Indian Empire, and Wolfe, at the cost of his life, added Canada to the English dominions beyond the sea—he was still in the Chair. He witnessed the rise and fall of the Pelhams, and he lived to see Pitt temporarily supplanted by Lord Bute. He was also directly interested in a movement which has exercised enormous influence on the House of Commons and the management of parties—the rise of the power of the newspaper press.

The Parliament of 1728 returned a large and docile majority for Walpole, and one of the first questions which agitated the minds of its members was the illicit reporting of the debates. A publisher, who had extended and amplified the summaries of speeches given by Boyer[2] since the reign of Queen Anne, was summoned to the Bar and imprisoned; but still the practice grew. In the *Gentleman's Magazine*, which first appeared in 1731, the reporting of the debates became a prominent

[1] As M.P. for Old Sarum, 1734-35.
[2] In his monthly publication the *Political State of Great Britain*.

feature, as it did in the *London Magazine*, wherein they were compiled by Gordon, the translator of Tacitus. When the next Parliament met the Speaker himself called the attention of the House to the subject, and in so doing allowed it to be seen that he was personally strongly opposed to the proceedings of the House being made public. Few historical writers have taken any notice of this debate.

In the course of an interesting discussion, in which Sir William Wyndham, Pulteney, and Sir Robert Walpole took part, the most sensible view was that taken by the leader of the Opposition. He, Wyndham, contended that the public had a right to know something more of the proceedings of the House than appeared in the votes. But the majority, who seem to have lived in dread of their constituents discovering what passed within the walls of St. Stephen's Chapel, declared that it was a high indignity and a notorious breach of privilege to print the debates at all. The official record of the day's proceedings runs as follows :—

" Thursday, 13 April, 1738.

" *Privilege.* A complaint being made to the House, That the Publishers of several written and printed News Letters and Papers had taken upon them to give accounts therein of the Proceedings of this House ; . . .

" Resolved, That it is an high indignity to, and a notorious Breach of the Privilege of this House, for any News Writer, in Letters, or other Papers (as Minutes, or under any other Denomination), or for any Printer or Publisher of any printed News Paper, of any Denomination, to presume to insert in the said Letters or Papers, or to give therein any account of the Debates, or other Proceedings, of this House, or any Committee thereof, as well during the Recess as the Sitting of Parliament ; and that this House will proceed with the utmost severity against such offenders." [1]

The account in Cobbett's *Parliamentary History* of the speeches delivered on this occasion is valuable from its containing an early reference to the custom of the Government and the Opposition sitting on opposite sides of the House. Some doubt has been expressed as to the date at which this practice was first introduced, but it is evident that in 1738 it was well established. Mr. Thomas Winnington, a member who was all in favour of drastic treatment of offending newspapers and magazines, alluded to his being in complete agreement with " the honourable gentleman over the way."

Sir Robert Walpole, in the course of his remarks on the supposed iniquities of the Press, declared that all the debates in which he had taken part which he had had an opportunity of reading in print were so garbled as to convey an entirely contrary meaning to that which he had intended. As to the charge frequently brought against him that he had instigated the publication of newspaper articles, in order to suit the policy of the Government, he only wished to say that, so far as he was able to judge, four pages were written against the Government for every one in its favour.

" No Government, I will venture to say, ever punished so few Libels, and no Government ever had provocation to punish so many. For my own part, I am extremely indifferent what opinion some gentlemen may form of the writers in favour of the Government, but I shall never have the worse opinion of them for that ; there is

[1] *Commons Journals*, Vol. XXIII, p. 148.

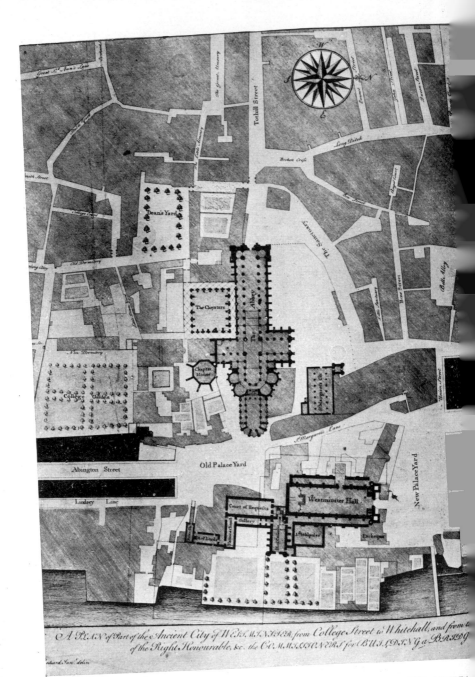

A PLAN of Part of the Ancient City of WESTMINSTER, from College Street to Whitehall, and from the Right Honourable, &c. the COMMISSIONERS for BUILDING a BRIDGE

Richard Iun.ᵗ delin.

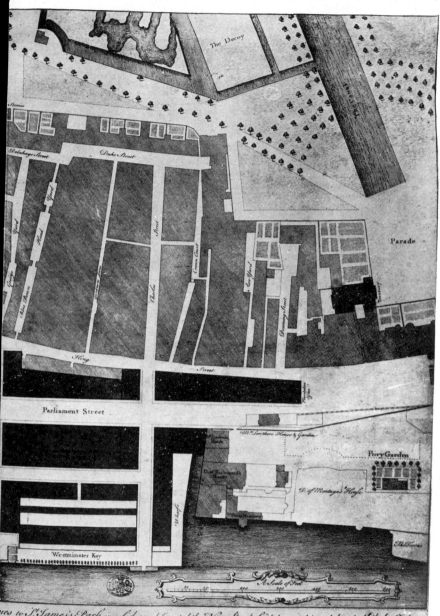

The Decoy

Parade

Duke Street

Delahaye Street

Stories

George Street · Axe Yard · Head Yard

Charles Street

Cross Court

New Yard

Downing Street

Treasury

King   Street

Parliament Street

Mr. Lowthers House & Garden

Fludyers House

Duke of Richmonds House

D. of Montagu's House

Privy Garden

Whitehall

The Ferries

Westminster Kay

A Scale of Feet

...mes to St. James's Park, in which are delineated the New Streets, laid down and intended to be built, by Order ...ESTMINSTER.   Survey'd Ao. 1740. by

Thomas Lediard Esqr. Agent and Surveyor of ye Streets & Ways for ye said Commissioners.   Fourdrinier Sculp.

NSLOW KNEW IT IN 1740
Fourdrinier's Map

nothing more easy than to raise a laugh : it has been the common practice of all minorities, when they were driven out of every other argument."

About this time a systematic attempt was first made to classify the members of both Houses according to their political convictions. Probably owing to an increasing interest on the part of the outside public in Parliamentary proceedings, the *Court Kalendar* for 1732 specified the members who were protesters against the Hessian troops in 1730 ; and a rival publication, *The Court and City Register*, in its issue for 1742, which was probably printed and circulated immediately after Walpole's defeat, divided the list of Peers into those who voted for and against the Convention ; whilst those members of the Commons " who are supposed to be in the country interest at the creation of Robert, Earl of Orford," have their names marked with an asterisk.[1] By passing a drastic Resolution against the printing and publishing of its debates the House was only acting on the principle observed since the time of Elizabeth, when Hooker wrote :—

" Every person of the Parliament ought to keep secret and not to disclose the secrets and things done and spoken in the Parliament House to any manner of person,

[1] These lists, of which those printed before 1740 are now very scarce, were probably first issued soon after the accession of George II. Watson's *Court Kalendar* for 1732, with a full list of both Houses of Parliament and the London addresses of the members, in the author's own collection, is the earliest hitherto met with. The British Museum Library contains the 1733 and many subsequent issues, and a fairly complete series of *The Court and City Register* from 1742 onwards. The better-known *Royal Kalendar* first appeared in 1767, and is still published annually.

unless he be one of the same House, upon pain to be sequestered out of the House, or otherwise punished as by the order of the House shall be appointed."

Notwithstanding the efforts of Sir Symonds D'Ewes and others to spread the light, and the journals kept by private members in the seventeenth century, our knowledge of the actual sayings and doings of Parliament from day to day remained extremely limited until the periodical magazine and the daily newspaper had come to stay. For a century after Speaker Onslow directed attention to the subject the unequal struggle between the Press and the Commons went on. Prosecutions, usually abortive, of offending newspapers and magazines were instituted from time to time, but the publications of Almon, Debrett, and Woodfall attained too much popularity with the outside world to be effectually suppressed. In 1771 the whole question was threshed out in the House, when the Press was so far successful that, from that date forward, the Commons tacitly acquiesced in the claim that the constituencies had a right to be informed of the proceedings of their Parliamentary representatives.

With the growth of the modern newspaper—both the *Morning Post* and *The Times* from their earliest issues have continued to supply a tolerably complete record of the speeches delivered in both Houses—came the shorthand reporters, who, as Speaker Abbot noted in his diary, gained a footing in St. Stephen's as early as 1786. In 1803 they occupied the back bench in the Strangers' Gallery without molestation, though, by one of those curious anomalies which abound in connection with Parliamentary institutions, the Press had still no official recognition at Westminster. An earlier entry in the same diary shows the scant regard entertained for the newspaper press a century ago. Speaker Onslow could not have been more emphatic in his disapproval of what has been called the fourth estate of the realm :—

" 19 December, 1798. Went to the Cockpit in the evening to hear the King's Speech. Two thirds of the room were filled with strangers and blackguard news-writers."

When, in 1836, the House of Commons began the publication of its own division lists (a reform which had been advocated by Burke in 1770) the battle was virtually won. The earliest instance known to the present writer of the publication of a division list, or something closely resembling one—a minority protest—was when the names of the members who voted against Strafford's attainder in May, 1641, were posted up outside Westminster Hall and headed : " These are the Straffordians, Betrayers of their Country."

The names of the Lords who voted against the occasional Conformity Bill in 1703 were published surreptitiously, as were those who voted for Sacheverell's impeachment in 1710. From that time forth more or less accurate particulars of the more important divisions in both Houses, compiled in the first instance by Abel Boyer, are to be found in the volumes of Cobbett's *Parliamentary History*. It should be mentioned that before the adoption of the present system of taking divisions a trial had been made in 1834 of a very primitive plan by which the names were called out by a member in the House and another in the lobby outside, and recorded by the Clerks.

After the great fire of 1834 reporters were admitted to the temporary building used by the Commons, and when, in 1852, the representatives of the people took possession of their new chamber in the Palace of Westminster,[1] the Press was at last officially recognised, and the reporters' gallery, as it at present exists, was an acknowledged fact. So voluminous have the *verbatim* reports of speeches become, and so vivid the descriptions of "scenes" in the House within the last few years, that one is sometimes tempted to wish that the penal regulations of the eighteenth century could once more be enforced ; for there is some reason to believe that there would be little or no obstruction of business if there were no picturesque reporting of the scenes to which obstruction gives rise. It is only fair to add that *The Times* has been an honourable exception amongst its competitors in the purveying of sensational reports.[2]

During the long years in which Onslow ruled the House many improvements were introduced in the keeping of its official records, all of them tending to regularise and simplify its procedure. The Journals, which had for centuries been kept in a haphazard manner, according to the capacity or incapacity of the Clerk of the House for the time being, assumed a more intelligible shape after 1750, in which year the Clerk of the Journals is first heard of. His office was from the first one of trust

---

[1] 3 February, 1852, after an experimental sitting in the spring of 1850.

[2] The whole history of Parliamentary reporting has been ably summarised by Mr. Porritt in Chapter XXX of *The Unreformed House of Commons*, 1903, a work of consummate ability and vast research.

and responsibility, and, as the House had no library of
its own until early in the nineteenth century, he had the
custody of all books and papers relating to the business
of the House. He fulfilled, in addition to the compilation of the Journals, which have always been accepted
as authoritative evidence in the courts of law, many of
the duties which now appertain exclusively to the Libra-
rian. It was owing to Speaker Onslow's exertions that
the House, in 1742, first ordered its Journals to be
printed.

On the recommendation of a Select Committee,
Nicholas Hardinge, then Clerk of the House, entrusted
the printing of the Manuscript Journals, from the commencement in 1547, to Samuel Richardson, printer and
novelist, then in the first bloom of *Pamela, or Virtue
Rewarded*, in " whose skill and integrity," as the Committee reported, Mr. Hardinge could safely confide. They
were printed in Roman letter upon " fine English Demy
worth fifteen shillings a ream." By 1825, when another
report was made to the House on the same subject, the
outlay had reached a grand total of between £160,000
and £170,000.[1]

It is certain that Journal books of an earlier date than
1547 were formerly in existence, as a statute passed in
the sixth year of Henry VIII provided that members of
Parliament who absented themselves without the licence
of the Speaker and of the House, " entered of record in
the book of the Clerk of the Parliament appointed for
the Commons," should be deprived of their wages.
Many instances could be cited of quaint entries made

[1] Report of the Select Committee appointed to consider of printing
the Journals of the House. (*Commons Journals*, Vol. XXIV, p. 262.)

by the earlier Clerks of the House in its official Journals, but two must suffice :—

" 31 May, 1604.   Prohibitions Bill.   During the argument on this Bill a young Jack Daw flew into the House, called *Malum Omen* to the Bill."

" 14 May, 1606.   A strange spanyell of mouse colour came into the House." [1]

The earliest issue of the printed *Votes and Proceedings* now in the Journal Office is that of 21 March, 1681 (the Oxford Parliament). But the daily proceedings of the House had certainly been published prior to that date, and the author had in his own possession a single sheet of earlier date in the reign of Charles II. This solitary issue is, unfortunately, no longer in existence, it having been accidentally destroyed by fire some years ago.   It was reserved for Sir Thomas Erskine May (Lord Farnborough) to compile a general index to the whole series of Journals from 1547 to the death of Queen Anne, an invaluable work of reference containing many thousands of cross references which, had he never written a line of his better-known *Treatise on the Law and Practice of Parliament*, would entitle him to rank amongst the very highest authorities on this complex subject.

The form in which the Journals, which are elaborated each day from the shorter minutes known as the *Votes and Proceedings* (compiled in the first instance from the Minute Books kept by the Clerks at the table), are now produced and indexed leaves little to be desired. Yet such was the slavish adherence to precedent which formerly characterised the compilation of these

[1] *Commons Journals*, Vol. I, pp. 229, 309.

JEREMIAH DYSON, CLERK OF THE HOUSE OF COMMONS
From a portrait by Sir Joshua Reynolds in the possession of Mrs. Myddelton

valuable records that not until November, 1890, were the names of members moving amendments to questions inserted in their pages, although this convenient practice had been followed in the Votes at least as early as 1837, when Mr. Speaker Abercromby was in the Chair. In February, 1866, an alteration was made in the form of the printing of the Votes, whereby the Latin names of the days of the week were replaced by their English equivalents.[1]

In 1750, when the Clerk of the Journals instituted a better method of preserving the official acts of the House, Jeremiah Dyson was Clerk of the House. He purchased the office in 1748, but he was the first to discontinue the objectionable practice of selling the subordinate clerkships to the highest bidder. Dyson left the service of the House to re-enter it as the Tory member for Yarmouth, Isle of Wight, after Onslow's retirement from the Chair. He became a Lord of the Treasury and a Privy Councillor, and, from his acknowledged authority on questions of Parliamentary procedure, he acquired the nickname of " Mungo " Dyson.[2]

Disorderly scenes were comparatively rare in the House of Commons in the middle of the eighteenth century, but in 1751 the authority of the Speaker was defied by a Mr. Alexander Murray, brother to the Lord Elibank of that day, who was summoned to the bar to be reprimanded for riotous behaviour in Covent Garden during a recent Westminster election, and for threatening the high bailiff in the execution of his duty. He is said to

[1] The Lords still adhere to the use of Latin names of week days in their Journals.
[2] The ubiquitous negro slave in Isaac Bickerstaffe's *Padlock*.

have called repeatedly to his followers, " Will nobody kill the dog ? " and to have incited them to other acts of violence.

When Murray was brought to the bar he refused to kneel in obedience to the Speaker's order, whereupon the House marked its sense of his contumacy and the enormity of his original offence by committing him to Newgate.

There he caught gaol fever, and, after having declined to avail himself of an offer for his transference to the milder custody of the Serjeant-at-Arms, he languished in durance vile until the prorogation brought with it his release. He then made a kind of triumphal progress through the streets of London, escorted to his home by a noisy mob, after which, like many another comet, blazing for a brief hour in the Parliamentary firmament, nothing more was heard of him.

In this same year [1751] Arthur Onslow spoke, of course in Committee, in opposition to the clause in the Regency Bill establishing a Council. Horace Walpole thought his speech " noble and affecting," and it was also warmly praised by Bubb Dodington. The Speaker favoured the House with an historical retrospect of the question from the Regency of the Earl of Pembroke *temp.* Henry III to the Hanoverian era, contending that, though the royal power might with advantage be limited, it could not be divided without grave injury to the State. The Bill, however, received the Royal Assent, at the close of the session, without material alteration.[1]

Onslow was a determined opponent of late sittings

[1] *Commons Journals*, XXVI, p. 32, and Cobbett's *Parliamentary History*, Vol. XIV, p. 1017.

and late hours of meeting, for which he was inclined to blame the Government of the day.

" This," he wrote, " is shamefully grown of late, even to Two of the Clock. I have done all in my power to prevent it, and it has been one of the griefs and burdens of my life. It has innumerable inconveniences attending it. The Prince of Wales that now is [1] has mentioned it to me several times with concern, and did it again this very day, 7 October, 1759, and it gives me hopes that, as in King William's time, those of his ministers who had the care of the Government business in the House of Commons were dismissed by him to be there by eleven o'clock.

" But it is not the fault of the present King ; his hours are early. It is the bad practice of the higher offices, and the members fall into it, as suiting the late hours of pleasure, exercise, or other private avocations.

" The modern practice, too, of long adjournments at Christmas and Easter, and the almost constant adjournment over Saturdays, are a great delay of business and of the sessions.

" This last was begun by Sir Robert Walpole for the sake of his hunting, and was then much complained of, but now everybody is for it." [2]

Onslow was a whole-hearted supporter and fearless advocate of the privileges of the House of Commons whenever it chanced to come into conflict with the Lords. It was, in his opinion, within his province, in presenting Money Bills, to advert not only to measures which had received the Royal Assent or were in readiness

[1] George III.
[2] Speaker Abbot, Lord Colchester, also raised a wail in his diary over the protracted sittings of the House, as is mentioned more particularly hereafter.

to receive it, but also to those which, after having occupied the attention of the Commons, had failed to pass the House of Lords. In the last Parliament of George II, when several Bills had been thrown out by the Peers, he thought it his right and duty to have animadverted upon their failure and their value and importance to the Constitution, and, as appears by a copy of his intended speech endorsed in his own hand, he was only prevented from delivering his opinion at the Bar of the House of Lords by the accident of the King's sudden indisposition, which disabled him from coming in person to prorogue Parliament.[1]

Onslow took leave of the House of Commons, two days before the dissolution, on 18 March, 1761, in the following simple words, spoken straight from his heart :—

" I was never under so great a difficulty in my life to know what to say in this place as I am at present—Indeed it is almost too much for me—I can stand against misfortunes and distresses : I have stood against misfortunes and distresses ; and I may do so again : But I am not able to stand this overflow of good will and honour to me. It overpowers me ; and had I all the strength of language, I could never express the full sentiments of my heart upon this occasion, of thanks and gratitude. If I have been happy enough to perform any services here, that are acceptable to the House, I am sure I now receive the noblest reward for them : the noblest that any man can receive for any merit, far superior, in my estimation, to all the other emoluments of this world. I owe everything to this House. I not only owe to this House that I am in this place, but that I have had their constant support in it ; and to their good

---

[1] *Vide* Lord Colchester's Diary.

will and assistance, their tenderness and indulgence towards me in my errors, it is, that I have been able to perform my duty here to any degree of approbation : Thanks therefore are not so much due to me for these services, as to the House itself, who made them to be services in me.

" When I began my duty here, I set out with a resolution and promise to the House, to be impartial in everything, and to show respect to everybody. The first I know I have done, it is the only merit I can assume : If I have failed in the other, it was unwillingly, it was inadvertently ; and I ask their pardon, most sincerely, to whomsoever it may have happened—I can truly say the giving satisfaction to all has been my constant aim, my study, and my pride.

" And now, sirs, I am to take my last leave of you. It is, I confess, with regret, because the being within these walls has ever been the chief pleasure of my life : But my advanced age and infirmities, and some other reasons, call for retirement and obscurity.

" There I shall spend the remainder of my days ; and shall only have power to hope and to pray, and my hopes and prayers, my daily prayer will be, for the continuance of the Constitution in general, and that the freedom, the dignity and authority of this House may be perpetual."[1]

The ex-Speaker died of a gradual decay in Great Russell Street on February 17th, 1768. He had removed there, on quitting the Chair, in order to be near the British Museum, of which he was one of the founders. In his retirement he found his principal solace in his well-stored library, and in the visits of politicians of both parties who desired the benefit of his advice and experience. He was buried first at Thames Ditton, near a former

---

[1] *Commons Journals*, Vol. XXVIII, p. 1108.

T

residence of his at Imber Court,[1] but his remains
were subsequently removed to Merrow, near Guildford.
There are two portraits of him in the Speaker's House,
and another at Clandon Park. A likeness of him, as a
young man, habited in his Speaker's robes, attributed
to Sir Godfrey Kneller, is in the National Portrait
Gallery. But unless Kneller was a prophet as well
as a painter this ascription must be incorrect, for
Sir Godfrey died in 1723, and Onslow did not become
Speaker until 1727–28. The story, which originated with
Lord Colchester, that the chairs in which he and his uncle,
Richard Onslow, sat were removed to Clandon is apocryphal, though Speaker Addington, in the next century,
claimed the chair as his personal property and took it
away with him. The chair occupied by Manners-Sutton
at the time of the great Reform Bill, is however preserved at Melbourne.

In Onslow's time a proposal was set on foot to
build a new House for the Commons, and plans were
even prepared for it and for a new House of Lords by
Lord Burlington, in consultation with the Speaker.
As early as 1719 the condition of many parts of the
old Palace of Westminster was considered to be dangerous, and the Speaker, after consultation by the Office of
Works, was requested to report on the repairs which were
necessary to make secure the passage leading from St.
Stephen's Chapel to the Painted Chamber, the roof and
gable end of the Court of Requests, the roof of the
Speaker's private chambers and those belonging to the
Clerk of the House, Paul Jodrell.[2] The condition of the

[1] Speaker's Lane is still known locally.
[2] *Commons Journals*, Vol. XIX, p. 65.

Cottonian Library was inquired into at the same time, and it was eventually condemned as ruinous. Nothing came of Lord Burlington's scheme of 1733, yet from time to time the demand for an enlarged Chamber is renewed, and even quite recently the congested state of the House on occasions of important divisions has been put forward as an argument in favour of Home Rule for Ireland !

The first Parliament of George III, which met for business on 3 November, 1761, chose as its Speaker Sir John Cust, of Belton, Lincolnshire, the ancestor of the Earls Brownlow, and the Tory member for Grantham. Horace Walpole, who was naturally critical of the successor to the really great man whom Sir Robert had selected to fill the Chair, wrote a few days later :—

" Sir John Cust is Speaker, and baiting his nose, the Chair seems well filled."

He was by no means a success, and he allowed great licence in debate. During the hearing of John Wilkes's case he sat in the Chair for sixteen hours, which was considered a great feat in those days.

" Think of the Speaker, Nay, think of the Clerks taking most correct minutes for sixteen hours and reading them over to every witness ; and then let me hear of fatigue ! Do you know, not only my Lord Temple—who you may swear never budged as spectator—but old Will Chetwynd, now past eighty, and who had walked to the House, did not stir a single moment out of his place, from three in the afternoon till the division at seven in the morning." [1]

On 17 January, 1770, Cust was taken ill and could not attend the sitting of the House; he resigned on

[1] Horace Walpole to the Earl of Hertford, 15 February, 1764.

22 January, and died five days later from a paralytic seizure at an age when men are still considered young. Educated at Eton, he lived in Argyll Buildings, Great Marlborough Street, in 1761 and 1762, but removed to Downing Street after the latter year. He is buried in St. George's Church, Stamford.[1] Hogarth, who had already painted the interior of the House of Commons with Speaker Onslow in the Chair, introduced Cust's portrait in *The Times*, Plate 2. Drawn in 1762, the plate, for some unexplained reason, was not issued until after the artist's death.

Lord North, in looking for another Speaker, reverted to the practice of appointing an experienced lawyer. His choice fell upon Sir Fletcher Norton, who, after having been leader of the northern circuit, had been Solicitor-General in the Bute Administration, and Attorney-General in that of George Grenville. He was dismissed from the latter post on the formation of the Rockingham Cabinet in July, 1765. He was talked of for the Mastership of the Rolls, but the Lord Chancellor objected to the appointment being made. If it had been, he would have been the last Speaker who ever held that office. At the Bar he earned the reputation of being a bold pleader rather than a learned counsel, and his greed of money gained him the nickname of "Sir Bull Face Double

---

[1] Of Speakers known to have been educated at Eton, Cust was the first, though in the absence of the earlier school lists it is not possible to say with certainty whether any of his predecessors were trained at Henry's "holy shade." Speakers Grenville, Manners-Sutton, Denison, Brand, Peel, and Lowther were all at Eton, whilst Harley, Hanmer, and Abbot were Westminster boys; and Arthur Onslow, Cornwall, Addington, Mitford, and Shaw-Lefevre received their early education at Winchester. No Harrow man has ever filled the Chair.

SIR JOHN CUST
1761, 1768
From a painting in the Speaker's House

Fee." His demeanour, both in public and private, was over-bearing, and his manners coarse; and he showed his contempt for his fellow-members when on one occasion he told the House that in debating a point of law he should value their opinion no more than that of a parcel of drunken porters.

Mrs. Piozzi, in her autobiography, quotes one of the many satirical verses made on this Speaker :—

> "Careless of censure, and no fool to fame,
>   Firm in his double post and double fees,
> Sir Fletcher, standing without fear or shame,
>   Pockets the cash, and lets them laugh that please."

Junius was even more severe in his strictures. "This," he said, "is the very lawyer described by Ben Jonson," who

> " 'Gives forked counsel; takes provoking gold
> On either hand, and puts it up.
> So wise, so grave, of so perplexed a tongue
> And loud, withal, that would not wag, nor scarce lie
>   still, without a fee.' "

He fell foul of the elder Pitt in 1766, and accused him, during the debates on the petition of the Stamp Act, of "sounding the trumpet to rebellion," whereon Pitt intimated that he would be ready to fight a duel with him "when his blood was warm." Naturally the Whigs opposed his elevation to the Chair, but Norton was successful by 237 votes to 121 recorded for Mr. Thomas Townshend, who had been put forward, against his will, as a protest against the nominee of the Court. Horace Walpole had a strong aversion to Norton, though he was quick to see that he would rule the House more firmly than Speaker Cust had been able to do:

" Sir Fletcher Norton consented to be Speaker of the House of Commons. Nothing can exceed the badness of his character, even in this bad age ; yet I think he can do less hurt in the Speaker's Chair than anywhere else. He has a roughness and insolence, too, which will not suffer the licentious speeches of these last days, and which the poor creature his predecessor did not dare to reprimand." [1]

If ever a Court nursed a viper in its bosom, it was Sir Fletcher Norton. No sooner was he installed in the Chair than he entered into unseemly wrangles with private members, and in a peculiarly offensive article, " The Memoirs of Sir Bull Face Double Fee and Mrs. G—h—m," [2] which appeared in the *Town and Country Magazine* for May, 1770, it was said that he persistently used his position to browbeat the minority. When some disorder arose in debate, he cried, " Pray, gentlemen, be orderly : you are almost as bad as the other House." On 11 February, 1774, he called the attention of the House to a letter written by Horne Tooke in the *Public Advertiser*, reflecting on his conduct in the Chair, but in a truly magnanimous spirit the House vindicated its Speaker and ordered Woodfall, the printer of the letter, to appear at the Bar.

In the next Parliament, despite his unpopularity with the Court, Norton was re-elected to the Chair and without a contest, as his very audacity prevented men from placing themselves in competition with such a notorious bully. In presenting to the Lords the Bill for the better support of the Royal Household on 7 May, 1777, he

[1] Horace Walpole to Mann, 19 January, 1770.
[2] Goreham.

SIR FLETCHER NORTON
1770, 1774
From a painting by Sir Wm. Beechy in the possession of Lord Grantley

made an extraordinary speech, recalling some of the utterances of the mediæval Speakers in drawing attention to the extravagance of the Plantagenet kings. He said that the Commons had granted to His Majesty a very great additional revenue, " great beyond example, great beyond Your Majesty's highest expense." [1] Some contemporary reports gave the last word as " wants " instead of " expense," but the Speaker denied their accuracy.

The Court was, naturally, highly indignant, and Richard Rigby was put up in the House to arraign the conduct of the Speaker, which he did in a speech of great acrimony, declaring that the general sense of the House had been grossly misrepresented by its official spokesman. Thurlow, who was Attorney-General at the time, also contended that the Speaker had given utterance to his own sentiments, and not those of the House at all. But on this occasion Fox came to his rescue, and, by a skilful piece of special pleading, induced the House to assent to a motion exonerating the Speaker whilst stultifying its previous action.

During the debate on Burke's Establishment Bill[2] the Speaker made a violent attack on Lord North : " There was a strange scene of Billingsgate between the Speaker and the Minister ; the former stooping to turn informer, and accusing the latter of breach of promise on a lucrative job, in which Sir Fletcher was to have been advantaged." [3] As the Speaker continued to act in hostility to the Court, George III was determined that, if he could

[1] Cobbett's *Parliamentary History*, Vol. XIX, p. 213.
[2] 13 March, 1780.
[3] Horace Walpole to Mann, 14 March, 1780.

prevent it, he should not be voted to the Chair a third time. It was during Norton's tenure of office that women were excluded from the gallery of the House in consequence of a disturbance which took place in the year 1778. After that date they were only permitted to view the proceedings from a ventilator in the roof of St. Stephen's Chapel. Twenty-five tickets for this apartment were issued every night by the Serjeant-at-Arms. Wraxall relates that he had seen the Duchess of Gordon habited as a man sitting in the Strangers' Gallery, and the beautiful Mrs. Sheridan is said to have adopted the same disguise in order to listen to her husband's oratory.

In the middle of the eighteenth century the House of Commons presented a much more picturesque appearance than it does at the present day. Members wore their orders, stars glittered on the front benches, and after the revival of the Order of the Bath red ribands were contrasted with blue. Lord North was always spoken of as " the noble lord in the blue ribbon." It was the etiquette of Parliament to wear orders, as at Court, and the lace cravat and ruffle, the powdered hair worn in a *queue*, were all but universal.

The members for the City of London were the last to preserve a trace of the former splendour of vestment when on the first day of a new session they took their seats on the Treasury Bench in all the gorgeousness of mazarine robes and gold chains. The last Speaker of the unreformed House, Manners-Sutton, with the red riband of the Bath thrown across his manly figure, looked the impersonation of grandeur in apparel. Even Fox, before he adopted the blue frock-coat and buff waistcoat, was seen in the House by the all-observant Wraxall in a hat and feather.

Published 7 June 1782 by C. Bretherton

SIR FLETCHER NORTON
A caricature by Ingleby lent by Lord Grantley

The American Revolution swept away Court suits, swords, and bag wigs ; and Pitt dealt a mortal blow at the wearing of hair powder. With the French Revolution came a more sombre taste in dress, levelling all distinctions ; and with an occasional eccentricity of attire, adopted, as a rule, for the sake of acquiring notoriety, the House presents at the present time a depressing uniformity of sartorial art, relieved only by the uniforms of the Mover and Seconder of the Address in answer to the gracious Speech from the Throne, and the periodical appearances of an officer of the Household when bearing a message from the Crown.

Sir Fletcher Norton lived in Lincoln's Inn Fields till his death on 1 January, 1789. He bought his house there, No. 63, in 1758 for £1721, and when sold in 1884 it realized £13,000. Its windows were broken by a mob on 8 May, 1771, when the town went mad because the House had committed Brass Crosby and Richard Oliver to the Tower in connection with Wilkes's agitation for the liberty of the Press. An even greater crowd attacked Lord North's house in the Cockpit at Whitehall and threatened to pull it down.

After Speaker Norton's transference to the House of Lords, as Baron Grantley of Markenfield,[1] he exhibited the same instability of political principle which had marked his earlier career ; but he ultimately returned to the Tory fold when his capacity for inflicting serious harm on his party had vanished. On the meeting of George III's fourth Parliament he had persuaded himself

---

[1] John Wilkes said, when he heard of the title which Norton had selected, that it was most appropriate since it was composed of his two favourite objects—a grant and a lie.

into believing that he would again be nominated for the Chair, and he professed to be highly indignant when the House chose Mr. Charles Wolfran Cornwall, member of a respectable Herefordshire family and a Gray's Inn lawyer without much practice at the Bar, in his place. "Sir Fletcher Norton, who never haggles with shame, published his own disgrace, and declared that he had been laid aside without notice. Courts do not always punish their own profligates so justly," were the scathing words in which Horace Walpole pronounced his presidential epitaph.

Mr. Cornwall's political complexion was supposed to have been determined when he married, in 1764, Lord Liverpool's sister. But for a time he attached himself to Lord Shelburne and acted with the Whigs. Later on he found political salvation under Lord North, from whom he accepted the post of a Lord of the Treasury. The new Speaker possessed a sonorous voice and an imposing presence, two extremely valuable Parliamentary assets, but he was by nature of a shy and retiring disposition, and was described by Walpole—a not altogether unprejudiced critic—as "blushing up to the eyes from a crimson conscience."

One of the minor economies in Burke's Bill for the reduction of the Civil List produced a curious situation at the close of the session of 1782. The Jewel Office had recently been abolished in the general process of retrenchment, and when the King signified his intention of proroguing Parliament in person the officials hitherto responsible for the conveyance of the Regalia from the Tower were found to be non-existent. No one seemed to know exactly whose business it was to issue the order

CHARLES WOLFRAN CORNWALL
1780, 1784
From a painting by Gainsborough in the Speaker's House

for the production of the crown and sceptre, or how they were to be transported to Westminster. Neither the Lord Chancellor or the Speaker could solve the riddle ; but the Home Secretary [1] rose to the occasion at the last moment, and, dispensing with a military escort, empowered the Bow Street magistrates to convey the Regalia of England in two hackney coaches with blinds closely drawn, and guarded only by a handful of police officers. They took a circuitous and unfrequented route by the New Road down Great Portland Street and thence to Westminster, returning the same way in the afternoon without attracting the slightest public attention. Had the secret of these unpretentious vehicles been revealed a dozen armed desperadoes could easily have overpowered the police and emulated the far more hazardous exploit of Colonel Blood in the reign of Charles II. And had any mishap occurred to the Crown jewels the severest censure would justly have been cast upon a system of economy fraught with such disastrous consequences at the outset.

On 27 February, 1786, Cornwall gave a casting vote against the Government on the question of the proposed fortification of Portsmouth and Plymouth at what was then considered the huge cost of a million of money. The plan was condemned in the House by General Burgoyne, Sheridan, and Fox, and the dawn had begun to stream in through the windows of St. Stephen's Chapel when the division was called. The members were found to be 169 on each side, and an uproar arose unparalleled since the defeat of Lord North in 1782. Silence having

[1] The Rt. Hon. Thomas Townshend. Previously to 1782 he was officially styled Secretary of State for the Northern Department.

been restored Cornwall stood up, and, after declaring the numbers, added that at so late an hour he was too exhausted to enter into the merits of a subject already fully discussed. " I shall therefore content myself with voting against the original motion, and declaring that the Noes have carried the question." Caricatures were issued representing the Duke of Richmond, the Master of the Ordnance and the real author of the scheme, attempting to apply a match to a battery of artillery, while the Speaker, in his robes, extinguished the fire by the same means which Gulliver adopted when he succeeded in quenching the flames which broke out in the royal apartments of Lilliput.

In the Coalition Ministry, headed by the Duke of Portland in 1783, Cornwall was unanimously re-elected, and he remained in the Chair till his death, which, by a singular coincidence, occurred within twenty-four hours of his old opponent, Sir Fletcher Norton.[1]

History has recorded the name of one, at least, of those who have attained the great position of the Chair whom the House was constrained to expel on the ground of corruption proved up to the hilt ; of others, like Dudley, Empson, and Rich, who deserve the contempt of posterity in an even higher degree. A Speaker has been known to burst into tears in the Chair ; but, up till such a comparatively recent period as 1780, no case had occurred in which a Speaker has been chiefly remembered for his having been addicted to drink.

A new precedent was set in an easy-going age, when Mr. Speaker Cornwall relieved the tedium of long debates

[1] Lord Grantley died on 1 January, and Mr. Cornwall on 2 January, 1789.

by copious draughts of porter, a flagon of which was
placed conveniently at his elbow.

> "Like sad Prometheus fastened to the rock,
> In vain he looks for pity to the clock,
> In vain th' effects of strengthening porter tries,
> And nods to Bellamy's for fresh supplies." [1]

Cornwall had the advantage of hearing the greatest
oratorical triumphs of Pitt and Fox, the thunders of
Burke, and the lightning-like flashes of Sheridan's wit.
Was it Sheridan, or Lord Hervey, who said of a fellow-
member of Parliament that he was evidently bent upon
doing his party all the harm he could, since he spoke *for*
them and voted *against* them? Yet not one of these
giants of debate could keep the Speaker from falling
asleep in his Chair.

Once when David Hartley, the worthy member for
Hull, but a portentously dull speaker, whose rising was
usually the signal for a general exodus, asked the Speaker's
permission to read a clause in the Riot Act, Burke exclaimed, before the Speaker could intervene, " You have
read it already ; the mob is dispersed." Another story
of the same unconscionable talker against time is that
Mr. Jenkinson, afterwards Lord Liverpool, leaving the
house as Hartley rose to speak, once rode down to
Wimbledon, dined there, rode back, and found him still
on his legs prosing to a select and patient few.

On his first entry into Parliament Cornwall lived in
Golden Square, then a fashionable quarter of the town,
but on being called to the Chair he removed to the Privy
Garden, Whitehall. His portrait, by Gainsborough, at

---

[1] *The Rolliad.*

the Speaker's House is one of the best in the whole collection. Wraxall, whose memoirs of contemporary notabilities are especially valuable at this period, snappishly said of him : " Never was any man in a public situation less regretted or sooner forgotten."

When the necessity arose for appointing a successor to Cornwall, and the younger Pitt looked round the ministerial benches, he bethought himself of his cousin, William Wyndham Grenville, who was exactly of his own age. When only twenty-two he had been appointed Chief Secretary for Ireland, his brother, Earl Temple, being the Lord-Lieutenant, for it was an axiom in the Pitt family that the Grenvilles must be taken care of. It was an age of young men, and even whilst he was at Eton Grenville had attracted the attention of the outside world. There was a rebellion in the school, and two hundred boys left Eton for an inn at Maidenhead. They observed great order and method in their proceedings, choosing officers and keeping accounts of their expenditure. Young Grenville was asked whether he would be treasurer or captain. Without hesitation he said he would rather be treasurer. Whilst the young rebels were awaiting events Grenville received a letter from his father[1] ordering him to return to Eton immediately on pain of never seeing his face again. Much perplexed at the receipt of the letter, for before it reached him the boys had taken an oath to stand by one another, he determined to obey his father and quit the confederacy.

Showing his companions his accounts, he asked that they might be examined to see if they were correct. Whereupon young Montagu, a son of Lord Sandwich,

[1] George Grenville, First Lord of the Treasury 1763-65.

WILLIAM WYNDHAM GRENVILLE
1789
From a painting in the National Portrait Gallery

who was captain, told him that he had made a good treasurer, but a miserable leader of a party, and that he did not doubt that they would meet again in some other place, where Grenville might depend upon his being reproached for the desertion of his friends. Young Grenville was sent back to Eton by his father for a few hours (probably in order to be flogged), and was then taken away from the school. Lord Granby, who had two sons in the rebellion, sent them to the play, saying : " You shall go there to-night for your pleasure, and to-morrow you shall return to Dr. Foster and be flogged for mine ! " Lord Sandwich's son was a good prophet, for a cold and unsympathetic manner prevented Grenville in after life from kindling the enthusiasm so necessary to successful leadership, be his industry and integrity what it may. That he was quite conscious of this defect is apparent from a letter he wrote to his brother years later : " I am not competent to the management of men. I never was so naturally, and toil and anxiety more and more unfit me for it."

Few men have reached the Speaker's Chair at such an early age, at any rate since the Middle Ages, as Grenville. He was not thirty at the time of his election by 215 votes to 144 recorded for Sir Gilbert Elliot. On this occasion, as the King was ill, the new Speaker did not go up to the House of Peers for the royal approbation. Had the King's illness continued, and the Regency Bill passed in 1788, the Whigs, on entering office, would have dissolved Parliament, and it was generally understood that Michael Angelo Taylor would have been appointed Speaker. But the recovery of the King extinguished Taylor's brilliant prospects.

One of Gillray's clever caricatures satirises his disappointment: "The New Speaker between the Hawks and the Buzzards" depicts the opposing parties uniting in preventing Taylor from ascending the Chair. Michael Angelo Taylor, if remembered at all at the present day, is rescued from Parliamentary oblivion by an Act which he was instrumental in passing for the improvement of the London streets, and which is always called by his name.

Grenville only held office for five months, as he became Home Secretary in the summer of 1789. The next year he was made a peer, and when, on the death of Pitt, the Tory party was rent into a multitude of fortuitous atoms, he became Prime Minister of "all the Talents," the ministry which did indeed abolish the slave trade, but failed in nearly everything else which it attempted. The rewards which were showered on the Grenville family during a long series of years, and especially under Lord Liverpool, were so considerable as to give rise to Lord Holland's witty saying: "All articles are now to be had at low prices, except Grenvilles." William Wyndham Grenville, it must be admitted, was as great an offender in this respect as any member of his family, for he held the post of Auditor of the Exchequer, a sinecure worth £4000 a year, for forty years, though much blamed for retaining it after he became Prime Minister.

For calling the Grenvilles "a family of cormorants" the Duke of Buckingham challenged the Duke of Bedford of that day to a duel in Kensington Gardens. His Grace of Stowe, who was of enormous bulk, should have presented an excellent target to his adversary, but though shots were exchanged on both sides, honour professed itself satisfied without the shedding of a drop of blood. The seconds were Lord Lynedoch and Sir Watkin Wynn, and a caricature of the scene was published, entitled " The Bloodless Rencontre," 1822.[1]

Speaker Grenville's knowledge of the procedure of the House of Commons cannot have been extensive, and he was probably content to rely upon the advice of Hatsell, an acknowledged authority on the subject, and Clerk of the House from 1768 to 1797. His clerk assistant, John Ley, one of an old Devonshire family which has served the House of Commons in an official capacity for 150 years, became Clerk in 1797 (at first as deputy to Hatsell), and retained the post until his death in 1814. To him succeeded Jeremiah Dyson, 1814–20 ; John Henry Ley, 1820–50 ; Sir Denis Le Marchant, 1850–71 ; Sir Thomas Erskine May (Lord Farnborough), 1871–86 ; Sir Reginald Palgrave, 1886–1900 ; Sir Archibald Milman, 1900–02, who was succeeded in the latter year by Sir Courtenay Ilbert, transferred to Westminster from the Treasury. Before becoming Speaker Grenville lived at the Pay Office in Whitehall, and on resigning the Chair he removed to 20, St. James's Square (Sir Watkin Wynn's beautiful Adam house), where he lived with his widowed sister. His widow, Lord Camelford's daughter, survived him until 1864, a remarkable link with the past.

Pitt's next choice for the Chair was Henry Addington, the son of his father's regular medical attendant, and,

---

[1] This anecdote was told to the author by the Rt. Hon. G. W. E. Russell, grandson of the sixth Duke of Bedford, who had heard it from his father, Lord Charles Russell, Serjeant-at-Arms to the House of Commons from 1848 to 1875.

U

like the previous Speaker, still in the prime of youth. Sir Gilbert Elliot was again put forward by the Opposition, and though by a strange coincidence exactly the same number of votes were recorded for Addington as there had been for Grenville, Elliot's supporters fell off by two. When old Addington heard of his son's success he is said to have remarked: "Depend upon it this is but the beginning of that boy's career." On three subsequent occasions he was re-elected unanimously. "The doctor," as he was facetiously called, had not sat long in the House, and his voice was almost unknown in it, but he had applied himself diligently to the study of the procedure and practice of Parliament. A new departure was made in 1790, when he was voted a fixed salary of £6000 a year, in place of the old system of remuneration by fees and sinecure offices.

A genial mediocrity, he was very popular with the country party, and Pitt had a high opinion of him, which posterity has not altogether shared. On the other hand spiteful Whigs, like Creevey, always spoke of him as "the cursed apothecary." In the celebrated altercation which took place between Pitt and Tierney in May, 1798, his personal predilection for the former overbore his impartiality. When he learnt that a duel was to take place, not only did he make no attempt to put a stop to it, but he went to Wimbledon Common to be an eye-witness of the encounter. On the following Sunday [1] two shots were exchanged on either side without a hit, when the seconds pronounced that honour was satisfied. Pitt's opponents declared that he had indulged not wisely but too well in

[1] 27 May, 1798.

G. *Richmond, pinxt.*   *E. Scriven sculpt.*

HENRY ADDINGTON
1789, 1790, 1796, 1801
From a print

the convivialities of the dinner table on the afternoon of the debate, which gave rise to the duel. However this may be, such symposia were not uncommon at the close of the eighteenth century, and *The Rolliad* contains a pointed allusion to a scene of this description in an epigram on Pitt and Dundas :—

> "I can't see the Speaker, Hal; can you ?"
> "Not see the Speaker, Will! I see two."

Old John Ley, the Clerk of the House in succession to Hatsell, was so disturbed at Pitt's condition on one occasion that he declared he had not been able to sleep all night for thinking of it.

But when the Prime Minister was told of this, he laughed it off by saying :

"Could there possibly have been a fairer division ? I had the wine, and the Clerk, poor man, had the headache !"

In February, 1801, Addington resigned the Speakership, and in March he became First Lord of the Treasury in an administration which was only noteworthy for the Peace of Amiens. The periodical recurrence of mediocrity in high places, counterbalancing and correcting the achievements of genius, is a curious and persistent feature of English political life. Not easy to account for but patent to all, it is probably not without advantage to a community temporarily satiated with the heroic element in public affairs, and, when an Addington succeeds a Pitt, or a Wilmington replaces a Walpole as leading minister of the Crown, it is often found that the Parliamentary machine runs all the smoother from not being driven at full speed. Almost wholly uninformed upon foreign affairs, for he had never visited the Continent or studied diplomatic interests, Addington's mind was not attuned to the ready comprehension of international politics. " Home-keeping youth have ever homely wits," and, whilst he had a fair knowledge of finance and a conciliatory Parliamentary manner, he was conspicuously lacking in that elevation of mind and loftiness of character which so distinguished the younger Pitt.

" As London is to Paddington
So is Pitt to Addington,"

ran a couplet which was composed at the time of his being called to the head of the Administration.

When the war with France broke out again in 1803 the Prime Minister's opponents said that his gaze was directed exclusively to the Channel and to that, to him, unknown French coast, in abject terror at the thought of the threatened invasion of England's shores by Napoleon. No sooner did Pitt weary of the seclusion of Walmer Castle and evince a desire to resume his former position than Addington's power dissolved into thin air. He subsided for a time into private life, soon, however, to reappear in a subordinate position. It was then that his great opponent Canning said of him : " Addington is like the chicken-pox or the measles. Ministers are bound to have him at least once in their lives." During his tenure of the Chair the House voted the buildings formerly occupied by the Auditor of the Exchequer as an official residence for the Speaker. Addington seems to have taken up his abode in the Palace in 1795. The crypt of St. Stephen's Chapel, which had been used in the time of Lord Halifax as a coal-

Sketch of the Interior of St. Stephens, as it now Stands.

SKETCH OF THE INTERIOR OF ST. STEPHEN'S WITH PORTRAITS OF
ADDINGTON, SPEAKER ABBOT, AND JOHN LEY (CLERK OF THE HOUSE)
From a print by Js. Gillray

cellar, was converted into a state dining-room, and, as "the doctor" was of a convivial nature, and wont to describe himself as the "last survivor of the port-wine faction," he entertained there frequently. An account of one of these banquets will be found at a later page.[1]

His daughter-in-law, the second Lady Sidmouth, who only died in 1894 at the great age of ninety-nine, lived much in her youth with her father-in-law, and with Mr. Hatsell, the Clerk of the House. She retained in her old age a vivid recollection of Pitt and Fox, and well remembered hearing Wilberforce speak on the abolition of the Slave Trade. But probably her most interesting reminiscence was in connection with Nelson : she distinctly recollected his coming to dine at the White Lodge in Richmond Park[2] in 1805, and explaining the plan of his operations which ended with the glorious victory of Trafalgar. The Admiral traced the probable course of his fleet on the dinner table, dipping his finger in a glass of wine to illustrate his meaning. This table is still preserved as an heirloom at Up Ottery Manor, the family place, in Devonshire.

It has been well said that genius has no ancestry. Yet mediocrity can often successfully lay claim to a long pedigree. Old Dr. Addington, prior to his retirement to Reading, had practised the healing art first in Bedford Row, in which unfashionable street the future Speaker and Prime Minister was born in 1757, and afterwards in

---

[1] In 1798 the House voted £2542 10s. 6d. for the expense of fitting up the houses occupied by the Speaker and the Serjeant-at-Arms. (*Commons Journals*, 24 April, 1798.)

[2] Of which her father-in-law, the ex-Speaker, was Deputy Ranger.

Clifford Street, Burlington Gardens. On his son's being raised to the Peerage he astonished his friends by proving his descent from a Devonshire family seated at Up Ottery since the seventeenth century. The new peer adopted as his motto the words "Libertas sub rege pio," which "Bobus" Smith impudently translated into "Our pious king has got liberty under."

Of Speaker Addington there is a likeness by Phillips in the official residence at Westminster. The formation of the collection there was due to his initiative; it fortunately escaped destruction in the great fire of 1834, and since his time it has been considerably augmented both by purchase and by the munificence of private donors. The portrait of the next Speaker, Sir John Mitford, afterwards Lord Redesdale, was thrown out of the window in the hurry and confusion of the fire, but not till it had been charred and singed by the flames, and it bears the marks of this rough usage to the present day.

On the death of Lord Clare, Mitford was made Lord Chancellor of Ireland, with a salary of £10,000 and a retiring pension of £4000, and a peer of the United Kingdom. He was the last Speaker to be transferred to the Judicial Bench on vacating the Chair. According to Sir Egerton Brydges, he was "a sallow man, with a round face and blunt features, of a middle height, thickly and heavily built, and had a heavy, drawling, tedious manner of speech." His election to the Chair was opposed by Sheridan, though he did not press his objection to a division. Mitford's attention had been directed to the office of Speaker by Hatsell at the time of Addington's election, but, as he naively told his successor, what he really had

SIR JOHN MITFORD
1801
From a painting in the Speaker's House

in view was the more lucrative Mastership of the Rolls. When Mitford was chosen he conferred with Abbot, telling him that he did not think the position was so arduous as some chose to represent it, and that he was of opinion that it only required diligence, civility, and firmness. Abbot was also informed by Addington that though Mitford had accepted the chair, it might not be for long, and that he wished him to qualify himself as far as possible to succeed him on the next vacancy.[1]

With the appreciative eye of a new member Abbot recorded in his diary his impressions of a state dinner given by his friend "the doctor" in February, 1796. Nothing seems to have escaped his attention with the exception of the hour at which the banquet began.

"Dined at the Speaker's. We were twenty in number, Lord Bridport, Sir George Beaumont, Sir A. Edmonstone, Sir W. Scott Lascelles, Colonel Beaumont, Mr. Adams, Sir H. G. Calthorpe, Bankes, Burton, Wilberforce, Powys, Parker, Coke, Metcalfe, E. Bouverie, Bramston, and Mr. Gipps and the chaplain.

"We dined in a vaulted room under the House of Commons, looking towards the river,—an ancient crypt of St. Stephen's Chapel.

"We were served on plate bearing the King's arms. Three gentlemen out of livery and four men in full liveries and bags. The whole party full-dressed, and the Speaker himself so, except that he wore no sword.

"The style of the dinner was soups at top and bottom,

[1] Lord Colchester's diary alludes to his meeting Mitford to discuss the Speakership at "the Coffee House." This must have been Howard's Coffee House which immediately adjoined the upper end of Westminster Hall. It was not burnt in the fire, but removed on the erection of the ne w Houses of Parliament.

changed for fish, and afterwards changed for roast saddle of mutton and roast loin of veal.

" The middle of the table was filled with a painted plateau ornamented with French white figures and vases of flowers. Along each side were five dishes, the middle centres being a ham and boiled chicken.

" The second course had a pig at top, a capon at bottom, and the two centre middles were turkey and a larded guinea-fowl. The other dishes, puddings, pies, puffs, blancmanges, etc. The wine at the corners in ice pails during the dinner. Burgundy, champagne,[1] hock, and hermitage. The dessert was served by drawing the napkins and leaving the cloth on. Ices at top and bottom ; the rest of the dessert oranges, apples, ginger wafers, etc. Sweet wine was served with it.

" After the cloth was drawn a plate of thin biscuits was placed at each end of the table and the wine sent round, viz. claret, port, Madeira, and sherry. Only one toast given—' The King.' [2]

" The room was lighted by patent lamps on the chimney and upon the side tables. The dinner-table had a double branch at top and at bottom, and on each side of the middle of the table. Coffee and tea were served on waiters at eight o'clock. The company gradually went out of the room, and the whole broke up at nine."

On 11 November, 1800, in consequence of some repairs which were in progress in St. Stephen's Chapel, the Commons, after the lapse of centuries, met once more in the Painted Chamber.[3] The Speaker acquainted the House on the opening day of the session that he had received a letter from the Lord Steward, in which he was

[1] An early notice of its use in England.
[2] A custom still observed on these occasions.
[3] Sometimes called St. Edward's Chamber.

commanded to inform the House that, as the chamber in which they usually assembled was not in a fit state to receive them, His Majesty had given orders that the Painted Chamber should be fitted up for their accommodation during the ensuing session.

In adapting this venerable apartment—for it was probably of even earlier date than the Great Hall—to its temporary purpose the interesting discovery was made that its walls, like those of the neighbouring Chapel, were entirely covered under the tapestry hangings with historical paintings of considerable artistic merit. The subjects represented were the Wars of the Maccabees and scenes from the life of Edward the Confessor, with explanatory inscriptions in Norman-French. These paintings were probably executed to the order of Henry III, and, though careful drawings were made of them at the time of their discovery, the authorities who should have taken steps to preserve them promptly covered them with a coat of whitewash! The very existence of these mural decorations had been forgotten, and they would probably have escaped notice, until their final destruction by fire in 1834, had it not been for the accidental use, for the last time in its long history, by the Commons of the room in which, by tradition, the Confessor is said to have breathed his last. Once more its doors were flung open to receive the body of the younger Pitt, who lay in state there before his interment in the Abbey.[1]

[1] Lord Colchester notes the meeting of the House in the Painted Chamber in his diary for 1800, and *The Times*, in its Parliamentary report, 12 November, 1800, also alludes to the unwonted place of assembly.

The procession of Tory Speakers was continued by Charles Abbot, who was created Lord Colchester on his retirement, with a pension of £4000 a year and £3000 to his successor in the title. From his earliest entry into Parliament in 1795 he enjoyed the confidence of Addington, who told him to make the Chair the goal of his ambition. Gillray is responsible for a "Sketch of the Interior of St. Stephen's as it now stands," with portraits of Addington, Abbot, and John Ley in the clerk's seat. It was Speaker Abbot who gave his casting vote against Pitt[1] when Whitbread brought forward a motion for the impeachment of Lord Melville on account of peculation in the administration of the Navy. Ministers made no attempt to screen Lord Melville, if he were guilty, from public censure; but they contended that, upon a subject of such magnitude, affecting as it did, not only the character of Parliament, but of every individual member of the House, the fullest investigation should precede a final decision.

Pitt proposed the appointment of a Select Committee to inquire into the charges brought with irresistible force against Lord Melville, but on the numbers being found to be equal, 216 to 216, the Speaker, pale with emotion and after ten minutes of terrible suspense, during which the dropping of a pin might have been heard in the crowded House, gave his vote against the Government. When the decision of the Chair was made known Pitt burst into tears, and at past five in the morning hurried from the House. The next day Lord Melville resigned.

Speaker Abbot was the inventor of the Census; he introduced many improvements in the form and printing

[1] 8 April, 1805.

THE RIGHT HON: CHARLES ABBOT, D.C.L. & F.R.S.
Speaker of the House of Commons
From an original Picture by J. NORTHCOTE, ESQ. R.A. in the Possession of the
Hon: Society of the Middle Temple
Drawn by J. Jackson & engraved by C. Picart

CHARLES ABBOT
1802-2, 1806, 1807, 1812
From a print

of the official records, and he left an interesting Parliamentary diary. In it is a valuable note on the hours of meeting of the House, which had steadily been growing later, in unison with the dinner-hour of London society.

" Mr. Pitt asked me at parting what would be the proper time for beginning public business every day. I said I thought half-past four, if he could come. He said by all means, it was just as easy for him to come at that hour as at any other. He actually came at five." [1]

Some mention has already been made of the early hour at which the House was accustomed to meet in Elizabethan times. During the Commonwealth and in the reign of Charles II it was usual for the House to stand adjourned at its rising until the following morning at 9 a.m. This continued to be the practice until 1770, when the nominal hour of meeting was altered to 10 a.m. This, with an occasional variation to 11 a.m., continued till the year 1810 ; but it will be seen that there was a considerable difference between the nominal and the actual time for commencing public business.

From 1811 to 1835 no hour is mentioned in the Votes for resumption on the following day, but from the latter year the time at which the Speaker would take the Chair is usually notified as three or half-past. On 18 July, 1835, it was appointed to meet at a quarter to four, at which hour it remained until 1888, when three o'clock was reverted to. The present time of meeting is a quarter of an hour earlier. At the close of the session of 1808 Lord Colchester wrote :—

" The most laborious session for hours of sitting ever

[1] *Diary of Lord Colchester*, Vol. I, p. 543.

known within living memory of the oldest members or officers of the House. There were III sitting days, amounting to 829 hours, averaging 7½ hours a day. Since Easter to the close of the session rarely less than 10 or 11 hours every day."

What would he have thought of 1887, when the House sat on 160 days, and for 277 hours after midnight !

On 24 May, 1803, the Speaker wrote in his diary :—

" Settled with the Serjeant-at-Arms and Mr. Ley that the gallery door should be opened, every day if required, at twelve ; and the Serjeant would let the House Keeper understand that the ' news writers ' might be let in their usual places (the back row of the gallery), as being understood to have the order of particular members like any other strangers."

This Speaker persuaded the Government to spend £70,000 in improving his official residence between 1802 and 1808, and the alterations and additions were carried out by Wyatt, the fashionable architect of the day, but one of the greatest Vandals his profession has ever known when engaged on the restoration of ancient buildings. Worse than " Blue Dick," who " rattled down proud Becket's glassy bones " at Canterbury from mistaken religious conviction, Wyatt, at Salisbury, in addition to other enormities, carted into the town ditch the mediæval glass which had escaped the Reformation and the Commonwealth.

" The King talked to me at length about the forms of the House of Commons, and the conversion of the Speaker's house in Palace Yard. He looked remarkably well ; rather grown larger within the last twelvemonth, and very cheerful. The King having asked me very particularly about the Speaker's house, and its' being finished, I wrote to the Duke of Portland to desire he would ask the King for his portrait, to be placed as the only picture in the principal of those apartments which the members of the House of Commons are accustomed to visit in the course of the session." [1]

The picture was given, and it was painted by Sir Thomas Lawrence, but it is nowhere to be found at Westminster now. The large expenditure on the official residence was much commented upon at the time, and Tierney, who voiced the opinion of the economists, threatened to bring the matter before the House ; but the Speaker referred him to the architect, and the storm blew over. Wyatt probably destroyed far more than he preserved, as is painfully evident from the additional plates in Smith's *Antiquities of Westminster*, in which Plates 24 and 26, 27 and 28, show extensive demolitions in progress on the east side of the old House of Lords and the vicinity of the Princes' Chamber ; but a curious oak door, painted and gilt with arabesque ornaments, which was found plastered up in the crypt of St. Stephen's Chapel, escaped wanton destruction, only to perish in the fire of 1834. [2]

On the debate on the Address, at the opening of the session of 1810, the Speaker showed that he was no respecter of persons in his official capacity. " We had a grand fuss in telling the House. The Princess of Wales, who had been present the whole time, would stay it out to know the numbers, and so remained in her place in the gallery. The Speaker very significantly

---

[1] *Diary*, 20 January, 1808.
[2] This door is figured in the body of Smith's *Antiquities of Westminster*, which, with the additional plates, is the most valuable pictorial representation of the Palace, as it existed a century ago.

called several times for strangers to withdraw ; which she defied, and sat on. At last the little fellow became irritated, started from his chair, and, looking up plump in the faces of her and her female friend, halloaed out most fiercely, ' If there are any strangers in the House they must withdraw.' They being the only two, they struck and withdrew." [1]

After the triumphant return of the Tory party from the polls in 1812 Abbot was unanimously re-elected to the Chair ; but a speech which he delivered at the Bar of the House of Lords in the course of the following year brought upon him a motion of censure by Lord Morpeth, on account of his having introduced into it the subject of Roman Catholic aggression. After mention of the supplies granted, the financial measures adopted, and anticipations of future prosperity, the Speaker went on to say, in a passage which immediately aroused the hostility of the Opposition :—

" But, sir, these are not the only subjects to which our attention has been called. Other monstrous charges have been proposed for our consideration. Adhering, however, to those laws by which the Throne, the Parliament, and the Government of this country are made fundamentally Protestant, we have not consented to allow that those who acknowledge a foreign jurisdiction should be authorised to administer the powers and jurisdiction of this realm ; willing as we are, nevertheless, and willing as I trust we ever shall be, to allow the largest scope to religious toleration."

After a heated debate, Lord Morpeth's motion was defeated by 274 to 106.

[1] *Creevey Papers*, Vol. I, p. 123.

" I remarked," says the Speaker in his diary, " to Lord Castlereagh, Vansittart, and Bathurst that the House had repeatedly refused to instruct the Speaker what he should say ; that they left it to him to collect the sense of the House from its proceedings ; and that as to pleasing everybody I had long ago given up that attempt."

The earliest speech made by any Speaker which is recorded in the Journals of the House of Lords is one of Sir Thomas Englefield in 1509–10. At first the entries only state the general substance of the Speaker's remarks, but in the reign of Elizabeth some are given by Sir Symonds D'Ewes at greater length. There is a speech of Speaker Lenthall, in 1641, given in some detail, and several more in the reign of Charles II. In 1689 two such speeches are entered in the Journals, but none during the reigns of William III or Anne. There are four by Sir Spencer Compton in the reign of George I, and one in the Commons Journals. From 1721 there is no prorogation speech entered at length in either Journal, except one by Speaker Onslow in 1745 reviewing the whole state of public affairs both in and out of Parliament.

Abbot died in Spring Gardens on 8 May, 1829, and was buried without a monument, by the side of his mother, in Westminster Abbey, the first Speaker to be so honoured since Trussell, Puckering, and Richardson, and also the last in the Abbey's roll of fame. His portrait, by Sir Thomas Lawrence, is one of the ornaments of the Speaker's collection.

The name is now reached of the only man who has ever been Speaker seven times, though his actual tenure of office was exceeded in length by both Arthur Onslow and Shaw - Lefevre. This was Charles Manners-Sutton, a son of the Archbishop of Canterbury who crowned George IV. But for his open connection with the Tory party outside the House he would undoubtedly have been re-elected an eighth time in 1835. Such an exceptional Parliamentary career deserves somewhat detailed examination. Manners-Sutton was originally intended for the Law. He entered Parliament for the first time in November, 1806, shortly after the death of Fox, and when the Ministry of " All the Talents " was hastening to its close to be replaced by the Duke of Portland as the nominal head of the Tory party.

At the time of his entering the House young Manners-Sutton was living in Stone Buildings, Lincoln's Inn, and though he never had very much practice at the Bar, his commanding voice and presence soon attracted the attention of his fellow-members, and especially of Castlereagh, George Canning, and Spencer Perceval. As became the son of an archbishop, his maiden speech was made on the Clergy Residence Bill, introduced by himself.[1] A little later on he was found supporting the retention of flogging in the army. At the early age of twenty-seven he had been made Judge Advocate-General, and was speaking as the mouthpiece of the Government. In 1812 he made a forcible speech in opposition to Lord Morpeth's motion for inquiry into the state of Ireland, veiling the demand for Catholic Emancipation. It was a long debate, and Grattan did not rise to address the House until four in the morning,

---

[1] " There was no point," he said, " in which so much improvement had taken place in the last twenty years as in the arrangements for the examination of candidates for Holy Orders."

H. W. *Pickersgill, R.A.*   *Samuel Cousins, sculpt.*

HENRY CHARLES MANNERS-SUTTON
1817, 1819, 1820, 1826, 1830, 1831, 1833
From a print

E.

nor did it adjourn until half-past five, after defeating
Lord Morpeth's motion by a majority of ninety-four.

Five years later Manners-Sutton's reputation was so
well established, that on the resignation of Speaker Abbot,
in June, 1817, little surprise was expressed when he was
put forward by the Ministry of the day to fill the vacant
Chair. The Opposition proposed C. W. Williams Wynn, the
member for Merionethshire, who was heavily handicapped
by a high falsetto voice, and in the *Creevey Papers* there
is a complimentary reference to the successful candidate
in the contest.

" We all like our new Speaker most extremely ; he
is gentlemanlike and obliging. The would-be Speaker [1]
(*alias* Squeaker) has, as I suppose you have heard,
moved down to my old anti-Peace of Amiens bench.
I rejoice sincerely that I did not vote for said Squeaker,
but some of those who did are, I hear, very much
ashamed of themselves for it." [2]

Mr. Wynn's brother, Sir Watkin, was also a member
of the House, and from the peculiarity of their voices
the two were commonly known as " Bubble and Squeak."
At the election referred to Manners-Sutton had been
chosen by a majority of one hundred votes, and some
spiteful wit said that if Williams Wynn had minded his
P's and Q's he might have been Speaker instead of
Squeaker ! Once in the Chair, not even the most bitter
Radical found cause to complain of the Speaker's partiality. He " rode the House with a snaffle rein, and not
with a curb," as one of his political opponents remarked.
Some colour is lent to his understanding of the changing

[1] Wynn.
[2] Lord Folkestone to Creevey, 23 February 1818.

X

relations between the House and the Chair by the fact that when he intervened in the debates in Committee on the Catholic Relief Bill of 1825, he prefaced his remarks with an apology for joining in the discussions. In 1827, in Canning's Administration, he could have been Home Secretary for the asking, but he preferred to remain where he was.

Tom Moore's *Diary* for May, 1829, reveals a glimpse of Manners-Sutton's private life in the old official residence on the banks of the Thames. Daniel O'Connell, the " Liberator," had made a dramatic appearance at the Bar of the House, to claim the seat for Clare denied to him as a Roman Catholic, a circumstance which convinced the Duke of Wellington that Catholic Emancipation could not be much longer delayed.

" Went to the House of Commons early, having begged Mr. Speaker yesterday to put me on the list for under the gallery. An immense crowd in the lobby, Irish agitators, etc. ; got impatient and went round to Mr. Speaker, who sent the train-bearer to accompany me to the lobby, and after some little difficulty I got in. The House enormously full. O'Connell's speech good and judicious. Sent for by Mrs. Manners-Sutton at seven o'clock to have some dinner ; none but herself and daughters, Mr. Lockwood, and Mr. Sutton. Amused to see her in all her state, the same hearty, lively Irishwoman still. Walked with her in the garden ; the moonlight rising on the river, the boats gliding along it, the towers of Lambeth rising on the opposite bank, the lights of Westminster Bridge gleaming on the left ; and then, when we turned round to the House, that beautiful, Gothic structure, illuminated from within, and at that moment containing within it the council of the nation— all was most picturesque and striking."

The Speaker's second wife, a Miss Ellen Power, from the county of Waterford, was only a recent bride at the time of Moore's visit. His first wife was Miss Denison, of the Nottinghamshire family which gave another Speaker to the House in after years.

The worst fault that could be laid to Manners-Sutton's charge was that he was never able wholly to dissociate himself from old party ties and obligations. Lord Grey has left it on record that as early as 1831 the opponents of Reform met at a party at the Speaker's house to discuss the plan of campaign, and " looked with confidence to its affording them the means of striking an effectual blow at the Administration " whenever the question should come before the House.

On Lord Grey's resignation in May, 1832, whilst the Duke of Wellington was endeavouring to form an administration, a short-lived intrigue was got up to offer the post of Prime Minister to Manners-Sutton. The idea seems to have originated with Lord Lyndhurst, aided and abetted by Vesey Fitzgerald and Arbuthnot. Peel, if we may believe Greville, also favoured the scheme, and, animated by a singular mixture of ambition and caution, he desired to make Manners-Sutton a second Addington, whilst he was to be another Pitt. But at a meeting held at Apsley House, at which Peel was not present, Manners-Sutton made a bad impression. He " talked infernal nonsense " for three hours, and Lyndhurst and the Duke were convinced of the impossibility of forming a Government under such leadership. The idea, so hastily conceived, was as promptly abandoned. As all the world knows, the Duke of Wellington declined to take office, and Lord Grey returned.

Nettled perhaps at the turn of events, Manners-Sutton intimated to the House his wish to retire.[1] A vote of thanks was accorded to him, and his pension of £4000 a year settled.

Merely to state that Speaker Manners-Sutton saw the Reform Bill of 1832 carried through all its stages would be to give a very inadequate idea of the strain imposed upon his physical powers and those of the responsible officers of the House. From 1830 the length of the sittings of the Commons went up with a bound. In that year the hours after midnight totalled 126; in 1831 they rose to 156; and in 1832, the crucial year, they amounted to no less than 223, a figure never exceeded or approached until 1881, when, at the beginning of the serious agitation for Home Rule in Ireland, they reached the unprecedented total of 238, a figure only since exceeded in the memorable session of 1887, when Speaker Peel was in the Chair. When, at last, in June, 1832, exactly five hundred years after the generally accepted date of the separation of the two Houses,[2] Manners-Sutton went up to the House of Lords to hear the Royal Assent given to Bills agreed upon by both Houses, it was to the provisions of a measure more far-reaching in its after effects upon English political life than any embodied in a statute of the realm since the origin of Parliaments.

When Reform was carried the Whig leaders played into the Speaker's hands. Nervous at the prospect of meeting the first Parliament to be elected under the new system, they implored Manners-Sutton to serve yet

---

[1] 30 July, 1832.
[2] 1332.

another term of office. Lord Althorp wrote him what Greville calls " a very flummery letter," and he accepted the offer.[1] On 29 January, 1833, he was voted to the Chair by 210 votes over Edward John Littleton,[2] who was put forward as a candidate by the Radicals. In the course of the year the King conferred upon him the Order of the Bath, an honour not enjoyed by any of his predecessors since Speaker Compton.[3]

Manners-Sutton was rather short-sighted, and when the new Parliament assembled, like the strong party man that he was, he affected not to be able to distinguish the new Whig members' faces, nor to remember their names. When he had to call on Mr. Bulteel to speak he made a great pretence of looking at the name through his glass before he cried out, " Mister Bull Tail," at which the House laughed loud and long. One of the first of the new members returned in the Tory interest was the young representative of the Duke of Newcastle's pocket borough of Newark—William Ewart Gladstone.

" The first time," he wrote to a correspondent many years later, " that business required me to go to the arm of the Chair to say something to the Speaker, Manners-Sutton—the first of seven whose subject I have been— who was something of a Keate, I remember the revival in me bodily of the frame of mind in which the school-boy stands before his master."

Mr. Gladstone had been at Eton under Dr. Keate, and

[1] *Greville Memoirs*, 11 January, 1833.

[2] Afterwards Lord Hatherton.

[3] " At Court yesterday, the Speaker was made a Knight of the Bath, to his great delight. It is a reward for his conduct during the session, in which he has done Government good and handsome service." (*Greville Memoirs*, 5 September, 1833.)

he retained a lively recollection of the methods of persuasion favoured by that well-known advocate of the birch. He took his seat in January, 1833, in the old House of Commons, which was soon afterwards to be destroyed by fire. On his first entry into Parliament the future Prime Minister took rooms in Jermyn Street, lodging over the shop of a corn-chandler named Crampern, a few doors west of York Street, St. James's Square. The corn-chandler in question was a relation of some of his constituents at Newark. Removing soon after to the Albany, Mr. Gladstone retained a lifelong partiality for St. James's, and during the session of 1890 he lived at No. 10, St. James's Square, the former home of Chatham. Lord Derby, the " Rupert of Debate," lived in the same house from 1837 to 1854.[1]

Lord John Russell admitted in after years that he had supported the candidature of Manners-Sutton in 1833 because he felt exceedingly solicitous and somewhat diffident concerning the reformed House of Commons. For the purpose of securing the advantage of his long experience he was willing to depart from the general rule that the Speaker should be the representative of the majority. During Manners-Sutton's last term of office Sir Thomas Erskine May, the greatest authority on Parliamentary Procedure that the House has ever known, first became officially connected with the Commons. Placed at first in the library, he undertook, whilst a mere youth, the enormous labour of indexing the whole series of Journals

---

[1] The London County Council has recently placed a memorial tablet on the front of the house to commemorate its association with the names of three Prime Ministers. Mr. Gladstone personally informed the present writer of the circumstances attending his early connection with the neighbourhood.

from the year 1547 to the reign of Queen Anne. As an illustration of the changed habits of the House within his personal recollection, Sir Thomas Erskine May told the present writer that he remembered the Speaker leaving the Chair, some time in the 'thirties, followed by the great majority of members, and proceeding in haste to the riverside in order to watch the race for Doggett's Coat and Badge as it passed by Westminster. There was then a pleasant garden, fringed with tall trees on the river bank, attached to the Speaker's house.

The most memorable incident of Manners-Sutton's last Speakership was the destruction of the old Houses of Parliament by fire on 16 October, 1834. The Speaker was with his family at Brighton at the time, recuperating his energies after the fatigues of the session. Recalled by an express, he arrived in town the next morning to find the flames still raging and his own house a smoking heap of ruins. Having witnessed the destruction of the whole Palace, with the exception of Westminster Hall, the Star Chamber, and a few unimportant exceptions, it was suggested to him that it was his duty to write to the King, informing him of the actual state of affairs, so far as it was in his power to form a judgment ; the more so as, by the gracious permission of the Crown, he was living in a portion of a royal palace. He waited upon the King at St. James's to discuss the expedients necessary to secure another place of meeting for the Parliament. William IV commanded him to survey Buckingham House and its gardens, with a view to the erection of a temporary building, and to take Blore, the royal architect, with him. It is necessary to mention these facts because his interviews with the King at this period were later on made the foundation of a groundless charge against his conduct in the Chair.

During the great fight to save Westminster Hall from the flames the Speaker's house was stripped of its contents, and even the furniture, china and mirrors, were thrown out of the windows. The official residence of Mr. Ley, the Clerk of the House, fared even worse, everything in it being destroyed, even to his wig and gown. It was one of the many misfortunes of that calamitous night that the tide was very low throughout the earlier hours of the conflagration, so that the floating fire-engines on the Thames were unable to render any service during the time when by their help the spread of the flames might have been checked. A strong south-west wind blew the fire into the heart of the ancient buildings, and added to the fears of the bystanders that the Great Hall would be destroyed. So great was the glare in the heavens that the King and Queen saw it at Windsor, twenty miles away. Thus perished in a single night the historic chamber replete with memories of Raleigh, Hampden, Coke, and Cromwell; the arena in which Chatham delivered his immortal eloquence.; where Pulteney and Walpole, Pitt and Fox, Canning and Brougham, in turn confronted one another; where Burke threw down the dagger, and Castlereagh walked proudly to his seat with the Treaty of Paris in his hand.

" By the Clerk's table in that ancient chapel the brow of the boldest warrior had grown pale as he stood up to receive the thanks of the House and a grateful nation. There Blake and Marlborough, and that hero of a hundred fights, the Duke of Wellington, drank in the pealing applause which foreshadowed Westminster Abbey, and there the noblest sons of genius, Bacon, Newton, Addison, and Gibbon sat ' mute but not inglorious.' Its historic walls rang with the shout of triumph when the slave trade went down in its iniquity ; there Grattan poured forth his matchless eloquence, and Meredith and Romilly pleaded, against capital punishments, that criminals still were men." [1]

After the fire it became necessary further to prorogue Parliament, and if ever a prorogation took place under difficulties it was this one, owing to the difficulty of finding any habitable room in the precincts of the Palace in which to perform the ceremony. An eye-witness of the scene wrote :—

" The two Mr. Leys (the Clerk of the House and the second Clerk Assistant) called on Saturday. They desired Mr. Rickman to attend the Prorogation because they have lost their wigs, and Mr. William Ley says : ' We shall follow you to the Bar in plain clothes, but where the Bar is to be we know not.' "

When the Houses met again in 1835 it was in temporary chambers hastily improvised for the occasion. The House of Lords was installed in a room on the site of the Painted Chamber, and the Commons in an apartment to the south of Westminster Hall improvised out of the ruins of the House of Lords. Gladstone made his maiden speech in the old chapel of St. Stephen's, but Disraeli's " The time will come when you shall hear me " was uttered in the temporary building in use until 1852.

After Lord Melbourne's summary dismissal by the King,[2] Sir Robert Peel undertook to form an administra-

---

[1] Townsend's *Memoirs of the House of Commons*, 1844, Vol. II, p. 465.   [2] In November, 1834.

tion, and, though unsuccessful in obtaining a majority at the polls, he pluckily determined to face Parliament, and allowed it to be known that it was his intention once more to propose Manners-Sutton for the Chair. Grave charges were circulated against the late Speaker in the Press and on the platform, some of them undoubtedly founded upon fact, whilst others were devoid of any solid foundation. For weeks before the date fixed for the opening of the session the newspapers were filled with arguments for and against Manners-Sutton's claim to the renewed confidence of the House.

Great excitement prevailed as to the issue of the coming contest for the Chair, but Manners-Sutton waited patiently and submissively under imputations affecting his honesty and integrity until such time as he could refute them in his place. The *gravamen* of the accusations of his enemies was that, being Speaker, he had busied himself in the subversion of Lord Melbourne's Government, that he had assisted, with others, in the formation of the new Cabinet, and that he had advised the dissolution of the late Parliament for party purposes.

Charles Greville, who, though he never entered Parliament, was perhaps better informed than any man of his time as to the secret springs of politics, has left a vivid picture of the intense interest excited by the promulgation of these charges against the late Speaker. He made a book on the event, and having at first favoured the chances of Manners-Sutton, he eventually leant to the side of his opponent and made £55 by backing his opinion.

On 19 February, 1835, the opening day of the session,

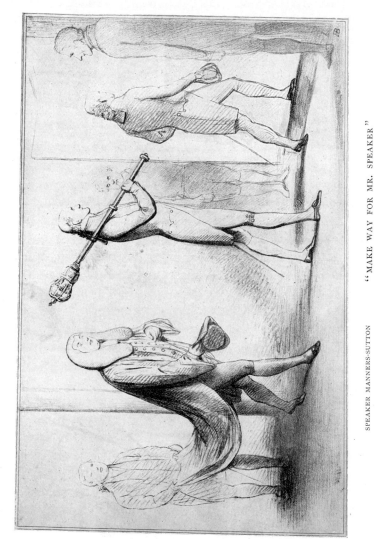

SPEAKER MANNERS-SUTTON

"MAKE WAY FOR MR. SPEAKER"

Manners-Sutton replied to his accusers in the fullest House ever known. The first charge, he was able to show, grew out of the fact (alluded to on a previous page) that he had been commanded by the King to attend him during the autumn, and he read a letter which he had addressed to His Majesty proving that it had reference solely to the burning of the Houses of Parliament. To the second and graver charge he admitted that he had been in communication with the Duke of Wellington during Peel's absence abroad, and that, on the latter's return, he had paid him a visit at the Prime Minister's own request. The only other occasion on which he visited Peel was when he waited on him for the purpose of obtaining the sanction and signature of the Chancellor of the Exchequer, in order to make good the payment of the Clerks of the House.

" He had never advised, had never suggested, never was in any way consulted, and he never knew of the appointment of any one individual member of the Government until after it had taken place. He admitted, however, that he did attend the meeting of the Privy Council after William IV had dismissed Lord Melbourne. So little did he know of the last charge, that of having counselled a dissolution, that he did not attend the meeting of the Privy Council from which the proclamation for dissolution emanated.

" He was not at it, he was not summoned to it, he was never consulted with regard to it, he never had anything to do with the dissolution, and so little did he know of the steps that had been taken, that he did not even know it had been resolved upon, until he read it in the *Gazette*."

Lord John Russell, in spite of these emphatic disclaimers, insinuated that for Manners-Sutton to have attended any meeting of the Privy Council at such a juncture was conduct unbecoming the Speaker of the House of Commons. Versed as Lord John was in the dead lore of the Constitution, he quoted from speeches made by Sir Harbottle Grimston and Mr. Speaker Williams in the seventeenth century, with a view to showing that if Manners-Sutton was elected, and the majority of the House gave up its right for the sake of a compliment, they might say farewell to the choosing of a Speaker for all time ; but, as Peel was quick to remark, Lord John must have selected his precedent when he thought that the charge of having counselled a dissolution could be proved, for the only part of his speech which extorted the faintest cheer from the House was that in which it was insinuated that, if he should be re-elected, the Speaker would do as he had done before.

Although Manners-Sutton had completely vindicated himself, the combination of Whigs, Radicals, and the Irish members under Daniel O'Connell carried the election of Abercromby, in the fullest House ever known, by the narrow majority of ten votes. It cannot be said that the Whigs triumphed out of their turn, for they had not had a Speaker of their own political complexion since Arthur Onslow's distinguished rule. Grenville, though he came of a Whig stock, was a supporter of Pitt when called to the Chair in 1789, and to all intents and purposes a member of the Tory fold.

" The great battle is over," wrote Greville on 20 February, " and the Government defeated by 316 to 306. Such a division never was known before in the House of

Commons, and the accuracy of the calculations is really surprising. Mulgrave told me three days ago that they had 317 people, which with the Teller makes the exact number.

" Holmes went over the other list and made it 307, also correct. In the House so justly had they reckoned, that when the numbers first counted (306) were told to Duncannon in the lobby, he said : ' Then we shall win by 10.' Burdett and Cobbett went away, which with Tellers makes a total of 626 members in the House. All the Irish members voted but four, all the Scotch but three, and all the English but 25. The Irish and Scotch, in fact, made the majority."

So disappeared Manners-Sutton from the Commons. He spoke but seldom in the House of Lords, though he lived for ten years after his ungenerous dismissal from the Chamber he had ruled so wisely and so well.

The only Speaker who ever came from north of the Tweed was James Abercromby, third son of General Sir Ralph Abercromby. Nicknamed by Brougham " Young Cole," in contradistinction to Tierney, " Old Cole," he had sat in the House for over a quarter of a century without attracting much attention or making many enemies. Creevey, indeed, calls him, in 1809, " as artificial as the devil," and a few years later " factious and violent," but the censure seems to have been undeserved. His career in the Chair was not marked by any incidents calling for the display of those higher qualities by which the office of Speaker acquires importance in emergencies. If he did not succeed in entirely repressing the tendency to disorder in the House which had grown up under the somewhat lax rule of Manners-Sutton in his later years, his impartiality was never called in question. His chief claim to remembrance rests upon his unremitting efforts to reform the conduct of the private business of the House.

Before Abercromby's time the passage of a Private Bill through the Commons was attended with much jobbing and confusion, and he succeeded in placing some salutary restrictions upon the expenses attending the promotion of many useful measures of routine. On the occasion of his re-election, on 7 November, 1837, he was proposed by his successor in the Chair—Mr. Charles Shaw-Lefevre. Abercromby was treated with marked rudeness by William IV, who took every opportunity of showing his resentment at the treatment of Manners-Sutton in 1835, and his general distrust of the Whigs.

" Tavistock told me a day or two ago that His Majesty's ministers are intolerably disgusted at his behaviour to them and his studied incivility to everybody connected with them. The other day the Speaker was treated by him with shocking rudeness at the drawing-room. He not only took no notice of him, but studiously over-looked him while he was standing opposite, and called up Manners-Sutton and somebody else to mark the difference by extreme graciousness to the latter. Seymour, who was with him as Serjeant-at-Arms, said he had never seen a Speaker so used in the five-and-twenty years he had been there, and that it was most painful. The Speaker asked him if he had ever seen a man in his situation so received at Court.

" Since he has been Speaker the King has never taken the slightest notice of him. It is monstrous, equally undignified and foolish." [1]

Speaker Abercromby, on his retirement in 1839, was created Lord Dunfermline, with a pension of £4000.

[1] *The Greville Memoirs*, 15 July, 1835.

John Jackson, R.A.   *Wm. Walker*

JAMES ABERCROMBY
1835, 1837
From a print

There is a portrait of him in the collection at Westminster. He wrote a memoir of his father, Sir Ralph Abercromby, published, after Lord Dunfermline's death, in 1861.

The first Lord Monteagle, Chancellor of the Exchequer in the Melbourne Administration,[1] had set his heart on the Speaker's Chair, and when Abercromby informed Lord Melbourne of his wish to resign, the then Prime Minister virtually promised Spring-Rice the reversion of the place, but finding that he would not be acceptable to the Radicals, Mr. Shaw-Lefevre was preferred in order to maintain the unity of the party. With the appointment of the latter, in 1839, the evolution of the non-partisan Speaker was all but complete. Born in London in February, 1794, the eldest son of a Hampshire squire, Shaw-Lefevre was predestined to become one of the most conspicuous successes in the Chair whom the House of Commons has ever known. His father, a man of tall and imposing figure, though of somewhat pompous manners, entered Parliament in 1796, and elicited from Canning the somewhat malicious remark that " there are only two great men in the world, Shah Abbas and Shaw-Lefevre." After being educated at Winchester and at Trinity College, Cambridge, the son was destined for the Bar by his father.

In 1819 he was admitted to Lincoln's Inn, but though by no means idle, his heart was in the healthy pursuits of a country gentleman rather than in the mysteries of the law. So keen a sportsman and so accomplished a shot did he become that his father once regretfully observed, " As for Charles, he is only fit to be a game-

[1] Thomas Spring-Rice.

keeper." After his father's death the young squire acquired a definite position in the county as a magistrate, a member of quarter sessions, and an officer of yeomanry. But he was perhaps even better known as the best shot in all that sporting county. In 1830, through the influence of a relative, Lord Radnor, he was put forward as the Whig candidate for the pocket borough of Downton, a seat which he soon exchanged[1] for his own county of Hants. He attracted the favourable notice of Lord Althorp, who asked him to move the Address at the opening of the session of 1834. Like his father before him, Shaw-Lefevre applied himself to the study of the rules and practice of the House, and to those useful but modest labours on Committees, which do so much to train the mind of the young member.

By 1837 his position was so far established that he was selected to propose Abercromby for re-election to the Chair. Two years later Abercromby suddenly retired, and Lord Eversley used, in after years, to relate how, standing behind the chair surrounded by a group of county members, one of the number said to him, "Now, Lefevre, we mean to have *you* as our Speaker." The friendly jest was found to express the general sentiment of the country gentlemen in the ministerial ranks. Ministers who had hitherto favoured the claims of Spring-Rice were forced to defer to the unmistakable desire of the bulk of their supporters. Nature had marked out Shaw-Lefevre as the fittest representative of an assembly of English gentlemen. His manly bearing, his handsome features and frank and open countenance commanded the ready confidence of men of his own class.

[1] i.e. in 1831.

John Jackson, R.A.   Wm. Ward, A.R.A., sculpt.

CHARLES SHAW LEFEVRE
1839, 1841, 1847, 1852
From a print

On 27 May he was formally proposed for the Chair, though on this occasion his election was not allowed to pass unchallenged. Goulburn, the rival candidate, had had longer experience of the House, had held office under the Crown, and he was, moreover, proposed by the greatest living authority on Parliamentary lore,[1] who had himself been spoken of as not unworthy to fill the post. In form and feature Goulburn presented an infelicitous contrast to his young rival, but, as usually happens in these contests, the ultimate verdict depended upon the relative strength of parties, and Shaw-Lefevre secured a majority of eighteen votes.

From the first his conduct in the Chair won the approval of all parties. He could call unruly members to order with a smile which disarmed anger. He knew how to rule them without giving offence to their *amour propre*. But when he was compelled to exercise a sterner authority his manner could be both resolute and unbending. In his intercourse with men of all shades of opinion he displayed the genial humour of his healthy nature. When twenty members sprang to their feet at once, someone asked him how he contrived to single out his man. " Well," he replied, " I have not been shooting rabbits all my life for nothing, and I have learnt to mark the right one." His firm rule was greatly needed in the stormy times of O'Connell's agitation for the repeal of the Union and during the great debates on the Corn Laws. Re-elected unanimously in 1841,[2] 1847,

---

[1] Mr. Williams Wynn.

[2] " The Tories were beginning to quarrel about the Speakership, some wanting to oust Lefevre, but the more sensible and moderate, with Peel and the leaders, desiring to keep him. The latter carried

Y

and 1852, he did not finally vacate the Chair he adorned until March, 1857.

The Commons met, experimentally, in the present House on Thursday, 30 May, 1850—whilst it was still in an unfinished state—in order to test the acoustic properties of the building. It might have been so utilised even sooner, but as no provision had been made for artificial warmth, and the season was an unusually cold one, it was deemed prudent to wait for a fine day. Mr. Speaker, accompanied by Sir Robert Peel, so soon to be snatched away from public life and usefulness, took the Chair at twelve o'clock, accompanied by upwards of 200 members. Hume, Cobden, and Bright were amongst those present, and below the Bar Hallam the historian and the architect Barry were provided with seats. The fittings of the House were still incomplete ; there was no stained glass in the windows, no heraldic decoration on the panels, and the benches were nothing but common deal and green baize knocked together with rough-and-ready haste. The primary idea of the architect had been not to produce a great hall, in which 656 gentlemen could lounge at their ease, but rather a compact house of business, in which 200 or 300 working members could enjoy reasonable facilities for transacting the public affairs.

Mr. Wilson Patten was the first member to raise his voice in the new chamber, and Mr. Sullivan, an Irishman,

their point without much difficulty. Peel wrote to four or five and twenty of his principal supporters and asked their opinions. All, except Lowther, concurred in not disturbing Lefevre, and he said that he would not oppose the opinions of the majority. So Peel wrote to Lefevre and gave him notice that he would not be displaced." (*Greville Memoirs*, 10 August, 1841.)

the first to present a petition. This was from the mayor and corporation of Kilkenny, " praying to be relieved from the odious tax of ministers' money." Mr. Gladstone also spoke, and amongst those present on this historic occasion in the annals of Parliament may have been the veteran Earl of Wemyss, now in his ninety-second year, for he was then, as Lord Elcho, a member of the Lower House. Sir Robert Peel took a seat in the galleries, as well as on both sides of the floor, being anxious to ascertain the tone of voice which members who desired to be audible without being noisy should in future adopt. The experiment was not altogether satisfactory, as every one who could, members and strangers alike, entered into loud and earnest conversation with his neighbour. Many groups talked all at once ; in vain, therefore, did the orators of the assembly, who affected to debate the questions under consideration, strain their lungs to raise a shout which might be heard above, not the murmurs, but the roar of general conversation. One member, addressing the Speaker from the gallery, said that he did not know whether the Speaker could hear him, but this he knew—that he could not himself hear what was passing on the floor of the House. At three o'clock the Speaker proceeded to the old House of Lords, which had been used by the Commons as a temporary home since the fire, and finished the business of the day there. This was assuredly the only time in its history when the House has occupied two separate chambers on one and the same day.

" Shaw-Lefevre was the best Speaker I ever knew," said Lord John Russell ; " when there was not a precedent, he made one," adding, so as to prevent any further discussion, "according to the well-known practice of the House," a formula which pleased everyone and permitted of no further discussion. This remarkable man maintained his vigour at an age when most men have retired from all outdoor pursuits. He bought a new pair of guns after he had passed his ninetieth birthday. He refused a pension of £2000 a year for two lives on the ground that he could not bear the thought of being a burden to posterity ; but he consented to accept £4000 for his own life, and enjoyed it for over thirty years. Lord Eversley's portrait, by Sir Martin Shee, is at the Speaker's House. Up to 1839 every Speaker on taking office had been provided with an ample service of plate, but, on the motion of Hume, the most persistent economist the House has ever known, it was henceforth attached to the office and no longer made personal to the holder.

It is within the knowledge of the writer that Lord Palmerston consulted Delane and asked him informally to adjudicate upon the credentials of the various candidates for the Chair, and they were not few, when, in 1857, Mr. Shaw-Lefevre retired. The qualifications which the editor of *The Times* held to be essential were : (1) imperturbable good temper, tact, patience, and urbanity ; (2) a previous legal training, if possible ; (3) absence of bitter partisanship in his previous career ; (4) the possession of innate gentlemanly feelings which involuntarily command respect and deference ; (5) personal dignity in voice and manner. To these indispensable requirements Delane might have added the importance of a sense of humour in the holder of the office, for many a delicate situation has been saved, especially in recent times, by the Speaker's possessing this precious gift of nature.

It would be invidious to mention the names of other candidates on whose merits Delane was asked to pronounce. But he made no secret of his opinion that the fittest man to succeed Mr. Shaw-Lefevre was Mr. Evelyn Denison, who had sat in the House for more than thirty years, and whose experience of its procedure dated from before the passing of the great Reform Bill. In after years Speaker Denison occasionally wrote in *The Times* for Delane, and one of his contributions to the paper was an article comparing the French legislative assembly with the English House of Commons.

On 7 April Lord Palmerston wrote as follows :—

" My dear Denison,

" We wish to be allowed to propose you for the Speakership of the House of Commons. Will you agree ? "

On the 30th of the same month he was unanimously chosen. The retiring Speaker, when asked if there was any one whom he could call to his assistance in a difficulty, said, " No one ; you must learn to rely entirely upon yourself." " I spent the first few years of my Speakership like the captain of a steamer on the Thames," Denison wrote in his interesting Journal,[1] " standing on the paddle-box, ever on the look out for shocks and collisions. The House is always kind and indulgent, but it expects its Speakers to be right. If he should be found often tripping, his

---

[1] First privately printed in 1900, and since re-issued for general circulation.

authority would soon be at an end." Disraeli, in congratulating Denison on his re-election in 1859, spoke of him as combining in his person the purity of an English judge and the spirit of an English gentleman.

He had a great admiration for Palmerston, and when he attended in state the opening of the International Exhibition of 1862 he bore witness to the great popularity which the veteran minister enjoyed with the people. On arriving at South Kensington, taking Lord Charles Russell, the Serjeant-at-Arms, and the mace and his train-bearer with him in his coach, the Speaker had to walk first in the procession ; but seeing the Prime Minister, he asked him to accompany him, when Palmerston replied, " No, the Speaker of the House should walk alone ; I will follow." And on Denison saying, " I should think it a great honour if we might proceed together," they entered the building side by side.

The moment Lord Palmerston came in sight shouts of welcome were raised : " Palmerston for ever ! " and so on throughout the whole building. One voice cried, " I wish you may be Minister for the next twenty years," at which Lord Taunton, who was standing by, drily remarked, " Well, he would only then be a little more than a hundred ! " Some men, it has been frequently proved, reach the maturity of their intellect at twenty-one, and some, like Lord Palmerston, the typical statesman of the Victorian era, at seventy-one.

Denison was in the Chair at the time of Lord Derby's and Disraeli's famous " leap in the dark "—the Reform Bill of 1867, the era from which pessimists date the declension of the usefulness of the Lower House, during the

Joseph Slater, delt.   F. C. Lewis, sculpt,

JOHN EVELYN DENISON
1857, 1859, 1866, 1868
From a print

period of the fiercest strife between Gladstone and his great rival. He was Speaker when the former became the first Minister of the Crown, though he did not live to see Disraeli head a triumphant majority at the polls. Age and ill-health compelled him to resign in 1872, too late, indeed, for his own welfare, for the long-deferred rest did not restore his overtaxed strength, and he died early in the following year. He possessed in an eminent degree the qualities of tact, discrimination, and justice so essential to the successful performance of his duties, and when his epitaph came to be written in the columns of *The Times*, Delane did no more than justice to a friend of many years' standing in causing it to be said of him :—

" As the House of Commons is the home where the English nature exhibits itself with the most absolute reality, Speaker Denison was the clear, unsullied mirror of that simple nobleness which we think Englishmen may claim as the ideal of our national character. Hence it was that he so exactly appreciated the feeling and disposition of the assembly over which he was called upon to preside, the sources to which he could look for aid, and the exact limits and sphere of his authority. He knew also that English gentlemen possessed, as he did, an unusual aptitude to conform to the spirit of traditionary law. He knew that hence he could rely for support on all who sat around him." [1]

[1] It was Delane's practice periodically to revise the obituary notices of public men which he kept ready standing in type, " necrologies awaiting their victims," as he called them. He took them home with him and made additions and alterations within his personal knowledge, during the brief intervals of leisure which he permitted himself at Ascot Heath. In this way the admirably lucid biography of Disraeli, though not required until 1881, eighteen months after his own death, was mainly his own work.

In view of recent occurrences affecting the relations of the two Houses, it may not be inappropriate to remark that when the House of Lords rejected the Bill for the repeal of the paper duty in May, 1860, Speaker Denison denounced in energetic language a practice by which he considered that the Upper House indirectly infringed on the special function of the Commons—the grant of public money—as one calculated to break down the broad line of distinction between the duties and powers of the two Chambers.

It often becomes the duty of the Speaker to decide, on the spur of the moment, what is and what is not a Parliamentary expression. Mr. Denison was appealed to in 1864 by Mr. Layard, then Under Secretary for Foreign Affairs, the House being in a very excited state at the time, to know whether it was competent for another member[1] to say that he had made " calumnious charges " against the Opposition. The Speaker said that he saw no ground for his intervention, whereon Mr. Gladstone looked reproachfully at the Chair and urged Lord Palmerston to get up. The Prime Minister then rose and said that, in his opinion, the imputation of motives was hardly in order, and that the expression used implied motives. A long discussion ensued, in which Mr. Disraeli, amongst others, took part, but before the incident closed the Speaker was reminded by Mr. Otway that Mr. Layard, of all people, should remember something about the use of the word " calumnious " in the House, for he had been accused of making false and calumnious charges in the year 1845, and by

---

[1] Mr. Gathorne Hardy, afterwards Earl of Cranbrook.

no other than the noble lord who had just spoken. And on Hansard being referred to, it appeared that though Lord Palmerston, at Mr. Gladstone's request, was protesting in 1864 against the use of the phrase, he had applied the very same words to charges made by the same Mr. Layard nearly twenty years before. Lord Eversley, on his attention being called to the expression, gave it as his opinion that " calumnious " was not a word to which exception could be taken. Since that date at least one Speaker has had constantly by his side for ready reference a list of admissible Parliamentary expletives. From time to time new adjectives and nouns have to be adjudicated upon ; but it is within the discretion of the Chair to determine how far they must be taken with the context and the circumstances of the moment, since it is quite possible for a word to be used in a manner calculated to give offence which, on another occasion, would pass without objection from any quarter of the House.

It has sometimes been said that nearly every Parliamentary contingency which can possibly arise has had its antecedent parallel, and is accordingly governed by a precedent, so that a Speaker cannot go far astray in a decision if he be thoroughly acquainted with the forms and procedure of the House and the rulings of his predecessors. But this is no longer strictly accurate. Formerly it was customary to give the Speaker notice of questions on points of order, but of late years the occasions have been numerous when the most weighty decisions have been required to be taken by the Chair on its being suddenly confronted with an absolutely unprecedented situation. In the case of the last three occupants of the Chair these decisions have required, in addition to exceptional tact, firmness, and courage, the prompt exercise of that peculiar authority which the confidence and respect of the House at large can alone confer. It is no exaggeration to say that the difficulties which Speakers Shaw-Lefevre and Denison, both of them admittedly strong and able men, had to contend with have increased tenfold since their day of power, owing to a multiplicity of causes which have fundamentally changed the temper and spirit of the House of Commons. Within the last twenty years the control and initiative in legislation have gradually been passing from the House to the executive Government—in other words, to the Cabinet, or a committee of that body which usually dominates the Cabinet considered as a whole.

Changes in the composition of the House, rendered inevitable by the " leap in the dark " of 1867, accentuated by Mr. Gladstone's Franchise Act of 1884 ; the claims of labour to separate representation and organisation successfully asserted in recent years ; the categorical demand by a majority of the representatives of Ireland for separation from the parent assembly, a demand annually restated, in spite of the abortive offers of settlement in 1886 and 1893 ; the formation of small subsidiary parties acting independently of the official whips ; the heavy strain of practically continuous sessions ; the altered rules of procedure all tending to enhance the power of the Government of the day at the expense of the independent member ; and, lastly, the application of the closure at the discretion of the Chair— all these have increased the ever-growing responsibilities of the Speaker.

When Speaker Denison presided over the House the practice of addressing questions to ministers was in its infancy, whereas at the present day the printed interrogatories to the Government on every conceivable topic of public and private interest run into thousands in the course of a single session, to say nothing of those, often the most difficult to deal with, which are sprung upon the attention of the Chair without notice. Mr. Denison was the last Speaker to exercise his right of speaking and voting in Committee. He had no liking for the financial methods of Mr. Lowe, and on 9 June, 1870, on a Budget proposal of the then Chancellor of the Exchequer, he formed one of a majority of four which inflicted a defeat on the Government. By a singular coincidence Mr. Speaker Abbot, who was strongly opposed to the removal of Catholic disabilities, carried an amendment in Committee in 1813 by the same narrow majority. The amendment was to omit the vital words " to sit and vote in either House of Parliament " from Grattan's Bill qualifying Roman Catholics for election as members of Parliament.

The Speakers of the House of Commons have not, on the whole, been conspicuous for literary ability. The notorious Dudley, as has been mentioned on an earlier page, wrote the *Tree of Commonwealth* during his imprisonment in the Tower. With this exception, a few volumes of law reports, of which the most notable example is that of Sir Edward Coke, and the writings of the great Sir Thomas More, whose *Utopia* will never die, are the only contributions to periodical literature emanating from the pen of a Speaker. Bulstrode Whitelocke was a painstaking and accurate historian, and Harley was a successful pamphleteer before he became a minister of the Crown. Sir Thomas Hanmer was a conscientious Shakespearean critic, and his predecessor, Speaker Bromley, wrote an amusing volume of travels. But both in fiction and poetry the Chair is otherwise unrepresented.

Speaker Denison, however, deserves to be remembered for his painstaking share in the field of Biblical criticism, known to posterity as the *Speaker's Commentary*. So impressed was he with the necessity that existed for an explanation of the Bible in accordance with the spirit of the age in which he lived, and the scientific knowledge accumulated during the nineteenth century, that he induced Archbishop Thomson of York and over forty other scholars and Biblical students to engage in the production of what is still recognised as a valuable book of reference. The Archbishop wrote the historical introduction to the whole work, which Denison, unfortunately, did not live to see completed.

On his retirement from the Chair in 1872, though he accepted a Peerage[1] Mr. Denison refused to accept the customary pension of £4000. "Though without any pretensions to wealth," he wrote to Mr. Gladstone, "I have a private fortune which will suffice, and for the few years of life which remain to me I should be happier in feeling that I am not a burden to my fellow-countrymen." There is a portrait of Lord Ossington, by Sir Francis Grant, in the Speaker's House. The official residence at Westminster was first occupied by him, and his coat of arms is sculptured over the entrance doorway in Speaker's Court.

---

[1] An honour conferred on every Speaker since Lord Colchester. The title which he selected was that of Viscount Ossington.

Having now reached a period in the history of the Speaker's office within the memory of many still living, it will be unnecessary to recapitulate facts which are within the knowledge of all who have studied the history of Parliament and parties during the last half-century. In treating of Mr. Speaker Denison's successors it would be unbecoming in one who, like the present writer, entered the service of the House of Commons when Mr. Speaker Brand still sat in the Chair, to consider in detail the political aspect of questions which await the impartial verdict of a later age—questions, moreover, which are apt to assume such a totally different complexion when viewed from the Government or from the Opposition benches.

When the inflammable and ephemeral matter which feeds the fires of debate has utterly burnt out, and when the sound and fury with which every step of political progress is wont to be discussed has been extinguished by the merciful hand of time, those who dwell on the fertile soil formed by those volcanic upheavals will be in a better position to appraise the ability and boldness, the success or failure, of rival English statesmen, and to recognise at their true value causes which agitated the length and breadth of the Kingdom whilst they were in the making.

Mr. Brand was three times unanimously called to the Chair, and will be long remembered for his *coup d'état* of February, 1881, when, after a sitting of nearly thirty hours, he declared the state of business to be so urgent as to justify him in summarily closing the debate. The story is told at length by Lord Morley in his *Life of Gladstone*. During this and the following session urgency resolutions were agreed to by the House, by which its powers could, in respect of a particular Bill, be vested in the Speaker, who accordingly laid rules upon the table prescribing the manner in which the Bill should be dealt with. At the same time obstruction was checked by the power given to the Speaker to put the question, " That the question be now put." If this question was agreed to in a House of not less than 200 members, the question was put forthwith without further debate.

Speaker Brand was reputed to have the best French cook in London, Cost by name. The title was disputed by Beguinot, successively *chef* to Lord Granville and his brother, Mr. F. Leveson-Gower, and by Mr. Russell Sturgis's *cordon bleu.* The first of them said " nous sommes trois," and opinions still vary as to their respective merits. Mr. Brand was a man of slight stature, with the fresh pink of a winter apple in his cheeks, of remarkable dignity, and sound judgment, and, though Disraeli was sceptical at the time of his appointment as to the expediency of promoting a former whip, his retirement, in 1884, was received with real regret by the majority of the House. Mr. Brand was once asked if in his long experience of Parliamentary life he had ever known or heard of money passing for the vote of a member. He said: "No, never. The nearest approach to it I have ever known was the finding of a suit of clothes for an M.P. who stated that without them he would be unable to attend the House at a critical division."[1]

Of his successor, Mr. Arthur Wellesley Peel, the worthy

[1] *Recollections of Sir Algernon West.*

HENRY BOUVERIE WILLIAM BRAND
1872, 1874, 1880
From an engraving in the possession of the Serjeant-at-Arms after F. Sargent

inheritor of an illustrious Parliamentary name, it will be unnecessary to say more at present than that he maintained to the full the high traditions of the Chair during a period of unexampled difficulty. Such was his command of the House that the mere rustle of his robes, as he rose to rebuke a breach of order, was sufficient to awe the most unruly member into prompt submission to his ruling.[1]

Mr. Speaker Brand's tenure of office will always be regarded as a landmark in the history of Parliamentary institutions, if only for the great change adopted by the House in entrusting the Chair with the power of closure by a bare majority, a necessary change which, more than any other, has tended to aggrandise the power of the Government of the day, though with a corresponding decline in the usefulness and efficiency of the private member.[2]

In 1887, under Mr. Speaker Peel, the Chair was relieved of the initial responsibility for the closure. Power was then conferred upon any member to move that the question be now put, the Chair being directed to put such question forthwith, unless the rights of the minority seemed to him to be infringed or the rules of the House abused. One hundred members must now vote in the majority to make the motion effective. When the motion for closure has been carried, and the question on

[1] Mr. Gladstone had offered the post, in the first instance, to the late Lord Goschen, who felt himself obliged to decline the honour on account of defective eyesight.

[2] The principle of closure of debate, first adopted in 1882, was never actually put in practice until February, 1885, when Mr. Speaker Peel was in the Chair. In March, 1888, the Chair was invested with increased powers for maintaining order and checking irrelevancy in debate, while a fixed hour for the adjournment of the House, subject to certain exceptions, was also agreed to.

which it has been moved has been decided, any question already proposed from the Chair may be put forthwith without a further closure motion.

Another innovation designed to facilitate the despatch of business has been the passing of Orders regulating the procedure on certain stages of Bills. These have differed from one another in their scope and severity, but their general object has been to fix the time at which certain stages or parts of a stage should be brought to a conclusion, and to provide a special form of procedure for the summary disposal of that part of the stage which has not been concluded at the prescribed time. As a rule, the " guillotine," as it has come to be called, has taken the form of directing the Chair to put at a prescribed hour the question then under discussion, and to put any questions necessary to dispose of the allotted portion or stage of the Bill without debate, and when amendments are admissible, to put the question only on amendments moved by the Government. Since 1887 this procedure has been adopted occasionally in order to dispose of the necessary supply before the close of the financial year.

Mr. Speaker Peel[1] during his whole term of office kept a diary, which it is to be hoped will one day be given to the world, far exceeding, as it does, in interest similar journals kept by Speaker Denison and Speaker Abbot. From his entry into Parliament, in 1865, Mr. Peel familiarised himself with the features and idiosyncrasies of the members over whom he was one day to be called upon to preside. On one occasion, he told the present writer, he was asked by Mr. Gladstone if he could

_____
[1] Now Viscount Peel of Sandy, Beds.

ARTHUR WELLESLEY PEEL
1884, 1886 (2), 1892

tell him the name of a gentleman who had walked into the House and seated himself on the front Opposition bench. For once he was at fault, and, as neither the Speaker,[1] on being applied to, nor the doorkeepers could solve the mystery, a messenger was sent to the intruder to ask his name. It transpired that he had mistaken the House of Commons for the House of Lords (to which assembly he was an infrequent visitor), and had imagined that he was sitting amongst his peers. Mr. Gladstone, whose eagle eye had at once spotted an unfamiliar face, remarked to Mr. Peel that he should have thought the colour of the benches might have suggested to him that he had taken the wrong turning from the Central Hall. An elaboration of this anecdote, for which, however, we do not vouch, was to the effect that, after listening for some time to the debate, the intruder asked his neighbour, in perfect good faith, whether the noble lord who was addressing the House was Lord Salisbury !

Mr. Peel was in the seat of power all through the period of the dynamite outrages which disgraced London and baffled the police in 1884. Once word was brought to him that a desperado, disguised as a woman, had obtained admission to the ladies' gallery immediately above his head, no doubt with the intention of hurling a bomb into the crowded chamber. But fortunately the necessary courage was lacking, and no outrage took place, though it was not without a feeling of relief that the Speaker put the question " That this House do now

[1] Then Mr. Denison.

z

adjourn " at the conclusion of an anxious sitting.
À *propos* of the reign of terror, the present writer has
excellent reasons for remembering the dastardly outrage
in Westminster Hall on 24 January, 1885, when a bomb
was placed on the staircase leading to the crypt by a
miscreant who deliberately chose a Saturday for his
fiendish purpose, when the Houses of Parliament are
usually thronged with visitors. The writer walked
through the Hall a few minutes before the per-
petration of the outrage, returning later on to find
every pane of glass blown out of the great stained
window by the terrific force of the explosion, and the
Hall itself smoking from end to end with the dust of ages
which had been shaken from its rafters.

Of Mr. Speaker Gully it would be unbecoming to speak
at any length, owing to his recent untimely decease.
Recommended to the attention of the Government in
the first instance by the late Lord Herschell, his election
to the Chair on April 10, 1895, was the closest contest
of the kind ever known, with the exceptions of Harley
in December, 1710, and Abercromby in 1835. Whereas
Abercromby was successful by ten votes, Mr. Gully
received only eleven more than Sir Matthew White-
Ridley in 1895. By his winning manner and unfailing
courtesy he gained the respect and affection of every
quarter of the House during the ten years in which he
filled the Chair. In August, 1895, and December, 1900,
his re-election was unanimous, nor was he again put to the
trouble of a contest at the latter appeal to the country.

There can be no indiscretion in mentioning in these
pages that, on the occasion of Mr. Gully's promotion,

WILLIAM COURT GULLY
1895 (2), 1900

the late Sir Henry Campbell-Bannerman would have liked to succeed Mr. Peel ; but it may not be generally known that, though he was fortified by the opinion of Mr. Gladstone to the effect that ample precedent existed for his projected transference from the ministerial bench, the then ruling powers in the Cabinet thought otherwise, with the result that he stood aside, to attain, in after years, an even more strenuous position in the State. With the advent of Mr. James William Lowther to the Chair of the House of Commons in June, 1905, exactly six hundred years after a member of his family sat as Knight of the Shire for Westmorland,[1] this record perforce ceases, to be taken up hereafter, it may be, by some more skilful hand.

Politicians and parties may come and go, changes may, and must, occur in the aims and aspirations of the democracy of England, which will affect the relations of the House of Commons towards the parent assembly; but the Speaker's office, unfettered by the exigencies of party, and administered in the lofty and impartial spirit which has characterised the later years of its existence, will endure as long as the Constitution itself.

Tradition binds the Commons together with amazing strength, and so long as the peculiar and essential functions of the Chair, in ruling by general consent rather than by compulsion, in upholding freedom of speech without ever allowing it to degenerate into licence, are adhered to by the successors of the great Englishmen whose names have been recorded in these inadequate pages, it is safe to predict that the proud heritage of seven centuries of liberty and progress will be handed

[1] XXXIII Edward I, 1305.

on unimpaired to many future generations of a free and self-governing nation.

In bidding farewell to Westminster and to the " well-ordered inheritance " of the Speaker's Chair, it only remains to add those two words so familiar and so dear to all of Eton's sons—

ESTO PERPETUA

JAMES WILLIAM LOWTHER
1905, 1906, 1910, 1911 .

CATALOGUE OF SPEAKERS OF THE HOUSE OF COMMONS FROM THE EARLIEST TIMES TO THE PRESENT DAY : :

Parliament	Speaker or other Presiding Officer	Authority	Date of Appointment
XLII Henry III, 11 June, 1258, at Oxford. The "Mad Parliament"	*Peter de Montfort*	Register Book of St. Alban, Cottonian Library, British M u s e u m, now illegible through damage by fire. H a k e w i l, 1641, p. 106	
XX Edward II, and 27th Parliament summoned to meet at Westminster 7 January, 1326–7	*William Trussell*	Styled Procurator of Parliament in Henry of Knighton's chronicle contained in Twysden's *Decem Scriptores*	
VI Edward III, and 10th Parliament summoned to meet at Westminster, 16 March, 1331–2, "Le lundi prechein apres la Feste de Seint Gregoir."	*Henry Beaumont*	Browne - Willis, and *Rot.Parl.*, Vol. II, p. 64	
VI Edward III, and 11th Parliament summoned to meet at Westminster, 9 September, 1332, "Le Lendemayn de la Nativité Nre Dame"	*Sir Geoffrey Le Scrope*	*Rot. Parl.*, Vol. II, p. 66	

Close of Office	Constituency	Subsequent Rank or Style	Remarks
			Said to have consented " vice totius communitatis " to the banishment of Aymer de Valence, 1259–60. (?) Died 1287. Owned the manor house of Ilmington, Warwickshire, where traces of thirteenth-century work remain.
			One of this name was Knight of the Shire for Leicester in 1314. Buried in Westminster Abbey, *circa* 1346
			" Lesqueux Comtes Barouns & autres Grantz puis revindrent & repondirent touz au Roi par la bouche [de] Mons* Henri de Beaumont "
			Probably the same man who was Chief Justice of the King's Bench from 1324 to 1338, and Secretary to Edward III in 1339. He was a Trier of Petitions as early as 1320. These important officials are first heard of in 1304. *Rot. Parl.*, Vol. I, p. 159. Le Scrope died in 1340

SPEAKERS OF THE HOUSE OF COMMONS

Parliament	Speaker or other Presiding Officer	Authority	Date of Appointment
XIV Edward III, and 26th Parliament summoned to meet at Westminster, 29 March, 1340. " Aujour de meskerdy prochein apres la fest de la Translation de Seint Thomas le Martir "	*William Trussell* again	*Rot. Parl.*, Vol. II, p. 118	
XV Edward III, 1341			
XVII Edward III, and 30th Parliament summoned to meet at Westminster, 28 April, 1343. " A la quinzeme de Pask "	*William Trussell* again	*Rot. Parl.*, Vol. II, p. 136	
XXI Edward III, 1347	*William de Thorpe*	Elsynge, *Rot. Parl.*, Vol. II, 164	
XXII Edward III, 1348	*William de Thorpe* again	Elsynge and *Rot. Parl.*, Vol. II, p. 200	

Close of Office	Constituency	Subsequent Rank or Style	Remarks
			Announced a naval victory to the Commons and undertook to raise wools for the King's aid. "Apres grand trete & parlance eue entre les Grantz & les dits Chivalers & autre les Communes"
			"Les ditz Grantz & autres de la Commune qu ils se traissent ensemble, & s'avisent entre eux c'est assaver les grantz de p. eux & les Chivalers des Counteez & Burgeys de p. eux"
			"Et puis vindrent les Chivalers de Counteez et les Communes & responderent pᵣ Monsᵣ William Trussell [to a communication from the Pope]. The Commons met in the Chambre Depeint or Painted Chamber and the Lords in the Chambre Blanche
		Chief Justice 1346	Elsynge considered that the Chief Justice habitually acted as Speaker temp. Edward III, though the cause of summons was occasionally delivered by the Chancellor. Thorpe was a Trier of English and Irish Petitions in 1346
		Baron of the Exchequer, 1352	

Parliament	Speaker or other Presiding Officer	Authority	Date of Appointment
XXV Edward III, and 36th Parliament summoned to meet at Westminster, 9 February, 1350–51	*William de Shareshull*	*Rot. Parl.,* Vol. II, p. 226	
XXV Edward III, and 37th Parliament summoned to meet at Westminster, 13 January, 1351–52	*William de Shareshull* again	*Rot. Parl.,* Vol. II, p. 237	

In 1354 *William de Shareshull* again declared the cause of summons, and in 1355 he stated that the King was pleased to command the cause to be delivered by Monsieur Walter de Manny, " overtement a totes gentz."

In 1362 the cause of summons was delivered by Monsieur *Henry Green* in *English.*

In 1363 *Sir Henry Green,* Chief Justice, told the Parliament in *English* (in the Painted Chamber) that the King was ready to begin his Parliament, but the cause of summons was subsequently delivered by the Bishop of Ely.

In 1372 the Chancellor, *John Knyvet* (in the Painted Chamber), and the next day *Sir Guy Brian* (in the Chambre Blanche), " more particularly," declared the cause of summons.

Parliament	Speaker or other Presiding Officer	Authority	Date of Appointment
L Edward III, 55th Parliament summoned to meet at Westminster, 28 April, 1376	The Chancellor, *John Knyvet,* again declared the cause of summons		

Close of Office	Constituency	Subsequent Rank or Style	Remarks
		Chief Justice 1350	Pronounced the cause of summons to Parliament and considered by Elsynge to have acted as Speaker. He was a Trier of Petitions from Flanders in 1340
			The Commons now meet in the Chapter House of the Abbey. The Lords in the Chambre Blanche. " Et q le remenant des Communes se trahissent el Chapitre de Westminster." (A committee of the Commons) *Rot.Parl.*, Vol. II, p. 237
			So early as 1347 Walter de Manny had been a Trier of Petitions
		Chief Justice 1361	In 1354 Green acted as a Trier of Petitions for England
		Chancellor of England 1372–77	Died 1381. As early as 1362 Knyvet had been a Trier of Petitions for foreign parts, whilst Brian acted in a similar capacity for England in 1354
			In this Parliament the Commons were under the leadership of Sir Peter de la Mare, though there is no mention in the Rolls of his having been formally elected to the chair.

Parliament	Speaker	Authority	Date of Appointment
LI Edward III, and 56th Parliament summoned to meet at Westminster, 27 January, 1376–77 ; sat till 2 March	Sir Thomas Hungerford	*Rot. Parl.*, Vol. II, p. 374	January, 1376–7
I Richard II, and 1st Parliament summoned to meet at Westminster, 13 October, 1377	Sir Peter de la Mare	*Rot. Parl.*, Vol. III, p. 5	October, 1377
II Richard II, and 2nd Parliament summoned to meet at Gloucester, 20 October, 1378	Sir James Pickering	*Rot. Parl.*, Vol. III, p. 34	22 October, 1378
III Richard II, and 4th Parliament summoned to meet at Westminster, 16 January, 1379–80	Sir John Guildesborough	*Rot. Parl.*, Vol. III, p. 73	January, 1379–80
IV Richard II, and 5th Parliament summoned to meet at Northampton, 5 November, 1380	Sir John Guildesborough again	*Rot. Parl.*, Vol. III, p. 89	November, 1380
V Richard II, and 6th Parliament summoned to meet at Westminster, 16 September, 1381, and his prorogation, 3 November, 1381	Sir Richard Waldegrave	*Rot. Parl.*, Vol. III, p. 100	18 November, 1381
VI Richard II, and 9th Parliament summoned to meet at Westminster, 23 February, 1382–83	Sir James Pickering again	*Rot. Parl.*, Vol. III, p. 145	23 February, 1382–83

Close of Office	Constituency	Subsequent Rank or Style	Remarks
2 March, 1376–7	Wilts		Died 1398 and was buried at Farleigh Hungerford, in the county of Somerset. Described in the Rolls as the "Chivaler qi avoit les paroles pur les Communes d'Engleterre en cest Parlement"
28 Nov., 1377	Hereford		
16 Nov., 1378	Westmorland		See also 1382–83
3 Mar., 1379–80	Essex		Sometimes erroneously called Goldesborough, but he does not appear to have been related to the Yorkshire family of that name
6 Dec., 1380	Essex		
25 Feb., 1381–2	Suffolk		Died 1402. Waldegrave may also have been Speaker in the two next Parliaments, but the Rolls are defective at this period
10 Mar., 1382–3	Yorkshire		He sat in Parliament altogether for thirty-five years

Parliament	Speaker	Authority	Date of Appointment

From 1383 to 1393 the Rolls of Parliament are defective, and it is not definitely known who was Speaker in Richard II's 10th, 11th, 12th, 13th, 14th, 15th, 16th, 17th, 18th, 19th, 20th, or 21st Parliament; but as Sir James Pickering sat for Yorkshire in 1384, 1388, 1389–90, and 1390, he probably acted as Speaker in one or more of them.

Parliament	Speaker	Authority	Date of Appointment
XVII Richard II, and 22nd Parliament summoned to meet at Westminster, 27 January, 1393–94	Sir John Bussy	*Rot. Parl.*, Vol. III, p. 310	28 Jan., 1393–94
XVIII Richard II, and 23rd Parliament summoned to meet at Westminster, 27 January, 1394 – 95. Sat till 15 February.	Probably Bussy again Speaker, though not mentioned in the Rolls		
XX Richard II, and 24th Parliament summoned to meet at Westminster, 22 January, 1396–97	Sir John Bussy again	*Rot. Parl.*, Vol. III, p. 338	22 Jan., 1396–97
XXI Richard II, and 25th Parliament summoned to meet at Westminster, 17 September, 1397, and adjourned to Shrewsbury, 27 January, 1397–98, and sat till 31 January, when it resigned its authority to a Committee of 18, 12 peers and 6 commoners, of whom the Speaker was one	Sir John Bussy again	*Rot. Parl.*, Vol. III, p. 357	17 Sept., 1397

Close of Office	*Constituency*	*Subsequent Rank or Style*	*Remarks*
			VII Richard II, 1384. The Commons are directed to choose a Speaker : " la personne qi'auroit les paroles en cest Parlement pur la Cõe." The cause of summons was delivered by Monsʳ Michel de la Pole, Chancellor
6 Mar., 1393–94	Lincolnshire		Beheaded 29 July, 1399. He lived at H o u g h a m , near G r a n t h a m , a n d several memorials of his family remain in the parish church. Styled " Commune Parlour" in the Rolls
			The Commons were charged by the Chancellor to assemble either in the Chapter House or the Refectory of Westminster, to choose a Speaker (*Rot. Parl.*, Vol. III, p. 329)
12 February, 1396–97	Lincolnshire		
31 Jan., 1397–8	Lincolnshire		

Parliament	Speaker	Authority	Date of Appointment
XXIII Richard II, and 26th Parliament, met 30 September, 1399, but sat only one day to depose the King	None chosen		
I Henry IV, and 1st Parliament, met at Westminster, 6 October, 1399	Sir John Cheyne or Cheney	*Rot. Parl.*, Vol. III, p. 424	14 October, 1399
Ditto	John Dorewood	*Rot. Parl.*, Vol. III, p. 424	15 October, 1399
II Henry IV, and 2nd Parliament summoned to meet at York, 27 October, 1400, and by prorogation at Westminster, 20 January, 1400–1. [The cause of summons was, however, still declared by the Chief Justice, Sir William Thurning.]	Sir Arnold Savage	*Rot. Parl.*, Vol. III, p. 455	21 Jan., 1400–1
III Henry IV, and 3rd Parliament summoned to meet at Westminster, 30 January, 1401–02			
III Henry IV, and 4th Parliament summoned to meet at Westminster (in the Painted Chamber), 15 September, 1402, and by prorogation on 30 September	Sir Henry Redford	*Rot. Parl.*, Vol. III, p. 486	3 October, 1402

Close of Office	Constituency	Subsequent Rank or Style	Remarks
Filled the Chair for only two days	Gloucestershire		(Not mentioned in the *D.N.B.*) Hakewil makes him Speaker again in 1405–6, but this is inaccurate. He was still living in 1409
9 Nov., 1399	Essex		See also 1413
0 March, 1400–01	Kent		Again Speaker in 1403–4, and died in 1410. Memorial brass in Bobbing Church, Kent
			Possibly Savage was again Speaker, but the Rolls do not mention him at this date
Nov., 1402	Lincolnshire		Died *circa* 1404. He owned lands at Heyling, Lincolnshire

2 A

Parliament	Speaker	Authority	Date of Appointment
V Henry IV, and 5th Parliament summoned to meet at Coventry, 3 December, 1403, and actually met there, and at Westminster, after prorogation, 14 January, 1403–04	Sir Arnold Savage again	*Rot. Parl.*, Vol. III, p. 523	15 Jan., 1403–
VI Henry IV, and 6th Parliament summoned to meet at Coventry, 6 October, 1404	Sir William Sturmy, or Esturmy	*Rot. Parl.*, Vol. III, p. 546	7 October, 140
VII Henry IV, and 7th Parliament summoned to meet at Coventry, 15 February 1405–06 (afterwards at Gloucester), and, after prorogation, met at Westminster, 1 March, 1405–06	Sir John Tiptoft	*Rot. Parl.*, Vol. III, p. 568	2 March, 1405–
IX Henry IV, and 8th Parliament summoned to meet at Gloucester, 20 October, 1407	Thomas Chaucer	*Rot. Parl.*, Vol. III, p. 609	25 October, 140
XI Henry IV, and 9th Parliament summoned to meet at Westminster, 27 January, 1409–10	Thomas Chaucer again	*Rot. Parl.*, Vol. III, p. 623	28 Jan., 1409–
XIII Henry IV, and 10th Parliament summoned to meet at Westminster, 3 November, 1411	Thomas Chaucer again	*Rot. Parl.*, Vol. III, p. 648	5 Nov., 1411

Close of Office	Constituency	Subsequent Rank or Style	Remarks
C. 10 April, 1403–4	Kent		Died 1410
14 November, 1404	Devon		" Parliamentum indoctorum " or Laymen's Parliament
22 December, 1406	Huntingdonshire	Baron Tiptoft 1426	The first Speaker to be raised to the Peerage. Died 1443
December, 1407	Oxfordshire		Believed to be son of the poet. Died 1434. Buried at Ewelme, Oxon. The Commons were directed to assemble in the Fratry of the Abbey at eight o'clock
May, 1410	Oxfordshire		
9 December, 1411	Oxfordshire		The King, in replying to the Speaker's excuse on presentation for the royal acceptance, said : " Qar il ne vorroit aucunement avoir nulle maniere de Novellerie en cest Parlement "

Parliament	Speaker	Authority	Date of Appointment
XIV Henry IV, and 11th Parliament summoned to meet at Westminster, 3 February, 1412–13	Speaker unknown		
I Henry V, and 1st Parliament summoned to meet at Westminster, 14 May 1413	William Stourton. "Gisoit cy malades en son lyt qu'il ne purroit pluis outre entendre d'occupier le dit office de Parlour"	*Rot. Parl.*, Vol. IV, pp. 4, 5	18 May, 1413
Ditto	John Dorewood again	*Rot. Parl.*, Vol. IV, p. 5	3 June, 1413
II Henry V, and 2nd Parliament summoned to meet at Leicester, 30 April, 1414	Sir Walter Hungerford	*Rot. Parl.*, Vol. IV, p. 16	1 May, 1414
II Henry V, and 3rd Parliament summoned to meet at Westminster, 19 November, 1414	Thomas Chaucer again	*Rot. Parl.*, Vol. IV, p. 35	19 Nov., 1414
III Henry V, and 4th Parliament summoned to meet at Westminster, 21 Oct., 1415, and, by prorogation, on 4 Nov.	Richard Redman, or Redmayne	*Rot. Parl.*, Vol. IV, p. 63	5 Nov., 1415
III Henry V, and 5th Parliament summoned to meet at Westminster, 16 Mar. 1415–16	Sir Walter Beauchamp	*Rot. Parl.*, Vol. IV, p. 71	18 Mar., 1415–1

Close of Office	Constituency	Subsequent Rank or Style	Remarks
3 June, 1413	Dorset		(?) Died 1417. Ancestor of Baron Stourton
9 June, 1413	Essex		
29 May, 1414	Wilts	Baron Hunger-ford, 1425–26	Son of Sir Thomas Hungerford (Speaker in 1377), died 1449, and was buried in Salisbury Cathedral
Date of dissolution not ascertained	Oxfordshire		
Sat less than a fortnight	Yorkshire		Died 1426
May, 1416	Wiltshire		Styled " Prolocutor "

Parliament	Speaker	Authority	Date of Appointment
IV Henry V, and 6th Parliament summoned to meet at Westminster, 19 October 1416	Roger Flower	*Rot. Parl.*, Vol. IV, p. 95	October, 1416
V Henry V, and 7th Parliament summoned to meet at Westminster, 16 November, 1417	Roger Flower again	*Rot. Parl.*, Vol. IV, p. 107	November, 1417
VII Henry V, and 8th Parliament summoned to meet at Westminster, 16 October, 1419	Roger Flower again	*Rot. Parl.*, Vol. IV, p. 117	October, 1419
VIII Henry V, and 9th Parliament summoned to meet at Westminster, 2 Dec., 1420	Roger Hunt	*Rot. Parl.*, Vol. IV, p. 123	4 Dec., 1420
IX Henry V, and 10th Parliament summoned to meet at Westminster, 2 May, 1421	Thomas Chaucer again	*Rot. Parl.*, Vol. IV, p. 130	May, 1421
IX Henry V, and 11th Parliament summoned to meet at Westminster, 1 December, 1421	Richard Baynard	*Rot. Parl.*, Vol. IV, p. 151	3 December 1421
I Henry VI, and 1st Parliament summoned to meet at Westminster, 9 Nov., 1422	Roger Flower again	*Rot. Parl.*, Vol. IV, p. 170	11 Nov., 1422
II Henry VI, and 2nd Parliament summoned to meet at Westminster, 20 October, 1423	Sir John Russell	*Rot. Parl.*, Vol. IV, p. 198	21 Oct., 1423

Close of Office	Constituency	Subsequent Rank or Style	Remarks
18 November, 1416	Rutland		Died 1428
17 December, 1417	Rutland		
November, 1419	Rutland		
Date of close of this Parliament unascertained	Bedfordshire		Omitted by Hakewil at this date. An eminent lawyer and a Baron of the Exchequer. Memorial brass dated 1473 at Gt. Linford, Bucks, may represent him or his son
Date of close of Parliament unascertained	Oxfordshire		First to be five times Speaker. Died 1434 and was buried at Ewelme, Oxfordshire, where his monument and brass remain
Date of close of Parliament unascertained	Essex		(Not mentioned in *Dictionary of National Biography*)
18 December, 1422	Rutland		
28 February, 1423–24	Herefordshire		

Parliament	Speaker	Authority	Date of Appointment
III Henry VI, and 3rd Parliament summoned to meet at Westminster, 30 April, 1425	Sir Thomas Walton, or Wauton	*Rot. Parl.*, Vol. IV, p. 262	2 May, 1425
IV Henry VI, and 4th Parliament summoned to meet at Leicester, 18 February, 1425–26	Sir Richard Vernon	*Rot. Parl.*, Vol. IV, p. 296	28 Feb., 1425-26
VI Henry VI, and 5th Parliament summoned to meet at Westminster, 13 October, 1427	Sir John Tyrrell	*Rot. Parl.*, Vol. IV, p. 317	15 October,1427
VIII Henry VI, and 6th Parliament summoned to meet at Westminster, 22 September, 1429	William Alington	*Rot. Parl.*, Vol. IV, p. 336	23 Sept., 1429
IX Henry VI, and 7th Parliament summoned to meet at Westminster, 12 January, 1430–31	Sir John Tyrrell again	*Rot. Parl.*, Vol. IV, p. 368	13 Jan., 1430-31
X Henry VI, and 8th Parliament summoned to meet at Westminster, 12 May, 1432	Sir John Russell again	*Rot. Parl.*, Vol. IV, p. 389	14 May, 1432
XI Henry VI, and 9th Parliament summoned to meet at Westminster, 8 July, 1433	Roger Hunt again	*Rot. Parl.*, Vol. IV, p. 420	10 July, 1433
XIV Henry VI, and 10th Parliament summoned to meet at Westminster, 10 October, 1435	John Bowes	*Rot. Parl.*, Vol. IV, p. 482	12 October,1435

Close of Office	Constituency	Subsequent Rank or Style	Remarks
14 July, 1425	Bedfordshire		Died 1437. Owned lands at Great Staughton, Hunts
1 June, 1426	Derbyshire		Died 1451. Ancestor of Lord Vernon
25 March, 1428	Herts		Died 1437
23 Feb., 1429-30	Cambridgeshire		
20 March, 1430–31	Essex		
17 July, 1432	Herefordshire		
21 December, 1433	Huntingdon- shire		
23 December, 1435	Nottingham- shire		(Not mentioned in *Dictionary of Nationa Biography*)

Parliament	Speaker	Authority	Date of Appointment
XV Henry VI, and 11th Parliament summoned to meet at Westminster, 21 January, 1436–37	Sir John Tyrrell again	*Rot. Parl.*, Vol. IV, p. 496	23 Jan., 1436–37
Ditto	William Burley, or Boerley	*Rot. Parl.*, Vol. IV, p. 502	19 Mar.,1436–37
XVIII Henry VI, and 12th Parliament summoned to meet at Westminster, 12 November, 1439	William Tresham	*Rot. Parl.*, Vol. V, p. 4	13 Nov., 1439
XX Henry VI, and 13th Parliament summoned to meet at Westminster, 25 January, 1441–42	William Tresham again	*Rot. Parl.*, Vol. V, p. 36	26 Jan.,1441–42
XXIII Henry VI, and 14th Parliament summoned to meet at Westminster, 25 February, 1444–45	William Burley again	*Rot. Parl.*, Vol. V, p. 67 ; and Appendix to *Return of Names of Members of Parliament*, p. xxiii, where he is styled "Prolocutor"	26 Feb., 1444-45
XXV Henry VI, and 15th Parliament summoned to meet at Bury St. Edmunds, 10 February, 1446–47	William Tresham again	*Rot. Parl.*, Vol. V, p. 129	11 Feb., 1446-47
XXVII Henry VI, and 16th Parliament summoned to meet at Westminster, 12 February, 1448–49	Sir John Say	*Rot. Parl.*, Vol. V, p. 141	13 Feb.,1448–49

Close of Office	Constituency	Subsequent Rank or Style	Remarks
March	Essex		
27 March, 1437	Salop		
1440	Northants		Murdered at Thorpland, Northants, 1450. Owned lands at Sywell, Northants. Leland, in his Itinerary, gives a circumstantial account of his death
27 May, 1442	Northants		
9 April, 1445	Salop		
3 March, 1446–47	Northants		
16 July, 1449	Cambridgeshire		Died 1478. Buried in Broxbourne Church, Herts, where his memorial brass remains

Parliament	Speaker	Authority	Date of Appointment
XXVIII Henry VI, and 17th Parliament summoned to meet at Westminster, 6 November, 1449	Sir John Popham	*Rot. Parl.*, Vol. V, p. 171	8 Nov., 1449
Ditto	William Tresham again	*Rot. Parl.*, Vol. V, p. 172	8 Nov., 1449
XXIX Henry VI, and 18th Parliament summoned to meet at Westminster, 6 November, 1450	Sir William Oldhall	*Rot. Parl.*, Vol. V, p. 210	7 Nov., 1450
XXXI Henry VI, and 19th Parliament summoned to meet at Reading, 6 Mar., 1452-53	Thomas Thorpe	*Rot. Parl.*, Vol. V, p. 227	8 Mar., 1452–53
XXXII Henry VI, and 19th Parliament —*continued*	Sir Thomas Charlton	*Rot. Parl.*, Vol. V, p. 240	16 Feb., 1453-54
XXXIII Henry VI, and 20th Parliament summoned to meet at Westminster, 9 July, 1455	Sir John Wenlock	*Rot. Parl.*, Vol. V, p. 280; and Appendix to *Return of Names of Members of Parliament*, p. xxiii, where he is styled "Prolocutor"	10 July, 1455

Close of Office	Constituency	Subsequent Rank or Style	Remarks
Excused on ground of ill-health	Hants		Died *c.* 1463
Spring, 1450	Northants		This Parliament, after being prorogued over Christmas, reassembled 22 January, and was sitting on 17 March. In April it met again at Leicester
May, 1451	Herefordshire		Died 1460. Buried in St. Michael, Paternoster Royal, London
16 February, 1453–54	Essex		Beheaded at Haringay Park, Middlesex, 1461
April, 1454	Middlesex		In place of Thorpe imprisoned. (Not mentioned in *D.N.B.*)
January, 1455–56	Bedfordshire	Lord Wenlock 1461	Killed at the battle of Tewkesbury, 1471

Parliament	Speaker	Authority	Date of Appointment
XXXVIII Henry VI, and 21st Parliament summoned to meet at Coventry, 20 November, 1459	Sir Thomas Tresham	*Rot. Parl.*, Vol. V, p. 345 ; and Appendix to *Return of Names of Members of Parliament*, p. xxiv, where he is styled " Prolocutor "	21 Nov., 1459
XXXIX Henry VI, and 22nd Parliament summoned to meet at Westminster, 7 October, 1460	John Green	*Rot. Parl.*, Vol. V, p. 373	8 October, 1460
I Edward IV, and 1st Parliament summoned to meet at Westminster, 4 November, 1461	Sir James Strangeways	*Rot. Parl.*, Vol. V, p. 462 ; and Appendix to *Names of Members of Parliament*, p. xxiv, where he is styled " Prolocutor "	5 Nov., 1461
III Edward IV, and 2nd Parliament summoned to meet at Westminster, 29 April, 1463	Sir John Say again	*Rot. Parl.*, Vol. V, p. 497 ; and Appendix to *Names of Members of Parliament*, p. xxv, where he is styled " Prolocutor "	30 April, 1463
VII Edward IV, and 3rd Parliament summoned to meet at Westminster, 3 June, 1467	Sir John Say again	*Rot. Parl.*, Vol. V, p. 572	5 June, 1467
IX Edward IV, and 4th Parliament summoned to meet at York, 22 Sept., 1469	No Speaker chosen		

Close of Office	*Constituency*	*Subsequent* *Rank or Style*	*Remarks*
20 December, 1459	Northants		Beheaded at Tewkesbury, 1471
Only sat about ten days	Essex		(Not mentioned in *D. N.B.*)
6 May, 1461–62	Yorkshire		Introduced a new precedent. Besides making the customary " excuse " on election he offered a formal address to Crown on the political situation. Buried in St. Mary Overy's, Southwark
1465	Herts		
May, 1468	Herts		

Parliament	Speaker	Authority	Date of Appointment
X Edward IV, and 5th Parliament summoned to meet at Westminster, 26 November, 1470			
XII Edward IV, and 6th Parliament summoned to meet at Westminster, 6 Oct., 1472	William Alington	*Rot. Parl.*, Vol. VI, p. 4	7 October, 1472
XVII Edward IV, and 7th Parliament summoned to meet at Westminster, 16 January, 1477–78	William Alington again	*Rot. Parl.*, Vol. VI, p. 168	17 Jan., 1477–78
XXII Edward IV, and 8th Parliament summoned to meet at Westminster, 20 January, 1482–83	John Wood, or Wode	*Rot. Parl.*, Vol. VI, p. 197; and Appendix to *Return of Names of Members of Parliament*, p. xxv, where he is styled " Prolocutor"	21 Jan., 1482–83
I Richard III, and 1st Parliament summoned to meet at Westminster, 23 January, 1483–84	William Catesby	*Rot. Parl.*, Vol. VI, p. 238; and Appendix to *Return of Names of Members of Parliament*, p. xxv, where he is styled " Prolocutor"	24 Jan., 1483-84

Close of Office	Constituency	Subsequent Rank or Style	Remarks
			No particulars known. Henry VI again temporarily dominant, and records, if any were kept, probably destroyed by order of Edward IV
14 March, 1474–75	Cambridgeshire		
Date of close of Parliament unascertained but it sat about five weeks	Cambridgeshire		Believed to have been buried in Bottisham Church, Cambridgeshire, in an altar tomb from which the brass has disappeared
February, 1482–83	Sussex (probably)		There is some doubt as to whether he represented Surrey or Sussex, but the latter appears to be more probable
20 February, 1483–84	Northants		Beheaded 1485, after the Battle of Bosworth. Memorial brass in the church at Ashby St. Ledgers, Northants

2 B

Parliament	Speaker	Authority	Date of Appointment
I Henry VII, and 1st Parliament summoned to meet at Westminster, 7 Nov., 1485	Sir Thomas Lovell	*Rot. Parl.*, Vol. VI, p. 268; and Appendix to *Return of Names of Members of Parliament*, p. xxvi, where he is styled "Prolocutor"	8 Nov., 1485
III Henry VII, and 2nd Parliament summoned to meet at Westminster, 9 Nov., 1487	Sir John Mordaunt	*Rot. Parl.*, Vol. VI, p. 386; and Appendix to *Return of Names of Members of Parliament*, p. xxvi, where he is styled "Prolocutor"	10 Nov., 1487
IV Henry VII, and 3rd Parliament summoned to meet at Westminster, 13 January, 1488–89	Sir Thomas Fitzwilliam	*Rot. Parl.*, Vol. VI, p. 410; and Appendix to *Return of Names of Members of Parliament*, p. xxvi, where he is styled "Prolocutor"	14 Jan.,1488–89
VII Henry VII, and 4th Parliament summoned to meet at Westminster, 17 October, 1491	Sir Richard Empson	*Rot. Parl.*, Vol. VI, p. 440; and Appendix to *Return of Names of Members of Parliament*, p. xxvi, where he is styled "Prolocutor"	18 October,1491

Close of Office	Constituency	Subsequent Rank or Style	Remarks
March, 1486	Northants		The last of the martial Speakers. Died 1524. Bronze medallion portrait by Torregiano now placed in Henry VII's Chapel, Westminster Abbey
Date of close of Parliament unascertained	Bedfordshire	Chancellor of the Duchy of Lancaster	Died 1506. Monumental effigy at Turvey, Beds.
Feb. 27, 1490	Yorkshire		(Not mentioned in D.N.B.) Died 1495
March, 1491–92	Northants	Chancellor of the Duchy of Lancaster	Beheaded with Dudley 1510

Parliament	Speaker	Authority	Date of Appointment
XI Henry VII, and 5th Parliament summoned to meet at Westminster, 14 October, 1495	Sir Robert Drury	*Rot. Parl.*, Vol. VI, p. 458; (Choice of Speaker declared by a Committee without naming the person elected)	15 October, 1495
XII Henry VII, on 24 October, 1496, a great Council, rather than a Parliament, met at Westminster	Sir Reginald Bray (President or Chairman)	Appendix to *Return of Names of Members of Parliament*, p. xxvii	
XII Henry VII, and 6th Parliament summoned to meet at Westminster, 16 January, 1496–97	Sir Thomas Englefield	*Rot. Parl.*, Vol. VI, p. 510; and Appendix to *Return of Names of Members of Parliament*, p. xxvii	19 Jan., 1496–97
XIX Henry VII, and 7th Parliament summoned to meet at Westminster, 25 January, 1503–04	Edmond Dudley	*Rot. Parl.*, Vol. VI, p. 521; and Appendix to *Return of Names of Members of Parliament*, p. xxvii, where he is styled "Prolocutor"	26 Jan., 1503–04
I Henry VIII, and 1st Parliament summoned to meet at Westminster, 21 January, 1509–10	Sir Thomas Englefield again	Appendix to official *Return of Names of Members of Parliament*, p. xxviii, where he is styled "Prolocutor"	23 Jan., 1509–10

Close of Office	Constituency	Subsequent Rank or Style	Remarks
Date of the close of this Parliament unas certained	Suffolk		Died 1536. Monumental effigy in St. Mary's Church, Bury St. Edmund's
	Bedfordshire or Northants in Parliament of 495	Chancellor of the Duchy of Lancaster	Died 1503, and was buried in St.George's Chapel, Windsor Castle, but without a monument
Date of close of this Parliament unascertained	Berkshire		(Not mentioned in D.N.B.) Died 1514
Date of close of this Parliament unascertained	Staffordshire		Advocate of absolute monarchy. Beheaded with Empson 1510
23 February, 1509–10	Berkshire		Died 1514

Parliament	Speaker	Authority	Date of Appointment
III Henry VIII, and 2nd Parliament summoned to meet at Westminster, 4 Feb., 1511–12	Sir Robert Sheffield	Appendix to official *Return of Names of Members of Parliament*, p. xxviii, where he is styled "Prolocutor"	5 Feb., 1511–12
VI Henry VIII, and 3rd Parliament summoned to meet at Westminster, 5 Feb., 1514–15, but met ultimately at Blackfriars	Sir Thomas Nevill	Appendix to official *Return of Names of Members of Parliament*, p. xxviii, where he is styled "Prolocutor"	6 Feb., 1514–15
XIV Henry VIII, and 4th Parliament summoned to meet at Black Friars, 15 April, 1523	Sir Thomas More	Appendix to official *Return of Names of Members of Parliament*, p. xxviii, where he is styled " Prolocutor"	16 April, 1523
XXI Henry VIII, and 5th Parliament summoned to meet at Westminster, 3 Nov., 1529	Sir Thomas Audley	Appendix to *Return of Names of Members of Parliament*, p. xxix, where he is styled " Prolocutor"	5 Nov., 1529
Ditto	Sir Humphrey Wingfield	Cobbett's *Parliamentary History*, Vol. I, p. 524	9 Feb., 1533
XXVIII Henry VIII, and 6th Parliament summoned to meet at Westminster, 8 June, 1536	Sir Richard Rich	Cobbett's *Parliamentary History*, Vol. I, p. 529	9 June, 1536

Close of Office	Constituency	Subsequent Rank or Style	Remarks
? Dec., 1513	Lincolnshire		Died 1518. Buried in the Church of the Augustinian Friars, London
22 Dec., 1515	Kent		Died 1542. Memorial brass in Mereworth Church, Kent
13 August, 1523	Middlesex	Lord Chancellor	Beheaded 1535
26 Jan., 1533	Essex	Lord Chancellor. Lord Audley 1538	Died 1544
4 April, 1536	Great Yarmouth		The first Speaker to sit for a borough constituency. Died 1545. This was the longest Parliament known to this date
18 July, 1536	Colchester	Lord Chancellor 1547–51. Lord Rich	Died 1567

Parliament	Speaker	Authority	Date of Appointment
XXXI Henry VIII, and 7th Parliament summoned to meet at Westminster, 28 April, 1539	Sir Nicholas Hare	Cobbett's *Parliamentary History*, Vol. I, p. 536	28 April, 1539
XXXIII Henry VIII, and 8th Parliament summoned to meet at Westminster, 16 January, 1541–42	Sir Thomas Moyle	Cobbett's *Parliamentary History*, Vol. I, p. 550	19 Jan., 1541-42
XXXVII Henry VIII, and 9th Parliament summoned to meet at Westminster, 23 November, 1545	Sir John Baker	*Acts of the Privy Council* (edited by Sir J. R. Dasent), Vol. II, p. 24	November, 1545
I Edward VI, and 1st Parliament met in St. Stephen's Chapel, Westminster, 4 November, 1547	Sir John Baker again	*Commons Journals*, Vol. I, p. 1	4 Nov., 1547
VII Edward VI, and 2nd Parliament summoned to meet at Westminster, 1 Mar., 1552–53	Sir James Dyer	*Commons Journals*, Vol. I, p. 24	2 Mar., 1552–53
I Mary, and 1st Parliament summoned to meet at Westminster, 5 October, 1553	Sir John Pollard	Cobbett's *Parliamentary History*, Vol. I, p. 607	5 October, 1553
I Mary, and 2nd Parliament summoned to meet at Westminster, 2 April, 1554	Sir Robert Brooke	Cobbett's *Parliamentary History*, Vol. I, p. 613	2 April, 1554
I and II Philip and Mary, and 1st Parliament summoned to meet at Westminster, 12 Nov., 1554	Sir Clement Heigham	Cobbett's *Parliamentary History*, Vol. I, p. 617	12 Nov., 1554

Close of Office	Constituency	Subsequent Rank or Style	Remarks
24 July, 1540	Norfolk	Master of the Rolls 1553	Died 1557
28 March, 1544	Kent		Died 1560
31 Jan.,1546–47	Huntingdon-shire	Chancellor of the Exchequer	Died 1558
15 April, 1552	Huntingdon-shire		Died 1558
31 March	Cambridgeshire	Chief Justice of the Common Pleas	Died 1582
5 December	Oxfordshire		Died 1557
5 May	London	Chief Justice of the Common Pleas	Died 1558. The first Speaker to represent the City of London. Monument in Claverley Church, near Wolverhampton
16 Jan.,1554–55	West Looe	Chief Baron of the Exchequer	Died 1570. Memorial brass in Barrow Church, Suffolk

Parliament	Speaker	Authority	Date of Appointment
II and III Philip and Mary, and 2nd Parliament summoned to meet at Westminster, 21 October, 1555	Sir John Pollard again	Commons Journals, Vol. I, p. 42	21 Oct., 1555
IV and V Philip and Mary, and 3rd Parliament summoned to meet at Westminster, 20 January, 1557–58	Sir William Cordell	Commons Journals, Vol. I, p. 47	20 Jan., 1557-58
I Elizabeth, and 1st Parliament summoned to meet at Westminster, 25 January, 1558–59	Sir Thomas Gargrave	Commons Journals, Vol. I, p. 53	25 Jan., 1558-59
V Elizabeth, and 2nd Parliament summoned to meet at Westminster, 11 January, 1562–63	Thomas Williams	Symonds D'Ewes, Journals, p. 79	12 Jan., 1562-63
VIII Elizabeth, and 2nd Parliament. Second session began 30 September, 1566	Richard Onslow	Symonds D'Ewes, Journals, p. 121	1 October, 1566
XIII Elizabeth, and 3rd Parliament summoned to meet at Westminster, 2 April, 1571	Sir Christopher Wray	Symonds D'Ewes, Journals, p. 156	2 April, 1571

Close of Office	Constituency	Subsequent Rank or Style	Remarks
9 December, 1555	Exeter or Chippenham. The latter is the more probable as the official return gives the name as Johannes Pollard "Armiger," whereas the member for Exeter is called ' Miles,' and the Speaker was not a knight in 1555		Died 1557
17 November, 1558	Suffolk	Master of the Rolls	Died 1581
8 May, 1559	Yorkshire	Vice-President of the Council of the North	Died 1579
10 April, 1563	Exeter		Died 1566. Buried in Harford Church, Co. Devon
2 Jan., 1566–67	Steyning		Died 1571
29 May, 1571	Ludgershall	Chief Justice of the Queen's Bench	Died 1592

Parliament	Speaker	Authority	Date of Appointment
XIV Elizabeth, and 4th Parliament summoned to meet at Westminster, 8 May, 1572.	Sir Robert Bell	Symonds D'Ewes, *Journals,* p. 205 *Commons Journals,* Vol. I, p. 94, which gives the date of his election as 10 May	8 May, 1572
Ditto—*continued.* 4th and last session began 16 January, 1580-81	Sir John Popham	*Commons Journals,* Vol. I, p. 117	18 Jan., 1580-81
XXVII Elizabeth, and 5th Parliament summoned to meet at Westminster, 23 November, 1584	Sir John Puckering	Symonds D'Ewes, *Journals,* p. 333	23 Nov., 1584
XXVIII Elizabeth, and 6th Parliament summoned to meet at Westminster, 29 Oct. 1586	Sir John Puckering again	Symonds D'Ewes, *Journals,* p. 392	29 Oct., 1586
XXXI Elizabeth, and 7th Parliament summoned to meet at Westminster, 4 Feb., 1588-89	Thomas Snagge	Symonds D'Ewes, *Journals,* p. 428	4 Feb., 1588-89
XXXV Elizabeth, and 8th Parliament summoned to meet at Westminster, 19 February, 1592-93	Sir Edward Coke	Symonds D'Ewes, *Journals,* p. 469	19 Feb., 1592-93

Close of Office	Constituency	Subsequent Rank or Style	Remarks
1576	Lyme Regis	Chief Baron of the Exchequer	Died 1577
19 April, 1583, but the House did not sit after 18 Mar., 1580-81	Bristol	Chief Justice of the King's Bench	Died 1607
14 Sept., 1586	Carmarthen	Lord Keeper of the Great Seal 1592	Died 1596
23 March, 1586–87	Gatton		
29 March, 1589	Bedford		Died 1593. (The *Dictionary of National Biography* says he was chosen on 12 November, 1588, but there was no Parliament in session at that date)
10 April, 1593	Norfolk	Chief Justice of the Common Pleas 1606, Chief Justice of the King's Bench 1613-16	Died 1634

Parliament	Speaker	Authority	Date of Appointment
XXXIX Elizabeth,and 9th Parliament summoned to meet at Westminster, 24 Oct. 1597	Sir Christopher Yelverton	Symonds D'Ewes, *Journals*, p. 550	24 Oct., 1597
XLIII Elizabeth, and 10th Parliament summoned to meet at Westminster, 27 October, 1601	Sir John Croke	Symonds D'Ewes, *Journals*, p. 621	27 October, 1601
I James I, and 1st Parliament summoned to meet at Westminster, 19 March, 1603–04	Sir Edward Phelips	*Commons Journals*, Vol. I, p. 141	19 Mar., 1603-4
XII James I, and 2nd Parliament summoned to meet at Westminster, 5 April, 1614	Sir Randolph Crewe	*Commons Journals*, Vol. I, p. 455	5 April, 1614
XVIII James I, and 3rd Parliament summoned to meet at Westminster, 16 Jan. 1620–21	Sir Thomas Richardson	*Commons Journals*, Vol. I, p. 507	30 Jan.,1620–21
XXI James I, and 4th Parliament summoned to meet at Westminster, 12 February, 1623–24. King's speech delivered 19 February	Sir Thomas Crewe	*Commons Journals*, Vol. I, p. 670	19 Feb., 1623-24
I Charles I, and 1st Parliament summoned to meet at Westminster, 17May, 1625. (Adjourned to Oxford)	Sir Thomas Crewe again	There is no mention in the *Journals* of his re-election to the Chair. Cobbett's *Parliamentary History*, Vol. II, p. 3	18 June, 1625

Close of Office	Constituency	Subsequent Rank or Style	Remarks
9 Feb., 1597–98	Northants	Justice of the Queen's Bench	Died 1612
19 December, 1601	London	Judge and Recorder of London	Died 1620
9 Feb., 1610–11	Somerset	Master of the Rolls 1611	Died 1614
7 June, 1614	? Brackley	Chief Justice of the King's Bench	Died 1646
8 Feb., 1621–22	St. Albans	Chief Justice of the Common Pleas 1626	Died 1635
27 March, 1625, but the House did not sit after 29 May, 1624	Aylesbury		Died 1634
12 August, 1625	Gatton		

Parliament	Speaker	Authority	Date of Appointment
I Charles I, and 2nd Parliament summoned to meet at Westminster, 6 Feb., 1625–26	Sir Heneage Finch	Commons Journals, Vol. I, p. 816	6 Feb., 1625–26
III Charles I, and 3rd Parliament summoned to meet at Westminster, 17 March, 1627–28	Sir John Finch	Commons Journals, Vol. I, p. 872	17 Mar., 1627-28
XVI Charles I, 4th or " Short " Parliament summoned to meet at Westminster 13 April, 1640	Sir John Glanville	Commons Journals, Vol. II, p. 3	13 April, 1640
XVI Charles I, 5th or " Long " Parliament summoned to meet at Westminster 3 November, 1640. Dispersed by Cromwell, 20 April, 1653	William Lenthall	Commons Journals, Vol. II, p. 20	3 Nov., 1640
1647—continued	Henry Pelham	Commons Journals, Vol. V, p. 259	30 July, 1647
" Long " Parliament and " Rump " Parliament	William Lenthall again	Commons Journals, Vol. V, p. 268	6 August, 1647 ; returned to the Chair
" Barebones " or Little Parliament met 4 July, 1653. (Lenthall not a member of it)	Rev. Francis Rous	Commons Journals, Vol. VII, p. 281	5 July, 1653
First Parliament of Oliver, Protector, assembled 3 September 1654	William Lenthall again	Commons Journals, Vol. VII, p. 365	4 Sept., 1654
Second Parliament of Oliver, Protector, assembled 17 September, 1656	Sir Thomas Widdrington	Commons Journals, Vol. VII, p. 423	17 Sept., 1656

Close of Office	Constituency	Subsequent Rank or Style	Remarks
15 June, 1626	London		Died 1631
10 March, 1628–29	Canterbury	Lord Keeper of the Great Seal 1639–40 Baron Finch of Fordwich	Died 1660
5 May, 1640	Bristol		Died 1661
Held office till 26 July, 1647, when he abandoned the post to join the Army	Woodstock	Master of the Rolls, and a Commissioner of the Great Seal	Died 1662
5 August, 1647	Grantham		(Not mentioned by Manning or *D.N.B.*)
20 April, 1653	Woodstock		
12 December, 1653	? Devonshire	Sat in Cromwell's House of Lords	Died 1659
22 Jan., 1654-55	Oxfordshire		
4 Feb.,1657–58	Northumberland	Chief Baron of the Exchequer 1658–60	Died 1664. Buried in St. Giles's-in-the-Fields

2 C

Parliament	Speaker	Authority	Date of Appointment
Second Parliament of Oliver, Protector—continued	Bulstrode Whitelocke	Commons Journals, Vol. VII, p. 482	27 Jan., 1656-57 appointed pro tem. during the absence of Widdrington from indisposition
Parliament of Richard Cromwell, Protector, assembled 27 Jan., 1658–59	Chaloner Chute	Commons Journals, Vol. VII, p. 594	27 Jan., 1658-59
Ditto	Sir Lislebone Long	Commons Journals, Vol. VII, p. 612	9 Mar., 1658–59
Ditto	Thomas Bampfylde	Commons Journals, Vol. VII, p. 613	16 Mar., 1658-59 and formally chosen, 15 April, 1659, after the death of Chute
" Rump," or that portion of the Long Parliament which had continued sitting till ejected by Cromwell, recalled	William Lenthall again	Commons Journals, Vol. VII, p. 797	7 May, 1659
The Rump restored a second time	William Lenthall again	Cobbett's Parliamentary History, Vol. III, p. 1571	26 Dec., 1659
	William Say	Commons Journals, Vol. VII, p. 811	13 Jan., 1659-60 (during Lenthall's absence from indisposition)
Whole surviving body of the Long Parliament recalled after Monk's arrival in London	William Lenthall again		21 Jan., 1659-60

Close of Office	Constituency	Subsequent Rank or Style	Remarks
	Buckingham-shire	Commissioner of the Great Seal 1648 and 1659	Died 1675
9 March, 1658–59	Middlesex		Died 1659
14 March, 1658–59	Wells		Died 1659
22 April, 1659	Exeter		(Not mentioned in *D.N.B.*) Died October 8, 1693, and was buried in St. Stephen's Church, Exeter
October 13, 1659, when the Rump was expelled by Lambert	Oxfordshire		
13 Jan., 1659-60	Oxfordshire		
21 January, 1659–60	Camelford		Died 1665 ?
16 March, 1659–60	Oxfordshire		

Parliament	Speaker	Authority	Date of Appointment
XII Charles II, and 1st or Convention Parliament summoned to meet at Westminster, 25 April, 1660	Sir Harbottle Grimston	Commons Journals, Vol. VIII, p. 1	25 April, 1660
XIII Charles II, and 2nd or "Pensionary" Parliament summoned to meet at Westminster, 8 May, 1661	Sir Edward Turnour	Commons Journals, Vol. VIII, p. 245	8 May, 1661
Ditto	Sir Job Charlton	Commons Journals, Vol. IX, p. 245	4 Feb., 1672–73
Ditto	Sir Edward Seymour	Commons Journals, Vol. IX, p. 253	18 Feb., 1672–73
Ditto	Sir Robert Sawyer	Commons Journals, Vol. IX, p. 463	11 April, 1678
Ditto	Sir Edward Seymour again	Commons Journals, Vol. IX, p. 476	6 May, 1678
XXXI Charles II, and 3rd Parliament summoned to meet at Westminster, 6 Mar., 1678–79	Sir Edward Seymour again	Cobbett's Parl. Hist., Vol. IV	6 Mar., 1678–79
Ditto	Sir William Gregory	Cobbett's Parl. Hist., Vol. IV	15 Mar., 1678–79
XXXI Charles II, and 4th Parliament summoned to meet at Westminster, 17 October, 1679. Met for business 21 October, 1680	Sir William Williams	Commons Journals, Vol. IX, p. 636	21 Oct., 1680

Close of Office	Constituency	Subsequent Rank or Style	Remarks
29 December, 1660	Colchester	Master of the Rolls	Died 1685
23 May, 1671	Hertford	Chief Baron of the Exchequer	Died 1676
15 February, 1672–73	Ludlow	Justice of the Common Pleas	Died 1697
11 April, 1678	Totnes	A Lord of the Treasury	Died 1708
6 May, 1678	Wycombe	Attorney-General 1681-87	Died 1692
24 Jan., 1678-79	Totnes		
15 March, 1678–79, when his re-election to the Chair was refused by the King	Devonshire		
12 July, 1679	Weobley	Baron of the Exchequer	Died 1696
18 Jan., 1680-81	Chester	Solicitor-General 1687	Died 1700

Parliament	Speaker	Authority	Date of Appointment
XXXIII Charles II, and 5th Parliament summoned to meet at Oxford, 21 Mar., 1680–81	Sir William Williams again	Commons Journals, Vol. IX, p. 705	21 Mar., 1680-81
I James II, and 1st Parliament summoned to meet at Westminster, 19 May, 1685	Sir John Trevor	Commons Journals, Vol. IX, p. 713	19 May, 1685
Convention Parliament summoned to meet at Westminster, 22 January, 1688–89	Henry Powle	Commons Journals, Vol. X, p. 9	22 Jan., 1688-89
II William and Mary, and 1st Parliament summoned to meet at Westminster, 20 March, 1689–90	Sir John Trevor again	Commons Journals, Vol. X, p. 347	20 Mar., 1689-90
Ditto	Paul Foley	Commons Journals, Vol. XI, p. 272	14 Mar., 1694-95
VII William and Mary, and 2nd Parliament summoned to meet at Westminster, 22 November, 1695	Paul Foley again	Commons Journals, Vol. XI, p. 334	22 Nov., 1695
X William III, and 3rd Parliament summoned to meet at Westminster, 24 August, 1698, and met for despatch of business 6 December	Sir Thomas Littleton	Commons Journals, Vol. XII, p. 347	6 Dec., 1698
XII William III, and 4th Parliament summoned to meet at Westminster, 6 Feb., 1700–01	Robert Harley	Commons Journals, Vol. XIII p. 325	10 Feb., 1700-1

Close of Office	Constituency	Subsequent Rank or Style	Remarks
28 March, 1681	Chester		
2 July, 1687	Denbigh Borough	Master of the Rolls	Expelled the House for taking bribes, 16 March, 1694–95. Died 1717
6 February, 1688–89	Windsor (Whig)	Master of the Rolls	Died 1692
14 March, 1694–95	Yarmouth, Isle of Wight (Whig)		
11 October, 1695	Hereford (Tory)		Died 1699
7 July, 1698	Hereford (Tory)		
19 Dec., 1700	Woodstock (Whig)	Treasurer of the Navy	Died 1710. He requested to be excused from executing the office on the ground that he suffered from the stone
11 Nov., 1701	New Radnor (Tory)	Chancellor of the Exchequer, Earl of Oxford 1711	Died 1724

Parliament	Speaker	Authority	Date of Appointment
XIII William III, and 5th Parliament summoned to meet at Westminster, 30 December, 1701	Robert Harley again	*Commons Journals*, Vol. XIII p. 645	30 Dec., 1701
I Anne, and 1st Parliament summoned to meet at Westminster, 20 August, 1702, and met for despatch of business 20 October	Robert Harley again	Cobbett's *Parliamentary History*, Vol. VI, p. 46.	20 Oct., 1702
IV Anne, and 2nd Parliament summoned to meet at Westminster, 14 June, 1705, and met for despatch of business 25 October. Declared First Parliament of Great Britain, 29 April, 1707	John Smith	*Commons Journals*, Vol. XV, pp. 5 and 393	25 Oct., 1705
VI Anne, and 1st Parliament of Great Britain met at Westminster, 23 October, 1707	Ditto	*Commons Journals*, Vol. XV, p. 393	23 Oct., 1707
VII Anne, and 3rd Parliament summoned to meet at Westminster, 8 July, 1708, and met for despatch of business 16 November	Sir Richard Onslow	*Commons Journals*, Vol. XVI, p. 4	16 Nov., 1708
IX Anne, and 4th Parliament summoned to meet at Westminster, 25 Nov. 1710	William Bromley	*Commons Journals*, Vol. XVI, p. 401	25 Nov., 1710

Close of Office	Constituency	Subsequent Rank or Style	Remarks
2 July, 1702	New Radnor (Tory)		Elected by a majority of four votes over Sir Thomas Littleton
5 April, 1705	New Radnor (Tory)		
13 April, 1708	Andover (Whig)	Chancellor of the Exchequer 1708–10	Died 1723
	Andover (Whig)		
21 Sept., 1710	Surrey (Whig)	Chancellor of the Exchequer 1714–15. Baron Onslow	Died 1717
8 August, 1713	Oxford University (Tory)	Secretary of State 1713–14	Died 1732

Parliament	Speaker	Authority	Date of Appointment
XII Anne, and 5th Parliament summoned to meet at Westminster, 12 November, 1713; and met for despatch of business 16 Feb., 1713–14. Queen's speech delivered 2 March	Sir Thomas Hanmer	*Commons Journals*, Vol. XVII, p. 472	16 Feb., 1713-14
I George I, and 1st Parliament summoned and met for business at Westminster, 17 March, 1714–15	Sir Spencer Compton	*Commons Journals*, Vol. XVIII, p. 16	17 Mar.,1714–15
VIII George I, and 2nd Parliament summoned to meet at Westminster,10May, 1722; met for business 9 October	Sir Spencer Compton again	*Commons Journals*,Vol. XX, p. 8	9 Oct., 1722
I George II, and 1st Parliament summoned to meet at Westminster, 28 November, 1727; met for despatch of business 23 January, 1727–28	Arthur Onslow	*Commons Journals*,Vol.XXI p. 20	23 Jan., 1727-28
VIII George II, and 2nd Parliament summoned to meet at Westminster, 13 June, 1734; met for despatch of business 14 January, 1734–35	Arthur Onslow again	*Commons Journals*, Vol. XXII, p. 324	14 Jan., 1734-35

Close of Office	Constituency	Subsequent Rank or Style	Remarks
15 Jan., 1714-15	Suffolk (Tory)		Died 1746.
10 Mar., 1721–22	Sussex (Whig)	First Lord of the Treasury 1742, and Earl of Wilmington	Died 1743.
5 August, 1727	Sussex (Whig)		
17 April, 1734	Surrey (Whig)		Died 1768, having been Speaker for the record number of years
27 April, 1741	Surrey (Whig)		

Parliament	Speaker	Authority	Date of Appointment
XV George II, and 3rd Parliament summoned to meet at Westminster, 25 June, 1741 ; met for despatch of business 1 Dec., 1741	Arthur Onslow again	*Commons Journals*, Vol. XXIV, p. 8	1 Dec., 1741
XXI George II, and 4th Parliament summoned to meet at Westminster, 13 August, 1747 ; met for despatch of business 10 Nov., 1747	Arthur Onslow again	*Commons Journals*, Vol. XXV, p. 416	10 Nov., 1747
XXVII George II, and 5th Parliament summoned to meet at Westminster, and met for despatch of business 31 May, 1754	Arthur Onslow again	*Commons Journals*, Vol. XXVII, p. 7	31 May, 1754
I George III, and 1st Parliament summoned to meet at Westminster, 19 May, 1761. King's speech delivered 3 November	Sir John Cust	*Commons Journals*, Vol. XXIX, p. 8	3 Nov., 1761
VIII George III, and 2nd Parliament summoned to meet at Westminster, and met for despatch of business 10 May, 1768	Sir John Cust again	*Commons Journals*, Vol. XXXII, p. 6	10 May, 1768
Ditto	Sir Fletcher Norton	*Commons Journals*, Vol. XXXII, p. 613	22 Jan., 1770

Close of Office	Constituency	Subsequent Rank or Style	Remarks
18 June, 1747	Surrey (Whig)		
8 April, 1754	Surrey (Whig)		
20 March, 1761	Surrey (Whig)		
11 March, 1768	Grantham (Tory)		Died 1770.
17 Jan., 1770	Grantham (Tory)		Died five days after his resignation.
30 Sept., 1774	Guildford (Tory)	Baron Grantley 1782	Died 1789.

Parliament	Speaker	Authority	Date of Appointment
XV George III, and 3rd Parliament summoned to meet at Westminster, and met for despatch of business 29 November, 1774	Sir Fletcher Norton again	Commons Journals, Vol. XXXV, p. 5	29 Nov., 1774
XXI George III, and 4th Parliament summoned to meet at Westminster, and met for despatch of business 31 October, 1780	Charles Wolfran Cornwall	Commons Journals, Vol. XXXVIII, p. 6	31 Oct., 1780
XXIV George III, and 5th Parliament summoned to meet at Westminster, and met for despatch of business 18 May, 1784	Charles Wolfran Cornwall again	Commons Journals, Vol. XL, p. 5	18 May, 1784
Ditto	William Wyndham Grenville	Commons Journals, Vol. XLIV, p. 45	5 Jan., 1789
Ditto	Henry Addington	Commons Journals, Vol. XLIV, p. 434	8 June, 1789
XXX George III, and 6th Parliament summoned to meet at Westminster, 10 August, 1790; met for despatch of business 25 November, 1790	Henry Addington again	Commons Journals, Vol. XLVI, p. 6	25 Nov., 1790

Close of Office	Constituency	Subsequent Rank or Style	Remarks
1 Sept., 1780	Guildford(Tory)	Baron Grantley 1782	
25 March, 1784	Winchelsea (Tory)		Died 1789
2 January, 1789	Rye (Tory)		
7 June, 1789	Buckinghamshire. Of a Whig family but a supporter of Pitt	Prime Minister "All the Talents." Baron Grenville 1790	Died 1834
11 June, 1790	Truro (Tory)	Prime Minister. Viscount Sidmouth 1805	Died 1844
20 May, 1796	Devizes (Tory)		

Parliament	Speaker	Authority	Date of Appointment
XXXVI George III, and 7th Parliament summoned to meet at Westminster, 12 July, 1796; and met for despatch of business 27 September	Henry Addington again	*Commons Journals,* Vol. LII, p. 8	27 Sept., 1796
(XLI George III, by proclamation of 5 November, 1800. Members then sitting were declared members of the First Parliament of the United Kingdom, to meet 22 January, 1801. King's speech delivered 2 February, 1801)	ditto	*Commons Journals,* Vol. LVI, p. 6	22 Jan., 1801
7th Parliament—*continued*	Sir John Mitford	*Commons Journals,* Vol. LVI, p. 33	11 Feb., 1801
Ditto	Charles Abbot	*Commons Journals,* Vol. LVII, p. 93	10 Feb., 1802
XLII George III, and 8th Parliament summoned to meet at Westminster, 31 August, 1802; and met for despatch of business 16 November. King's speech delivered 23 November	Charles Abbot again	*Commons Journals,* Vol. LVIII, p. 8	16 Nov., 1802
XLVII George III, and 9th Parliament summoned to meet at Westminster, and met for despatch of business 15 December, 1806. King's speech delivered 19 December	Charles Abbot again	*Commons Journals,* Vol. LXII, p. 4	15 Dec., 1806

Close of Office	Constituency	Subsequent Rank or Style	Remarks
16 Feb., 1801	Devizes (Tory)		
	Devizes (Tory)		
9 February, 1802	Northumberland (Tory)	Baron Redesdale 1802. Lord Chancellor of Ireland 1802	Died 1830
29 June, 1802	Woodstock (Tory)	Baron Colchester 1817	Died 1829. Buried in Westminster Abbey. The last Speaker to be so honoured
29 April, 1807	Woodstock (Tory)		
29 April, 1807	Oxford University (Tory)		

2 D

Parliament	Speaker	Authority	Date of Appointment
XLVII George III, and 10th Parliament summoned to meet at Westminster, and met for despatch of business 22 June, 1807. King's speech delivered 26 June	Charles Abbot again	*Commons Journals*, Vol. LXII, p. 560	22 June, 1807
LIII George III, and 11th Parliament summoned to meet at Westminster, and met for despatch of business 24 November, 1812. Prince Regent's speech delivered 30 Nov.	Charles Abbot again	*Commons Journals*, Vol. LXVIII, p. 4	24 Nov., 1812
Ditto	Charles Manners-Sutton	*Commons Journals*, Vol. LXXII, p. 307	2 June, 1817
LVIII George III, and 12th Parliament summoned to meet at Westminster, 4 August, 1818; met for despatch of business 14 January, 1819. King's speech delivered 21 Jan.	Charles Manners-Sutton again	*Commons Journals*, Vol. LXXIV, p. 8	14 Jan., 1819
I George IV, and 1st Parliament summoned to meet at Westminster, and met for despatch of business 21 April, 1820. King's speech delivered 27 April	Charles Manners-Sutton again	*Commons Journals*, Vol. LXXV, p. 108	21 April, 1820

Close of Office	Constituency	Subsequent Rank or Style	Remarks
29 Sept., 1812	Oxford University (Tory)		
2 June, 1817	Oxford University (Tory)		
10 June, 1818	Scarborough (Tory)	Viscount Canterbury 1835	Died 1845
29 Feb., 1820	Scarborough (Tory)		
2 June, 1826	Scarborough (Tory)		

Parliament	Speaker	Authority	Date of Appointment
VII George IV, and 2nd Parliament summoned to meet at Westminster, 25 July, 1826; met for despatch of business 14 November. King's speech delivered 21 November	Charles Manners-Sutton again	*Commons Journals,* Vol. LXXXII p. 8	14 Nov., 1826
I William IV, and 1st Parliament summoned to meet at Westminster, 14 September, 1830; met for despatch of business 26 October. King's speech delivered 2 November	Charles Manners-Sutton again	*Commons Journals,* Vol. LXXXVI, p. 6	26 Oct., 1830
I William IV, and 2nd Parliament summoned to meet at Westminster, and met for despatch of business 14 June, 1831. King's speech delivered 21 June	Charles Manners-Sutton again	*Commons Journals,* Vol. LXXXVI, p. 522	14 June, 1831
III William IV, and 3rd Parliament summoned to meet at Westminster, and met for despatch of business 29 January, 1833. King's speech delivered 5 February	Charles Manners-Sutton again	*Commons Journals,* Vol. LXXXVIII p. 5	29 Jan., 1833
V William IV, and 4th Parliament summoned to meet at Westminster, and met for despatch of business 19 February, 1835. King's speech delivered 24 February	James Abercromby	*Commons Journals,* Vol. XC, p. 5	19 Feb., 1835

Close of Office	Constituency	Subsequent Rank or Style	Remarks
24 July, 1830	Scarborough (Tory)		
23 April, 1831	Scarborough (Tory)		
3 Dec., 1832	Scarborough (Tory)		
29 Dec., 1834	Cambridge University (Tory)		
17 July, 1837	Edinburgh (Whig)	Baron Dunfermline 1839	The only Speaker to come from north of the Tweed. Died 1858

Parliament	Speaker	Authority	Date of Appointment
I Victoria, and 1st Parliament summoned to meet at Westminster, 11 September, 1837; and met for despatch of business 15 November. Queen's speech delivered 20 November	James Abercromby again	*Commons Journals,* Vol. XCIII, p. 7	15 Nov., 1837
Ditto,	Charles Shaw-Lefevre	*Commons Journals,* Vol. XCIV, p. 274	27 May, 1839
V Victoria, and 2nd Parliament summoned to meet at Westminster, and met for despatch of business 19 August, 1841. Queen's speech delivered 24 August	Charles Shaw-Lefevre again	*Commons Journals,* Vol. XCVI, p. 465	19 August, 1841
XI Victoria, and 3rd Parliament summoned to meet at Westminster, 21 September, 1847; and met for despatch of business 18 November. Queen's speech delivered 23 November	Charles Shaw-Lefevre again	*Commons Journals,* Vol. CIII, p. 7	18 Nov., 1847
XVI Victoria, and 4th Parliament summoned to meet at Westminster, 20 August, 1852. Met for despatch of business 4 November. Queen's speech delivered 11 November	Charles Shaw-Lefevre again	*Commons Journals,* Vol. CVIII, p. 7	4 Nov., 1852

Close of Office	Constituency	Subsequent Rank or Style	Remarks
15 May, 1839	Edinburgh (Whig)		
23 June, 1841	North Hampshire (Liberal)	Viscount Eversley 1857	Died 1888
23 July, 1847	North Hampshire (Liberal)		
1 July, 1852	North Hampshire (Liberal)		
21 March, 1857	North Hampshire (Liberal)		

Parliament	Speaker	Authority	Date of Appointment
XX Victoria, and 5th Parliament summoned to meet at Westminster, and met for despatch of business 30 April, 1857. Queen's speech delivered 7 May	John Evelyn Denison	*Commons Journals,* Vol. CXII, p. 119	30 April, 1857
XXII Victoria, and 6th Parliament summoned to meet at Westminster, and met for despatch of business 31 May, 1859. Queen's speech delivered 7 June	John Evelyn Denison again	*Commons Journals,* Vol. CXIV, p. 191	31 May, 1859
XXIX Victoria, and 7th Parliament summoned to meet at Westminster, 15 August, 1865 ; and met for despatch of business 1 February, 1866. Queen's speech delivered 6 February	John Evelyn Denison again	*Commons Journals,* Vol. CXXI, p. 9	1 Feb., 1866
XXXII Victoria, and 8th Parliament summoned to meet at Westminster, and met for despatch of business 10 December, 1868. Queen's speech delivered 16 February, 1869	John Evelyn Denison again	*Commons Journals,* Vol. CXXIV, p. 5	10 Dec., 1868
Ditto	Henry Bouverie William Brand	*Commons Journals,* Vol. CXXVII, p. 23	9 Feb., 1872

Close of Office	Constituency	Subsequent Rank or Style	Remarks
23 April, 1859	North Notts (Liberal)	Viscount Ossington 1872	Died 1873. His election to the Chair was unanimous on each occasion
6 July, 1865	North Notts (Liberal)		
11 Nov., 1868	North Notts (Liberal)		
7 Feb., 1872	North Notts (Liberal)		
26 Jan., 1874	Cambridgeshire (Liberal)	Viscount Hampden 1884	Died 1892. His election to the Chair was unanimous on each occasion

Parliament	Speaker	Authority	Date of Appointment
XXXVIII Victoria, and 9th Parliament summoned to meet at Westminster, and met for despatch of business 5 March, 1874. Queen's speech delivered 19 March	Henry Bouverie William Brand again	*Commons Journals,* Vol. CXXIX, p. 5	5 Mar., 1874
XLIII Victoria, and 10th Parliament summoned to meet at Westminster, and met for despatch of business 29 April, 1880. Queen's speech delivered 20 May	Henry Bouverie William Brand again	*Commons Journals,* Vol. CXXXV, p. 5	29 April, 1880
Ditto	Arthur Wellesley Peel	*Commons Journals,* Vol. CXXXIX, p. 74	26 Feb., 1884
XLIX Victoria, and 11th Parliament summoned to meet at Westminster, and met for despatch of business 12 January, 1886. Queen's speech (delivered in person by Her Majesty) 21 January	Arthur Wellesley Peel again	*Commons Journals,* Vol. CXLI, p. 5	12 Jan., 1886
L Victoria, and 12th Parliament summoned to meet at Westminster, and met for despatch of business 5 August, 1886. Queen's speech delivered 19 August	Arthur Wellesley Peel again	*Commons Journals,* Vol. CXLI, p. 315	5 August, 1886

Close of Office	Constituency	Subsequent Rank or Style	Remarks
24 March, 1880	Cambridgeshire (Liberal)		
25 Feb., 1884	Cambridgeshire (Liberal)		
18 Nov., 1885	Warwick and Leamington (Liberal)	Viscount Peel, 1895	His election to the Chair was unanimous on each occasion
26 June	Warwick and Leamington (Liberal)		
28 June, 1892	Warwick and Leamington (Liberal)		

Parliament	Speaker	Authority	Date of Appointment
LVI Victoria, and 13th Parliament summoned to meet at Westminster, and met for despatch of business 4 August, 1892. Queen's speech delivered 8 August	Arthur Wellesley Peel again	Commons Journals, Vol. CXLVII, p. 412	4 August, 1892
Ditto	William Court Gully	Commons Journals, Vol. CL, p. 149	10 April, 1895
LIX Victoria, and 14th Parliament summoned to meet at Westminster, and met for despatch of business 12 August, 1895. Queen's speech delivered 15 August	William Court Gully again	Commons Journals, Vol. CL, p. 340	12 August, 1895
LXIV Victoria, and 15th Parliament summoned to meet at Westminster, 1 November, 1900 ; and met for despatch of business 3 December. Queen's speech delivered 6 Dec.	William Court Gully again	Commons Journals, Vol. CLV, p. 406	3 Dec., 1900
And I Edward VII, and 1st Parliament summoned to hear the King's speech 14 February, 1901			
Ditto—continued	James William Lowther	Commons Journals, Vol. CLX, p. 249	8 June, 1905

Close of Office	Constituency	Subsequent Rank or Style	Remarks
9 April, 1895	Warwick and Leamington (Liberal)		
8 July, 1895	Carlisle(Liberal)	Viscount Selby, 1905	Died 1909.
25 Sept., 1900	Carlisle(Liberal)		
7 June, 1905	Carlisle(Liberal)		
8 Jan., 1906	Cumberland (Penrith Div.) (Conservative)		

Parliament	Speaker	Authority	Date of Appointment
VI Edward VII, and 2nd Parliament summoned to meet at Westminster, and met for despatch of business 13 Feb., 1906. King's speech delivered 19 Feb.	James William Lowther again	*Commons Journals,* Vol. CLXI, p. 5	13 Feb., 1906
X Edward VII, and 3rd Parliament summoned to meet at Westminster, and met for despatch of business, 15 Feb., 1910. King's speech delivered 21 Feb. And I George V, 7 May, 1910	James William Lowther again	*Commons Journals,* Vol. CLXV, p. 5	15 Feb., 1910
I George V, and 1st Parliament summoned to meet at Westminster, and met for despatch of business 31 January, 1911. King's speech delivered 6 Feb.	James William Lowther again	*Commons Journals,* Vol. CLXVI, p. 5	31 Jan., 1911

It will be noticed that the dates of several elections to the Chair and the sequence of names do not, in all cases, correspond with the list of Speakers inscribed on the panels of the Library of the House of Commons. They, unfortunately, contain many inaccuracies, and it has been the Author's endeavour to correct them as far as possible in these pages.

Close of Office	Constituency	Subsequent Rank or Style	Remarks
10 Jan., 1910	Cumberland (Penrith Div.) (Conservative)		
28 Nov., 1910	Cumberland (Penrith Div.) (Conservative)		
	Cumberland (Penrith Div.) (Conservative		

APPENDICES

pleaseth you . . . to the number of xxiiij, and they to
goo togedir unto my Lord Chaunceler, and there to show
unto his lordship that they have doon the Kyngs com-
maundement in the chosyn of our Speker, desyring his
lordship if that he wold shew it unto the Kyng's grace.
And . . . whan it plesith the King to commaunde us
when, we shall present hym afore his high grace. Yt
pleased the Kyng that we shuld present hym upon the
ix day of Novembre. That same day, at x of the cloke,
sembled Maister Speker and all the Knyghts, sitteners,[1]
and burgeyses in the parlement house, and so departed
into the parlement chamber before the Kyngs grace and
all his lords spirituall and temporall and all his Juggs,[2]
and so presented our Speker before the Kyngs grace and
all his lords spirituall and temporall.' "

The Lord Chancellor referred to was John Russell,
Bishop of Lincoln, and the Recorder of London was
Thomas Fitzwilliam, who was himself Speaker in 1488–89.
Speaker Lovell was a contemporary of Abbot Islip,
the last of the great monastic builders to stamp his
individuality on the fabric of the Abbey. As Treasurer
of the Royal Household Lovell probably assisted at the
laying of the foundation stone of Henry the Seventh's
Chapel, in which, after the lapse of four centuries, his
noble medallion portrait by Torregiano has, with singular
appropriateness, recently been placed. (See illustration
in this volume.)

[1] Citizens.   [2] Judges.

APPENDIX II

Sir Thomas More's Speech on presentation for the Royal Approval, 1523. Translated from the original Latin.

"ON Saturday the 18th day of April, the 4th day of Parliament, the Commons from their House, appearing before our Lord the King in full Parliament, presented to our Lord the King Thomas More, knight, as their Speaker ; whom our aforesaid Lord the King was graciously pleased to accept.

" Whereupon Thomas, after making his excuse before our Lord the King, inasmuch as his excuse could not be admitted on the part of our Lord the King, made his most humble supplication, that, with the like liberty of speech, he might publish and declare all and singular things to be by him published and declared in the Parliament aforesaid, in the name of the said Commons ; but that if he declared any things enjoined on him by his Fellows otherwise than they themselves were agreed upon, either by adding or diminishing, he might be enabled to correct and amend the things so declared by his Fellows aforesaid ; and that his Protestation to this effect might be entered on the Roll of the Parliament aforesaid.

" To whom, by the King's command, answer was made

INDEX

A

Abbey of Westminster, *v.* Westminster Abbey

Abbot, Charles (afterwards Lord Colchester), Speaker in 1802, 1806, 1807, and 1812, xxviii, xxx, xxxi, xxxv, 264, 295, 298, 299, 300, 301, 302, 303, 331, 400, 402

Abbots of Abingdon, 14

Abbots of Furness, 13

Abbots of Westminster, 12, 20, 37, 46, 47, 59, 161

  William of Colchester, 46, 47, 48

  Thomas Henley, 37 ; John Islip, 420

  Simon Langham, 42, 43, 44, 45, 47

  Nicholas Litlington, 44, 45, 47

  Thomas Millyng, 95

  Richard Ware, 42

Abbot's School, Westminster, King Edward V educated at, 95

Abercorn, Earl of, 206

Abercromby, James (Lord Dunfermline), Speaker in 1835 and 1837, xxx, xxxi, 269, 316, 317, 318, 319, 320, 404, 406

Abingdon, Abbots of, 14

Abingdon Street, xxxix

Addington, Dr., the Speaker's father, 293

Addington, Henry (Lord Sidmouth), Speaker in 1789, 1790, 1796, and 1801, xxviii, xxx, xxxi, 289, 291, 292, 293, 294, 398, 400

"Addled Parliament," 170

Adjournment, fixed hour for, adopted by the House of Commons in 1888, 335

Agincourt, Battle of, a Speaker fights at, 75

Album of water-colour drawings of Speakers in the National Portrait Gallery, xxiv, xxvii, xxviii

Alexander IV, Pope, 34

Alington, William, Speaker in 1429, xxiii, xxxvi, 79, 360

Alington, William, the younger, Speaker in 1472 and 1477-78, xxxvi, 91, 368

"All the Talents," Ministry of, 288

Almon, printer of Parliamentary debates, 264

Althorp, Lord, 308

Amiens, 7, 291

Anne, Queen of England, 234, 244, 245

Argyll Buildings, London residence of Speaker Cust, 276

Argyll, Duke of, 257

Armstrong, Sir Thomas, 226

Arundel, Thomas, Archbishop of Canterbury, 62

Ashby St. Ledger's, Northants, church of, xxv ; burial place of Speaker Catesby, 369

Askew, Mr., 197

"Assenters as well as Petitioners," Commons so described in the Rolls of 1414, 75

Audley, Sir Thomas (afterwards Lord Audley), Speaker in 1529, xxviii, xxx ; painting by Holbein, xxxiii ; 124, 125, 374

Audley End, Essex, said to be the largest private house in England, 124

Austin Friars, burial place of Speaker Sheffield, 117

Aye Bourne, 10

Ayles, Rev. Dr. H. H. B., xl

Aymer de Valence, Bishop Elect of Winchester, 34, 343

Ayremine, William de, Clerk in Chancery, records the doings of both Houses, *temp.* Edward II, 32

425

Carteret, Lord, 253
Carey Street, Lincoln's Inn Fields, 237
Caricatures of Speakers, 284, 288
Cartwright, Thomas, 162
Casting Votes of Speakers, 160, 196, 223, 283
"Cat, the Rat and Lovell the Dog," 96
Catesby, Robert, 96
Catesby, William, Speaker in 1483–84, xxxvi, 96, 97, 368; memorial brass of, xxv
Caxton, William, 48, 150
Cecil, Sir Robert, 153, 169
Chair, Speaker Lenthall's, canopy of, preserved at Radley, Berks, 195
Chamber of the Chauntor of St. Stephen's Chapel, Palace of Westminster, 17
Chamber of the Cross in the old Palace of Westminster, 18
Chamberlayne's *Angliæ Notitia*, 219, 220
Chambers, John, Dean of St. Stephen's Chapel, Westminster, 119
Chambre Blanche, or White Hall, in the old Palace of Westminster, 42, 43
Chancery Lane, 103, 202
Chapel of St. Benedict, Westminster Abbey, 44
Chapel of St. Erasmus, Westminster Abbey, 95
Chapel of the Pyx, Westminster Abbey, 58
Chapel of St. Michael, Westminster Abbey, Wm. Trussell's tomb in, 40
Chapel of St. Stephen, in the old Palace of Westminster, *v.* St. Stephen, Chapel of; Chapel, Henry VII's, in Westminster Abbey, 94, 105, 109, 110, 111
Chaplain of the House of Commons, in the reign of Queen Anne, 245
Chapter House of the Abbey, 41, 45, 46, 47, 48, 49
Charles I, King of England, 7, 190, 191,
Charles II, King of England, 215, 226, 227, 228
Charlton, Sir Job, Speaker in 1672–73, xxx, 222, 388
Charlton, Sir Thomas, Speaker, in 1453–54, xxiii, xxxvii, 81, 83, 364

Chaucer, Geoffrey, 53, 71
Chaucer, Thomas, Speaker in 1407, 1409-10, 1411, 1414, and 1421, 71, 72, 354, 356, 358; memorial brass of, xxv
Checkenden, Bucks, xxxiv
Cheney, *v.* Cheyne
Cheyne, Sir John, Speaker in 1399, xxiii, xxxvii, 62, 352
Chope, Mr. R. P., xl
Christ Church College, Oxford, xxix, xxxv
Church and State, symbol of the Union of, in Plantagenet times, 48
Church, spoliation of the, proposed by the House of Commons in 1404, 69
Chute, Chaloner, Speaker in 1658-59, xxix, 213, 386
Chute, Mr. Charles, of The Vyne, Basingstoke, xxix
Cinque Ports, 25
City of London, Sir Robert Brooke the first Speaker to represent it in Parliament, 134
Clarence, Duke of, 92
Claverley, near Wolverhampton, burial place of Speaker Brooke, xxxiv, 134
Clement's Lane, 230
Clergy Residence Bill, introduced by Speaker Manners-Sutton, 304
Clerk of the House of Commons, 33, 159, 168, 267, 315
Clerk Assistant of the House of Commons, print disproving the belief that John Rushworth was the first, xxxviii
Clerk of the Parliaments, 33
Cleuderre, William, a craftsman employed on Westminister Hall, *temp.* Richard II, 59
Clifford Street, Burlington Gardens, 294
Clive, Lord, 260
Clock for use of the House of Commons, first mention of, 157
Clock Tower of the old Palace of Westminister, 118
Cloister Court of St. Stephen's Chapel, Palace of Westminister, 118, 119
Closure of Debate, institution of, 335
Cloth Fair, Smithfield, 126
Coalition Ministry of 1783, 284

Cobbett's *Parliamentary History*, 265, 374, 376, 382, 386, 388, 392
Cockpit in Whitehall, 199, 265, 281
Coe, Rev. C. H., xl
Coke, Sir Edward, Speaker in 1592–93, xxviii, xxix, xxxi, 31, 147, 148, 149–158, 171, 172, 178, 179, 184, 331, 380
Colchester, Lord, *v.* Abbot, Charles
College Street, Great, Westminster, viii, 10, 12
Coldham, xxviii
Commercial Treaty with France, 1713, 247
"Committee of Safety," 213
Committee of the whole House, Speaker formerly votes in, 331
Commons, House of—
Plantagenet Period—
Dawn of the English Constitution, at Westminster, 4
Barones Minores, or lesser Tenants in Chief, separate from the House of Lords, 22
Simon de Montfort and the writ of summons, 23
The Writ becomes a right, instead of, as in the case of the House of Lords, a privilege, 25
Transition of the principle of representation from tenure to selection, 23
Knights of the Shire, when first summoned to Westminster, 24
Novelties and experiments introduced into the Parliamentary system in the thirteenth century, 27
Burgesses, when first summoned to Westminster, 28 ; seldom attend in person, contenting themselves with petitioning the Crown, 23
End of the experimental stage and permament establishment of an assembly comprising three estates of the realm, 28
Separation of the two Houses, *temp.* Edward III, 30 ; notwithstanding some uncertainty as to Lords and Commons having, at any time, deliberated in the same Chamber, 31

Commons, House of—
Plantagenet Period—
Lords and Commons make separate grants in 1332 and 1339, 31
Earliest mouthpieces of the Commons, the precursors of the formally elected Speakers mentioned in the Rolls of Parliament, 33
Important constitutional assembly at Westminster in February, 1304–05, 29
In 1322 the Commons obtain from Edward II an acknowledgment of the supremacy of a representative assembly, virtually amounting to a written Constitution, 32
Maintenance of order within the Palace of Westminster, *temp.* Edward III, 31
Clerk of the House of Commons appointed in 1338, 33
Peter de Montfort said to have acted "*vice totius communitatis*" in the "Mad Parliament," held at Oxford, 1258, a restricted assembly of Barons and Prelates, 35
Differences between Lords and Commons in 1339 lead to the summoning of a new Parliament, 39
Commons assemble in the Painted Chamber in the Easter Parliament of 1343, 42 ; in the Chapter House of the Abbots of Westminster in 1351–52, during the rule of Simon Langham, 43
A Parliamentary leader, holding a position not dissimilar to that of Speaker (William Trussell), buried in Westminster Abbey, *temp.* Edward III, 44
Commons assemble in the Refectory of the Monks of Westminster in 1397, 48
Sir Thomas Hungerford, the first Speaker whose name is entered on the Rolls, calls the attention of the King to the grievances of his subjects, both male and female, 53

Commons, House of—
Tudor Period—
A growing spirit of self-reliance manifests itself in the Commons towards the close of Elizabeth's reign, 163
The right of argument recognised when responsible Ministers of the Crown sit in the House and take part in debate on equal terms with the general body of members, 163
Stuart Period—
The great struggle between the Commons and the Crown—
Notwithstanding the advent of a generation which valued privilege more than prerogative Parliamentary progress is retarded, temp. James I, 165
The important case of Privilege of Sir Thomas Shirley carries the amount of protection afforded by the House to its members a step further than in the instances of Haxey and Strode, 166
Rules made for the guidance of the House and its Speaker, 168
Old or discredited system of raising money by benevolences, the sale of honours, and the creation of monopolies, resorted to by the King, 170
The Commons make formal assertion of their liberties in 1621, 171; whereon the King tears the page out of the Journal with his own hand, 172
The refusal of supplies in Charles I's first Parliament leads to its summary dismissal, 175
Increasing boldness of the Commons instanced by the impeachment of the Duke of Buckingham, 175
Oliver Cromwell enters the House at the age of 29, 176
A committee appointed by the Commons to draw up the preamble of the Bill of Supply, 177
A conference held between the two Houses, 1628, and a threatened deadlock averted by the Lords passing the Bill as it stood, 180

Commons, House of—
Stuart Period—
The Long Parliament assembles, 184
Lenthall chosen Speaker, 184; owes his election to an accident, 184; the opinion of most of his contemporaries unfavourable, 185; derives great assistance from Henry Elsynge, the Clerk of the House, 186; the latter resigns his post in 1648 rather than it should be said that he even tacitly approved of the trial and condemnation of the King, 186
Quorum of the House fixed at forty, 188
Long hours of sitting cause the Speaker to think of resigning office, 189
Attempted arrest of the Five Members, 3 January, 1641–42, 190
A King of England enters the House of Commons and takes the Speaker's Chair, 190
Lenthall's memorable reply to Charles I, 192
Incidents of the day described, 192, 193
Lenthall abandons his post on the military party becoming absolute masters of the situation, 195; but returns to the Chair a few days later, 196
"Pride's Purge" effected without articulate protest from the Speaker, 196
Lenthall gives a casting vote on a question connected with the Isle of Wight Treaty with the King, 197
The rift between the Army and the Parliament broadens, 198
The nation not truly represented at Westminster, 198
The uncontrolled rule of a single Chamber proves distasteful to many of Cromwell's supporters, 198
Expulsion of the Long Parliament by Cromwell, 199
The Speaker pulled out of his Chair and the mace removed, 199

Commons, House of—
Stuart Period—
"Barebones" or Little Parliament, Lenthall not a member of it, 200
This assembly, known as "The Reign of the Saints," having served its purpose, is cajoled by its Speaker (Francis Rous) into summary abdication, 200
Lenthall unanimously re-elected in the first Parliament of Oliver, Protector, but replaced by Sir Thomas Widdrington in his second, 200
Lenthall takes his seat in the caricature of the House of Lords set up by Cromwell in January, 1658, 201
Lenthall consents to preside over the restored "Rump" in May, 1659, 201
The 'Rump' violently dispersed by General Lambert, 202
The whole surviving body of the Long Parliament having been restored by the army, Lenthall again takes the Chair, 202
Military and Parliamentary rule having alike become distasteful to the country, the way is paved for the Restoration of the Monarchy, 202
Proposal to exclude lawyers from the House, Speaker Bulstrode Whitelocke's sarcastic remarks upon, 213
The "Pensionary Parliament" of Charles II shows itself extremely jealous of the privileges of the Commons, 216
The House of Commons as seen by French eyes in 1663, 220, 221
Formal contention of the House of Commons in 1671 that the Lords are unable to amend a Money Bill, 221
The struggle between the two Houses renewed over a Money Bill for the disbandment of troops, 222

2 F

Commons, House of—
Stuart Period—
The Commons pass a resolution debarring the Lords from amending, though not of rejecting or suspending, a Money Bill, 222
A grave disturbance in committee of the whole House quelled by the prompt action of the Speaker, 224
The reorganisation of Danby's supporters in the House of Commons leads to a cleavage of parties, out of which sprang the Whigs and Tories of later days, 225
The relations of the two Houses become once more strained (the precedent of Henry IV again quoted), 225
Evolution of the non-partisan Speaker foreshadowed, 227
The terms Whig and Tory first generally applied, 227
The Commons seek to curtail the prerogative of the Crown, 228
Parliament summoned to meet at Oxford, 228
Speaker Trevor expelled the House for taking bribes, 229
Importance of the Speaker's office enters upon a new phase after the Revolution of 1688, 231
Position of the Speaker, as first Commoner of the Realm, defined by the Legislature, 231
The Speakership of Paul Foley, *temp.* William III, marks a stage in the evolution of the independence of the Chair, 233
Reaction, in 1695, from the custom of promoting lawyers to the Chair, 234
"Tacking," in 1699 and 1700, 235
A quarrel between the two Houses leads to a better understanding between William III and the Tory party, 236
Speaker Littleton's antipathy to the legal profession in Parliament, 237

Commons, House of—
Stuart Period—

Speaker Harley, by birth and education a Whig, develops, by imperceptible stages, into the leader of the Tory party, 238; said to have been the inventor of the newspaper press as an instrument of party warfare, 239

A Speaker confronted in the House of Commons by no less than three previous holders of the office (1708), 242

Sir Thomas Hanmer, Speaker in 1713-14, a popular leader before his elevation to the Chair, 246; makes the speech of his life in 1713, 247-49

A Tariff Reform debate in the reign of Queen Anne, 247

The Speakership assumes a permanent character, hitherto unknown in its annals, *temp.* George I, 251

Under Sir Robert Walpole the House of Commons becomes the real seat of power, with a corresponding increase in the dignity and importance of the Chair, 252

Arthur Onslow, Speaker for the record number of years, elected to the Chair, 255; embraces the orthodox Whig creed, 255; the first Speaker to realise the paramount importance of the impartiality of the Chair, 258; his conception of the duties and responsibilities of his office, contributes to the shaping of the modern system of Party Government, 259

Hanoverian and Saxe-Coburg Period—

Rise of the system of Cabinet Government coupled with ministerial responsibility to Parliament, 260

The Speaker brings to the notice of the House the illicit reporting of its Debates, 260–66

Rise of the influence of the newspaper press, 260–66

Commons, House of—
Hanoverian and Saxe-Coburg Period—

Speaker Arthur Onslow's authority defied by a culprit at the bar in 1751, 269

The Speaker opposes, in committee of the whole House, a measure promoted by the Government, 270

His fearless advocacy of the privileges of the Commons and his opposition to late sittings and late hours of meeting, 271

His farewell speech to the House, quoted *in extenso*, 272

Proposals for building a new House of Commons, 274

Speaker Cust sits in the Chair for sixteen hours, 275

The Commons revert to the practice of appointing a law officer of the Crown to the Chair, 276; the experiment not altogether successful, 277–79

Speaker Norton's extraordinary speech to the Throne on presenting a Bill for the better support of the Royal Household, 279

The Speaker makes a violent attack on the Prime Minister (Lord North), in the debate on Burke's Establishment Bill, 279

Picturesque appearance of the House in the middle of the eighteenth century, as compared with the present day, 280

Ladies excluded from the gallery in consequence of a disturbance in 1778, 280

Speaker Cornwall gives a casting vote against the Government of the day, 283

William Wyndham Grenville, (Pitt's cousin) raised to the Chair at the early age of 29, 286

Speaker Addington, a genial mediocrity, owes his election to the Chair to the influence of Pitt, 290; becomes Prime Minister, 291; replaced by Pitt, 292

Commons, House of—
Hanoverian and Saxe - Coburg Period—
The Speaker takes up his official residence at Westminster, 292 ; and gives his State dinners in the crypt of St. Stephen's Chapel, which had long been used as a coal-cellar, 295
The procession of Tory Speakers continued by Charles Abbot (the inventor of the Census), 298 ; his conversation with Pitt as to the most convenient hour for beginning public business, 299 ; induces the Government to spend £70,000 on his official residence, 300 ; incurs a motion of censure for having introduced the subject of Roman Catholic aggression into his speech to the Throne, 320 ; his action exonerated by the House by a substantial majority, 302
Speaker Abbot, the last Speaker to be buried in Westminster Abbey, 303
Speaker Manners-Sutton fills the Chair of the Commons on seven separate occasions, 303 ; is offered the post of Prime Minister, 307 ; in the Chair at the passing of the great Reform Bill, 308 ; is asked by the Whigs to retain the Speakership after the Reform Bill had been carried, 308
Destruction of the old Houses of Parliament by fire in 1834, 311
Manners-Sutton is superseded by Abercromby in 1835 by a combination of minorities voting with the Whigs, 316
Speaker Abercromby, the first Whig to occupy the Chair since Arthur Onslow, and the only Speaker from north of the Tweed, 317
Speaker Shaw-Lefevre, one of the conspicuous successes of the Chair, and the first nonpartisan Speaker of modern times, 319 ; wins the approval of all parties in the House, 321

Commons, House of—
Hanoverian and Saxe - Coburg Period—
The Commons meet, experimentally, in the present Chamber, May 30, 1850, 322
Changing conditions of the House of Commons, its causes described, 330
Lord Palmerston consults Delane as to the choice of a successor to Speaker Shaw-Lefevre, 324
John Evelyn Denison, first chosen in 1857, 325 ; the last Speaker to exercise his right of voting in Committee, 331, and the first to occupy the new official residence in the Palace of Westminster, 332
Mr. Speaker Brand's *coup d'état* of February, 1881, declaring the state of public business to be so urgent as to justify him in closing the debate, 333
Urgency resolutions adopted by the House and power given to the Speaker to put the question forthwith, 334
The principle of Closure of Debate adopted in 1882, and further powers for maintaining order and checking irrelevancy, conferred on the Chair in 1888, 335
A fixed hour for the adjournment of the House adopted in 1888, 335
Orders regulating procedure on certain stages of Bills introduced by the Government, generally known as "Guillotine" Resolutions, 336
Since 1887 occasionally applied in order to dispose of the necessary supply before the close of the financial year, 336
Dynamite explosions at Westminster in 1884, 337
Control and initiative in legislation gradually passing from the House to the executive Government, with a corresponding decline in the power and usefulness of the private member, 330

Commons, House of—
Hanoverian and Saxe - Coburg
Period—
  Altered rules of procedure in the
  last two decades tend to enhance the power of the
  Government, 330
  The Speaker's office, unfettered
  by the exigencies of party,
  and administered in the impartial spirit characterising
  the later years of its existence,
  will endure as long as the
  Constitution itself, 339
Compton, Sir Spencer, Earl of Wilmington, Speaker in 1714–15, and
  1722, xxviii, xxx, xxxi, 252, 253,
  254, 394
Compton Wynyates, Warwickshire,
  burial place of Speaker Compton,
  254
Conferences between Lords and
  Commons, 152–55, 178, 225
Contests for the Chair, early instance
  of, 137
Convention Parliament of 1660,
  215; 1688–89, 231
Convocation House, Oxford, fitted up
  for the House of Commons in
  1680–81, 228
Conway, Mr. L. Hussell Conway,
  xxxviii
Cordell, Sir William, Speaker in
  1557–58, xxix, 135, 378
Cornwall, Charles Wolfran, Speaker
  in 1780 and 1784, xxviii, xxx, 282,
  283, 284, 285, 286, 398
Cornwall, Earl of, Richard, 24
Corrupt Practices Act, 1883, 116
Cottonian Library, Westminster, 275
Council Chamber in old Palace of
  Westminster, 17
County Franchise, qualification for,
  in 1429–30, 79
Coup d'état of February, 1881, under
  Speaker Brand, 333
Court and City Register, addresses
  of Members of Parliament, pub-
  lished in, 263
Court and Country Parties, rise of, in
  English political history, 173
Court Kalendar, 263
Courts of Law, establishment of, in
  the old Palace of Westminster, 21
Coventry, Lord Keeper, 181, 182

Coventry, Parliament at, in 1404,
  69; in 1459, 83
Coverham Church, Yorks, xxxiv
Cranbrook, Kent, burial place of
  Speaker Baker, 130
Creevey, Thomas, 290, 302, 305, 317
Crewe, Earl of, xxxv, xl
Crewe, Sir Randolph, Speaker in
  1614, xxviii, xxx, xxxv, 169, 382
Crewe, Sir Thomas, Speaker in 1623–
  24 and 1625, xxviii, xxx, xxxv,
  169, 173, 382
Croke, Sir John, Speaker in 1601,
  xxvii, 160, 161, 162, 382
Cromwell, Mary, v. Falconbergh,
  Lady
Cromwell, Oliver, 176, 196, 198, 199,
  200, 201, 212, 224, 256; House
  of Lords set up by, in 1658, 200,
  201
Cromwell, Richard, 201
Cromwell, Thomas, 122, 125
Crosby Hall, 96
Crypt of St. Stephen's Chapel, 18;
  (formerly used as a coal-cellar) as
  the Speaker's State dining-room,
  292, 293; attempted destruction
  of, by dynamite, in 1884, 338
Cullum, Mr. George Gery Milner-
  Gibson, xxix
Cust, Sir John, Speaker in 1761 and
  1768, xxviii, xxx, 275, 276, 396

D

Dahl, Michael, painter, xxxv
Danby, Lord, Thomas Osborne,
  afterwards 1st Duke of Leeds, 223,
  225
Dasent, Sir John Roche, Editor of
  the Acts of the Privy Council
  mentioned, 376
Dasent, Sir George Webbe, the
  author's father, mentioned, x
Davis, Moll, 254
Dean's Yard, Westminster, viii, 20
Debrett, John, printer of Parliamen-
  tary Debates, 264
Declaration of Gloucester in 1407,
  72
D'Ewes, Sir Symonds, 34, 137, 156,
  185, 264, 378, 380, 382
Defoe, Daniel, 247
De la Mare, Peter, v. Mare, De la
De La Hay Street, 10

Delane, John, Editor of *The Times*, 123, 324, 325, 327 ; on the Speaker's office, 327
De L'Isle, Robert, 37
Denison, John Evelyn (Viscount Ossington), Speaker in 1857, 1859, 1866 and 1868, xxx, xxxi, 160, 325, 326, 327, 328, 330, 331, 332
De Thorpe, William, xxxvii
Desmond's rebellion in Ireland, 145
Despencer, Le, Hugh, 37
Dickenson, Dr., of Merton College, Oxford, 202, 209
Dictionary of National Biography, important names added to, xxiii
Digges, Dudley, 175
Dignity of the Peerage, Report of Lord Shaftesbury's Committee on, 23,
Dillon Sir Lucas, Chief Baron of Ireland, *temp.* Elizabeth, 144
Dining-room in the House of Commons, contains portrait of Speaker William Williams by Kneller, xxx ; collection of paintings being formed there, xxx
Disagreements between Lords and Commons, in 1399, 38 ; in 1407, 72 ; in 1592-93, 151, 152, 153, 154 ; in 1628, 177 ; in 1671, 221 ; in 1675, 225 ; in 1700, 236 ; in 1909, 38
Disorder having arisen in committee of the whole House, Speaker resumes the Chair, 224
Disraeli, Benjamin, Earl of Beaconsfield, 313, 328, 332, 334
Division of Lords and Commons into two bodies, *temp.* Edward III, 31
Divisions of the House of Commons, officially recorded since 1836, 265
Doggett's Coat and Badge, Speaker leaves the Chair to witness the race for, 311
Dorewood, John, Speaker in 1399 and 1413, xxiii, xxxvii, 63, 352
Downing Street, Speaker Cust lives in, 276
Dress in the House of Commons, 220, 280, 281
Drury, Sir Robert, Speaker in 1495, xxvi, 106, 107, 372
Drury Lane, 107
Dublin, letter from Speaker Snagge at, 144

Dudley, Edmond, Speaker in 1503-04, xxxvi, 107, 113, 331, 372
Duel between Pitt and Tierney on Wimbledon Common in 1798, witnessed by the Speaker, 290
Duncombe, Anthony, 256
Dundas, Henry, afterwards Viscount Melville, 291
Dunfermline, Lord, *v.* Abercromby
Dyer, Sir James, Speaker in 1552-53, xxvii, xxviii, 132, 376
Dynamite explosions in Palace of Westminster, 1884, 337
Dyson, Jeremiah, Clerk of the House of Commons, 1747-62, xxxiii, 269, 289

E

Earle, Mr. J. G., xl
Easton Mauduit, Northants, 158
Eastwell Church, Kent, xxxiv
Ebury, or Eybury, 10
Edenestowe, Henry de, Clerk of the Parliaments in 1330, 33
Edward, The Black Prince, 39, 50, 51, 52
Edward the Confessor, 5, 17, 18
Edward I, King of England, 27, 121
Edward II, King of England, 16, 36
Edward III, King of England, 50
Edward IV, King of England, 91, 92, 93
Edward V, King of England, 95
Edward VI, King of England, 129, 132, 133
Edward VII, King of England, 93
Eland, Rev. C. T., xl
Elcho, Lord, now Earl of Wemyss, 323
Eleanor of Provence, 24
Eliot, Sir John, 175, 176
Elizabeth, Queen of England, 130, 139, 141, 142, 144, 148, 150, 151, 161, 163
Elliot, Sir Gilbert, a candidate for the Chair in 1789, 287, 290
Elms, The, (Dean's Yard, Westminster) ; 20
Elsynge, Henry, Clerk of the House of Commons 1640-48, 41, 174, 186, 188, 193
Ely Cathedral ; tomb of John Tiptoft, Earl of Worcester, in, xxxii, 70
Embankment, the Thames, 12

Empson, Sir Richard, Speaker in 1491, xxxvi, 105, 106, 107, 113, 370
Englefield, Sir Thomas, Speaker in 1496–97 and 1509–10, xxiii, xxxvii, 107, 113, 303, 372
English Primitives, paintings by, in country houses, xxii
Erskine, Mr. H. D., of Cardross (Serjeant-at-Arms), xxx, xxxix, xl
Erskine-May, Sir Thomas, v. May
Esturmy, or Sturmy, Sir William, Speaker in 1404, 69, 354
Étaples, Peace of, 105
Eton, 76, 211, 276, 286, 287
Evans, Elizabeth, wife of Speaker Lenthall, 184
Evelyn, John, 225
Evelyn, George, 227
Evelyn, Sir Edward, 227
Eversley, Viscount, v. Shaw-Lefevre, Charles
Ewelme, Oxfordshire, burial place of Speaker Chaucer, xxv, 71
Exchequer, Office of, 7, 119
Exclusion Bill of 1860, 228
Eye, or Aye, Cross, 10
Exeter, burial place of Speaker Bampfylde, 387
Experimental meeting of the House in the new Chamber, May 30, 1850, 322

F

Faber, Johann, engraver, xxxv
Fairfax, General, brother-in-law of Speaker Widdrington, 21
Faithorne, William, engraver, xxxv
Falconbergh House, Soho Square, former residence of Speaker Arthur Onslow, xxxix, 256
Falconbergh, Mary, Lady, Oliver Cromwell's daughter, 256
Falkland, Viscount, Lucius Cary, 184, 206
Farleigh Castle, Somerset, seat of the Hungerford family, xxiv, 53
Farleigh - Hungerford, Somerset, burial place of Sir Thomas Hungerford, Speaker in 1376-77, xxiv, xxvi, 53
Fawkes, Guy, 169
Felstead Church, Essex, xxxiv; burial place of Speaker Rich, 127
Felton, John, 171

Fenwick, Sir John, 237
Fermerie at Leicester, meeting-place of the House of Commons 1414, 74
Fiennes, Mr, 193
Financial supremacy of the House of Commons, asserted in the Declaration of Gloucester, 1407, 72
Finch, Sir Heneage, Speaker in 1625-26, xxviii, xxix, xxxiv, 175, 384
Finch, Sir John, Speaker in 1627-28, xxviii, xxix, xxxi, xxxv, 176, 177, 182, 384
Fire at old Palace of Westminster in 1512, 118 ; in 1834, 17, 311, 312, 313
FitzWilliam, Sir Thomas, Speaker in 1488-89, xxiii, xxxvii, 105, 370, 420
Five members, attempted arrest of, by Charles I, 190
Fleet Ditch, 119
Fleet Prison, 83
Flower, Roger, Speaker in 1417, 1419, 1422, xxxvii, 75, 358
Foley, Mr. Paul Henry, xxii
Foley, Paul, Speaker in 1694-95 and 1695, xxviii, 223 ; miniature of, xxii
Foley, Richard, 232
Foley, Thomas, 232
Forster, John, "biographer of Dickens," 193
Fortescue, Sir John, 206
Fox, Charles James, 279, 280, 285
Frankland, Sir Thomas, 256
Franchise Act of 1884, 330
Free Trade and Protection in the reign of Queen Anne, 248
Furness, abbot of, 13

G

Gainsborough, Thomas, xxx
Gallows, the new, beyond the Temple Gate, 75
Gardener's Lane, 10, 12
Gardiner, S. R., Dr., opinion of Lenthall, 187
Gardiner, Sir Thomas, 184
Gargrave, Sir Thomas, Speaker in 1558-59, xxix, 378
Gascony, 17, 24
Gasquet's Henry III and the Church, referred to, 35

Gatton, Surrey, 175
Gaunt, John of, 50, 51
Gentlemen Errant, by Mrs. Henry Cust, quoted, 118
"George," The, by Paul's Wharf, 89
George I, King of England, 251, 253
George II, King of England, 253
George III, King of England, 271, 275, 279, 287, 300, 301
George IV, King of England, 50
Gillray, James, caricature by, xxxix
Gladstone, Rt. Hon. W. E., 309, 313, 323, 335, 336, 337, 339
Glanville, Sir John, Speaker in 1640, xxvii, xxxi, 182, 183, 384
Gloucester, Parliament held at, in 1407, 72
Golden Square, town residence of Speaker Cornwall, 285
"Good" Parliament of 1376, 49
Gordon, Thomas, translator of Tacitus, compiles Parliamentary Debates for the London Magazine, 261
Gorhambury, estate purchased by Sir Harbottle Grimston, 214
Goring House, now Buckingham Palace, occupied by Speaker Lenthall, 190, 196
Goring, Lord, afterwards Earl of Norwich, 198
Goschen, Lord, 335
Goulburn, Henry, a candidate for the Chair in 1839, 321
Government and Opposition Benches in Elizabethan times, 138; in the reign of George II, 262
Grant, Sir F., xxxi
Grant, Sir William, 136
Grantley, Lord, xxix
Granville, 2nd Earl, 334;
Grattan, Henry, 304, 331
Gray's Inn, Speaker Snagge at, with Walsingham and Burghley, 143
Great College Street, 7, 10, 12
Great George Street, 19
Great Linford Church, Bucks, xxv
Great Russell Street, death of Speaker Arthur Onslow in, 273
Great Smith Street, 10
"Great Tom" of Westminster, 104
Green, Sir Henry (Chief Justice), xxxvii, 41, 57, 346
Green, John, Speaker in 1460, xxiii, xxxvii, 81, 85, 366

Greensted, Mr. Henry, xl
Gregory, Mr., xxviii
Gregory, Sir William, Speaker in, 1678-79, xxviii, xxx, 227, 388
Grenville, George, 276
Grenville, William Wyndham (Lord Grenville), Speaker in 1789, xxvii, xxviii, xxxi, xxxv, 286, 287, 288, 289, 398
Greville, Charles, 307, 314
Greville Memoirs quoted, 309, 314, 316, 318
Grey, Lady Jane, 133
Grey de Ruthyn, Lord, 80
Grimston, Sir Harbottle, Speaker in 1660, xxvii, xxviii, xxxi, xxxv, 214, 215, 388
Grimthorpe, Lord, 163
Guildesborough, Sir John, Speaker in 1379-80, xxiii, xxxvii, 33, 54, 348
Guildhall, the, xxviii
Guillotine orders, regulating the procedure of the House on Bills and Supply, 336
Gully, William Court (Viscount Selby), Speaker in 1895 (2), 1900, xxxi, 338, 412
Gunpowder Plot, The, 166, 169
Gwynne, Nell, 206

H

Habeas Corpus Act, of 1679, 388
Haden, Sir Francis Seymour, the late, xxxviii
Hakewil, William, 30, 34, 178
Hale, Sir Matthew, 183
Halifax, Earl of, Charles Montagu, 235
Hall, Sir Benjamin, First Commissioner of Works, 103
Halloran, Rev. J. A., xl
Hampden, John, 177, 183, 190
Hampden, Viscount, v. Brand, Henry
Hampton Court Palace, proposals between Charles I and the Parliament, 1647, 196
Hampton Court, Herefordshire, property of Speaker Lenthall, 195
Hanbury-Williams, Sir Charles, 253
Hanmer, Sir Thomas, Speaker in 1713-14, xxviii, xxx, xxxi, 246, 248, 249, 250, 332, 394
Harbord, Mr., 223

Harding, S. P., xxvii

Harding, Sylvester, v. Harding, S. P.

Hardinge, Nicholas, Clerk of the House of Commons, 267

Hare, Sir Nicholas, Speaker in 1539, xxxvii, 127, 376

Haringay, Speaker Thorpe beheaded at, 83

Harford, North Devon, burial place of Speaker Thomas Williams, xxv, 379

Harley, Robert (Earl of Oxford), Speaker in 1700-01, 1701, and 1702, xxvii, xxviii, xxxi, 236, 238, 239, 240, 246, 331, 390, 392

Harling, East, Norfolk, home of Speaker Lovell, 105

Harman, family of, owners of Burford Priory, 205, 206

Hartley, David, 285

Hasely, Oxfordshire, birthplace of Speaker Lenthall, 184

Hastings, Sir Francis, 165

Hatton, Sir Christopher, 141, 163, 169

Hatfield House, Herts, plans of Westminster Palace in 1593 preserved at, 119

Hatsell, John, Clerk of the House of Commons, xxxviii, 253, 258, 289

Haxey, Sir Thomas, 56, 166

Hay or Aye Hill, 10

Hazlerig, Arthur, 190, 201

H. B., caricatures by, xxxix

Heigham, Sir Clement, Speaker in 1554, xxvii, xxxiv, 133, 134, 376

Henley in Arden, 36

Henley, Thomas, Abbot of Westminster, 37

Henry III, King of England, 4, 5, 6, 7, 11, 19, 24, 28, 45

Henry IV, King of England, 56, 57, 59, 60, 61, 62, 64, 66, 67, 68, 69, 72, 73, 74, 161

Henry V, King of England, 74, 76

Henry VI, King of England, 76, 79, 81, 83, 85, 86

Henry VII, King of England, 99, 100, 101, 102, 104, 105, 107, 109, 110; with Empson and Dudley, painting of, xxvi; Chapel, Westminster, xxii

Henry VIII, King of England, 113, 114, 117, 121, 122, 126, 128, 129

Henry of Knighton's Chronicle, 36

Herbary, The, "between the King's Chamber and the Church," 11

Herschell, Lord, 338

Hervey, Lord, 253

Higham, Mr. John, of Bedford, xxvii

Highclere, Hants, seat of Sir Robert Sawyer, Speaker in 1678, 226

High Gate of the Palace of Westminster, 19

Hoby, Sir Edward, 165

Hogarth, William, paints interior of the House of Commons, xxxiv, 276

Holbein, Hans, drawing after, xxviii; portrait of Sir Thomas More, 194

Holl, Frank, xxxi

Holland, Rev. C. W., xl

Hollar, Wenceslaus, engraver, xxxviii

Holles, Denzil, 190

Holmes, Mr. C. J., xl

Holywell, Nunnery of, Shoreditch, 105

Hooker's description of the House of Commons in the reign of Elizabeth, 138; remarks on publication of proceedings of the House, 263

Hours of meeting of the House of Commons in former times—at sunrise in the fourteenth century, 49; at 6 a.m., 159; at 7 a.m., 159

House of Commons, v. Commons

House of Lords, v. Lords

Howard's Coffee House, at upper end of Westminster Hall, 295

"Hudibras," quoted in connection with Speaker Lenthal, 201

Hulton, Rev. C. B., xl

Hume, Joseph, 324

Humphreys, Mr. A. L., xl

Hungerford, Sir Thomas, Speaker in 1376-77; first Speaker mentioned in the Rolls, xxiv; monumental effigy of, xxvi; portrait of, xxvi; xxvii, 33, 52, 53, 348

Hungerford, Sir Walter (Lord Hungerford), Speaker in 1414, xxiv, 74, 75, 356

Hunsdon House, Herts, seat of Speaker Oldhall, 82

Hunt, Roger, Speaker in 1420 and 1433, 358, 360; memorial brass of, xxv

Hustings in Trafalgar Square, x

Hutton-Hall, Rev. E., xl
Hylton, Lord, xl
Hysing, Hans, painter, xxxv

I

Iddesleigh, Earl of, xl
Ilbert, Sir Courtenay, Clerk of the House of Commons, from 1902, xi, 289
Ilmington, Warwickshire, owned by Peter de Montfort, 343
Imber Court, Thames Ditton, residence of Speaker Arthur Onslow, 274
Impeachment of Lord Melville, Speaker Abbot's casting vote, 298
Income Tax, sought to be imposed on all owners of land and house property, *temp.* Henry IV, 66; institution of, in an inquisitorial form, by Edward IV, 92
Infirmary garden of St. Peter's Monastery, 12
Inner Palace of Westminster, Constable of England's apartments in, 70
Inns, wretched accommodation afforded by, in the Middle Ages, 26
" Instrument of Government," 200
Intimidation of voters in mediæval times, 114
Inundations of the Thames at Westminster in former times, 12
Ireland, early mention of in English Parliament, 29; Speaker of the Irish House of Commons, 97, 138; great debate on the state of, in 1812, 304, 305; demand for Home Rule, rejected in 1886 and 1893, 330
Irish House of Commons, Speakers of, 97
Islip, John, Abbot of Westminster, 420
Ivy Bridge, Strand, 142

J

James I, King of England, 165, 172
James II, King of England, 229, 230
Jeffreys, Judge, 222, 229, 230
Jermyn Street, residence of Mr. Gladstone in, on first entry into Parliament, 310

Jerusalem Chamber, Westminster Abbey, 74
Jewel Office, 282
Jewel Tower of the Palace of Westminster, the, illustration of, from a drawing, xxxviii; view of the interior, xxxviii, 7
"Jew's Harp," Marylebone Fields, 259
Jodrell, Paul, Clerk of the House of Commons, 242, 274
John, King of England, 4
Jonson, Ben, his description of a dishonest lawyer applied to Sir Fletcher Norton by " Junius," 277
Journals of the House of Commons, defaced by James I, 172; ordered to be printed in 1742, under Speaker Arthur Onslow, 267; Sir Symonds D'Ewes prints portions of Elizabethan Journals, 147; antiquity of, 267; curious entries in, *temp.* James I, 268; improvements in, 269; indexed by Sir T. Erskine May, 268
Journals, Clerk of the, first mention of, in 1750, 266
"Junius" and Sir Fletcher Norton, 277

K

Katherine of Arragon, Queen of England, 123
Keate, Dr., head master of Eton, 309
Kenilworth, 37
Kettle, Mr. Bernard, of the Guildhall Library, xxix
Kew, residence of Speaker Puckering, 142
King Street, Covent Garden, 190
Kingston, Jamaica, mace at, 215
King Street, Westminster, 11
Kneller, Sir Godfrey, portrait of Speaker William Williams, in the Dining-room of the House of Commons, xxx; portrait of Speaker Arthur Onslow in National Portrait Gallery, erroneously attributed to, 274
Knightsbridge, Speaker Trevor's estate at, 230
Knights of the Shire, the aristocracy of the Lower House, 18, 22, 23, 25, 79

Knollys, Sir Francis, 150
Knyvet, Sir John (Chancellor), 51, 346

L

Labouchere, Henry, Rt. Hon., his house in Old Palace Yard, 8
Labour, representation of, in the House of Commons, 330
Ladies' Gallery of House of Commons, 280, 301, 337
Lambe, John, Dr., 181
Lambert, John, Parliamentary General, 199, 201, 202
Lambeth Palace, xxxi ; fall of engraving at, xxxii, 14
Landor, Walter Savage, *Imaginary Conversations*, 67
Land taxes, early unpopularity of the principle, 43, 66, 235
Langham, Simon, Abbot of Westminster, Cardinal and Archbishop, Preface, viii, 42, 43
Langland's " Richard the Redeless," 80
Late hours in the House of Commons and late hours of meeting strenuously opposed by Speaker Arthur Onslow, 270, 271
La Terriere, Colonel, restores Burford Priory, Lenthall's former house, 204
Latimer, Lord, impeachment of, in 1376, 51
Laud, William, Archbishop of Canterbury, xxxii, 189, 213
Law, firm grip of the Speaker's Chair by the legal profession, 135
Law and Practice of Parliament, by Sir Thomas Erskine-May, 268
Law in Ireland, Speaker Snagge's opinion of, *temp.* Elizabeth, 144, 145
Lawrence, Sir Thomas, xxxi, xxxiv, 303 ; portrait of George III by, formerly at Westminster, 301
Lawson, Wilfrid, Mr., 157
Layard, Sir Austen Henry, 328, 329
Lefevre-Shaw, Charles (Viscount Eversley), Speaker in 1839, 1841, 1847, and 1852, 318, 319, 320, 321, 322, 323, 324, 325, 329, 406
Leicester, Earl of, *v.* Montfort, De, Simon
Leicester, Earl of, xxix

Leicester, Parliament held at, in 1414, 74
Leicester Street, Leicester Square, Speaker Arthur Onslow's house in, 255
Lely, Sir Peter, xxix, xxxi
Le Marchant, Sir Denis, Clerk of the House of Commons from 1850 to 1871, 289
Lenthall, Sir John, 190, 203, 206
Lenthall, Sir Roland, 195
Lenthall, William, Speaker in 1640 1647, 1654, 1659, 1659–60, xxvii, xxxi, xxxiii, 184–210, 384, 386
Le Scrope, Sir Geoffrey, xxxiv, xxxvii
Le Sueur, Hubert, sculptor, xxxiii, 173
Lesser Tenants in Chief, or *Barones Minores*, 22
Leveson-Gower, Frederick, 334
Lewin, William, 150
Lewkenor, Mr. 181
Ley, John, Clerk of the House of Commons from 1797 to 1814, 289, 291
Ley, John Henry, Clerk of the House of Commons from 1820 to 1850, 289, 312, 313
Ley, William, 313
Ley, a Devonshire family of that name connected with the House of Commons for 150 years, 289, 313
Library of the House of Commons, books and papers formerly in the custody of the Clerk of the Journals, 267
Lincoln, 4
Lincoln's Inn, the gateway of, built by Speaker Lovell, 103
Lincoln's Inn Fields, 202, 215, 281
Litlington, Nicholas, Abbot of Westminster, 44, 45, 47
Little Hall, in old Palace of Westminster, 17, 48
Littleton, Edward John (afterwards Lord Hatherton), a candidate for the Chair in 1833, 309
Littleton, Sir Thomas, Speaker in 1698, xxx, 223, 233, 234, 236, 237, 238, 239, 390
Liverpool, Earl of, 285
Livery and maintenance, evils of, 81
Lollards, The, 69

London, Sir Robert Brooke, the first Speaker to represent the City of, 134

Long Ditch, Westminster, 11, 12

Long Parliament assembles, 183

Long, Sir Lislebone, Speaker in, 1658–59, xxxvii, 213, 386

Longford, Lord, 227

Lords—

Lords, House of, viii ; the parent assembly, 22

A body lineally descended from the feudal Norman *Curia*, 22

The writ of summons to, a privilege to be issued or withheld at the will of the Sovereign, 25

Constitution of in Plantagenet times, the non-hereditary element a moiety of the whole until the Reformation, 28

Separation of the two Houses, usually accepted date of, 31

The Upper House appoints its own Clerk in 1330, 33

"The Mad Parliament" of Oxford in 1258, a restricted assembly of Barons and Prelates, 35

Grants made by the Lords in 1339, and disagreement with the Commons, lead to the calling of a New Parliament, 39

The Deadlock of 1339 not dissimilar to that of 1909, 39

The Lords meet in the Chambre Blanche of the Palace of Westminster in 1368, 43

The Speaker of the House of Commons (Sir Thomas Hungerford) delivers seven Bills to the Clerk of the Parliament in 1376–77, but the Lords vouchsafe no reply, the session having come to an end, 53

Consolidation of the Peerage, *temp.* Henry IV, and a remarkable unanimity prevailing between Lords and Commons, 63

Establishment of a permanent hereditary Chamber acting as a Court of Appeal in civil cases, 64

Lords, House of—

King Henry IV invites both Lords and Commons to dine with him at Westminster in 1402, 65

Social reunion of the two Houses in Plantagenet times contrasted with the recent scheme for two Chambers sitting as one deliberative body, in cases of deadlock, 65

The Declaration of Gloucester, in 1407, defines the functions of the Lords in assenting to money grants, 72, 73

Exhaustion of the English nobility consequent on the Wars of the Roses, 87

Depletion of the numbers of the House of Lords at the commencement of the Tudor era, 99

Only twenty-nine temporal peers entitled to sit at the accession of Henry VII, 100

The peerages created in the sixteenth century lay the foundations of a new aristocracy, 100

Henry VII relegates the House of Lords to a position of legislative impotence, at the same time desiring to be independent of the Lower House, 101

The temporary eclipse of the Lords as a legislative body continued under Henry VIII, 114

A serious disagreement with the Commons in 1593, in connection with a Money Bill, 151

Sir Francis Bacon, on behalf of the Commons, opposes a conference with the Lords, as contrary to their privileges, 152

The conference held, and the wording of the preamble of the Bill decided in favour of the Lords, 155

The Bill hurriedly passed by the Commons through the action of its Speaker (Sir Edward Coke), 156

Lords, House of—
In 1625 the Lords concur in a
Money Bill, founded upon a
grant to which their assent
had not been specified in the
preamble, 178
In 1628 the wording of the preamble of a Money Bill again
gives rise to serious disagreement between the two Houses,
a deadlock averted by the
Lords passing the Bill as presented to them, after a conference with the Commons,
180
A message sent to the Lords by
the Commons declaring that
"the good concurrence be-
tween the two Houses is the
very heart-string of the Commonwealth, and that they shall
be ever as zealous of their
Lordships' privileges as of
their own rights," 180
Cromwell's House of Lords meets
in January, 1658, Lenthall, the
Speaker of the Long Parliament, takes his place in it,
together with Fleetwood, Monk
and Pride, 201
In 1671 the Pensionary Parliament of Charles II passes a
formal resolution to the effect
that the Lords are unable to
amend a Money Bill, 221
In 1675 the relations of the two
Houses again become strained,
and the Lords accuse the representative Chamber of infringing their privileges, 225
Queen Anne creates a dozen
peers to ensure a Tory majority
in the House of Lords, 234;
Lord Wharton's sarcastic observations upon, 234
The House of Lords most compact body in the State at
the accession of George I,
251
Several bills having been rejected
by the Lords in the last Parliament of George II, the Speaker
of the House of Commons desired to have animadverted
upon the cause of their failure,

Lords, House of—
but was prevented from doing
so by the accidental absence of
the Sovereign, 272
A Bill for the repeal of the paper
duty having been rejected by
the Lords in 1860, Speaker
Denison deprecates the action
of the Peers as calculated
to break down the distinction between the duties and
powers of the two Chambers,
328
Lovell, Sir Thomas, Speaker in 1485,
102, 103, 104, 105, 370, 419, 420;
medallion portrait of, by Torregiano, in Westminster Abbey, xxii,
420
Lowe, Robert (Viscount Sherbrooke),
33
Lowther, Right Hon. James William,
Speaker in 1905, 1906, 1910, and
1911, xxx, 339, 412, 414

M

Macaulay, Lord, on conferences be-
tween the two Houses, 155
Mace of the House of Commons;
description of, xxxix; 215
"Mad" Parliament of 1258, held at
Oxford, 35, 342
Maiden Bradley, xxxv
Maitland, Professor, his introduction
to the *Memoranda de Parlia-
mento*, 29
Mall, The, 112
Manners, Lady Victoria, xl
Manners-Sutton, Charles (Viscount
Canterbury), Speaker in 1817, 1819,
1820, 1826, 1830, 1831, and 1833,
xxix, xxx, xxxi, 281, 301, 304, 305,
306, 307, 308, 309, 310, 311, 314,
315, 316, 317, 402, 404
Marculph's Tower, Palace of West-
minster, 17
Mare, Sir Peter De la, Speaker in
1377, xxxvii, 33, 50, 51, 52, 53,
54, 348
Margaret of Anjou, Queen of Henry
VI, 86
Marlowe's *Edward II*, reference
to Trussell in, 37
Marshall, Master, 189

Marston Morteyne, Beds, burial place of Speaker Snagge, xxvi, 146

Mary, Queen of England, 133, 134, 135

Mary, Queen of Scots, 139, 141

Maud, Empress, 12

Maundy, Thomas, goldsmith in Fetter Lane, maker of the mace removed by Cromwell, 215

May-Erskine, Sir Thomas (Lord Farnborough), Clerk of the House of Commons from 1871 to 1886, x, 242, 268, 289, 310, 311

Mayo, Rev. Canon, of Long Burton, xxvii

Melbourne, Lord, 313

Melville, Lord, Impeachment of, decided by casting vote of Speaker Abbot, 298

Member of Parliament, early uses of the term, 75, 128

Memoranda de Parliamento, 1304–05, 29

Memorial Brasses, xxii, xxv

Meres, Sir Thomas, 226

Mereworth, Kent, burial place of Speaker Nevill, xxv, 375

Merchant Taylors Company, 168

Merrow, near Guildford, burial place of Speaker Arthur Onslow, 274

"Michael Ritus," *v.* John Michael Wright

Middlesex, Earl of, impeachment, 174

Mildmay, Sir H., 185

Mileham, near Swaffham, Norfolk. birthplace of Sir Edward Coke, house in which he was born, xxxix

Millbank, 10, 19

Millyng, Thomas, Abbot of Westminster, 95

Milman, Sir Archibald, Clerk of the House of Commons from 1900 to 1902, 289

Milner, Mr. J. D., xl

Mitford, Sir John (Lord Redesdale), Speaker in 1801, xxviii, xxx, 294, 295, 400

Mompesson, Sir Giles, 171

"Model" Parliament of 1295, 27

Monastery of Blackfriars, *v.* Blackfriars

Monastery of Westminster, *v.* Westminster

Monconys, description of the House of Commons in 1663, 220, 221

Money Bills, Speaker Arthur Onslow's attitude on presentation to the House of Lords, 272

Money grants, differences between Lords and Commons as to, in Gloucester Parliament of 1407, 72 ; in 1593, 152 ; in 1628, 178 ; in 1671, 221

Monk, General, 201, 202, 203

Monopolies, 136, 137, 171

Montacute, co. Somerset, built by Speaker Phelips, xxxix, 165, 166

Montagu, Sir Henry, 165

Monteagle, Lord, Thomas Spring Rice, 319

Montfort, de, Peter, xxiii, xxxvii, 33, 34, 35

Montfort, de, Simon, 5, 23, 24, 27, 35, 36 ; his coat of arms remaining in the Abbey, 5

Monumental Effigies of Speakers, xxii

Moore, Thomas, 306

Mordaunt, Sir John, Speaker in 1487, monumental effigy of, xxvi ; 105, 370

Morecambe Bay, 13

More, Sir Thomas, Speaker in 1523, xxviii, xxx, xxxv, xxxvi, 49, 120, 121, 122, 123, 124, 331, 374, 421, 422 ; portrait of, formerly at Burford Priory, 194

Morley's *Life of Gladstone*, 333

Morpeth, Lord, 302

Morris, Mr., 150

"Mother of Parliaments, The," xxxv

Mowbray, John, Earl-Marshal of England, 78

Moyle, Sir Thomas, Speaker in 1541– xxxiv, xxxvii, 42, 128, 376

Murray, Alexander, defies Speaker Arthur Onslow in 1751, 269

Myddleton, Mrs., of Chirk Castle, xxxiii

N

National Portrait Gallery : library of, xxiv, xxvii ; album of water-colour drawings of Speakers in, xxiv, xxvii, xxxviii

Nelson, Horatio, Admiral, memorial to, in Trafalgar Square, 113; Lady Sidmouth's ancedote of, 293

Nevill, Sir Henry, 165

Nevill, Sir Thomas, Speaker in 1514-15, 119, 173, 374; memorial brass of, xxv

Newcastle, Duke of, 253

Newgate Prison, 270

New Palace Yard, Westminster, view of, xxxviii; 9, 20

Newspaper Press, rise of the power of, 260

Neyte, Manor House of, belonging to the Abbots of Westminster, 51

Norfolk, Thomas Howard, 3rd Duke of, 129

Norman masonry remaining in Westminster Hall, 8

North, Lord, 276, 279, 280, 281

North, Roger, 222, 233

North, Mr. Stanley, xxiv

Northampton, Mary, Countess of, 254

Northcote, James, painter and engraver, xxxv

Northumberland, Duke of, 133

Northumberland, Earl of, thanked by Parliament in 1402, 64

Norton, Sir Fletcher (Lord Grantley), Speaker in 1770 and 1774, xxviii, xxix, 276, 277, 278, 279, 280, 281, 282, 396, 398

Nottingham Castle, Sir Peter de la Mare imprisoned in, 52

O

Occasional Conformity Bill of 1703, 265

O'Connell, Daniel, 306, 316

Official residence of the Speaker, in 1511-12, 117; in the seventeenth century, 136; in 1795, 292; in 1802, 300; new house, designed by Sir Charles Barry, first occupied by Speaker Denison, 332

Oglethorpe, Mr., 241

Old and new peerages, Selden's opinion of, 177

Oldcastle, Sir John, 75

"Old Cole," a nickname bestowed on Tierney, 317

Oldhall, Sir William, Speaker in 1450, xxxvii, 81, 82, 83, 364

Old Palace Yard, Westminster, 19, 20, 71, 169

Oliver Isaac, 123

Onslow, Arthur, grandfather of the Speaker of that name, 227

Onslow, Arthur, Speaker in 1727-28, 1734-35, 1741, 1747, and 1754, xxvii, xxviii, xxxi, xxxiv, xxxv, xxxviii; view of his house in Soho Square, xxxix; 255-274, 394, 396

Onslow, Earl of, xxxiii, xl

Onslow, Fulk, Clerk of the House of Commons, 137, 160

Onslow, Richard, Speaker in 1566, xxviii, xxx, 137, 139, 378

Onslow, Sir Richard, Speaker in 1708, xxviii, xxx, 239, 241, 242, 392

Opposition, early rise of a constitutional, *temp.* Henry VI, 81

Orchardson, Sir W. Q., xxxi

Order in debate, rules adopted in 1888, 335

Order, maintenance of, in the Palace of Westminster, regulations, *temp.* Edward III, 31

Orders regulating the procedure of the House on Bills and Supply, 336

Oriel College, Oxford, xxxv

Ossington, Viscount, *v.* Denison, John Evelyn

Otway, Mr., 328

Owen, William, painter, xxxv

Oxford, xxxii, xxxv; a colloquium held there in 1204, 4; provisions of, 35; assizes at, 139; Parliaments at, 35, 228, 342, 390

P

Painted Chamber in the Old Palace of Westminister, 17, 48, 49, 96, 118, 155, 178, 218, 225, 274, 296, 297, 313

Paisley, Lord, James Hamilton, 207

Palace of Westminster, *v.* Westminster

Palace Gate, Westminster, 17

Palgrave, Sir Reginald, Clerk of the House of Commons from 1886 to 1900, 289

Pall Mall, 246
Palmerston, Viscount, x, 324, 325, 326, 328, 329
Paris, Matthew, 12
Parliament held at Blackfriars, 119, 120, 374; Bury St. Edmund's, 362; Coventry, 69, 354, 366; Gloucester, 72, 348, 354; Leicester, 74, 356, 360; Lincoln, 4; Northampton, 348; Oxford, 4, 35, 228, 342, 390; Reading, 364; Shrewsbury, 350; Winchester, 45; York, 32, 352, 366
"Parliamentary Indoctorum," or Laymen's Parliament, held at Coventry, 1404, 355
Parliament Street, xxxix
Parndon, Little, Essex, burial place of Speaker Turnour, 219
Party government, rise of, 225, 236
Paston family, co. Norfolk, 15, 87 Agnes, 82; Elizabeth, 83; John, 88–89; Margaret, 15
Patten-Wilson, Mr., 322
Payment of members in the Middle Ages, 88
Pearson, J. L., architect employed on Westminster Hall, temp. Queen Victoria, 8, 9
Peart, Henry, pupil of Vandyck, xxxi, 210
Peel, Arthur Wellesley (Viscount Peel), Speaker in 1884, 1886 (2), and 1892, xxxi, xl, 224, 334, 335, 336, 337, 410, 412
Peel, Sir Robert, 160, 313, 315, 322, 323
Peerage and Pedigree, by J. Horace Round, 23
Peerages, created by Queen Anne in 1712 to secure a Tory majority in the House of Lords, 234
Peerages old and new, Selden's opinion of the comparative value set upon them, 177
Pelham, Dr., chaplain to Speaker Bromley, 245
Pelham, Henry, Speaker in 1647, xxiii, xxix, 210, 214, 384
Pembroke, 8th Earl of, 226
Pembroke College, Oxford, xxviii, xxxv
"Pensionary Parliament," 216, 222
Pepys, Samuel, 216, 217, 218

Perrers, Alice, 50, 52, 53
Pery, Edmond Sexten, Speaker of the Irish House of Commons, 1772–85, 97
Petite Salle in the old Palace of Westminster, 43
Petition of Right, 177
Petitions, gradually replaced by Bills, 75
Petitions, triers of (first mentioned in 1304), 17, 343
Peyton, Sir Robert, 228
Phelips, Sir Edward, Speaker in 1603–04, xxviii, xxix, xxxi, 165, 166, 167, 168
Phelips, Mr. William Robert, of Montacute, xxix
Philip II of Spain, husband of Queen Mary, 133, 134, 135
Phillips, Thomas, painter, xxxi, xxxv
Picart, Charles, engraver, xxxv
Pickering, Sir James, Speaker in 1378, xxxvii, 33, 54, 55, 56, 348
Pimlico, 19
Pinkerton's Iconographica Scotica, plate in, supposed to represent Edward I sitting in Parliament, 121
Piozzi, Mrs., 277
Pitt, William, Earl of Chatham, 260, 277
Pitt, William, the younger, 290, 297, 298, 299, 310
Play House Yard, Blackfriars, 123
Plate, service of, used by the Speaker, formerly his personal property, but now attached to the holder of the office for the time being, 246, 250, 295, 324
"Pleine Parlement," proposed reversion to, in case of disagreement between the two Houses, 65
Plough Inn, Lincoln's Inn Fields, 237
Podlicote, Richard, robs the Royal Treasury in Westminster Abbey in 1303, 58
Pole, Cardinal, 134
Pole, William de la, 37
Pollard, Sir John, Speaker in 1553 and 1555, xxxvii, 133, 134, 376, 378
Pollen, Richard, xxiv
Poltimore, Lady, xl

Poltimore, Lord, descended from Speaker Bampfylde, 213

Poole, Mrs. S. L., xl

Popham, Sir John, Speaker in 1449, 364

Popham, Sir John, Speaker in 1580–81, xxvii, xxxiv, xxxvii, 139, 140, 380

Porritt's *Unreformed House of Commons* quoted, 233, 266

Portmore, Lord, 254

Portraits, from church windows, xxii; historical collection at Lambeth Palace, xxxi; ignorance of owners regarding their possessions, xxi; list of Speakers of whom no portraits can be traced, xxxvi; many unidentified in country-houses, xxii; reasons why the present collection is of such interest, xxii

Portsmouth and Plymouth, fortification of, in 1786, debate and casting vote of the Speaker, 283

Powerscourt, Viscount, xl

Powle, Henry, Speaker in 1688–89, xxviii, xxx, 231, 232, 390

Poynings, Robert, sword-bearer to Jack Cade, 83

Prayers in the House of Commons, 159

Præmunire, Statute of, passed at Winchester in 1393, 45

Preamble of Bills of Supply, wording of, gives rise to differences between Lords and Commons, 152, 177

Prerogative of the Crown, 75, 163, 165, 174, 175, 178, 234

Press Gallery, House of Commons, 264, 266

Pride, Thomas, 201

Prideaux family, the, brass in colours to the memory of, xxv

Pride's Purge, 196

Primogeniture and Selection, evolution of the Writ of Summons, 22

Prince's Chamber, Palace of Westminster, 301

Prince's Street, 10

Princess of Wales requested to withdraw from the Gallery by Speaker Abbot, 301

Printing House Square, Blackfriars, 123

Priory Church, Malvern, xxvi

Prior John, of Burford, murdered in 1697, 207

Priory, Great Hall of, in Blackfriars, Parliaments held in, 120, 123

Private Bill Office, instituted by Speaker Abbot in 1811 and developed by Speaker Abercromby, 318

Privilege, 261; v. Commons, House of

Privy Garden, Whitehall, 285

Procurator of Parliament, a title bestowed on some of the earlier presiding officers of the Commons, 36

Prolocutor, a title bestowed on some of the earlier Speakers, 36

"Provisions of Oxford," 35

Prynne, William, 24, 25

Public Record Office, 230

Puckering, Sir John, Speaker in 1584 and 1586, 140, 141, 142, 380; tomb of, xxvi

Pulteney, Sir William, Earl of Bath, 69, 261

Purbrick, Father Edward, at Lambeth Palace, xxxii

Purveyance, 15

Pym, John, 172, 175, 190, 191, 192, 193

Pyx, Chapel of the, in Westminster Abbey, 27, 58

Q

Queen Anne's creation of peers in 1712 to secure a Tory majority in the House of Lords, 234

Quenington, Gloucestershire, burial place of Speaker Powle, 232

Question to be put forthwith by the Chair, rules adopted in 1881 and 1882, and extended in 1887, 335

Quorum of the House of Commons fixed by the Long Parliament, 188

R

Radley, Berks, Canopy of Speaker Lenthall's chair preserved at, 195

Radnor, Earl of, xl

Raleigh, Sir Walter, 153, 154, 158, 160

Reading, Parliament held at, 364
Redesdale, Lord, *v.* Mitford, Sir John
Redesdale, Lord, xxxiv, xl
Redford, Sir Henry, Speaker in 1402, xxxvii, 64, 352
Redman, or Redmayne, Richard, xxxvii, Speaker in 1415, 356
Redress of grievances to precede the granting of supplies, *temp.* Henry IV, 66
Refectory of the Monks of Westminster, meeting-place of the Commons in 1397, 1403-4, 1414, 1415, and 1416, 48
Reformation of Religion Act, 128
Reform Bill of 1832, 308; of 1867, 326
"Regale of France," a diamond stolen from Becket's shrine by Henry VIII, 126
Regency Bill of 1751, opposed by Speaker Arthur Onslow, 270
Roid, Sir George, xxxi
"Reign of the Saints," a name bestowed on the "Barebone's" Parliament, 200
Remarks on the Grand Tour of France and Italy by Speaker Bromley, 243
"Remonstrance, The Grand," 189
Repeal of the Paper Duty, Bill rejected by the House of Lords 1860, 328
Reporters' Gallery, House of Commons, first officially recognised, 266
Reporting of debates, recorded in *The Times* since its establishment, 264
Reporting of debates in the House of Commons, 263, 264, 265, 266
Representative system, origin of, 6, 23, 24, 25, 26, 27, 28, 29, 30, 31, 32, 35
Reunion of the two Houses of Parliament in 1402 for a social purpose, 65
Reynell, Mr., a candidate for the Chair in 1658-59, 213
Reynolds, Sir Joshua, xxxiii
Rheims, 7
Rich, Sir Richard, (afterwards Lord Rich), Speaker in 1536, xxviii, xxx, xxxiv, 125, 126, 374

Richard II, King of England, 9, 13, 55, 57, 59, 60
Richard III, King of England, 95, 96, 97
Richardson, Samuel, author of *Pamela*, 267; printing of the Journals of the House of Commons entrusted to, in 1742, 267
Richardson, Sir Thomas, Speaker in 1620-21, xxvii, xxxiii, 170, 171, 173, 382
Rickman, John, Clerk-Assistant of the House of Commons, 313
Ridley, White, Sir Matthew, a candidate for the Chair, 338
Rigby, Richard, 279
Ripperda, 257
Robinson, Mr. George, xl
Robinson, Sir Charles, xxii
Rockingham Administration, 276
Rolliad, The, and Speaker Cornwall, 285; on Pitt and Dundas, 291
Rolls Chapel, 230
Rolls House, Chancery Lane, former residence of many Speakers (as Masters of the Rolls), 136
Rolls of Parliament (Rotuli Parliamentorum), 30, etc. etc.
Rome, engraving of, xxxii
Rosamond, Fair, 92
Rosebery, Earl of, 175
Rothschild, Messrs., 106
Round, Mr. J. H., xl
Round, Rt. Hon. James, xxxv
Rous, Francis, Speaker in 1653, xxviii, xxx, xxxi, xxxv, 200, 384
Royal Commission on Historical Portraits, the necessity for, xxi
Rules of the House of Commons adopted, *temp.* James I, 168; great alterations in, adopted in 1882 and 1888, 334, 335
"Rump" Parliament, 196, 384, 386
Rushworth, John, Clerk-Assistant of the House of Commons, xxiii, xxxviii, 7, 174, 193
Russell, Lord Charles, Serjeant-at-Arms to the House of Commons, 289, 326
Russell, Rt. Hon. G. W. E., 289
Russell, Lord John, afterwards Earl Russell, 315, 323
Russell, Sir John, Speaker in 1423 and 1432, xxxvii, 77, 78, 358, 360

2 G

Russell, John, Bishop of Lincoln and Lord Chancellor, 420
Russell House, Strand, town residence of Speaker Puckering, 142
Rutland, Duke of, xxvi
Rutland, Dukes of, xxxiii
Rutley, Mr. J. L., xl

S

St. Albans, 84
St. Albans, Duke of, 206
St. Bartholomew's, Smithfield, 126
St. Benedict's Chapel, Westminster Abbey, tomb of Simon Langham in, 44
St. Chad's Church, Shrewsbury, burial place of Speaker Richard Onslow in 1571, 139
St. Edward's Chamber, Palace of Westminster. Painted Chamber sometimes so called, 296
St. Erasmus' Chapel, Westminster Abbey, 95
St. George's Chapel, Windsor Castle, 94, 109
— burial place of Sir Reginald Bray, 109
St. George's Church, Stamford, burial place of Speaker Cust, 276
St. Giles-in-the-Fields, Church of, xxvii; burial place of Speaker Widdrington, 385
St. James's Park, 11, 19, 112
St. James's Square, town residence of Speaker Compton, 254
— town residence of Speaker Grenville, 289
St. John, Oliver, 150
St. John's College, Oxford, the President of, xxix
St. Martin's Church, Canterbury, burial place of Speaker John Finch, 182
St. Mary Overy's, Southwark, 90
St. Mary's Church, Bury St. Edmunds, burial place of Speaker Drury, xxvi, 373
St. Maur, Mr. Harold, xxxiv
St. Michael, Paternoster Royal, burial place of Speaker Oldhall, 365
St. Michael's Chapel, Westminster Abbey, Wm. Trussell's tomb in, 40

St. Paul's Chapel, Westminster Abbey, Speaker Puckering's tomb in, 142
St. Stephen's Chapel, Palace of Westminster, xxxviii; 17, 44, 48, 93, 131, 138, 156, 201, 295, 296, 301, 306, 313
St. Swithin's Lane, 106
Sac, Le, M., 239
Sacheverell, Dr., 242
Saffron Walden, Essex, burial place of Speaker Audley, 124
Salisbury Cathedral, xxiv, 300; burial place of Speaker Walter Hungerford, 357
Salle Blanche, or White Hall in the old Palace of Westminster, 18, 42, 43
Salter's Hall, 106
Sanctuary, The, Westminster, ix, 95
Sandys, Lord, 213
Sanitation in Westminster in the Middle Ages, 16
Saturday holiday of House of Commons, due to Sir Robert Walpole, 160
Saunders, Sir Edward, 139
Savage, Sir Arnold, Speaker in 1400–01 and 1403–04, 64, 65, 66, 67, 68, 352, 354; memorial brass of, xxv
Sawyer, Margaret, 226
Sawyer, Sir Robert, Speaker in 1678, xxviii, 225, 226, 388
Say, Sir John, Speaker in 1448–49, 1463 and 1467, 80, 81, 84, 125, 362, 366; memorial brass of, xxv
Say, William, Speaker in 1659–60, xxxvii, 214, 386
Scardesburgh, John de, Clerk of the House of Commons 1388, 33
Scobell, Henry, Clerk of the House of Commons, 139, 174, 199
Scotch members at Westminster in 1707, 240
Scott, Sir Gilbert, architect, 112
Scrope, Geoffrey Le, 33, 40, 342, 343
Scrope, William Le, (Earl of Wiltshire), 57
Selby, Viscount, v. Gully, William Court

Selden, John, on peerages old and new, 177

"Self-Denying Ordinance," Eton exempted from, 211

Separation of Lords and Commons, supposed date of, 32, 45

Serjeant-at-Arms of the House of Commons, The, xl, 140, 156, 157

Serjeant's Inn, 157

Seymour, Sir Edward, Speaker in 1678 and 1678-79, xxvii, xxxi, xxxiv; 55, 223, 224, 225, 226, 231, 236, 388

Seymour, John, Clerk of the House of Commons, *temp.* Elizabeth, 132

Shaftesbury, 1st Earl of, Anthony Ashley-Cooper, 225; 3rd Earl, 242

Shaftesbury, 6th Earl of, Cropley Ashley-Cooper, Chairman of the Lords Committee on the Dignity of the Peerage, 23

Shakespeare, William, 57, 123; on Sir John Bussy, Speaker in 1393-94, 1396-97, 57

Shareshull, Sir William, Chief Justice, xxxvii, 41, 346

Shaw-Lefevre, Charles (Viscount Eversley), Speaker in 1839, 1841, 1847 and 1852, xxx, xxxi, 318, 319, 320, 321, 322, 323, 324, 325, 329, 406

Shee, Sir Martin Archer, xxxi

Sheffield, Sir Robert, Speaker in 1511-12, xxx, 117, 118, 374

Shelburne, Lord, 282

Shere, Manors at, xxvi

Sheridan, Richard Brinsley, 283, 285

Shirley, Evelyn Philip, 154

Shirley, Sir Thomas, 166, 167

Shore, Jane, 91

"Short" Parliament of 1640, 182

Shottesbrooke, Berks, 40

Shovell, Sir Cloudesley, 257

Shrewsbury, Duke of, the "favourite of the nation," 234

Shrine of Edward the Confessor in Westminster Abbey, 126

Sidmouth, Lord, *v.* Addington

Sidmouth, Lady, the second, anecdote of Nelson, 293

Sidney, Henry, Lord Deputy of Ireland, *temp.* Elizabeth, 143

Simco, Mr., xxviii

Simon de Montfort, *v.* Montfort

Single Chamber system, proposed reunion of Lords and Commons as one deliberative body, 65; contrast between 1402 and 1911, 65; Cromwell's adherents chafe under the uncontrolled rule of, 198

Sissinghurst Castle, near Cranbrook, Kent, built by Speaker Baker, 129, 130

Skelton, Sir John, 127

Smallbridge, Suffolk, 54

Smith, "Bobus," his translation of Speaker Addington's motto, 294

Smith, John, Speaker in 1705 and 1707, xxvii, xxxi, 240, 392

Smith, William Henry, Rt. Hon., 253

Smith's *Antiquities of Westminster*, 301

Snagge, Thomas, Speaker in 1588-89, xxvi; 142, 143, 144, 145, 146, 380

Snagge, Sir Thomas, a direct descendant of the Speaker of that name, xxvi, 146, 147

Soho Square, Speaker Arthur Onslow's house in, 256, 257

Somerset, Dukes of, 84, 224

Somerset, Duchess of, at Burford Priory, 206

Speaker's Commentary, 332

Speaker, *v.* Commons, House of, and under individual names; earliest painting of, xxvii; of the Irish Parliament, 97, 138

Speakers executed, xxxvi

Speaker's house, collection of portraits at, xxx, xxxi; parlour at Clandon, xxxiv; residence, xxxvi; salary, xxxvi

Speeches of the Speakers, 303

Spring Gardens, 303

Stamford, St. George's Church, burial place of Speaker Cust, 276

Stanhope, General, 247, 248

Stanhope, Sir Walter Spencer, Bart., xxxv

Stanley, Arthur Penrhyn, Dean of Westminster, x, 5, 6, 40, 41, 94

Staple in Westminster, 17

State dinner in the Crypt of St. Stephen's Chapel, described by Speaker Abbot, 296

Star Chamber, in Palace of Westminster, 17, 101, 118, 178, 311
—— Court of, 101
Statute "De hæretico comburendo," 68
Steele, Rev. J. T., xl
Stew Lane, 21
"Stiff Dick," a nickname of Sir Richard Onslow, Speaker in 1708, 241
Stoke Edith, Herefordshire, built by Speaker Foley, 232, 233; view of, xxxix
Stone Buildings, Lincoln's Inn, 304
Stone, Sir Benjamin, xxxviii
Storey's Gate, 10, 11
Stourton, William, Speaker in 1413, xxiii, xxxvii, 63, 356
Strangers in the House, temp. Elizabeth, 156
Strangeways, Sir James, Speaker in 1461, xxxvii, 89, 366
Strangways, Colonel, 223
Strafford, Thomas Wentworth, 1st Earl of, 183, 189
Stratford, John, Archbishop of Canterbury, 37
Strange, John, 115
Strode, William, 166, 190
Sturgis, Russell, Mr., 334
Sturmy, or Esturmy, Sir William, Speaker in 1404, xxxvii, 69, 354
Subsidy Bills, disputes between Lords and Commons in 1593, 152; as to preamble of the Bill of Supply in 1628, 178
Suffolk, Duchess of, daughter of Speaker Chaucer, 72
Suffolk, Duke of, William de la Pole, 79
Supplies, granting of, to follow redress of grievances, temp. Henry IV, 66
Supply, modern procedure of, foreshadowed in 1380, 54
Supply, Bills of, 73; disputes between Lords and Commons in connection with, 152, 178
Sutton Street, Soho Square, 257
Swift, Jonathan, 240, 246
Symonds, John, 119

T

"Tacking," temp. William III, 235
Talbot, Gilbert, 37
Tanfield, Sir Lawrence, owner of Burford Priory, 206
Tariff Reform in the reign of Queen Anne, 247
Taunton, Lord, 326
Taxes on House and Land Property, unpopularity of, in the Middle Ages, 43, 66
Taylor, Michael Angelo, a possible candidate for the Chair, 287
Temple Bar, 16, 17
Temple Church, burial place of Speaker Hare, 127
Temple Gate, The New Gallows beyond, 75
Temporary Chambers for Lords and Commons, improvised after the great fire of 1834, 313
Tenants in Chief, Lesser, become merged in the Knights of the Shire, 23
Tewkesbury, Battle of, two former Speakers killed at, 86, 365, 367
Thames Ditton, former residence of Speaker Arthur Onslow, 273
Thirty-nine Articles, The, legalised by Parliament of 1571, 162
Thomas, Sir Alfred, 229
Thomond, Murrough O'Brien, 1st Earl of, 128
Thompson, Mr. H. Y., xl
Thomson, William, Archbishop of York, 332
Thorney Island, Westminster, 10, 12, 13, 18, 19, 20, 21, 46
Thornhill, Sir James, xxxiv, 234
Thorpe, Thomas, Speaker in 1452–53, xxxvi, xxxvii, 83, 364
Thorpe, William (Chief Justice), 41, 344
Thurloe, John, 212
Thurlow, Lord, 279
Tierney, George, 290, 301
Tillotson, John, Archbishop of Canterbury, 230
Times, The, Editor of, (John Delane), on qualifications for the Speaker's office, 324; on Speaker Denison's retirement, 327

INDEX

Times Office, Blackfriars, 120, 123

Tiptoft, Sir John, (Lord Tiptoft), Speaker in 1405–06, 34, 69, 70, 354

Tiptoft, Sir John, (Earl of Worcester), son of the Speaker of that name, xxxiii, xxxvii, 69, 70, 71; called "The butcher of England," 70

Tong, Shropshire, burial place of Speaker Vernon, xxxvi, 360

Tooke, John Horne, 278

Torel, William, sculptor, 58

Torregiano's medallion portrait of Speaker Lovell, now in Henry VII's Chapel, xxii, 105, 420

Tory and Whig, early growth of two parties so called, 225, 227

Tothill Fields, 11, 17, 21

Tower Hill, 71

Tower of London, 26, 57, 83, 167, 282

Townshend, Thomas, the Rt. Hon., 277, 283

Trafalgar Square, proposed reconstruction of, 112, 113

Treasury, Royal, in Westminster, 42, 58; at Winchester, 7

"Tree of Commonwealth," 331

Trenchard, Sir Thomas, of Wolfeton, Dorset, 77

Tresham, Sir Thomas, Speaker in 1459, xxxvi, xxxvii, 80, 366

Tresham, William, Speaker in 1439, 1441–42, 1446–47, and 1449, xxxvi, xxxvii, 79

Trevor, Arthur, 229

Trevor, Sir John, Speaker in 1685 and 1689–90, xxx, 136, 229, 230, 390

Triennial Bill of 1640, 189

Triers of Petitions, 17

Trussell, William, xxxvii, 33, 40, 342, 344; his tomb in Westminster Abbey, 40

Turnour, Sir Edward, Speaker in 1661, xxviii, xxx, 216, 217, 218, 219, 388

Turvey, Beds, burial place of Speaker Mordaunt, xxvi, 371

Tyburn, 10

Tydder, Cadwallader, Clerk of the House of Commons, *temp.* Elizabeth, 160

Tylney, Lord, 256

Tyrrell, Sir John, Speaker in 1427, 1430–31, and 1436–37, xxxvii, 360

U

Uniformity, Act of, 1549, 132

Union of Scotland, the Scotch members sit at Westminster for the first time, 240

Up Ottery, Devon, seat of Lord Sidmouth, 293

Utopia, by Sir Thomas More, 331

Utrecht, Treaty of, 247

V

Valence, Aymer de, Bishop-Elect of Winchester, and half-brother to King Henry III, 34, 343

Vandyck, Anthony, portrait by, at Raby Castle, xxviii, xxxi, 123

Vernon, Sir Richard, Speaker in 1425–26, xxvi, 360

Vertue, Robert, architect of Henry VII's Chapel, Westminster Abbey, 109

Victoria Tower, Palace of Westminster, designed by Sir Charles Barry, 9

Votes and Proceedings of the House of Commons, earliest issue of, 268

Vyne, The, Hampshire, property of Speaker Chute, 213

W

Wadham College, Oxford, xxxv

Wake, William, Archbishop of Canterbury, 14

Wakefield, Battle of, 85, 86

Walbrook, 106

Waldegrave, Earl, xl

Waldegrave, Sir Richard, Speaker in 1381, xxxvii, 33, 54, 55, 348

Wall, Rev. R., xl

Walpole, Horace, 270, 275, 278, 282

Walpole, Sir Robert, 69, 160, 251, 255, 260, 261, 262, 271; portrait of, xxxiv

Walter, John, founder of *The Times*, 123

Walsingham, Sir Francis, 143, 144, 146

Walton, or Wauton, Sir Thomas, Speaker in 1425, xxxvii, 78, 360

Warden of the Fleet Prison, 167
Ware, Richard, Abbot of Westminster, 42
Warfield, Berks, 40
Warham, William, Archbishop of Canterbury, 113
"War Parliament" of 1511–12, 117
Wars of the Roses arrest constitutional progress, 81
Warwick House, Cloth Fair, town residence of Speaker Rich, 126
Warwick, the "King-maker," 86
Wauton, v. Walton
Webster, T. L., Second Clerk-Assistant of the House of Commons, xi
Wellington Church, Somerset, xxxiv
Wenlock, Sir John (Lord Wenlock), Speaker in 1455, xxxvi, xxxvii, 81, 84, 364
Wentworth, Peter, 249
Westminster Abbey, x, xxii, xxvi, xxviii, 5, 6, 7, 8, 9, 10, 11, 13, 18, 19, 20, 21, 27, 36, 40, 41, 42, 43, 44, 45, 46, 47, 48, 49, 58, 59, 62, 85, 94, 95, 105, 109, 110, 111, 118, 126, 135, 142, 173, 303
Westminster Hall, 8, 9, 64, 93, 338
Westminster Palace, great fires at, in 1512, 118; in 1834, 311
Westminster Stairs, 191
Westmorland, Earl of, Ralph Nevill, 100
Wharton, Lord, 234
Whig and Tory, early growth of rival parties, 225, 227
"Whimsicals," The, 250
"Whip with six strings," 127
White, Sir Thomas, xxix
White-Ridley, Sir Matthew, v. Ridley
Whitehall, 14, 112, 199, 232
White Hall or Salle Blanche in the old Palace of Westminster, 18, 42, 43
"White House" in Soho Square, 257
White Lodge in Richmond Park, residence of Speaker Addington when Lord Sidmouth, 293
Whitelocke, Bulstrode, Speaker in 1656–57, xxvii, 212, 213, 231, 386

Widdrington, Sir Thomas, Speaker in 1656, xxvii, 211, 212, 384
Wilkes, John, 275, 281
William III, King of England, 224, 231, 234, 235, 236, 238
William IV, King of England, 311, 313, 315, 318
William of Colchester, Abbot of Westminster, 46, 47, 48
Williams, Thomas, Speaker in 1562–63, 378; epitaph on, xxv; memorial brass of, xxv
Williams, Sir William, Speaker in 1680 and 1680–81, xxx, 228, 229, 388, 390
Wilmington, Earl of, v. Compton, Sir Spencer
Windsor, 93, 161
Wingfield, Major, xxix
Wingfield, Sir Humphrey, Speaker in 1533, xxix, 124, 125, 374
Winnington Bridge, 202
Witley, Worcestershire, 232
Wolfeton, Dorset, seat of Sir Thomas Trenchard, 77
Wolsey, Cardinal, 121, 122, 125
Wood, John, Speaker in 1482–83, xxxvii, 93, 368
Woodfall, H. S., Printer of Parliamentary debates etc., 278
Woolley, Sir John, 149
Worcester, Earl of, John Tiptoft, son of the Speaker of 1405–06, xxxii, 70; execution of, xxxvi
Worsop, William, 115
Wraxall, Sir Nathaniel, on Speaker Cornwall, 286
Wray, Sir Christopher, Speaker in 1571, xxvii, xxviii, xxxi, 162, 378
Wright, John Michael, xxix
Wriothesley, Sir Thomas, 1st Earl of Southampton, 129
Writ of summons, origin of the issue to Members of Parliament, 22
Wyatt, James, architect and Surveyor-General to the Board of Works, 300, 301
Wyndham, Sir William, 261
Wynn, Sir Watkin, 289, 305
Wynn, Williams, C., a candidate for the Speakership in 1817, 305

Y

Yarborough, Earl of, xxix
Yelverton, Sir Christopher, Speaker
  in 1597, xxx, 158, 159, 382
York, 86
  Archbishop of York, William
    Thomson, 332

York—
  Archbishops of, resident at White-
    hall until the fall of Wolsey, 14
  Parliaments held at, 32, 352, 356
York, Richard Duke of, 85, 86
"Young Cole," nickname bestowed
  on Speaker Abercromby by Lord
  Brougham, 317

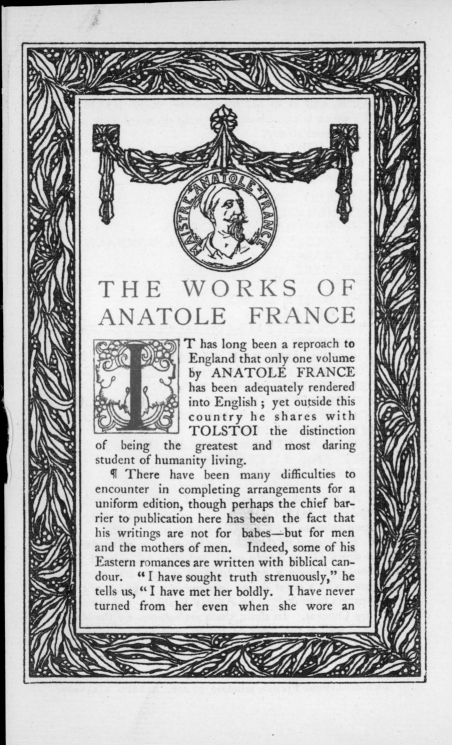

THE WORKS OF
ANATOLE FRANCE

IT has long been a reproach to England that only one volume by ANATOLE FRANCE has been adequately rendered into English ; yet outside this country he shares with TOLSTOI the distinction of being the greatest and most daring student of humanity living.

¶ There have been many difficulties to encounter in completing arrangements for a uniform edition, though perhaps the chief barrier to publication here has been the fact that his writings are not for babes—but for men and the mothers of men. Indeed, some of his Eastern romances are written with biblical candour. " I have sought truth strenuously," he tells us, " I have met her boldly. I have never turned from her even when she wore an unexpected aspect." Still, it is believed that the day has come for giving English versions of all his imaginative works, as well as of his monumental study JOAN OF ARC, which is undoubtedly the most discussed book in the world of letters to-day.

¶ MR. JOHN LANE has pleasure in announcing that the following volumes are either already published or are passing through the press.

THE RED LILY
MOTHER OF PEARL
THE GARDEN OF EPICURUS
THE CRIME OF SYLVESTRE BONNARD
BALTHASAR
THE WELL OF ST. CLARE
THAÏS
THE WHITE STONE
PENGUIN ISLAND
THE MERRIE TALES OF JACQUES TOURNE
    BROCHE
JOCASTA AND THE FAMISHED CAT
THE ELM TREE ON THE MALL
THE WICKER-WORK WOMAN
AT THE SIGN OF THE REINE PEDAUQUE
THE OPINIONS OF JEROME COIGNARD
MY FRIEND'S BOOK
THE ASPIRATIONS OF JEAN SERVIEN
LIFE AND LETTERS (4 vols.)
JOAN OF ARC (2 vols.)

¶ All the books will be published at 6/- each with the exception of JOAN OF ARC, which will be 25/- net the two volumes, with eight Illustrations.

¶ The format of the volumes leaves little to be desired. The size is Demy 8vo (9 × 5¾), and they are printed from Caslon type upon a paper light in weight and strong of texture, with a cover design in crimson and gold, a gilt top, end-papers from designs by Aubrey Beardsley and initials by Henry Ospovat. In short, these are volumes for the bibliophile as well as the lover of fiction, and form perhaps the cheapest library edition of copyright novels ever published, for the price is only that of an ordinary novel.

¶ The translation of these books has been entrusted to such competent French scholars as MR. ALFRED ALLINSON,

THE WORKS OF ANATOLE FRANCE

MR. FREDERIC CHAPMAN, MR. ROBERT B. DOUGLAS, MR. A. W. EVANS, MKS. FARLEY, MR. LAFCADIO HEARN, MRS. W. S. JACKSON, MRS. JOHN LANE, MRS. NEWMARCH, MR. C. E. ROCHE, MISS WINIFRED STEPHENS, and MISS M. P. WILLCOCKS.

¶ As Anatole Thibault, *dit* Anatole France, is to most English readers merely a name, it will be well to state that he was born in 1844 in the picturesque and inspiring surroundings of an old bookshop on the Quai Voltaire, Paris, kept by his father, Monsieur Thibault, an authority on eighteenth-century history, from whom the boy caught the passion for the principles of the Revolution, while from his mother he was learning to love the ascetic ideals chronicled in the Lives of the Saints. He was schooled with the lovers of old books, missals and manuscript; he matriculated on the Quais with the old Jewish dealers of curios and *objets d'art;* he graduated in the great university of life and experience. It will be recognised that all his work is permeated by his youthful impressions; he is, in fact, a virtuoso at large.

¶ He has written about thirty volumes of fiction. His first novel was JOCASTA & THE FAMISHED CAT (1879). THE CRIME OF SYLVESTRE BONNARD appeared in 1881, and had the distinction of being crowned by the French Academy, into which he was received in 1896.

¶ His work is illuminated with style, scholarship, and psychology; but its outstanding features are the lambent wit, the gay mockery, the genial irony with which he touches every subject he treats. But the wit is never malicious, the mockery never derisive, the irony never barbed. To quote from his own GARDEN OF EPICURUS : "Irony and Pity are both of good counsel; the first with her smiles makes life agreeable, the other sanctifies it to us with her tears. The Irony I invoke is no cruel deity. She mocks neither love nor beauty. She is gentle and kindly disposed. Her mirth disarms anger and it is she teaches us to laugh at rogues and fools whom but for her we might be so weak as to hate."

¶ Often he shows how divine humanity triumphs over mere asceticism, and with entire reverence; indeed, he might be described as an ascetic overflowing with humanity, just as he has been termed a "pagan, but a pagan constantly haunted by the pre-occupation of Christ." He is in turn—like his own Choulette in THE RED LILY—saintly and Rabelaisian, yet without incongruity.

THE WORKS OF ANATOLE FRANCE

At all times he is the unrelenting foe of superstition and hypocrisy. Of himself he once modestly said : "You will find in my writings perfect sincerity (lying demands a talent I do not possess), much indulgence, and some natural affection for the beautiful and good."

¶ The mere extent of an author's popularity is perhaps a poor argument, yet it is significant that two books by this author are in their HUNDRED AND TENTH THOUSAND, and numbers of them well into their SEVENTIETH THOUSAND, whilst the one which a Frenchman recently described as "Monsieur France's most arid book" is in its FIFTY-EIGHT-THOUSAND.

¶ Inasmuch as M. FRANCE'S ONLY contribution to an English periodical appeared in THE YELLOW BOOK, vol. v., April 1895, together with the first important English appreciation of his work from the pen of the Hon. Maurice Baring, it is peculiarly appropriate that the English edition of his works should be issued from the Bodley Head.

ORDER FORM.

.... 19

To Mr... ....
Bookseller.

Please send me the following works of Anatole France:

THAÏS   PENGUIN ISLAND
BALTHASAR   THE WHITE STONE
THE RED LILY   MOTHER OF PEARL
THE GARDEN OF EPICURUS
THE CRIME OF SYLVESTRE BONNARD
THE WELL OF ST. CLARE
THE MERRIE TALES OF JACQUES TOURNE-
    BROCHE
THE ELM TREE ON THE MALL
THE WICKER—WORK WOMAN
JOCASTA AND THE FAMISHED CAT
JOAN OF ARC (2 VOLS.)
LIFE AND LETTERS (4 VOLS.)

for which I enclose..

    Name..

    Address..

JOHN LANE, Publisher The Bodley Head, Vigo St., London, W.

A CATALOGUE OF MEMOIRS, BIOGRAPHIES, ETC.

WORKS UPON NAPOLEON

NAPOLEON & THE INVASION OF ENGLAND:

The Story of the Great Terror, 1797–1805. By H. F. B. WHEELER and A. M. BROADLEY. With upwards of 100 Full-page Illustrations reproduced from Contemporary Portraits, Prints, etc.; eight in Colour. Two Volumes. 32s. net.

Outlook.—"The book is not merely one to be ordered from the library; it should be purchased, kept on an accessible shelf, and constantly studied by all Englishmen who love England."

DUMOURIEZ AND THE DEFENCE OF ENGLAND AGAINST NAPOLEON. By J. HOLLAND ROSE, Litt.D. (Cantab.), Author of "The Life of Napoleon," and A. M. BROADLEY, joint-author of "Napoleon and the Invasion of England." Illustrated with numerous Portraits, Maps, and Facsimiles. Demy 8vo. 21s. net.

NAPOLEON IN CARICATURE : 1795–1821. By A. M. BROADLEY, joint-author of "Napoleon and the Invasion of England," etc. With an Introductory Essay on Pictorial Satire as a Factor in Napoleonic History, by J. HOLLAND ROSE, Litt.D. (Cantab.). With 24 full-page Illustrations in colour and upwards of 200 in black and white from rare and often unique originals. In 2 vols. Demy 8vo (9 × 5¾ inches.) 42s. net.

THE FALL OF NAPOLEON. By OSCAR BROWNING, M.A., Author of "The Boyhood and Youth of Napoleon." With numerous Full-page Illustrations. Demy 8vo (9 × 5¾ inches). 12s. 6d. net.

Spectator.—"Without doubt Mr. Oscar Browning has produced a book which should have its place in any library of Napoleonic literature."

Truth.—"Mr. Oscar Browning has made not the least, but the most of the romantic material at his command for the story of the fall of the greatest figure in history."

THE BOYHOOD & YOUTH OF NAPOLEON, 1769–1793. Some Chapters on the early life of Bonaparte. By OSCAR BROWNING, M.A. With numerous Illustrations, Portraits, etc. Crown 8vo. 5s. net.

Daily News.—"Mr. Browning has with patience, labour, careful study, and excellent taste given us a very valuable work, which will add materially to the literature on this most fascinating of human personalities."

THE LOVE AFFAIRS OF NAPOLEON. By
JOSEPH TURQUAN. Translated from the French by JAMES L. MAY.
With 32 Full-page Illustrations. Demy 8vo (9 × 5½ inches).
12s. 6d. net.

THE DUKE OF REICHSTADT (NAPOLEON II.)
By EDWARD DE WERTHEIMER. Translated from the German.
With numerous Illustrations. Demy 8vo. Cheap Edition. 5s. net.

Times.—"A most careful and interesting work which presents the first complete and
authoritative account of the life of this unfortunate Prince."

Westminster Gazette.—"This book, admirably produced, reinforced by many additional
portraits, is a solid contribution to history and a monument of patient, well-applied
research."

NAPOLEON'S CONQUEST OF PRUSSIA, 1806.
By F. LORAINE PETRE. With an Introduction by FIELD-
MARSHAL EARL ROBERTS, V.C., K.G., etc. With Maps, Battle
Plans, Portraits, and 16 Full-page Illustrations. Demy 8vo
(9 × 5¾ inches). 12s. 6d. net.

Scotsman.—"Neither too concise, nor too diffuse, the book is eminently readable. It is the
best work in English on a somewhat circumscribed subject."

Outlook.—"Mr. Petre has visited the battlefields and read everything, and his monograph is
a model of what military history, handled with enthusiasm and literary ability, can be."

NAPOLEON'S CAMPAIGN IN POLAND, 1806–
1807. A Military History of Napoleon's First War with Russia,
verified from unpublished official documents. By F. LORAINE
PETRE. With 16 Full-page Illustrations, Maps, and Plans. New
Edition. Demy 8vo (9 × 5¾ inches). 12s. 6d. net.

Army and Navy Chronicle.—"We welcome a second edition of this valuable work. . .
Mr. Loraine Petre is an authority on the wars of the great Napoleon, and has brought
the greatest care and energy into his studies of the subject."

NAPOLEON AND THE ARCHDUKE
CHARLES. A History of the Franco-Austrian Campaign in
the Valley of the Danube in 1809. By F. LORAINE PETRE.
With 8 Illustrations and 6 sheets of Maps and Plans. Demy 8vo
(9 × 5¾ inches). 12s. 6d. net.

RALPH HEATHCOTE. Letters of a Diplomatist
During the Time of Napoleon, Giving an Account of the Dispute
between the Emperor and the Elector of Hesse. By COUNTESS
GÜNTHER GRÖBEN. With Numerous Illustrations. Demy 8vo
(9 × 5¾ inches). 12s. 6d. net.

⁎⁎ *Ralph Heathcote, the son of an English father and an Alsatian mother, was for
some time in the English diplomatic service as first secretary to Mr. Brook Taylor, minister
at the Court of Hesse, and on one occasion found himself very near to making history.
Napoleon became persuaded that Taylor was implicated in a plot to procure his assassina-
tion, and insisted on his dismissal from the Hessian Court. As Taylor refused to be
dismissed, the incident at one time seemed likely to result to the Elector in the loss of his
throne. Heathcote came into contact with a number of notable people, including the Miss
Berrys, with whom he assures his mother he is not in love. On the whole, there is much
interesting material for lovers of old letters and journals.*

MEMOIRS OF THE COUNT DE CARTRIE.
A record of the extraordinary events in the life of a French Royalist during the war in La Vendée, and of his flight to South-ampton, where he followed the humble occupation of gardener. With an introduction by Frédéric Masson, Appendices and Notes by Pierre Amédée Pichot, and other hands, and numerous Illustra-tions, including a Photogravure Portrait of the Author. Demy 8vo. 12s. 6d. net.

Daily News.—"We have seldom met with a human document which has interested us as so much."

THE JOURNAL OF JOHN MAYNE DURING A TOUR ON THE CONTINENT UPON ITS RE-OPENING AFTER THE FALL OF NAPOLEON, 1814. Edited by his Grandson, JOHN MAYNE COLLES. With 16 Illustrations. Demy 8vo (9 × 5¾ inches). 12s. 6d. net.

WOMEN OF THE SECOND EMPIRE.
Chronicles of the Court of Napoleon III. By Frédéric Loliée. With an introduction by Richard Whiteing and 53 full-page Illustrations, 3 in Photogravure. Demy 8vo. 21s. net.

Standard.—"M. Frédéric Loliée has written a remarkable book, vivid and pitiless in its description of the intrigue and dare-devil spirit which flourished unchecked at the French Court. . . . Mr. Richard Whiteing's introduction is written with restraint and dignity."

LOUIS NAPOLEON AND THE GENESIS OF THE SECOND EMPIRE. By F. H. Cheetham. With Numerous Illustrations. Demy 8vo (9 × 5¾ inches). 16s. net.

MÉMOIRS OF MADEMOISELLE DES ÉCHEROLLES. Translated from the French by Marie Clothilde Balfour. With an Introduction by G. K. Fortescue, Portraits, etc. 5s. net.

Liverpool Mercury.—". . . this absorbing book. . . . The work has a very decided historical value. The translation is excellent, and quite notable in the preservation of idiom."

JANE AUSTEN'S SAILOR BROTHERS. Being the Life and Adventures of Sir Francis Austen, G.C.B., Admiral of the Fleet, and Rear-Admiral Charles Austen. By J. H. and E. C. Hubback. With numerous Illustrations. Demy 8vo. 12s. 6d. net.

Morning Post.—". . . May be welcomed as an important addition to Austeniana . . .; it is besides valuable for its glimpses of life in the Navy, its illustrations of the feelings and sentiments of naval officers during the period that preceded and that which followed the great battle of just one century ago, the battle which won so much but which cost us—Nelson."

SOME WOMEN LOVING OR LUCKLESS.
By Teodor de Wyzewa. Translated from the French by C. H. Jeaffreson, m.a. With Numerous Illustrations. Demy 8vo (9 × 5¾ inches). 7s. 6d. net.

THE TRUE STORY OF MY LIFE: an Auto-
biography by Alice M. Diehl, Novelist, Writer, and Musician. Demy 8vo. 10s. 6d. net.

GIOVANNI BOCCACCIO: A BIOGRAPHICAL
STUDY. By Edward Hutton. With a Photogravure Frontis-piece and numerous other Illustrations. Demy 8vo (9 × 5¾ inches). 16s. net.

MINIATURES: A Series of Reproductions in
Photogravure of Eighty-Five Miniatures of Distinguished Person-ages, including the Queen Mother and the three Princesses of the House. Painted by Charles Turrell. The Edition is limited to One Hundred Copies (many of which are already subscribed for) for sale in England and America, and Twenty-five Copies for Pre-sentation, Review, and the Museums. Each will be Numbered and Signed by the Artist. Large Quarto. £15 15s. net.

COKE OF NORFOLK AND HIS FRIENDS:
The Life of Thomas William Coke, First Earl of Leicester of the second creation, containing an account of his Ancestry, Surroundings, Public Services, and Private Friendships, and including many Unpublished Letters from Noted Men of his day, English and American. By A. M. W. Stirling. With 20 Photogravure and upwards of 40 other Illustrations reproduced from Contemporary Portraits, Prints, etc. Demy 8vo. 2 vols. 32s. net.

The Times.—"We thank Mrs. Stirling for one of the most interesting memoirs of recent years."

Daily Telegraph.—"A very remarkable literary performance. Mrs. Stirling has achieved a resurrection. She has fashioned a picture of a dead and forgotten past and brought before our eyes with the vividness of breathing existence the life of our English ancestors of the eighteenth century."

Pall Mall Gazette.—"A work of no common interest; in fact, a work which may almost be called unique."

Evening Standard.—"One of the most interesting biographies we have read for years."

THE LIFE OF SIR HALLIDAY MACART-
NEY, K.C.M.G., Commander of Li Hung Chang's trained
force in the Taeping Rebellion. Secretary and Councillor to
the Chinese Legation in London for thirty years. By DEMETRIUS
C. BOULGER, Author of the "History of China," the "Life of
Gordon," etc. With Illustrations. Demy 8vo. Price 21s. net.

Daily Graphic.—"It is safe to say that few readers will be able to put down the book without feeling the better for having read it . . . not only full of personal interest, but
tells us much that we never knew before on some not unimportant details."

DEVONSHIRE CHARACTERS AND STRANGE
EVENTS. By S. BARING-GOULD, M.A., Author of "Yorkshire
Oddities," etc. With 58 Illustrations. Demy 8vo. 21s. net.

Daily News.—"A fascinating series . . . the whole book is rich in human interest. It is
by personal touches, drawn from traditions and memories, that the dead men surrounded
by the curious panoply of their time, are made to live again in Mr. Baring-Gould's pages."

CORNISH CHARACTERS AND STRANGE
EVENTS. By S. BARING-GOULD, M.A., Author of "Devonshire
Characters and Strange Events," etc. With 62 full-page Illus-
trations reproduced from old prints, etc. Demy 8vo. 21s. net.

ROBERT HERRICK : A BIOGRAPHICAL AND
CRITICAL STUDY. By F. W. MOORMAN, B.A., Ph. D.,
Assistant Professor of English Literature in the University of
Leeds. With 9 Illustrations. Demy 8vo (9 × 5¾ inches).
12s. 6d. net.

THE MEMOIRS OF ANN, LADY FANSHAWE.
Written by Lady Fanshawe. With Extracts from the Correspondence of Sir Richard Fanshawe. Edited by H. C. FANSHAWE.
With 38 Full-page Illustrations, including four in Photogravure
and one in Colour. Demy 8vo. 16s. net.

*** This Edition has been printed direct from the original manuscript in the possession
of the Fanshawe Family, and Mr. H. C. Fanshawe contributes numerous notes which
form a running commentary on the text. Many famous pictures are reproduced, including paintings by Velazquez and Van Dyck.*

THE LIFE OF JOAN OF ARC. By ANATOLE
FRANCE. A Translation by WINIFRED STEPHENS. With 8 Illustrations. Demy 8vo (9 × 5¾ inches). 2 vols. Price 25s. net.

THE DAUGHTER OF LOUIS XVI. Marie-Thérèse-Charlotte of France, Duchesse D'Angoulême. By. G. LENOTRE. With 13 Full-page Illustrations. Demy 8vo. Price 10s. 6d. net.

WITS, BEAUX, AND BEAUTIES OF THE GEORGIAN ERA. By JOHN FYVIE, author of "Some Famous Women of Wit and Beauty," "Comedy Queens of the Georgian Era," etc. With a Photogravure Portrait and numerous other Illustrations. Demy 8vo (9 × 5¾ inches). 12s. 6d. net.

LADIES FAIR AND FRAIL. Sketches of the Demi-monde during the Eighteenth Century. By HORACE BLEACKLEY, author of "The Story of a Beautiful Duchess." With 1 Photogravure and 15 other Portraits reproduced from contemporary sources. Demy 8vo (9 × 5½ inches). 12s. 6d. net.

MADAME DE MAINTENON : Her Life and Times, 1635–1719. By C. C. DYSON. With 1 Photogravure Plate and 16 other Illustrations. Demy 8vo (9 × 5¼ inches). 12s. 6d. net.

DR. JOHNSON AND MRS. THRALE. By A. M. BROADLEY. With an Introductory Chapter by THOMAS SECCOMBE. With 24 Illustrations from rare originals, including a reproduction in colours of the Fellowes Miniature of Mrs. Piozzi by Roche, and a Photogravure of Harding's sepia drawing of Dr. Johnson. Demy 8vo (9 × 5¾ inches). 12s. 6d. net.

THE DAYS OF THE DIRECTOIRE. By ALFRED ALLINSON, M.A. With 48 Full-page Illustrations, including many illustrating the dress of the time. Demy 8vo (9 × 5¾ inches). 16s. net.

A PRINCESS OF INTRIGUE : A Biography of Anne Louise Benedicte, Duchesse du Maine. Translated from the French of GENERAL DE PIÈPAPE by J. LEWIS MAY. With a Photogravure Portrait and 16 other Illustrations. Demy 8vo (9 × 5¾ inches). 12s. 6d. net.

PETER THE CRUEL: The Life of the Notorious Don Pedro of Spain, together with an Account of his Relations with the famous Maria de Padilla. By Edward Storer. With a Photogravure Frontispiece and 16 other Illustrations. Demy 8vo (9 × 5¾ inches). 12s. 6d. net.

CHARLES DE BOURBON, CONSTABLE OF FRANCE: " THE GREAT CONDOTTIERE." By Christopher Hare. With a Photogravure Frontispiece and 16 other Illustrations. Demy 8vo (9 × 5¾ inches). 12s. 6d. net.

HUBERT AND JOHN VAN EYCK: Their Life and Work. By W. H. James Weale. With 41 Photogravure and 95 Black and White Reproductions. Royal 4to. £5 5s. net.

Sir Martin Conway's Note.

Nearly half a century has passed since Mr. W. H. James Weale, then resident at Bruges, began that long series of patient investigations into the history of Netherlandish art which was destined to earn so rich a harvest. When he began work Memlinc was still called Hemling, and was fabled to have arrived at Bruges as a wounded soldier. The van Eycks were little more than legendary heroes. Roger Van der Weyden was little more than a name. Most of the other great Netherlandish artists were either wholly forgotten or named only in connection with paintings with which they had nothing to do. Mr. Weale discovered Gerard David, and disentangled his principal works from Memlinc's, with which they were then confused.

VINCENZO FOPPA OF BRESCIA, FOUNDER OF THE LOMBARD SCHOOL, His Life and Work. By Constance Jocelyn Ffoulkes and Monsignor Rodolfo Majocchi, D.D., Rector of the Collegio Borromeo, Pavia. Based on research in the Archives of Milan, Pavia, Brescia, and Genoa, and on the study of all his known works. With over 100 Illustrations, many in Photogravure, and 100 Documents. Royal 4to. £3 11s. 6d. net.

*** No complete Life of Vincenzo Foppa has ever been written: an omission which seems almost inexplicable in these days of over-production in the matter of biographies of painters, and of subjects relating to the art of Italy. The object of the authors of this book has been to present a true picture of the master's life based upon the testimony of records in Italian archives. The authors have unearthed a large amount of new material relating to Foppa, one of the most interesting facts brought to light being that he lived for twenty-three years longer than was formerly supposed. The illustrations will include several pictures by Foppa hitherto unknown in the history of art.*

MEMOIRS OF THE DUKES OF URBINO. Illustrating the Arms, Art and Literature of Italy from 1440 to 1630. By James Dennistoun of Dennistoun. A New Edition edited by Edward Hutton, with upwards of 100 Illustrations. Demy 8vo. 3 vols. 42s. net.

*** For many years this great book has been out of print, although it still remains the chief authority upon the Duchy of Urbino from the beginning of the fifteenth century. Mr. Hutton has carefully edited the whole work, leaving the text substantially the same, but adding a large number of new notes, comments and references. Wherever possible the reader is directed to original sources. Every sort of work has been laid under contribution to illustrate the text, and bibliographies have been supplied on many subjects. Besides these notes the book acquires a new value on account of the mass of illustrations which it now contains, thus adding a pictorial comment to an historical and critical one.*

SIMON BOLIVAR, " EL LIBERTADOR." A
Life of the Chief Leader in the Revolt against Spain in Venezuela,
New Granada and Peru. By F. LORAINE PETRE. Author of
" Napoleon and the Conquest of Prussia," " Napoleon's Campaign
in Poland," and " Napoleon and the Archduke Charles." With
2 Portraits, one in Photogravure, and Maps. Demy 8vo (9 × 5¾
inches). 12s. 6d. net.

THE DIARY OF A LADY-IN-WAITING. By
LADY CHARLOTTE BURY. Being the Diary Illustrative of the
Times of George the Fourth. Interspersed with original Letters
from the late Queen Caroline and from various other distinguished
persons. New edition. Edited, with an Introduction, by A.
FRANCIS STEUART. With numerous portraits. Two Vols.
Demy 8vo. 21s. net

THE LAST JOURNALS OF HORACE WAL-
POLE. During the Reign of George III from 1771 to 1783.
With Notes by Dr. DORAN. Edited, with an Introduction, by
A. FRANCIS STEUART, and containing numerous Portraits (2 in
Photogravure) reproduced from contemporary Pictures, Engravings,
etc. 2 vols. Uniform with " The Diary of a Lady-in-Waiting."
Demy 8vo (9 × 5¾ inches). 25s. net.

JUNIPER HALL : Rendezvous of certain illus-
trious Personages during the French Revolution, including Alexander D'Arblay and Fanny Burney. Compiled by CONSTANCE HILL.
With numerous Illustrations by ELLEN G. HILL, and reproductions
from various Contemporary Portraits. Crown 8vo. 5s. net.

JANE AUSTEN : Her Homes and Her Friends.
By CONSTANCE HILL. Numerous Illustrations by ELLEN G. HILL,
together with Reproductions from Old Portraits, etc. Cr. 8vo. 5s. net.

THE HOUSE IN ST. MARTIN'S STREET.
Being Chronicles of the Burney Family. By CONSTANCE HILL,
Author of " Jane Austen, Her Homes and Her Friends," " Juniper
Hall," etc. With numerous Illustrations by ELLEN G. HILL, and
reproductions of Contemporary Portraits, etc. Demy 8vo. 21s. net.

STORY OF THE PRINCESS DES URSINS IN
SPAIN (Camarera-Mayor). By CONSTANCE HILL. With 12
Illustrations and a Photogravure Frontispiece. New Edition.
Crown 8vo. 5s. net.

MARIA EDGEWORTH AND HER CIRCLE IN THE DAYS OF BONAPARTE AND BOURBON.

By Constance Hill. Author of "Jane Austen: Her Homes and Her Friends," "Juniper Hall," "The House in St. Martin's Street," etc. With numerous Illustrations by Ellen G. Hill and Reproductions of Contemporary Portraits, etc. Demy 8vo (9 × 5¾ inches). 21s. net.

NEW LETTERS OF THOMAS CARLYLE.

Edited and Annotated by Alexander Carlyle, with Notes and an Introduction and numerous Illustrations. In Two Volumes. Demy 8vo. 25s. net.

Pall Mall Gazette.—"To the portrait of the man, Thomas, these letters do really add value; we can learn to respect and to like him the more for the genuine goodness of his personality."

Literary World.—"It is then Carlyle, the nobly filial son, we see in these letters; Carlyle, the generous and affectionate brother, the loyal and warm-hearted friend, . . . and above all, Carlyle as the tender and faithful lover of his wife."

Daily Telegraph.—"The letters are characteristic enough of the Carlyle we know: very picturesque and entertaining, full of extravagant emphasis, written, as a rule, at fever heat, eloquently rabid and emotional."

NEW LETTERS AND MEMORIALS OF JANE WELSH CARLYLE.

A Collection of hitherto Unpublished Letters. Annotated by Thomas Carlyle, and Edited by Alexander Carlyle, with an Introduction by Sir James Crichton Browne, m.d., ll.d., f.r.s., numerous Illustrations drawn in Litho-graphy by T. R. Way, and Photogravure Portraits from hitherto unreproduced Originals. In Two Volumes. Demy 8vo. 25s. net.

Westminster Gazette.—"Few letters in the language have in such perfection the qualities which good letters should possess. Frank, gay, brilliant, indiscreet, immensely clever, whimsical, and audacious, they reveal a character which, with whatever alloy of human infirmity, must endear itself to any reader of understanding."

World.—"Throws a deal of new light on the domestic relations of the Sage of Chelsea. They also contain the full text of Mrs. Carlyle's fascinating journal, and her own humorous and quaintly candid narrative of her first love-affair."

THE LOVE LETTERS OF THOMAS CAR-LYLE AND JANE WELSH.

Edited by Alexander Carlyle, Nephew of Thomas Carlyle, editor of "New Letters and Memorials of Jane Welsh Carlyle," "New Letters of Thomas Carlyle," etc. With 2 Portraits in colour and numerous other Illustrations. Demy 8vo (9 × 5¾ inches). 2 vols. 25s. net.

CARLYLE'S FIRST LOVE. Margaret Gordon—

Lady Bannerman. An account of her Life, Ancestry and Homes; her Family and Friends. By R. C. Archibald. With 20 Portraits and Illustrations, including a Frontispiece in Colour. Demy 8vo (9 × 5¾ inches). 10s. 6d. net.

THE FOUNDATIONS OF THE NINE-
TEENTH CENTURY. By HOUSTON STEWART CHAMBER-
LAIN. A Translation from the German by JOHN LEES, M.A.,
D.Litt. (Edin.). With an Introduction by LORD REDESDALE,
G.C.V.O., K.C.B. 2 vols. Demy 8vo (9 × 5¾ inches). 32s. net.

MEMOIRS OF THE MARTYR KING: being a
detailed record of the last two years of the Reign of His Most
Sacred Majesty King Charles the First, 1646-1648-9. Compiled by ALLAN FEA. With upwards of 100 Photogravure
Portraits and other Illustrations, including relics. Royal 4to.
105s. net.

Mr. M. H. SPIELMANN in *The Academy*.—"The volume is a triumph for the printer and
publisher, and a solid contribution to Carolinian literature."

Pall Mall Gazette.—"The present sumptuous volume, a storehouse of eloquent associations
.. comes as near to outward perfection as anything we could desire."

MEMOIRS OF A VANISHED GENERATION
1813-1855. Edited by Mrs. WARRENNE BLAKE. With numerous
Illustrations. Demy 8vo. 16s. net.

*** This work is compiled from diaries and letters dating from the time of the Regency
to the middle of the nineteenth century. The value of the work lies in its natural un-
embellished picture of the life of a cultured and well-born family in a foreign environment
at a period so close to our own that it is far less familiar than periods much more remote.
There is an atmosphere of Jane Austen's novels about the lives of Admiral Knox and his
family, and a large number of well-known contemporaries are introduced into Mrs. Blake's
pages.*

THE LIFE OF PETER ILICH TCHAIKOVSKY
(1840-1893). By his Brother, MODESTE TCHAIKOVSKY. Edited
and abridged from the Russian and German Editions by ROSA
NEWMARCH. With Numerous Illustrations and Facsimiles and an
Introduction by the Editor. Demy 8vo. 7s. 6d. net. Second
edition.

The Times.—"A most illuminating commentary on Tchaikovsky's music."

World.—"One of the most fascinating self-revelations by an artist which has been given to
the world. The translation is excellent, and worth reading for its own sake."

Contemporary Review.—"The book's appeal is, of course, primarily to the music-lover; but
there is so much of human and literary interest in it, such intimate revelation of a
singularly interesting personality, that many who have never come under the spell of
the Pathetic Symphony will be strongly attracted by what is virtually the spiritual
autobiography of its composer. High praise is due to the translator and editor for the
literary skill with which she has prepared the English version of this fascinating work ...
There have been few collections of letters published within recent years that give so
vivid a portrait of the writer as that presented to us in these pages."

CÉSAR FRANCK : A Study. Translated from the
French of Vincent d'Indy, with an Introduction by Rosa Newmarch. Demy 8vo. 7s. 6d. net.

₊ *There is no purer influence in modern music than that of César Franck, for many years ignored in every capacity save that of organist of Sainte-Clotilde, in Paris, but now recognised as the legitimate successor of Bach and Beethoven. His inspiration "rooted in love and faith" has contributed in a remarkable degree to the regeneration of the musical art in France and elsewhere. The now famous "Schola Cantorum," founded in Paris in 1896, by A. Guilmant, Charles Bordes and Vincent d'Indy, is the direct outcome of his influence. Among the artists who were in some sort his disciples were Paul Dukas, Chabrier, Gabriel Fauré and the great violinist Ysäye. His pupils include such gifted composers as Benoît, Augusta Holmès, Chausson, Ropartz, and d'Indy. This book, written with the devotion of a disciple and the authority of a master, leaves us with a vivid and touching impression of the saint-like composer of "The Beatitudes."*

GRIEG AND HIS MUSIC. By H. T. Finck,
Author of Wagner and his Works," etc. With Illustrations.
Crown 8vo. 7s. 6d. net.

THE OLDEST MUSIC ROOM IN EUROPE :
A Record of an Eighteenth-Century Enterprise at Oxford. By
John H. Mee, M.A., D.Mus., Precentor of Chichester Cathedral,
(sometime Fellow of Merton College, Oxford). With 25 full-page
Illustrations. Demy 8vo (9 × 5¾ inches). 10s. 6d. net.

EDWARD A. MACDOWELL : A Biography.
By Lawrence Gilman, Author of "Phases of Modern Music,"
"Straus's 'Salome '," "The Music of To-morrow and Other
Studies," etc. Profusely Illustrated. Crown 8vo. 5s. net.

THE KING'S GENERAL IN THE WEST,
being the Life of Sir Richard Granville, Baronet (1600–1659).
By Roger Granville, M.A., Sub-Dean of Exeter Cathedral.
With Illustrations. Demy 8vo. 10s. 6d. net.

Westminster Gazette.—"A distinctly interesting work ; it will be highly appreciated by historical students as well as by ordinary readers."

THE SOUL OF A TURK. By Mrs. de Bunsen.
With 8 Full-page Illustrations. Demy 8vo. 10s. 6d. net.

₊ *We hear of Moslem "fanaticism" and Christian "superstition," but it is not easy to find a book which goes to the heart of the matter. "The Soul of a Turk" is the outcome of several journeys in Asiatic and European Turkey, notably one through the Armenian provinces, down the Tigris on a raft to Baghdad and across the Syrian Desert to Damascus. Mrs. de Bunsen made a special study of the various forms of religion existing in those countries. Here, side by side with the formal ceremonial of the village mosque and the Christian Church, is the resort to Magic and Mystery.*

THE LIFE AND LETTERS OF ROBERT
Stephen Hawker, sometime Vicar of Morwenstow in Cornwall.
By C. E. Byles. With numerous Illustrations by J. Ley
Pethybridge and others. Demy 8vo. 7s. 6d. net.

Daily Telegraph.—" . . . As soon as the volume is opened one finds oneself in the presence of a real original, a man of ability, genius and eccentricity, of whom one cannot know too much. . . . No one will read this fascinating and charmingly produced book without thanks to Mr. Byles and a desire to visit—or revisit—Morwenstow."

THE LIFE OF WILLIAM BLAKE. By ALEXANDER
GILCHRIST. Edited with an Introduction by W. GRAHAM ROBERTSON.
Numerous Reproductions from Blake's most characteristic and
remarkable designs. Demy 8vo. 10s. 6d. net. New Edition.

Birmingham Post.—"Nothing seems at all likely ever to supplant the Gilchrist biography.
Mr. Swinburne praised it magnificently in his own eloquent essay on Blake, and there
should be no need now to point out its entire sanity, understanding keenness of critical
insight, and masterly literary style. Dealing with one of the most difficult of subjects,
it ranks among the finest things of its kind that we possess."

GEORGE MEREDITH : Some Characteristics.
By RICHARD LE GALLIENNE. With a Bibliography (much en-
larged) by JOHN LANE. Portrait, etc. Crown 8vo. 5s. net. Fifth
Edition. Revised.

Punch.—"All Meredithians must possess 'George Meredith; Some Characteristics,' by
Richard Le Gallienne. This book is a complete and excellent guide to the novelist and
the novels, a sort of Meredithian Bradshaw, with pictures of the traffic superintendent
and the head office at Boxhill. Even Philistines may be won over by the blandishments
of Mr. Le Gallienne."

LIFE OF LORD CHESTERFIELD. An Account
of the Ancestry, Personal Character, and Public Services of the
Fourth Earl of Chesterfield. By W. H. CRAIG, M.A. Numerous
Illustrations. Demy 8vo. 12s. 6d. net.

Times.—"It is the chief point of Mr. Craig's book to show the sterling qualities which
Chesterfield was at too much pains in concealing, to reject the perishable trivialities of
his character, and to exhibit him as a philosophic statesman, not inferior to any of his
contemporaries, except Walpole at one end of his life, and Chatham at the other."

A QUEEN OF INDISCRETIONS. The Tragedy
of Caroline of Brunswick, Queen of England. From the Italian
of G. P. CLERICI. Translated by FREDERIC CHAPMAN. With
numerous Illustrations reproduced from contemporary Portraits and
Prints. Demy 8vo. 21s. net.

The Daily Telegraph.—"It could scarcely be done more thoroughly or, on the whole, in
better taste than is here displayed by Professor Clerici. Mr Frederic Chapman himself
contributes an uncommonly interesting and well-informed introduction."

**LETTERS AND JOURNALS OF SAMUEL
GRIDLEY HOWE.** Edited by his Daughter LAURA E.
RICHARDS. With Notes and a Preface by F. B. SANBORN, an
Introduction by Mrs. JOHN LANE, and a Portrait. Demy 8vo
(9 × 5¾ inches). 16s. net.

Outlook.—"This deeply interesting record of experience. The volume is worthily produced
and contains a striking portrait of Howe."

THE WAR IN WEXFORD. An Account of the
Rebellion in the South of Ireland in 1798, told from Original
Documents. By H. F. B. WHEELER and A. M. BROADLEY,
Authors of "Napoleon and the Invasion of England," etc. With
numerous Reproductions of contemporary portraits and engravings.
Demy 8vo (9 × 5¾ inches). 12s. 6d. net.

THE LIFE OF ST. MARY MAGDALEN.
Translated from the Italian of an Unknown Fourteenth-Century
Writer by VALENTINA HAWTREY. With an Introductory Note by
VERNON LEE, and 14 Full-page Reproductions from the Old Masters.
Crown 8vo. 5s. net.

Daily News.—"Miss Valentina Hawtrey has given a most excellent English version of this
pleasant work."

**LADY CHARLOTTE SCHREIBER'S
JOURNALS** : Confidences of a Collector of Ceramics and
Antiques throughout Britain, France, Germany, Italy, Spain,
Holland, Belgium, Switzerland, and Turkey. From the Year
1869 to 1885. Edited by MONTAGUE GUEST, with Annotations
by EGAN MEW. With upwards of 100 Illustrations, including
8 in colour and 2 in photogravure. Royal 8vo. 2 Volumes.
42s. net.

WILLIAM MAKEPEACE THACKERAY. A
Biography by LEWIS MELVILLE. With 2 Photogravures and
numerous other Illustrations. Demy 8vo (9 × 5¾ inches). 25s. net.

** In compiling this biography of Thackeray Mr. Lewis Melville, who is admittedly
the authority on the subject, has been assisted by numerous Thackeray experts. Mr.
Melville's name has long been associated with Thackeray, not only as founder of the
Titmarsh Club, but also as the author of "The Thackeray Country" and the editor of the
standard edition of Thackeray's works and "Thackeray's Stray Papers." For many
years Mr. Melville has devoted himself to the collection of material relating to the life and
work of his subject. He has had access to many new letters, and much information has
come to hand since the publication of "The Life of Thackeray." Now that everything
about the novelist is known, it seems that an appropriate moment has arrived for a new
biography. Mr. Melville has also compiled a bibliography of Thackeray that runs to
upwards 1300 items, by many hundreds more than contained in any hitherto issued.
This section will be invaluable to the collector. Thackeray's sketches, including several
never before republished, have also been collected. There is a list of portraits of the
novelist, and a separate index to the Bibliography.

A LATER PEPYS. The Correspondence of Sir
William Weller Pepys, Bart., Master in Chancery, 1758–1825,
with Mrs. Chapone, Mrs. Hartley, Mrs. Montague, Hannah More,
William Franks, Sir James Macdonald, Major Rennell, Sir
Nathaniel Wraxall, and others. Edited, with an Introduction and
Notes, by ALICE C. C. GAUSSEN. With numerous Illustrations.
Demy 8vo. In Two Volumes. 32s. net.

DOUGLAS SLADEN in the *Queen.*—"This is indisputably a most valuable contribution to the
literature of the eighteenth century. It is a veritable storehouse of society gossip, the
art criticism, and the *mots* of famous people."

**MEMORIES OF SIXTY YEARS AT ETON,
CAMBRIDGE AND ELSEWHERE.** By OSCAR BROWNING,
M.A., University Lecturer in History, Senior Fellow and sometime
History Tutor at King's College, Cambridge, and formerly Assistant
Master at Eton College. Illustrated. Demy 8vo (9 × 5¾ inches).
14s. net.

RUDYARD KIPLING : a Criticism. By RICHARD LE GALLIENNE. With a Bibliography by JOHN LANE. Crown 8vo. 3s. 6d. net.

Scotsman—"It shows a keen insight into the essential qualities of literature, and analyses Mr. Kipling's product with the skill of a craftsman . . . the positive and outstanding merits of Mr. Kipling's contribution to the literature of his time are marshalled by his critic with quite uncommon skill."

ROBERT LOUIS STEVENSON, AN ELEGY; AND OTHER POEMS, MAINLY PERSONAL. By RICHARD LE GALLIENNE. Crown 8vo. 4s. 6d. net.

Globe—"The opening Elegy on R. L. Stevenson includes some tender and touching passages, and has throughout the merits of sincerity and clearness."

JOHN LOTHROP MOTLEY AND HIS FAMILY : Further Letters and Records. Edited by his daughter and Herbert St. John Mildmay, with numerous Illustrations. Demy 8vo (9 × 5¾ inches). 16s. net.

THE LIFE OF W. J. FOX, Public Teacher and Social Reformer, 1786–1864. By the late RICHARD GARNETT, C.B., LL.D., concluded by EDWARD GARNETT. Demy 8vo. (9 × 5¾ inches.) 16s. net.

* W. J. Fox was a prominent figure in public life from 1820 to 1860. From a weaver's boy he became M.P. for Oldham (1847-1862), and he will always be remembered for his association with South Place Chapel, where his Radical opinions and fame as a preacher and popular orator brought him in contact with an advanced circle of thoughtful people. He was the discoverer of the youthful Robert Browning and Harriet Martineau, and the friend of J. S. Mill, Horne, John Forster, Macready, etc. As an Anti-Corn Law orator, he swayed, by the power of his eloquence, enthusiastic audiences. As a politician, he was the unswerving champion of social reform and the cause of oppressed nationalities, his most celebrated speech being in support of his Bill for National Education, 1850, a Bill which anticipated many of the features of the Education Bill of our own time. He died in 1863. The present Life has been compiled from manuscript material entrusted to Dr. Garnett by Mrs. Bridell Fox.

ROBERT DODSLEY : POET, PUBLISHER, AND PLAYWRIGHT. By RALPH STRAUS. With a Photogravure and 16 other Illustrations. Demy 8vo (9 × 5¾ inches). 21s. net.

THE LIFE AND TIMES OF MARTIN BLAKE, B.D. (1593-1673), Vicar of Barnstaple and Prebendary of Exeter Cathedral, with some account of his conflicts with the Puritan Lecturers and of his Persecutions. By JOHN FREDERICK CHANTER, M.A., Rector of Parracombe, Devon. With 5 full-page Illustrations. Demy 8vo (9 × 5¾ inches). 10s. 6d. net.

WILLIAM HARRISON AINSWORTH AND HIS FRIENDS. By S. M. ELLIS. With upwards of 50 Illustrations, 4 in Photogravure. 2 vols. Demy 8vo (9 × 5¾ inches). 32s. net.

THE SPENCER STANHOPES OF YORK-
SHIRE; FROM THE PAPERS OF A MACARONI
AND HIS KINDRED. By A. M. W. STIRLING, Author of
"Coke of Norfolk," etc. With numerous Illustrations reproduced
from contemporary prints, etc. 2 vols. Demy 8vo. 32s. net.

THE SPEAKERS OF THE HOUSE OF
COMMONS from the Earliest Times to the Present Day,
with a Topographical Account of Westminster at various Epochs,
Brief Notes on the Sittings of Parliament, and a Retrospect of
the principal Constitutional Changes during Seven Centuries. By
ARTHUR IRWIN DASENT, Author of "The Life and Letters of
JOHN DELANE," "The History of St. James's Square," etc. With
numerous Portraits. Demy 8vo. 21s.

JUNGLE BY-WAYS IN INDIA : Leaves from
the Note-book of a Sportsman and a Naturalist. By E. P.
STEBBING, I.F.S., F.Z.S., F.R.G.S. With upwards of 100 Illustrations
by the Author and others. Demy 8vo (9 × 5¾ inches). 12s. 6d.
net.

A TRAMP IN THE CAUCASUS. By STEPHEN
GRAHAM. With 16 full-page Illustrations. Demy 8vo (9 × 5¾
inches). 12s. 6d. net.

SERVICE AND SPORT IN THE SUDAN : A
Record of Administration in the Anglo-Egyptian Sudan. With
some Intervals of Sport and Travel. By D. C. E. FF.COMYN,
F.R.G.S. (late of the Black Watch). With 16 full-page Illustrations
and 3 Maps. Demy 8vo (9 × 5¾ inches). 12s. 6d. net.

FRENCH NOVELISTS OF TO-DAY : Maurice
Barrès, René Bazin, Paul Bourget, Pierre de Coulevain, Anatole
France, Pierre Loti, Marcel Prévost, and Edouard Rod. Bio-
graphical, Descriptive, and Critical. By WINIFRED STEPHENS.
With Portraits and Bibliographies. Crown 8vo. 5s. net.

** *The writer, who has lived much in France, is thoroughly acquainted with French
life and with the principal currents of French thought. The book is intended to be a
guide to English readers desirous to keep in touch with the best present-day French
fiction. Special attention is given to the ecclesiastical, social, and intellectual problems
of contemporary France and their influence upon the works of French novelists of to-day.*

MEN AND LETTERS. By HERBERT PAUL, M.P.
Fourth Edition. Crown 8vo. 5s. net.

Daily News.—"Mr. Herbert Paul has done scholars and the reading world in general a
high service in publishing this collection of his essays."

JOHN LANE, THE BODLEY HEAD, VIGO STREET, LONDON, W.